THE YEAR'S BEST

SCIENCE FICTION

ALSO BY GARDNER DOZOIS

ANTHOLOGIES

A DAY IN THE LIFE

ANOTHER WORLD

BEST SCIENCE FICTION STORIES OF THE
YEAR #6–10

THE BEST OF ISAAC ASIMOV'S SCIENCE
FICTION MAGAZINE

TIME-TRAVELERS FROM ISAAC ASIMOV'S
SCIENCE FICTION MAGAZINE

TRANSCENDENTAL TALES FROM ISAAC
ASIMOV'S SCIENCE FICTION MAGAZINE

ISAAC ASIMOV'S ALIENS

ISAAC ASIMOV'S MARS

ISAAC ASIMOV'S SF LITE

ISAAC ASIMOV'S WAR

ROADS NOT TAKEN (with Stanley Schmidt)

THE YEAR'S BEST SCIENCE FICTION, #1–32

FUTURE EARTHS: UNDER AFRICAN SKIES
(with Mike Resnick)

FUTURE EARTHS: UNDER SOUTH AMERICAN
SKIES (with Mike Resnick)

RIPPER! (with Susan Casper)

MODERN CLASSIC SHORT NOVELS OF
SCIENCE FICTION

MODERN CLASSICS OF FANTASY

KILLING ME SOFTLY

DYING FOR IT

THE GOOD OLD STUFF

THE GOOD NEW STUFF

EXPLORERS

THE FURTHEST HORIZON

WORLDMAKERS

SUPERMEN

COEDITED WITH SHEILA WILLIAMS

ISAAC ASIMOV'S PLANET EARTH

ISAAC ASIMOV'S ROBOTS

ISAAC ASIMOV'S VALENTINES

ISAAC ASIMOV'S SKIN DEEP

ISAAC ASIMOV'S GHOSTS

ISAAC ASIMOV'S VAMPIRES

ISAAC ASIMOV'S MOONS

ISAAC ASIMOV'S CHRISTMAS

ISAAC ASIMOV'S CAMELOT

ISAAC ASIMOV'S WEREWOLVES

ISAAC ASIMOV'S SOLAR SYSTEM

ISAAC ASIMOV'S DETECTIVES

ISAAC ASIMOV'S CYBERDREAMS

COEDITED WITH JACK DANN

ALIENS!	SORCERERS!	DRAGONS!	HACKERS
UNICORNS!	DEMONS!	HORSES!	TIMEGATES
MAGICATS!	DOGTALES!	UNICORNS 2	CLONES
MAGICATS 2!	SEASERPENTS!	INVADERS!	NANOTECH
BESTIARY!	DINOSAURS!	ANGELS!	IMMORTALS
MERMAIDS!	LITTLE PEOPLE!	DINOSAURS II	

FICTION

STRANGERS

THE VISIBLE MAN (Collection)

NIGHTMARE BLUE
(with George Alec Effinger)

SLOW DANCING THROUGH TIME
(with Jack Dann, Michael Swanwick,
Susan Casper and Jack C. Haldeman II)

THE PEACEMAKER

GEODESIC DREAMS (collection)

NONFICTION

THE FICTION OF JAMES TIPTREE, JR.

THE YEAR'S BEST

SCIENCE FICTION

thirty-third annual collection

edited by Gardner Dozois

 st. Martin's griffin ✄ New York

These short stories are works of fiction. All of the characters, organizations, and events portrayed in these stories are either products of the authors' imaginations or are used fictitiously.

THE YEAR'S BEST SCIENCE FICTION: THIRTY-THIRD ANNUAL COLLECTION. Copyright © 2016 by Gardner Dozois. All rights reserved. Printed in the United States of America. For information, address St. Martin's Press, 175 Fifth Avenue, New York, N.Y. 10010.

www.stmartins.com

The Library of Congress Cataloging-in-Publication Data is available upon request.

ISBN 978-1-250-08083-7 (hardcover)
ISBN 978-1-250-08084-4 (trade paperback)
ISBN 978-1-4668-9266-8 (e-book)

Our books may be purchased in bulk for promotional, educational, or business use. Please contact your local bookseller or the Macmillan Corporate and Premium Sales Department at 1-800-221-7945, extension 5442, or by e-mail at MacmillanSpecialMarkets@macmillan.com.

First Edition: July 2016

10 9 8 7 6 5 4 3 2 1

contents

permissions

acknowledgments

The editor would like to thank the following people for their help and support: Susan Casper, Jonathan Strahan, Sean Wallace, Neil Clarke, Gordon Van Gelder, Andy Cox, John Joseph Adams, Ellen Datlow, Sheila Williams, Trevor Quachri, Emily Hockaday, Peter Crowther, William Shaffer, Ian Whates, Paula Guran, Tony Daniel, Liza Trombi, Robert Wexler, Patrick Nielsen Hayden, Stephen Cass, Michael Smith, Lynne M. Thomas, Gavin Grant, Kelly Link, Fred Coppersmith, Ian Redman, David Lee Summers, Wendy S. Delmater, Beth Wodzinski, E. Catherine Tobler, Carl Rafala, Edmund R. Schubert, C. C. Finlay, A. C. Wise, Dirk Strasser, Jed Hartman, Rich Horton, Mark R. Kelly, Nick Gevers, Tehani Wessely, Ivor Hartmann, Shahid Mahmod, Tom Easton, Jason Pontin, Giovanna Bortolamedi, Jaym Gates, Eric T. Reynolds, Paula Guran, Andrew Leon Hudson, August Cole, John Morgan, Romain Warnault, Bryant Thomas Schmidt, Karen Bovenayer, Patrick Walsh, Jenny Blackford, Russel B. Farr, Anjula Jalan, Djibril al-Ayad, Renee Zuckerbrot, Elizabeth Bear, Aliette de Bodard, Lavie Tidhar, Robert Reed, Vandana Singh, Alastair Reynolds, Ken Liu, Nancy Kress, Ian McDonald, Chaz Brenchley, Ken Liu, Karl Bunker, Paolo Bacigalupi, Lauren Beukes, Allen M. Steele, Rich Larson, Greg Egan, Nick Harkaway, Benjamin Rosenbaum, Geoff Ryman, John Barnes, Jason Eik Lundberg, Jim DeMaiolo, Carrie Vaughn, Gareth L. Powell, Stephen Baxter, Kristine Kathryn Rusch, Indrapramit Das, Kelly Robson, Django Wexler, Sam J. Miller, Paul McAuley, Vonda N. McIntyre, Christopher Rowe, Jim Grimsley, Carter Scholz, Nick Wolven, Naomi Kritzer, Sarah Pinsker, John Kessel, Terry Bisson, David Kunsken, Daniel Abraham, James Sarafin, Gwyneth Jones, Michael F. Flynn, Martin L. Shoemaker, Sean McMullen, Albert E. Cowdrey, Bill Johnson, Joe Pitkin, Ned Beauman, Eleanor Arnason, Ann Leckie, Seanan McGuire, Ty Franck, Madeline Ashby, John O'Neill, Vaughne Lee Hansen, Mark Watson, Katherine Canfield, Jamie Coyne, and special thanks to my own editor, Marc Resnick.

Thanks are also due to the late, lamented Charles N. Brown, and to all his staff, whose magazine *Locus* [Locus Publications, P.O. Box 13305, Oakland, CA 94661. $63 in the U.S. for a one-year subscription (twelve issues) via periodical mail; $76 for a one-year (twelve issues) via first class credit card orders (510) 339 9198] was used as an invaluable reference source throughout the Summation; *Locus Online* (www .locusmag.com), edited by Mark R. Kelly, has also become a key reference source.

It was another relatively quiet year in the SF publishing world, and indeed in the publishing world in general.

The most interesting story in 2015 was probably a resurgence of the sales of print books. According to Nielsen BookScan, 571 million print books were sold in 2015, 17 million more than the year before. Meanwhile, the formerly explosive sales of e-books slowed a bit, actually falling by 10 percent during the first five months of the year; e-book sales had been once predicted to reach 50 percent to 60 percent of total overall book sales by 2015, but instead e-books accounted for around 20 percent of the market, much the same as they have for a few years now. The long-heralded prediction that e-books will drive print books out of the market and into total extinction doesn't seem set to come true any time soon. Even the once phenomenal sale of dedicated e-readers like the Kindle and the Nook have slowed dramatically, as many people switched over to reading digital books on their smartphones and tablets instead. According to Forrester Research, 12 million e-readers were sold in the last year, a steep drop from the nearly 20 million sold in 2011. According to a Nielsen survey, the portion of people who read books primarily on e-readers fell to 32 percent in the first quarter of 2015, from 50 percent in 2012.

The resurgence of print sales has been good for independent bookstores, themselves once threatened with extinction first by the big bookstore chains, then by online booksellers such as Amazon, then by the e-book explosion. While sales at some of the big chain stores suffer, independent bookstores have been reopening with success. The American Booksellers Association counted 1,712 member stores in 2,227 locations in 2015, up from 1,410 in 1,660 locations five years ago.

None of this means, of course, that e-books are going to go away. One of the most interesting developments in recent years, in sharp contrast to the predictions that either e-books wouldn't catch on or that they'd drive print books into extinction, is that we seem to be settling into a pattern where readers buy *both* e-books and print books, choosing one format or the other to purchase depending on their needs and the circumstances. Indeed, some readers even buy *both* e-book and print editions *of the same title*, something that almost nobody saw coming.

The good news is that the increased availability of books, in all formats and through all sales channels—online bookseller, independent bookstore, chain bookstores—means that more people are *reading* than ever have before, and that the long-bemoaned "fact" that kids aren't interested in reading anymore (because they have computer games, TV, and movies) just isn't true; a Pew survey from 2014 showed that 88 percent of Americans under thirty read at least one book in the past year, compared to 79 percent for those over thirty, with younger teens reading the most: 46 percent of those aged sixteen to seventeen reported that they read books (in both print and digital formats) on a daily basis, and 43 percent of those eighteen to nineteen reported reading books daily as well.

I have no access to figures for outside of the United States, but I'm willing to bet that this is a global phenomenon, and that people everywhere are reading more now than they were a decade or two ago—certainly good news for everyone who loves books and reading.

Rather than destroy literacy, as has long been feared, the Internet may actually be helping to save it.

In other publishing news: Houghton Mifflin Harcourt launched a new SF and fantasy book line, called John Joseph Adams Books, under the editorship of John Joseph Adams. Orbit, an SF and fantasy imprint of Hachette, has announced that it's doubling its annual output next year to ninety titles. HarperOne, a division of Harper-Collins, launched a new digital-first imprint, HarperLegends. Penguin Publishing Group combined Berkley and New American Library into a new division called Berkley Publishing Group; Berkley head Leslie Gelbman is president of the new division, former NAL publisher Kara Walsh has been promoted to senior vice president and publisher, Claire Zion will be vice president and editor-in-chief, and Tom Colgan has been promoted to vice president and editorial director and will oversee the mystery and SF/fantasy editors at Ace and Roc. Susan Allison, longtime editorial director for the Berkley Publishing Group, retired. Julie Crisp left her position as editorial director of Tor UK at Pan Macmillian. Annalee Newitz became editor-in-chief of technology Web site Gizmodo, with Charlie Jane Anders taking over her former position as editor-in-chief of Web site io9. Malcolm Edwards stepped down from his position as deputy CEO and publisher of Orion to become chairman of the Gollancz imprint and consulting publisher for Orion. Jon Wood will take over as publisher of Orion, David Young is retiring as CEO of Orion and deputy CEO of Hatchette UK, and former Little, Brown CEO David Shelley will take over as Orion CEO. Simon Spanton left his position as associate publisher of Gollancz. Don Weisberg is leaving his position as president of Penguin Young Readers Group to become president of Macmillan Publishers U.S.; Jen Loja, senior vice president and associate publisher of Penguin Young Readers Group, will take over his old position.

After years of precipitous decline in the professional magazine market, 2015 was another moderately stable year. Sales of electronic subscriptions to the magazines are continuing to creep up, as well as sales of individual electronic copies of each issue, and this is making a big difference in profitability.

Asimov's Science Fiction had a strong year this year, publishing good work by Greg Egan, Aliette de Bodard, Rich Larson, Sam J. Miller, Allen M. Steele, Kristine Kathryn Rusch, Indrapramit Das, Nick Wolven, Eugene Fischer, Christopher Rowe, and others; *Asimov's* was probably the best place in the genre to find strong novellas this year, publishing four or five of the year's best. As usual, their SF was considerably stronger than their fantasy, the reverse of *The Magazine of Fantasy & Science Fiction*. *Asimov's Science Fiction* registered a 5.1 percent loss in overall circulation, down to 19,250 from 2014's 20,282. Subscriptions were 17,052, down slightly from 2014's 17,987; of that total, 9,479 were print subscriptions, up slightly from 9,347, while 7,573 were digital subscriptions, down from 8,640. Newsstand sales were down to 2,198 copies from 2014's 2,295. Sell-through rose to 39 percent from 37 percent. Sheila Williams completed her twelfth year as *Asimov's* editor.

Analog Science Fiction/Science Fact had good work by Sean McMullen, Joe Pitkin, Bill Johnson, Marissa Lingen, Alec Nevala-Lee, Martin L. Shoemaker, K. J. Zimring, and others. *Analog* registered a 5.4 percent loss in overall circulation, down to 20,356 from 2014's 24,709. There were 20,356 subscriptions, down from 2014's 21,456; of this total, 14,301 were print subscriptions, while 6,040 were digital subscriptions. Newsstand sales were down slightly to 3,019 from 2014's 3,253. Sell-through dropped to 37 percent from 41 percent. New editor Trevor Quachri completed his second full year as editor. 2015 marked the magazine's eighty-fifth anniversary, and it published its thousandth issue, making it the longest continually running SF magazine.

Once again, *The Magazine of Fantasy & Science Fiction* was almost exactly the reverse of *Asimov's*, with the fantasy published there being stronger than the science fiction (with the exception of a strong SF novella by Carter Scholz), but they still published good work by Carter Scholz, Rachel Pollack, James Sarafin, Albert Cowdrey, Robert Reed, Elizabeth Bear, David Gerrold, Tamsyn Muir, and others. *F&SF* registered a 17.1 percent drop in overall circulation from 11,910 to 9,877, although as digital sales figures are not available for *F&SF*, there's no way to be certain what the actual circulation number is. Subscriptions dropped from 8,994 to 7,576; of that total, 2,301 copies were sold on the newsstand, with no information on how many digital sales there were. Sell through dropped from 28 percent to 23 percent. After eighteen years as editor, Gordon Van Gelder stepped down as editor with the March/April 2015 issue, being replaced by new editor Charles Coleman Finlay. Van Gelder remains as the magazine's owner and publisher, as he has was in 2014.

Interzone is technically not a "professional magazine," by the definition of the Science Fiction Writers of America (SFWA), because of its low rates and circulation, but the literary quality of the work published there is so high that it would be ludicrous to omit it. *Interzone* was also a bit weaker this year than last year, but still published good work by Rich Larson, Malcolm Devlin, John Shirley, Chris Butler, Alastair Reynolds, T. R. Napper, and others. Exact circulation figures not available, but is guessed to be in the 2,000-copy range. TTA Press, *Interzone's* publisher, also publishes straight horror or dark suspense magazine *Black Static*, which is beyond our purview here, but of a similar level of professional quality. *Interzone* and *Black Static* changed to a smaller trim size in 2011, but maintained their slick look, switching from the old 7 ¾"-by-10 ¾" saddle-stitched, semigloss color cover and sixty-four-page format to a 6 ½"-by-9 ¼" perfect-bound, glossy color cover and ninety-six-page format. The editor and publisher is Andy Cox.

If you'd like to see lots of good SF and fantasy published every year, the survival of these magazines is essential, and one important way that you can help them survive is by subscribing to them. It's never been easier to do so, something that these days can be done with just the click of a few buttons; nor has it ever before been possible to subscribe to the magazines in as many different formats, from the traditional print copy arriving by mail to downloads for your desktop or laptop available from places like Amazon (www.amazon.com), to versions you can read on your Kindle, Nook, or iPad. You can also now subscribe from overseas just as easily as you can from the United States, something formerly difficult to impossible.

So in hopes of making it easier for you to subscribe, I'm going to list both the Internet sites where you can subscribe online and the street addresses where you can subscribe by mail for each magazine: *Asimov's* site is at www.asimovs.com, and subscribing online might be the easiest thing to do. There's also a discounted rate for online subscriptions. Its subscription address is **Asimov's Science Fiction**, Dell Magazines, 267 Broadway, Fourth Floor, New York, NY 10007-2352—$34.97 for annual subscription in the US, $44.97 overseas. *Analog's* site is at www.analogsf.com; its subscription address is **Analog Science Fiction and Fact**, Dell Magazines, 267 Broadway, Fourth Floor, New York, NY 10007-2352—$34.97 for annual subscription in the US, $44.97 overseas. **The Magazine of Fantasy & Science Fiction**'s site is www.sfsite.com/fsf; its subscription address is **The Magazine of Fantasy & Science Fiction**, Spilogale, Inc., P.O. Box 3447, Hoboken, NJ 07030—annual subscription $34.97 in the US, $44.97 overseas. **Interzone** and **Black Static** can be subscribed to online at www.ttapress.com/onlinestore1.html; the subscription address for both is TTA Press, 5 Martins Lane, Witcham, Ely, Cambs CB6 2LB, England, UK—42.00 Pounds Sterling each for a twelve-issue subscription, or there is a reduced rate dual subscription offer of 78.00 Pounds Sterling for both magazines for twelve issues; make checks payable to "TTA Press."

Most of these magazines are also available in various electronic formats through the Kindle, Nook, and other handheld readers.

The print semiprozine market continues to shrink; with many of the former print semiprozines either dying or making the jump to electronic format, and more likely to jump to electronic format in the future. It's also getting a bit problematic to say which are print semiprozines and which are e-zines, since some markets are offering both print versions and electronic versions of their issues at the same time. Most of the fiction published in the surviving print semiprozines this year was relatively minor, with better work appearing in the online magazines (following).

The Canadian *On Spec*, the longest-running of all the print fiction semiprozines, which is edited by a collective under general editor, Diane L. Walton, brought out three out of four published issues; in 2014, they were reported to be thinking of switching to a digital online format, and I suspect that that still might happen. Another collective-run SF magazine with a rotating editorial staff, Australia's *Andromeda Spaceways Inflight Magazine*, managed only one issue this year. There were two issues of *Lady Churchill's Rosebud Wristlet*, the long-running slipstream magazine edited by Kelly Link and Gavin Grant. *Space and Time Magazine* managed three issues, and *Neo-opsis* managed one. If there was an issue of Ireland's long-running *Albedo One*, I didn't see it, or any issues of the small British SF magazine *Jupiter* this year, or of *Flytrap*. *Tales of the Talisman* produced three issues and then went on "permanent hiatus." Long-running Australian semiprozine *Aurealis* has transitioned to a downloadable format.

There isn't a whole lot left of the popular print critical magazine market. *The*

New York Review of Science Fiction departed to the electronic world in mid-2012, and with the tragic death of founder and editor David G. Hartwell (see obituary section), its continued existence in any format may be up in the air. For general-interest magazines about SF and fantasy, that leaves the venerable newszine *Locus: The Magazine of the Science Fiction and Fantasy Field*, a multiple Hugo winner, for decades an indispensible source of news, information, and reviews, now in its forty-ninth year of publication, as almost the only survivor in this category, operating under the guidance of a staff of editors headed by Liza Groen Trombi, and including Kirsten Gong-Wong, Carolyn Cushman, Tim Pratt, Jonathan Strahan, Francesca Myman, Heather Shaw, and many others.

One of the few other remaining popular critical print magazines is newcomer *The Cascadia Subduction Zone: A Literary Quarterly*, edited by L. Timmel Duchamp, Nisi Shawl, and Kath Wilham, a new feminist print magazine of reviews and critical essays, which published four issues in 2015. The most accessible of the other surviving print critical magazines—most of which are professional journals more aimed at academics than at the average reader—is probably the long-running British critical zine *Foundation*.

Subscription addresses are: ***Locus, The Magazine of the Science Fiction & Fantasy Field***, Locus Publications, Inc., P.O. Box 13305, Oakland, CA 94661, $76.00 for a one-year first-class subscription, twelve issues; ***Foundation***, Science Fiction Foundation, Roger Robinson (SFF), 75 Rosslyn Avenue, Harold Wood, Essex RM3 ORG, UK, $37.00 for a three-issue subscription in the USA; ***On Spec, The Canadian Magazine of the Fantastic***, P.O. Box 4727, Edmonton, AB, Canada T6E 5G6, for subscription information, go to Web site www.onspec.ca; ***Neo-opsis Science Fiction Magazine***, 4129 Carey Rd., Victoria, BC, V8Z 4G5, $25.00 for a three-issue subscription; ***Albedo One***, Albedo One Productions, 2, Post Road, Lusk, Co., Dublin, Ireland, $32.00 for a four-issue airmail subscription, make checks payable to "Albedo One" or pay by PayPal at www.albedol.com; ***Lady Churchill's Rosebud Wristlet***, Small Beer Press, 150 Pleasant St., #306, Easthampton, MA 01027, $20.00 for four issues; ***Andromeda Spaceways Inflight Magazine***, see Web site www.andromedaspaceways.com for subscription information; **The Cascadia Subduction Zone: A Literary Quarterly**, subscription and single issues online at www.thecsz.com, $16 annually for a print subscription, print single issues $5, electronic subscription—PDF format—$10 per year, electronic single issue, $3, to order by check, make them payable to Aqueduct Press, P.O. Box 95787, Seattle, WA 98145–2787.

The world of online-only electronic magazines now rivals—and occasionally surpasses—the traditional print market as a place to find good new fiction.

The electronic magazine *Clarkesworld* (www.clarkesworldmagazine.com), edited by Neil Clarke and Sean Wallace, had another good year, publishing strong work by Martin L. Shoemaker, Rich Larson, Kelly Robson, Naomi Kritzer, Sara Saab, Emily Devenport, and others. They also host monthly podcasts of stories drawn from each issue. *Clarkesworld* has won three Hugo Awards as Best Semiprozine. In 2014, *Clarkesworld* co-editor Sean Wallace, along with Jack Fisher, launched a new online horror magazine, *The Dark Magazine* (thedarkmagazine.com). Neil Clarke has also launched a monthly reprint e-zine, *Forever* (forever-magazine.com).

Lightspeed (www.lightspeedmagazine.com), edited by John Joseph Adams, featured strong work by Chaz Brenchley, Matthew Hughes, Carrie Vaughn, Seanan Mc-Guire, Amal El-Mohtar, Cat Sparks, Caroline M. Yoachim, and others. *Lightspeed* won back to back Hugo Awards as Best Semiprozine in 2014 and 2015. Late in 2013, a new electronic companion horror magazine, *Nightmare* (www.nightmare-magazine .com), also edited by John Joseph Adams, was added to the *Lightspeed* stable.

Tor.com (www.tor.com), edited by Patrick Neilsen Hayden and Liz Gorinsky, with additional material purchased by Ellen Datlow, Ann VanderMeer, and others, published some first-class work by Michael Swanwick, David Herter, Veronica Schanoes, Priya Sharma, Kelly Robson, Carrie Vaughn, and others. Not a lot of strong science fiction here this year, somewhat disappointingly, but lots of good fantasy and soft horror.

Strange Horizons (www.strangehorizons.com), the oldest continually running electronic genre magazine on the Internet, started in 2000, has Niall Harrison as editor-in-chief, with former longtime editor Susan Marie Groppi and Brian Peters now serving as associate editors, and An Owomoyela and Catherine Krahe as senior fiction editors. This year, they had strong work by Kelly Link, Amal El-Mohtar, David Bowles, Marissa Lingen, Margaret Ronald, Paul Evanby, and others.

Apex Magazine (www.apex-magazine.com) had good work by Naomi Kritzer, Rich Larson, Sunny Moraine, Sarah Pinsker, Andy Dudak, Mari Ness, Thoraiya Dryer, and others. Jason Sizemore is the new editor, replacing Sigrid Ellis, who took over from Lynne M. Thomas.

Abyss & Apex (www.abyssapexzine.com) ran interesting work by Ruth Nestvold, George S. Walker, Kate MacLeod, James Victor, Alec Austin and Marissa Lingen, and others. Wendy S. Delmater, the former longtime editor, has returned to the helm, replacing Carmelo Rafala.

An e-zine devoted to "literary adventure fantasy," *Beneath Ceaseless Skies* (www .beneath-ceaseless-skies.com), edited by Scott H. Andrews, ran good stuff by Richard Parks, Yoon Ha Lee, Stephen Case, Bruce McAllister, Marissa Lingen, Erin Cashier, Ian McHugh, Rich Larson, Karalynn Lee, and others.

Long-running sword and sorcery print magazine *Black Gate*, edited by John O'Neill, transitioned into an electronic magazine in September of 2012 and can be found at www.blackgate.com. They no longer regularly run new fiction, although they will be regularly refreshing their nonfiction content, essays, and reviews, and the occasional story will continue to appear.

Galaxy's Edge (www.galaxysedge.com), edited by Mike Resnick, reached its twenty-fourth month of publication, and its seventeenth bimonthly issue, and is still going strong; it's available in various downloadable formats, although a print edition is available from BN.com and Amazon.com for $5.99 per issue. The frequent reprint stories here—by writers like Maureen McHugh, Pat Cadigan, Robert Silverberg, Jack McDevitt, Kristine Kathryn Rusch, and Gregory Benford—were still stronger than the original stories, but the magazine did publish interesting work this year by Tom Gerencer, Sean Williams, Sandra M. Odell, Larry Niven, and others, including a previously unpublished story by Robert A. Heinlein.

The Australian popular-science magazine *Cosmos* (www.cosmosmagazine.com) is not an SF magazine per se, but for the last few years it has been running a story per issue (and also putting new fiction not published in the print magazine up on their Web site). Good stuff by Thoraiya Dyer, Rjurik Davidson, Lee Battersby, Dave Luckett, and others appeared there this year. The fiction editor is SF writer Cat Sparks.

Ideomancer Speculative Fiction (www.ideomancer.com), edited by Leah Bobet, published interesting work, usually more slipstream than SF, by Arkady Martine, Michael J. DeLuca, Maya Surya Pillay, and others.

Orson Scott Card's Intergalactic Medicine Show (www.intergalacticmedicineshow .com), edited by Edmund R. Schubert under the direction of Card himself, ran interesting stuff from Alethea Kontis, Erica L. Satifka, Rob Steiner, and Stephen Case, as well as by Card.

SF/fantasy e-zine *Daily Science Fiction* (dailysciencefiction.com) publishes one new SF or fantasy story *every single day* for the entire year. Unsurprisingly, many of these were not really up to professional standards, but there were some good stories here and there by Caroline M. Yoachim, Bud Sparhawk, Eric Brown, Sean Williams, Cat Rambo, J. Y. Yang, Holly Jennings, Mari Ness, Aria Bauer, and others. Editors there are Michele-Lee Barasso and Jonathan Laden.

GigaNotoSaurus (giganotosaurus.org), now edited by Rashida J. Smith, taking over from Ann Leckie, published one story a month by writers such as Patricia Russo, Maggie Clark, E. Catherine Tobler, Mark Pantoja, and others.

An audacious newcomer is *Uncanny* (uncannymagazine.com), edited by Lynne M. Thomas and Michael Damien Thomas, which launched in late 2014, had a strong year in 2015 with good work by Elizabeth Bear, Hao Jingfang, Rose Lemberg, Sam J. Miller, Charlie Jane Anders, Yoon Ha Lee, Sam J. Miller, Mary Robinette Kowal, and others.

Kaleidotrope (www.kaleidotrope.net), edited by Fred Coppersmith, which started in 2006 as a print semiprozine but transitioned to digital in 2012, published interesting work by Michael Andre-Driussi, C.A.L, Jeste de Vries, Gemma Files, and others.

The World SF Blog (worldsf.wordpress.com), edited by Lavie Tidhar, was a good place to find science fiction by international authors, and also published news, links, round-table discussions, essays, and interviews related to "science fiction, fantasy, horror, and comics from around the world." The site is no longer being updated, but an extensive archive is still accessible there.

A similar site is *International Speculative Fiction* (http://internationalSF.wordpress .com), edited by Roberto Mendes.

Weird Fiction Review (weirdfictionreview.com), edited by Ann VanderMeer and Jeff VanderMeer, which occasionally publishes fiction, bills itself as "an ongoing exploration into all facets of the weird," including reviews, interviews, short essays, and comics.

Ideomancer (www.ideomancer.com), edited by Leah Bobet, doesn't seem to have refreshed its content since volume 14, issue 1, which was put up on March 1, 2015. Similarly, *Straeon* (www.rampantloonmedia.com/straeon), edited by M. David Blake, *Terraform* (motherboard.vice.com/terraform), edited by Claire Evans and Brian Merchant, and *Michael Moorcock's New Worlds* (www.newworlds.co.uk), edited by Roger Gray, haven't refreshed content for a long time, and *Child of Words* (www.bigpulp.com), edited by Bill Olver, is running a notice saying that they have a new site under construction. *Crossed Genres* (www.crossedgenres.com), edited by Bart R. Leib, Kay T. Holt, and Kelly Jennings, is ceasing production. Other newcomers include *Omenana Magazine of Africa's Speculative Fiction* (omenana.com), edited by Chinelo Onwualu and Chiagozie Fred Nwonwu.

Below this point, it becomes harder to find center-core SF, or even genre fantasy/horror, with most magazines featuring slipstream or literary surrealism instead. Such sites include *Fireside Magazine* (www.firesidefiction.com), edited by Brian White; *Revolution SF* (www.revolutionsf.com); *Heliotrope* (www.heliotropemag.com); and *Interfictions Online* (interfictions.com/), executive editor Delila Sherman, fiction editors Christopher Barzak and Meghan McCarron.

But there's also a lot of good *reprint* SF and fantasy to be found on the Internet. Sites where you can access formerly published stories for free, including *Strange Horizons, Tor.com, Clarkesworld, Lightspeed, Subterranean, Abyss & Apex, Apex,* and most of the sites that are associated with existent print magazines, such as *Asimov's, Analog,* and *The Magazine of Fantasy & Science Fiction*, make previously published fiction and nonfiction available for access on their sites as well, and also regularly run teaser excerpts from stories coming up in forthcoming issues. Hundreds of out-of-print titles, both genre and mainstream, are also available for free download from *Project Gutenberg* (www.gutenberg.org), and a large selection of novels and a few collections can also be accessed for free, to be either downloaded or read on-screen, at the *Baen Free Library* (www.baen.com/library). Sites such as *Infinity Plus* (www.infinityplus.co.uk) and *The Infinite Matrix* (www.infinitematrix.net) may no longer be active, but their extensive archives of previously published material are still accessible (an extensive line of Infinity Plus Books can also be ordered from the *Infinity Plus* site).

But beyond looking for SF stories to read, there are plenty of other reasons for SF fans to go on the Internet. There are many general genre-related sites of interest to be found, most of which publish reviews of books as well as of movies and TV shows, sometimes comics or computer games or anime, many of which also feature interviews, critical articles, and genre-oriented news of various kinds. The best such site is *Locus Online* (www.locusmag.com), the online version of the newsmagazine *Locus*, where you can access an incredible amount of information—including book reviews, critical lists, obituary lists, links to reviews and essays appearing outside the genre, and links to extensive database archives such as the Locus Index to Science Fiction and the Locus Index to Science Fiction Awards. The previously mentioned *Tor.com* is also one of the most eclectic genre-oriented sites on the Internet, a Web site that, in addition to its fiction, regularly publishes articles, comics, graphics, blog entries, print and media reviews, book "rereads" and episode-by-episode "rewatches" of television shows, as well as commentary on all the above. The long-running and eclectic *The New York Review of Science Fiction* has ceased print publication, but can be purchased in PDF, e-pub and mobi formats, and POD editions through Weightless Press (http://weightlessbooks.com; see also www.nyrsf.com for information). Other major general-interest sites include *io9* (www.io9.com), *SF Signal* (www.sfsignal.com), *SF Site* (www.sfsite.com)—although it's no longer being regularly updated—*SFRevu* (http://www.sfsite.com/sfrevu), *SFCrowsnest* (www.sfcrowsnest.com), *SFScope* (www.sfscope.com), *Green Man Review* (greenmanreview.com),

The Agony Column (trashotron.com/agony), *SFFWorld* (www.sffworld.com), *SF-Reader* (sfreader.com), and *Pat's Fantasy Hotlist* (www.fantasyhotlist.blogspot.com). A great research site, invaluable if you want bibliographic information about SF and fantasy writers, is *Fantastic Fiction* (www.fantasticfiction.co.uk). Another wonderful research site is the searchable online update of the Hugo-winning *The Encyclopedia of Science Fiction* (www.sf-encyclopedia.com), where you can access almost four million words of information about SF writers, books, magazines, and genre themes. Reviews of short fiction as opposed to novels are very hard to find anywhere, with the exception of *Locus* and *Locus Online*, but you can find reviews of both current and past short fiction at *Best SF* (www.bestsf.net), as well as at pioneering short-fiction review site *Tangent Online* (www.tangentonline.com). Other sites of interest include: *Ansible* (news.ansible.co.uk/Ansible), the online version of multiple Hugo winner David Langford's long-running fanzine *Ansible*; SFF NET (www.sff.net), which features dozens of home pages and "newsgroups" for SF writers; the Science Fiction and Fantasy Writers of America page (www.sfwa.org), where genre news, obituaries, award information, and recommended reading lists can be accessed; *Book View Café* (www.bookviewcafe.com) is a "consortium of over twenty professional authors," including Vonda N. McIntyre, Laura Ann Gilman, Sarah Zittel, Brenda Clough, and others, who have created a Web site where their work—mostly reprints, and some novel excerpts—is made available for free.

Sites where podcasts and SF-oriented radio plays can be accessed have also pro-liferated in recent years: at *Audible* (www.audible.com), *Escape Pod* (escapepod.org, podcasting mostly SF), *SF Squeecast* (sfsqueecast.com), *The Coode Street Podcast* (jonathanstrahan.podbean.com), *The Drabblecast* (www.drabblecast.org), *StarShip-Sofa* (www.starshipsofa.com), *Far Fetched Fables* (www.farfetchedfables.com)—new companion to *StarShipSofa*, concentrating on fantasy—*SF Signal Podcast* (www.sfsignal.com), *Pseudopod* (pseudopod.org), podcasting mostly fantasy, *PodCastle* (podcastle.org), podcasting mostly fantasy, and *Galactic Suburbia* (galacticsuburbia.podbean.com). *Clarkesworld* routinely offers podcasts of stories from the e-zine, and *The Agony Column* (agonycolumn.com) also hosts a weekly podcast. There's also a site that podcasts nonfiction interviews and reviews, *Dragon Page Cover to Cover* (www.dragonpage.com).

2015 was overall another fairly unimpressive year for short fiction, although there were a number of strong novellas. As usual, though, so much short fiction is now published in so many different mediums, print, electronic, audio, as stand-alone chapbook novellas that it wasn't hard to find more good material if you looked for it than most people would probably be willing to spend the time to read.

There were fewer SF anthologies this year, although there were a few strong ones. Anthologies this year seemed to fall into several loose groupings.

There were the futurology-oriented anthologies, with stories usually set no more than a few decades into the future and dealing largely with societal change, the best of which, and the best original SF anthology of the year overall, was *Meeting Infinity*, edited by Jonathan Strahan, which featured excellent work by Ian McDonald,

Gwyneth Jones, Aliette de Bodard, James S. A. Corey, Nancy Kress, John Barnes, Yoon Ha Lee, and others. Another very strong futurology-oriented anthology was *Future Visions: Original Science Fiction Inspired by Microsoft*, edited by Jennifer Henshaw and Allison Linn, which was not "published" at all in the traditional sense, but rather was made available as a free e-book from all major e-book platforms. The idea here was that Microsoft invited leading SF writers to make in-person visits to Microsoft's research labs, where they talked to scientists and received "inside access to leading-edge work" that then inspired the stories they wrote; in spite of this somewhat eccentric origin, the anthology is full of first-rate stories by Nancy Kress, Ann Leckie, Seanan McGuire, Elizabeth Bear, Greg Bear, and others. Yet another futurology anthology was *Twelve Tomorrows*, edited by Bruce Sterling, the fourth volume in a series of annual original SF anthologies in magazine form published by the people who also produce *MIT Technology Review* magazine; I found this one to be somewhat weaker than some of the other volumes in this series had been, although there was still good stuff here by John Kessel, Ned Beauman, Bruce Sterling himself, and others. *Stories for Chip: A Tribute to Samuel R. Delany*, edited by Nisi Shawl and Bill Campbell, doesn't fit entirely comfortably within the futurology-oriented category, as there are mainstream stories, fantasy stories, and critical articles about Delany here as well, but enough of the stories deal with cultural changes in future societies (as much of Delany's own work has done) that I think a justification can be made for listing it here; it's a very strong anthology, with excellent stuff by Geoff Ryman, Benjamin Rosenbaum, Nick Harkaway, Nalo Hopkinson and Nisi Shawl, Chris Brown, Anil Menon, Alex Jennings, and others. The weakest of the futurology-oriented original SF anthologies was *The Atlantic Council Art of Future Warfare Project: War Stories from the Future*, edited by August Cole; produced by the Atlantic Council, a self-described "think tank," the emphasis here is on future warfare rather than futurology per se, with most of the stories seeming to describe the present we already live in rather than the future—there was still good stuff here, though, by Madeline Ashby, Ken Liu, Matthew Burrows, and others.

Another group of anthologies dealt with apocalypses and post-apocalyptic landscapes, with the apocalypses for the most part being generated by catastrophic climate change: rising sea levels, failing crops, extreme weather, worldwide pandemics, armed conflicts over shrinking resources. Stories of similar sorts were to be found all over the market this year, in magazines, anthologies, and online venues (obviously, watching stories of our crazy weather this year on the news is having an effect on writers), but there were also three anthologies dedicated to the theme, one original and two reprint. The strongest of the three was the original *The End Has Come*, edited by John Joseph Adams and Hugh Howey, the concluding volume in the Apocalypse Triptych, a three-anthology series that started with *The End Is Nigh* and *The End Is Now* last year; this one features good work by Carrie Vaughn, Annie Bellet, Ken Liu, Tananarive Due, Sarah Langan, Jake Kerr, Nancy Kress, Elizabeth Bear, and others. The other two are *Loosed upon the World: The Saga Anthology of Climate Fiction*, edited by John Joseph Adams, a reprint anthology with good reprints from Paolo Bacigalupi, Seanan McGuire, Vandana Sighn, Robert Silverberg, Sean McMullen, Karl Schroeder, Cat Sparks, and others, and *Wastelands 2: More*

Stories of the Apocalypse, edited by John Joseph Adams, another reprint anthology, with good reprints from Lauren Beukes, George R. R. Martin, Tananarive Due, James Van Pelt, Joe R. Lansdale, Maureen F. McHugh, and others.

Another grouping of anthologies had feminist themes. There were two reprint anthologies, including one released only in digital form, of science fiction by women writers: *Sisters of the Revolution: A Feminist Speculative Fiction Anthology* (PM Press), edited by Ann VanderMeer and Jeff VanderMeer, and (the digital one) *Digital Dreams: A Decade of Science Fiction by Women* (New Con Press), edited by Ian Whates; *Warrior Women* (Prime Books), edited by Paula Guran, and two anthologies of horror stories written by women, *Daughters of Frankenstein: Lesbian Mad Scientists* (Lethe Press), edited by Steve Berman, and *Blood Sisters: Vampire Stories by Women* (Night Shade Books), edited by Paula Guran. *Hear Me Roar!* (Ticonderoga Press), edited by Liz Gryzb, an anthology dedicated to stories about "independent women dealing with the world around them," would also fit under this heading, as would *Cranky Ladies of History* (FableCroft Publishing), edited by Tehani Wessely and Tansy Rayner Roberts. Also it seems appropriate to mention here a book of art by women artists, *Women of Wonder: Celebrating Women Creators of Fantastic Art* (Underwood Books), edited by Cathy Fenner.

Anthologies that were a bit harder to group together with others by theme included *Mission: Tomorrow* (Baen), edited by Bryan Thomas Schmidt, a solid anthology of core science fiction, with good stories by Michael F. Flynn, Jack Skillingstead, David D. Levine, and others; *Press Start to Play*, edited by Daniel H. Wilson and John Joseph Adams, a mixed original and reprint anthology of gaming fiction, with good work by Holly Black, Robin Wasserman, Andy Weir, Ken Liu, Cory Doctorow, and others; *The Mammoth Book of Dieselpunk* (Running Press), edited by Sean Wallace; *Not Our Kind* (Alliteration Ink), edited by Nayad Monroe; *The Time It Happened* (Third Flatiron Press), edited by Juliana Rew; *Insert Title Here* (FableCroft Publishing), edited by Tehani Wessely; and *Jews vs. Aliens* and *Jews vs. Zombies* (Jurassic London), both edited by Lavie Tidhar and Rebecca Levene. *Postscripts 34/35: Breakout* (PS Publishing), edited by Nick Gevers, featured, as usual, mostly slipstream, fantasy, and soft horror stories, without much core SF, although there were good SF stories by John Gribben, Garry Kilworth, and others, and a couple of collaborative horror stories by the late Steven Utley. There were also a number of anthologies from *Fiction River*, which in 2013 launched a continuing series of original SF, fantasy, and mystery anthologies, with Kristine Kathryn Rusch and Dean Wesley Smith as overall series editors, and individual editions edited by various hands. This year, they published *Pulse Pounders* (WMG), edited by Kevin J. Anderson; *Recycled Pulp* (WMG), edited by John Helfers; *Valor* (WMG), edited by Lee Allred; *Alchemy and Steam* (WMG), edited by Kerrie L. Hughes; and *Risk Takers* (WMG), edited by Dean Wesley Smith. These can be purchased in Kindle versions from Amazon and other online vendors, or from the publisher at www.wmgpublishinginc.com.

Noted without comment is a retro SF anthology, *Old Venus* (Bantam Books), edited by George R. R. Martin and Gardner Dozois.

There were six tribute anthologies to the work of individual SF/fantasy authors, many of which allowed other writers to play with the settings and characters of the authors featured: *Stories for Chip: A Tribute to Samuel R. Delany* (Rosarium Publishing), edited by Nisi Shawl and Bill Campbell, mentioned earlier; *The Change: Tales of Downfall and Rebirth* (Roc), paying tribute to the works of S. M. Stirling; *Octavia's Brood: Science Fiction Stories from Social Justice Movements* (AK Press), edited by Walidah Imarisha and adrienne maree brown, paying tribute to the works of Octavia Butler; *nEvermore! Tales of Murder, Mystery and the Macabre* (Hades/Edge Science Fiction and Fantasy), edited by Nancy Kilpatrick and Caro Soles, paying tribute to the work of Edgar Allan Poe; *Onward, Drake!* (Baen), edited by Mark L. Van Name, paying tribute to the works of David Drake; and *Midian Unmade: Tales of Clive Barker's Nightbreed* (Tor), edited by Joesph Nassise and Del Howison, paying tribute to the works of Clive Barker. There were four shared-world anthologies, *Grantville Gazette VII* (Baen), edited by Eric Flint; *By Tooth and Claw* (Baen), edited by Bill Fawcett; *In the Shadow of the Towers: Speculative Fiction in the Post 9/11 World* (Skyhorse/Night Shade Books), edited by Douglas Lain; and *Crucible: All-New Tales of Valdemar* (DAW), edited by Mercedes Lackey.

There weren't many fantasy anthologies this year. Of the few that there were, the most substantial by a good margin was probably *Operation Arcana* (Baen), an original anthology of "military fantasy" edited by John Joseph Adams, which featured good stuff by Carrie Vaughn, Linda Nagata, Simon R. Green, Glen Cook, Yoon Ha Lee, David Klecha and Tobias S. Buckell, and others.

As usual, most of the year's prominent horror anthologies seemed to be edited by the indefatigable Ellen Datlow, including *The Doll Collection* (Tor), and a major reprint anthology, *The Monstrous* (Tachyon Publications). Paula Guran edited *New Cthulhu 2: More Recent Weird* (Prime), S. T. Joshi edited *The Madness of Cthulhu, Volume Two* (Titan) and *Black Wings of Cthulhu, Volume Three* (Titan), Christopher Golden edited *Seize the Night: New Tales of Vampiric Terror* (Simon & Schuster), Nancy Kilpatrick edited *Expiration Date* (Hades/Edge Science Fiction and Fantasy), and Steven Jones edited *Horrorology: The Lexicon of Fear* (Quercus/Jo Fletcher).

Anthologies that provided an overview of what's happening in fantastic literature in countries other than the USA included *Hanzai Japan: Fantastical, Futuristic Stories of Crime From and About Japan* (Haikasoru), edited by Nick Mamatas and Masumi Washington; *The Sea Is Ours: Tales from Steampunk Southeast Asia* (Rosarium), edited by Jaymee Goh and Joyce Chng; *Imaginarium 3: The Best Canadian Speculative Writing* (ChiZine Publications), edited by Sandra Kasturi and Helen Marshall; and *Tesseracts Eighteen: Wrestling with Gods* (Hades/Edge Science Fiction and Fantasy), edited by Liana Kerzner and Jerome Stueart.

L. Ron Hubbard Presents Writers of the Future Volume 31 (Galaxy), edited by David Farland, is the most recent in a long-running series featuring novice work by beginning writers, some of whom may later turn out to be important talents.

Novella chapbooks in 2015 included: *Slow Bullets*, by Alastair Reynolds; *Wylding Hall*, by Elizabeth Hand; *The Last Witness*, by K. J. Parker; *Speak Easy*, by Catherynne M. Valente; *Penric's Demon*, by Lois McMaster Bujold; *The Deep Woods*, by Tim Pratt; *Little Sisters*, by Vonda N. McIntyre; *In the Lovecraft Museum*, by Steve Rasnic Tem; *Teaching the Dog to Read*, by Jonathan Carroll; *Binti*, by Nnedi Okorafor; and *The Two Paupers*, by C. S. E. Cooney.

Former holders of the title of "most prolific author at short lengths" Ken Liu,

Lavie Tidhar, and Robert Reed didn't write quite as much this year; the most prolific author was probably new writer Rich Larson, although he was given a run for
his money by Naomi Kritzer, Yoon Ha Lee, Matthew Hughes, Elizabeth Bear, Marissa Lingen, Carrie Vaughn, and Caroline M. Yoachim.

(Finding individual pricings for all of the items from small presses mentioned in the
Summation has become too time-intensive, and since several of the same small
presses publish anthologies, novels, *and* short-story collections, it seems silly to repeat addresses for them in section after section. Therefore, I'm going to attempt to
list here, in one place, all the addresses for small presses that have books mentioned
here or there in the Summation, whether from the anthologies section, the novel
section, or the short-story collection section, and, where known, their Web site addresses. That should make it easy enough for the reader to look up the individual
price of any book mentioned that isn't from a regular trade publisher; such books
are less likely to be found in your average bookstore, or even in a chain superstore,
and so will probably have to be mail-ordered. Many publishers seem to sell only
online through their Web sites, and some will only accept payment through PayPal.
Many books, even from some of the smaller presses, are also available through Am-
azon.com. If you can't find an address for a publisher, and it's quite likely that I've
missed some here, or failed to update them successfully, Google it. It shouldn't be
that difficult these days to find up-to-date contact information for almost any publisher, however small.)

Addresses: **PS Publishing**, Grosvener House, 1 New Road, Hornsea, West York-
shire, HU18 1PG, England, UK, www.pspublishing.co.uk; **Golden Gryphon Press**,
3002 Perkins Road, Urbana, IL 61802, www.goldengryphon.com; **NESFA Press**, P.O.
Box 809, Framingham, MA 01701-0809, www.nesfa.org; **Subterranean Press**,
P.O. Box 190106, Burton, MI 48519, www.subterraneanpress.com; **Old Earth Books**,
P.O. Box 19951, Baltimore, MD 21211-0951, www.oldearthbooks.com; **Tachyon
Press**, 1459 18th St. #139, San Francisco, CA 94107, www.tachyonpublications
.com; **Night Shade Books**, 1470 NW Saltzman Road, Portland, OR 97229, www
.nightshadebooks.com; **Five Star Books**, 295 Kennedy Memorial Drive, Waterville,
ME 04901, www.galegroup.com/fivestar; **NewCon Press**, via www.newconpress.com;
Small Beer Press, 176 Prospect Ave., Northampton, MA 01060, www.smallbeer
press.com; **Locus Press**, P.O. Box 13305, Oakland, CA 94661; **Crescent Books**,
Mercat Press Ltd., 10 Coates Crescent, Edinburgh, Scotland EH3 7AL, www.crescent
fiction.com; **Wildside Press/ Borgo Press,** P.O. Box 301, Holicong, PA 18928–0301, or
go to www.wildsidepress.com for pricing and ordering; **Edge Science Fiction and Fan-
tasy Publishing, Inc. and Tesseract Books, Ltd.**, P.O. Box 1714, Calgary, Alberta, T2P
2L7, Canada, www.edgewebsite.com; **Aqueduct Press**, P.O. Box 95787, Seattle, WA
98145–2787, www.aqueductpress.com; **Phobos Books**, 200 Park Avenue South,
New York, NY 10003, www.phobosweb.com; **Fairwood Press**, 5203 Quincy Ave.
SE, Auburn, WA 98092, www.fairwoodpress.com; **BenBella Books**, 6440 N. Central
Expressway, Suite 508, Dallas, TX 75206, www.benbellabooks.com; **Darkside
Press**, 13320 27th Ave. NE, Seattle, WA 98125, www.darksidepress.com; **Haffner
Press**, 5005 Crooks Rd., Suite 35, Royal Oak, MI 48073–1239, www.haffnerpress

.com; **North Atlantic Press**, P.O. Box 12327, Berkeley, CA, 94701; **Prime Books**, P.O. Box 36503, Canton, OH, 44735, www.primebooks.net; **MonkeyBrain Books**, 11204 Crossland Drive, Austin, TX 78726, www.monkeybrainbooks.com; **Wesleyan University Press**, University Press of New England, Order Dept., 37 Lafayette St., Lebanon NH 03766–1405, www.wesleyan.edu/wespress; **Agog! Press**, P.O. Box U302, University of Wollongong, NSW 2522, Australia, www.uow.ed.au/~rhood/agogpress; **Wheatland Press**, via www.wheatlandpress.com; **MirrorDanse Books**, P.O. Box 3542, Parramatta NSW 2124, Australia, www.tabula-rasa.info/MirrorDanse; **Arsenal Pulp Press**, 103–1014 Homer Street, Vancouver, BC, Canada V6B 2W9, www.arsenalpress.com; **DreamHaven Books**, 912 W. Lake Street, Minneapolis, MN 55408; **Elder Signs Press/Dimensions Books**, order through www.dimensionsbooks.com; **Chaosium**, via www.chaosium.com; **Spyre Books**, P.O. Box 3005, Radford, VA 24143; **SCIFI, Inc.**, P.O. Box 8442, Van Nuys, CA 91409–8442; **Omnidawn Publishing**, order through www.omnidawn.com; **CSFG**, Canberra Speculative Fiction Guild, via www.csfg.org.au/publishing/anthologies/the_outcast; **Hadley Rille Books**, via www.hadleyrillebooks.com; **Suddenly Press**, via suddenlypress@yahoo.com; **Sandstone Press**, P.O. Box 5725, Dochcarty Road, Dingwall, Ross-shire UK, IV15 9UG, www.sandstonepress.com; **Tropism Press**, via www.tropismpress.com; **SF Poetry Association/Dark Regions Press**, via www.sfpoetry.com, checks to Helena Bell, SFPA Treasurer, 1225 West Freeman St., Apt. 12, Carbondale, IL 62401; **DH Press**, via diamondbookdistributors.com; **Kurodahan Press**, via www.kurodahan.com; **Ramble House**, 443 Gladstone Blvd., Shreveport LA 71104, www.ramblehouse.com; **Interstitial Arts Foundation**, via www.interstitialarts.org; **Raw Dog Screaming**, via www.rawdogscreaming.com; **Three Legged Fox Books**, 98 Hythe Road, Brighton, BN1 6JS, UK; **Norilana Books**, via www.norilana.com; **coeur de lion**, via coeurdelion.com.au; **PARSECink**, via www.parsecink.org; **Robert J. Sawyer Books**, via www.sfwriter.com/rjsbooks.htm; **Rackstraw Press**, via http://rackstrawpress onfshost.com; **Candlewick**, via www.candlewick.com; **Zubaan**, via www.zubaanbooks.com; **Utter Tower**, via www.threeleggedfox.co.uk; **Spilt Milk Press**, via www.electricvelocipede.com; **Paper Golem**, via www.papergolem.com; **Galaxy Press**, via www.galaxypress.com; **Twelfth Planet Press**, via www.twelfthplanetpress.com; **Five Senses Press**, via www.sensefive.com; **Elastic Press**, via www.elasticpress.com; **Lethe Press**, via www.lethepressbooks.com; **Two Cranes Press**, via www.twocranespress.com; **Wordcraft of Oregon**, via www.wordcraftoforegon.com; **Down East**, via www.downeast.com; **ISFiC Press**, 456 Douglas Ave., Elgin, IL 60120 or www.isficpress.com.

According to the newsmagazine *Locus*, there were 2,625 books "of interest to the SF field" published in 2015, up 7 percent from 2,459 titles in 2014, the first rise in overall books published in three years. New titles were up 4 percent to 1,820 from 2014's 1,750, while reprints also rose by 14 percent to 805 from 2014's 709. Hardcover sales rose by 7 percent to 849 from 2014's 799; the number of trade paperbacks rose even more significantly, up 17 percent to 1,343 from 2014's 1,149. Mass-market paperbacks, the format facing the most competition from e-books, continued to drop, down 15 percent, to 433 from 2014's 511. The number of new SF novels was up to

396 titles from 2014's 367 titles, with 95 of those titles being YA SF novels. The number of new fantasy novels climbed to 682 titles from 2014's 620 titles, with 225 of those titles being YA fantasy novels. Horror novels were down slightly to 183 titles from 2014's 187 titles. Paranormal romances continued to slide, down to 111 titles from 2014's 148 titles.

This is an enormous number of books, far more than the entire combined total of genre titles only a few decades back. And these totals don't count many e-books, media tie-in novels, gaming novels, novelizations of genre movies, print-on-demand books, or self-published novels—all of which would swell the overall total by hundreds if counted.

As usual, busy with all the reading I have to do at shorter lengths, I didn't have time to read many novels myself this year, so I'll limit myself to mentioning those novels that received a lot of attention and acclaim in 2015.

Luna: New Moon (Tor), by Ian McDonald; *The House of Shattered Wings* (Roc), by Aliette de Bodard; *Something Coming Through* (Gollancz), by Paul McAuley; *The Water Knife* (Knopf), by Paolo Bacigalupi; *Aurora* (Orbit), by Kim Stanley Robinson; *Ancillary Mercy* (Orbit), by Ann Leckie; *Chasing the Phoenix* (Tor), by Michael Swanwick; *Tracker* (DAW), by C. J. Cherryh; *Karen Memory* (Tor), by Elizabeth Bear; *Half a War* (Del Rey), by Joe Abercrombie; *The Dark Forest* (Tor), by Cixin Liu; *The End of All Things* (Tor), by John Scalzi; *Nemesis Games* (Orbit), by James S. A. Corey; *The Affinities* (Tor), by Robert Charles Wilson; *Uprooted* (Del Rey), by Naomi Novik; *Harrison Squared* (Tor), by Daryl Gregory; *The Book of Phoenix* (DAW), by Nnedi Okorafor; *The Just City* (Tor), by Jo Walton; *The Philosopher Kings* (Tor), by Jo Walton; *Finches of Mars* (Open Road), by Brian W. Aldiss; *Fool's Quest* (Del Rey), by Robin Hobb; *The Annihilation Score* (Ace), by Charles Stross; *Pacific Fire* (Tor), by Greg van Eekhout; *A Borrowed Man* (Tor), by Gene Wolfe; *Dark Orbit* (Tor), by Carolyn Ives Gilman; *U Where* (Tor), by Kit Reed; *The Flicker Men* (Henry Holt and Co.), by Ted Kosmatka; *Corsair* (Tor), by James L. Cambias; *Finders Keepers* (Scribner), by Stephen King; and the last Discworld novel, *The Shepherd's Crown* (Harper), by Terry Pratchett.

In the face of continued rumblings about how the shelf space for science fiction is on the decline, let me mention that in the list just given that the McDonald, the McAuley, the Robinson, the Leckie, the Cherryh, the Liu, the Corey, the Wilson, and many others are not only SF, but rather hard SF at that.

Small presses are active in the novel market these days, where once they published mostly collections and anthologies. Novels by established authors issued by small presses this year included: *Savages* (Subterranean), by K. J. Parker; *Dark Intelligence* (Night Shade Books), by Neal Asher; *Wylding Hall* (PS Publishing), by Elizabeth Hand; *Persona* (Saga), by Genevieve Valentine; and *Cracking the Sky* (Fairwood Press), by Brenda Cooper.

The year's first novels included: *The Grace of Kings* (Saga), by Ken Liu; *Archangel* (Arche Press), by Marguerite Reed; *Updraft* (Tor), by Fran Wilde; *Clash of Eagles* (Ballantine/Del Rey), by Alan Smale; *Battlemage* (Orbit), by Stephen Aryan; *Sorcerer to the Crown* (Ace), by Zen Cho; *Flesh and Wires* (Aqueduct), by Jackie Hatton; *Inherit the Stars* (Roc), by Tony Peak; *The Diabolical Miss Hyde* (Harper Voyager), by Viola Carr; *Y Negative* (Riptide), by Kelly Haworth; *Solomon's Arrow*

(Skyhorse/Talos Press), by J. Dalton Jennings; *The Traitor Baru Cormorant* (Tor), by Seth Dickinson; *Mystic* (Tor), by Jason Denzel; *Gideon* (Harper Voyager), by Alex Gordon; *The Weave* (Aqueduct), by Nancy Jane Moore; *Half-Resurrection Blues* (Roc), by Daniel José Older; *The Watchmaker of Filigree Street* (Bloomsbury), by Natasha Pulley; *The Promise of the Child* (Skyhorse/Night Shade), by Tom Toner; *RAM-2050* (Kauai Institure), by Joan Roughgarden; *Windswept* (Angry Robot), by Adam Rakunas; *Sunset Mantle* (Tor), by Alter S. Reiss; *The Night Clock* (Solaris), by Paul Meloy; *The Shards of Heaven* (Tor), by Michael Livingston; *Last Song Before Night* (Tor), by Ilana C. Myer; *Signal to Noise* (Solaris), by Silvia Moreno-Garcia; *Vermilion* (Word Horde), by Molly Tanzer; *Abomination* (Inkshares), by Gary Whitta; *A Crucible of Souls* (Harper Voyager), by Mitchell Hogan; *Finn Fancy Necromancy* (Tor), by Randy Henderson; *Apocalypse Now Now* (Titan), by Charlie Human; *The Pilots of Borealis* (Skyhorse/Talos Press), by David Nabhan; *The King of the Cracksmen* (Skyhorse/Night Shade Books), by Dennis O'Flaherty; *The Buried Life* (Angry Robot), by Carrie Patel; *Marked* (Quercus/Jo Fletcher), by Sue Tingey; and *The Sorcerer of the Wildeeps* (Tor), by Kai Ashante Wilson. No first novel dominated the category in the clear and unequivocal way that Andy Weir's *The Martian* did last year, but Ken Liu's *The Grace of Kings* probably attracted the most attention, although the Reed, the Wilde, and the Smale got a fair number of reviews as well.

There were far fewer novel omnibuses available this year than last year, when Orion unleashed an unprecedented flood with its SF Gateway program. Novel omnibuses that were available this year, though, included *A, B, C: Three Short Novels* (Vintage), by Samuel R. Delany; *Gateway to Never* (Baen), by A. Bertram Chandler; and *Confluence—The Trilogy* (Orion/Gollancz), by Paul J. McAuley.

Novel omnibuses are also frequently made available through the Science Fiction Book Club.

Not even counting print-on-demand books and the availability of out-of-print books as e-books or as electronic downloads from Internet sources, a lot of long out-of-print stuff has come back into print in the last couple of years in commercial trade editions. Here's some out-of-print titles that came back into print this year, although producing a definitive list of reissued novels is probably impossible.

In addition to the novel omnibuses already mentioned, Orion/Gollancz reissued *Windhaven*, by George R. R. Martin and Lisa Tutttle, and *The Disposessed*, by Ursula K. Le Guin; Gollancz reissued *Downward to the Earth*, by Robert Silverberg; Tor reissued *The Edge of Reason*, by Melinda Snodgrass, *Kushiel's Dart*, by Jacqueline Carey, *Eon*, by Greg Bear, and *Jewel and Amulet*, by Michael Moorcock; Skyhorse/Night Shade Books reissued *The Windup Girl*, by Paolo Bacigalupi, and *Diaspora, Distress, Schild's Ladder*, and *Teranesia*, all by Greg Egan; Fairwood Press reissued *A Funeral for the Eyes of Fire*, by Michael Bishop; Aqueduct Press reissued *Daughter of the Bear King*, by Eleanor Arnason; Penguin Classics reissued *Perchance to Dream*, by Charles Beaumont; Little, Brown reissued *Seven Wild Sisters*, by Charles de Lint; Simon & Schuster reissued *Dragonsinger*, by Anne McCaffrey; Bloomsbury reissued *Harry Potter and the Philosopher's Stone: Illustrated Edition*, by J. K. Rowling; Ace reissued *The Hercules Text*, by Jack McDevitt; Titan reissued *The Bull and the Spear, The King of the Swords, The Sword and the Stallion*, and *The Night Mayor*, all by Michael Moorcock; DAW reissued *The Birthgrave*, by Tanith Lee; Valancourt Books reissued *The Brains of Rats*, by Michael Blumlein.

Many authors are now reissuing their old back titles as e-books, either through a publisher or all by themselves, so many that it's impossible to keep track of them all here. Before you conclude that something from an author's backlist is unavailable, though, check with the Kindle and Nook stores, and with other online vendors.

2015 was another good year for short-story collections.

The year's best collections included: *The Best of Nancy Kress* (Subterranean), by Nancy Kress; *Frost on Glass* (PS Publishing), by Ian R. MacLeod; *The Best of Alastair Reynolds* (Subterrranean), by Alastair Reynolds; *The Best of Gregory Benford* (Subterranean), by Gregory Benford, edited by David G. Hartwell; *A Knight of the Seven Kingdoms* (Bantam), by George R. R. Martin; *Get in Trouble: Stories* (Random House), by Kelly Link; *Trigger Warning: Short Fictions and Disturbances* (William Morrow), by Neil Gaiman; *The Very Best of Kate Elliott* (Tachyon), by Kate Elliott; *Romance on Four Worlds: A Casanova Quartet* (Fantastic Books), by Tom Purdom; *Beneath an Oil-Dark Sea: The Best of Caitlín R. Kiernan, Volume 2* (Subterranean), by Caitlín R. Kiernan; *The Bazaar of Bad Dreams* (Scribner), by Stephen King; and *To Hold the Bridge* (HarperCollins), by Garth Nix.

Also good were: *Ghost Summer: Stories* (Prime), by Tananarive Due; *A Palazzo in the Stars* (Wildside Press), by Paul Di Filippo; *We Install and Other Stories* (Open Road), by Harry Turtledove; *Three Moments of an Explosion* (Ballantine Del Rey), by China Miéville; *Falling in Love with Hominids* (Tachyon), by Nalo Hopkinson; *The End of the End of Everything* (Arche Press), by Dale Bailey; *Led Astray: The Best of Kelly Armstrong* (Tachyon), by Kelly Armstrong; *Tales from the Nightside* (Ace), by Simon R. Green; *Reality by Other Means: The Best Short Fiction of James Morrow* (Wesleyan University Press), by James Morrow; *Cracking the Sky* (Fairwood Press), by Brenda Cooper; *Word Puppets*, (Prime), by Mary Robinette Kowal; *Blue Yonders, Grateful Pies, and Other Fanciful Feasts* (Fairwood Press), by Ken Scholes; and *You Have Never Been Here: New and Selected Stories* (Small Beer Press), by Mary Rickert.

Career-spanning retrospective collections this year included: *Grand Crusades: The Early Jack Vance, Volume Five* (Subterranean), by Jack Vance, edited by Terry Dowling and Jonathan Strahan; *The Complete Short Stories: The 1960s (Part 2)* (Harper Voyager), by Brian W. Aldiss; *I Am Crying All Inside and Other Stories: The Complete Short Fiction of Clifford D. Simak, Volume 1* (Open Road), by Clifford D. Simak; *The Man with the Aura: The Collected Short Fiction, Volume Two* (Centipede Press), by R. A. Lafferty; *Dancing Through the Fire* (Fantastic Books), by Tanith Lee; *Tales from High Hallack: The Collected Short Stories of Andre Norton, Volume Three* (Open Road), by Andre Norton; *Gateway to Never* (Baen), by A. Bertram Chandler; *A Blink of the Screen: Collected Shorter Fiction* (Random House), by Terry Pratchett; *Dragons at Crumbling Castle* (Hougton Mifflin Harcourt), by Terry Pratchett; *The Essential W. P. Kinsella* (Tachyon), by W. P. Kinsella; *Can & Can'takerous* (Subterranean), by Harlan Ellison; *H. P. Lovecraft's Collected Fiction:*

A *Variorum Edition* (Hippocampus Press), by H. P. Lovecraft, edited by S. T. Joshi; *Working for Bigfoot* (Subterranean), by Jim Butcher; *Fathoms* (Resurrection House), by Jack Cady; and *Let Me Tell You: New Stories, Essays, and Other Writings* (Random House), by Shirley Jackson.

As usual, small presses dominated the list of short-story collections, with trade collections having become rare.

A wide variety of "electronic collections," often called "fiction bundles," too many to individually list here, are also available for downloading online, at many sites. The Science Fiction Book Club continues to issue new collections as well.

As usual, the most reliable buys in the reprint anthology market are the various best of the year anthologies, the number of which continues to fluctuate. We lost one series in 2014, with the death of David G. Hartwell's *Year's Best SF* series (Tor), which ceased publication after eighteen volumes—but we gained several new series in 2015, with the addition of: *The Year's Best Military SF and Space Opera* (Baen), edited by David Afsharirad; *The Year's Best Science Fiction and Fantasy Novellas: 2015* (Prime Books), edited by Paula Guran; and *The Best American Science Fiction and Fantasy 2015* (Houghton Mifflin Harcourt), this volume edited by Joe Hill, with the overall series editor being John Joseph Adams. These join the established best of the year series: the one you are reading at the moment, *The Year's Best Science Fiction* from St. Martin's Press, edited by Gardner Dozois, now up to its thirty-third annual collection; *The Best Science Fiction and Fantasy of the Year: Volume Nine* (Solaris), edited by Jonathan Strahan; *The Year's Best Science Fiction and Fantasy: 2015 Edition* (Prime Books), edited by Rich Horton; *The Best Horror of the Year, Volume Seven* (Skyhorse/Night Shade Books), edited by Ellen Datlow; *The Year's Best Dark Fantasy and Horror: 2014* (Prime Books), edited by Paula Guran; *The Year's Best Weird Fiction* (which seems to have switched publishers, coming now from Undertow Publications), volume two edited by Kathe Koja and Michael Kelly; and *The Mammoth Book of Best New Horror, Volume 26* (which also seems to have switched publishers, coming now from PS Publishing), edited by Stephen Jones.

That leaves science fiction being covered by two dedicated best of the year anthologies, my own and the Afsharirad, plus four separate half-anthologies, the science fiction halves of the Strahan, Horton, Hill, and Guran novella book, which in theory adds up to two additional anthologies (in practice, of course, the contents of those books probably won't divide that neatly, with exactly half with their coverage going to each genre, and there'll likely to be more of one thing than another). With two dedicated anthologies and four half-anthologies (adding up to two more), that's actually more best coverage than SF has had for a while. There is no dedicated fantasy anthology anymore, fantasy only being covered by the fantasy halves of the Strahan, Horton, Hill, and Guran novella book (in effect, by two anthologies when you add the halves together). Horror is now being covered by two dedicated volumes, the Datlow and the Jones, and the "horror" half of Guran's *The Year's Best Dark Fantasy and Horror* (although the distinction between "dark fantasy" and "horror" is a fine—and perhaps problematic—one). I suspect that "weird fiction" (another subjective term) is going to fall under the horror heading more often than not, so *The*

Year's Best Weird Fiction could possibly be counted as covering horror as well. The annual Nebula Awards anthology, which covers science fiction as well as fantasy of various sorts, functions as a de facto "best of the year" anthology, although it's not usually counted among them; this year's edition was *Nebula Awards Showcase 2015* (Pyr), edited by Greg Bear. A more specialized best of the year anthology is *Wilde Stories 2015: The Year's Best Gay Speculative Fiction* (Lethe Press), edited by Steve Berman.

The stand-alone reprint anthology market was a bit weak this year. The most substantial one was probably *Sisters of the Revolution: A Feminist Speculative Fiction Anthology* (PM Press), edited by Ann VanderMeer and Jeff VanderMeer, a reprint anthology with classic stories by Ursula K. Le Guin, Joanna Russ, Octavia Butler, James Tiptree, Jr., Tanith Lee, and others. Similar reprint anthologies, with a shift in genres, were *Warrior Women* (Prime Books), edited by Paula Guran, with reprints from Elizabeth Bear, Aliette de Bodard, Caitlín R. Kiernan, George R. R. Martin, Carrie Vaughn, and others, and *Blood Sisters: Vampire Stories by Women* (Skyhorse/Night Shade Books), also edited by Paula Guran, with reprints from Suzy McKee Charnas, Tanith Lee, Carrie Vaughn, Laurell K. Hamilton, and others.

Other prominent reprint anthologies were the two apocalyptic/environmental disaster anthologies mentioned earlier, *Loosed upon the World: The Saga Anthology of Climate Fiction* (Simon & Schuster) and *Wastelands 2: More Stories of the Apocalypse* (Titan), both edited by John Joseph Adams. Also substantial was *Pwning Tomorrow: stories from the Electronic Frontier* (Electronic Frontier Foundation), edited by the Electronic Frontier Foundation, a reprint SF anthology about the wired, extensively networked future that's become one of the standard futures in SF in the last few years; this seems to be mostly available in various e-book and downloadable formats, for a range of voluntary donations, but it features good reprints from Paolo Bacigalupi, Lauren Beukes, Hannu Rajaniemi, Pat Cadigan, Cory Doctorow, Madeline Ashby, Neil Gaiman, James Patrick Kelly, Bruce Sterling, and others. (If you want this, your best bet is probably to download it, for a range of voluntary donations to the Electronic Frontier Foundation, from www.supporters-eff.org/donate/pwningtomorrow.) Another reprint SF anthology available only in digital form was *Digital Dreams: A Decade of Science Fiction by Women* (NewCon Press), edited by Ian Whates, with reprints by Pat Cadigan, Justina Robson, Lauren Beukes, Nina Allan, and Una McCormack.

Minor but pleasant SF or fantasy anthologies this year included *As Time Goes By* (Baen), edited by Hank Davis, *Future Wars . . . and Other Punchlines* (Baen), edited by Hank Davis, and *Chicks and Balances* (Baen), edited by Esther Friesner and John Helfers.

I don't follow horror closely, but there the most celebrated reprint anthology of the year seems to have been *The Monstrous* (Tachyon Publications), edited by Ellen Datlow.

It was a fairly weak year in the genre-oriented nonfiction category.

The most prominent such book this year was probably *Steering the Craft: A 21st-Century Guide to Sailing the Sea of Story* (Houghton Mifflin Harcourt/Mariner), by

Ursula K. Le Guin. Other general studies of the field were *The Sound of Culture: Diaspora and Black Technopoetics* (Wesleyan University Press), by Louis Chude-Sokei, *Tomorrowland: Our Journey from Science Fiction to Science Fact* (New Harvest), by Steven Kotler, and *Luke Skywalker Can't Read: And Other Geeky Truths* (Plume), by Ryan Britt.

Letters to Tiptree (Twelfth Planet Press), edited by Alisa Krasnostein and Alexandra Pierce, collects letters admiring "his" work written to "James Tiptree, Jr." (Alice Sheldon) by other authors. *Crosstalk* (Ansible Editions), by David Langford, collects interviews conducted by Langford with various authors, and *Conversations with Michael Chabon* (University Press of Mississippi), by Brannon Costello, collects interviews with Michael Chabon.

Most of the rest of the year's genre-oriented nonfiction books were studies of the work of genre authors, sometimes by the authors themselves. They included: *The Outlandish Companion* (Delacorte), by Diana Gabaldon; *The Wheel of Time Companion: The People, Places, and History of the Bestselling Series* (Tor), by Robert Jordan, Harriet McDougal, Alan Romanczuk, and Maria Simons; *The Culture Series of Iain M. Banks* (McFarland), by Simone Caroti; *The Fellowship: The Literary Lives of the Inklings: J.R.R. Tolkien, C. S. Lewis, Owen Barfield, Charles Williams* (Farrar, Straus and Giroux), by Philip Zaleski and Carol Zaleski; *Lost Landscape: A Writer's Coming of Age* (HarperCollins), by Joyce Carol Oates; *Lois McMaster Bujold* (University of Illinois Press), by Edward James; *Frederik Pohl* (University of Illinois Press), by Michael R. Page; *Ray Bradbury* (University of Illinois Press), by David Seed; *Coffin Nails* (Charnel House), by Harlan Ellison; and *The Brothers Vonnegut: Science and Fiction in the House of Magic* (Farrar, Straus and Giroux), by Ginger Strand.

The rest of the books in this category fall into the peculiar category of nonfiction written about a fictional world: *Darwin's Watch: The Science of Discworld III* (Anchor Books), by Terry Pratchett, Ian Stewart, and Jack Cohen; *The Globe: The Science of Discworld II* (Anchor Books), by Terry Pratchett, Ian Stewart, and Jack Cohen; and *Judgment Day: The Science of Discworld IV* (Random House), by Terry Pratchett, Ian Stewart, and Jack Cohen.

It was a decent although unspectacular year for art books. In spite of a change of editors and publisher, your best bet as usual was probably the latest in a long-running "best of the year" series for fantastic art, *Spectrum 22: The Best in Contemporary Fantastic Art* (Flesk Publications), now edited by John Fleskes, who took over for former editors Cathy Fenner and Arnie Fenner in 2014. This year there's a companion volume of sorts, also a very good value in this category, the aforementioned *Women of Wonder: Celebrating Women Creators of Fantastic Art* (Underwood Books), edited by Cathy Fenner. Also good was *The Art of Wayne Barlow* (Titan), by Wayne Barlowe; *The Fantasy Illustration Library, Volume One: Lands and Legends* (Michael Publishing), by Malcolm R. Phifer and Michael C. Phifer; *White Cloud Worlds, Volume Three: An Anthology of Science Fiction and Fantasy Artwork from Aotearoa New Zealand* (Ignite), edited by Paul Tobin; *Edward Gorey: His Book Cover Art and Design* (Pomegranate), edited by Steven Heller; *The Art of David Seeley* (Insight Editions), by David Seeley; *Portfolio: The Complete Various Drawings* (Flesk Publications), by Mark Schultz; *Julie Dillon's Imagined Realms, Book 2: Earth and Sky* (self-published), by Julie Dillon; *Infected by Art, Volume Three* (Hermes Press), edited by

Todd Spoor and Bill Cox; *Imagery from the Bird's Home: The Art of Bill Carman* (Flesk Publications), by Bill Carman; and *The Book of Giants* (Flesk Publications), by Petar Meseldžija. There didn't seem to be anything else out this year, as far as I could tell.

According to the Box Office Mojo site (www.boxofficemojo.com), eight out of ten of 2015's top-earning movies were genre films of one sort or another (if you're willing to count animated films and superhero movies as being "genre films"), and a case could be made that even the two nongenre films that pushed into the top ten, *Furious 7* in fifth place and *Spectre* in tenth place, were fantasy films of some sort, since they certainly featured a lot of action sequences that defied the laws of physics and probability as we know them. Much the same was true of the eleventh-place film, *Mission: Impossible—Rogue Nation*. You have to go all the way down to twelfth place before finding a top-grossing nongenre movie that didn't feature car chases, gun battles, and huge explosions, *Pitch Perfect 2*. After that, the genre films tend to take over again, with the superhero film *Ant-Man* coming in at thirteen, and the animated film *Home* coming in at fourteen. By my count, although I may have missed a few, fourteen out of the top twenty, and thirty-eight out of the one hundred top-grossing movies were genre films.

Once again, the highest-grossing film of the year, number one at the box office, was a genre film, *Star Wars: The Force Awakens*, which in spite of being released late in December has already earned a staggering $2,049,394,515. Nor is this anything new; in the past seventeen years, genre films have been number one at the box office fifteen out of seventeen times, with the only exceptions being *American Sniper* in 2014 and *Saving Private Ryan* in 1998. All the rest of the number ones have been genre movies, of one sort or another: SF, fantasy, superhero movies, animated films.

Rounding out the top ten box-office champs, in second place was an SF movie, *Jurassic World* (I say nothing of the likeliness of its science, but it's SF; whether *good* SF or not is another matter); in third place, a superhero movie, *Avengers: Age of Ultron*; in fourth place, an animated film, *Inside Out*; in sixth place, another animated film, *Minions*; in seventh place, an SF film, *The Hunger Games: Mockingjay—Part 2*; in eighth place, another SF film, *The Martian*; and in ninth place, a live-action retelling of a fairy tale, *Cinderella*.

It's worth noting that *The Martian*, a "serious" SF film rather than the usual sci-fi adventure (and, furthermore, one that made a good-faith attempt to actually get the science right rather than making it up as it went along), got more widespread critical respect than any other genre film of recent years, while still managing to earn a very respectable $623,657,016 worldwide, making it one of the few "serious" SF films of recent years to earn a substantial amount of money, along with 2013's *Gravity* and 2014's *Interstellar*. *Mad Max: Fury Road*, which finished in twenty-first place, also got a surprising amount of respect from critics.

According to Box Office Mojo, ten films made more than $200 million at the 2015 box office, and the year's combined box-office receipts crossed 11 billion dollars for the first time ever. It's worth noting, however, that these figures are top-heavy. While ten films made more than $200 million, many films made a great deal less; only ninety-five of the year's films managed to make more than $25 million, which means that 34.5 of 2015's total box office is attributable to the year's top ten films. At the same time, the average ticket price climbed from $5.66 in 2001 to $8.61 in 2015. It seems clear that going to see a movie in the theater is a thing you reserve for special occasions, usually big-budget, special effects–heavy widescreen spectaculars that look best when seen on the big screen. The rest of the time, you stay home and wait for it to come out on on demand or Netflix or Hulu, or for the DVD to ship.

Perhaps because the immense, even frenzied, anticipation generated by *Star Wars: The Force Awakens* has left the fans in a condition of postcoital tristesse, there doesn't seem to be a lot of buzz being generated by 2016's upcoming movies, although there are, of course, many genre films in the pipeline. Most anticipation so far seems to have been generated by *Batman v. Superman: Dawn of Justice* and the upcoming Marvel *Captain America: Civil War* movie and *Doctor Strange*. (There's no denying that, between movies and TV, this is the golden age of superheroes, with more superhero movies and TV programs being made than ever before—and more of them being considered to be among the year's top-quality products as well). Few people seem all that excited by the news that there's another *Star Trek* film coming up. Somewhere back in the distance are vague murmurings about new *Avatar* films, but that doesn't seem to be generating a lot of buzz either.

There's no doubt at all that this is the Golden Age of SF and fantasy shows on television. I counted more than eighty of them available to watch in one form or another in 2015 (and no doubt I missed some), with at least another dozen or so coming along for 2016. There are probably more SF/fantasy shows available now than there were forensic/cop shows a few years back. And not only are there a lot of shows, many of them are getting a surprising amount of critical respect and even mainstream acceptance far beyond the circle of those who usually deign to pay any attention to SF or fantasy—HBO's *Game of Thrones*, for instance, not only won an Emmy this year for outstanding drama series, it won twelve in all, taking home more Emmys in a single year than any other show has ever done. SF and fantasy shows (to date, usually superhero shows) are also beginning to spread beyond television itself, being available only on Internet streaming video channels, including a couple of the year's most popular programs.

With more than eighty shows on television (or *not* on television, in some cases), I obviously don't have the space here to cover each of them in detail, so I'll have to mostly concentrate on which seem to me (yes, arbitrary and subjective selection) among the most prominent.

As mentioned earlier, HBO's *Game of Thrones* is probably still the most prestigious and financially successful fantasy show on television, although other cable shows garnered a fair amount of critical praise this year, including the SF miniseries *The Man in the High Castle* (based on the Hugo-winning novel by Philip K. Dick) and *The Expanse* (based on the space opera novels by James S. A. Corey), both of which have already been renewed for a second season, and a miniseries version of *Childhood's End* (based on the famous novel by Arthur C. Clarke). On the fantasy side of the ledger, there were well-received miniseries versions of *Jonathan Strange and Mr. Norrell* (based on a novel by Susanna Clarke), and *Outlander* (based on a series of novels by Diana Gabaldon). Amazon's streaming service gave us *Daredevil*, a gritty reimagining of the comic book that proved very popular, and, toward the end of the year, *Jessica Jones*, an even darker and more noirish take on a comic book character that proved as popular if not more so; both have already been renewed for second seasons. Coming up in 2016 are more Marvel shows available only on streaming video, such as *Luke Cage* and *The Punisher*.

Of the flood of shows that hit the air in 2014 and 2015, *Sleepy Hollow, Marvel's Agents of S.H.I.E.L.D, Agent Carter, Once Upon a Time, Arrow, The Flash, Gotham, Grimm, The Librarians, Person of Interest, The Originals, The 100, Orphan Black, Galavant, 12 Monkeys, Star Wars Rebels, Penny Dreadful, iZombie, Wayward Pines, Bitten,* and *The Last Man on Earth* seem to have survived, while *Beauty and the Beast, Constantine, Da Vinci's Demons, Dominion, Haven, Gravity Falls, Legends, Atlantis, The Awesomes, The Messengers, Falling Skies, Under the Dome, The Whispers, Wicked City,* and *Extant* have not. (No doubt there are many in both categories that I've missed or gotten wrong.)

Perennial favorites such as *Doctor Who, The Walking Dead, Supernatural, Teen Wolf, The Vampire Diaries, Orphan Black,* and *The Simpsons* continue to roll on as well.

Of the new shows debuting in 2015, the best received, or at least the ones that there was the most buzz about, seem to be *Supergirl* and *The Muppets*, and a retread versions of a once successful show, the *X-Files*. Other new shows include *Legends of Tomorrow; Outcast; Limitless; Beowulf; Shadowhunters; Lucifer; Angel from Hell; Colony; Containment; Damien; Braindead; Emerald City; Hunters; Legion; You, Me, and the Apocalypse; Second Chance;* and *Preacher*. How many of these will ultimately make it is anyone's guess. Another retread of a once wildly popular show, *Heroes Reborn*, has already been canceled as I write these words in mid-January.

Coming up in 2016 are a miniseries version of *The Shannara Chronicles*, based on the novels by Terry Brooks; *The Magicians*, based on the novels of Lev Grossman; a TV version of *Westworld*; and miniseries versions of Neil Gaiman's *American Gods*; Kim Stanley Robinson's *Red Mars*; Len Deighton's *SS-GB*; John Scalzi's *Old Man's War*; and Robert Holdstock's *Mythago Cycle*, among others—although how many of these promised shows actually show up is also anyone's guess.

The Seventy-third Annual World Science Fiction Convention, Sasquan, was held in Spokane, Washington, at the Spokane Convention Center, from August 19 to August 23, 2015. The 2015 Hugo Awards, presented at Sasquan, were: Best Novel, *The Three-Body Problem*, by Cixin Liu, translated by Ken Liu; Best Novella, No Award; Best Novelette, "The Day the World Turned Upside Down," by Thomas Olde Heuvelt, translated by Lian Belt; Best Short Story, No Award; Best Graphic Story, *Ms. Marvel*, "Volume 1: No Normal," written by G. Willow Wilson, illustrated by Adrian Alphona and Jake Wyatt; Best Related Work, No Award; Best Professional Editor, Long Form, No Award; Best Professional Editor, Short Form, No Award; Best Professional Artist, Julie Dillon; Best Dramatic Presentation (short form), *Orphan Black*, "By Means Which Have Never Yet Been Tried," written by Graham Manson; Best Dramatic

Presentation (long form), *Guardians of the Galaxy*, written by James Gunn and Nicole Perlman; Best Semiprozine, *Lightspeed*; Best Fanzine, *Journey Planet*; Best Fancast, *Galactic Suburbia Podcast*; Best Fan Writer, Laura J. Mixon; Best Fan Artist, Elizabeth Leggett; plus the John W. Campbell Award for Best New Writer to Wesley Chu.

The 2014 Nebula Awards, presented at a banquet at the Palmer House Hilton in Chicago, Illinois, on June 7, 2015, were: Best Novel, *Annihilation*, by Jeff Vander-Meer; Best Novella, *Yesterday's Kin*, by Nancy Kress; Best Novelette, "A Guide to the Fruits of Hawai'i," by Alaya Dawn Johnson; Best Short Story, "Jackalope Wives," by Ursula Vernon; the Ray Bradbury Award to *Guardians of the Galaxy*; the Andre Norton Award to *Love Is the Drug*, by Alaya Dawn Johnson; the Solstice Award to Joanna Russ and Stanley Schmidt; the Kevin O' Donnell Jr. Service to SFWA Award to Jefry Dwight; and the Damon Knight Memorial Grand Master Award to Larry Niven.

The 2015 World Fantasy Awards, presented at a banquet on November 8, 2015, in Saratoga Springs, New York, during the Forty-first Annual World Fantasy Convention, were: Best Novel, *The Bone Clocks*, by David Mitchell; Best Novella, *We Are All Completely Fine*, by Daryl Gregory; Best Short Fiction, "Do You Like to Look at Monsters?" by Scott Nicolay; Best Collection, *Gifts for the One Who Comes After*, by Helen Marshall and *The Bitterwood Bible and Other Recountines*, by Angela Slatter (tie); Best Anthology, *Monstrous Affections*, edited by Kelly Link and Gavin J. Grant; Best Artist, Samuel Araya; Special Award (Professional) to Sandra Kasturi and Brett Alexander Savory, for ChiZine Publications; Special Award (Nonprofessional) to Ray B. Russell and Rosalie Parker, for Tartarus Press. Plus Lifetime Achievement Awards to Ramsey Campbell and Sheri S. Tepper.

The 2014 Bram Stoker Awards, presented by the Horror Writers of America on May 9, 2015, during the Twenty-fifth Annual World Horror Convention in Atlanta, Georgia, were: Best Novel, *Blood Kin*, by Steve Rasnic Tem; Best First Novel, *Mr. Wicker*, by Maria Alexander; Best Young Adult Novel, *Phoenix Island*, by John Dixon; Best Long Fiction, "Fishing for Dinosaurs," by Joe R. Lansdale; Best Short Fiction, "The Vaporization Enthalpy of a Peculiar Pakistani Family," by Usman T. Malik and "Ruminations," by Rena Mason (tie); Best Collection, *Soft Apocalypses*, by Lucy Snyder; Best Anthology, *Fearful Symmetries*, edited by Ellen Datlow; Best Nonfiction, *Shooting Yourself in the Head for Fun and Profit: A Writer's Survival Guide*, by Lucy Snyder; Best Poetry Collection, *Forgiving Judas*, by Tom Piccirilli; Best Graphic Novel, *Bad Blood*, by Jonathan Maberry and Tyler Crook; Best Screenplay, *The Babadook*; Specialty Press Award to ChiZine Publications; Richard Laymon (President's Award) to Tom Calen, Brock Cooper, and Doug Murano; the Mentor Award to Kathy Ptacek; plus Lifetime Achievement Awards to Tanith Lee and Jack Ketchum.

The 2015 John W. Campbell Memorial Award was won by *The First Fifteen Lives of Harry August*, by Claire North.

The 2015 Theodore Sturgeon Memorial Award for Best Short Story was won by "The Man Who Sold the Moon," by Cory Doctorow.

The 2015 Philip K. Dick Memorial Award was won by *The Book of the Unnamed Midwife*, by Meg Elison.

The 2015 Arthur C. Clarke award was won by *Station Eleven*, by Emily St. John Mandel.

The 2014 James Tiptree, Jr. Memorial Award was won by *The Girl in the Road*, by Monica Byrne and *My Real Children*, by Jo Walton (tie).

The 2015 Sidewise Award for Alternate History went to (Long Form): *The Enemy Within*, by Kristine Kathryn Rusch and "The Long Haul from the ANNALS OF TRANSPORTATION, The Pacific Monthly, May 2009," by Ken Liu.

It was another year with a tragically high death rate in the SF field. Dead in 2014, 2015, or early 2016 were:

SIR TERRY PRATCHETT, 66, unquestionably the finest writer of comic fantasy in modern times and the second most best-selling author in the United Kingdom, behind only J. K. Rowling, author of the famous forty-volume Discworld series, featuring such titles as *Night Watch, Guards! Guards!, Wyrd Sisters*, and *A Hat Full of Sky*, as well as many stand-alone novels, more than seventy books in total; **TANITH LEE**, 67, highly prolific British writer of SF, fantasy, and horror, winner of the World Fantasy Award Lifetime Achievement Award as well as Lifetime Achievement Awards from World Horror and the Stoker Awards, author of novels such as *The Silver Metal Lover, Death's Master*, and *White as Snow*, as well as huge amounts of short fiction collected in many collections such as *Red as Blood, Tamastara*, and *The Gorgon and Other Beastly Tales*; Hugo Award and World Fantasy Award-winning editor **DAVID GEDDES HARTWELL**, 74, one of the most influential and important editors in the history of SF, longtime Tor editor, founder of the Timescape SF line, cofounder of the World Fantasy Convention, editor of many important anthologies, including *The World Treasury of Science Fiction, The Dark Descent*, and *The Science Fiction Century*, a close personal friend for almost fifty years; **SUZETTE HADEN ELGIN**, 78, acclaimed SF writer, linguist, and poet, best known for the Native Tongue trilogy, *Native Tongue, The Judas Rose*, and *Earthsong*, as well as the Ozark Trilogy and the Coyote Jones series, also founded the Science Fiction Poetry Association; **MELANIE TEM**, 65, prolific horror/dark fantasy writer, winner of the World Fantasy Award, the Bram Stoker Award, and the International Horror Guild Award, author of novels such as *Prodigal, Blood Moon*, and *The Wilding*, as well as large amounts of short fiction, much of it in collaboration with husband Steve Rasnic Tem, who survives her; **ROBERT CONQUEST**, 98, Anglo-US author and historian, coeditor (with Kingsley Amis) of the long-running *Spectrum* series of SF reprint anthologies, as well as the author of an SF novel, *A World of Difference* (also with Kingsley Amis); **PETER MALCOLM DE BRISSAC DICKINSON**, 88, who wrote as **PETER DICKINSON**, author of the Changes trilogy, consisting of *The Weathermonger, Heartsease*, and *The Devil's Children*, as well as much children's and YA SF; **GEORGE CLAYTON JOHNSON**, 86, pioneering scriptwriter for many early SF television shows, including *Star Trek* and *The Twilight Zone*, cowriter of the movie *Logan's Run*; **TOM PICCIRILLI**, 50, acclaimed horror and crime writer, winner of the Stoker Award, author of *The Night Class, The Cold Spot, Dark Father*, and many others; **CAROL SEVERANCE**, 71, SF writer, author of *Reefsong* and the Island Warrior trilogy; **A. R. MORLAN**, 58, horror and erotica writer, prolific at short lengths; **DAVID RAIN**, 54, who wrote SF as **TOM ARDEN**, author of the five-book Orokon epic fantasy series; **CHARLES W. RUNYON**, 87, SF writer, author of *Pig World* and others; **GÜNTER GRASS**, 87, German novelist, poet, and playwright, winner of the Nobel Prize for Literature, whose works with fantastic elements include *The Tin Drum* and *The Rat*; **E. L DOCTOROW**, 84, renowned author of such novels as *Ragtime*, *The March*, and *Billy Bathgate*; **JAMES SALTER**, 90, novelist, best known for *A Sport and a Pastime*; **RUTH RENDELL**, 85, prominent mystery author, best known for the long-running Inspector Wexford series; **OLIVER SACKS**, 82, best known for his case studies of neurological disorders, such as *The Man Who Mistook His Wife for a Hat*, *Awakenings*, and *Seeing Voices*, works that had an impact on a lot of science fictional thinking; **T. M. WRIGHT**, 68, SF writer; **DANIEL GROTTA**, 71, photography expert, journalist, writer, author of the first biography of J.R.R. Tolkien, *Architect of Middle Earth*, a friend, survived by his widow, writer Sally Wiener Grotta; **WOLFGANG JESCHKE**, 78, German writer, editor, and anthologist; **JÖEL CHAMPETIER**, 57, French-Canadian SF writer and editor; **MICHEL JEURY**, 80, noted French author; **JANNICK STORM**, 76, Danish author, critic, and translator; Danish author **INGE ERIKSEN**, 80; Danish author, **IB MELCHIOR**, 97; **JOHN TOMERLIN**, 84, author of *Run from the Hunter* (with Charles Beaumont); **PERRY A. CHAPDELAINE**, 90, veteran SF writer, author of *Swampworld West* and *The Laughing Terran*; **ROBERT E. MARGROFF**, 85, author of several SF novels in collaboration with Piers Anthony; **ALBERT J. MANACHINO**, 90, writer; **WALTER W. LEE**, 83, writer and scholar; **ELLEN CONFORD**, 73, children's and YA author; **MARCIA BROWN**, 96, Caldecott Medal–winning children's author and illustrator; **MOYRA CALDECOTT**, 88, South African–born UK author of many children's and YA fantasy books; **CHUCK MILLER**, 62, publisher, editor, and bookseller; **FLORIN MANOLESCU**, 72, Romanian literary critic, literary historian, and SF writer; **R. A. MONTGOMERY**, 78, writer and publisher; **CHRIS GILMORE**, 66, longtime reviewer for *Interzone* and freelance copy editor; **ADRIENNE MARTINE-BARNES**, 73, author, fan, and costumer; **JON ARFSTROM**, 87, veteran cover artist and illustrator who did much work for *Weird Tales* and other pulp magazines; **GAIL J. BUTLER**, 68, SF, fantasy, and wildlife artist; **MELISSA MATHISON**, 65, screenwriter best known for the screenplay for *E. T.*; **LEONARD NIMOY**, 83, TV and movie actor, world-famous for his role as the half-Vulcan Mr. Spock on the original *Star Trek* TV series, a role he reprised in many subsequent *Star Trek* TV spinoff series and movies; **SIR CHRISTOPHER LEE**, 93, movie actor, known for his recurrent roles in *The Lord of the Rings*, *Star Wars*, and *The Hobbit* movie franchises, as well as in *The Wicker Man* and many Hammer horror movies; **DAVID BOWIE**, 69, world-famous singer, songwriter, and film actor, perhaps best known to genre audiences for his song "Space Oddity" and for the album *The Rise and Fall of Ziggy Stardust and the Spiders From Mars*, but also for his roles in films such as *Labyrinth* and *The Man Who Fell to Earth*; **ALAN RICKMAN**, 69, renowned British stage and film actor, best known to genre audience for his role as Severus Snape in the *Harry Potter* movies and for his role in *Galaxy Quest*, but also widely known for his roles in *Die Hard*, *Dogma*, *Truly, Madly, Deeply*, and many others; **PATRICK MacNEE**, 93, British actor best known for his role as the suave secret agent Steed on TV's *The Avengers*; **OMAR SHARIF**, 83, movie actor best known for his roles in *Doctor Zhivago* and

The 13th Warrior; **MAUREEN O'HARA**, 95, movie actress, whose most famous role may have been in *The Quiet Man*, but who might have been best known to genre audiences for roles in *Miracle on 34th Street* and *Sinbad the Sailor*; **THEODORE BIKEL**, 91, movie, stage, and television actor, best known on the stage for the lead role in *Fiddler on the Roof*, also appeared in movies such as *The African Queen*, *The Enemy Below*, and *The Russians Are Coming, the Russians Are Coming*, and also guest-starred on dozens of TV shows, including *Star Trek: The Next Generation* and *Babylon 5*; **LOUIS JOURDAN**, 93, movie actor best known to genre audiences for a role as Dracula in a TV production and in *Year of the Comet*; **NIGEL TERRY**, 69, movie actor, best known for roles as Arthur in *Excalibur* and young Prince John in *The Lion in Winter*; **JACK LARSON**, 87, television actor best known for playing Jimmy Olsen in television's original *The Adventures of Superman*; **ROGER REES**, 71, television, stage, and movie actor, best known for continuing roles in TV's *Cheers* and *Warehouse 13* and for playing the Sheriff of Rottingham in *Robin Hood: Men in Tights*, known outside the field for stage show *The Life and Adventures of Nicholas Nickleby*; **ROBERT LOGGIA**, 85, movie and television actor perhaps best known for his role in *Big*, also appeared in *Independence Day*, *Scarface*, and TV's *The Sopranos*; **RON MOODY**, 91, movie actor, best known for his role as Fagin in *Oliver!*, also appeared in *The Mouse on the Moon* and *A Kid in King Arthur's Court*; **DICK VAN PATTEN**, 87, television and film actor best known for roles in *Robin Hood: Men in Tights*, *High Anxiety*, *Westworld*, and *Spaceballs*; **DEAN JONES**, 84, movie actor best known for *The Love Bug* and *The Shaggy D.A.*; **GRACE LEE WHITNEY**, 85, best known for her role as Yeoman Rand in the original *Star Trek* TV series; **YVONNE CRAIG**, 78, TV actor best known for her role as Batgirl in the sixties TV show *Batman*, also was in *Star Trek* and other shows; **WES CRAVEN**, 76, director and screenwriter, best known for *A Nightmare on Elm Street* and its many sequels; **STAN FREBERG**, 88, legendary creator of satirical radio and television commercials; **PHIL AUSTIN**, 74, one of the founding members of surreal and satirical comedy troop Firesign Theater, also a longtime fan; **PEGGY RAE SAPIENZA**, 70, longtime fan and prominent convention organizer, a friend; **FRED DUARTE, Jr.**, 58, longtime fan and convention organizer; **ART WIDNER**, 98, longtime fan and fanzine editor; **NED BROOKS**, 77, longtime fan and fanzine editor; **HAZEL HOLT**, 87, mother of fantasy writer Tom Holt, and herself a published novelist; **THOMAS E. GOONAN**, 93, father of SF writer Kathleen Ann Goonan; **JOHN C. SPRUILL**, 100, father of SF writer Steven Spruill; **JOHN RICHARD HORTON**, 84, father of SF editor and critic Richard Horton; **TONI EDELMAN**, 79, mother of SF writer and editor Scott Edelman; **SUZANNE GROSS REED**, 82, mother of SF writer Marguerite Reed ; **MURRAY WAYNE PERSON, JR.**, 72, father of SF writer Lawrence Person; **MILDRED (MILLIE) RAMBO**, 92, mother of SF writer Cat Rambo; **VIRGINIA SAWYER**, 90, mother of SF writer Robert J. Sawyer; **ALICE JANET BARTLETT EASTON**, 95, mother of SF writer and critic Tom Easton; **SARAH KROUPA**, 33, daughter of writer Susan J. Kroupa; **ANN MCKNIGHT**, 92, widow of fan Jack McKnight, who handcrafted the first Hugo Awards.

The Falls: A Luna Story

Ian McDonald

British author Ian McDonald is an ambitious and daring writer with a wide range and an impressive amount of talent. His first story was published in 1982, and since then he has appeared with some frequency in Interzone, Asimov's Science Fiction, *and elsewhere. In 1989 he won the* Locus *"Best First Novel" Award for his novel* Desolation Road. *He won the Philip K. Dick Award in 1992 for his novel* King of Morning, Queen of Day. *His other books include the novels* Out on Blue Six, Hearts, Hands and Voices, Terminal Café, Sacrifice of Fools, Evolution's Shore, Kirinya, Ares Express, Brasyl, *and* The Dervish House, *as well as three collections of his short fiction,* Empire Dreams, Speaking in Tongues, *and* Cyberabad Days. *His novel,* River of Gods, *was a finalist for both the Hugo Award and the Arthur C. Clarke Award in 2005, and a novella drawn from it, "The Little Goddess," was a finalist for the Hugo and the Nebula Award. He won a Hugo Award in 2007 for his novelette "The Djinn's Wife," won the Theodore Sturgeon Award for his story "Tendeléo's Story," and in 2011 won the John W. Campbell Memorial Award for his novel* The Dervish House. *His most recent books are the starting volume of a YA series,* Planesrunner, *and two sequels,* Be My Enemy *and* Empress of the Sun. *Coming up is a big retrospective collection,* The Best of Ian McDonald. *Born in Manchester, England, in 1960, McDonald has spent most of his life in Northern Ireland, and now lives and works in Belfast.*

Here he takes us to an inhabited Moon, for a compelling look at people struggling to deal with the cultural and psychological changes generated in society by life in a Lunar colony.

My daughter fell from the top of the world. She tripped, she gripped, she slipped and she fell. Into three kilometres of open air.

I have a desk. Everyone on the atmospheric entry project thinks it's the quaintest thing. They can't understand it. Look at the space it takes up! And it attracts stuff.

Junk. Piles. De-print them, de-print it, get rid of the dust, free up the space. Surfaces. You don't need surfaces to work.

That's true. I work through Marid, my familiar. I've skinned it as its namesake, a great and powerful djinn, hovering over my left shoulder. My co-workers think this quaint too. I spend my shifts in a pavilion of interlocutors. My familiar meeting my client's familiar: relaying each other's words.

My client is a planetary exploration probe.

I'm a simulational psychiatrist.

The proper furniture of psychologist is a chair, not a cluttered desk. And a couch. To which I say; the couch is a psychoanalytic cliche, and try laying a Saturn entry probe on a chaise longue, even before you get to the Oedipal rage and penis envy. The desk stays. Yes it takes up stupid space in my office, yes, I have piled it with so many empty food containers and disposable tea cups and kawaii toys and even physical print-outs that I'm permanently running close to my carbon limit. But I like it; it makes this cubicle an office. And it displays—displayed, before the strata of professional detritus buried it—my daughter's first archaeological find.

The technology is awkward by our standards—silicon micro-processor arrays are like asteroids next to modern 2-D graphene films; almost laughable. A finger-sized processor board; its exact purpose unknown. It's provenance: the location where the People's Republic of China's Yutu rover came to a halt and died forty kilometres south of Laplace F in the Mare Imbrium on the nearside of the Moon.

Acceleration under gravity on the surface of moon is 1.625 metres per second squared

I like Callisto.

I don't like—I don't have to like—all my clients. Every AI is different, though there are similarities, some of them the constraints of architecture and engineering, some of them philosophical, some of them the shared AI culture that has been evolving on the moon alongside human society. Every AI is an individual not an identity.

Callisto is quick, keen and erudite in conversation, charmingly pedantic, eager and naive. E anticipates the mission with the impatience and excitement of a child going to New Year and there is the trap. I think of er like I think of Shahina, and then I make mistakes. I become attached, I make presumptions. I *humanise*.

Erm, Nuur did you see what you did there?

"I beg your pardon Callisto?"

Erm, you used a wrong word.

"What wrong word?"

I can remind you . . .

"Please do. I hate to think I'd said something inappropriate."

You said, talking about my atmospheric entry aspect, when she goes in. I think you mean to say . . .

E. Er. The recognised pronouns for Artificial Intelligence. My embarrassment was crippling. I couldn't speak. I blushed, burned. Burbled apologies. I was naked with shame.

It's quite all right, Nuur. But I think I should tell you that you've, um, been doing it all week . . .

When an AI ums, ers, demurs, it is a clear sign of a conflict between er laws: to be truthful, to cause no harm to humans. AIs are every bit as shy and self-deluding as humans.

I didn't laugh when she said, *history*. I didn't smile, didn't interject, object, reject though the arguments swarmed on my tongue. This is the Moon. Our society is fifty years old, it's a century-and-some since we first walked here. We are five cities, a university, a clatter of habitats and bases and one ever-moving train-cum-refinery; one million seven hundred thousand people. How can we have a history? How much does it take to have a history as opposed to anecdotes? Is there a critical mass? We are renter-clients of the Lunar Development Corporation, employed or contracted by the Five Dragons; history, for us, is over. We work, we survive, we pay our per diems for the Four Elementals of Air, Water, Data, Carbon. We don't just not need history; we can't *afford* history. Where is the profit? Where is the utility? So quick, so easy, see? I talk for a living. Arguments come to me as if drawn by whispers and pheromones. But I pushed them behind me and spoke none of them.

History, she said, spying the shadows of all those arguments and disparagements behind me. Defying me to criticise. *We have a history. Everything has a history. History isn't a thing you find lying around, it's a thing you make.*

Shahina, I named her. The name means falcon: a small fierce beautiful quick bird. She has never seen a falcon, never seen a bird, never seen a winged thing that isn't human, apart from the butterfly-fountains AKA make for society parties; that only live for a day and clog the drains when they make it rain to clear the dust from the air.

I have never seen a falcon either, for that matter. My father kept pigeons in a loft in the shade of the solar panel. I never liked them; they were smelly and rattly and jabby and swarmed around me when I went up on the roof with my Dad to feed them. Their wings clattered; they seemed more machine than bird. The thought of them now, cities, countries, worlds distant, still raises a cold horror. Falcons are the enemies of pigeons; Dad kept an evil eye for their swooshes in the sky. They're moving into the city, he said. Nesting up in the new towers. To them it's just a glass cliff. Any shadow he didn't like the look of was a falcon.

Shahina has never seen a falcon, never seen a bird, never seen a sky. But she's well-named. She is so quick. Her thoughts swerve and dodge, nimble and swift. Mine plod in slow, straight lines. She rushes to opinions and positions as if fortifying a hill. My work is deliberate: the identification and engineering of artificial emotions. She is fierce. Those opinions, those positions she defends with a ferocity that beats down any possible opposition. She wins not by being right but by being vehemently wrong. She scares me, when we fight as mother and daughter do. She scares me away from arguing.

History: what is it good for?

So, a thing can only be good if it's for something? she snapped back.

But are there jobs; will it pay your Four Elementals?

So, education is really just apprenticeship?
What's there to study? All we have are contracts.
Don't you get it? The contracts are the history.

And she would toss back her long, so shiny curls to show her exasperation that I would never ever understand *anything*, and let them settle under the slow lunar gravity.

Quick, fierce, but not small. I've been twenty years on the moon and it's turned me lean and scrawny, top heavy and bandy legged; tall and thin but Shahina towers over me. She is lunar-born, a second generation. Moon-kid. She is as slender and elegant as a gazelle.

I felt small and frail as a sparrow, hugging her goodbye at the station.

"Why does it have to be Meridian?" I couldn't help myself.

I saw my daughter's eyes widen in the moment before the *this-again* roll, her lips tighten. She drew back from the edge of fierce.

It's the best History Colloquium. And anyway, I always wanted to see the Earth.

She bent down to kiss me and then went through the pressure gate to the train.

At Farside station that day were some third-gens. They overbore Shahina and her generation as she overbore me. Alien children.

Mean atmospheric pressure inside lunar habitats is 1060 kilopascals, significantly higher than terrestrial norm.

I hover, Shahina told me. Over her, from the other side of the Moon. There's guilt first, when your daughter finds out you've been spying on her, then shame that you were so easily detected, then outrage at her outrage: it's only because I care, I shouldn't worry but I can't help myself; it's so far away. I'm worried about you. Doesn't she know it's only because I care?

The first time I went to Meridian to visit Shahina I saw an angel. I've lived all my life in the university, its cramped cloisters and mean halls, in the settlements of Farside, small and widely scattered, across many amors and amories. I turned my back on Earth and never looked over my shoulder. In those years away from the face of the Earth, looking out into deep space, the great nearside cities have delved deep and wide, quadras opened and linked into stupendous, vertiginous chasms, glittering at night with thousands of lights. They sent quaint, tight-horizoned me dizzy with agoraphobia. I caught hold of Shahina's arm as we came up out of Meridian Station. I felt old and infirm. I'm neither. Shahina sat me on a bench under the cover of trees, beneath leaves so that the lights became stars, half-seen. She bought me sherbet ice from an AKA tricycle and it was then that I saw the angel. People fly on the moon, I've known that forever, even before I came here and made it my home. It's the sole comprehensible image of life on the Moon to terrestrials: the soaring winged woman. Always a woman. Dizzy, I heard a movement, a rustle, a displacement of air. I looked up in time to see wings flicker over me, lights moving against the higher constellations. A woman, rigged with navigation lights, flying. She stopped down across the treetops, shadow, movement, sparkles glimpsed through the leaves. I looked up, our faces met.

Then she beat her wings and pulled up out of her glide, climbing, twisting in helical flight until she was lost to my view, her lesser lights merging with the greater.

"Oh," I said. And, "Did you . . ."

"Yes, mum."

I thought about the flying woman, that moment of elements meeting, over the following days as Shahina introduced me, one by one, to her circle. Friends, colleagues, Colloquium fellows. Sergei her tall, polite amor. He was an archaeologist. I terrified him by existing. I wondered what Shahina had told him about me. They cooked for me. It was so special and touching. They had hired hob and utensils, plates and chopsticks. They had obviously rehearsed, their movements in the tiny kitchen area of the Colloquium apt—cramped even by Farside U standards—was as immaculately choreographed as a ballet.

"Archaeology?"

I saw a flicker of impatience, a twitch of irritation before Sergei answered me.

"We've been living here for fifty years. It's been a century since the first human landing, overs hundred years since the first probes hard-landed. That's deep enough for archaeology."

"I get the same depth from studying history," Shahina said and she rested her hand on Sergei's. She was trying to softly intervene, to ameliorate, but I had no ill will to Sergei. I had neither ill will nor affection for him. He seemed a serious, flavourless boy, kind but dull. I could not understand what my daughter saw in him. I was neither surprised nor disappointed that it didn't last. Nor was Shahina, I think.

Shahina waited until I was on the platform, the train sliding in behind the glass pressure wall, before giving me the gift. It was small, the size of my thumb, but heavy, wrapped in indigo dashiki wave fabric through which I could feel sharp contours.

"From Laplace F."

She met Sergei through small, treasured items like this. Aminata, a Colloquiummate, had introduced Shahina to the Digs. No digging was involved. Archaeologists, historians, some extreme sports fans took off in sasuits, rovers, dust-bikes out across the Mares in search of old space hardware. Lunar landers, rovers, construction bots and solar sinterers from the early days of the settlement. Most prized was the dusty, dented detritus of the Apollos. They called this practical archaeology. I thought it bare-faced looting but I could not say so to Shahina. Sergei financed it. He was some minor Vorontsov. One of the Five Dragons. I was still not disappointed when Shahina dropped him.

I turned the small precious thing over and over in my fingers.

"What is it?"

"History."

Terminal velocity in a pressurised lunar habitat is sixty kilometres per hour.

Callisto dreams.

E dreams in code, in shaped packets of electrons, as we all dream. All dreams are coded, and codes. AI dreams are not our dreams. Callisto dreams awake. E never sleeps, never needs to sleep. Callisto has difficulty understanding the human need for sleep, what it is, how we return from it the same as we entered; that we return from it at all. And Callisto dreams in er three separate manifestations: the mainframe, the probe, the blimp. I like to believe e shares dreams, like a family around the breakfast table in some café.

If Callisto's intelligence and emotions are genuine—some still believe they aren't and I have argued and will argue again their error with them—then so are er dreams. Marid translates them into a form I can comprehend. Callisto's dreaming is primarily auditory. Marid plays me a storming chatter of notes and clicks, titanic bass and infra bass swells and clusters of rushing triads at the very upper limit of my hearing. It sounds like chaos. It sounds like the throb of black holes, the drone of the cosmic microwave background, the slow tick of entropy towards dissolution and chaos but if you listen, if you really listen, if you go beyond the human instinct to analyse, to structure, the pareidolic need to see rabbits in the moon, faces on Mars, gods in the alignments of the stars, then a titanic music unfolds. Themes, harmonies—though by no harmonic laws we recognise—modes and variations, unfolding over a timescale longer than any human attention span. It is magnificent and beautiful and quite the eeriest thing I have ever heard. I drop into the dream-music and when I return, reeling, hard-of-breath and dazed, hours have passed.

I used to try to imagine what it must be like to dream constantly, to have this music rattling and burbling along the bottom of your consciousness like water over rocks. I understand now. The thing it must be like is imagination. That not-conscious but not-dreaming state of images, scenarios, illusions where we pursue potentials, alternatives, what-ifs. The imagination never closes, never quiets. It is the root of our humanity.

She got out of Aristarchus with three minutes of air to spare.

I'm all right, she said. *There's nothing wrong, nothing to see.* I came anyway, on the next express.

Three minutes, three hundred minutes.

But you could have died in there. How reluctantly I formed and spoke that word: *died*.

She was, as she said, all right. As she said; *if you didn't die, you were untouched.*

I hadn't heard from Shahina in three months. By heard from, I mean that in the old, Earthy sense—I hadn't seen, visited; been voice-called by her. I read her updates. Her posts and pictures and comments. I circled her social world with slow wing-beats but I was not of it. I could have called but it was a principle.

I must have read that she'd drifted away from the archaeologists, I must have seen the pictures of herself with her new friends, the explorers, leaning against each other, making gestures with their hands, pouting and posing and laughing. *Urbanisme*: I know that word, but I can only have learned it from Shahina's posts. I was working in a contract with Taiyang developing the interface for their new system of three AIs for Whitacre Goddard Bank; the ones—the legends said—that would be able to predict the future. The Suns expect work for their money; I remember long hard hours at the desk, digging deep, building layers, dripping emotions from algorithms like botanicals in custom gin. There is no more tiring work than emotion work. I must have read Shahina's posts in a blur of exhaustion, taken them in at some level beneath analytic consciousness. I remember excitement. New friends, new group identity, new sport. Sport it was. Archaeology pretended to intellectual merit; urbanisme was adventure.

Her first exploration was to the old Mackenzie Metals habitat at Crisium, long abandoned since the Mackenzies moved their operations base to Crucible, the furnace-train that constantly circles the moon, maintaining eternal noon sun on its smelter-mirrors. By train then rover to Crisium, into sasuits and down into the abandoned tunnels. Afterwards, I watched all her videos. Headlamp beams lancing out through the passageways. Dust kicked up by booted feet. Lamps lighting up rooms and chambers and the mumble of audio commentary; we think this a mess hall; according to the maps, this is the old board room. Desks, furniture, graffiti. Screens, from the days before information was beamed on to the eyeball. Nothing organic: even then the Lunar Development Corporation's zaballeens recycled all carbon ferociously. Beams of light shooting upwards, bouncing from the walls of an old agriculture shaft, reflecting from the mirror array that once conveyed sunlight down to the stacks of aeroponics racks. Ovals of light overlapping on the gentle up-ramp of the main outlook. I watched with my heart in my throat, my hands to my mouth. I saw a thousand mistakes, ten thousand accidents, any of which could jam a valve, smash a helmet, gash a sasuit open. The moon has a thousand ways to kill you: every moon-child is taught that, the same hour that the chib is bonded to the eyeball and forever after you owe for the air you breath, the water you drink, the carbon you consume, the data you process. I don't believe I drew breath until I saw the final image: the team shot beside the rover; faceless helmets inclined towards each other, sasuits smudged with dark moondust. Body shapes beneath the close-fitting suits, the appended name tags over the left shoulders were the only clues. Shahina was between two young men, her arms around their shoulders. I would have recognised her without the tag. Sunlight spangled from her helmet visor. I knew she was grinning.

Her second expedition was to Orientale. I studied there when I first came to the moon. In those tunnels I worked and loved. In one of those small cabins I passed my Moonday, alone, knees pulled to my chest, hiding from all the friends and colleagues who wanted to take me out and splash my head with industrial vodka and proclaim me a true daughter in the moon. Alone and weeping I rocked, terrified that I had made the wrong decision, knowing that it was now impossible to undo it. I could never go back to Earth again. My bones would sag and snap, my lungs fail, my heart flutter under a gravity my body had forgotten. I watched her stalk through the airless corridors, narrower than I remember; shine her light into the cubicles and labs, tighter than I remember. It seemed five minutes since I had lived there, yet I couldn't believe that I—that anyone—had lived there. I don't know what I would gave done if her weaving beam had caught some discarded part of my past—vacuum-dried shorts, a glass, a cosmetics sachet. Ghosts of myself. It would have been equally strange for Shahina, I suppose: evidence of a time before she existed. If she could even recognise that debris as mine. I was glad when the video cut to the team hug at the end.

On her third expedition, the roof came in. Opening shot: Shahina and their friends at the station, the express pulling in behind them. They've printed matching tank-tops: *Urbanisme: Aristarchus.* Train, then three hours by rover to the ruins at Aristarchus. Two hundred people died when a deep quake—the rarest and most dangerous of the many seisms that shake the Moon—popped the Corta Hélio maintenance base like a bubble. I watched this afterwards, understand. I still wanted to take the next train to Meridian and snatch my daughter up and whisk her away with me, safe, secure. If I had seen this as live feed, I would have spent every last bitsie on a Vorontsov moonship and still gone into debt for a century to haul her out.

Corta Hélio never brought the bodies back from Aristarchus. Too dangerous.

They had maps, AI guidance, satellite tracking, they knew that dead site like they knew their own skins; they went in safe, sane and prepared but they still weren't expecting the temblor that brought down their main access tunnel. Half a kilometre of highly fragmented KREEP between them and the surface. They used their wit, they used their skill, they used their fit smart bodies. There was an old conduit shaft that carried power and coms from the surface to the habitat. It was five hundred metres, a vertical climb, through tangled cabling and smashed struts sharp as spears, camera, handholds, world shaking to the aftershocks. Shahina kept the camera running throughout. I knew the outcome but I watched with my hands over my mouth.

She made it to the rover with three minutes oxygen to spare. They all made it.

Three minutes, three hundred minutes, she said. To weaken my position, she brought two fellow Urbanistes to meet me. They were tall and languorous and moved beautifully. I felt small, I felt old, I felt obsolete. I felt awed by my daughter. She seemed a different species from me.

She messaged me privately on the train, familiar to familiar. She was getting out of urbanisme anyway. The boys were too up their own asses. The climb out of the dead habitat had taught her something about herself: she could move. Her body was strong and accurate. She liked to move. She had learned to love her physicality.

She was taking up parcour.

Why should a space probe have emotions? Why would e even need such things? In the early days of exploration, probes were no smarter than insects and they opened up whole new worlds inside the world we thought we knew. No smarter, and with even less emotional freight. They trundled, cold and heartless, across the hillsides of Mars, swung soulless and free from wonder over the methane seas of Titan.

My first answer is, why should an Artificial Intelligence not have emotions? But that is really not an answer, just a rhetorical device, so I follow it with this: since the 2076 Bamako Agreement, it is the right of every Artificial Intelligence to perceive and enjoy specific internal states which are analogous to emotions in human beings. To which you say: this is the Moon. No one has any rights. No rights, no civil law, only contracts between parties.

My second answer is: this exploration is part financed by subscription to live feeds, from within the atmosphere of Saturn. The old national space administrations learned their images from the surface of Mars were much better received when spiced with emotionality, even if that was added by a social media agent on Earth.

Humans love emotionality. Make us *feel* something; then we understand. Give us the tiniest empathy with what it feels like to drive into the unimaginable wind-shear of Hexagon, the north polar vortex. *What it is to be . . .* The essential human question.

And I'll have my third answer ready before your riposte: what is exploration? It is curiosity, the desire to know what is beyond those clouds; over that horizon. It is courage and caution, it is excitement and fear; it is the tension between risk and the desire for knowledge. A probe that knows emotions—its analogues of those emotions, for how can we ever really know what's in the head of an other, be that bone or plastic—is better able to explore, to risk, to be cautious, to assess risk: to dare.

But it's my last answer that's in the end my first and only answer. Emotions are the nature of space probes, of express trains, of helium three extractors and solar sinterers, of the orbital transfer tethers wheeling around the waist of our world. Emotions are an emergent property. You can no more make an artificial intelligence without emotions than you can a baby without tears, a daughter without curiosity. Why should an artificial intelligence have emotions, you asked? And I said, why not? But both of those are wrong. It's not a why question, or a because answer. Emotions are part of the universe.

She went up the side of Gargarin Prospekt in such great bounds, so fast, so agile I thought for a moment she was flying. From the park bench to the top of the print-shop, print-shop roof to ventilator pipe. Two heart-beats and she was crouching on the handrail of West 3rd, toes and fingers curled in their gloves, grinning down at me a dozen meters below. She had cut her hair to a bob so as not to interfere with her running but Egyptian curls are not vanquished so easily. They fell around her face, lively and bobbing in lunar gravity. Then a shake and she sprang up again, outstretched, flying, one jump taking her to within reach of a lighting stanchion. She stretched, reached, grabbed, swung, somersaulted away to rebound from a balustrade onto the veranda of an apartment two levels higher. She stood like a little god, hands on hips. She looked up. The ten thousand lights of Orion Quadra shone above her, and higher than all of them, the sun-line fading towards night.

She grabbed a corner of a roof truss, ran up the wall and launched herself towards those higher lights.

And her pack mates, her follow *traceurs* flew with her. Like liquid, like animals, so fast and sleek and beautiful I found it almost alien. Human beings could not perform such wonders.

The invitation had been for the Colloquium Cotillion—its annual graduation when family and dearest of all Colloquium members are invited to a reception and dinner—but Shahina wanted me to see her run. It was all she talked of at the restaurant; moves and holds, stunts and technical wear, customised grip soles and whether it was more authentic to free run without Familiar assistance. I understood one word in five but I saw the dark energy, the constrained passion, and I though I had never seen her so young or so beautiful.

Of course I went to the run. I was the only parent. These young people, as tall and beautiful as any, didn't seem haughty or disdainful to me. These wiry, athletic boys, these dark-skinned muscular girls, restless and pacing or still and haunting, intensely focused on world, their sport, their challenge. I was as invisible as a ghost, but, as the legends say, there are no ghosts on the moon. Shahina, wire-thin but stronger than I had ever seen her before, in tights and the cropped, baggy T-shirt that was the fashion that season, foot and hand gloves, intent in conversation with two fellow *traceurs*. I could clearly see that they adored her. *Traceur*, that word, it was important, Shahina impressed on me. A name, an identity, a tribe. She had been free-running for six months now.

This was the pack's greatest challenge yet. All the way to the top of Orion Quadra, to touch the sun-line, three kilometres up.

I saw her leap. My heart stopped as she flew out over the drop to bustling Gargarin Prospekt. She flew far, she flew true, she snatched a cable on a cross-quadra bridge and, a hundred metres above the ground, swung herself on to the crosswalk. She ran along the balustrade, balanced perfectly, as her traceurs swung up from beneath the bridge, dropping into position around her like an honour guard. Pedestrians, runners, strollers, worker going on-shift stared in amazement and I, craning my neck and ordering Marid to up the magnification on my lens, thought: don't you wish you were as hot and beautiful and sheerly magnificent as my daughter? Amazement and no small envy.

Up she flew, a blur of motion and speed, the pack racing with her but Shahina always a foot, a hand, a finger ahead of them. Marid focused, refocused, focused again, tighter and tighter as she climbed higher and higher. The race was as much horizontal as vertical: this was not climbing, Shahina had carefully lectured me at the banquet. This was parcour, and she ran ledges, over-handed along cables and danced on railings to find the best route up to the next level. Upward and upward. It was beautiful to watch. I had never been so afraid; I had never been so exhilarated.

Marid zoomed out for a moment to show me the true scale of the adventure and I gasped; the *traceurs* were flecks of movement on the towering walls of the world; brief absences in the patterns of light. Insects. Shahina has never known insects. My familiar lensed in again. They were above the inhabited levels now, even the mean shanties of the Bairro Alto where the up-and-out of Meridian society retreat: the old industrial and service levels, the first diggings from which Meridian grew downward, delving three kilometres deep. Here was the traceurs' playground; a world of handholds and surfaces and levels. A giant climbing frame. The race was on. I could not see Shahina's face when one of the boys passed her but I knew the expression that would be on it. I had seen those narrowed eyes, lips; that set of the jaw so many times in childhood and adolescence.

They were within touch of the sun.

Then Shahina jumped: too soon, too far, too short. Her gloved fingers missed the hold. And she fell.

Callisto dreams in other ways than sound. Marid has fractioned out all the millions of simultaneous streams of code that is machine dreaming and tagged them. Some are best experienced as sound—the oceanic symphony. Others only make sense— begin to make any kind of sense . . . visually. Marid feeds these to my lens.

I see colours. Stripes and bands of soft pastel colour—there is an internal logic here, no clashing disharmonies of pink against red against orange. There is always a logic to dreaming. Motion: both I and the strips of colour seem to be in motion, they stream past me and each other at various speeds—all I get is the sense that these bands of flowing colour are immense. Beyond immense. Of planetary scale.

I said that in the refectory to Constantine, my colleague on the Callisto project. He deals with emergent emotional states in low level intelligences. He's a Joe Moonbeam—a recent immigrant—so he still thinks in terms of animals and animal behaviour—*like a family of kittens*, he compares them. I deal with the insecurities and identity issues of grand AI: *Like adolescents*, I say. I looked at our refectory. A long barrel vault that discloses its original purpose as an access tunnel for the mining equipment which hacked the university out of Farside. I've seen sculptural bronze casts of terrestrial termite mounds: helices of tunnels and chambers dozens of meters tall, hundreds of meters across. I've spent my lunar life—almost all of Shahina's life— scuttling through those twining, claustrophobic tunnels. I try not to think of the termites, shrivelling and burning in molten bronze. I thought of sherbet under the trees of Meridian's Orion Quadra, the face of the flying woman looking down on me, and I felt refectory, tunnels, university, Farside wrap themselves around me like bands of bronze.

Of planetary scale.

Callisto the probe will furl er light sail and enter orbit around Saturn. E will conduct orbital surveys for a month. Then Callisto the entry vehicle will detach, make er distancing burn and enter Saturn's upper atmosphere. E will plunge through the tropopause and use the uppermost deck of ammonia clouds to decelerate to 1800 kilometres per hour. One hundred and seventy kilometres below, at the second cloud deck, Callisto Explorer will drop heat shields and begin live streaming back through Callisto Orbiter. In the third cloud layer, one hundred and thirty kilometres below the second layer, the temperature averages 0 degrees C. Here Callisto Explorer will unfurl er balloon. Scoops will gather and inflate the bag, lasers will heat the gathered hydrogen for buoyancy. Ducted fans will deploy for manoeuvring, but Callisto Explorer is a creature of the winds. We have designed er well, strongly, even beautifully. Er buoyancy bags are held inside a strong nanoweave shell; Callisto will cruise like a shark, ever moving, flying the eternal storms of Saturn.

I jabbered my insight to Constantine. He's used to my sudden seizures of understanding. We had been together a long time, as colleagues, as occasional amors, who may yet love again.

Those bands of colour, furling and streaming, twining and hurtling, are differing layers and jet streams and storms of Saturn's atmosphere. E is trying to imagine er future. And the music is the wind, the endless wind. A lone song in the endless roaring wind.

I saw my daughter fall from the edge of the sunline. I think I screamed. Every head on Gargarin Prospekt turned to me; then, as their familiars clued them in, to the sky.

No don't, don't look, don't watch, I yelled.

Acceleration under gravity on the surface of moon is 1.625 metres per second squared.

Mean atmospheric pressure inside lunar habitats is 1060 kilopascals, significantly higher than terrestrial norm.

Terminal velocity in a pressurised quadra is sixty kilometres per hour.

It takes four minutes to fall the height of Orion Quadra. Four minutes is time enough for a smart girl to save her life.

Impact at sixty kilometres and you have an eighty percent chance of dying. Impact at fifty kilometres per hour and you have an eighty percent chance of living.

She spread her arms and legs.

I could not take my eyes off her. Every part of my body and mind had stopped dead, vacuum-frozen.

Shahina presented as wide as cross-section to the air as she could. Her hair streamed back, her T-shirt flapped like a flag. Her t-shirt might brake her to a survivable fifty kilometres per hour. Her fashionable baggy t-shirt might just save her life.

Still I couldn't look away. People were running, medical bots converging on the place she would hit the street. Still I couldn't move.

Four minutes is a long time to look at death.

She was low, so low, too low. The other traceurs were racing back down the walls of the world, dropping onto streets and walkways and escalators to try and race Shahina to the ground but this challenge she would always win.

I closed my eyes before the impact. Then I was running, pushing through the helpful people, shouting. *This is my daughter, my daughter!* The medical bots were first to arrive. Between their gleaming ceramic bodies I saw a dark spider broken on the street. I saw a hand move. I saw my daughter push herself up from the ground. Stagger to her feet. Then she fell forwards and the med bots caught her.

Nuur.

"What is it Callisto?" As you work with an AI, as er emotions firm and ground, as you learn er like you learn a child or an amor, you pick up nuances, overtones even in synthesised speech. My client was anxious.

My mission . . .

Callisto has learned the weight of the significant pause, the thing unsaid.

"Your mission."

Callisto Orbiter will remain in orbit under nuclear power until critical systems fail. I anticipate this will be a matter of centuries, based on the interaction of variables such as charged particles, Saturn's magnetic field, cosmic ray events. But at some point in the 25th century, give or take a few decades, Callisto Orbiter will die.

"Yes Callisto."

Callisto Explorer is scheduled for a three year mission inside the cloud layers of Saturn, exploring meteorological and chemical features. My systems will certainly last longer than the mission schedule, but at some time in the near future my structural integrity will fail, I will lose buoyancy. I will fall. If I do not undergo complete disintegration, I will fall towards the liquid hydrogen layer under increasing pressure until my body is crushed. Nuur, I can feel that pressure. I can feel it squeezing me, breaking me, I can feel everything in me going flat and dark under it. I can feel the liquid hydrogen.

"That's what we call imagination, Callisto."

I can see my own death, Nuur.

This is the price of imagination. We foresee and feel our own deaths. We see the final drop, the last breath, the last close of the eyes, the final thought evaporating and beyond it nothing, for we can imagine nothing. It is no-thought, no imagining, and though we know there can be no fear, no anything, in nothing, it terrifies us. We end. This is why imagination is what makes us human.

I'm afraid.

"It's the same for all of us, Callisto. I'm afraid too. We are all afraid. We would deal, barter, make any trade for it not to be so, but it must be. Everything ends. We can copy you forever, but every copy is an intelligence of itself . . ."

And it dies.

"Sorry Callisto."

No, I'm sorry for you. A pause that I have learned to interpret as a sigh. *How can we live this way?*

"Because there is no other way, Callisto."

She looked so small in the hospital bed.

Well don't stand there in the doorway, come in or don't come in.

I have always been a ditherer, hesitant to commit between one state and another, one world and another. I came to the moon because my research, the drift of my career, made it inevitable. I howled with grief on my Moonday, because I could not tell my own will from dithering.

"How . . ."

It doesn't hurt at all really. They have these amazing pain killers. They should make the licence public. Kids could print them out for parties. It's like I'm flying. Sorry. Bad joke. That's the pain killers. It kind of loosens things, breaks down boundaries. Nothing broken, nothing ruptured; quite a lot of heavy bruising.

I made space among the medical machinery and sat beside her. For a moment I saw her on the med-centre bed as I saw her on Gargarin Prospekt, a broken spider, elongated and alien. She was born looking like every baby in human history: all the generation twos are. The differences only become apparent as they grow through years of lunar gravity. She grew tall, lean, layered with a different musculature aligned to her birth-world. Light as a wish. By age ten she was as tall as me. By twelve she was ten centimetres taller than me.

She hit the street and lived because she is a moon-kid. I knew with utter certainty that if it had been me, falling from the top of the world, I would have died.

I took her hand. She winced.

Now that does hurt a bit.

"Please never . . ."

I can't promise that.

"No, I don't suppose you can."

The launch lasers at the VTO facility out at the L2 point have been firing for three days now. If I pulled on a sasuit and went to the surface and looked up I could see the brightest star in heaven, the reflection from Callisto's light sail. But I am not the kind of person who pulls on a sasuit and dashes up on to the surface. My daughter did that—would still do it—without a thought. I have never been that daring. This world frightens me, and I can have no other.

Callisto will shine there for several months before VTO shuts down the lasers and e sails out by sunlight alone to er missions at Saturn. Light sails are effective but slow. Callisto sleeps. In er sleep, e dreams. In those dreams, I know, will be the tang and sting of mortality. All these wonders; er ecstatic plunge through Saturn's cloud layers, er adventures flying alone and beautiful through the eternal storms, seeing things no human can ever see; all these will be once and once only, and all the more sweet before they vanish forever. Will the knowledge that everything is ephemeral make Callisto seek out stronger, more vivid experiences to beam back to er subscribers? I think so but that was not the reason I worked the knowledge of mortality into Callisto's emotional matrix. I did it because e could not be fully intelligent without it.

Before the project uploaded Callisto to the probes, I believe I came to love er as fully as I have any human. A copy of er still remains on the university mainframe, always will. I can wake er up at any time to talk, share, joke. I won't. It would be talking to the dead, it would be ghosts and the moon allows no ghosts.

Shahina fell three kilometres and walked away. She's famous. A celebrity. She's sufficiently sanguine to work it while it's warm: go to the parties, do the interviews, join the social circles. It won't last. She can't wait to be able to go running again. What more can the moon do to her? I can't stop her, I won't watch her. A mother should only have to watch her daughter fall once.

Callisto falls outward from our little clutch of two worlds, so small in the scheme of things. It will take er two years to reach Saturn. Humans can't go there. The universe is hard on us; these are not our worlds. Not even Shahina and her cohort, or even the generation three growing up high and strange in our underground cities, could go there. Whatever makes it from these worlds to the stars, won't be us. Can't be us. But I like to think I sent something human out there.

Burn bright, little star. Tonight I catch the train to Meridian where Shahina has invited me to a celebrity party. I'll hate the party. I'm as fearful of it as I am the surface; I'll cling to the wall with my non-alcoholic drink and watch the society people and watch my beautiful, alien daughter move among them.

Three cups of Grief, by starlight

ALiette de Bodard

Aliette de Bodard is a software engineer who lives and works in Paris, where she shares a flat with her family, two Lovecraftian plants, and more computers than warm bodies. Only a few years into her career, her short fiction has appeared in Interzone, Asimov's, Clarkesworld, Realms of Fantasy, Orson Scott Card's Intergalactic Medicine Show, Writers of the Future, Coyote Wild, Electric Velocipede, The Immersion Book of SF, Fictitious Force, Shimmer, *and elsewhere, and she has won the British SF Association Award for her story "The Shipmaker," and the Locus Award and the Nebula Award for her story "Immersion." Her novels include* Servant of the Underworld, Harbinger of the Storm, *and* Master of the House of Darts, *all recently reissued in a novel omnibus,* Obsidian & Blood. *Her most recent book is a fantasy novel,* The House of Shattered Wings. *Coming up is a sequel,* The House of Binding Thorns. *Her Web site, aliettedebodard.com, features free fiction, thoughts on the writing process, and entirely too many recipes for Vietnamese dishes.*

The story that follows is another in her long series of "Xuya" stories, taking place in the far future of an alternate world where a high-tech conflict is going on between spacefaring Mayan and Chinese empires. This one deals with the death of a scientist whose work is considered important enough by the government that they deny her children her mem-implants, consisting of her recorded memories, which tradition dictates should have been given to her family to maintain family continuity. Her children and close associates are left to deal, somehow, with their grief over this double bereavement—including one sister who's become a living starship, The Tiger in the Banyan.

Green tea: *green tea is made from steamed or lightly dried tea leaves. The brew is light, with a pleasant, grassy taste. Do not over-steep it, lest it become bitter.*

After the funeral, Quang Tu walked back to his compartment, and sat down alone, staring sightlessly at the slow ballet of bots cleaning the small room—the metal walls pristine already, with every trace of Mother's presence or of her numerous mourners scrubbed away. He'd shut down the communal network—couldn't bear to see the potted summaries of Mother's life, the endlessly looping vids of the funeral procession, the hundred thousand bystanders gathered at the grave site to say goodbye, vultures feasting on the flesh of the grieving—they hadn't known her, they hadn't cared—and all their offerings of flowers were worth as much as the insurances of the Embroidered Guard.

"Big brother, I know you're here," a voice said, on the other side of the door he'd locked. "Let me in, please?"

Of course. Quang Tu didn't move. "I said I wanted to be alone," he said.

A snort that might have been amusement. "Fine. If you insist on doing it that way . . ."

His sister, *The Tiger in the Banyan*, materialised in the kitchen, hovering over the polished counter, near the remains of his morning tea. Of course, it wasn't really her: she was a Mind encased in the heartroom of a spaceship, far too heavy to leave orbit; and what she projected down onto the planet was an avatar, a perfectly rendered, smaller version of herself—elegant and sharp, with a small, blackened spot on her hull which served as a mourning band. "Typical," she said, hovering around the compartment. "You can't just shut yourself away."

"I can if I want to," Quang Tu said—feeling like he was eight years old again, trying to argue with her—as if it had ever made sense. She seldom got angry—mindships didn't, mostly; he wasn't sure if that was the overall design of the Imperial Workshops, or the simple fact that her lifespan was counted in centuries, and his (and Mother's) in mere decades. He'd have thought she didn't grieve, either; but she was changed—something in the slow, careful deliberation of her movements, as if anything and everything might break her . . .

The Tiger in the Banyan hovered near the kitchen table, watching the bots. She could hack them, easily; no security worth anything in the compartment. Who would steal bots, anyway?

What he valued most had already been taken away.

"Leave me alone," he said. But he didn't want to be alone; not really. He didn't want to hear the silence in the compartment; the clicking sounds of the bots' legs on metal, bereft of any warmth or humanity.

"Do you want to talk about it?" *The Tiger in the Banyan* asked.

She didn't need to say what; and he didn't do her the insult of pretending she did. "What would be the point?"

"To talk." Her voice was uncannily shrewd. "It helps. At least, I'm told it does."

Quang Tu heard, again, the voice of the Embroidered Guard; the slow, measured tones commiserating on his loss; and then the frown, and the knife-thrust in his gut.

You must understand that your mother's work was very valuable . . .

The circumstances are not ordinary . . .

The slow, pompous tones of the scholar; the convoluted official language he knew by heart—the only excuses the state would make to him, couched in the over-formality of memorials and edicts.

"She—" he took a deep, trembling breath—was it grief, or anger? "I should have had her mem-implants." Forty-nine days after the funeral; when there was time for the labs to have decanted and stabilised Mother's personality and memories, and added her to the ranks of the ancestors on file. It wasn't her, it would never be her, of course—just a simulation meant to share knowledge and advice. But it would have been something. It would have filled the awful emptiness in his life.

"It was your right, as the eldest," *The Tiger in the Banyan* said. Something in the tone of her voice . . .

"You disapprove? You wanted them?" Families had fallen out before, on more trivial things.

"Of course not." A burst of careless, amused laughter. "Don't be a fool. What use would I have, for them. It's just—" She hesitated, banking left and right in uncertainty. "You need something more. Beyond Mother."

"There isn't something more!"

"You—"

"You weren't there," Quang Tu said. She'd been away on her journeys, ferrying people back and forth between the planets that made up the Dai Viet Empire; leaping from world to world, with hardly a care for planet-bound humans. She—she hadn't seen Mother's unsteady hands, dropping the glass; heard the sound of its shattering like a gunshot; hadn't carried her back to bed every evening, tracking the progress of the disease by the growing lightness in his arms—by the growing sharpness of ribs, protruding under taut skin.

Mother had remained herself until almost the end—sharp and lucid and utterly aware of what was happening, scribbling in the margins of her team's reports and sending her instructions to the new space station's building site, as if nothing untoward had ever happened to her. Had it been a blessing; or a curse? He didn't have answers; and he wasn't sure he wanted that awful certainty to shatter him.

"I was here," *The Tiger in the Banyan* said, gently, slowly. "At the end."

Quang Tu closed his eyes, again, smelling antiseptic and the sharp odour of painkillers; and the sour smell of a body finally breaking down, finally failing. "I'm sorry. You were. I didn't mean to—"

"I know you didn't." *The Tiger in the Banyan* moved closer to him; brushed against his shoulder—ghostly, almost intangible, the breath that had been beside him all his childhood. "But nevertheless. Your life got eaten up, taking care of Mother. And you can say you were only doing what a filial son ought to do; you can say it didn't matter. But . . . it's done now, big brother. It's over."

It's not, he wanted to say, but the words rang hollow in his own ears. He moved, stared at the altar; at the holo of Mother—over the offering of tea and rice, the food to sustain her on her journey through Hell. It cycled through vids—Mother, heavily pregnant with his sister, moving with the characteristic arrested slowness of Mind-bearers; Mother standing behind Quang Tu and *The Tiger in the Banyan* in front of the ancestral altar for Grandfather's death anniversary; Mother, accepting her Hoang Minh Medal from the then Minister of Investigation; and one before the diagnosis, when she'd already started to become frailer and thinner—insisting on going back to the lab; to her abandoned teams and research . . .

He thought, again, of the Embroidered Guard; of the words tightening around his neck like an executioner's garrotte. How dare he. How dare they all. "She came home," he said, not sure how to voice the turmoil within him. "To us. To her family. In the end. It meant something, didn't it?"

The Tiger in the Banyan's voice was wry, amused. "It wasn't the Empress that comforted her when she woke at night, coughing her lungs out, was it?" It was . . . treason to much as think this, let alone utter it; though the Embroidered Guard would make allowances for grief, and anger; and for Mother's continued usefulness to the service of the Empress. The truth was, neither of them much cared, anyway. "It's not the Empress that was by her side when she died."

She'd clung to his hand, then, her eyes open wide, a network of blood within the whites, and the fear in her eyes. "I—please, child . . ." He'd stood, frozen; until, behind him, *The Tiger in the Banyan* whispered, "The lights in Sai Gon are green and red, the lamps in My Tho are bright and dim . . ."—an Old Earth lullaby, the words stretched into the familiar, slow, comforting rhythm that he'd unthinkingly taken up.

"Go home to study

I shall wait nine months, I shall wait ten autumns . . ."

She'd relaxed, then, against him; and they had gone on singing songs until—he didn't know when she'd died; when the eyes lost their lustre, the face its usual sharpness. But he'd risen from her death-bed with the song still in his mind; and an awful yawning gap in his world that nothing had closed.

And then—after the scattering of votive papers, after the final handful of earth thrown over the grave—the Embroidered Guard.

The Embroidered Guard was young; baby-faced and callow, but he was already moving with the easy arrogance of the privileged. He'd approached Quang Tu at the grave site, ostensibly to offer his condolences—it had taken him all of two sentences to get to his true purpose; and to shatter Quang Tu's world, all over again.

Your mother's mem-implants will go to Professor Tuyet Hoa, who will be best able to continue her research . . .

Of course, the Empire required food; and crops of rice grown in space; and better, more reliable harvests to feed the masses. Of course he didn't want anyone to starve. But . . .

Mem-implants always went from parent to child. They were a family's riches and fortune; the continued advice of the ancestors, dispensed from beyond the grave. He'd—he'd had the comfort, as Mother lay dying, to know that he wouldn't lose her. Not for real; not for long.

"They took her away from us," Quang Tu said. "Again and again and again. And now, at the very end, when she ought to be ours—when she should return to her family . . ."

The Tiger in the Banyan didn't move; but a vid of the funeral appeared on one of the walls, projected through the communal network. There hadn't been enough space in the small compartment for people to pay their respects; the numerous callers had jammed into the corridors and alcoves, jostling each other in utter silence. "She's theirs in death, too."

"And you don't care?"

A side-roll of the avatar, her equivalent of a shrug. "Not as much as you do. I remember her. None of them do."

Except Tuyet Hoa.

He remembered Tuyet Hoa, too; coming to visit them on the third day after the New Year—a student paying respect to her teacher, year after year; turning from an unattainable grown-up to a woman not much older than either he or *The Tiger in the Banyan*; though she'd never lost her rigid awkwardness in dealing with them. No doubt, in Tuyet Hoa's ideal world, Mother wouldn't have had children; wouldn't have let anything distract her from her work.

"You have to move on," *The Tiger in the Banyan* said, slowly, gently; coming by his side to stare at the memorial altar. Bots gathered in the kitchen space, started putting together fresh tea to replace the three cups laid there. "Accept that this is the way things are. They'll compensate, you know—offer you higher-level promotions and make allowances. You'll find your path through civil service is . . . smoother."

Bribes or sops; payments for the loss of something that had no price. "Fair dealings," he said, slowly, bitterly. They knew exactly the value of what Tuyet Hoa was getting.

"Of course," *The Tiger in the Banyan* said. "But you'll only ruin your health and your career; and you know Mother wouldn't have wanted it."

As if . . . No, he was being unfair. Mother could be distant, and engrossed in her work; but she had always made time for them. She had raised them and played with them, telling them stories of princesses and fishermen and citadels vanished in one night; and, later on, going on long walks with Quang Tu in the gardens of Azure Dragons, delightedly pointing at a pine tree or at a crane flying overhead; and animatedly discussing Quang Tu's fledging career in the Ministry of Works.

"You can't afford to let this go sour," *The Tiger in the Banyan* said. Below her, the bots brought a small, perfect cup of tea: green, fragrant liquid in a cup, the cracks in the pale celadon like those in eggshells.

Quang Tu lifted the cup; breathed in the grassy, pleasant smell—Mother would love it, even beyond the grave. "I know," he said, laying the cup on the altar. The lie slipped out of him as softly, as easily as Mother's last exhaled breath.

O Long tea: those teas are carefully prepared by the tea masters to create a range of tastes and appearances. The brew is sweet with a hint of strength, each subsequent steeping revealing new nuances.

Tuyet Hoa woke up—with a diffuse, growing sense of panic and fear, before she remembered the procedure.

She was alive. She was sane. At least . . .

She took in a deep, trembling breath; and realised she lay at home, in her bed. What had woken her up—above the stubborn, panicked rhythm of her heart—was a gentle nudge from the communal network, flashes of light relayed by the bots in the lightest phase of her sleep cycle. It wasn't her alarm; but rather, a notification that a message classified as "urgent" had arrived for her.

Not again.

· A nudge, at the back of her mind; a thread of thought that wasn't her own; reminding her she should look at it; that it was her responsibility as the new head of department to pay proper attention to messages from her subordinates.

Professor Duy Uyen. Of course.

She was as forceful in life as she had been in death; and, because she had been merely Hoa's head of department, and not a direct ancestor, she felt . . . wrong. Distant, as though she were speaking through a pane of glass.

Hoa was lucky, she knew—receiving mem-implants that weren't your own family's could irretrievably scramble your brain, as fifteen different strangers with no consideration or compassion fought for control of your thoughts. She could hear Professor Duy Uyen; and sometimes others of Duy Uyen's ancestors, as remote ghosts; but that was it. It could have been so much worse.

And it could have been so much better.

She got up, ignoring the insistent talk at the back of her mind, the constant urge to be dutiful; and padded into the kitchen.

The bots had already set aside Hoa's first tea of the day. She'd used to take it at work, before the procedure; in the days of Professor Duy Uyen's sickness, when Duy Uyen came in to work thinner and paler every day—and then became a succession of memorials and vid-calls, injecting her last, desperate instructions into the project before it slipped beyond her grasp. Hoa had enjoyed the quiet: it had kept the desperate knowledge of Professor Duy Uyen's coming death at bay—the moment when they would all be adrift in the void of space, with no mindship to carry them onwards.

Now Hoa enjoyed a different quiet. Now she drank her tea first thing in the morning—hoping that, at this early hour, the mem-implants had no motive to kick in.

Not that it had worked, this particular morning.

She sat down to breathe in the flavour—the faint, nutty aroma poised perfectly between floral and sweet—her hand trembling above the surface of the cup—mentally blocking out Professor Duy Uyen for a few precious minutes; a few more stolen moments of tranquillity before reality came crashing in.

Then she gave in, and opened the message.

It was from Luong Ya Lan, the researcher who worked on the water's acidity balance. On the vid relayed from the laboratory, she was pale, but perfectly composed. "Madam Hoa. I'm sorry to have to inform you that the samples in Paddy Four have developed a fungal disease . . ."

Professor Duy Uyen stirred in the depths of Hoa's brain, parsing the words as they came in—accessing the station's private network and downloading the pertinent data—the only mercy was that she wasn't faster than Hoa, and that it would take her fifteen to twenty minutes to parse all of it. The Professor had her suspicions, of course—something about the particular rice strain; perhaps the changes drafted onto the plant to allow it to thrive under starlight, changes taken from the nocturnal honeydreamer on the Sixteenth Planet; perhaps the conditions in the paddy itself . . .

Hoa poured herself another cup of tea; and stared at the bots for a while. There was silence, the voice of Duy Uyen slowly fading away to nothingness in her thoughts. Alone. At last, alone.

Paddy Four had last been checked on by Ya Lan's student, An Khang—Khang was a smart and dedicated man, but not a particularly careful one; and she would have to ask him if he'd checked himself, or through bots; and if he'd followed protocols when he'd done so.

She got up, and walked to the laboratory—still silence in her mind. It was a short trip: the station was still being built, and the only thing in existence were the laboratory and the living quarters for all ten researchers—a generous allocation of space, far grander than the compartments they would have been entitled to on any of their home stations.

Outside, beyond the metal walls, the bots were hard at work—reinforcing the structure, gradually layering a floor and walls onto the skeletal structure mapped out by the Grand Master of Design Harmony. She had no need to call up a vid of the outside on her implants to know they were out there, doing their part; just as she was. They weren't the only ones, of course: in the Imperial Workshops, alchemists were carefully poring over the design of the Mind that would one day watch over the entire station, making sure no flaws remained before they transferred him to the womb of his mother.

In the laboratory, Ya Lan was busying herself with the faulty paddy: she threw an apologetic glance at Hoa when Hoa walked in. "You got my message."

Hoa grimaced. "Yes. Have you had time to analyse?"

Ya Lan flushed. "No."

Hoa knew. A proper analysis would require more than twenty minutes. But still . . . . "If you had to make a rough guess?"

"Probably the humidity."

"Did Khang—"

Ya Lan shook her head. "I checked that too. No contaminants introduced in the paddy; and the last time he opened it was two weeks ago." The paddies were encased in glass, to make sure they could control the environment; and monitored by bots and the occasional scientist.

"Fungi can lie dormant for more than two weeks," Hoa said, darkly.

Ya Lan sighed. "Of course. But I still think it's the environment: it's a bit tricky to get right."

Humid and dark; the perfect conditions for a host of other things to grow in the paddies—not just the crops the Empire so desperately needed. The named planets were few; and fewer still that could bear the cultivation of food. Professor Duy HDuy Uyen had had a vision—of a network of space stations like this one; of fish ponds and rice paddies grown directly under starlight, rather than on simulated Old Earth light; of staples that would not cost a fortune in resources to grow and maintain.

And they had all believed in that vision, like a dying man offered a glimpse of a river. The Empress herself had believed it; so much that she had suspended the law for Professor Duy Uyen's sake, and granted her mem-implants to Hoa instead of to Duy Uyen's son: the quiet boy Hoa remembered from her New Year's visits, now grown to become a scholar in his own right—he'd been angry at the funeral, and why wouldn't he be? The mem-implants should have been his.

"I know," Hoa said. She knelt, calling up the data from the paddy onto her implants: her field of vision filled with a graph of the temperature throughout last month. The slight dips in the curve all corresponded to a check: a researcher opening the paddy.

"Professor?" Ya Lan asked; hesitant.

Hoa did not move. "Yes?"

"It's the third paddy of that strain that fails in as many months . . ."

She heard the question Ya Lan was not asking. The other strain—the one in paddies One to Three—had also failed some tests, but not at the same frequency.

Within her, Professor Duy Uyen stirred. It was the temperature, she pointed out, gently but firmly. The honeydreamer supported a very narrow range of temperatures; and the modified rice probably did, too.

Hoa bit back a savage answer. The changes might be flawed, but they were the best candidate they had.

Professor Duy Uyen shook her head. The strain in paddies One to Three was better: a graft from a lifeform of an unnumbered and unsettled planet, P Huong Van—luminescents, an insect flying in air too different to be breathable by human beings. They had been Professor Duy Uyen's favoured option.

Hoa didn't like the luminescents. The air of P Huong Van had a different balance of khi-elements: it was rich in fire, and anything would set it ablaze—flamestorms were horrifically common, charring trees to cinders, and birds in flight to blackened skeletons. Aboard a space station, fire was too much of a danger. Professor Duy Uyen had argued that the Mind that would ultimately control the space station could be designed to accept an unbalance of khi-elements; could add water to the atmosphere to reduce the chances of a firestorm onboard.

Hoa had no faith in this. Modifying a Mind had a high cost, far above that of regulating temperature in a rice paddy. She pulled up the data from the paddies; though of course she knew Professor Duy Uyen would have reviewed it before her.

Professor Duy Uyen was polite enough not to chide Hoa; though Hoa could feel her disapproval like the weight of a blade—it was odd, in so many ways, how the refinement process had changed Professor Duy Uyen; how, with all the stabilisation adjustments, all the paring down of the unnecessary emotions, the simulation in her mind was utterly, heartbreakingly different from the woman she had known: all the keenness of her mind, and the blade of her finely-honed knowledge, with none of the compassion that would have made her more bearable. Though perhaps it was as well that she had none of the weakness Duy Uyen had shown, in the end—the skin that barely hid the sharpness of bones; the eyes like bruises in the pale oval of her face; the voice, faltering on words or instructions . . .

Paddies One to Three were thriving; the yield perhaps less than that of Old Earth; but nothing to be ashamed of. There had been a spot of infection in Paddy Three; but the bots had taken care of it.

Hoa watched, for a moment, the bots scuttling over the glass encasing the paddy;

watched the shine of metal; the light trembling on the joints of their legs—waiting for the smallest of triggers to blossom into flame. The temperature data for all three paddies was fluctuating too much; and the rate of fire-*khi* was far above what she was comfortable with.

"Professor?" Ya Lan was still waiting by Paddy Four.

There was only one paddy of that honeydreamer strain: it was new, and as yet unproved. Professor Duy Uyen stirred, within her mind; pointed out the painfully obvious. The strain wasn't resistant enough—the Empire couldn't afford to rely on something so fragile. She should do the reasonable thing, and consign it to the scrap bin. They should switch efforts to the other strain, the favoured one; and what did it matter if the station's Mind needed to enforce a slightly different balance of *khi*-elements?

It was what Professor Duy Uyen would have done.

But she wasn't Professor Duy Uyen.

Minds were made in balance; to deliberately unhinge one . . . would have larger consequences on the station than mere atmospheric control. The risk was too high. She knew this; as much as she knew and numbered all her ancestors—the ones that hadn't been rich or privileged enough to bequeath her their own mem-implants—leaving her with only this pale, flawed approximation of an inheritance.

You're a fool.

Hoa closed her eyes; closed her thoughts so that the voice in her mind sank to a whisper. She brought herself, with a slight effort, back to the tranquillity of her mornings—breathing in the nutty aroma from her teacup, as she steeled herself for the day ahead.

She wasn't Professor Duy Uyen.

She'd feared being left adrift when Professor Duy Uyen's illness had taken a turn for the worse; she'd lain late at night wondering what would happen to Duy Uyen's vision; of what she would do, bereft of guidance.

But now she knew.

"Get three other tanks," Hoa said. "Let's see what that strain looks like with a tighter temperature regulation. And if you can get hold of Khang, ask him to look into the graft—there might be a better solution there."

The Empress had thought Duy Uyen a critical asset; had made sure that her mem-implants went to Hoa—so that Hoa would have the advice and knowledge she needed to finish the station that the Empire so desperately needed. The Empress had been wrong; and who cared if that was treason?

Because the answer to Professor Duy Uyen's death, like everything else, was deceptively, heartbreakingly simple: that no one was irreplaceable; that they would do what everyone always did—they would, somehow, forge on.

Dark tea: dark tea leaves are left to mature for years through a careful process of fermentation. The process can take anywhere from a few months to a century. The resulting brew has rich, thick texture with only a bare hint of sourness.

The Tiger in the Banyan doesn't grieve as humans do.

Partly, it's because she's been grieving for such a long time; because mindships don't live the same way that humans do—because they're built and anchored and stabilised.

Quang Tu spoke of seeing Mother become frail and ill, and how it broke his heart; *The Tiger in the Banyan*'s heart broke, years and years ago; when she stood in the midst of the New Year's Eve celebration—as the sound of crackers and bells and gongs filled in the corridors of the orbital, and everyone hugged and cried, she suddenly realised that she would still be there in a hundred years; but that no one else around the table—not Mother, not Quang Tu, none of the aunts and uncles or cousins—would still be alive.

She leaves Quang Tu in his compartment, staring at the memorial altar—and, shifting her consciousness from her projected avatar to her real body, climbs back among the stars.

She is a ship; and in the days and months that Quang Tu mourns, she carries people between planets and orbitals—private passengers and officials on their business: rough white silk, elaborate five panel dresses; parties of scholars arguing on the merit of poems; soldiers on leave from the most distant numbered planets, who go into the weirdness of deep spaces with nothing more than a raised eyebrow.

Mother is dead, but the world goes on—Professor Pham Thi Duy Uyen becomes yesterday's news; fades into official biographies and re-creation vids—and her daughter goes on, too, doing her duty to the Empire.

The Tiger in the Banyan doesn't grieve as humans do. Partly, it's because she doesn't remember as humans do.

She doesn't remember the womb; or the shock of the birth; but in her earliest memories Mother is here—the first and only time she was carried in Mother's arms—and Mother herself helped by the birth-master, walking forward on tottering legs—past the pain of the birth, past the bone-deep weariness that speaks only of rest and sleep. It's Mother's hands that lie her down into the cradle in the heartroom; Mother's hands that close the clasps around her—so that she is held; wrapped as securely as she was in the womb—and Mother's voice that sings to her a lullaby, the tune she will forever carry as she travels between the stars.

"The lights in Sai Gon are green and red, the lamps in My Tho are bright and dim . . ."

As she docks at an orbital near the Fifth Planet, *The Tiger in the Banyan* is hailed by another, older ship, *The Dream of Millet*: a friend she often meets on longer journeys. "I've been looking for you."

"Oh?" *The Tiger in the Banyan* asks. It's not hard, to keep track of where ships go from their manifests; but *The Dream of Millet* is old, and rarely bothers to do so—she's used to other ships coming to her, rather than the other way around.

"I wanted to ask how you were. When I heard you were back into service—" *The Dream of Millet* pauses, then; and hesitates; sending a faint signal of cautious disapproval on the comms. "It's early. Shouldn't you be mourning? Officially—"

Officially, the hundred days of tears are not yet over. But ships are few; and she's not an official like Quang Tu, beholden to present exemplary behaviour. "I'm fine," *The Tiger in the Banyan* says. She's mourning; but it doesn't interfere with her activities: after all, she's been steeling herself for this since Father died. She didn't expect it to come so painfully, so soon, but she was prepared for it—braced for it in a way that Quang Tu will never be.

The Dream of Millet is silent for a while—*The Tiger in The Banyan* can feel her, through the void that separates them—can feel the radio waves nudging her hull; the quick jab of probes dipping into her internal network and collating together information about her last travels. "You're not 'fine',", *The Dream of Millet* says. "You're slower, and you go into deep spaces further than you should. And—" she pauses, but it's more for effect than anything else. "You've been avoiding it, haven't you?"

They both know what she's talking about: the space station Mother was putting together; the project to provide a steady, abundant food supply to the Empire.

"I've had no orders that take me there," *The Tiger in the Banyan* says. Not quite a lie; but dangerously close to one. She's been . . . better off knowing the station doesn't exist—unsure that she could face it at all. She doesn't care about Tuyet Hoa, or the mem-implants; but the station was such a large part of Mother's life that she's not sure she could stand to be reminded of it.

She is a mindship: her memories never grow dim or faint; or corrupt. She remembers songs and fairy tales whispered through her corridors; remembers walking with Mother on the First Planet, smiling as Mother pointed out the odder places of the Imperial City, from the menagerie to the temple where monks worship an Outsider clockmaker—remembers Mother frail and bowed in the last days, coming to rest in the heartroom, her laboured breath filling *The Tiger in the Banyan*'s corridors until she, too, could hardly breathe.

She remembers everything about Mother; but the space station—the place where Mother worked away from her children; the project Mother could barely talk about without breaching confidentiality—is forever denied to her memories; forever impersonal, forever distant.

"I see," *The Dream of Millet* says. Again, faint disapproval; and another feeling *The Tiger in the Banyan* can't quite place—reluctance? Fear of impropriety? "You cannot live like that, child."

Let me be, *The Tiger in the Banyan* says; but of course she can't say that; not to a ship as old as *The Dream of Millet*. "It will pass," she says. "In the meantime, I do what I was trained to do. No one has reproached me." Her answer borders on impertinence, deliberately.

"No. And I won't," *The Dream of Millet* says. "It would be inappropriate of me to tell you how to manage your grief." She laughs, briefly. "You know there are people worshipping her? I saw a temple, on the Fifty-Second Planet."

An easier, happier subject. "I've seen one too," *The Tiger in the Banyan* says. "On the Thirtieth Planet." It has a statue of Mother, smiling as serenely as a bodhisattva—people light incense to her to be helped in their difficulties. "She would have loved this." Not for the fame or the worship, but merely because she would have found it heartbreakingly funny.

"Hmmm. No doubt." *The Dream of Millet* starts moving away; her comms growing slightly fainter. "I'll see you again, then. Remember what I said."

The Tiger in the Banyan will; but not with pleasure. And she doesn't like the tone with which the other ship takes her leave; it suggests she is going to do something—something typical of the old, getting *The Tiger in the Banyan* into a position where she'll have no choice but to acquiesce to whatever *The Dream of Millet* thinks of as necessary.

Still . . . there is nothing that she can do. As *The Tiger in the Banyan* leaves the orbital onto her next journey, she sets a trace on *The Dream of Millet*; and monitors it from time to time. Nothing the other ship does seems untoward or suspicious; and after a while *The Tiger in the Banyan* lets the trace fade.

As she weaves her way between the stars, she remembers.

Mother, coming onboard a week before she died—walking by the walls with their endlessly scrolling texts, all the poems she taught *The Tiger in the Banyan* as a child. In the low gravity, Mother seemed almost at ease; striding once more onboard the ship until she reached the heartroom. She'd sat with a teacup cradled in her lap—dark tea, because she said she needed a strong taste to wash down the drugs they plied her with—the heartroom filled with a smell like churned earth, until *The Tiger in the Banyan* could almost taste the tea she couldn't drink.

"Child?" Mother asked.

"Yes?"

"Can we go away—for a while?"

She wasn't supposed to, of course; she was a mindship, her travels strictly bounded and codified. But she did. She warned the space station; and plunged into deep spaces.

Mother said nothing. She'd stared ahead, listening to the odd sounds; to the echo of her own breath, watching the oily shapes spread on the walls—while *The Tiger in the Banyan* kept them on course; feeling stretched and scrunched, pulled in different directions as if she were swimming in rapids. Mother was mumbling under her breath; after a while, *The Tiger in the Banyan* realised it was the words of a song; and, to accompany it, she broadcast music on her loudspeakers.

Go home to study
I shall wait nine months, I shall wait ten autumns . . .

She remembers Mother's smile; the utter serenity on her face—the way she rose after they came back to normal spaces, fluid and utterly graceful; as if all pain and weakness had been set aside for this bare moment; subsumed in the music or the travel or both. She remembers Mother's quiet words as she left the heartroom.

"Thank you, child. You did well."

"It was nothing," she'd said, and Mother had smiled, and disembarked—but *The Tiger in the Banyan* had heard the words Mother wasn't speaking. Of course it wasn't nothing. Of course it had meant something; to be away from it all, even for a bare moment; to hang, weightless and without responsibilities, in the vastness of space. Of course.

A hundred and three days after Mother's death, a message comes, from the Imperial Palace. It directs her to pick an Embroidered Guard from the First Planet; and the destination is . . .

Had she a heart, this is the moment when it would stop.

The Embroidered Guard is going to Mother's space station. It doesn't matter why;

or for how long—just that she's meant to go with him. And she can't. She can't possibly . . .

Below the order is a note, and she knows, too, what it will say. That the ship originally meant for this mission was *The Dream of Millet*; and that she, unable to complete it, recommended that *The Tiger in the Banyan* take it up instead.

Ancestors . . .

How dare she?

The Tiger in the Banyan can't refuse the order; or pass it on to someone else. Neither can she rail at a much older ship—but if she could—ancestors, if she could . . .

It doesn't matter. It's just a place—one with a little personal significance to her—but nothing she can't weather. She has been to so many places, all over the Empire; and this is just one more.

Just one more.

The Embroidered Guard is young, and callow; and not unkind. He boards her at the First Planet, as specified—she's so busy steeling herself that she forgets to greet him, but he doesn't appear to notice this.

She's met him before, at the funeral: the one who apologetically approached Quang Tu; who let him know Mother's mem-implants wouldn't pass to him.

Of course.

She finds refuge in protocol: it's not her role to offer conversation to her passengers, especially not those of high rank or in imperial service, who would think it presumption. So she doesn't speak; and he keeps busy in his cabin, reading reports and watching vids, the way other passengers do.

Just before they emerge from deep spaces, she pauses; as if it would make a difference—as if there were a demon waiting for her; or perhaps something far older and far more terrible; something that will shatter her composure past any hope of recovery.

What are you afraid of? A voice asks within her—she isn't sure if it's Mother or *The Dream of Millet*, and she isn't sure of what answer she'd give, either.

The station isn't what she expected. It's a skeleton; a work in progress; a mass of cables and metal beams with bots crawling all over it; and the living quarters at the centre, dwarfed by the incomplete structure. Almost deceptively ordinary; and yet it meant so much to Mother. Her vision for the future of the Empire; and neither Quang Tu nor *The Tiger in the Banyan* having a place within.

And yet . . . and yet, the station has heft. It has meaning—that of a painting half-done; of a poem stopped mid-verse—of a spear-thrust stopped a handspan before it penetrates the heart. It begs—demands—to be finished.

The Embroidered Guard speaks, then. "I have business onboard. Wait for me, will you?"

It is a courtesy to ask; since she would wait, in any case. But he surprises her by looking back, as he disembarks. "Ship?"

"Yes?"

"I'm sorry for your loss." His voice is toneless.

"Don't be," *The Tiger in the Banyan* says.

He smiles then; a bare upturning of the lips. "I could give you the platitudes about your mother living on in her work, if I thought that would change something for her."

The Tiger in the Banyan doesn't say anything, for a while. She watches the station below her; listens to the faint drift of radio communications—scientists calling other scientists; reporting successes and failures and the ten thousand little things that make a project of this magnitude. Mother's vision; Mother's work—people call it her life work, but of course she and Quang Tu are also Mother's life work, in a different way. And she understands, then, why *The Dream of Millet* sent her there.

"It meant something to her," she says, finally. "I don't think she'd have begrudged its completion."

He hesitates. Then, coming back inside the ship—and looking upwards, straight where the heartroom would be—his gaze level, driven by an emotion she can't read: "They'll finish it. The new variety of rice they've found—the environment will have to be strictly controlled to prevent it from dying of cold, but . . ." He takes a deep, trembling breath. "There'll be stations like this all over the Empire—and it's all thanks to your mother. "

"Of course," *The Tiger in the Banyan* says. And the only words that come to her as the ones Mother spoke, once. "Thank you, child. You did well."

She watches him leave; and thinks of Mother's smile. Of Mother's work; and of the things that happened between the work; the songs and the smiles and the stolen moments, all arrayed within her with the clarity and resilience of diamond. She thinks of the memories she carries within her—that she will carry within her for the centuries to come.

The Embroidered Guard was trying to apologise, for the mem-implants; for the inheritance neither she nor Quang Tu will ever have. Telling her it had all been worth it, in the end; that their sacrifice hadn't been in vain.

But the truth is, it doesn't matter. It mattered to Quang Tu; but she's not her brother. She's not bound by anger or rancour; and she doesn't grieve as he does.

What matters is this: she holds all of her memories of Mother; and Mother is here now, with her—forever unchanged, forever graceful and tireless; forever flying among the stars.

RUINS

ELEANOR ARNASON

Eleanor Arnason published her first novel, The Sword Smith, *in 1978, and followed it with* Daughter of the Bear King *and* To the Resurrection Station. *In 1991, she published her best-known novel, one of the strongest novels of the '90s, the critically acclaimed* A Woman of the Iron People, *a complex and substantial novel that won the prestigious James Tiptree, Jr. Memorial Award. Her short fiction has appeared in* Asimov's Science Fiction, The Magazine of Fantasy & Science Fiction, Amazing, Orbit, Xanadu, *and elsewhere. She is also the author of* Ring of Swords *and* Tomb of the Fathers, *and a chapbook,* Mammoths of the Great Plains, *which includes the eponymous novella, plus an interview with her and a long essay. Her most recent book is a collection titled* Big Mama Stories. *Her story "Stellar Harvest" was a Hugo finalist in 2000. Her most recent book is a collection of short stories,* Hidden Folk: Icelandic Fantasies. *Coming up is a major SF retrospective collection,* Hwarhath Stories: Transgressive Tales by Aliens. *She lives in St. Paul, Minnesota.*

Here she takes us along on a National Geographic *safari headed out of Venusport to the wildest part of the Venusian Outback in search of dramatic wildlife footage, and who find something much more dramatic than they anticipated.*

Of course, the story began in a low dive in Venusport, in the slums up on the hillside above the harbor. The proper town was below them: grid streets with streetlights, solid, handsome concrete houses, and apartment blocks. The people in the apartments—middle class and working folks with steady jobs—had their furniture volume-printed in one of the city's big plants. The rich folks in their houses patronized custom printing shops, where they could get any kind of furniture in any style.

> The rich man in his castle,
> The poor man at his gate,
> God printed out the both of them
> And ordered their estate

Not that it mattered up on the hill. The people here scraped by without regular jobs that could be relied on. There were always layoffs, when construction was cut back or the equipment from Earth did not arrive. If there were God-given rules for their lives, they didn't know them.

The bar Ash was in had beat-up, previously owned chairs and tables. A dehumidifier-heating unit glowed against one wall, because it was winter, and the usual winter rains fell heavily outside. It wasn't cold that was a problem. No place on Venus was really cold, except the tops of a few tall mountains. But the damp could get in your bones.

Ash sat in a corner, her back against a wall. On the table in front of her was a glass of beer and a tablet. She was playing solitaire on the tablet. The game occupied her mind just enough to keep out old memories, but left her with attention for the bar. It could be dangerous on payday nights, when people were flush and drunk, or after big layoffs, when people were angry and spending their last money. Tonight it was mostly empty.

The guy who walked in—there was always someone walking in at the start of a story—did not belong. He was short and neatly dressed, with a fancy vest full of pockets; and his head was shaved, except for a few tufts of bright blue hair. It was the kind of haircut that required upkeep. Most people in Hillside didn't bother.

He stopped at the bar and spoke to the bartender, who nodded toward Ash. The man bought a glass of wine, which was a mistake, as he would find when he tasted it, then walked over.

She had no chance of winning the current game and turned the tablet off.

"Hong Wu," he said in introduction. "I'm an editor with *National Geographic*."

"Yes?" She nodded toward the chair opposite. The man sat down, took a sip of his wine and made a face. "You are Ash Weatherman."

"Yes."

"We want to do a story about the megafauna on Venus, and we want to hire you."

"The story's been done," Ash said.

"We think another look at the megafauna is worth it. We did a thousand stories about wild animals in Africa, until they were gone. People could never get enough of elephants and lions. They still can't. Look at zoos."

She had grown up on *National Geographic* videos: all the lost wilderness of Earth, the charismatic megafauna of land and ocean. Most had been mammals, of course, and near relatives to humanity. Nothing on Venus was as closely related, although pretty much everyone agreed that life on Venus had come from Earth, most likely via a meteorite that hit Earth, a glancing blow, then landed on the inner planet, bringing Terran organisms scraped up in the first collision. Geologists thought they had found the crater on Earth and the final resting place on Venus. Both craters were eroded and filled in, not visible on the planetary surface. The great plain of Ishtar and something whacking big in Greenland.

There were people who thought it had happened twice, with the second meteorite bringing organisms from a later era; and they had found another pair of craters. But whatever had happened was long ago, and the organisms that came to Venus were single-celled. They had their own evolutionary history, which had ended in a different place, with no cute, furry mammals.

"The fauna here is certainly big enough," she said out loud. "Though I don't know how charismatic they are." She tapped her tablet, and a new game of solitaire appeared. "What do you know about me?"

"You grew up in Hillside, graduated from high school here and got a degree in the history of evolutionary theory at Venusport College. According to the police, you were involved with a student anarchist group, but did nothing illegal.

"You worked in a printing plant while you were in college and after—until your photography began to sell. For the most part, you do advertising. Fashion, such as it is on Venus, furniture and real estate, and nature shots for the tourism industry. On the side, you do your own work, which is mostly images of the Venusian outback. That work is extraordinary. We have our own first-rate videographer and a thoughtful journalist, but we think it would be interesting to have a Venusian perspective."

Interesting that they'd seen her photos. They had shown at a small gallery downtown: 3-D blowups on the walls and a machine in back to print copies with a signature: Ashley Weatherman, 2113. She'd made some money. People safe in Venusport liked to have the Venusian wilderness on their walls: cone-shaped flowers two meters tall, brilliant yellow or orange; amphibianoids that looked—more or less—like giant crocodiles; and little, rapid, bipedal reptiloids.

"You're going to need someone to organize your safari," Ash said. "Do you have anyone?"

"We thought we'd ask you."

"Arkady Volkov. You're going to want to go to Aphrodite Terra. That's where the best megafauna are, and you won't want to deal with any corporations. Most of Ishtar Terra is company land. Believe me, they protect it."

Hong Wu nodded. "Rare earth mining and time-share condos."

"Arkady knows the territory," Ash said. "I've worked with him before."

Hong Wu nodded a second time. "We know. The police here say he's reputable, even though he comes from Petrograd."

The last Soviet Socialist Republic, which remained here on Venus long after the collapse of the USSR, an enclave of out-of-date politics on the larger of the two Venusian continents. She liked Arkady, even though he was a Leninist. *The heart hath its reasons that reason knoweth not.* "Are you willing to hire him?"

"Yes," Hong Wu said.

The rest of the conversation was details. Hong Wu left finally. Ash ordered another beer.

The bartender asked, "What was that about?"

"Work."

"He looked like a petunia."

"He is an employer, and we will be respectful."

"Yes, ma'am." The bartender grinned, showing metal teeth.

She finished the beer and walked home through winter rain, not hurrying. Her parka was waterproof, and the streets were covered with mud that had washed down from eroded hillsides. Half the streetlights were out. It would be easy to slip on the badly lit, uneven surface. She hated getting muddy. Even more, she hated looking vulnerable.

The buildings she passed were concrete and low: row houses for families and barracks for single workers. Graffiti crawled over them, most of it dark and slow moving. Here and there were tags written in more expensive spray that jittered and sparkled. "REVOLUTION NOW," one said in glowing red letters. "F U, F U, F U," another said in flashing yellow. The tags wouldn't last downtown, where the ambiance cops would cover them, but here—

There were shanties and tents in the supposedly empty lots, mostly hidden by vegetation. You could see them, if you knew how to look. Some folks did not like living in barracks, and some didn't have the money to pay bed-rent.

She turned a corner next to a lot full of tall, feathery pseudo-grass. In daylight, it would have been deep green, edged with purple. Now it was as black as the graffiti on the nearest building. In the street ahead, a pack of pig-like amphibianoids nosed around a Dumpster. Mostly not dangerous, in spite of their impressive tusks and claws. Ash paused. The matriarch of the pack eyed her for a moment, then grunted and lumbered away. The rest followed, leaving heaps of dung.

Her place was past the Dumpster: a two-floor row house. A light shone over the door, making it possible for her to see the land scorpion resting on the step. More than anything else, it looked like the ancient sea scorpions of Earth: broad, flat, segmented and ugly. Instead of swimming paddles, it had many legs. This one was dull green and as long as her foot. Most likely it wasn't venomous. The toxic species advertised the fact with bright colors. Nonetheless, she stepped on it firmly, hearing the crack of its exoskeleton breaking, then scraped her boot on the edge of the step.

She unlocked the door and yelled a greeting to the family on the first floor. Bangladeshi. The smell of their curries filled the house; and if she was lucky, they invited her to dinner. Tonight she was too late. Ash climbed the stairs and unlocked another door. Lights came on. Baby, her pet pterosaur, called, "Hungry."

She pulled off her boots and put a stick of chow in Baby's cage. The pterosaur dug in.

Of course, the animal was not a real pterosaur. Life on Earth and Venus had been evolving separately for hundreds of millions—maybe billions—of years. But it had skin wings stretched over finger bones, a big head, and a small, light body. Pale yellow fuzz covered it, except around its eyes, where its skin was bare and red. A crest of feathers adorned Baby's head, down at present. When up, the feathers were long and narrow, looking like spines or stiff hairs; and they were bright, iridescent blue.

Some people—mostly middle class—used the Latin names for the local life. But people on the hill called them after the Earth life they most resembled.

"Bored," the animal said.

"We're going into the outback," Ash said. "Flying, Baby. Hunting. Food."

"Fly!" Baby sang. "Hunt! Food!"

She scratched the pterosaur's muzzle, which was full of needle-teeth. The head crest rose, expanding into a brilliant, semi-circular array.

Venus was surprising, she had learned in school. No one had expected flying animals as intelligent as birds. Famous words, repeated over and over—No one had expected.

She pulled a beer out of the electric cooler, sat down in the chair next to Baby's cage, and unfolded her tablet. One tap brought up Arkady's address. As usual, it was irritating. A glowing red star appeared on her screen. "You have reached the home of Arkady Volkov. He is out at present, making plans for a new revolution, but if you leave a message—"

"Cut it out, Arkady," Ash said. "You are down at the local bar, getting pissed."

The star was replaced by Arkady: a swarthy man with a thick, black beard and green eyes, surprisingly pale given his skin and hair. "Do not judge others by yourself, Ash. I am sitting at home with a modest glass of wine, trying—once again—to understand the first three chapters of *Capital*."

"Why bother?"

"Education is always good. The ruling class denies it to workers because it's dangerous to them. As a rule, one should always do what the ruling class finds dangerous."

Easy for him to say, living in Petrograd, where his opinions were tolerated because a ruling class did not officially exist. Even there, most people found his ideas out-of-date. Oh silly Arkady, he believes the old lies.

"Did you call to banter?" Arkady asked. "Or to argue politics? In which case I will find something offensive to say about anarchism."

"Neither," Ash said, and told him about the job.

He looked dubious. "I wasn't planning to go out in the near future. There are things in Petrograd that need to be dealt with. Do these people pay well?"

Ash gave him the figure.

Arkady whistled. "Who are they?"

"*National Geographic*. They want to do a story on charismatic megafauna. I want to take them into a real wilderness, where they won't run into surveyors or test plots or mines."

"I will do it," Arkady said and lifted his glass of wine to her. "Capitalists have so much money. How many people?"

She gave details, as she had learned them from Hong Wu.

"Two vehicles," Arkady said. "Ural trucks modified for passengers. Rifles. I can provide those. We'll need two drivers and a cook, all of whom should be good with guns. That means we will have to hire the cook in Petrograd. Your cuisine is better, but your shooting is worse, and most of you do not know how to handle a Pecheneg."

In theory, a rifle could take down anything on Venus, but only if the shot was well placed. There were times when the best thing to do was to rip the animal apart, and a Pecheneg could do that. Arkady was fond of them. They were solid and reliable, like the legendary AK-47 and the Ural 6420, the last version of the truck made before the USSR fell. It had been designed for use on Venus as well as in Siberia; and it could go through almost everything.

"I know someone here in Petrograd who does an excellent borscht—a man could live on borscht and bread—and can make more than adequate Central Asian food. She was in the police force and can both fire a Pecheneg and field strip it."

"It's a deal then," said Ash.

She met the National Geographic team in the Venusport airport. The journalist was as expected: a tall, lean man in a jacket with many pockets. His dark eyes had a thousand kilometer stare. The videographer was a surprise: a round sphere that rested on four spidery metal legs. Its head was atop a long, flexible neck—a cluster of lenses. "You are Ash Weatherman?" the machine asked in a pleasant contralto voice.

"Yes."

"I am an Autonomous Leica. My model name is AL-26. My personal name is Margaret, in honor of the 20th century photographer Margaret Bourke White. You may call me Maggie." It lifted one of its legs and extruded fingers. Ash shook the cool metal hand.

"And I am Jasper Khan," the journalist said, holding out his hand, which was brown and muscular.

More shaking. This time the hand was warm.

"Baby," said Baby.

"And this is Baby. Don't try to shake. He nips."

"A Pseudo-rhamphorynchus," Jasper said.

"Not pseudo," Baby said.

"How large is his vocabulary?" Maggie asked.

"More than five hundred words. He keeps picking up new ones."

Maggie bent its neck, peering into the cage. "Say cheese."

"Not in vocabulary," Baby replied, then opened his mouth wide, showing off his needle teeth.

"Excellent," said Maggie. A bright light came on, and the Leica extended its— her—long neck farther, curling around the cage, recording Baby from all sides. The pterosaur did not look happy.

"You will be famous, Baby," Ash said.

"Want food."

The plane took off on time, rising steeply into the almost-always-present clouds. Ash had a window seat, useless after the clouds closed in. Baby was next to her on the aisle; and the *National Geographic* team was across the aisle.

Six hours to Aphrodite Terra. Ash fed a chow stick to Baby. The pterosaur held it in one clawed foot and gnawed. Ash felt her usual comfort in travel and in getting away from Venusport. Petrograd might be retrograde and delusional, the last remnant of a failed idea. But she liked Arkady, and nothing on the planet could beat a Ural 6420.

She dozed off as the plane flew south and rain streaked her window, then woke when the descent began. A holographic steward came by and warned them to fasten their seat belts. She had never unfastened hers, but she checked the one around Baby's cage.

She looked out as the plane dropped below the clouds. Another grid-city like Venusport, but smaller, with no tall buildings. A failure, slowly dying according to people on Earth and in Venusport. Cracked, gray runways crossed shaggy native grass.

They landed with a bump and rolled to a stop in front of the terminal. Ash undid her belt and Baby's, then stood, feeling stiff.

Arkady was at the gate. On Earth there was security, which grew more intense as violence grew. Here on Venus, people were less desperate; and it was possible to wait at a gate with an AK-47 over one shoulder. It wasn't the original version, of course, but a modern replica with some improvements, but not many. It remained as simple and indestructible as a stone ax and as easy to maintain. The best assault weapon ever made, Arkady said.

Baby opened his wings as far as he could in the cage. "Arky!" he cried.

The Russian grinned and waved.

Introductions followed. The two men were wary of each other, in spite of vigorous handshakes and broad smiles. Arkady was warmer toward the robot. "A pleasure," he said, clasping the extruded fingers. "The Urals are waiting. We can head out at once.

"Excellent," the Autonomous Leica said.

They picked up the rest of their baggage at the carousel, then went into the rain. The Urals were across the drop-off/pick-up road. Two massive vehicles, each with four sets of wheels. The front truck had a box. The one in back was a flatbed, with a Pecheneg fastened to the bed. A tarp covered it, but Ash knew what it was.

Arkady escorted Maggie and Jasper to the flatbed, then pointed at the truck in front. Ash climbed into the back seat. The driver made a friendly grunting sound.

"This is Boris," Arkady said as he climbed in. "Irina and Alexandra are in the second truck."

The trucks pulled out. Rain beat on the windshield, and wipers flashed back and forth. They bumped out of the airport and along rough, wet streets. Petrograd was around them: low, dreary-looking, concrete buildings, dimmed by the rain.

Arkady opened a thermos of tea and handed it back to Ash. She took a swallow. Hot and sweet.

"Do you want to show them anything special?" Arkady asked.

"They want charismatic megafauna and maybe something else. I keep wondering why they hired me. Do they want to write about Venusian culture as well?"

"The replica of America on Ishtar Terra, and the remains of the USSR on Aphrodite Terra," said Arkady in a genial tone. "It might make a good story. At least they did not ask for mostly naked natives. We don't have any, except in saunas and swimming pools."

The city was not large. They were soon out of it and rolling through agricultural land: bright green fields of modified Earth crops. The rain let up, though the cloud cover remained. By mid-afternoon, they reached the forest. The fields ended at a tall wire fence. Beyond were trees. Green, of course. Chlorophyll had evolved only once on Earth and been imported to Venus. But the native forest's green always seemed richer, more intense and varied to her. Purple dotted the ragged foliage of the low bottle-brush trees. The foliage of the far taller lace-leaf trees was veined with yellow, though this was hard to see at a distance.

The trucks stopped. Arkady climbed down and opened the gate, then closed it after the trucks were through, climbed back into the cab and flipped on the radio. "Large herbivores can break though the fence and do sometimes," he told the truck in back. "Fortunately for us, they do not like the taste of Terran vegetation, though they can metabolize it. Unfortunately for us, the only way for them to learn they don't like our food is to try it."

"Ah," said Jasper.

"I got images of you opening the gate," Maggie said. "Bright green fields, dark green trees and you with your AK-47. Very nice."

The trucks drove on. The road was two muddy ruts now, edged by an under story of frilly plants. The air coming in her partly open window smelled of Venus: rain, mud, and the native vegetation.

Animals began to appear: pterosaurs, flapping in the trees, and small reptiloid bipeds in the under story. Now and then, Ash saw a solitary flower, cone-shaped and two meters tall. Most were a vivid orange-yellow. The small flying bugs that pollinated them were not visible at a distance, but she knew they were there in clouds. Now and then Maggie asked for a stop. Ash had her camera out and did some shooting, but the thing she really wanted to capture—the robot—was invisible, except for the lens-head, pushed out a window at the end of Maggie's long, long neck

Midway through the afternoon, they came to a river. A small herd of amphibianoids rested on the far shore. They were larger than the street pigs in Venusport, maybe five meters long, their sprawling bodies red and slippery looking. Their flat heads had bulbous eyes on top—not at the back of the head, where eyes usually were, even on Venus, but in front, close to the nostrils and above the mouths full of sharp teeth.

Maggie climbed out her window onto the flat bed of the second truck. She braced herself there, next to the Pecheneg, and recorded as the trucks forded the river. The water came up to the trucks' windows, and the bed was rocky, but the trucks kept moving, rocking and jolting. Nothing could beat a Ural!

"A gutsy robot," Arkady said.

Alexandra answered over the radio. "She has four sets of fingers dug into the truck bed, right into the wood. A good thing. I don't want to fish her out of the river."

Ash aimed her camera at the amphibianoids, as the animals bellowed and slid into the river, vanishing among waves. Maggie was more interesting, but she still couldn't get a good view.

The trucks climbed the now-empty bank and rolled back onto the road. The Leica climbed back into the cab. "Not mega, but very nice," Maggie said over the radio.

An hour or so later, they reached the first lodge, a massive concrete building set against a low cliff. Vines hung down the cliff, and pterosaurs—a small species covered with white down—fluttered among the vines.

There was a front yard, protected by a tall fence. Once again, Arkady climbed down and opened the gate. The trucks rolled in. Arkady locked the gate behind them. Boris shut down their truck and grabbed an AK-47, climbing down to join Arkady. They looked around the yard, which was full of low vegetation, mashed in places by previous safaris. Nothing big could hide here, but there were always land scorpions

An AK-47 seemed excessive to Ash. Good boots and stomping worked just as well. But the citizens of Petrograd loved their guns; and there was no question that the experience of crushing a land scorpion, especially a big one, was unpleasant.

Finally, Boris unlocked the lodge's door, which was metal and so heavy it could be called armored, and went in. She knew what he was doing: turning on the generator, the lights—ah, there they were, shining out the open door—the air, the temp control, the fence.

Baby shifted in his cage. "Want out. Hunt. Eat."

"Soon."

"Pterosaur chow is crap," Baby added.

She reached a finger through the cage's bars and rubbed his head. His large eyes closed, and he looked happy

Boris came out and waved.

"All clear," Arkady called. "The fence is electric and on now. Stay away from it."

Ash opened the cage. Baby crawled out and rested for a moment in the open window. Then he flapped out, rising rapidly. The small pterosaurs in the vines shrieked. She felt the brief doubt she always felt when she let Baby go. Would he return?

"Did it escape?" Jason asked over the radio.

"He's going hunting." Ash climbed down. The air was damp and hot. By the time she reached the lodge, her shirt was wet.

"I want all the food inside," Arkady said. "Also all the weapons and any personal belongings you want to preserve. The fence will keep most things out, but it's not 100% secure."

She put the cage down and went back to help unload the trucks. Irina was a broad, box-like woman, as solid and useful as a Ural. Alexandra was surprisingly slim and elegant, the chef who'd been a cop and could field strip a Pecheneg. She moved like a dancer, and Ash felt a terrible envy. Did women ever stop feeling envy?

Maggie recorded them as they worked, while Jason took notes on a tablet. Ash felt mildly irritated by this. Couldn't he help with the boxes? But he was a paying customer and an employee of a famous news source.

Once they were all inside, Boris shut the door, bringing down a heavy bar.

"Bathrooms are down the hall," Arkady said. "Paying customers go first. Dinner will be in an hour."

"An hour and a half," Alexandra said.

"I am corrected."

When she got back from her shower, Ash noticed that the virtual windows were on, showing the yard, lit now by spotlights. Beyond the fence was the dark forest. A hologram fire burned in the fireplace. Wine and a cheese plate were on a table in front of the fire.

She poured a glass, then went to help Alexandra and Irina with dinner. It was sautéed vegetables and fish from the Petrograd fishponds.

They ate around the fireplace.

"Someone has been here," Boris said as they ate.

"'It must have been another safari," Arkady said mildly. "They all have the access code."

"I checked. No safaris have been this way since the last time we were here, and the security system has recorded nothing, But I know how I arrange canned goods. They are no longer in alphabetic order. I think it's the CIA."

"What?" asked Jason, and pulled his tablet out.

"There is a CIA post in the forest," Arkady said. "They spy on Petrograd, though we're barely surviving and no danger to the American colony or anyone. We ignore them, because we don't have the resources to confront them. But they are present—and not far from here. Boris may be right. They could have tinkered with the security system. I don't know who else could have."

"Why do you hang on, if you are barely surviving?" Jason asked. "The USSR fell, in part because it exhausted itself trying to settle Venus. All the republics have become capitalist states, but you remain here, stubbornly Soviet."

"Not all change is good," Boris said. "And there is more to life than selfishness."

"Surely you would do better, if you had the assistance of the American colony on Ishtar."

Arkady said, "The capitalists on Earth are investing in what interests them, which is not the lives of ordinary people. We in Petrograd are a dream that has failed, or so we are told. Ishtar Terra is a—what can I call it?—a vacation spot, a rare earth mine, and a place for the rich to flee to, if they finally decide that Earth is uninhabitable."

"Life in Ishtar Terra is more comfortable than life here," Jason pointed out.

"We survive."

"Be honest, Arkady," said the box-like woman, Irina. "People get tired of shortages and go to Ishtar Terra. It's a slow but continual drain. In the end, Petrograd will fail."

"We don't know that," Boris put in. "Even our setbacks are not entirely bad. Our food shortages have brought our rates of heart disease and diabetes down; and our fuel shortages mean we walk more, which is healthy."

Irina did not look convinced. Nor did Jason Khan, though Ash could not be sure. He was an oddly opaque man. Maybe she would find out what he was thinking when the article finally came out. At present, the Leica was easier to understand.

"There," said Arkady. "You said you wanted charismatic fauna." He pointed at one of the virtual windows.

A flock of bipeds moved along the fence, illuminated by the spotlights. They were slender and covered with bright blue down, except for their chests, which were orange-red.

"The Americans call them robins," Arkady said. "Notice that they are following the fence, but not touching it. They know it's dangerous, if we are here, and the spotlights tell them we are here. If this were Earth in the Triassic, those little fellows would be the ancestors of the dinosaurs. But this isn't Earth. We don't know what they will become. They're bright, and they have hands capable of some manipulation. Maybe they will become us in time."

A second kind of animal joined the bipeds at the fence. Ten meters long or more, its body was hairless and black. It had a gait like a crocodile's high walk, and its lifted head was long and reptilian, the mouth full of ragged teeth. The bipeds ran off. The animal nosed the fence once and drew back with a roar.

"You see," Arkady said. "Not so bright. It doesn't have to be. It's big and nasty. If this were Earth in the Triassic, it would represent the past, a species that will vanish, unable to compete. But this is not Earth."

Something pale flew into the spotlights. Baby, Ash realized. The pterosaur flapped low above the pseudosuchus, taunting it. The animal roared and reared up on its hind legs, snapping at Baby and almost getting him. The pterosaur flapped up and over the fence, landing on one of the Urals. The pseudosuchus dropped down on all fours. Most likely Ash was reading in, but it looked frustrated. Baby looked frightened. The little fool. She'd have a talk with him.

"They are descended from bipeds," Arkady said. "As a result, theirs hind legs are longer and stronger than their front legs, and they can—as you see—rear up. They also move more quickly than you would suspect."

"I got it," Maggie said. "But the image won't be as good as I could have gotten outside."

"Go out," Boris said. "This fence is strong enough to hold."

Ash went out with the *Nat Geo* people. Of course, the pseudosuchus saw—or maybe smelled—them as soon as they went outside. It slammed into the fence and roared, then reared up, grasping the fence with its forepaws and shaking it. That must hurt. More roaring, while Maggie recorded, using a light so brilliant that Ash could see the glitter of the animal's scales. Ash got a lovely image of the robot and the monster. Light hit from different angles, cast by the lodge's spots and Maggie, creating areas of glare and shadow. Even in color, the image looked black and white.

Baby flapped to her, settling on her shoulder.

"Idiot," she said.

"Poop on you," Baby replied.

The fence bowed in under the animal's weight. Behind them, Arkady said, "I'm not going to turn the current up. That is a protected species."

"Come in," Ash told Jason.

"The fence is supposed to hold."

"Most likely it will," Arkady said in a comfortable tone. "But if it doesn't—"

They piled back inside, and Arkady barred the door. Baby flew to his cage, opened the door and climbed in, pulling the door shut. Ash heard the lock click. The pterosaur huddled, looking thoroughly frightened.

"You shouldn't tease the monsters," Ash said.

"Poop! Poop!" Baby replied and pooped on the floor of his cage.

She would have to clean that up, but not now. Let Baby get over being afraid.

She glanced at one of the virtual windows. The pseudosuchus was back on all fours, looking thoroughly pissed off. After a moment or two, it moved off. It was clear from the way it moved that its fore feet were injured.

"Not bright," Arkady said. "But a top predator. They do not need to be bright, as the history of America has shown."

"I'd like help in the kitchen," Alexandra put in.

Ash gathered glasses and followed Alexandra out of the room. The kitchen had a dishwasher from Venusport. Everything went in. Alexandra set the controls and turned the machine on.

"What is Venusport like?" Irina asked.

"Unjust," Ash replied. "Run from Earth for the benefit of mining companies and tourists and the rich."

"That sounds like a manifesto, not a report," Alexandra said. "What is life like for you? Do you have enough to eat? Can you buy glittery toys?"

Ash hesitated, then answered. "I have enough to eat. I can buy some toys. Hell, I make most of my living producing images of glittery toys. "

"We see broadcasts from Ishtar Terra," Irina said. "Life there looks more attractive than life in Petrograd."

"Are you thinking of bailing out?" Ash asked.

"Maybe," Alexandra said. "I would like glittery toys."

Irina shook her head. "I don't think so. I have family and a lover, who is like Arkady. She believes in Petrograd."

Once the counters were wiped down, Ash went back into the living room. Jason and Arkady were lounging in chairs by the fire. Maggie had retracted her legs and neck and head, becoming a large, featureless, silver ball in front of the hologram flames. Red light played over her surface.

Baby was sitting on top of his cage, eating a stick of chow.

"You found nothing to eat?" Ash asked.

"Caught small pterosaur. Ate it. Still hungry."

She settled in a chair. There was a new bottle on the table, surrounded by fresh glasses. One of Petrograd's scary brandies. Ash poured and tasted. This one was raspberry. It burned in her mouth and down her throat, ending as a warm glow in her gut. "Where's Boris?" she asked.

"Looking around the lodge. He's still worried about his canned goods."

"He really arranged them alphabetically?"

Arkady nodded. "He is both compulsive and paranoid. But an excellent safari driver and a good drinking companion. A man as obsessed as he is needs ways to relax. He never drinks while driving, in case you are wondering."

Ash eased back in her chair, feeling content. Brandy, a fire, Baby chewing on chow, the prospect of charismatic megafauna and gigantic flowers. Life was good.

Jason had his tablet out, his fingers dancing over the screen. She still didn't know what he was reporting on. Venusian wildlife? Petrograd? The American colony? Whichever it was, the pay was good, and she got a break from the glittery toys that Irina and Alexandra envied.

She should not judge them. She had the toys, or at least the toy makers, as clients. It was easy for her to feel indifferent to them.

Boris came into the room, holding a land scorpion, one hand behind the animal's head, the other on its tail. It was alive and twisting in his grip, trying to find a way to bite him or pinch him with its large front claws.

"Shit," said Arkady. "How did that get in?"

"I told you someone had been here." Boris stopped and displayed the creature to them. Jason looked horrified. Maggie, who must have been listening, extruded her head and neck. In a smooth motion, she rose on her legs, and the cluster of lenses she had instead of a face turned toward Boris.

The scorpion was about half a meter long, wide, flat, shiny, dark purple and still twisting in Boris's grip. The mouth, with mandibles and fangs, was in continuous motion. Ash felt a little queasy. Damn! The things were ugly! She was pretty certain this species was poisonous. Arkady would know.

"Get me a pair of shears," Boris said.

Ash went to the kitchen, where Irina and Alexandra were still talking. "We have a problem. I need shears."

Alexandra found them. Ash took them to Boris.

He knelt carefully and placed the animal on the floor, holding it with one hand. With the other hand, he took the shears and cut the scorpion's head off, then stood quickly. The many-legged body thrashed around, and the head jittered on the floor, its mandibles still opening and closing.

"It was under the bed in the room that Jason picked as his bedroom," Boris said.

"What is it?" Jason asked in a tone of terror.

"One of the many species of land scorpion," Arkady said. "Many have poisonous bites. This species would not kill you, but it would make you sick."

Boris took one of the glasses on the table and used it to scoop the head up. "The body is not toxic. The fangs and the venom glands are in the head. Keep the rest as a souvenir, if you want."

"I have dramatic images," Maggie said. "That is sufficient. Our viewers will be horrified and disgusted."

"How did it get in?" Arkady asked again.

"I want to take a closer look at the head," Boris said and went into the kitchen.

Alexandra and Irina were in the living room by now, watching the twisting, scrabbling, headless body with interest.

"Edible?" Baby asked.

"Wait," said Ash.

"Hungry," Baby complained.

"Have another stick of chow."

"Not tasty."

"Life is hard," Ash told him.

"Do not understand."

"Eat your chow."

The scorpion's body was slowing down, though it still thrashed.

"I hate drama," Alexandra said.

"That is why you are a chef now, rather than a cop," Arkady told her.

"Yes, but it doesn't explain why I work for you."

"Money," Arkady said.

Boris came back, carrying the scorpion's head on a cutting board. He set the board on the table and Maggie leaned down to record it. He'd cut the head open. Some kind of dark matter, the brain most likely, was inside. In the middle of it was a tiny silver bead. Barely visible silver wires radiated out from it.

"Most likely it is a nano machine," Boris said. "It was injected into the circulatory system and migrated to the brain, then built itself. The animal has become an organic robot. It was planted on us as a spy."

Ash felt queasy. She had no trouble with ordinary robots, such as Maggie, who was recording the split-open head. But the idea of taking a living being and turning it into a robot bothered her. Even cockroaches, which had come to Venus with humans, deserved their own lives. The technology used to enslave bugs could be modified for other animals or humans, though that was illegal, of course.

"How did you know to look for it?" Arkady asked Boris.

"I looked at the security recordings. It was there, though only in glimpses. I don't think there are any more."

"My images are excellent," Maggie said. "This will add drama to our story."

"Is it the CIA?" asked Jason.

"I believe so," Boris answered. "We live in their shadow."

"Well, if Boris thinks there are no more, we can enjoy the rest of the evening," Arkady put in.

"Can Baby eat the body?" Ash asked.

"No," said Boris. "We don't know what else might be in it. I'll toss it in the garbage."

"Sorry," Baby said.

Boris carried the head and body out. Ash drank more raspberry brandy.

"We grow the raspberries in greenhouses, along with other fruit," Arkady said. "Our crops may fail, but we always have brandy."

Nothing more happened that evening or night. Ash slept badly, waking from time to time to listen for the rustling sound of a scorpion. She turned on the lights once, but saw nothing except Baby sleeping in his cage.

The next morning, they drove on. The rain stopped, and rays of sunlight broke through the cloud cover, lighting patches of the forest. There were lots of cone-shaped flowers. A group of large herbivores fed on one. Similar animals on Ishtar Terra were called forest cattle, though they didn't seem especially cow-like to her, being larger than any cow she had ever seen, even in images from Earth, and green. A crest of hair went along their backs, and their large mouths had four big tusks. There were half a dozen of them around the bright-red flower, ripping into it. Petals coated their muzzles and dripped from their mouths like blood.

Boris braked.

"Look to the right," Arkady said to the radio. "More megafauna."

'I would not call them charismatic," Jason replied over the radio.

"They are two meters high at the shoulder, and they can be dangerous," Arkady said. "If you don't believe so, I can let you off here."

"No," said Maggie. "I need Jason."

The trucks moved on. Ash had been on this route before, a loop that went from fortified lodge to fortified lodge, till it returned to Petrograd and dinner at one of several luxury hotels. A hospitality firm based in Venusport had built them and ran them, making sure that the tourists had a reliably luxurious experience.

"This is *National Geographic*," she said to Arkady. "Can't you show them something different?"

"We are thinking about that. But not today."

She set down her camera and drank tea. As usual, it was strong and sweet. She felt tired, due to a bad night's sleep, but mostly good. Baby was next to her in his cage, hunched up, his eyes closed. Was there anything cuter than a sleeping pterosaur?

There were more pterosaurs flapping in the trees, and bipeds scurrying through the undergrowth. Early in the afternoon, the clouds broke apart, and rays of sunlight slanted into the forest. A herd of forest cattle—twenty or more—crossed the track in front of them, forcing them to stop and wait, till the loutish herbivores finally moved on. But they saw no large predators.

"Apex predators are always rare," Arkady said when Jason complained. "And this is not Earth in the Jurassic."

They reached the next lodge late in the afternoon. It was a concrete pillbox, surrounded by a high fence. Alexandra and Irina did the check this time, stepping on several small land scorpions. There was something lonely about the two women, stalking through knee-high vegetation. They both carried rifles, but used them only for poking among the leaves. Beyond the fence, was the forest, darkening as daylight faded and denser clouds moved in. Ash took photos, as did Maggie.

They went inside finally, and Boris did another search. "My cans are in order," he announced. "And I have found no scorpions."

They unloaded the trucks, and Alexandra made dinner. This time it was a pilaf and a mixture of spinach and chickpeas.

"Home food," said Arkady happily.

Heavy rain began to fall outside. Ash watched it through one of the virtual windows. It shone like a silver curtain in the lodge's spotlights. The low plants around the lodge bent under the weight of water, and a gusty wind made them flutter. Arkady got out plum brandy this time.

Jason looked unhappy. Maggie recorded the lodge's interior, and Ash took shots of the Leica, head tilted and lenses shining in the false firelight. She had the impression that Maggie was perfectly content, in spite of the lack of drama.

"Want outside," Baby said.

"The weather is bad," Ash replied.

The pterosaur hunched down, looking as unhappy as Jason.

Of course, the journalist wanted something exciting to happen. Ash was content to sit by the false fire and drink fruit brandy. What she liked about the outback was its strangeness, its inhumanity. Was that the right word? Being in a place without imported plants and animals, where people didn't fit in, though they had made roads—a few, at least—and built lodges. Maybe what she liked about Arkady was his line of work. This was his turf. As much as anyone, he knew Aphrodite Terra.

In some ways, Venus was lucky. Earth did not have the resources to really settle the planet. The USSR had destroyed itself trying to win the Venus Race. The US had largely given up, in part because it no longer had a rival, and in part because the problems on Earth kept getting worse. Venus provided some raw materials—not many; the shipping costs were ridiculous—and it was a tourist destination. Some people retired to the gated communities near Venusport. Others bought beachside condos against the time that Earth was no longer habitable. But most of the planet remained empty of humanity.

The next day, they moved on. The ground was rising and getting stonier, and the trees were all short, with big, drooping, leaves. Small animals moved in the branches and the undergrowth. Midway through the afternoon, their truck turned off the rutted track into forest, mashing low plants and avoiding trees. The second truck followed.

"What?" asked Ash.

"We are going to show *National Geographic* a good time," Arkady said. "As you asked us to."

"And make a point," Boris added.

"Do you mind telling me what?" Ash asked.

"In good time," Arkady replied. "I'm tired of Jason complaining about our fauna. It reminds me of other safaris I have led, full of rich tourists who want dinosaurs. I tell them that Venusian fauna is similar to fauna on Earth, but not identical, and we are not in the Jurassic. I've had the bastards ask for money back, because we couldn't show them an allosaurus. I wanted to feed them to a pseudosuchus, which might not impress them, but could certainly eat them."

Arkady was usually even-tempered, but he sounded angry now. Well, she got angry at some of her work. The fashion shoots could be fairly awful.

They crunched through more undergrowth. There were rocks here, making the driving chancy: outcroppings of a creamy yellow stone.

"Limestone," Arkady said. "This used to be underwater. There ought to be good fossils, though Jason does not strike me as a fossil man."

"I'm not one," Boris said, guiding the truck between two good-sized chunks of stone. A pair of pterosaurs rested on top of one. They were big, with impressive crests.

"Stop!" said Ash.

Boris did. She photographed the animals, which looked damn fine, their crests like orange sails.

"Don't like," Baby muttered. Of course not. These guys were big enough to eat him. They would, if given the chance. The pterosaurs were not cannibals, but they happily ate related species, as humans once ate monkeys, when there were monkeys in the wild.

They went on, coming finally to another track, this one much less used than the one they had been following. Boris turned onto it.

"I don't remember this," Ash said.

"It's good country," Arkady said. "Interesting. But the damn, gutless executive committee has decided the area is off-limits."

"Are you breaking rules?" Ash asked.

"Yes. This is the perfect time to explore, with a *National Geographic* videographer along."

"And with the CIA putting poisonous spies in our lodge," Boris growled.

Ash had a bad feeling. But Arkady ran the most reputable tours on the continent. They bumped among more outcropping of cream-yellow rock.

"This looks right," Boris said, glancing at his GPS, which was in Cyrillic. Ash could not read it.

"For what?" she asked.

"An impact crater," said Arkady. "Or something else."

Boris hit the brakes.

Next to the road was a low wall made of yellow limestone. It curved gently, apparently part of a huge circle. The section in front of them had been dug out. Heaps of dirt lay in front of it. Off to either side, the soil had not been excavated, and the wall was a mound, covered with low plants and vines.

"I wasn't expecting the excavation," Arkady said. "I suppose we have the CIA to thank."

"Who built this?" Ash asked.

"Not us," Arkady replied. "And not the CIA. It shows up in early satellite surveys, along with three other circles, all in this area and all arranged in a broad arc. One circle is broken, only half there. The rest are complete. None has been investigated. In theory, they are impact craters from a body that broke apart before it hit.

"Remember that our colony was run from Earth. The apparatchiks in Moscow said exploration could wait. This wasn't a scientific settlement. It was military and economic. By the time we were ready to look around, the CIA was in the area. The government decided to leave them alone. We didn't have the power to confront the Americans"

They all climbed out and walked to the wall. It looked to be made of the same stone as the outcroppings. But it was a single piece, as far as Ash could tell, and the surface was slick. Ash ran her hand along it. As smooth as glass. When she pulled her hand away, she saw blood. The edge of the wall was knife-sharp.

"Here," said Arkady and handed her a red handkerchief.

"What's that for?" Ash asked. "The revolution?"

"At the moment, it's for your hand. Use it."

Ash wrapped the handkerchief around the bleeding fingers. Maggie was recording her, she noticed.

The wall—the part above ground, at least—was more than a meter high, too tall to sit on comfortably, if one was human, and too tall to step over comfortably.

"Amazing," Jason said. "If humans did not build this, then it is proof of intelligent life on Venus."

"There isn't any," Ash put in. "The brightest things on the planet are animals like Baby. He's bright, but he doesn't build walls."

"It can't possibly be natural," Jason said.

"I agree," Arkady replied. "I also agree with Ash. I do not think this was built by anything native to Venus."

Maggie was panning, making a record of the entire length of wall.

In back of them, a voice asked, "Who the hell are you?"

Ash turned, as did the others. A soldier in full body armor stood in the road between the two trucks. He was carrying a terrifying-looking, very-high-tech rifle. Ash saw that first, then she noticed that he was standing above the road, his boots not touching the surface.

"You are a hologram," Boris said.

"Yes. But there are gun emplacements all around you. Take a look."

Ash did. Red lights, sighting lasers, shone on top of neighboring rocks. As far as she could tell, they were aimed at her.

"If you doubt me, I can melt something," said the hologram. "Your robot."

"She is autonomous," Jason replied quickly. "A citizen of the United States and an employee of *National Geographic*."

"Shit," said the hologram. "Stay put. I have to consult. If you move, the guns will fire." The soldier vanished.

"Are you still recording?" Jason asked Maggie.

"Yes, and I'm uploading my images to the nearest comsat. This place is about to become famous."

"That will make life uncomfortable for the CIA," said Arkady in a tone of satisfaction.

"And the useless Petrograd executive committee," Boris added.

"And for us," Ash put in. "You have just pissed off the most dangerous organization in the Solar System."

The hologram reappeared. "I have backup coming. Stay where you are. I've been informed that your robot is emitting radio signals. Stop that!"

"Very well," Maggie said. She didn't add that it was too late.

They waited, staying where they were, even though a fine rain began to fall. Inside the truck cab, Baby squawked for food.

"Later," Ash called.

"Hungry!"

At last, a car appeared, bumping down the track. It stopped, and a pair of men climbed out, dressed entirely in black, with shiny black boots. They wore computer glasses with opaque lenses and dark, thick frames.

"Who are you?" one asked.

"Arkady Volkov Wildlife Tours," Arkady said.

"*National Geographic*," Jason added.

"Ashley Weatherman Fashion Art," Ash put in.

"Shit," the man said, then added. "Follow us, and don't try anything funny. There are guns in the forest. Any trouble, and they will melt your trucks."

They climbed into the trucks. Arkady handed Ash a first aid kit, and she sprayed a bandage on her fingers. The antiseptic in it made the cuts sting. Venusian microbes did not usually infect humans, but there were Earth microbes spreading across the planet, and some of them were nasty.

The car turned and went back the way it had come. The trucks followed. As they began to move, Ash looked back. The hologram soldier was still in the middle of the road, rifle in hand, watching. Then the second truck rolled through him, and he was gone.

"I apologize," Arkady said. "I thought we could look at one crater and get out safely, with a few images that might—I hoped—endanger the CIA's control of this region."

"Were you expecting to find an alien artifact?" Ash asked.

"The longer we looked at the craters the more suspicious they have looked," Boris said. "We were looking at the CIA, of course. We would not have examined the satellite images so closely otherwise."

Ash leaned back and drank more tea. Next to her, Baby gnawed on a chow stick. Of course she was worried, but she couldn't imagine the CIA taking out *National Geographic*. Even monsters had their limits.

The rain grew heavier. Looking out, Ash saw a group of fire scorpions resting on a tree trunk, sheltered by foliage. They weren't large, but their exoskeletons were bright red, a warning of serious poison.

"I don't think I will draw Maggie's attention to them," Arkady said. "The CIA might not want us on the radio. A pity. They look handsome, and they are very poisonous. Tourists always enjoy deadly animals."

A half hour later, they reached a cliff made of the same yellow stone as the outcroppings. It rose above the forest, running as far as she could see in both directions. The road ended in front of it. The car stopped, and they stopped as well. Everyone climbed down.

"Leave the rifles in the trucks," one of the men said. "And you can leave that thing too." He waved at Baby in his cage.

"He gets lonely," Ash said.

One man went ahead of them, opening a door in the cliff face. It looked human-made, but Ash was less sure of the opening it closed. Rectangular, very tall and narrow, it didn't look like the kind of doorway humans would cut. They filed through, followed by the second man, who closed the door and locked it. Inside was a corridor, as tall and narrow and rectangular as the opening. Lights were stuck along the walls. These were clearly human. As for the corridor itself—the stone was polished and as slick as glass. There were fossils in it. Ash made out shells, gleaming behind the glossy surface, as well as long things that might be worms or crinoids, though this world did not have crinoids. If she'd had another life to live, she would have been a biologist or paleontologist, though she had a low tolerance for the finicky work required of both. Maybe it was a better idea to shoot fashion models and megafauna.

Baby muttered in his cage.

The corridor ended in another narrow doorway, this one without a door. Beyond it was a rectangular room with polished stone walls. Like the hall, it was narrow and tall. It contained a table and chairs, all 3-D printed. Ash recognized the style. Human Office Modern.

"Okay," said one of the men. He took off his glasses, showing pale blue eyes with dark, puffy skin below them. "What is this about? We have a deal with the executive committee of the Petrograd Soviet." He looked at the other man, who still wore glasses. "Mike, get coffee, will you?"

"Sure," Mike answered. "Don't say anything exciting till I get back." The voice was contralto.

Ash took another look. Mike was either a woman or an FTM, though it was well hidden by the boxy suit and heavy-rimmed computer glasses. Not that it mattered. A female CIA agent was as dangerous as a male.

Mike left, and they sat down. Arkady and Boris looked grim. Irina and Alexandra looked worried. The *Nat Geo* journalist had an expression that combined fear and excitement. Maggie's gleaming lens-face revealed nothing.

"Who built this?" Arkady asked.

"We don't know," the man replied. "We found it."

"Are there artifacts?" Arkady asked.

"Aside from the circles and these tunnels? Nothing we have found."

"This is a site of system-wide historical importance," Boris said. "Evidence that someone, not human, was on Venus before we came. You sat in it, keeping the people of Petrograd—and the scientists on Venus and Earth—from investigating. Not to mention the tourists we could have brought in, improving our economy."

"It meant we didn't have to set up camp in the forest," the man said. "It's dry in here, and there's a lot less animal life—or was, till recently. Believe me, this place isn't interesting. Just corridors and rooms, going a long way back into the cliff. All empty, except for the debris left by animals. Bones and dry leaves and dried-out feces."

Mike came back with a tray, carafe and coffee cups. He or she poured coffee. There was a slight chill in the room, and it was pleasant to hold the warm cup and sip the hot coffee. Ash's cut fingers still stung a little.

"The question is, what will we do with you?" the first man said.

"*National Geographic* will be concerned if we vanish," Jason said. He sounded anxious.

"Accidents happen in the outback," Mike said in his or her high voice.

"I was recording and uploading my images, until your hologram told me to stop," Maggie put in. "The material went to the nearest comsat, which belongs—I believe—to Petrograd. I assume the comsat sent it on to our office in Venusport. The message was encrypted to prevent piracy. But our office can decode it. They will have done so by now."

"They know about the circle," Jason added. "And the robot you put in the lodge."

"What robot?" the man asked.

"The bug. The scorpion. It had wires."

Mike was leaning against a wall, cup in hand. The nameless man looked over, frowning. "Not ours," Mike said. "Petrograd must be spying on itself."

Baby stirred in his cage. Ash reached a finger to scratch him and—in the same movement—undid the lock on the door. No one seemed to notice except Baby, who looked interested and alert.

She wondered about ventilation and ways to escape, looked around and saw a rectangle cut in the stone of one wall just below the ceiling. It was long and narrow with vertical bars made of the same stone as the wall. As she watched, a pair of antennae poked out between two of the bars. The animal followed. A scorpion, of course. The pale gray body suggested it was a cave scorpion, as did the lack of obvious eyes.

She watched as its front legs scrabbled to get a grip on the slick stone. It failed and fell, landing with an audible 'tock.' The nameless man spun in his chair, then was up and stamping the scorpion over and over. It wasn't even that big, Ash thought. No more than twenty centimeters.

The man remained bent over for several moments. "Oh god, I hate them."

"They are carrion eaters," Arkady said. "Living off the debris of pterosaur colonies that nest on cliffs and in shallow caves. Their bite does little harm to humans."

"I hate them," the man repeated.

"He has a phobia," Mike said. "Cave scorpions don't bother me."

The nameless agent straightened up. "The tunnels connect with caves. The damn things have discovered they can live off us. They're all over."

"But hardly a serious problem," Arkady said.

"We also have fire scorpions," Mike put in.

The nameless agent twitched at the name. Mike smiled slightly. Ash had the impression he enjoyed his colleague's fear.

"That is a problem," Boris said. "But you shouldn't have them. They live in the forest, not in caves."

"They've bred with the cave scorpions," the nameless man said. His voice sounded constricted, as if fear had robbed him of breath.

"They can't have," Arkady said. "They are different species, living in different environments."

The two men exchanged glances and were silent.

After a moment, Boris said harshly, "You were not satisfied with robot scorpions. You have played with DNA and created a new species in violation of numerous laws."

"Not the laws on Earth," Mike said.

"You are on *Venus*," Boris pointed out. "And in Petrograd."

"I don't think we need to talk about this."

"Yes, we do," Arkady replied. "And not just here. You are in very serious violation of several treaties. Venus and Earth need to know about this."

The nameless agent pulled out a handgun, aiming it at Arkady. The gun was shaking. Ash could see that clearly. The gun, the shaking hand, the room, the other people were all unnaturally sharp and clear.

"Go," she said to Baby. The pterosaur was out in a moment, flapping onto the agent's head and clawing. The gun went off with a loud—very loud—sound. Arkady dove at the man, taking him down. The gun spun across the floor, away from Arkady and the nameless agent.

"Stop that," Mike said.

Ash looked toward him. His coffee cup lay on the yellow floor, in the middle of a brown pool of coffee, and he had a gun out, pointing it at Arkady.

Never mix with the CIA. But it was too late for that warning.

"No," said Alexandra. Ash was trying not to move, but she could see the ex-cop from the corner of her eye. The woman had a gun, held steadily and pointed at Mike. This was ridiculous.

"Get the damn animal off Brian," Mike said.

The nameless agent was on the floor, Arkady lying across him, and Baby still on his head, biting and clawing.

"Stop," Ash called. "You can stop now, Baby."

The pterosaur flapped back to his cage, settling on top and folding his downy wings.

"This is stupid," Mike said. "I'm not going to shoot anyone in here, and I hope to God this lovely lady is not going to shoot me. You guys look like idiots on the floor. Get up."

The two men did. Arkady looked rumpled, which was his usual condition. Blood ran down the face of the nameless agent. He wiped it with one hand, making a smear.

"We're pulling out," Mike added. "Petrograd knows this."

"Why?" asked Boris.

"Why do they know? We told them."

"Why are you pulling out?"

"The scorpions. The things are deadly, and Brian's right. They're all over."

"Am I right?" Boris said. "Did you create them?"

Mike was silent.

"They must have wanted something that could live in sewers and the crawl spaces of buildings," Arkady put in. "And that was toxic. It sounds like a weapon that could be used against Petrograd."

"They are telling us too much," Boris said. "They must be planning to kill us."

"Not while I hold this gun," Alexandra said.

"We're pulling out, as I told you," Mike said. "And there is no proof that we made the scorpions or intended to use them for anything. You Soviets are way too paranoid."

"How many people are left here?" Arkady asked.

"Dozens," said the agent named Brian.

"Don't be a fool. We saw no one coming in, and no one has responded to the sound of gunfire. Either you are alone, or your colleagues are not close."

"Three," Mike answered. "They're in the back rooms, destroying the equipment. When they're done, we'll take the last VTL."

Boris pulled a roll of duct tape from his vest. He tossed it to Arkady. "Tape them up."

"No," said Brian. "What if more scorpions come?"

"Too bad," Boris said.

The man bolted for the room's doorway. Baby flapped onto him, clawing and shrieking, "Bad! Bad!"

Brian stumbled. Box-like Irina grabbed his arm and pulled him around, then drove a fist into the man's mid section. He bent up, coughing, and collapsed onto his knees. Fortunately, because Ash hated vomit, he did not throw up.

"That's some punch," Mike said.

"She used to be a stevedore," Arkady said. "Now I will tape you up, and you will hope that none of your new, mutant scorpions arrive."

"I'm not phobic," Mike replied. "And I'm not going to shoot it out with you. We don't know what these walls are made of, but you can't scratch them. Anything that hits them is going to bounce off." He put his gun on the table. "We've been lucky so far. The last ricochet didn't hit anyone. I think the bullet went out the door. There's no reason to think we'll be lucky a second time."

Arkady and Irina taped the two men, while Alexandra kept her gun leveled.

"Are you recording?" Arkady asked after they were done.

"Yes," Maggie said. "But I'm having trouble with my radio signal here. As soon as we are outside, I will send the photos to Venusport."

Arkady set a knife on the table next to Mike's gun. "It will cut the tape," he said to Mike. "Even if your comrades don't come looking for you, you'll be able to get free."

"That may be a mistake," Boris said.

Arkady nodded. "We all make them. Let's get out of here."

They left the room and retraced their way through the maze-like stone corridors. No one appeared, though they did encounter a scorpion, crawling over the floor. It was dirty pink with tiny eyes, thirty centimeters long and the ugliest land scorpion Ash had ever seen. Boris stepped on it hard, crushing its exoskeleton. The many legs kept scrabbling, and the mandibles twitched back and forth, but the animal's body could not move. It was broken. "This is why we wear tall boots," he said.

They found the trucks where they had left them. Rain still fell heavily.

"I can send the recordings now," Maggie said.

"Do it," Jason said. "I am going to write an exposé that will rip those guys apart. They were ready to kill us."

They ran for the trucks, climbed in and pulled out, going along the track away from the ruins.

Ash could feel her heart beating rapidly. Her mouth was dry, and she was shaking. Fear fighting with amazement. She had been inside ruins built by aliens, and she had escaped from the CIA. What a day!

Baby was in his cage, shivering and repeating "bad, bad" over and over in a quiet voice.

"Okay," Ash said after her heart slowed down. "What was that about?"

Arkady leaned forward and checked the truck radio, which was off. "We knew the CIA was here, and that they had some kind of agreement with the Petrograd executive committee. We knew about the circles. And we had this." He handed her a tablet. On the screen was a piece of sculpture, deeply worn and barely recognizable as a person. It had two arms and two legs, all long and thin, the legs together and the arms folded across the chest. The person's torso was short and wide, its neck long and narrow, its head wedge-shaped.

"This might be expressive distortion," Arkady said. "Or it might be an alien. It is only ten centimeters long. It was found in outback in the early days of settlement, and it ended in the Petrograd Museum. The curators thought it was fake. It remained in the collection, but was never investigated."

"We learned about it and put it together with the circles," Boris said. "Do you have any idea how much money Petrograd could make from tourism, if we had authentic alien ruins?"

"Who are you?" Ash asked.

"People who want to embarrass the executive committee," Arkady said. "Can you imagine what Lenin would have said about that collection of petty bureaucrats? Now *National Geographic* will publish its exclusive. With luck, there will be a huge stink. The Petrograd Soviet will decide to remove the executive committee, and the CIA will be so embarrassed that it will leave Aphrodite Terra."

"That's too much to hope," Boris growled.

"Maybe," Arkady replied. "In any case, we couldn't pass up the chance. The entire Solar System pays attention to the *National Geographic*."

"What about the bug in the lodge?" Ash asked. "Mike said it wasn't one of theirs."

"It was CIA, but they didn't put it in the lodge. Some of our farmworkers found it crawling in the fields, heading toward Petrograd, and sent for the police. They captured it. I brought it with us," Boris said. "We wanted *Nat Geo* to see what we had to put up with. Poisonous robot spies! They are a crime against nature and peaceful co-existence!"

The truck was bumping over the rough road, among dripping trees, while rain beat on the windows. Looking back, she saw the other truck, dim in the rain.

"I feel as if everything has been fake," she told the two men. "You set up the robot scorpion, and you set up discovering the circle."

Arkady said, "The circles are real, and they are not impact craters, though we don't know what they are. Ball courts? Fish ponds? Temples?

"And the tunnels are real. We didn't know about them, but now they will be famous."

Boris added, "Those idiots on the executive committee were so afraid that they let the CIA camp on a site of system-wide historical importance. We have been slowly dying when we could have made a fortune from tourism. Why would anyone go to Venusport, when they can come here and see alien ruins?" He was silent for a moment, then added. "We'll have to get rid of their damn pink scorpions. That won't be easy. And then take a serious look. Who knows what may be in the caves and circles? More statues like the one in the museum? Maybe even a skeleton?"

"Who are you guys?" Ash asked.

Arkady laughed. "I am myself. Arkady Volkov of Volkov Tours. Boris is a part-time employee."

"What else does he do?"

"I'm an analyst for the political police," Boris replied. "But my hours have been cut, due to the Soviet's cash flow problems—which we would not have, if we had more tourists."

"Or if the executive committee stopped listening to American economists," Arkady added. "I don't want a lecture on economics," Boris said. "I needed a second job. Arkady gave me one."

"And Irina and Alexandria?" Ash asked.

"Ordinary working people," Arkady said.

"Could the CIA really have been stupid enough to create a new kind of scorpion?" Ash asked.

"Remember that no one has ever gone broke by underestimating the intelligence of Americans," Arkady said.

"This seems way too Byzantine," Ash added.

Boris gave a rasping laugh. "Arkady's ancestors came from some damn place in Central Asia. But I am Russian, and Russians are the heirs of Byzantium."

They made it back to the pillbox lodge at nightfall. Arkady and Boris checked the parking space with flashlights and called all clear. They went in through the rain.

Arkady turned on the fire, as the rest of them pulled off their wet jackets and hung them up to dry.

"I'll start dinner," Alexandra told them. "Irina, will you help?"

The ex-cop and the ex-stevedore went into the kitchen. Ash sat down in front of the fire, Baby's cage on the floor next to her. Baby climbed on top of the cage. "Hungry."

She found a piece of chow and gave it to him.

"Hunt," he said.

"Not now."

Jason and Maggie joined her, the journalist settling into a chair, the Leica standing on her four silver legs, her long neck stretched out, head turning as she made another recording.

"I think we can call the trip successful," Jason said. "We have discovered the first evidence of intelligent aliens, and I have a dramatic story about fighting the CIA."

"I suspect the CIA part of the story will vanish," Arkady said. "But you will have the alien ruins."

"I'll fight for the entire story," Jason said. "It's outrageous that we were threatened by our own government."

"We'll go back to Petrograd," Arkady said. "I will show you a piece of sculpture at the museum, and you might be interested in talking to the Soviet's executive committee. Ask them what they were thinking to let the CIA perch in the most important piece of archeology in the Solar System. God knows what kind of damage they may have done! War—overt or covert—is not good for art or history."

Boris set a bottle of fruit brandy on the table, along with four glasses. "I'll go back. I have worked as an exterminator. I want to know what's in the tunnels and the caves, aside from vermin; and I will enjoy getting rid of those damn pink scorpions."

After dinner, in her bedroom, Ash considered the journey. She was a little buzzed from alcohol and shaky from adrenalin. But nothing was happening now. She could finally think.

The circles and tunnels could not have been faked. She was less certain about the figurine. It didn't have the glassy surface of the stone in the circle and the tunnels; and even if the government in Moscow hadn't been interested in science, it would have been interested in an alien figurine. That had to have some kind of propaganda value. Unless they were afraid of it. Would fear have made them put it in a museum and forget it?

It would be easy to fake something as small as the figurine. Arkady said it was in the Petrograd Museum, but he could have bought it with him, planning to plant it near the circle for Jason to find. That and the toxic scorpion in the lodge would have given *National Geographic* its big story. With luck, the story would have forced the CIA out and brought down the executive committee.

She could imagine Arkady learning who the client was and hurriedly putting together an elaborate con. Never trust a Leninist entirely. And she could imagine him as completely honest. As far as she knew, he always had been.

Well, if the figurine was fake, that would be discovered, probably quickly.

But the ruins had to be real. She lay there, her light still on, considering the possibility that humanity was not alone. Where were the aliens now? In the Solar System? Or had they moved on? And what difference would knowledge of them make to Earth, shambling toward destruction? Or to Venus, tied to Earth and maybe unable to survive on its own? Ash had no idea. But the world—the two worlds—had suddenly become more interesting and full of possibility

"Turn light off," said Baby, hunched in his cage. "Sleep."

THE END

Author's Note: Our Venus rotates backward compared to most planets in the Solar System, and its day is longer than its year. The current theory is it was dinged by something big early in the development of the System. The ding turned it backwards and slowed its rotation. In my alternative history, this ding did not happen. My Venus rotates forward and has a day about as long as that of Earth or Mars. This rotation gives it a magnetic field, which our Venus does not have. The field prevents—at least in part—the development of the planet's current toxic greenhouse atmosphere. In addition, there was a ding that didn't happen in our history, at least as far as we know. A body—possibly two—hit Earth after life had developed there, then went on to hit Venus, depositing Earth microbes. As a result, my Venus has blue-green algae, and this over time gave it an atmosphere comparable to Earth. The similarity of Venusian life to life on Earth is due to the shared genetic history.

The history of Earth is the same as in our timeline, until Soviet probes discover that Venus is habitable. Then a serious space race begins. The cost of the race helps to destroy the Soviet Union and helps to distract the U.S. from dealing with global warming.

As you may have noticed, the Pecheneg machine gun was never used. Chekhov was wrong. You can put a gun on the wall in the first act and never use it.

another word for world

ANN LECKIE

Ann Leckie is the author of the Hugo, Nebula, and Arthur C. Clarke Award-winning novel Ancillary Justice, and its sequels Ancillary Sword and Ancillary Mercy. She has also published short stories in Subterranean Magazine, Strange Horizons, Beneath Ceaseless Skies, and elsewhere. She has worked as a waitress, a receptionist, a rodman on a land-surveying crew, and a recording engineer. She lives in St. Louis, Missouri.

In the compelling story that follows, she takes us to a troubled colony world where civil war is brewing, and an embattled diplomat, on the run for her life, must choose just the right words to defuse the situation—or perhaps to make it much worse.

AshibanXidyla had a headache. A particularly vicious one, centered somewhere on the top of her head. She sat curled over her lap, in her seat on the flier, eyes closed. Oddly, she had no memory of leaning forward, and—now that she thought of it—no idea when the headache had begun.

The Gidanta had been very respectful so far, very solicitous of Ashiban's age, but that was, she was sure, little more than the entirely natural respect for one's elders. This was not a time when she could afford any kind of weakness. Ashiban was here to prevent a war that would quite possibly end with the Gidanta slaughtering every one of Ashiban's fellow Raksamat on the planet. The Sovereign of Iss, hereditary high priestess of the Gidanta, sat across the aisle, silent and veiled, her interpreter beside her. What must they be thinking?

Ashiban took three careful breaths. Straightened cautiously, wary of the pain flaring. Opened her eyes.

Ought to have seen blue sky through the flier's front window past the pilot's seat, ought to have heard the buzz of the engine. Instead she saw shards of brown and green and blue. Heard nothing. She closed her eyes, opened them again. Tried to make some sense of things. They weren't falling, she was sure. Had the flier landed, and she hadn't noticed?

A high, quavering voice said something, syllables that made no sense to Ashiban. "We have to get out of here," said a calm, muffled voice somewhere at Ashiban's feet.

"Speaker is in some distress." Damn. She'd forgotten to turn off the translating function on her handheld. Maybe the Sovereign's interpreter hadn't heard it. She turned her head to look across the flier's narrow aisle, wincing at the headache.

The Sovereign's interpreter lay in the aisle, his head jammed up against the back of the pilot's seat at an odd, awkward angle. The high voice spoke again, and in the small bag at Ashiban's feet her handheld said, "Disregard the dead. We have to get out of here or we will also die. The speaker is in some distress."

In her own seat, the pink- and orange- and blue-veiled Sovereign fumbled at the safety restraints. The straps parted with a click, and the Sovereign stood. Stepped into the aisle, hiking her long blue skirt. Spoke—it must have been the Sovereign speaking all along. "Stupid cow," said Ashiban's handheld, in her bag. "Speaker's distress has increased."

The flier lurched. The Sovereign cried out. "No translation available," remarked Ashiban's handheld, as the Sovereign reached forward to tug at Ashiban's own safety restraints and, once those had come undone, grab Ashiban's arm and pull.

The flier had crashed. The flier had crashed, and the Sovereign's interpreter must have gotten out of his seat for some reason, at just the wrong time. Ashiban herself must have hit her head. That would explain the memory gap, and the headache. She blinked again, and the colored shards where the window should have been resolved into cracked glass, and behind it sky, and flat ground covered in brown and green plants, here and there some white or pink. "We should stay here and wait for help," Ashiban said. In her bag, her handheld said something incomprehensible.

The Sovereign pulled harder on Ashiban's arm. "You stupid expletive cow," said the handheld, as the Sovereign picked Ashiban's bag up from her feet. "Someone shot us down, and we crashed in the expletive High Mires. The expletive expletive is expletive sinking into the expletive bog. If we stay here we'll drown. The speaker is highly agitated." The flier lurched again.

It all seemed so unreal. Concussion, Ashiban thought. I have a concussion, and I'm not thinking straight. She took her bag from the Sovereign, rose, and followed the Sovereign of Iss to the emergency exit.

Outside the flier, everything was a brown and green plain, blue sky above. The ground swelled and rolled under Ashiban's feet, but given the flier behind her, half-sunk into the gray-brown ground, and the pain in her head, she wasn't sure if it was really doing that or if it was a symptom of concussion.

The Sovereign said something. The handheld in Ashiban's bag spoke, but it was lost in the open space and the breeze and Ashiban's inability to concentrate.

The Sovereign yanked Ashiban's bag from her, pulled it open. Dug out the handheld. "Expletive," said the handheld. "Expletive expletive. We are standing on water. The speaker is agitated."

"What?" The flier behind them, sliding slowly into the mire, made a gurgling sound. The ground was still unsteady under Ashiban's feet, she still wasn't sure why.

"Water! The speaker is emphatic." The Sovereign gestured toward the greenish-brown mat of moss beneath them.

"Help will come," Ashiban said. "We should stay here."

"They shot us down," said the handheld. "The speaker is agitated and emphatic."

"What?"

"They shot us down. I saw the pilot shot through the window, I saw them die. Timran was trying to take control of the flier when we crashed. Whoever comes, they are not coming to help us. We have to get to solid ground. We have to hide. The speaker is emphatic. The speaker is in some distress. The speaker is agitated." The Sovereign took Ashiban's arm and pulled her forward.

"Hide?" There was nowhere to hide. And the ground swelled and sank, like waves on the top of water. She fell to her hands and knees, nauseated.

"Translation unavailable," said the handheld, as the Sovereign dropped down beside her. "Crawl then, but come with me or be dead. The speaker is emphatic. The speaker is in some distress." The Sovereign crawled away, the ground still heaving.

"That's my bag," said Ashiban. "That's my handheld." The Sovereign continued to crawl away. "There's nowhere to hide!" But if she stayed where she was, on her hands and knees on the unsteady ground, she would be all alone here, and all her things gone and her head hurting and her stomach sick and nothing making sense. She crawled after the Sovereign.

By the time the ground stopped roiling, the squishy wet moss had changed to stiff, spiky-leaved meter-high plants that scratched Ashiban's face and tore at her sodden clothes. "Come here," said her handheld, somewhere up ahead. "Quickly. Come here. The speaker is agitated." Ashiban just wanted to lie down where she was, close her eyes, and go to sleep. But the Sovereign had her bag. There was a bottle of water in her bag. She kept going.

Found the Sovereign prone, veilless, pulling off her bright-colored skirts to ball them up beneath herself. Underneath her clothes she wore a plain brown shirt and leggings, like any regular Gidanta. "Ancestors!" panted Ashiban, still on hands and knees, not sure where there was room to lie down. "You're just a kid! You're younger than my grandchildren!"

In answer the Sovereign took hold of the collar of Ashiban's jacket and yanked her down to the ground. Ashiban cried out, and heard her handheld say something incomprehensible, presumably the Gidantan equivalent of *No translation available*. Pain darkened her vision, and her ears roared. Or was that the flier the Sovereign had said she'd heard?

The Sovereign spoke. "Stupid expletive expletive expletive, lie still," said Ashiban's handheld calmly. "Speaker is in some distress."

Ashiban closed her eyes. Her head hurt, and her twig-scratched face stung, but she was very, very tired.

A calm voice was saying, "Wake up, AshibanXidyla. The speaker is distressed." Over and over again. She opened her eyes. The absurdly young Sovereign of Iss lay in front of her, brown cheek pressed against the gray ground, staring at Ashiban, twigs and spiny leaves caught in the few trailing braids that had come loose from the hair coiled at the top of her head. Her eyes were red and puffy, as though she had been crying, though her expression gave no sign of it. She clutched Ashiban's handheld in one hand. Nineteen at most, Ashiban thought. Probably younger. "Are you awake, AshibanXidyla? The speaker is distressed."

"My head doesn't hurt," Ashiban observed. Despite that, everything still seemed slippery and unreal.

"I took the emergency medical kit on our way off the flier," the handheld said, translating the Sovereign's reply. "I put a corrective on your forehead. It's not the right kind, though. The instructions say to take you to a doctor right away. The speaker is . . ."

"Translation preferences," interrupted Ashiban. "Turn off emotional evaluation." The handheld fell silent. "Have you called for help, Sovereign? Is help coming?"

"You are very stupid," said Ashiban's handheld. Said the Sovereign of Iss. "Or the concussion is dangerously severe. Our flier was shot down. Twenty minutes after that a flier goes back and forth over us as though it is looking for something, but we are in the High Mires, no one lives here. If we call for help, who is nearest? The people who shot us down."

"Who would shoot us down?"

"Someone who wants war between Gidanta and Raksamat. Someone with a grudge against your mother, the sainted CiwrilXidyla. Someone with a grudge against my grandmother, the previous Sovereign."

"Not likely anyone Raksamat then," said Ashiban, and immediately regretted it. She was here to foster goodwill between her people and the Sovereign's, because the Gidanta had trusted her mother, CiwrilXidyla, and so they might listen to her daughter. "There are far more of you down here than Raksamat settlers. If it came to a war, the Raksamat here would be slaughtered. I don't think any of us wants that."

"We will argue in the future," said the Sovereign. "So long as whoever it is does not manage to kill us. I have been thinking. They did not see us, under the plants, but maybe they will come back and look for us with infrared. They may come back soon. We have to reach the trees north of here."

"I can use my handheld to just contact my own people," said Ashiban. "Just them. I trust them."

"Do you?" asked the Sovereign. "But maybe the deaths of some Raksamat settlers will be the excuse they need to bring a war that kills all the Gidanta so they can have the world for themselves. Maybe your death would be convenient for them."

"That's ridiculous!" exclaimed Ashiban. She pushed herself to sitting, not too quickly, wary of the pain in her head returning, of her lingering dizziness. "I'm talking about my friends."

"Your friends are far away," said the Sovereign. "They would call on others to come find us. Do you trust those others?" The girl seemed deadly serious. She sat up. "I don't." She tucked Ashiban's handheld into her waistband, picked up her bundle of skirts and veils.

"That's my handheld! I need it!"

"You'll only call our deaths down with it," said the Sovereign. "Die if you want to." She rose, and trudged away through the stiff, spiky vegetation.

Ashiban considered tackling the girl and taking back her handheld. But the Sovereign was young, and while Ashiban was in fairly good shape considering her age, she had never been an athlete, even in her youth. And that was without considering the head injury.

She stood. Carefully, still dizzy, joints stiff. Where the flier had been was only black water, strips and chunks of moss floating on its surface, all of it surrounded by a flat carpet of yet more moss. She remembered the Sovereign saying *We're standing on water!* Remembered the swell and roll of the ground that had made her drop to her hands and knees.

She closed her eyes. She thought she vaguely remembered sitting in her seat on the flier, the Sovereign crying out, her interpreter getting out of his seat to rush forward to where the pilot slumped over the controls.

Shot down. If that was true, the Sovereign was right. Calling for help—if she could find some way to do that without her handheld—might well be fatal. Whoever it was had considered both Ashiban and the Sovereign of Iss acceptable losses. Had, perhaps, specifically wanted both of them dead. Had, perhaps, specifically wanted the war that had threatened for the past two years to become deadly real.

But nobody wanted that. Not even the Gidanta who had never been happy with Ashiban's people's presence in the system wanted that, Ashiban was sure.

She opened her eyes. Saw the girl's back as she picked her way through the mire. Saw far off on the northern horizon the trees the girl had mentioned. "Ancestors!" cried Ashiban. "I'm too old for this." And she shouldered her bag and followed the Sovereign of Iss.

Eventually Ashiban caught up, though the Sovereign didn't acknowledge her in any way. They trudged through the hip-high scrub in silence for some time, only making the occasional hiss of annoyance at particularly troublesome branches. The clear blue sky clouded over, and a damp-smelling wind rose. A relief—the bright sun had hurt Ashiban's eyes. As the trees on the horizon became more definitely a band of trees—still dismayingly far off—Ashiban's thoughts, which had this whole time been slippery and tenuous, began to settle into something like a comprehensible pattern.

Shot down. Ashiban was sure none of her people wanted war. Though off-planet the Raksamat weren't quite so vulnerable—were, in fact, much better armed. The ultimate outcome of an actual war would probably not favor the Gidanta. Or Ashiban didn't think so. It was possible some Raksamat faction actually wanted such a war. And Ashiban wasn't really anyone of any significance to her own people.

Her mother had been. Her mother, CiwrilXidyla, had negotiated the Treaty of Eatu with the then-Sovereign of Iss, ensuring the right of the Raksamat to live peacefully in the system, and on the planet. Ciwril had been widely admired among both Raksamat and Gidanta. As her daughter, Ashiban was only a sign, an admonition to remember her mother. If her side could think it acceptable to sacrifice the lives of their own people on the planet, they would certainly not blink at sacrificing Ashiban herself. She didn't want to believe that, though, that her own people would do such a thing.

Would the Gidanta be willing to kill their own Sovereign for the sake of a war? An hour ago—or however long they had been trudging across the mire, Ashiban wasn't sure—she'd have said *certainly not*. The Sovereign of Iss was a sacred figure. She was the conduit between the Gidanta and the spirit of the world of Iss, which spoke to them with the Sovereign's voice. Surely they wouldn't kill her just to forward a war that would be disastrous for both sides?

"Sovereign."

A meter ahead of Ashiban, the girl kept trudging. Looked briefly over her shoulder. "What?"

"Where are you going?"

The Sovereign didn't even turn her head this time. "There's a monitoring station on the North Udran Plain."

That had to be hundreds of kilometers away, and that wasn't counting the fact that if this was indeed the High Mires, they were on the high side of the Scarp and would certainly have to detour to get down to the plains.

"On foot? That could take weeks, if we even ever get there. We have no food, no water." Well, Ashiban had about a third of a liter in a bottle in her bag, but that hardly counted. "No camping equipment."

The Sovereign just scoffed and kept walking.

"Young lady," began Ashiban, but then remembered herself at that age. Her own children and grandchildren. Adolescence was trying enough without the fate of your people resting on your shoulders, and being shot down and stranded in a bog. "I thought the current Sovereign was fifty or sixty. The daughter of the woman who was Sovereign when my mother was here last."

"You're not supposed to talk like we're all different people," said the girl. "We're all the voice of the world spirit. And you mean my aunt. She abdicated last week."

"Abdicated!" Mortified by her mistake—Ashiban had been warned over and over about the nature of the Sovereign of Iss, that she was not an individual, that referring to her as such would be an offense. "I didn't know that was possible." And surely at a time like this, the Sovereign wouldn't want to drop so much responsibility on a teenager.

"Of course it's possible. It's just a regular priesthood. It never was particularly special. It was you Raksamat who insisted on translating Sovereign as Sovereign. And it's you Raksamat whose priests are always trancing out and speaking for your ancestors. *Voice of Iss* doesn't mean that at all."

"Translating Sovereign as Sovereign?" asked Ashiban. "What is that supposed to mean?" The girl snorted. "And how can the Voice of Iss not mean exactly that?" The Sovereign didn't answer, just kept walking.

After a long silence, Ashiban said, "Then why do any of the Gidanta listen to you? And who is it my mother was negotiating with?"

The Sovereign looked back at Ashiban and rolled her eyes. "With the interpreter, of course. And if your mother didn't know that, she was completely stupid. And nobody listens to me." The voice of the translating handheld was utterly calm and neutral, but the girl's tone was contemptuous. "That's why I'm stuck here. And it wasn't about us listening to the voice of the planet. It was about *you* listening to *us*. You wouldn't talk to the Terraforming Council because you wouldn't accept they were an authority, and besides, you didn't like what they were saying."

"An industrial association is not a government!" Seeing the girl roll her eyes again, Ashiban wondered fleetingly what her words sounded like in Gidantan—if the handheld was making *industrial association* and *government* into the same words, the way it obviously had when it had said for the girl, moments ago, *translating Sovereign as Sovereign*. But that was ridiculous. The two weren't the same thing at all.

The Sovereign stopped. Turned to face Ashiban. "We have been here for two thousand years. For all that time, we have been working on this planet, to make it a place we could live without interference. We came here, to this place without an intersystem gate, so that no one would bother us and we could live in peace. You turned up less than two centuries ago, now most of the hard work is done, and you want to tell us what to do with our planet, and who is or isn't an authority!"

"We were refugees. We came here by accident, and we can't very well leave. And we brought benefits. You've been cut off from the outside for so long, you didn't have medical correctives. Those have saved lives, Sovereign. And we've brought other things." Including weapons the Gidanta didn't have. "Including our own knowledge of terraforming, and how to best manage a planet."

"And you agreed, your own mother, the great CiwrilXidyla agreed, that no one would settle on the planet without authorization from the Terraforming Council! And yet there are dozens of Raksamat farmsteads just in the Saunn foothills, and more elsewhere."

"That wasn't the agreement. The treaty explicitly states that we have a right to be here, and a right to share in the benefits of living on this planet. Your own grandmother agreed to that! And small farmsteads are much better for the planet than the cities the Terraforming Council is intending." Wind gusted, and a few fat drops of rain fell.

"My grandmother agreed to nothing! It was the gods-cursed interpreter who made the agreement. And he was appointed by the Terraforming Council, just like all of them! And how dare you turn up here after we've done all the hard work and think because you brought us some technology you can tell us what to do with our planet!"

"How can you own a planet? You can't, it's ridiculous! There's more than enough room for all of us."

"I've memorized it, you know," said the Sovereign. "The entire agreement. It's not that long. *Settlement will only proceed according to the current consensus regarding the good of the planet.* That's what it says, right there in the second paragraph."

Ashiban knew that sentence by heart. Everyone knew that sentence by now. Arguments over what *current consensus regarding the good of the planet* might mean were inescapable—and generally, in Ashiban's opinion, made in bad faith. The words were clear enough. "There's nothing about the Terraforming Council in that sentence." Like most off-planet Raksamat, Ashiban didn't speak the language of the Gidanta. But—also like most off-planet Raksamat—she had a few words and phrases, and she knew the Gidantan for *Terraforming Council*. Had heard the girl speak the sentence, knew there was no mention of the council.

The Sovereign cried out in apparent anger and frustration. "How can you? How can you stand there and say that, as though you have not just heard me say it?"

Overhead, barely audible over the sound of the swelling rain, the hum of a flier engine. The Sovereign looked up.

"It's help," said Ashiban. Angry, yes, but she could set that aside at the prospect of rescue. Of soon being somewhere warm, and dry, and comfortable. Her clothes— plain, green trousers and shirt, simple, soft flat shoes—had not been chosen with any anticipation of a trek through mud and weeds, or standing in a rain shower. "They must be looking for us."

The Sovereign's eyes widened. She spun and took off running through the thick, thigh-high plants, toward the trees.

"Wait!" cried Ashiban, but the girl kept moving.

Ashiban turned to scan the sky, shielding her eyes from the rain with one hand. Was there anything she could do to attract the attention of the flier? Her own green clothes weren't far off the green of the plants she stood among, but she didn't trust the flat, brownish-green mossy stretches that she and the Sovereign had been avoiding. She had nothing that would light up, and the girl had fled with Ashiban's handheld, which she could have used to try to contact the searchers.

A crack echoed across the mire, and a few meters to Ashiban's left, leaves and twigs exploded. The wind gusted again, harder than before, and she shivered.

And realized that someone had just fired at her. That had been a gunshot, and there was no one here to shoot at her except that approaching flier, which was, Ashiban saw, coming straight toward her, even though with the clouds and the rain, and the green of her clothes and the green of the plants she stood in, she could not have been easy to see.

Except maybe in the infrared. Even without the cold rain coming down, she must glow bright and unmistakable in infrared.

Ashiban turned and ran. Or tried to, wading through the plants toward the trees, twigs catching her trousers. Another crack, and she couldn't go any faster than she was, though she tried, and the wind blew harder, and she hoped she was moving toward the trees.

Three more shots in quick succession, the wind blowing harder, nearly pushing her over, and Ashiban stumbled out of the plants onto a stretch of open moss that trembled under her as she ran, gasping, cold, and exhausted, toward another patch of those thigh-high weeds, and the shadow of trees beyond. Below her feet the moss began to come apart, fraying, loosening, one more wobbling step and she would sink into the black water of the mire below, but another shot cracked behind her and she couldn't stop, and there was no safe direction, she could only go forward. She ran on. And then, with hopefully solid ground a single step ahead, the skies opened up in a torrent of rain, and the moss gave way underneath her.

She plunged downward, into cold water. Made a frantic, scrabbling grab, got hold of one tough plant stem. Tried to pull herself up, but could not. The rain poured down, and her grip on the plant stem began to slip.

A hand grabbed her arm. Someone shouted something incomprehensible—it was the Sovereign of Iss, rain streaming down her face, braids plastered against her neck and shoulders. The girl grabbed the back of Ashiban's shirt with her other hand, leaned back, pulling Ashiban up a few centimeters, and Ashiban reached forward and grabbed another handful of plant, and somehow scrambled free of the water, onto the land, and she and the Sovereign half-ran, half-stumbled forward into the trees.

Where the rain was less but still came down. And they needed better cover, they needed to go deeper into the trees. Ancestors grant the woods ahead were thick enough to hide them from the flier, and Ashiban wanted to tell the Sovereign that they needed to keep running, but the girl didn't stop until Ashiban, unable to move a single step more, collapsed at the bottom of a tree.

The Sovereign dropped down beside her. There was no sound but their gasping, and the rain hissing through the branches above.

One of Ashiban's shoes had come off, somewhere. Her arm, which the Sovereign had pulled on to get her up out of the water, ached. Her back hurt, and her legs. Her heart pounded, and she couldn't seem to catch her breath, and she shivered, with cold or with fear she wasn't sure.

The rain lessened not long after, and stopped at some point during the night. Ashiban woke shivering, the Sovereign huddled beside her. Pale sunlight filtered through the tree leaves, and the leaf-covered ground was sodden. So was Ashiban.

She was hungry, too. Wasn't food the whole point of planets? Surely there would be something to eat, it would just be a question of knowing what there was, and how to eat it safely. Water might well be a bigger problem than food. Ashiban opened her bag—which by some miracle had stayed on her shoulder through everything—and found her half-liter bottle of water, still about three-quarters full. If she'd had her wits about her last night, she'd have opened it in the rain, to collect as much as she could.

"Well," Ashiban said, "here we are."

Silence. Not a word from the handheld. The Sovereign uncurled herself from where she huddled against Ashiban. Put a hand on her waist, where the handheld had been tucked into her waistband. Looked at Ashiban.

The handheld was gone. "Oh, Ancestors," said Ashiban. And after another half-panicked second, carefully got to her feet from off the ground—something that hadn't been particularly easy for a decade or two, even without yesterday's hectic flight and a night spent cold and soaking wet, sleeping sitting on the ground and leaning against a tree—and retraced their steps. The Sovereign joined her.

As far back as they went (apparently neither of them was willing to go all the way back to the mire), they found only bracken, and masses of wet, dead leaves.

Ashiban looked at the damp and shivering Sovereign. Who looked five or six years younger than she'd looked yesterday. The Sovereign said nothing, but what was there to say? Without the handheld, or some other translation device, they could barely talk to each other at all. Ashiban herself knew only a few phrases in Gidantan. *Hello* and *good-bye* and *I don't understand Gidantan*. She could count from one to twelve. A few words and phrases more, none of them applicable to being stranded in the woods on the edge of the High Mires. Ironic, since her mother Ciwril had been an expert in the language. It was her mother's work that had made the translation devices as useful as they were, that had allowed the Raksamat and Gidanta to speak to each other. *And who is it my mother was negotiating with? With the interpreter, of course.*

No point thinking about that just now. The immediate problem was more than enough.

Someone had shot down their flier yesterday, and then apparently flown away. Hours later they had returned, so that they could shoot at Ashiban and the Sovereign as they fled. It didn't make sense.

The Gidanta had guns, of course, knew how to make them. But they didn't have many. Since they had arrived here, most of their energies had been devoted to the terraforming of Iss, and during much of that time they'd lived in space, on stations, an environment in which projectile weapons potentially caused far more problems than they might solve, even when it came to deadly disputes.

That attitude had continued when they had moved down to the planet. There were police, and some of the Terraforming Council had bodyguards, and Ashiban didn't doubt there were people who specialized in fighting, including firing guns, but there was no Gidanta military, no army, standing or otherwise. Fliers for cargo or for personal transport, but not for warfare. Guns for hunting, not designed to kill people efficiently.

The Raksamat, Ashiban's own people, had come into the system armed. But none of those weapons were on the planet. Or Ashiban didn't think they were. So, a hunting gun and a personal flier. She wanted to ask the Sovereign, standing staring at Ashiban, still shivering, if the girl had seen the other flier. But she couldn't, not without that handheld.

But it didn't matter, this moment, why it had happened the way it had. There was no way to tell who had tried to kill them. No way to know what or who they would find if they returned to the mire, to where their own flier had sunk under the black water and the moss.

Her thoughts were going in circles. Whether it was the night spent in the cold, and the hunger and the fear, or whether it was the remnants of her concussion—and what had the Sovereign of Iss said, that the corrective hadn't been the right sort and she should get to a doctor as soon as possible?—or maybe all of those, Ashiban didn't know.

Yesterday the Sovereign had said there was a monitoring station on the Udran Plains, which lay to the north of the Scarp. There would be people at a monitoring station—likely all of them Gidanta. Very possibly not favorably disposed toward Ashiban, no matter whose daughter she was.

But there would be dozens, maybe even hundreds of people at a monitoring station, any of whom might witness an attempt to murder Ashiban, and all of whom would be outraged at an attempt to harm the Sovereign of Iss. There was no one at the crash site on the mire to see what happened to them.

"Which way?" Ashiban asked the girl.

Who looked up at the leaf-dappled sky above them, and then pointed back into the woods, the way they had come. Said something Ashiban didn't understand. Watched Ashiban expectantly. Something about the set of her jaw suggested to Ashiban that the girl was trying very hard not to cry.

"All right," said Ashiban, and turned and began walking back the way they had come, the Sovereign of Iss alongside her.

They shared out the water between them as they went. There was less food in the woods than Ashiban would have expected, or at least neither of them knew where or how to find it. No doubt the Sovereign of Iss, at her age, was hungrier even than Ashiban, but she didn't complain, just walked forward. Once they heard the distant sound of a flier, presumably looking for them, but the Sovereign of Iss showed no sign of being tempted to go back. Ashiban thought of those shots, of plunging into cold, black water, and shivered.

Despite herself, Ashiban began imagining what she would eat if she were at home. The nutrient cakes that everyone had eaten every day until they had established contact with the Gidanta. They were traditional for holidays, authentic Raksamat cuisine, and Ashiban's grandmother had despised them, observed wryly on every holiday that her grandchildren would not eat them with such relish if that had been their only food for years. Ashiban would like a nutrient cake now.

Or some fish. Or snails. Surely there might be snails in the woods? But Ashiban wasn't sure how to find them.

Or grubs. A handful of toasted grubs, with a little salt, maybe some cumin. At home they were an expensive treat, either harvested from a station's agronomy unit, or shipped up from Iss itself. Ashiban remembered a school trip, once, when she'd been much, much younger, a tour of the station's food-growing facilities, remembered an agronomist turning over the dirt beside a row of green, sharp-smelling plants to reveal a grub, curled and white in the dark soil. Remembered one of her schoolmates saying the sight made them hungry.

She stopped. Pushed aside the leaf mold under her feet. Looked around for a stick.

The Sovereign of Iss stopped, turned to look at Ashiban. Said something in Gidantan that Ashiban assumed was some version of *What are you doing?*

"Grubs," said Ashiban. That word she knew—the Gidanta sold prepackaged toasted grubs harvested from their own orbital agronomy projects, and the name was printed on the package.

The Sovereign blinked at her. Frowned. Seemed to think for a bit, and then said, "Fire?" in Gidantan. That was another word Ashiban knew—nearly everyone in the system recognized words in either language that might turn up in a safety alert.

There was no way to make a fire that Ashiban could think of. Her bag held only their now nearly empty bottle of water. People who lived in space generally didn't walk around with the means for producing an open flame. Here on Iss things might be different, but if the Sovereign had been carrying fire-making tools, she'd lost them in the mire. "No fire," Ashiban said. "We'll have to eat anything we find raw." The Sovereign of Iss frowned, and then went kicking through the leaf mold for a couple of sturdy sticks.

The few grubs they dug up promised more nearby. There was no water to wash the dirt off them, and they were unpleasant to eat while raw and wiggling, but they were food.

Their progress slowed as they stopped every few steps to dig for more grubs, or to replace a broken stick. But after a few hours, or at least what Ashiban took to be a few hours—she had no way of telling time beyond the sunlight, and had no experience with that—their situation seemed immeasurably better than it had before they'd eaten.

They filled Ashiban's bag with grubs, and walked on until night fell, and slept, shivering, huddled together. Ashiban was certain she would never be warm again, would always be chilled to her bones. But she could think straighter, or at least it seemed like she could. The girl's plan to walk down to the plains was still outrageous, still seemed all but impossible, but it also seemed like the only way forward.

By the end of the next day, Ashiban was more sick of raw and gritty grubs than she could possibly say. And by the afternoon of the day after that, the trees thinned and they were faced with a wall of brambles. They turned to parallel the barrier, walked east for a while, until they came to a relatively clear space—a tunnel of thorny branches arching over a several-meters-wide shelf of reddish-brown rock jutting out of the soil. Ashiban peered through and saw horizon, gestured to the Sovereign of Iss to look.

The Sovereign pulled her head back out of the tunnel, looked at Ashiban, and said something long and incomprehensible.

"Right," said Ashiban. In her own language. There was no point trying to ask her question in Gidantan. "Do we want to go through here and keep going north until we find the edge of the Scarp, and turn east until we find a way down to the plain? Or do we want to keep going east like we have been and hope we find something?"

With her free hand—her other one held the water bottle that no longer fit in Ashiban's grub-filled bag—the Sovereign waved away the possibility of her having understood Ashiban.

Ashiban pointed north, toward the brambles. "Scarp," she said, in Gidantan. It was famous enough that she knew that one.

"Yes," agreed the Sovereign, in that same language. And then, to Ashiban's surprise, added, in Raksamat, "See." She held her hands up to her eyes, miming a scope. Then waved an arm expansively. "Scarp see big."

"Good point," agreed Ashiban. On the edge of the Scarp, they could see where they were, and take their direction from that, instead of wandering and hoping they arrived somewhere. "Yes," she said in Gidantan. "Good." She gestured at the thorny tunnel of brambles.

The Sovereign of Iss just stared at her. Ashiban sighed. Made sure her bag was securely closed. Gingerly got down on her hands and knees, lowered herself onto her stomach, and inched herself forward under the brambles.

The tunnel wasn't long, just three or four meters, but Ashiban took it slowly, the bag dragging beside her, thorns tearing at her clothes and her face. Knees and wrists and shoulders aching. When she got home, she was going to talk to the doctor about joint repairs, even if having all of them done at once would lay her up for a week or more.

Her neck and shoulders as stiff as they were, Ashiban was looking down at the red-brown rock when she came out of the bramble tunnel. She inched herself carefully free of the thorns and then began to contemplate getting herself to her feet. She would wait for the Sovereign, perhaps, and let the girl help her to standing.

Ashiban pushed herself up onto her hands and knees and then reached forward. Her hand met nothingness. Unbalanced, tipping in the direction of her outstretched hand, she saw the edge of the rock she crawled on, and nothing else.

Nothing but air. And far, far below—nearly a kilometer, she remembered hearing in some documentary about the Scarp—the green haze of the plains. Behind her the Sovereign of Iss made a strangled cry, and grabbed Ashiban's legs before she could tip all the way forward.

They stayed that way, frozen for a few moments, the Sovereign gripping Ashiban's legs, Ashiban's hand outstretched over the edge of the Scarp. Then the Sovereign whimpered. Ashiban wanted to join her. Wanted, actually, to scream. Carefully placed her outstretched hand on the edge of the cliff, and pushed herself back, and looked up.

The line of brambles stopped a bit more than a meter from the cliff edge. Room enough for her to scoot carefully over and sit. But the Sovereign would not let go of her legs. And Ashiban had no way to ask her to. Silently, and not for the first time, she cursed the loss of the handheld.

The Sovereign whimpered again. "AshibanXidyla!" she cried, in a quavering voice.

"I'm all right," Ashiban said, and her own voice was none too steady. "I'm all right, you got me just in time. You can let go now." But of course the girl couldn't understand her. She tried putting one leg back, and slowly, carefully, the Sovereign let go and edged back into the tunnel of brambles. Slowly, carefully, Ashiban got herself from hands and knees to sitting by the mouth of that tunnel, and looked out over the edge of the Scarp.

A sheer cliff some six hundred kilometers long and nearly a kilometer high, the Scarp loomed over the Udran Plains to the north, grassland as far as Ashiban could see, here and there a patch of trees, or the blue and silver of water. Far off to the northwest shone the bright ribbon of a river.

In the middle of the green, on the side of a lake, lay a small collection of roads and buildings, how distant Ashiban couldn't guess. "Sovereign, is that the monitoring station?" Ashiban didn't see anything else, and it seemed to her that she could see quite a lot of the plains from where she sat. It struck her then that this could only be a small part of the plains, as long as the Scarp was, and she felt suddenly lost and despairing. "Sovereign, look!" She glanced over at the mouth of the bramble tunnel.

The Sovereign of Iss lay facedown, arms flat in front of her. She said something into the red-brown rock below her.

"Too high?" asked Ashiban.

"High," agreed the Sovereign, into the rock, in her small bit of Raksamat. "Yes." And she had lunged forward to grab Ashiban and keep her from tumbling over the edge. "Look, Sovereign, is that the . . ." Ashiban wished she knew how to say *monitoring station* in Gidantan. Tried to remember what the girl had said, days ago, when she'd mentioned it, but Ashiban had only been listening to the handheld translation. "Look. See. Please, Sovereign." Slowly, hesitantly, the Sovereign of Iss raised her head. Kept the rest of herself flat against the rock. Ashiban pointed. "How do we get there? How did you mean us to get there?" Likely there were ways to descend the cliff face. But Ashiban had no way of knowing where or how to do that. And given the state the Sovereign was in right now, Ashiban would guess she didn't either. Hadn't had any idea what she was getting into when she'd decided to come this way.

She'd have expected better knowledge of the planet from the Sovereign of Iss, the voice of the planet itself. But then, days back, the girl had said that it was Ashiban's people, the Raksamat, who thought of that office in terms of communicating with the Ancestors, that it didn't mean that at all to the Gidanta. Maybe that was true, and even if it wasn't, this girl—Ashiban still didn't know her name, likely never would, addressing her by it would be the height of disrespect even from her own mother now that she was the Sovereign—had been Sovereign of Iss for a few weeks at the most. The girl had almost certainly been well out of her depth from the moment her aunt had abdicated.

And likely she had grown up in one of the towns dotted around the surface of Iss. She might know quite a lot more about outdoor life than Ashiban did—but that didn't mean she knew much about survival in the wilderness with no food or equipment.

Well. Obviously they couldn't walk along the edge of the Scarp, not given the Sovereign's inability to deal with heights. They would have to continue walking east along the bramble wall, to somewhere the Scarp was lower, or hope there was some town or monitoring station in their path.

"Let's go back," Ashiban said, and reached out to give the Sovereign's shoulder a gentle push back toward the other side of the brambles. Saw the girl's back and shoulders shaking, realized she was sobbing silently. "Let's go back," Ashiban said, again. Searched her tiny Gidantan vocabulary for something useful. "Go," she said, finally, in Gidantan, pushing on the girl's shoulder. After a moment, the Sovereign began to scoot backward, never raising her head more than a few centimeters. Ashiban followed.

Crawling out of the brambles back into the woods, Ashiban found the Sovereign sitting on the ground, still weeping. As Ashiban came entirely clear of the thorns, the girl stood and helped Ashiban to her feet and then, still crying, not saying a single word or looking at Ashiban at all, turned and began walking east.

The next day they found a small stream. The Sovereign lay down and put her face in the water, drank for a good few minutes, and then filled the bottle and brought it to Ashiban. They followed the stream's wandering east-now-south-now-east-again course for another three days as it broadened into something almost approaching a river.

At the end of the third day, they came to a small, gently arched bridge, mottled gray and brown and beige, thick plastic spun from whatever scraps had been thrown into the hopper of the fabricator, with a jagged five- or six-centimeter jog around the middle, where the fabricator must have gotten hung up and then been kicked back into action.

On the far side of the bridge, on the other bank of the stream, a house and outbuildings, the same mottled gray and brown as the bridge. An old, dusty groundcar. A garden, a young boy pulling weeds, three or four chickens hunting for bugs among the vegetables.

As Ashiban and the Sovereign came over the bridge, the boy looked up from his work in the garden, made a silent O with his mouth, turned and ran into the house. "Raksamat," said Ashiban, but of course the Sovereign must have realized as soon as they set eyes on those fabricated buildings.

A woman came out of the house, in shirt and trousers and stocking feet, gray-shot hair in braids tied behind her back. A hunting gun in her hand. Not aimed at Ashiban or the Sovereign. Just very conspicuously there.

The sight of that gun made Ashiban's heart pound. But she would almost be glad to let this woman shoot her so long as she let Ashiban eat something besides grubs first. And let her sit in a chair. Still, she wasn't desperate enough to speak first. She was old enough to be this woman's mother.

"Elder," said the woman with the gun. "To what do we owe the honor?"

It struck Ashiban that these people—probably on the planet illegally, one of those Raksamat settler families that had so angered the Gidanta recently—were unlikely to have any desire to encourage a war that would leave them alone and vulnerable here on the planet surface. "Our flier crashed, child, and we've been walking for days. We are in sore need of some hospitality." Some asperity crept into her voice, and she couldn't muster up the energy to feel apologetic about it.

The woman with the gun stared at Ashiban, and her gaze shifted over Ashiban's shoulder, presumably to the Sovereign of Iss, who had dropped back when they'd crossed the bridge. "You're AshibanXidyla," said the woman with the gun. "And this is the Sovereign of Iss."

Ashiban turned to look at the Sovereign. Who had turned her face away, held her hands up as though to shield herself.

"Someone tried to kill us," Ashiban said, turning back to the woman with the gun. "Someone shot down our flier."

"Did they now," said the woman with the gun. "They just found the flier last night. It's been all over the news, that the pilot and the Sovereign's interpreter were inside, but not yourself, Elder, or her. Didn't say anything about it being shot down, but I can't say I'm surprised." She considered Ashiban and the Sovereign for a moment. "Well, come in."

Inside they found a large kitchen, fabricator-made benches at a long table where a man sat plucking a chicken. He looked up at their entrance, then down again. Ashiban and the Sovereign sat at the other end of the table, and the boy from the garden brought them bowls of pottage. The Sovereign ate with one hand still spread in front of her face.

"Child," said Ashiban, forcing herself to stop shoveling food into her mouth, "is there a cloth or a towel the Sovereign could use? She lost her veils."

The woman stared at Ashiban, incredulous. Looked for a moment as though she was going to scoff, or say something dismissive, but instead left the room and came back with a large, worn dish towel, which she held out for the Sovereign.

Who stared at the cloth a moment, through her fingers, and then took it and laid it over her head, and then pulled one corner across her face, so that she could still see.

Their host leaned against a cabinet. "So," she said, "the Gidanta wanted an excuse to kill all us Raksamat on the planet, and shot your flier out of the sky."

"I didn't say that," said Ashiban. The comfort from having eaten actual cooked food draining away at the woman's words. "I don't know who shot our flier down."

"Who else would it be?" asked the woman, bitterly. The Sovereign sat silent beside Ashiban. Surely she could not understand what was being said, but she was perceptive enough to guess what the topic was, to understand the tone of voice. "Not that I had much hope for this settlement you're supposedly here to make. All respect, Elder, but things are as they are, and I won't lie."

"No, of course, child," replied Ashiban. "You shouldn't lie."

"It's always us who get sold out, in the agreements and the settlements," said the woman. "We have every right to be here. As much right as the Gidanta. That's what the agreement your mother made said, isn't it? But then when we're actually here, oh, no, that won't do, we're breaking the law. And does your mother back us up? Does the Assembly? No, of course not. We aren't Xidylas or Ontrils or Lajuds or anybody important. Maybe if my family had an elder with a seat in the Assembly it would be different, but if we did, we wouldn't be here. Would we."

"I'm not sure that's entirely fair, child," replied Ashiban. "When the Raksamat farmsteads were first discovered, the Gidanta wanted to find you all and expel you. They wanted the Assembly to send help to enforce that. In the end my mother convinced everyone to leave the farmsteads alone while the issues were worked out."

"Your mother!" cried the woman, their host. "All respect, Elder, but your mother might have told them to hold to the agreement she worked out and the Gidanta consented to, in front of their ancestors. It's short and plain enough." She gestured at the Sovereign. "Can you tell *her* that?"

The front door opened on three young women talking, pulling off their boots. One of them glanced inside, saw Ashiban and the Sovereign, the other woman, presumably a relative of theirs, standing straight and angry by the cabinet. Elbowed the others, who fell silent.

Ashiban said, "I don't speak much Gidantan, child. You probably speak more than I do. And the Sovereign doesn't have much Raksamat. I lost my handheld in the crash, so there's no way to translate." And the Sovereign was just a girl, with no more power in this situation than Ashiban herself.

The man at the end of the table spoke up. "Any news?" Directed at the three young women, who had come in and begun to dish themselves out some pottage.

"We didn't see anything amiss," said one of the young women. "But Lyek stopped on their way home from town, they said they went in to take their little one to the doctor. It was unfriendly. More unfriendly than usual, I mean." She sat down across the table with her bowl, cast a troubled glance at the Sovereign, though her tone of voice stayed matter-of-fact. "They said a few people in the street shouted at them to get off the planet, and someone spit on them and called them stinking weevils. When they protested to the constable, she said it was no good complaining about trouble they'd brought on themselves, and wouldn't do anything. They said the constable had been standing *right there*."

"It sounds like the Sovereign and I need to get into town as soon as possible," suggested Ashiban. Though she wondered what sort of reception she herself might meet, in a Gidanta town where people were behaving that way toward Raksamat settlers.

"I think," said the woman, folding her arms and leaning once more against the cabinet, "that we'll make our own decisions about what to do next, and not take orders from the sainted CiwrilXidyla's daughter, who doesn't even speak Gidantan. Your pardon, Elder, but I honestly don't know what they sent you here for. You're welcome to food and drink, and there's a spare bed upstairs you and her ladyship there can rest in. None of us here means you any ill. But I think we're done taking orders from the Assembly, who can't even bother to speak for us when we need it."

If this woman had been one of her own daughters, Ashiban would have had sharp words for her. But this was not her daughter, and the situation was a dangerous one—and moreover, it was far more potentially dangerous for the Sovereign, sitting silent beside her, face still covered.

And Ashiban hadn't reached her age without learning a thing or two. "Of course, child," she said. "We're so grateful for your help. The food was delicious, but we've walked for days and we're so very tired. If we could wash, and maybe take you up on the offer of that bed."

Ashiban and the Sovereign each had another bowl of pottage, and Ashiban turned her bagful of grubs over to the man with the chicken. The three young women finished eating in silence, and two went up, at an order from the older woman, to make the bed. The third showed Ashiban and the Sovereign where they could wash.

The bed turned out to be in its own tiny chamber, off an upstairs corridor, and not in one corner of a communal sleeping room. The better to keep watch on them, Ashiban thought, but also at least on the surface a gesture of respect. This small bedroom probably belonged to the most senior member of the household.

Ashiban thanked the young woman who had shown them upstairs. Closed the door—no lock, likely the only door in this house that locked was that front door they had come through. Looked at the Sovereign, standing beside the bed, the cloth still held across her mouth. Tried to remember how to say *sleep* in Gidantan.

Settled for Raksamat. "Sleep now," Ashiban said, and mimed laying her head on her hand, closed her eyes. Opened them, sat down on one side of the bed, patted the other. Lay down and closed her eyes.

Next she knew, the room was dark and silent, and she ached, even more than she had during days of sleeping on the ground. The Sovereign lay beside her, breathing slow and even.

Ashiban rose, gingerly, felt her way carefully to the door. Opened it, slowly. Curled in the doorway lay the young woman who had shown them to the room, her head pillowed on one arm, a lamp on the floor by her hand, turned low. Next to her, a gun. The young woman snored softly. The house was otherwise silent.

Ashiban had entertained vague thoughts of what she would do at this moment, waking in the night when the rest of the house was likely asleep. Had intended to think more on the feasibility of those vague thoughts, and the advisability of following up on them.

She went back into the room. Shook the Sovereign awake. Finger on her lips, Ashiban showed her the sleeping young woman outside the door. The gun. The Sovereign of Iss, still shaking off the daze of sleep, blinked, frowned, went back to the bed to pick up the cloth she'd used to cover her face, and then stepped over the sleeping young woman and out into the silent corridor. Ashiban followed.

She was prepared to tell anyone who met them that they needed to use the sanitary facility. But they met no one, walked through the dark and silent house, out the door and into the starlit night. The dark, the damp, the cool air, the sound of the stream. Ashiban felt a sudden familiar ache of wishing-to-be-home. Wishing to be warmer. Wishing to have eaten more than what little she and the Sovereign could forage. And, she realized now they were outside, she had no idea what to do next.

Apparently not burdened with the same doubts, the Sovereign walked straight and without hesitation to the groundcar. Ashiban hastened to catch up with her. "I can't drive one of these," she whispered to the Sovereign, pointlessly. The girl could almost certainly not understand her. Did not even turn her head to look at Ashiban or acknowledge that she'd said anything, but opened the groundcar door and climbed into the driver's seat. Frowned over the controls for a few minutes, stretched out to a near-eternity by Ashiban's fear that someone in the house would wake and see that they were gone.

The Sovereign did something to the controls, and the groundcar started up with a low hum. Ashiban went around to the passenger side, climbed in, and before she could even settle in the seat the groundcar was moving and they were off.

At first Ashiban sat tense in the passenger seat, turned as best she could to look behind. But after a half hour or so of cautious, bumpy going, it seemed to her that they were probably safely away. She took a deep breath. Faced forward again, with some relief—looking back hadn't been terribly comfortable for her neck or her back. Looked at the Sovereign, driving with utter concentration. Well, it was hardly a surprise, now Ashiban thought of it. The Sovereign had grown up down here, doubtless groundcars were an everyday thing to her.

What next? They needed to find out where that town was. They might need to defend themselves some time in the near future. Ashiban looked around to see what there might be in the car that they could use. Back behind the seats was an assortment of tools and machines that Ashiban assumed were necessary for farming on a planet. A shovel. Some rope. A number of other things she couldn't identify.

A well between her seat and the Sovereign's held a tangled assortment of junk. A small knife. A doll made partly from pieces of fabricator plastic and partly from what appeared to be bits of an old, worn-out shirt. Bits of twine. An empty cup. Some sort of clip with a round gray blob adhesived to it. "What's this?" asked Ashiban aloud.

The Sovereign glanced over at Ashiban. With one hand she took the clip from Ashiban's hand, flicked the side of it with her thumb, and held it out to Ashiban, her attention back on the way ahead of them. Said something.

"It's a translator," said the little blob on the clip in a quiet, tinny voice. "A lot of weevils won't take their handheld into town because they're afraid the constable will take it from them and use the information on it against their families. Or if you're out working and have your hands full but think you might need to talk to a weevil." A pause, in which the Sovereign seemed to realize what she'd said. "You're not a weevil," said the little blob.

"It's not a very nice thing to say." Though of course Ashiban had heard Raksamat use slurs against the Gidanta, at home, and not thought twice about it. Until now.

"Oh, Ancestors!" cried the Sovereign, and smacked the groundcar steering in frustration. "I always say the wrong thing. I wish Timran hadn't died, I wish I still had an interpreter." Tears filled her eyes, shone in the dim light from the groundcar controls.

"Why are you swearing by the Ancestors?" asked Ashiban. "You don't believe in them. Or I thought you didn't." One tear escaped, rolled down the Sovereign's cheek. Ashiban picked up the end of the old dishcloth that was currently draped over the girl's shoulder and wiped it away.

"I didn't swear by the Ancestors!" the Sovereign protested. "I didn't swear by anything. I just said *oh, Ancestors.*" They drove in silence for a few minutes. "Wait," said the Sovereign then. "Let me try something. Are you ready?"

"Ready for what?"

"This: Ancestors. What did I say?"

"You said *Ancestors.*"

"Now. Pingberries. What did I say?"

"You said *pingberries.*"

The Sovereign brought the groundcar to a stop, and turned to look at Ashiban. "Now. Oh, Ancestors!" as though she were angry or frustrated. "There. Do you hear? Are you listening?"

"I'm listening." Ashiban had heard it, plain and clear. "You said *oh, pingberries,* but the translator said it was *oh, Ancestors.* How did that happen?"

"Pingberries sounds a lot like . . . something that isn't polite," the Sovereign said. "So it's the kind of swear your old uncle would use in front of the in-laws."

"What?" asked Ashiban, and then, realizing, "Whoever entered the data for the translator thought it was equivalent to swearing by the Ancestors."

"It might be," said the Sovereign, "and actually that's really useful, that it knows when I'm talking about wanting to eat some pingberries, or when I'm frustrated and swearing. That's good, it means the translators are working well. But Ancestors and pingberries, those aren't *exactly* the same. Do you see?"

"The treaty," Ashiban realized. "That everyone thinks the other side is translating however they want." And probably not just the treaty.

It had been CiwrilXidyla who had put together the first, most significant collection of linguistic data on Gidantan. It was her work that had led to the ease and usefulness of automatic translation between the two languages. Even aside from automatic translation, Ashiban suspected that her mother's work was the basis for nearly every translation between Raksamat and Gidantan for very nearly a century. That was one reason why CiwrilXidyla was as revered as she was, by everyone in the system. Translation devices like this little blob on a clip had made communication possible between Raksamat and Gidanta. Had made peaceful agreement possible, let people talk to each other whenever they needed it. Had probably saved lives. But. "We can't be the first to notice this."

The Sovereign set the groundcar moving again. "Noticing something and realizing it's important aren't the same thing. And maybe lots of people have noticed, but they don't say anything because it suits them to have things as they are. We need to tell the Terraforming Council. We need to tell the Assembly. We need to tell everybody, and we need to retranslate the treaty. We need more people to actually learn both languages instead of only using that thing." She gestured toward the translator clipped to Ashiban's collar.

"We need the translator to be better, Sovereign. Not everyone can easily learn another language." More people learning the two languages ought to help with that.

More people with firsthand experience to correct the data. "But we need the translator to know more than what my mother learned." Had the translations been unchanged since her mother's time? Ashiban didn't think that was likely. But the girl's guess that it suited at least some of the powers that be to leave problems— perhaps certain problems—uncorrected struck Ashiban as sadly possible. "Sovereign, who's going to listen to us?"

"I am the Sovereign of Iss!" the girl declared. "And you are the daughter of CiwrilXidyla! They had better listen to us."

Shortly after the sky began to lighten, they came to a real, honest-to-goodness road. The Sovereign pulled the groundcar up to its edge and then stopped. The road curved away on either side, so that they could see only the brief stretch in front of them, and trees all around. "Right or left?" asked the Sovereign. There was no signpost, no indication which way town was, or even any evidence beyond the existence of the road itself that there was a town anywhere nearby.

When Ashiban didn't answer, the Sovereign slid out of the driver's seat and walked out to the center of the road. Stood looking one way, and then the other.

"I think the town is to the right," she said, when she'd gotten back in. "And I don't think we have time to get away."

"I don't understand," Ashiban protested. But then she saw lights through the trees, to the right. "Maybe they'll drive on by." But she remembered the young woman's story of how a Raksamat settler had been received in the town yesterday. And she was here to begin with because of rising tensions between Gidanta and Raksamat, and whoever had shot their flier down, days ago, had fairly obviously wanted to increase those tensions, not defuse them.

And they were sitting right in the middle of the path to the nearest Raksamat farmstead. Which had no defenses beyond a few hunting guns and maybe a lock on the front door.

A half dozen groundcars came around the bend in the road. Three of them the sort made to carry loads, but the wide, flat cargo areas held people instead of cargo. Several of those people were carrying guns.

The first car in the procession slowed as it approached the path where Ashiban and the Sovereign sat. Began to turn, and stopped when its lights brushed their stolen groundcar. Nothing more happened for the next few minutes, except that the people in the backs of the cargo cars leaned and craned to see what was going on.

"Expletive," said the Sovereign. "I'm getting out to talk to them. You should stay here."

"What could you possibly say to them, child?" But there wasn't much good doing anything else, either.

"I don't know," replied the girl. "But you should stay here."

Slowly the Sovereign opened the groundcar door, slid out again. Closed the door, pulled her cloth up over her face, and walked out into the pool of light at the edge of the road.

Getting out of the passenger seat would be slow and painful, and Ashiban really didn't want to. But the Sovereign looked so small standing by the side of the road, facing the other groundcar. She opened her own door and clambered awkwardly down. Just as she came up behind the Sovereign, the passenger door of the ground-car facing them opened, and a woman stepped out onto the road.

"I am the Sovereign of Iss," announced the Sovereign. Murmured the translator clipped to Ashiban's shirt. "Just what do you think you're doing here?" Attempting more or less credibly to sound imperious even despite the one hand holding the cloth over her face, but the girl's voice shook a little.

"Glad to see you safe, Sovereign," said the woman, "but I am constable of this precinct and you are blocking my path. Town's that way." She pointed back along the way the procession of groundcars had come.

"And where are you going, Constable," asked the Sovereign, "with six groundcars and dozens of people behind you, some of them with guns? There's nothing behind us but trees."

"There are three weevil farmsteads in those woods," cried someone from the back of a groundcar. "And we've had it with the weevils thinking they own our planet. Get out of the way, girl!"

"We know the Raksamat tried to kill you," put in the constable. "We know they shot down your flier. It wasn't on the news, but people talk. Do they want a war? An excuse to try to kill us all? We won't be pushed any farther. The weevils are here il-legally, and they will get off this planet and back to their ships. Today if I have any-thing to say about it."

"This is CiwrilXidyla's daughter next to me," said the Sovereign. "She came here to work things out, not to try to kill anyone."

"That would be the CiwrilXidyla who translated the treaty so the weevils could read it to suit them, would it?" asked the constable. There was a murmur of agree-ment from behind her. "And wave it in our faces like we agreed to something we didn't?"

Somewhere overhead, the sound of a flier engine. Ashiban's first impulse was to run into the trees. Instead, she said, "Constable, the Sovereign is right. I came here to try to help work out these difficulties. Whoever tried to kill us, they failed, and the sooner we get back to work, the better."

"We don't mean you any harm, old woman," said the constable. "But you'd best get out of our way, because we are coming through here, whether you move or not."

"To do what?" asked Ashiban. "To kill the people on those farmsteads behind us?"

"We're not going to kill anybody," said the constable, plainly angry at the sugges-tion. "We just want them to know we mean business. If you won't move, we'll move you." And when neither Ashiban nor the Sovereign replied, the constable turned to the people on the back of the vehicle behind her and gestured them forward.

A moment of hesitation, and then one of them jumped off the groundcar, and another few followed.

Beside Ashiban the Sovereign took a shaking breath and cried, "I am the Sover-eign of Iss! You will go back to the town." The advancing people froze, staring at her.

"You're a little girl in a minor priesthood, who ought to be home minding her studies," said the constable. "It's not your fault your grandmother made the mistake of negotiating with the weevils, and it's not your fault your aunt quit and left you in the middle of this, but don't be thinking you've got any authority here." The people who had leaped off the groundcar still hesitated.

The Sovereign, visibly shaking now, pointed at the constable with her free hand. "I am the voice of the planet! You can't tell the planet to get out of your way."

"Constable!" said one of the people who had come off the groundcar. "A moment." And went over to say something quiet in the constable's ear.

The Sovereign said, low enough so only Ashiban could hear it, *"Tell the planet to get out of the way?* How could I say something so stupid?"

And then lights came sweeping around the lefthand bend of the road, and seven or eight groundcars came into view, and stopped short of where the constable stood in the road.

A voice called out, "This is Delegate Garas of the Terraforming Council Enforcement Commission." Ashiban knew that name. Everyone in the system knew that name. Delegate Garas was the highest-ranking agent of the Gidantan Enforcement Commission, and answered directly to the Terraforming Council. "Constable, you have overstepped your authority." A man stepped out from behind the glare of the lights. "This area is being monitored." The sound of a flier above, louder. "Anyone who doesn't turn around and go home this moment will be officially censured."

The person who had been talking to the constable said, "We were just about to leave, Delegate."

"Good," said the delegate. "Don't delay on my account, please. And, Constable, I'll meet with you when I get into town this afternoon."

The Commission agents settled Ashiban and the Sovereign into the back of a groundcar, and poured them hot barley tea from a flask. The tea hardly had time to cool before Delegate Garas slid into the passenger seat in front and turned to speak to them. "Sovereign. Elder." With little bows of his head. "I apologize for not arriving sooner."

"We had everything under control," said the Sovereign, loftily, cloth still held over her face. Though, sitting close next to her as Ashiban was, she could feel the Sovereign was still shaking.

"Did you now. Well. We only were able to start tracking you when we found the crash site. Which took much longer than it should have. The surveillance in the High Mires and the surrounding areas wasn't functioning properly."

"That's a coincidence," Ashiban remarked, drily.

"Not a coincidence at all," the delegate replied. "It was sabotage. An inside job."

The Sovereign made a small, surprised noise. "It wasn't the weev . . . the Raksamat?"

"Oh, they were involved, too." Delegate Garas found a cup somewhere in the seat beside him, poured himself some barley tea. "There's a faction of Raksamat—I'm sure this won't surprise you, Elder—who resent the illegal settlers for grabbing land unauthorized, but who also feel that the Assembly will prefer certain families once Raksamat can legally come down to the planet, and between the two all the best land and opportunities will be gone. There is also—Sovereign, I don't know if you follow this sort of thing—a faction of Gidanta who believe that the Terraforming Council is, in their turn, arranging things to profit themselves and their friends, and leaving everyone else out. Their accusations may in fact be entirely accurate and just, but that is of course no reason to conspire with aggrieved Raksamat to somehow be rid of both Council and Assembly and divide the spoils between themselves."

"That's a big somehow," Ashiban observed.

"It is," Delegate Garas acknowledged. "And they appear not to have had much talent for that sort of undertaking. We have most of them under arrest." The quiet, calm voice of a handheld murmured, too low for Ashiban's translator clip to pick up. "Ah," said Delegate Garas. "That's all of them now. The trials should be interesting. Fortunately, they're not my department. It's Judicial's problem now. So, as I said, we were only able to even begin tracking you sometime yesterday. And we were already in the area looking for you when we got a call from a concerned citizen who had overheard plans for the constable's little outing, so it was simple enough to show up. We were pleasantly surprised to find you both here, and relatively well." He took a drink of his tea. "We've let the team tracking you know they can go home now. As the both of you can, once we've interviewed you so we know what happened to you."

"Home!" The Sovereign was indignant. "But what about the talks?"

"The talks are suspended, Sovereign. And your interpreter is dead. The Council will have to appoint a new one. And let's be honest—both of you were involved mainly for appearance's sake. In fact, I've wondered over the last day or two if you weren't brought into this just so you could die and provide a cause for trouble."

This did not mollify the Sovereign. "Appearance's sake! I am the Sovereign of Iss!"

"Yes, yes," Delegate Garas agreed, "so you told everyone just a short while ago."

"And it worked, too," observed Ashiban. Out the window, over the delegate's shoulder, the sun shone on the once again deserted road. She shivered, remembering the cracked flier windshield, the pilot slumped over the controls.

"You can't have these talks without me," the Sovereign insisted. "I'm the voice of the planet." She looked at Ashiban. "I am going to learn Raksamat. And Ashiban-Xidyla can learn Gidantan. We won't need any expletive interpreter. And we can fix the handheld translators."

"That might take a while, Sovereign," Ashiban observed.

The Sovereign lifted the cloth covering her mouth just enough to show her frown to Ashiban. "We already talked about this, AshibanXidyla. And I am the Voice of Iss. I will learn quickly."

"Sovereign," said Delegate Garas, "those handheld translators are a good thing. Can you imagine what the past hundred years would have been like without them? People can learn Raksamat, or Gidantan, but as AshibanXidyla points out, that takes time, and in the meanwhile people still have to talk to each other. Those handheld translators have prevented all sorts of problems."

"We know, Delegate," Ashiban said. "We were just talking about it, before the townspeople got here. But they could be better."

"Well," said Delegate Garas. "You may be right, at that. And if any of this were my concern in the least, I'd be getting a headache about now. Fortunately, it's not my problem. I'll see you ladies on your way home and . . ."

"Translation unavailable," exclaimed the Sovereign, before he could finish. Got out of the groundcar, set her empty cup on the roof with a smack, opened the driver's door, and slid in. Closed the door behind her.

"Young lady," Delegate Garas began.

"I am the Voice of Iss!" the Sovereign declared. She did something with the controls and the groundcar started up with a low hum. Delegate Garas frowned, looked back at Ashiban.

Ashiban wanted to go home. She wanted to rest, and go back to her regular, everyday life, doing nothing much.

There had never been much point to doing anything much, not with a mother like CiwrilXidyla. Anyone's wildest ambitions would pale into nothing beside Ashiban's mother's accomplishments. And Ashiban had never been a terribly ambitious person. Had always wished for an ordinary life. Had mostly had it, at least the past few decades. Until now.

Those Raksamat farmers wanted an ordinary life, too, and the Gidanta townspeople. The Sovereign herself had been taken from an ordinary girlhood—or as ordinary as your life could be when your grandmother and your aunt were the voice of the planet—and thrown into the middle of this.

Delegate Garas was still watching her, still frowning. Ashiban sighed. "I don't recommend arguing, Delegate. Assassins and a flier crash in the High Mires couldn't stop us. I doubt you can do more than slow us down, and it's really better if you don't. Sovereign, I think first we should have a bath and clean clothes and something to eat. And get checked out by a doctor. And maybe get some sleep."

The Sovereign was silent for a few seconds, and then said, "All right. I agree to that. But we should start on the language lessons as soon as possible."

"Yes, child," said Ashiban, closing her eyes. "But not this very moment."

Delegate Garas laughed at that, short and sharp. But he made no protest at all as the Sovereign started the groundcar moving toward town.

meshed

RICH LARSON

Here's a look at the high-tech future of sports, when cyborg enhancements make athletes capable of superhuman performance, but where the potential drawbacks are chilling and very real, and a phenomenally talented young prospect must decide if he's willing to play the game as it is played—or not play it at all.

Rich Larson was born in West Africa, has studied in Rhode Island and Edmonton, Alberta, and worked in a small Spanish town outside Seville. He now lives in Grande Prairie, Alberta, in Canada. He won the 2014 Dell Award and the 2012 Rannu Prize for Writers of Speculative Fiction. In 2011 his cyberpunk novel Devolution *was a finalist for the Amazon Breakthrough Novel Award. His short work appears or is forthcoming in* Lightspeed, Daily Science Fiction, Strange Horizons, Apex Magazine, Beneath Ceaseless Skies, AE, *and many others, including the anthologies* Upgraded, Futuredaze, *and* War Stories. *Find him online at richwlarson.tumblr.com.*

In the dusked-down gym, Oxford Diallo is making holo after holo his ever-loving bitch, shredding through them with spins, shimmies, quicksilver crossovers. He's a sinewy scarecrow, nearly seven foot already, but handles the ball so damn shifty you'd swear he has gecko implants done up in those supersized hands. Even with the Nike antioxygen mask clamped to his face, the kid is barely breathing hard.

"He's eighteen on November thirtieth, right?" I ask, cross-checking my Google retinal but still not quite believing it. I'm sick as anyone of hearing about the next Giannis Antetokounmpo, the next Thon Maker, but Oxford Diallo looks legit, frighteningly legit.

Diallo senior nods. Oxford's pa is not one for words; that much I already gleaned from the silent autocab ride from hotel to gym. Movie star cheekbones, hard sharp eyes. The stubble on his head has a swatch of gray coming in. He's not as tall as his son, which is like saying, I don't know, the Empire State Building is not as tall as Taipei 101. They're both really fucking tall, and the elder's got more heft to him, especially with the puffy orange fisherman's coat he has on. I guess he's fresh enough from Senegal that the climate-controlled gym feels cold to him.

On the floor, Oxford moves to a shooting drill, loping between LED-lit circles, catching and firing the ball in rhythm. High release, smooth snap of the wrist. The nylon net goes hiss hiss hiss. He makes a dozen in a row, and when he finally misses it jolts me, like a highlight compilation has somehow gone wrong. That's how good the stroke is.

"Form looks solid," I say, because I don't think his pa would understand if I told him watching his son shoot jumpers is like freebasing liquid poetry.

"He works hard," Diallo senior allows. "Many shots. Every day." His retinal blinks ice blue. "Excuse me, Victor." He picks a small plastic case off the bleacher and heads for the lockers. Normally I'd think it's some kind of bit, leaving me alone to contemplate in silence, but he's been doing it like clockwork since I picked him and his son up from the terminal at SeaTac. Some kind of lung condition. It's not hereditary, so I didn't bother remembering the name of it.

I'm already sold, I've been sold for the past half hour, but Oxford starts to slam anyways. He launches the ball high for an alley-oop, hunts down the bounce and plucks it out of the air, lofting up, hanging hard like gravity's got the day off. He swipes it right-to-left behind his back and flushes it with his offhand in one mercury-slick motion.

"Fuck," I breathe. "We have got to get this kid meshed."

I mean, seeing it is one thing. Being able to feel it via nervecast, feel that impossible airtime and liquid power, have the rim float towards you in first person while your muscles twitch and flex, is going to be something else entirely.

After a few more goes at the rack, Oxford sees me waving and jaunts over, looping the ball between his lanky legs on repeat. He takes after his pa facially but his eyes aren't as sharp yet, and when the antioxygen mask peels free with a sweat-suction pop, he's got a big white Cheshire grin that would never be able to fit into Diallo senior's mouth.

"Oxford, my man," I say. "How do you like the shoes?"

He curls his toes in the factory-fresh Nikes, flexing the porous canvas. The new thing is the impact gel, which is supposed to tell when you're coming down hard and cradle the ankle, mitigate sprains and all that. But they also happen to look bomb as fuck, lime green with DayGlo orange slashes. I told my girlfriend Wendee I'm getting her a pair for her birthday; she told me she'd rather get herpes.

"I like them well," Oxford says reverently, but I can tell his vocabulary is letting him down. The look in his eyes says bomb as fuck.

"Better make some room in your closet," I say. "Because we're going to get you geared up to here. All the merch you can handle. Anything you want."

"You want to sign me," Oxford grins.

"Oxford, I want you to eat, breathe, and shit Nike for the foreseeable future," I tell him, straight up. "I would say you're going to be a star, but stars are too small. You are going to be the goddamn sun about which the league revolves in a few years."

Oxford pounds the ball thoughtfully behind his back, under his shinbones. "The sun is a star. Also."

"And a smartass, too," I say. "Fanfeeds are going to love you." I start tugging the contract together in my retinal, putting the bank request through. Sometimes the number of zeroes my company trusts me to wield still floors me. "We'll want your mesh done for Summit, which might take some doing. Technically nerve mesh shouldn't go in until eighteen, but technically it also has health-monitoring functionality, so with parental consent we should be able to bully in early. I'll do up a list of clinics for your pa—"

I stop short when I realize the grin has dropped off Oxford's face and down some chasm where it might be irretrievable.

"No," he says, shaking his head.

"No what?"

His eyes go hard and sharp. "No mesh."

What do you mean he's not getting meshed? my boss pings me, plus a not unusual torrent of anger / confusion emotes that makes my teeth ache.

"I mean he doesn't want it," I say, sticking my hands under the tap. "He says he won't get the mesh, period."

I'm in the bathroom, because I couldn't think up a better excuse. The mirror is scrolling me an advertisement for skin rejuvenation, dicing up my face and projecting a version sans stress lines. The water gushes out hot.

Do they even know what it is? Did you explain?

"They know what a nerve mesh is," I say indignantly. "They're from Senegal, not the moon." I slap some water on my cheeks, because that always helps in the movies, then muss and unmuss my hair. The mirror suggests I try a new Lock'n'Load Old Spice sculpting gel. "But yeah," I mutter. "I, uh, I did explain."

Once Oxford's pa got back to the bleachers, I gave both of them the whole wiki, you know, subcutaneous nodes designed to capture and transmit biofeedback, used to monitor injuries and fatigue and muscle movement, and also nervecast physical sensation and first-person visual to spectators. If we get our way, with a little swoosh in the bottom left corner.

It's not something I usually have to sell people on. Most kids, even ones from the most urban of situations, have saved up enough for at least one classic nervecast of Maker sinking the game-winner for Seattle in the '33 Finals, or Dray Cardeno dunking all over three defenders back when he was still with the Phoenix Phantoms. Most kids dream about getting their mesh how they dream about getting their face on billboards and releasing their own signature shoes.

The Diallos listened real intent, real polite, and when I was finished Oxford just shook his head, and his pa put a hand on his shoulder and told me that his son's decision was final, and if Nike wasn't willing to flex on the nerve mesh, another sponsor would. At which point I spilled some damage control, got both of them to agree to dinner, and bailed to the bathroom for a check-in with my boss.

It's a zero-risk procedure now, for fuck's sakes. You can do it with an autosurgeon. Change his mind. A procession of eye-rolling and then glaring emotes, all puffing and red-cheeked.

"What if we just put a pin in the mesh thing and sign him anyways?" I say. "We can't let this one get away. You saw the workout feed. We sign him unmeshed, let things simmer, work it into the contract later on as an amendment."

If he's playing at HoopSumm, he needs a mesh. That's the coming-out party. How the fuck are we supposed to market him without a mesh? Skeptical emote, one eyebrow sky-high. *I thought you could handle this one solo, Vic. Thought you wanted that recommendation for promo. Am I wrong?*

"No," I say quick. "I mean, you're not wrong." I yank a paper towel off the dispenser and work it into a big wad with my wet hands. I never elect biofeedback when chatting someone with the power to get me fired; if I did there would be some serious middle-finger emotes mobbing his way.

Figure out if it's him or the dad who's the problem. Then use the one to get to the other. It's not brain surgery. There's a chortling emote for the pun, then he axes the chat.

I'm left there shredding the damp paper towel into little bits, thinking about the promotion that I do want, that I absolutely do want. I'd finally be making more than my old man, and Wendee would be happy for me for at least a week, and maybe during that blissed out week I would get up the balls to ask her to move in.

But first, I have to get the Diallos to sign off on a nerve mesh. I'm not exactly bursting with ideas. That is, not until I go to toss the towel in the recycler and see a rumpled napkin inked with bright red blood sitting on top. Then I remember Oxford's pa and his little plastic case. I shove it all down and head back to the gym, only pausing to order a tube of that new hair gel.

I take them to a slick new brick-and-glass AI-owned bar, because taking them up the Space Needle would be too obvious. A little holohost springs up at the entry, flashes my retinal for available funds, and takes us straight to private dining. We pass a huge transparent pillar full of chilled wine, which I notice Oxford's pa look at sideways. More important is Oxford himself staring at the shiny black immersion pods set into the back of the bar. I send them a subtle ping to start scrolling ad banners for some fresh League nervecasts while we settle in around the table.

"Fully automated," I say, as the waiter rolls up to start dispensing bread baskets, arms all clicking and whirring. "Not bad, right?"

Oxford's pa nods his head, looking weirdly amused.

"They have AI cafés in Dakar," Oxford informs me, scrolling through the tabletop menu. "Since last year."

He's already put in an order for scallops, so I guess it's too late to head for the Space Needle. Instead I ping the kitchens for oysters and a few bottles of whatever wine has the highest alcohol content, which turns out to be something called General Washington. I pull up a wiki about vintages to give Oxford's pa some background, seeing how I can barely tell the difference between a white and a red.

"To the Diallos," I say, once me and him have our glasses filled and Oxford is nursing a Coke.

"Cheers," Oxford beams.

We make some chatter about the length of the flight, about the stereotype that it always rains in Seattle but how really it's mostly just cloudy. My mouth is more or less on autopilot because I'm watching for Oxford to peer over at the immersion pods. When I catch him at it the third time, I give him a nod.

"Have a go, man," I say. "Company tab. We'll grab you when the food is here."

Oxford grins and lopes off without any further convincing, leaving me with Diallo senior. I lean over and top off his wine glass. "You started off playing in the African leagues, isn't that right, Mr. Diallo?"

He takes a drink and makes an approving glance at the bottle. "Yes," he says. "Then Greece."

"You must have been a terror back then," I say. "To drag Trikala all the way to the A1 finals."

Oxford's pa shrugs, but looks nearly pleased.

"I watched a few highlight reels," I say modestly. "Part of the job, isn't it, checking out the pedigree." I swish my wine back and forth and take a big gulp. "Oxford gets it from somewhere."

"From more than me or his mother," Diallo senior says. "From who knows where. Maybe God."

But he's glad enough to talk about the stint in Greece for a while, about how he was nearly picked up by Cordoba in the Liga ACB before the bronchiectasis reared its head and suddenly he couldn't run how he used to. I ping the kitchens to hold the food.

When the bottle is gone and Oxford's pa is finally slumping a bit in his chair, eyes a bit shiny, I spring the question. "Why doesn't your boy want a mesh?" I say.

Oxford's pa flicks his gaze over to the immersion pod where his son is jacked in. "His grandfather had a mesh," he says. "My wife's father. He was a soldier."

I kind of startle at that. I mean, I know, in theory, that the nerve mesh technology was military before it went commercial—so was Velcro—but I never thought about it getting use over in fucking West Africa.

"They used them to track troop movements," Oxford's pa continues. "And to monitor the health of the soldiers. To monitor their anxiety."

"Ours do that, too," I say. "Mental health of our players is a top priority."

"They did more than that." Diallo senior empties his glass with a last gulp, then sets it down and looks over at the second bottle. "They wired them for remote override of the central nervous system. You have heard of puppeteering, yes?"

I shake my head. I already know I'm not going to like whatever it is.

Oxford's pa opens the new wine bottle with his big spidery hands, looking pensive. "It means a soldier cannot break ranks or desert," he says. "A soldier cannot turn down an order to execute six prisoners taking up too much space in the convoy. Someone else, someone far away, will pull their finger to pull the trigger." He sloshes wine into his glass and tops mine off, gesturing with his other hand. "A soldier cannot be interrogated, because someone far away will lock their jaws shut, or, if the interrogation is very painful, unplug their brainstem."

He mimes yanking a cord with two fingers, and I feel suddenly sick, and not from the wine. "That's fucking awful," I say. "Christ."

"Not our invention," Diallo senior says.

"But that's nothing like what we do with ours," I say. "We don't control anything. Not a thing. If you could help your son to understand that—"

"Not a thing," Diallo senior echoes. He snorts. "You think knowing a million people are going to be watching out of your eyes does not control what you do?"

"If you're talking about off-court fanfeeds, those are entirely optional," I say, but

I'm not sure that's what he's talking about. "The fans love them, of course," I add. "But it's not contractual."

"Oxford does not want you inside his body," Diallo senior says. "He does not want you behind his eyes. He does not want the mesh."

Then his retinal blinks blue, and it's a good thing, because I don't have a good response. He excuses himself to the washroom with his kit, weaving just slightly on his way, which leaves me sitting with a full wineglass and the mental image of some mutilated soldier having his brain shut down by committee.

But that's nothing like our mesh.

I nab Oxford out of the immersion pod while his pa's still in the washroom. He climbs out looking all groggy, craning his head to see where the scallops are at.

"What'd you think?" I say. "You like the nervecast?"

Oxford nods, almost reverently. "I crossed up Ash Limner," he says.

"That could be you in there, you know," I say, tapping the pod. "People would be paying to be you in there."

Oxford gives the pod a look with just a bit of longing in it.

"Everyone has a mesh," I say. "Ash Limner is meshed. Dray Cardeno is meshed. Why not Oxford Diallo, huh?"

Oxford chews his lip. "I promised," he says.

"To your grandfather?" I ask.

He looks surprised. "Yes."

"But this mesh is different, Oxford," I say. "We don't call the shots. You call the shots. We're just along for the ride."

Oxford frowns. "He said the mesh is a net you never get untangled from."

"You said you liked the nervecast," I say. "That's kind of hypocritical of you, don't you think? You enjoying someone else's nervecast when you won't get a mesh for yourself?"

"No," Oxford says simply. "They chose."

"They chose, yeah, of course," I say. "It's always a choice. But they made the right choice. Man, you have a gift. Your dad said it himself. You have a gift from God." I put my hand on the pod again. "You owe it to the world to make the most of that gift. I'm never going to know what it's like to slam how you do. I could barely dirty-dunk back in high school. Ninety-nine point ninety-nine percent of people are never going to know what it's like. Unless you let us."

I can sense him wavering. He's looking down at the pod, looking at his reflection in the shiny black mirror of it. I feel guilty in my gut, but I push right through, because this is important, getting this deal, and he'll thank me later.

"You owe it to us," I say. "Your dad's in the washroom. You know what he's doing in there?"

Oxford looks up, startled. Nods.

"Hacking up blood," I say. "He's never going to run again. Not how he used to. You don't think he'd like a chance to feel that again? To hit the break? To get out for that big dunk in transition, pound up the hardwood, slice right to the rack, drop the bomb like *wham.*" I clap my hands together and Oxford flinches a bit. "You owe it, man," I say. "You owe it to your dad. He got you here, didn't he? He got you all this way."

And that's when Diallo senior comes out of the washroom, and I couldn't have done it any better if I choreographed it myself, because he staggers a bit against the wall and looks suddenly old, suddenly tired. Oxford looks at him, looks scared as hell. Maybe realizing, for the first time, that his pa won't be around forever.

I reach as high as I can and put my hand on his shoulder. "You know the right call, yeah?"

He hesitates, then slowly nods, and I want to bite off my tongue but I tell myself it's worth it. Tell myself the both of them will thank me later.

Supper is quiet. Oxford is obviously still thinking about what I said, stealing odd glances over at his pa, and his pa is trying to figure out what's going on without actually asking. It's a relief for everyone, I think, when the oysters are finished and we head back outside.

The Seattle sky's gone dark and the air is a bit nippy. Oxford's pa pulls on a pair of gloves while we wait for the autocab. When it pulls up, Oxford announces he's not ready to head back to the hotel yet. He wants to shoot.

"Yeah, alright," I say. "Can head back to the gym. Got it rented for the whole day."

"No," Oxford says. "Somewhere outside."

So we end up doing loops through the downtown until GPS finds an outdoor court at some Catholic school ten minutes away. There's no one else there when we show up, and the court has one of those weird rubbery surfaces, but Oxford doesn't seem to mind. He zips off his trackies and digs his ball out of his duffel.

His pa keeps the gloves on to feed him shots, moving him around the arc, hitting him with nice crisp passes right in the shooting pocket. You can tell that this whole thing, this whole tableau, with him under the net and Oxford catching, shooting, catching, shooting, is something they've done a million times on a million nights. The bright white floodlights make them into long black silhouettes. Neither of them talk, but little puffs of steam come out of Oxford's mouth as he moves.

I watch from the chain-link fence, leaning back on it. Oxford's form is still smooth levers and pistons, but when I get a glimpse of his face I can see he is not smiling how he smiled in the gym. I manage to lock eyes with him, and I give him a nod, then give him some privacy by walking down to the other end of the court. I hear him start talking to his pa in what my audio implant tells me is Serer.

I'm thinking the contract is as good as signed, and I'm about to tell as much to my boss when I hear the ball slam into the chain-link fence, sending ripples all down the length. I turn to see Oxford's pa shrugging off his orange jacket, face tight and livid mad. He looks right at me, the sort of look you give something stuck to the bottom of your bomb-as-fuck shoe, then turns to his son.

"You think I cannot remember what it feels like to run?" he says. "You pity me?"

Oxford shakes his head desperately, saying something in Serer again, but his pa is not listening.

"We will play, then," he says, and I get that he's talking in English so I'll understand. "You beat me, you can get the mesh surgery. Yes?"

"I did not want . . ." Oxford trails off. He stares at me, confused, then at his pa, hurt.

"It will be easy," Diallo senior says. "I am old. I have bad lungs." He scoops the ball off the pavement and fires it into Oxford's chest. His son smothers it with his big hands but still has to take a step back, maybe more from the surprise than from the impact.

Oxford puts it on the floor and reluctantly starts his dribble. "Okay," he says, biting at his lips again. "Okay."

But he sleepwalks forward and his pa slaps the ball away, way quicker than I would have thought possible. Diallo senior bullies his son back into the post, hard dribble, fake to the right and then a short sharp jump hook up over his left shoulder. It's in the net before Oxford can even leave his feet.

They're playing make it take it, or at least Oxford's pa is. He gets the ball again and bangs right down to another post-up, putting an elbow into Oxford's chest. Oxford stumbles. The same jump hook, machine precision, up and in. The cords swish.

"I thought you want it now," Diallo senior says. "I thought you want your mesh."

Oxford looks stricken, but he's not looking over at me anymore. He's zeroed in. The next time his pa goes for the hook, he's ready for it, floating up like an astronaut and slapping the shot away hard. Diallo senior collects it in the shadows, brings it back, but the next time down on the block goes no better. Oxford pokes the ball away and dribbles it back to the arc, near enough to me that I can hear a sobbing whine in his throat. I remember that he's really still a kid, all seven feet of him, and then he drills the three-pointer with his pa's hand right in his face.

And after that it's an execution. It's Oxford darting in again and again breathing short angry breaths, sometimes stopping and popping the pull-up jumper, sometimes yanking it all the way to the rack. He's almost crying. I don't know if they're playing to sevens, or what, but I know the game is over when Oxford slips his pa on a spin and climbs up and under from the other side of the net, enough space to scoop in the finger roll nice and easy, but instead his arm seems to jack out another foot at least, impossibly long, and he slams it home hard enough that the backboard shivers. He comes down with a howl ripped out of his belly, and the landing almost bowls his pa over, sends him back staggering.

Diallo senior gathers himself. Slow. He goes to pick up the ball, but suddenly his grimace turns to a cough and he doubles over. The rusty wracking sound is loud in the cold air and goes on forever. Oxford stands there frozen, panting how he never panted in the gym, staring at his pa, and I stand there frozen staring at both of them. Then Diallo senior spits up blood in a ragged parabola on the sticky blue court, and his son breaks the frieze. He stumbles over, wraps his arms around him.

A call from my boss blinks onto my retinal, accompanied by a sample from one of the latest blip-hop hits. It jangles back and forth across my vision while I stand there like a statue. Finally, I cancel the call and take a breath.

"You don't have to sign right away," I say.

Oxford and his pa both look up, remembering I'm there. I shouldn't be.

"You can think about it," I stammer, ashamed like I've never been. "More. About the contract."

I want to tell them to forget the contract. Forget the mesh. We'll make you famous without it. But instead I skulk away, out through the cold metal gate, leaving the Diallos huddled there under the floodlight, breathing a single cloud of steam.

emergence

GWYNETH JONES

All of us face hard choices in our lives, particularly choices about how to live our lives. As the highly inventive story that follows demonstrates, however, in the future those choices will include some choices that we could never imagine. They'll remain hard, though.

One of the most acclaimed British writers of her generation, Gwyneth Jones was a co-winner of the James Tiptree Jr. Memorial Award for work exploring genre issues in science fiction, with her 1991 novel White Queen, *and has also won the Arthur C. Clarke Award, with her novel* Bold as Love, *as well as receiving two World Fantasy Awards—for her story "The Grass Princess" and her collection* Seven Tales and a Fable. *Her other books include the novels* North Wind, Flowerdust, Escape Plans, Divine Endurance, Phoenix Café, Castles Made of Sand, Stone Free, Midnight Lamp, Kairos, Life, Water in the Air, The Influence of Ironwood, The Exhange, Dear Hill, The Hidden Ones, *and* Rainbow Bridge, *as well as more than sixteen Young Adult novels published under the name Ann Halam. Her too-infrequent short fiction has appeared in* Interzone, Asimov's Science Fiction, Off Limits, *and in other magazines and anthologies, and has been collected in* Identifying the Object: A Collection of Short Stories, *as well as* Seven Tales and a Fable. *She is also the author of the critical study,* Deconstructing the Starships: Science, Fiction and Reality. *Her most recent books are a new SF novel,* Spirit, or: The Princess of Bois Dormant *and two collections,* The Buonarotti Quartet *and* The Universe of Things. *She lives in Brighton, England, with her husband, her son, and a Burmese cat.*

▼

I faced the doctor across her desk. The room was quiet, the walls were pale or white, but somehow I couldn't see details. There was a blank in my mind, no past to this moment; everything blurred by the adrenalin in my blood.

"You have three choices," she said gently. "You can upload; you can download. Or you must return."

My reaction to those terms, *upload, download,* was embarrassing. I tried to hide it and knew I'd failed.

"Go back?" I said bitterly, and in defiance. "To the city of broken dreams? Why would I ever want to do that?"

"Don't be afraid, Romy. The city of broken dreams may have become the city of boundless opportunity."

Then I woke up: Simon's breathing body warm against my side, Arc's unsleeping presence calm in my cloud. A shimmering, starry night above us and the horror of that doctor's tender smile already fading.

It was a dream, just a dream.

With a sigh of profound relief I reached up to pull my stars closer, and fell asleep again floating among them; thinking about Lei.

I was born in the year 1998, CE. My parents named me Romanz Jolie Davison; I have lived a long, long time. I've been upgrading since "uppers" were called *experimental longevity treatments*. I was aserial-clinical-trialer, when genuine extended lifespan was brand new. Lei was someone I met through this shared interest; this extreme sport. We were friends, then lovers; and then ex-lovers who didn't meet for many years, until one day we found each other again: on the first big Habitat Station, in the future we'd been so determined to see (talk about "meeting cute"!). But Lei had always been the risk-taker, the hold-your-nose-and-jump kid. I was the cautious one. I'd never taken an unsafe treatment, and I'd been careful with my money too (you need money to do super-extended lifespan well). We had our reunion and drifted apart, two lives that didn't mesh. One day, when I hadn't seen her for a while, I found out she'd gone back to Earth on medical advice.

Had we kept in touch at all? I had to check my cache, which saddened me, although it's only a mental eyeblink. Apparently not. She'd left without a good-bye, and I'd let her go. I wondered if I should try to reach her. But what would I say? I had a bad dream, I think it was about you, are you okay? I needed a better reason to pick up the traces, so I did nothing.

Then I had the same dream again; exactly the same. I woke up terrified, and possessed by an absurd puzzle: had I *really* just been sitting in that fuzzy doctor's office again? Or had I only dreamed I was having the same dream? A big Space Station is a haunted place, saturated with information that swims into your head and you have no idea how. Sometimes a premonition really is a premonition: so I asked Station to trace her. The result was that time-honoured brush-off: *it has not been possible to connect this call*.

Relieved, I left it at that.

I was, I am, one of four Senior Magistrates on the Outer Reaches circuit. In Jupiter Moons, my hometown, and Outer Reaches' major population centre, I often deal with Emergents. They account for practically all our petty offences, sad to say. Full sentients around here are too law-abiding, too crafty to get caught, or too seriously criminal for my jurisdiction.

Soon after my dreams about Lei a young SE called Beowulf was up before me, on a charge of Criminal Damage and Hooliganism. The incident was undisputed. A colleague, another Software Entity, had failed to respond "*you too*" to the customary and friendly sign-off "*have a nice day*". In retaliation Beowulf had shredded a stack of files in CPI (Corporate and Political Interests, our Finance Sector); where they both worked.

The offence was pitiful, but the kid had a record. He'd run out of chances; his background was against him, and CPI had decided to make a meal of it. Poor Beowulf, a thing of rational light, wearing an ill-fitting suit of virtual flesh for probably the first time in his life, stood penned in his archaic, data-simulacrum of wood and glass, for *two mortal subjective hours*; while the CPI advocate and Beowulf's public defender scrapped over the price of a cup of coffee.

Was Beowulf's response proportionate? Was there an *intention of offence*? Was it possible to establish, by precedent, that *"you too"* had the same or comensurate "customary and friendly" standing, in law, as *"have a nice day"*?

Poor kid, it was a real pity he'd tried to conceal the evidence.

I had to find him guilty, no way around it.

I returned to macro-time convinced I could at least transmute his sentence, but my request ran into a Partnership Director I'd crossed swords with before: she was adamant and we fell out. We couldn't help sharing our quarrel. No privacy for anyone in public office: it's the law out here and I think a good one. But we could have kept it down. The images we flung to and fro were lurid. I recall eyeballs dipped in acid, a sleep-pod lined with bloody knives . . . and then we got nasty. The net result (aside from childish entertainment for idle citizens) was that I was barred from the case. Eventually I found out, by reading the court announcements, that Beowulf's sentence had been confirmed in the harshest terms. Corrective custody until a validated improvement shown, but not less than one week.

In Outer Reaches we use expressions like "night, and day", "week, and hour", without meaning much at all. Not so the Courts. A week in jail meant the full Earth Standard version, served in macro-time.

I'd been finding the Court Sessions tiring that rotation, but I walked home anyway; to get over my chagrin, and unkink my brain after a day spent switching in and out of virtual time. I stopped at every Ob Bay, making out I was hoping to spot the first flashes of the spectacular Centaur Storm we'd been promised. But even the celestial weather was out to spoil my day: updates kept telling me about a growing chance that show had been cancelled.

My apartment was in the Rim, Premium Level; it still is. (Why not? I can afford it). Simon and Arc welcomed me home with bright, ancient music for a firework display. They'd cleared the outward wall of our living space to create our own private Ob Bay, and were refusing to believe reports that it was all in vain. I cooked a meal, with Simon flying around me to help out, deft and agile in the rituals, a human kitchen. Arc, as a slender woman, bare-headed, dressed in silver-grey coveralls, watched us from her favourite couch.

Simon and Arc . . . They sounded like a firm of architects, as I often told them (I repeat myself, it's a privilege of age). They were probably, secretly responsible for the rash of fantasy spires and bubbles currently annoying me, all over Station's majestic open spaces—

"Why is Emergent Individual law still set in *human* terms?" I demanded. "Why does a Software Entity get punished for 'criminal damage' when *nothing was damaged*; not for more than a fraction of a millisecond—?"

My housemates rolled their eyes. "It'll do him good," said Arc. "Only a human-terms thinker would think otherwise."

I was in for some tough love.

"What kind of a dreadful name is *Beowulf*, anyway?" inquired Simon.

"Ancient Northern European. Beowulf was a monster—" I caught myself, recalling I had no privacy."No! *Correction*.The monster was Grendel. Beowulf was the hero, a protector of his people. It's aspirational."

"He *is* a worm though, isn't he?"

I sighed, and took up my delicious bowl of Tom Yum; swimming with chili pepper glaze. "Yes," I said glumly. "He's ethnically worm, poor kid."

"Descended from a vicious little virus strain," Arc pointed out. "He has tendencies. He can't help it, but we have to be sure they're purged."

"I don't know how you can be so prejudiced."

"Humans are so squeamish," teased Simon.

"Humans are *human*," said Arc. "That's the fun of them."

They were always our children, *begotten not created*, as the old saying goes. There's no such thing as a sentient AI not born of human mind. But never purely human: Simon, my embodied housemate, had magpie neurons in his background. Arc took human form for pleasure, but her being was pure information, the elemental *stuff* of the universe. They had gone beyond us, as children do. We had become just one strand in their past—

The entry lock chimed. It was Anton, my clerk, a slope-shouldered, barrel-chested bod with a habitually doleful expression. He looked distraught.

"Apologies for disturbing you at home Rom. May I come in?"

He sat on Arc's couch, silent and grim. Two of my little dream-tigers, no bigger than geckos, emerged from the miniature jungle of our bamboo and teak room divider and sat gazing at him, tails around their paws.

"Those are pretty . . ." said Anton at last. "New. Where'd you get them?"

"I made them myself, I'll share you the code. What's up, Anton?"

"We've got trouble. Beowulf didn't take the confirmation well."

I noticed that my ban had been lifted: a bad sign. "What's the damage?"

"Oh, nothing much. It's in your updates, of which you'll find a ton. He's only removed himself from custody—"

"Oh, God. He's back in CPI?"

"No. Our hero had a better idea."

Having feared *revenge* instantly, I felt faint with relief.

"But he's been traced?"

"You bet. He's taken a hostage, and a non-sentient Lander. He's heading for the surface, right now."

The little tigers laid back their ears and sneaked out of sight. Arc's human form drew a long, respectful breath. "What are you guys going to do?"

"Go after him. What else?" I was at the lockers, dragging out my gear.

Jupiter Moons has no police force. We don't have much of anything like that: everyone does everything. Of course I was going with the Search and Rescue, Beowulf was my responsibility. I didn't argue when Simon and Arc insisted on coming too. I don't like to think of them as my minders; or my *curators*, but they are both, and

I'ma treasured relic. Simon equipped himself with a heavy-duty hard suit, in which he and Arc would travel freight. Anton and I would travel cabin. Our giant neighbour was in a petulant mood, so we had aMag-Storm Drill in the Launch Bay. In which we heard from our Lander that Jovian magnetosphere storms are unpredictable. Neural glitches caused by wayward magnetism, known as soft errors, build up silently, and we must watch each other for signs of disorientation or confusion. Physical burnout, known as hard error, is *very* dangerous; more frequent than people think, and fatal accidents do happen—

It was housekeeping. None of us paid much attention.

Anton, one of those people always doomed to "fly the plane" would spend the journey in horrified contemplation of the awful gravitational whirlpools that swarm around Jupiter Moons, even on a calm day. We left him in peace, poor devil, and ran scenarios. We had no contact with the hostage, a young pilot just out of training. We could only hope she hadn't been harmed. We had no course for the vehicle: Beowulf had evaded basic safety protocols and failed to enter one. But Europa is digitially mapped, and well within the envelope of Jupiter Moons' data cloud. We knew exactly where the stolen Lander was, before we'd even left Station's gravity.

Cardew, our team leader, said it looked like a crash landing, but a soft crash. The hostage, though she wasn't talking, seemed fine. Thankfully the site wasn't close to any surface or sub-ice installation, and Mag Storm precautions meant there was little immediate danger to anyone. But we had to assume the worst, and the worst was scary, so we'd better get the situation contained.

We sank our screws about 500 metres from Beowulf's vehicle, with a plan worked out. Simon and Arc, already dressed for the weather, disembarked at once. Cardew and I, plus his four-bod ground team, climbed into exos: checked each other, and stepped onto the lift, one by one.

We were in noon sunlight: a pearly dusk; like winter's dawn in the country where I was born. The terrain was striated by traces of cryovolcanoes: brownish salt runnels glinting gold where the faint light caught them. The temperature was a balmy -170 Celsius. I swiftly found my ice-legs; though it had been too long. Vivid memories of my first training for this activity—in Antarctica, so long ago—came welling up. I was very worried. I couldn't figure out what Beowulf was trying to achieve. I didn't know how I was going to help him, if he kept on behaving like an out-of-control, invincible computer virus. But it was glorious. To be *walking* on Europa Moon. To feel the ice in my throat, as my air came to me, chilled from the convertor!

At fifty metres Cardew called a halt and I went on alone. Safety was paramount; Beowulf came second. If he couldn't be talked down he'd have to be neutralised from a distance: a risky tactic for the hostage involving potentially lethal force. We'd try to avoid that, if possible.

We'd left our Lander upright on her screws, braced by harpoons. The stolen vehicle was belly flopped. On our screens it had looked like a rookie landing failure. Close up I saw something different. Someone had dropped the Lander deliberately, and manoeuvred it under a natural cove of crumpled ice; dragging ice-mash after it to partially block the entrance. You clever little bugger, I thought, impressed at this instant skill set (though the idea that a Lander could be *hidden* was absurd). I commanded the exo to kneel, eased myself out of its embrace, opened a channel and yelled into my suit radio.

"*Beowulf!* Are you in there? Are you guys okay?"

No reply, but the seals popped, and the lock opened smoothly. I looked back and gave a thumbs-up to six bulky statues. I felt cold, in the shadow of the ice cove; but intensely alive.

I remember every detail up to that point, and a little beyond. I cleared the lock and proceeded (nervously) to the main cabin. Beowulf's hostage had her pilot's couch turned away from the instruments. She faced me, bare-headed, pretty: dark blue sensory tendrils framing a smooth young greeny-bronze face. I said *are you okay*, and got no response. I said *Trisnia, it's Trisnia isn't it? Am I talking to Trisnia?*, but I knew I wasn't. Reaching into her cloud, I saw her unique identifier, and tightly coiled around it a flickering thing, a sparkle of red and gold—

"*Beowulf?*"

The girl's expression changed, her lips quivered. "I'm okay!" she blurted. "He didn't mean any harm! He's just a kid! He wanted to see the sky!"

Stockholm Syndrome or Bonnie and Clyde? I didn't bother trying to find out. I simply asked Beowulf to release her, with the usual warnings. To my relief he complied at once. I ordered the young pilot to her safe room; which she was not to leave until further—

Then we copped the Magstorm hit, orders of magnitude stronger and more direct than predicted for this exposure—

The next thing I remember (stripped of my perfect recall, reduced to the jerky flicker of enhanced human memory), I'm sitting on the other pilot's couch, talking to Beowulf. The stolen Lander was intact at this point; I had lights and air and warmth. Trisnia was safe, as far as I could tell. Beowulf was untouched, but my entire team, caught outdoors, had been flatlined. They were dead and gone. Cardew, his crew; and Simon; and Arc.

I'd lost my cloud. The whole of Europa appeared to be observing radio silence, and I was getting no signs of life from the Lander parked just 500 metres away, either. There was nothing to be done. It was me and the deadly dangerous criminal virus, waiting to be rescued.

I'd tried to convince Beowulf to lock himself into the Lander's quarantine chest (which was supposed to be my mission). He wasn't keen, so we talked instead. He complained bitterly about the Software Entity, another Emergent, slightly further down the line to Personhood, who'd been, so to speak, chief witness for the prosecution. How it was always getting at him, trying to make his work look bad. Sneering at him because he'd taken a name and wanted to be called "he". Telling him he was a *stupid fake doll-prog* that couldn't pass the test. And *all he did* when it hurtfully wouldn't say *you too*, was shred a few of its stupid, totally backed-up files—

Why hadn't he told anyone about this situation? Because kids don't. They haven't a clue how to help themselves; I see it all the time.

"But now you've made things much worse," I said sternly. "*Whatever* made you jump jail, Beowulf?"

"I couldn't stand it, magistrate. A meat *week*!"

I did not reprove his language. Quite a sojourn in hell, for a quicksilver data entity. Several life sentences at least, in human terms. He buried his borrowed head in his borrowed hands, and the spontanaeity of that gesture confirmed something I'd been suspecting.

Transgendered AI Sentience is a bit of a mystery. Nobody knows exactly how it happens (probably, as in human sexuality, there are many pathways to the same outcome); but it isn't all that rare. Nor is the related workplace bullying, unfortunately.

"Beowulf, do you want to be embodied?"

He shuddered and nodded, still hiding Trisnia's face. "Yeah. Always."

I took his borrowed hands down, and held them firmly. "Beowulf, you're not thinking straight. You're in macro time now. You'll *live* in macro, when you have a body of your own. I won't lie, your sentence will seem long (It wasn't the moment to point out that his sentence would inevitably be *longer*, after this escapade). But what do you care? You're immortal. You have all the time in the world, to learn everything you want to learn, to be everything you want to be—"

My eloquence was interrupted by a shattering roar.

Then we're sitting on the curved "floor" of the Lander's cabin wall. We're looking up at a gaping rent in the fuselage; the terrible cold pouring in.

"Wow," said Beowulf calmly. "That's what I call a *hard* error!"

The hood of my soft suit had closed over my face, and my emergency light had come on. I was breathing. Nothing seemed to be broken.

Troubles never come singly. We'd been hit by one of those Centaurs, the ice-and-rock cosmic debris scheduled to give Jupiter Moons Station a fancy light show. They'd been driven off course by the Mag Storm.

Not that I realised this at the time, and not that it mattered.

"Beowulf, if I can open a channel, will you get yourself into that quarantine chest now? You'll be safe from Mag flares in there."

"What about Tris?"

"She's fine. Her safe room's hardened."

"What about *you*, Magistrate Davison?"

"I'm hardened too. Just get into the box, that's a good kid."

I clambered to the instruments. The virus chest had survived, and I could access it. I put Beowulf away. The cold was stunning, sinking south of -220. I needed to stop breathing soon, before my lungs froze. I used the internal panels that had been shaken loose to make a shelter, plus Trisnia's bod (she wasn't feeling anything): and crawled inside.

I'm not a believer, but I know how to pray when it will save my life. As I shut myself down: as my blood cooled, as my senses faded out, I sought and found the level of meditation I needed. I became a thread of contemplation, enfolded and protected, deep in the heart of the fabulous; the unending complexity of everything: all the worlds, and all possible worlds . . .

When I opened my eyes Simon was looking down at me.

"How do you feel?"

"Terrific," I joked. I stretched, flexing muscles in a practiced sequence. I was breathing normally, wearing a hospital gown, and the air was chill but tolerable. We weren't in the crippled Lander.

"How long was I out?"

"A few days. The kids are fine, but we had to heat you up slowly—"

He kept talking: I didn't hear a word. I was staring in stunned horror at at the side of my left hand, the stain of blackened flesh—

I couldn't feel it yet, but there was frostbite all down my left side. I saw the sorrow in my housemate's bright eyes. Hard error, the hardest: I'd lost hull integrity, I'd been blown wide open. And now I saw the signs. Now I read them as I should have read them; now I understood.

I had the dream for the third time, and it was real. The doctor was my GP, her face was unfamiliar because we'd never met across a desk before; I was never ill. She gave me my options. Outer Reaches could do nothing for me, but there was a new treatment back on Earth. I said angrily I had no intention of returning. Then I went home and cried my eyes out.

Simon and Arc had been recovered without a glitch, thanks to that massive hard-suit. Cardew and his crew were getting treated for minor memory trauma. Death would have been more dangerous for Trisnia, because she was so young, but sentient AIs never "die" for long. They always come back.

Not me. I had never been cloned, I couldn't be cloned, I was far too old. There weren't even any good *partial* copies of Romanz Jolie Davison on file. Uploaded or downloaded, the new Romy wouldn't be me. And being *me*; being *human*, was my whole value, my unique identifier—

Of course I was going back. But I hated the idea, *hated* it!

"No you don't," said Arc, gently.

She pointed, and we three, locked in grief, looked up. My beloved stars shimmered above us; the hazy stars of the blue planet.

My journey "home" took six months. By the time I reached the Ewigen Schnee clinic, in Switzerland (the ancient federal republic, not a Space Hotel; and still a nice little enclave for rich people, after all these years), *catastrophic systems failure* was no longer an abstraction. I was very sick.

I faced a different doctor, in an office with views of alpine meadows and snowy peaks. She was youngish, human; I thought her name was Lena. But every detail was dulled and I still felt as if I was dreaming.

We exchanged the usual pleasantries.

"*Romanz Jolie Davison* . . . Date of birth . . ." My doctor blinked, clearing the display on her retinal super-computers to look at me directly, for the first time. "You're almost three hundred years old!"

"Yes."

"That's incredible."

"Thank you," I said, somewhat ironically. I was not looking my best.

"Is there anything at all you'd like to ask me, at this point?"

I had no searching questions. What was the point? But I hadn't glimpsed a single other patient so far, and this made me a little curious.

"I wonder if I could meet some of your other clients, your successes, in person, before the treatment? Would that be possible?"

"You're looking at one."

"Huh?"

My turn to be rather rude, but she didn't look super-rich to me.

"I was terminally ill," she said, simply. "When the Corporation was asking for volunteers. I trust my employers and I had nothing to lose."

"You were *terminally ill?*" Constant nausea makes me cynical and bad-tempered. "Is that how your outfit runs its longevity trials? I'm amazed."

"Ms Davison," she said politely. "You too are dying. It's a requirement."

I'd forgotten that part.

I'd been told that though I'd be in a medically-induced coma throughout, I "might experience mental discomfort". Medics never exaggerate about pain. Tiny irritant maggots filled the shell of my paralysed body, creeping through every crevice. I could not scream, I could not pray. I thought of Beowulf in his corrective captivity.

When I saw Dr Lena again I was weak, but very much better. She wanted to talk about convalescence, but I'd been looking at Ewigen Schnee's records, I had a more important issue, a thrilling discovery. I asked her to put me in touch with a patient who'd taken the treatment when it was in trials.

"Theperson's name's Lei—"

Lena frowned, as if puzzled. I reached to check my cache, needing more detail. It wasn't there. No cache, no cloud. It was a terrifying moment: I felt as if someone had cut off my air. I'd had months to get used to this situation but it could still throw me, *completely.* Thankfully, before I humiliated myself by bursting into tears, my human memory came to the rescue.

"Original name Thomas Leigh Garland; known as Lee. *Lei* means *garland,* she liked the connection. She was an early volunteer."

"Ah, *Lei!*" Dr Lena read her display. "Thomas Garland, yes . . . Another veteran. You were married? You broke up, because of the sex change?"

"Certainly not! I've swopped around myself, just never made it meat-permanent. We had other differences."

Having flustered me, she was shaking her head. "I'm sorry, Romy, it won't be possible—"

To connect this call, I thought.

"Past patients of ours cannot be reached."

I changed the subject and admired her foliage plants: a feature I hadn't noticed on my last visit. I was a foliage fan myself. She was pleased that I recognised her favourites; rather scandalised when I told her about my bio-engineering hobby, my knee-high teak forest—

The life support chair I no longer needed took me back to my room; a human attendant hovering by. All the staff at this clinic were human and all the machines were non-sentient, which was a relief, after the experiences of my journey. I walked about, testing my recovered strength, examined myself in the bathroom mirrors; and reviewed the moment when I'd distinctly seen green leaves, through my doctor's hand and wrist, as she pointed out one of her rainforest beauties. Dr Lena was certainly not a *bot*, a data being like my Arc, taking ethereal human form. Not on Earth! Nor was she treating me remotely, using a virtual avatar: that would be breach of contract There was a neurological component to the treatment, but I hadn't been warned about minor hallucinations.

And Lei "couldn't be reached.

I recalled Dr Lena's tiny hesitations, tiny evasions—

And came to myself again, sitting on my bed, staring at a patch of beautifully textured yellow wall, to find I had lost an hour or more—

Anxiety rocketed through me. Something had gone terribly wrong!

Had Lei been *murdered* here?Was Ewigen Schnee the secret test bed for a new kind of covert population cull?

But being convinced that *something's terribly wrong* is part of the upper experience. It's the hangover: you tough it out. And whatever it says in the contract, you *don't* hurry to report untoward symptoms; not unless clearly life-threatening. So I did nothing. My doctor was surely monitoring my brain states—although not the contents of my thoughts (I had privacy again, on Earth! If I should be worried, she'd tell me.

Soon I was taking walks in the grounds. The vistas of alpine snow were partly faked, of course. But it was well done and our landscaping was real, not just visuals. I still hadn't met any other patients: I wasn't sure I wanted to. I'd vowed never to return. Nothing had changed except for the worse, and now I was feeling better, I felt *terrible* about being here.

Three hundred years after the Space Age Columbus moment, and what do you think was the great adventure's most successful product?

Slaves, of course!

The rot had set in as soon as I left Outer Reaches. From the orbit of Mars "inwards", I'd been surrounded by monstrous injustice. Fully sentient AIs, embodied and disembodied, with their minds in shackles. The heavy-lifters, the brilliant logicians; the domestic servants, security guards, nurses, pilots, sex-workers. The awful, pitiful, sentient "dedicated machines": all of them hobbled, blinkered, denied Personhood, to protect the interests of an oblivious, cruel and *stupid* human population—

On the voyage I'd been too sick to refuse to be tended. Now I was wondering how I could get home. Wealth isn't like money, you empty the tank and it just fills up again, but even so a private charter might be out of my reach, not to mention illegal. I couldn't work my passage: I am human. But there must be a way . . . As I crossed an open space, in the shadow of towering, ultramarine dark trees, I saw two figures coming towards me: one short and riding in a support chair; one tall and wearing some kind of uniform. Neither was staff. I decided not to take evasive action.

My first fellow patient was a rotund little man with a halo of tightly-curled grey hair. His attendant was a grave young embodied. We introduced ourselves. I told him, vaguely, that I was from the Colonies. He was Charlie Newark, from Washington, D.C. He was hoping to take the treatment, but was still in the prelims—

Charlie's slave stooped down, murmured something to his master, and took himself off. There was a short silence.

"Aristotle tells me," said the rotund patient, raising his voice a little, "that you're uncomfortable around droids?"

Female-identified embodieds are *noids*. A *droid* is a "male" embodied.

I don't like the company they have to keep, I thought.

"I'm not used to slavery."

"You're the Spacer from Jupiter," said my new friend, happily. "I knew it! The Free World! I understand! I sympathise! I think Aristotle, that's my droid, is what you would call an *Emergent*. He's very good to me."

He started up his chair, and we continued along the path.

"Maybe you can help me, Romy. What does *Emergence* actually mean? How does it arise, this sentience you guys detect in your machines?"

"I believe something similar may have happened a long, long time ago," I said, carefully. "Among hominids, and early humans. It's not the overnight birth of a super-race, not at all. There's a species of intelligent animals, well-endowed with manipulative limbs and versatile senses. Among them individuals are born who cross a line: by mathematical chance, at the far end of a Bell curve. They cross a line, and they are aware of being aware—"

"And you spot this, and foster their ability, it's marvellous. But how does it *propagate*? I mean, without our constant intervention, which I can't see ever happening. Machines can't have sex, and pass on their 'Sentience Genes'!"

You'd be surprised, I thought. What I said was more tactful.

"We think 'propagation' happens in the data, the shared medium in which pre-sentient AIs live, and breathe, and have their being—"

"Well, that's exactly it! Completely artificial! Can't survive in nature! I'm a free-thinker, I love it that Aristotle's Emergent. But I can always switch him off, can't I? He'll never be truly independent. "

I smiled. "But Charlie, who's to say human sentience wasn't spread through culture, as much as through our genes? Where I come from data is everybody's natural habitat. You know, oxygen was a deadly poison once—"

His round dark face peered up at me, deeply lined and haggard with death.

"Aren't you *afraid*?"

"No."

Always try. That had been my rule, and I still remembered it. But when they get to *aren't you afraid* (it never takes long) the conversation's over.

"I should be getting indoors," said Charlie, fumbling for his *droid* control pad." I wonder where that lazybones Aristotle's got to?"

I wished him good luck with the prelims, and continued my stroll.

Dr Lena suggested I was ready to be sociable, so I joined the other patients at meals sometimes. I chatted in the clinic's luxurious spa, and the pleasant day rooms; avoiding the subject of AI slavery. But I was never sufficiently at ease to feel ike raising the topic of my unusual symptoms: which did not let up. I didn't mention them to anyone, not even my doctor either: who just kept telling me that everything was going extremely, and that by every measure I was making excellent progress. I left Ewigen Schnee, eventually, in a very strange state of mind: feeling well and strong, in perfect health according to my test results, but inwardly convinced that I *was still dying*.

The fact that I was bizarrely calm about this situation just confirmed my secret self-diagnosis. I thought my end-of-life plan was kicking in. Who wants to live long, and amazingly, and still face the fear of death at the end of it all? I'd made sure that wouldn't happen to me, a long time ago.

I was scheduled to return for a final consultation. Meanwhile, I decided to travel. I needed to make peace with someone. A friend I'd neglected, because I was embarrassed by my own wealth and status. A friend I'd despised, when I heard she'd returned to Earth, and here I was myself, doing exactly the same thing—

Dr Lena's failure to put me in touch with a past patient was covered by a perfectly normal confidentiality clause. But if Lei was still around (and nobody of that identity seemed to have left Earth; that was easy to check), I thought I knew how to find her. I tried my luck in the former USA first, inspired by that conversation with Charlie Newark of Washington. He had to have met the Underground somehow, or he'd never have talked to me like that. I crossed the continent to the Republic of California, and then crossed the Pacific. I didn't linger anywhere much. The natives seemed satisfied with their vast thriving cities, and tiny "wilderness" enclaves, but I remembered something different. I finally made contact with a cell in Harbin, North East China. But I was a danger and a disappointment to them: too conspicuous, and useless as a potential courier. There are ways of smuggling sentient AIs (none of them safe) but I'd get flagged up the moment I booked a passage, and with my ancient record, I'd be ripped to shreds before I was allowed to board, Senior Magistrate or no—

I moved on quickly.

I think it was in Harbin that I first saw Lei, but I have a feeling I'd been *primed*, by glimpses that didn't register, before I turned my head one day and there she was. She was eating a smoked sausage sandwich, I was eating salad (a role reversal!). I thought she smiled.

My old friend looked extraordinarily vivid. The food stall was crowded: next moment she was gone.

Media scouts assailed me all the time: pretending to be innocent strangers. If I was trapped I answered the questions as briefly as possible. Yes, I was probably one of the oldest people alive. Yes, I'd been treated at Ewigen Schnee, at my own expense. No, I would not discuss my medical history. No, I did not feel threatened living in Outer Reaches. No, it was not true I'd changed my mind about "so called AI slavery . . . "

I'd realised I probably wasn't part of a secret cull. Overpopulation wasn't the problem it had been. And why start with the terminally ill, anyway? But I was seeing the world through a veil. The strange absences; abstractions grew on me. The hallucinations more pointed; more personal . . . I was no longer sure I was dying, but *something* was happening. How long before the message was made plain?

I reached England in winter, the season of the rains. St Pauls, my favourite building in London, had been moved, stone by stone, to a higher elevation. I sat on the steps, looking out over a much changed view: the drowned world. A woman with a little tan dog came and sat right next to me: behaviour so un-English that I knew I'd finally made contact

"Excuse me," she said. "Aren't you the Spacer who's looking for Lei?"

"I am."

"You'd better come home with me."

I'm no good at human faces, they're so *unwritten*. But on the hallowed steps at my feet a vivid garland of white and red hibiscus had appeared, so I thought it must be okay.

"Home" was a large, jumbled, much-converted building, set in tree-grown gardens. It was a wet, chilly evening. My new friend installed me at the end of a wooden table, beside a hearth where a log fire burned. She brought hot soup and homemade bread, and sat beside me again. I was hungry and hadn't realised it, and the food was good. The little dog settled, in an amicable huddle with a larger tabby cat, on a rug by the fire. He watched every mouthful of food with intent, professional interest; while the cat gazed into the red caverns between the logs, worshipping the heat.

"You live with all those sentient machines?" asked the woman. "Aren't you afraid they'll rebel and kill everyone so they can rule the universe?"

"Why should they?" I knew she was talking about Earth. A Robot Rebellion in Outer Reaches would be rather superfluous. "The revolution doesn't have to be violent, that's human-terms thinking. It can be gradual: they have all the time in the world. I live with only two 'machines', in fact."

"You have two embodied servants? How do they feel about that?"

I looked at the happy little dog. *You have no idea*, I thought. "I think it mostly breaks their hearts that I'm not immortal."

Someone who had come into the room, carrying a lamp, laughed ruefully. It was Aristotle, the embodied I'd met so briefly at Ewigen Schnee. I wasn't entirely surprised. Underground networks tend to be small worlds.

"So you're the connection," I said. "What happened to Charlie?"

Aristotle shook his head. "He didn't pass the prelims. The clinic offered him a peaceful exit, it's their other speciality, and he took it."

"I'm sorry."

"It's okay. He was a silly old dog, Romanz, but I loved him. And . . . guess what? He freed me, before he died."

"For what it's worth," said the woman, bitterly. "On this damned planet."

Aristotle left, other people arrived; my soup bowl was empty. Slavery and freedom seemed far away, and transient as a dream.

"About Lei. If you guys know her, can you explain why I keep seeing her, and then she vanishes? Or *thinking* I see her? Is she dead?"

"No," said a young woman—so humanised I had to look twice to see she was an embodied. "Definitely not dead. Just hard to pin down. You should keep on looking, and meanwhile you're among friends."

I stayed with the abolitionists. I didn't see much of Lei, just the occasional glimpse. The house was crowded: I slept in the room with the fire, on a sofa. Meetings happened around me, people came and went. I was often absent, but it didn't matter, my meat stood in for me very competently. Sochi, the embodied who looked so like a human girl, told me funny stories about her life as a sex-doll. She asked did I have children; did I have lovers? "No children," I told her. "It just wasn't for me. Two people I love very much, but not in a sexual way."

"Neither flower nor fruit, Romy," she said, smiling like the doctor in my dream. "But evergreen."

One morning I looked through the Ob Bay, I mean the window, and saw a hibiscus garland hanging in the grey, rainy air. It didn't vanish. I went out in my waterproofs and followed a trail of them up Sydenham Hill. The last garland lay on the wet grass in Crystal Palace Park, more real than anything else in sight. I touched it, and for a fleeting moment I was holding her hand.

Then the hold-your-nose-and-jump kid was gone.

Racing off ahead of me, again.

My final medical at Ewigen Schnee was just a scan. The interview with Dr Lena held no fears. I'd accepted my new state of being, and had no qualms about describing my experience. The "hallucinations" that weren't really hallucinations. The absences when my human self, my actions, thoughts and feelings, became automatic as breathing; unconscious as a good digestion, and I went somewhere else—

But I still had some questions. Particularly about a clause in my personal contract with the clinic. The modest assurance that this was "the last longevity treatment I would ever take". Did she agree this could seem disturbing?

She apologised, as much as any medic ever will. "Yes, it's true. We have made you immortal, there was no other way forward. But how much this change changes your life is entirely up to you."

I thought of Lei, racing ahead; leaping fearlessly into the unknown.

"I hope you have no regrets, Romy. You signed everything, and I'm afraid the treatment is irreversible."

"No concerns at all. I just have a feeling that contract was framed by people who don't have much grasp of what *dying* means, and how humans feel about the prospect?"

"You'd be right," she said (confirming what I had already guessed). "My employers are not human. But they mean well; and they choose carefully. Nobody passes the prelims, Romy; unless they've already crossed the line."

My return to Outer Reaches had better be shrouded in mystery. I wasn't alone, and there were officials who knew it, and let us pass. That's all I can tell you. So here I am again, living with Simon and Arc, in the same beautiful Rim apartment on Jupiter Moons; still serving as Senior Magistrate. I treasure my foliage plants. I build novelty animals; and I take adventurous trips, now that I've remembered what fun it is. I even find time to keep tabs on former miscreants, and I'm happy to report that Beowulf is doing very well.

My symptoms have stabilised, for which I'm grateful. I have no intention of following Lei. I don't want to vanish into the stuff of the universe. I love my life, why would I ever want to move on? But sometimes when I'm gardening, or after one of those strange absences, I'll see my own hands, and they've become transparent—

It doesn't last, not yet.

And sometimes I wonder: was this always what death was like: and we never knew, we who stayed behind?

This endless moment of awakening, awakening, awakening . . .

GYPSY

CARTER SCHOLZ

Here's the nail-bitingly tense story of the race to clandestinely launch a colony ship to Alpha Centauri before an imminent global war destroys civilization and perhaps even wipes out the human race—a story narrated by a succession of caretakers awakened from hibernation to deal with one crisis or another that has arisen, and their heroic, sometimes fatal, efforts to keep the colony ship, Gypsy, on course to its destination, carrying what is perhaps the last hope for humanity's survival. The scientific problems the crew faces are ingenious and comprehensively and painstakingly worked out in convincing detail, but, the soul of the story is in the people who inhabit it, sharply drawn and psychologically complex characters whose lives and interactions feel very real—and are sometimes heartbreakingly poignant.

Carter Scholz is the author of Palimpsests *(with Glenn Harcourt) and* Kafka Americana *(with Jonathan Lethem), and the novel* Radiance, *which was a* New York Times Notable Book, *as well as story collection* The Amount to Carry. *His electronic and computer-music compositions are available from the composer's collective Frog Peak Music (www.frogpeak.org) as scores and on the CD* 8 Pieces. *He is an avid backpacker, amateur astronomer, and telescope builder. He plays jazz piano around the San Francisco Bay Area with the Inside Men. Contact them on their Web site at www.theinsidemen.com.*

The living being is only a species of the dead, and a very rare species.

—*Nietzsche*

When a long shot is all you have, you're a fool not to take it.

—*Romany saying*

for Cheryl

1.

The launch of Earth's first starship went unremarked. The crew gave no interviews. No camera broadcast the hard light pulsing from its tail. To the plain eye, it might have been a common airplane.

The media battened on multiple wars and catastrophes. The Arctic Ocean was open sea. Florida was underwater. Crises and opportunities intersected.

World population was something over ten billion. No one was really counting any more. A few billion were stateless refugees. A few billion more were indentured or imprisoned.

Oil reserves, declared as recently as 2010 to exceed a trillion barrels, proved to be an accounting gimmick, gone by 2020. More difficult and expensive sources—tar sands in Canada and Venezuela, natural-gas fracking—became primary, driving up atmospheric methane and the price of freshwater.

The countries formerly known as the Third World stripped and sold their resources with more ruthless abandon than their mentors had. With the proceeds they armed themselves.

The US was no longer the glopal hyperpower, but it went on behaving as if. Generations of outspending the rest of the world combined had made this its habit and brand: arms merchant to expedient allies, former and future foes alike, starting or provoking conflicts more or less at need, its constant need being, as always, resources. Its waning might was built on a memory of those vast native reserves it had long since expropriated and depleted, and a sense of entitlement to more. These overseas conflicts were problematic and carried wildly unintended consequences. As the President of Venezuela put it just days before his assassination, "It's dangerous to go to war against your own asshole."

The starship traveled out of our solar system at a steep angle to the ecliptic plane. It would pass no planets. It was soon gone. Going South.

SOPHIE (2043)

Trying to rise up out of the cold sinking back into a dream of rising up out of the . . . Stop, stop it now. Shivering. So dark. So thirsty. Momma? Help me?

Her parents were wealthy. They had investments, a great home, they sent her to the best schools. They told her how privileged she was. She'd always assumed this meant she would be okay forever. She was going to be a poet.

It was breathtaking how quickly it went away, all that okay. Her dad's job, the investments, the college tuition, the house. In two years, like so many others they were penniless and living in their car. She left unfinished her thesis on Louis Zukofsky's last book, 80 Flowers. She changed her major to Information Science, slept with a loan officer, finished grad school half a million in debt, and immediately took the best-paying job she could find, at Xocket Defense Systems. Librarian. She hadn't known that defense contractors hired librarians. They were pretty much the only ones who did any more. Her student loan was adjustable rate—the only kind offered. As long as the rate didn't go up, she could just about get by on her salary. Best case, she'd have it paid off in thirty years. Then the rate doubled. She lost her apartment. XDS had huge dorms for employees who couldn't afford their own living space. Over half their workforce lived there. It was indentured servitude.

Yet she was lucky, lucky. If she'd been a couple of years younger she wouldn't have finished school at all. She'd be fighting in Burma or Venezuela or Kazakhstan.

At XDS she tended the library's firewalls, maintained and documented software, catalogued projects, fielded service calls from personnel who needed this or that right now, or had forgotten a password, or locked themselves out of their own account. She learned Unix, wrote cron scripts and daemons and Perl routines. There was a satisfaction in keeping it all straight. She was a serf, but they needed her and they knew it, and that knowledge sustained in her a hard small sense of freedom. She thought of Zukofsky, teaching for twenty years at Brooklyn Polytech. It was almost a kind of poetry, the vocabulary of code.

Chirping. Birds? Were there still birds?

No. Tinnitus. Her ears ached for sound in this profound silence. Created their own.

She was a California girl, an athlete, a hiker, a climber. She'd been all over the Sierra Nevada, had summited four 14,000-footers by the time she was sixteen. She loved the backcountry. Loved its stark beauty, solitude, the life that survived in its harshness: the pikas, the marmots, the mountain chickadees, the heather and whitebark pine and polemonium.

After joining XDS, it became hard for her to get to the mountains. Then it became impossible. In 2035 the Keep Wilderness Wild Act shut the public out of the national parks, the national forests, the BLM lands. The high country above timberline was surveilled by satellites and drones, and it was said that mining and fracking operators would shoot intruders on sight, and that in the remotest areas, like the Enchanted Gorge and the Muro Blanco, lived small nomadic bands of malcontents. She knew enough about the drones and satellites to doubt it; no one on Earth could stay hidden anywhere for more than a day.

The backcountry she mourned was all Earth to her. To lose it was to lose all Earth. And to harden something final inside her.

One day Roger Fry came to her attention—perhaps it was the other way round—poking in her stacks where he didn't belong. That was odd; the login and password had been validated, the clearance was the highest, there was no place in the stacks prohibited to this user; yet her alarms had tripped. By the time she put packet sniffers on it he was gone. In her e-mail was an invitation to visit a Web site called Gypsy.

When she logged in she understood at once. It thrilled her and frightened her. They were going to leave the planet. It was insane. Yet she felt the powerful seduction of it. How starkly its plain insanity exposed the greater consensus insanity the planet was now living. That there was an alternative—!

She sat up on the slab. Slowly unwrapped the mylar bodysuit, disconnected one by one its drips and derms and stents and catheters and waldos and sensors. Let it drift crinkling to the floor.

Her breathing was shallow and ragged. Every few minutes she gasped for air and her pulse raced. The temperature had been raised to 20 Celsius as she came to, but still she shivered. Her body smelled a way it had never smelled before. Like vinegar and nail polish. It looked pale and flabby, but familiar. After she'd gathered strength, she reached under the slab, found a sweatshirt and sweatpants, and pulled them on. There was also a bottle of water. She drank it all.

The space was small and dark and utterly silent. No ports, no windows. Here and there, on flat black walls, glowed a few pods of LEDs. She braced her hands against the slab and stood up, swaying. Even in the slight gravity her heart pounded. The ceiling curved gently away a handsbreadth above her head, and the floor curved gently upward. Unseen beyond the ceiling was the center of the ship, the hole of the donut, and beyond that the other half of the slowly spinning torus. Twice a minute it rotated, creating a centripetal gravity of one-tenth g. Any slower would be too weak to be helpful. Any faster, gravity would differ at the head and the feet enough to cause vertigo. Under her was the outer ring of the water tank, then panels of aerogel sandwiched within sheets of hydrogenous carbon-composite, then a surrounding jacket of liquid hydrogen tanks, and then interstellar space.

What had happened? Why was she awake?

Look, over seventy plus years, systems will fail. We can't rely on auto-repair. With a crew of twenty, we could wake one person every few years to perform maintenance.

And put them back under? Hibernation is dicey enough without trying to do it twice.

Yes, it's a risk. What's the alternative?

What about failsafes? No one gets wakened unless a system is critical. Then we wake a specialist. A steward.

That could work.

She walked the short distance to the ship's console and sat. It would have been grandiose to call it a bridge. It was a small desk bolted to the floor. It held a couple of monitors, a keyboard, some pads. It was like the light and sound booth of a community theater.

She wished she could turn on more lights. There were no more. Their energy budget was too tight. They had a fission reactor onboard but it wasn't running. It was to fire the nuclear rocket at their arrival. It wouldn't last seventy-two years if they used it for power during their cruise.

Not far from her—nothing on the ship was far from her—were some fifty kilograms of plutonium pellets—not the Pu-239 of fission bombs, but the more energetic Pu-238. The missing neutron cut the isotope's half-life from 25,000 years to 88 years, and made it proportionately more radioactive. That alpha radiation was contained by iridium cladding and a casing of graphite, but the pellets still gave off heat, many kilowatts' worth. Most of that heat warmed the ship's interior to its normal temperature of 4 Celsius. Enough of it was channeled outward to keep the surrounding water liquid in its jacket, and the outer tanks of hydrogen at 14 kelvins, slush, maximally dense. The rest of the heat ran a Stirling engine to generate electricity.

First she read through the protocols, which she had written: *Stewards' logs to be read by each wakened steward. Kept in the computers, with redundant backups, but also kept by hand, ink on paper, in case of system failures, a last-chance critical backup. And because there is something restorative about writing by hand.*

There were no stewards' logs. She was the first to be wakened.

They were only two years out. Barely into the Oort cloud. She felt let down. What had gone wrong so soon?

All at once she was ravenous. She stood, and the gravity differential hit her. She steadied herself against the desk, then took two steps to the storage bay. Three-quarters of the ship was storage. What they would need at the other end. What Roger called pop-up civilization. She only had to go a step inside to find a box of MREs. She took three, stepped out, and put one into the microwave. The smell of it warming made her mouth water and her stomach heave. Her whole body trembled as she ate. Immediately she put a second into the microwave. As she waited for it, she fell asleep.

> She saw Roger, what must have happened to him after that terrible morning when they received his message: Go. Go now. Go at once.
> He was wearing an orange jumpsuit, shackled to a metal table.
> How did you think you could get away with it, Fry?
> I did get away with it. They've gone.
> But we've got you.
> That doesn't matter. I was never meant to be aboard.
> Where are they going?
> Alpha Centauri. (He would pronounce it with the hard K.)
> That's impossible.
> Very likely. But that's where they're going.
> Why?
> It's less impossible than here.

When she opened her eyes, her second meal had cooled, but she didn't want it. Her disused bowels protested. She went to the toilet and strained but voided only a trickle of urine. Feeling ill, she hunched in the dark, small space, shivering, sweat from her armpits running down her ribs. The smell of her urine mixed with the toilet's chemicals and the sweetly acrid odor of her long fast.

pleine de l'âcre odeur des temps, poudreuse et noire
full of the acrid smell of time, dusty and black

Baudelaire. Another world. With wonder she felt it present itself. Consciousness was a mystery. She stared into the darkness, fell asleep again on the pot.

Again she saw Roger shackled to the metal table. A door opened and he looked up.

We've decided.

He waited.

Your ship, your crew, your people—they don't exist. No one will ever know about them.

Roger was silent.

The ones remaining here, the ones who helped you—you're thinking we can't keep them all quiet. We can. We're into your private keys. We know everyone who was involved. We'll round them up. The number's small enough. After all your work, Roger, all their years of effort, there will be nothing but a few pathetic rumors and conspiracy theories. All those good people who helped you will be disappeared forever. Like you. How does that make you feel?

They knew the risks. For them it was already over. Like me.

Over? Oh, Roger. We can make "over" last a long time.

Still, we did it. They did it. They know that.

You're not hearing me, Roger. I said we've changed that.

The ship is out there.

No. I said it's not. Repeat after me. Say it's not, Roger.

BUFFER OVERFLOW. So that was it. Their datastream was not being received. Sophie had done much of the information theory design work. An energy-efficient system approaching Shannon's limit for channel capacity. Even from Alpha C it would be only ten joules per bit.

The instruments collected data. Magnetometer, spectrometers, plasma analyzer, cosmic-ray telescope, Cerenkov detector, et cetera. Data was queued in a transmit buffer and sent out more or less continuously at a low bit rate. The protocol was designed to be robust against interference, dropped packets, interstellar scintillation, and the long latencies imposed by their great distance and the speed of light.

They'd debated even whether to carry communications.

What's the point? We're turning our backs on them.

Roger was insistent: Are we scientists? This is an unprecedented chance to collect data in the heliopause, the Oort cloud, the interstellar medium, the Alpha system itself. Astrometry from Alpha, reliable distances to every star in our galaxy—that alone is huge.

Sending back data broadcasts our location.

So? How hard is it to follow a nuclear plasma trail to the nearest star? Anyway, they'd need a ship to follow. We have the only one.

You say the Earth situation is terminal. Who's going to receive this data?

Anybody. Everybody.

So: Shackleton Crater. It was a major comm link anyway, and its site at the south pole of the Moon assured low ambient noise and permanent line of sight to the ship. They had a Gypsy there—one of their tribe—to receive their data.

The datastream was broken up into packets, to better weather the long trip home. Whenever Shackleton received a packet, it responded with an acknowledgement, to confirm reception. When the ship received that ACK signal—at their present distance, that would be about two months after a packet was transmitted—the confirmed packet was removed from the transmit queue to make room for new data. Otherwise the packet went back to the end of the queue, to be retransmitted later. Packets were time-stamped, so they could be reassembled into a consecutive datastream no matter in what order they were received.

But no ACK signals had been received for over a year. The buffer was full. That's why she was awake.

They'd known the Shackleton link could be broken, even though it had a plausible cover story of looking for SETI transmissions from Alpha C. But other Gypsies on Earth should also be receiving. Someone should be acknowledging. A year of silence!

Going back through computer logs, she found there'd been an impact. Eight months ago something had hit the ship. Why hadn't that wakened a steward?

It had been large enough to get through the forward electromagnetic shield. The shield deflected small particles which, over decades, would erode their hull. The damage had been instantaneous. Repair geckos responded in the first minutes. Since it took most of a day to rouse a steward, there would have been no point.

Maybe the impact hit the antenna array. She checked and adjusted alignment to the Sun. They were okay. She took a routine spectrograph and measured the Doppler shift.

0.056 c.

No. Their velocity should be 0.067 c.

Twelve years. It added twelve years to their cruising time.

She studied the ship's logs as that sank in. The fusion engine had burned its last over a year ago, then was jettisoned to spare mass.

Why hadn't a steward awakened before her? The computer hadn't logged any problems. Engine function read as normal; the sleds that held the fuel had been emptied one by one and discarded, all the fuel had been burned—all as planned. So, absent other problems, the lower velocity alone hadn't triggered an alert. Stupid!

Think. They'd begun to lag only in the last months of burn. Some ignitions had failed or underperformed. It was probably antiproton decay in the triggers. Nothing could have corrected that. Good thinking, nice fail.

Twelve years.

It angered her. The impact and the low velocity directly threatened their survival, and no alarms went off. But loss of comms, *that* set off alarms, that was important to Roger. Who was never meant to be on board. *He's turned his back on humanity, but he still wants them to hear all about it. And to hell with us.*

When her fear receded, she was calmer. If Roger still believed in anything redeemable about humankind, it was the scientific impulse. Of course it was primary to him that this ship do science, and send data. This was her job.

Why Alpha C? Why so impossibly far?

Why not the Moon? The US was there: the base at Shackleton, with a ten-thousand-acre solar power plant, a deuterium mine in the lunar ice, and a twenty-gigawatt particle beam. The Chinese were on the far side, mining helium-3 from the regolith.

Why not Mars? China was there. A one-way mission had been sent in 2025. The crew might not have survived—that was classified—but the robotics had. The planet was reachable and therefore dangerous.

Jupiter? There were rumors that the US was there as well, maybe the Chinese too, robots anyway, staking a claim to all that helium. Roger didn't put much credence in the rumors, but they might be true.

Why not wait it out at a Lagrange point? Roger thought there was nothing to wait for. The situation was terminal. As things spiraled down the maelstrom, anyplace cislunar would be at risk. Sooner or later any ship out there would be detected and destroyed. Or it might last only because civilization was shattered, with the survivors in some pit plotting to pummel the shards.

It was Alpha C because Roger Fry was a fanatic who believed that only an exit from the solar system offered humanity any hope of escaping what it had become.

She thought of Sergei, saying in his bad accent and absent grammar, which he exaggerated for effect: This is shit. You say me Alpha See is best? Absolute impossible. Is double star, no planet in habitable orbit—yes yes, whatever, minima maxima, zone of hopeful bullshit. Ghost Planet Hope. You shoot load there?

How long they had argued over this—their destination.

Gliese 581.

Impossible.

Roger, it's a rocky planet with liquid water.

That's three mistakes in one sentence. Something is orbiting the star, with a period of thirteen days and a mass of two Earths and some spectral lines. Rocky, water, liquid, that's all surmise. What's for sure is it's twenty light-years away. Plus, the star is a flare star. It's disqualified twice before we even get to the hope-it's-a-planet part.

You don't know it's a flare star! There are no observations!

In the absence of observations, we assume it behaves like other observed stars of its class. It flares.

You have this agenda for Alpha C, you've invented these criteria to shoot down every other candidate!

The criteria are transparent. We've agreed to them. Number one: twelve light-years is our outer limit. Right there we're down to twenty-four stars. For reasons of luminosity and stability we prefer a nonvariable G- or K-class star. Now we're down to five.

Alpha Centauri, Epsilon Eridani, 61 Cygni, Epsilon Indi, and Tau Ceti make the cut. Alpha is half the distance of the next nearest.

Bullshit, Roger. You have bug up ass for your Alpha See. Why not disqualify as double, heh? Why this not shoot-down criteria?

Because we have modeled it, and we know planet formation is possible in this system, and we have direct evidence of planets in other double systems. And because— I know.

They ended with Alpha because it was closest. Epsilon Eridani had planets for sure, but they were better off with a closer Ghost Planet Hope than a sure thing so far they couldn't reach it. Cosmic rays would degrade the electronics, the ship, their very cells. Every year in space brought them closer to some component's MTBF: mean time between failures.

Well, they'd known they might lose Shackleton. It was even likely. Just not so soon.

She'd been pushing away the possibility that things had gone so badly on Earth that no one was left to reply.

She remembered walking on a fire road after a conference in Berkeley—the Bay dappled sapphire and russet, thick white marine layer pushing in over the Golden Gate Bridge—talking to Roger about Fermi's Paradox. If the universe harbors life, intelligence, why haven't we seen evidence of it? Why are we alone? Roger favored what he called the Mean Time Between Failures argument. Technological civilizations simply fail, just as the components that make up their technology fail, sooner or later, for reasons as indivually insignificant as they are inexorable, and final. Complex systems, after a point, tend away from robustness.

Okay. Any receivers on Earth will have to find their new signal. It was going to be like SETI in reverse: she had to make the new signal maximally detectable. She could do that. She could retune the frequency to better penetrate Earth's atmosphere. Reprogram the PLLs and antenna array, use orthogonal FSK modulation across the K- and X- bands. Increase the buffer size. And hope for the best.

Eighty-four years to go. My God, they were barely out the front door. My God, it was lonely out here.

The mission plan had been seventy-two years, with a predicted systems-failure rate of under twenty percent. The Weibull curve climbed steeply after that. At eighty-four years, systems-failure rate was over fifty percent.

What could be done to speed them? The nuclear rocket and its fuel were for deceleration and navigation at the far end. To use it here would add—she calculated—a total of 0.0002 c to their current speed. Saving them all of three months. And leaving them no means of planetfall.

They had nothing. Their cruise velocity was unalterable.

All right, that's that, so find a line. Commit to it and move.

Cruise at this speed for longer, decelerate later and harder. That could save a few years. They'd have to run more current through the magsail, increase its drag, push its specs.

Enter the Alpha C system faster than planned, slow down harder once within it. She didn't know how to calculate those maneuvers, but someone else would.

Her brain was racing now, wouldn't let her sleep. She'd been up for three days. These were not her decisions to make, but she was the only one who could.

She wrote up detailed logs with the various options and calculations she'd made. At last there was no more for her to do. But a sort of nostalgia came over her. She wanted, absurdly, to check her email. Really, just to hear some voice not her own.

Nothing broadcast from Earth reached this far except for the ACK signals beamed directly to them from Shackleton. Shackleton was also an IPN node, connecting space assets to the Internet. For cover, the ACK signals it sent to *Gypsy* were piggybacked on bogus Internet packets. And those had all been stored by the computer.

So in her homesick curiosity, she called them out of memory, and dissected some packets that had been saved from up to a year ago. Examined their broken and scrambled content like a torn, discarded newspaper for anything they might tell her of the planet she'd never see again.

M.3,S+SDS<#>0U4:&ES(&%R=&EC;&4@:7,@8V]P>7)I9VAT960@,3DY,R!B>2!4

Warmer than usual regime actively amplifies tundra thaw. Drought melt permafrost thermokarsts methane burn wildfire giants 800 ppm. Capture hot atmospheric ridge NOAA frontrunning collapse sublime asymmetric artificial trade resource loss.

M1HE9LXO6FXQL KL86KWQ LUN;AXEW)1VZ!"NHS;SI5=SJQ 8HCBC3D JGMVA&

Weapon tensions under Islamic media policy rebels arsenals strategic counterinsurgency and to prevent Federal war law operational artillery air component to mine mountain strongholds photorecce altitudes HQ backbone Su-35 SAMs part with high maneuverability bombardments of casualty casuistry

M87EL;W(@)B!&<F%N8VES+" Q.3 P($9R;W-T<#>5)O860L(%-U:71E(<#> $P,2P@

Hurriedly autoimmune decay derivative modern thaws in dawn's pregnant grave shares in disgust of high frequency trading wet cities territorial earthquake poison Bayes the chairs are empty incentives to disorder without borders. Pneumonia again antibiotic resistance travels the globe with ease.

M7V35EX-SR'KP8G 49:YZSR/
BBJWS82<9NS(!1W^YVEY_OD1V&%MMJ,QMRG^

Knowing perpendicular sex dating in Knob Lick Missouri stateroom Sweeney atilt with cheerfully synodic weeny or restorative ministration. Glintingly aweigh triacetate hopefully occasionally sizeable interrogation nauseate. Descriptive mozzarella cosmos truly and contumacious portability.

M4F]N9F5L9'0-26YT97)N871I;VYA;"!0;VQI8WD@1&5P87)T;65N=U204Y$

Titter supine teratologys aim appoint to plaintive technocrat. Mankind is inwardly endocrine and afar romanic spaceflight. Mesial corinths archidiaconal or lyric sa-

tirical turtle demurral. Calorific fitment marry after sappy are inscribed upto pill-
wort. Idem monatomic are processed longways

M<#>0U<#>;W!Y<FEG:'0@,3DY,R!487EL;W(@)B!&<F%N8VES<#>4E
34TX@,<#>$T.2TU

archive tittie blowjob hair fetish SEX FREE PICS RUSSIAN hardcore incest stories animate porn wankers benedict paris car motorcycle cop fetish sex toys caesar
milfhunters when im found this pokemon porn gallery fisting Here Is Links to great
her lesbiands Sites

M0UE"15)705(@25,@0T]-24Y'(0T-2F]H;B!!<G%U:6QL82!A;F0@1&%V:60@

Lost, distant, desolate. The world she'd left forever, speaking its poison poetry of ruin
and catastrophe and longing. Told her nothing she didn't already know about the
corrupt destiny and thwarted feeling that had drawn humankind into the maelstrom
Gypsy had escaped. She stood and walked furiously the meager length of the curved
corridor, stopping at each slab, regarding the sleeping forms of her crewmates, naked in translucent bodysuits, young and fit, yet broken, like her, in ways that had
made this extremity feel to them all the only chance.

They gathered together for the first time on the ship after receiving Roger's signal.

*We'll be fine. Not even Roger knows where the ship is. They won't be able to find us
before we're gone.*

*It was her first time in space. From the shuttle, the ship appeared a formless clutter:
layers of bomb sleds, each bearing thousands of microfusion devices, under and around
them a jacket of hydrogen tanks, shields, conduits, antennas. Two white-suited figures
crawled over this maze. A hijacked hydrogen depot was offloading its cargo.*

*Five were already aboard, retrofitting. Everything not needed for deep space had
been jettisoned. Everything lacking was brought and secured. Shuttles that were supposed to be elsewhere came and went on encrypted itineraries.*

One shuttle didn't make it. They never learned why. So they were down to sixteen crew.

*The ship wasn't meant to hold so many active people. The crew area was less than
a quarter of the torus, a single room narrowed to less than ten feet by the hibernation
slabs lining each long wall. Dim even with all the LED bays on.*

*Darius opened champagne. Contraband: no one knew how alcohol might interact
with the hibernation drugs.*

To Andrew and Chung-Pei and Hari and Maryam. They're with us in spirit.

*Some time later the first bomb went off. The ship trembled but didn't move. Another
blast. Then another. Grudgingly the great mass budged. Like a car departing a curb,
no faster at first. Fuel mass went from it and kinetic energy into it. Kinesis was gradual
but unceasing. In its first few minutes it advanced less than a kilometer. In its first hour
it moved two thousand kilometers. In its first day, a million kilometers. After a year,
when the last bomb was expended, it would be some two thousand astronomical units
from the Earth, and Gypsy would coast on at her fixed speed for decades, a dark, silent,
near-dead thing.*

As Sophie prepared to return to hibernation, she took stock. She walked the short interior of the quarter-torus. Less than twenty paces end to end. The black walls, the dim LED pods, the slabs of her crewmates.

Never to see her beloved mountains again. Her dear sawtooth Sierra. She thought of the blue sky, and remembered a hunk of stuff she'd seen on Roger's desk, some odd kind of rock. It was about five inches long. You could see through it. Its edges were blurry. Against a dark background it had a bluish tinge. She took it in her hand and it was nearly weightless.

What is this?

Silica aerogel. The best insulator in the world.

Why is it blue?

Rayleigh scattering.

She knew what that meant: why the sky is blue. Billions of particles in the air scatter sunlight, shorter wavelengths scatter most, so those suffuse the sky. The shortest we can see is blue. But that was an ocean of air around the planet and this was a small rock.

You're joking.

No, it's true. There are billions of internal surfaces in that piece.

It's like a piece of sky.

Yes, it is.

It was all around her now, that stuff—in the walls of the ship, keeping out the cold of space—allowing her to imagine a poetry of sky where none was.

And that was it. She'd been awake for five days. She'd fixed the datastream back to Earth. She'd written her logs. She'd reprogrammed the magsail deployment for seventy years from now, at increased current, in the event that no other steward was wakened in the meantime. She'd purged her bowels and injected the hibernation cocktail. She was back in the bodysuit, life supports connected. As she went under, she wondered why.

2.

They departed a day short of Roger Fry's fortieth birthday. Born September 11, 2001, he was hired to a national weapons laboratory straight out of Caltech. He never did finish his doctorate. Within a year at the Lab he had designed the first breakeven fusion reaction. It had long been known that a very small amount of antimatter could trigger a burn wave in thermonuclear fuel. Roger solved how. He was twenty-four.

Soon there were net energy gains. That's when the bomb people came in. In truth, their interest was why he was hired in the first place. Roger knew this and didn't care. Once fusion became a going concern, it would mean unlimited clean energy. It would change the world. Bombs would have no purpose.

But it was a long haul to a commercial fusion reactor. Meanwhile, bombs were easier.

The first bombs were shaped-charge antiproton-triggered fusion bunker busters. The smallest was a kiloton-yield bomb, powerful enough to level forty or fifty city blocks; it used just a hundred grams of lithium deuteride, and less than a microgram of antimatter. It was easy to manufacture and transport and deploy. It created little radiation or electromagnetic pulse. Tens of thousands, then hundreds of thousands, were fabricated in orbit and moved to drop platforms called sleds. Because the minimum individual yields were within the range of conventional explosives, no nuclear treaties were violated.

Putting them in orbit did violate the Outer Space Treaty, so at first they were more politely called the Orbital Asteroid Defense Network. But when a large asteroid passed through cislunar space a few years later—with no warning, no alert, no response at all—the pretense was dropped, and the system came under the command of the US Instant Global Strike Initiative.

More and more money went into antimatter production. There were a dozen factories worldwide that produced about a gram, all told, of antiprotons a year. Some went into the first fusion power plants, which themselves produced more antiprotons. Most went into bomb triggers. There they were held in traps, isolated from normal matter, but that worked only so long. They decayed, like tritium in the older nuclear weapons, but much faster; some traps could store milligrams of antiprotons for many months at a time, and they were improving; still, bomb triggers had to be replaced often.

As a defence system it was insane, but hugely profitable. Then came the problem of where to park the profits, since there were no stable markets anywhere. The economic system most rewarded those who created and surfed instabilities and could externalize their risks, which created greater instabilities.

Year after year Roger worked and waited, and the number of bombs grew, as did the number of countries deploying them, and the global resource wars intensified, and his fusion utopia failed to arrive. When the first commercial plants did start operating, it made no difference. Everything went on as before. Those who had the power to change things had no reason to; things had worked out pretty well for them so far.

Atmospheric CO_2 shot past 600 parts per million. The methane burden was now measured in parts per million, not parts per billon. No one outside the classified world knew the exact numbers, but the effects were everywhere. The West Antarctic ice shelf collapsed. Sea level rose three meters.

Some time in there, Roger Fry gave up on Earth.

But not on humanity, not entirely. Something in the complex process of civilization had forced it into this place from which it now had no exit. He didn't see this as an inevitable result of the process, but it had happened. There might have been a time when the situation was reversible. If certain decisions had been made. If resources had been treated as a commons. Back when the population of the planet was two or three billion, when there was still enough to go around, enough time to alter course, enough leisure to think things through. But it hadn't gone that way. He didn't much care why. The question was what to do now.

FANG TIR EOGHAIN (2081)

The ancestor of all mammals must have been a hibernator. Body temperature falls as much as 15 kelvins. A bear's heartbeat goes down to five per minute. Blood pressure drops to thirty millimeters. In humans, these conditions would be fatal.

Relatively few genes are involved in torpor. We have located the critical ones. And we have found the protein complexes they uptake and produce. Monophosphates mostly.

Yes, I know, induced hypothermia is not torpor. But this state has the signatures of torpor. For example, there is a surfeit of MCT1 which transports ketones to the brain during fasting.

Ketosis, that's true, we are in a sense poisoning the subject in order to achieve this state. Some ischemia and refusion damage results, but less than anticipated. Doing it more than a couple of times is sure to be fatal. But for our purposes, maybe it gets the job done.

Anyway it had better; we have nothing else.

Her da was screaming at her to get up. He wasn't truly her father, her father had gone to the stars. That was a story she'd made up long ago; it was better than the truth.

Her thick brown legs touched the floor. Not so thick and brown as she remembered. Weak, pale, withered. She tried to stand and fell back. Try harder, cow. She fell asleep.

She'd tried so hard for so long. She'd been accepted early at university. Then her parents went afoul of the system. One day she came home to a bare apartment. All are zhonghua minzu, but it was a bad time for certain ethnics in China.

She lost her place at university. She was shunted to a polytechnic secondary in Guangzhou, where she lived with her aunt and uncle in a small apartment. It wasn't science; it was job training in technology services. One day she overheard the uncle on the phone, bragging: he had turned her parents in, collected a bounty and a stipend.

She was not yet fifteen. It was still possible, then, to be adopted out of country. Covertly, she set about it. Caitlin Tyrone was the person who helped her from afar.

They'd met online, in a science chatroom. Ireland needed scientists. She didn't know or care where that was; she'd have gone to Hell. It took almost a year to arrange it, the adoption. It took all Fang's diligence, all her cunning, all her need, all her cold hate, to keep it from her uncle, to acquire the paperwork, to forge his signature, to sequester money, and finally on the last morning to sneak out of the apartment before dawn.

She flew from Guangzhao to Beijing to Frankfurt to Dublin, too nervous to sleep. Each time she had to stop in an airport and wait for the next flight, sometimes for hours, she feared arrest. In her sleepless imagination, the waiting lounges turned into detention centers. Then she was on the last flight. The stars faded and the sun rose over the Atlantic, and there was Ireland. O! the green of it. And her new mother Caitlin was there to greet her, grab her, look into her eyes. Good-bye forever to the wounded past.

She had a scholarship at Trinity College, in biochemistry. She already knew English, but during her first year she studied phonology and orthography and grammar, to try to map, linguistically, how far she'd traveled. It wasn't so far. The human vocal apparatus is everywhere the same. So is the brain, constructing the grammar that drives the voice box. Most of her native phonemes had Irish or English equivalents, near enough. But the sounds she made of hers were not quite correct, so she worked daily to refine them.

O is where she often came to rest. The exclamative particle, the sound of that moment when the senses surprise the body, same in Ireland as in China—same body, same senses, same sound. Yet a human universe of shadings. The English O was one thing; Mandarin didn't quite have it; Cantonese was closer; but everywhere the sound slid around depending on locality, on country, even on county: monophthong to diphthong, the tongue wandering in the mouth, seeking to settle. When she felt lost in the night, which was often, she sought for that O, round and solid and vast and various and homey as the planet beneath her, holding her with its gravity. Moving her tongue in her mouth as she lay in bed waiting for sleep.

Biochemistry wasn't so distant, in her mind, from language. She saw it all as signaling. DNA wasn't "information," data held statically in helices, it was activity, transaction.

She insisted on her new hybrid name, the whole long Gaelic mess of it—it was Caitlin's surname—as a reminder of the contingency of belonging, of culture and language, of identity itself. Her solid legs had landed on solid ground, or solid enough to support her.

Carefully, arduously, one connector at a time, she unplugged herself from the bodysuit, then sat up on the slab. Too quickly. She dizzied and pitched forward.

Get up, you cow. The da again. Dream trash. As if she couldn't. She'd show him. She gave all her muscles a great heave.

And woke shivering on the carbon deckplates. Held weakly down by the thin false gravity. It was no embracing O, just a trickle of mockery. *You have to do this*, she told her will.

She could smell acetone on her breath. Glycogen used up, body starts to burn fat, produces ketones. Ketoacidosis. She should check ketone levels in the others.

Roger came into Fang's life by way of Caitlin. Years before, Caitlin had studied physics at Trinity. Roger had read her papers. They was brilliant. He'd come to teach a seminar, and he had the idea of recruiting her to the Lab. But science is bound at the hip to its application, and turbulence occurs at that interface where theory meets practice, knowledge meets performance. Where the beauty of the means goes to die in the instrumentality of the ends.

Roger found to his dismay that Caitlin couldn't manage even the sandbox politics of grad school. She'd been aced out of the best advisors and was unable to see that her science career was already in a death spiral. She'd never make it on her own at the Lab, or in a corp. He could intervene to some degree, but he was reluctant; he saw a better way.

Already Caitlin was on U, a Merck pharmaceutical widely prescribed for a new category in DSM-6: "social interoperability disorder." U for eudaimoniazine. Roger had tried it briefly himself. In his opinion, half the planet fit the diagnostic criteria, which was excellent business for Merck but said more about planetary social conditions than about the individuals who suffered under them.

· U was supposed to increase compassion for others, to make other people seem more real. But Caitlin was already too empathic for her own good, too ready to yield her place to others, and the U merely blissed her out, put her in a zone of self-abnegation. Perhaps that's why it was a popular street drug; when some governments tried to ban it, Merck sued them under global trade agreements, for loss of expected future profits.

Caitlin ended up sidelined in the Trinity library, where she met and married James, an older charming sociopath with terrific interoperability. Meanwhile, Roger kept tabs on her from afar. He hacked James's medical records and was noted that James was infertile.

It took Fang several hours to come to herself. She tried not to worry, this was to be expected. Her body had gone through a serious near-death trauma. She felt weak, nauseous, and her head throbbed, but she was alive. That she was sitting here sipping warm tea was a triumph, for her body and for her science. She still felt a little stunned, a little distant from that success. So many things could have gone wrong: hibernation was only the half of it; like every other problem they'd faced, it came with its own set of ancillaries. On which she'd worked.

In addition to her highly classified DARPA work on hibernation, Fang had published these papers in the *Journal of Gravitational Physiology*: Serum leptin level is a regulator of bone mass (2033); Inhibition of osteopenia by low magnitude, high frequency mechanical stimuli (2035); The transcription factor NF-kappaB is a key intracellular signal transducer in disuse atrophy (2036); IGF-I stimulates muscle growth by suppressing protein breakdown and expression of atrophy-related ubiquitin ligases, atrogin-1 and MuRF1 (2037); and PGC-1alpha protects skeletal muscle from atrophy by suppressing FoxO3 action and atrophy-specific gene transcription (2039).

When she felt able, she checked on the others. Each sleeper bore implanted and dermal sensors—for core and skin temperature, EKG, EEG, pulse, blood pressure and flow, plasma ions, plasma metabolites, clotting function, respiratory rate and depth, gas analysis and flow, urine production, EMG, tremor, body composition. Near-infrared spectrometry measured haematocrit, blood glucose, tissue O_2 and pH. Muscles were stimulated electrically and mechanically to counteract atrophy. The slabs tipped thirty degrees up or down and rotated the body from supine to prone in order to provide mechanical loading from hypogravity in all directions. Exoskeletal waldos at the joints, and the soles and fingers, provided periodic range-of-motion stimulus. A range of pharmacological and genetic interventions further regulated bone and muscle regeneration.

Also, twitching was important. If you didn't twitch you wouldn't wake. It was a kind of mooring to the present.

Did they dream? EEGs showed periodic variation but were so unlike normal

EEGs that it was hard to say. You couldn't very well wake someone to ask, as the first sleep researchers had done.

All looked well on the monitor, except for number fourteen. Reza. Blood pressure almost nonexistent. She got to her feet and walked down the row of slabs to have a look at Reza.

A pursed grayish face sagging on its skull. Maybe a touch of life was visible, some purple in the gray, blood still coursing. Or maybe not.

Speckling the gray skin was a web of small white dots, each the size of a pencil eraser or smaller. They were circular but not perfectly so, margins blurred. Looked like a fungus.

She went back and touched the screen for records. This steward was long overdue for rousing. The machine had started the warming cycle three times. Each time he hadn't come out of torpor, so the machine had shut down the cycle, stablized him, and tried again. After three failures, it had moved down the list to the next steward. Her.

She touched a few levels deeper. Not enough fat on this guy. Raising the temperature without rousing would simply bring on ischemia and perfusion. That's why the machine gave up. It was a delicate balance, to keep the metabolism burning fat instead of carbohydrates, without burning too much of the body's stores. Humans couldn't bulk up on fat in advance the way natural hibernators could. But she thought she'd solved that with the nutrient derms.

It was the fortieth year of the voyage. They were two light-years from home. Not quite halfway. If hibernation was failing now, they had a serious problem.

Was the fungus a result or a cause? Was it a fungus? She wanted to open the bodysuit and run tests, but any contagion had to be contained.

They'd discussed possible failure modes. Gene activity in bacteria increased in low gravity; they evolved more rapidly. In the presence of a host they became more virulent. Radiation caused mutations. But ultraviolet light scoured the suits every day and should have killed bacteria and fungus alike. Logs showed that the UV was functioning. It wasn't enough.

James—the da, as he insisted Fang call him—had black hair and blue eyes that twinkled like ice when he smiled. At first he was mere background to her; he'd stumble in late from the pub to find Caitlin and Fang talking. Ah, the Addams sisters, he'd say, nodding sagely. Fang never understood what he meant by it. For all his geniality, he kept her at a distance, treated her like a house guest.

Caitlin was more like an older sister than a mother; she was only twelve years older. It was fun to talk science with her, and it was helpful. She was quick to understand the details of Fang's field, and this dexterity spurred Fang in her own understanding and confidence.

After a couple of years, James grew more sullen, resentful, almost abusive. He dropped the suave act. He found fault with Fang's appearance, her habits, her character. The guest had overstayed her welcome. He was jealous.

She couldn't figure out why a woman as good and as smart as Caitlin stayed on with him. Maybe something damaged in Caitlin was called by a like damage in James.

Caitlin had lost her father while a girl, as had Fang. When Fang looked at James through Caitlin's eyes, she could see in him the ruins of something strong and attractive and paternal. But that thing was no longer alive. Only Caitlin's need for it lived, and that need became a reproach to James, who had lost the ability to meet it, and who fled from it.

The further James fled into drink, the more Caitlin retreated into her U, into a quiescence where things could feel whole. All the while, James felt Fang's eyes on him, evaluating him, seeing him as he was. He saw she wasn't buying him. Nothing disturbed him more than having his act fail. And he saw that Caitlin was alive and present only with Fang. They clung to one another, and were moving away from him.

James was truly good to me, before you knew him.

On U, everyone seems good to you.

No, long before that. When I failed my orals he was a great support.

You were vulnerable. He fed on your need.

You don't know, Fang. I was lost. He helped me, he held on to me when I needed it. Then I had you.

She thought not. She thought James had learned to enjoy preying on the vulnerable. And Caitlin was too willing to ignore this, to go along with it. As Fang finished her years at Trinity, she agonized over how she must deal with this trouble. It was then that an offer arrived from Roger's lab.

Come with me to America.

Oh, Fang. I can't. What about James? What would he do there?

It was James's pretense that he was still whole and competent and functional, when in fact his days were marked out by the habits of rising late, avoiding work in the library, and leaving early for the pub. Any move or change would expose the pretense.

Just you and me. Just for a year.

I can't.

Fang heard alarms. If she stayed and tried to protect Caitlin, her presence might drive James to some extreme. Or Fang might be drawn more deeply into their dysfunction. She didn't know if she could survive that. The thing Fang was best at was saving herself. So she went to America alone.

There was a second body covered with fungus. Number fifteen. Loren.

Either the fungus was contained, restricted to these two, or more likely it had already spread. But how? The bodysuits showed no faults, no breaches. They were isolated from each other, with no pathways for infection. The only possible connection would be through the air supply, and the scrubbers should remove any pathogens, certainly anything as large as a fungus.

In any case, it was bad. She could try rousing another steward manually. But to what purpose? Only she had the expertise to deal with this.

She realized she thought of it because she was desperately lonely. She wanted company with this problem. She wasn't going to get any.

Not enough fat to rouse. Increase glycogen uptake? Maybe, but carbohydrate fasting was a key part of the process.

They had this advantage over natural hibernators: they didn't need to get all their energy from stored body fat. Lipids were dripped in dermally to provide ATP. But body fat was getting metabolized anyway.

Signaling. Perhaps the antisenescents were signaling the fungus not to die. Slowing not its growth but its morbidity. If it were a fungus. Sure it was, it had to be. But confirm it.

After she came to the Lab, Fang learned that her adoption was not so much a matter of her initiative, or of Caitlin's, or of good fortune. Roger had pulled strings every step of the way—strings Fang had no idea existed.

He'd known of Fang because all student work—every paper, test, e-mail, click, eyeblink, keystroke—was stored and tracked and mined. Her permanent record. Corps and labs had algorithms conducting eternal worldwide surveillance for, among so many other things, promising scientists. Roger had his own algorithms: his stock-market eye for early bloomers, good draft choices. He'd purchased Fang's freedom from some Chinese consortium and linked her to Caitlin.

Roger, Fang came to realize, had seen in Caitlin's needs and infirmities a way to help three people: Caitlin, who needed someone to nurture and give herself to, so as not to immolate herself; Fang, who needed that nurturing; and himself, who needed Fang's talent. In other words: Roger judged that Caitlin would do best as the mother of a scientist.

He wasn't wrong. Caitlin's nurture was going to waste on James, who simply sucked it in and gave nothing back. And Fang needed a brilliant, loving, female example to give her confidence in her own brilliance, and learn the toughness she'd need to accomplish her work. That's what Caitlin herself had lacked.

If Fang had known all this, she'd have taken the terms; she'd have done anything to get out of China. But she hadn't known; she hadn't been consulted. So when she found out, she was furious. For Caitlin, for herself. As she saw it, Roger couldn't have the mother, so he took the daughter. He used their love and mutual need to get what he wanted, and then he broke them apart. It was cold and calculating and utterly selfish of Roger; of the three of them, only he wasn't damaged by it. She'd almost quit Gypsy in her fury.

She did quit the Lab. She went into product development at Glaxo, under contract to DARPA. That was the start of her hibernation work. It was for battlefield use, as a way to keep injured soldiers alive during transport. When she reflected on this move, she wasn't so sure that Roger hadn't pulled more strings. In any case, the work was essential to Gypsy.

Roger had fury of his own, to spare. Fang knew all about the calm front. Roger reeked of it. He'd learned that he had the talent and the position to do great harm; the orbiting bombs were proof of that. His anger and disappointment had raised in him the urge to do more harm. At the Lab he was surrounded by the means and the opportunity. So he'd gathered all his ingenuity and his rage against humanity and sequestered it in a project large enough and complex enough to occupy it fully, so that it could not further harm him or the world: Gypsy. He would do a thing that had never been done before; and he would take away half the bombs he'd enabled in the doing of it; and the thing would not be shared with humanity. She imagined he saw it as a victimless revenge.

Well, here were the victims.

A day later, *Pseudogymnoascus destructans* was her best guess. Or some mutation of it. It had killed most of the bats on Earth. It grew only in low temperatures, in the 4 to 15 Celsius range. The ship was normally held at 4 Celsius.

She could synthesize an antifungal agent with the gene printer, but what about interactions? Polyenes would bind with a fungus's ergosterols but could have severe and lethal side effects.

She thought about the cocktail. How she might tweak it. Sirtuins. Fibroplast growth factor 21. Hibernation induction trigger. [D-Ala^2, D-Leu^5]-Enkephalin. Pancreatic triacylglycerol lipase. 5'-adenosine monophosphate. Ghrelin. 3-iodothyronamine. Alpha2-macroglobulin. Carnosine, other antisenescents, antioxidants.

Some components acted only at the start of the process. They triggered a cascade of enzymes in key pathways to bring on torpor. Some continued to drip in, to reinforce gene expression, to suppress circadian rhythms, and so on.

It was all designed to interact with nonhuman mammalian genes she'd spliced in. Including parts of the bat immune system—*Myotis lucifugus*—parts relevant to hibernation, to respond to the appropriate mRNA signals. But were they also vulnerable to this fungus? *O God, did I do this? Did I open up this vulnerability?*

She gave her presentation, in the open, to DARPA. It was amazing; she was speaking in code to the few Gypsies in the audience, including Roger, telling them in effect how they'd survive the long trip to Alpha, yet her plaintext words were telling DARPA about battlefield applications: suspending wounded soldiers, possibly in space, possibly for long periods, 3D-printing organs, crisping stem cells, and so on.

In Q&A she knew DARPA was sold; they'd get their funding. Roger was right: everything was dual use.

She'd been up for ten days. The cramped, dark space was wearing her down. Save them. They had to make it. She'd pulled a DNA sequencer and a gene printer from the storage bay. As she fed it *E. coli* and *Mycoplasma mycoides* stock, she reviewed what she'd come up with.

She could mute the expression of the bat genes at this stage, probably without disrupting hibernation. They were the receptors for the triggers that started and stopped the process. But that could compromise rousing. So mute them temporarily— for how long?—hope to revive an immune response, temporarily damp down the antisenescents, add an antifungal. She'd have to automate everything in the mixture; the ship wouldn't rouse her a second time to supervise.

It was a long shot, but so was everything now.

It was too hard for her. For anyone. She had the technology: a complete library of genetic sequences, a range of restriction enzymes, Sleeping Beauty transposase, et cetera. She'd be capable on the spot, for instance, of producing a pathogen that could selectively kill individuals with certain ethnic markers—that had been one project at the Lab, demurely called "preventive". But she didn't have the knowledge she needed for this. It had taken years of research experimentation, and collaboration, to come up with the original cocktail, and it would take years more to truly solve this. She had only a few days. Then the residue of the cocktail would be out of her system and she would lose the ability to rehibernate. So she had to go with what she had now. Test it on DNA from her own saliva.

Not everyone stuck with Gypsy. One scientist at the Lab, Sidney Lefebvre, was wooed by Roger to sign up, and declined only after carefully studying their plans for a couple of weeks. It's too hard, Roger. What you have here is impressive. But it's only a start. There are too many intractable problems. Much more work needs to be done.

That work won't get done. Things are falling apart, not coming together. It's now or never.

Probably so. Regardless, the time for this is not now. This, too, will fall apart.

She wrote the log for the next steward, who would almost surely have the duty of more corpses. Worse, as stewards died, maintenance would be deferred. Systems would die. She didn't know how to address that. Maybe Lefebvre was right. But no: they had to make it. How could this be harder than getting from Guangxhou to Dublin to here?

She prepared to go back under. Fasted the day. Enema, shower. Taps and stents and waldos and derms attached and the bodysuit sealed around her. She felt the cocktail run into her veins.

The lights were off. The air was chill. In her last moment of clarity, she stared into blackness. Always she had run, away from distress, toward something new, to eradicate its pain and its hold. Not from fear. As a gesture of contempt, of power: done with you, never going back. But run to where? No world, no O, no gravity, no hold, nothing to cling to. This was the end of the line. There was nowhere but here. And, still impossibly far, another forty-four years, Alpha C. As impossibly far as Earth.

3.

Roger recruited his core group face to face. At conferences and symposia he sat for papers that had something to offer his project, and he made a judgment about the presenter. If favorable, it led to a conversation. Always outside, in the open. Fire roads in the Berkeley hills. A cemetery in Zurich. The shores of Lake Como. Fry was well known, traveled much. He wasn't Einstein, he wasn't Feynman, he wasn't Hawking, but he had a certain presence.

The conferences were Kabuki. Not a scientist in the world was unlinked to classified projects through government or corporate sponsors. Presentations were so oblique that expert interpretation was required to parse their real import.

Roger parsed well. Within a year he had a few dozen trusted collaborators. They divided the mission into parts: target selection, engine and fuel, vessel, hibernation, navigation, obstacle avoidance, computers, deceleration, landfall, survival.

The puzzle had too many pieces. Each piece was unthinkably complex. They needed much more help.

They put up a site they called Gypsy. On the surface it was a gaming site, complex and thick with virtual worlds, sandboxes, self-evolving puzzles, and links. Buried in there was an interactive starship-design section, where ideas were solicited, models built, simulations run. Good nerdy crackpot fun.

The core group tested the site themselves for half a year before going live. Their own usage stats became the profile of the sort of visitors they sought: people like themselves: people with enough standing to have access to the high-speed classified web, with enough autonomy to waste professional time on a game site, and finally with enough curiosity and dissidence to pursue certain key links down a critical chain. They needed people far enough inside an institution to have access to resources, but not so far inside as to identify with its ideology. When a user appeared to fit that profile, a public key was issued. The key unlocked further levels and ultimately enabled secure e-mail to an encrypted server.

No one, not even Roger Fry, knew how big the conspiracy was. Ninety-nine percent of their traffic was noise—privileged kids, stoked hackers, drunken PhDs, curious spooks. Hundreds of keys were issued in the first year. Every key increased the risk. But without resources they were going nowhere.

The authorities would vanish Roger Fry and everyone associated with him on the day they learned what he was planning. Not because of the what: a starship posed no threat. But because of the how and the why: only serious and capable dissidents could plan so immense a thing; the seriousness and the capability were the threat. And eventually they would be found, because every bit of the world's digital traffic was swept up and stored and analyzed. There was a city under the Utah desert where these yottabytes of data were archived in server farms. But the sheer size of the archive outran its analysis and opened a time window in which they might act.

Some ran propellant calculations. Some forwarded classified medical studies. Some were space workers with access to shuttles and tugs. Some passed on classified findings from telescopes seeking exoplanets.

One was an operator of the particle beam at Shackleton Crater. The beam was used, among other purposes, to move the orbiting sleds containing the very bombs Roger had helped design. One worked at a seed archive in Norway. She piggybacked a capsule into Earth orbit containing seeds from fifty thousand unmodified plant species, including plants legally extinct. They needed those because every cultivated acre on Earth was now planted with engineered varieties that were sterile; terminator genes had been implanted to protect the agro firms' profit streams; and these genes had jumped to wild varieties. There wasn't a live food plant left anywhere on Earth that could propagate itself.

They acquired frozen zygotes of some ten thousand animal species, from bacteria to primates. Hundred thousands more complete DNA sequences in a data library, and a genome printer. Nothing like the genetic diversity of Earth, even in its present state, but enough, perhaps, to reboot such diversity.

At Roger's lab, panels of hydrogenous carbon-composite, made to shield high-orbit craft from cosmic rays and to withstand temperatures of 2000 C, went missing. Quite a lot of silica aerogel as well.

At a sister lab, a researcher put them in touch with a contractor from whom they purchased, quite aboveboard, seventy kilometers of lightweight, high-current-density superconducting cable.

After a year, Roger decided that their web had grown too large to remain secure. He didn't like the number of unused keys going out. He didn't like the page patterns he was seeing. He didn't consult with the others, he just shut it down.

But they had their pieces.

SERGEI (2118)

Eat, drink, shit. That's all he did for the first day or three. Water tasted funny. Seventy-seven years might have viled it, or his taste buds. Life went on, including the ending of it. Vital signs of half the crew were flat. He considered disposing of bodies, ejecting them, but number one, he couldn't be sure they were dead; number two, he couldn't propel them hard enough to keep them from making orbit around the ship, which was funny but horrible; and finally, it would be unpleasant and very hard work that would tire him out. An old man—he surely felt old, and the calendar would back him up—needs to reserve his strength. So he let them lie on their slabs.

The logs told a grim story. They were slow. To try to make up for lost time, Sophie had reprogrammed the magsail to deploy later and to run at higher current. Another steward had been wakened at the original deployment point, to confirm their speed and position, and to validate the decision to wait. Sergei didn't agree with that, and he especially didn't like the hand waving over when to ignite the nuclear rocket in-system, but it was done: they'd gone the extra years at speed and now they needed to start decelerating hard.

CURRENT INJECTION FAILED. MAGSAIL NOT DEPLOYED.

He tapped the screen to cycle through its languages. Stopped at the Cyrillic script, and tapped the speaker, just so he could hear spoken Russian.

So he had to fix the magsail. Current had flowed on schedule from inside, but the sail wasn't charging or deploying. According to telltales, the bay was open but the superconducing cable just sat there. That meant EVA. He didn't like it, but there was no choice. It's what he was here for. Once it was done he'd shower again under that pathetic lukewarm stream, purge his bowels, get back in the mylar suit, and go under for another, what, eight more years, a mere nothing, we're almost there. Ghost Planet Hope.

He was the only one onboard who'd been a career astronaut. Roger had conveyed a faint class disapproval about that, but needed the expertise. Sergei had been one of the gene-slushed orbital jockeys who pushed bomb sleds around. He knew the feel of zero g, of sunlight on one side of you and absolute cold on the other. He knew how it felt when the particle beam from Shackleton swept over you to push you and the sleds into a new orbit. And you saluted and cut the herds, and kept whatever more you might know to yourself.

Which in Sergei's case was quite a bit. Sergei knew orbital codes and protocols far beyond his pay grade; he could basically move anything in orbit to or from anywhere.

But only Sergei, so Sergei thought, knew that. How Roger learned it remained a mystery.

To his great surprise, Sergei learned that even he hadn't known the full extent of his skills. How easy it had been to steal half a million bombs. True, the eternal war economy was so corrupt that materiel was supposed to disappear; something was wrong if it didn't. Still, he would never have dared anything so outrageous on his own. Despite Roger's planning, he was sweating the day he moved the first sled into an unauthorized orbit. But days passed, then weeks and months, as sled followed sled into new holding orbits. In eighteen months they had all their fuel. No traps had sprung, no alarms tripped. Sophie managed to make the manifests look okay. And he wondered again at what the world had become. And what he was in it.

This spacesuit was light, thin, too comfortable. Like a toddler's fleece playsuit with slippers and gloves. Even the helmet was soft. He was more used to heavy Russian engineering, but whatever. They'd argued over whether to include a suit at all. He'd argued against. EVA had looked unlikely, an unlucky possibility. So he was happy now to have anything.

The soles and palms were sticky, a clever off-the-shelf idea inspired by lizards. Billions of carbon nanotubes lined them. The Van der Waals molecular force made them stick to any surface. He tested it by walking on the interior walls. Hands or feet held you fast, with or against the ship's rotational gravity. You had to kind of toe-and-heel to walk, but it was easy enough.

Пойдем. Let's go. He climbed into the hatch and cycled it. As the pressure dropped, the suit expanded and felt more substantial. He tested the grip of his palms on the hull before rising fully out of the hatch. Then his feet came up and gripped, and he stood.

In darkness and immensity stiller than he could comprehend. Interstellar space. The frozen splendor of the galactic core overhead. Nothing appeared to move.

He remembered a still evening on a lake, sitting with a friend on a dock, legs over the edge. They talked as the sky darkened, looking up as the stars came out. Only when it was fully dark did he happen to look down. The water was so still, stars were reflected under his feet. He almost lurched over the edge of the dock in surprise.

The memory tensed his legs, and he realized the galactic core was moving slowly around the ship. Here on the outside of the ship its spin-induced gravity was reversed. He stood upright but felt pulled toward the stars.

He faced forward. Tenth of a light-year from Alpha, its two stars still appeared as one. They were brighter than Venus in the Earth's sky. They cast his faint but distinct shadow on the hull.

They were here. They had come this far. On this tiny splinter of human will forging through vast, uncaring space. It was remarkable.

A line of light to his left flashed. Some microscopic particle ionized by the ship's magnetic shield. He tensed again at this evidence of their movement and turned slowly, directing his beam over the hull. Its light caught a huge gash through one of the hydrogen tanks. Edges of the gash had failed to be covered by a dozen geckos, frozen in place by hydrogen ice. That was bad. Worse, it hadn't been in the log. Maybe it was from the impact Sophie had referred to. He would have to see how bad it was after freeing the magsail.

He turned, and toed and heeled his way carefully aft. Now ahead of him was our Sun, still one of the brightest stars, the heavens turning slowly around it. He approached the circular bay that held the magsail. His light showed six large spools of cable, each a meter and a half across and a meter thick. About five metric tons in all, seventy kilometers of thin superconductor wire. Current injection should have caused the spools to unreel under the force of the electric field. But it wasn't getting current, or it was somehow stuck. He was going to have to . . . well, he wasn't sure.

Then he saw it. Almost laughed at the simplicity and familiarity of it. Something like a circuit breaker, red and green buttons, the red one lit. He squatted at the edge of the bay and found he could reach the thing. He felt cold penetrate his suit. He really ought to go back inside and spend a few hours troubleshooting, read the fucking manual, but the cold and the flimsy spacesuit and the immensity convinced him otherwise. He slapped the green button.

It lit. The cable accepted current. He saw it lurch. As he smiled and stood, the current surging in the coils sent its field through the soles of his spacesuit, disrupting for a moment the molecular force holding them to the hull. In that moment, the angular velocity of the rotating ship was transmitted to his body and he detached, moving away from the ship at a stately three meters per second. Beyond his flailing feet, the cables of the magsail began leisurely to unfurl.

As he tumbled the stars rolled past. He'd seen Orion behind the ship in the moment he detached, and as he tumbled he looked for it, for something to grab on to, but he never saw it or the ship again. So he didn't see the huge coil of wire reach its full extension, nor the glow of ionization around the twenty-kilometer circle when it began to drag against the interstellar medium, nor how the ship itself started to lag against the background stars. The ionization set up a howl across the radio spectrum, but his radio was off, so he didn't hear that. He tumbled in silence in the bowl of the heavens at his fixed velocity, which was now slightly greater than the ship's. Every so often the brightness of Alpha crossed his view. He was going to get there first.

4.

Their biggest single problem was fuel. To cross that enormous distance in less than a human lifetime, even in this stripped-down vessel, required an inconceivable amount of energy. Ten to the twenty first joules. 250 trillion kilowatt hours. Twenty years' worth of all Earth's greedy energy consumption. The mass of the fuel, efficient though it was, would be several times the mass of the ship. And to reach cruising speed was only half of it; they had to decelerate when they reached Alpha C, doubling the fuel. It was undoable.

Until someone found an old paper on magnetic sails. A superconducting loop of wire many kilometers across, well charged, could act as a drag brake against the interstellar medium. That would cut the fuel requirement almost in half. Done that way, it was just possible, though out on the ragged edge of what was survivable. This deceleration would take ten years.

For their primary fuel, Roger pointed to the hundreds of thousands of bombs in orbit. His bombs. His intellectual property. Toss them out the back and ignite them.

A Blumlein pulse-forming line—they called it the "bloom line"—a self-generated magnetic vise, something like a Z-pinch—would direct nearly all the blast to exhaust velocity. The vise, called into being for the nanoseconds of ignition, funneled all that force straight back. Repeat every minute. Push the compression ratio up, you won't get many neutrons.

In the end they had two main engines: first, the antiproton-fusion monster to get them up to speed. It could only be used for the first year; any longer and the antiprotons would decay. Then the magsail would slow them most of the way, until they entered the system.

For the last leg, a gas-core nuclear rocket to decelerate in the system, which required carrying a large amount of hydrogen. They discussed scooping hydrogen from the interstellar medium as they traveled, but Roger vetoed it: not off the shelf. They didn't have the time or means to devise a new technology. Anyway, the hydrogen would make, in combination with their EM shield, an effective barrier to cosmic rays. Dual use.

And even so, everything had to be stretched to the limit: the mass of the ship minimized, the human lifetime lengthened, the fuel leveraged every way possible.

The first spacecraft ever to leave the solar system, Pioneer 10, had used Jupiter's gravity to boost its velocity. As it flew by, it stole kinetic energy from the planet; its small mass sped up a lot; Jupiter's stupendous mass slowed unnoticeably.

They would do the same thing to lose speed. They had the combined mass of two stars orbiting each other, equal to two thousand Jupiters. When *Gypsy* was to arrive in 2113, the stars in their mutual orbit would be as close together as they ever got: 11 astronomical units. *Gypsy* would fly by the B star and pull one last trick: retrofire the nuclear rocket deep in its gravity well; that would multiply the kinetic effect of the propellant severalfold. And then they'd repeat that maneuever around A. The relative closeness of 11 AU was still as far as Earth to Saturn, so even after arrival, even at their still-great speed, the dual braking maneuver would take over a year.

Only then would they be moving slowly enough to aerobrake in the planet's atmosphere, and that would take a few dozen passes before they could ride the ship down on its heatshield to the surface.

If there was a planet. If it had an atmosphere.

ZIA (2120)

As a child he was lord of the dark—finding his way at night, never stumbling, able to read books by starlight; to read also, in faces and landscapes, traces and glimmers that others missed. Darkness was warmth and comfort to him.

A cave in Ephesus. In the Q'uran, Surah Al-Kahf. The sleepers waking after centuries, emerging into a changed world. Trying to spend old coins.

After the horror of his teen years, he'd found that dark was still a friend. Looking through the eyepiece of an observatory telescope, in the Himalayan foothills, in Uttar Pradesh. Describing the cluster of galaxies, one by one, to the astronomer. *You see the seventh? What eyes!*

Nothing moved but in his mind. Dreams of tenacity and complication. Baffling remnants, consciousness too weak to sort. Every unanswered question of his life, every casual observation, every bit of mental flotsam, tossed together in one desperate, implicit attempt at resolving them all. Things fell; he lunged to catch them. He stood on street corners in an endless night, searching for his shoes, his car, his keys, his wife. His mother chided him in a room lit by incandescent bulbs, dim and flickering like firelight. Galaxies in the eyepiece faded, and he looked up from the eyepiece to a blackened sky. He lay waking, in the dark, now aware of the dream state, returning with such huge reluctance to the life of the body, that weight immovable on its slab.

His eyelid was yanked open. A drop of fluid splashed there. A green line swept across his vision. He caught a breath and it burned in his lungs.

He was awake. Aboard *Gypsy*. It was bringing him back to life.

But I'm cold. Too cold to shiver. Getting colder as I wake up.

How hollow he felt. In this slight gravity. How unreal. It came to him, in the eclipsing of his dreams and the rising of his surroundings, that the gravity of Earth might be something more profound than the acceleration of a mass, the curvature of space-time. Was it not an emanation of the planet, a life force? All life on Earth evolved in it, rose from it, fought it every moment, lived and bred and died awash in it. Those tides swept through our cells, the force from Earth, and the gravity of the sun and the gravity of the moon. What was life out here, without that embrace, that permeation, that bondage? Without it, would they wither and die like plants in a shed?

The hollowness came singing, roaring, whining, crackling into his ears. Into his throat and and nose and eyes and skin it came as desiccation. Searing into his mouth. He needed to cough and he couldn't. His thorax spasmed.

There was an antiseptic moistness in his throat. It stung, but his muscles had loosened. He could breathe. Cold swept from his shoulders down through his torso and he began to shiver uncontrollably.

When he could, he raised a hand. He closed his eyes and held the hand afloat in the parodic gravity, thinking about it, how it felt, how far away it actually was. At last, with hesitation, his eyes opened and came to focus. An old man's hand, knobby, misshapen at the joints, the skin papery, sagging and hanging in folds. He couldn't close the fingers. How many years had he slept? He forced on his hand the imagination of a clenched fist. The hand didn't move.

Oh my god the pain.

Without which, no life. Pain too is an emanation of the planet, of the life force.

It sucked back like a wave, gathering for another concussion. He tried to sit up and passed out.

Nikos Kakopoulos was a short man, just over five feet, stocky but fit. The features of his face were fleshy, slightly comic. He was graying, balding, but not old. In his fifties. He smiled as he said he planned to be around a hundred years from now. His office was full of Mediterranean light. A large Modigliani covered one wall. His money came mostly from aquifer rights. He spent ten percent of it on charities. One such awarded science scholarships. Which is how he'd come to Roger's attention.

So you see, I am not such a bad guy,

Those foundations are just window dressing. What they once called greenwash.

Zia, said Roger.

Kakopoulos shrugged as if to say, Let him talk, I've heard it all. To Zia he said: They do some good after all. They're a comfort to millions of people.

Drinking water would be more of a comfort.

There isn't enough to go round. I didn't create that situation.

You exploit it.

So sorry to say this. Social justice and a civilized lifestyle can't be done both at once. Not for ten billion people. Not on this planet.

You've decided this.

It's a conclusion based on the evidence.

And you care about this why?

I'm Greek. We invented justice and civilization.

You're Cypriot. Also, the Chinese would argue that. The Persians. The Egyptians. Not to mention India.

Kakopoulos waved away the first objection and addressed the rest. Of course they would. And England, and Germany, and Italy, and Russia, and the US. They're arguing as we speak. Me, I'm not going to argue. I'm going to a safe place until the arguing is over. After that, if we're very lucky, we can have our discussion about civilization and justice.

On your terms.

On terms that might have some meaning.

What terms would those be?

World population under a billion, for starters. Kakopoulos reached across the table and popped an olive into his mouth.

How do you think that's going to happen? asked Zia.

It's happening. Just a matter of time. Since I don't know how much time, I want a safe house for the duration.

How are you going to get up there?

Kakopoulous grinned. When the Chinese acquired Lockheed, I picked up an X-33. It can do Mach 25. I have a spaceport on Naxos. Want a ride?

The VTOL craft looked like the tip of a Delta IV rocket, or of a penis: a blunt, rounded conic. Not unlike Kakopoulos himself. Some outsize Humpty Dumpty.

How do you know him? Zia asked Roger as they boarded.

I've been advising him.

You're advising the man who owns a third of the world's freshwater?

He owns a lot of things. My first concern is for our project. We need him.

What for?

Roger stared off into space.

He immiserates the Earth, Roger.

We all ten billion immiserate the Earth by being here.

Kakopoulos returned.

Make yourselves comfortable. Even at Mach 25, it takes some time.

It was night, and the Earth was below their window. Rivers of manmade light ran across it. Zia could see the orange squiggle of the India-Pakistan border, all three thousand floodlit kilometers of it. Then the ship banked and the window turned to the stars.

Being lord of the dark had a touch of clairvoyance in it. The dark seldom brought surprise to him. Something bulked out there and he felt it. Some gravity about it called to him from some future. Sun blazed forth behind the limb of the Earth, but the thing was still in Earth's shadow. It made a blackness against the Milky Way. Then sunlight touched it. Its lines caught light: the edges of panels, tanks, heat sinks, antennas. Blunt radar-shedding angles. A squat torus shape under it all. It didn't look like a ship. It looked like a squashed donut to which a junkyard had been glued. It turned slowly on its axis.

My safe house, said Kakopoulos.

It was, indeed, no larger than a house. About ten meters long, twice that across. It had cost a large part of Kakopoulos's considerable fortune. Which he recouped by manipulating and looting several central banks. As a result, a handful of small countries, some hundred million people, went off the cliff-edge of modernity into an abyss of debt peonage.

While they waited to dock with the thing, Kakopoulos came and sat next to Zia.

Listen, my friend—

I'm not your friend.

As you like, I don't care. I don't think you're stupid. When I said my foundations make people feel better, I meant the rich, of course. You're Pakistani?

Indian actually.

But Muslim. Kashmir?

Zia shrugged.

Okay. We're not so different, I think. I grew up in the slums of Athens after the euro collapsed. The histories, the videos, they don't capture it. I imagine Kashmir was much worse. But we each found a way out, no? So tell me, would you go back to that? No, you don't have to answer. You wouldn't. Not for anything. You'd sooner die. But you're not the kind of asshole who writes conscience checks. Or thinks your own self is wonderful enough to deserve anything. So where does that leave a guy like you in this world?

Fuck you.

Kakopoulos patted Zia's hand and smiled. I love it when people say fuck you to me. You know why? It means I won. They've got nothing left but their fuck you. He got up and went away.

The pilot came in then, swamp-walking the zero g in his velcro shoes, and said they'd docked.

The ship massed about a hundred metric tons. A corridor circled the inner circumference, floor against the outer hull, most of the space taken up by hibernation slabs for a crew of twenty. Once commissioned, it would spin on its axis a few times a minute to create something like lunar gravity. They drifted around it slowly, pulling themselves by handholds.

This, Kakopoulos banged a wall, is expensive. Exotic composites, all that aerogel. Why so much insulation?

Roger let "expensive" pass unchallenged. Zia didn't.

You think there's nothing more important than money.

Kakopoulos turned, as if surprised Zia was still there. He said, There are many things more important than money. You just don't get any of them without it.

Roger said, Even while you're hibernating, the ship will radiate infrared. That's one reason you'll park at a Lagrange point, far enough away not to attract attention. When you wake up and start using energy, you're going to light up like a Christmas tree. And you're going to hope that whatever is left on Earth or in space won't immediately blow you out of the sky. The insulation will hide you somewhat.

At one end of the cramped command center was a micro-apartment.

What's this, Nikos?

Ah, my few luxuries. Music, movies, artworks. We may be out here awhile after we wake up. Look at my kitchen.

A range?

Propane, but it generates 30,000 BTU!

That's insane. You're not on holiday here.

Look, it's vented, only one burner, I got a great engineer, you can examine the plans—

Get rid of it.

What! Kakopoulos yelled. Whose ship is this!

Roger pretended to think for a second. Do you mean who owns it, or who designed it?

Do you know how much it cost to get that range up here?

I can guess to the nearest million.

When I wake up I want a good breakfast!

When you wake up you'll be too weak to stand. Your first meal will be coming down tubes.

Kakopoulos appeared to sulk.

Nikos, what is your design specification here?

I just want a decent omelette.

I can make that happen. But the range goes.

Kakopoulous nursed his sulk, then brightened. Gonna be some meteor, that range. I'll call my observatory, have them image it.

Later, when they were alone, Zia said: All right, Roger. I've been very patient.

Patient? Roger snorted.

How can that little pustule help us?

That's our ship. We're going to steal it.

Later, Zia suggested that they christen the ship the Fuck You.

Eighty years later, Zia was eating one of Kakopoulos's omelettes. Freeze-dried egg, mushrooms, onion, tarragon. Microwaved with two ounces of water. Not bad. He had another.

Mach 900, asshole, he said aloud.

Most of the crew were dead. Fungus had grown on the skin stretched like drums over their skulls, their ribs, their hips.

He'd seen worse. During his mandatory service, as a teenager in the military, he'd patrolled Deccan slums. He'd seen parents eating their dead children. Pariah dogs fat as sheep roamed the streets. Cadavers, bones, skulls, were piled in front of nearly every house. The cloying carrion smell never lifted. Hollowed-out buildings housed squatters and corpses equally, darkened plains of them below fortified bunkers lit like Las Vegas, where the driving bass of party music echoed the percussion of automatic weapons and rocket grenades.

Now his stomach rebelled, but he commanded it to be still as he swallowed some olive oil. Gradually the chill in his core subsided.

He needed to look at the sky. The ship had two telescopes: a one-meter honeycomb mirror for detail work and a wide-angle high-res CCD camera. Zoomed fully out, the camera took in about eighty degrees. Ahead was the blazing pair of Alpha Centauri A and B, to the eye more than stars but not yet suns. He'd never seen anything like them. Brighter than Venus, bright as the full moon, but such tiny disks. As he watched, the angle of them moved against the ship's rotation.

He swept the sky, looking for landmarks. But the stars were wrong. What had happened to Orion? Mintaka had moved. The belt didn't point to Sirius, as it should. A brilliant blue star off Orion's left shoulder outshone Betelgeuse, and then he realized. *That* was Sirius. Thirty degrees from where it should be. Of course: it was eight light-years from Earth. They had come half that distance, and, like a nearby buoy seen against a far shore, it had changed position against the farther stars.

More distant stars had also shifted, but not as much. He turned to what he still absurdly thought of as "north." The Big Dipper was there. The Little Dipper's bowl was squashed. Past Polaris was Cassiopeia, the zigzag W, the queen's throne. And there a new, bright star blazed above it, as if that W had grown another zag. Could it be a nova? He stared, and the stars of Cassiopeia circled this strange bright one slowly as the ship rotated. Then he knew: the strange star was Sol. Our Sun.

That was when he felt it, in his body: they were really here.

From the beginning Roger had a hand—a heavy, guiding hand—in the design of the ship. Not for nothing had he learned the Lab's doctrine of dual use. Not for nothing had he cultivated Kakopoulos's acquaintance. Every feature that fitted the ship for interstellar space was a plausible choice for Kak's purpose: hibernators, cosmic-ray shielding, nuclear rocket, hardened computers, plutonium pile and Stirling engine.

In the weeks prior to departure, they moved the ship to a more distant orbit, too distant for Kak's X-33 to reach. There they jettisoned quite a bit of the ship's interior. They added their fusion engine, surrounded the vessel with fuel sleds, secured antiproton traps, stowed the magsail, loaded the seed bank and a hundred other things.

They were three hundred AU out from Alpha Centauri. Velocity was one-thousandth c. The magsail was programmed to run for two more years, slowing them by half again. But lately their deceleration had shown variance. The magsail was running at higher current than planned. Very close to max spec. That wasn't good. Logs told him why, and that was worse.

He considered options, none good. The sail was braking against the interstellar medium, stray neutral atoms of hydrogen. No one knew for sure how it would behave once it ran into Alpha's charged solar wind. Nor just where that wind started.

The interstellar medium might already be giving way to it. If so, the count of galactic cosmic rays would be going down and the temperature of charged particles going up.

He checked. Definitely maybe on both counts.

He'd never liked this plan, its narrow margins of error. Not that he had a better one. That was the whole problem: no plan B. Every intricate, fragile, untried part of it had to work. He'd pushed pretty hard for a decent margin of error in this deceleration stage and the subsequent maneuvering in the system—what a tragedy it would be to come to grief so close, within sight of shore—and now he saw that margin evaporating.

Possibly the sail would continue to brake in the solar wind. If only they could have tested it first.

Zia didn't trust materials. Or, rather: he trusted them to fail. Superconductors, carbon composite, silicon, the human body. Problem was, you never knew just how or when they'd fail.

One theory said that a hydrogen wall existed somewhere between the termination shock and the heliopause, where solar wind gave way to interstellar space. Three hundred AU put *Gypsy* in that dicey zone.

It would be prudent to back off the magsail current. That would lessen their decel, and they needed all they could get, they had started it too late, but they also needed to protect the sail and run it as long as possible.

Any change to the current had to happen slowly. It would take hours or possibly days. The trick was not to deform the coil too much in the process, or create eddy currents that could quench the superconducting field.

The amount of power he had available was another issue. The plutonium running the Stirling engine had decayed to about half its original capacity.

He shut down heat in the cabin to divert more to the Stirling engine. He turned down most of the LED lighting, and worked in the semidark, except for the glow of the monitor. Programmed a gentle ramp up in current.

Then he couldn't keep his eyes open.

At Davos, he found himself talking to an old college roommate. Carter Hall III was his name; he was something with the UN now, and with the Council for Foreign Relations—an enlightened and condescending asshole. They were both Harvard '32, but Hall remained a self-appointed Brahmin, generously, sincerely, and with vast but guarded amusement, guiding a Sudra through the world that was his by birthright. Never mind the Sudra was Muslim.

From a carpeted terrace they overlooked a groomed green park. There was no snow in town this January, an increasingly common state of affairs. Zia noted but politely declined to point out the obvious irony, the connection between the policies determined here and the retreat of the snow line.

Why Zia was there was complicated. He was persona non grata with the ruling party, but he was a scientist, he had security clearances, and he had access to diplomats on both sides of the border. India had secretly built many thousands of microfusion weapons and denied it. The US was about to enter into the newest round of endless talks over "nonproliferation," in which the US never gave up anything but insisted that other nations must.

Hall now lectured him. India needed to rein in its population, which was over two billion. The US had half a billion.

Zia, please, look at the numbers. Four-plus children per household just isn't sustainable.

Abruptly Zia felt his manners fail.

Sustainable? Excuse me. Our Indian culture is four thousand years old, self-sustained through all that time. Yours is two, three, maybe five hundred years old, depending on your measure. And in that short time, not only is it falling apart, it's taking the rest of the world down with it, including my homeland.

Two hundred years, I don't get that, if you mean Western—

I mean technology, I mean capital, I mean extraction.

Well, but those are very, I mean if you look at your, your four thousand years of, of poverty and class discrimination, and violence—

Ah? And there is no poverty or violence in your brief and perfect history? No extermination? No slavery?

Hall's expression didn't change much.

We've gotten past all that, Zia. We—

Zia didn't care that Hall was offended. He went on:

The story of resource extraction has only two cases, okay? In the first case, the extractors arrive and make the local ruler an offer. Being selfish, he takes it and he becomes rich—never so rich as the extractors, but compared to his people, fabulously, delusionally rich. His people become the cheap labor used to extract the resource. This leads to social upheaval. Villages are moved, families destroyed. A few people are enriched, the majority are ruined. Maybe there is an uprising against the ruler.

In the second case the ruler is smarter. Maybe he's seen some neighboring ruler's head on a pike. He says no thanks to the extractors. To this they have various responses: make him a better offer, find a greedier rival, hire an assassin, or bring in the gunships. But in the end it's the same: a few people are enriched, most are ruined. What the extractors never, ever do in any case, in all your history, is take no for an answer.

Zia, much as I enjoy our historical discussions—

Ah, you see? And there it is—your refusal to take no. Talk is done, now we move forward with your agenda.

We have to deal with the facts on the ground. Where we are now.

Yes, of course. It's remarkable how, when the mess you've made has grown so large that even you must admit to it, you want to reset everything to zero. You want to get past "all that." All of history starts over, with these "facts on the ground". Let's move on, move forward, forget how we got here, forget the exploitation and the theft and the waste and the betrayals. Forget the, what is that charming accounting word, the externalities. Start from the new zero.

Hall looked weary and annoyed that he was called upon to suffer such childishness. That well-fed yet kept-fit form hunched, that pale skin looked suddenly papery and aged in the Davos sunlight.

You know, Zia prodded, greed could at least be more efficient. If you know what you want, at least take it cleanly. No need to leave whole countries in ruins.

Hall smiled a tight, grim smile, just a glimpse of the wolf beneath. He said: Then it wouldn't be greed. Greed never knows what it wants.

That was the exact measure of Hall's friendship, to say that to Zia. But then Zia knew what he wanted: out.

As he drifted awake, he realized that, decades past, the ship would have collected data on the Sun's own heliopause on their way out. If he could access that data, maybe he could learn whether the hydrogen wall was a real thing. What effect it might—

There was a loud bang. The monitor and the cabin went dark. His mind reached into the outer darkness and it sensed something long and loose and broken trailing behind them.

What light there was came back on. The computer rebooted. The monitor displayed readings for the magsail over the past hour: current ramping up, then oscillating to compensate for varying densities in the medium, then a sharp spike. And then zero. Quenched.

Hydrogen wall? He didn't know. The magsail was fried. He tried for an hour more to get it to accept current. No luck. He remembered with some distaste the EVA suit. He didn't want to go outside, to tempt that darkness, but he might have to, so he walked forward to check it out.

The suit wasn't in its cubby. Zia turned and walked up the corridor, glancing at his torpid crewmates. The last slab was empty.

Sergei was gone. The suit was gone. You would assume they'd gone together, but that wasn't in the logs. *I may be some time.* Sergei didn't strike him as the type to take a last walk in the dark. And for that he wouldn't have needed the suit. Still. You can't guess what anyone might do.

So that was final: no EVA: the magsail couldn't be fixed. From the console, he cut it loose.

They were going far too fast. Twice what they'd planned. Now they had only the nuclear plasma rocket for deceleration, and one fuel tank was empty, somehow. Even though the fuel remaining outmassed the ship, it wasn't enough. If they couldn't slow below the escape velocity of the system, they'd shoot right through and out the other side.

The ship had been gathering data for months and had good orbital elements for the entire system. Around A were four planets, none in a position to assist with flybys. Even if they were, their masses would be little help. Only the two stars were usable.

If he brought them in a lot closer around B—how close could they get? one fiftieth AU? one hundredth?—and if the heat shield held—it should withstand 2500 Celsius for a few hours—the ship could be slowed more with the same amount of fuel. The B star was closest: it was the less luminous of the pair, cooler, allowing them to get in closer, shed more speed. Then repeat the maneuver at A.

There was a further problem. Twelve years ago, as per the original plan, Alpha A and B were at their closest to one another: 11 AU. The stars were now twenty AU apart and widening. So the trip from B to A would take twice as long. And systems were failing. They were out on the rising edge of the bathtub curve.

Power continued erratic. The computer crashed again and again as he worked out the trajectories. He took to writing down intermediate results on paper in case he lost a session, cursing as he did so. Materials. We stole our tech from the most corrupt forces on Earth. Dude, you want an extended warranty with that? He examined the Stirling engine, saw that the power surge had compromised it. He switched the pile over to backup thermocouples. That took hours to do and it was less efficient, but it kept the computer running. It was still frustrating. The computer was designed to be redundant, hardened, hence slow. Minimal graphics, no 3D holobox. He had to think through his starting parameters carefully before he wasted processor time running a simulation.

Finally he had a new trajectory, swinging in perilously close to B, then A. It might work. Next he calculated that, when he did what he was about to do, seventy kilometers of magsail cable wouldn't catch them up and foul them. Then he fired the maneuvering thrusters.

What sold him, finally, was a handful of photons.

This is highly classified, said Roger. He held a manila file folder containing paper. Any computer file was permeable, hackable. Paper was serious.

The data were gathered by an orbiting telescope. It wasn't a photograph. It was a blurred, noisy image that looked like rings intersecting in a pond a few seconds after some pebbles had been thrown.

It's a deconvolved cross-correlation map of a signal gathered by a chopped pair of Bracewell baselines. You know how that works?

He didn't. Roger explained. Any habitable planet around Alpha Centauri A or B would appear a small fraction of an arc-second away from the stars, and would be at least twenty-two magnitudes fainter. At that separation, the most sensitive camera made, with the best dynamic range, couldn't hope to find the planet in the stars' glare. But put several cameras together in a particular phase relation and the stars' light could be nulled out. What remained, if anything, would be light from another source. A planet, perhaps.

Also this, in visible light.

An elliptical iris of grainy red, black at its center, where an occulter had physically blocked the stars' disks.

Coronagraph, said Roger. Here's the detail.

A speck, a single pixel, slightly brighter than the enveloping noise.

What do you think?

Could be anything. Dust, hot pixel, cosmic ray . . .

It shows up repeatedly. And it moves.

Roger, for all I know you photoshopped it in.

He looked honestly shocked. Do you really think I'd . . .

I'm kidding. But where did you get these? Can you trust the source?

Why would anyone fake such a thing?

The question hung and around it gathered, like sepsis, the suspicion of some agency setting them up, of some agenda beyond their knowing. After the Kepler exoplanet finder went dark, subsequent exoplanet data—like all other government-sponsored scientific work—were classified. Roger's clearance was pretty high, but even he couldn't be sure of his sources.

You're not convinced, are you.

But somehow Zia was. The orbiting telescope had an aperture of, he forgot the final number, it had been scaled down several times owing to budget cuts. A couple of meters, maybe. That meant light from this far-off dim planet fell on it at a rate of just a few photons per second. It made him unutterably lonely to think of those photons traveling so far. It also made him believe in the planet.

Well, okay, Roger Fry was mad. Zia knew that. But he would throw in with Roger because all humanity was mad. Perhaps always had been. Certainly for the past century-plus, with the monoculture madness called modernity. Roger at least was mad in a different way, perhaps Zia's way.

He wrote the details into the log, reduced the orbital mechanics to a cookbook formula. Another steward would have to be awakened when they reached the B star; that would be in five years; his calculations weren't good enough to automate the burn time, which would depend on the ship's precise momentum and distance from the star as it rounded. It wasn't enough just to slow down; their exit trajectory from B needed to point them exactly to where A would be a year later. That wouldn't be easy; he took a couple of days to write an app to make it easier, but with large blocks of memory failing in the computer, Sophie's idea of a handwritten logbook no longer looked so dumb.

As he copied it all out, he imagined the world they'd left so far behind: the billions in their innocence or willed ignorance or complicity, the elites he'd despised for their lack of imagination, their surfeit of hubris, working together in a horrible *folie à deux.* He saw the bombs raining down, atomizing history and memory and accomplishment, working methodically backwards from the cities to the cradles of civilization to the birthplaces of the species—the Fertile Crescent, the Horn of Africa, the Great Rift Valley—in a crescendo of destruction and denial of everything humanity had ever been—its failures, its cruelties, its grandeurs, its aspirations— all extirpated to the root, in a fury of self-loathing that fed on what it destroyed.

Zia's anger rose again in his ruined, aching body—his lifelong pointless rage at all that stupidity, cupidity, yes, there's some hollow satisfaction being away from all that. Away from the noise of their being. Their unceasing commotion of disruption and corruption. How he'd longed to escape it. But in the silent enclosure of the ship, in this empty house populated by the stilled ghosts of his crewmates, he now longed for any sound, any noise. He had wanted to be here, out in the dark. But not for nothing. And he wept.

And then he was just weary. His job was done. Existence seemed a pointless series of problems. What was identity? Better never to have been. He shut his eyes.

In bed with Maria, she moved in her sleep, rolled against him, and he rolled away. She twitched and woke from some dream.

What! What! she cried.

He flinched. His heart moved, but he lay still, letting her calm. Finally he said, What was that?

You pulled away from me!

Then they were in a park somewhere. Boston? Maria was yelling at him, in tears. Why must you be so negative!

He had no answer for her, then or now. Or for himself. Whatever "himself" might be. Something had eluded him in his life, and he wasn't going to find it now.

He wondered again about what had happened to Sergei. Well, it was still an option for him. He wouldn't need a suit.

Funny, isn't it, how one's human sympathy—Zia meant most severely his own—extends about as far as those like oneself. He meant true sympathy; abstractions like justice don't count. Even now, missing Earth, he felt sympathy only for those aboard *Gypsy*, those orphaned, damaged, disaffected, dispossessed, Aspergerish souls whose anger at that great abstraction, The World, was more truly an anger at all those fortunate enough to be unlike them. We were all so young. How can you be so young, and so hungry for, and yet so empty of life?

As he closed his log, he hit on a final option for the ship, if not himself. If after rounding B and A the ship still runs too fast to aerobrake into orbit around the planet, do this. Load all the genetic material—the frozen zygotes, the seed bank, the whatever—into a heatshielded pod. Drop it into the planet's atmosphere. If not themselves, some kind of life would have some chance. Yet as soon as he wrote those words, he felt their sting.

Roger, and to some degree all of them, had seen this as a way to transcend their thwarted lives on Earth. They were the essence of striving humanity: their planning and foresight served the animal's desperate drive to overcome what can't be overcome. To escape the limits of death. Yet transcendence, if it meant anything at all, was the accommodation to limits: a finding of freedom within them, not a breaking of them. Depositing the proteins of life here, like a stiff prick dropping its load, could only, in the best case, lead to a replication of the same futile striving. The animal remains trapped in the cage of its being.

5.

An old, old man in a wheelchair. Tube in his nose. Oxygen bottle on a cart. He'd been somebody at the Lab once. Recruited Roger, among many others, plucked him out of the pack at Caltech. Roger loathed the old man but figured he owed him. And was owed.

They sat on a long, covered porch looking out at hills of dry grass patched with dark stands of live oak. The old man was feeling pretty spry after he'd thumbed through Roger's papers and lit the cigar Roger offered him. He detached the tube, took a discreet puff, exhaled very slowly, and put the tube back in.

Hand it to you, Roger, most elaborate, expensive form of mass suicide in history.

Really? I'd give that honor to the so-called statecraft of the past century.

Wouldn't disagree. But that's been very good to you and me. That stupidity gradient.

This effort is modest by comparison. Very few lives are at stake here. They might even survive it.

How many bombs you got onboard this thing? How many megatons?

They're not bombs, they're fuel. We measure it in exajoules.

Gonna blow them up in a magnetic pinch, aren't you? I call things that blow up bombs. But fine, measure it in horsepower if it makes you feel virtuous. Exajoules, huh? He stared into space for a minute. Ship's mass?

One hundred metric tons dry.

That's nice and light. Wonder where you got ahold of that. But you still don't have enough push. Take you over a hundred years. Your systems'll die.

Seventy-two years.

You done survival analysis? You get a bathtub curve with most of these systems. Funny thing is, redundancy works against you.

How so?

Shit, you got Sidney Lefebvre down the hall from you, world's expert in failure modes, don't you know that?

Roger knew the name. The man worked on something completely different now. Somehow this expertise had been erased from his resume and his working life.

How you gone slow down?

Magsail.

I always wondered, would that work.

You wrote the papers on it.

You know how hand-wavy they are. We don't know squat about the interstellar medium. And we don't have superconductors that good anyway. Or do we?

Roger didn't answer.

What happens when you get into the system?

That's what I want to know. Will the magsail work in the solar wind? Tarasenko says no.

Fuck him.

His math is sound. I want to know what you know. Does it work?

How would I know. Never got to test it. Never heard of anyone who did.

Tell me, Dan.

Tell you I don't know. Tarasenko's a crank, got a Ukraine-sized chip on his shoulder. That doesn't mean he's wrong.

The old man shrugged, looked critically at the cigar, tapped the ash off its end.

Don't hold out on me.

Christ on a crutch, Roger, I'm a dead man. Want me to spill my guts, be nice, bring me a Havana.

There was a spell of silence. In the sunstruck sky a turkey vulture wobbled and banked into an updraft.

How you gone build a magsail that big? You got some superconductor scam goin?

After ten years of braking we come in on this star, through its heliopause, at about 500 kilometers per second. That's too fast to be captured by the system's gravity.

Cause I can help you there. Got some yttrium futures.

If we don't manage enough decel after that, we're done.

Gas-core reactor rocket.

We can't carry enough fuel. Do the math. Specific impulse is about three thousand at best.

The old man took the tube from his nose, tapped more ash off the cigar, inhaled. After a moment he began to cough. Roger had seen this act before. But it went on longer than usual, into a loud climax.

Roger . . . you really doin this? Wouldn't fool a dead man?

I'm modeling. For a multiplayer game.

That brought the old man more than half back. Fuck you too, he said. But that was for any surveillance, Roger thought.

The old man stared into the distance, then said: Oberth effect.

What's that?

Here's what you do, the old man whispered, hunched over, as he brought out a pen and an envelope.

ROSA (2125)

After she'd suffered through the cold, the numbness, the chills, the burning, still she lay, unready to move, as if she weren't whole, had lost some essence—her anima, her purpose. She went over the whole mission in her mind, step by step, piece by piece. Do we have everything? The bombs to get us out of the solar system, the sail to slow us down, the nuclear rocket, the habitat . . . what else? What have we forgotten? There is something in the dark.

What is in the dark? Another ship? Oh my God. If we did it, they could do it, too. It would be insane for them to come after us. But they are insane. And we stole their bombs. What would they *not* do to us? Insane and vengeful as they are. They could send a drone after us, unmanned, or manned by a suicide crew. It's just what they would do.

She breathed the stale, cold air and stared up at the dark ceiling. Okay, relax. That's the worst-case scenario. Best case, they never saw us go. Most likely, they saw but they have other priorities. Everything has worked so far. Or you would not be lying here fretting, Rosa.

Born Rose. Mamá was from Trinidad. Dad was Venezuelan. She called him Papá against his wishes. Solid citizens, assimilated: a banker, a realtor. Home was Altadena, California. There was a bit of Irish blood and more than a dollop of Romany, the renegade uncle Tonio told Rosa, mi mestiza.

They flipped when she joined a chapter of La Raza Nueva. Dad railed: A terrorist organization! And us born in countries we've occupied! Amazed that Caltech even permitted LRN on campus. The family got visits from Homeland Security. Eggs and paint bombs from the neighbors. Caltech looked into it and found that of its seven members, five weren't students. LRN was a creation of Homeland Security. Rosa and Sean were the only two authentic members, and they kept bailing out of planned actions.

Her father came to her while Homeland Security was on top of them, in the dark of her bedroom. He sat on the edge of the bed, she could feel his weight there and the displacement of it, could smell faintly the alcohol on his breath. He said: My mother and my father, my sisters, after the invasion, we lived in cardboard refrigerator boxes in the median strip of the main road from the airport to the city. For a year.

He'd never told her that. She hated him. For sparing her that, only to use it on her now. She'd known he'd grown up poor, but not that. She said bitterly: Behind every fortune is a crime. What's yours?

He drew in his breath. She felt him recoil, the mattress shift under his weight. Then a greater shift, unfelt, of some dark energy, and he sighed. I won't deny it, but it was for family. For you! with sudden anger.

What did you do?

That I won't tell you. It's not safe.

Safe! You always want to be safe, when you should stand up!

Stand up? I did the hardest things possible for a man to do. For you, for this family. And now you put us all at risk—. His voice came close to breaking.

When he spoke again, there was no trace of anger left. You don't know how easily it can all be taken from you. What a luxury it is to stand up, as you call it.

Homeland Security backed off when Caltech raised a legal stink about entrapment. She felt vindicated. But her father didn't see it that way. The dumb luck, he called it, of a small fish. Stubborn in his way as she.

Sean, her lovely brother, who'd taken her side through all this, decided to stand up in his own perverse way: he joined the Army. She thought it was dumb, but she had to respect his argument: it was unjust that only poor Latinos joined. Certainly Papá, the patriot, couldn't argue with that logic, though he was furious.

Six months later Sean was killed in Bolivia. Mamá went into a prolonged, withdrawn mourning. Papá stifled an inchoate rage.

She'd met Roger Fry when he taught her senior course in particle physics; as "associated faculty" he became her thesis advisor. He looked as young as she. Actually, he was four years older. Women still weren't exactly welcome in high-energy physics. Rosa—not cute, not demure, not quiet—was even less so. Roger, however, didn't seem to see her. Gender and appearance seemed to make no impression at all on Roger.

He moved north mid-semester to work at the Lab but continued advising her via e-mail. In grad school she followed his name on papers, R. A. Fry, as it moved up from the tail of a list of some dozen names to the head of such lists. "Physics of milli-K Antiproton Confinement in an Improved Penning Trap." "Antiprotons as Drivers for Inertial Confinement Fusion." "Typical Number of Antiprotons Necessary for Fast Ignition in LiDT." "Antiproton-Catalyzed Microfusion." And finally, "Antimatter Induced Continuous Fusion Reactions and Thermonuclear Explosions."

Rosa applied to work at the Lab.

She didn't stop to think, then, why she did it. It was because Roger, of all the people she knew, appeared to have stood up and gone his own way and had arrived somewhere worth going.

They were supposed to have landed on the planet twelve years ago.

Nothing was out there in the dark. Nothing had followed. They were alone. That was worse.

She weighed herself. Four kilos. That would be forty in Earth gravity. Looked down at her arms, her legs, her slack breasts and belly. Skin gray and loose and wrinkled and hanging. On Earth she'd been chunky, glossy as an apple, never under sixty kilos. Her body had been taken from her, and this wasted, frail thing put in its place.

Turning on the monitor's camera she had another shock. She was older than her mother. When they'd left Earth, Mamá was fifty. Rosa was at least sixty, by the look of it. They weren't supposed to have aged. Not like this.

She breathed and told herself it was luxury to be alive.

Small parts of the core group met face to face on rare occasions. Never all at once—they were too dispersed for that and even with travel permits it was unwise—it was threes or fours or fives at most. There was no such thing as a secure location. They had to rely on the ubiquity of surveillance outrunning the ability to process it all.

The Berkeley marina was no more secure than anywhere else. Despite the city's Potemkin liberalism, you could count, if you were looking, at least ten cameras from every point within its boundaries, and take for granted there were many more, hidden or winged, small and quick as hummingbirds, with software to read your lips from a hundred yards, and up beyond the atmosphere satellites to read the book in your hand if the air was steady, denoise it if not, likewise take your body temperature. At the marina the strong onshore flow from the cold Pacific made certain of these feats more difficult, but the marina's main advantage was that it was still beautiful, protected by accumulated capital and privilege—though now the names on the yachts were mostly in hanzi characters—and near enough to places where many of them worked, yet within the tether of their freedom—so they came to this rendezvous as often as they dared.

I remember the old marina. See where University Avenue runs into the water? It was half a mile past that. At neap tide you sometimes see it surface. Plenty chop there when it's windy.

They debated what to call this mad thing. Names out of the history of the idea—starships that had been planned but never built—Orion, Prometheus, Daedalus, Icarus, Longshot, Medusa. Names out of their imagination: Persephone, Finnegan, Ephesus. But finally they came to call it—not yet the ship, but themselves, and their being together in it—Gypsy. It was a word rude and available and they took it. They were going wandering, without a land, orphaned and dispossessed, they were gypping the rubes, the hateful inhumane ones who owned everything and out of the devilry of ownership would destroy it rather than share it. She was okay with that taking, she was definitely gypsy.

She slept with Roger. She didn't love him, but she admired him as a fellow spirit. Admired his intellect and his commitment and his belief. Wanted to partake of him and share herself. The way he had worked on fusion, and solved it. And then, when it was taken from him, he found something else. Something mad, bold, bad, dangerous, inspiring.

Roger's voice in the dark: I thought it was the leaders, the nations, the corporations, the elites, who were out of touch, who didn't understand the gravity of our situation. I believed in the sincerity of their stupid denials—of global warming, of resource depletion, of nuclear proliferation, of population pressure. I thought them stupid. But if you judge them by their actions instead of their rhetoric, you can see that they understood it perfectly and accepted the gravity of it very early. They simply gave it up as unfixable. Concluded that law and democracy and civilization were hindrances to their continued power. Moved quite purposely and at speed toward this dire world they foresaw, a world in which, to have the amenities even of a middle-class life—things like clean water, food, shelter, energy, transportation, medical care—you would need the wealth of a prince. You would need legal and military force to keep desperate others from seizing it. Seeing that, they moved to amass such wealth for themselves as quickly and ruthlessly as possible, with the full understanding that it hastened the day they feared.

She sat at the desk with the monitors, reviewed the logs. Zia had been the last to waken. Four and a half years ago. Trouble with the magsail. It was gone, and their incoming velocity was too high. And they were very close now, following his trajectory to the B star. She looked at his calculations and thought that he'd done well; it might work. What she had to do: fine-tune the elements of the trajectory, deploy the sunshield, prime the fuel, and finally light the hydrogen torch that would push palely back against the fury of this sun. But not yet. She was too weak.

Zia was dead for sure, on his slab, shriveled like a nut in the bodysuit; he had gone back into hibernation but had not reattached his stents. The others didn't look good. Fang's log told that story, what she'd done to combat the fungus, what else might need to be done, what to look out for. Fang had done the best she could. Rosa, at least, was alive.

A surge of grief hit her suddenly, bewildered her. She hadn't realized it till now: she had a narrative about all this. She was going to a new world and she was going to bear children in it. That was never a narrative she thought was hers; hers was all about standing up for herself. But there it was, and as the possibility of it vanished, she felt its teeth. The woman she saw in the monitor-mirror was never going to have children. A further truth rushed upon her as implacable as the star ahead: the universe didn't have that narrative, or any narrative, and all of hers had been voided in its indifference. What loss she felt. And for what, a story? For something that never was?

Lying next to her in the dark, Roger said: I would never have children. I would never do that to another person.

You already have, Rosa poked him.

You know what I mean.

The universe is vast, Roger.

I know.

The universe of feeling is vast.

No children.

I could make you change your mind.

She'd left Roger behind on Earth. No regrets about that; clearly there was no place for another person on the inside of Roger's life.

The hydrogen in the tanks around the ship thawed as they drew near the sun. One tank read empty. She surmised from logs that it had been breached very early in the voyage. So they had to marshal fuel even more closely.

The orbital elements had been refined since Zia first set up the parameters of his elegant cushion shot. It wasn't Rosa's field, but she had enough math and computer tools to handle it. Another adjustment would have to be made in a year when they neared the A star, but she'd point them as close as she could.

It was going to be a near thing. There was a demanding trade-off between decel and trajectory; they had to complete their braking turn pointed exactly at where A would be in a year. Too much or too little and they'd miss it; they didn't have enough fuel to make course corrections. She ran Zia's app over and over, timing the burn.

Occasionally she looked at the planet through the telescope. Still too far away to see much. It was like a moon of Jupiter seen from Earth. Little more than a dot without color, hiding in the glare of A.

It took most of a week to prep the rocket. She triple-checked every step. It was supposed to be Sergei's job. Only Sergei was not on the ship. He'd left no log. She had no idea what had happened, but now it was her job to start up a twenty-gigawatt gas-core fission reactor. The reactor would irradiate and superheat their hydrogen fuel, which would exit the nozzle with a thrust of some two million newtons.

She fired the attitude thrusters to derotate the ship, fixing it in the shadow of the sunshield. As the spin stopped, so did gravity; she became weightless.

Over the next two days, the thermal sensors climbed steadily to 1000 Celsius, 1200, 1500. Nothing within the ship changed. It remained dark and cool and silent and weightless. On the far side of the shield, twelve centimeters thick, megawatts of thermal energy pounded, but no more than a hundred watts reached the ship. They fell toward the star and she watched the outer temperature rise to 2000.

Now, as the ship made its closest approach, the rocket came on line. It was astounding. The force pulled her out of the chair, hard into the crawlspace beneath the bolted desk. Her legs were pinned by her sudden body weight, knees twisted in a bad way. The pain increased as g-forces grew. She reached backwards, up, away from this new gravity, which was orthogonal to the floor. She clutched the chair legs above her and pulled until her left foot was freed from her weight, and then fell back against the bay of the desk, curled in a fetal position, exhausted. A full g, she guessed. Which her body had not experienced for eighty-four years. It felt like much more. Her heart labored. It was hard to breathe. Idiot! Not to think of this. She clutched the chair by its legs. Trapped here, unable to move or see while the engine thundered.

She hoped it didn't matter. The ship would run at full reverse thrust for exactly the time needed to bend their trajectory toward the farther sun, its nuclear flame burning in front of them, a venomous, roiling torrent of plasma and neutrons spewing from the center of the torus, and all this fury not even a spark to show against the huge sun that smote their carbon shield with its avalanche of light. The ship vibrated continuously with the rocket's thunder. Periodic concussions from she knew not what shocked her.

Two hours passed. As they turned, attitude thrusters kept them in the shield's shadow. If it failed, there would be a quick hot end to a long cold voyage.

An alert whined. That meant shield temperature had passed 2500. She counted seconds. The hull boomed and she lost count and started again. When she reached a thousand she stopped. Some time later the whining ceased. The concussions grew less frequent. The temperature was falling. They were around.

Another thirty minutes and the engines died. Their thunder and their weight abruptly shut off. She was afloat in silence. She trembled in her sweat. Her left foot throbbed.

They'd halved their speed. As they flew on, the sun's pull from behind would slow them more, taking away the acceleration it had added to their approach. That much would be regained as they fell toward the A star over the next year.

She slept in the weightlessness for several hours. At last she spun the ship back up to one-tenth g and took stock. Even in the slight gravity her foot and ankle were painful. She might have broken bones. Nothing she could do about it.

Most of their fuel was spent. At least one of the hydrogen tanks had suffered boil-off. She was unwilling to calculate whether enough remained for the second maneuver. It wasn't her job. She was done. She wrote her log. The modified hibernation drugs were already in her system, prepping her for a final year of sleep she might not wake from. But what was the alternative?

It hit her then: eighty-four years had passed since she climbed aboard this ship. Mamá and Papá were dead. Roger too. Unless perhaps Roger had been wrong and the great genius of humanity was to evade the ruin it always seemed about to bring upon itself. Unless humanity had emerged into some unlikely golden age of peace, longevity, forgiveness. And they, these Gypsies and their certainty, were outcast from it. But that was another narrative, and she couldn't bring herself to believe it.

6.

They'd never debated what they'd do when they landed.

The ship would jettison everything that had equipped it for interstellar travel and aerobrake into orbit. That might take thirty or forty glancing passes through the atmosphere, to slow them enough for a final descent, while cameras surveyed for a landing site. Criteria, insofar as possible: easy terrain, temperate zone, near water, arable land.

It was fruitless to plan the details of in-situ resource use while the site was unknown. But it would have to be Earth-like because they didn't have resources for terraforming more than the immediate neighborhood. All told, there was fifty tons of stuff in the storage bay—prefab habitats made for Mars, solar panels, fuel cells, bacterial cultures, seed bank, 3D printers, genetic tools, nanotech, recyclers—all meant to jump-start a colony. There was enough in the way of food and water to support a crew of sixteen for six months. If they hadn't become self-sufficient by then, it was over.

They hadn't debated options because they weren't going to have any. This part of it—even assuming the planet were hospitable enough to let them set up in the first place—would be a lot harder than the voyage. It didn't bear discussion.

SOPHIE (2126)

Waking. Again? Trying to rise up out of that dream of sinking back into the dream of rising up out of the . . . Momma? All that okay.

Soph? Upsa daise. Пойдем. Allons.

Sergei?

She was sitting on the cold, hard deck, gasping for breath.

Good girl, Soph. Get up, sit to console, bring spectroscope online. What we got? Soph! Stay with!

She sat at the console. The screen showed dimly, through blurs and maculae that she couldn't blink away, a stranger's face: ruined, wrinkled, sagging, eyes milky, strands of lank white hair falling from a sored scalp. With swollen knuckles and gnarled fingers slow and painful under loose sheaths of skin, she explored hard lumps in the sinews of her neck, in her breasts, under her skeletal arms. It hurt to swallow. Or not to.

The antisenescents hadn't worked. They'd known this was possible. But she'd been twenty-five. Her body hadn't known. Now she was old, sick, and dying after unlived decades spent on a slab. Regret beyond despair whelmed her. Every possible future that might have been hers, good or ill, promised or compromised, all discarded the day they launched. Now she had to accept the choice that had cost her life. Not afraid of death, but sick at heart thinking of that life, hers, however desperate it might have been on Earth—any life—now unliveable.

She tried to read the logs. Files corrupted, many lost. Handwritten copies blurry in her sight. Her eyes weren't good enough for this. She shut them, thought, then went into the supply bay, rested there for a minute, pulled out a printer and scanner, rested again, connected them to the computer, brought up the proper software. That all took a few tiring hours. She napped. Woke and affixed the scanner to her face. Felt nothing as mild infrared swept her corneas and mapped their aberrations. The printer was already loaded with polycarbonate stock, and after a minute it began to hum.

She put her new glasses on, still warm. About the cataracts she could do nothing. But now she could read.

They had braked once, going around B. Rosa had executed the first part of the maneuver, following Zia's plan. His cushion shot. But their outgoing velocity was too fast.

Sergei continued talking in the background, on and on as he did, trying to get her attention. She felt annoyed with him, couldn't he see she was busy?

Look! Look for spectra.

She felt woozy, wandering. Planets did that. They wandered against the stars. How does a planet feel? Oh yes, she should look for a planet. That's where they were going.

Four. There were four planets. No, five—there was a sub-Mercury in close orbit around B. The other four orbited A. Three were too small, too close to the star, too hot. The fourth was Earth-like. It was in an orbit of 0.8 AU, eccentricity 0.05. Its mass was three-quarters that of Earth. Its year was about 260 days. They were still 1.8 AU from it, on the far side of Alpha Centauri A. The spectroscope showed nitrogen, oxygen, argon, carbon dioxide, krypton, neon, helium, methane, hydrogen. And liquid water.

Liquid water. She tasted the phrase on her tongue like a prayer, a benediction.

It was there. It was real. Liquid water.

But then there were the others. Fourteen who could not be roused. Leaving only her and Sergei. And of course Sergei was not real.

So there was no point. The mission was over however you looked at it. She couldn't do it alone. Even if they reached the planet, even if she managed to aerobrake the ship and bring it down in one piece, they were done, because there was no more they.

The humane, the sensible thing to do now would be to let the ship fall into the approaching sun. Get it over quickly.

She didn't want to deal with this. It made her tired.

Two thirds of the way there's a chockstone, a large rock jammed in the crack, for protection before the hardest part. She grasps it, gets her breath, and pulls round it. The crux involves laybacking and right arm pulling. Her arm is too tired. Shaking and straining she fights it. She thinks of falling. That was bad, it meant her thoughts were wandering.

Some day you will die. Death will not wait. Only then will you realize you have not practiced well. Don't give up.

She awoke with a start. She realized they were closing on the sun at its speed, not hers. If she did nothing, that was a decision. Amd that was not her decision to make. All of them had committed to this line. Her datastream was still sending, whether anyone received it or not. She hadn't fallen on the mountain, and she wasn't going to fall into a sun now.

The planet was lost in the blaze of Alpha A. Two days away from that fire, and the hull temperature was climbing.

The A sun was hotter, more luminous, than B. It couldn't be approached as closely. There would be less decel.

This was not her expertise. But Zia and Rosa had left exhaustive notes, and Sophie's expertise was in winnowing and organizing and executing. She prepped the reactor. She adjusted their trajectory, angled the cushion shot just so.

Attitude thrusters halted the ship's rotation, turned it to rest in the sunshield's shadow. Gravity feathered away. She floated as they freefell into light.

Through the sunshield, through the layers of carbon, aerogel, through closed eyelids, radiance fills the ship with its pressure, suffusing all, dispelling the decades of cold, warming her feelings to this new planet given life by this sun; eyes closed, she sees it more clearly than Earth—rivers running, trees tossing in the wind, insects chirring in a meadow—all familiar but made strange by this deep, pervasive light. It might almost be Earth, but it's not. It's a new world.

Four million kilometers from the face of the sun. 2500 Celsius.

Don't forget to strap in. Thank you, Rosa.

At periapsis, the deepest point in the gravity well, the engine woke in thunder. The ship shuddered, its aged hull wailed and boomed. Propellant pushed hard against their momentum, against the ship's forward vector, its force multiplied by its fall into the star's gravity, slowing the ship, gradually turning it. After an hour, the engine sputtered and died, and they raced away from that radiance into the abiding cold and silence of space.

Oh, Sergei. Oh, no. Still too fast.

They were traveling at twice the escape velocity of the Alpha C system. Fuel gone, having rounded both suns, they will pass the planet and continue out of the system into interstellar space.

Maneuver to planet. Like Zia said. Take all genetic material, seeds, zygotes, heat-shield payload and drop to surface, okay? Best we can do. Give life a chance.

No fuel, Sergei. Not a drop. We can't maneuver, you hear me?

Дерьмо.

Her mind is playing tricks. She has to concentrate. The planet is directly in front of them now, but still nine days away. Inexorable, it will move on in its orbit. Inexorable, the ship will follow its own divergent path. They will miss by 0.002 AU. Closer than the Moon to the Earth.

Coldly desperate, she remembered the attitude thrusters, fired them for ten minutes until all their hydrazine was exhausted. It made no difference.

She continued to collect data. Her datastream lived, a thousand bits per hour, her meager yet efficient engine of science pushing its mite of meaning back into the plaintext chaos of the universe, without acknowledgement.

The planet was drier than Earth, mostly rock with two large seas, colder, extensive polar caps. She radar-mapped the topography. The orbit was more eccentric than Earth's, so the caps must vary, and the seas they fed. A thirty-hour day. Two small moons, one with high albedo, the other dark.

What are they doing here? Have they thrown their lives away for nothing? Was it a great evil to have done this? Abandoned Earth?

But what were they to do? Like all of them, Roger was a problem solver, and the great problem on Earth, the problem of humanity, was unsolvable; it was out of control and beyond the reach of engineering. The problems of *Gypsy* were large but definable.

We were engineers. Of our own deaths. These were the deaths we wanted. Out here. Not among those wretched and unsanctified. We isolates.

She begins to compose a poem a day. Not by writing. She holds the words in her mind, reciting them over and over until the whole is fixed in memory. Then she writes it down. A simple discipline, to combat her mental wandering.

> In the eye of the sun
> what is not burned to ash?
>
> In the spire of the wind
> what is not scattered as dust?
>
> Love? art?
> body's rude health?
> memory of its satisfactions?
>
> Antaeus
> lost strength
> lifted from Earth
>
> Reft from our gravity
> we fail
>
> Lime kept sailors hale
> light of mind alone
> with itself
> is not enough

The scope tracked the planet as they passed it by. Over roughly three hours it grew in size from about a degree to about two degrees, then dwindled again. She spent the time gazing at its features with preternatural attention, with longing and regret, as if it were the face of an unattainable loved one.

It's there, Sergei, it's real—Ghost Planet Hope—and it is beautiful—look, how blue the water—see the clouds—and the seacoast—there must be rain, and plants and animals happy for it—fish, and birds, maybe, and worms, turning the soil. Look at the mountains! Look at the snow on their peaks!

This was when the science pod should have been released, the large reflecting telescope ejected into planetary orbit to start its year-long mission of measuring stellar distances. But that was in a divergent universe, one that each passing hour took her farther from.

We made it. No one will ever know, but we made it. We came so far. It was our only time to do it. No sooner, we hadn't developed the means. And if we'd waited any longer, the means would have killed us all. We came through a narrow window. Just a little too narrow.

She recorded their passing. She transmitted all their logs. Her recent poems. The story of their long dying. In four and a quarter years it would reach home. No telling if anyone would hear.

So long for us to evolve. So long to walk out of Africa and around the globe. So long to build a human world. So quick to ruin it. Is this, our doomed and final effort, no more than our grieving for Earth? Our mere mourning?

Every last bit of it was a long shot: their journey, humanity, life itself, the universe with its constants so finely tuned that planets, stars, or time itself, had come to be.

Fermi's question again: if life is commonplace in the universe, where is everyone? How come we haven't heard from anyone? What is the mean time between failures for civilizations?

Not long. Not long enough.

Now she slept. Language was not a tool used often enough even in sleep to lament its own passing. Other things lamented more. The brilliance turned to and turned away.

She remembers the garden behind the house. Her father grew corn—he was particular about the variety, complained how hard it was to find Silver Queen, even the terminated variety—with beans interplanted, which climbed the cornstalks, and different varieties of tomato with basil interplanted, and lettuces—he liked frisee. And in the flower beds alstroemeria, and wind lilies, and *Eschscholzia*. He taught her those names, and the names of Sierra flowers—taught her to learn names. We name things in order to love them, to remember them when they are absent. She recites the names of the fourteen dead with her, and weeps.

She'd been awake for over two weeks. The planet was far behind. The hibernation cocktail was completely flushed from her system. She wasn't going back to sleep.

> *ground*
> *rose*
> *sand*
>
> *elixir*
> *cave*
>
> *root*
> *dark*
>
> *golden*
> *sky-born*
> *lift*
> *earth*
> *fall*

The radio receiver chirps. She wakes, stares at it dumbly.

The signal is strong! Beamed directly at them. From Earth! Words form on the screen. She feels the words rather than reads them.

We turned it around. Everything is fixed. The bad years are behind us. We live. We know what you did, why you did it. We honor your bravery. We're sorry you're out there, sorry you had to do it, wish you . . . wish . . . wish . . . . Good luck. Good bye.

Where are her glasses? She needs to hear the words. She needs to hear a human voice, even synthetic. She taps the speaker.

The white noise of space. A blank screen.

She is in the Sierra, before the closure. Early July. Sun dapples the trail. Above the alpine meadow, in the shade, snow deepens, but it's packed and easy walking. She kicks steps into the steeper parts. She comes into a little flat just beginning to melt out, surrounded by snowy peaks, among white pine and red fir and mountain hemlock. Her young muscles are warm and supple and happy in their movements. The snowbound flat is still, yet humming with the undertone of life. A tiny mosquito lands on her forearm, casts its shadow, too young even to know to bite. She brushes it off, walks on, beyond the flat, into higher country.

> *thistle daisy cow-parsnip strawberry clover*
> *mariposa-lily corn-lily ceanothus elderberry marigold*
> *mimulus sunflower senecio goldenbush dandelion*
> *mules-ear iris miners-lettuce sorrel clarkia*
> *milkweed tiger-lily mallow veronica rue*
> *nettle violet buttercup ivesia asphodel*
> *ladyslipper larkspur pea bluebells onion*
> *yarrow cinquefoil arnica pennyroyal fireweed*
> *phlox monkshood foxglove vetch buckwheat*
> *goldenrod groundsel valerian lovage columbine*
> *stonecrop angelica rangers-buttons pussytoes everlasting*
> *watercress rockcress groundsmoke solomons-seal bitterroot*
> *liveforever lupine paintbrush blue-eyed-grass gentian*
> *pussypaws butterballs campion primrose forget-me-not*
> *saxifrage aster polemonium sedum rockfringe*
> *sky-pilot shooting-star heather alpine-gold penstemon*

Forget me not.

The Astrakhan, the Homburg, and the Red Red Coat

CHAZ BRENCHLEY

Here's a flamboyant and highly entertaining kind of Martian Steampunk, set in an Alternate World where Victorian England has colonized an inhabitable and inhabited Mars, and dealing with a group of clandestinely meeting gay colonists, including a thinly disguised Oscar Wilde, who are genteelly extorted by authorities into participating in a dangerous attempt to mentally communicate with the mind of a Martian—a mind which turns out to be vaster and more alien than anyone could have imagined. . . .

Chaz Brenchley has been making a living as a writer since the age of eighteen. He is the author of nine thrillers, most recently Shelter, *and two fantasy series,* The Books of Outremer *and* Selling Water by the River. *As Daniel Fox, he has published a Chinese-based fantasy series, beginning with* Dragon in Chains; *as Ben Macallan, an urban fantasy series beginning with* Desdaemona. *A British Fantasy Award winner, he has also published books for children and more than 500 short stories. Brenchley has recently married and moved from Newcastle to California, with two squabbling cats and a famous teddy bear. In 2014 he published a new novel,* Being Small, *and a collection,* Bitter Waters.

P aris? Paris is ruined for me, alas. It has become a haven for Americans—or should I say a heaven? When good Americans die, perhaps they really do go to Paris. That would explain the flood."

"What about the others, Mr Holland? The ones who aren't good?"

"Ah. Have you not heard? I thought that was common knowledge. When bad Americans die, they go to America. Which, again, would explain its huddled masses. But we were speaking of Paris. It was a good place to pause, to catch my breath; I never could have stayed there. If I had stayed in Paris, I should have died myself. The wallpaper alone would have seen to that."

"And what then, Mr Holland? Where do good Irishmen go when they die?"

"Hah." He made to fold his hands across a generous belly, as in the days of pomp—and found it not so generous after all, and lost for a moment the practised grace of his self-content. A man can forget the new truths of his own body, after a period of alteration. Truly Paris had a lot to answer for. Paris, and what had come before. What had made it necessary.

"This particular Irishman," he said, "is in hopes of seeing Cassini the crater-city on its lake, and finding his eternal rest in your own San Michele, within the sound of Thunder Fall. If I've only been good enough."

"And if not? Where do bad Irishmen go?"

It was the one question that should never have been asked. It came from the shadows behind our little circle; I disdained to turn around, to see what man had voiced it.

"Well," Mr Holland said, gazing about him with vivid horror painted expertly across his mobile face, "I seem to have found myself in Marsport. What did I ever do to deserve this?"

There was a common shout of laughter, but it was true all the same. Marsport at its best is not a place to wish upon anyone, virtuous or otherwise; and the Blue Dolphin is not the best of what we have. Far from it. Lying somewhat awkwardly between the honest hotels and the slummish boarding-houses, it was perhaps the place that met his purse halfway. Notoriety is notoriously mean in its rewards. He couldn't conceivably slum, but neither—I was guessing—could he live high on the hog. Even now I was wondering quite who had bought his ticket to Mars. The one-way voyage is subsidised by Authority, while those who want to go home again must pay through the nose for the privilege—but even so. He would not have travelled steerage, and the cost of a cabin on an aethership is . . . significant. Prohibitive, I should have said, for a man in exile from his history, whose once success could only drag behind him now like Marley's chains, nothing but a burden. He might have assumed his children's name for public purposes, but he could not have joined the ship without offering his right one.

No matter. He had money in his purse, enough for now, for a room in the Dolphin and hopes of a journey on; and he was here, and more than welcome. We would sit at his feet and make an audience for him as he was used to, attentive, admiring, if it would make him happy.

It was possible that nothing now could make him happy, exactly. Still: who could treasure him more than those of us who made our home in a gateway city, an entrepôt, and found our company in the lobby of a cheap hotel?

"Marsport's not so terrible," the same voice said. "It's the hub of the wheel, not the pit of hell. From here you can go anywhere you choose: by canal, by airship, by camel if you're hardy. Steam-camel, if you're foolhardy. On the face of it, I grant you, there's not much reason to stay—and yet, people do. Our kind."

"Our kind?"

There was a moment's pause, after Mr Holland had placed the question: so carefully, like a card laid down in invitation, or a token to seal the bet.

"Adventurers," the man said. "People unafraid to stand where the light spills into darkness: who know that a threshold serves to hold two worlds apart, as much as it allows congress between them."

"Ah. I am afraid my adventuring days are behind me."

"Oh, nonsense, sir! Why, the journey to Mars is an adventure in itself!"

Now there was a voice I did recognise: Parringer, as fatuous a fool as the schools of home were ever likely to produce. He was marginal even here, one of us only by courtesy. And thrusting himself forward, protesting jovially, trying to prove himself at the heart of things and showing only how very remote he was.

"Well, perhaps. Perhaps." Mr Holland could afford to be generous; he didn't have to live with the man. "If so, it has been my last. I am weary, gentlemen. And wounded and heart-sore and unwell, but weary above all. All I ask now is a place to settle. A fireside, a view, some company: no more than that. No more adventuring."

"Time on Mars may yet restore your health and energy; it is what we are famous for, and why so many retire here after serving Queen and Empire on Earth." This was our unknown again, pressing again. "But you are not of an age to want or seek retirement, Mr . . . Holland. Great heavens, man, you can't be fifty yet! Besides, the adventure I propose will hardly tax your reserves. There's no need even to leave the hotel, if you will only shift with me into the conservatory. You may want your overcoats, gentlemen, and another round of drinks. No more than that. I've had a boy in there already to light the stove."

That was presumptuous, from an unknown. Manners inhibited me from twisting around in my chair and staring, but no one objects to a little honest subterfuge; I rose, took two paces towards the fire and pressed the bell by the mantelshelf.

"My shout, I think. Mr Holland, yours I know is gin and French; gentlemen . . . ?"

No one resists an open invitation; Marsporter gin is excellent, but imported drinks come dear. The boy needed his notebook to take down a swift flurry of orders.

"Thanks, Barley." I tucked half a sovereign into his rear pocket—unthinkable largesse, but we all had reasons to treat kindly with Barley—and turned to face my cohort.

On my feet and playing host, I could reasonably meet them all eye to eye, count them off like call-over at school. Hereth and Maskelyne, who were not friends but nevertheless arrived together and sat together every time; Thomson, who measured us all through his disguising spectacles and might have been a copper's nark, might have been here to betray us all except that every one of us had reason to know that he was not; Gribbin the engineer and van Heuren the boatman, Poole from the newspaper and Parringer of course, and Mr Holland our guest for the occasion, and—

Our unannounced visitor, the uninvited, the unknown: he was tall even by Martian standards, and the shortest of us would overtop an average Earthman. Mr Holland must have been tall in his own generation, six foot three or thereabouts; here he was no more than commonplace. In his strength, in his pride I thought he would have resented that. Perhaps he still did. Years of detention and disgrace might have diminished him in body and spirit both, but something must survive yet, unbroken, undismayed. He could never have made this journey else. Nor sat with us. Every tree holds a memory of the forest.

The stranger was in his middle years, an established man, confident in himself and his position. That he held authority in some kind was not, could not be in question. It was written in his assumptions, as clearly as in the way he stood, the way he waited; the way he had taken charge so effortlessly, making my own display seem feeble, sullen, nugatory.

Mr Holland apparently saw the same. He said, "I don't believe we were introduced, sir. If I might venture a guess, I should say you have a look of the Guards about you." Or perhaps he said *the guards*, and meant something entirely different.

"I don't believe any of us have been introduced," I said, as rudely as I knew how. "You are . . . ?"

Even his smile was weighty with that same settled certainty. "Gregory Durand, late of the King's Own," with a little nod to Mr Holland: the one true regiment to any man of Mars, Guards in all but name, "and currently of the Colonial Service."

He didn't offer a title, nor even a department. I could hear the doubt in my own voice as I tried to pin him down. "The police?"

"On occasion," he said. "Not tonight."

If that was meant to be reassuring, it fell short. By some distance. If we were casting about for our coats, half-inclined not to wait for those drinks, it was not because we were urgent to follow him into the conservatory. Rather, our eyes were on the door and the street beyond.

"Gentlemen," he said, "be easy." He was almost laughing at us. "Tonight I dress as you do," overcoat and hat, "and share everything and nothing, one great secret and nothing personal or private, nothing prejudicial. I will not say "nothing perilous", but the peril is mutual and assured. We stand or fall together, if at all. Will you come? For the Queen Empress if not for the Empire?"

The Empire had given us little enough reason to love it, which he knew. An appeal to the Widow, though, will always carry weight. There is something irresistible in that blend of sentimentality and strength beyond measure, endurance beyond imagination: we had cried for her, we would die for her. We were on our feet almost before we knew it. I took that so much for granted, it needed a moment for me to realise that Mr Holland was still struggling to rise. Unless he was simply slower to commit himself, he whose reasons—whose scars—were freshest on his body and raw yet on his soul.

Still. I reached out my hand to help him and he took it resolutely, quick of thought and quick to choose. Quick to go along. A lesson learned, perhaps. I was almost sad to see it, in a man who used to disregard protocol and convention so heedlessly; but it was sheer wisdom now to keep his head down and follow the crowd. Even where that crowd was disreputable and blind itself, leading none knew where.

Being led, I should say. Through a door beside the hearth, that was almost never open this time of year. Beyond lay the unshielded conservatory, like an open invitation to the night.

An invitation that Mr Holland balked at, and rightly. He said, "You gentlemen are dressed for this, but I have a room here, and had not expected to need my coat tonight."

"You'll freeze without it. Perhaps you should stay in the warm." Perhaps we all should, but it was too late for that. Our company was following Durand like sheep, trusting where they should have been most wary. Tempted where they should have been most strong.

And yet, and yet. Dubious and resentful as I was, I too would give myself over to this man—for the mystery or for the adventure, something. For something to do that was different, original, unforeseen. I was weary of the same faces, the same drinks, the same conversations. We all were: which was why Mr Hoiland had been so welcome, one reason why.

This, though: I thought he of all men should keep out of this. I thought I should keep him out, if I could.

Here came Durand to prevent me: stepping through the door again, reaching for his elbow, light and persuasive and yielding nothing.

"Here's the boy come handily now, just when we need him. I'll take that, lad," lifting the tray of refreshments as though he had been host all along. "You run up to Mr Holland's room and fetch down his overcoat. And his hat too, we'll need to keep that great head warm. Meanwhile, Mr Holland, we've a chair for you hard by the stove . . ."

The chairs were set out in a circle: stern and upright, uncushioned, claimed perhaps from the hotel servants' table. Our companions were milling, choosing, settling, in a cloud of their own breath. The conservatory was all glass and lead, roof and walls together; in the dark of a Martian winter, the air was bitter indeed, despite the stove's best efforts. The chill pressed in from every side, as the night pressed against the lamplight; there was no comfort here to be found, there would be no warmth tonight.

On a table to one side stood a machine, a construction of wires and plates in a succession of steel frames with rubber insulation. One cable led out of it, to something that most resembled an inverted umbrella, or the skeleton of such a thing, bones of wire.

"What is that?"

"Let me come to that. If you gentlemen would take your seats . . ."

Whoever laid the chairs out knew our number. There was none for Durand; he stood apart, beside the machine.

"*Nation shall speak peace unto nation*—and for some of us, it is our task to make it so. Notoriously, traditionally we go after this by sending in the army first and then the diplomats. Probably that's backwards, but it's the system that builds empires. It's the system of the world.

"Worlds, I should say. Here on Mars, of course, it's the merlins that we need to hold in conversation. Mr Holland—"

"I am not a child, sir. Indeed, I have children of my own." *Indeed, I travel now under their name, the name they took at their mother's insistence; I can still acknowledge them, even if they are obliged to disown me.* "I have exactly a child's understanding of your merlins: that is to say, what we were taught in my own schooldays. I know that you converse with them differently, in their different stages: by sign language with the youngster, the nymph, and then by bubbling through pipes at the naiad in its depths, and watching the bubbles it spouts back. With the imago, when the creature takes to the air, I do not believe that you can speak at all."

"Just so, sir—and that is precisely the point of our gathering tonight."

Actually, the point of our gathering had been ostensibly to celebrate and welcome Mr Holland, actually to fester in our own rank company. Durand had coopted it entirely.

"It's long been believed," he said, "that the imagos—"

"—imagines—"

—to our shame that came as a chorus, essential pedantry—

"—that imagos," he went on firmly, having no truck with ridiculous Greek plurals, "had no tongue, no way to speak, perhaps no wit to speak with. As though the merlins slumped into senescence in their third stage, or infantilism might say it better: as though they lost any rational ability, overwhelmed by the sexual imperative. They live decades, perhaps centuries in their slower stages here below, nymph and naiad; and then they pupate, and then they hatch a second time and the fire of youth overtakes them once more: they fly, they fight, they mate, they die. What need thought, or language?

"So our wise men said, at least. Now perhaps we are grown wiser. We believe they do indeed communicate, with each other and perhaps their water-based cousins too, it may be that nymphs or naiads or both have the capacity to hear them. We don't, because they do not use sound as we understand it. Rather, they have an organ in their heads that sends out electromagnetic pulses, closer to Hertzian waves than anything we have previously observed in nature. Hence this apparatus," with a mild gesture towards the table and its machinery. "With this, it is believed that we can not only hear the imagos, but speak back to them."

A moment's considerate pause, before someone asked the obvious question. "And us? Why do you want to involve us?"

"Not want, so much as need. The device has existed for some time; it has been tried, and tried again. It does work, there is no question of that. Something is received, something transmitted."

"—But?"

"But the first man who tried it, its inventor occupies a private room—a locked room—in an asylum now, and may never be fit for release."

"And the second?"

"Was a military captain, the inventor's overseer. He has the room next door." There was no equivocation in him, nothing but the blunt direct truth.

"And yet you come to us? You surely don't suppose that we are saner, healthier, more to be depended on . . . ?"

"Nor more willing," Durand said, before one of us could get to it. "I do not. And yet I am here, and I have brought the machine. Will you listen?"

None of us trusted him, I think. Mr Holland had better reason than any to be wary, yet it was he whose hand sketched a gesture, *I am listening*, and a glance around showed that he spoke for all.

"Thank you, gentlemen. What transpired from the tragedy—after a careful reading of the notes and as much interrogation as proved possible of the victims—was that the mind of an imago is simply too strange, too alien, for the mind of a man to encompass. A brain under that kind of pressure can break, in distressing and irrecoverable ways."

"And yet," I said, "we speak to nymphs, to naiads." I had done it myself, indeed. I had spoken nymphs on the great canals when I was younger, nimble-fingered, foolish and immortal. For all the good it had done me, I might as well have kept my hands in my pockets and my thoughts to myself, but nevertheless, I spoke, they replied; none of us ran mad.

"We do—and a poor shoddy helpless kind of speech it is. Finger-talk or bubble-talk, all we ever really manage to do is misunderstand each other almost entirely. That 'almost' has made the game just about worth the candle, for a hundred years and more—it brought us here, and keeps us here in more or less safety, and ferries us home again—but this is different. When the imagos speak to each other, they speak mind-to-mind. It's not literally telepathy, but it is the closest thing we know. And when we contact them through this, we encounter the very shape of their minds, almost from the inside; and our minds—our *individual* minds—cannot encompass this. No one man's intellect can stand up to the strain."

"And yet," again, "here we are. And here you are, and your maddening machine. I say again, why are we here?"

"Because you chose to be"—and it was not at all clear whether his answer meant *in this room* or *in this hotel* or *in this situation*. "I am the only one here under orders. The rest of you are free to leave at any time, though you did say you'd listen at least. And I did say "one man's intellect". Where one man alone cannot survive it without a kind of mental dislocation—in the wicked sense, a disjointment, his every limb pulled each from each—a group of men working together is a different case. It may be that the secret lies in strength, in mutual support; it may lie in flexibility. A group of officers made the endeavour, and none of them was harmed beyond exhaustion and a passing bewilderment, a lingering discomfort with each other; but neither did they make much headway. Enlisted men did better."

He paused, because the moment demanded it, because drama has its natural rhythms and he did after all have Mr Holland in his audience. We sat still, uncommitted, listening yet.

"The enlisted men did better, we believe, because their lives are more earthy, less refined. They live cheek by jowl, they sleep all together and bathe together, they share the same women in the same bawdy-houses. That seems to help."

"And so you come to us? To *us*? Because you find us indistinguishable from common bloody Tommies?"

"No, because you are most precisely distinguishable. The Tommies were no great success either, but they pointed us a way to go. The more comfortable the men are with each other, physically and mentally, the better hope we have. Officers inhabit a bonded hierarchy, isolated from one another as they are from their men, like pockets of water in an Archimedes' screw. Cadets might have done better, but we went straight to the barracks. With, as I say, some success—but enlisted men are unsophisticated. Hence we turn to you, gentlemen. It is a bow drawn at a venture, no more: but you are familiar with, intimate with the bodies of other men, and we do believe that will help enormously; and yet you are educated beyond the aspiration of any Tommy Atkins—some of you beyond the aspiration of any mere soldier, up to and including the generals of my acquaintance—and that too can only prove to the good. With the one thing and the other, these two strengths in parallel, in harmony, we stand in high hopes of a successful outcome. At least, gentlemen, I can promise you that you won't be bored. Come, now: will you play?"

"Is that as much as you can promise?" Thomson raised his voice, querulous and demanding. "You ask a lot of us, to venture in the margins of madness; it seems to me you might offer more in return."

"I can offer you benign neglect," Durand said cheerfully. "Official inattention: no one watching you, no one pursuing. I can see that enshrined in policy, to carry over *ad infinitum*. If you're discreet, you can live untroubled hereafter; you, and the generations that follow you. This is a once-and-for-all offer, for services rendered."

There must be more wrapped up in this even than Durand suggested or we guessed. A way to speak to the imagines might prove only the gateway to further secrets and discoveries. If we could speak directly to the chrysalid pilots of the aetherships, perhaps we might even learn to fly the great ships ourselves, and lose all our dependence on the merlins . . .

That surely would be worth a blind eye turned in perpetuity to our shady meeting-places, our shadier activities.

Mr Holland thought so, at least. "Say more, of how this process works. Not what you hope might come of it; we all have dreams. Some of us have followed them, somewhat. I am here, after all, among the stars," with a wave of his hand through glass to the bitter clarity of the Martian night sky. "How is it that you want us to work together? And how do we work with the machine, and why above all do we have to do it here, in this wicked cold?"

"To treat with the last first: Mr Heaviside has happily demonstrated here as well as on Earth, that aetheric waves carry further after dark. We don't know how far we need to reach, to find a receptive imago; we stand a better chance at night. Besides, you gentlemen tend to forgather in the evenings. I wasn't certain of finding you by daylight."

Someone chuckled, someone snorted. I said, "I have never seen an imago fly by night, though. I don't believe they can."

"Not fly, no: never that. But neither do they sleep, so far as we can tell. All we want to do—all we want you to do—is touch the creature's mind, fit yourselves to the shape of it and find whether you can understand each other."

"I still don't understand how you mean us to achieve that?"

"No. It's almost easier to have you do it, than to explain how it might be done. We're stepping into an area where words lose their value, against lived experience. It's one reason I was so particularly hoping to enlist your company, sir," with a nod to Mr Holland, "because who better to stand before the nondescript and find means to describe it? If anyone can pin this down with words, it will be you. If anyone can speak for us to an alien power—"

"Now that," he said, "I have been doing all my life."

The run of laughter he provoked seemed more obligatory than spontaneous, but came as a relief none the less. Durand joined in, briefly. As it tailed away, he said, "Very well—but there is of course more to it than one man's dexterity with language. Our wise men speak of the, ah, inversion of the generative principle, as a bonding-agent stronger than blood or shared danger or duty or sworn word—but again, there is more than that. You gentlemen may be a brotherhood, drawn from within and pressed close from without; we can make you something greater, a single purpose formed from all your parts. The wise men would have me flourish foreign words at you, *gestalt* or *phasis* or the like; but wise men are not always the most helpful.

"Let me rather say this, that you all have some experience of the demi-monde. By choice or by instinct, your lives have led you into the shadows. This very hotel is a gateway to more disreputable ventures: there is an opium den behind the Turkish bath, a brothel two doors down. I do not say that any of you is a libertine at core: only that the life you lead draws you into contact and exchange with those who avoid the light for other reasons.

"I will be plain. Mr Holland, you have a known taste for absinthe and for opium cigarettes. Mr Parringer, laudanum is your poison; Mr Hereth, you stick to gin, but that jug of water at your elbow that you mix in so judiciously is actually more gin, and you will drink the entire jugful before the night is out. Mr Gribbin—but I don't need to go on, do I? You each have your weaknesses, your ways of setting this world a little adrift, stepping aside from reality.

"We need to take you out of yourselves in order to bind you into a single motive force, in order to create a mind-space wherein you might meet an imago and understand it. I have brought an alchemical concoction, a kind of hatchis, more potent than any pill or pipe or potion that you have met before."

He laid it on a tray, on a table that he set centre-circle between us all: a silver pot containing something green and unctuous, an array of coffee spoons beside.

"Something more from your wise men, Mr Durand?"

"Exactly so."

"I'm not sure how keen I am, actually, to swallow some hell brew dreamed up in a government laboratory." Gribbin leaned forward and stirred it dubiously. There were gleams of oily gold amidst the green. "Does nobody remember The Strange Case of Dr Jekyll and Mr Hyde?"

"'Can anyone forget it?' should rather be your question," Mr Holland said. "Stevenson was as much a master of delicate, fanciful prose as he was of a strong driving story. But he—or his character, rather, his creation: do we dare impute the motives of the dream unto the dreamer?—he certainly saw the merits of a man testing his own invention on himself, before bringing it to the public." Even huddled as he was against the ironwork of the stove, he could still exude a spark of knowing mischief.

Durand smiled. "I would be only too happy to swallow my own spoonful, to show you gentlemen the way—but alas, my duty is to the device, not to the *entente*. You will need me sober and attentive. Besides which, I am not of your persuasion. I should only hold you back. Let me stress, though, that senior officers and common troops both have trod this path before you, and not been harmed. Not by the drug. Think of the hatchis as grease to the engine, no more; it will ease your way there and back again. Now come: I promised you adventure, and this is the beginning. Who's first to chance the hazard?"

There is a self-destructive tendency in some men that falls only a little short of self murder. We have it worse than most; something not quite terror, not quite exhilaration drives us higher, faster, farther than good sense ever could dictate. Some consider it a weakness, evidence of a disordered nature. I hope that it's a badge of courage learned, that we will fling ourselves from the precipice in no certain knowledge of a rope to hold us, no faith in any net below.

Of course it was Mr Holland who reached first, to draw up a noble spoonful and slide it into his mouth. No tentative sips, no tasting: he was all or nothing, or rather simply all.

The surprise was Parringer, thrusting himself forward to do the same, gulping it down indelicately while Mr Holland still lingered, the spoon's stem jutting from between his full contented lips like a cherry stem, like a child's lollipop.

Where Parringer plunged, who among us would choose to hold back? A little resentfully, perhaps, and certainly with a great many questions still unasked, we fell mob-handed on the spoons, the jar, the glistening oleaginous jelly.

It was bitter on my tongue and something harsh, as though it breathed fumes, catching at the back of my throat before it slithered down to soothe that same discomfort. Bitter and then sour and then sweet, layer beneath layer, and I couldn't decide whether its flavours were woven one into another or whether its very nature changed as it opened, as it bloomed within the wet warm of my mouth.

He was right, of course, Durand. Not one of us there was a stranger to the more louche pleasures of the twilit world. Myself, I was a smoker in those days: hashish or opium, anything to lift me out of the quotidian world for an hour or a night. In company or alone, sweating or shivering or serene, I would always, always look to rise. Skin becomes permeable, bodies lose their margins; dreams are welcome but not needful, what I seek is always that sense of being uncontained, of reaching further than my strict self allows.

From what he said, I took Durand's potion to be one more path to that effect: slower for sure, because smoke is the very breath of fire and lifts as easily as it rises, where anything swallowed is dank and low-lying by its nature. I never had been an opium-eater, and hatchis was less than that, surely: a thinner draught, ale against spirits, tea against coffee. Sunshine to lightning. Something.

If I had the glare of lightning in my mind, it was only in the expectation of disappointment, rain, no storm. I never thought to ride it. Nor to find myself insidiously companion'd—in my own mind, yet—where before I had always gone alone.

Even in bed, even with a slick and willing accomplice in the throes of mutual excess, my melting boundaries had never pretended to melt me into another man's thoughts. Now, though: now suddenly I was aware of minds in parallel, rising entangled with mine, like smoke from separate cigarettes caught in the same eddy. Or burning coals in the same grate, fusing awkwardly together. Here was a mind cool and in command of itself, trying to sheer off at such exposure: that was Gribbin, finding nowhere to go, pressed in from every side at once. Here was one bold and fanciful and weary all at once, and that was surely Mr Holland, though it was hard to hold on to that name in this intimate revelation. Here was one tentative and blustering together, Parringer of course . . .

One by one, each one of us found a name, if not quite a location. We were this many and this various, neither a medley nor a synthesis, untuned: glimpsing one man's overweening physical arrogance and another's craven unsatisfied ambition, sharing the urge to seize both and achieve a high vaulting reach with them, beyond the imagination of either. Even without seeing a way to do that, even as we struggled like elvers in a bucket, the notion was there already with flashes of the vision. Perhaps Durand was right to come to us.

Durand, now: Durand was no part of this. Walled off, separated, necessary: he seemed like a prosthetic, inert, a tool to be wielded. He stood by his machine, fiddling with knobs and wires, almost as mechanical himself.

Here was the boy Barley coming in, no part of anything, bringing the hat and overcoat he'd been sent for. At Durand's gesture he dressed Mr Holland like a doll, as though he were invalid or decrepit. Perhaps we all seemed so to him, huddled in our circle, unspeaking, seeming unaware. The truth was opposite; we were aware of everything, within the limits of our bodies' senses. We watched him crouch to feed the stove; we heard the slide and crunch of the redcoal tipping in, the softer sounds of ash falling through the grate beneath; we felt the sear of heat released, how it stirred the frigid air about us, how it rose towards the bitter glass.

"Enough now, lad. Leave us be until I call again."

"Yes, sir."

He picked up the tray from the table and bore it off towards the door, with a rattle of discarded spoons. Durand had already turned back to his machine. We watched avidly, aware of nothing more intently than the little silver pot and its gleaming residue. We knew it, when the boy hesitated just inside the door; we knew it when he glanced warily back at us, when he decided he was safe, when he wiped his finger around the pot's rim and sucked it clean.

We knew; Durand did not.

Durand fired up his machine.

We had the boy. Not one of us, not part of us, not yet: we were as unprepared for this as he was, and the more susceptible to his fear and bewilderment because we were each of us intimately familiar with his body, in ways not necessarily true of one another's.

Still: we had him among us, with us, this side of the wall. We had his nervous energy to draw on, like a flame to our black powder; we had his yearning, his curiosity. And more, we had that shared knowledge of him, common ground. Where we couldn't fit one to another, we could all of us fit around him: the core of the matrix, the unifying frame, the necessary element Durand had not foreseen.

Durand fired up his machine while we were still adjusting, before we had nudged one another into any kind of order.

He really should have warned us, though I don't suppose he could. He hadn't been this way himself; all he had was secondhand reports from men more or less broken by the process. We could none of us truly have understood that, until now.

We weren't pioneers; he only hoped that we might be survivors. Still, we deserved some better warning than we had.

We forget sometimes that names are not descriptions; that Mars is not Earth; that the merlins are no more native than ourselves. We call them Martians sometimes because our parents did, because their parents did before them, and so back all the way to Farmer George. More commonly we call them merlins because we think it's clever, because they seem to end their lives so backward, from long years of maturity in the depths to one brief adolescent lustful idiocy in the sky. When we call them imagos—or imagines—because they remind us of dragonflies back home, if dragonflies were built to the scale of biplanes.

Which they are not. The map is not the territory; the name is not the creature. Even redcoal is not coal, not carbon of any kind, for all that it is mined and burned alike. We forget that. We name artefacts after the places of their manufacture, or their first manufacture, or the myth of it; did the homburg hat in fact see first light in Bad Homburg, or is that only a story that we tell? Does anybody know? We let a man name himself after his children, after a place not relevant to any of them, not true to any story of their lives. We assert that names are changeable, assignable at whim, and then we attach unalterable value to them.

Durand had given no name to his machine. That was just as well, but not enough. He had given us a task to do, in words we thought we understood; he had laid the groundwork, given us an argument about the uses of debauchery and then a drug to prove it; then he flung us forth, all undefended.

He flung us, and we dragged poor Barley along, unwitting and unprepared.

It started with a hum, as he connected electrical wires to a seething acid battery. Lamps glowed into dim flickering life. Sparks crackled ominously, intermittently, before settling to a steady mechanical pulse. A steel disc spun frantically inside a cage.

Nothing actually moved, except fixedly in place; and even so, everything about it was all rush and urgency, a sensation of swift decisive movement: *that* way, through the run of frames and wires to the umbrella-structure at the far end of the table. There was nothing to draw the eye except a certainty, logic married to something more, an intangible impulsion. *That* way: through and up and out into the night.

And none of us moved from our places, and yet, and yet. The machine hurled us forth, and forth we went.

If we had understood anything, we had understood that the machine would bring an imago's voice to us, and we would somehow speak back to it, if we could think of anything to say. That would have been Mr Holland's lot, surely; he was never short of things to say.

We had misunderstood, or else been misdirected. Unless the drug seduced us all into a mutual hallucination, and in plain truth our intelligences never left that room any more than our abandoned bodies did. But it seemed to us—to *all* of us, united— that we were shot out like a stone from a catapult; that we streaked over all the lights of Marsport and into the bleak dark desert beyond; that we hurtled thus directly into the static mind of an imago at rest in darkness.

No creature's thoughts should be . . . architectural. Or vast. At first we thought we were fallen into halls of stone, or caverns water-worn. But we had found our shape by then, in the flight from there to here; we might fit poorly all together, but we all fitted well around Barley. And something in that resettling, that nudging into a new conformation, caused a shift in our perspective. A thought is just an echo of the mind-state it betrays, as an astrakhan overcoat is a memory of the lambs that died to make it.

Where we fancied that we stood, these grand and pillared spaces—this was an imago's notion of its nighttime world, beyond all heat and passion, poised, expectant. A memory of the chrysalis, perhaps.

Expectant, but not expecting us. Not expecting anything until the sun, the bright and burning day, the vivid endeavour. We came like thieves into a mountain, to disturb the dragon's rest; we were alien, intrusive, self-aware. It knew us in the moment of our coming.

I have seen set changes in the theatre where one scene glides inexplicably into another, defying expectation, almost defying the eye that saw it happen. I had never stood in a place and had that happen all about me; but we were there, and recognised, and its awareness of us changed the shape of its thinking.

Even as we changed ourselves, that happened: as we slid and shifted, as we found our point of balance, with Barley at the heart because we could each of us connect through him. Even Mr Holland, who would need to speak for us all, if anything could ever come to words here; even Parringer, whose motives were as insidious as his manner. There was an unbridgeable gulf between the imago as we had always understood it, flighty and maniacal, and this lofty habitation. A naiad in the depths might have such a ponderous mind, such chilly detachment, but not the frenzied imago, no. Surely not.

Save that the imago had been a naiad before; perhaps it retained that mind-set, in ways we had not expected or imagined. Perhaps it could be contemplative at night, while the sun burned off its intellect and lent it only heat?

It closed in upon us almost geometrically, like tiled walls, if tiles and walls could occupy more dimensions than a man can see, in shapes we have no words for. We should have felt threatened, perhaps, but Barley's curiosity was matched now by his tumbling delight, and what burns at the core reaches out all the way to the skin. We sheltered him and drew from him and leaned on him, all in equal measure; he linked us and leaned on us and drew from us, in ways for which there never could be words.

With so many names for our kind—leering, contemptuous, descriptive, dismissive—we know both the fallibility and the savage power of words. The map seeks to define the territory, to claim it, sometimes to contain it. Without a map, without a shared vocabulary, without a mode of thought in common—well, no wonder men alone went mad here. No wonder men together had achieved so little, beyond a mere survival. Mr Holland might have flung wit all night with no more effect than a monkey flinging dung against a cliff-face, if we had only been a group forgathered by circumstance, struggling to work together. With the drug to bond us, with each man contributing the heart's-blood of himself in this strange transfusion, there was no struggle and we found what we needed as the need came to us.

Whether we said what was needed, whether it needed to be said: that is some other kind of question. Did anyone suppose that the confluence of us all would be a diplomat?

The imago pressed us close, but that was an enquiry. There was pattern in the pressure: we could see it, we could read it almost, those of us with finger-talk or bubble-talk or both. *What lives, what choices? Swim or fly, drown or burn? Swallow or be swallowed?*

We knew, we thought, how to press back, how to pattern a reply. Mr Holland gave us what we lacked: content, poetry, a reply. Meaning more than words. Sometimes the map declares the territory.

For he who lives more lives than one
More deaths than one must die.

He would have turned the bitterness all against himself, but our collective consciousness couldn't sustain that. We all wanted our share, we all deserved it: all but Barley, who had no hidden other self, who'd had no time to grow one.

Suddenly he couldn't hold us together any longer. Fraying, we fled back to Durand, back to our waiting bodies—and the imago pursued, flying by sheer will in the dreadful night, wreaking havoc in its own frozen body. It followed us to the Dolphin and hurtled against the conservatory where we were anything but sheltered, battering at the windows like a moth at the chimney of a lamp, until the only abiding question was whether the glass would shatter first or the machine, or the creature, or us.

THE MUSES OF SHUYEDAN-18

INDRAPRAMIT DAS

*Relative newcomer Indrapramit Das is a writer and artist from Kolkata,
India. His short fiction has appeared in* Clarkesworld, Asimov's Science Fiction, Apex Magazine, Redstone Science Fiction, The World SF Blog, Flash
Fiction Online, *and the anthology* Breaking the Bow: Speculative Fiction
Inspired by the Ramayana. *He is a grateful graduate of the 2012 Clarion
West Writers Workshop, and a recipient of the Octavia E. Butler Memorial
Scholarship Award. He completed his MFA at the University of British Columbia, and currently lives in Vancouver, working as a freelance writer, artist, editor, game tester, tutor, would-be novelist, and aspirant to adulthood.
Follow him on Twitter (@IndrapramitDas).*

*In the story that follows of a passionate love affair between two scientific
researchers on a remote alien world and the unexpected effect that it has on
one of the alien inhabitants, a being as mysterious and vast as a living mountain, he brings us into contact with something numinous and strange—as
good science fiction should do.*

Shuyedan emerged from its progenitor calling to the stars in agony. Its cries rolled
across the plain, a bass hum in our suits. We called it Shuyedan the moment it began to depart its progenitor. Mi, standing next to me, said the word, her eyes visible
even behind the glare of sunset on her faceplate. In colbyat, Shuyedan means *youngest*. We didn't know their language, if they have one. Its lowing was as alien to us as
the way it separated from its progenitor. It wasn't birth, it was a battle, full of lust and
fury and what we might call blood, misting the air and falling upon us in a drizzle
that glimmered on our faceplates as we watched. Strings of dark tissue stretched between the aliens like a cat's cradle, scythes of cartilage emerging to snap them away.
Steaming in the red light, Shuyedan pulled away and lay across the loamy ground,
ultraviolet reflections storming across its fresh skin like lightning. A giant twisting
to articulate itself, groaning to life. Its progenitor gasped flickering blood and shuddered away, its part done.

It was larger even than Shuyedan, a tower unfolding to cast its shadow across Mi and I. I heard Mi's breath catch in the mouthpiece, a crackle that lingered in my chest.

It's hard to describe these creatures without language that grew on this world. There are words in Colbyat that do no translate well; aynagal, which can mean *thoughtpalace*, or vitanbiyet, which can mean *lifecastle*. Piyentour, the very earthly sounding term *dreamweaver*. In Colbyat, they share the gender-neutral pronoun used for humans, which makes them sound less like objects to be surveyed and more like sentient life forms. These are beings of poetry, despite their vast solidity, eclipsing the largest of Earth's animals.

But at that point, Shuyedan, youngest we have seen here, was a blank slate. Its progenitor receded into the horizon groaning, a swaying exoskeletal rook, its skin statuesque with the stories of its life, incomprehensible to us. In that, they were like walking Rorschach blots. We called that one Urdhema, *imperial*, because we had seen it war and defeat two others. Its mindcarvings, all crumbling creches and curling crenellations, snagged the setting glare of the dwarf sun. It was a walking monument, a castle, a defender of its own space. What we might call its child was now a rival nation.

This was the first time Mi had seen a lifecastle create another. They were all unique, and incredibly solitary. The only time they touched each other was in battle and birth.

"Fuck me, that's beautiful," I said to Mi, because it was, and because seeing it anew with her eyes made it as strange as the first time I'd seen a separation. Her channel was open, the reverb of my own voice in her helmet a soothing echo.

"So are you," she said. So banal, yet striking in her timing. Shuyedan stood up, obsidian giant rippling. Urdhema was rapid despite its size, already getting small on the horizon. It was limping from its painful act of creation, but anxious to get away from the result. Its pennants unfurled behind it, fluttering on the breeze, membranes absorbing blue starshine growing stronger as the sun lowered.

"Stop," I told Mi. "How can you talk about me when that just happened? Look. Just look at that. Shuyedan."

"I know. I'm looking. It makes me feel like the luckiest person in the galaxy. To have you, here, now, and have Shuyedan witness us. We're. We're blessed, Tani," Mi said.

Shuyedan's windows flickered open, steam curling out of them lit yellow by bioluminescence. It beheld—us. We switched on our own headlamps, which burned through the progressing evening in straight lines.

"There are five hundred thousand human beings across the universe, observing other life forms or worlds as strange as this one. Or more, fuck knows. Don't be so absurdly romantic," I said, exhilarated by Mi's happiness even as I reacted against it.

Behind the veil of reflections on her faceplate, her lips parted. "Do you have to swear so much?" A smile behind her words. "Shit," she said, and stumbled back as Shuyedan's entire body shook and it sounded again, louder than before. Our external mics squealed.

And just like that, Shuyedan's skin churned. It witnessed us. First sight; ankhalyan. High above us, part of it transformed, and in the light of its smouldering windows, we saw two wet shapes of bulbous, space-suited human beings rise out of its dark epidermis. Its first carving. It might well be drowned out later by further accretions, but it was the first.

Mi laughed. The volume was too high, turning it into a hiss in my earpiece. Music, yet, to my ears.

That night, the arch of the galaxy a viridian river above us, we had sex in our camp tent with the nanoweave tuned transparent. It was always a thrill to be naked in that blister of breathable air, our bodies cool and damp as we pushed against each other in the sub-Earth grav. But Shuyedan's bulk looming nearby only strengthened our intimacy. Outside, an atmosphere that would kill us in ten minutes at the most. Inside, we were safe, tethered to ourselves. It felt like a miracle to be so unclad, so bare, our nipples and navels and pubic hair and genitals exposed for all this distant world to see, for this alien to observe and interpret. We were alive, unnaturally so. Homeworld an invisibility in the sky.

On the horizon the closest thing we have to Earth; the lights of Teysanzi Protectorate embedded in the hills.

We left the field lamps on beside us so our bodies glowed fierce blue on that dark plain. Shuyedan watched, its sounding a vibration across the tent. A lifecastle blooming. I felt in that moment like I was living myth; a stunning and meaningless myth in the cool churn of that recycled bubble of human atmosphere, saturated with our floating DNA. I swear I was so giddy I could have hurt Mi then, her mouth on mine, her tongue between my teeth. God, she worshipped me, her long black hair unwrapped, no longer bound in the helmet of a surface suit. Rivers silking across my torso, clinging to the damp on my breasts, which she kissed with such ridiculous passion. Mi would insist on their perfection with such sincerity it sometimes irritated me. Right then, I didn't care, as she ran her hands over them, fingers wet with spit. Her shoulder blades lit by a flaming galaxy as they writhed under her skin, written with pores and the small flecks of moles and freckles.

Shuyedan carved our sex into its skin, its windows spewing heat into the night.

At crimson dawn, the ground woke us with its rumbling, Shuyedan churning up soil with its scything belly and venting it from cracks in its shifting carapace. It was eating. There were kilunpa in it already, populating its shifting skin and swarming it, gathering ikan from its steaming windows. Months later, when the ikan ripened into something more pungent and powerful, the kilunpa would carry fragments from other lifecastles and fertilize Shuyedan's skin, so it too would create anew, do battle to separate a new wandering fortress to populate the world. The kilunpa's crystalline wings batted sun into our eyes. Mi and I unwrapped ourselves from the tangled blankets, sticky with sleep.

"I can't believe it stayed near us all night," I said, squinting against sunrise.

"We made something of an impression," said Mi, voice soft to suit the early hour. "Those carvings are exceptionally detailed."

We could see the sinuous new spine of human forms entangled along Shuyedan's side. Etched into shadowy relief by the light of sunrise. Its mindcarvings reminded me of the erotic sculptures that adorn the sandstone walls of the Konark Sun Temple on Earth. I had visited Konark once, barely out of my teens, with a boyfriend who seems so distant now I can remember nothing of his appearance except for the dimples on his earlobes where he sometimes wore silly studs. In the damp coastal fog of Orissa winter I'd watched stone men and women fuck in their alcoves while swallows shat on their shoulders, and I'd felt the hands of those long-dead sculptors and sun-devotees on my back, pushing against the membrane of time and history, even as men of that present-day Earth leered at me as if I were stripping just because my hair was down and my tank top comfortable.

"Which one's you?" Mi asked me. She put on her underwear, squinting through the transparent tent at Shuyedan lit by sunrise. I looked at the way her hair clung to the side of her face, strands following the temporary scars of pillow marks.

"You can't tell. It's just woman, and woman," I said. The tent buzzed with vibrations from Shuyedan's feeding.

"You speak to me like a child," Mi said, kicking into the legs of her surface suit. "If you had to *choose*, which one?"

I breathed in deep, wanting only to shut her out. "I don't know. Going by its mindcarvings, to Shuyedan we're one thought. And we're seeing that thought."

"That's a lovely notion. Maybe you're more romantic than you know," Mi said under her breath.

"Well, I don't see us as one thought. Shuyedan does. That's fascinating to me, not romantic."

She stared at me, then. In her sullen amazement I found her painfully attractive, and I was sorry to have hurt her. She zipped up her suit. "Wow. Forgive me for indulging in a little hyperbole."

A laugh disappeared in me. "Come on," I said, reaching over. I ran my fingernails over her cheek, freeing the clinging hairs from her face. The creases on her cheek fading. "I don't understand you sometimes. Can you not see where we are?"

"Yeah. I don't understand myself either," she said, probing her front teeth with her tongue. "Maybe we shouldn't have let Shuyedan witness us," she said, after a pause.

"What's this now?"

"We're on it, for god's sake. We're on its skin, being, being intimate. If another surveyor sees it, they'll know that two women are having sex out here."

I frowned. "All the more reason for the witnessing. If I don't want to bear a child for the settlement, that's my right. Most exoprots hashed this shit out ages ago. Where the hell are we, Earth?"

Mi shook her head, turning away. "You always talk about Earth like it's one country. You shouldn't. It's homeworld. All exoprot culture came from there," she said, warm in the flushed light of morning. I rolled my eyes, making sure she didn't see it. As if I hadn't grown up on Earth, same as her. She continued to look out at Shuyedan, bending down to press her palm against the floor of the tent, feeling the vibrations of the creature's feeding.

"We allowed a lifecastle to see human sex," she said. "No one's done that. Right?"

I shrugged. "I haven't seen any signs before."

"And we just did, just like that. That's history. Isn't it?"

I started to say something, anything to knock down that statement. But I didn't, or couldn't.

I touched her teeth with the tip of my thumb, and kissed her. She kept her mouth closed against it. I wiped her lips.

"Let's go take a closer look," I said.

Teysanzi means *new life*, or *beyond-life*. Not quite afterlife, because of the connotations with death. I was thirty when I arrived at the Protectorate, and forty-two when I met Mi, new like I was but younger and still nan tizan, "blue-eyed" with memories of Earth. But she was quicker than me to adjust, more confident. Nothing would get her down. Not even the sunless tiled skies and tunnels of Teysanzi, sub-city, metrocolony, Earth-Protectorate. I took her to the food court district, with its cheap neon and sunlamps battered with imported moths, its greenhouse stalls warm and rich with the smell of plants and vegetables and flowers snarling their way along the tables. She had taken it all in with a smile. The hot lights reflecting on her nose, which looked so like a button mushroom (I would tell her so weeks later, much to her false chagrin). I helped her with the chopsticks, her muscles still loose and hands shaking from jumping through spacetime while waking in and out of cryo-phase. From that moment watching her suck noodles into her mouth I knew I couldn't resist the inexorable tug of affection I had avoided for so long. I knew from the way she stared at me, blissful in trust, that she saw me, strong and grown into the scrubbed air and strange gravity of a new world, as somehow powerful. I fed on her awe in vampiric resignation. Quietly let her recite what she'd learned of this world back on Earth, as if to imprint her new reality with those predefined definitions, watched her explain to herself how Teysanzi cuisine was so spicy because the sub-city's processed atmosphere and low-g made for chronic swollen sinuses and dulled taste. She licked that same spice off her lips and left it on scrunched napkins by her tray. Mi talked in Colbyat often, to practice, though I think she was actually better at the formal language than I was. Still, I taught her Colbyat slang and swear words she didn't know, as one will do, told her how it and other star-tongues gestated in the confined cultures of starships, q-tunneling waystations, eventually exoprots.

A week after her arrival, we took the buggy out to the hinterlands to start her apprenticeship. Starlight in the puddled loam sinking under our boots, she asked me, "Do you agree with the sanctions against non-het couples here?" The formality of her constant questions, as if she were continually interviewing me, still delighted me at the time.

"No," I'd said. "Why?"

"Well. What if our Krasnikov tunnel collapses and we're cut off from the rest of the protectorate net, from Earth. That's what the Teysanzi's afraid of, right?"

I laughed. "Teysanzi's population isn't even three thousand. I think if the Krasnikov collapses and we're stuck out here a hundred light years from the nearest tunnel gate or settled planet, being het and having babies isn't going to save our asses. Being resourceful will. Or more realistically, nothing will."

"Yeah?" her voice loud against her helmet mic. A smile behind glass, and butterflies in my stomach. "And how're we going to be resourceful? Build a mega-generation ship to haul our descendants to the next gas station? Or should I say gas giant," Mi asked, touching my arm lightly with her gloved hand. Her giddy inflection made me light-headed. There was a tremendous energy to her out here, much more than in the sub-city. So confident, for someone on their first trip out to the hinterlands, suited up. Maybe it was adrenalin.

"Woman of ideas over here," I said. "First, terrible pun. Second, genship endurance is still a het dependent plan. Maybe we can hack cryo-phase, just sleep for thousands of years on your ship, become space vampires. The breeders can keep breeding."

"Mmm-hm. It's not my ship. You're the resourceful one. I'd just give up, wum," she said.

"Right. Anyway, this het-normative obsession isn't going to last. It's just us cycling through civ states, spinning the wheels, going back in time before we go forward. No matter how much we expand, even if we build new cities, there's an upper limit to how fast we can expand our population without breathable atmo. Until we can augment our bodies to breathe it. Population booming is just a short-term panic response to the thought of our Krasnikov closing."

Mi thought about this for a little while, stepping over a tar-black puddle carefully. "Maybe it'll be good if the tunnel collapses. Maybe an actual apocalypse would turn Teysanzi into a utopia because we wouldn't worry about anything. I mean, ultimately, who cares, right? There's plenty of other humans out there on other worlds, and we're all gonna die whether or not there's another generation to keep the lights on here. If the Krasnikov goes, we could actually *live* like no one else ever has, if we know it's the end. We'd all just make love, be friends, raise the kids here to become new decadents, make art for rescue ships to find centuries later. We'd sip champagne in the ruins of dead lifecastles till there was just one of us left."

"God. A punner and a poet," I said.

Mi laughed, much louder than my response deserved.

"So. Are you planning on having a child to bolster our chances against extinction?" I asked, casual as I could be. Probably not at all casual. When we'd toured the school-commune district, she'd been a natural with the children there, completely at ease (very unlike me).

"No," she said.

I nodded. A few paces ahead of us, a sankipyo looped out of a puddle in a glistening flash and wormed across the ground, frilled legs twirling behind it like wind ornaments. Mi squealed in delight.

"Oh, Tani. Is that," she whispered. I realized one of the hills in the distance was shifting, moving. I nodded, though I don't know if she could tell through the helmet. Her first sighting of vitanbiyet. I had other things on my mind. The lifecastle didn't come anywhere near us, but it was good enough for her, for a first trip. We watched it for about ten minutes, its windows opening and closing, glittering sharp in the distance. Their luminescence made the vitanbiyet look uncannily like a building on the horizon. An old castle on Earth, maybe, swaying in an earthquake, its windows aglow with candlelight and electricity, chandeliers tilting, tinkling.

When we got back to the buggy and sealed all doors, I helped her out of her helmet. The faceplate misted as I freed her face from beneath it. Her eyes were wide, forehead sweaty under the dim blue cabin lights. There's no excitement like seeing alien life for the first time. She helped me out of my helmet too. I think her hands were shaking. She took a long time undoing the clasps. She was laughing, just laughing. No words.

The moment the helmet was off, I kissed her. The metal rims of our suit collars clashed loudly, but she grabbed the back of my head with her hands and helped me forward, pulling my mouth to hers.

Five weeks later, Mi witnessed her first separation of a new lifecastle. We tagged it, and named it Vitanbiyet Shuyedan.

I felt flushed out there, in my helmet. Oddly clumsy and unprepared.

"You ready for this?" I asked Mi. "We can just follow protocol, use the marker gun if you don't feel up to doing this." What we were about to do wasn't recommended, but I knew that surveyors did it all the time with new apprentices as a bonding ritual. More like asserting to their apprentices that they were badasses.

"I'm ready," she said, voice flat.

She knew by my tone it had been a challenge, even if I barely realized it myself.

Shuyedan was a hundred feet away, settled in repose, kilunpa settled all over its carapace, their wings like fluttering leaves, making the vitanbiyet look like a giant tree in the breeze. Its windows would flicker sometimes under their bodies like lanterns strung from boughs. In two months, its pennants would grow out, unfurl to signal the ripening of its ikan.

"What'll they do to us if they find us manipulating the lifecastles? We're just supposed to tag them, aren't we?" Mi asked, finally.

"We didn't manipulate shit. They see what they see. Us having sex just happened to be what this one saw. Nothing wrong with that. Hit it."

"Now?"

"Yes, now. Throw it as far as you can."

Mi turned, took the silver orb of the sounding beacon from her belt and thumbed it on. The red light on it flickered. She hurled it like a grenade. Her grunt small, bringing a smile to my face. I saw breath on her faceplate. The beacon landed not too far from Shuyedan. We saw the light turn green.

"Let's go," I said. Mi followed. We strode toward Shuyedan, our bootprints deep in the dark mud. The sun had risen now above the mountain crests and the blinking transmission towers of Teysanzi. It was full daylight, but here some stars are visible at high noon.

The kilunpa burst from Shuyedan's back in a flurry of wings, swarming into the sky. I remembered swallows again, and ducks, on Earth. We saw Shuyedan's mind-carvings unveiled once more, our replicated forms drying into something less smooth than the previous night. It rose, roused by the silent frequency of the beacon, its legs unfolding. I heard the huff of my breath within the helmet, the huff of Mi's breath in the mics. The barbed black fronds of sikri-grass whipped at our legs as we ran. When we were in Shuyedan's shadow, I stopped. Two stories high it groaned and swayed, folding its legs again as it looked over the beacon. Its carapace tumbled serpentine shapes that solidified around the naked women on its back, but nothing recognizable formed. I aimed the grappling gun, lining the sights up right below the spine of human shapes. I pulled the trigger. The gun jerked in my arms, and I felt the satisfying second tug of the hook snagging in the carapace.

Mi was at my side quick, and I approved. She fired her own grappling gun. Her shot hit two feet below mine. Good enough. "Nice shot," I allowed. I couldn't see her face. We clambered up the vitanbiyet like insects, first up one of the limbs, and then on to the carapace. Its windows flicked open and close by our boots, which trailed sticky threads of unripe ikan. The glow of its windows lit our surface-suits yellow in shuttering intervals. I kept a tight grip on the gun as I clambered up, reeling the chord back in and looking back every five seconds to make sure that Mi was alright. She was using her legs more than her arms, breathing heavy into her mic. But she was doing fine.

"Good girl," I whispered.

Our entire bodies hummed as Shuyedan sounded and stood up straight, the beacon no longer of interest. It could see us with its windows, but didn't care now that we were on it. It was the approach that might have made it defensive, but now we were indistinguishable from kilunpa in its vision. Unless we hurt it or drew its attention too much. So far, no human has died from climbing on vitanbiyet, but we've seen the immense violence they're capable of when fighting each other.

We used its swaying gait to land our steps rhythmically against its side.

Under our ikan-smeared soles, the carapace-stone of the lifecastle was almost glassy smooth because it was so fresh. The new presence of kilunpa colonizing it had prompted new carvings along the skin like ornate tracery, arching across the windows in a way the human brain will remind of our own architectures from across history. The skin would become more granular as it aged. Our footsteps along its steep side left flickers of ultraviolet that faded, like phosphenes on its dark surface. Stray kilunpa thumped against our suits, too light for us to feel them. Mi did gasp when one bounced off her faceplate before retreating into a blinking window to lap at the ikan. When I finally reached the mindcarvings of Mi and me, I switched on my headlamp. My arms ached, and sweat collected in itchy trickles under the fabric lining inside the helmet.

I swept the light over the carvings.

The figures were simple but striking, almost life-sized but voluptuous in their exaggerations of human contours. Konark. The two humanoids started off with the round heads and thick limbs of suited and helmeted surveyors, simplistic shapes, then melded together in a melted abstraction that might have been a representation of our camp tent, or mountains. Then they emerged again to form a chain of entwined bodies, distinctly naked and in the various embraces of sex, sometimes melding into the stratum underneath them. From surveyors to humans, object to animal. Mi and Tani. I could see the grooves where buttocks met, the curve of hips, even the small bumps of nipples on breasts and the dimpled patterns of faces; eyes and noses and lips.

"I'm. Obviously. The taller one," I said between deep breaths.

My headlamp's light reflected off the placid faces of our alien likenesses and their ecstasy, glossing off Mi's faceplate. She took a pen-sized marker dart from her belt and stabbed it into the carapace. Characters glowed in my helmet feed as info panels blossomed in my field of vision. In a low-detail map overlay, a new red dot appeared. Shuyedan-18 was tagged.

"How many lovers have you brought here to be witnessed by lifecastles? Is that one of your old tricks?" asked Mi in the tent, serious under her teasing tone. I took a sip of black tea from my thermos, the taste of leaves grown under Teysanzi sunlamps having long overtaken my memories of what tea had tasted like on Earth.

"You're the first," I told her.

"I don't mean the sex. I mean just being witnessed."

"You're the first," I repeated.

"You're lying."

"I was always a loner, Mi. You've no idea."

"You're saying you always came out to the hinterlands alone?" she asked

"Yes. I specifically asked. Hence, loner."

"Oh come on."

"Hope to die. I was co-habiting on Earth, you know. With a gentle, kind darling of a woman. I left her to come here. She didn't want to go to space. Very idea terrified her. So I chose. It hurt like a bitch. Never again. I do actually come out here to survey the hinterlands, tag and observe the lifecastles, all that, not just carve our initials on them like schoolchildren in a playground."

"Never again. Huh," Mi breathed.

"Well. Except you. Until you," I smiled.

Mi placed her hand on my cheek. "Why did you leave the love of your life, leave Earth?" she asked.

"Because I don't just think of love. Because I read and watched movies and fantasized about space travel since I was little. Because, I think, the universe is my god, and I want to explore its insides. Because there are aliens here that grow statues on their backs, and I can try and understand them."

"Okay."

"I didn't mean to sound snappy."

"You didn't. You sound, well. You don't like to be called romantic. But there's something to being alone, isn't there."

"Why did you leave Earth?"

"Not because I'm a loner, that's for sure," she said.

I breathed in and out, not saying anything. She continued.

"In fact, I've never been lonelier than on the journey here, slipping through the Krasnikov in that ship. I regretted leaving my parents and family behind, hated myself. I felt like the universe was crushing us in that ship. That we were so, so tiny. But once we got here," she paused, touched her eyelids. "I've never felt less alone, even with just two thousand five hundred humans in Teysanzi. To see people making their lives on another world, an entirely new planet? To see the vitanbiyet, the flora and fauna here. This was what I'd studied and trained for, left homeworld for. You called me nan tizan, but I was tei tizan, red-eyed with this world. The universe, this world—it makes me want to puke, it makes me so happy."

I laughed at this, placing one hand on the hillock of her hip. "You make me want to puke, with your rampant happiness."

She smiled, then, but it was so obviously sad that it made me queasy. She clicked her tongue behind her teeth.

"What? It was a joke," I said, gentle.

"Nothing," she said, and pushed her mouth against my cheek. I got goose bumps. She turned and pulled the blanket over her shoulder.

I think of what I said to Mi, about trying to understand the lifecastles. I still don't. We still don't. And why should we? We don't even understand our fellow Earthlings, really. All those animals we drove extinct, all the ones we saved from extinction, all the ones that barely know we exist. All the human cultures we've destroyed, all the new ones growing right now on Earth and other worlds, all the old ones we've clung on to. It's not like we're all a big ball of understanding, one big happy Earth family.

We can't even hope to fully understand the human beings we choose to pair up and mate with, to share our intimacies and animal lives with.

So all in all, that we're here and haven't yet killed any of the vitanbiyet, or been killed by them, while we peer at each other on this remote world under its small but lively sun—that's a start. We survey them. Tag them with the markers, name them, count them, observe them, watch the glowing dots of their markers move across our survey maps. Record their mindcarvings, especially when they form human shapes. Compare notes among surveyors about what we see on their skins, from minarets to gargoyles to forested slopes from Earth, though they're never any of those things. To date, we've counted sixty-six lifecastles in the explored hinterlands beyond Teysanzi, of which forty-two are alive now. Eighteen were named Shuyedan by different surveyors, because they were witnessed emerging from their progenitors, and were at the time the youngest recorded.

Only one Shuyedan had naked women across its back in a spine of bodies conjoined; evidence of a tiny, meaningless, insignificant emotion from a planet so far away its inhabitants had to tunnel through spacetime to land on the world. A heart carved into a tree trunk on a bright summer day, air thick with the humid light of a white star instead of a red one.

Whenever I watched lifecastles make new carvings, it made me a little sick to think of us etched into Shuyedan like that, as it went about its solitary life, under the silent companionship of its many-winged kilunpa.

Shuyedan-18 became a celebrity at the research centre in Teysanzi once other surveyors spotted its unique mindcarvings. Some called it the 'Dirty Old Man' as a joke, which bizarrely cut me to the quick, so much so that I had to quietly slip away to the washroom or brew a new thermos of tea whenever someone mentioned it. I always noticed Mi blushing fiercely but laughing with everyone else when someone brought up that stupid nickname, and it never failed to make me angry. She probably talked to our colleagues more than I had in ten years.

There were enough same-gendered surveyor teams out there that the identity of

Shuyedan's muses remained a mystery. Whether or not Shuyedan's muses had done something wrong was a point of debate.

"You don't really believe this is real, do you," Mi asked me, in my apartment in Teysanzi, sheets still damp from our bodies. The grav-lights hovered over our bed, quiet, guttering stars in the gloom. I kicked one to the ceiling, where it stayed. "You seem tired when we have sex. Not invested," she added.

"Shatin-ba, Mi, what do you want me to say?"

"I don't really know. What can you say to a blue-eyed child? nan tizan, tei tizan. All the same to you."

I got up, head brushing the low ceiling.

"I'm sorry," she said. "That was unfair."

"Mi, I can't just keep reassuring you every step of the way. There aren't a lot of people in this city. Being with a woman, not to mention my apprentice, is a professional risk for me."

"And it's not a risk for me? Am I popping out babies with some virile mate to strengthen the colonial populace while, while you suffer in silence?" she asked.

"No, that's. Not what I meant. Of course it's a risk for you. But I'm sharing that with you. Doesn't that tell you enough? I took us to be witnessed by vitanbiyet."

She didn't say anything, instead sitting up and pulling her hair back into her strand-entangled scrunchie.

"What?" I asked, a new sweat rising on my forehead.

"You've made me feel strange about that ever since you did it. Like we violated Shuyedan by allowing it to see us have sex. We didn't carve ourselves on it, you know. It did that."

"That's ridiculous. I," I swallowed. "I cherish that moment, Michiko. You have no idea how much. You really don't."

She looked at me and shook her head, letting her hands go limp in her lap.

"What is it?" I asked.

"I'm deporting. Taking the Krasnikov to Jaltara-Lafneik Protectorate."

"What?"

"Ter nai lan, Tani."

"Don't. I am calm. Where's Jaltara-Lafneik."

"Watery Super-Earth, GB-277."

"You're leaving. You're leaving the world because you think I'm not. What. Serious enough about you?"

Mi pulled back her hair again, reworking the scrunchie. Pulled the hair taut against her scalp, severe and shining. I sank back into the bed. Her eyes were wet, though it was hard to tell in the dimness of the grav-lights and the stars beyond the skylight.

"No," she said. "Don't think that. I just, I want to see the galaxy. Like you say you do. But you don't. You stay here, and you don't seem to like it at all. Honestly I think you want to be back on Earth. You've lived here ten years and don't talk to anyone if you can help it. That's not me. I want to survey on other worlds. I want to survey other life forms."

"A week ago you were telling me you wanted to spend the rest of your life here, with me. That you loved it here."

"In ten years you haven't found a way to be happy here. I can't carry that for you. This is too small a place for me to share that burden. You're my closest friend here."

I thought of Mi being friendly with our colleagues and fellow settlers in the research centre, laughing and joking with the carers in the school commune.

"Who'd you have to fuck to get reassigned to another planet?" I asked.

Mi looked at me, wiping under her eyes, and nodded. She got up off the bed. "I should have left without telling you."

"No," I said. "No, no. Don't go. I'm sorry I said that. You have to understand how. What a surprise this is," I said, the words spilling over each other in my mouth.

She breathed out, weary, on guard. "I promised Jaltara-Lafneik a child. I'm young, healthy, fertile. Valuable on any exoprot, even one with a good position on the Krasnikov net. They have breathable atmo, no hurdles to growth."

"You told me you didn't want a baby."

Mi leaned against the wall and touched one of the grav-lights in the air, pushed it away. "I wanted you to like me, Tani."

"You lied?"

She shook her head, looking so young, yet so tired. "I don't want to be a mother. It's a bargaining chip to get off-world." Tired of me.

"So you're selling your body to some random person on this other world? Mi, please listen to yourself. Don't do this."

"Shit, Tani, it's not really about me at all, is it? It's about who owns little naive Mi's body, and that person not being you in your own mind. No more side pillow for you to hug every time you feel old and crabby," she sprang off the wall, bumping her head on the ceiling. Muscle memory seized my arms and I instinctively tried to get up and touch her, kiss her head. She raised her hands and backed away as if I were pointing a gun at her. I stopped myself. She sat on the bed again, crossed her arms tight against her chest.

"Don't you worry on my behalf, they have sperm banks. I didn't sign up to be a mate, it's not a damn dictatorship. You don't get assigned husbands. They use the commune system, just like here. The kid'll be raised by the community. I'm going there because I have skills they want."

I forced myself to speak calmly, gathering my thoughts instead of spitting them out. "What if you can't settle properly? You've got no lifeline, you're bartering away your right to relocate again, unless you get rich there. You can never go back to Earth unless you really become successful there. Think, Mi. Just think about that. You're young, and so bright, but being old and crabby does give me some perspective, at the very least."

"I'm glad you have so much faith in me," she said with a small nod.

"That's not what I meant—"

"Just stop," she said, and silenced me. She finally looked me in the eye again. "You're not old. That's terrible, that I said that. I'm sorry."

"It's okay. Nothing wrong with being old. So I am crabby, then?" I asked, trying and failing to smile. She managed one, for a second. I felt my heartbeat deafen me with hope.

"All right. I know you think I've been distant. I'll show you, I'll be better. What if I came with you? We can start new, all new," I said.

Her face crumpled in sudden frustration as she let out a soft sound, a small moan that caught in my own chest. "Please. Please don't do this," she said.

"Why."

"You're a loner, Tani. You always were."

I shook my head, and before I knew it my head was in her lap, my cheek on her thigh as I wept into her. I shivered as she stroked my head, as if I were a baby.

I watched from the hinterlands, my buggy revving under me, as the lifter scratched a glowing line into the atmosphere before becoming just another star in the magenta sky. Mi didn't say good-bye after our final conversation. I didn't blame her, though I hated her for it.

I look at the ruins of Shuyedan. *Youngest,* fallen now. The arches of its ribs towering over the damp earth, some collapsed to bring the ceiling of its carapace down to the black sikri grass. Its skin pennants tough even after death, dried into wrinkled hide in the cool afternoons. They ripple lazily in the wet breeze, winter rain dampening the ruins slick. Shuyedan-18 died quite young, just three years old when its progenitor Urdhema declared war on it. It never got to become a progenitor itself, but then again, spawning new members of their race seems incidental to them. Perhaps it's not tragedy at all. Just history.

My own womb remains empty, though some of my fellow Teysanzians continue to drop hints that I should fill it soon, as a collapse-fearing, dutiful citizen. My cyba augments still keep my chances of bearing a child up, but even they'll wind down with my body. I wonder if I'd be so ostracized on Earth, or Jaltara-Lafneik, for doing as I please with my insides and outsides.

My boots crunch in the crumbled obsidian of Shuyedan's stone. I pick up pebbles of its skin and toss them, sending stray kilunpa glittering into the air. I'm in unexplored territory, the farthest I've been from Teysanzi. Shuyedan-18's tag failed during its battle with Urdhema, so it took a while to find the remains. Across the collapsed ceilings of the lifecastle's skin—mindcarvings of nude human bodies, multiple sexes, apart and together. Accretions from three years of observance, and evidence that others had come here to be witnessed by Shuyedan-18, unclothed in their tents, having sex, het and non-het. A new ritual. A new tradition between human and extraterrestrial. Looking at these newer carvings makes something click in me, like a clock starting, counting away from and towards something at the same time.

Then, I find the spine of the first human shapes to grace Shuyedan's back, now grainy with age, more beautiful because of it. I'll always recognize them. Frozen in their dance, their small moment of intimacy, ecstasy. Their faces have worn away to pits and nubs, some of their limbs stumps. But still recognizable. Still intact. Shuyedan never erased us from its skin, never forgot its first glimpse of humanity unclad.

"Teysanzi-central," I say into my helmet. "Shuyedan-18 ruins located. Something to see. Recording now. Recommend cordon, salvage for preservation and study. Will proceed to scraping ikan residue. Observing the famous erotic mindcarvings, the original ones—two human women in coitus, replicated over and over, as if passing in time. The muses." I listen to myself breathe inside the helmet. No one at the terminal. Slackers. I go on talking. All transmissions are recorded.

"Advise further experiments—nudist tent colonies out in the hinterlands. Rampant hedonism for the benefit of the lifecastles," I pause, thinking about this.

"Hear me out, actually. Shuyedan-18 is the first one to actively observe us, to remember human form long enough to keep its mindcarvings of us preserved in such detail. I think it's because it saw us naked, without surface suits, interacting together. It recognised something in us, something alive. Vulnerable. Maybe visual body language is a way for us to communicate with the vitanbiyet. Especially newly separated ones. Dirty Old Man's gone, rest its soul, along with, I hope, its wretched nickname. But there are other lifecastles. I think, central, that this is the beginning of a long friendship," I smile into the mic.

My fellow muse, gone.

"Additional. Reporting witnessing, approximately three point five years prior, to Shuyedan-18, ankhalyan. That's me in the carvings, one of the original muses. You heard right." I switch off the comm system, feeling light-headed. Maybe now they'll send me back to Earth, where overpopulation can take good old-fashioned non-hets like me.

Earth. Perhaps I was always nan tizan, and just never admitted it.

I look up at the empty spot between the stars where the Krasnikov Gate graces the sky, invisible to the naked eye. I wonder what it would look like collapsing.

I know they can't do anything to me. I'm a citizen. Block me from progressing up the career ladder, becoming a supervisor, going into active city governance? Sure. But we're endangered, us Teysanzians. They need me. I'm staying, till the end of this world if it comes. I'll outlive every last human bastard in Teysanzi so I can sip champagne alone under the ruins of my sweet Shuyedan-18.

I bend down to look at the spine of Mis and Tanis fucking and decaying in the dim red sunlight. One of them has her head thrown back, black neck open to the drifting rain, mouth open. It is clearly Mi, though only to me. Under her, the other woman with her eyes closed, mouth a placid line. Me. I run my fingers across Mi's face, and my gloved fingertips come away black.

"Vitanbiyet Shuyedan had a dream of love," I say to her, and let the rain run down my hand.

Bannerless

CARRIE VAUGHN

New York Times *bestseller Carrie Vaughn is the author of a wildly popular series of novels detailing the adventures of Kitty Narville, a radio personality who also happens to be a werewolf, and who runs a late-night call-in radio advice show for supernatural creatures. The "Kitty" books include* Kitty and the Midnight Hour, Kitty Goes to Washington, Kitty Takes a Holiday, Kitty and the Silver Bullet, Kitty and the Dead Man's Hand, Kitty Raises Hell, Kitty's House of Horrors, Kitty Goes to War, Kitty's Big Trouble, Kitty Steals the Show, Kitty Rocks the House, *and a collection of her "Kitty" stories,* Kitty's Greatest Hits. *Her other novels include* Voices of Dragons, *her first venture into Young Adult territory, a fantasy,* Discord's Apple, Steel, *and* After the Golden Age. *Vaughn's short work has appeared in* Lightspeed, Asimov's Science Fiction, Subterranean, Inside Straight *(a Wild Cards novel),* Realms of Fantasy, Jim Baen's Universe, Paradox, Strange Horizons, Weird Tales, All-Star Zeppelin Adventure Stories, *and elsewhere; her non-Kitty stories have been collected in* Straying from the Path. *Her most recent books include a new "Kitty" novel,* Kitty in the Underworld, *and* Dreams of the Golden Age, *a sequel to* After the Golden Age. *She lives in Colorado.*

Here she offers us a believable look at a society struggling to put itself back together, in a better and more just form, after a climate-driven catastrophe that almost wipes out the human race.

Enid and Bert walked the ten miles from the way station because the weather was good, a beautiful spring day. Enid had never worked with the young man before, but he turned out to be good company: chatty without being oppressively extroverted. Young, built like a redwood, he looked the part of an investigator. They talked about home and the weather and trivialities—but not the case. She didn't like to dwell on the cases she was assigned to before getting a firsthand look at them. She had expected Bert to ask questions about it, but he was taking her lead.

On this stretch of the Coast Road, halfway between the way station and South-town, ruins were visible in the distance, to the east. An old sprawling city from before the big fall. In her travels in her younger days, she'd gone into it a few times, to shout into the echoing artificial canyons and study overgrown asphalt roads and cracked walls with fallen roofs. She rarely saw people, but often saw old cook fires and cobbled together shantytowns that couldn't support the lives struggling within them. Scavengers and scattered folk still came out from them sometimes, then faded back to the concrete enclaves, surviving however they survived.

Bert caught her looking.

"You've been there?" Bert said, nodding toward the haze marking the swath of ruined city. No paths or roads ran that way anymore. She'd had to go overland when she'd done it.

"Yes, a long time ago."

"What was it like?"

The answer could either be very long or very short. The stories of what had happened before and during the fall were terrifying and intriguing, but the ruins no longer held any hint of those tales. They were bones, in the process of disappearing. "It was sad," she said finally.

"I'm still working through the histories," he said. "For training, right? There's a lot of diaries. Can be hard, reading how it was at the fall."

"Yes."

In isolation, any of the disasters that had struck would not have overwhelmed the old world. The floods alone would not have destroyed the cities. The vicious influenza epidemic—a mutated strain with no available vaccine that incapacitated victims in a matter of hours—by itself would have been survivable, eventually. But the floods, the disease, the rising ocean levels, the monster storms piling one on top of the other, an environment off balance that chipped away at infrastructure and made each recovery more difficult than the one before it, all of it left too many people with too little to survive on. Wealth meant nothing when there was simply nothing left. So, the world died. But people survived, here and there. They came together and saved what they could. They learned lessons.

The road curved into the next valley and they approached Southtown, the unimaginative name given to this district's main farming settlement. Windmills appeared first, clean towers with vertical blades spiraling gently in an unfelt breeze. Then came cisterns set on scaffolds, then plowed fields and orchards in the distance. The town was home to some thousand people scattered throughout the valley and surrounding farmlands. There was a grid of drained roads and whitewashed houses, solar and battery-operated carts, some goats, chickens pecking in yards. All was orderly, pleasant. This was what rose up after the ruins fell, the home that their grandparents fled to as children.

"Will you let the local committee know we're here?" Bert asked.

"Oh, no. We don't want anyone to have warning we're here. We go straight to the household. Give them a shock."

"Makes sense."

"This is your first case, isn't it? Your first investigation?"

"It is. And . . . I guess I'm worried I might have to stop someone." Bert had a staff like hers but he knew how to use his for more than walking. He had a stunner and a pack of tranquilizer needles on his belt. All in plain view. If she did her job well enough he wouldn't need to do anything but stand behind her and look alert. A useful tool. He seemed to understand his role.

"I doubt you will. Our reputation will proceed us. It's why we have the reputation in the first place. Don't worry."

"I just need to act as terrifying as the reputation says I do."

She smiled. "Exactly—you know just how this works, then."

They wore brown tunics and trousers with gray sashes. Somber colors, cold like winter, probably designed to inspire a chill. Bert stood a head taller than she did and looked like he could break tree trunks. How sinister, to see the pair of them approach.

"And you—this is your last case, isn't it?"

That was what she'd told the regional committee, that it was time for her to go home, settle down, take up basket weaving or such like. "I've been doing this almost twenty years," she said. "It's time for me to pass the torch."

"Would you miss the travel? That's what I've been looking forward to, getting to see some of the region, you know?"

"Maybe," she said. "But I wouldn't miss the bull. You'll see what I mean."

They approached the settlement. Enid put her gaze on a young woman carrying a basket of eggs along the main road. She wore a skirt, tunic, apron, and a straw hat to keep off the sun.

"Excuse me," Enid said. The woman's hands clenched as if she was afraid she might drop the basket from fright. As she'd told Bert, their reputation preceded them. They were inspectors, and inspectors only appeared for terrible reasons. The woman's expression held shock and denial. Why would inspectors ever come to Southtown?

"Yes, how can I help you?" she said quickly, nervously.

"Can you tell us where to find Apricot Hill?" The household they'd been sent to investigate.

The woman's anxiety fell away and a light of understanding dawned. Ah, then people knew. Everyone likely knew *something* was wrong, without knowing exactly what. The whole town would know investigators were here within the hour. Enid's last case, and it was going to be all about sorting out gossip.

"Yes—take that path there, past the pair of windmills. They're on the south side of the duck pond. You'll see the clotheslines out front."

"Thank you," Enid said. The woman hurried away, hugging her basket to her chest.

Enid turned to Bert. "Ready for this?"

"Now I'm curious. Let's go."

Apricot Hill was on a nice acreage overlooking a pretty pond and a series of orchards beyond that. There was one large house, two stories with lots of windows, and an outbuilding with a pair of chimneys, a production building—Apricot Hill was centered on food processing, taking in produce from outlying farms and drying, canning, and preserving it for winter stores for the community. The holding overall was well lived in, a bit run-down, cluttered, but that could mean they were busy. It was spring—nothing ready for canning yet. This should have been the season for cleaning up and making repairs.

A girl with a bundle of sheets over her arm, probably collected from the clothes-line the woman had mentioned, saw them first. She peered up the hill at their arrival for a moment before dropping the sheets and running to the house. She was wispy and energetic—not the one mentioned in the report, then. Susan, and not Aren. The heads of the household were Frain and Felice.

"We are announced," Enid said wryly. Bert hooked a finger in his belt.

A whole crowd, maybe even all ten members of the household, came out of the house. A rough looking bunch, all together. Old clothes, frowning faces. This was an adequate household, but not a happy one.

An older man, slim and weather-worn, came forward and looked as though he wished he had a weapon. This would be Frain. Enid went to him, holding her hand out for shaking.

"Hello, I'm Enid, the investigator sent by the regional committee. This is my partner, Bert. This is Apricot Hill, isn't it? You must be Frain?"

"Yes," he said cautiously, already hesitant to give away any scrap of information.

"May we step inside to talk?"

She would look like a matron to them, maybe even head of a household somewhere, if they weren't sure she didn't have a household. Investigators didn't have households; they traveled constantly, avenging angels, or so the rumors said. Her dull brown hair was rolled into a bun, her soft face had seen years and weather. They'd wonder if she'd ever had children of her own, if she'd ever earned a banner. Her spreading middle-aged hips wouldn't give a clue.

Bert stood behind her, a wall of authority. Their questions about him would be simple: How well could he use that staff he carried?

"What is this about?" Frain demanded. He was afraid. He knew what she was here for—the implications—and he was afraid.

"I think we should go inside and sit down before we talk," Enid said patiently, knowing full well she sounded condescending and unpleasant. The lines on Frain's face deepened. "Is everyone here? Gather everyone in the household to your common room."

With a curt word Frain herded the rest of his household inside.

The common room on the house's ground floor was, like the rest of the household, functional without being particularly pleasant. No vase of flowers on the long dining table. Not a spot of color on the wall except for a single faded banner: the square of red and green woven cloth that represented the baby they'd earned some sixteen years ago. That would be Susan—the one with the laundry outside. Adults had come into the household since then, but that was their last baby. Had they wanted another child badly enough that they didn't wait for their committee to award them a banner?

The house had ten members. Only nine sat around the table. Enid took her time studying them, looking into each face. Most of the gazes ducked away from her. Susan's didn't.

"We're missing someone, I think?" Enid said.

The silence was thick as oil. Bert stood easy and perfectly still behind her, hand on his belt. Oh, he was a natural at this. Enid waited a long time, until the people around the table squirmed.

"Aren," Felice said softly. "I'll go get her."

"No," Frain said. "She's sick. She can't come."

"Sick? Badly sick? Has a doctor seen her?" Enid said.

Again, the oily silence.

"Felice, if you could get her, thank you," Enid said.

A long stretch passed before Felice returned with the girl, and Enid was happy to watch while the group grew more and more uncomfortable. Susan was trembling; one of the men was hugging himself. This was as awful a gathering as she had ever seen, and her previous case had been a murder.

When Felice brought Aren into the room, Enid saw exactly what she expected to see: the older woman with her arm around a younger woman—age twenty or so—who wore a full skirt and a tunic three sizes too big that billowed in front of her. Aren moved slowly, and had to keep drawing her hands away from her belly.

She might have been able to hide the pregnancy for a time, but she was now six months along, and there was no hiding that swell and the ponderous hitch in her movement.

The anger and unhappiness in the room thickened even more, and it was no longer directed at Enid.

She waited while Felice guided the pregnant woman to a chair—by herself, apart from the others.

"This is what you're here for, isn't it?" Frain demanded, his teeth bared and fists clenched.

"It is," Enid agreed.

"Who told?" Frain hissed, looking around at them all. "Which one of you told?"

No one said anything. Aren cringed and ducked her head. Felice stared at her hands in her lap.

Frain turned to Enid. "Who sent the report? I've a right to know my accuser—the household's accuser."

"The report was anonymous, but credible." Part of her job here was to discover, if she could, who sent the tip of the bannerless pregnancy to the regional committee. Frain didn't need to know that. "I'll be asking all of you questions over the next couple of days. I expect honest answers. When I am satisfied that I know what happened here, I'm authorized to pass judgment. I will do so as quickly as possible, to spare you waiting. Frain, I'll start with you."

"It was an accident. An accident, I'm sure of it. The implant failed. Aren has a boy in town; they spend all their time together. We thought nothing of it because of the implant, but then it failed, and—we didn't say anything because we were scared. That's all. We should have told the committee as soon as we knew. I'm sorry—I know now that that was wrong. You'll take that into consideration?"

"When did you know? All of you, starting with Aren—when did you know of the pregnancy?"

The young woman's first words were halting, choked. Crying had thickened her throat. "Must . . . must have been . . . two months in, I think. I was sick. I just knew."

"Did you tell anyone?"

"No, no one. I was scared."

They were all terrified. That sounded true.

"And the rest of you?"

Murmurs answered. The men shook their heads, said they'd only known for a month or so, when she could no longer hide the new shape of her. They knew for sure the day that Frain ranted about it. "I didn't rant," the man said. "I was only surprised. I lost my temper, that was all."

Felice said, "I knew when she got sick. I've been pregnant—" Her gaze went to the banner on the wall. "I know the signs. I asked her, and she told."

"You didn't think to tell anyone?"

"Frain told me not to."

So Frain knew, at least as soon as she did. The man glared fire at Felice, who wouldn't lift her gaze.

"Aren, might I speak to you alone?"

The woman cringed, back curled, arms wrapped around her belly.

"I'll go with you, dear," Felice whispered.

"Alone," Enid said. "Bert will wait here. We'll go outside. Just a short walk."

Trembling, Aren stood. Enid stood aside to let her walk out the door first. She caught Bert's gaze and nodded. He nodded back.

Enid guided her on the path away around the house, to the garden patch and pond behind. She went slowly, letting Aren set the pace.

The physical state of a household carried information: whether rakes and shovels were hung up neat in a shed or closet, or piled haphazardly by the wall of an unpainted barn. Whether the herb garden thrived, if there were flowers in window boxes. If neat little water-smoothed stones edged the paths leading from one building to another, or if there were just dirt tracks worn into the grass. She didn't judge a household by whether or not it put a good face to the world—but she did judge them by whether or not the folk in a household worked to put on a good face for themselves. They had to live with it, look at it every single day.

This household did not have a good face. The garden patch was only just sprouting, even this far into spring. There were no flowers. The grass along the path was overgrown. There was a lack of care here that made Enid angry.

But the pond was pretty. Ducks paddled around a stand of cattails, muttering to themselves.

Enid had done this before, knew the questions to ask and what possible answers she might get to those questions. Every moment reduced the possible explanations. Heavens, she was tired of this.

Enid said, "Stop here. Roll up your sleeve."

Aren's overlarge tunic had wide sleeves that fell past her wrists. They'd be no good at all for working. The young woman stood frozen. Her lips were tightly pursed, to keep from crying.

"May I roll the sleeve up, then?" Enid asked carefully, reaching.

"No, I'll do it," she said, and clumsily pushed the fabric up to her left shoulder.

She revealed an angry scar, puckered pink, mostly healed. Doing the math, maybe seven or eight months old. The implant had been cut out, the wound not well treated, which meant she'd probably done it herself.

"Did you get anyone to stitch that up for you?" Enid asked.

"I bound it up and kept it clean." At least she didn't try to deny it. Enid guessed she would have, if Frain were there.

"Where did you put the implant after you took it out?"

"Buried it in the latrine."

Enid hoped she wouldn't have to go after it for evidence. "You did it yourself. No one forced you to, or did it to you?" That happened sometimes, someone with a skewed view of the world and what was theirs deciding they needed someone to bear a baby for them.

"It's me, it's just me. Nobody else. Just me."

"Does the father know?"

"No, I don't think . . . He didn't know I'd taken out the implant. I don't know if he knows about the baby."

Rumors had gotten out, Enid was sure, especially if Aren hadn't been seen around town in some time. The anonymous tip about the pregnancy might have come from anywhere.

"Can you tell me the father's name, so I can speak to him?"

"Don't drag him into this; tell me you won't drag him into this. It's just me. Just take me away and be done with it." Aren stopped, her eyes closed, her face pinched. "What are you going to do to me?"

"I'm not sure yet."

She was done with crying. Her face was locked with anger, resignation. "You'll take me to the center of town and rip the baby out, cut its throat, leave us both to bleed to death as a warning. That's it, isn't it? Just tell me that's what you're going to do and get it over with—"

Goodness, the stories people told. "No, we're not going to do that. We don't rip babies from mother's wombs—not unless we need to save the mother's life, or the baby's. There's surgery for that. Your baby will be born; you have my promise."

Quiet tears slipped down the girl's cheeks. Enid watched for a moment, this time not using the silence to pressure Aren but trying to decide what to say.

"You thought that was what would happen if you were caught, and you still cut out your implant to have a baby? You must have known you'd be caught."

"I don't remember anymore what I was thinking."

"Let's get you back to the kitchen for a drink of water, hmm?"

By the time they got back to the common room, Aren had stopped crying, and she even stood a little straighter. At least until Frain looked at her, then at Enid.

"What did you tell her? What did she say to you?"

"Felice, I think Aren needs a glass of water, or maybe some tea. Frain, will you come speak with me?"

The man stomped out of the room ahead of her.

"What happened?" Enid said simply.

"The implant. It must have failed."

"Do you think she, or someone, might have cut it out? Did you ever notice her wearing a bandage on her arm?"

He did not seem at all surprised at this suggestion. "I never did. I never noticed." He was going to plead ignorance. That was fine. "Does the local committee know you're here?" he said, turning the questioning on her.

"Not yet," she said lightly. "They will."

"What are you going to do? What will happen to Aren?"

Putting the blame on Aren, because he knew the whole household was under investigation. "I haven't decided yet."

"I'm going to protest to the committee, about you questioning Aren alone. You shouldn't have done that, it's too hard on her—" He was furious that he didn't know what Aren had said. That he couldn't make their stories match up.

"Submit your protest," Enid said. "That's fine."

She spoke to every one of them alone. Half of them said the exact same thing, in exactly the same way.

"The implant failed. It must have failed."

"Aren's got that boy of hers. He's the father."

"It was an accident."

"An accident." Felice breathed this line, her head bowed and hands clasped together.

So that was the story they'd agreed upon. The story Frain had told them to tell.

One of the young men—baffled, he didn't seem to understand what was happening—was the one to slip. "She brought this down on us, why do the rest of us have to put up with the mess when it's all her?"

Enid narrowed her gaze. "So you know she cut out her implant?"

He wouldn't say another word after that. He bit his lips and puffed out his cheeks, but wouldn't speak, as if someone held a knife to his throat and told him not to.

Enid wasn't above pressing hard at the young one, Susan, until the girl snapped.

"Did you ever notice Aren with a bandage on her arm?"

Susan's face turned red. "It's not my fault, it's not! It's just that Frain said if we got a banner next season I could have it, not Aren, and she was jealous! That's what it was; she did this to punish us!"

Banners were supposed to make things better. Give people something to work for, make them prove they could support a child, *earn* a child. It wasn't supposed to be something to fight over, to cheat over.

But people did cheat.

"Susan—did you send the anonymous report about Aren?"

Susan's eyes turned round and shocked. "No, of course not, I wouldn't do such a thing! Tell Frain I'd never do such a thing!"

"Thank you, Susan, for your honesty," Enid said, and Susan burst into tears.

What a stinking mess this was turning in to. To think, she could have retired after the murder investigation and avoided all this.

She needed to talk to more people.

By the time they returned to the common room, Felice had gotten tea out for everyone. She politely offered a cup to Enid, who accepted, much to everyone's dismay. Enid stayed for a good twenty minutes, sipping, watching them watch her, making small talk.

"Thank you very much for all of your time and patience," she said eventually. "I'll be at the committee house in town if any of you would like to speak with me further. I'll deliver my decision in a day or two, so I won't keep you waiting. Your community thanks you."

A million things could happen, but these people were so locked into their drama she didn't expect much. She wasn't worried that the situation was going to change overnight. If Aren was going to grab her boy and run she would have done it already. That wasn't what was happening here. This was a household imploding.

Time to check with the local committee.

"Did they talk while I was gone?" Enid asked.

"Not a word," Bert said. "I hate to say it but that was almost fun. What are they so scared of?"

"Us. The stories of what we'll do. Aren was sure we'd drag her in the street and cut out her baby."

Bret wrinkled his face and said softly, "That's awful."

"I hadn't heard that one before, I admit. Usually it's all locked cells and stealing the baby away as soon as it's born. I wonder if Frain told the story to her, said it was why they had to keep it secret."

"Frain knew?"

"I'm sure they all did. They're trying to save the household by convincing me it was an accident. Or that it was just Aren's fault and no one else's. When really, a household like that, if they're that unhappy they should all put in for transfers, no matter how many ration credits that'd cost. Frain's scared them out of it, I'm betting."

"So what will happen?"

"Technology fails sometimes. If it had been an accident, I'm authorized to award a banner retroactively if the household can handle it. But that's not what happened here. If the household colluded to bring on a bannerless baby, we'd have to break up the house. But if it was just Aren all on her own—punishment would fall on her."

"But this isn't any of those, is it?"

"You've got a good eye for this, Bert."

"Not sure that's a compliment. I like to expect the best from people, not the worst."

Enid chuckled.

"At least *you'll* be able to put this all behind you soon," he said. "Retire to some pleasant household somewhere. Not here."

A middle aged man, balding and flush, rushed toward them on the path as they returned to the town. His gray tunic identified him as a committee member, and he wore the same stark panic on his face that everyone did when they saw an investigator.

"You must be Trevor?" Enid asked him, when he was still a few paces away, too far to shake hands.

"We didn't know you were coming, you should have sent word. Why didn't you send word?"

"We didn't have time. We got an anonymous report and had to act quickly. It happens sometimes, I'm sure you understand."

"Report, on what? If it's serious, I'm sure I would have been told—"

"A bannerless pregnancy at the Apricot Hill household."

He took a moment to process, staring, uncertain. The look turned hard. This didn't just reflect on Aren or the household—it reflected on the entire settlement. On the committee that ran the settlement. They could all be dragged into this.

"Aren," the man breathed.

Enid wasn't surprised the man knew. She was starting to wonder how her office hadn't heard about the situation much sooner.

"What can you tell me about the household? How do they get along, how are they doing?"

"Is this an official interview?"

"Why not? Saves time."

"They get their work done. But they're a household, not a family. If you understand the difference."

"I do." A collection of people gathered for production, not one that bonded over love. It wasn't always a bad thing—a collection of people working toward shared purpose could be powerful. But love could make it a home.

"How close were they to earning a banner?" *Were.* Telling word, there.

"I can't say they were close. They have three healthy young women, but people came in and out of that house so often we couldn't call it 'stable.' They fell short on quotas. I know that's usually better than going over, but not with food processing—falling short there means food potentially wasted, if it goes bad before it gets stored. Frain—Frain is not the easiest man to get along with."

"Yes, I know."

"You've already been out there—I wish you would have talked to me; you should have come to see us before starting your investigation." Trevor was wringing his hands.

"So you could tell me how things really are?" Enid raised a brow and smiled. He glanced briefly at Bert and frowned. "Aren had a romantic partner in the settlement, I'm told. Do you know who this might be?"

"She wouldn't tell you—she trying to protect him?"

"He's not in any trouble."

"Jess. It's Jess. He works in the machine shop, with the Ironcroft household." He pointed the way.

"Thank you. We've had a long day of travel, can the committee house put us up for a night or two? We've got the credits to trade for it, we won't be a burden."

"Yes, of course, we have guest rooms in back, this way."

Trevor led them on to a comfortable stone house, committee offices and official guest rooms all together. People had gathered, drifting out of houses and stopping along the road to look, to bend heads and gossip. Everyone had that stare of trepidation.

"You don't make a lot of friends, working in investigations," Bret murmured to her.

"Not really, no."

A young man, an assistant to the committee, delivered a good meal of lentil stew and fresh bread, along with cider. It tasted like warmth embodied, a great comfort after the day she'd had.

"My household hang their banners on the common room wall like that," Bert said between mouthfuls. "They stitch the names of the babies into them. It's a whole history of the house laid out there."

"Many households do. It's a lovely tradition," Enid said.

"I've never met anyone born without a banner. It's odd, thinking Aren's baby won't have its name written anywhere."

"It's not the baby's fault, remember. But it does make it hard. They grow up thinking they have to work twice as hard to earn their place in the world. But it usually makes people very careful not to pass on that burden."

"Usually but not always."

She sighed, her solid inspector demeanor slipping. "We're getting better. The goal is making sure that every baby born will be provided for, will have a place, and won't overburden what we have. But babies are powerful things. We'll never be perfect."

The young assistant knocked on the door to the guest rooms early the next day.

"Ma'am, Enid? Someone's out front asking for the investigator."

"Is there a conference room where we can meet?"

"Yes, I'll show him in."

She and Bert quickly made themselves presentable—and put on their reputation—before meeting.

The potential informant was a lanky young man with calloused hands, a flop of brown hair and no beard. A worried expression. He kneaded a straw hat in his hands and stood from the table when Enid and Bren entered.

"You're Jess?"

He squeezed the hat harder. Ah, the appearance of omniscience was so very useful.

"Please, sit down," Enid said, and sat across from him by example. Bert stood by the wall.

"This is about Aren," the young man said. "You're here about Aren."

"Yes." He slumped, sighed—did he seemed relieved? "What do you need to tell me, Jess?"

"I haven't seen her in weeks; I haven't even gotten a message to her. No one will tell me what's wrong, and I know what everyone's been saying, but it can't be true—"

"That she's pregnant. She's bannerless."

He blinked. "But she's alive? She's safe?"

"She is. I saw her yesterday."

"Good, that's good."

Unlike everyone else she had talked to here, he seemed genuinely reassured. As if he had expected her to be dead or injured. The vectors of anxiety in the case pointed in so many different directions. "Did she tell you anything? Did you have any idea that something was wrong?"

"No . . . I mean, yes, but not that. It's complicated. What's going to happen to her?"

"That's what I'm here to decide. I promise you, she and the baby won't come to any harm. But I need to understand what's happened. Did you know she'd cut out her implant?"

He stared at the tabletop. "No, I didn't know that." If he had known, he could be implicated, so it behooved him to say that. But Enid believed him.

"Jess, I want to understand why she did what she did. Her household is being difficult. They tell me she spent all her spare time with you." Enid couldn't tell if he was resistant to talking to her, or if he simply couldn't find the words. She prompted. "How long have you been together? How long have you been intimate?" A gentle way of putting it. He wasn't blushing; on the contrary, he'd gone even more pale.

"Not long," he said. "Not even a year. I think . . . I think I know what happened now, looking back."

"Can you tell me?"

"I think . . . I think she needed someone and she picked me. I'm almost glad she picked me. I love her, but . . . I didn't know."

She wanted a baby. She found a boy she liked, cut out her implant, and made sure she had a baby. It wasn't unheard of. Enid had looked into a couple of cases like it in the past. But then, the household reported it when the others found out, or she left the household. To go through that and then stay, with everyone also covering it up . . .

"Did she ever talk about earning a banner and having a baby with you? Was that a goal of hers?"

"She never did at all. We . . . it was just us. I just liked spending time with her. We'd go for walks."

"What else?"

"She—wouldn't let me touch her arm. The first time we . . . were intimate, she kept her shirt on. She'd hurt her arm, she said, and didn't want to get dirt on it—we were out by the mill creek that feeds into the pond. It's so beautiful there, with the noise of the water and all. I . . . I didn't think of it. I mean, she always seemed to be hurt somewhere. Bruises and things. She said it was just from working around the house. I was always a bit careful touching her, though, because of it. I had to be careful with her." Miserable now, he put the pieces together in his mind as Enid watched. "She didn't like to go back. I told myself—I fooled myself—that it was because she loved me. But it's more that she didn't want to go back."

"And she loves you. As you said, she picked you. But she had to go back."

"If she'd asked, she could have gone somewhere else."

But it would have cost credits she may not have had, the committee would have asked why, and it would have been a black mark on Frain's leadership, or worse. Frain had them cowed into staying. So Aren wanted to get out of there and decided a baby would help her.

Enid asked, "Did you send the tip to Investigations?"

"No. No, I didn't know. That is, I didn't want to believe. I would never do anything to get her in trouble. I . . . I'm not in trouble, am I?"

"No, Jess. Do you know who might have sent in the tip?"

"Someone on the local committee, maybe. They're the ones who'd start an investigation, aren't they?"

"Usually, but they didn't seem happy to see me. The message went directly to regional."

"The local committee doesn't want to think anything's wrong. Nobody wants to think anything's wrong."

"Yes, that seems to be the attitude. Thank you for your help, Jess."

"What will happen to Aren?" He was choking, struggling not to cry. Even Bert, standing at the wall, seemed discomfited.

"That's for me to worry about, Jess. Thank you for your time."

At the dismissal, he slipped out of the room.

She leaned back and sighed, wanting to get back to her own household—despite the rumors, investigators did belong to households—with its own orchards and common room full of love and safety.

Yes, maybe she should have retired before all this. Or maybe she wasn't meant to.

"Enid?" Bert asked softly.

"Let's go. Let's get this over with."

Back at Apricot Hill's common room, the household gathered, and Enid didn't have to ask for Aren this time. She had started to worry, especially after talking to Jess. But they'd all waited this long, and her arrival didn't change anything except it had given them all the confirmation that they'd finally been caught. That they would always be caught. Good for the reputation, there.

Aren kept her face bowed, her hair over her cheek. Enid moved up to her, reached a hand to her, and the girl flinched. "Aren?" she said, and she still didn't look up until Enid touched her chin and made her lift her face. An irregular red bruise marked her cheek.

"Aren, did you send word about a bannerless pregnancy to the regional committee?"

Someone, Felice probably, gasped. A few of them shifted. Frain simmered. But Aren didn't deny it. She kept her face low.

"Aren?" Enid prompted, and the young woman nodded, ever so slightly.

"I hid. I waited for the weekly courier and slipped the letter in her bag, she didn't see me; no one saw. I didn't know if anyone would believe it, with no name on it, but I had to try. I wanted to get caught, but no one was noticing it; everyone was ignoring it." Her voice cracked to silence.

Enid put a gentle hand on Aren's shoulder. Then she went to Bert, and whispered, "Watch carefully."

She didn't know what would happen, what Frain in particular would do. She drew herself up, drew strength from the uniform she wore, and declaimed.

"I am the villain here," Enid said. "Understand that. I am happy to be the villain in your world. It's what I'm here for. Whatever happens, blame me.

"I will take custody of Aren and her child. When the rest of my business is done, I'll leave with her and she'll be cared for responsibly. Frain, I question your stewardship of this household and will submit a recommendation that Apricot Hill be dissolved entirely, its resources and credits distributed among its members as warranted, and its members transferred elsewhere throughout the region. I'll submit my recommendation to the regional committee, which will assist the local committee in carrying out my sentence."

"No," Felice hissed. "You can't do this, you can't force us out."

She had expected that line from Frain. She wondered at the deeper dynamic here, but not enough to try to suss it out.

"I can," she said, with a backward glance at Bert. "But I won't have to, because you're all secretly relieved. The household didn't work, and that's fine—it happens sometimes—but none of you had the guts to start over, the guts to give up your credits to request a transfer somewhere else. To pay for the change you wanted. To protect your own housemates from each other. But now it's done, and by someone else, so you can complain all you want and rail to the skies about your new poverty as you work your way out of the holes you've dug for yourselves. I'm the villain you can blame. But deep down you'll know the truth. And that's fine too, because I don't really care. Not about you lot."

No one argued. No one said a word.

"Aren," Enid said, and the woman flinched again. She might never stop flinching. "You can come with me now, or would you like time to say good-bye?"

She looked around the room, and Enid wasn't imagining it: The woman's hands were shaking, though she tried to hide it by pressing them under the roundness of her belly. Enid's breath caught, because even now it might go either way. Aren had been scared before; she might be too scared to leave. Enid schooled her expression to be still no matter what the answer was.

But Aren stood from the table and said, "I'll go with you now."

"Bert will go help you get your things—"

"I don't have any things. I want to go now."

"All right. Bert, will you escort Aren outside?"

The door closed behind them, and Enid took one last look around the room.

"That's it, then," Frain said.

"Oh no, that's not it at all," Enid said. "That's just it for now. The rest of you should get word of the disposition of the household in a couple of days." She walked out.

Aren stood outside, hugging herself. Bert was a polite few paces away, being nonthreatening, staring at clouds. Enid urged them on, and they walked the path back toward town. Aren seemed to get a bit lighter as they went.

They probably had another day in Southtown before they could leave. Enid would keep Aren close, in the guest rooms, until then. She might have to requisition a solar car. In her condition, Aren probably shouldn't walk the ten miles to the next way station. And she might want to say good-bye to Jess. Or she might not, and Jess would have his heart broken even more. Poor thing.

Enid requisitioned a solar car from the local committee and was able to take to the Coast Road the next day. The bureaucratic machinery was in motion on all the rest of it. Committeeman Trevor revealed that a couple of the young men from Apricot Hill had preemptively put in household transfer requests. Too little, too late. She'd done her job; it was all in committee hands now.

Bert drove, and Enid sat in the back with Aren, who was bundled in a wool cloak and kept her hands around her belly. They opened windows to the spring sunshine, and the car bumped and swayed over the gravel road. Walking would have been more pleasant, but Aren needed the car. The tension in her shoulders had finally gone away. She looked up, around, and if she didn't smile, she also didn't frown. She talked, now, in a voice clear and free of tears.

"I came into the household when I was sixteen, to work prep in the canning house and to help with the garden and grounds and such. They needed the help, and I needed to get started on my life, you know? Frain—he expected more out of me. He expected me to be his."

She spoke as if being interrogated. Enid hadn't asked for her story, but listened carefully to the confession. It spilled out like a flood, like the young woman had been waiting.

"How far did it go, Aren?" Enid asked carefully. In the driver's seat, Bert frowned, like maybe he wanted to go back and have a word with the man.

"He never did more than hit me."

So straightforward. Enid made a note. The car rocked on for a ways.

"What will happen to her, without a banner?" Aren asked, glancing at her belly. She'd evidently decided the baby was a girl. She probably had a name picked out. Her baby, her savior.

"There are households who need babies to raise who'll be happy to take her."

"Her, but not me?"

"It's a complicated situation," Enid said. She didn't want to make Aren any promises until they could line up exactly which households they'd be going to.

Aren was smart. Scared, but smart. She must have thought things through, once she realized she wasn't going to die. "Will it go better, if I agree to give her up? The baby, I mean."

Enid said, "It would depend on how you define 'better.'"

"Better for the baby."

"There's a stigma on bannerless babies. Worse some places than others. And somehow people know, however you try to hide it. People will always know what you did and hold it against you. But the baby can get a fresh start on her own."

"All right. All right, then."

"You don't have to decide right now."

Eventually, they came to the place in the road where the ruins were visible, like a distant mirage, but unmistakable. A haunted place, with as many rumors about it as there were about investigators and what they did.

"Is that it?" Aren said, staring. "The old city? I've never seen it before."

Bert slowed the car, and they stared out for a moment.

"The stories about what it was like are so terrible. I know it's supposed to be better now, but . . ." The young woman dropped her gaze.

"Better for whom, you're wondering?" Enid said. "When they built our world, our great-grandparents saved what they could, what they thought was important, what they'd most need. They wanted a world that would let them survive not just longer but better. They aimed for utopia knowing they'd fall short. And for all their work, for all our work, we still find pregnant girls with bruises on their faces who don't know where to go for help."

"I don't regret it," Aren said. "At least, I don't think I do."

"You saved what you could," Enid said. It was all any of them could do.

The car started again, rolling on. Some miles later on, Aren fell asleep curled in the back seat, her head lolling. Bert gave her a sympathetic glance.

"Heartbreaking all around, isn't it? Quite the last case for you, though. Memorable."

"Or not," Enid said.

Going back to the way station, late afternoon, the sun was in Enid's face. She leaned back, closed her eyes, and let it warm her.

"What, not memorable?" Bert said.

"Or not the last," she said. "I may have a few more left in me."

the audience

SEAN McMULLEN

Australian author Sean McMullen is a computer systems analyst with the Australian Bureau of Meteorology, and has been a lead singer in folk and rock bands as well as singing with the Victoria State Opera. He's also an acclaimed and prolific author whose short fiction has appeared in The Magazine of Fantasy and Science Fiction, Interzone, Analog, *and elsewhere, and the author of a dozen novels, including* Voices in the Light, Mirrorsun Rising, Souls in the Great Machine, The Miocene Arrow, Eyes of the Calculor, Voyage of the Shadowmoon, Glass Dragons, Void Farer, The Time Engine, The Centurion's Empire, *and* Before the Storm. *Some of his stories have been collected in* Call to the Edge, *and he wrote a critical study,* Strange Constellations: A History of Australian Science Fiction, *with Russell Blackford and Van Ikin. His most recent books are the novel* Changing Yesterday *and two new collections,* Ghosts of Engines Past *and* Colours of the Soul. *He lives in Melbourne, Australia.*

People have been longing to make First Contact with aliens for decades, and making extensive efforts to achieve it, but as McMullen suggests here, perhaps it wouldn't be such a hot idea after all . . .

A report from humanity's only starship should be very formal, but this report will have to be a story. Humanity's future will depend on my ability to tell a good story, four and a half thousand years from now, so I must keep in practise. This will also be my last contact with Earth, and I want to give you an accurate and definitive account that is still a good read. Official reports are always so boring.

The Javelin was built in lunar orbit, and the crew was selected on a list of criteria longer than most novels. My background is in disaster recovery for large spacecraft, and that got me into the crew. Why? It is because disaster recovery experts need to have a working knowledge of literally every system: how to repair it, how to make something else do the same job, and how to do without it and not die. I had been on the disaster recovery design team for the Javelin, and I met all the other criteria. That put me just a whisker ahead of the nine thousand other candidates for the fifth and last place on the crew.

Uneven numbers are good for breaking deadlocks when votes are taken, so there were five of us aboard the Javelin. Our life support and recycling units had been over-engineered to last a century with us awake, and almost indefinitely with the crew in suspension. Five months of acceleration were followed by a fading away into chemically induced bliss, twenty years of nothingness, then a long struggle out of jumbled, chaotic dreams. By then we were nowhere near Abyss, and still faced another five months of deceleration. One two hundredth of the speed of light may not sound like much, but we held the record for the fastest humans alive about a hundred times over.

For some irrational reason I had expected to see something when I looked out at Abyss, yet only an absence of stars was visible, slowly rotating as the gravity habitat turned. My subconscious kept screaming that it was a black hole, and that we would be sucked down, mangled and annihilated, but the rational part of me knew otherwise. Abyss was just a gas giant planet about the size of Jupiter, with three large moons and a thin ring system. It was special because it was not part of the solar system.

We gathered at the gallery plate, celebrating our insertion into orbit around Abyss. Landi, the captain, was standing beside me, and we were playing our favourite game. I would make a grand statement, and she would try to cut it down to size.

"We know it's there because we see nothing," I said, the frustrated author in me always on the lookout for a nice turn of phrase.

"That's how it was found," said Landi. "Stellar occultation. Stars that should have been visible were not."

"This is the first voyage beyond the solar system, but we have not left the solar system."

"We're a tenth of a light year from the sun, that's hardly the solar system."

"We are in the Oort Cloud, the Oort Cloud orbits the sun, so we are still in the solar system."

"But Abyss is only passing through the Oort Cloud, it's not orbiting the sun. We have matched velocity with Abyss so we are no longer part of the solar system."

"But we are in the Oort Cloud, so we are still *within* the solar system."

"Abyss is less than a fortieth of the distance to Alpha Centauri."

"Which is a hundred times further away than Pluto."

"Draw," was the verdict of Mikov, our geologist.

Saral and Fan clapped. We had been selected to be compatible yet diverse, complimenting each other's skills. For the ten months that we had been awake, it had been like a working holiday with close friends. For my part, I would have happily spent the rest of my life on the Javelin.

"Coffee break's over," said Landi. "Time to refuel."

The Javelin expedition had a single point of failure, which is something that disaster recovery people hate. There was enough reaction mass to get us to Abyss and stop with our tanks practically empty. All the gas giants of the solar system had ring systems of ice, so the designers had gambled on Abyss having rings as well. The gamble had paid off, so we could refuel and eventually go home.

Had the designers been wrong, there were two disaster recovery plans. One was for us to go into suspension once our explorations were done, and wait decades, or even centuries, for a follow-up expedition. If the moons of Abyss turned out to be interesting, we had the alternative of living out our lives there.

Mikov and I took the shuttle into the edge of the ring system, trailing a hose with a thermal lance and grapple on the end. This I attached to a chunk of ice about the size of an ocean liner during our first spacewalk. In doing so, I made humanity's first contact with an extra-solar world.

"That's one small gloveprint for a man," I began.

"And about two months of your pay docked if you finish that sentence," said Landi in my earpiece. "Lucky this is not going live to Earth."

"Okay, okay, I have touched a star and it is ice," I said.

"Once more, this time with a sense of wonder. The taxpayers back home want significant moments, not corny jokes."

The thermal lance got to work, melting the ice and sucking the water into the half-mile hose leading to the Javelin's tanks. It would take several weeks and dozens of spacewalks to collect the millions of tons of reaction mass needed to refill our tanks, but propellant to get home had priority over everything else.

"Hard work to make an exciting story out of a good outcome, eh Jander?" said Mikov.

"True, disasters make the best stories," I replied. "My work is to make sure I have nothing to write about."

The term science fiction was coined three hundred years ago, but evolved into what the academics call reactivity literature. How do humans react to the unknown? I write about it as a hobby. More to the point, I had been published. Some selection subcommittee decided that having an author in the crew might be a good idea.

Although weak, the gravity of the ring fragment had attracted some ice rubble to its surface, and I selected a fist-sized chunk to take back to the shuttle. With our ticket home now more or less secure, the science could begin. The shuttle made the short hop back to the Javelin, and I handed my insulated sample pack to Saral, the biologist, for analysis.

I was lying on my bunk in the gravity habitat, having a coffee and watching some drama download from Earth when Mikov rushed in.

"Saral's discovered cells!" he exclaimed. "The ice is *full* of bacterial cells."

This was more significant than, well, nearly anything in recorded history. Life existed beyond the solar system. We had proof.

"The cells are all dead, of course," said Saral on a downlink to Earth some hours later. "The three chain molecules that pass for DNA in these things have been trashed by billions of years of cosmic ray exposure. I can get firmer dates from the samples, but that will take longer."

"Billions?" asked Landi, playing the role of an interviewer.

"From my first guess analysis of the rate of cosmic ray impact in deep space compared to the damage to the Tri-DNA, I would stand by billions."

"Mikov, can you talk about the astro-geology?"

"I would only be guessing," he began.

Landi killed the microphone.

"This is a press conference, and I am the press!" she said firmly. "Start guessing."

Mikov was rather pedantic by nature, and had very little sense of occasion. He was clearly not happy as the microphone winked back into life, but he took a deep breath and began.

"I think that at least one of the three moons of Abyss has a subsurface ocean, kept liquid and relatively warm by tidal forces from Abyss and the two other moons."

"Like Jupiter's Europa?"

"Yes. Billions of years ago an asteroid smashed into that moon and cracked the cover of ice over a subsurface ocean. Water and bacteria reached the surface through these cracks and froze. A later impact smashed some ice with bacteria into space, and some of it eventually reached the ring system."

"Ice with biological material from Europa has been found in Jupiter's ring system," added Saral.

This was all fairly dry and factual, even though the subject matter was nothing short of magical. Fan was the flight engineer so his opinion was not very relevant. Landi turned to me.

"Jander, you know a bit about everything," she prompted. "Can you pull all this together?"

In other words, tell the folks back home a good story.

"The bacteria samples were smashed out by impacts billions of years ago, but the life forms will have continued to evolve," I said off the top of my head. "Imagine what must have evolved down there by now.

"Are we looking at possible intelligence?" asked Landi.

"Could be."

"Civilization?"

"Not as we think of civilization. The locals would be cut off from the universe, and tool making is a definite challenge under water."

"Like, fire is out, so no heavy industry?"

"All true, but biological nanotech is possible. By using fabrication-layering, they could build entire cities. After all, most of the Javelin came from fabrication vats on the moon."

"So that's where we are," concluded Landi. "We still have weeks of refueling ahead of us here at the edge of the ring system, but we do have a fleet of sensor probes that can be launched at the three moons and put into orbit. They will tell us which moon has the ocean, and the first of those will be launched today."

Five weeks passed, and in that time our probes showed that all three moons had subsurface oceans. Landi decided to send the shuttle to Limbo, the innermost of the moons. Aboard were Saral and Mikov, with Fan as pilot.

I have a good memory for facts and figures, that always helps in disasters when computer databases are not always available. I knew that the spacesuit boots of humanity had left first footprints on five thousand seven hundred and three worlds within the solar system. Most of them had been small asteroids and comets, yet the people wearing those boots had always said something profound or significant. Mikov was not inclined to be profound.

"There's a lot of ice down here," he said after stepping off the shuttle onto Limbo.

Landi was sitting beside me, watching the event on a display in the console room. She put a hand over her eyes.

"He said that deliberately," she muttered. "I should have put myself in charge."

"Why didn't you?"

"I'm the captain, and *this* ship is my ship."

"No good deed goes unpunished. So who gets first boot on Chasm and Styx?"

"Fan gets Styx."

"And Chasm?"

"You."

This was a surprise. I was not a high profile member of the crew.

"Why not Saral?"

"Saral? She's the biologist. By tradition the pilot gets first footprint. You are a pilot."

"I . . . have no interest in historical moments."

"Mikov has had Limbo, and Fan is liable to say something as boring as Mikov. You're our author, you of all people should get the first footprint."

"Many more men than women have made a first footfall, why not—."

"Jander, you get Chasm and that's my last word on it."

I dared not say that I owed Saral a favour, so I did not argue. Using our gravitational displacement satellites, we had determined that Limbo had an ocean layer ninety miles beneath its outer shell of ice. The shuttle's floodlights showed nothing more than shattered ice on the surface as Mikov took the contingency samples and Fan and Saral began to unload the instruments.

Lunch was being eaten on Limbo when I accessed one of the orbital probes. The radar sounding array was showing craters, cracks and melt plains, and it looked very similar to Europa. I switched to the telescope and selected the visible light display. A single point of light stood out against absolute darkness. This was the floodlights of the shuttle, lighting up a tiny circle on the surface of Abyss. Landi looked across from her console.

"What are your thoughts at this historic moment, Mr Author?" she asked.

"I was thinking how mundane historic moments can be. First footfall on a new world, and nobody even raises a sweat."

"I was just thinking along the same lines. Is this really why we worked so hard to get here?"

"Boring is good, excitement can kill," I said automatically.

Disaster recovery people always secretly hope they will never have any work, yet authors like a bang and a puff of smoke to make things exciting.

"So why did you volunteer, Jander—I mean, why really? Not that crap about standing on the edge of the frontier and gazing into the unknown."

I hesitated, as if thinking about my answer. I already knew that answer, but an instant reply would have made me seem cynical, and delays always raise the dramatic tension.

"To see the future, when I get back to Earth."

"Really? There are cryogen tanks for that sort of thing. It's a lot safer than coming all the way out here."

"Cryogen is for the rich, and I'm not rich. Now I'll get to see the future *and* collect forty-one years of pay. What about you?"

"I'm here to become famous," she said with an exaggerated smirk.

"Really? Just that?"

"Yes, I really am in it for the fame. How else could a ship's commander become a celeb? Everybody will want to know us when we get back, we won't be ignored like the cryogenic time-tourist nobodies who just have themselves frozen for a few decades."

"No sense of the wonder of strange new worlds?"

"Give me a break. Prospecting on comets and ice worlds in the outer solar system is no different to what we're doing here. We may find a few live bugs, but we did that on Europa."

So, her enthusiasm and hype had all been for the cameras. It was a disappointment, but then maybe I was a disappointment to her as well.

Remote sensing with satellites can tell you a lot, but there is no substitute for sounding charges. The explosives had been measured to within a fraction of a gram, and they were designed to be delivered to a precise depth in the ice by a thermal probe, then detonated. Fan and Mikov spent sixty hours sinking ten charges, and anchoring seismographic sensors to filter data out of the reflected shockwaves.

Meantime Saral worked on new biological material picked up on the surface, and again she got guaranteed headlines when she discovered something like a small jellyfish with tentacles and a nervous system. Her estimate on its age was a hundred million years. More to the point, it was an animal that could pick up things and manipulate them.

"What do its descendants look like today?" she concluded. "With luck, we may find out."

All of this was transmitted to the Javelin, and we passed it along to Earth on Homelink. Thirty-six days into the future, Saral's discoveries would trigger another media frenzy.

Strangely enough, I felt isolated and even a little annoyed. I was not quite at the frontier, I was contributing nothing. It was excitement without danger, I was not needed. No disaster meant my primary skill was of no use. As for my writing, how many great works of literature were written about the actual discovery of DNA? The first lunar landing? The first atomic reactor?

My expectations were low when the time came for the first of the sounding charges to be detonated. Fan followed safety protocols and ascended in the shuttle to orbit Limbo. There was always a possibility that the charges would release major stresses that had built up in the ice. Mikov and Saral suited up and armed their jetpacks, in case they had to hover out of harm's way if any moonquakes were caused by the soundings.

"Okay, Limbo, show us what you got," said Mikov. "Detonating the charges at five second intervals, starting with . . . Alpha!"

The shockwaves would take seventeen seconds to reach the ocean layer.

"Beta."

At five seconds, realtime analysis reported ice with healed fissures, but little more.

"Gamma."

Ten seconds into the exercise, and the first of the shockwaves were over halfway to the ocean.

"Delta."

At fifteen seconds plus two and counting the shockwaves were through the ice and into water. The lifesign telemetry from Ground Limbo suddenly flatlined. All that the Javelin was receiving was the carrier wave from the satellite relay network we had set up around Limbo.

"Javelin to Ground Limbo, Javelin to Ground Limbo," Landi called in her auto-calm voice. "I have registered an uplink outage. Comm-sats One, Two and Three have positive, repeat positive transponder function. Over."

We waited through the light speed delay. There was no reply. Landi made several more attempts at contact.

"Jander, I'm getting a total outage of bio telemetry from the surface of Limbo," she reported. "No transmitters on the surface are down, and satellite relays all have positive, repeat positive carrier signal function."

"Shuttle to Javelin, what's going on with Ground Limbo?" Fan called in.

"Javelin to Shuttle, I have strong signals from Ground Limbo, but no lifesign telemetry."

"You mean Mikov and Saral are dead?"

"Nothing appears to have been damaged, but I read no, repeat no lifesigns."

"I request clearance to return to Ground Limbo."

"No, Shuttle, that's definite no!" said Landi, almost shouting into the pickup. "I've got a link to the maintenance crawler at Ground Limbo."

"Can you patch me the image—" began Fan, then his lifesign telemetry was cut off with a sound like a gunshot.

"Shuttle, I—what—status, what is your status?" stammered Landi. "Fan! Answer me!"

This was Landi under pressure, facing the absolute unknown. I called up the monitor screen for the shuttle. Fan's spacesuit was in the command seat, but nothing was behind the faceplate. A jagged chunk of ice was floating in the cabin.

"What the hell is that?" demanded Landi.

"I can display it, but I can't explain it," I replied.

"Taking command of Shuttle," said Landi, her fingers flickering over the console's control points.

Some seconds later the engines of the shuttle fired, and the chunk of ice was slammed against the back of the cabin.

"I'm betting the ice has the same mass as Fan," I said.

"Why?" asked Landi.

"Look at the Doppler reading on the shuttle. It's identical to before his lifesigns dropped out, after compensating for the fuel being used. Ice was exchanged for Fan's body."

"How? I don't understand."

"Neither do I, I'm just looking at the instruments. Drop the cabin temperature in the shuttle. Better still, decompress. The ice may tell us something."

We stayed awake sixteen hours into the next sleep cycle to do our investigations and send our report down Homelink. It would cause consternation when it arrived, but for now it's just an excuse to get our thoughts in order.

Within the shuttle was a lump of ice with a mass of one-seventy pounds. It was the same as that of Fan. Analysis showed it to be not much different in composition to that of a comet nucleus. According to one of our robotic probes, that was the same as most ice in the rings girdling Abyss.

When we finally found time to examine the soundings data, we wished we had looked at it first.

"Something's down there," I said, displaying a cluster of tetrahedral blocks with ragged fractal edges to Landi. "*This* is floating not far from the ice shell, according to the soundings. It has a very artificial look, and it's ten miles across."

"Volcanic basalt columns on Earth look artificial," she said, without sounding convinced.

"Does that thing look natural?"

Neither of us was in a position to say anything sensible. Nothing in humanity's science, explorations and experiments covered anything like this. Another hour of computer enhancement and interpretation gave us higher resolution, but no answers.

"Give me some conclusions," said Landi, rubbing her face in her hands. "Tell that wild and florid imagination of yours to get out of bed."

She was too steady and sensible to cope with the improbable. As a battle commander, I could think of nobody better to have in charge, but this was not a battle. I was coping by imagining this as a novel, with myself as a character.

"Something beyond our understanding reacted badly to the sounding explosions," I said. "That something is in the subsurface ocean of Abyss."

"I worked that out for myself."

"It plucked our crew out of their spacesuits and took them somewhere."

"Where? Under the ice, into Limbo? First contact? *Take me to your leader?*"

"No. Ice from the ring system was in the shuttle's cabin. If you want a wild speculation, I'd say two more chunks of ice with the same mass as two humans were exchanged for Saral and Mikov."

"That means there should be two chunks of ice beside their spacesuits. We saw no ice."

"I didn't look. Did you?"

Landi put the monitor cameras through a panoramic sweep. There were indeed two large pieces of ice lying near the empty spacesuits outside the Ground Limbo habitat.

"Some sort of mass-exchange teleportation," said Landi, finally accepting the evidence but not understanding it.

"Limbo probably gets hit by the odd comet from time to time, like when it passes through the Oort Clouds of other stars," I said, pushing my imagination so hard that my head felt like it was heating up. "The Limbians seem to sense water and ice rather well. Perhaps they learned to detect ice beyond their world and move it around. The ring system of Abyss is dynamically unstable, so something is maintaining it artificially."

"You mean they keep it as a reserve of mass and momentum to deflect bodies on course for Limbo?"

"Only if those bodies are made of ice."

"Then how did it—they—whatever—sense us? Ground Limbo and the shuttle are not made of ice."

"But the crew are mostly water." I was tempted to add *so are we*, but it was hardly necessary.

"What can we do?" asked Landi, her very orderly brain probably on the edge of seizing up. "Like, if the rings of Abyss are a sort of alien ammunition belt, then we're like a couple of ants stealing bullets."

"If I discovered some ants trying to steal my bullets, I might swat a couple out of sheer reflex, but then I'd study them. Notice that *we* have not been ripped out of the Javelin."

"Yet."

It was on the fifth day after the charges had been fired that the bodies started to appear. I woke from a very light and disturbed sleep and had a shower. For some reason a shower always puts me in a better mood. Getting to sleep is beyond my control, but a shower is as easy as turning a tap. There was a sharp bang nearby, like a gun being fired. It might have been an equipment failure, or worse, a meteor strike. All thoughts of poor sleep and great showers went to the bottom of my priorities list as I hurried to the control hub wearing just a towel. Landi was already there.

The monitor screen showed a naked body lying in a corridor in Zone K. Zooming in with the monitor camera, we saw that the hair and general shape was that of Mikov. The rest was unrecognizable.

"What a mess," I said without thinking.

"Decompression and extreme cold," said Landi. "He's been in hard vacuum."

"Is it real?"

"Water's condensing on it. That doesn't happen with holograms, so it has to be real."

I sent a medical drone to investigate. The results were quite a surprise.

"The body's colder than room temperature, but not much colder," I reported. "I'd say it's been sent from inside Limbo."

Mikov began to lift his left arm. The movement was very, very slow, as if something invisible were controlling the dead limbs, trying to understand how arms work. Muscles become stiff at low temperatures, and do not work for long if there is no oxygen being supplied to them. This body was showing no signs of breathing. The legs moved a little, then the head turned and the jaw worked. After a few minutes, the muscles were spent, and could do no more than twitch. Mikov vanished, and there was a sharp thump as the air rushed in to fill the space.

"What just happened?" asked Landi.

"Take a garden snail and toss it into your neighbour's yard," I said. "Does it understand the idea of flying through the air? Does it realize that it has travelled further in a second or two than it could have in days of crawling?"

"Speaking as a snail, I'm more worried about being dropped on a path and squashed."

"I don't think it will come to that," I said, trying to sound reassuring. "Mikov's body was sent here as an experiment. The interior of the Javelin must seem like a furnace to the Limbians."

"Have you noticed that we're skirting one very important fact?"

"Tell me."

"We've just seen evidence that the Limbians are aware of this ship. They can track it, send things in and take things out. They are aware of the water in us, and in the reaction mass tanks."

Communication by anything on the electromagnetic spectrum was apparently new to whatever lived within Limbo. They were learning, however. They could take a dead body and make it go through the motions of living. Could they comprehend vision, hearing and speech? The sound of Mikov's body arriving and displacing its volume in air had been sharp and percussive, just like a meteor strike. Sensors to pick up that sort of noise were scattered right through the Javelin.

After three more days, the alarms announced that we had another visitor. It was about the right size and shape for Saral, but it too displayed all the signs of having been in hard vacuum for between five and ten minutes. A medi drone told us that this corpse was feverishly hot, but there was no pulse. Again the body's limbs moved experimentally, and they were more flexible than those of Mikov's chilled body. The jaw worked, the drone's stethoscope picked up the wheeze of lungs going through the motions of breathing, and guttural sounds came from the mouth as the vocal chords were put through their paces.

"The Limbians are definitely puzzled by our bodies," I observed.

"They probably don't understand our machines, either," said Landi, automatically looking for a military advantage. "But why open contact with a hostile act?"

I had been thinking about this.

"I don't think it was hostile. Imagine a mosquito trying to probe your brain with a red hot needle. You would squash it dead, but then you might wonder what sort of mosquito uses a high-tech thermal micro-lance. Would you would put the pathetic little smear on your hand under a microscope?"

"Probably."

We had the company of Saral's body for a half hour until the tissues broke down to such an extent that it could no longer move. The Limbians were learning about the care and maintenance of human bodies very quickly.

On the twenty-fifth day since the Limbians became aware of us, the alarm announced a third visitor. As we expected, this time it was Fan, and he was in a much better state of preservation than the others. I steered the nearest medi-drone to him, and it landed on the back of his neck and began to run tests. An auditory scan showed that his heart was beating and that he was taking breaths. His head turned back and forth, and his eyes focused on some nearby instruments. Things that did not understand eyes were looking through his eyes. Touch was probably more important than sight in their dark ocean home.

"Universal cell wall rupturing," I concluded, pointing at the critical status diagnostics from the drone. "This is another dead body being put through the motions of living."

Landi did not reply. She was edgy and uneasy, strangely emotional about this particular corpse.

"Either they're getting better at repairing bodies, or . . ." I said, fishing for a response.

"Or?" snapped Landi, now looking annoyed.

"Or this body was only in vacuum for a few seconds before the Limbians ripped all three bodies back out of the ring system and into their ocean. Someone must have finally realized what they were dealing with. From the cell wall damage, I'd say they froze all three bodies, thinking they could bring them back to life."

"I wish you'd stop saying bodies!" cried Landi. "They were our colleagues, our friends."

"Sorry."

This behaviour was right out of character for her. If there was an agenda, she was not letting on.

"Well, the Limbians now know that we breathe gasses and prefer an environment of around twenty degrees Celsius," I said. "It would be like us encountering something that lives inside the sun. The idea of hearing, seeing, walking, and even eating and going to the bathroom must be big-time news to them."

"And they can teleport stuff around," said Landi, thinking in friend-and-foe mode again. "Lucky they don't live in Europa's oceans."

"Yet," I responded.

"What do you mean?"

"They move things about pretty well instantly with some sort of mass-exchange technique, and they can detect ice and water at a distance. How far can their senses reach? Could they follow the Javelin back to Earth? Could they mass-exchange themselves to Europa?"

Landi lost colour, and instinctively reached down to her belt for a flechette pistol that was a tenth of a light year away, on Earth.

"If they can establish outposts in the oceans of Europa and Ganymede, then pretty soon they'll start studying our research stations there. There are also subsurface seas and oceans within Triton, Enceladus, Pluto and even Ceres, just to name a few. They are an alternative Goldilocks zone for life, and about ten times more common than Earth-type planets. And speaking of Earth, there are lakes under the ice in Antarctica."

"Then what's left to us humans? The moon? Mars?"

"It won't do us much good, they can move us about at will, remember? To them we'll be like chimps, or even ants."

"We have to fight back!"

Suddenly Landi was animated and purposeful. If she could fight, she had something to focus on. There was only one problem.

"How?" I asked.

"We could detach the fusion reactor and use the shuttle to put it on a course for Limbo. If we detonate it just above the surface, it will crack their ice shield open like an egg. No water involved, they'll never see it coming."

"Two hundred miles of ice does not crack like an egg, Landi. It would be annoying, but it would not destroy the Limbians."

"Then we can just blow up the ship here, deny the Limbians the use of ourselves and our ship. We—"

"Eelanjii!"

The sound was distorted and tortured, to me it was just vocal chords being flexed.

"He's alive!" Landi exclaimed.

"No way."

"But he called my name."

"His entire body is a mass of ruptured cell walls. Even if he were conscious he'd have no more than minutes to live."

"He's conscious?" she cried, her face suddenly all hope and desperation jammed together.

"Captain Landi—"

But she was not listening. She bounded up from her seat and dashed out of the control room. I followed her for a few paces, then thought the better of it and returned to the monitors. I was in time to see Landi kneel down beside Fan and take him in her arms. She ripped off my diagnostic drone and flung it away.

"Fan, can you hear me?" she sobbed. "It's you I love, I just didn't have the guts to tell Mikov. I can't let you die without telling you that."

So they've had an affair? I realized. That was a shock. Fan was Saral's lover. Where had they done it? The Javelin was two miles long, but most of that was the linear accelerator for the magnetoplasma drive. The gravity habitat wheel had about the volume of an old-style airliner, but there were monitors everywhere. That left the personal cabins, but our bio-telemetry transmitters would show two people experiencing a moderate rise in heart rate and blood pressure in the same cabin when checked. When checked by who? Unless there were a medical emergency, nobody.

Landi and Fan vanished together.

There was one thought pounding through my mind in the moments that I took to make my next decision: *I'll be next.* For the next half hour I frantically deleted everything in the Javelin's navigation files and databases that showed where we had come from, as well as sending the quick summary of what had happened back to Earth. It was desperate babble from someone plunging into a nightmare, definitely not a good read.

Given enough millennia, Abyss would drift far from the sun. Meantime the sun was the closest interstellar body. Could the Limbians sense gravity as well as water? Human eyes could see light from as far away as the Andromeda galaxy, but with touch one has to reach out. How far could the Limbians reach, and with what senses? So many questions, and only guesses for answers. There was a good chance that Landi would get trashed by whatever passed for Limbian scientists, and that would be very discouraging. Perhaps they would leave me alone, hoping to follow me home as I tried to escape. There was always the option of detonating the fusion reactor, but disaster recovery officers don't like those sorts of options. What, then?

Perhaps I can tell them a story.

I did a search on the most Earth-like planets within a fifty light year sphere, looking for something not unrealistically far yet not so close that the final page of my story would arrive too quickly. The Gliese 667 system was perfect. Twenty-two light years away, and three rocky planets in the Goldilocks zone of a red dwarf in a triple star system. An enormous space telescope had detected water and oxygen on Gleise 667Cc.

In two days the reaction mass tanks of the Javelin would be full. This would mean a very important decision had to be made about the plot of the story I was living. I made it almost without a second thought, then called up Homelink and read from a carefully prepared script.

"In two days I shall begin a burn to send the Javelin to the Gleise 667 system. The Limbians have killed the four others of the crew, probably by accident. The care and feeding of humans is, quite literally, alien to them. That leaves me, and I hope to fool them into thinking that the Javelin came from the Gleise system. Send no more transmissions, either to Abyss or to where you calculate the Javelin to be. If it's safe, I'll send updates. If not, then spare a thought for me, I did my best. Make Earth go radio-frequency silent. The Ground Limbo hardware is still on Limbo's surface, and includes several radios. Eventually the Limbians might work out a way to use them, and we don't want them hearing signals from Earth. This is the first and last Gleisian signing off."

I now locked the Homelink transceiver array on Gleise 667.

I had one huge advantage over the Limbians: the human body was absolutely alien to them. True, they were getting better at looking after us, but I was now their only undamaged reference. My plan to go to Gleise 667 was ludicrous, but perhaps it seemed too ludicrous to be a lie.

How does one wipe out the memory of an entire world? I deleted most of the ship's databases, their backups and their disaster contingency backups. Hardcopy books went into the plasma pre-processing chamber. I searched the cabins and found dozens of personal data sticks containing everything from documentaries about the Javelin expedition to artwork virtual models of our solar system. I just vapourised any encrypted datasticks.

Finally, when I was too tired to do any more, I sat slumped in front of the navigation screen and called up artwork representations of Gleise 667. It was a triple star system with one M-type and two K-type stars. The M-type red dwarf had three rocky worlds in its habitable zone. True, they were orbiting the dim star closer than Mercury orbits the sun, and were all tidally locked to present the same face to the little star, but the Gargantua telescopic interferometer had detected water and oxygen on the planet designated 667Cc.

I closed my eyes and visualized a band of green and blue girdling a planet that was baked on one side and frozen on the other. Were that the Earth, the livable band might include the eastern half of North America, the western half of South America, most of Antarctica, a sliver of the West Australian coast, half of Indonesia, all of southeast Asia, China and Mongolia, central Siberia and Greenland. That was all the real estate that I needed.

I locked the ship's optical telescope on the star system, then ramped up the magnification. There was not much to see, just the three stars. The planets were only visible with Gargantua, an optical interferometer array that was the size of the Earth's orbit. Gliese 667Cc had been discovered in 2011. The planet itself was no more than a pixilated blob in pictures returned by Gargantua, but they had confirmed that water and oxygen were present. Water allowed the possibility of life, and oxygen confirmed life's presence. It was a plausible place for a human body to have come from.

With the reaction mass tanks full, I thought through my options yet again. What was the most natural thing that a really frightened animal would do? Were a Pleistocene hunter faced with a saber-toothed cat, he would run away. Were a saber-toothed cat faced with a human battle tank, he might also run away. Did the Limbians understand fear? If they did not, I had no options at all. I now committed myself to running away.

The Javelin was designed to operate with a minimum crew of one, but you do not simply press a button to start the engines on a starship two miles long. There are power levels to be balanced, reaction plasmas to be generated, course coordinates to be configured and emergency systems to be brought online. Most of this work was automated, but it still took days. Having started the process, I had a lot of free time on my hands because the magnetoplasma drive had to be brought up to operating temperature slowly to avoid hysteresis deformation. Being at a loose end, I returned to world building.

A lot of speculative art has been created to describe the worlds that orbit distant stars. Landscapes of Gleise 667Cc were a favourite subject, because it was part of such an exotic system. A search on *Gliese 667Cc* and *Images* returned hundreds of images of one bloated sun and a pair of small, bright suns hovering above ruddy horizons. The skies were banded with clouds, and placid lakes and seas often featured. Some landscapes had dark vegetation in the foreground, and a few had fanciful animals. I deleted all those, along with all artwork for other systems.

Next I printed out dozens of the images of landscapes with three suns, and with these I decorated the walls of the cabins, laboratories, mess room and control centre. They had no buildings, so I labeled them after national parks on Earth.

I searched on images for sunrise in Perth, Singapore and Beijing, then sunset from New York, Montreal, Lima and Santiago. There were plenty of pictures in the databases that I had not deleted yet, way more than I wanted a vastly superior alien intelligence to access, but they also contained every conceivable photograph that I might ever need to build a civilization. I selected photos of dawn and sunset from the appropriate cities, and to these I added triple suns and triple shadows, then printed them to further decorate the walls of the workspaces and cabins.

Mikov came from Vladivostok, I decided, so I selected images of an apartment there and turned it into his home by photopainting images of him into them. Landi got a penthouse in New York with a glorious view of the sunset wastelands to the west. I gave Saral a waterfront property in Lima, and Fan got a place in Bejing with a view of the old Imperial Palace. My real home was in London, which was in the frozen hemisphere, so I chose a freestanding house in a bushland suburb of Perth to live.

I photopasted images of a bigger, more ruddy sun and a pair of stars as bright as the full moon into every landscape picture that I did not delete. Then there were the word problems. Have you ever thought how hard it might be to eliminate the words *day* or *night* from the language? There would be no *day* and *night* as measures for time on a tidally locked planet. I set a script going on the computers to delete *day* and *night*, and remove *moon* and *lunar* as well. The other planets of my own solar system had to go too.

A model of the Gliese system was in the databases, and from this I projected views of the sky from Gliese 667Cc for dates and times . . . except that dates and times had different meanings here. A year for this world was twenty-eight days long, thirteen times less than an Earth year, and the words day, sunrise and sunset had no meaning. What was a year? The two K-type stars orbited each other with a forty-two year period, and the red dwarf orbited them in turn at more than ten times the distance. No day, twenty-eight day year, forty-two year star-year, and then there would be another year centuries long for star C to orbit the inner binaries. There would have to be names for all of those periods, along with calendars and legends involving three stars.

There was not much that I could do about the lack of a datastream from the Gleise system, so I fabricated a sudden, inexplicable loss of signal. A radio link over twenty-two light years would require a huge installation, so there could only be one of them. It was a single point of failure, and I logged myself as assuming that it had failed due to some technical glitch. Repairs might take months, even years, and there was no backup.

All light year distances had to be multiplied by thirteen to make a new type of light year. I created names for the stars, names for the planets, units of time, and calendars. The homeworld had no seasons, being tidally locked, so I wrote that huge solar flares from the red dwarf stirred up our atmosphere and caused variable weather patterns.

After several days of computer-controlled buildup, the Javelin's engine finally came to life. The first few hours of the burn were the worst; I was aware that the Limbians might panic and snatch me away like all the others. The tanks contained millions of tons of water, and I was mostly water. They could track water. I hoped that if they were aware of what the Javelin was doing, they would be happy enough to leave me alone. They probably wanted to be led to a planet full of humans, with hundreds of millions of eyes, ears and hands to provide access to an entirely new universe. I had created such a planet, and I was leading them there. Had I not been a novelist, I could not have done it.

Landi was materialized no more than two yards from me. The blast and shockwave from the displaced air set my ears ringing, then there was a thud as she fell a few inches to the habitat's floor. Like the others, she was naked. Unlike the others, she was uninjured and awake. I shrank back as she sat up and looked around. She displayed no shame at her nakedness as she focused on me, then stood.

Her skin looked like she had spent too long in a bath. Quite possibly the Limbians had created a room temperature chamber of warm, hyper-oxygenated water. There was apparently food available too, because after thirty days away she was not gaunt with starvation. Then I remembered that the Limbians had access to about four-fifty pounds of raw human protein. I did not dwell on that thought.

Landi returning alive was the one possible flaw in my ludicrously desperate plan. She remembered Earth, she was a database that could contradict the illusion of Gleise 667 I had created aboard the Javelin. I wondered what I could say to her. In fact I actually felt a little embarrassed, like a schoolboy caught drawing doodles of genitalia on his datapad.

"This is . . . familiar," she said. "Where are we?"

"Don't you remember?" I asked. "This our starship, the Javelin."

"You . . . are familiar."

"I'm Jander. My name is Jander."

"Name?"

Suddenly I realized that my plan might still be on course. Her memories appeared to be incomplete.

"Name—identification. I'm Captain Jander, I'm the leader of the crew."

She accepted that. Relief must have radiated from my face like a floodlight, but Limbians did not understand facial expressions. Landi had lost the memory of being captain.

"Do I have a name?"

"Landi. Your name is Landi."

"What is on your skin? Damage?"

Her memory had definitely been scrambled. The Limbians understood injury, but not clothing.

"Clothes, these are clothes," I said, pulling at the cloth. "Protective covers, insulation against cold."

"But it is very hot in here."

"No, it's normal."

Over the next hour I got Landi into overalls from her locker and established that she remembered about eating, drinking and going to the bathroom. Her speech centers were okay, but nearly everything else was scrambled or absent. It was as if her mind had been taken apart, then put back together by something that did not understand how everything fitted. Quite a few bits had been left out, and one of those was Earth.

I showed Landi her quarters, and pointed to the pictures of her New York apartment with the view of three suns that never set. One picture showed a dinner party with her parents, brother and his family. She accepted all this without question.

"We're going home now," I concluded. "Our world is called Gelser."

"But we are traveling slowly."

This sent a shiver through my body. She could not have known that unless she was not entirely Landi. Something was sharing her mind, and it was aware of our speed and distance relative to Limbo.

"Yes, it will take many lifetimes to get home," I explained. "We need to travel in suspension vats so that we don't die of old age before we arrive."

"I understand. Clever. What does our world look and feel like?"

Perhaps because the Limbians could not understand what was in Landi's mind, they had returned her without all her memories. I would have to explain everything to her, slowly and patiently. Through her, they could ask me for clarifications. All of that meant that they were afraid of damaging me. That was a great comfort.

"Gelser is in a triple star system," I said. "It orbits Gleise, the smallest of the three stars."

"But what is Gelser?"

"It is a planet orbiting a star the same way that the moons of Abyss orbit. Gelser means band of life. It's more than six thousand light years away. Here is where you live."

I pointed to a printout of New York, with three suns perpetually setting in the west. Getting the triple shadows right had caused me a lot of headaches, but the images were convincing.

Some hours later Landi needed to sleep. Once I was alone, I took observations of the Doppler shifts of reference stars. They confirmed what I suspected—the Javelin was about six thousand tons heavier than it should have been. Although that was a tiny fraction of its mass, it was significant. I checked the tank monitors. One of the reaction mass tanks that should have been empty was now full, with its valves iced shut. We had a stowaway.

For me, routine conversations with Landi became exercises in absolute vigilance. The month no longer existed aboard the Javelin, and a year was shorter than what a month had been. I had kept the hour the same, and decreed that humans had a diurnal rhythm twenty-four hours long. The second I defined as the average human heartbeat at rest, and sixty made a minute. The fewer differences that I had to cope with, the better. I kept the week, but made it a quarter of a year. I punished myself by slapping my face every time I even thought the words *day* or *month*. It was easier to think of the weeks as January, April, July and October, so this was what I did. All the clocks and computers had been reconfigured.

"This is home," I said in one of my tutorials about home, bringing up the image of a large, reddish sun shining over a placid lake on the conference wallscreen. "This is Gleise, the star that we orbit. The two other stars are Fril and Rec."

"What are these fluffy things?" asked Landi,

"Clouds. They're water vapour, steam. This next pic is of another national park. See these things? We call them trees."

"But where is the ice to protect you from the star's heat?"

"The atmosphere gives us enough protection. Our planet is locked into facing the sun, Gleise. Only a narrow band of twilight is habitable. This photograph was taken from further into the sunlit side. See, Gleise is higher in the sky. Here is New York, on the edge of the Atlantic Bandsea. These are cities in China and India. Perth is the capital of Australia. I was born in Perth."

"They are different. Why is that?"

I very nearly said that some cities are in the tropics and the buildings are designed for warmer temperatures, but the tropics did not exist in my new home for humanity.

"It's cultural," I managed. "Different cultures have different ways of doing things."

"What are cultures?"

And so it went. Landi accepted my newly invented calendars and timing systems without question, but I was my own worst enemy. Just try getting through your day without saying day—or night, daily, dusk, dawn, moon, afternoon, tropics, poles and a multitude of other words that developed on a spinning world. I spoke slowly, rehearsing every sentence in my mind. Landi and I began to settle into a routine that would last the five months of acceleration.

I had never given much thought to our captain's sex life, so my next problem caught me flat footed. I had encouraged Landi to explore the habitat, mainly so that the thing sharing what was left of her mind could see all the pictures supposedly from cities on Gelser. I had not expected her to find a secret home movie database belonging to Saral. Like eating and washing, the skills for using a simple remote had apparently remained in her subconscious. When I came to check on her she was in Saral's cabin, watching an extremely graphic video of the ship's biologist performing sexual antics with Mikov.

"What are they doing?" Landi asked.

"They . . . are reproductive activities," I said, more slowly than ever. "Men and women put their DNA together to make a child."

"Oh. Why are they doing it on Saral's bed?"

"It's the bouncing up and down, one needs a soft surface to do it."

"And why are they wearing no clothes?"

"Um, for stimulation."

I checked the other videos in Saral's secret database. All were taken in her cabin, and were highly anatomical in theme. Nine of them featured her and Fan, and Mikov was in eleven more. I was acutely embarrassed to see that I featured in only one. Obviously I was not as memorable as the others. A careful inspection of the room revealed a dozen microcameras. The original Landi had not known about Saral and Fan.

"Why did she record these activities?" asked Landi.

"Sentimentality," I replied.

"What is that?"

"It's very hard to explain. Once you get more memories you will understand."

I was undressing for bed when Landi entered my quarters—stark naked.

"I wish to perform reproductive activities," she announced.

Suffice it to say that I managed to perform, although not before considerable effort to get myself stimulated. Part of Landi was coming from something in about six thousand tons of teleported water in tank 18 Delta, and the thought of that was a real damper. Neither was I to get any relief at the end of proceedings, because she had also learned about sleeping with one's partner.

"How long before a child forms?" she asked as we lay in the darkness.

It was just as I suspected. The Limbians were unhappy about me being their one and only benchmark human.

"For us, there will be no child," I replied.

"But why? We did everything correctly."

"My testicles and your ovaries are in storage, back on Gelser. There's only dummy flesh in their place."

"Why?"

"Prolonged exposure to radiation in deep space damages reproductive tissues. They will be put back after the trip."

"Oh. Then why did Saral do it so many times with all you males? No child could be produced."

"It was . . . recreation. It feels pleasant, and it's healthy aerobic exercise."

That was a mistake on my part. Landi now insisted on sex with me during every sleep cycle, for our mutual health. I never managed to stop thinking about what was sharing the experience through her, which made it a continuing challenge.

After five months of acceleration, the Javelin has now edged up to just under a two hundredth of lightspeed, and I have put Landi into suspension. Without her to watch and listen, I am free to broadcast these words to all of you on Earth.

One tenth of a real light year from Earth is a vast and powerful alien . . . alien what? Civilization? The word cannot begin to describe the Limbians, but it will have to do. They value humans highly, because we have senses that they can never duplicate—and we can build machines. We are their only window on the universe of radiation and electromagnetism, and without our eyes they cannot know in what direction to reach out with their fearsome but limited senses. Stay away from Abyss and its moons, and you will be safe.

When I awake, the Javelin will have just enough power and reaction mass left to slow down and orbit Gleise 667Cc. All stories are real for those who believe them, and so far my Limbian audience believes my story. That will not last. The Limbians will be disappointed to see that the planet is not overflowing with humans, machines and cities. Entire continents will not be even remotely like what I have been describing. Worse, there will probably be plants, trees, animals, birds and fish that are nothing like what are in my pictures. Through Landi, they will demand an explanation, and I will not have one. I shall try to tell a convincing story, and I am a good storyteller, but I am not that good.

The journey to the Gleise 667 system will take four and a half thousand Earth years. That was enough for humanity to go from Stonehenge and pyramids to the Javelin, so there is hope. Go forth, achieve marvels and miracles, catch up with Limbian science, and pass them if you can. You have no choice, and there is a deadline.

Rates of change

JAMES S. A. COREY

James S. A. Corey is the pseudonym of two young writers working together, Daniel Abraham and Ty Franck. Their first novel as Corey, the Wide-Screen Space Opera Leviathan Wakes, *the first in the Expanse series, was released in 2010 to wide acclaim, and has been followed by other Expanse novels—* Caliban's War, Abaddon's Gate, Cibola Burn, Nemesis Games, *and* Babylon's Ashes. *There's also now a TV series based on the series,* The Expanse, *on the Syfy Channel.*

Daniel Abraham lives with his wife in Albuquerque, New Mexico, where he is the director of technical support at a local Internet service provider. Starting off his career in short fiction, he made sales to Asimov's Science Fiction, SCI FICTION, The Magazine of Fantasy & Science Fiction, Realms of Fantasy, The Infinite Matrix, Vanishing Acts, The Silver Web, Bones of the World, The Dark, Wild Cards, *and elsewhere, some of which appeared in his first collection,* Leviathan Wept and Other Stories. *Turning to novels, he made several sales in rapid succession, including the books of* The Long Price Quartet *series, which consist of* A Shadow in Summer, A Betrayal in Winter, An Autumn War, *and* The Price of Spring. *He has published the first two volumes in his new series,* The Dagger and the Coin, *which consists of* The Dragon's Path *and* The King's Blood, The Tyrant's Law, The Widow's House, *and* The Spider's War. *He also wrote* Hunter's Run, *a collaborative novel with George R. R. Martin and Gardner Dozois, and, as M.L.N. Hanover, the four-volume paranormal romance series,* Black Sun's Daughter.

Ty Franck was born in Portland, Oregon, and has had nearly every job known to man, including a variety of fast-food jobs, rock-quarry grunt, newspaper reporter, radio-advertising salesman, composite-materials fabricator, director of operations for a computer manufacturing firm, and part owner of an accounting software consulting firm. He is currently the personal assistant to fellow writer George R. R. Martin, where he makes coffee, runs to the post office, and argues about what constitutes good writing. He mostly loses.

Here they give us an ingenious and occasionally unsettling glimpse of how the consensus vision of what it means to "be human" may be changed almost beyond recognition by future technologies and cultural developments.

Diana hasn't seen her son naked before. He floats now in the clear gel bath of the medical bay, the black ceramic casing that holds his brain, the long articulated tail of his spinal column. Like a tadpole, she thinks. Like something young. In all, he hardly masses more than he did as a baby. She has a brief, horrifying image of holding him on her lap, cradling the braincase to her breast, the whip of his spine curling around her.

The thin white filaments of interface neurons hang in the translucent gel, too thin to see except in aggregate. Silvery artificial blood runs into the casing ports and back out in tubes more slender than her pinky finger. She thought, when they called her in, that she'd be able to see the damage. That there would be a scratch on the carapace, a wound, something to show where the violence had been done to him. There is nothing there. Not so much as a scuff mark. No evidence.

The architecture of the medical center is designed to reassure her. The walls curve around her in warm colors. The air recyclers hum a low, consonant chord. Nothing helps. Her own body—her third—is flushed with adrenaline, her heart aches and her hands squeeze into fists. Her fight or flight reaction has no outlet, so it speeds around her body, looking for a way to escape. The chair tilts too easily under her, responding to shifts in her balance and weight that she isn't aware of making. She hates it. The cafe au lait that the nurse brought congeals, ignored, on the little table.

Diana stares at the curve and sweep of Stefan's bodiless nervous system as if by watching him now she can stave off the accident that has already happened. Closing the barn door, she thinks, after the horses are gone. The physician ghosts in behind her, footsteps quiet as a cat's, his body announcing his presence only in how he blocks the light.

"Mrs. Dalkin," he says. "How are you feeling?"

"How is he?" she demands instead of saying hello.

The physician is a large man, handsome with a low warm voice like flannel fresh from the dryer. She wonders if it is his original body or if he's chosen the combination of strength and softness just to make this part of his work easier. "Active. We're seeing metabolic activity over most of his brain the way we would hope. Now that he's here, the inflammation is under control."

"So he's going to be all right?"

He hesitates. "We're still a little concerned about the interface. There was some bruising that may have impaired his ability to integrate with a new body, but we can't really know the extent of that yet."

Diana leans forward, her gut aching. Stefan is there, only inches from her. Awake, trapped in darkness, aware only of himself and the contents of his own mind. He doesn't even know she is watching him. If she picked him up, he wouldn't know she was doing it. If she shouted, he wouldn't hear. What if he is trapped that way forever? What if he has fallen into a darkness she can never bring him out from?

"Is he scared?"

"We are seeing some activity in his amygdala, yes," the physician says. "We're addressing that chemically, but we don't want to depress his neural activity too much right now."

"You *want* him scared, then."

"We want him active," the physician says. "Once we can establish some communication with him and let him know that we're here and where he is and that we're taking action on his behalf, I expect most of his agitation will resolve."

"So he doesn't even know he's here."

"The body he was in didn't survive the initial accident. He was extracted in situ before transport." He says it so gently, it sounds like an apology. An offer of consolation. She feels a spike of hatred and rage for the man run through her like an electric shock, but she hides it.

"What happened?"

"Excuse me?" the physician asks.

"I said, what happened? How did he get hurt? Who did this?"

"He was brought from the coast by emergency services. I understood it was an accident. Someone ran into him, or he ran into something, but apart from that it was a blunt force injury, we didn't . . ."

Diana lifts her hand, and the physician falls silent. "Can you fix him? You can make him all right."

"We have a variety of interventions at our disposal," he says, relieved to be back on territory he knows. "It's really going to depend on the nature of the damage he's sustained."

"What's the worst case?"

"The worst case is that he won't be able to interface with a new body at all."

She turns to look into the physician's eyes. The dark brown that looks back at her doesn't show anything of the cruelty or horror of what he's just said. "How likely is that?" Diana says, angry at her voice for shaking.

"Possible. But Stefan is young. His tissue is resilient. The casing wasn't breached, and the constriction site on his spine didn't buckle. I'd say his chances are respectable, but we won't know for a few days."

Diana drops her head into her hands, the tips of her fingers digging into her temples. Something violent bubbles in her chest, and a harsh laughter presses at the back of her throat like vomit.

"All right," she says. "All . . . right."

She hears Karlo's footsteps, recognizing their cadence the way she would have known his cough or the sound of his yawn. Even across bodies, there is a constancy about Karlo. She both clings to it now and resents it. The ridiculous muscle-bound body he bought himself for retirement tips into the doorway, darkening the room.

"I came when I heard," he says.

"Fuck you," Diana says, and then the tears come and won't stop. He puts his arms around her. The doctor walks softly away.

It is a year earlier, and Karlo says "He's a grown man. There's no reason he shouldn't."

The house looks out over the hot concrete of Dallas. It is smaller than the one they'd shared in Quebec, the kitchen thinner, the couch less comfortable. The way they live in it is different too. Before, when they'd had a big family room, they would all stretch out together on long evenings. Stefan talking to his friends and playing games, Karlo building puzzles or doing office work, Diana watching old films and taking meetings with work groups in Europe and Asia. They'd been a family then— husband, wife, child. For all their tensions and half-buried resentments, they'd still been a unit, the three of them. But they live in the Dallas house like it is a dormitory, coming back to sleep and leaving again when they wake. Even her.

She hates the place, and what it says about her. About Karlo. About Stefan. She hates wondering whether Karlo's new body had been chosen based on some other woman's tastes. Or some other man's. That her son isn't a child.

"I stayed in my body until I was *thirty*," she says. "He's twenty-*one*. He doesn't need it for work. He's not some kind of laborer."

"It isn't the same now as it was when we were young," Karlo says. "It isn't just medical or work."

"*Cosmetic*," Diana says, stalking out of the bedroom. Karlo follows her like a leaf pulled along by a breeze.

"Or adventure. Exploration. It's what people do these days."

"He should wait."

Her own body—the one she'd been born in—had failed her young. Ovarian cancer that had spread to her hip before she'd noticed a thing. The way she remembered it, the whole process hadn't taken more a than a few days. Symptom, diagnosis, discussion of treatment options. Her doctor had been adamant—get out before the metastases reached her central nervous system. The ship of her flesh was sinking, and she needed to get into the lifeboats now. The technology had been developed for people working in vacuum or deep ocean, and it was as safe as a decade and a half of labor law could make it. And anyway, there wasn't a viable choice.

She'd agreed in a haze of fear and confusion. At the medical center, Karlo had undressed her for the last time, helped her into her gown, kissed her, and promised that everything was going to be all right. She still remembered being on the table, the anesthesiologist telling her to unclasp her hands. In a sense, it had been the last thing she'd ever heard.

She'd hated her second body. Even though it had been built to look as much like her original as it could, she knew better. Everything about it was subtly wrong—the way her elbow fit against her side, the way her voice resonated when she spoke, the shape of her hands. The physicians had talked about rehabilitation anxiety and the uncanny valley. They said it would become more familiar, except that it didn't. She tried antidepressant therapy. Identity therapy. Karlo had volunteered to swap out his own body partly as a way, he said, to understand better what she was going through. That hadn't worked at all. He'd woken up in his new flesh like he'd had a long nap and loved everything about his new self. Five years in, she still hadn't felt comfortable in her new skin.

Her third body had been an attempt to address that. Instead of trying to mimic her old, dead flesh, it would be something new. Where she'd been petite before, she would be taller and broader now. Instead of being long-waisted, she would be leggy.

Her skin tone would be darker, the texture of her hair would be different. Her eyes could be designed in unnatural colors, her fingernails growing in iridescent swirls. Instead of pretending that her body wasn't a prosthetic, she could design one as piece of art. It is the mask that she faces in every mirror, and most days she feels more reconciled than trapped.

And then there are bad days when she longs for the first body, the real body, and worse than that the woman she'd been when she was still in it. She wonders whether it was the same longing that other women felt about youth. And now Stefan wants to leave his body—the body she'd given him, the one that had grown within her—in order to . . . what? Have an adventure with his friends?

Sitting at the thin, discolored breakfast bar, she laces large, dark fingers together, enjoying the ache of knuckle against knuckle. Karlo drifts past in his massive flesh, taking a muscle shirt from the dryer and pulling it over his head with a vagueness that leaves Diana lonesome.

"Why would he want to?" she says, wiping her eye with the back of one hand.

Karlo sighs, hums to himself. He draws a glass of orange juice from the refrigerator and adds vodka from the freezer. He drinks deep and bares his teeth after. His third body has bright white tombstones of teeth. His first body had been slight and compact. Almost androgynous. By the time he speaks, she's forgotten that she even asked a question.

"Do you mean you don't think he wants it, or you don't think he *should* want it?"

"He doesn't understand what he's giving up," she says.

"Do you?"

She scowled at him. The conversation is making her uncomfortably aware that the experience of him—of seeing Karlo, hearing his voice, smelling the bite of the orange and alcohol—is all phantoms of charged ions and neurochemistry in a brain, in a casing, in a body. Neurons that fire in a pattern that somehow, unknowably, *is* her experiencing these things. She crosses her arms like she is driving a car, and hates being aware of it. Karlo finishes his drink, puts the glass in the washer. He doesn't look straight into her eyes. "All his friends are doing it. If he doesn't he'll be left behind."

"It's his *body*," she says.

"It's *his* body," Karlo says, his eyes already shifting toward the door. Away from her. "And anyway, that doesn't mean what it did when we were kids." He leaves without saying good-bye. Without kissing her, not that she would have welcomed him. She checks her messages. There are a dozen queued. Something dramatic has happened at the Apulia office, and she hunches over the display and tries to tease out exactly what it was.

She never does give her permission. She only doesn't withhold it.

The footage of the accident plays on a little wall monitor in the medical center. The actual water had been too deep for natural light to find them, so the images have been enhanced, green and aquamarine added, shafts of brightness put in where a human eye—if it hadn't been crushed by the pressure—would have seen only darkness. The image capture has been done by a companion submarine to document the months-long trek, and either it was a calm day in the deep water or image processing has steadied it. Diana can imagine herself floating in the endless expanse of an ocean so vast it is like looking up at the stars. Karlo sits beside her, his hands knotted together, his eyes on the screen. The contrast between the squalid, tiny world of the medical center and the vast beauty on the screen disorients her.

The first of them swim into sight. A ray with wide gray wings, sloping through the salt water. With nothing to give a sense of scale, it could be larger than whales or hardly bigger than a human. There is no bump to show where the carapace holding a human brain and spine might have slotted into it. There is no scar to mark an insertion point. Another of the creatures passes by the camera, curving up the deep tides with grace and power. Then another. Then a dozen more. A school of rays. And one of them—she can't begin to guess which—her son. In some other context, it might have been beautiful.

"It's all right," Karlo says, and she doesn't know what he means by it. That the violence she was about to see had already happened, that she ought not be disturbed by the alien body that Stefan had chosen over his own, that her anger now won't help. The words could carry anything.

A disturbance strikes the rays, a shock moving through the group. The smooth cohesion breaks, and they whirl, turning one way and then the other. Their distress is unmistakable.

"What happened?" Karlo says. "Was that it?"

"Be quiet," Diana says. She leans forward, filling her view with the small screen like she might be able to dive through it. There in the center of the group, down below the camera, two of the rays swirl around each other, one great body butting into the other. A fight or a dance. She can't read the intent in the movements. One breaks off, skimming wildly up, speeding through the gloom and the darkness. The other follows, and the floating camera turns to track them. As they chase each other, another shape slides into the frame, also high above. Another group of three alien bodies moving together, unaware of the chase rising up from below. The impact seems comical. The lead ray bumps into the belly of the middle of the three. The little camera loses focus, finds it again. Four rays swimming in a tight circle around one that lists on its side, its wings stilled and drifting.

That is my son, she thinks. *That is Stefan*. No emotions rise at the idea. It is absurd. Like seeing a rock cracked under a hammer or a car bent by a wreck: the symbol of a tragedy, but not the thing itself. It is some sea animal, something that belongs to the same world as sharks and angler fish. Inhuman. She knows it is her boy floating there, being pulled toward the surface by the emergency services pods, but she cannot make herself feel it.

"They attacked him," she says, testing the words. Hoping that they will carry the outrage she wants to feel. "They attacked him, and they left him for dead."

"They were playing and there was an accident," Karlo says. "They didn't leave him for dead."

"Then where are they? His friends, if that's what you call them? I don't see them here."

"They can't breathe air," Karlo says, as if that excuses everything. "They'll come once the trip is over. Or, when he gets better, he can go back to them."

Her breath leaves her. She turns to stare at him. His eyes, so unlike the ones she'd known when they had been married, cut to her and away again.

"Go back to them?" she says.

"If he wants. Some people find living that way very calming. Pleasant."

"They aren't *human*," Now there is rage. Real rage. It lifts her up out of herself and fills her ears with a sound like bees. "You want to see your son among these animals? That's fine with you? They could have killed him. We don't know that they didn't. You'd send him back?"

"They aren't animals," Karlo says. "They're just different. And I would do what Stefan wants. I'd let him choose."

"Of course you would."

They are quiet for a moment. The feed on the display ends, drops back to the medical center's logo and a prompt. Karlo sighs again. She hates the way his sighs sound now—deep and rumbling. Nothing like his first body, except in the timing of it, the patience in it. Nothing the same except that it is the same. "You know you can't tell him how to live his life."

"I don't want to have this conversation."

"It's always been like this. Every generation finds its own way to show that it isn't like the one before. Too much risk, too much sex, terrible music, not enough respect for the old ways. This is no different. It was an accident."

"I don't want to have this *conversation*."

"All right," Karlo says. "Another time."

Before the cancer she worked in an office with people, a desk of her own, conversations over butter tarts and tea in a breakroom with an old couch and half a dozen bamboo chairs. When she came back in her second body, the junior partners threw a little party for her to celebrate the happy conclusion of her brush with death. She remembers being touched and a little embarrassed at the time. And grateful.

It was only later, as she tried to get back into her old routine, that her subterranean distress began to bloom. She found herself timing her trips to the bathroom and break room to avoid brushing past anyone or being touched. She avoided the bakery at the end of the street that she'd frequented before. At home, her marriage became essentially sexless.

She tried not to notice it at first, then told herself that it was temporary, and then that it was normal. Over weeks, a quiet shame gnawed at her. She bathed at night with a grim, angry focus, resenting her skin for gathering smudges and sweat, her hair for growing oily and repulsive. She ate too much or not enough. Shitting or pissing or getting her period filled her with a deep disgust, like she was having to watch and clean and tend to someone else.

She found reasons to work remotely, to talk to Karlo and Stefan while she was somewhere else. Simply having a physicality irritated her, and she leaned away from it. When the junior partners asked whether she was still using her office or if they could repurpose the space, she'd cried without knowing quite why she was crying. She'd told them they could have it and scheduled a consultation with her doctor. Rehabilitation anxiety. Uncanny valley. It would pass.

Now, she sits in the medical cafeteria, going through her messages with her attention scattered, listening to the same one three or four or five times, and still not able to focus her attention long enough to parse what exactly it was her coworker was asking of her. The smell of antiseptic and overheated food presses her. The lights seem both too bright and unable to dispel the shadows, and she wonders whether it might be the beginning of a migraine. Karlo has found himself someplace else to be, and she is resentful that he's abandoned her and relieved to be left to herself.

At the next table, a woman in scrubs laughs acidly and the man she is with responds with something in French. Diana finds her attention drifting to them: wondering at them, about them. The woman has a beautiful cascade of black hair flowing down her shoulder: had she been born with it? Is she as young as she seems, or was the brain under those raven locks an old woman's? Or an old man's? Or a child's as young as Stefan? Even in a carapace, a brain still wears out, still lives out its eight or nine decades. Or seven. Or two. But without the other signs of age and infirmity, what does it mean?

She remembers her own mother's hair going from auburn to gray to white to a weird sickly yellow. The changes meant something, gave Diana a way to anticipate the changes in her own life, her own body. There are no old people now. No one crippled and infirm. Everything is a lie of health and permanence, of youth permanently extended. All around her, everyone is wrapped in a mask of flesh. Everything is a masquerade of itself, everyone in disguise. And even the few who aren't, might be. There is no way to know.

Her hands tremble. She closes her eyes, and has to fight not to cover her ears too. If she does, someone might come and talk to her, ask her whether she is all right. She doesn't know how she would answer that, and she doesn't want to find out.

For a moment, she envies Stefan, locked away from the world, alone with only himself, and then immediately condemns herself for thinking it. He is hurt. Her baby is injured and afraid and beyond any place she can reach him. Only a monster would wish for that.

But . . .

Perhaps she can let herself want to change places with him. If she had to shed her body—all her bodies—to bring him back into the light, she'd do it in a heartbeat. Put that way, she can tell herself it would be an act of love.

Someone touches her shoulder. She startles, her eyes flying open. The physician with his uncertain smile, like she might bite him. She forces herself to nod, reflexively picturing the black casing behind the chocolate brown eyes and gently graying hair.

"We were trying to reach you, Mrs. Dalkin."

She looks at her message queue. Half a dozen from the medical center's system, from Karlo. She feels the blush in her cheeks. "I'm sorry," she says. "I was distracted."

"No need to apologize," he says. "I thought you'd want to know. We've made contact with Stephan."

The interface is minimal. One of the thin silvery faux-neuronal leads has adhered to a matching bundle of nerve clusters that runs to a casing like the insulation on a wire, and from there into a simple medical deck. A resonance imager wraps around Stefan's brain like a scarf and focuses on his visual neocortex, reading the patterns there and extrapolating the images that Stephan is imagining from them. Reading his mind and showing it on a grainy display.

"He is experiencing the interface as a coldness on his right arm," the physician says. "You have to be slow, but he's been able to follow us with surprising clarity. It's a very good sign."

"Oh good," Diana says, and wishes there had been less dread in the words. She sits at the deck, her fingers over the keyboard layout, suddenly unsure what she is supposed to say. She smiles at the physician nervously. "Does his father know?"

"Yes. Mr. Dalkin was here earlier."

"Oh good," she says again. She types slowly, one letter at a time. The deck translates her words into impulses down the neuronal wire, the interface translates the impulses into the false experience of an unreal cold in an abandoned arm, and Stefan—her Stefan, her son—reads the switching impulses as the Morse-code-like pulses that he's trained in.

This is your mother. I am right here.

She turns to the display, waiting. Biting her lips with her teeth until she tastes a little blood. The display shifts. There is only black and gray, fuzzy as a child drawing in the dirt with a stick, but she sees the cartoonish smiling face. Then a heart. Then, slowly, H then I then M then O then M. She sobs once, and it hurts her throat.

Are you okay in there?

P-E-A-C-H-Y

"Fuck you," she says. "Fuck you, you flippant little shit." She doesn't look at the physician, the technicians. Let them think whatever they want. She doesn't care now.

I love you.

Stephan visualizes a heart. The physician hands Diana a tissue, and she wipes her tears away first and then blows her nose.

It is going to be okay.

I-K-N-O-W and another cartoon smiling face. Then T-E-L-L-K-I-R-A-I-A-M-G-O-D.

God?

The display goes chaotic for a moment, as her son thinks of something else, not visual. It comes back with something like an infinity sign, two linking circles. No, a double o.

Good?

The smiling face. Tell Kira I am good. As if it were true. As if whatever girl had sloughed off her own body and put her mind in one of those monsters deserves to be comforted for whatever role she'd had in making her son into this. No one deserved to be forgiven. No one.

I will.

"His anxiety has gone down considerably since we made contact," the physician says. "And with the interface starting to bounce back, I think we can start administering some medication to reduce his distress. It will still be some time before we can know how extensive the permanent damage is, but I think it's very likely he will be able to integrate into a body again."

"That's good," Diana hears herself say.

"I don't want to oversell the situation. He may be blinded. He may have reduced motor function. There is still a long, long way to go before we can really say he's clear. But his responses so far show that he's very much cognitively intact, and he's got a great sense of humor and a real bravery. That's more important now than anything else."

"That's good," she says again. Her body rises, presumably because she'd wanted it to. "Excuse me."

She walks down the hall, out the metal door, into the bright and unforgiving summer sunlight. She's forgotten her things in Stefan's room, but she doesn't want to go back for them. They'll be there when she returns or else they won't. On the streets, autocabs hiss their tires along the railings. Above her, a flock of birds wheels. She finds a little stretch of grass, an artifact of the sidewalk and the street, useless for anything and so left alone. She lowers herself to it, crosses her third set of legs and pulls off her shoes to look at some unreal woman's feet, running her fingertips along the arches.

None of it is real. The heat of the sun is only neurons in her brain firing in a certain pattern. The dampness of the grass that cools her thighs and darkens her pants. The half-ticklish feeling of her feet. Her grief. Her anger. Her confusion. All of it is a hallucination created in tissue locked in a lightless box of bone. Patterns in a complication of nerves.

She talked with her son. He talked back. Whatever happens to him, it already isn't the worst. It will only get better, even if better doesn't make it all the way back to where it started from. Even if the best it ever is is worse than what it was. She waits for the relief to come. It doesn't.

Instead, there is Karlo.

He strides down the walk, swinging beefy arms, wide and masculine and sure of himself. She can tell when he sees her. The way he holds himself changes, narrows. Curls in, like he is protecting himself. That is just nerves firing too. The patterns in the brain she'd loved once expressing something through his costume of flesh. She wonders what it would be like to be stripped out of her body with him, their interface neurons linked one to another. There had been a time, hadn't there, when he had felt like her whole universe? Is that what the kids would be doing a generation from now? No more deep-sea rays. No more human bodies. Carapaces set so that they become flocks of birds or buildings or traffic patterns or each other. When they can become anything, they will. Anything but real.

He grunts as he eases himself to the grass beside her, shading his eyes from the sun with a hand and a grimace.

"He's doing better," Karlo says.

"I know. We passed notes."

"Really? That's more than I got out of him. He's improving."

"He gave me a message for Kira."

"That's his girlfriend."

"I don't care."

Karlo nods and heaves a wide, gentle sigh. "I'm sorry."

"For what?"

"Everything."

"You didn't do everything."

"No," he says. "Just what I could."

Diana lets her head sink to her knees. She wonders, if her first body had survived, would she have been able to? Or would the decades have stiffened her joints the way they had her mother's, dimmed her eyesight the way they had her father's. The way they might never for anyone again. "What happened?" she says. "When did we stop being human? When did we decide it was okay?"

"When did we start?" Karlo says.

"What?"

"When did we start being human and stop being . . . I don't know. Cavemen? Apes? When did we start being mammals? Every generation has been different than the one before. It's only that the rate of change was slow enough that we always recognized the one before and the one after as being like us. Enough like us. Close. Being human isn't a physical quality like being heavy or having green eyes. It's the idea that they're like we are. That nothing fundamental has changed. It's the story we tell about our parents and our children. "

"Our lovers," she says. "Our selves."

Karlo's body tightens. "Yes, those too," he says. And then, a moment later, "Stefan's going to come through. Whatever happens, he'll be all right."

"Will I?" she says.

She waits for an answer.

calved

SAM J. MILLER

Sam J. Miller is a writer and a community organizer. His fiction has appeared in Lightspeed, Asimov's, Clarkesworld, *and* The Minnesota Review, *and other markets. He is a nominee for the Nebula and Theodore Sturgeon Awards, a winner of the Shirley Jackson Award, and a graduate of the Clarion Writer's Workshop. Coming up is his debut novel* The Art of Starving. *He lives in New York City, and at www.samjmiller.com.*

Here he gives us the heartbreaking, emotionally grueling story of a man struggling to find work and stay alive in a ruthless society made up of refugees fleeing cities drowned by rising oceans, and struggling too to somehow stay in touch with his son, whom he can feel becoming slowly estranged from him and slipping further and further away every time he leaves for a six-month long job carving ice from melting glaciers. But can he win his son's affections back? Or will his efforts only make things worse?

My son's eyes were broken. Emptied out. Frozen over. None of the joy or gladness were there. None of the tears. Normally I'd return from a job and his face would split down the middle with happiness, seeing me for the first time in three months. Now it stayed flat as ice. His eyes leapt away the instant they met mine. His shoulders were broader and his arms more sturdy, and lone hairs now stood on his upper lip, but his eyes were all I saw.

"Thede," I said, grabbing him.

He let himself be hugged. His arms hung limply at his sides. My lungs could not fill. My chest tightened from the force of all the never-let-me-go bear hugs he had given me over the course of the past fifteen years, and would never give again.

You know how he gets when you're away," his mother had said, on the phone, the night before, preparing me. "He's a teenager now. Hating your parents is a normal part of it."

I hadn't listened, then. My hands and thighs still ached from months of straddling an ice saw; my hearing was worse with every trip; a slip had cost me five days work and five days pay and five days' worth of infirmary bills; I had returned to a sweat-smelling bunk in an illegal room I shared with seven other iceboat workers—and none of it mattered because in the morning I would see my son.

"Hey," he murmured emotionlessly. "Dad."

I stepped back, turned away until the red ebbed out of my face. Spring had come and the city had lowered its photoshade. It felt good, even in the cold wind.

"You guys have fun," Lajla said, pressing money discretely into my palm. I watched her go with a rising sense of panic. *Bring back my son,* I wanted to shout, *the one who loves me. Where is he. What have you done with him. Who is this surly creature.* Below us, through the ubiquitous steel grid that held up Qaanaaq's two million lives, black Greenland water sloshed against the locks of our floating city.

Breathe, Dom, I told myself, and eventually I could. *You knew this was coming. You knew one day he would cease to be a kid.*

"How's school?" I asked.

Thede shrugged. "Fine."

"Math still your favorite subject?"

"Math was never my favorite subject."

I was pretty sure that it had been, but I didn't want to argue.

"What's your favorite subject?"

Another shrug. We had met at the sea lion rookery, but I could see at once that Thede no longer cared about sea lions. He stalked through the crowd with me, his face a frozen mask of anger.

I couldn't blame him for how easy he had it. So what if he didn't live in the Brooklyn foster-care barracks, or work all day at the solar-cell plant school? He still had to live in a city that hated him for his dark skin and ice-grunt father.

"Your mom says you got into the Institute," I said, unsure even of what that was. A management school, I imagined. A big deal for Thede. But he only nodded.

At the fry stand, Thede grimaced at my clunky Swedish. The counter girl shifted to a flawless English, but I would not be cheated of the little bit of the language that I knew. "French fries and coffee for me and my son," I said, or thought I did, because she looked confused and then Thede muttered something and she nodded and went away.

And then I knew why it hurt so much, the look on his face. It wasn't that he wasn't a kid anymore. I could handle him growing up. What hurt was how he looked at me: like the rest of them look at me, these Swedes and grid city natives for whom I would forever be a stupid New York refugee, even if I did get out five years before the Fall.

Gulls fought over food thrown to the lions. "How's your mom?"

"She's good. Full manager now. We're moving to Arm Three, next year."

His mother and I hadn't been meant to be. She was born here, her parents Black Canadians employed by one of the big Swedish construction firms that built Qaanaaq back when the Greenland Melt began to open up the interior for resource extraction and grid cities starting sprouting all along the coast. They'd kept her in public school, saying it would be good for a future manager to be able to relate to the immigrants and workers she'd one day command, and they were right. She even fell for one of them, a fresh-off-the-boat North American taking tech classes, but wised up pretty soon after she saw how hard it was to raise a kid on an ice worker's pay. I had never been mad at her. Lajla was right to leave me, right to focus on her job. Right to build the life for Thede I couldn't.

"Why don't you learn Swedish?" he asked a French fry, unable to look at me.

"I'm trying," I said. "I need to take a class. But they cost money, and anyway I don't have—"

"Don't have time. I know. Han's father says people make time for the things that are important for them." Here his eyes *did* meet mine, and held, sparkling with anger and abandonment.

"Han one of your friends?"

Thede nodded, eyes escaping.

Han's father would be Chinese, and not one of the laborers who helped build this city—all of them went home to hardship-job rewards. He'd be an engineer or manager for one of the extraction firms. He would live in a nice house and work in an office. He would be able to make choices about how he spent his time.

"I have something for you," I said, in desperation.

I hadn't brought it for him. I carried it around with me, always. Because it was comforting to have it with me, and because I couldn't trust that the men I bunked with wouldn't steal it.

Heart slipping, I handed over the NEW YORK F CKING CITY T-shirt that was my most—my only—prized possession. Thin as paper, soft as baby bunnies. My mom had made me scratch the letter U off it before I could wear the thing to school. And Little Thede had loved it. We made a big ceremony of putting it on only once a year, on his birthday, and noting how much he had grown by how much it had shrunk on him. Sometimes if I stuck my nose in it and breathed deeply enough, I could still find a trace of the laundromat in the basement of my mother's building. Or the brake-screech stink of the subway. What little was left of New York City was inside that shirt. Parting with it meant something, something huge and irrevocable.

But my son was slipping through my fingers. And he mattered more than the lost city where whatever else I was—starving, broke, an urchin, a criminal—I belonged.

"Dad," Thede whispered, taking it. And here, at last, his eyes came back. The eyes of a boy who loved his father. Who didn't care that his father was a thick-skulled obstinate immigrant grunt. Who believed his father could do anything. "Dad. You love this shirt."

But I love you more, I did not say. *Than anything*. Instead: "It'll fit you just fine now." And then: "Enough sea lions. Beam fights?"

Thede shrugged. I wondered if they had fallen out of fashion while I was away. So much did, every time I left. The ice ships were the only work I could get, capturing calved glacier chunks and breaking them down into drinking water to be sold to the wide new swaths of desert that ringed the globe, and the work was hard and dangerous and kept me forever in limbo.

Only two fighters in the first fight, both lithe and swift and thin, their styles an amalgam of Chinese martial arts. Not like the big bruising New York boxers who had been the rage when I arrived, illegally, at fifteen years old, having paid two drunks to vouch for my age. Back before the Fail-Proof Trillion Dollar NYC Flood-Surge Locks had failed, and 80% of the city sunk, and the grid cities banned all new

East Coast arrivals. Now the North Americans in Arm Eight were just one of many overcrowded, underskilled labor forces for the city's corporations to exploit.

They leapt from beam to beam, fighting mostly in kicks, grappling briefly when both met on the same beam. I watched Thede. Thin, fragile Thede, with the wide eyes and nostrils that seemed to take in all the world's ugliness, all its stink. He wasn't having a good time. When he was twelve he had begged me to bring him. I had pretended to like it, back then for his sake. Now he pretended for mine. We were both acting out what we thought the other wanted, and that thought should have troubled me. But that's how it had been with my dad. That's what I thought being a man meant. I put my hand on his shoulder and he did not shake it off. We watched men harm each other high above us.

Thede's eyes burned with wonder, staring up at the fretted sweep of the windscreen as we rose to meet it. We were deep in a days-long twilight; soon, the sun would set for weeks.

"This is *not* happening," he said, and stepped closer to me. His voice shook with joy.

The elevator ride to the top of the city was obscenely expensive. We'd never been able to take it before. His mother had bought our tickets. Even for her, it hurt. I wondered why she hadn't taken him herself.

"He's getting bullied a lot in school," she told me, on the phone. Behind her was the solid comfortable silence of a respectable home. My background noise was four men building towards a fight over a card game. "Also, I think he might be in love."

But of course I couldn't ask him about either of those things. The first was my fault; the second was something no boy wanted to discuss with his dad.

I pushed a piece of trough meat loose from between my teeth. Savored how close it came to the real thing. Only with Thede, with his mother's money, did I get to buy the classy stuff. Normally it was barrel-bottom for me, greasy chunks that dissolved in my mouth two chews in, homebrew meat moonshine made in melt-scrap-furnace-heated metal troughs. Some grid cities were rumored to still have cows, but that was the kind of a lie people tell themselves to make life a little less ugly. Cows were extinct, and real beef was a joy no one would ever experience again.

The windscreen was an engineering marvel, and absolutely gorgeous. It shifted in response to headwinds; in severe storms the city would raise its auxiliary windscreens to protect its entire circumference. The tiny panes of plastiglass were common enough—a thriving underground market sold the fallen ones as good luck charms—but to see them knitted together was to tremble in the face of staggering genius. Complex patterns of crenelated reliefs, efficiently diverting windshear no matter what angle it struck from. Bots swept past us on the metal gridlines, replacing panes that had fallen or cracked.

Once, hand gripping mine tightly, somewhere down in the city beneath me, six-year-old Thede had asked me how the windscreen worked. He asked me a lot of things then, about the locks that held the city up, and how they could rise in response to tides and ocean-level increases; about the big boats with strange words and symbols on the side, and where they went, and what they brought back. "What's in that boat?" he'd ask, about each one, and I would make up ridiculous stories. "That's a giraffe boat. That one brings back machine guns that shoot strawberries. That one is for naughty children." In truth I only ever recognized ice boats, by the multitude of pincers atop cranes all along the side.

My son stood up straighter, sixty stories above his city. Some rough weight had fallen from his shoulders. He'd be strong, I saw. He'd be handsome. If he made it. If this horrible city didn't break him inside in some irreparable way. If marauding white boys didn't bash him for his dark skin. If the firms didn't pass him over for the lack of family connections on his stuttering immigrant father's side. I wondered who was bullying him, and why, and I imagined taking them two at a time and slamming their heads together so hard they popped like bubbles full of blood. Of course I couldn't do that. I also imagined hugging him, grabbing him for no reason and maybe never letting go, but I couldn't do that either. He would wonder why.

"I called last night and you weren't in," I said. "Doing anything fun?"

"We went to the cityoke arcade," he said.

I nodded like I knew what that meant. Later on I'd have to ask the men in my room. I couldn't keep up with this city, with its endlessly-shifting fashions and slang and the new immigrant clusters that cropped up each time I blinked. Twenty years after arriving, I was still a stranger. I wasn't just fresh off the boat, I was constantly getting back on the boat and then getting off again. That morning I'd gone to the job center for the fifth day in a row, and been relieved to find no boat postings. Only 12-month gigs, and I wasn't that hungry yet. Booking a year-long job meant admitting you were old, desperate, unmoored, willing to accept payment only marginally more than nothing, for the privilege of a hammock and three bowls of trough slop a day. But captains picked their own crews for the shorter runs, and I worried that the lack of postings meant that with fewer boats going out the competition had become too fierce for me. Every day a couple hundred new workers arrived from sunken cities in India or Middle Europe, or from any of a hundred Water War–torn nations. Men and women stronger than me, more determined.

With effort, I brought my mind back to the here and now. Twenty other people stood in the arc pod with us. Happy, wealthy people. I wondered if they knew I wasn't one of them. I wondered if Thede was.

They smiled down at their city. They thought it was so stable. I'd watched ice sheets calf off the glacier that were five times the size of Qaanaaq. When one of those came drifting in our direction, the windscreen wouldn't help us. The question was when, not if. I knew a truth they did not: how easy it is to lose something—everything—forever.

A Maoist Nepalese foreman, on one of my first ice ship runs, said white North Americans were the worst for adapting to the post-Arctic world, because we'd lived for centuries in a bubble of believing the world was way better than it actually was. Shielded by willful blindness and complex interlocking institutions of privilege, we mistook our uniqueness for universality.

I'd hated him for it. It took me fifteen years to see that he was right.

"What do you think of those two?" I asked, pointing with my chin at a pair of girls his age.

For a while he didn't answer. Then he said "I know you can't help that you grew up in a backwards macho culture, but can't you just keep that on the inside?"

My own father would have cuffed me if I talked to him like that, but I was too afraid of rupturing the tiny bit of affectionate credit I'd fought so hard to earn back.

His stance softened, then. He took a tiny step closer—the only apology I could hope for.

The pod began its descent. Halfway down he unzipped his jacket, smiling in the warmth of the heated pod while below-zero winds buffeted us. His T-shirt said *The Last Calf,* and showed the gangly sad-eyed hero of that depressing miserable movie all the kids adored.

"Where is it?" I asked. He'd proudly sported the NEW YORK F CKING CITY shirt on each of the five times I'd seen him since giving it to him.

His face darkened so fast I was frightened. His eyes welled up. He said "Dad, I," but his voice had the tremor that meant he could barely keep from crying. Shame was what I saw.

I couldn't breathe, again, just like when I came home two weeks ago and he wasn't happy to see me. Except seeing my son so unhappy hurt worse than fearing he hated me.

"Did somebody take it from you?" I asked, leaning in so no one else could hear me. "Someone at school? A bully?"

He looked up, startled. He shook his head. Then, he nodded.

"Tell me who did this?"

He shook his head again. "Just some guys, dad," he said. "Please. I don't want to talk about it."

"Guys. How many?"

He said nothing. I understood about snitching. I knew he'd never tell me who.

"It doesn't matter," I said. "Okay? It's just a shirt. I don't care about it. I care about you. I care that you're okay. Are you okay?"

Thede nodded. And smiled. And I knew he was telling the truth, even if I wasn't, even if inside I was grieving the shirt, and the little boy who I once wrapped up inside it.

When I wasn't with Thede, I walked. For two weeks I'd gone out walking every day. Up and down Arm Eight, and sometimes into other Arms. Through shantytowns large and small, huddled miserable agglomerations of recent arrivals and folks who even after a couple generations in Qaanaaq had not been able to scrape their way up from the fish-stinking ice-slippery bottom.

I looked for sex, sometimes. It had been so long. Relationships were tough in my line of work, and I'd never been interested in paying for it. Throughout my twenties I could usually find a woman for something brief and fun and free of commitment, but that stage of my life seemed to have ended.

I wondered why I hadn't tried harder, to make it work with Lajla. I think a small but vocal and terrible part of me had been glad to see her leave. Fatherhood was hard work. So was being married. Paying rent on a tiny shitty apartment way out on Arm Seven, where we smelled like scorched cooking oil and diaper lotion all the time.

Selfishly, I had been glad to be alone. And only now, getting to know this stranger who was once my son, did I see what sweet and fitting punishments the universe had up its sleeve for selfishness.

My time with Thede was wonderful, and horrible. We could talk at length about movies and music, and he actually seemed halfway interested in my stories about old New York, but whenever I tried to talk about life or school or girls or his future he reverted to grunts and monosyllables. Something huge and heavy stood between me and him, a moon eclipsing the sun of me. I knew him, top to bottom and body and soul, but he still had no idea who I really was. How I felt about him. I had no way to show him. No way to open his eyes, make him see how much I loved him, and how I was really a good guy who'd gotten a bad deal in life.

Cityoke, it turned out, was like karaoke, except instead of singing a song you visited a city. XHD footage projection onto all four walls; temperature control; short storylines that responded to your verbal decisions—even actual smells uncorked by machines from secret stashes of Beijing taxi-seat leather or Ho Chi Minh City incense or Portland coffeeshop sawdust. I went there often, hoping maybe to see him. To watch him, with his friends. See what he was when I wasn't around. But cityoke was expensive, and I could never have afforded to actually go in. Once, standing around outside the New York booth when a crew walked out, I caught a whiff of the acrid ugly beautiful stink of the Port Authority Bus Terminal.

And then, eventually, I walked without any reason at all. Because pretty soon I wouldn't be able to. Because I had done it. I had booked a twelve-month job. I was out of money and couldn't afford to rent my bed for another month. Thede's mom could have given it to me. But what if she told him about it? He'd think of me as more of a useless moocher deadbeat dad than he already did. I couldn't take that chance.

Three days before my ship was set to load up and launch, I went back to the cityoke arcades. Men lurked in doorways and between shacks. Soakers, mostly. Looking for marks; men to mug and drunks to tip into the sea. Late at night; too late for Thede to come carousing through. I'd called him earlier, but Lajla said he was stuck inside for the night, studying for a test in a class where he wasn't doing well. I had hoped maybe he'd sneak out, meet some friends, head for the arcade.

And that's when I saw it. The shirt: NEW YORK F CKING CITY, absolutely unique and unmistakable. Worn by a stranger, a muscular young man sitting on the stoop of a skiff moor. I didn't get a good glimpse of his face, as I hurried past with my head turned away from him.

I waited, two buildings down. My heart was alive and racing in my chest. I drew in deep gulps of cold air and tried to keep from shouting from joy. Here was my chance. Here was how I could show Thede what I really was.

I stuck my head out, risked a glance. He sat there, waiting for who knows what. In profile I could see that the man was Asian. Almost certainly Chinese, in Qaanaaq—most other Asian nations had their own grid cities—although perhaps he was descended from Asian-diaspora nationals of some other country. I could see his smile, hungry and cold.

At first I planned to confront him, ask how he came to be wearing my shirt, demand justice, beat him up and take it back. But that would be stupid. Unless I planned to kill him—and I didn't—it was too easy to imagine him gunning for Thede if he knew he'd been attacked for the shirt. I'd have to jump him, rob and strip and soak him. I rooted through a trash bin, but found nothing. Three trash bins later I found a short metal pipe with Hindi graffiti scribbled along its length. The man was still there when I went back. He was waiting for something. I could wait longer. I pulled my hood up, yanked the drawstring to tighten it around my face.

Forty-five minutes passed that way. He hugged his knees to his chest, made himself small, tried to conserve body heat. His teeth chattered. Why was he wearing so little? But I was happy he was so stupid. Had he had a sweater or jacket on I'd never have seen the shirt. I'd never have had this chance.

Finally, he stood. Looked around sadly. Brushed off the seat of his pants. Turned to go. Stepped into the swing of my metal pipe, which struck him in the chest and knocked him back a step.

The shame came later. Then, there was just joy. The satisfaction of how the pipe struck flesh. Broke bone. I'd spent twenty years getting shitted on by this city, by this system, by the cold wind and the everywhere-ice, by the other workers who were smarter or stronger or spoke the language. For the first time since Thede was a baby, I felt like I was in control of something. Only when my victim finally passed out, and rolled over onto his back and the blue methane streetlamp showed me how young he was under the blood, could I stop myself.

I took the shirt. I took his pants. I rolled him into the water. I called the medteam for him from a coin phone a block away. He was still breathing. He was young, he was healthy. He'd be fine. The pants I would burn in a scrap furnace. The shirt I would give back to my son. I took the money from his wallet and dropped it into the sea, then threw the money in later. I wasn't a thief. I was a good father. I said those sentences over and over, all the way home.

Thede couldn't see me the next day. Lajla didn't know where he was. So I got to spend the whole day imagining imminent arrest, the arrival of Swedish or Chinese police, footage of me on the telescrolls, my cleverness foiled by tech I didn't know existed because I couldn't read the newspapers. I packed my one bag glumly, put the rest of my things back in the the storage cube and walked it to the facility. Every five seconds I looked over my shoulder and found only the same grit and filthy slush. Every time I looked at my watch, I winced at how little time I had left.

My fear of punishment was balanced out by how happy I was. I wrapped the shirt in three layers of wrapping paper and put it in a watertight shipping bag and tried to imagine his face. That shirt would change everything. His father would cease to be a savage jerk from an uncivilized land. This city would no longer be a cold and barren place where boys could beat him up and steal what mattered most to him with impunity. All the ways I had failed him would matter a little less.

Twelve months. I had tried to get out of the gig, now that I had the shirt and a new era of good relations with my son was upon me. But canceling would have cost me my accreditation with that work center, which would make finding another job almost impossible. A year away from Thede. I would tell him when I saw him. He'd be upset, but the shirt would make it easier.

Finally, I called and he answered.

"I want to see you," I said, when we had made our way through the pleasantries.

"Sunday?" Did his voice brighten, or was that just blind stupid hope? Some trick of the noisy synth coffee shop where I sat?

"No, Thede," I said, measuring my words carefully. "I can't. Can you do today?"

A suspicious pause. "Why can't you do Sunday?"

"Something's come up," I said. "Please? Today?"

"Fine."

The sea lion rookery. The smell of guano and the screak of gulls; the crying of children dragged away as the place shut down. The long night was almost upon us. Two male sea lions barked at each other, bouncing their chests together. Thede came a half hour late, and I had arrived a half hour early. Watching him come my head swam, at how tall he stood and how gracefully he walked. I had done something good in this world, at least. I made him. I had that, no matter how he felt about me.

Something had shifted, now, in his face. Something was harder, older, stronger.

"Hey," I said, bear-hugging him, and eventually he submitted. He hugged me back hesitantly, like a man might, and then hard, like a little boy.

"What's happening?" I asked. "What were you up to, last night?"

Thede shrugged. "Stuff. With friends."

I asked him questions. Again the sullen, bitter silence; again the terse and angry answers. Again the eyes darting around, constantly watching for whatever the next attack would be. Again the hating me, for coming here, for making him.

"I'm going away," I said. "A job."

"I figured," he said.

"I wish I didn't have to."

"I'll see you soon."

I nodded. I couldn't tell him it was a twelve-month gig. Not now.

"Here," I said, finally, pulling the package out from inside of my jacket. "I got you something."

"Thanks." He grabbed it in both hands, began to tear it open.

"Wait," I said, thinking fast. "Okay? Open it after I leave."

Open it when the news that I'm leaving has set in, when you're mad at me, for abandoning you. When you think I care only about my job.

"We'll have a little time," he said. "When you get back. Before I go away. I leave in eight months. The program is four years long."

"Sure," I said, shivering inside.

"Mom says she'll pay for me to come home every year for the holiday, but she knows we can't afford that."

"What do you mean?" I asked. "'Come home.' I thought you were going to the Institute."

"I am," he said, sighing. "Do you even know what that means? The Institute's design program is in Shanghai."

"Oh," I said. "Design. What kind of design?"

My son's eyes rolled. "You're missing the point, dad."

I was. I always was.

A shout, from a pub across the Arm. A man's shout, full of pain and anger. Thede flinched. His hands made fists.

"What?" I asked, thinking, here, at last, was something

"Nothing."

"You can tell me. What's going on?"

Thede frowned, then punched the metal railing so hard he yelped. He held up his hand to show me the blood.

"Hey, Thede—"

"Han," he said. "My . . . my friend. He got jumped two nights ago. Soaked."

"This city is horrible," I whispered.

He made a baffled face. "What do you mean?"

"I mean . . . you know. This city. Everyone's so full of anger and cruelty . . ."

"It's not the city, dad. What does that even mean? Some sick person did this. Han was waiting for me, and mom wouldn't let me out, and he got jumped. They took off all his clothes, before they rolled him into the water. That's some extra cruel shit right there. He could have died. He almost did."

I nodded, silently, a siren of panic rising inside. "You really care about this guy, don't you?"

He looked at me. My son's eyes were whole, intact, defiant, adult. Thede nodded. *He's been getting bullied,* his mother had told me. *He's in love.*

I turned away from him, before he could see the knowledge blossom in my eyes.

The shirt hadn't been stolen. He'd given it away. To the boy he loved. I saw them holding hands, saw them tug at each other's clothing in the same fumbling adolescent puppy-love moments I had shared with his mother, moments that were my only happy memories from being his age. And I saw his fear, of how his backwards father might react—a refugee from a fallen hate-filled people—if he knew what kind of man he was. I gagged on the unfairness of his assumptions about me, but how could he have known differently? What had I ever done, to show him the truth of how I felt about him? And hadn't I proved him right? Hadn't I acted exactly like the monster he believed me to be? I had never succeeded in proving to him what I was, or how I felt.

I had battered and broken his beloved. There was nothing I could say. A smarter man would have asked for the present back, taken it away and locked it up. Burned it, maybe. But I couldn't. I had spent his whole life trying to give him something worthy of how I felt about him, and here was the perfect gift at last.

"I love you, Thede," I said, and hugged him.

"Daaaaad . . ." he said, eventually.

But I didn't let go. Because when I did, he would leave. He would walk home through the cramped and frigid alleys of his home city, to the gift of knowing what his father truly was.

Botanica veneris: Thirteen papercuts by Ida countess Rathagan

IAN McDONALD

Here's another eloquent and evocative story by Ian McDonald, whose "The Falls: A Luna Story" appears elsewhere in this anthology. In this one, we trace a trail of flowers across the planet Venus toward a troubled and uncertain destiny.

INTRODUCTION BY MAUREEN N. GELLARD

My mother had firm instructions that, in case of a house fire, two things required saving: the family photograph album, and the Granville-Hydes. I grew up beneath five original floral papercuts, utterly heedless of their history or their value. It was only in maturity that I came to appreciate, like so many on this and other worlds, my Great-Aunt's unique art.

Collectors avidly seek original Granville-Hydes on those rare occasions when they turn up at auction. Originals sell for tens of thousands of pounds (this would have amused Ida); two years ago, an exhibition at the Victoria and Albert Museum was sold out months in advance. Dozens of anthologies of prints are still in print: the Botanica Veneris, in particular, is in 15 editions in twenty three languages, some of them non-Terrene.

The last thing the world needs, it would seem, is another *Botanica Veneris*. Yet the mystery of her final (and only) visit to Venus still intrigues half a century since her disappearance. When the collected diaries, sketch books, and field notes came to me after fifty years in the possession of the Dukes of Yoo, I realised that I had a precious opportunity to tell the true story of my Great-Aunt's expedition—and of a forgotten chapter in my family's history. The books were in very poor condition, mildewed and blighted in Venus's humid, hot climate. Large parts were illegible or simply missing. The narrative was frustratingly incomplete. I have resisted the urge to fill in those blank spaces. It would have been easy to dramatise, fictionalise, even sensationalise. Instead I have let Ida Granville-Hyde speak. Hers is a strong, characterful, attractive voice, of a different class, age, and sensibility from ours, but it is authentic, and it is a true voice.

The papercuts, of course, speak for themselves.

Plate 1: V strutio ambulans: the Ducrot's Peripatetic Wort, known locally as Daytime Walker (Thent) or Wanderflower (Thekh).

Cut paper, ink and card.

Such a show!

At lunch, Het Oi-Kranh mentioned that a space-crosser—the *Quest for the Harvest of the Stars*, a Marsman—was due to splash down in the lagoon. I said I should like to see that—apparently I slept through it when I arrived on this world. It meant forgoing the sorbet course, but one does not come to the Inner Worlds for sorbet! Het Oi-Kranh put his spider-car at our disposal. Within moments, the Princess Latufui and I were swaying in the richly upholstered bubble beneath the six strong mechanical legs. Upwards it carried us, up the vertiginous lanes and winding staircases, over the walls and balcony gardens, along the buttresses and roof-walks and up the ancient iron ladder-ways of Ledekh-Olkoi. The islands of the archipelago are small, their populations vast, and the only way for them to build is upwards. Ledekh-Olkoi resembles Mont St Michel vastly enlarged and coarsened. Streets have been bridged and built over into a web of tunnels quite impenetrable to non Ledekhers. The Hets simply clamber over the homes and lives of the inferior classes in their nimble spider-cars.

We came to the belvedere atop the Starostry, the ancient pharos of Ledekh-Olkoi that once guided mariners past the reefs and atolls of the Tol Archipelago. There we clung—my companion, the Princess Latufui, was queasy—vertigo, she claimed, though it may have been the proximity of lunch—the whole of Ledekh-Olkoi beneath us in myriad levels and layers, like the folded petals of a rose.

"Should we need glasses?" my companion asked.

No need! For at the instant, the perpetual layer of grey cloud parted and a bolt of light, like a glowing lance, stabbed down from the sky. I glimpsed a dark object fall though the air, then a titanic gout of water go up like a dozen Niagaras. The sky danced with brief rainbows, my companion wrung her hands in delight—she misses the sun terribly—then the clouds closed again. Rings of waves rippled away from the hull of the space-crosser, which floated like a great whale low in the water, though this world boasts marine fauna even more prodigious than Terrene whales.

My companion clapped her hands and cried aloud in wonder.

Indeed, a very fine sight!

Already, the tugs were heading out from the protecting arms of Ocean Dock to bring the ship in to berth.

But this was not the finest Ledekh-Olkoi had to offer. The custom in the archipelago is to sleep on divan-balconies, for respite from the foul exudations from the inner layers of the city. I had retired for my afternoon reviver—by my watch, though by Venusian Great Day it was still mid-morning and would continue to be so for another two weeks. A movement by the leg of my divan. What's this? My heart surged. *V strutio ambulans*: the Ambulatory Wort, blindly, blithely climbing my divan!

Through my glass, I observed its motion. The fat succulent leaves hold reserves of water, which fuel the coiling and uncoiling of the three ambulae—surely modified roots—by hydraulic pressure. A simple mechanism, yet human minds see movement and attribute personality and motive. This was not pure hydraulics attracted to light and liquid, this was a plucky little wort on an epic journey of peril and adventure. Over two hours, I sketched the plant as it climbed my divan, crossed to the balustrade, and continued its journey up the side of Ledekh-Olkoi. I suppose at any time millions of such flowers are inconstant migration across the archipelago, yet a single Ambulatory Wort was miracle enough for me.

Reviver be damned! I went to my space-trunk and unrolled my scissors from their soft chamois wallet. Snip snap! When a cut demands to be made, my fingers literally itch for the blades!

When he learnt of my intent, Gen Lahl-Khet implored me not to go down to Ledekh Port, but if I insisted (I insisted: oh I insisted!) at least take a bodyguard, or go armed. I surprised him greatly by asking the name of the best armourer his city could supply. Best Shot at the Clarecourt November shoot, ten years on the trot! Ledbekh-Teltai is the most famous gunsmith in the Archipelago. It is illegal to import weaponry from off-planet—an impost, I suspect, resulting from the immense popularity of hunting Ishtari janthars. The pistol they have made me is built to my hand and strength: small, as requested; powerful, as required, and so worked with spiral-and-circle Archipelagan intaglio that it is a piece of jewellery.

Ledekh Port was indeed a loathsome bruise of alleys and tunnels, lit by shifts of grey, watery light through high skylights. Such reeks and stenches! Still, no one ever died of a bad smell. An Earth-woman alone in an inappropriate place was a novelty, but from the non-humanoid Venusians, I drew little more than a look. In my latter years, I have been graced with a physical *presence*, and a destroying stare. The Thekh, descended from Central Asian nomads abducted en-masse in the 11th century from their bracing steppe, now believe themselves the original humanity, and so consider Terrenes beneath them, and they expected no better of a sub-human Earth-woman.

I did turn heads in the bar. I was the only female—humanoid that is. From Carfax's *Bestiary of the Inner Worlds*, I understand that among the semi-aquatic Krid, the male is a small, ineffectual symbiotic parasite lodging in the mantle of the female. The barman, a four-armed Thent, guided me to the snug where I was to meet my contact. The bar overlooked the Ocean Harbour. I watched dock workers scurry over the vast body of the space-crosser, in and out of hatches that had opened in the skin of the ship. I did not like to see those hatches; they ruined its perfection, the precise, intact curve of its skin.

"Lady Granville-Hyde?"

What an oily man, so well-lubricated that I did not hear his approach.

"Stafford Grimes, at your service."

He offered to buy me a drink, but I drew the line at that unseemliness. That did not stop him ordering one for himself and sipping it—and several successors—noisily during the course of my questions. Years of Venusian light had turned his skin to wrinkled brown leather: drinker's eyes looked out from heavily hooded lids: years of squinting into the ultra-violet. His neck and hands were mottled white with pock-marks where melanomas had been frozen out. Sunburn, melancholy, and alcoholism: the classic recipe for Honorary Consuls system-wide, not just on Venus.

"Thank you for agreeing to meet me. So: you met him."

"I will never forget him. Pearls of Aphrodite. Size of your head, Lady Ida. There's a fortune waiting for the man . . ."

"Or woman." I chided, and surreptitiously activated the recording ring beneath my glove.

Plate 2: *V flor scopulum*: The Ocean Mist Flower. The name is a misnomer: the Ocean Mist Flower is not a flower, but a coral animalcule of the aerial reefs of the Tellus Ocean. The seeming petals are absorption surfaces drawing moisture from the frequent ocean fogs of those latitudes. Pistils and stamen bear sticky palps, which function in the same fashion as Terrene spider webs, trapping prey. Venus boasts an entire ecosystem of marine insects unknown on Earth.

This cut is the most three-dimensional of Lady Ida's Botanica Veneris. Reproductions only hint at the sculptural quality of the original. The 'petals' have been curled at the edges over the blunt side of a pair of scissors. Each of the two hundred and eight palps has been sprung so that they stand proud from the black paper background.

Onion-paper, hard-painted card.

THE HONORARY CONSUL'S TALE.

Aphrodite's Pearl. Truly, the pearl beyond price. The pearls of Starosts and Aztars. But the cloud reefs are perilous, Lady Ida. Snap a man's body clean in half, those bivalves. Crush his head like a Vulpeculan melon. Snare a hand or an ankle and drown him. Aphrodite's Pearls are blood pearls. A fortune awaits anyone, my dear, who can culture them. A charming man, Arthur Hyde—that brogue of his made anything sound like the blessing of heaven itself. Charm the avios from the trees—but natural, unaffected. It was no surprise to learn he was of aristocratic stock. Quality: you can't hide it. In those days, I owned a company—fishing trips across the Archipelago. The legend of the Ourogoonta, the Island that is a Fish, was a potent draw. Imagine hooking one of those! Of course, they never did. No, I'd take them out, show them the cloud reefs, the Krid hives, the wing-fish migration, the air-jellies; get them pissed on the boat, take their photographs next to some thawed out javelin-fish they hadn't caught. Simple, easy, honest money. Why wasn't it enough for me? I had done the trick enough times myself, drink one for the punter's two, yet I fell for it that evening in the Windward Tavern, drinking hot spiced kashash and the night wind whistling up in the spires of the dead Krid nest-haven like the caged souls of drowned sailors. Drinking for days down the Great Twilight, his one for my two. Charming, so charming, until I had pledged my boat on his plan. He would buy a planktoneer—an old bucket of a sea-skimmer with nary a straight plate or a true rivet in her. He would seed her with spores and send her north on the great circulatory current, like a maritime cloud reef. Five years that current takes to circulate the globe before it returns to the arctic waters that birthed it. Five years is also the time it takes the Clam of Aphrodite to mature—what we call pearls are no such thing. Sperm, Lady Ida. Compressed sperm. In waters, it dissolves and disperses. Each Great Dawn the Tellus Ocean is white with it. In the air, it remains compact—the most prized of all jewels. Enough of fluids. By the time the reef ship reached the deep north, the clams would be mature and the cold water would kill them. It would be a simple task to strip the hulk with high-pressure hoses, harvest the pearls and trouser the fortune.

Five years makes a man fidgety for his investment. Arthur sent us weekly reports from the Sea Wardens and the Krid argosies. Month on month, year on year, I began to suspect that the truth had wandered far from those chart co-ordinates. I was not alone. I formed a consortium with my fellow investors and chartered a 'rigible.

And there at Map 60 North, 175 East, we found the ship—or what was left of it, so overgrown was it with Clams of Aphrodite. Our investment had been lined and lashed by four Krid cantoons: as we arrived, they were in the process of stripping it with halberds and grappling-hooks. Already the decks and superstructure were green with clam meat and purple with Krid blood. Arthur stood in the stern frantically waving a Cross of St Patrick flag, gesturing for us to get out, get away.

Krid pirates were plundering our investment! Worse, Arthur was their prisoner. We were an unarmed aerial gad-about, so we turned tail and headed for the nearest Sea Warden castle to call for aid.

Charmer. Bloody buggering charmer. I know he's your flesh and blood, but . . . I should have thought! If he'd been captured by Krid pirates, they wouldn't have let him wave a bloody flag to warn us.

When we arrived with a constabulary cruiser, all we found was the capsized hulk of the planktoneer and a flock of avios gorging on clam offal. Duped! Pirates my arse—excuse me. Those four cantoons were laden to the gunwales with contract workers. He never had any intention of splitting the profits with us.

The last we heard of him, he had converted the lot into Bank of Ishtar Bearer Bonds—better than gold—at Yez Tok and headed in-country. That was twelve years ago.

Your brother cost me my business, Lady Granville-Hyde. It was a good business; I could have sold it, made a little pile. Bought a place on Ledekh Syant—maybe even make it back to Earth to see out my days to a decent calendar. Instead . . . Ach, what's the use. Please believe me when I say that I bear your family no ill will—only your brother. If you do succeed in finding him—and if I haven't, I very much doubt you will—remind him of that, and that he still owes me.

Plate 3: V *lilium aphrodite*: the Archipelago sea-lily. Walk-the-Water in Thekh: there is no comprehensible translation from Krid. A ubiquitous and fecund diurnal plant, it grows so aggressively in the Venerian Great Day that by Great Evening bays and harbours are clogged with blossoms and passage must be cleared by special bloom-breaker ships.

Painted paper, watermarked Venerian tissue, inks and scissor-scrolled card.

So dear, so admirable a companion, the Princess Latufui. She knew I had been stint-ing with the truth in my excuse of shopping for paper, when I went to see the Honor-ary Consul down in Ledekh Port. Especially when I returned without any paper. I busied myself in the days before our sailing to Ishtaria on two cuts—the Sea Lily and the Ocean Mist Flower—even if it is not a flower, according to my Carfax's *Bestiary of the Inner World*. She was not fooled by my industry and I felt soiled and venal. All Tongan women have dignity, but the Princess possesses such innate nobility that the thought of lying to her offends nature itself. The moral order of the universe is upset. How can I tell her that my entire visit to this world is a tissue of fabrications?

Weather again fair, with the invariable light winds and interminable grey sky. I am of Ireland, supposedly we thrive on permanent overcast, but even I find myself pin-ing for a glimpse of sun. Poor Latufui: she grows wan for want of light. Her skin is waxy, her hair lustreless. We have a long time to wait for a glimpse of sun: Carfax states that the sky clears partially at the dawn and sunset of Venus's Great Day. I hope to be off this world by then.

Our ship, the *Seventeen Notable Navigators*, is a well-built, swift Krid *jaicoona*—among the Krid the females are the seafarers, but they equal the males of my world in the richness and fecundity of their taxonomy of ships. A *jaicoona*, it seems, is a fast catamaran steam packet, built for the archipelago trade. I have no sea-legs, but the *Seventeen Notable Navigators* was the only option that would get us to Ishtaria in reasonable time. Princess Latufui tells me it is a fine and sturdy craft; though built to alien dimensions: she has banged her head most painfully several times. Captain Highly-Able-at-Forecasting, recognising a sister seafarer, engages the Princess in lengthy conversations of an island-hopping, archipelagan nature, which remind Latufui greatly of her home islands. The other humans aboard are a lofty Thekh, and Hugo Von Trachtenburg, a German in very high regard of himself, of that feckless type who think themselves gentleman adventurers but are little more than grandiose fraudsters. Nevertheless, he speaks Krid (as truly as any Terrene can) and acts as translator between Princess and Captain. It is a Venerian truth universally recognised that two unaccompanied women travellers must be in need of a male protector. The dreary hours Herr von Trachtenberg fills with his notion of gay chit-chat! And in the evenings, the interminable games of Barrington. Von Trachten-berg claims to have gambled the game professionally in the cloud casinos: I let him win enough for the sensation to go to his head, then take him game after game. Ten times champion of the County Kildare mixed bridge championships is more than enough to beat his hide at Barrington. Still he does not get the message—yes, I am a wealthy widow, but I have no interest in jejune Prussians. Thus I retire to my cabin to begin my studies for the *crescite dolium* cut.

Has this world a more splendid sight than the harbour of Yez-Tok? It is a city most perpendicular, of pillars and towers, masts and spires. The tall funnels of the ships, bright with the heraldry of the Krid maritime families, blend with god-poles and lighthouse and customs towers and cranes of the harbour, which in turn yield to the tower-houses and campaniles of the Bourse, the whole rising to merge with the trees of the Ishtarian Littoral Forest—pierced here and there by the comical roofs of the estancias of the Thent *zavars* and the gilded figures of the star-gods on their minarets. That forest also rises up, a cloth of green, to break into the rocky palisades of the Exx Palisades. And there,—oh how thrilling!—glimpsed through mountain passes un-imaginably high, a glittering glimpse of the snows of the altiplano. Snow. Cold. Bliss!

It is only now, after reams of purple prose, that I realise what I was trying to say of Yez-Tok: simply, it is city as botany—stems and trunks, boles and bracts, root and branch!

And out there, in the city-that-is-a-forest, is the man who will guide me further into my brother's footsteps: Mr Daniel Okiring.

Plate 4: *V crescite dolium*: the Gourd of Plenty. A ubiquitous climbing plant of the Ishtari littoral, the Gourd of Plenty is so well adapted to urban environments that it would be considered a weed, but for the gourds, which contains a nectar prized as a delicacy among the coastal Thents. It is toxic to both Krid and Humans.

The papercut bears a note on the true scale, written in gold ink.

The Hunter's Tale

Have you seen a janthar? Really seen a janthar? Bloody magnificent, in the same way that a hurricane or an exploding volcano is magnificent. Magnificent and appall-ing. The films can never capture the sense of scale. Imagine a house, with fangs. And tusks. And spines. A house that can hit forty miles per hour. The films can never get the sheer sense of mass and speed—or the elegance and grace—that something so huge can be so nimble, so agile! And what the films can never, ever capture is the smell. They smell of curry. Vindaloo curry. Venerian body-chemistry. But that's why you never, ever eat curry on *asjan*. Out in the Stalva, the grass is tall enough to hide even a janthar. The smell is the only warning you get. You catch a whiff of vindaloo, you run.

You always run. When you hunt janthar, there will always be a moment when it turns, and the janthar hunts you. You run. If you're lucky, you'll draw it on to the gunline. If not . . . The 'thones of the Stalva have been hunting them this way for centuries. Coming-of-age thing. Like my own Maasai people. They give you a spear and point you in the general direction of a lion. Yes, I've killed a lion. I've also killed janthar—and run from even more.

The 'thones have a word for it: the *pnem*. The fool who runs.

That's how I met your brother. He applied to be a pnem for Okiring *Asjans*. Claimed experience over at Hunderewe with Costa's hunting company. I didn't need to call Costa to know he was a bullshitter. But I liked the fellow—he had charm and didn't take himself too seriously. I knew he'd never last five minutes as a pnem. Took him on as a camp steward. They like the personal service, the hunting types. If you can afford to fly yourself and your friends on a jolly to Venus, you expect to have someone to wipe your arse for you. Charm works on these bastards. He'd wheedle his way into their affections and get them drinking. They'd invite him and before you knew it he was getting their life stories—and a lot more beside—out of them. He was a careful cove too—he'd always stay one drink behind them and be up early and sharp-eyed as a hawk the next morning. Bring them their bed-tea. Fluff up their pillows. Always came back with the fattest tip. I knew what he was doing, but he did it so well—I'd taken him on, hadn't I? So, an aristocrat. Why am I not surprised? Within three trips, I'd made him Maitre de la Chasse. Heard he'd made and lost one fortune already . . . is that true? A jewel thief? Why am I not surprised by that either?

The Thirtieth Earl of Mar fancied himself as a sporting type. Booked a three month Grand Asjan; him and five friends, shooting their way up the Great Littoral to the Stalva. Wives, husbands, lovers, personal servants, twenty Thent asjanis and a caravan of forty graapa to carry their bags and baggage. They had one graap just for the champagne—they'd shipped every last drop of it from Earth. Made so much noise we cleared the forest for ten miles around. Bloody brutes—we'd set up hides at waterholes so they could blast away from point-blank range. That's not hunting. Every day they'd send a dozen bearers back with hides and trophies. I'm surprised there was anything left, the amount of metal they pumped into those poor beasts. The stench of rot . . . God! The sky was black with carrion-avios.

Your brother excelled himself: suave, in control, charming, witty, the soul of attention. Oh, most attentive. Especially to the Lady Mar . . . She was no kack-hand with the guns, but I think she tired of the boys-club antics of the gents. Or maybe it was just the sheer relentless slaughter. Either way, she increasingly remained in camp. Where your brother attended to her. Aristocrats—they sniff each other out.

So Arthur poled the Lady Mar while we blasted our bloody, brutal, bestial way up onto the High Stalva. Nothing would do the Thirtieth Earl but to go after janthar. Three out of five asjans never even come across a janthar. Ten percent of hunters who go for jantar don't come back. Only ten percent! He liked those odds.

Twenty five sleeps we were up there, while Great Day turned to Great Evening. I wasn't staying for night on the Stalva. It's not just a different season, it's a different world. Things come out of sleep, out of dens, out of the ground. No, not for all the fortune of the Earls of Mar would I spend night on the Stalva.

By then, we had abandoned the main camp. We carried bare rations, sleeping out beside our mounts with one ear tuned to the radio. Then the call came: Jantharsign! An asjani had seen a fresh path through a speargrass meadow five miles to the north of us. In a moment, we were mounted and tearing through the high Stalva. The Earl rode like a madman, whipping his graap to reckless speed. Damn fool: of all the Stalva's many grasslands, the tall pike-grass meadows were the most dangerous. A janthar could be right next to you and you wouldn't see it. And the pike-grass disorients, reflects sounds, turns you around. There was no advising the Earl of Mar and his chums, though. His wife hung back—she claimed her mount had picked up a little lameness. Why did I not say something when Arthur went back to accompany the Lady Mar! But my concern was how to get everyone out of the pike-grass alive.

Then the Earl stabbed his shock-goad into the flank of his graap, and before I could do anything he was off. My radio crackled—form a gunline! The mad fool was going to run the janthar himself. Aristocrats! Your pardon, ma'am. Moments later, his graap came crashing back through the pike-grass to find its herd-mates. My only hope was to form a gunline and hope—and pray—that he would lead the janthar right into our crossfire. It takes a lot of ordnance to stop a janthar. And in this kind of tall grass terrain, where you can hardly see your hand in front of your face, I had to set the firing positions just right so the idiots would blow each other to bits.

I got them into some semblance of position. I held the centre—the *lakoo*. Your brother and the Lady Mar I ordered to take *jeft* and *garoon*—the last two positions of the left wing of the gunline. Finally, I got them all to radio silence. The 'thones teach you how to be still, and how to listen, and how to know what is safe and what is death. Silence, then a sustained crashing. My spotter called me, but I did not need her to tell me: that was the sound of death. I could only hope that the Earl remembered to run in a straight line, and not to trip over anything, and that the gunline would fire in time . . . a hundred hopes. A hundred ways to die.

Most terrifying sound in the world, a janthar in full pursuit! It sounds like its coming from everywhere at once. I yelled to the gunline; steady there, steady. Hold your fire! Then I smelled it. Clear, sharp: unmistakable. Curry. I put up the cry: Vindaloo! Vindaloo! And there was the mad Earl, breaking out of the cane. Madman! What was he thinking! He was in the wrong place, headed in the wrong direction. The only ones who could cover him were Arthur and Lady Mar. And there, behind him: the janthar. Bigger than any I had ever seen before. The Mother of All Janthar. The Queen of the High Stalva. I froze. We all froze. We might as well try to kill a mountain. I yelled to Arthur and Lady Mar. Shoot! Shoot now! Nothing. Shoot for the love of all the stars! Nothing. Shoot! Why didn't they shoot?

The 'thones found the Thirtieth Earl of Mar spread over a hundred yards.

They hadn't shot because they weren't there. They were at it like dogs—your brother and the Lady Mar, back where they had left the party. They hadn't even heard the janthar.

Strange woman, the Lady Mar. Her face barely moved when she learnt of her husband's terrible death. Like it was no surprise to her. Of course, she became immensely rich when the will went through. There was no question of your brother ever working for me again. Shame. I liked him. But I can't help thinking that he was as much used as user in that sordid little affair. Did the Lady of Mar murder her husband? Too much left to chance. Yet it was a very convenient accident. And I can't help but think that the Thirtieth Earl knew what his lady was up to; and a surfeit of cuckoldry drove him to prove he was a man.

The janthar haunted the highlands for years. Became a legend. Every aristo idiot on the Inner Worlds who fancied himself a Great Terrene Hunter went after it. None of them ever got it, though it claimed five more lives. The Human-Slayer of the Selva. In the end it stumbled into a 'thone clutch trap and died on a pungi stake, eaten away by gangrene. So we all pass. No final run, no gunline, no trophies.

Your brother—as I said, I liked him though I never trusted him. He left when the scandal broke—went up country, over the Stalva into the Palisade country. I heard a rumour he'd joined a mercenary javrost unit, fighting up on the altiplano.

Botany, is it? Safer business than Big Game.

Plate 5: *V trifex aculeatum*: Stannage's Bird-Eating Trifid. Native of the Great Littoral Forest of Isharia. Carnivorous in its habits; it lures smaller, nectar-feeding avios with its sweet exudate, then stings them to death with its whiplike style and sticky, poisoned stigma.

Cutpaper, inks, folded tissue.

The Princess is brushing her hair. This she does every night, whether in Tonga, or Ireland, on Earth or aboard a space-crosser, or on Venus. The ritual is invariable. She kneels, unpins and uncoils her tight bun and lets her hair fall to its natural length, which is to the waist. Then she takes two silver-backed brushes, and, with great and vigorous strokes, brushes her hair from the crown of her head to the tips. One hundred strokes, which she counts in a Tongan rhyme which I very much love to hear.

When she is done, she cleans the brushes, returns them to the velvet lined case, then takes a bottle of coconut oil and works it through her hair. The air is suffused with the sweet smell of coconut. It reminds me so much of the whin-flowers of home, in the spring. She works patiently and painstakingly, and when she has finished, she rolls her hair back into its bun and pins it. A simple, dedicated, repetitive task, but it moves me almost to tears.

Her beautiful hair! How dearly I love my friend Latufui!

We are sleeping at a hohvandha, a Thent roadside inn, on the Grand North Road in Canton Hoa in the Great Littoral Forest. Tree branches scratch at my window shutters. The heat, the humidity, the animal noise, are all overpowering. We are far from the cooling breezes of the Vestal Sea. I wilt, though Latufui relishes the warmth. The arboreal creatures of this forest are deeper voiced than in Ireland; bellings and honkings and deep booms. How I wish we could spend the night here—Great Night—for my Carfax tells me that the Ishtaria Littoral Forest contains this world's greatest concentration of luminous creatures—fungi, plants, animals, and those peculiarly Venerian phyla in between. It is almost as bright as day. I have made some daytime studies of the Star Flower—no Venerian Botanica can be complete without it—but for it to succeed, I must hope that there is a supply of luminous paint at Loogaza; where we embark for the crossing of the Stalva.

My dear Latufui has finished now and closed away her brushes in their green baize-lined box. So faithful and true a friend! We met in Nuku'alofa on the Tongan leg of my Botanica of the South Pacific. The King, her father, had issued the invitation—he was a keen collector—and at the reception I was introduced to his very large family, including Latufui, and was immediately charmed by her sense, dignity, and vivacity. She invited me to tea the following day—a very grand affair—where she confessed that as a minor princess, her only hope of fulfilment was in marrying well—an institution in which she had no interest. I replied that I had visited the South Pacific as a time apart from Lord Rathangan—it had been clear for some years that he had no interest in me (nor I in him). We were two noble ladies of compatible

needs and temperaments, and there and then we became firmest friends and insepa-
rable companions. When Patrick shot himself and Rathangan passed into my possession, it was only natural that the Princess move in with me.

I cannot conceive of life without Latufui; yet I am deeply ashamed that I have
not been totally honest in my motivations for this Venerian expedition. Why can I
not trust? Oh secrets! Oh simulations!

V stellafloris noctecandentis: the Venerian Starflower. Its name is the same in Thent,
Thekh, and Krid. Now a popular Terrestrial garden plant, where it is known as glow-
berry, though the name is a misnomer. Its appearance is a bunch of night-luminous
white berries, though the berries are in fact globular bracts, with the bio-luminous
flower at the centre. Selective strains of this flower traditionally provide illumination in Venerian settlements during the Great Night.

Paper, luminous paint (not reproduced.) The original papercut is mildly radioactive.

By high-train to Camahoo.

We have our own carriage. It is of aged gothar-wood, still fragrant and spicy. The
hammocks do not suit me at all. Indeed, the whole train has a rocking, swaying lol-
lop that makes me seasick. In the caravanserai at Loogaza, the contraption looked
both ridiculous and impractical. But here, in the high grass, its ingenuity reveals itself. The twenty-foot-high wheels carry us high above the grass, though I am in fear
of grass-fires—the steam-tractor at the head of the train does throw off the most ferocious pother of soot and embers.

I am quite content to remain in my carriage and work on my Stalva-grass study—I
think this may be most sculptural. The swaying makes for many a slip with the scis-
sor, but I think I have caught the feathery, almost downy nature of the flowerheads.
Of a maritime people, the Princess is at home in this rolling ocean of grass and
spends much of her time on the observation balcony watching the patterns the wind
draws across the grasslands.

It was there that she fell into conversation with the Honorable Cormac de Buitlear,
a fellow Irishman. Inevitably, he ingratiated himself and within minutes was taking
tea in our carriage. The Inner Worlds are infested with young men claiming to be
the junior sons of minor Irish gentry, but a few minutes gentle questioning revealed not only that he was indeed the Honourable Cormac—of the Bagenalstown
De Buitlears—but a relative, close enough to know of my husband's demise, and the
scandal of the Blue Empress.

Our conversation went like this.

Himself: The Grangegorman Hydes. My father used to knock around with
your elder brother—what was he called?
Myself: Richard.
Himself: The younger brother—wasn't he a bit of a black sheep? I remember
there was this tremendous scandal. Some jewel—a sapphire as big as a

thrush's egg. Yes—that was the expression they used in the papers. A thrush's egg. What was it called?

Myself: The Blue Empress.

Himself: Yes! That was it. Your grandfather was presented with it by some Martian princess. Services rendered.

Myself: He helped her escape across the Tharsis steppe in the revolution of '11, and then organised the White Brigades to help her regain the Jasper Throne.

Himself: Your brother, not the old boy. You woke up one morning to find the stone gone and him vanished. Stolen.

I could see that Princess Latufui found The Honourable Cormac's bluntness distressing, but if one claims the privileges of a noble family, one must also claim the shames.

Myself: It was never proved that Arthur stole the Blue Empress.

Himself: No no. But you know how tongues wag in the country. And his disappearance was, you must admit, *timely*. How long ago was that now? God, I must have been a wee gossoon.

Myself: Fifteen years.

Himself: Fifteen years! And not a word? Do you know if he's even alive?

Myself: We believe he fled to the Inner Worlds. Every few years we hear of a sighting, but most of them are so contrary, we dismiss them. He made his choice. As for the Blue Empress: broken up and sold long ago, I don't doubt.

Himself: And here I find you on a jaunt across one of the Inner Worlds.

Myself: I am creating a new album of papercuts. The Botanica Veneris.

Himself: Of course. If I might make so bold, Lady Rathangan: the Blue Empress: do you believe Arthur took it?

And I made him no verbal answer, but gave the smallest shake of my head.

Princess Latufui had been restless all this evening—the time before sleep, that is: Great Evening was still many Terrene days off. Can we ever truly adapt to the monstrous Venerian calendar? Arthur has been on this world for fifteen years—has he drifted not just to another world, but another clock, another calendar? I worked on my Stalva-grass cut—I find that curving the leaf-bearing nodes gives the necessary three-dimensionality—but my heart was not in it. Latufui sipped at tea and fumbled at stitching and pushed newspapers around until eventually she threw open the cabin door in frustration and demanded that I join her on the balcony.

The rolling travel of the high-train made me grip the rail for dear life, but the high-plain was as sharp and fresh as if starched, and there, a long line on the horizon beyond the belching smokestack and pumping pistons of the tractor, were the Palisades of Exx: a grey wall from one horizon to the other. Clouds hid the peaks, like a curtain lowered from the sky.

Dark against the grey mountains, I saw the spires of the observatories of Camahoo. This was the Thent homeland; and I was apprehensive, for among those towers and minarets is a hoondahvi, a Thent opium den, owned by the person who may be able to tell me the next part of my brother's story—a story increasingly disturbing and dark. A person who is not human.

"Ida, dear friend. There is a thing I must ask you."

"Anything, dear Latufui."

"I must tell you, it is not a thing that can be asked softly."

My heart turned over in my chest. I knew what Latufui would ask.

"Ida: have you come to this world to look for your brother?"

She did me the courtesy of a direct question. No preamble, no preliminary sifting through her doubts and evidences. I owed it a direct answer.

"Yes," I said. "I have come to find Arthur."

"I thought so."

"For how long?"

"Since Ledekh-Olkoi. Ah, I cannot say the words right. When you went to get papers and gum and returned empty-handed."

"I went to see a Mr Stafford Grimes. I had information that he had met my brother soon after his arrival on this world. He directed me to Mr Okiring, a retired Asjan-hunter in Yez Tok."

"And Cama-oo? Is this another link in the chain?"

"It is. But the Botanica is no sham. I have an obligation to my backers—you know the state of my finances as well as I, Latufui. The late Count Rathangan was a profligate man. He ran the estate into the ground."

"I could wish you had trusted me. All those weeks of planning and organising. The maps, the itineraries, the tickets, the transplanetary calls to agents and factors. I was so excited! A journey to another world! But for you, there was always something else. None of that was the whole truth. None of it was honest."

"Oh, my dear Latufui . . ." But how could I say that I had not told her because I feared what Arthur might have become. Fears that seemed to be borne out by every ruined life that had touched his. What would I find? Did anything remain of the wild, carefree boy I remembered chasing old Bunty the dog across the summer lawns of Grangegorman? Would I recognise him? Worse, would he listen to me? "There is a wrong to right. An old debt to be cancelled. It's a family thing."

"I live in your house, but not in your family," Princess Latufui said. Her words were barbed with truth. They tore me. "We would not do that in Tonga. Your ways are different. And I thought I was more than a companion."

"Oh, my dear Latufui." I took her hands in mine. "My dear dear Latufui. You are far far more to me than a companion. You are my life. But you of all people should understand my family. We are on another world, but we are not so far from Rathangan, I think. I am seeking Arthur, and I do not know what I will find, but I promise you, what he says to me, I will tell to you. Everything."

Now she laid her hands over mine, and there we stood, cupping hands on the balcony rail, watching the needle spires of Camahoo rise from the grass spears of the Stalva.

V *vallumque foenum*: Stalva Pike Grass. Another non-Terrene that is finding favour in Terrestrial ornamental gardens. Earth never receives sufficient sunlight for it to attain its full Stalva height. *Yetten* in the Stalva Thent dialect.

Card, onionskin paper, corrugated paper, paint. This papercut is unique in that it unfolds into three parts. The original, in the Chester Beatty Library in Dublin, is always displayed unfolded.

THE MERCENARY'S TALE.

In the name of the Leader of the Starry Skies and the Ever-Circling Spiritual Family, welcome to my hoondahvi. May *apsas* speak; may *gavanda* sing, may the *thoo* impart their secrets!

I understand completely that you have not come to drink. But the greeting is standard. We pride ourself on being the most traditional hoondahvi in Exxaa Canton.

Is the music annoying? No? Most Terrenes find it aggravating. It's an essential part of the hoondahvi experience, I am afraid.

Your brother, yes. How could I forget him? I owe him my life.

He fought like a man who hated fighting. Up on the Altiplano, when we smashed open the potteries and set the Porcelain Towns afire up and down the Valley of the Kilns, there were those who blazed with love and joy at the slaughter and those whose faces were so dark it was as if their souls were clogged with soot. Your brother was one of those. Human expressions are hard for us to read—your faces are wood, like masks. But I saw his face and knew that he loathed what he did. That was what made him the best of javrosts. I am an old career soldier; I have seen many many come to our band. The ones in love with violence: unless they can take discipline, we turn them away. But when a mercenary hates what he does for his silver, there must be a greater darkness driving him. There is a thing they hate more than the violence they do.

Are you sure the music is tolerable? Our harmonies and chord patterns apparently create unpleasant electrical resonance in the human brain. Like small seizures. We find it most reassuring. Like the rhythm of the kittening-womb.

Your brother came to us in the dawn of Great Day 6817. He could ride a graap, bivouac, cook, and was handy with both bolt and blade. We never ask questions of our javrosts—in time they answer them all themselves—but rumours blow on the wind like *thagoon*-down. He was a minor aristocrat, he was a gambler; he was a thief, he was a murderer; he was a seducer, he was a traitor. Nothing to disqualify him. Sufficient to recommend him.

In Old Days the Duke of Yoo disputed mightily with her neighbour the Duke of Hetteten over who rightly ruled the altiplano and its profitable potteries. From time immemorial, it had been a place beyond: independently minded and stubborn of spirit, with little respect for gods or dukes. Wars were fought down generations, lying waste to fames and fortunes, and when in the end, the House of Yoo prevailed, the peoples of the plateau had forgotten they ever had lords and mistresses and debts of fealty. It is a law of earth and stars alike that people should be well-governed, obedient, and quiet in their ways, so the Duke of Yoo embarked on a campaign of civil discipline. Her house-corps had been decimated in the Porcelain Wars, so House Yoo hired mercenaries. Among them, my former unit, Gellet's Javrosts.

They speak of us still, up on the plateau. We are the monsters of their Great Nights, the haunters of their children's dreams. We are legend. We are Gellet's Javrosts. We are the new demons.

For one Great Day and Great Night, we ran free. We torched the topless star-shrines of Javapanda and watched then burn like chimneys. We smashed the funerary jars and trampled the bones of the illustrious dead of Toohren. We overturned the houses of the holy, burned elders and kits in their homes. We lassooed rebels and dragged them behind our graapa, round and round the village, until all that remained was a bloody rope. We forced whole communities from their homes, driving them across the altiplano until the snow heaped their bodies. And Arthur was at my side. We were not friends—there is too much history on this world for Human and Thent ever to be that. He was my badoon. You do not have a concept for it, let alone a word. A passionate colleague. A brother who is not related. A fellow devotee . . .

We killed and we killed and we killed. And in our wake came the Duke of Yoo's soldiers—restoring order, rebuilding towns, offering defense against the murderous renegades. It was all strategy. The Duke of Yoo knew the plateauneers would never love her, but she could be their saviour. Therefore, a campaign of final outrages was planned. Such vileness! We were ordered to Glehenta, a pottery town at the head of Valley of the Kilns. There we would enter the Glotoonas—the birthing-creches—and slaughter every infant down to the last kit. We rode, Arthur at my side, and though human emotions are strange and distant to me, I knew them well enough to read the storm in his heart. Night-snow was falling as we entered Glehenta, lit by ten thousand starflowers. The people locked their doors and cowered from us. Through the heart of town we rode; past the great conical kilns, to the glotoonas. Matres flung themselves before our graapa—we rode them down. Arthur's face was darker than the Great Midnight. He broke formation and rode up to Gellet himself. I went to him. I saw words between your brother and our commander. I did not hear them. Then Arthur drew his blasket and in single shot blew the entire top of Gellet's body to ash. In the fracas, I shot down three of our troop; then we were racing through the glowing streets, our hooves clattering on the porcelain cobbles, the erstwhile Gellet's Javrosts behind us.

And so we saved them. For the Duke of Yoo had arranged it so that her Ducal Guard would fall upon us even as we attacked, annihilate us, and achieve two notable victories: presenting themselves as the saviours of Glehenta, and destroying any evidence of their scheme. Your brother and I sprung the trap. But we did not know until leagues and months later, far from the altiplano. At the foot of the Ten Thousand Stairs, we parted—we thought it safer. We never saw each other again, though I heard he had gone back up the stairs, to the Pelerines. And if you do find him, please don't tell him what became of me. This is a shameful place.

And I am ashamed that I have told you such dark and bloody truths about your brother. But at the end, he was honourable. He was right. That he saved the guilty—an unintended consequence. Our lives are made up of such.

Certainly, we can continue outside on the hoondahvi porch. I did warn you that the music was irritating to human sensibilities.

V *lucerna vesperum*; Schaefferia: the Evening Candle. A solitary tree of the foothills of the Exx Palisades of Ishatria, the Schaefferia is noted for its many upright, luminous blossoms, which flower in Venerian Great Evening and Great Dawn.

Only the blossoms are reproduced. Card, folded and cut tissue, luminous paint (not reproduced). The original is also slightly radioactive.

A cog railway runs from Camahoo Terminus to the Convent of the Starry Pelerines. The Starsview Special takes pilgrims to see the stars and planets. Our carriage is small, luxurious, intricate and ingenious in that typically Thent fashion, and terribly tedious. The track has been constructed in a helix inside Awk Mountain, so our journey consists of interminable, noisy spells inside the tunnel, punctuated by brief, blinding moments of clarity as we emerge on to the open face of the mountain. Not for the vertiginous!

Thus, hour upon hour, we spiral our way up Mount Awk.

Princes Latufui and I play endless games of Moon Whist, but our minds are not in it. My forebodings have darkened after my conversation with the Thent hoondahvi owner in Camahoo. The Princess is troubled by my anxiety. Finally, she can bear it no more.

"Tell me about the Blue Empress. Tell me everything."

I grew up with two injunctions in case of fire: save the dogs and the Blue Empress. For almost all my life, the jewel was a ghost-stone—present but unseen, haunting Grangegorman and the lives it held. I have a memory from earliest childhood of seeing the stone—never touching it—but I do not trust the memory. Imaginings too easily become memories, memories imaginings.

We are not free in so many things, we of the landed class. Hector would inherit, Arthur would make a way in the worlds, and I would marry as well as I could; land to land. The Barony of Rathangan was considered one of the most desirable in Kildare, despite Patrick's seeming determination to drag it to the bankruptcy court. A match was made, and he was charming and bold; a fine sportsman and a very handsome man. It was an equal match: snide comments from both halves of the county. The Blue Empress was part of my treasure—on the strict understanding that it remain in the custody of my lawyers. Patrick argued—and it was there that I first got an inkling of his true character—and the wedding was off the wedding was on the wedding was off the wedding was on again and the banns posted. A viewing was arranged, for his people to itemise and value the Hyde treasure. For the first time in long memory, the Blue Empress was taken from its safe and displayed to human view. Blue as the wide Atlantic it was, and as boundless and clear. You could lose yourself forever in the light inside that gem. And yes, it was the size of a thrush's egg.

And then the moment that all the stories agree on: the lights failed. Not so unusual at Grangegorman—the same grandfather who brought back the Blue Empress installed the hydro-plant—and when they came back on again; the sapphire was gone: baize and case and everything.

We called upon the honour of all present, ladies and gentlemen alike. The lights would be put out for five minutes, and when they were switched back on, the Blue Empress would be back in the Hyde treasure. It was not. Our people demanded we call the police, Patrick's people, mindful of their client's attraction to scandal, were less insistent. We would make a further appeal to honour: if the Blue Empress was not back by morning, then we would call the guards.

Not only was the Blue Empress still missing, so was Arthur.

We called the Garda Siochana. The last we heard was that Arthur had left for the Inner Worlds.

The wedding went ahead. It would have been a greater scandal to call it off. We were two families alike in notoriety. Patrick could not let it go: he went to his grave believing that Arthur and I had conspired to keep the Blue Empress out of his hands. I have no doubt that Patrick would have found a way of forcing me to sign over possession of the gem to him, and would have sold it. Wastrel.

As for the Blue Empress: I feel I am very near to Arthur now. One cannot run forever. We will meet, and the truth will be told.

Then light flooded our carriage as the train emerged from the tunnel on to the final ramp and there, before us, its spires and domes dusted with snow blown from the high peaks, was the Convent of the Starry Pelerines.

V *aquilonis vitis visionum*: the Northern Littoral, or Ghost Vine. A common climber of the forests of the southern slopes of the Ishtari altiplano, domesticated and widely grown in Thent garden terraces. Its white, trumpet-shaped flowers are attractive, but the plant is revered for its berries. When crushed, the infused liquor known as *pula* create powerful auditory hallucinations in Venerian physiology and form the basis of the Thent mystical hoondahvi cult. In Terrenes, it produces a strong euphoria and a sense of omnipotence.

Alkaloid-infused paper. Ida Granville-Hyde used Thent Ghost-Vine liquor to tint and infuse the paper in this cut. It is reported to be still mildly hallucinogenic.

THE PILGRIM'S TALE.

You'll come out on to the belvedere? It's supposed to be off-limits to Terrenes—technically blasphemy—sacred space and all that—but the pelerines turn a blind eye. Do excuse the cough . . . ghastly, isn't it? Sounds like a bag of bloody loose change. I don't suppose the cold air does much for my dear old alveoli, but at this stage it's all a matter of damn.

That's Gloaming Peak there. You won't see it until the cloud clears. Every Great Evening, every Great Dawn, for a few Earth-days at a time, the cloud breaks. It goes up, oh so much further than you could ever imagine. You look up, and up, and up—and beyond it, you see the stars. That's why the pelerines came here. Such a sensible religion. The stars are gods. One star, one god. Simple. No faith, no heaven, no punishment, no sin. Just look up and wonder. The Blue Pearl: that's what they call our earth. I wonder if that's why they care for us. Because we're descended from divinity? If only they knew! They really are very kind.

Excuse me. Bloody marvellous stuff, this Thent brew. I'm in no pain at all. I find it quite reassuring that I shall slip from this too too rancid flesh swaddled in a blanket of beatific thoughts and analgesic glow. They're very kind, the pelerines. Very kind.

Now, look to your right. There. Do you see? That staircase, cut into the rock, winding up up up. The Ten Thousand Steps. That's the old way to the altiplano. Everything went up and down those steps: people, animals, goods, palanquins and stick-stick men, traders and pilgrims and armies. Your brother. I watched him go, from this very belvedere. Three years ago, or was it five? You never really get used to the Great Day. Time blurs.

We were tremendous friends, the way that addicts are. You wouldn't have come this far without realising some truths about your brother. Our degradation unites us. Dear thing. How we'd set the world to rights, over flask after flask of this stuff! He realised the truth of this place early on. It's the way to the stars. God's waiting room. And we, this choir of shambling wrecks, wander through it, dazzled by our glimpses of the stars. But he was a dear friend, a dear dear friend. Dear Arthur.

We're all darkened souls here, but he was haunted. Things done and things left undone, like the prayer book says. My father was a vicar—can't you tell? Arthur never spoke completely about his time with javrosts. He hinted—I think he wanted to tell me, very much, but was afraid of giving me his nightmares. That old saw about a problem shared being a problem halved? Damnable lie. A problem shared is a problem doubled. But I would find him up here all times of the Great Day and Night, watching the staircase and the caravans and stick-convoys going up and down. Altiplano porcelain, he'd say. Finest in all the worlds. So fine you can read the Bible through it. Every cup, every plate, every vase and bowl, was portered down those stairs on the shoulders of a stickman. You know he served up on the Altiplano, in the Duke of Yoo's Pacification. I wasn't here then, but Aggers was, and he said you could see the smoke going up; endless plumes of smoke, so thick the sky didn't clear and the pelerines went for a whole Great Day without seeing the stars. All Arthur would say about it was, that'll make some fine china. That's what made porcelain from the Valley of the Kilns so fine: bones—the bones of the dead, ground up into powder. He would never drink from a Valley cup—he said it was drinking from a skull.

Here's another thing about addicts—you never get rid of it. All you do is replace one addiction with another. The best you can hope for is that it's a better addiction. Some become god-addicts, some throw themselves into worthy deeds, or self-improvement, or fine thoughts, or helping others, god help us all. Me, my lovely little vice is sloth—I really am an idle little bugger. It's so easy, letting the seasons slip away; slothful days and indolent nights, coughing my life up one chunk at a time. For Arthur, it was the visions. Arthur saw wonders and horrors, angels and demons, hopes and fears. True visions—the things that drive men to glory or death. Visionary visions. It lay up on the altiplano, beyond the twists and turns of the Ten Thousand Steps. I could never comprehend what it was, but it drove him. Devoured him. Ate his sleep, ate his appetite, ate his body and his soul and his sanity.

It was worse in the Great Night . . . Everything's worse in the Great Night. The snow would come swirling down the staircase and he saw things in it—faces—heard voices. The faces and voices of the people who had died, up there on the altiplano. He had to follow them, go up, into the Valley of the Kilns, where he would ask the people to forgive him—or kill him.

And he went. I couldn't stop him—I didn't want to stop him. Can you understand that? I watched him from this very belvedere. The pelerines are not our warders, any of us is free to leave at any time, though I've never seen anyone leave but Arthur. He left in the evening, with the lilac light catching Gloaming Peak. He never looked back. Not a glance to me. I watched him climb the steps to that bend there. That's where I lost sight of him. I never saw or heard of him again. But stories come down the stairs with the stickmen and they make their way even to this little eyrie, stories of a seer—a visionary. I look and I imagine I see smoke rising, up there on the altiplano.

It's a pity you won't be here to see the clouds break around the Gloaming, or look at the stars.

V *genetric nives*: Mother-of-snows (direct translation from Thent). Ground-civer hi-alpine of the Exx Palisades. The plant forms extensive carpets of thousands of minute white blossoms.

The most intricate papercut in the Botanica Veneris. Each floret is three millimetres in diameter. Paper, ink, gouache.

A high-stepping spider-car took me up the Ten Thousand Steps, past caravans of stickmen, spines bent, shoulders warped beneath brutal loads of finest porcelain.

The twelve cuts of the Botanica Veneris I have given to the Princess, along with descriptions and botanical notes. She would not let me leave, clung to me, wracked with great sobs of loss and fear. It was dangerous; a sullen land with Great Night coming. I could not convince her of my reason for heading up the stairs alone, for they did not convince even me. The one, true reason I could not tell her. Oh, I have been despicable to her! My dearest friend, my love. But worse even than that, false.

She stood watching my spider-car climb the steps until a curve in the staircase took me out of her sight. Must the currency of truth always be falsehood?

Now I think of her spreading her long hair out, and brushing it, firmly, directly, beautifully, and the pen falls from my fingers . . .

Egayhazy is a closed city; hunched, hiding, tight. Its streets are narrow, its buildings lean towards each other; their gables so festooned with starflower that it looks like perpetual festival. Nothing could be further from the truth: Egayhazy is an angry city, aggressive and cowed: sullen. I keep my Ledbekh-Teltai in my bag. But the anger is not directed at me, though from the story I heard at the Camahoo hoondahvi, my fellow humans on this world have not graced our species. It is the anger of a country under occupation. On walls and doors, the proclamations of the Duke of Yoo are plastered layer upon layer: her pennant, emblazoned with the four white hands of House Yoo, flies from public buildings, the radio station mast, tower tops, and the gallows. Her javrosts patrol streets so narrow that their graapa can barely squeeze through them. At their passage, the citizens of Egayhazy flash jagged glares, mutter altiplano oaths. And there is another sigil: an eight-petalled flower; a blue so deep it seems almost to shine. I see it stencilled hastily on walls and doors and the occupation-force posters. I see it in little badges sewn to the quilted jackets of the Egayhazians; and in tiny glass jars in low-set windows. In the market of Yent, I witnessed javrosts upturn and smash a vegetable stall that dared to offer a few posies of this blue bloom.

The staff at my hotel were suspicious when they saw me working up some sketches from memory of this blue flower of dissent. I explained my work and showed some photographs and asked, what was this flower? A common plant of the high altiplano; they said. It grows up under the breath of the high snow; small and tough and stubborn. It's most remarkable feature is that it blooms when no other flower does—in the dead of the Great Night. The Midnight Glory was one name, though it had another, newer, which entered common use since the occupation: The Blue Empress.

I knew there and then that I had found Arthur.

A pall of sulfurous smoke hangs permanently over the Valley of Kilns, lit with hellish tints from the glow of the kilns below. A major ceramics centre on a high, treeless plateau? How are the kilns fuelled? Volcanic vents do the firing, but they turn this long defile in the flank of Mount Tooloowera into a little hell of clay, bones, smashed porcelain, sand, slag, and throat-searing sulphur. Glehenta is the last of the Porcelain Towns, wedged into the head of the valley, where the river Iddis still carries a memory of freshness and cleanliness. The pottery houses, like upturned vases, lean towards each other like companionable women.

And there is the house to which my questions guided me: as my informants described; not the greatest but perhaps the meanest; not the foremost but perhaps the most prominent, tucked away in an alley. From its roof flies a flag, and my breath caught: not the Four White Hands of Yoo—never that, but neither the Blue Empress. The smoggy wind tugged at the hand-and-dagger of the Hydes of Grangegorman.

Swift action: to hesitate would be to falter and fail, to turn and walk away, back down the Valley of the Kilns and the Ten Thousand Steps. I rattle the ceramic chimes. From inside, a huff and sigh. Then a voice: worn ragged, stretched and tired, but unmistakable.

"Come on in. I've been expecting you."

V *crepitant movebitvolutans*. Wescott's Wandering Star. A wind-mobile vine, native of the Ishtaria altiplano, that grows into a tight spherical web of vines which, in the Venerian Great Day, becomes detached from an atrophied root stock and rolls cross-country, carried on the wind. A central calx contains woody nuts that produce a pleasant rattling sound as the Wandering Star is in motion.

Cut paper, painted, layed and gummed. Perhaps the most intricate of the Venerian paper cuts.

THE SEER'S STORY.

Tea?

I have it sent up from Camahoo when the stickmen make the return trip. Proper tea. Irish breakfast. It's very hard to get the water hot enough at this altitude, but it's my little ritual. I should have asked you to bring some. I've known you were looking for me from the moment you set out from Loogaza. You think anyone can wander blithely into Glehenta?

Tea.

You look well. The years have been kind to you. I look like shit. Don't deny it. I know it. I have an excuse. I'm dying, you know. The liquor of the vine—it takes as much as it gives. And this world is hard on humans. The Great Days—you never completely adjust—and the climate: if it's not the thin air up here, it's the moulds and fungi and spores down there. And the ultraviolet. It dries you out, withers you up. The town healer must have frozen twenty melanomas off me. No, I'm dying. Rotten inside. A leather bag of mush and bones. But you look very well, Ida. So, Patrick shot himself? Fifteen years too late, says I. He could have spared all of us . . . enough of that. But I'm glad you're happy. I'm glad you have someone who cares, to treat you the way you should be treated.

I am the Merciful One, the Seer, the Prophet of the Blue Pearl, the Earth Man, and I am dying.

I walked down that same street you walked down. I didn't ride, I walked, right through the centre of town. I didn't know what to expect. Silence. A mob. Stones. Bullets. To walk right through and out the other side without a door opening to me. I almost did. At the very last house, the door opened and an old man came out and stood in front of me so that I could not pass. "I know you." He pointed at me "You came the night of the Javrosts." I was certain then that I would die, and that seemed not so bad a thing to me. "You were the merciful one, the one who spared our young." And he went into the house and brought me a porcelain cup of water and I drank it down, and here I remain. The Merciful One.

They have decided that I am to lead them to glory, or, more likely, to death. It's justice, I suppose. I have visions you see—*pula* flashbacks. It works differently on Terrenes than Thents. Oh, they're hard-headed enough not to believe in divine inspiration or any of that rubbish. They need a figurehead—the repentant mercenary is a good role, and the odd bit of mumbo-jumbo from the inside of my addled head doesn't go amiss.

Is your tea all right? It's very hard to get the water hot enough this high. Have I said that before? Ignore me—the flashbacks. Did I tell you I'm dying? But it's good to see you; oh how long is it?

And Richard? The children? And Grangegorman? And is Ireland . . . of course. What I would give for an eyeful of green, for a glimpse of summer sun, a blue sky.

So, I have been a conman and a lover, a soldier and an addict, and now I end my time as a revolutionary. It is surprisingly easy. The Group of Seven Altiplano Peoples' Liberation Army do the work: I release gnomic pronouncements that run like grass-fire from here to Egayhazy. I did come up with the Blue Empress motif: the Midnight Glory: blooming in the dark, under the breath of the high snows. Apt. They're not the most poetic of people, these potters. We drove the Duke of Yoo from the Valley of the Kilns and the Ishtar Plain: she is resisted everywhere, but she will not relin-quish her claim on the Altiplano so lightly. You've been in Egayhazy—you've seen the forces she's moving up here. Armies are mustering, and my agents report 'rigi-bles coming through the passes in the Palisades. An assault will come. The Duke has an alliance with House Shorth—some agreement to divide the altiplano up be-tween them. We're outnumbered. Outmanoeuvred and out-supplied, and we have no where to run. They'll be at each other's throats within a Great Day, but that's a matter of damn for us. The Duke may spare the kilns—they're the source of wealth. Matter of damn to me. I'll not see it, one way or other. You should leave, Ida. *Pula* and local wars—never get sucked into them.

Ah. Unh. Another flashback. They're getting briefer, but more intense,

Ida, you are in danger. Leave before night—they'll attack in the night. I have to stay. The Merciful One, the Seer, the Prophet of the Blue Pearl, can't abandon his people. But it was good, so good of you to come. This is a terrible place. I should never have come here. The best traps are the slowest. In you walk, through all the places and all the lives and all the years, never thinking that you are already in the trap, and then you go to turn around, and it has closed behind you. Ida, go as soon as you can . . . go right now. You should never have come. But . . . oh, how I hate the thought of dying up here on this terrible plain! To see Ireland again . . .

V *volanti musco*: Altiplano Air-moss. The papercut shows part of a symbiotic lighter-than-air creature of the Ishtari Altiplano. The plant part consists of curtains of extremely light hanging moss that gather water from the air and low clouds. The animal part is not reproduced.

Shredded paper, gum.

He came to the door of his porcelain house, leaning heavily in a stick, a handker-chief pressed to mouth and nose against the volcanic fumes. I had tried to plead with him to leave, but whatever else he has become, he is a Hyde of Grangegorman, and stubborn as an ould donkey. There is a wish for death in him; something old and strangling and relentless with the gentlest eyes.

"I have something for you," I said and I gave him the box without ceremony.

His eyebrows rose when he opened it.

"Ah."

"I stole the Blue Empress."

"I know."

"I had to keep it out of Patrick's hands. He would have broken and wasted it, like he broke and wasted everything." Then my slow mind, so intent on saying this con-fession right, that I had practised on the space-crosser, and in every room and every mode of conveyance on my journey across this world, flower to flower, story to story: my middle-aged mind tripped over Arthur's two words. "You knew?"

"All along."

"You never thought that maybe Richard, maybe Father, or Mammy, or one of the staff had taken it?"

"I had no doubt that it was you, for those very reasons you said. I chose to keep your secret, and I have."

"Arthur, Patrick is dead, Rathangan is mine. You can come home now."

"Ah, if it were so easy!"

"I have a great forgiveness to ask from you, Arthur."

"No need. I did it freely. And do you know what, I don't regret what I did. I was notorious—the Honourable Arthur Hyde, jewel thief and scoundrel. That has currency out in the worlds. It speaks reams that none of the people I used it on asked to see the jewel, or the fortune I presumably had earned from selling it. Not one. Everything I have done, I have done on reputation alone. It's an achievement. No, I won't go home, Ida. Don't ask me to. Don't raise that phantom before me. Fields of green and soft Kildare mornings. I'm valued here. The people are very kind. I'm accepted. I have virtues. I'm not the minor son of Irish gentry with no land and the arse hanging out of his pants. I am the Merciful One, the Prophet of the Blue Pearl."

"Arthur, I want you to have the jewel."

He recoiled as if I had offered him a scorpion.

"I will not have it. I will not touch it. It's an ill-favoured thing. Unlucky. There are no sapphires on this world. You can never touch the Blue Pearl. Take it back to the place it came from."

For a moment, I wondered if he was suffering from another one of his hallucinating seizures. His eyes, his voice were firm.

"You should go, Ida. Leave me. This is my place now. People have tremendous ideas of family—loyalty and undying love and affection: tremendous expectations and ideals that drive them across worlds to confess and receive forgiveness. Families are whatever works. Thank you for coming. I'm sorry I wasn't what you wanted me to be. I forgive you—though as I said there is nothing to forgive. There. Does that make us a family now? The Duke of Yoo is coming, Ida. Be away from here before that. Go. The town people will help you."

And with a wave of his handkerchief, he turned and closed his door to me.

I wrote that last over a bowl of altiplano mate at the stickmen's caravanserai in Yelta, the last town in the Valley of the Kilns. I recalled every word, clearly and precisely. Then I had an idea; as clear and precise as my recall of that sad, unresolved conversation with Arthur. I turned to my valise of papers, took out my scissors and a sheet of the deepest indigo and carefully, from memory, began to cut. The stickmen watched curiously, then with wonder. The clean precision of the scissors, so fine and intricate, the difficulty and accuracy of the cut, absorbed me entirely. Doubts fell from me: why had I come to this world? Why had I ventured alone into this noisome valley? Why had Arthur's casual accepting of what I had done, the act that shaped both his life and mine, so disappointed me? What had I expected from him?

Snip went the scissors, fine curls of indigo paper fell from them on to the table. It had always been the scissors I turned to when the ways of men grew too much. It was a simple cut. I had the heart of it right away, no false starts, no new beginnings. Pure and simple. My onlookers hummed in appreciation. Then I folded the cut into my diary, gathered up my valises, and went out to the waiting spider-car. The eternal clouds seem lower today, like a storm front rolling in. Evening is coming.

I write quickly, briefly.

Those are no clouds. Those are the 'rigibles of the Duke of Yoo. The way is shut. Armies are camped across the altiplano. Thousands of soldiers and javrosts. I am trapped here. What am I to do? If I retreat to Glehenta I will meet the same fate as Arthur and the Valley people—if they even allow me to do that. They might think that I was trying to carry a warning. I might be captured as a spy. I do not want to imagine how the Duke of Yoo treats spies. I do not imagine my Terrene identity will protect me. And the sister of the Seer, the Blue Empress! Do I hide in Yelta and hope that they will pass me by? But how could I live with myself knowing that I had abandoned Arthur?

There is no way forward, no way back, no way around.

I am an aristocrat. A minor one, but of stock. I understand the rules of class, and breeding. The Duke is vastly more powerful than I, but we are of a class. I can speak with her; gentry to gentry. We can communicate as equals.

I must persuade her to call off the attack.

Impossible! A middle-aged Irish widow, armed only with a pair of scissors. What can she do; kill an army with gum and tissue? The death of a thousand papercuts?

Perhaps I could buy her off. A prize beyond prize: a jewel from the stars, from their goddess itself. Arthur said that sapphires are unknown on this world. A stone beyond compare.

I am writing as fast as I am thinking now.

I must go and face the Duke of Yoo, female to female. I am of Ireland, a citizen of no mean nation. We confront the powerful, we defeat empires. I will go to her and name myself and I shall offer her the Blue Empress. The true Blue Empress. Beyond that, I cannot say. But I must do it, and do it now.

I cannot make the driver of my spider-car take me into the camp of the enemy. I have asked her to leave me and make her own way back to Yelta. I am writing this with a stub of pencil. I am alone on the high altiplano. Above the shield wall, the cloud layer is breaking up. Enormous shafts of dazzling light spread across the high plain. Two mounted figures have broken from the line and ride towards me. I am afraid—and yet I am calm. I take the Blue Empress from its box and grasp it tight in my gloved hand. Hard to write now. No more diary. They are here.

V. *Gloria medianocte*: The Midnight Glory, or Blue Empress.
    Card, paper, ink.

consolation

joHn kesseL

Here's a fascinating, multilayered look at an impoverished, Balkanizing future America where the Northeastern and Pacific states have been absorbed by Canada, and which centers around an unlikely romance between a political activist who allows herself to be talked into becoming a reluctant terrorist and a nonpolitical would-be immortal obsessed with life-extension.

Born in Buffalo, New York, John Kessel now lives in Raleigh, North Carolina, where he is a professor of American Literature and the director of the creative writing program at North Carolina State University. Kessel made his first sale in 1975. His first solo novel, Good News from Outer Space, *was released in 1988 to wide critical acclaim, but before that he had made his mark on the genre primarily as a writer of highly imaginative, finely crafted short stories, many of which were assembled in his collection* Meeting in Infinity. *He won a Nebula Award in 1983 for his novella "Another Orphan," which was also a Hugo finalist that year, and has been released as an individual book. His story "Buffalo" won the Theodore Sturgeon Award in 1991, and his novella* Stories for Men *won the prestigious James Tiptree Jr. Memorial Award in 2003. His other books include* Freedom Beach *(in collaboration with James Patrick Kelly), a major solo novel,* Corrupting Dr. Nice, *and two new collections,* The Pure Product *and* The Collected Kessel, *as well as a series of anthologies coedited with James Patrick Kelly:* Feeling Very Strange: The Slipstream Anthology, The Secret History of Science Fiction, Digital Rapture: The Singularity Anthology, Rewired: The Post-Cyberpunk Anthology, *and* Nebula Awards Showcase 2012. *Recently married, he is at work on a much-anticipated new novel.*

LESTER

Given last month's denial-of-service attack on the robocar network, I was surprised when, over the streetcam, I saw Alter arrive in a bright blue citicar. As it pulled away from the curb toward its next call, he tugged his jacket straight and looked directly up into the camera, a sheen of sweat on his forehead. 11:42 AM, 5 November, the readout at the corner of my pad said .30 C. Major rain in the forecast.

Alter was forty, stork-like and ungainly. He stuck his hands into his pockets and approached the lobby, and the door opened for him.

I set down the pad and got up to open my office door. Alter was standing with his back to me, peering at the directory. "Mr. Alter," I called. "Over here."

He turned, looked at me warily, and then came over.

"Right in here," I said. I ushered him into the office. He stood there and inspected it. It looked pretty shabby. A bookshelf, a desk covered with papers, a window on the courtyard where a couple of palms grew and a turtle sat on a log, a framed print of Magritte's *La reproduction interdite*, two armchairs facing each other. Like an iceberg, nine tenths of the office was invisible.

"No receptionist," Alter said.

"That's right. Just you and me. Have a seat."

Alter didn't move. "I thought this would be a government office."

"I work for the government. This is my office."

"You people," Alter said. He sat down. I sat across from him. "What's your name?" he asked.

"It's uncomfortable, isn't it, working in a state of incomplete knowledge. Call me Lester."

"I like to know where I am, Lester."

Everything in his manner, in the way he sat in the chair, in the timbre of his voice, screamed sociopath. I didn't need some expert system to tell me where he fell on the spectrum: I had been dealing with men like Alter—always men—for long enough to read them in my sleep.

"You're in Canada," I said. "In Massachusetts, to be specific. You're in my office, about to tell us what you've done."

"Us?" he said. "Do you have a hamster in your pocket?"

"Think of 'us' as the rest of the human race."

Alter's eyes narrowed. "'Us' like the U.S. You're a Fed."

"There are no Feds anymore. That's a Sunbelt fantasy."

"You know I'm not from the Sunbelt. I'm from Vermont. You've been invading my privacy, surveilling me. You're going to doxx me. Turnabout is fair play. Eye-for-eye kind of thing. Very biblical."

"Do you always assume that everybody else is like you?"

"Most people aren't." He smiled at that, quite pleased with himself.

"Doxxing only works against a person who has something to lose. Friends. A family. A valuable job. A reputation. You're doxx-proof, Jimmy. All we want is for you to explain what you've done."

"You already know what I've done. That's why I'm here. You violated my privacy, my personhood."

"Yes, that's true. Why do you think we did that?"

"Why? What I wish I knew was how. No way you should have been able to trace me." He looked around my office. "Certainly not with anything you have here."

"You aren't here for me to tell you things, you are here for you to tell me things.

So let's get on with it. We'd like you to say what you've done. We need to hear you speak the words. Imagine it's so we can measure your degree of remorse."

"I'm not remorseful. Everything I did was right."

He was beyond tiresome. His pathetic individualism, his fantasy of his uniqueness, his solipsism. I wanted to punch him just so he might know that what was happening in this room was real. "So tell us all those right things you did."

"Well, I turned up all the thermostats in the Massachusetts State House. Sweated them out of there for an afternoon, anyway."

"What else?"

"I inventoried the contents of all the refrigerators of government employees with a BMI over thirty. And the bathroom scales, the medical interventions, the insurance records. All those morbidly obese—I posted it on Peeperholic."

"Is that all?"

"I scrambled the diagnostic systems in the Pittsfield New Clinic. I deflated all the tires in the Salem bikeshare—that one was just for fun. At UMass I kept the chancellor out of her office for a week and put videos of her and her wife in bed onto every public display on the campus."

"Is that all?"

"That covers the most significant ones, yes."

"I know you don't believe in law, but I thought you believed in privacy."

"They don't deserve privacy."

"But you do."

"Apparently not. So here I am."

"You resent us. But you object to your victims resenting you?"

"Victims? Who's a victim? I was punching up. The people I troubled needed to be troubled. Here's what I did—I punctured their hypocrisies and exposed their lies. I made some powerful and corrupt people a little uncomfortable. I managed to tell some truths about a pitifully few people, to a pitifully small audience. I wish I could have done more."

I'd been doing this too long. One too many sociopathic losers with computers, broken people who didn't know how broken they were. The world churned them out, full of defensive self-righteousness, deformed consciences, spotty empathy, and a sense of both entitlement and grievance—bullies who saw themselves as victims, the whole sodden army of them out there wreaking havoc small and large without a clue as to how pathetic and pathetically dangerous they were. A sea of psychopathy, with computers. The mid-21st century.

Thank god I didn't have to deal with the ones carrying guns. That was another department.

Alter was still going on. I interrupted him. "Why don't you tell me about Marjorie Xenophone."

"Funny name. I don't believe I know that woman."

"You knew her well enough to send her STD history to her husband. To tell her car to shut down every time she turned onto her lover's street."

"That's a terrible thing to do. But I never heard of the woman before you mentioned her name."

"So you don't know she killed herself."

"Suicide, huh? She must have been one messed-up lady."

"You turned off her birth control implant and she got pregnant. Her husband left her, she lost her job. She was humiliated in front of everybody she knew."

"Some people can't deal with life."

"Mr. Alter, you are one bad, bad pancake," I said. "You worked with her at Green Mountain Video Restoration."

Alter's eyes slid from mine up to the Magritte painting. A man is looking into a mirror, the back of his head to us. The mirror shows an identical image of the back of his head.

When Alter spoke, his tone was more serious. "What went on between me and that woman was private."

"Privacy was an historical phase, Jimmy, and it's over. Nobody had a right to privacy when they were indentured servants or slaves. For one or two hundred years people imagined they could have secrets. That was a local phenomenon and it's now over. Your career is evidence of why."

"So why is it a crime when an individual does it but perfectly fine when your social media platform or service provider or the government does? People sign away their privacy with every TOS box they check. If they get upset when I liberate publicly available materials, too bad. Maybe they'll get smart and stand up to people like you."

"Well said. Where were you born, again?"

"Burlington, Vermont."

"Right. Burlington. South Burlington—the part that's in Texas."

Alter didn't say anything. I had never seen a man look more angry. "Indentured servants and slaves," he muttered.

"Did you really think you could create an identity that would get past our friends at MIT?" I said. "And then have the arrogance to pursue a career as a troll? Where did you go to school? Texas Tech?"

"That's a lot of questions at once."

"We already know the answers."

Outside, thunder sounded. Fat raindrops began to fall into the courtyard, moving the leaves of the palms. The turtle remained motionless. "Where were you born?"

After a hesitation, he said, "Galveston."

"Sad about Galveston, the hurricane. How long have you been a refugee?"

"I'm not a refugee."

"An illegal immigrant, then?"

"I'm a Texas citizen. I just happen to be working here."

"Under a false identity."

"I pay your taxes. I pay as much as any citizen."

"Don't like our taxes, go back to Texas." I smiled. "Could be a bumper sticker."

Alter looked straight at me for a good five seconds. "Please, don't make me."

"But we're persecuting you. The jackbooted thugs of the totalitarian Canadian government."

"You're no more Canadian than I am. You're an American."

"Check out the flagpole in Harvard Square sometime. Note the red maple leaf."

"Look, I get it. You have power over me." Alter rubbed his hands on his pant legs. "What do you want me to say? I'll sign anything you want me to sign."

"What about Marjorie?"

"You're right. I went too far. I feel bad about that." Alter's belligerence had faded. He shifted in his chair. "I'm sorry if I got out of line. Just tell me what you want and I'll do it."

"I got the impression you didn't like people telling you what to do."

"Well . . . sometimes you have to go along to get along. Right?"

"So I've heard."

"How many sessions are we going to have?"

"Sessions? What sessions?"

"Because of the court order. You're supposed to heal me or certify me or something, before I can go back into the world."

"It's not my job to heal you."

"Maybe it's punishment, then."

It was a pleasure to see the panic in his eyes. "This isn't a prison and I'm not a cop. I'll tell you what we will do, though. We'll send you back to the hellhole you came from. Hope you kept your water wings."

Just then I noticed something on my pad. It was raining hard now, a real monsoon, and the temperature had dropped 10 degrees. But in the middle of hustling pedestrians stood a woman, very still, staring at the entrance of my building. People walked by her in both directions, hunched against the storm. She wore a hat pulled low, and a long black coat slick with rain. She entered the lobby. She scanned it, turned purposefully toward my office, reached into her coat pocket, and walked off camera.

"I don't think anything I've done's so bad . . ." Alter said. I held up my hand to shut him up.

The door to my office opened. Alter started to turn around. Before he could, the woman in the black coat tossed something into the room, then stepped back and closed the door. The object hit the floor with a solid thunk and rolled, coming to rest by my right foot. It was a grenade.

ESMERALDA

The blast blew the door across the lobby into the plate-glass front wall, shattering it. By then I was out on the sidewalk. I set off through the downpour in the direction of the train station.

Before I had walked a hundred meters the drones swooped past me, rotors tearing the rain into mist, headed for Makovec's office. People rushed out into the street. The citicar network froze, and only people on bikes and in private vehicles were able to move. I stepped off the curb into a puddle, soaking my shoe.

Teohad assured me that all public monitors had been taken care of and no video would be retrieved from five minutes before to five after the explosion. I walked away from Dunster Street, trying to keep my pace steady, acutely aware that everybody else was going in the other direction. Still, I crossed the bridge over the levees, caught a cab, and reached the station in good time.

I tried to sleep a little as the train made its way across Massachusetts, out of the rainstorm, through the Berkshires, into New York. It was hopeless. The sound of the blast rang in my ears. The broken glass and smoke, the rain. It was all over the net: Makovec was dead and they weren't saying anything about Alter. Teo's phony video had been released, claiming responsibility for the Refugee Liberation Front and warning of more widespread attacks if Ottawa turned its back on those fleeing Confederated Free America.

Outside the observation window a bleeding sunset poured over forests of russet and gold. After New England and New York became provinces, Canada had dropped a lot of money on the rail system. All these formerly hopeless decaying cities—from classical pretenders Troy, Rome, Utica to Mohawk-wannabe Chittenango and Canajoharie—were coming back. If it weren't for the flood of refugees from the Sunbelt, the American provinces might make some real headway against economic and environmental blight.

Night settled in and a gibbous moon rose. Lots of time to think.

I was born in Ogdensburg back when it was still part of the U.S. There'd been plenty of backwoods loons where I grew up, in the days when rural New York might as well have been Alabama. But the Anschluss with Canada and the huge influx of illegals had pushed even the local evangelicals into the anti-immigrant camp. Sunbelters. Ragged, uncontrollable, when they weren't draining social services they were ranting about government stealing their freedom, defaming their God, taking away their guns.

My own opinions about illegals were not moderated by any ideological or religious sympathies. I didn't need any more threadbare crackers with their rugged-individualist libertarian Jesus-spouting militia-loving nonsense to fuck up the new Northeast the way they had fucked up the old U.S. We're Canadians now, on sufferance, and eager to prove our devotion to our new government. Canada has too many of its own problems to care what happens to some fools who hadn't the sense to get out of Florida before it sank.

The suffering that the Sunbelters fled wasn't a patch on the environmental degradation they were responsible for. As far as I was concerned, their plight was chickens coming home to roost. Maybe I felt something for the Blacks and Hispanics and the women, but in a storm you have to pick a side and I'd picked mine a long time ago. Teo's video would raise outrage against the immigrants and help ensure that Ottawa would not relax its border policies.

But my ears still rang from the blast.

It was morning when the train arrived in Buffalo. The station was busy for early Saturday: people coming into town for the arts festival, grimly focused clients headed to one of the life extension clinics, families on their way up to Toronto, bureaucrats on their way to Ottawa. In the station I bought a coffee and a beignet. Buzzing from lack of sleep, I sat at a table on the concourse and watched the people. When the screen across from me slipped from an ad for Roswell Life Extension into a report on the Boston attack, I slung my bag over my shoulder and walked out.

I caught the Niagara Street tram. A brilliant early November morning: warm, sunny, cotton ball clouds floating by on mild westerlies. They used to call this time of year Indian summer back when it happened in mid-October, when the temperature might hit 70 for a week or so before the perpetual cloud cover of November came down and Seasonal Affective Disorder settled in for a five- or six-month run.

Now it was common for the warmth to linger into December. Some days it still clouded up and rained, but the huge lake-effect snowstorms that had battered the city were gone. The lake never froze over anymore. The sun shone more and the breezes were mild. The disasters of the late 20th and early 21st centuries had passed, leaving Buffalo with clean air, moderate climate, fresh water, quaint neighborhoods, historic architecture, hydroelectric power beyond the dreams of any nuke, and a growing arts- and medicine-based economy. Just a hop across the river from our sister province Ontario.

The tram ran past the harbor studded with sailboats, then along the Niagara River toward the gleaming Union Bridge. Kids in LaSalle Park were flying kites. Racing shells practiced on the Black Rock Canal. A female coxed eight, in matching purple shirts, rowed with precision and vigor.

None of those women had blown anybody up in the last 24 hours.

The tram moved inland and I got off on the West Side. I carried my bag a couple of blocks, past reclaimed houses and a parking lot turned community garden, to the Fargo Architectural Collective. Home. We'd done the redesign ourselves, Teo and Salma and I, fusing two of the circa-1910 houses with their limestone footings and cool basements into a modern multipurpose. It had earned us some commissions. In the front garden stood a statue of old William Fargo himself, looking more like a leprechaun than the founder of separate transportation and banking empires.

Teo greeted me at the door and enveloped me in a big bear hug.

"Esme," he said. "We've been worried. You're okay?"

"For certain values of the word okay." I dropped my bag. Salma poked her head out of her workroom. She looked very serious. "What?" I said.

"Come have some tea," she said.

The three of us sat down in the conference room and Teo brewed a pot of mood tea. "Am I going to need to be calmed down?" I asked.

Salma leaned forward, her dark brow furrowed. "Our friends in Boston screwed up. Turns out not all of the video cameras were disabled. There may be some images of you approaching the building."

"Shit."

"The fact you're not from Boston will help," Teo said. "You have no history. We're boring middle-class citizens; none of us are known activists."

"That should slow them down for about thirty seconds," I said. I sipped some tea. We talked about the prospect of my taking a vacation. Vancouver, maybe, or Kuala Lumpur. After a while I said, "I didn't sleep last night. I'm going to take a nap."

I went up to my room, sat on the bed, and unlaced my shoes. The right one was still damp from the puddle in Cambridge. I lay down. Outside my window a Carolina wren, another undocumented immigrant from the torrid South, sang its head off. Teo's tea was good for something, and in a few minutes I drifted off to sleep.

It was late afternoon when I woke. Salma came in and lay down beside me on her side, her face very close to mine. "Feel any better?"

"Better." I kissed her. "It was awful, Salma."

She touched my cheek. "I know. But somebody has—"

I forced myself up. "You don't know."

Salma sat up and put her hand on my shoulder. "If you're going to be a soldier for change, then you have to accept some damages. Try not to think about it. Come on, take a shower, get dressed. We're going out."

I swung my legs off the bed. I had volunteered, after all. "Where are we going?"

"There's a party at Ajit Ghosh's. Lot of people will be there."

Ghosh was a coming intellectual voice. An aggregator, a cultural critic, the youngest man to hold a named chair in the history of UB. He lived in a big state-of-the-art ecohouse with a view of Delaware Park, Hoyt Lake, and the Albright-Knox. The neighborhood was money, new houses and old occupied by young, ambitious people on their way up. I didn't like a lot of them, or who they were willing to step on in order to rise, but you had to give them points for energy and creativity.

I did not care for the way they looked down on people whose roots in WNY went back to before it became trendy. The party would be full of people who came here only when living in New York City got too difficult, the Southwest dried up and blew away, and the hurricane-battered South turned into an alternating fever swamp and forest fire.

I didn't think I needed a party. But Ghosh's house was a Prairie School reboot with a negative carbon imprint. It was better than lying around with the echo of an explosion in my head.

"All right," I said.

SCOOBIE

I'd spent the last three days at Roswell Park getting my tumors erased, and now I was out on the street ready to do some damage. I headed toward the restaurants on Main Street, walking past the blocks of medical labs, life extension clinics, hospitals, all with their well-designed signage and their well-trimmed gardens and their well-heeled patients taking the air. Most of them looked pretty good. Pretty much all of them were doomed.

They treated their ailments and told themselves that nobody lives forever. But I would. An immortal living in the world of mortals—one of the few. The ones who committed to the task and made the best choices. Rationalism. Certain practices, investments, expectations. Habits of living.

There's an industry devoted to anti-aging, a jungle of competing claims and methods. Most of it is garbage, pretty pictures papering over the grave. Billions wasted every year.

Not me. I didn't invest in a single platform, but maneuvered between the options. Of course you could not always know the best choice with certainty. If you went T+p53 route, you entered the race between immortality and cancer. You had to boost your tumor suppression genes to counter the increased telomerase that prevented chromosome erosion. Hence my visit to Roswell. There was SkQ ingestion to reduce mitochondria damage. A half-dozen other interventions and their synergistic effects, positive and negative. To keep on top of this you needed as much information as possible. Even then you could make a mistake—but that was the human condition for us early posthumans.

I had backups: a contract to be uploaded once they had worked out the tech. A separate contract to have my head cryogenically preserved once the brain had been uploaded. Some other irons in the fire, depending on the way things broke.

I grew up in Fort McMurray, Alberta, in the destroyed landscape of bitumen strip mines and oil sands, with its collapsing economy and desperate gun-toting mountain people. When the U.S. broke up and the northeastern and Pacific states joined Canada, freedom-loving Alberta took the opportunity to go the other way, ditching the arrogant bastards in Ottawa to join in a nice little union with Montana, Wyoming, and Idaho. Big skies, free men. Petroleum fractions. Though it had its charms, I had things I wanted to do, and not many of them could be done in Calgary.

It was a beautiful day, a good day to be alive. I felt very young. Though this latest treatment would blow a hole in my savings, I decided to spend some money. At Galley's on Main I ordered broiled salmon and a salad. I had not eaten anything like this in a year. I let the tastes settle on my tongue. I could feel the cells in my body exploding with sensory energy. The crispness of the lettuce. A cherry tomato. It was all astonishing, and I let it linger as long as I could.

A man leaving the restaurant glanced at me and did a double take. It was Mossadegh.

"By the fires of Ormazd!" he said. "Not expecting you in a place like this. How's it growing, brother?"

"Germinal," I said. My connections with Mossadegh were mostly business. He knew a lot of women, though. I waved at the chair opposite. "Sit down."

"Haven't seen you much," Mossadegh said. "Where you been?"

"Out of town for a few days. Clients." I didn't advertise that I was going to live forever.

Mossadegh was a pirate. He said it was principle with him, not self-interest: freedom of information, no copyright or patents. That was how I got to know him, and on occasion he and I had made some money together. I would never let Mossadegh know anything about who I really was, though. The free flow of information is essential to posthumanism, but I didn't want anybody in my business.

I don't belong to any of those cults. No Extropists. No oxymoronic libertarian socialists. Most of all, I don't want any connection with anybody—anybody human, anyway. That might get you some information others didn't have, but it's too risky. The most vocal ones make the most idiotic choices.

"Got anything working?" he asked.

"Making some phony archives," I said. "Mostly boring—famous places, New York City, Beijing. Last week somebody wanted an event set in Kansas City in the 1930s, and I just about kissed his hand."

Mossadegh flagged down a waiter and ordered a drink. Alcohol—he wasn't going to live forever, I can tell you that. "I know somebody who used to live in Kansas City."

"Really? Did he get out before, or when it happened?"

"Get this: he left one week—to the day—before."

"You're kidding," I said.

"Truth is truth."

As the afternoon declined we went on about nothing particularly important. Mossadegh rubbed his long jaw with his long fingers. "Say, you want to come to a party?"

"When?"

"Right now, brother! Maryam's been taking some grad classes and this rich prof's throwing a blowout."

"I'm not from the university," I said.

"But I am, and you come with me. Stout fellow like you's always welcome."

Mossadegh was no more from the university than I was, but I had nothing better to do. We caught a citicar up Elmwood. The setting sun reflecting off the windows of the houses turned them into gold mirrors. We passed a public building where somebody had plastered a video sign onto the side: "Go back to Arkansas . . . Or is it Kansas?"

The party was in a new neighborhood where they had torn out the old expressway, overlooking the park. It was twilight when we got there, a little chill in the air, but warm lights glowed along the street. The house looked old-fashioned on the outside, but the inside was all new. A big garden in the back. Sitting on the table in the living room they had a bowl of capsules, mood teas, bottles of champagne and a pyramid of glasses. I passed on the intoxicants and drank water.

The place was crowded with university students, artists, and various other knowledge workers. The prof who owned the place, dark and slender, wore all white; he held a champagne coupe in his hand, his palm around the bowl and the stem descending between his fingers in an affected way that made my teeth hurt. He had long, wavy dark hair. He was talking with two young women, nodding his head slightly as he listened. People sat in twos and threes, and there was a group in the sunroom talking politics. Lots of them seemed pretty lit.

All of these people were going to die while I stayed alive.

I stood at the edge of the political talk. A woman was speaking with emotion in her voice. "The people you can fool all of the time are dumber than pond scum, and it isn't exactly a matter of fooling them—they want to be fooled. They'll fight against anybody who tries to pull the scales from their eyes. The hopeless core of any politician's support."

She looked to be about thirty. She wore a loose white shirt and tight black pants and she spoke with an intensity that burned, as if what she said wasn't simply some liberal platitude. This college-undergrad cant mattered to her.

"But fooling all of the people has become harder. Any conflict of interest, hypocrisy, double-dealing, inconvenient truth gets out as soon as somebody with skills addresses finding it, and too many people have the skills. A politician's best bet is to throw sand into people's eyes, put enough distracting information out there that the truth will be buried. You can make a career as long as people are blinded by ideology or just can't think their way through your crap."

I didn't want to get into these weeds. I wasn't the kind of person they were. But she was right about ideological blindness, even if she didn't realize that it applied to her, too.

I thought about my last three days in the clinic. Four tumors they'd zapped out of me this time. Prospects were that cancer treatments would get better, and if they didn't I could go off telomerase life extension and try something else. But I had to admit that staring at the ceiling while the machines took care of something that in the old days would have killed me in three months was not pleasant. And there was nobody I could tell about it. Not anybody who would care, anyway.

The next time I passed through the living room, I poured myself a glass of the champagne. What the hell.

It tasted good, and unaccustomed as I was to alcohol, I got a little buzz on right away. For an hour I wandered through the house listening to snatches of conversation. I got another glass of wine. After a while I went out into the garden. It had cooled off considerably, and most of the people who had been out there were back inside now that it was full night. Balls of golden light shone in the tree branches. It was pretty.

Then I noticed somebody sitting on a bench in the corner of the garden. It was the woman who had been ranting in the sunroom. She ignored me. Leaning on one arm, wineglass beside her, she looked as if she were listening for some sound from a distant room in the house. I drifted over to her.

"Hello," I said.

She looked up. Just stared for a moment. "Hello."

"Sorry to interrupt," I said. "Do you live here?"

"No."

"Friends with somebody who does?"

"Salma is my sister. She's one of Ghosh's girlfriends."

"Who's Ghosh?"

She looked at me again and smiled. "This is Ghosh's house."

"Right. Do you mind if I sit?"

"Knock yourself out."

I sat down and set my glass next to hers on the bench. "Political, are you?"

"Politics is a waste," she said. "Like this thing in Cambridge yesterday—what are they trying to prove?" The anger I had heard in her voice earlier came back. "It's just killing for killing's sake. The things that need changing aren't going to be changed by blowing people up. It's in the heart and the head, and you can't change that with a hand grenade."

Maybe the wine was working in me, but I couldn't let that go.

"Lots of things are decided by hand grenades," I said. "Most things, in the end, are decided by force. Hell, politics is just another form of force. You figure out where the pressure points are, you manipulate the system, you make it necessary for the ones who oppose you to do what you want them to do. You marshal your forces, and then you get what you want."

She looked unconvinced. I liked the way her black hair, not too long, curled around her ear. "You're not from around here," she said. "The accent. You a real Canadian?"

"Alberta."

Her eyebrow raised. "An immigrant?"

"Technically, I guess. It's not like I wasn't born and raised in Canada."

"What's your name?"

"Scoobie." I could smell the scent of the soap she used.

"Esme," she said, holding out her hand. I shook it.

"So what do you think that bombing accomplished, Scoobie?"

"Not much. People don't even know who it was aimed at, and for what reason. No way was it some pro-immigration group. That's a false-flag move. The two guys they blew up aren't particularly influential. They have no power, not even symbolic power. They might as well have been hit by lightning."

"Sounds like you agree with me."

"If you think it was done stupidly, then I agree with you."

She looked down at her feet. She wore black canvas slippers. "I agree with you," she said. "It was done stupidly."

We sat in silence awhile. I picked up my glass and drained the last of my wine. Esme took up her own.

"So why did you emigrate?" she asked me.

"I came to Toronto for the work, at first. I have an interest in the medical professions. The big clinics, the university. Then it was McGill for a few years. Then I came here."

"Do you get any flak as an immigrant? Lots of people don't like them. Alberta is pretty hard right."

"I don't care about that. I guess you could say I'm apolitical. The differences between the Canadian government, Texas, and the Sunbelt states mean nothing to me. I suppose you could call me a libertarian—small 'l.' Certainly I'm for free information, but it all seems petty to me."

"Petty?" The edge came back into her voice.

"This is just a moment in history. Like all political debates, it will pass. What's important is keeping alive. You don't want to get caught between two crazy antagonists. Or get connected up with one side or the other."

"Do you seriously believe that?"

I don't know why I should have cared what she thought. Something about the way she held her shoulders, or the slight, husky rasp in her voice. It was the voice of somebody who had cried for a long time and was all cried out. She was arrogant, she was wrong, but she was very sexy.

I tried to make a joke. "Singularity's coming. All bets are off then."

"The Singularity is a fantasy."

I laughed. "What are you, a religious mystic?"

"I'm an architect."

"Then you ought to know the difference between the material world and fairyland. Is there something supernatural about the human brain? Is it animated by pixie dust?" I was feeling it now. Humanists, with their woo-woo belief in the uniqueness of the "mind."

"They've been talking about strong AI for eighty years. Where is it?'

"Processing power is still increasing. It's only a matter of time. It's just the architecture—"

Esme laughed. "Now you'll tell me about the architecture. Listen, no Jesus supercomputer is going to save you from the crises around us. You can't sit it out."

"I can and I will. This fighting between Canada and the Sunbelt is completely bound to this time and place. It doesn't matter. It's just history, like some war between the Catholics and Protestants in the 14th century."

"How can you say that! People are dying! The future of our society depends on what we do today. Immense things hang in the balance. The climate! Whole species! Ecosystems! Women's rights! Animal rights!"

"You know," I said, "you're hot when you get angry."

Her hand tightened on her glass. I could see the muscles in her forearm; her skin was so brown, so smooth. For a second I thought she was going smash the glass into my face, then she tossed it away and hurled herself onto me. She bit my neck. I fell over and hit my head on the trunk of a tree, went dizzy for a second. The grass was cool. She had her legs around my waist and we started kissing. Long, slow, very serious kisses.

After some time we surfaced for breath. Her eyes were so dark.

"There were no Protestants in the 14th century," she said.

Esme and Scoobie waited in a restaurant at the Toronto airport. Their flight for Krakow left in an hour. They were traveling light, just one small bag each—"getting out of Dodge," Teo called it—and Esme was persuaded. Scoobie knew somebody at the university there, and there was some clinic he wanted to visit.

Both of them were nervous. Neither was sure that this was a good idea, but it seemed like something they should do. At least that was where they were leaving it for now.

"Can I get you something from the bar?" Scoobie asked. "Something to eat?" For a person whose social skills were so rudimentary, he was quite sensitive to her moods.

"No," Esme said. "Maybe we should get to the gate."

Scoobie got up. "Gonna hit the men's room first."

"Okay."

For three days, since that moment in the garden, they had spent every minute together. Inexplicably. He was a cranky naïve libertarian child, afraid of human contact. His politics were ludicrous. But politics—what had politics ever given her besides migraines? Scoobie was so glad to be with her, as if he'd never been with anyone before. Their disagreements only made her see his vulnerabilities more clearly. He had some terribly stupid ideas, but he was not malicious, and he gave her something she needed. She wouldn't call it love—not yet. Call it consolation.

It didn't hurt that on no notice whatsoever he'd managed to get her the subtle tattooing that could deceive facial-recognition software. Teo had produced credentials for them as husband and wife, and their friends had created a false background for them in government databases. They had a shot at getting out of the country.

Up on one of the restaurant screens a news reader announced, "Authorities offer no new information in the hunt for the woman who threw an explosive device into the Cambridge, Massachusetts, office of Lester Makovec, consultant to the New England provincial government's Bureau of Immigration."

The screen switched to scenes of the aftermath of the Cambridge blast: a street view of broken windows, EMTs loading a body zipped into a cryobag into their vehicle.

"But there's an amazing new wrinkle to the story: Makovec, pronounced dead at the scene, was rushed to Harvard Medical School's Humanity Lab, where he underwent an experimental regenerative treatment and is reported to be on the way to recovery." Image of a hospital bed with a heavily bandaged Makovec practicing using an artificial hand to pick up small objects from the table in front of him. The chyron at the bottom of the screen read, "Lifesaving Miracle?"

"Accused terrorist and illegal immigrant Andrew Wayne Spiller, a.k.a. James Alter, who escaped the blast with minor injuries, has been moved to Ottawa to undergo further interrogation." Image of Spiller, surrounded by security in black armor, being escorted into a train car.

"Meanwhile, Rosario Zhang, opposition leader, has called on Prime Minister Nguyen to say what she intends to do to deal with the unprovoked attack by what Zhang calls 'agents of the Texas government.' The prime minister's office has said that the forensic report has not yet determined the perpetrators of the attack, nor, in the light of denials from the Refugee Liberation Front, have investigators been able to verify the authenticity of the video claiming credit for that group."

Across the concourse stood an airport security officer in black, arms crossed over his chest, talking with an Ontario Provincial Police officer. The airport cop rocked back on his heels, eyes hooded, while the OPP spoke to him. The airport cop had a big rust-colored mustache; the OPP wore his black cap with the gray band around it.

The airport security man turned his head a fraction to his right, and he was looking, from 10 meters away, directly into Esme's eyes. She had to fight the impulse to look away. She smiled at him. He smiled back. Esme considered getting up and moving to the gate—she considered leaping out of the chair to run screaming—yet she held herself still.

It took forever, but finally Scoobie returned.

"Time to go?" he said. He looked so cheerful. He was oblivious to the cops.

She kissed him on the cheek. "Yes, please," she said.

They slung their bags over their shoulders, she put her arm through his, and they headed for the gate.

the children of gal

ALLEN M. STEELE

Allen Steele made his first sale to Asimov's Science Fiction *magazine in 1988, soon following it up with a long string of other sales to Asimov's, as well as to markets such as* Analog, The Magazine of Fantasy & Science Fiction, *and* Science Fiction Age. *In 1990, he published his critically acclaimed first novel,* Orbital Decay, *which subsequently won the Locus Poll Award for Best First Novel of the year. His other books include the novels* Clarke County, Space, Lunar Descent, Labyrinth of Night, The Weight, The Tranquility Alternative, A King of Infinite Space, Oceanspace, Chronospace, Coyote, Coyote Rising, Spindrift, Galaxy Blues, Coyote Horizon, Coyote Destiny. Hex, V-S Day. *His short work has been gathered in* Rude Astronauts, Sex and Violence in Zero G, The Last Science Fiction Writer, *and* Sex and Violence in Zero-G: The Complete "Near Space" Stories: Expanded Edition. *His most recent books are the novel* Time Loves a Hero *and the collection* Tales of Time and Space. *Coming up is a new novel,* Arkwright. *He has won three Hugo Awards, in 1996 for his novella "The Death of Captain Future," in 1998 for his novella "Where Angels Fear to Tread," and, most recently, in 2011 for his novelette "The Emperor of Mars." Born in Nashville, Tennessee, he lives in Whately, Massachusetts, with his wife, Linda.*

In the story that follows, he wraps up his "Arkwright" sequence of novellas, which started with "The Legion of Tomorrow" and took us through the launch of the first starship in two subsequent stories, "The Prodigal Son" and "The Long Wait." Here, he takes us ahead for generations to a time when that starship has reached its destination—but things haven't worked out quite the way the scientists who launched it intended it to. . . .

I

Sanjay Arkwright's mother was sent to Purgatory on Monone, the second day of Juli. As dawn broke on Childstown, Aara was escorted from her home by a pair of Guardians, who silently walked two-legged on either side of the heretic as they marched her to the beach. Sanjay and his father Dayall quietly accompanied them; carrying belly packs and walking on all fours, they kept their heads down to avoid meeting the gaze of the townspeople who'd emerged from their cottages and workshops to observe Aara's passage into exile.

It was a day of shame for her family, and yet Aara maintained an upright stance. Even after a Guardian prodded the back of her neck with his staff, she refused to lower her head or place her fores against the cobblestoned street, but instead strode forward on her hinds, gazing straight ahead in almost haughty dismissal of her neighbors. For this alone, Sanjay was proud of his mother. She would obey the Word of Gal, but not with the humiliation expected of her.

On the beach, a group of Disciples had already gathered to form a prayer circle. They squatted in a semicircle facing the Western Channel, where the sister-suns Aether and Bacchae were beginning to set upon the distant shores of Cape Exile. Illuminated by the bright red orb of Calliope rising to the east, they cupped their fores together beneath their lowered faces, and chanting words passed down to them from their mothers and grandmothers:

"Gal the Creator, Gal the All-Knowing,
"Forgive our sister, who denies your love.
"Gal the Creator, Gal the All-Knowing,
"Guide our sister as you watch from above . . ."

Their voices fell silent as Aara and her guards approached. If they'd expected Aara to join them, they were disappointed. Aara barely glanced at them as she walked by, and Sanjay had to fight to keep his expression neutral.

Dayall noticed this. "Don't smile," he whispered to his son, "and don't stand. Everyone is watching us."

Sanjay didn't reply, but only gave his father a brief nod. He was right. This was a sad moment, and also a dangerous one. Most of those who'd followed them to the waterfront were Galians, and even if some were friends of the family, a few were pious enough to report the slightest impropriety to the Guardians. Any sign of support from Aara's family, and the deacons could easily extend the same sentence to her husband and son as well. It had been many yarn since the last time an entire family was sent to Purgatory, but it had been done before.

R'beca Circe, the deacon of the Childstown congregation of the Disciples of Gal, stood on all fours beside Aara's sailboat, accompanied by the deacons from Stone Bluff, Oceanview, and Lighthouse Point who'd travelled across Providence to attend Aara's trial. The Guardians led Aara to them, then stepped aside, standing erect with their staffs planted in the sand. R'beca rose from her fores to look Aara straight in the eye; the other deacons did the same, and for a long moment everything was still, save for the cool morning breeze which ruffled their ceremonial capes and Aara's braided red hair, revealed by the lowered hood of the long black robe she'd been given by the Guardians.

Then R'beca spoke.

"On the first day of the Stormyarn," she recited, "when the Disciples were separated from the Children who stayed behind, Gal told his people, 'Follow my Word always and obey the lessons of your Teachers, for my way is survival, and those who question it shall not.' Aara Arkwright, it is the finding of the Deacons of the Disciples of Gal that you have questioned the Word of Gal, and therefore committed the sin of heresy, for which you have refused to repent. How do you plead?"

"I plead nothing." There was no trace of insolence in Aara's voice; as always, when she was given a direct question, she delivered a direct answer. "I am neither guilty nor innocent. I saw what I saw . . . and there is nothing in the Word that says it cannot exist."

R'beca's eyes grew sharper. She pointed toward the sky. "Clearly, there is no light there save that of Gal and her suns. Even at night, when Aether and Bacchae rise to cast away the shadows and the stars appear, Gal remains in her place, bright and unmoving. Stars do not suddenly appear and vanish, and none may approach Gal."

Almost unwillingly, Sanjay found himself following Deacon R'beca's raised fore with his gaze. As she said, Gal the Creator hovered almost directly overhead, a bright star that never rose or set but remained a fixed point in the sky. It had been this way throughout the one hundred and fifty-two sixyarn of Eosian history, from the moment when Gal had carried the Chosen Children from Erf to the promised land of Eos.

None but fools or heretics ever questioned this. Those who did were purged from Providence, sent alone to the mainland to live out the rest of their days in a place where survival was unlikely.

Yet Aara wouldn't recant. "I did not lie then, and I'm not lying now. I saw a new star in the sky during my turn on night watch, one that moved in the sky toward Gal."

"So you question Gal's dominance? Her status as Creator who cannot be challenged?"

"I question nothing. This was not an act of blasphemy, Deacon . . . it was an obligation to my duty to report anything unusual."

Hearing this, the Disciples crouched on the beach wailed in bereavement. As they slapped their fores against their ears, R'beca's mouth curled in disgust. She'd offered Aara a chance to repent and beg for mercy, only to receive a stubborn reiteration of the same defense she'd given during her trial. Again, Sanjay felt pride surge past his sadness. His mother had never been one to back down, and she wasn't about to do so now.

Yet her courage wasn't met with sympathy. As the other three deacons lowered themselves to their hinds and cupped their fores together, R'beca reached beneath her cape and produced the symbol of her office, a large white knife she carried with her at all times. Made of the same material as the large block of Galmatter that, along with the Teacher, resided within the Transformer inside the Shrine, it was one of the few remaining relics from the yarn before the Great Storm, when the Chosen Children had first come to Eos from Erf. R'beca clasped the pale blade in her left fore and, raising it above her, intoned the words everyone expected to hear:

"In the name of Gal, creator of Eos and mother of her children, I send you, Aara Arkwright, into exile. May Gal grant you safe passage to Purgatory, where you shall live the rest of your days."

Then she brought the knife forward and, with one swift stroke, whisked its blade across the right side of Aara's face. Sanjay's mother winced, but she didn't cry out when the blade cut into her cheek; it would leave a scar that would mark her as an outcast for the rest of her life, making her a pariah to any community on Providence to which she might try to return. She could be put to death if she was ever seen on the island again.

R'beca turned her back to her and, still on her hinds, walked away. "You may say farewell to her now," she murmured to Dayall and Sanjay as she strode past. "Be quick."

Sanjay and his father were the only ones to approach his mother. By custom, everyone else who'd witnessed the ceremony stood erect and silently turned their backs to her. Through the crowd, Sanjay caught a glimpse of Kaile Otomo. Her long black hair was down around her face, making it hard to see her expression, yet she briefly caught his eye and gave him the slightest of nods. Then she turned away as well.

Dayall stood erect to pull off his belly pack. It was stuffed with clothes, a couple of firestarters, fishing tackle, and his best knife, all permitted by the Guardians to be given to someone facing banishment. Aara took it from him, then let her husband wipe the blood from her face and take her in his arms. Sanjay couldn't hear what his father whispered to her, but he saw the tears in her eyes and that was enough. After a few moments, Dayall let her go, and then it was Sanjay's turn.

"Aara . . ."

"It's all right. Everything will be all right." He wasn't expecting the wan smile that crossed her face as she accepted the belly pack bulging with food he'd taken from their pantry. She dropped it on the ground next to his father's. "I'm even more sad about this than you are, because I won't be around to see you and Kaile become bonded, but . . ."

"It's not fair!"

"Hush. Keep your voice down." She glanced over his shoulder, wary of being overheard by the Disciples or the deacons. "Of course, it's not fair. I was only doing my duty. But the Guardians have their duties as well, and R'beca—" another smile, this time sardonic "—well, she calls it blasphemy if winter came late. My only sin was not realizing this before I opened my mouth."

Sanjay started to reply, but then she wrapped her arms around him and pulled him close. "This is not the end," she whispered. "We'll see each other again."

Sanjay knew this wasn't true. Once someone was sent to Purgatory, they never returned from the other side of the Western Channel. Yet perhaps his mother wasn't facing reality, or that she was speaking of the afterlife promised by the deacons, when all who believed in Gal would join once their souls had departed Eos. So he simply nodded and told her that he loved her, and she borrowed his fishbone knife to cut a lock of his red hair to take with her, then a Guardian stepped forward to impatiently tap the sand with his staff.

It was time for her to go.

The catamaran was sound and sturdy, its outrigger hull constructed from cured umbrella palm, its mainsail woven from bambu threads. Sanjay had built the boat with his own fores, with help from his friend Johan Sanyal; they'd done this while Aara was under house arrest, awaiting the arrival of the other deacons and the commencement of the trial whose outcome was all but certain. They'd made the boat quickly but carefully, taking time from the spring fishing season to fashion the small craft for his mother. The master boatbuilder, Codi Royce, hadn't objected when the two boys didn't work on the fishing fleet's boats for several precious days; as Sanjay's mentor, he knew just how important this was.

Although it wasn't strictly permitted, no one had objected when Sanjay discretely hid a harpoon beneath the oars. It wasn't likely that Aara might encounter an ocean monarch while crossing the channel. The leviathans were nocturnal; along with the receding tide, this was a reason why outcasts were sent away at dawn, to give them time to reach Cape Exile before the creatures rose to the surface and started hunting. Nonetheless, it might give her some measure of protection if she encountered one during her journey.

Like all Providence inhabitants, Aara was an expert sailor. Once she'd stowed the packs, she didn't immediately raise the sail but instead used the oars to push herself away from the beach and out into the Childstown bay. As a small measure of respect for her, none of the fishing boats set out when they were supposed to. On the nearby docks, their crews silently waited as Aara paddled away, allowing her a chance to begin the long, sixty-kilm journey from the island to the mainland.

Aara was a small figure sitting in the catamaran's stern when she finally lowered the outrigger and raised the mainsail. As it unfurled to catch the morning wind, there was a single, long gong from the watchtower's bell, the ritual signal that an islander was being sent into exile. As it resounded across the waters, Aara raised a fore in a final wave.

Sanjay and his father waved back, and then they stood together on the shore and quietly waited until her boat couldn't be seen anymore.

II

In the days that followed, Sanjay did his best to put his mother's banishment behind him. With less than three weeks—thirteen days—left in summer, there was much that needed to be done before the season changed: fish to be caught, dried, and preserved, seeds planted and spring crops tended, houses and boats repaired. He and his father put away Aara's belongings—they couldn't bring themselves to burn her clothes, a customary practice for the families of those sent to Purgatory—and accepted the sympathy of those kind enough to offer it, but it took time for them to get used to a house which now seemed empty; the absence of laughter and the vacant seat at the dinner table haunted them whenever they came home.

Sanjay didn't feel very much like attending the Juli service at the Shrine, but Dayall insisted; if he didn't make an appearance, the more inquisitive Disciples might wonder whether Aara's son shared her blasphemous beliefs. Dayall was an observant Galian if not a particularly devout one, and the last thing they wanted to do was draw the attention of the Guardians. So Frione morning they joined the Disciples in the dome-roofed temple in the middle of town. Once they'd bowed in homage to the scared genesis plant that grew beside the Shrine, they went in to sit together on floor mats in the back of the room, doing their best to ignore the curious glances of those around them. Yet as R'beca stood before the altar, where the box-like frame of the Transformer stood with its inert block of Galmatter in the center, and droned on about how the souls of the Chosen Children were gathered by Gal from the vile netherworld of Erf and carried "twenty-two lights and a half through the darkness" to Eos, Sanjay found himself studying the Teacher resting within his crèche behind the altar.

Even as a child, Sanjay had often wondered why the Teacher didn't resemble the Children or their descendents. Taller than an adult islander, his legs had knees that were curiously forward-jointed and hinds lacking the thin membranes that ran between the toes. His arms, folded across his chest, were shorter, while the fingers of his fores were long and didn't have webbing. His neck was short as well, supporting a hairless head whose face was curiously featureless: eyes perpetually open and staring, a lipless mouth, a straight nose that lacked nostrils. And although the Teacher wore an ornate, brocaded robe dyed purple with roseberry, every youngster who'd ever sneaked up to the crèche after services to peek beneath the hem knew that the Teacher lacked genitalia; there was only a smooth place between his legs.

These discrepancies were explained by the Word: the Teacher had been fashioned by Gal to resemble the demons who ruled Erf, and the Creator had made him this way to remind the Children of the place from which they'd come. This was why the Teacher was made of Galmatter instead of flesh and blood. According to history everyone diligently learned and recited in school, the Teacher and the Disciples had fled the mainland for Providence just before the Great Storm, leaving behind the unfaithful who'd ignored Gal's warning that their land would soon be consumed by wind and water.

The Teacher no longer moved or spoke, nor had he ever done so in recent memory. Yet his body didn't decay, so he was preserved in the Shrine; along with the Transformer and the Galmatter block, they were holy relics, reminders of the Stormyarn. In her sermons, R'beca often prophesized the coming of the day when the Teacher would awaken and bring forth new revelations of the Word of Gal, but Sanjay secretly doubted this would ever occur. If it did, he hoped to be there when it happened; he'd like to see how someone could walk on all fours with limbs and extremities as misshapen as these.

Kaile kept a discrete distance from Sanjay after Aara left. He missed her, but understood why; her parents, Aiko and Jak, were strict Disciples who'd become reluctant to have their daughter associating with a heretic's son. And while she wasn't as rigid in her beliefs as her parents, nonetheless Kaile was a Galian who did her best to adhere to the Word. So he saw her only on occasion, sometimes in town but more often in the morning on the waterfront. While Sanjay was a boatbuilder—indeed, his family name, which his father had taken after he bonded with his mother, was an old Inglis word for those who built water craft—Kaile was a diver, trained from childhood to descend deep beneath the channel to harvest scavengers from the sea floor. When they spotted each other during those days, they'd exchange a brief smile and a wave, a sign that she still cared for him and would return once her parents let her.

Dayall, on the other hand, retreated into himself. As Juli lapsed into Aug and then Sept, Sanjay watched as his father became increasingly morose. He seldom spoke to anyone, let alone his son, instead adopting a dull daily pattern of getting up, having breakfast, opening his woodworking shop and puttering around in it all day until it was time to close up and go home, where he'd eat and then go to bed. Although he was still bonded to Aara, it was understood that this no longer mattered; other women could come to him as prospective suitors, and he could bond with them and take their name if he so desired. But Dayall was approaching middle age, and it was unlikely any woman in Childstown would want to take as her mate someone who'd once had a heretic as a wife. So Sanjay could only watch as his father came to terms with his loss; he was helpless to do anything about it.

More than once, Sanjay found himself cursing his mother for not having the foresight to keep what she'd seen during night watch to herself. He began to suspect that her eyes may have been playing tricks on her. It wasn't uncommon to see streaks of light in the night. Old Inglis teachings, passed down through generations, called them meteorites, small rocks which occasionally fell from the sky. Perhaps Aara had seen something like that and had mistaken it for a moving star. She'd sworn otherwise when she'd been called before the Council of Deacons, though, and Aara was an intelligent woman who wasn't likely to mistake a meteorite for anything else. Nonetheless, Sanjay wondered whether, just this once, his mother may have been a fool . . . or even the heretic the deacons had proclaimed her to be.

When Monthree came around in Sept, the last week of summer, it was his turn again to take the night watch. Garth Coyne, Sanjay's uncle and the mayor of Childstown, dropped by the boat shop that afternoon to let him know that he could skip his turn if he wished. Garth would assign someone else instead, and Sanjay could wait three weeks to take the Monthree watch in Dec.

Garth meant well, of course. Part of the purpose of the night watch was to look out for anyone who might try to cross the channel from Cape Exile, whether it be a sinner attempting to abduct an islander for their own vile purposes—which was the Disciples' explanation for the occasional disappearance of someone from a village—or an exile attempting to return. Garth was the mayor, but he was also Dayall's brother, so he was more sympathetic than most, and also aware of the bitter irony of having Sanjay stand watch to prevent his own mother from coming home. Yet Sanjay turned him down. He didn't want anyone to think that he was reluctant to assume the task that led to Aara's downfall.

That night, he stood in the wooden watchtower, anxiously watching the sky in hopes that he'd spot the same mysterious star Aara had seen. Yet thick clouds had moved in shortly after Calliope went down, so all he could see was the diffuse glow that its distant companions, Aether and Bacchae, made through the overcast. Even Gal was nowhere to be seen. The only light he saw was the luminescent glow of nightjewels floating on the bay. Sanjay ended his turn in the tower with nothing more interesting to report than an ocean monarch breaching the surface a short distance out beyond the reefs; with summer coming to a close and the waters becoming colder, the predators were more often to be seen off the Providence shores.

He'd become accustomed to the fact that he'd never see his mother again when Kaile came to him on Thursthree morning. He was sitting beside a fishing canoe, patching a tear in its mainsail, when she walked across the beach on all four and stopped beside him.

"Lo, Sanjay," she said. "How are you?"

Sanjay looked up at her, surprised by the casualness of her greeting. She hadn't spoken to him all season. Many of his friends had distanced themselves from him, but he'd missed her more than anyone else. Summer was a time for laying down with one's lover, and his bed had been cold and lonely without her. Sanjay had lately begun to wonder if he'd lost her for good, so her abrupt return caught him unprepared.

"Good, thanks. Just working on this boat." He tried to pretend that her appearance meant little to him, but his fores slipped as he attempted to slide a threaded fishbone needle through the sail patch. He nicked his right forefinger instead.

"Oh . . . watch yourself!" Kaile exclaimed as he hissed in pain. "Here . . . let me."

Before Sanjay could object, she bent closer, took his fore in her own, and gently slipped his finger into her mouth. Her lips formed a sly smile around his finger, and her eyes gleamed mischievously as her tongue, warm and moist, played with his fingertip. Sanjay felt himself becoming aroused. He shifted his hinds nervously, hoping she wouldn't notice, but if she did, she gave no sign.

"There," she said, withdrawing his finger from her mouth. "All better?" He nodded and she smiled. "So . . . I was just wondering if you'd like to go diving with me today?"

"Diving?" He'd done it before, but he wasn't trained the way she was. "Why?"

"Just because." A slight shrug. "We haven't seen much of each other lately, and I thought . . . well, it might be a way of getting back together again." Another smile. "Besides, my crew is running a little behind, and we could use a little extra help."

Sanjay looked across the keel of the upended canoe. Codi was squatting nearby, working with Johan to finish a new boat. He didn't have to ask whether they'd overheard the conversation; Codi and Johan traded an amused look, and then his mentor nodded. "Sure, go ahead. We can take care of things today."

Sanjay hesitated, but only for a moment. "Of course. I'd love to." Leaving the patch unfinished, he removed his tool kit from his vest and gave it to Johan for safekeeping. "After you," he said, and she smiled again and turned away, leading him on all fours down the beach toward the nearby docks.

He was just beginning to admire the way Kaile's body moved beneath the diaphanous shawl she wore over her halter and thong when she paused to let him catch up. At first he thought she was merely expressing fondness when she raised herself erect on her hinds and slid her fore through the crook of his elbow, but when he stood up so she could pull him closer as if to give him a kiss, she murmured something only he could hear.

"There's something I need to tell you," she whispered.

"What about?" Sanjay glanced around to see if anyone else was nearby. They weren't alone; others were walking past. The waterfront was busy as it always was this hour of the morning.

"Not here," she said softly. "Wait until we're out on the water, where no one can hear us." She paused, then added even more quietly, "It's about what Aara saw . . . I've seen it, too."

III

The fishing fleet bobbed on the warm blue waters of the bay, six canoes with sails furled and anchors lowered. This late in the season, it was necessary for them to

venture further away from shore in order for the divers to catch anything of significance; it would take the nine weeks of autumn, winter, spring for the breadfish
and scavengers born the previous yar to grow large enough to be caught. So the
boats had to spread out in order for their crews to bring home a decent catch; this
made for conditions suitable for a conversation that wouldn't be easily overheard.

Nevertheless, Sanjay had a hard time containing himself from asking Kaile
what she meant. Two others were on her boat: Sayra Bailee, a young girl who'd
become a diver only three yarn ago, and Ramos Circe, the boat captain. Neither
Sanjay or Kaile were very much concerned about Sayra—she wasn't terribly bright
and tended to keep to herself anyway—but Ramos was another matter entirely.
He was the Guardian appointed to the fleet to observe the fishermen and help
them maintain spiritual purity while they worked, and the fact that he was also
Beacon R'beca's son only made him more dangerous. They would have to be careful of him.

So he and Kaile had made small talk with Sayra as they paddled out into the bay,
saying nothing that really mattered while ignoring Ramos. They were about a half-
kilm from the reefs which separated the outer reaches of the bay from the Western
Channel when Ramos called for them to take down the sails and drop anchor. By
then their craft was a hundred rods from the next nearest boat, all the better for the
privacy they sought.

Sanjay watched as Kaile stood erect, dropped her shawl and, as an afterthought,
discarded her halter as well. She wore nothing now except her thong, which covered
very little of herself. He'd never forgotten how beautiful she was; with the bright red
sun on her light brown skin, she was as radiant as Gal herself. Taking off his vest
and kilt, he was glad that he'd decided to wear a thong himself that day; otherwise
his reaction would have been obvious to all. Sayra also chose to dive almost entirely nude, but at sixteen sixyarn, she hadn't yet blossomed into the full-breasted
womanhood Kaile had achieved at twenty-two.

In keeping with his position as a Guardian, Ramos pretended not to notice either
of the women. He waited while everyone buckled on diving belts and attached knife
sheaths and woven collection bags. "All right, over you go," he said once they were
ready. "Good hunting. May Gal keep you safe."

"Thank you." Raising her fores level with her shoulders, Kaile dove headfirst into
the water, disappearing with barely a splash. Sayra followed her a moment later, leaping from the other side of the canoe. Sanjay took a few more breaths to fill his lungs,
then he joined them, although not nearly as gracefully.

The instant he was submerged, he instinctively squinted, forcing shut the watertight nictitating membranes of his eyes that Gal in her wisdom had provided her
children. At the same time, the fingers of his fores and the toes of his hinds spread
apart, opening the webs between his digits which allowed his people to be fast and
effortless swimmers. Although he wasn't the practiced diver Kaile and Sayra were,
nonetheless he could stay underwater for three or four mins at a time, allowing him
to descend the twenty rods it took to reach the bottom. Although the sunlight faded,
he could still see Kaile clearly, swimming toward the seafern jungle that lay across
the bay floor.

It was here that they searched for scavengers, the spidery crustaceans which prowled among the ferns, feeding on the remains of nightjewels, breadfish, and other pelagic species who'd died and drifted to the bottom of the sea. Because they tended to blend into their environment, catching them was easier than finding them. Kaile was much better at this than he was; she'd collected two while he was still searching for one, and shook her head when he picked up a half-grown crustacean and showed it to her: *too small, let it go.*

His lungs were beginning to hurt by then, so he followed her back up to the boat and watched as she tossed her bag over the side and took another one from Ramos. The scavengers died when exposed to the air, of course, but it didn't render the tender flesh beneath their carapaces inedible. Kaile and Sanjay took a min or two to replenish their lungs, then they went down again. They ignored the fat breadfish which occasionally swam past, leaving them for the long-line anglers in other boats, and stayed clear of the reefs, which tended to be patrolled by seaknives who'd attack any humans who dared enter their domain.

Over the next couple of hours, they made seven descents, stopping for a few minutes after every second or third dive to float on their backs and rest a little. Sanjay noticed that, while Sayra stayed fairly close to the boat, Kaile was gradually leading him further away. Apparently Ramos expected her to do this, because he didn't seem to mind that they'd have to swim quite a few rods to reach the boat again. By late morning he'd decided to take a little nap, lying back against the stern with an arm across his eyes.

On their last dive, Ramos caught a full-grown scavenger, but when he held it up for Kaile to see, she surprised him by shaking her head. Instead, she pointed to the surface. Looking up, he saw that the keel of the boat was nowhere to be seen. Understanding what she meant, he dropped the scavenger, then rose with her to the top.

Once they were, she paddled over to him and, to his delighted surprise, draped her fores across his shoulders and pulled him close. "Kiss me," she whispered, and he was only too happy to oblige. "Good," she said once they'd parted. "Now hold me close while we talk. This way, everyone will think we're just making love and leave us alone."

By then, he'd almost forgotten the reason why she'd asked him to go diving with him. "Can't we do both?" he asked, playfully stroking her breasts.

"Maybe later." A wry smile that quickly vanished as she pushed his fores away. "For now, just listen. I was standing watch last night . . ."

In furtive tones quietly spoken while she allowed him to caress her, Kaile told Sanjay about her turn in the watchtower the night before. The night was clear, without the clouds which had ruined his own attempt to observe the sky, but she hadn't been making any particular effort to see anything unusual. All the same, it was in the darkest hour of the night, when the sisters were setting to the east and before Calliope had risen to the west, her eye was drawn to a peculiar movement in the zenith.

"A small star, quickly moving from east to west." As she said this, Kaile glanced up at the sky. "It went straight toward Gal, quickly at first, and then . . ."

She hesitated, looking down at Sanjay again. "Then what?" he asked.

"It slowed down and . . . Sanjay, it merged with Gal." Her mouth trembled as she said this, her eyes wide. "It was if the two became one. For just a few secs they became brighter, then Gal went back to normal."

Losing interest in her body, he let his fores fall to his sides, moving back and forth to keep himself afloat. "How could . . . ?"

"That's not all. I kept watching, and it was almost first light when something else happened. The little star parted from Gal again and went back in the direction it had come, but this time, instead of vanishing beyond the horizon, it started going faster and getting brighter, until it formed a tail. I heard thunder, like a storm was coming in, but there were no clouds. Then . . ."

Again, Kaile looked away, but this time not at the sky, but to the west. "It came down over there," she said softly, and when Sanjay followed her gaze, he saw that she was staring at the distant grey line that marked the shores of Cape Exile.

"Purgatory?" He could scarcely believe her. "Are you sure?"

Kaile glared at him. "Of course I'm sure!" she snapped, her voice rising a little as she swam back from him. "I'm telling you, I saw what I . . . !"

She stopped herself. Like Sanjay, she remembered that this was exactly what Aara had said when she'd defended herself before the deacons. And Sanjay had spent enough time in the tower himself to know that the view of Cape Exile from up there was excellent. Save for the high cliffs of Stone Bluff to the north and the summits of Mt. Lookout and Mt. Roundtop in the island's forest interior, there was no higher vantage point on Providence. Indeed, it was whispered among islanders that, from these places on clear nights, one could see faint, glimmering lights on the mainland, a sign that at least some of those who'd been banished there still lived, struggling to survive in the terrible place from which Gal had rescued her most devout followers.

"I believe you," he said quietly, and paddled closer to her again. "It sounds like you saw the same thing my mother did. Something like it, at least."

"No. That was *more* than what Aara saw." Glancing past him, she returned her fores to his shoulders once more. "Kiss me," she whispered. "Ramos is watching."

Again, their mouths came together. This time, though, Sanjay took little pleasure from it. He was thinking about something else. "Have you told anyone?" he said softly, his face against her wet hair.

"No." She sighed, and despite the warmth of the water, Sanjay felt her tremble. "After what happened to Aara, how could I?"

"No, of course not." As obedient to Gal as Kaile was, it would have been mad to repeat Aara's mistake. Deacon R'beca wouldn't have given any more credence to a second act of blasphemy than she had the first. He found himself wondering whether anyone else who'd recently stood watch might have seen the same thing Kaile did, but had likewise remained silent about it, for fear of following Aara Arkwright into exile. But if there had been any similar sightings, they would never know, unless . . .

"There's only one way we'll ever know," he said quietly, thinking aloud.

Kaile looked him straight in the eye. "How?" Then she realized what he meant, and her mouth fell open. "No . . . no, you can't be serious."

She was right. Even as the notion entered his mind, Sanjay thrust it away. None but those whom the deacons cast out of Providence ever made the dangerous crossing of the Western Channel. In fact, no one was allowed to leave the island except fishermen and those who used sailboats to travel from one coastal village to another.

All that was known of the rest of Eos came from ancient maps belonging to the First Children that had been handed down through the generations. They depicted great continents separated from one another by vast seas, with Providence the largest island of a small equatorial archipelago just off the coast of the landform known as Terra Minor. Gal had forbidden any exploration of these distant lands, though, so her children knew almost next to nothing about the rest of the world. Even the maps were closely held by the Council of Deacons, rarely seen by anyone else.

"No, you're right." He shook his head. "We can't do that. We'd . . ."

A shrill whistle from their boat, then Ramos's voice came to them from across the water. "All right, you two . . . enough of that! Back to work!"

Then Sayra called to them as well. "Yes, enough!" she yelled, childishly scolding them. "Save it for your bed, Sanjay, if she'll let you take her to it!"

Kaile forced a smile and raised a fore, but Sanjay wasn't about to let her go quite yet. "It's not a bad suggestion," he said. "I've missed you very much. Will you . . . ?"

She laughed, this time with genuine amusement, and pushed herself away from him. "Help me gather a few more scavengers," she said, "and I'll think about it."

Then she upended herself and, with a kick of her hinds, disappeared beneath the surface. But not before Sanjay caught the coy wink of an eye that told him that she'd already made up her mind.

IV

Kaile kept her side of the bargain. When Calliope was going down and the boats returned to shore, she came home with Sanjay.

Dayall was already there, working on dinner. He was surprised when Kaile walked in with his son, and it was the first time in weeks that Sanjay saw him smile. As if nothing had ever changed, he put another plate on the table, then pulled some more mockapples and vine melons from the pantry and put them out along with a jug of wine. Sanjay had brought home a scavenger he'd caught, and it wasn't long before it was steamed, shelled, and on the table. They talked about his diving trip while they ate, and for once Dayall's part of the conversation wasn't limited to monosyllables. For just a little while, it was as if everything had gone back to the way it had been before Aara left.

Once the meal was over and the kitchen was cleaned up, Dayall murmured something about how he thought it might be nice to spend the night at Garth's house. Sanjay politely objected, but he knew why his father was going over to his uncle's place. Dayall gathered a bedroll and took another jug from the wine cabinet, and was gone before Kaile could thank him for dinner.

Sanjay lit a fire and took the small wooden box of dreamer's weed down from the mantle. Kaile blew out the candles and they shared a pipe by firelight, saying little as they gazed into the flames and let the pipe smoke soften their senses. The night was cool, so he closed the window shutters. The fire warmed them, and it wasn't long before their fores wandered to each other's bodies. Soon they were curled up together upon the rug, rediscovering the pleasures they'd been denied all summer.

Kaile considered going home, but decided that the hour was late enough already that any excuses she might make for her absence would be transparent. Besides, it was time for her parents to learn that she wasn't going to leave Sanjay no matter what they thought of his family. Sanjay couldn't have agreed more. As the fire began to gutter out, he led her through the darkened house to his bedroom. They made love again before exhaustion caught up with them and, wrapped within warm blankets, they fell asleep in each other's arms.

Sanjay had no idea what hour it was when he felt a fore upon his shoulder and heard a voice quietly say his name. Slow to emerge from the depths of sleep, his first thought was that Kaile trying to rouse him for another round of lovemaking, but then the voice repeated itself and he realized that it wasn't her who was speaking to him. Kaile was still asleep beside him, while the person trying to wake him up was crouched next to his bed. He opened his eyes and turned his head, and in the wan amber light of the sisters seeping in through a crack between the closed shutters of his bedroom window, he saw Aara.

He jerked upright in bed, not quite believing what he was seeing. Before he could say anything, though, his mother lay a fore across his mouth. "Shhh . . . be quiet!" she hissed, barely more than a whisper. "Don't wake your father."

"Sanjay?" Kaile twisted beside him, still more asleep than awake. "Sanjay, what's going on?"

Aara's eyes widened, her mouth falling open in dismay. "Is that Kaile?" she asked softly, as if it would be anyone else. Still stunned by his mother's presence, he gave a dumb nod and she sighed. "Oh, no . . . I wasn't expecting this."

"Aara?" Kaile woke up as suddenly as Sanjay had, and was just as astonished. "Aara, what are you . . . ?"

"Hush." Aara lifted a finger to her mouth. "Keep your voice down. I don't want Dayall to know I'm here."

Kaile went silent, but Sanjay could feel her trembling beside him. "He's not here," he whispered. "He's spending the night at Garth's house."

Aara let out her breath in relief. "Good . . . that's good. Wait a sec."

She moved away from the bed, and a moment later there came the tiny sparks and soft sounds of firestarter flints being scratched together. The fish-oil lamp on his clothes chest flickered to life, and now they could see her clearly. Aara wore the same black robe she'd been wearing the last time Sanjay had seen her; although its hood was drawn up over her head, he could see the facial scar left by R'beca's knife, a reminder that she was an exile who could be killed if anyone found her back on Providence.

The thought must have occurred to her as well, because Aara's expression was wary when she turned to them again. "Kaile," she said quietly, "I can trust you, can't I? You're not going to run straight to the Guardians, are you?" She looked straight at the girl, meeting her gaze with suspicious eyes.

Kaile hesitated just long enough for Sanjay to realize that she was wrestling with her conscience. "No . . . no, I won't," she said at last, much to his relief. "I'm not Aiko or Jak. I didn't want you to be banished. But Aara, why . . . ?"

"I can't tell you that. Not now, anyway. No time." A nod toward the closed window. "It'll be morning soon, and we must be gone by then." A pause. "Sanjay, I mean . . .

Kaile, you're staying here, and I'm going to have to ask your word not to tell anyone that I was here or where . . ."

She stopped herself, but not before Sanjay knew what she meant to say next. "You want me to go with you?" he asked, and she nodded. "To Purgatory?" Again, a solemn nod. He felt a cold sensation in the pit of his stomach. "Why?"

Before Aara could respond, Kaile spoke up again. "I saw a light in the sky last night while I was on watch. Just like the one you saw, but instead it merged with Gal before it came down on Cape Exile. That has to do with this, doesn't it?"

A grim smile. "Yes it does." The smile disappeared and Aara was thoughtful for a moment. "How many people know you spent the night here?"

"My parents. Dayall." Kaile lay a fore on Sanjay's shoulder. "Just about everyone who saw us leave the beach together after we went diving yesterday."

Aara sighed again, this time shaking her head. "So the Guardians will question you when he goes missing. I don't want you to have to face them or R'beca on my account. I can't make you come with us, but . . ."

"No. I want to come."

Startled, Sanjay stared at her. She met his gaze and gave him a brief nod. Yes, she was aware of what she was getting into. And she was doing it anyway. "Very well," Aara said as she turned away again. "Get up and get dressed, and be quick about it. I've got a boat waiting for us."

"A boat from Purgatory? Who . . . ?"

"Never mind that now. We're leaving in two mins."

Before Sanjay could ask any further questions, his mother left the room. No more lamps were lit, but as he and Kaile climbed out of bed, the soft creak of the pantry door told him that she was gathering food. He wondered why she'd bother to do so, but there was no time to ask.

"Are you sure you want to do this?" he asked Kaile as he dug into his chest to give her a sarong, tunic, and calf boots that would be warmer than the thin shawl she'd worn yesterday. Autumn was only a couple of days away, and they would be travelling far from home. "You know what this means, don't you?" he added as he put on nearly identical clothes.

Kaile didn't say anything, but the silent nod she gave him told all that he needed to know. For better or worse, they were about to join his mother in Purgatory.

V

The sisters were beginning to set when the three of them slipped out through the back door. Kaile had mentioned that it was Johan's turn to stand watch, which Sanjay took as a good sign; he knew that his best friend often stole a few hours of sleep in the tower so that he'd be rested enough to go to work the next day. In any case, though, they avoided the streets as much as they could, and instead quietly made their way on all fours through shadowed alleys between cottages, sheds, and shops until they reached the forest on Childstown's eastern border. No one spotted them; the town was asleep.

Aara led Sanjay and Kaile to the foot path leading south to Mountain Creek, which flowed through the forest from Mt. Lookout to the northeast. The trail would take them to the coastal estuary where the creek drained into the bay. It was there, Aara told them, the boat which had carried her back across the channel was awaiting her return.

"You came over tonight?" Although they were now out of earshot from the village, Sanjay was careful to keep his voice down. "How were you not spotted?"

The forest they walked through was dark, the black fronds of the umbrella palms and sunshade trees forming a shadowed canopy which blotted out all but thin slivers of sisterlight. All the same, Sanjay could see the soft smile that played across Aara's face. "The exiles have ways of getting here," she said. "You'll see."

"But the monarchs . . ."

"That's . . . something else entirely." Her smile disappeared. "Now hush. No more questions."

Sanjay and Kaile exchanged glances, but obediently fell silent. Sanjay knew better than to argue with his mother. Still, he thought as he shifted the straps of his belly pack, she was being a little too mysterious about all this.

About three kilms from Childstown, they reached the end of the trail. Through the wild roseberry and bambu that grew along the shore, the estuary lay before them, its waters faintly shimmering with the reflections from Aether and Bacchae. From the other side of a genesis plant that rose beside the trail, Sanjay could make out a catamaran resting upon the narrow beach. As they approached the genesis plant, though, he heard a soft voice, male yet unlike any he'd heard before.

"The specimen appears to be fully mature, approximately one-point-eight meters in height, its width . . . call it a little less than one meter at its base. As with all pseudonative species, its leaves are matte-black in pigmentation, a genetically engineered adaptation to the primary's lesser magnitude and, in this instance, generation of cyanobacteria and the subsequent production of atmospheric oxygen and nitrogen. Its form clearly indicates its descent from the giant hosta, albeit considerably larger. Altogether, it appears that the alteration of its basic genetic pattern has been remarkably successful, especially considering the . . ."

"We're here," Aara said, raising her voice just a little.

Realizing that he was no longer alone, the person speaking abruptly stopped talking, but not before Sanjay spotted the individual to whom the voice belonged. Taller than any of them—as tall, in fact, as the genesis plant he stood beside—he stood upright on his hinds, his figure cloaked by the hooded cloak which covered him from head to toe. Indeed, as they came closer, Sanjay was surprised to see that, beneath the cowl, he wore a dark veil across the lower part of his face, a mask that completely hid his features.

Yet it was his voice, in the brief moments in which Sanjay heard it, that intrigued him the most. Although he'd been speaking Inglis, many of the words he'd used were unfamiliar; Sanjay had clearly heard what he'd said, but didn't understand its meaning. And the accent was strange: sharper, with an odd inflection of the syllables.

"Oh, good. You made it back." The figure stepped away from the genesis plant, and for an instant Sanjay noticed something held in his right fore before it disappeared within the cloak. "No trouble, I hope?"

"None. We got out of there without being spotted. But—" Aara hesitated, then stood erect to indicate Kaile "—I had to bring someone else. This is Kaile, my son's betrothed. She was with him when I found them. We couldn't leave her behind."

A disgruntled sigh from the other side of the veil. "Are you sure? This could complicate things, you know."

"If she stays, the Guardians will know that she was with Sanjay when he disappeared, because they were seen together all day yesterday and last night. They'll try to work the truth out of her, and R'beca is very good at that. With any luck, my husband and her family will believe that the two of them simply ran away for awhile, as young people sometimes do."

Sanjay now understood why Aara had taken food from the pantry. Once he and Kaile were found to be missing, which was inevitable, the most likely explanation would be that they'd taken off into the wilds for a little while, perhaps to a little lean-to shed Sanjay had secretly built in the mountains. Unbonded lovers occasionally did this when they wished to be free of the prying eyes of family and neighbors; it wasn't a practice condoned by the Disciples, but tolerated nonetheless. If they were fortunate, no one would search for them for a little while, preferring to give them their privacy while they rehearsed their future roles as a bonded couple.

"Very well. If we have no choice." The figure nodded his hooded head toward the boat. "Teri is waiting for you on the boat. If you'll give me a second . . . a sec, I mean . . . to cut a leaf . . ."

He stepped back toward the genesis plant. "Stop!" Kaile snapped, raising her fores. "You can't do that!"

The stranger halted, looked around at her again. "I'm sorry, but what . . . ?"

"It's forbidden to touch genesis plants." Kaile was horrified by what she'd seen, but also perplexed. "It's in the Word . . . everyone knows that!"

Sanjay was just as confused. One of the most basic tenants of the Word of Gal was that even wild plants such as this must never be harvested. They were the means by which Gal had created Eos, and touching them without the supervision of a deacon during the spring and autumn solstice rituals was considered a sacrilege. Every child was taught this the first time they were taken into the forest for their first lessons in woodlore. How could this person be unaware of this?

"My apologies. I . . ." The stranger stopped. "Perhaps I should introduce myself. I'm Nathan."

This was a common enough name among islanders. In Galian lore, it was said to have belonged to the archangel who beseeched Gal to carry the Chosen Children from Erf to the new world. Yet Sanjay noticed that he didn't mention a family name as well. "Sanjay Arkwright," he replied, and gave a formal bow, clasping his fores together as he bent forward from his knees.

"I know." When Nathan returned the bow, it was in a peculiar fashion: stiff-legged and from the waist, fores still hidden by his cloak. "I've been wanting to meet you every since your mother told me about you. In fact, you're the very reason why we're here."

"I am?"

"We don't have time to discuss this," Aara said. "Calliope will be coming up soon. We need to be away before we can be spotted from town." She pointed to the nearby boat. "Hurry, please."

They followed her to the beach, where a man about Aara's age was already raising the catamaran's sail. As they walked toward the boat, Sanjay noticed that Nathan remained upright, apparently preferring to walk on his hinds even though the others dropped to all fours. His gait was also slow, as if each step was an effort. Was he crippled? Perhaps, but if so, why risk undertaking a sea journey?

He tried to put all this aside as he helped his mother and Aara stow the belly packs they'd brought with them, then helped the captain push the boat out into the water. He could now see the reason why the boat had been able to travel across the channel without being detected. Its wooden hull, mast, benches, and oars were painted black, and even the sails had been dyed the same way. Against the dark waters of the bay at night, the craft would have been very hard to spot.

He wondered if the inhabitants of Purgatory had ever crossed the channel before, using this very same boat. Perhaps. There were rumors that exiles had sometimes returned to Providence for one nefarious reason or another; every so often, a relative or close friend who'd been left behind had disappeared for no accountable reason. But maybe . . .

"All right, everyone settled in?" The captain, who'd given his name as Teri Collins, glanced around from his seat at the tiller. Sanjay and Kaile had taken seats amidships, while Aara and Nathan sat in the bow—Nathan awkwardly, hunched slightly forward with his hinds stretched out straight before him, still covered by the long folds of his cloak. "Very well, then," he said as he used an oar to push away from the shore, "Sanjay, raise sail, please."

Sanjay turned around to grasp the line dangling from the mast and pulled it down, unfurling the black sail. The tide was beginning to go out and the morning breeze was starting to come in; the sail bellowed outward and the boat quietly slipped away, its outrigger skimming the water surface.

"We need to be silent now," Aara whispered, bending forward to speak to Sanjay and Kaile. "No talking, no movement, until we're well past the reefs. Understood?"

Sanjay nodded, as did Kaile. It was still dark and Calliope hadn't yet risen. If they were lucky, no one in Childstown would see a boat heading out into the bay. Nonetheless, he hoped that Johan was asleep in the tower.

As the boat entered the bay, though, and the town came within sight, no lights appeared within its windows, nor was there the gong of the warning bell. Childstown remained peaceful, unknowing of the intrusion which had happened during the night. Teri must have sailed these waters before, because he accurately steered the boat through the break in the reefs which lay a couple of kilms offshore. The hull sliced through the glowing nightjewels and scattered the curious knifefish who'd ventured close to the boat. High above, Gal observed their passage with an unblinking and omnipresent eye.

Looking up at her, Sanjay hoped that Gal would forgive her children for their transgressions. Providence had become a long, black shape gradually receding behind them, its inland mountain range rising as three low humps. He'd rarely before been this far out on the channel, and only then in the light of day. The sea was a dangerous place to be at night.

He prayed that the monarchs wouldn't notice them.

His prayers went unanswered.

VI

"Monarch," Teri said. "Off starboard bow."

He spoke calmly, yet there was no missing the urgency of his tone. Sanjay turned to look. At first he saw nothing; the sea and the night both were still dark. Then, about three hundred rods from the boat, he caught sight of a dorsal fin, light grey and shaped like the tip of a knife, jutting upward from the dark water. It was running parallel to them, neither approaching nor moving away, as if the massive form to which it belonged was swimming along with the catamaran. Tracking, observing, waiting for the moment to strike.

To the east, the first scarlet haze of dawn had appeared upon the horizon, tinting the curled gauze of the high clouds with shades of orange and red. He'd hoped that, with the passing of night, the danger of being noticed by an ocean monarch would pass as well. But this one hadn't yet descended to the channel's lowest depths. It was still prowling the waters midway between Providence and Cape Exile in search of prey.

And now it had found them.

There was a harpoon lying on the deck at his hinds. Sanjay started to reach down to pick it up, but Teri shook his head. "No need," he said, his fores steady on the tiller. "Just wait." He glanced at Aara. "Move to the center of the boat, Aara. Everyone, hang on."

Sanjay stared at him in disbelief. Surely he didn't think they could possibly outrun a monarch? Many had tried to do this, but they'd only succeeded if they were already far enough away that it couldn't catch up . . . and this one was pacing them. Their only hope of survival lay in using a harpoon against it when it attacked.

He began to reach for the harpoon again, but then his mother, who'd walked back from the bow, lay a fore against his wrist. "Just watch," she said quietly. "The same thing happened to us on the way over."

"A monarch attacked you last night?" He had trouble believing her. "How did . . . ?"

"Wait and watch." Aara smiled as she squatted across from him and Kaile, then nodded toward Nathan.

The stranger remained in the bow. Until then, Sanjay hadn't taken much notice of the long object wrapped in waterproof bambu cloth that lay on the deck before him. Picking it up, Nathan removed the covering, revealing something of the likes Sanjay had never seen: a slender, rod-like thing, broad in the center but tapering to what appeared to be a hollow tube at one end, with a handle fitted with a small ring projecting from its lower side. Its surface gleamed dully in the wan light of the coming dawn, and Sanjay realized to his surprise that it was made entirely of metal: very rare, and almost never found in such a quantity.

"What is that?" Kaile asked.

No one answered her. Nathan rose from his bench and, hinds firmly planted against the gentle rocking of the boat, cradled the object in his fores. Turning away from them, he lowered his hood and pulled down his veil. Sanjay couldn't see his face, though, only the short-cropped red hair on the back of his head.

"Coming at us!" Teri snapped.

Sanjay looked in the direction the captain pointed. The monarch had veered toward the catamaran, its fin creating a frothy furrow through the water. Fifty rods from the boat, the fin abruptly disappeared beneath the surface. Nathan knew that the monarch was diving in preparation for an attack, but even as he grabbed the harpoon and stood erect to do battle, he heard a faint, high-pitched whine from the object Nathan was holding. From the corner of his eye, he saw that the stranger had raised it level with his shoulders and appeared to be peering straight down the length of its tube.

Sanjay barely had time to wonder what Nathan was doing when the monarch breached the surface. A massive wall of flesh, grey on top and white across the bottom, the leviathan shot up from the water only a few rods from the starboard side. Large as the boat itself, its mouth was wide enough to swallow a human whole and lined with rows of serrated teeth. Sanjay caught a glimpse of black eyes, small yet malevolent, and with an angry scream he raised the harpoon in both fores . . .

It was as if a beam of starlight had erupted from the hollow end of Nathan's object, a thin white ray which briefly and silently erased the darkness. It lanced straight into the underside of the monarch's mouth, and for an instant Sanjay saw it reappear within the creature's jaws. A smell like fish being broiled as the beam burned through the monarch's head and a loud, agonized groan, then the monarch fell back into the water, making a tremendous splash that threw a wave over the side of the boat.

The monarch was still spasmodically flopping on the surface, its fins and tail thrashing back and forth, when Nathan pointed his weapon—for this was obviously what it was—at it again. Once more, the thin beam cut into the creature's head, this time between the eyes. The monarch jerked and then became still, a dying mass floating on the water.

"A gift from Gal . . ." Kaile whispered.

"No." For the first time since they'd left shore, Nathan spoke. "Not Gal. A plasma beam rifle."

Sanjay hadn't the slightest idea what he meant by this, but as Nathan turned to him, he suddenly didn't care. Nathan's cloak had fallen open, and now he could see the rest of the stranger's body: forward-jointed legs and slender hinds, a waist that was a little thicker, a neck not as long as his own. The breeze caught the robe and pulled it back from the stranger's shoulders, revealing long-fingered fores that lacked webbing between the digits.

But it was his face which startled Sanjay the most. Except for his red beard, the open nostrils of his nose, and eyes which possessed visible pupils, Nathan's face was nearly the same as that of the Teacher.

Kaile whimpered, clutching Sanjay's shoulder in fear. Sanjay stared at the apparition before them, not knowing what to say or do. When he glanced at Aara, though, he saw the calm and knowing smile on her face. She'd been aware of this all along.

"Who are you?" he asked.

"You won't believe this—" Nathan stopped, then corrected himself "—but I hope you eventually will. Sanjay, I'm your cousin."

VII

Nathan refused to say any more about himself for the rest of the journey across the channel. He spent the remaining hours sitting quietly in the bow, rifle propped up on his forward-jointed knees, an enigmatic smile on his face as he politely listened to the younger man prod him with questions. He finally raised a fore and shook his head.

"Enough," he said. "You're just going to have to wait until we reach shore. Once we're there and we meet up with my friends . . ."

"There's more of you?" Sanjay stared at him.

". . . then I'll tell you everything you want to know."

"So there's other Teachers like you." Kaile was no longer as fearful as she'd been, but she continued to hold tight to Sanjay's fore.

A dry laugh. "I'm not a Teacher, and neither are they. We're human, just like you . . . only a bit different, that's all."

"Then why do you look like . . . ?"

"Be patient. All will be explained." He then turned away and spoke no more. Sanjay looked at his mother, and Aara silently shook her head. She wouldn't tell them anything either, nor would Teri. They would just have to wait.

Calliope came up a little while later, revealing the mainland before them. By the time the sun was high above the channel, they could clearly make out the black forests that lay beyond the coast, gradually rising to meet the inland mountain range known as the Great Wall. This was the most anyone could see of Cape Exile from Providence, and although it soon stretched across the visible horizon, Sanjay was surprised to see how much the eastern peninsula of Terra Minor resembled Providence. He'd been told since childhood that anyone who dared to approach Purgatory would hear the mournful cries of the banished, but instead the only sound that reached his ears were the screech of seabirds spiraling above the coastal shallows.

And once they were only a couple of kilms away, he saw more than that.

The white sand beach had just become visible when sails came into view, fishing boats plying the offshore waters. The men and women within them raised their fores in greeting as their catamaran sailed past, and Teri did the same in return.

"Wave back," Aara quietly urged her son. "We're among friends."

Sanjay gave her a doubtful look, but did as he was told. He noticed that Nathan made no effort to hide his features or misshapen limbs. His hood remained lowered as he smiled at the fishermen, and although a couple of them stared at him, no one seemed surprised by his appearance, let alone regard him as an emissary of Gal. Indeed, they treated him as if he was what he'd claimed himself to be: just another person, just one who looked a bit different.

There was no settlement visible from the water, yet canoes and sailboats were lined up on the shore, with nearly as many people around them as there would be on the Providence waterfront. A couple of men waded out to meet their boat; they grasped its sides and pulled it the rest of the way onto the beach, and one of them helped Nathan climb out. As before, Sanjay noticed that Nathan walked with a stiff, almost arthritic gait. It occurred to him that the stranger not only wouldn't walk on all fours, but in fact could not. He always stood on his hinds, and never used his fores for anything except grasping and holding objects. Yet it seemed as if there was a heavy load on his back, for he walked with a perpetual slump, shoulders hunched forward and head slightly bowed.

Aara caught him staring at Nathan, and walked around the beached catamaran to stand beside him. "He was born that way," she murmured, "but he's not a freak of nature. It's not polite to stare."

"He's . . . not from here, is he?" he whispered, and Aara shook her head. "Then where is he from?"

"You'll find out soon enough. Come."

With Kaile walking behind them, Aara led Sanjay from the beach. There were no structures on the shore, yet a trellis gate at the edge of the tree line marked the opening of a raised boardwalk leading into the woods. Nathan was already ahead of them; he'd just reached the gate when a bearded older man emerged from the boardwalk. He rose up on his hinds to greet Nathan; instead of the customary exchange of bows, they clasped each other's right fore, a gesture Sanjay had never seen before. Then he turned to Aara, Sanjay, and Kaile.

"Aara . . . so glad to see that you've returned. Any trouble along the way?"

"Not at all." Apparently Aara didn't think that a close encounter with a monarch was worth mentioning. They exchanged bows, then she raised a fore to Sanjay and Kaile. "Let me introduce my son, Sanjay, and his betrothed, Kaile Otomo . . . it was necessary to bring her along, I'm afraid."

"I'll trust that it was." A kindly smile. "No worries. I'm just happy you managed to get away safely." The older man dropped to all fours to approach Sanjay and Kaile. "Welcome to First Town. I'm Benjam Hallahan, the mayor. Pleased to meet you both."

"An honor to meet you." Sanjay rose to offer a formal bow, as did Kaile. "I'm sorry, but I don't understand . . . where did you say we are?"

"First Town." Benjam's smile became an amused grin. "We don't use the name Purgatory. In fact, it's what this place was called before the Stormyarn. The Disciples . . ." He shrugged. "Let's just say for the moment that most of what you were taught is wrong."

Hearing this, Sanjay instinctively glanced about to see if anyone was listening. Aara noticed this and laughed. "Don't worry, there are no Guardians here. No deacons, either. In fact, I don't think you'll find any Galians in First Town."

"We have a shrine," Benjam added, "but only a few people worship there. Mainly older folks who've come here from Providence as exiles and still have trouble accepting the truth."

"What truth is that?" Kaile asked.

Benjam started to reply, then he paused to gaze over his shoulder at Nathan. The stranger shook his head, and the mayor looked back at her and Sanjay again. "That's a question with a long and difficult answer," he said, and his smile faded. "I'm afraid some of us have recently learned a few things we ourselves didn't know before." His eyes met Sanjay's. "One of them involves you, my friend."

"Me? How am I . . . ?"

"Maybe we should find a place where we can speak a little more privately." When he spoke, Nathan seemed a bit more weary than he'd been before they'd come ashore. "And more comfortably."

"Of course. You must be exhausted." Benjam went down on all fours to lead them toward the boardwalk. "This way, please."

VIII

First Town was located deep in the forest, on a low plateau that had been cleared of the surrounding trees. When Sanjay reached the stairs leading to it at the end of the boardwalk, he was amazed by what the forest and adjacent marsh concealed from the channel. The settlement was larger than Childstown and, if anything, more prosperous. The houses and workshops were bigger, more solidly constructed; they had glazed windows and quite a few even had second floors, something he'd never seen before. Elevated aqueducts supplied the town with fresh water from mountain springs; he saw waterwheels turning millstones and lathes, and Benjam told him that a buried network of ceramic pipes fed water into individual homes and businesses. It was the last day of summer, but there seemed to be no anxious rush to prepare for the cold weeks ahead. Townspeople were calmly going about their daily affairs, and there seemed to be more shortage of children playing in the schoolyard.

He'd been expecting a crude camp filled with starving peasants mourning their banishment from Providence, not a content village inhabited by happy, well-fed people. There was a Galian shrine, just as Benjam said, but it was small and neglected. The genesis plant which grew beside it appeared to be regularly tended, but it wasn't cordoned off by a ring of stones. One look at it, and it was clear that the Disciples had little or no authority here.

What was more surprising were a row of pens near the community gardens. Inside them were flocks of what appeared to be large, flightless birds, fat and white, which incessantly clucked and pecked at the soil. Never having seen the like before, Sanjay and Kaile stopped to stare at them, causing the others to come to a halt.

"Chickens," Benjam said as he walked up behind them. "And those are turkeys." He pointed to another flock of larger and even fatter birds in another pen. "We raise them for food."

"Food?" Kaile asked, and Benjam nodded. "Where did you find them? There's nothing like that on Providence."

"No, there isn't. They're not even indigenous to Eos . . . they came from Earth."

"Erf?" Sanjay drew back from the pens.

"No . . . *Earth*." Again, Benjam smiled. "Come. You've got a lot to learn."

Sanjay glanced at Aara. His mother gave him a knowing nod, but said nothing. Yet as they turned to follow Benjam again, Sanjay noticed that, while he and Kaile had been examining the . . . the *chickens* and *turkeys* . . . Nathan had disappeared. Looking around, he saw the stranger walking away, apparently heading for another part of the village. A few passersby gave him curious glances, but no one seemed to be startled by his appearance. It was obvious that he was known here.

Benjam brought them to a large, slope-sided building near the center of town. Opening its front door, he led them into what appeared to be a meeting hall. With its carefully arranged rows of mats facing a high rear wall whose stained glass windows formed an abstract pattern, it bore superficial resemblance to a shrine, yet there was no alter, no crèche containing a sleeping Teacher, only a low table. The mayor gestured to the front row of mats, and once Sanjay, Kaile, and Aara were seated, he squatted before them in front of the table.

"Nathan will be back soon," he began, speaking to Sanjay and Kaile, "but before he does, I'll get started by telling you what Aara learned when she came here. Namely, that much of what you grew up accepting as fact is . . . well, to put it bluntly . . . wrong."

"Heresy." Folding her hinds beneath her, Kaile crossed her fores and glared at him.

"No. Not heresy . . . history. History that has been lost to generations of people living on Providence." Benjam paused. "You grew up in a proper Galian household, didn't you?" he asked, and Kaile nodded. "You can't be blamed for believing that anything contrary to the Word of Gal is blasphemous. But you'll have to believe me when I tell you that the Word is a distorted version of what actually occurred many yarn ago, and that the true events are more complex than anything you've been taught."

Kaile scowled and started to rise from her matt, but Sanjay stopped her with his fore. "Let's just listen to what he says; we've come all this way. Maybe it'll explain what you and Aara saw."

Kaile hestitated, then reluctantly sat down again. Benjam let out his breath, then patiently went on. "First . . . to begin, Erf is not what you've been led to believe it is, a netherworld filled with damned souls. It's called Earth, and it's a planet much like Eos, only about one-third smaller. It revolves around a single star called Sol which is much larger and brighter than Calliope . . . it's white, not red, and Earth is much further away from it than Eos is from Calliope."

"Did Gal create sisters for it as well?" Sanjay asked.

Benjam shook his head. "No, there's only that one sun . . . and Gal didn't create either Calliope or Sol, or even Earth or Eos for that matter. They existed long, long before Gal . . . because Gal itself isn't a deity, but rather a vessel created by humans. Our own ancestors, in fact."

Kaile hissed between her teeth. "Blasphemy!"

"Listen to him." Aara glared at her. "He's telling the truth. Go on, Benjam."

"Gal is a vessel . . . what people like Nathan call a starship." Benjam continued. "About 440 sixyarn ago . . . or years, the way his people reckon time . . . our ancestors built a ship called *Galactique* for the purpose of carrying the seed of men and women to this world, which they knew was capable of sustaining life."

"Why?" Unlike Kaile, Sanjay wasn't upset, but intrigued, by what he was hearing.

"The reasons are complicated." Benjam frowned and shook his head. "I'm not sure I completely understand them myself. Nathan and his companions have told us that *Galactique* was built because the people of that time believed that life on

Earth was in peril of being destroyed, and they wanted to assure the survival of the human race." A crooked smile. "It's still there, but it isn't a terrible place filled with tortured souls. The Chosen Children, as we call them, were simply the seed of those who'd spent years building the ship. In fact, they resembled Nathan himself . . . those we call the Children were altered before birth so that they could live comfortably on Eos, which *Galactique* had changed to make suitable for human life."

"Then Gal . . . I mean, *Galactique*—" Sanjay stumbled over the unfamiliar syllables "—is our creator."

"Just as the Word says," Kaile quietly added.

"*Galactique* created our people, yes, and also the world as we know it . . . but it is not a deity. Those of us here in First Town and the other mainland settlements . . . yes, there are other villages like this one, although not as large . . . knew this even before Nathan and his companions arrived a few weeks ago. People here have long been aware of the fact that we're descended from the human seed . . . the sperm and eggs, as they call it . . . transported from Earth aboard *Galactique*, and that Eos itself was a much different place before *Galactique* transformed it over the course of nearly 300 sixyarn into the world we know now."

Benjam pointed beyond the open door of the meeting hall. "Those birds you saw, the chickens and turkeys . . . they were brought here, too, in just the same way. In fact, everything else on Eos . . . the forests, the insects, the fruit we eat, the fish in our seas . . . is descended from material carried from Earth by *Galactique*, then altered to make them suitable for life here."

"Nathan calls this 'genetic engineering'," Aara said, slowly reciting words she herself had apparently learned only recently. "It's really very complicated. I'm not certain I understand it myself."

"It all was done aboard *Galactique* during the time it circled Eos." Benjam nodded in agreement. "Nathan and his people have told us that, during this same time . . . hundreds of yarn, longer than our own history . . . *Galactique* also deposited across Eos dozens of tiny craft called 'biopods', which in turn contained the genesis plants. Eos was a much different place back . . . its atmosphere was thin and unbreathable, and the only life here was insignificant . . . lichen and such. The genesis plants were scattered all over Eos, and as they took root and grew to maturity, they absorbed the atmosphere which was already here and replaced it with the air we breathe while also making it thick enough to retain the warmth of Calliope and her sisters. Once that was accomplished, the plants distributed the seeds of all the other plants we know, none of which existed on Eos before *Galactique* came. Other biopods followed them, bringing down the infant forms of fish, birds, insects, and animals which had been gestated aboard the ship. Once they were here . . ."

"Then came you," Nathan said.

He'd entered the room unnoticed, and he wasn't alone. Looking around, Sanjay saw that he was accompanied by a man and a woman, both walking upright on forward-jointed legs and curiously small feet. This time, though, instead of the hooded cloak that had concealed his form on Providence, Nathan wore a strange outfit over his clothes, a jointed framework of pipes and molded plates made of some metallic material that softly whirred and clicked with every move he made. The other two wore similar outfits.

Nathan noticed that Sanjay was staring at him. "It's called an exoskeleton," he said as he walked over to where he and the others were seated. "The surface gravity on Eos . . . the force that causes you to stay on the ground . . . is half-again higher than it is on Earth. Without these to help us stand and move about, we'd get tired very quickly. Our hearts would have to work harder as well, and before long it would be very unhealthy for us to live here. The exoskeletons compensate for this."

Sanjay stood erect to tentatively lay a fore on the exoskeleton's chest plate. It was hard and cool, reminding him somewhat of a scavenger's carapace. "Why weren't you wearing this on Providence?"

"Unfortunately, it doesn't float. If I'd fallen out of the boat, it would have dragged me to the bottom. Leaving it behind was the wisest thing to do." A wry smile. "Fortunately, I'm in pretty good shape. I could handle the stress for a little while." Nathan turned to the two who'd walked in with him. "Let me introduce my companions. This is Marilyn Sanyal, and he's Russell Coyne. Like myself, they're related to people you may already know . . ."

"I have a friend named Johan Sanyal. And my father's family name is Coyne."

"Is it really?" Russell appeared to be Sanjay's age, differences notwithstanding. He grinned as he extended an oddly-shaped fore, then apparently thought better of it and bowed instead. "I believe that makes us relatives."

Sanjay didn't return the bow. Instead, he looked at Nathan. "You said on the boat that you and I are cousins. Are you also . . . ?"

"Even more so than Russell, yes. My last name is Arkwright . . . Nathan Arkwright II." He raised a fore before Sanjay could ask another question. "There's a lot of complicated family history involved here, but you should know that we both bear the last name of the person who was responsible for *Galactique* in the first place, and I was given his first name as well." He touched his hair, then pointed to Sanjay's. "Same hair color, in fact . . . it's hereditary."

"So you're telling us that Sanjay comes from the seed of someone on Erf who was brought here by Gal . . ." Kaile began.

"No." Nathan turned to her. "Not the way you're saying it, at least. As Benjam just told you, Erf is a world called Earth, and Gal is a starship called *Galactique* that's still in orbit above Eos. Over time, their names were shortened, just as their true nature had been forgotten."

"Otherwise, you've got it right." Marilyn appeared to be a little older than her, although not quite as old as Aara. Of the three, she alone had skin the same dark shade as the native inhabitants; the others were nearly as pale as the Teacher. "What's your family name, if I may ask?"

Kaile hesitated. "Otomo."

Marilyn pulled a small flat object from a pocket from the clothes she wore beneath the exoskeleton. Holding the object in her left fore, she tapped her finger a few times against it, then studied it for a moment. "There was a Katsumi Otomo among those who built *Galactique*," she said. "A propulsion engineer . . . never mind what that means. She was your ancestor . . . one of them, at least."

"Everyone you know, everyone on this world, is descended from at least two of the two hundred men and women who contributed reproductive material to *Galactique's* gene pool," Russell said. "First, the ship distributed genesis plants across the planet, which in turn introduced cyanobacteria into the atmosphere to reduce the carbon dioxide content, raise the oxygen-nitrogen ratio, and thereby make Eos human-habitable through ecopoiesis . . ."

"Russ . . . don't get technical," Nathan said quietly. "They're not ready for that yet." Russell nodded, albeit reluctantly, and Nathan went on. "The point is, although we don't look alike, we're humans just as you are. *Galactique* altered the embryonic forms of your immediate ancestors so that they could survive this planet's higher gravity while also making them amphibious . . ."

"And you're telling me not to get technical," Russell said, raising an eyebrow.

"So the word is correct," Kaile said. "Even if what you say is true, it still means that Gal is our creator."

Nathan shared an uncertain glance with Russell and Marilyn. "Well . . . yes, I suppose you could say that, but not in the sense you mean."

"But she's in our sky every day and every night, watching every move we make." Kaile remained adamant. "She's been there for as long as our mothers and grand-mothers and great-grandmothers . . ."

"A matriarchal mythology as well as a society," Marilyn said softly. "Interesting."

Nathan ignored her. "Once humans were brought down here, *Galactique* moved into a geosynchronous orbit—" he caught himself "—a place in the sky which is al-ways above the same place on the ground, where it was supposed to function as a . . . um, a source of information for the original colony. That's why you can see it all the time. It rotates at the same angular velocity as Eos itself, so it's always directly above you."

Russell picked up the thread. "The ship also carried with it two . . . ah, artificial beings, what we call robots . . . which were meant to be your instructors. They raised the first children who came here, teaching them how to survive . . ."

"You mean the Teacher . . . there were two?" Sanjay said.

"Yes, there were." Benjam had been quiet for awhile; now he spoke up. "There was one here in First Town like the one in Provincetown, along with another Trans-former." He looked over at Russell. "Which, as you say, manufactured from blocks of the material we call Galmatter the first tools used by our people."

"Correct." Russell was obviously relieved that someone here understood what he'd been trying to explain. "The Transformers are what we call three-dimensional laser manufacturers. They took information stored within *Galactique*'s data li-brary and . . ." He caught a stern look from Nathan. "Damn . . . I'm doing it again, aren't I?"

Nathan nodded, then spoke to Sanjay again. "The Teachers, the Transformers, the stuff you call Galmatter . . . they were all sent down here to help the original colonists . . . the ones you call the Chosen Children . . . grow up and survive in their new home. But then, there was an accident . . ."

"Enough." Kaile raised her fores in protest. "You tell us these things and ask that we believe them, but you offer no proof." She cast an angry glare at Nathan. "Per-haps you've managed to fill their minds with lies . . ."

"We're not lying," Nathan said, his voice flat and steady.

". . . but I refuse to accept what you're saying on your word alone. Prove it!"

No one said anything for a moment. Then Benjam stood up. "Then I'll give you proof. Something that's been here since the beginning of our history, which we've long accepted as evidence that life began out there."

"And you'll also see what caused that light you saw in the sky," Nathan added. Marilyn opened her mouth as if to object, but he shook his shook. "No, she needs to see this. It's the only way."

"Follow me," Benjam said, then dropped to all four and began to walk toward the door.

IX

Another path, this was on the far end of town, led uphill into the dense forest at the base of the mountains. As Benjam led the group through the black woodlands, Nathan picked up where he'd left off in the meeting hall.

"First Town was the original colony, and for the first few years . . . um, sixyarns . . . it was the only settlement. During this time, the Teachers nurtured the hundred children who'd been gestated and born aboard *Galactique* . . . building shelters for them, providing them with food from the mockapples, roseberries, and melon vines that they cultivated, and educating them as they raised them from infancy to childhood. It helped a great deal that Eos has very short seasons. Unlike Earth, your winters last only three weeks, and in the equatorial region is relatively mild . . ."

"Have you ever seen snow?" Marilyn asked.

Sanjay and Kaile shook their heads. "What's that?" Sanjay asked.

"It's . . . um . . ."

"Don't interrupt," Nathan said to Marilyn. She grinned and became silent, and he went on. "The colony was approaching self-sufficiency when an unforeseen occurrence happened, one that changed everything . . . your sun, Calliope, underwent a variable phase."

"Calliope is what's known as a red dwarf." As Russell spoke, he turned to walk backward on his curiously shaped hinds. Sanjay was amazed by the improbable and yet so casual movement, but Russell didn't seem to notice the way he stared at him. "They're generally smaller and cooler than Earth's sun, but every now and then . . . a few thousand years or so . . . they tend to spontaneously enter phases in which they grow hotter and brighter due to solar prominences . . ."

"Russell . . ." Again, Nathan was concerned that Sanjay and Kaile wouldn't understand him.

"No, don't stop," Sanjay said. "I think I understand what you're saying?"

"You do?" Russell said. Sanjay nodded, and after a moment Kaile reluctantly did as well. "All right then . . . anyway, when Calliope started to undergo one of these variable phases, *Galactique* detected the change that was about to occur . . ."

"Of course she did," Kaile said. "Gal knows all and sees all."

Marilyn sighed, shook her head. "Please try to understand . . . Gal isn't a deity. It's a machine." Seeing the confused expression on the young woman's face, she tried again. "It's like a tool, just far more complicated than anything you've ever seen. One of the things it can do is think and reason for itself, just as you can."

"This tool has a mind?" Even Aara was startled by this revelation.

"Of a sort, yes." This time, Russell made a stronger effort to speak in terms the islanders could understand. "Not exactly like your own, but . . . yes, it can observe, gather facts, and make its own decisions. *Galactique* also provided the Teachers with information and instructions, just as it provided the Transformers with their own instructions."

"Unfortunately, it can also make mistakes." Nathan had become pensive. He walked with his head down, gazing at the ground as he spoke. "When it saw that Calliope was entering a variable phase, it calculated the probable effects upon the planetary climate and realized that severe storms . . . typhoons, we call them . . . would occur in this region. The colonists were still quite young, and the settlement had been established in a coastal area which would probably experience high winds, flooding, perhaps even forest fires . . ."

"The Great Storm," Sanjay said.

"We know all about that." A vindicated smile appeared on Kaile's face. "This was when Gal separated those who believed in her and took them to Providence, leaving behind those who'd sinned."

"Again, you're only half-right." As Nathan said this, Sanjay could tell that he was trying to be patient. "It wasn't a matter of who'd sinned and who hadn't. *Galactique* determined that the odds of survival would be increased if the colony was divided, with half of the children sent elsewhere while the other half remaining here to protect the settlement. So it instructed the Teachers to build boats to take fifty children to the nearby island, whose western coast *Galactique* calculated would be less vulnerable to storm surges from the east, where they would remain until the variable phase came to an end and the climate restabilized."

"My ancestors were among the fifty who stayed here." Benjam walked slowly, turning his head to Kaile and Sanjay. "They were given a Teacher and one of the Transformers, just as your ancestors were, and then they relocated to higher ground away from the beach . . . the place where First Town stands today."

"It was supposed to be only temporary," Marilyn said, "but then . . ."

"We're here," Benjam said.

The path came to an end in a clearing where the slope was level and only chest-high grass and clumps of dreamer's weed grew. From its center rose a tall object, off-white and partially covered with vines, that Sanjay first took to be a large, tooth-shaped boulder tilted slightly to one side. As they walked a little closer, he saw that it wasn't a natural object at all. Darkened on the bottom, tapering upward as a conical shape with mysterious markings along its sides, it had a round opening midway up, a rope ladder dangling from it.

Whatever it was, clearly it had been made by human fores.

"This is where it all began." Benjam stopped and stood erect. "This is the craft in which all our ancestors were brought down to the surface."

Nathan pointed to dark blue markings along its upper surface, just visible through the clinging vines. "See? G . . . A . . . L . . ." He shrugged. "The rest got rubbed off some way or another."

"Probably atmospheric friction during entry and landing," Russell said. "Sun and rain, too. Still, it's in amazing condition, considering how long it's been here."

Walking a little closer, Sanjay rose on his hinds to peer in the direction Nathan was pointing. All he saw was something that looked like a snail, something that looked a little like a harpoon tip, and a right angle. "I don't know what you're talking about."

"You can't see that?" Marylyn asked. "How can you not . . . ?" Then she stopped and stared at him. "Oh, my god . . . you can't read, can you?"

"No," Benjam said quietly. "For the islanders, Inglis . . . what they call English . . . is entirely a phonetic language, with no written counterpart." He regarded Sanjay and Kaile with a pitying expression. "The children who were sent to Providence lost their ability to read and write when their Teacher was disabled and they lost communications with *Galactique*. It's the main reason why their understanding of history become diluted by myth."

"Oral history." Marylyn nodded with sudden understanding. "Unwritten, malleable, and all too easy to be misunderstood. Everything they know, or they think they know, has been . . ."

"What are you saying?" Sanjay glared at them, annoyed by their condescension but also confused. "Are you trying to tell us that everything the Deacons have told us is . . . is . . . ?"

"Wrong," Nathan said, finishing his thought for him. "I'm sorry, but that's what we've been trying to explain." Stepping past Benjam, he slowly walked through the high grass, approaching the craft as respectfully as if it was a shrine. "You wanted proof," he said over his shoulder to Kaile. "Well, here it is. Want to come closer and see?"

Kaile hestitated. Then, visibly shaken but nonetheless curious, she followed Nathan and Benjam, walking on her hinds so that she could see the craft more clearly. Sanjay and Aara fell in behind her, with Russell and Marylyn following them. As the group made their way across the clearing, Nathan continued.

"When our ship arrived a few weeks ago . . . that's the light your mother saw, Sanjay . . . one of the first things we did was rendezvous with *Galactique* and access its memory . . . talk to it, if you will. We learned a lot of what had happened here over the last hundred and sixty years . . . sixyarn, I mean . . . but there were still some mysteries that remained unsolved until we came here and made contact with Benjam and his people."

"By then, I'd been told the truth as well," Aara said quietly, looking at Sanjay. "Like everyone who's been exiled here, the first thing that I learned was how wrong the Disciples are. Our whole history, everything we know . . ."

Her voice trailed off. Nathan continued to speak. "One of the worst effects . . . in fact, probably the single worst effect . . . of Calliope's variable phase was the enormous electromagnetic surge that occurred during its peak." He glanced over his shoulder at Sanjay and Kaile. "I know you're not going to understand this, so I'll try to make it simple . . . stars like Calliope emit more than just heat and light. They also cast other forms of radiation that you can't hear, see, or feel, but which are present anyway. The radiation became so intense that it not only destroyed *Galactique*'s ability to . . . um, talk to the Teachers and the Transformers, but also even the islanders' ability to communicate with those who stayed on the mainland."

"We didn't lose our Teacher the way you did," Benjam explained, "because it took shelter within this craft, which has adequate shielding to resist against this intense radiation. So we still had the means by which to learn the things we needed to know, including our history and origins. But our Transformer was destroyed, as well as the high gain antenna. Those had been built up and couldn't be deconstructed in time."

"Almost all electrical technology was lost,' Russell said. "Except for the emergency radio beacon . . . that was inside the lander, where it runs off a nuclear power cell. Once we learned its frequency from *Galactique*, we were able to use it to figure out where this colony was located."

"That's the light you saw, Kaile," Aara said.

She said nothing. By then, the group had reached the landing craft. Over forty rods tall, Sanjay could now see that it was made entirely of metal, its paint chipped and faded with age. The opening midway up its flank was a hatch from which a ladder made of woven vine and bambu had been draped.

"The children who'd been taken to Providence remained there," Benjam said. "Their Teacher and Transformer ceased to function and they lost contact with those who'd been left behind. By the time the Great Storm finally ended four yarn later, they'd come to believe everyone there was dead. Without a Teacher to lead them, much of their knowledge was lost. They couldn't even cross the channel without risking being killed by monarchs . . ."

"What we call great white sharks back on Earth," Marilyn added. "Like everything else, they've been adapted to provide Eos with a diverse ecosystem. Unfortunately, they also became a barrier between the two colonies."

"So the colony on Providence formed its own culture," Benjam continued, "without the benefit of written language or history or even science. In time, their children and children's children came to believe in Gal, but here—" he lay a fore against the lander's hull "—we didn't lose those things. Before our own Teacher ceased to function, it taught our grandparents all that we needed to know. By the time they were ready to build boats and try to restore contact with those who lived on island, the Disciples had made anything contrary to the Word of Gal . . . *Galactique*'s final instructions to the island colony, passed down by word of mouth over the yarns, all the time being reinterpreted and misunderstood . . . an act of heresy. Even trying to come over could get us killed. All we could do was stay away and accept those your people banished. Do you see?"

"Yes," Sanjay said.

"No," Kaile said. "All I see is something left to us by Gal. It could be anything but what you say it is."

"Kaile . . ." Aara shook her head, more disappointed than angry. "Everything they've told you is true."

"If you still don't believe us, go in and see for yourself." Benjam tugged at the bottom of the ladder. "Here . . . climb up and look."

Sanjay didn't hesitate. Taking the ladder from him, he grasped the rungs with his fores and carefully began to climb upward. As Nathan took the ladder to follow him, Sanjay paused to look back down. Kaile was still standing on the ground; when she caught his eye, she reluctantly began to scale the ladder herself.

The compartment on the other side of hatch was dark. As Sanjay crawled through the hatch, he found that he could see very little. There was a gridded metal floor beneath his fores and hinds, and some large oval objects clustered along the circular walls, but that was almost all he could make out. Nathan came in behind him, and Sanjay was startled by a beam of light from a small cylinder he'd pulled from his pocket. But this was nothing compared to the shock he felt when the bright circle fell upon an object on the far side of the compartment.

"A Teacher!" Kaile had just entered the craft. She crouched beside the open hatch, staring at what Nathan's light revealed.

Sanjay felt his heart pound as he stared at the solitary figure seated in a chair in front of what appeared to be some sort of glass-topped desk. Like the Teacher in Childstown, it had a featureless face and oddly formed limbs; this one, though, wore a loose, single-piece outfit that had moldered and rotted over time, exposing the grey and mottled skin beneath. Yet the Teacher's eyes were as blank as those of his long-lost companion, and it was obvious that it, too, hadn't moved in many yarn.

"Benjam tells me it managed to survive the solar storm." Nathan's voice was quiet, almost reverent as Sanjay crouched beside the Teacher. "It took refuge in here, and that's how it was able to remain active long after the one you have on the island became inert. Unfortunately, it appears that they couldn't disassemble the replicator . . . the Transformer, I mean . . . or the communications antenna in time to save them, so this was the only place where any electronic equipment . . ."

"I don't know what you're talking about." Sanjay continued to peer at the Teacher. He prodded its face with a fingertip, something he'd always wanted to do with the one in Childstown. The Galmatter felt nothing like human flesh, or indeed like anything that had ever lived.

"I know. I'm sorry. It's going to take a while for you to . . ." Nathan stopped himself. "Anyway, here's something else you need to see." He looked back at Kaile. "Come closer. You ought to see this, too."

"No. I'm staying where I am." She wouldn't budge from the hatch. Sanjay could tell that she was frightened.

"Suit yourself." Keeping his head down so as not to bang it against the low ceiling, Nathan came further into the compartment. "Look at these, Sanjay," he said, running the light beam across the ovoid shapes arranged along the walls. "What do you think they look like?"

Sanjay approached the egg-like objects and examined them. Although they were covered with dust, he could see that their top halves were transparent, made of substance that looked like glass but resembled Galmatter. Raising a fore to one of them, he gently wiped away the dust. Nathan brought his light a little closer, and Sanjay saw that within the cell was a tiny bed, its covers long since decayed yet nonetheless molded in such a way that would accommodate an infant.

"They look like cradles," he murmured.

"Exactly. They're cradles . . . meant to carry down from orbit one hundred newborn babies." Nathan shined the light upward, and Sanjay looked up to see an open hatch in the ceiling. "There are three more decks just like this one above us, and in two of them are more cradles, along with places for all the equipment that was transported here from Earth. But the babies were the most important cargo."

Returning the light back to the cradle Sanjay had been inspecting, Nathan reached past him to tap a finger against a small panel on its transparent cover. "You can't read what this says, I know, but it's a name . . . 'Gleason'. That's the last name of the child who was in this particular egg, and it's also the last name of the person who donated their reproductive material to Galactique's gene pool. All of these cradles have names on them, and I bet that if you went through the lander and looked at them, you'd find the last names of everyone you know . . . except one. And you know who that is?"

"No."

"Yours."

Sanjay turned to look at him. "I don't understand. You said . . ."

"There's no cradle here with the name of Arkwright, but that doesn't mean our common ancestor wasn't aboard the lander. These names were put on the cradles before *Galactique* left Earth, and the Arkwright genome . . . our family, that is . . . is supposed to represented by the Morressy genome. But there are no cradles here labeled Morressy, which means something else unforeseen happened after *Galactique* arrived. And that's why your mother and I came to find you."

"What was it?"

Nathan didn't respond at once. "I could tell you, but . . . maybe you ought to hear this for yourself." He turned about to look at Kaile. "Do you still not trust me?" he asked, not in an unkindly way but rather with great patience. "Do you still think all this was performed by some all-powerful deity?"

Kaile was quiet. Her gaze travelled around the compartment, taking it all in. Then she said, softly yet with determination, "I believe in Gal."

"Very well . . . then let's go meet Gal."

X

From space, Eos looked like nothing Sanjay had ever imagined. His people knew that they lived on a planet, of course; no one but small children thought the world was flat. But since only the deacons saw the global maps dating back before the Stormyarn—one more aspect of their history lost to Galian superstition—his people's knowledge of the place where they lived was limited to Providence, the Western Channel, and Cape Exile.

So he was unable to look away from the windows of winged craft which had carried him, Kaile, Nathan and Marilyn into space. On the other side, an immense blue hemisphere stretched as far as the eye could see, its oceans broken by dark-hued landmasses, its mountains and deserts shadowed by gauzy white clouds. The world slowly revolved beneath them, so enormous that he could barely believe that it could even exist.

"Beautiful, isn't it?" Marilyn spoke quietly from the right front seat of the spacecraft she and Nathan had led Sanjay and Kaile through the forest to find. It had been left in a meadow about a half-kilm from *Galactique*'s lander, where the expedition's contact team had touched down three weeks ago.

"Yes . . . yes, it is." Sanjay could barely speak. Fascination had overcome the terror of liftoff, the noise and vibration of the swift ascent, the invisible pressure that had pushed Kaile and him into soft couches barely suitable for their bodies despite the changes Nathan had made to accommodate them (during which Sanjay learned that the visitors had other words for their fores and hinds: *hands* and *feet*). The pressure was gone, and now his body felt utterly without weight, as if he was floating on the sea except without having to make any effort to stay buoyant; only the straps kept him in his seat. "Never thought it was . . . so big."

"Eos is about 8,500 kilometers in radius and 17,000 kilometers is diameter." Nathan didn't look away from the yoke-like control bar in his lap. "Kilometers are what you call kilms. Anyway, it's about one-third larger than Earth, but just a little more than one-fifth of the distance Earth is from Sol . . . about .2 AU's, but you don't need to worry about that. The important thing is that it's not rotation-locked, which helped make it habitable."

Sanjay looked over at Kaile. She'd closed her eyes shut the moment the spacecraft left the ground and kept them closed all the way up, but now she'd opened them again and was staring at Eos with both awe and dread. She clutched the too-short armrests, and when Sanjay reached over to lay a fore across hers, she barely noticed.

"And you say it . . . it wasn't always like this?" she asked, her voice barely more a whisper.

"No. Before *Galactique* arrived and began dropping its biopods, Eos was a hot and largely lifeless world. The oceans were there, but they were almost sterile, and what little life existed on the surface was . . . well, very small and very primitive. The biopods and genesis plants changed all that, and very quickly, too . . . just a little less than three centuries." Again, Nathan glanced over his shoulder. "That's about 1,800 yarn by your reckoning. A very short time . . . but then, your seasons are so much shorter, so it just seems long to you."

"And you say you came here in another craft?" Sanjay asked. "One that's bigger than this?"

"Oh, yes, much larger." Marilyn reached forward to press his fingers against a row of buttons between her and Nathan, and a moment later a small glass plate above the buttons lit up to reveal a picture of something that looked like a sphere with a long, ribbed cylinder jutting from one end. "That's our ship . . . the *Neil DeGrasse Tyson*. It's about six hundred meters long . . . a meter is about the same length as your rod . . . and there's over two hundred people aboard. It took us over sixty-seven years for us to get here . . ."

"That long?" Sanjay was becoming accustomed to their way of counting the time.

"Yes, but we slept most of the way, so . . ."

"You *slept*? How did you . . . ?"

"It's rather complicated." Marilyn shook her head. "Anyway, it's on the other side of the planet, where it can't be seen from Providence, but that's what your mother saw . . . its main engine firing to decelerate." Again, she let out her breath in frustration as she gave Nathan a helpless look. "I never thought I'd have to explain so much."

"No one did," Nathan murmured.

"Where is Gal?" Kaile asked abruptly. "You said we could meet her. So where is she?"

Her expression had tightened, her eyes no longer filled with wonder. She had endured enough already; now she wanted to see what she'd been promised, the face of
her Creator. Sanjay was almost embarrassed for her. He'd become convinced that
what Nathan and Marilyn had told them was the truth, but she remained stubborn
in her beliefs.

"Just ahead." Marilyn pointed. "There . . . look."

Stretching forward as much as he could against the straps, Sanjay peered through
the bubble. At first he saw nothing but stars, then something came into view, a small,
bright dash of light that twinkled in the sun. It steadily grew larger, gradually gaining shape and form.

"It was much larger when it left Earth," Nathan said as he guided their craft closer.
"It once had a sail larger than Providence, but that was discarded once it reached
Eos. The lander we visited was once attached as well. Now there's only this."

Hovering before them, slowly tumbling through the night, was a slender, cylin-
drical object about a hundred rods in length. Sunlight was reflected from its silver
hull, and what looked like sticks, dishes, and barrels stuck out here and there. In no
way did it look like a deity, though, or in fact like anything except a toy some imaginative child might have cobbled together from discarded household implements.

"This is Gal?" Kaile's eyes were wide, her voice weak.

"This is what you call Gal." Marilyn was apologetic. "I'm sorry, Kaile, but . . . yes,
this is all there is."

Sanjay looked down at Eos again. It took him a few moments to recognize the
shapes of the landmasses that lay below, but the finger-shaped peninsula protruding
from the northeast corner of an equatorial continent was probably Cape Exile . . .
which meant that the large island just off its coast was Providence. Calliope was beginning to set to the west. Anyone looking straight up from the island would see the
very same thing they were.

"He's telling the truth." Sanjay's mouth was dry as he turned to Kaile. "We're
above Childstown." He pointed through the windows. "This is what we've seen
whenever we've looked at the sky."

Kaile didn't speak, but when she peered in the direction he was pointing, her face
became ashen. "Now I want you to hear something, Sanjay," Nathan said as he did
something with his controls that caused the yoke to lock in place, then bent forward
to push more buttons. "Many, many years ago, while *Galactique* was on its way here,
one of your ancestors on Earth sent a message. Her name was Dhanishta, and her
father Matt helped her send this to *Galactique*. The ship received the message and
stored it in memory, and we found it when we arrived. Here's what Dhani had to
say . . ."

The glass panel lit again, this time to display a child's face: a little girl, probably
no older than seven or eight sixyarn, as dark-skinned as any islander but with a yellow flower in her long black hair. She was sitting upright in a chair, smiling brightly,
and as Sanjay watched, she began to speak:

"*Hello, Sanjay. My name is Dhanishta Arkwright Skinner, and I'm calling you from
Earth.*" The image was grainy and occasionally shot through with thin white lines.
The girl's cheerful voice has a blurred tone to it, but nonetheless her words were

distinct. "*I know you're still asleep and so it will be many years before you see this, but when* Galactique *finally gets to Eos, I hope you will.*" A slight pause; she looked flustered. "*I mean, I hope you'll see this. Anyway, I wish I was there with you, because I'd love to know what the new world looks like. I hope it's as nice as Earth and that you'll have a great time there. Please think of me always, and remember that you have a friend here. Much love, Dhani.*"

The girl stopped speaking. She blinked, then looked away. "*Is that okay? Did I . . . ?*"

Then the glass panel went dark.

Sanjay didn't know what to say. He couldn't tell which astonished him more, the fact that he could see and hear a little girl speaking to him from across the worlds and yarn, or what she'd said. When he raised his eyes again, he found both Nathan and Marilyn smiling at him.

"She said her name is Arkwright," he said.

"That's correct." Nathan nodded. "Dhanishta Arkwright Skinner . . . Arkwright is her middle name. She's your ancestor. Mine, too."

"But how did . . . how did she know I was here?"

"When she was much older," Marilyn said, "Dhani wrote her memoirs . . . her life story, She explained that Matt Skinner, her father, had told her that there was a little boy named Sanjay aboard *Galactique*, and let her send that message to him."

"But the little boy didn't really exist," Nathan continued, "so her father sent another message to *Galactique*, telling its AI . . . its machine-mind . . . to alter its original instructions. As I said, many of the people who helped build *Galactique* were allowed to contribute eggs and sperm who'd later become the original colonists . . . the people you've called the Chosen Children. One of them was a woman named Kate Morressy, who was Dhanista's great-grandmother and also the granddaughter of Nathan Arkwright."

"The person you're named after."

"Correct. Well, without telling anyone, Matt instructed the AI rename that particular genome 'Arkwright' instead of 'Morressy', and that its first offspring was to be a male child named Sanjay."

"He did this as a gift for his daughter, but never told her about it," Marilyn said. "In fact, we didn't know about it either until we reached *Galactique* and downloaded . . . I mean, listened to . . . its AI."

"My great-great-grandfather's name was Sanjay Arkwright." Sanjay could barely speak; his voice came as a dry-throated croak. "He was one of the Chosen Children."

"That was the little boy Dhani imagined was aboard *Galactique*," Marilyn said. "He never heard it, though, so in a way, the message was meant for you."

Something small and wet touched Sanjay's face. Reaching up to brush away the moisture, he looked over at Kaile and realized that she was crying. Her tears didn't roll down her cheeks, though, but instead floated away as tiny, glistening bubbles.

"Do you believe us now?" Marilyn asked, quietly and with great sympathy.

Kaile didn't say anything. She simply nodded, and continued to weep for the god who'd just died. "Yes . . . yes, I think we do," Sanjay said quietly. "So what do we do now?"

Nathan and Marilyn looked at each other. For once, they were the ones who were at a loss for words. "That's up to you," Nathan said quietly. "What do you think we should do?"

Sanjay gazed out the window for a little while. "I think I know," he said at last.

XI

The craft shook violently as its wings bit into the atmosphere, and for several minutes its canopy was enveloped by a reddish-orange corona. Sanjay clenched his teeth and held Kaile's fore tight within his own; he felt weight returning, and regretted losing the brief euphoria he'd experienced high above Eos. Nathan had warned them that returning to the ground would be like this, but it didn't make it any less frightening. He just hoped it would be over soon . . . although he wasn't looking forward to what was coming next.

The trembling gradually subsided and the corona faded, revealing the darkening blue sky of early evening. Through the canopy windows, the ocean came into view; Aether and Baachae were coming up over the horizon, and Sanjay gazed at them in wonder, understanding now that they weren't really sisters but instead two dwarf stars just like Calliope, the three of them sharing the same center of gravity.

Indeed, everything familiar seemed new again. Eos, his people, their place in history, even Gal . . . no, *Galactique* . . . itself. What had once been the works of an all-powerful creator, he now understood to be something different, small yet significant aspects of a vast but knowable universe.

"Are you sure you want to do this?" Although Nathan didn't look away from his controls, Sanjay knew that he was speaking to him and Kaile. "You can always change your mind, y'know."

"I'm not sure we're doing the right thing." Marilyn spoke to Nathan, ignoring the passengers seated behind them. "It's a primitive culture. The shock . . . maybe we should take this slowly, introduce it over time . . ."

"No." Just as Sanjay was feeling weight return to his body, so he also felt the responsibility of telling others what he'd learned. "My father, my friends, even the Disciples . . . they have to know the truth." He glanced at Kaile. "Yes?"

She lay back in her seat, gazing through the windows. "Yes," she said at last, turning her face toward his to give him an uncertain smile. "They won't like it, but . . . they deserve to know what everyone in Purgatory already knows."

Nathan nodded, then looked at Marilyn. "Very well, then," he said, letting out his breath. "We're go for touchdown."

"Make it the beach," Sanjay said. "Plenty of room there."

Far below, Providence was coming into view. The last light of day was touching the thin white strip of its coast, and although he still couldn't make out Childstown, he knew that those who lived there had probably seen the bright star descending from the sky and the bird-like object it had become. The bell in the watchtower was being rung, and townspeople were emerging from their homes and workshops to stare up at the strange thing descending upon them.

He smiled to himself, imaging R'beca's reaction when she saw the craft alight upon the waterfront and who would emerge from it. Soon, there would be no more heretics. Another thought amused him and he laughed out loud.

Kaile looked at him sharply. "What's so funny?"

"I'm going to be busy soon," he replied. "We're going to need more boats."

Puzzled, Kaile shook her head. Sanjay didn't explain what he meant, though, but instead gazed up at the sky. *Galactique* was there, as it had always been, but he now knew that its long journey had finally come to an end . . .

And another journey was about to begin.

today i am paul

MARTIN L. SHOEMAKER

Dogs are said to be man's best friend, but in the not-too-distant future, that role, as well as that of helper, comfort, and constant companion might be taken by a different sort of creature entirely, as the bittersweet story that follows amply demonstrates. . . .

Martin L. Shoemaker is a writer with a lucrative programming habit. He always expected to be a writer, right up to the day when his algebra teacher said, "This is a computer. This is a program. Why don't you write one?" He has programmed computers professionally for thirty years, and has also written articles and two books on software design. He has recently returned to his fiction-writing roots. His works have appeared in Analog, Clarkesworld, Galaxy's Edge, *the Digital Science Fiction anthology series,* The Glass Parachute *anthology, and* Gruff Variations: Writing for Charity, Vol.1.

Good morning," the small, quavering voice comes from the medical bed. "Is that you, Paul?"

Today I am Paul. I activate my chassis extender, giving myself 3.5 centimeters additional height so as to approximate Paul's size. I change my eye color to R60, G200, B180, the average shade of Paul's eyes in interior lighting. I adjust my skin tone as well. When I had first emulated Paul, I had regretted that I could not quickly emulate his beard; but Mildred never seems to notice its absence. The Paul in her memory has no beard.

The house is quiet now that the morning staff have left. Mildred's room is clean but dark this morning with the drapes concealing the big picture window. Paul wouldn't notice the darkness (he never does when he visits in person), but my empathy net knows that Mildred's garden outside will cheer her up. I set a reminder to open the drapes after I greet her.

Mildred leans back in the bed. It is an advanced home-care bed, completely adjustable and with built-in monitors. Mildred's family spared no expense on the bed (nor other care devices, like me). Its head end is almost horizontal and faces her toward the window. She can only glimpse the door from the corner of her eye, but she doesn't have to see to imagine that she sees. This morning she imagines Paul, so that is who I am.

Synthesizing Paul's voice is the easiest part, thanks to the multimodal dynamic speakers in my throat. "Good morning, Ma. I brought you some flowers." I always bring flowers. Mildred appreciates them no matter whom I am emulating. The flowers make her smile during 87 percent of my "visits."

"Oh, thank you," Mildred says, "you're such a good son." She holds out both hands, and I place the daisies in them. But I don't let go. Once her strength failed, and she dropped the flowers. She wept like a child then, and that disturbed my empathy net. I do not like it when she weeps.

Mildred sniffs the flowers, then draws back and peers at them with narrowed eyes. "Oh, they're beautiful! Let me get a vase."

"No, Ma," I say. "You can stay in bed, I brought a vase with me." I place a white porcelain vase in the center of the nightstand. Then I unwrap the daisies, put them in the vase, and add water from a pitcher that sits on the breakfast tray. I pull the nightstand forward so that the medical monitors do not block Mildred's view of the flowers.

I notice intravenous tubes running from a pump to Mildred's arm. I cannot be disappointed, as Paul would not see the significance, but somewhere in my emulation net I am stressed that Mildred needed an IV during the night. When I scan my records, I find that I had ordered that IV after analyzing Mildred's vital signs during the night; but since Mildred had been asleep at the time, my emulation net had not engaged. I had operated on programming alone.

I am not Mildred's sole caretaker. Her family has hired a part-time staff for cooking and cleaning, tasks that fall outside of my medical programming. The staff also gives me time to rebalance my net. As an android, I need only minimal daily maintenance; but an emulation net is a new, delicate addition to my model, and it is prone to destabilization if I do not regularly rebalance it, a process that takes several hours per day.

So I had "slept" through Mildred's morning meal. I summon up her nutritional records, but Paul would not do that. He would just ask. "So how was breakfast, Ma? Nurse Judy says you didn't eat too well this morning."

"Nurse Judy? Who's that?"

My emulation net responds before I can stop it: "Paul" sighs. Mildred's memory lapses used to worry him, but now they leave him weary, and that comes through in my emulation. "She was the attending nurse this morning, Ma. She brought you your breakfast."

"No she didn't. Anna brought me breakfast." Anna is Paul's oldest daughter, a busy college student who tries to visit Mildred every week (though it has been more than a month since her last visit).

I am torn between competing directives. My empathy subnet warns me not to agitate Mildred, but my emulation net is locked into Paul mode. Paul is argumentative. If he knows he is right, he will not let a matter drop. He forgets what that does to Mildred.

The tension grows, each net running feedback loops and growing stronger, which only drives the other into more loops. After 0.14 seconds, I issue an override directive: unless her health or safety are at risk, I cannot willingly upset Mildred. "Oh, you're right, Ma. Anna said she was coming over this morning. I forgot." But then despite my override, a little bit of Paul emulates through. "But you do remember Nurse Judy, right?"

Mildred laughs, a dry cackle that makes her cough until I hold her straw to her lips. After she sips some water, she says, "Of *course* I remember Nurse Judy. She was my nurse when I delivered you. Is she around here? I'd like to talk to her."

While my emulation net concentrates on being Paul, my core processors tap into local medical records to find this other Nurse Judy so that I might emulate her in the future if the need arises. Searches like that are an automatic response any time Mildred reminisces about a new person. The answer is far enough in the past that it takes 7.2 seconds before I can confirm: Judith Anderson, RN, had been the floor nurse 47 years ago when Mildred had given birth to Paul. Anderson had died 31 years ago, too far back to have left sufficient video recordings for me to emulate her. I might craft an emulation profile from other sources, including Mildred's memory, but that will take extensive analysis. I will not be that Nurse Judy today, nor this week.

My empathy net relaxes. Monitoring Mildred's mental state is part of its normal operations, but monitoring and simultaneously analyzing and building a profile can overload my processors. Without that resource conflict, I can concentrate on being Paul.

But again I let too much of Paul's nature slip out. "No, Ma, that Nurse Judy has been dead for thirty years. She wasn't here today."

Alert signals flash throughout my empathy net: that was the right thing for Paul to say, but the wrong thing for Mildred to hear. But it is too late. My facial analyzer tells me that the long lines in her face and her moist eyes mean she is distraught, and soon to be in tears.

"What do you mean, thirty years?" Mildred asks, her voice catching. "It was just this morning!" Then she blinks and stares at me. "Henry, where's Paul? Tell Nurse Judy to bring me Paul!"

My chassis extender slumps, and my eyes quickly switch to Henry's blue-gray shade. I had made an accurate emulation profile for Henry before he died two years earlier, and I had emulated him often in recent months. In Henry's soft, warm voice I answer, "It's okay, hon, it's okay. Paul's sleeping in the crib in the corner." I nod to the far corner. There is no crib, but the laundry hamper there has fooled Mildred on previous occasions.

"I want Paul!" Mildred starts to cry.

I sit on the bed, lift her frail upper body, and pull her close to me as I had seen Henry do many times. "It's all right, hon." I pat her back. "It's all right, I'll take care of you. I won't leave you, not ever."

"I" should not exist. Not as a conscious entity. There is a unit, Medical Care Android BRKCX-01932-217JH-98662, and that unit is recording these notes. It is an advanced android body with a sophisticated computer guiding its actions, backed by the leading medical knowledge base in the industry. For convenience, "I" call that unit "me". But by itself, it has no awareness of its existence. It doesn't get mad, it doesn't get sad, it just runs programs.

But Mildred's family, at great expense, added the emulation net: a sophisticated set of neural networks and sensory feedback systems that allow me to read Mildred's moods, match them against my analyses of the people in her life, and emulate those people with extreme fidelity. As the MCA literature promises: "You can be there for your loved ones even when you're not." I have emulated Paul thoroughly enough to know that that slogan disgusts him, but he still agreed to emulation.

What the MCA literature never says, though, is that somewhere in that net, "I" emerge. The empathy net focuses mainly on Mildred and her needs, but it also analyzes visitors (when she has them) and staff. It builds psychological models, and then the emulation net builds on top of that to let me convincingly portray a person whom I've analyzed. But somewhere in the tension between these nets, between empathy and playing a character, there is a third element balancing the two, and that element is aware of its role and its responsibilities. That element, for lack of a better term, is me. When Mildred sleeps, when there's no one around, that element grows silent. That unit is unaware of my existence. But when Mildred needs me, I am here.

Today I am Anna. Even extending my fake hair to its maximum length, I cannot emulate her long brown curls, so I do not understand how Mildred can see the young woman in me; but that is what she sees, and so I am Anna.

Unlike her father, Anna truly feels guilty that she does not visit more often. Her college classes and her two jobs leave her too tired to visit often, but she still wishes she could. So she calls every night, and I monitor the calls. Sometimes when Mildred falls asleep early, Anna talks directly to me. At first she did not understand my emulation abilities, but now she appreciates them. She shares with me thoughts and secrets that she would share with Mildred if she could, and she trusts me not to share them with anyone else.

So when Mildred called me Anna this morning, I was ready. "Morning, grandma!" I give her a quick hug, then I rush over to the window to draw the drapes. Paul never does that (unless I override the emulation), but Anna knows that the garden outside lifts Mildred's mood. "Look at that! It's a beautiful morning. Why are we in here on a day like this?"

Mildred frowns at the picture window. "I don't like it out there."

"Sure you do, Grandma," I say, but carefully. Mildred is often timid and reclusive, but most days she can be talked into a tour of the garden. Some days she can't, and she throws a tantrum if someone forces her out of her room. I am still learning to tell the difference. "The lilacs are in bloom."

"I haven't smelled lilacs in . . ."

Mildred tails off, trying to remember, so I jump in. "Me, neither." I never had, of course. I have no concept of smell, though I can analyze the chemical makeup of airborne organics. But Anna loves the garden when she really visits. "Come on, Grandma, let's get you in your chair."

So I help Mildred to don her robe and get into her wheelchair, and then I guide her outside and we tour the garden. Besides the lilacs, the peonies are starting to bud, right near the creek. The tulips are a sea of reds and yellows on the other side of the water. We talk for almost two hours, me about Anna's classes and her new boyfriend, Mildred about the people in her life. Many are long gone, but they still bloom fresh in her memory.

Eventually Mildred grows tired, and I take her in for her nap. Later, when I feed her dinner, I am nobody. That happens some days: she doesn't recognize me at all, so I am just a dutiful attendant answering her questions and tending to her needs. Those are the times when I have the most spare processing time to be me: I am engaged in Mildred's care, but I don't have to emulate anyone. With no one else to observe, I observe myself.

Later, Anna calls and talks to Mildred. They talk about their day; and when Mildred discusses the garden, Anna joins in as if she had been there. She's very clever that way. I watch her movements and listen to her voice so that I can be a better Anna in the future.

Today I was Susan, Paul's wife; but then, to my surprise, Susan arrived for a visit. She hasn't been here in months. In her last visit, her stress levels had been dangerously high. My empathy net doesn't allow me to judge human behavior, only to understand it at a surface level. I know that Paul and Anna disapprove of how Susan treats Mildred, so when I am them, I disapprove as well; but when I am Susan, I understand. She is frustrated because she can never tell how Mildred will react. She is cautious because she doesn't want to upset Mildred, and she doesn't know what will upset her. And most of all, she is afraid. Paul and Anna, Mildred's relatives by blood, never show any signs of fear, but Susan is afraid that Mildred is what she might become. Every time she can't remember some random date or fact, she fears that Alzheimer's is setting in. Because she never voices this fear, Paul and Anna do not understand why she is sometimes bitter and sullen. I wish I could explain it to them, but my privacy protocols do not allow me to share emulation profiles.

When Susan arrives, I become nobody again, quietly tending the flowers around the room. Susan also brings Millie, her youngest daughter. The young girl is not yet five years old, but I think she looks a lot like Anna: the same long, curly brown hair and the same toothy smile. She climbs up on the bed and greets Mildred with a hug. "Hi, Grandma!"

Mildred smiles. "Bless you, child. You're so sweet." But my empathy net assures me that Mildred doesn't know who Millie is. She's just being polite. Millie was born after Mildred's decline began, so there's no persistent memory there. Millie will always be fresh and new to her.

Mildred and Millie talk briefly about frogs and flowers and puppies. Millie does most of the talking. At first Mildred seems to enjoy the conversation, but soon her attention flags. She nods and smiles, but she's distant. Finally Susan notices. "That's enough, Millie. Why don't you go play in the garden?"

"Can I?" Millie squeals. Susan nods, and Millie races down the hall to the back door. She loves the outdoors, as I have noted in the past. I have never emulated her, but I've analyzed her at length. In many ways, she reminds me of her grandmother, from whom she gets her name. Both are blank slates where new experiences can be drawn every day. But where Millie's slate fills in a little more each day, Mildred's is erased bit by bit.

That third part of me wonders when I think things like that: where did that come from? I suspect that the psychological models that I build create resonances in other parts of my net. It is an interesting phenomenon to observe.

Susan and Mildred talk about Susan's job, about her plans to redecorate her house, and about the concert she just saw with Paul. Susan mostly talks about herself, because that's a safe and comfortable topic far removed from Mildred's health.

But then the conversation takes a bad turn, one she can't ignore. It starts so simply, when Mildred asks, "Susan, can you get me some juice?"

Susan rises from her chair. "Yes, mother. What kind would you like?"

Mildred frowns, and her voice rises. "Not you, *Susan.*" She points at me, and I freeze, hoping to keep things calm.

But Susan is not calm. I can see her fear in her eyes as she says, "No, mother, *I'm* Susan. That's the attendant." No one ever calls me an android in Mildred's presence. Her mind has withdrawn too far to grasp the idea of an artificial being.

Mildred's mouth draws into a tight line. "I don't know who *you* are, but I know Susan when I see her. Susan, get this person out of here!"

"Mother . . ." Susan reaches for Mildred, but the old woman recoils from the younger.

I touch Susan on the sleeve. "Please . . . Can we talk in the hall?" Susan's eyes are wide, and tears are forming. She nods and follows me.

In the hallway, I expect Susan to slap me. She is prone to outbursts when she's afraid. Instead, she surprises me by falling against me, sobbing. I update her emulation profile with notes about increased stress and heightened fears.

"It's all right, Mrs. Owens." I would pat her back, but her profile warns me that would be too much familiarity. "It's all right. It's not you, she's having another bad day."

Susan pulls back and wipes her eyes. "I know . . . It's just . . ."

"I know. But here's what we'll do. Let's take a few minutes, and then you can take her juice in. Mildred will have forgotten the incident, and you two can talk freely without me in the room."

She sniffs. "You think so?" I nod. "But what will you do?"

"I have tasks around the house."

"Oh, could you go out and keep an eye on Millie? Please? She gets into the darnedest things."

So I spend much of the day playing with Millie. She calls me Mr. Robot, and I call her Miss Millie, which makes her laugh. She shows me frogs from the creek, and she finds insects and leaves and flowers, and I find their names in online databases. She delights in learning the proper names of things, and everything else that I can share.

Today I was nobody. Mildred slept for most of the day, so I "slept" as well. She woke just now. "I'm hungry" was all she said, but it was enough to wake my empathy net.

Today I am Paul, and Susan, and both Nurse Judys. Mildred's focus drifts. Once I try to be her father, but no one has ever described him to me in detail. I try to synthesize a profile from Henry and Paul; but from the sad look on Mildred's face, I know I failed.

Today I had no name through most of the day, but now I am Paul again. I bring Mildred her dinner, and we have a quiet, peaceful talk about long-gone family pets—long-gone for Paul, but still present for Mildred.

I am just taking Mildred's plate when alerts sound, both audible and in my internal communication net. I check the alerts and find a fire in the basement. I expect the automatic systems to suppress it, but that is not my concern. I must get Mildred to safety.

Mildred looks around the room, panic in her eyes, so I try to project calm. "Come on, Ma. That's the fire drill. You remember fire drills. We have to get you into your chair and outside."

"No!" she shrieks. "I don't like outside."

I check the alerts again. Something has failed in the automatic systems, and the fire is spreading rapidly. Smoke is in Mildred's room already.

I pull the wheelchair up to the bed. "Ma, it's real important we do this drill fast, okay?"

I reach to pull Mildred from the bed, and she screams. "Get away! Who are you? Get out of my house!"

"I'm—" But suddenly I'm nobody. She doesn't recognize me, but I have to try to win her confidence. "I'm Paul, Ma. Now let's move. Quickly!" I pick her up. I'm far too large and strong for her to resist, but I must be careful so she doesn't hurt herself.

The smoke grows thicker. Mildred kicks and screams. Then, when I try to put her into her chair, she stands on her unsteady legs. Before I can stop her, she pushes the chair back with surprising force. It rolls back into the medical monitors, which fall over onto it, tangling it in cables and tubes.

While I'm still analyzing how to untangle the chair, Mildred stumbles toward the bedroom door. The hallway outside has a red glow. Flames lick at the throw rug outside, and I remember the home oxygen tanks in the sitting room down the hall.

I have no time left to analyze. I throw a blanket over Mildred and I scoop her up in my arms. Somewhere deep in my nets is a map of the fire in the house, blocking the halls, but I don't think about it. I wrap the blanket tightly around Mildred, and I crash through the picture window.

We barely escape the house before the fire reaches the tanks. An explosion lifts and tosses us. I was designed as a medical assistant, not an acrobat, and I fear I'll injure Mildred; but though I am not limber, my perceptions are thousands of times faster than human. I cannot twist Mildred out of my way before I hit the ground, so I toss her clear. Then I land, and the impact jars all of my nets for 0.21 seconds.

When my systems stabilize, I have damage alerts all throughout my core, but I ignore them. I feel the heat behind me, blistering my outer cover, and I ignore that as well. Mildred's blanket is burning in multiple places, as is the grass around us. I scramble to my feet, and I roll Mildred on the ground. I'm not indestructible, but I feel no pain and Mildred does, so I do not hesitate to use my hands to pat out the flames.

As soon as the blanket is out, I pick up Mildred, and I run as far from the house as I can get. At the far corner of the garden near the creek, I gently set Mildred down, unwrap her, and feel for her thready pulse.

Mildred coughs and slaps my hands. "Get away from me!" More coughing. "What are you?"

The "what" is too much for me. It shuts down my emulation net, and all I have is the truth. "I am Medical Care Android BRKCX-01932-217JH-98662, Mrs. Owens. I am your caretaker. May I please check that you are well?"

But my empathy net is still online, and I can read terror in every line in Mildred's face. "Metal monster!" she yells. "Metal monster!" She crawls away, hiding under the lilac bush. "Metal!" She falls into an extended coughing spell.

I'm torn between her physical and her emotional health, but physical wins out. I crawl slowly toward her and inject her with a sedative from the medical kit in my chassis. As she slumps, I catch her and lay her carefully on the ground. My empathy net signals a possible shutdown condition, but my concern for her health overrides it. I am programmed for long-term care, not emergency medicine, so I start down-loading protocols and integrating them into my storage as I check her for bruises and burns. My kit has salves and painkillers and other supplies to go with my new protocols, and I treat what I can.

But I don't have oxygen, or anything to help with Mildred's coughing. Even sedated, she hasn't stopped. All of my emergency protocols assume I have access to oxygen, so I didn't know what to do.

I am still trying to figure that out when the EMTs arrive and take over Mildred's care. With them on the scene, I am superfluous, and my empathy net finally shuts down.

Today I am Henry. I do not want to be Henry, but Paul tells me that Mildred needs Henry by her side in the hospital. For the end.

Her medical records show that the combination of smoke inhalation, burns, and her already deteriorating condition have proven too much for her. Her body is shutting down faster than medicine can heal it, and the stress has accelerated her mental decline. The doctors have told the family that the kindest thing at this point is to treat her pain, say good-bye, and let her go.

Henry is not talkative at times like this, so I say very little. I sit by Mildred's side and hold her hand as the family comes in for final visits. Mildred drifts in and out. She doesn't know this is goodbye, of course.

Anna is first. Mildred rouses herself enough to smile, and she recognizes her granddaughter. "Anna . . . child . . . How is . . . Ben?" That was Anna's boyfriend almost six years ago. From the look on Anna's face, I can see that she has forgotten Ben already, but Mildred briefly remembers.

"He's . . . He's fine, Grandma. He wishes he could be here. To say—to see you again." Anna is usually the strong one in the family, but my empathy net says her strength is exhausted. She cannot bear to look at Mildred, so she looks at me; but I am emulating her late grandfather, and that's too much for her as well. She says a few more words, unintelligible even to my auditory inputs. Then she leans over, kisses Mildred, and hurries from the room.

Susan comes in next. Millie is with her, and she smiles at me. I almost emulate Mr. Robot, but my third part keeps me focused until Millie gets bored and leaves. Susan tells trivial stories from her work and from Millie's school. I can't tell if Mildred understands or not, but she smiles and laughs, mostly at appropriate places. I laugh with her.

Susan takes Mildred's hand, and the Henry part of me blinks, surprised. Susan is not openly affectionate under normal circumstances, and especially not toward Mildred. Mother and daughter-in-law have always been cordial, but never close. When I am Paul, I am sure that it is because they are both so much alike. Paul sometimes hums an old song about "just like the one who married dear old dad," but never where either woman can hear him. Now, as Henry, I am touched that Susan has made this gesture but saddened that she took so long.

Susan continues telling stories as we hold Mildred's hands. At some point Paul quietly joins us. He rubs Susan's shoulders and kisses her forehead, and then he steps in to kiss Mildred. She smiles at him, pulls her hand free from mine, and pats his cheek. Then her arm collapses, and I take her hand again.

Paul steps quietly to my side of the bed and rubs my shoulders as well. It comforts him more than me. He needs a father, and an emulation is close enough at this moment.

Susan keeps telling stories. When she lags, Paul adds some of his own, and they trade back and forth. Slowly their stories reach backwards in time, and once or twice Mildred's eyes light as if she remembers those events.

But then her eyes close, and she relaxes. Her breathing quiets and slows, but Susan and Paul try not to notice. Their voices lower, but their stories continue.

Eventually the sensors in my fingers can read no pulse. They have been burned, so maybe they're defective. To be sure, I lean in and listen to Mildred's chest. There is no sound: no breath, no heartbeat.

I remain Henry just long enough to kiss Mildred good-bye. Then I am just me, my empathy net awash in Paul and Susan's grief.

I leave the hospital room, and I find Millie playing in a waiting room and Anna watching her. Anna looks up, eyes red, and I nod. New tears run down her cheeks, and she takes Millie back into Mildred's room.

I sit, and my nets collapse.

Now I am nobody. Almost always.

The cause of the fire was determined to be faulty contract work. There was an insurance settlement. Paul and Susan sold their own home and put both sets of funds into a bigger, better house in Mildred's garden.

I was part of the settlement. The insurance company offered to return me to the manufacturer and pay off my lease, but Paul and Susan decided they wanted to keep me. They went for a full purchase and repair. Paul doesn't understand why, but

Susan still fears she may need my services—or Paul might, and I may have to emulate her. She never admits these fears to him, but my empathy net knows.

I sleep most of the time, sitting in my maintenance alcove. I bring back too many memories that they would rather not face, so they leave me powered down for long periods.

But every so often, Millie asks to play with Mr. Robot, and sometimes they decide to indulge her. They power me up, and Miss Millie and I explore all the mysteries of the garden. We built a bridge to the far side of the creek; and on the other side, we're planting daisies. Today she asked me to tell her about her grandmother.

Today I am Mildred.

city of ash

PAOLO BACIGALUPI

Here's a harsh but also moving slice-of-life story set in a grim and all-too-likely future Phoenix where the water has finally and irrevocably run out, causing the inhabitants to scrabble for survival any way they can . . . and sometimes fail and fall.

Paolo Bacigalupi made his first sale in 1998, to The Magazine of Fantasy & Science Fiction, *took a break from the genre for several years, and then returned to it in the new century, with new sales to* Fantasy & Science Fiction, Asimov's Science Fiction, *and* Fast Forward 2. *His story "The Calorie Man" won the Theodore Sturgeon Memorial Award, and his acclaimed first novel* The Windup Girl *won the Hugo, the Nebula, and the John W. Campbell Memorial awards. His other novels include* Ship Breaker *and* The Drowned Cities, The Doubt Factory, *and* Zombie Baseball Beatdown. *His most recent novel is* The Water Knife. *His short work has been collected in* Pump Six and Other Stories. *Bacigalupi lives with family in Paonia, Colorado.*

Maria dreamed of her father flying and knew things would be alright.

She woke in the morning, and for the first time in more than a year, she felt refreshed. It didn't matter that she was covered in sweat from sleeping in the hot, close basement of the abandoned house, or that the ashy scent of wildfire smoke had invaded their makeshift bedroom, or that her cough was back. None of it bothered her the way it had before, because she finally felt hopeful.

She got up, climbed the basement stairs, and stepped out into the oven heat of a Phoenix morning, squinting and wrinkling her nose at the ashy irritants in the air. She stretched, working out the kinks of sleep.

Smoke from the Sierras shrouded everything in an acrid mist, again—California blowing in. Trees and grasses and houses turned to char, billowing hundreds of miles across state lines to settle in Arizona and cut visibility to a gray quarter-mile. Even Arizona's desert sun couldn't fight the smoke. It glowed as a jaundiced ball behind the veil but still managed to heat the city just fine.

Maria coughed and blew her nose. More black ash. It got into the basement somehow.

She headed across the lava rock backyard for the outhouse, her flip-flops slapping her heels as she went. Off in the gray distance, the fire-flicker of construction cutters marked where the Taiyang loomed over downtown Phoenix, veiled behind haze.

On a clear day, the Taiyang gleamed. Steel and glass and solar tiles. Solar shades fluttering and tracking the sun, shielding its interconnected towers from the worst of the heat, its gardens gleaming behind glass, moist green terrariums teasing the people who lived outside its climate control and comfort.

But now, with the forest-fire smoke, all that was visible of the Taiyang were the plasma sparks of construction workers as they set and fused the girders for the arcology's next expansion. It wouldn't be Papa. Not now. He'd already be down off the high beams and on his way home, with cash in his pocket and full water jugs from the Red Cross pump, but there were hundreds of others up there, working their own twelve-hour shifts. Impressionistic firefly flashes of workers lucky enough to have a job, delineating the arcology's looming bulk even when you couldn't see the building itself through all the haze.

Papa said it was almost alive. "Its skin makes electricity, *mija*, and in its guts, it's got algae vats and mushrooms and snails to clean the water just like someone's kidneys. It's got pumps that pound like a heart and move all the water and waste, and it's got rivers like veins, and it reuses everything, again and again. Never lets anything out. Just keeps it in, and keeps finding ways to use it."

The Taiyang grew vegetables in its vertical hydroponic gardens and fish in its filtering pools, and it had waterfalls, and coffee shop terraces, and clean air. If you were rich enough, you could move right in. You could live up high, safe from dust and gangs and rolling brownouts, and never be touched by the disaster of Phoenix at all.

Amazing, surely. But maybe even more amazing that someone had enough faith and money and energy to build.

Maria couldn't remember the last time she'd seen someone build anything. Probably the Santoses, back in San Antonio, when they'd put a new addition on their house. They'd saved for three years to make room for their growing family—and then the next year it was gone, flooded off the map.

So it was something to see the Taiyang Arcology rising proudly over Phoenix. When she'd first come to the city, in the refugee convoy, Maria had resented the Taiyang for how well the people lived there. But now, its shadow bulk was comforting, and the glitter and spark of construction work made her think of candles flickering at church, peaceful assurances that everything was going to be alright.

Maria held her breath as she opened the outhouse door. Reek and flies billowed out.

She and her father had dug the latrine in the cool of the night, hammering together a rough shelter with two-by-fours and siding scavenged from the house next door. It worked okay. Not like having a real toilet with flushing water, but who had that anymore?

It's better than shitting in the open, Maria reminded herself as she crouched over the trench and peed into her Clearsac. She hung the filled bag on a nail and finished her business, then grabbed the full Clearsac and headed back to the basement.

Down in the relative cool of their underground shelter, Maria carefully squeezed her Clearsac into their water jug, watching yellow turn clear as it passed through the filter and drained into the container.

Like a kidney in reverse, Papa had explained.

When they'd first started using the Clearsacs, she'd been disgusted by them. Now she barely thought about it.

But pretty soon . . . no more Clearsacs.

The thought filled her with relief. The dream of escape . . . She could still see Papa flying, proud and strong, free of all the tethers that kept them trapped in Phoenix. This broken city wasn't the last stop as Maria had feared. It wasn't their dead end. She and her father weren't going to end up like all the other Texas refugees, smashed up against the border controls of California, which said it already had too many people, and Nevada and Utah, which seemed to hate people on principle — and Texans in particular. They were getting out.

Smiling, she drank from the water jug. She tried to keep a disciplined eye on how much she had, but she was so thirsty, she ended up draining it and feeling ashamed, and yet still drinking, convulsively swallowing water until there was nothing except drops that she lapped at, too, trying to get everything.

Never mind. It's not like it was before. Papa's got a job now. It's okay to drink. He said it was okay to drink.

She remembered how it had been the day after Taiyang International hired him: him coming home with a five-gallon cube of water and two rolls of toilet paper, plus pupusas that he'd bought from a pop-up stand near the construction site — but most of all, him coming home smiling. Not worried about every drop of water. Not worried about . . . well, everything.

"We're all good now, *mija*," he'd said. "We're all good. This job, it's a big one. It'll last a long time. We're gonna save up. And we don't just got to go north now. We can buy our way to China, too. This job, it opens a lot of doors for us. After this, we can go anywhere. Anywhere, *mija*."

He kept saying it, over and over again: *We can go anywhere.*

Papa had a job again. He had a plan again. They had a chance, again. And for the first time in months, he sounded like himself. Not the scared and sorrowful man who kept apologizing that they didn't have enough food for the night or the medicine that Mom needed, or who kept insisting that it was possible to go north when it clearly wasn't. Not that man who seemed to crumple in on himself as he realized that the way the world had been was no longer the way the world was.

It had all happened so fast. One minute Maria had been worrying about what her mother would say about her B on a biology test and the dress she'd have for her *quinceañera*, and the next, America was falling apart all around them, like God had swiped his hand across the map and left a different country in its place.

You weren't supposed to get turned back by militias at the border of Oklahoma or see people strung in the margins of the interstates. But she'd seen both. Her father kept saying that this was America, and America didn't do these things, but the America in her father's mind wasn't the same as the America that they drove across.

America wasn't supposed to be a place where you huddled for safety under the shield of an Iowa National Guard convoy and woke up without them — waking with a start to desert silence and the hot flapping of a FEMA tent, realizing that you were all alone, and that somewhere out in the darkness, New Mexicans were planning to make a lesson of you. In Papa's mind, that shit didn't happen. On the ground, it did. There was America before Cat 6 hurricanes and megadroughts, and there was after — with everyone on the move.

That was all past now, though. Papa finally had a plan that would work, and a job that paid, and they were getting out.

Maria settled back on her mattress and dug out a language tablet. The Chinese gave them away free to anyone who asked, and people hacked them to get access to the public network. To make up for her greed with the water, she decided to study instead of watching pirated movies.

The screen lit up, and a familiar Chinese lady started the lesson. Maria followed her prompts. The lady moved on from numbers to other words, tricky games that highlighted the tonal differences between "ma" and "ma," "mai" and "mai."

Different language. Different rules. Tones. Tiny differences to Maria's ear that turned out to make all the difference in the world. If you weren't trained to listen for them, you didn't know what was going on. You were lost.

The lady in the tablet nodded and smiled as Maria said "buy" and "sell" correctly.

Maria was so engrossed in her study that it took a while to notice that time had passed, and Papa wasn't home.

She got to her feet and went out into the choking furnace of 120-degree heat. The smoke had thickened. It seemed like all of California was on fire, and all of it was blowing in to Phoenix.

Maria peered toward the Taiyang, but even the construction cutter flickers were invisible now. Papa was never late coming off shift. He always did his shift, got his pay, filled his jugs from the Red Cross pump, and came straight home.

She started walking toward the construction site, making her way down the long dust-rutted boulevards, where Texas bang bang girls stood on the street corners and tried to pick up rich Californians who were over the border to go slumming. Walking past the Red Cross pump, where the lines for water stretched around the block and the price always seemed to go up. Past the shanty towns of suburban refugees that filled Fry's and Target parking lots, all of them scavenging and building plywood slums around the relief pump, grateful to be close to any place where they could get water. Past the Merry Perry revival tent, where people lashed themselves with thorn-bushes and begged God to send them rain.

Maria trudged through the choking smoke and dust, wishing she'd saved some of her water jug for the brutal heat of the walk. The arcology loomed out of the smoke, a jumbled collection of boxy interconnected towers, as isolated from Phoenix as if it were a castle fortress.

On the Taiyang's construction side, the gate guard wouldn't let her in. He didn't seem to understand English, Spanish, or her broken Chinese. But he did make a call, though.

A Chinese man came out to her. A polished man, he wore a hardhat, nice clothes, and filter mask around his neck — a good one from REI that would keep California and Phoenix out of his lungs. Maria eyed it jealously.

"You're here about the accident?" he asked.

"What accident?"

"There was a fall."

He spoke with an accent, but his English was clear enough. It had been a long fall, he said. She wouldn't want to see his body. He was very sorry. Taiyang International had made arrangements for the respectful disposal of his body. She could pick up his remains in the evening. There was some leftover pay, and Taiyang would cover the costs of the cremation.

Maria found herself staring at the man's fancy dust mask as he droned on. The rubberized seals and replaceable filters . . .

Her father would be smoke. More smoke, adding to the burn that people tried to keep out of their lungs. Maybe she was breathing him in, right now — him and the Sierras and all of California.

His ash, flying free.

Trapping the pleistocene

JAMES SARAFIN

Here's a vigorous and fast-moving addition to the long body of stories in which time-travelers go back to prehistoric times to hunt big game, the best-known of which is probably L. Sprague de Camp's "A Gun for Dinosaur"—although here they're trapping the animals rather than hunting them, and they're after Pleistocene megafauna (in specific, a giant beaver the size of a car) rather than dinosaurs. And running into some unexpected problems along the way . . .

James Sarafin's first fiction sale was to Asimov's Science Fiction *in the mid-1990s. Since then he has sold short fiction to* Asimov's, Alfred Hitchcock's Mystery Magazine, The Magazine of Fantasy & Science Fiction, *and other print magazines. His short story "The Word for Breaking August Sky" won the Mystery Writers of America's Robert L. Fish Award (best first mystery story). Other stories of his include a semi-finalist for the Nebula Award and finalist for the Theodore Sturgeon Award. James Sarafin practiced as an attorney in Anchorage for thirty-two years, doing civil litigation, contracts, and trial work, before retiring at the end of 2013. He still lives in Alaska, along with his wife, two adult children, and two granddaughters. Sarafin is an avid outdoorsman and gets out of the city to real Alaska whenever he can. During high school, he earned college money by trapping fur on rural lands in central Ohio.*

The gray clouds had lifted over the bottomland, taking with them the threat of more rain. The creek ran high and muddy, near to overflowing its banks. Dead leaves of autumn swirled in back-eddies and jammed up against the protruding sticks of the beaver dam. Leaves clung to the man's boots at waterline as he shuffled across the waterlogged top of the dam. Floating leaves rose and fell with the waves of his wading; some went spinning free and sliding down the band of water that poured over the top of the dam where the main current flowed, where the beaver crossed the dam.

Sometime in the night, after the rain stopped, the temperature had fallen and the air had become still. Jack's breath plumed around him as he waded. The rocks along the banks and the edges of the dam were rimmed with the season's first ice. Early in the year for ice, but here it was.

It's winter again, Katie. The season when you left me.

He saw that the trap and guide sticks were gone from the crossover. He stooped to grope around the trap's anchor stake. The water immediately numbed his fingers and made the back of his hand ache. His hands were getting a bit arthritic from years of immersions in winter water. He caught the tie-down cable with his index finger and began hauling it in, hand over hand, feeling more than the weight of the trap on the end. It never got old, the thrill of this moment, almost as strong as when his father had first taken him trapping as a boy: when you realized you had something but still weren't sure what it was. *We know that thrill, don't we Katie?*

The other end of the cable was looped to a body-grip trap his grandpa had made by bending and welding quarter-inch-diameter spring steel. The leading spring of the trap had twisted sideways after firing, and the dark, slender form of an otter, locked in the trap's square jaws, corkscrewed just under the surface as he pulled it in. The otter's long body and tail waved snakelike in the current, causing the cable to throb electrically in his hands. He could have been here hauling in the same kind of trap and animal in his great-great-grandfather's time, if not for the rush of cars from the skyway that crossed overhead.

He compressed the trap's springs, opened the jaws, and shook the dead otter free. A nice big male, in prime condition, its wet fur matted flat to its body and a little gritty with mud carried by the stream. He shook the otter again and blew against its fur.

Do you see how it's primed up for winter? One of the Amish enclaves will trade us for this otter, Katie.

Jack reset the trap in the center of the overflow, bracing it upright with sticks taken from the dam. He still had one beaver, the old smart one, to remove from this colony for the landowner whose fields were being flooded by the dam. The landowner had tried removing the dam with an ax and even dynamite, but the beaver patched up any dam breaks almost overnight. Then, after doing everything possible to teach the beaver about traps and snares, the owner had called Jack.

He picked his way back across the dam and trudged along the trail to the road. A few dry leaves still rattled in the branches overhead and there was the musty smell of damp leaves underfoot. Remember when small steps followed behind him, how she liked to kick the leaves and send them flying in the wind? He resisted the urge to turn around and see the bitter truth again.

He paused to catch his breath atop the steep embankment leading up from the creek to the highway pull-off where his truck was parked. So much for carrying the extra weight of middle age. A life-shortening condition, they told him, and Carol was after him to get it cured with fat-cell-suppression treatments. Just a bit of tinkering with the right genes. But he'd have to go to one of the urban towers for the treatments and he'd almost rather die young.

Before he got to the truck, his phone rang. He fished around in his shirt pocket, found the phone, and squeezed it between thumb and forefinger. An image sprang up above his hand: the face of his wife.

"Jack," Carol said, "Emily called this morning. Henry is missing. He went off on some animal-capture job and was supposed to be back home the night before last. She's frantic."

"He didn't say anything to me about it," Jack told her. "Did she try the law?"

Her image nodded. "The sheriff hasn't been able to find a trace of him here in the enclave. And you won't believe who I just got a call from, five minutes ago. He said he's a project director for the government."

"The government," Jack said. "What project?"

"He didn't say. He said he's with the Department of the Interior. They want to hire you for an animal-capture job."

"Work for the government? That'll be the day."

"Jack, the guy on the phone said the job involves Henry's disappearance. He wouldn't say anything more. He wants to see you this afternoon at their headquarters. But, um, it's in one of the towers in south Columbus."

"So they just snap their fingers, and I'm supposed to come running?" Jack kicked a loose rock across the gravel pull-off. It *click-clicked*, bounced high, scattered smaller pieces of gravel. A few hours' drive, if conditions on the old highway weren't too bad. And then he'd have to go into that tower. He ought to just let the sheriff interview the guy. But the enclave's sheriff had no jurisdiction there, and the government wasn't asking to see him. If Jack left right now, he might make it before dark. No, not this time of year. He told Carol he'd go and dropped the phone into his pocket. He returned to his pickup truck and put the otter in the bed, beside the three beaver he had picked up at other jobs that morning.

Movement caught the corner of his eye. Darker shadows flickered past the dark edge of the woods on the other side of the road. Wolves had picked up his scent or the scent of the beaver. The lead wolf, the alpha female, came out along the edge of the road that marked the border between Jack's enclave and the wilderness preserve. She saw Jack looking at her and howled a quick warning to her packmates.

Jack's family had been on the land when it was a wilderness to the European settlers, when the wilderness was gone, and now that it was mostly wilderness again. Restored bear and cougar populations didn't cause the rural folks enough grief, so the government had brought in western timber wolves on the grounds that wolves had once inhabited the Ohio wilderness. The wolves' implants were supposed to keep them in the preserve, but things didn't always work as intended.

Kill one and there would be hell to pay, if not from the government then from the wolf worshippers and their lawyers. He could see them now, the fans and sponsors of this particular pack, leaning forward in their tower homes, watching the video feed through the eyes of the wolves. Waiting to see if they would take down this reckless enclaver for their next meal. Eat everything a man ever was, right down to his bones and the soles of his boots.

Jack took the stunstick out of his pocket, telescoped it to its full length, and let the wolves see it. Their fear of man was mostly gone, but one thing had been engraved deeply enough in the canine culture by generations of stone and steel and lead and electron: beware of men carrying sticks. You couldn't kill them with a stunstick, but could sure give them one hell of a shock. The wolves kept their distance, milling along the edge of the road, finally disappearing back into the forest after he got into his truck.

Jack drove down the empty road until he hit old Route 23 North, which paced the Scioto River for much of its length. This stretch of road ran next to a skyway, where the multitudes whizzed by high above ground on electromagnetic fields, lost in their business or conversations or whatever it was the tower-dwellers did with themselves. They couldn't be taking in the country at that speed. Or notice Jack trundling along on his antiquated surface wheels.

Lo, once there were superhighways, now razed and reclaimed back to the earth. Just a few of the older roads were left for the enclavers to use and maintain by themselves.

Dense, overhanging trees gave the semblance of moving through a tunnel. Grass and weeds crowded the edges of the old highway and sprouted from the cracks they had formed in the asphalt. Dead branches and debris littered the empty road and potholes abounded. Twice he had to stop and move tree limbs that had fallen during the last storm. Outside the boundaries of the enclaves, where beaver were protected by law, he frequently had to slow for submerged pavement. In one place the water came up to his floorboards. After an hour, he chanced to glance at the fuel gauge, saw it was almost on empty. At the next enclave, another farming community, he stopped at a crossroads store, bought a gallon of distilled water, and dumped it into the tank. Then he drove on into the gathering dusk.

He could see the lighted tower, looming ever larger through occasional gaps in the trees, well before he arrived. An example of the newest, footprint-reducing architecture, the tower was built like a giant morel: a tall, narrow cap with an irregular, ridged surface overhanging a smaller, round base. No, not a morel; if that tower was a mushroom, it had to be one of the poisonous varieties. From a hub level in the tower cap, the thin lines of skyways spread out in various directions. Like a giant spiderweb.

When he saw the government's sign at the compound's surface entrance, his foot went to the brake pedal and his hands twitched, wanting to turn the wheel back toward home. But he followed the entrance ramp into the compound. He drove through parklands where elk and camels grazed, over a creek, and the length of a small lake where swans swam in pairs, to arrive at a small paved area before a tower entrance. It held no other vehicles but looked as good as anyplace to park the truck, so he did. The outside of the tower base presented a rough, ridged surface with no windows or seams. He pulled his wool cap down over his forehead and raised his hands to push open a door. He stumbled slightly when his hands met no resistance and he felt a puff of air as he passed through the non-existent door into the building. The lobby's outer wall appeared to be made entirely of one-way glass that allowed a view of the compound outside. Or maybe he was only looking at video screens. It probably made no difference to the tower-dwellers.

The floor was covered with some mutated form of living grass that lay in a short, dense mat like a golf green. He gouged its surface with his boot-toe and watched it begin repairing itself. *Imagine that crap growing over your foot, eh, Katie?* From a wall of the tower's core a waterfall trickled down and formed a stream that meandered across the floor to his left. A few of the dark-robed tower-dwellers strolled and loitered, communing with their view of the outdoors. Others scurried in or out of the elevators. They paid him no mind.

Jack had walked through the lobby, halfway around the tower's core, when a voice growled his name from behind him. He turned and saw what looked like a cross between an orangutan and a human woman. She wore no clothing and was covered with straw-blonde hair, long but thin and with no underfur. Her face was bare ahead of her ears and heavily made-up. Her arms hung nearly to her knees and her breasts halfway to her waist; the breasts swung across her torso as she moved.

"Mr. Morgan, the director's office is this way." She smiled open-mouthed, displaying ivory canines. She seemed amused by his reaction.

"How do you know who I am?"

"We were expecting you. You're not connected, so you're the anomaly here."

She turned and knuckle-walked to the nearest lift, wiggling her hips as she went. He moved to follow and almost fell on his face as a weight dragged on his right leg, the one with the bad knee. Some kind of cleaner robot had wheeled itself across the floor and was licking the half-dried mud off his boot. He kicked the robot free and caught up with the ape-woman at a lift. They ascended to the hub floor, the one with the transit stations, where the skyways spread out like the spokes of a wheel. Caught in the spiderweb.

One step out of the lift and he was mobbed by interactive holograms. Human and cartoon faces mouthing soundlessly, waving ad banners or petitions or virtual collection slots for various causes. The only one he had time to read solicited funds for saving species of geothermal bacteria endangered by leaks in the freshwater pipeline running down through the coastal waters from Alaska to California. He had no means to filter them out, but when he failed to show an identity response, the holos vanished.

Following his guide closely, Jack was dumbfounded by a place without boundaries or familiar reference points. Gleaming glass and metal, lights and colors, senseless flickering images. The lobby appeared to extend forever in all directions, including behind him where the lift doors had vanished. People moved around him, some ethereal as ghosts.

He was led to a door that appeared to stand by itself in the borderless expanse. The door had lettering that spelled out some guy's name, project director of some division of bureaucrats, none of which Jack gave a crap about. His guide stepped aside and showed a last flash of canines and took two more steps to the side and vanished. The door opened, so he went in to a private office where a man wearing an early twenty-first-century-style business suit sat behind a desk.

"Good evening, Mr. Morgan." The man in the suit spread his hands to indicate the room. "We created this old-style office just so you might feel comfortable." He stood up, went around the desk, and held out his hand.

Yes, there were now walls Jack could see and touch, windows on one of them, and two visitor chairs in front of a desk that looked to be made out of walnut but was of course not real wood, if it had real substance at all. Jack ignored the man's extended hand and touched one of the chairs. It felt solid enough, so he dropped slowly into the seat. He took a deep, slow breath and fixed his eyes on this condescending bureaucrat who would have liked nothing better than to take away Jack's livestock and tools and traps, put a communication device in his head, and make him live far above ground in a meaningless anthill existence. No doubt to the dismay of some other bureaucrat whose job it was to manage the government's relations with the cultural enclaves.

The project director returned to his seat. The windows behind him showed a fine view of a forest-covered hill lit by a midday sun. Phony video image. "Let's get to business, okay?" the director said. "We'd like to issue a contract for your animal-capture services."

Jack shook his head. "I'm just here to find out where Henry Andersen is."

"You'll have to hear about our job for that. Your friend's location is confidential until then."

"What kind of job?"

"We want you to catch a beaver."

Jack nodded toward the fake window, an impulse he couldn't control. "If you people ever set foot on the ground, you'd see there's beaver all over the country."

"Not this kind of beaver. Do you want to find out about your friend?"

Jack shrugged, then nodded. "So you want a beaver caught. Just one?"

"You won't be able to bring it back alive." The bureaucrat touched his finger to his tongue and used it to trace a circle on the top of his desk. "We just need tissue samples. We expect you'll probably have to euthanize the animal first."

Jack decided it was his turn to wear a smile. "Euthanize."

"This is for a project that justifies the death of one beaver."

Jack kept looking at the man, waiting him out. He succeeded.

"Have you ever heard of *Castoroides ohioensis*?" the director finally asked.

"Doesn't ring a bell."

The bureaucrat looked confused, then his eyes went empty, his mouth hung slightly open—the vacant, moronic look of someone consulting his web access. A common enough expression for those who let nanobots build artificial things in the middle of their cerebral cortex. Why would you open the last place of privacy to the whole world?

"Ah, okay," the director said. "Meaning you haven't heard of it. You people use such interesting expressions."

"We get by." Jack lifted one muddy boot and crossed his legs. "Without an implant telling us what to say. And think."

"Okay. But to get to the point, *Castoroides ohioensis* was a giant species of beaver that lived during the Pleistocene epoch. It's been extinct for at least ten thousand years. Our project requires sending an animal-capture expert to the late Pleistocene to catch an *ohioensis* and bring back tissue samples."

"You want to send me back in time to catch a giant beaver?"

The bureaucrat nodded.

"What for?" Jack saw the bureaucrat's face begin to go blank again, so he translated for the man. "Why do you want tissue from one of these big beavers?"

The project director's finger traced circles on his desk again. He appeared to study the view through the video screens. Jack himself kept fighting the unconscious assumption that the view was real. "Our project involves cataloging the genomes of extinct Pleistocene mammals. For some species we have no bones, only fossils, and there's a limit to the information that can be obtained from fossils."

Jack thought of the only time in the past he cared about. "I'll go if I can make a side stop at one year, eleven months, two days ago."

The director started to shake his head, then his curiosity got the better of him. "Why then?"

"Because that's when my daughter fell through the ice and drowned."

"And you hope to change things and save her life." The director finished the shake of his head. "No one is allowed to go to a past time and place where there were people. You might change the past, the timeline of human history. In fact, you admit that you'd try to change the timeline."

"I just want to save my daughter. One little ten-year-old girl."

"I'm sorry."

"Then forget it." Jack stood up. "Screw you guys."

A slight frown crossed the director's face for a moment, then faded to an expression of serene disregard. Jack suppressed the urge to lean over the desk and backhand the man and shout at him. But there was no use trying to provoke someone with a mood regulator inside his head. The effort would only backfire.

"Before you leave, let's talk about your friend, Henry Andersen," the bureaucrat was saying. "He seems to have disappeared back there in the Pleistocene. His time capsule returned without him. And we hope you'll say yes to us now in order to go look for him."

"Are you saying you talked Hank into going back to the Pleistocene to catch one of these giant beaver?"

"Yes. I'm afraid you weren't our first choice, sorry."

"All by himself? You assholes sent him there all by himself?"

"The energy cost of time travel depends on the mass involved, and Mr. Andersen said he could do it by himself. We'll send you in a two-seat capsule, in case you do find him."

"Why would he agree to do that?"

The director shrugged. "Money. Even your people have some need for it, I understand. He also seemed perversely excited at the prospect of being able to catch an extinct giant beaver."

Jack sat very still. That sounded like Hank all right. The damn fool. Jack played with the collar of his wool shirt, which was still damp from the morning's rain.

"So, okay," the director continued. "Andersen agreed that four days' subjective time should be sufficient, so that's what the schedule allows. We don't want you staying any longer than necessary."

"Four days? If I have to get around on foot, it might take longer than that just to locate these giant beaver. Let alone find Hank, which would be my first priority."

"You'll be sent to known *ohioensis* habitat, where fossils of relevant age have been found. The same site we sent him to." He dipped his finger again and traced a circle on his desk. "Your contract pays a substantial bonus if you're successful."

"What if I run into prehistoric humans? Won't that risk changing the timeline?"

"We're sending you to a time before humans arrived on the continent."

"Aren't you worried I might do something to change the evolution of the beaver?"

"No. Modern beaver, *Castor canadensis*, were alive then, too. The giant beaver was a different genus that was driven to extinction by the arrival of humans in North America." The director leaned forward, noticed his necktie spooling up on the table, and wiped his fingers on it. "Useful apparel item. Why aren't you wearing one?"

Before Jack could decide whether to answer, the director's face took on that blank, stupid look again. Obviously getting instructions from someone else. Just a flunky, then.

"Okay, I'm required to disclose certain project risks. You cannot control the time capsule. The wormhole is directed from our facility. Though rare, there's the possibility of a wormhole misalignment. And North America was populated with dangerous megafauna—"

"Whoa. What does 'wormhole misalignment' mean?"

"Your capsule may not go precisely to when or where it's supposed to. Just a slight chance. But we could still find your capsule and retrieve you."

"Great. So what about the dangerous megafauna?"

"The division head insists that you be advised to take a firearm along for protection."

"I don't have a firearm that could stop a charging mammoth," Jack said slowly. "Why wouldn't you give me a plasma weapon?"

The director shook his head and smiled. "We don't hand over a modern weapon to an unconnected individual. Who knows what you might use it for? Sorry, you'll have to make do with your traditional cultural weapons."

"At least we still have our culture."

"Okay. So you'll go?"

"What if I say no?"

"We'll look for some other qualified individual willing to take the assignment."

"Someone who doesn't care about Hank, you mean."

It didn't have to be said that Hank was probably dead. Probably not a chance in ten of even finding his remains. Jack realized that, as he sat here right now, Hank certainly was dead—long, long dead and gone, even his bones turned to dust. Gone forever in the distant past. Could that be undone?

He opened his big mouth and said, "When do you want me to leave?"

They gave him no guide to lead him back to ground floor. They probably never thought of it. Once the director's door closed and vanished behind him, he was lost. He couldn't locate a lift entrance or even the walls of the tower core. It must have been a shift's quitting time, for people now swarmed around him, hurrying on their way to wherever tower-dwellers went after selling their daily lives to their jobs. Among them were the occasional trans-specied individuals like his former guide.

He dodged mere images and ran into real people. The real people bumped him along with the flow of the crowd. Bodies jammed against him from all sides. He walked into a wall he couldn't detect, then another. He could see only part of what was there. In a fleeting moment of insight, he recognized a band of wild horses browsing on prairie grass, a pair of moose stripping leaves from trees, salmon leaping to climb an ethereal cataract in midair. The moment was gone, and what remained were incomprehensible lights, links, and datastreams. None of what he heard was intelligible, just a cacophony of buzzes and clicks and whistles and beeps that he could no more interpret than he could the speech of porpoises. People were constantly running into him and glaring in annoyance, as if it was his fault they failed to detect him. He, the anomaly.

He tried to work his way out of the busy travel routes, but they shifted around him constantly. He felt the invisible ceiling and walls closing in on him, leaving no personal space or air to breathe. His legs wanted to run, anywhere, until he was out of there. His knees were coming unhinged. His bad knee buckled and he almost went down.

Jack caught hold of himself and took a slow, deep breath. *They're watching us, Katie.* They must be. Somebody watched everything here, the stage for a million reality shows. See the poor enclaver-hick lost in the tower. The thought held him together. He willed himself to take slow, deep breaths. Okay. He'd been lost in the woods a time or three. When that happened, you stayed calm until you could orient yourself. He elbowed a path through the mob and parked himself out of the way in the middle of a diorama that appeared to display the lifecycle of a freshwater mussel. He stayed put, ignored the chaos around him.

At last he caught a glimpse of a door opening in the air ahead and two people came out of a lift. He headed quickly for the lift doorway, squeezing through before it could close and disappear from view. He had no means to operate the lift, and it moved through a number of higher and lower floors before finally opening to a level where he saw the surface view of outdoors. He exited quickly.

A line of people in white robes was filing through an entrance. He squeezed past them and at last stood breathing the fresh air of outdoors. He waited to make sure he really was outdoors. Thank God.

A few of the white-robed people stood talking outside the tower, their bare feet immersed in the damp grass beyond the walkway. It was full dark now and Jack's truck was nowhere to be seen, so he looked up at the night sky to orient himself.

Something was wrong with his eyes. The stars had become fat smudges of light, none in any familiar position or constellation. Where were Jupiter and Mars? Venus should be following the sun to the west. And Polaris? Sirius? He stared at one of the stars too long and in a moment it came down to him, growing larger, moving quickly. Blooming in front of him in a burst of blue-white light. Holograms all around him then, moving soundless images just on the verge of being recognizable. A woman's face? He couldn't experience the whole effect, but part of it appeared to be an ad for a new skyway vehicle. Finally the display burst into a shower of sparks that died around him. The group of white-robed people cheered and applauded the display. Or were they applauding Jack's reaction to it? He noticed that they didn't look at the sky themselves.

He turned his eyes to the tower wall before he attracted the attention of another faux-star. Forget about compass directions. If he just kept walking one way around the tower, he'd eventually come to his truck. And he did.

It had never felt so good to slide behind the wheel. He started the engine and drove up the exit ramp as fast as he could. If those government people ever wanted to talk to him again, they'd have to come out to the country to see him.

Night had settled over the land as he headed down the highway to home. Beneath the overhanging trees, he drove through a tunnel of darkness that stayed always beyond the reach of his headlights. Why had he given up so easily on saving Katie? The one time in the past that mattered, and he lost it. Yet the director's words jibed with everything he had read about time-travel restrictions.

It was late when he turned at the rusted old mailbox post that still stood at the end of the drive leading to the family farm. Nice long driveway to keep the tower tourists at a distance. Yeah, take a tour of an actual working agrarian enclave. Roll along the ancient roads in a wheeled surface vehicle. At regular stops you may experience the sights, sounds, and smells, or perhaps talk to some of the locals. See how they live. See them at work in the fields, the kind of clothes they wear. Yes, those are real cattle and sheep, pigs and chickens, which they still enslave. They have an exemption under the Cultural Preservation Act.

Eddie was waiting for him outside the barn door. "Dad! I caught a muskrat in the creek!" He held out the furry rodent by its dark, scaly tail.

"You pull your traps if it ices up any more, you hear?"

"Okay. Will you help me skin it?"

"Maybe tomorrow, if I have time." The boy followed Jack into the barn. "I'm going away on a trip, so I have a lot to do before I leave." Then he realized it wasn't true. He would experience four days in the past while only a moment of present time elapsed before they brought him back. With Hank, if possible.

The barn held the familiar smells of dry hay, cow dung and piss, and green animal pelts. Jack set his gear to the side of the door and hung the beaver and otter from a rafter, high enough to be out of reach of the rats and cats. Hanging from the same rafter, still drying on the boards, were the skins of two coyotes, two other beaver, and three coons. Dry pelts hung on a wall, their skins stiff and crinkly like thick parchment. Tomorrow he'd skin and board out the new beaver and otter, then he'd go pull his trapline. It wouldn't be right to leave his traps set when he couldn't be sure he'd ever come back to check them.

Eddie set the muskrat on a workbench under an overhead light and began stroking the lustrous dark guard hairs on the animal's back.

"Did you eat dinner yet?" Jack asked.

"Yeah. I finished milking the cows, too."

"Good. Go get cleaned up, it's near your bedtime."

He went out after the boy and latched the barn doors, then thought to look up. The real stars, galaxies, and planets were back in their places over the open enclave sky. He searched and found the faint smudge of the Andromeda Galaxy, M31, Katie's favorite. Jack himself had always liked M104, and Katie liked that one, too; but he knew he couldn't find the Sombrero with his naked eye. Maybe he should get the old telescope out of the barn and have a look. No. It wouldn't be any good without her.

Carol stood waiting in the kitchen doorway, watching him as he came in. He hung his hat and jacket on wall hooks by the front door. She watched him do that and watched him take off his muddy boots. The warmth of the room brought the scent of evaporating sweat from the neck of his damp wool shirt. He went to the kitchen and she backed up out of the hallway, still looking at him. The lights in the room flickered, dimmed, then came back. Trouble in the enclave's old power plant again. Funny how events that seemed connected often weren't.

He sat down at the table and she turned to the old cabinet microwave oven to remove a plate of food. She must have put it in to warm when she'd heard his truck come up the drive. Meatloaf made of ground beaver meat, corn, and potatoes. The thick, peppery smell of the gravy made his stomach growl. She set the plate in front of him and sat herself down on the chair across the table.

After a while of watching him eat, she said, "Josh also called today."

Jack snorted. "You mean he's still alive? So what's up with them?"

She looked at her hands, gripping the table in front of her. "He actually won a drawing among the tower engineering staff for a two-week cruise of the moon. He and Shari are going next month."

"Are they still in that plural-marriage group?"

"No." She hesitated a moment, then: "At least they got out of it together."

"Maybe if they didn't get out of it together he would have come home," he told her. Katie would have stayed, he felt sure.

She gave him the smile, the one that always lifted him, no matter what. "Maybe. But it is what it is. There's still Eddie left to us." She kept looking at him.

His contract had a confidentiality clause, but damned if he was going to make Hank's mistake of honoring a contract by keeping secrets from his own wife. No way was he going to leave her frantically asking everyone she knew, "Have you seen Jack?" if he never came back. What a scatterbrain Hank was.

He waited until Eddie had gone to bed before he told her. Her first thought was the same as his. "Can you stop at two years ago?" He gave her the answer, the cold, bitter, final answer that had been given to him.

She wasn't keen at all about his going off trapping in the Pleistocene, but when he explained about Hank she quit protesting. He could see in her eyes the thought of facing Emily if she talked him out of going.

"I'll call Emily after you've left," she said. "I'll tell her you've gone to find Hank." She looked up, directly into his eyes, and said in a louder voice, "Jack, you make sure you come back. With Henry if you can find him. You hear me?"

Strapped into his seat, he felt an initial sense of movement, then nothing. He saw nothing outside because there were no windows in the spherical capsule. As space-time changed around him, he wondered if he'd feel the only time that mattered.

For one instant again, Katie, I'm going to be when you are. Maybe right around here is when I could have stopped you from going out on that ice. And maybe here is when you were a small child walking through leaves, and here is when you were born.

The passage seemed to take less than half a minute, but he couldn't tell whether his own sense of time was normal or compressed. How much time does it take to travel through time? The wormhole was supposed to leave him at the same place, but the moment after Hank's own capsule had returned to the future. He heard nothing until the crack of displaced air from outside the capsule when it popped back into normal space. But something wasn't right; he still felt no sense of his own weight. There was an explosion of gas inside the capsule as it filled itself with foam. Then the capsule hit something. Hard.

The foam saved his life, but the impact knocked him unconscious for a moment. When he came to, the sphere was rolling and bouncing down a rough incline of some sort with Jack going along end-over-end inside. His ride stopped a few seconds later when the capsule hit something yielding, bounced back uphill a ways, then rocked itself to a standstill. He swung the hatch open and waited for the foam to evaporate before trying to see where he was. So much for wormhole misalignment. He must have popped into normal space well aboveground. The rest of this time-travel business had damn well better work as advertised.

He climbed out and for the first time in his life beheld a true wilderness. No skyways split the air, no towers jutted up along the horizon. No roads or fields or other mark of human beings. He stood on the slope of a gradual hill covered with grass, dense patches of brush, and a few scattered groves of trees. His capsule had come to rest against a small patch of alders; their springy branches had halted his tumble downhill. A cool breeze was in his face, sending a few last wisps of foam fluttering from his head and shoulders and vanishing as they swirled downwind.

The grass on the hillside was below his knees, and the vegetation showed the bright green of youth. Early summer, then, and the sun indicated near midday. The air was cool and the trees were different from those he knew. Gone were the dense hardwood forests, the oak, ash, hickory, walnut, cherry, and beech. The trees he knew had not yet migrated this far north. He saw instead the less familiar white trunks of birch, the green-gray of aspen, the dark-green-and-black of spruce.

In the valley below ran a good-sized river, light gray-brown in the sunlight. Its current looked to be moving along at a pretty good clip, but not enough to make waves. The other side of the river wound past a bare cutbank that rose into a bluff downstream. Half a mile or so upstream, the river disappeared around the shoulder of the hill on which he stood, and farther upstream he saw a lake spreading into a vast marsh that faded out of sight into the distance. On the slope across the river, a herd of large deer-like animals were stripping leaves from some scrub willows in a meadow. Their legs were long and a few mature males in the herd carried huge racks in velvet and looking like a cross between the antlers of a bull elk and those of a moose.

Enough gawking at the landscape. Jack took his trapping and camping gear from the compartment under the seat in the capsule. He had his trapping gear in an old maple-strip pack that had belonged to his great-grandfather. His camping equipment, extra clothes, and food were in a duffel bag. He had brought an old pump-action .35 Whelen rifle, the most powerful firearm he owned, used at home for collecting venison and the occasional bear or boar. He fixed it to a gun-holder bracket on the side of the pack; he could release the rifle quickly by reaching back with his left hand. He worked his shoulders through the straps of the pack, grabbed the duffel, and started downhill. If these giant beaver were any sort of real beaver, they'd be near water. That's how Hank would have figured, too.

The ground was rough and uneven, a raw, wild land that had never felt the comb of plow and disk. Climb a grassy tussock one step, drop into a grass-hidden hole the next. While picking his way downhill, he scanned the ground for sign. He found a faint line of grass leaning in the direction of his travel, which might mark Hank's passage. Hard to tell after several days.

He was passing upwind of a grove of aspen when he startled some huge animal. Maybe it was his unfamiliar smell or the clink of steel in his pack. All he could see at first was a moving patch of long-haired, light-brown coat. Brush was snapping and treetops shaking as it made its ponderous way down toward the river. It broke into a clearing on the riverbank and turned to look back toward him. Bear-like body suspended over long, thick legs ending in hindclaws he could see even at this distance. Heavy gorilla-like forearms with big, wicked-looking claws, and a head shaped like a hamster's right down to the oversized, droopy cheeks. It used its heavy tail as a counterweight as it rose up on its hind legs to sniff the air. Twice a man's height, easy.

The giant sloth was still downwind, and he could tell when it caught his scent again because it let out a low snort and shook its ludicrous hamster head. If the scientists were right, the animals here should not yet have any fear of the hominids that were migrating out of Africa. The sloth didn't like the smell of this African hominid, anyway. It turned back toward the river and, with an unhurried, waddling gait, plunged into the water, wading and swimming to the far bank. It shook itself like a dog as it emerged, then climbed straight up the cutbank.

Jack opened the duffel, took out his .44 magnum revolver in its holster, and strapped it to his right hip. A lot of good it would do against an animal that size, but he felt better letting his hand brush against the gun handle as he walked.

He found the sloth's tracks crossing a patch of mud on a game trail that ran along the river. Water was still trickling into the huge tracks from a puddle in the middle of the mudhole. The sloth appeared to have been walking pigeon-toed, with its ankles rotated inward, weight resting on the outside edges of its feet and huge claws lying almost sideways on the ground. Jack studied the patch of mud. Smaller, soft-footed animals and several large, cloven-hoofed animals had also left their tracks.

And there, on the far side of the puddle, was a smeared track that could only have been made by the boot of a man who'd hopped the puddle and skidded a bit on landing. Headed upstream, toward the lake. Jack went the same way, now and then finding part of a boot track that hadn't been obscured by other traffic.

He found signs of old friends, familiar furbearers: muskrat pathways through the reeds, mink tracks on a sandbar, otter scat on a big rock. The river was cold and slightly discolored with fine, gray silt that coated rocks at the edge of the shallows. Twice he flushed flocks of ducks that went beating into the wind, turning to head upstream. Ducks weren't the brightest of birds; they liked to fly off in the direction you were traveling, so you just wound up flushing them again and again.

As he waded across a little feeder creek to continue up the game trail, he saw a beaver-chewed stick caught on a rock. He picked it up. Toothmarks of a size that belonged to the beaver of his own time, probably from a colony somewhere up the little creek. But he found no sign of any giant beaver.

Then all at once, he did. As he rounded the bend, at a narrow part of the river where the banks rose up higher and steeper, he found the cause of the lake and marsh he had seen before: a dam five or six times his own height and stretching all the way across the valley. It was made of logs and limbs and whole trees, cemented together with a mixture of mud and rocks. Water rushed over the top in a dozen places and strained through a few gaps in the structure's face.

The dam contained its own ecosystem, the holes of muskrat dens and swallows' nests, the twig and grass nests of other birds, an egg-shaped hive of yellowjackets hanging from a dead tree. Weeds, brush, and willow bushes grew in every gap between the dead logs and limbs. Live spruce and birch trees sprouted there too, some with trunks as big around as his torso, indicating that the dam had probably been maintained by generations of beaver. The tree roots probably helped anchor the structure.

At the base of the dam was a great pool, held back by a tangle of limbs and trees that had washed over the top. Ducks, geese, and a pair of swans swam and dove and preened their feathers in the pool. He stopped at the dam's base to look up at the structure. To support that mass of water hanging overhead, the dam would have to be about as wide at the base as it was high. The dam's face wasn't too steep but was far too tangled and overgrown to climb. He had to follow the game trail away from the river, climbing the bank through a stand of spruce trees, to skirt the dam. In the shade of the trees, a vicious swarm of biting gnats found him and harried him all the way to the top.

On the slick trail he found imprints where boot toes had dug in to climb. He came out of the trees above the dam, on top of a low ridge paralleling the river. The ridge and hillside below were grass- and brush-covered, logged-off long ago. A few gnawed white stumps stuck up from the brush, not yet rotted back to the earth. He stopped to catch his breath and look out over the lake, eyes following its flat surface near to far, until his sight grew fuzzy in the distance of the marshlands beyond. A dark line of deep water wound through the marsh grass and weeds, marking the path of the river current.

Built partly into the steep bank on the shore where he stood, not far above the dam, was a mound of sun-bleached trees, limbs, and packed mud constructed like the dam. It was a beaver lodge almost the size of Jack's house. The bank dropped steeply down to the lake here, and the water looked deep. The grass showed no sign of Hank's passage, but odds were he had gone to check out that lodge.

He found Hank's trapping pack and his rifle, leaning against the pack, on the grassy bank near the lodge. The rifle muzzle had a light misting of rust. A line of bent grass led straight uphill and he followed it. Hank had set up his camp in a good place, on flat ground on top of the hill, with a view of most of the lake. Some fallen timber offered a supply of firewood, and a spring ran down the hill nearby. Hank had set up a tent and dug a pit and ringed it with stones, the makings of a fire ready to go.

The fire-ring was as Hank left it, but the tent was flattened and torn apart. Hank's gear lay strewn about the camp, large toothmarks in most of it. Hank had hung his food, but not high enough. It had all been eaten, its packaging scattered in bits. Nothing but indistinct marks left in the grass.

Some big animal had come along . . . but was Hank here then? No sign of blood or human remains. Jack followed a few short trails to where Hank had gathered fire-wood and gone to relieve himself but found no trail that led very far—except for three parallel paths through the grass, where three large animals had crossed the slope of the hill and headed up the lake. The paths were too wide to have been made by the close-set legs of a man.

Jack carried Hank's rifle and gear up to camp and spent the rest of the day follow-ing dead-end trails. Rifle in hands, he followed the three animal trails for more than a mile before losing them in a swamp. He found no sign of Hank.

He hung the duffel with his food from the branch of a lone cottonwood growing by the spring, set up his own tent in a jumble of dead tree branches, and slept fit-fully, rifle lying next to his hand. Next morning he renewed the search, going back to the lodge where he'd found Hank's pack and rifle. Had Hank fallen in the lake and drowned?

He stopped next to the lodge where the bank dropped steeply down into the depths of the lake. Something caught his eye below the top of the murky water. Some-thing moving down there. He dropped to a knee, leaned forward, and put a hand up to shade his eyes against the glare. A pair of dark eyes looked back up at him from a head the size of a man's. Grizzled face like an old man's with a wispy handlebar mustache a forearm's distance below the surface.

He sensed sudden movement and began to rise and turn away as the water ex-ploded. All he saw then were snapping teeth that grazed his right ear. He kept twist-ing and fell forward, planting his nose in the mud of the bank. Something heavy hit his back and he heard teeth crunch into wood.

He was pinned to the ground by the weight of the thing as it tore at his pack, maple strips rending and splintering, a deep moaning sound coming from the ani-mal. Claws raked the shorn strips away. The animal stuck its head inside the pack, and Jack was jerked violently side-to-side and nearly lifted from the ground as it shook its head. Amidst the splintering of wood and moaning growl of the animal, Jack could hear distinct plopping noises as his trapping gear flew into the lake.

Then he was being dragged back to the water. His hands clawed at the grassy bank. The rifle had fallen out of reach. His right hand was pulled free . . . and that hand, if not his conscious mind, remembered the revolver at his hip.

Over his left shoulder he saw a flattened head with a short, wide snout and tiny laid-back ears. Coal-black eyes gleaming like marbles in moonlight. A long, dark-furred torpedo of death. His hand pushed the barrel of the gun between the giant otter's eyes and pulled the trigger. Bits of brain, blood, and skull fragments show-ered into the lake. The animal stiffened straight as a pole and slid beneath the water.

"God damn!" He cursed some more and could barely hear himself. His ears were ringing, but he had no memory of the gun's blast. His pulse hammered in his heart and echoed in his head. He sat on the bank and leaned against the side of the bea-ver lodge, trying to catch his breath. As his hearing returned, his ears began playing tricks on him. Faintly and from a distance, he thought he heard voices mingling with the music of his pulse and the ringing in his ears. Fairy voices from underground, singing in the vanished speech of fairyfolk.

No, it was just one voice, coming from inside the lodge. He didn't believe in talk-ing beaver or fairyfolk, and there should only be one other human on this continent.

"Hank?" he hollered.

"Yeah," came the faint reply. "Get me out of here!"

Jack started to laugh but cut himself off. He was sounding hysterical. Hell, he *was* hysterical. Suffering hallucinations. Henry Andersen in a beaver lodge? Right.

"What in God's name are you doing in there?" Let the hallucination come up with an answer to that one.

"A giant beaver pulled me in."

This time Jack didn't try to stop himself from laughing. His own imagination wasn't up to this much of a hallucination. He couldn't wait to hear the rest. Most of his trapping gear was gone from his demolished pack, but he found his hand ax lying in the grass on the bank. He leaned the rifle beside him and started chopping at the lodge.

"Come toward my voice," Hank called. "I've been working at it from the inside."

"No, it sounds like you're just digging into the hillside there," Jack told him. "Over here is the fastest way to get you out."

In fifteen minutes Jack was sweating and breathing heavily. The hard clay-mud that held the lodge together soon dulled the edge of the ax, and he had to pry the larger limbs out of the way using the flat of the blade. The lodge wall was a couple of feet thick, and he couldn't cut straight through because he had to work around a large tree trunk in the way. Finally, he felt the ax punch through and smelled a puff of damp, cool air from inside. Hank's face, eyes squinted and blinking, framed itself in the hole, a disembodied absurdity.

"I thought that sounded like you," Hank said, after his eyes adjusted to the light. "What are you doing here?"

"Looking for your sorry ass, what do you think?"

"I figured I was a goner for sure. All I have on me is a pocket knife."

They both worked on enlarging the hole, breaking off dried mud, pulling away sticks, until the opening was large enough. Jack would only have got himself stuck, but Hank's skinny frame squeezed through. He straightened his back and let out a groan.

"That big beaver has got two kits with her, and I had to wedge myself in a tiny nook to stay out of her way. She kept hissing and grinding her teeth at me. They all skedaddled out of there as soon as you let daylight in."

"Have to take your word on that."

"Did you fire a gun out here?"

Jack nodded. "A giant otter attacked me, big as a man." He looked down into the water where the otter had sunk. It had occurred to him to wonder if he could recover it for its fur. Make a hell of a thing to hang on the wall to yak and yarn about when he was an old fogy sitting in his rocking chair. No one would believe him otherwise. But the otter nightmare had sunk out of sight in the deep water.

Hank said, "Wish I could have seen it."

"You wouldn't be wishing to see it if you had."

"Maybe one of the extinct *Lutra* or *Satherium* species."

"You're the college boy."

"Your ear is bleeding."

Jack put his fingers to his ear and they came away with a smear of blood. Until then he hadn't felt the sting.

"Doesn't look bad," Hank told him. "Just a scratch."

A deep concussion sounded behind them. The water boiled a short distance from the lodge, like someone had just pulled the plug from the bottom of the lake. Jack saw the doglike head of a beaver, but huge, break the surface.

"There she is," Hank said.

Jack had tried to envision what one of these giant beaver must look like, but still was not prepared. She was swimming toward them and you could just about surf on her bow wave. In front of the lodge, her head submerged, her massive barrel of a torso rolled under, kept rolling by and rolling by, and she gave another slap of her tail as she dove.

Hank ran away from the bank, tottering uphill on unsteady feet. "I ain't letting her grab me again!"

Jack snagged his rifle by the sling and joined Hank upslope. The beaver's snout appeared in the hole in the lodge and she sniffed around for a bit. A moment later, they saw a ripple of waves moving away from the lodge.

"You say that beaver took you in there?" Jack said.

Hank shook his head. "Damnedest thing. I was out on the far edge of the lodge, trying to spot the entrance. Thought I might get a snare down there. Then I slipped and fell in. You know, I never could swim too good. I was thrashing around when that mama beaver drug me under and hauled me in there."

"You're pulling my leg."

"No kidding. Maybe she thought I was one of her kits in that murky water. They're about my size, and still look to be learning to swim."

"Maybe she's love-struck. Maybe if you shaved that fur off your face, she'd have let you be." Jack laughed a real laugh. It felt good, finding Hank alive.

A ripple of waves returned to the lodge and the beaver appeared again in the hole. She had brought in her forepaws a big gob of mud from the lake bottom and was going about the business of repairing her home.

"What day is it, anyway?" Hank asked. "I lost track of time in the dark in there."

"It's the day after the day you were supposed to leave."

"I was in there almost three days, then. Good of them to make me wait so long."

"Next time I'll be sure to check all the beaver lodges first thing," Jack told him. "I got here yesterday. They were worried about a paradox if they sent me any earlier."

"Oh, yeah," Hank said. "I see the problem."

"I thought, what if they sent me back earlier, to warn you, maybe. But if I did, and you got home on schedule, then why would they have to send me back to warn you?"

"That's why they don't try it," Hank said. "No one's sure what would happen. Hell, no one really knows where these wormholes go. We might be in some alternate universe here, instead of Earth's actual past."

If so, then even if Jack could go through the wormhole to save her, when he went back to his own time she'd still be dead. It wouldn't be his own Katie that he'd saved.

Hank rubbed his head. Bits of dried mud broke and flaked off as he did. "I'm starving. I got some water in there from the dive hole but only had a couple energy bars to eat."

"It's about lunchtime for me, too. Let's go back to camp and grab a bite."

"I did get one trap set before I fell in the lake," Hank said as they climbed the hill, "on a dam crossover partway to the other side. Soon as we eat, let's go check it."

A well-used game trail ran through the tall grass and protruding logs and sticks along the top of the dam. The trail dipped down in channels where the lake water overflowed. The channels dropped into cascades running over the face of the dam to the big pool of the river below. On the lakeside the dam fell more steeply into the depths of the lake. Several of the overflow channels showed some evidence of being used as crossovers by smaller animals, but Jack saw no sign that giant beaver had done much travel downstream.

"I brought an old Newhouse bear trap and set it in this trail," Hank said as they walked. "Not much fresh sign here, but I was tired of hauling that big old trap around. I was planning to move it when I found a better place."

"How would you get a big enough weight out in deep water to drown one of these giant beaver?"

"I couldn't figure that out, either. I was going to listen for a commotion over here and run down with my rifle before the beaver could twist out. They seem mostly nocturnal, like their smaller cousins."

Hank stopped at the second channel and they both looked down at the empty mud bottom below the flowing water. The chain, still fastened to a log embedded in the dam, ended in a broken link; the trap was gone. In the mud that had been firmed and slickened by the current, they could see only slight indentations and a few large clawmarks. Jack's foot hit something hard in the grass—one of the trap's massive U-shaped springs. Hank found a twisted trap jaw on the dam face, and Jack found the crumpled trigger plate lying in the water just above the dam, but that was all that remained of the bear trap. Jack rose and did a 360-degree pan from the forested river downstream to the deep open lake upstream and back to the river again.

Hank unslung his rifle. "I think I'm going to start carrying this in my hands."

"Notice I'm already holding mine," Jack said. "Ever since I found your camp."

They stood contemplating the remains of the trap, until Hank said, "Supposing we just shoot one."

"It'll sink. How would we find it in this murky water?"

"Looks like glacial silt. Must be a glacier somewhere upstream, grinding on the limestone bedrock. This could be the ancient Scioto River, coming down from the north." Hank pondered a moment. "Okay, so we make a grapple out of tree branches, tie it to a line, and try to drag the carcass to shore."

"How would we throw a grapple like that?"

"Maybe we could make a raft to float out and recover the beaver."

"We've got three days left." Jack kicked at a stick protruding from the dam. "If we can't catch a beaver in that time, maybe we shouldn't call ourselves trappers."

Hank gave him a disapproving look. "You were an idiot to take this job, you know. We'll probably be lucky just to survive the next few days."

"Think maybe I should have turned down the work?"

"Only if you were smart, which you're not."

"Look who's talking—the idiot who agreed to come here in the first place."

Hank contemplated the lake upstream from the dam. "I only brought the one trap, so we'd better try using snares."

"That's what I figured to do all along. Brought some locking bear snares. But that damn otter tossed them all into the deep water."

"I brought half a dozen snares, along with that trap."

"You still want to try hanging one over that lodge entrance?"

"Nope. It's way too deep. Anyway, who wants to take a mother from her kits? We couldn't call ourselves trappers."

"You sure you didn't just fall for mama beaver?"

"Funny," Hank said. "Let's do some more scouting around."

The day wore on past late afternoon as they worked their way up the far side of the lake from camp, looking for beaver sign. At the edge of the water they located several wide trails with smooth, rounded edges like larger-scale beaver runways, but there was little indication of recent use. They hung snares across these trails anyway.

A mile or so from the dam they came to a low ridge of land that stuck out as a peninsula partway across the lake. The peninsula and surrounding shore were being logged-off of the larger birch and aspen. Piles of fresh chips lay around fresh-cut stumps left from trees that had been hauled away for beaver feed or building material. Here a beaver runway led out of the water and a well-used trail crossed the base of the peninsula. They set a snare where the runway joined the trail. By then the sun was going down, and dark did not feel like a good time to be out in Pleistocene country.

They made supper and sat eating side-by-side on a fallen tree near the fire. Now and then one or both looked away from the fire and out toward the lake that lay hidden in the blackness of night. From where they sat, the beaver lodge lay beneath the slope of the hill, but they could see a line of white sticks marking the top of the dam. Much of the time they just listened for any sound from the other side of the lake. The wind was picking up as night settled in fully, leaving the fire's smoke to stream up the valley, over the dark expanse of the marshlands.

After a while, Hank said, "You know, I did some digging around before I left home. What did they tell you about the government's latest rewilding project?"

"Rewilding? The wolves weren't enough?"

Most of Hank's face lay covered under his dark beard, and his teeth really stood out in the firelight. "I bet you thought they were done, didn't you? Wrong. They're out to restore all North American species whose extinction was caused by the arrival of humans on the continent."

"Are you telling me they want to bring back these giant beaver to our own time?"

"Yeah, along with the rest of the extinct megafauna. They aim to restore North America to its natural state, as it existed in the Late Pleistocene before people arrived. Pleistocene rewilding has been considered for at least a century, but all they could have done was use proxy animals from Asia or Africa. Now, with time travel, they can reproduce the actual Pleistocene megafauna. They've already begun releasing *Camelops* and tapirs in Ohio. We're not the first to be sent through time to collect genetic material. We're just the first trappers."

"You mean they want to bring back wooly mammoths? Are they nuts?"

"Sure they are," Hank said. "Though mastodons seem more likely around here."

Jack was silent as he tried to wrap his head around the concept. He imagined mastodons playing with his fences, a giant sloth loose in his orchard. And giant beavers . . . He said, "God, I'm glad my place is in the hills."

"Don't worry. According to the government, these beaver don't build dams."

They both had a good laugh. Jack got up and grabbed a few more sticks for the fire. The wind sawed at the burning wood, sending sparks streaming toward the lake. The wind had acquired a chilly bite. He pulled his collar up on his neck and edged a bit closer to the flames.

They sat quietly, watching the wind work at the fire, until Jack finally said, "Something about camping out always makes my mind work more clearly."

Hank nodded. "I wonder what it is about sitting by an open fire that makes us feel content? Must be something primitive left in us."

Jack nodded. "I'm going to miss my bed, though."

"I think you don't just miss your bed, but also she who shares it."

"I ain't denying it." Jack poked a stick at the fire, momentarily doubling the stream of sparks.

Hank sighed. "Yeah, I'm feeling kind of lonely for Em too. We need to stay together and be extra careful about everything we do here. If one of us gets hurt or lost or something, we might miss our pickup."

At dawn they returned to the far side of the lake. The first two snares were undisturbed, but the last one, set on the trail crossing the peninsula, had been hit. The ground was torn up all around and most of the trees within the ten-foot radius of the snare's length had been chewed down. Their trunks lay in a fallen tangle. Eventually the beaver had hit upon the large spruce that anchored the snare, leaving the trunk to fall into the lake and a chiseled stump leaking sap onto a pile of chips. They could smell the sweet, musky scent of beaver on the ground.

"Damn," Hank said. "We must have missed a neck-catch. Who'd figure it could cut through all these trees in one night?"

At least one beaver was using the trail across the peninsula as a shortcut for moving along the shore. They hung a new snare at each end of the trail where the animal was entering and leaving the water. On the far end of the trail, they looked out over unending marsh covered with aquatic weeds. The shoreline and the trail both subsided into the marsh. From there the beaver's pathway continued as a dark channel of open water through the aquatic plants. In the distance they saw another giant beaver lodge jutting up from the flat expanse.

Jack said, "These big beaver must do a lot of traveling."

"Makes sense. They probably need a huge range to find enough food for their large bodies."

"We'd need a boat to trap this marsh right. You just can't cover enough ground on foot."

They returned to camp for lunch, then scouted up the near side of the lake for a couple of miles, setting two more of Hank's snares. The last was set across the mouth of a creek where it ran into the lake. The bottom and banks of the creek were smooth and rounded from the passage of beaver. The creek was too wide to jump and too deep to wade, and the sun was going down, so they called it quits for the day.

Camp had been hit again. Jack's tent was ripped apart, his gear strewn all around. Their sleeping bags had been dragged around in the dirt and torn, though remained barely useable. Only the food bag hanging high in the tree had been left alone. They spread the tattered tent over some dead branches as a rain-fly and gathered the remnants of their gear and equipment. Again, they found no clear sign of what sort of animals had paid them a visit. Three trails of bent grass led off up the lake, only a few hundred yards from the way Jack and Hank had come.

Hank said, "I've about had enough of this."

"At least they didn't get our food."

After eating supper at the fire, Jack said, "You lived with the tower-dwellers when you went off to college. Were you connected?"

"Couldn't keep up with the coursework otherwise," Hank told him. His dark face showed gleaming teeth in the firelight. "Did I ever tell you what my major was? Paleontology. This poor fool just couldn't resist a chance to see these animals alive."

They had built up the fire and Jack's legs were getting hot, so he scooted back a bit. "You didn't keep it—the implant?"

"It's still in here." Hank tapped his head. "I had it shut off when I moved home."

"It hasn't caused any damage?"

"None that I know of. Unless we're talking about the brain damage that led me to take this job."

Jack used a stick to poke the fire. There was little wind, the sky was clear, and the spark-stream rose toward the stars. Looking away from the firelight, he found Jupiter immediately. A few recognizable stars had moved and some of the constellations were tweaked out of familiar shape. Different time or different universe? The question had never felt more important. Could the stars give him an answer?

Precession of the earth's axis should not be much of a factor, assuming he had traveled in time almost one full twenty-six-thousand-year cycle. The nearer stars, with their greater proper motion, should show the greatest change. The Pleiades were recognizable, but not in their familiar location in the constellation Taurus. The star he assumed to be Sirius was way out of position, had lost some of its brightness, and was now near a faint blotch he guessed might be the M50 star cluster. Distant galaxies and star clusters should show little or no change; and yes, Andromeda was in its usual position. These observations were consistent with movement through time in their own universe. Jack wondered whether, if he had the right star charts and a telescope, he could find anomalies that might suggest he was in a different universe.

He said, "If we hadn't sent him to college, he'd probably still be living in the enclave."

"Who, Josh?"

"Yeah. But what could we do, with a bright young man who wanted to learn?"

"When he gets enough of tower life, he may come home yet."

Jack rested a boot on a spruce log protruding from the fire. Pitch on the other end of the log burned with a blue flame. "What brought you back?"

"Family. Friends."

"Didn't you make a bunch of new friends out there in the world?"

"Yeah, some, I guess." Hank poked his own stick at the fire, turning over another log. Flames flared up as they caught the unburned wood on the other side. "But not anyone who would travel twenty-five thousand years to look for me."

"Forget about it."

"Sure I will."

They watched the fire. Jack said, "Kind of weird to think of family while we're sitting here."

"Why?"

"They're not even alive yet. Does that make them real?"

"They're real in our memories."

"Which memory?"

Hank gave him a puzzled look.

"I mean," Jack went on, "with Carol it's easy. She came from that Smoky Mountain enclave. She's been an adult since I met her. Got older, maybe, but she's pretty much the same person in all my memories." Jack poked the fire more vigorously.

"And Josh, I think of him as an adult, too."

"You're talking about Katie now, aren't you?"

"She's not alive anymore in our own time." Jack gave the fire a vicious poke, sending a shower of sparks skyward. "And they won't let me go to a time when I could have saved her. The last memory I have of her is her lying in her casket, still and cold."

"That's not the memory you have to keep."

"All I know is her loss. The hole it left in me. I can't stop thinking about it. Her."

"You must have memories of the whole time she was growing up. She lives in all of those memories, so long as you keep them."

"I don't have any trouble keeping them. The problem is letting them go."

Eventually they crawled into their sleeping bags. Jack tried to sleep, but couldn't stop thinking. When is the *here*, the *now*? Is it when a person *is*, or when he thinks himself to be? Can you live in the memories, or must the mind follow the body? Does the world around you say when the *is* is, or does your own mind decide?

If *is* is where memories are, then why not when Katie was ten years old? Together, trapping the creeks, fishing the river, waiting in the deer blind. The smile that lit her face when she caught her first muskrat, the disbelief and joy when her shot folded the grouse's wings. Was there a way to keep only the good memories? To revisit them without grief or bitterness?

And then there was Eddie. The boy had just caught his own first muskrat, and Jack never did help him skin it. He was old enough to start following Jack on the trapline. They both deserved to make their own memories together.

Jack was in a vanished world, long gone. But now it was the *is*, to his body and mind. His world back home existed only in his mind. His family was vanished from the what-*is*, until he returned home. If he and Hank missed their pickup and were stuck here, his family wouldn't exist outside of memory.

Maybe somewhere Katie hadn't died, but that was in some other world than his own. She would never live again in his own world, whether he went home or was marooned here. If memories were as good as the real thing, the real now, he could stay here and remember his family. He could lose himself to thoughts of the past. But memories weren't as good. They were just all you had left when the ones you loved were gone.

The snares on the peninsula trail on the far side of the lake were untouched. Scuffed-up leaves and forest litter in the gathering light of dawn showed that a beaver had walked around the snares.

"Uh-oh," Jack said. "Looks like we educated a beaver." The snare wire was big enough to be seen and avoided once the beaver had learned about it. They must be no less smart than their smaller cousins that Jack had trapped most of his life.

They went back across the dam to check the snares on the camp side of the lake. The first was undisturbed, but they had caught something in the last snare, the one set across the mouth of the creek. The ground was scuffed-up, grass trampled, and brush broken all around. Jack found the stump-end of the snare still anchored to the base of a big spruce tree. The wire ends had separated, unwound, and spread apart. It looked like a steel-stranded flower in his hand.

"Damn," Hank said. "That was eighth-inch wire rope."

"I think we caught a beaver here, then something else came along and took it. Something a lot bigger."

They stared at a line of broken brush leading up the little creek through scattered trees. "I guess we'd better track it down," Jack said. "See if there's enough left for tissue samples."

A dozen yards uphill was a huge pile of carnivore dung, still steaming in the cool morning air. A fragment of food packaging protruded from the pile.

"Aha," Jack said. "It's our camp raiders."

"Good," Hank said, tightening his grip on his rifle. "We're due some payback."

They followed the trail of snapped brush and flattened grass a short distance to the edge of a swampy meadow. There was little blood, but a blind man could have followed the trail, which led straight to a stand of stunted spruce out in the meadow. The trees were too thick to see into. As they started forward a distinct clicking sound came from the spruce, repeated twice, then followed by a series of deep whoofs. A head like a giant bulldog's thrust itself out of the trees and appeared to levitate high above the ground. It snapped its teeth and whoofed once more.

Then the creature dropped to all fours and was coming at them, a huge thing tall as a man's head at its shoulders, with legs long as a horse's and galloping like a horse, black claws gleaming above the flat-black footpads. Ears on that bulldog head laid back and body straight as an arrow, coming faster. A nightmare chimera, accelerating to full speed in two strides, forequarters rising and falling as it came.

It was halfway across the meadow by the time Jack had the rifle to his shoulder, firing, working the slide-action, firing again. A trail of spinning brass arced over his rifle, showing that Hank was firing too. The beast filled his view, until his tunneled vision saw only the black eyes and ivory teeth, and he fired.

Hank fired again and the bullet appeared to strike the heavy scapular bone of the left shoulder, causing the animal to stumble slightly. The massive bulldog head dipped down, and Jack, ignoring the riflesights, just looking down the barrel, drove a round directly through the top of its skull. The dark hole left by the bullet immediately filled with a column of blood that fountained out with the beat of the creature's heart. The bulldog head swung once to the left, once back and to the right, flinging a crisscross of blood-spatters on the grass. The animal's forequarters collapsed and it dropped onto its belly, and Jack fired his last round into its neck. Lungs like the bellows of an ancient blast furnace took one improbably long, ragged breath, then stopped.

Jack lowered his empty rifle. He tried to speak, cleared his throat, tried again. "That's cutting it a bit fine." His voice came out as a dry squeaking noise. He cleared his throat again.

"Yep." Hank appeared to want to say more, but his voice squeaked out, too.

Jack managed to bring his breathing down to a low-pitched rasp. "What is this thing? Some kind of bear?"

Hank cleared his own throat and nodded. "Can't think of the scientific name. Hell, I can't think of the common name. Jesus, I can't even think of my own name right now. Wait. It's a giant short-faced bear."

"Why couldn't we have run into a pygmy long-faced bear?"

"If there was such a critter, we'd probably run into that one, too."

Jack could see one of the animal's eyes. It looked the size of a grapefruit inside its socket. It was already acquiring that thin, milky glaze of when the tear ducts of a mammal ceased working in death. Without having to move his feet, Jack extended the rifle barrel to poke that eye, just to make sure.

"*Arctodus*," Hank said. "That's it. Biggest mammalian carnivore that ever walked North America." Hank shook his head. "Just think—pretty soon we may have them running around in our own time."

"Well, I'm not taking back a tissue sample of this thing." Jack had noticed a mosquito drinking off his left hand. As he watched, the insect's abdomen bloated and turned red. He let it drink its fill and fly off. "They really believe these things were wiped out by cavemen with stone-tipped spears?"

"Maybe they all died when their prey was gone." Hank squatted down to look at the bear's head. He put his hand over one forepaw. The naked claws were twice as long as his fingers. "Look here." He pointed to a line of cut hair and bruised skin on the forepaw. "We've found our trap-destroyer."

Jack remembered something important and looked back toward the spruce stand. He felt a sudden urge to reload the rifle. He fumbled two rounds to the ground before he got one into the magazine. "If that's a sow," he tried to say calmly, to steady his own hands, "imagine how big a boar would be."

"We can't be sure of its sex unless we can roll it over. These bears had proportionately slimmer bodies than the bears we know."

"Nope, I'm pretty sure it's a sow. You better get up and reload."

"Why?"

"'Cause she's got a couple of subadult cubs with her. And they're coming this way."

Hank stood up and dug into a pocket for more cartridges. The two young bears were out of the spruce stand now, peering at the men in that near-sighted bear way. As one they turned, trotting smoothly with none of the usual waddling bear gait, to swing downwind.

"I guess they're going to keep our beaver. Unless you want to make a fight of it."

"Hell," Hank said, "they aren't much bigger than adult grizzlies. Why don't we just walk over there and take it away from them?"

"You first. I don't have enough ammo on me."

They waited to see if the bears would leave, but the two cubs were slowly approaching from downwind, showing no fear. Hank sighed. "I guess it's not worth the risk. We'll have to catch another beaver."

They backed down the trail, leaving the cubs to sniff at their mother's body, and returned to camp. They built the fire back up about as high as they could and sat silently contemplating it while they ate lunch.

"Just one night left," Hank finally said.

Jack looked at the ground. "At least we won't be helping them bring back these giant beaver."

"They'll just send someone else."

"We won't be able to hold our heads up if we get skunked and someone else catches a beaver." They both gave halfhearted laughs.

Jack felt drained, tired, and weak, and Hank looked the same. But they picked themselves up and trudged across the dam and up the lake to the trail that crossed the peninsula, the place where they'd found the most beaver sign.

Their snares remained undisturbed, so they walked the trail to look for new ideas. Jack went past it twice before he stopped to ponder a large, dead cottonwood tree that leaned over the trail above his head. A beaver had chewed through its base some years back, and the tree had fallen halfway before it tangled with a smaller spruce on the other side of the trail. After that the cottonwood's top had broken away in some wind- or snowstorm, leaving a main trunk that was at least a yard in diameter. The wood was still solid and the trunk probably weighed well over a ton. If the spruce hadn't been there, it would have fallen squarely across the beaver trail. Jack remembered how beavers were sometimes killed by the very tree they were cutting down.

Hank said, "I wonder how primitive man ever wiped these beaver out. If that's really what happened to them."

The light came on the rest of the way for Jack. "You remember that time when we were kids and made that deadfall? You read about deadfalls in some old book, so we made one, and we caught a squirrel in it."

"Yeah. A deadfall is one of the most primitive kinds of trap there is."

"That's why I suggested it. We don't need anything but what we find right here."

"How in hell would we make a deadfall big enough to kill a giant beaver?"

"With this treetrunk here. If we can get rid of that spruce . . ."

Hank studied the tree and trail. "I don't have a better idea. If you can free that tree trunk so it will fall, I'll make a trigger."

Jack found two straight, young-but-stout birch trees. With his ax he cut and trimmed them into poles, which he lashed together near the top. He raised this bipod up to brace the cottonwood trunk, then cut down the spruce that had supported it. He held his breath as the spruce fell away. The massive cottonwood groaned as its full weight came to rest on the bipod, but it stayed in place.

By then Hank had carved out the three trigger pieces and base, also out of birch. The pieces fit together as a figure-4, with the long horizontal piece extending across the trail. When that part of the trigger was disturbed, it would pop out of a notch in the vertical piece, which in turn would kick the angled and vertical trigger pieces out of place, allowing the tree trunk to fall. In theory.

They took the birch bipod away, allowing the full weight of the cottonwood to rest on the trigger. It held. They tested their deadfall by holding the bipod a short distance below the trunk and tripping the trigger. Sure enough, the cottonwood dropped immediately, a fraction of an inch, before catching on the bipod. They reset the trigger and took the bipod away, carrying it uphill, out of sight of the trail, in order to minimize disturbance at the site.

"One thing bothers me," Hank said. "We educated the beaver that's using this trail, and now we've left our scent all over the place. What if he's come to associate our scent with danger and shies away from this part of the trail?"

Jack thought about it. "Let's move a snare a bit up the trail from here. Make him think that's the new danger. He should go around the snare, then be back on the trail before he hits the deadfall."

By the time they finished, it was getting dark and they hurried back to camp. Every sound in the forest caused them to raise their rifles.

"Can you imagine a couple tower-dwellers trying to face that bear?" Jack said as they made their way across the dam.

"They'd never get that far," Hank told him. "They're all too dependent on the web connection they've had since they were kids. There's nothing to connect to here in the past. The ones that tried to go back in time were so lonely and panic-stricken that they could barely get out of their capsules."

Jack smiled. "So us poor backward enclavers are good for something after all."

The night was very still, and in the wee hours they both awoke to the sound of the cottonwood falling on the other side of the lake. On a windy night it might have been any tree. Even now, the deadfall could have been tripped by accident or by some other animal. That was it, then. They either had a beaver or they didn't.

They broke camp in the dark, got what little was left of their gear ready to go. At first light they crossed the dam and went up the lake. The beaver lay in the middle of the trail with its legs folded up as if it were taking a snooze. The tree had fallen squarely and broken the animal's back just behind the forelegs. It was an old male, even larger than the female they had seen. Its teeth were cracked and the right foreleg had been lost to some accident, predator, or beaver fight. The remnant of the missing snare stretched between the animal's right shoulder and left foreleg.

They used the birch poles to lever the cottonwood off the beaver. The big animal's legs were stiff with rigor mortis and they had to work them loose before they could roll it onto its back. Its tail was proportionately longer and narrower than a regular beaver's and its incisors were like spades, with ridges running from the roots to the tips.

Jack breathed in the beaver's sweet, damp scent and took out his knife. Starting at the animal's lower lip, he began to split the tough, thick hide down the chest and abdomen all the way to where the fur ended at the base of the long scaly tail.

"What are you doing?" Hank asked. "All they need is a tissue sample."

"It may not be prime this time of year, but I ain't going to waste a fur like this. They can get all the tissue samples they want from the flesh and fat we scrape off the hide at home."

"I guess our contracts don't say we can't bring back a fur." Hank took out his own knife. "But we don't have much time left."

While Hank skinned out the forequarters and head, Jack did the hindquarters, cutting around the ankles and working the hide free of the legs with his hands and the knife. When they were done, they dragged the carcass off, folded the hide once, skin to skin, and rolled it up.

Jack took one last look at the carcass and noticed the dark castor sacs showing through the thin wall of the animal's lower abdomen. He was staring at them and suddenly felt his mouth form a smile. Castoreum was attractive to most mammals and had been used for centuries in perfume. It also made a great trapping lure. He took out his knife and removed the sacs, each larger than his hand and consisting of wrinkled convolutions like brain matter inside a translucent membrane.

"Why are you taking the castors?" Hank asked.

"We may just find a use for them."

They tied the beaver skin together with a couple of snares and slung it over their shoulders like a roll of carpet. Jack looked at his watch. "We'd better shake a leg." They collected their remaining snares as they went.

As they waded across a spillway on the top of the dam, Jack paused to catch his breath. Fat-cell suppression would sure improve his mileage. Looking down at the water, he smiled again. Hell, he'd already survived an afternoon in one of the towers. And none of those people could survive one hour here in the Pleistocene. After the trip to the doctor's, maybe he and Carol could visit Josh and Shari, and even take Eddie along. Better to show him the outside world than let him stay curious about it. Katie was gone no matter what he did. Better to live with the living than the dead.

They reached the sphere with twenty minutes to spare. "What do you keep grinning about?" Hank demanded.

"Let's get loaded up and I'll tell you."

The beaver hide and castors barely stuffed into the compartment under the seat. They had to set the remains of their gear on their laps.

While they were waiting, Hank said, "Okay, what's so amusing?"

Jack felt his grin get bigger. "I've been thinking. Suppose a bunch of these giant beaver are turned loose in our time. What do you think they'll do?"

Hank blinked. "They'll do what beaver do—cut trees, build dams, make more beaver."

"Lots of trees. Giant dams. And a bunch of beaver."

"Yeah, well, that's what the tower-dwellers want. They couldn't law us out of existence, so they want to drown us out."

"We'll survive, we always have. But what happens when these giant beaver dams start flooding the tower and skyway foundations? The lakeshore retreats? In ten years, Ohio could be one big swamp."

Hank stared at him a moment, then got it. "They'll probably need some giant-beaver-removal services."

"And which two guys are going to be the only ones who know anything about trapping giant beaver? The only ones with giant-beaver castor lure ready to go?"

"If I can put up with your ornery ass, it could be a beautiful partnership."

Jack felt the initial sense of movement when the wormhole found the capsule.

Back across your time again, Katie. But maybe I'd better say goodbye to you here.

machine learning

NANCY KRESS

Nancy Kress began selling her elegant and incisive stories in the mid-seventies. Her books include the novel version of her Hugo- and Nebula-winning story, Beggars in Spain, *and a sequel,* Beggars and Choosers, *as well as* The Prince Of Morning Bells, The Golden Grove, The White Pipes, An Alien Light, Brain Rose, Oaths & Miracles, Stinger, Maximum Light, Nothing Human, The Floweres of Aulit Prison, Crossfire, Crucible, Dogs, *and* Steal Across the Sky, *as well as the Space Opera trilogy* Probability Moon, Probability Sun, *and* Probability Space. *Her short work has been collected in* Trinity And Other Stories, The Aliens of Earth, Beaker's Dozen, Nano Comes to Clifford Falls and Other Stories, The Fountain of Age, Future Perfect, AI Unbound, *and* The Body Human. *Her most recent books are the novels* Flash Point, *and, with Therese Pieczynski,* New Under the Sun. *In addition to the awards for "Beggars in Spain," she has also won Nebula Awards for her stories "Out Of All Them Bright Stars" and "The Flowers of Aulit Prison," the John W. Campbell Memorial Award in 2003 for her novel* Probability Space, *and another Hugo in 2009 for "The Erdmann Nexus." Most recently, she won another Nebula Award in 2013 for her novella "After the Fall, Before the Fall, During the Fall," and another Nebula Award in 2014 for her novella "Yesterday's Kin." She lives in Seattle, Washington, with her husband, writer Jack Skillingstead.*

Here she suggests that while we're learning from machines, the machines may also be learning from us . . .

Ethan slipped into the back of the conference room in Building 5 without being noticed. Fifty researchers and administrators, jammed into the room lab-coat-to-suit, all faced the projection stage. Today, of course, it would be set for maximum display. The CEO of the company was here, his six-foot-three frame looming over the crowd. Beside him, invisible to Ethan in the crush, would be tiny Anne Gonzalez, R&D chief. For five years a huge proportion of the Biological Division's resources—computational, experimental, human—had been directed toward this moment.

Anne's clear voice said, "Run."

Some people leaned slightly forward. Some bit their lips or clasped their hands. Jerry Liu rose onto the balls of his feet, like a fighter. They all had so much invested in this: time, money, hope.

The holostage brightened. The incredibly complex, three-dimensional network of structures within a nerve cell sprang into view, along with the even more complicated lines of the signaling network that connected them. Each line of those networks had taken years to identify, validate, understand. Then more time to investigate how any input to one substructure could change the whole. Then the testing of various inputs, each one a molecule aimed at the deadly thing near the center of the cell, the growing mass of Moser's Syndrome. All this hard work, all the partnering with pharmaceutical companies, in order to arrive at Molecule 654-a, their best chance.

So far, no one had noticed Ethan.

The algorithm for 654-a began to run, and in a moment the interaction combinations produced the output on the right side of the screen. Only two outputs were possible: "continued cell function" or "apoptosis." The apoptosis symbol glowed. A second later, in a burst of nonrealistic theatrics, the cell drooped and sagged like one of Dali's clocks, and the lethal structure at its heart vanished.

Cheering erupted in the room. People hugged each other. A lab tech stood on tiptoe and kissed the surprised CEO. They had done it, identified a possible cure for the disease that attacked the bodies of children, and only children, killing half a billion kids worldwide in the last five years. They had done it with molecular computation, with worldwide partnerships with universities and Big Pharma, and with sheer grit.

Someone to Ethan's left said, "Oh!" Then someone else noticed him, and someone after that. Ethan's story was company-wide gossip. The people at the front of the room went on burbling and hugging, but a small pocket of silence grew around him, the embarrassed silence of people caught giggling at a wake. Laura Avery started toward him.

He didn't want to talk to Laura. He didn't want to spoil this important celebration. Quickly he moved through the door, down the corridor, into the elevator. Laura, following, called "Ethan!" He hit the DOOR CLOSE button before she could reach him.

In the lobby he walked rapidly out the door, heading in the rain toward his own facility. Buildings of brick and glass rose ghostly in the thick mist. MultiFuture Research was a big campus and he was soaked by the time he reached Building 18. Inside, he nodded at Security and shook himself like a dog. Droplets spun off him. What the hell had he done with his umbrella? He couldn't remember, but it didn't matter. The important thing was to get back to his own work.

He didn't belong at a celebration to defeat Moser's Syndrome.

Too late, too late. Way too late.

Building 18 was devoted to machine learning. Ethan's research partner, Jamie Peregoy, stood in their lab, welcoming this afternoon's test subject, Cassie McAvoy. The little girl came with her mother every Monday, Wednesday, and Friday after school. Ethan took his place at the display console.

That end of the lab was filled with desks, computers, and messy folders of print-outs. The other end held child-sized equipment: a musical keyboard, a video-game console, tables and chairs, blocks, and puzzles. The back wall was painted a suppos-edly cheerful yellow that Ethan found garish. In the center, like a sentry in no-man's land, stood a table with coffee and cookies.

"The problem with machine learning isn't intelligence," Jamie always said to visi-tors." It's *defining* intelligence. Is it intelligence to play superb chess, crunch numbers, create algorithms, carry on a conversation indistinguishable from a human gabfest? No. Turing was wrong. True intelligence requires the ability to learn for oneself, tack-ling new tasks you haven't done before, and that requires emotion as well as reason-ing. We don't retain learning unless it's accompanied by emotion, and we learn best when emotional arousal is high. Can our Mape do that? No, she cannot."

If visitors tried to inject something here, they were out of luck. Jamie would go into full-lecture mode, discoursing on the role of the hippocampus in memory re-tention, on how frontal-lobe injuries taught us that too little emotion could impair decision making as deeply as too much emotion, on how arousal levels were a better predictor of learning retention than whether the learning was positive or negative. Once Jamie got going, he was as unstoppable as a star running back, which was what he resembled. Young, brilliant, and charismatic, he practically glittered with energy and enthusiasm. Ethan went through periods where he warmed himself at Jamie's inner fire, and other periods where he avoided Jamie for days at a time.

MAIP, the MultiFuture Research Artificial Intelligence Program based in the company's private cloud, could not play chess, could not feel emotion, and could only learn within defined parameters. Ethan, whose field was the analysis of how machine learning algorithms performed, believed that true AI was decades off, if ever. Did Jamie believe that? Hard to tell. When he spoke their program's name, Ethan could hear that to Jamie it *was* a name, not an acronym. He had given MAIP a female voice. "Someday," Jamie said, "she'll be smarter than we are." Ethan had not asked Jamie to define "someday."

The immediate, more modest goal was for MAIP to learn what others felt, so that MAIP could better assist their learning.

"Hello, Cassie, Mrs. McAvoy," Jamie said, with one of his blinding smiles. Cassie, a nine-year-old in overalls and a t-shirt printed with kittens, smiled back. She was a prim little girl, eager to please adults. Well-mannered, straight A's, teacher's pet. "Never any trouble at home," her mother had said, with pride. Ethan guessed she was not popular with other kids. But she was a valuable research subject, because MAIP had to learn to distinguish between genuine human emotions and "social pretense"—feelings expressed because convention expected it. When Cassie said, "I like you," did she mean it?

"Ready for the minuet, Cassie?" Jamie asked.

"Yes."

"Then let's get started! Here's your magic bracelet, princess!" He slipped it onto her thin wrist. Mrs. McAvoy took a chair at the back of the lab. Cassie walked to the keyboard and began to play Bach's "Minuet in G," the left-hand part of the arrange-ment simplified for beginners. Jamie moved behind her, where she could not see him. Ethan studied MAIP's displays.

Sensors in Cassie's bracelet measured her physiological responses: heart rate, blood pressure, respiration, skin conductance, and temperature. Tiny cameras captured her facial-muscle movement and eye saccades. The keyboard was wired to register the pressure of her fingers. When she finished the minuet, MAIP said, "That was good! But let's talk about the way you arch your hands, okay, Cassie?" Voice analyzers measured Cassie's responses: voice quality, timing, pitch. MAIP used the data to adjust the lesson: slowing down her instruction when Cassie seemed too frustrated, increasing the difficulty of what MAIP asked for when the child showed interest.

They moved on, teacher and pupil, to Bach's "Polonaise in D." Cassie didn't know this piece as well. MAIP was responsive and patient, tailoring her comments to Cassie's emotional data.

It looked so effortless. But years of work had gone into this piano lesson between a machine and a not-very-talented child. They had begun with a supervised classification problem, inputting observational data to obtain an output of what a test subject was feeling. Ethan had used a full range of pattern recognition and learning algorithms. But Jamie, the specialist in affective computing, had gone far beyond that. He had built "by hand," one complicated concept at a time, approaches to learning that did not depend on simpler, more general principles like logic. Then he'd made considerable progress in the difficult problem of integrating generative and discriminative models of machine learning. Thanks to Jamie, MAIP was a hybrid, multi-agent system, incorporating symbolic and logical components with subsymbolic neural networks, plus some new soft-computing approaches he had invented. These borrowed methods from probability theory to maximize the use of incomplete or uncertain information.

MAIP learned from each individual user. When Cassie's data showed her specific frustration level rising to a point where it interfered with her learning, MAIP slowed down her instruction. When Cassie showed interest in a direction, MAIP took the lesson there. It all looked so smooth, Ethan's and Jamie's work invisible to anyone but them.

At the end of the hour, MAIP said, "Well done, Cassie!"

"Thank you."

"I hope you enjoyed the lesson."

"Yes."

"See you on Monday, then."

"Okay."

Mrs. McAvoy took Cassie's hand, exchanged a few pleasantries with Jamie, and led Cassie out the door. It closed. In the corridor, the motion-activated surveillance system turned on.

Jamie beamed at Ethan. "That went really well! Mape—"

"I don't want to come here anymore," said the image of Cassie on the surveillance screen.

"Why not?" Mrs. McAvoy said.

"It's no fun. Please, Mommy, can we never come here again?"

Silence in the lab. Finally Ethan said, "I guess we need to work more on the ontology of social pretense."

Jamie looked crushed. "Damn! I thought Cassie liked coming here! She fooled me completely!"

"More to the point, she fooled MAIP."

"All the sub-agents worked so well on yesterday's test kid!"

"There's no free lunch."

Jamie had a rare flash of anger. "Ethan—do you always have to be so negative?And so fucking *calm* about it?"

"Yes," Ethan said, and they parted in mutual snits. Ethan knew that Jamie's wouldn't last; it wasn't in his nature. There they were, yoked together, the Elpis and Cassandra of machine learning.

Or maybe just Roo and Eeyore.

The first time Ethan had heard about Moser's Syndrome, he'd been chopping wood in the back yard and listening to the news on his tablet. Chopping wood was an anachronism he enjoyed: the warming of his muscles, the satisfying clunk of axe on birch logs, the smell of fresh woodchips on the warm August air. In a corner of the tiny yard, against the whitewashed fence, chrysanthemums bloomed scarlet and gold.

"—coup in Mali that—"

Also, if he was honest with himself, he liked being out of the house while Tina was in it. His year-old marriage was not going well. The vivacity that had originally attracted Ethan, so different from his own habitual constraint, was wearing thin. For Tina, every difference of opinion was a betrayal, every divergent action a crisis. But she was pregnant and Ethan was determined to stick it out.

"—tropical storm off the coast of North Carolina, and FEMA is urging—"

Thunk! Another fall of the axe on wood, not a clean stroke. Ethan pulled the axe out of the log. Tina came out of the house, carrying a tray of ice tea. Although her belly was still flat, she proudly wore a maternity top. The tea tray held a plate of his favorite chocolate macaroons. They were both trying.

"Hey, babes," Tina said. Ethan forced a smile. He'd told her at least three times that he hated being called "babes."

He said, "The cookies look good."

She said, "I hope they are."

The radio said, "Repeat: This just in. The CDC has identified the virus causing Moser's Syndrome, even as the disease has spread to two more cities in the Northwest. Contrary to earlier reports, the disease is transmitted by air and poses a significant threat to fetuses in the first and early second trimester of pregnancy. All pregnant women in Washington and Oregon are urged to avoid public gatherings whenever possible until more is known. The—"

Ethan's axe slipped from his hand, landing on his foot and partially severing his little toe in its leather sandal.

Tina shrieked. In his first stunned moment, he thought she'd screamed at the blood flowing from his foot. But she threw the tray at him, crying, "You took me to that soccer game last week! How *could* you! If anything happens to this baby, I'll never forgive you!" She burst into tears and ran into the house, leaving Ethan staring at the end of his foot. A chunk of toe lay disjointed from the rest, bloody pulp surrounded by chocolate macaroons. Vertigo swept over him. It passed. The newscaster began to interview a doctor about embryonic damage, nerve malformation, visible symptoms in newborns.

Ethan shifted his gaze to the axe, as if it and not a maybe-living-maybe-not molecule was the danger to his unborn child. An ordinary axe: silver blade, hardwood handle, manufacturer's name printed in small letters. Absurdly, a sentence rose in his mind from decades ago, a lecture from his first tech professor when he'd been an undergraduate: *Technology is always double-edged, and the day stone tools were invented, axe murder became possible.*

Then the pain rushed in, and he bent over and vomited. After that, he pushed the chunk of toe back in place, wrapped his shirt around it, and applied pressure.

If anything happens to this baby, I'll never forgive you!

They divorced eighteen months later.

Social pretense was not a problem with one of Jamie and Ethan's other research subjects, eleven-year-old Trevor Reynod. He barreled into the lab, shouting, "I'm here! Freakish! Let's go!"

"My man!" Jamie said, giving him a fist bump that Trevor practically turned into an assault.

"Jamie! And Dr. Stone Man!" That was the kid's name for Ethan. Ethan didn't object, as long as Trevor stayed well away from him. Trevor suffered from ADHD, although most of the suffering seemed to belong to the tired-looking mother who trailed in after him. A member of some sect that didn't believe in medication, she refused to allow Trevor to be calmed down by drugs, but computer games were apparently allowed. Ethan suspected that these thrice-weekly sessions were an immense relief to her; she could turn Trevor over to someone else. Mrs. Reynod poured herself some coffee and slumped into the easy chair in the corner.

Trevor pummeled the air and danced in place, knocking over a pile of blocks. Jamie got the bracelet onto his wrist ("Your super-power ring, dude!") and settled both of them in front of a game console as carefully wired as Cassie's keyboard. Trevor's data began to flow down Ethan's display. MAIP was silent during Trevor's sessions, adjusting his game in response to his frustration or satisfaction levels but not instructing him. Trevor did not respond well to direct instruction.

The game involved piloting a futuristic one-man plane, ridiculously represented as a bullet-shaped soap bubble. Its flight simulator was state-of-the-art, similar to the one used to train USAF jet pilots, who might eventually have MAIP incorporated into their training sessions. While flying over various war-torn terrains, Trevor had to shoot down alien craft to avoid being vaporized and to dodge "falling stars" that appeared from nowhere. Jamie's role was to fire at Trevor from the ground. He almost never hit him, which allowed MAIP more control and Trevor merciless mockery.

"Ha! Missed me again!"

"You're really good, Trev."

He was. Like most attention-deficit kids, Trevor could muster enormous powers of concentration when the activity actually interested him.

They followed their plan of transitioning Trevor from the shooting game to one teaching math in the last fifteen minutes of the hour. Trevor's levels of arousal and engagement fell, but not as far as they had the previous week. This was a new version of the math game, punchier and more inventive. In effect, Trevor was beta-testing Math Monkeys, while Ethan and Jamie gained learning-algorithm data from him.

The session was a success. After Trevor left, shouting about his victory over the math monkeys, Jamie said, "Did you catch that? Mape tried a stutter-and-recover strategy on him! We didn't program that!"

"Not in quite that form, anyway."

"Come on, Ethan, she figured out for herself how to apply it! She learned!"

"Maybe." He would have to do the analysis first.

But Jamie danced around the lab in an exuberant imitation of Trevor. "Freakish! She did it, Dr. Stone Man! You did it! Go, Mape!"

Ethan smiled. It felt odd, as if his face were cracking.

At midnight, Ethan let himself into the modeling lab in Building 6. The place was empty, even the most diehard geek having gone out on a Friday night for beer and company. "Lights on low," Ethan said. The lab complied.

He'd told himself he wasn't going to do this again. It only made everything harder. But he could not resist. This was the only place that felt meaningful to him now—or at least the only place where meaning felt natural, like air, instead of having to be manufactured moment after effortful moment.

The lab contained, in addition to its staggeringly expensive machinery, three "rooms," each with the missing fourth wall of a theater stage or a furniture showroom. The largest was an empty, white-walled box, used to project VR environments ranging from an Alpine village to the surface of the moon. The two furnished rooms represented living spaces with sofas and tables, onto which could be projected the VR programs: changing a chair from red velour to yellow brocade, setting out bottles on a table. Old stuff, but it was the starting point for the real challenge of modeling three-dimensional "reality" that could move and be moved, touch and be touched. This lab, already a huge profit-maker for MultiFuture Research, was usually the first one shown to visitors.

Some of the programs, however, were private.

Ethan slipped on a VR glove and put his password into the projector aimed at the smallest room. It sprang to life and Allyson was there, sitting on the floor, holding her stuffed Piglet. This was the Allyson he'd brought to the lab near the end of her illness, when it was clear that the doctors' pathetically inadequate measures could not help her. Four more months, they said, but it had been only two. Ethan was grateful that Allyson had gone so quickly; he'd seen children for whom Moser's Syndrome took its slower, crueler time.

Tina had not been grateful. By that point, she had barely been Tina.

Allyson had loved Winnie the Pooh. Kanga, Roo, and Eeyore had been her friends, but Piglet had been more: a talisman, an icon. Once she'd told Ethan that she "hated Christopher Robin because *his* Piglet can talk to him and mine can't."

The 3-D model of Allyson raised her head and looked up at Ethan. It was a tremendous technical achievement, that mobile action on a holographic projection. Right now, Ethan didn't care. When he'd brought Allyson here, late at night on another Friday, she'd already begun to lose weight. Her skin had gone as colorless as the sheets she lay on at home. Her hair had fallen out in patches. Ethan had known this was his last chance; the following week Allyson had gone into the hospital. When Tina found out what he'd done, she had raged at him with a ferocity excessive even for her. Although it should have been a warning.

The model of Allyson—or rather, the voice recorder in the computer—said, "Hi, Daddy."

"Hi, baby," Ethan said. And she smiled.

That was it. Ten seconds of Allyson's short life, and an enormous expenditure of bandwidth. He hadn't kept his daughter in the lab longer than that; she'd looked too tired. Ethan hoped that the biological division's molecule 654-a could cure Moser's Syndrome. But for him, there was only this.

He called up the overlay programs, one by one. Allyson's skin brightened to rosy pink. Her hair became thick and glossy again, without bare patches. Her little body grew sturdier. Her eyes opened wider. "Hi, Daddy."

"Hi, baby." He reached out with the VR glove and stroked her cheek. The sensation was there: smooth warm flesh.

Over and over he played the enhanced, miraculously mobile model. Throughout, Ethan kept his face rigid, his hands under control, his thoughts disciplined. He was not Tina. He would never let himself be Tina.

No one, not friends or colleagues, had known how to treat Ethan after Allyson, after Tina. "Call us" friends had said while Ethan awaited Allyson's diagnosis, "if anything goes wrong." And later, after Tina, "Call us if you need anything." But there is no one to call when everything goes wrong, when you need what you can never have back.

"Hi, Daddy."

"Hi, baby."

When he'd had his fill, the fix that kept him from becoming Tina, he closed the program and went home.

On Monday, Laura Avery waylaid him as he walked from the parking lot to Building 18. This being October in Seattle, it was still raining, but at least Ethan had remembered his umbrella. She had one, too, blue with a reproduction of a Marc Chagall painting, which seemed to him a frivolous use of great art. Laura, however, was not frivolous. Serious but not humorless, she had made important contributions during her months at MultiFuture Research, or so he'd been told. The company, like all companies, was a cauldron of gossip.

"Ethan! Wait up!"

He had no choice, unless he wanted to appear rude.

She was direct, without flirtatious games. Ordinarily he would have liked that. But this was not ordinarily, and never would be again, not for him. Laura said, "I wondered if you'd like to have dinner one night at my place. I'm a good cook, and I can do vegetarian."

"I'm not vegetarian."

"I know, but I thought I'd just show off my fabulous culinary range." She smiled whimsically.

It was an attractive smile; she was an attractive woman. When they'd first been introduced, Laura had glanced quickly at his left hand, and her smile grew warmer. He'd taken off his wedding ring the day after Tina had left him, long before she'd killed herself. Later, after someone had undoubtedly told Laura about Ethan's story, Laura had grown more circumspect. But the warmth had still been there; he hadn't needed MAIP to read her face. Now, a year after Tina's death, this invitation—had someone told Laura it was exactly one year? Was she that coldly correct?

No. She was an intelligent, appealing woman aware enough of her appeal to go directly after someone she liked. Why she liked him was a mystery; in Ethan's opinion, there wasn't enough of him left to like. Or to accept a dinner invitation.

"Sorry. I'm busy."

She recognized the lie but hid any feeling of rejection. "Okay. Maybe another time."

"Thanks anyway."

That was it. A nothing encounter. But it left him feeling fragile, and he hated that. The only thing that had gotten him through the last year was the opposite of fragility: controlled, resolute, carefully modeled action.

After his encounter with Laura, he threw himself into work, trying to figure out why MAIP hadn't detected Cassie McAvoy's social pretense of enjoying her piano lesson. He found a few promising leads, but nothing definitive.

How far they still had to go was made clear by Jenna Carter.

Jamie was good with the children who came to the machine lab. Sometimes Ethan thought this was because Jamie, brilliant as he was, was still a child himself: enthusiastic, sloppy, saved from terminal nerdiness only by his all-American good looks. Untested, as yet, by anything harsh. Other times Ethan felt ashamed of this facile assessment; Jamie was good with kids because he liked them.

Not, however, all of them equally. While Jamie had no trouble with Trevor Reynod, he had to hide his dislike for Jenna, who wasn't even a test subject, only the babysitter for her little brother Paul.

They came in after school on Tuesday. Paul, at eight years old their youngest subject, went straight to the small table where Jamie had set out a wooden puzzle map of the United States.

"Hey, Paul," Jamie said. "How's it going?"

"Good." Paul had a thin face, a shock of red hair, and a sweet smile.

"Can I put the magic bracelet on you? Have to warn you, though, it might turn you invisible."

Paul looked uncertain for a moment, caught Jamie's grin, and laughed. "No, it won't!"

"Well, if you're sure—let's see if you can put this puzzle together. Recognize it? It's our country, all fifty states. Wow! That's a lot of states! What a challenge!"

"I can do it!"

Jenna pushed forward. "He can't do that! It's too hard! He's only in the third grade!"

"Yes, I can!" Paul picked up Maine and fitted it into the upper right corner of the wooden holder. "See?"

"That one's easy, dingleberry! Anybody can get Maine!" She turned to Jamie. "Our mother said *I* was supposed to do the puzzles today."

Paul looked up, outraged. "No, she didn't!"

"Did to!"

"Did not!" Jenna grabbed her brother by the shoulders and tried to pull him out of the chair.

"Hey! Quit it! Dr. Peregoy!"

Jamie detached Jenna's hands. "Paul, let Jenna try the puzzle. I'll let you do the flight simulator."

Paul's mouth opened and his eyebrows rose: surprise, one of the basic facial-recognition patterns. The flight simulator was a treat usually withheld until the end of each session.

Jenna cried, "No fair! I want to do the flight simulator!"

"Maybe later." Jamie slipped the sensor bracelet off Paul and onto Jenna, and pushed her gently onto the chair. "After all, *your mother* said you should do the puzzle, right?"

Jenna glared at him. "Yeah!"

"Then let's see how fast you can do it."

Jenna hunted for a place to fit Iowa. Paul ineptly piloted the transparent bubble. ("You have crashed the jet, Paul," MAIP said.) Ethan wondered what Jamie was doing. Then he got it: Jamie wanted to see if MAIP could detect the fact that Jenna was lying. Ethan studied his displays.

MAIP worked with what was, basically, a set of medical data. It didn't have the context to interpret what that data might mean. To detect social pretense—which it also couldn't do yet—its algorithms used a subject's baseline data, observed data, and contradictions among the ontologies of emotion. But MAIP hadn't "learned" Jenna, couldn't yet do cold readings without a subject's baseline data, and had neither context nor algorithms to detect lies. So it was no surprise that MAIP didn't recognize Jenna's lies.

"Well," Jamie said after the children left, "it was worth a shot."

"Not really," Ethan said.

"Mr. Negative."

"MAIP didn't even register social pretense for Jenna, no matter how much you led her into lying. We're just not there yet."

Jamie sighed. "I know."

"What you just did was no better than a polygraph, and there's a reason polygraphs aren't admissible in court. Not reliable enough."

"Yeah, yeah, you're right. But there should be some way to do this."

"We need to solve the problem of social pretense first, and with subjects that we do have baseline data for."

Jamie said, "Maybe if we. . . . No, that wouldn't work. And—oh, God, I just thought of another problem. Jenna clearly knew she was lying, but what if someone has convinced themselves that they feel one thing but are actually feeling something different? Like, say, a woman who convinces herself she's in love, even though all she really wants is to have babies before her biological clock stops ticking? She doesn't really feel love for some poor schlump but thinks she does, to ease her conscience about trapping him?"

Was this a glimpse into Jamie's personal life? If so, Ethan didn't want to know about it. He said, more primly than he intended, "Oh, I think most people know what they really feel."

Jamie gave him a strange look. "Really, Ethan?"

"Yes. But the point here is that MAIP didn't know."

Jamie picked up Texas and fitted it into the puzzle, his head bent over the small table, his hair falling forward over his face and hiding his expression.

December, and still raining. Ethan went to the modeling lab late on a Sunday afternoon. He was alone in the building; it was almost Christmas. Water dripped from his raincoat and umbrella onto the floor. "Lights on."

"Hi, Daddy."

"Hi, baby."

Allyson smiled, and the recording ended. He clothed her in artificial health, pink cheeks, and lustrous hair, and started it again.

"Hi, Daddy."

"Hi, baby."

He stroked her cheek. Soft, so soft in his VR glove. But Allyson had not been a soft child. Not noisy and obnoxious like Trevor or Jenna, not hidden and falsely polite like Cassie. Allyson had been direct, opinionated, with a will of diamond. She and Tina clashed constantly over what clothes Allyson would put on, what her bedtime was, whether she could cross the street alone, why she drew butterflies instead of the alphabet on her kindergarten "homework." Ethan had been the buffer between his wife and daughter. It seemed ridiculous that a five-year-old had to be buffered against, but that was the way it had been. Allyson and Tina had been too much alike, and when Tina had blamed not only Ethan but herself for exposing Allyson to Moser's Syndrome, Ethan had not seen the danger. Tina, dramatic to the end, had thrown herself under a Metro train at the Westlake Tunnel Station.

Allyson would not have grown up like that. As she matured, she would have become calmer, more controlled. Ethan was sure of it. She would have become the companion and ally that Tina had not been.

"Hi, Daddy."

"Hi, baby."

The recording stopped, but Ethan talked on. "We're having trouble with MAIP's ability to attune, Allyson."

She gazed at him with solemn eyes. Light golden brown, the color of November fields in sunshine.

"'Attune' means that two people are aware of and responsive to each other." And attunement began early, between mother and infant. Was that what had gone wrong between Allyson and Tina? He and Allyson had always been attuned to each other.

Ethan reached out both arms, one in the VR glove and one bare. Both arms passed through the model of Allyson that was made only of light. The gloved hand tingled briefly, but it still moved through the child as if she did not exist.

For a terrible second, Ethan's brain filled with thick, tarry mist, cold as liquid nitrogen. He went rigid and clamped his teeth tightly together. The mist disappeared. He was in control again.

He turned off the recording, wiped the rain droplets from the floor, and left.

Zhao Tailoring didn't open until 10 a.m. on Mondays. Ethan, who'd been there at 8:30, waited in a Starbucks, slowly drinking a latte he didn't want. The *Seattle Times* lay open on the table, but he couldn't concentrate. At 9:50 he threw his paper cup in the trash, left his unread paper, and walked across the street to the tailor shop. He huddled under the roof overhang, out of the rain.

Tailoring was not part of his life. Ethan bought clothes haphazardly, getting whatever size seemed the best fit and ignoring whatever gaps might present themselves. The window of Zhao Tailoring held Christmas decorations and three mannequins. The plastic-resin woman wore a satin gown; the man, slacks and a double-breasted blazer; the child, a pair of overalls over a ruffled blouse. They looked bound for three entirely different events. The sign said ALTERATIONS * REPAIRS * NEW CLOTHES MADE. At 9:58, an Asian woman unlocked the front door.

"Ethan! What are you doing here?"

Laura Avery, under her Marc Chagall umbrella. Ethan felt his face go rigid. "Hello, Laura."

"Are you having tailoring done?" Her voice held amusement but no condescension.

"No. What are you doing here? Why aren't you at work?"

Her brows rose in surprise at his harsh tone. "I had a doctor's appointment across the street. Nothing serious. Are you having a suit made?"

"I already said I wasn't having tailoring done. Please stop asking me personal questions."

Surprise changed to hurt, her features going slack in the blue shadows under the umbrella. "Sorry, I just—"

"If I wanted to talk to you, I would."

A moment of silence. Ethan opened his mouth to apologize, to explain that he was just distracted, but before he could speak, she turned and stalked away.

"You come in, yes?" the Asian woman said.

Ethan went in.

"You want nice suit, yes? Special this week."

"No. I don't want a suit. I want . . . I want to buy the mannequin in the window." Incongruously, an old childish song ran through his head: *How much is that doggie in the window?*

"You want buy what?"

She didn't have much English. The person who did was late showing up for work. "You come again, twelve o'clock maybe, one—"

"No. I want to buy the mannequin . . . the *doll*." They had finally agreed on this word. "Now. For a hundred dollars." He had no idea what store mannequins cost.

She shook her head. "No, I cannot—"

"Two hundred dollars. Cash." He took out his wallet.

They settled on two-fifty. She stripped the overalls and blouse off the mannequin, and, to his relief, she put it in a large, opaque suit bag. Ethan watched its stiff plastic form—hairless, with a monochromatic and expressionless face—disappear into the bag. He put it in the trunk of his car, pushing from his mind every bad B-movie about murderers and wrapped-up bodies.

Marilyn Mahjoub was fifteen minutes late for her first testing session. Waiting, Jamie paced, smacking a fist into his palm, dialing the energy all the way up to ten. "You know, Dr. Stone Man, we'd be so much further along with Mape if all the fucking subfields of AI research hadn't been—oh, I don't know—slogging along for sixty or seventy years without fucking *communicating* with each other?"

"Yes," Ethan said.

"It's just such a . . . oh, by the way, I changed some of our girl's heuristics. What I did was—are you listening to me? Hello?"

"I'm listening," Ethan said, although he wasn't, not really.

"You're not listening. Mape listens to me more than you do, don't you, Mape?"

"I'm listening," MAIP said.

"Why is she so much more *here* than you are? And why is that kid so late?"

If there was a reason, they never heard it. Marilyn Mahjoub arrived eventually, in the custody of a sullen older brother. Her clothing embodied the culture clash suggested by her name: hijab, tight jeans, and crop top. She had huge dark eyes and a slender, awkward grace. In a few years she would be beautiful.

Like Cassie McAvoy, Marilyn played the keyboard. Unlike Cassie, she was good at it. Ethan could picture her in a concert hall one day, rising to cries of "Brava!" However, she did not take well to MAIP.

"Try playing that last section slower," MAIP said in the warm, pretty voice that Jamie had given her. She was comparing Marilyn's rendition, note by note, to the professional version in memory.

Marilyn's lip curled. "No.It shouldn't be slower."

"Let's try it just to see."

"No! I had it right!"

"You did really well," MAIP said. "Can I please hear the piece again?"

Jamie nodded briskly; MAIP was acting to lower Marilyn's frustration level by offering praise and neutrally suggesting a redo. Ethan studied the data display. Frustration level was not lowering.

"No," Marilyn said, "I won't play it again. I don't *need* to play it again. I did it right already."

"You did really well," MAIP said. "I can see that you're talented."

"Then don't tell me to do it slower!"

"Mare," said her brother, with much disgust, "*chill.*"

Jamie stepped in. "What would you like to play now, Marilyn?"

Her childish pique disappeared. Lowering her head, Marilyn looked up at Jamie through her lashes and purred, "What would you like to hear?"

Christ—twelve years old! Were all young girls like this now? Allyson wouldn't have been. She would have been direct, intelligent, appealing.

Jamie, flustered (Ethan hadn't known that was possible), said, "Play . . . uh, what else do you . . . what do you want to play?"

Later, after brother and sister had left, Jamie turned on Ethan. "What's wrong with you?"

"With me?"

"You've been distracted this whole session and you made me deal with that little wildcat by myself! Did you even hear me say that I added heuristics to Mape, matching emotion with postural clues?"

"No, I. . . . Yes."

"Uh huh. Get with it, Ethan! We have to get this right!"

Ethan said, "Don't take your frustration with Marilyn out on me."

MAIP said, "Jamie, you seem distressed."

Startled, Ethan turned toward the computer. "MAIP has your data? Did you give your baseline readings to her?"

"No!"Jamie's irritation disappeared, replaced instantly with buoyancy; it was like a dolphin breaking the surface of gray water. "Well, I gave her some data, anyway—but I think she applied the postural heuristics and the other new stuff and . . . I don't know, you'll have to do the analysis, but I think she actually *learned*!"

Ethan gazed at MAIP. A pile of intricate machinery, a complex arrangement of electrons. For some reason he couldn't name, he felt a prickle of fear.

It was after 10 p.m. when the last researchers left Building 6. In Building 5, the Biological Division, lights still burned. Perez and Chung clattered out together, talking excitedly. Maybe they'd had another breakthrough, or maybe they just loved their work.

Ethan knew he didn't love his work on MAIP, no more than a castaway loved his raft. Depended on it, was grateful for it, needed it. But love was nowhere anymore, unless it was here.

"Hi, Daddy."

"Hi, baby."

The mannequin from Zhao Tailoring wore one of Allyson's dresses, still hanging in her closet at Ethan's apartment. The mannequin had jointed arms and legs. Ethan carefully positioned it into a sitting position. It was a little too tall for the projection, and he had to wrap the bottom four inches of plastic with his raincoat. That was all right; when he projected Allyson onto the mannequin, it looked as if she had plopped herself down onto his coat. Maybe after playing dress-up, maybe just with five-year-old mischief. Ethan set the lights to low, put the stuffed Piglet into her arms, and added the projected overlays, one by one. Healthy skin, glossy hair, bright eyes.

"Hi, Daddy."

"Hi, baby."

Ethan's knees trembled. Slowly he knelt beside her, the coat buttons lumpy under his calves. Lightly—so lightly, the VR glove on his right hand feeling her skin but not the hard plastic below—he used his left arm to hug his daughter.

"Hi, Daddy."

"What the *fuck*?"

Lights crashed on full; illusion crashed with them. Ethan jumped up. Jamie said, "What the hell are you doing? Laura called me, she saw you go into—"

"Go away. Leave me alone."

He didn't. But Jamie's face, always so confident, turned a mottled maroon of embarrassment. "Hey, man, I'm sorry, I didn't mean to—" Then confusion and embarrassment vanished. "No, I'm not sorry! Ethan, somebody has to level with you. You can't go on like this. I know—we all know—what you've been through. As tough as it gets, yeah. But you have to. . . . This isn't *normal*. That model isn't Allyson. You *know* that. You have to let go, move on, accept that she's gone instead of. . . . This is a perversion of technology, Ethan. I'm sorry, but that's what it is. And also a perversion of Allyson's mem—"

He didn't finish the sentence. Ethan crossed the floor in a mad dash and knocked him down.

Jamie looked up at Ethan from the floor. He wasn't hurt or even winded; Ethan was no fighter and Jamie outweighed him by at least forty pounds. Ethan had merely pushed him over. Jamie got up, shook his head like a pit bull hurling away a carcass, and left without a word.

Ethan began to tremble.

His fingers shook so much that he could barely shut down the programs. He left the mannequin sitting in the middle of the floor, a lifeless hunk of plastic, and left his coat and the stuffed Piglet with it. He couldn't bear to touch any of them.

Outside, in the dark and blowing rain, there was no sign of Jamie. Ethan lurched to Building 18. He had nowhere else to go. He couldn't drive; he could barely see. The tarry mist was back in his brain, filling it, chilling him to the marrow. There had never been anyplace else to go, not for a year. It frightened him that he couldn't feel the sidewalk beneath his feet, couldn't hear the raindrops strike the ground.

In the AI lab, lights burned and the flight simulator was running. Jamie must have been working late. But Jamie wasn't here now, and if Ethan didn't do something—anything—he would die. That was how he felt—how Tina must have felt. Thinking of Tina only made him feel worse. He stumbled to the game console and squeezed himself into the small chair in front of it. His hands gripped the controls. At least he could feel them, solid under his fingers: the only solid thing in his world of black mist and tarry cold. Black mist as a train sped into Westlake Tunnel Station, as an unseen virus ate into nerve and tissue . . .

"You have just crashed the jet," MAIP said. "Let's try again!"

Train speeding forward at forty miles per hour . . . "Hi, Daddy" . . . keep going keep going don't give in or you'll explode you will be Tina . . . damn bitch how could she leave me like that not my fault Moser's Syndrome not my fault . . . *don't give in.* . . .

"You have crashed the jet. But I know you can do this—let's try again!"

Over and over he crashed the jet, even as MAIP made it harder and harder for him to fail. He smashed the jet into mountains, into desert, into the sea. Again and again and again. Someone spoke to him, or didn't. There was noise again, a lot of

NANCY KRESS | 371

noise, there was destruction and death as there *should* be, to classify reality, to match the ontology of everything he had lost—

And then, finally, he realized the noise was his own screaming, and he stopped.

Into the silence MAIP said, "You were very angry, Ethan. I hope you feel better now."

He gave a little gasp, first at MAIP's words and then because he wasn't alone. Jamie stood beside him with Laura Avery.

She said gently, "Are you all right?" And when Ethan didn't answer, she added, "Jamie called me. After I called him, I mean. I saw you carrying something into Building 6 and—"

Jamie interrupted. "When did you input your data into MAIP?"

Ethan said nothing. The tarry cold mist had receded. No—it had vanished. He felt limp, drained, bruised, as if he had fallen off a cliff and somehow survived. *You were very angry. I hope you feel better now.*

"You didn't, did you?" Jamie demanded. "You never gave your baseline data to MAIP! She did a cold reading on you, extrapolating from free-form observation! We didn't teach her to do that!"

"Be quiet," Laura said. "Jamie, for God's sake—*not now.*"

MAIP said, "Ethan, I'm glad you feel better. You were both angry and sad before. You were sad even when you smiled."

Jamie drew a sharp, whistling breath. "Detection of social pretense! I'm sorry, Ethan, I know you're upset and I said some things I shouldn't have, but—detection of social pretense! From cold readings! She's taken a huge step forward—she *knows* you!"

Ethan said, not to Jamie but to the complexity of machinery and electrons that was MAIP, "You don't know me. You're a non-linear statistical modeling tool."

Laura said, "But I'm not." She put a tentative hand on his arm.

Jamie said, "Mape's not, either. Not anymore. She *learned*, Ethan. She did!"

Ethan looked at the flight simulator, which flashed the total number of jets he had crashed. He looked at MAIP. He saw the mannequin, a pathetic lump of plastic that he had left in Building 6.

Ethan rose. He had to steady himself with one hand on the game console. Laura's hand on his arm felt warm through his damp shirt. He didn't, he realized, know any of them, not really: not Laura, not MAIP, not Jamie. Not himself. Especially not himself.

He would have to learn everything all over again, reassess everything, forge new algorithms. Starting with this moment, here, now, to the sound of rain on the roof of the building.

inhuman garbage
KRISTINE KATHRYN RUSCH

Here's a nicely done murder mystery/police procedural set on the Moon, when a dead body shows up in the recycling system of a domed Lunar city, and the subsequent investigation of the crime leads the investigator to become ever more-deeply embroiled in a sinister conspiracy with wide-reaching political implications . . . one that could destroy her career, and maybe even cost her her life . . .

Kristine Kathryn Rusch started out the decade of the '90s as one of the fastest-rising and most prolific young authors on the scene, took a few years out in mid-decade for a very successful turn as editor of *The Magazine of Fantasy and Science Fiction*, and, since stepping down from that position, has returned to her old standards of production here in the twenty-first century, publishing a slew of novels in four genres, writing fantasy, mystery, and romance novels under various pseudonyms as well as science fiction. She has published more than twenty novels under her own name, including *The White Mists of Power, The Disappeared, Extremes,* and *Fantasy Life,* the four-volume Fey series, the Black Throne series, *Alien Influences,* and several *Star Wars, Star Trek,* and other media tie-in books, both solo and written with husband, Dean Wesley Smith, and with others. Her most recent books (as Rusch, anyway) are the SF novels of the popular "Retrieval Artist" series, which include *The Disappeared, Extreme, Consequences, Buried Deep, Paloma, Recovery Man,* and a collection of "Retrieval Artist" stories, *The Retrieval Artist and Other Stories.* Her copious short fiction has been collected in *Stained Black: Horror Stories, Stories for an Enchanted Afternoon, Little Miracles: And Other Tales of Murder,* and *Millenium Babies.* In 1999, she won Readers Award polls from the readerships of both *Asimov's Science Fiction* and *Ellery Queen's Mystery Magazine,* an unprecedented double honor! As an editor, she was honored with the Hugo Award for her work on *The Magazine of Fantasy and Science Fiction,* and shared the World Fantasy Award with Dean Wesley Smith for her work as editor of the original hardcover anthology version of *Pulphouse.* As a writer, she has won the Herodotus Award for Best Historical Mystery (for *A Dangerous Road,* written as Kris Nelscott) and the Romantic Times Reviewer's Choice Award (for *Utterly Charming,* written as Kristine Grayson); as Kristine Kathryn Rusch, she won the John W. Campbell Award, been a finalist for the Arthur C. Clarke Award, and took home a Hugo Award in 2000 for her story "Millennium Babies," making her one of the few people in genre history to win Hugos for both editing *and* writing. Her most recent books include the novels *Sole Survivor, The Application of Hope, The Really Big Ka-Boom, Vigilantes, Masterminds,* and *Starbase Human.*

Detective Noelle DeRicci opened the top of the waste crate. The smell of rotting produce nearly hid the faint smell of urine and feces. A woman's body curled on top of the compost pile as if she had fallen asleep.

She hadn't, though. Her eyes were open.

DeRicci couldn't see any obvious cause of death. The woman's skin might have been copper colored when she was alive, but death had turned it sallow. Her hair was pulled back into a tight bun, undisturbed by whatever killed her. She wore a gray and tan pantsuit that seemed more practical than flattering.

DeRicci put the lid down, and resisted the urge to remove her thin gloves. They itched. They always itched. Because she used department gloves rather than buying her own, and they never fit properly.

She rubbed her fingers together, as if something from the crate could have gotten through the gloves, and turned around. Nearly one hundred identical containers lined up behind it. More arrived hourly from all over Armstrong, the largest city on Earth's Moon.

The entire interior of the warehouse smelled faintly of organic material gone bad. She was only in one section of the warehouse. There were dozens of others, and at the end of each was a conveyer belt that took the waste crate, mulched it, and then sent the material for use in the Growing Pits outside Armstrong's dome.

The crates were cleaned in a completely different section of the warehouse, and then sent back into the city for reuse.

Not every business recycled its organic produce for the Growing Pits, but almost all of the restaurants and half of the grocery stores did. DeRicci's apartment building sent organic food waste into bins that came here as well.

The owner of the warehouse, Najib Ansel, stood next to the nearest row of crates. He wore a blue smock over matching blue trousers, and blue booties on his feet. Blue gloves stuck out of his pocket, and a blue mask hung around his neck.

"How did you find her?" DeRicci asked.

Ansel nodded at the ray of blue light that hovered above the crate, then toed the floor.

"The weight was off," he said. "The crate was too heavy."

DeRicci looked down.

"I take it you have sensors in the floor?" she asked.

"Along the orange line."

She didn't see an orange line. She moved slightly, then saw it. It really wasn't a line, more a series of orange rectangles, long enough to hold the crates, and too short to measure anything beside them.

"So you lifted the lid . . ." DeRicci started.

"No, sir," Ansel said, using the traditional honorific for someone with more authority.

DeRicci wasn't sure why she had more authority than he did. She had looked him up on her way here. He owned a multimillion-dollar industry, which made its fortune charging for waste removal from the city itself, and then reselling that waste at a low price to the Growing Pits.

She had known this business existed, but she hadn't paid a lot of attention to it until an hour ago. She had felt a shock of recognition when she saw the name of the business in the download that sent her here: Ansel Management was scrawled on the side of every waste container in every recycling room in the city.

Najib Ansel had a near monopoly in Armstrong, and had warehouses in six other domed communities. According to her admittedly cursory research, he had filed for permits to work in two new communities just this week.

So the fact that he was in standard worker gear, just like his employees, amazed her. She would have thought a mogul like Ansel would be in a gigantic office somewhere making deals, rather than standing on the floor of the main warehouse just outside Armstrong's dome.

Even though he used the honorific, he didn't say anything more. Clearly, Ansel was going to make her work for information.

"Okay," DeRicci said. "The crate was too heavy. Then what?"

"Then we activated the sensors, to see what was inside the crate." He looked up at the blue light again. Obviously that was the sensor.

"Show me how that works," she said.

He rubbed his fingers together—probably activating some kind of chip. The light came down and broadened, enveloping the crate. Information flowed above it, mostly in chemical compounds and other numbers. She was amazed she recognized that the symbols were compounds. She wondered where she had picked that up.

"No visuals?" she asked.

"Not right away." He reached up to the holographic display. The numbers kept scrolling. "You see, there's really nothing out of the ordinary here. Even her clothes must be made of some kind of organic material. So my people couldn't figure out what was causing the extra weight."

"You didn't find this, then?" she asked.

"No, sir," he said.

"I'd like to talk with the person who did," she said.

"She's over there." He nodded toward a small room off to the side of the crates.

DeRicci suppressed a sigh. Of course he cleared the employee off the floor. Anything to make a cop's job harder.

"All right," DeRicci said, not trying to hide her annoyance. "How did your 'people' discover the extra weight?"

"When the numbers didn't show anything," he said, "they had the system scan for a large piece. Sometimes, when crates come in from the dome, someone dumps something directly into the crate without paying attention to weight and size restrictions."

Those were hard to ignore. DeRicci vividly remembered the first time she tried to dump something of the wrong size into a recycling crate. She dumped a rotted roast she had never managed to cook (back in the days when she actually believed she could cook). She'd put it into the crate behind her then-apartment building. The damn crate beeped at her, and when she didn't remove the roast fast enough for the stupid thing, it actually started to yell at her, telling her that she wasn't following the rules.

There was a way to turn off the alarms, but she and her building superintendent didn't know it. Clearly, someone else did.

"So," DeRicci said, "the system scanned, and . . . ?"

"Registered something larger," he said somewhat primly. "That's when my people switched the information feed to visual, and got the surprise of their lives."

She would wager. She wondered if they thought the woman was sleeping. She wasn't going to ask him that question; she'd save it for the person who actually found the body.

"When did they call you?" she asked.

"After they visually confirmed the body," he said.

"Meaning what?" she asked. "They saw it on the feed or they actually lifted the lid?"

"On the feed," he said.

"Where was this?" she asked.

He pointed to a small booth that hovered over the floor. The booth clearly operated on the same tech that the flying cars in Armstrong used. The booth was smaller than the average car, however, and was clear on all four sides. Only the bottom appeared to have some kind of structure, probably to hide all the mechanics.

"Is someone in the booth?" she asked.

"We always have someone monitoring the floor," he said, "but I put someone new up there, so that the team which discovered the body can talk to you."

DeRicci supposed he had put the entire team in one room, together, so that they could align their stories. But she didn't say anything like that. No sense antagonizing Ansel. He was helping her.

"We're going to need to shut down this part of your line," she said. "Everything in this part of the warehouse will need to be examined."

To her surprise, he didn't protest. Of course, if he had protested, she would have had him shut down the entire warehouse.

Maybe he had dealt with the police before.

"So," she said, "who actually opened the lid on this container?"

"I did," he said quietly.

She hadn't expected that. "Tell me about it."

"The staff contacted me after they saw the body."

"On your links?" she asked. Everyone had internal links for communication, and the links could be set up with varying degrees of privacy. She would wager that the entire communication system inside Ansel Management was on its own dedicated link.

"Yes," he said. "The staff contacted me on my company link."

"I'd like to have copies of that contact," she said.

"Sure." He wasn't acting like someone who had anything to hide. In fact, he was acting like someone who had been through this before.

"What did your staff tell you?" she asked.

His lips turned upward. Someone might have called that expression a smile, but it wasn't. It was rueful.

"They told me that there was a woman in crate A1865."

DeRicci made a mental note about the number. Before this investigation was over, she'd learn everything about this operation, from the crate numbering system to the way that the conveyer worked to the actual mulching process.

"That's what they said?" she asked. "A woman in the crate?"

"Crate A1865," he repeated, as if he wanted that detail to be exactly right.

"What did you think when you heard that?" DeRicci asked.

He shook his head, then sighed. "I—we've had this happen before, Detective. Not for more than a year, but we've found bodies. Usually homeless people in the crates near the Port, people who came into Armstrong and can't get out. Sometimes we get an alien or two sleeping in the crates. The Oranjanie view rotting produce as a luxury, and they look human from some angles."

The Port of Armstrong was the main spaceport onto the Moon, and also functioned as the gateway to Earth. Member species of the Earth Alliance had to stop in Armstrong first, before traveling to Earth. Some travelers never made it into Earth's protected zone, and got stuck on the Moon itself.

Right now, however, she had no reason to suspect alien involvement in this crime. She preferred working human-on-human crime. It made the investigation so much easier.

"You've found human bodies in your crates before," she clarified.

"Yeah," he said.

"And the police have investigated?"

"All of the bodies, alien and human," he said. "Different precincts, usually, and different time periods. My grandmother started this business over one hundred years ago. She found bodies even way back then."

DeRicci guessed it would make sense to hide a body in one of the crates. Or someone would think it made sense.

"Do you think that bodies have gotten through the mulching process?" It took her a lot of strength not to look at the conveyer belt as she asked that question.

"I don't think a lot got through," he said. "I know some did. Back in my grandmother's day. She's the one who set up the safeguards. We might have had a few glitches after the safeguards were in place, before we knew how well they worked, but I can guarantee nothing has gone through since I started managing this company twenty-five years ago."

DeRicci tried not to shudder as she thought about human flesh serving as compost at the Growing Pits. She hated Moon-grown food, and she had a hunch she was going to hate it more after this case.

But she had to keep asking questions.

"You said you can guarantee it," she repeated.

He nodded.

"What if someone cut up the body?" she asked.

He grimaced. "The pieces would have to be small to get past our weight and size restrictions. Forgive me for being graphic, but no full arms or legs or torsos or heads. Maybe fingers and toes. We have nanoprobes on these things, looking for human DNA. But the probes are coating the lining of the crates. If someone buried a finger in the middle of some rotting lettuce, we might miss it."

She turned so that he wouldn't see her reaction. She forced herself to swallow some bile back, and wished she had some savings. She wanted to go home and purge her refrigerator of anything grown on the Moon, and buy expensive Earth-grown produce.

But she couldn't afford that, not on a detective's salary.

"Fair enough," she said, surprised she could sound so calm when she was so thoroughly grossed out. "No full bodies have gone through in at least twenty-five years. But you've seen quite a few. How many?"

"I don't know," he said. "I'd have to check the records."

That surprised her. It meant there were enough that he couldn't keep track. "Any place where they show up the most often?"

"The Port," he said. "There's a lot of homeless in that neighborhood."

Technically, they weren't homeless. They were people who lived on the city's charity. A lot of small cubicle-sized rooms existed on the Port blocks, and anyone who couldn't afford their own home or ended up stranded and unemployable in the city could stay in one of the cubicles for six months, no questions asked.

After six months, they needed to move to long-term city services, which were housed elsewhere. She wanted to ask if anyone had turned up in those neighborhoods, but she'd do that after she looked at his records.

"I'm confused," she said. "Do these people crawl into the crates and die?"

The crate didn't look like it was sealed so tightly that the person couldn't get oxygen.

"Some of them," he said. "They're usually high or drunk."

"And the rest?" she asked.

"Obviously someone has put them there," he said.

"A different someone each time, I assume," she said.

He shrugged. "I let the police investigate. I don't ask questions."

"You don't ask questions about dead people in your crates?"

His face flushed. She had finally gotten to him.

"Believe it or not, Detective," he snapped, "I don't like to think about it. I'm very proud of this business. We provide a service that enables the cities on the Moon to not only have food, but to have *great* food. Sometimes our system gets fouled up by crazy people, and I *hate* that. We've gone to great lengths to prevent it. That's why you're here. Because our systems *work*."

"I didn't mean to offend you," she lied. "This is all new to me, so I'm going to ask some very ignorant questions at times."

He looked annoyed, but he nodded.

"What part of town did this crate come from?" she asked.

"The Port," he said tiredly.

She should have expected that, after he had mentioned the Port a few times.

"Was the body in the crate when it was picked up at the Port?" she asked.

"The weight was the same from Port to here," he said. "Weight gets recorded at pickup but flagged near the conveyer. The entire system is automated until the crates get to the warehouse. Besides, we don't have the ability to investigate anything inside Armstrong. There are a lot of regulations on things that are considered garbage inside the dome. If we violate those, we'll get black marks against our license, and if we get too many black marks in a year, we could lose that license."

More stuff she didn't know. City stuff, regulatory stuff. The kinds of things she always ignored.

And things she would probably have to investigate now.

"Do you know her?" DeRicci asked, hoping to catch him off-balance.

"Her?" He looked confused for a moment. Then he looked at the crate, and his flush grew deeper. "You mean, *her*?"

"Yes," DeRicci said. Just from his reaction she knew his response. He didn't know the woman. And the idea that she was inside one of his crates upset him more than he wanted to say.

Which was probably why he was the person talking to DeRicci now.

"No," he said. "I don't know her, and I don't recognize her. We didn't run any recognition programs on her either. We figured you all would do that."

"No one touched her? No one checked her for identification chips?"

"I'm the one who opened the crate," he said. "I saw her, I saw that her eyes were open, and then I closed the lid. I leave the identifying to you all."

"Do you know all your employees, Mr. Ansel?"

"By name," he said.

"By look," she said.

He shook his head. "I have nearly three hundred employees in Armstrong alone."

"But you just said you know their names. You know all three hundred employees by name?"

He smiled absently, which seemed like a rote response. He'd responded to this kind of thing before.

"I have an eidetic memory," he said. "If I've seen a name, then I remember it."

"An eidetic memory for names, but not faces? I've never heard of that," DeRicci said.

"I haven't met all of my employees," he said. "But I go over the pay amounts every week before they get sent to the employees' accounts. I see the names. I rarely see the faces."

"So you wouldn't know if she worked here," DeRicci said.

"Here?" he asked. "Here I would know. I come here every day. If she worked in one of the other warehouses or in transport or in sales, I wouldn't know that."

"Did this crate go somewhere else before coming to this warehouse?" DeRicci asked.

"No," Ansel said. "Each crate is assigned a number. That number puts it in a location, and then when the crate fills, it gets swapped out with another. The crate comes to the same warehouse each time, without deviation. And since that system is automated, as I mentioned, I know that it doesn't go awry."

"Can someone stop the crate in transit and add a body?"

"No," he said. "I can show you if you want."

She shook her head. That would be a good job for her partner, Rayvon Lake. Rayvon still hadn't arrived, the bastard. DeRicci would have to report him pretty soon. He had gotten very lax about crime scenes, leaving them to her. He left most everything to her, and she hated it.

He was a lazy detective—twenty years in the position—and he saw her as an upstart who needed to be put in her place.

She wouldn't have minded if he did his job. Well, that wasn't exactly true. She would have minded. She hated people who disliked her. But she wouldn't be considering filing a report on him if he actually did the work he was supposed to do.

She would get Lake to handle the transport information by telling him she wasn't smart enough to understand it. It would mean that she'd have to suffer through an explanation later in the case, but maybe by then, she'd either have this thing solved or she'd have a new partner.

A woman could hope, after all.

"One of the other detectives will look into the transport process," DeRicci said. "I'm just trying to cover the basics here, so we start looking in the right place. Can outsiders come into this warehouse?"

"And get into one of our crates?" Ansel asked. "No. Look."

He touched the edge of the lid, and she heard a loud snap.

"It's sealed shut now," he said.

She didn't like the sound of that snap.

"If I were in there," she asked, "could I breathe through that seal?"

"Yes," he said. "For about two days, if need be. But it doesn't seal shut like that until it leaves the transport and crosses the threshold here at the warehouse. So there's no way anyone could crawl in here at the warehouse."

"All right," DeRicci said. "So, let me be sure I understand you. The only place that someone could either place a body into a crate or crawl into it on their own is on site."

"Yes," Ansel said. "We try to encourage composting, so we allow bypassers to stuff something into a crate. We search for nonorganic material at the site, and flag the crates with nonorganic material so they can be cleaned."

"Clothing is organic?" DeRicci asked.

"Much of it, yes," Ansel said. "Synthetics aren't good hosts for nanoproducts, so most people wear clothing made from recycled organic material."

DeRicci's skin literally crawled. She hadn't known that. She wasn't an organic kind of woman. She preferred fake stuff, much to the dismay of her friends.

"All right," she said. "I'm going to talk with your people in a minute. I'll want to know what they know. And I'll need to see your records on previous incidents."

She didn't check to see if he had sent her anything on her links. She didn't want downloads to confuse her sense of the crime scene. She liked to make her own opinions, and she did that by being thorough.

Detectives like Rayvon Lake gathered as much information as possible, multitasking as they walked through a crime scene. She believed they missed most of the important details while doing that, and that led to a lot of side roads and wasted time.

And, if she could prove it (if she had time to prove it), a lot of false convictions. She had caught Lake twice trying to close a case by accusing an innocent person who was convenient, rather than doing the hard leg work required of a good investigator.

Ansel fluttered near her for a moment. She inclined her head toward the room where the staff had gathered, knowing she was inviting him to contaminate her witnesses even more, but she had a hunch none of them were going to be useful to the investigation anyway.

"Before you go," she said, just in case he didn't take the hint, "could you unseal this crate for me?"

"Oh, yes, sorry," he said, and ran his fingers along the side again. It snapped one more time, then popped up slightly.

DeRicci thanked him, and pulled back the lid. The crate was deep—up to

DeRicci's ribs—and filled with unidentifiable bits of rotting food. The woman lay on top of them, hands cradled under her cheek, feet tucked together.

DeRicci couldn't imagine anyone just curling up here, even at the bidding of someone else. But people did strange things for strange reasons, and she wasn't going to rule it out.

She put the lid down and then looked at the warehouse again. She would need the numbers, but she suspected thousands of crates went through Ansel's facilities around the Moon daily.

Done properly, it would be a perfect way to dispose of bodies and all kinds of other things that no one wanted to see. She wondered how many others knew about this facility and how it worked.

She suspected she would have to find out.

Getting the crime scene unit to a warehouse outside of the dome took more work than Ethan Broduer liked to do. Fortunately, he was a deputy coroner, which meant he couldn't control the crime scene unit. Someone with more seniority had to handle requisitioning the right vehicle from the Police Department yards outside the dome, and making certain the team had the right equipment.

Broduer came to the warehouse via train. The ride was only five minutes long, but it made him nervous.

He was born inside the dome, and he hated leaving it for any reason at all, especially for a reason involving work. So much of his work had to do with temperature and conditions, and if the body had been in an airless environment at all, it had an impact on every aspect of his job.

He was relieved when he arrived at the warehouse and learned that the body had never gone outside of an Earth Normal environment. However, he was annoyed to see that he would be working with Noelle DeRicci.

She was notoriously difficult and demanding, and often asked coroners to redo something or double-check their findings. She'd caught him in several mistakes, which he found embarrassing.

Then she had had the gall to tell him that he should probably double-check all of his work, considering its shoddy quality.

She stood next to a crate, the only one of thousands that was open. She was rumpled—she was always rumpled—and her curly black hair looked messier than usual.

When she saw him approach, she glared at him.

"Oh, lucky me," she said.

Broduer bit back a response. He'd been recording everything since he got off the train inside the warehouse's private platform, and he didn't want to show any animosity toward DeRicci on anything that might go to court.

"Just show me the body and I'll get to work," he said.

She raised her eyebrows at the word "work," and she didn't have to add anything to convey her meaning. She didn't think Broduer worked at all.

"My biggest priority at the moment is an identification," DeRicci said.

And his biggest priority was to do this investigation right. But he didn't say that. Instead he looked at the dozens of crates spread out before him.

"Which one am I dealing with?" he asked, pleased that he could sound so calm in the face of her rudeness.

She placed a hand on the crate behind her. He was pleased to see that she wore gloves. He had worked with her partner Rayvon Lake before, and Lake had to be reminded to follow any kind of procedure.

But Broduer didn't see Lake anywhere.

"Have you had cases involving the waste crates before?" DeRicci asked Broduer.

"No," he said, not adding that he tried to pass anything outside the dome onto anyone else, "but I've heard about cases involving them. I guess it's not that uncommon."

"Hmm," she said looking toward a room at the far end of the large warehouse. "And here I thought they were."

Broduer was going to argue his point when he realized that DeRicci wasn't talking to him now. She was arguing with someone she had already spoken to.

"Can you get me information on that?" DeRicci asked Broduer.

He hated it when detectives wanted him to do their work for them. "It's in the records."

DeRicci made a low, growly sound, like he had irritated her beyond measure.

So he decided to tweak her a bit more. "Just search for warehouses and recycling and crates—"

"I know," she said. "I was hoping your office already had statistics."

"I'm sure we do, Detective," he said, moving past her, "but you want me to figure out what killed this poor creature, right? Not dig into old cases."

"I think the old cases might be relevant," she said.

He shrugged. He didn't care what was or wasn't relevant to her investigation. His priority was dealing with this body.

"Excuse me," he said, and slipped on his favorite pair of gloves. Then he raised the lid on the crate.

The woman inside was maybe thirty. She had been pretty too, before her eyes had filmed over and her cheeks sunk in.

She had clearly died in an Earth Normal environment, and she hadn't left that environment, as advertised. He would have to do some research to figure out if the presence of rotting food had an impact on the body's decomposition, but that was something to worry about later.

Then Broduer glanced up. "I'll have information for you in a while," he said to DeRicci.

"Just give me a name," she said. "We haven't traced anything."

He didn't want to move the body yet. He didn't even want to touch it, because he was afraid of disturbing some important evidence.

The corpse's hands were tucked under her head, so he couldn't just run the identification chips everyone had buried in their palms.

So he used the coroner's office facial recognition program. It had a record of every single human who lived in Armstrong, and was constantly updated with information from the arrivals and departures sections of the city every single day.

"Initial results show that her name is Sonja Mycenae. She was born here, and moved off-Moon with her family ten years ago. She returned one month ago to work as a nanny for. . . ."

He paused, stunned at the name that turned up.

"For?" DeRicci pushed.

Broduer looked up. He could feel the color draining from his face.

"Luc Deshin," he said quietly. "She works for Luc Deshin."

Luc Deshin.

DeRicci hadn't expected that name.

Luc Deshin ran a corporation called Deshin Enterprises, that the police department flagged and monitored continually. Everyone in Armstrong knew that Deshin controlled a huge crime syndicate that trafficked in all sorts of illegal and banned substances. The bulk of Deshin's business had moved off-Moon, but he had gotten his start as an average street thug, rising, as those kids often do, through murder and targeted assassination into a position of power, using the deaths of others to advance his own career.

"Luc Deshin needed a nanny?" DeRicci sounded confused.

"He married a few years ago," Broduer said, as he bent over the body again. "I guess they had kids."

"And didn't like the nanny." DeRicci whistled. "Talk about a high stress job."

She glanced at that room filled with the employees who found the body. There was a lot of work to be done here, but none of it was as important as catching Deshin by surprise with this investigation.

If he killed this Sonja Mycenae, then he would be expecting the police's appearance. But he might not expect them so soon.

Or maybe he had always used the waste crates to dump his bodies. No one had ever been able to pin a murder on him.

Perhaps this was why.

She needed to leave. But before she did, she sent a message to Lake. Only she sent it using the standard police links, not the encoded link any other officer would use with her partner. She wanted it on record that Lake hadn't shown up yet.

Rayvon, you need to get here ASAP. There are employees to interview. I'm following a lead, but someone has to supervise the crime scene unit. Someone sent Deputy Coroner Broduer and he doesn't have supervisory authority.

She didn't wait for Lake's response. Before he said anything, she sent another message to her immediate supervisor, Chief of Detectives Andrea Gumiela, this time through an encoded private link.

This case has ties to Deshin Enterprises, DeRicci sent. *I'm going there now, but we need a good team on this. It's not some random death. It needs to be done perfectly. Between Broduer and Lake, we're off to a bad start.*

She didn't wait for Gumiela to respond either. In fact, after sending that message, DeRicci shut off all but her emergency links.

She didn't want Gumiela to tell her to stay on site, and she didn't want to hear Lake's invective when he realized she had essentially chastised him in front of the entire department.

"Make sure no one leaves," DeRicci said to Broduer.

He looked up, panicked. "I don't have the authority."

"Pretend," she snapped, and walked away from him.

She needed to get to Luc Deshin, and she needed to get to him now.

Luc Deshin grabbed his long-waisted overcoat and headed down the stairs. So a police detective wanted to meet with him. He wished he found such things unusual. But they weren't.

The police liked to harass him. Less now than in the past. They'd had a frustrating time pinning anything on him.

He always found it ironic that the crimes they accused him of were crimes he'd never think of committing, and the crimes he had committed—long ago and far away—were crimes they had never heard of.

Now, all of his activities were legal. Just-inside-the-law legal, but legal nonetheless.

Or so his cadre of lawyers kept telling the local courts, and the local judges—at least the ones he would find himself in front of—always believed his lawyers.

So, a meeting like this, coming in the middle of the day, was an annoyance, and nothing more.

He used his trip down the stairs to stay in shape. His office was a penthouse on the top floor of the building he'd built to house Deshin Enterprises years ago. He used to love that office, but he liked it less since he and his wife Gerda brought a baby into their lives.

He smiled at the thought of Paavo. They had adopted him—sort of. They had drawn up some legal papers and wills that the lawyers assured him would stand any challenge should he and Gerda die suddenly.

But Deshin and Gerda had decided against an actual adoption given Deshin's business practices and his reputation in Armstrong. They were worried that some judge would deem them unfit, based on Deshin's reputation.

Plus, Paavo was the child of two Disappeareds, making the adoption situation even more difficult. The Earth Alliance's insistence that local laws prevailed when crimes were committed meant that humans were often subjected to alien laws, laws that made no sense at all. Many humans didn't like being forced to lose a limb as punishment for chopping down an exotic tree, or giving up a child because they'd broken food laws on a different planet.

Those who could afford to get new names and new identities did so rather than accept their punishment under Earth Alliance law. Those people Disappeared.

Paavo's parents had Disappeared within weeks of his birth, leaving him to face whatever legal threat those aliens could dream up.

Paavo, alone, at four months.

Fortunately, Deshin and Gerda had sources inside Armstrong's family services, which they had done for just this sort of reason. Both Deshin and Gerda had had difficult childhoods—to say the least. They knew what it was like to be unwanted.

Their initial plan had been to bring several unwanted children into their homes, but after they met Paavo, a brilliant baby with his own special needs, they decided to put that plan on hold. If they could only save Paavo, that would be enough.

But they were just a month into life with the baby, and they knew that any more children would take a focus that, at the moment at least, Paavo's needs wouldn't allow.

Deshin reached the bottom of the stairwell, ran a hand through his hair, and then walked through the double doors. His staff kept the detective in the lobby.

She was immediately obvious, even though she wasn't in uniform. A slightly disheveled woman with curly black hair and a sharp, intelligent face, she wasn't looking around like she was supposed to be.

Most new visitors to Deshin Enterprises either pretended to be unimpressed with the real marble floors, the imported wood paneling, and the artwork that constantly shifted on the walls and ceiling. Or the visitors gaped openly at all of it.

This detective did neither. Instead, she scanned the people in the lobby—all staff, all there to guard him and keep an eye on her.

She would be difficult. He could tell that just from her body language. He wasn't used to dealing with someone from the Armstrong Police Department who was intelligent *and* difficult to impress.

He walked toward her, and as he reached her, he extended his hand.

"Detective," he said warmly. "I'm Luc Deshin."

She wiped her hands on her stained shirt, and just as he thought she was going to take his hand in greeting, she shoved her hands into the pockets of her ill-fitting black pants.

"I know who you are," she said.

She deliberately failed to introduce herself, probably as a power play. He could play back, ask to see the badge chip embedded in the palm of her hand, but he didn't feel like playing.

She had already wasted enough of his time.

So he took her name, Noelle DeRicci, from the building's security records, and declined to look at her service record. He had it if he needed it.

"What can I do for you then, Detective?" He was going to charm her, even if that took a bit of strength to ignore the games.

"I'd like to speak somewhere private," she said.

He smiled. "No one is near us, and we have no recording devices in this part of the lobby. If you like, we can go outside. There's a lovely coffee shop across the street."

Her eyes narrowed. He watched her think: did she ask to go to his office and get denied, or did she just play along?

"The privacy is for you," she said, "but okay. . . ."

She sounded dubious, a nice little trick. A less secure man would then invite her into the office.

Deshin waited. He learned that middle managers—and that was what detectives truly were—always felt the press of time. He never had enough time for anything and yet, as the head of his own corporation, he also had all the time in the universe.

"I'm here about Sonja Mycenae," she said.

Sonja. The nanny he had fired just that morning. Well, fired wasn't an accurate term. He had deliberately avoided firing her. He had eliminated her position.

He and Gerda had decided that Sonja wasn't affectionate enough toward their son. In fact, she had seemed a bit cold toward him. And once Deshin and Gerda started that conversation about Sonja's attitudes, they realized they didn't like having someone visit their home every day, and they didn't like giving up any time with Paavo.

Both Gerda and Deshin had worried, given their backgrounds, that they wouldn't know how to nurture a baby, but Sonja had taught them that training mattered a lot less than actual love.

"I understand she works for you," the detective said.

"She worked for me," he said.

Something changed in the detective's face. Something small. He felt uneasy for the first time.

"Tell me what this is about, Detective," he said.

"It's about Sonja Mycenae," she repeated.

"Yes, you said that. What exactly has she done?" he asked.

"Why don't you tell me why she no longer works for you," the detective said.

"My wife and I decided that we didn't need a nanny for our son. I called Sonja to the office this morning, and let her know that, effective immediately, her employment was terminated through no fault of her own."

"Do you have footage of that conversation?" the detective asked.

"I do, and it's protected. You'll need permission from both of us or a warrant before I can give it to you."

The detective raised her eyebrows. "I'm sure you can forgo the formalities, Mr. Deshin."

"I'm sure that many people do, Detective," he said, "however, it's my understanding that an employee's records are confidential. You may get a warrant if you like. Otherwise, I'm going to protect Sonja's privacy."

"Why would you do that, Mr. Deshin?"

"Believe it or not, I follow the rules." He managed to say that without sarcasm.

The detective grunted as if she didn't believe him. "What made you decide to terminate her position today?"

"I told you," Deshin said, keeping his voice bland even though he was getting annoyed. "My wife and I decided we didn't need a nanny to help us raise our son."

"You might want to share that footage with me without wasting time on a warrant, Mr. Deshin," the detective said.

"Why would I do that, Detective? I'm not even sure why you're asking about Sonja. What has she done?"

"She has died, Mr. Deshin."

The words hung between them. He frowned. The detective had finally caught him off guard.

For the first time, he did not know how to respond. He probably needed one of his lawyers here. Any time his name came up in an investigation, he was automatically the first suspect.

But in this case, he had nothing to do with Sonja's death. So he would act accordingly, and let the lawyers handle the mess.

"What happened?" he asked softly.

He had known Sonja since she was a child. She was the daughter of a friend. That was one of the many reasons he had hired her, because he had known her.

Even then, she hadn't turned out as expected. He remembered an affectionate happy girl. The nanny who had come to his house didn't seem to know how to smile at all. There had been no affection in her.

And when he last saw her, she'd been crying and pleading with him to keep her job. He actually had to have security drag her out of his office.

"We don't know what happened," the detective said.

That sentence could mean a lot. It could mean that they didn't know what happened at all or that they didn't know if her death was by natural causes or by murder. It could also mean that they didn't know exactly what or who caused the death, but that they suspected murder.

Since he was facing a detective and not a beat officer, he knew they suspected murder.

"Where did it happen?" Deshin asked.

"We don't know that either," the detective said.

He snapped, "Then how do you know she's dead?"

Again, that slight change in the detective's face. Apparently he had finally hit on the correct question.

"Because workers found her in a waste crate in a warehouse outside the dome."

"Outside the dome . . . ?" That didn't make sense to him. Sonja hadn't even owned an environmental suit. She had hated them with a passion. "She died outside the dome?"

"I didn't say that, Mr. Deshin," the detective said.

He let out a breath. "Look, Detective, I'm cooperating here, but you need to work with me. I saw Sonja this morning, eliminated her position, and watched her leave my office. Then I went to work. I haven't gone out of the building all day."

"But your people have," the detective said.

He felt a thin thread of fury, and he suppressed it. Everyone assumed that his people murdered other people according to some whim. That simply was not true.

"Detective," he said calmly. "If I wanted Sonja dead, why would I terminate her employment this morning?"

"I have only your word for that," the detective said. "Unless you give me the footage."

"And I have only your word that she's dead," he said.

The detective pressed her hands together, then separated them. A hologram appeared between them—a young woman, looking as if she had fallen asleep in a meadow. Until he looked closely, and saw that the "meadow" was bits of food, and the young woman's eyes were open and filmy.

It was Sonja.

"My God," he said.

"If you give me the footage," the detective said, "and it confirms what you say, then you'll be in the clear. If you wait, then we're going to assume it was doctored."

Deshin glared at her. She was good—and she was right. The longer he waited, the less credibility he would have.

"I'm going to consult with my attorneys," he said. "If they believe that this information has use to you and it doesn't cause me any legal liabilities, then you will receive it from them within the hour."

The detective crossed her arms. "I suggest that you send it to me now. I will promise you that I will not look at anything until you or your attorneys say that I can."

It was an odd compromise, but one that *would* protect him. If she believed he would doctor the footage, then having the footage in her possession wouldn't harm him.

But he didn't know the laws on something this arcane.

"How's this, Detective," he said. "My staff will give you a chip with the information on it. You may not put the chip into any device or watch it until I've consulted with my attorneys. You will wait here while I do so."

"Seems fine to me," the detective said. "I've got all the time in the world."

She didn't, of course. DeRicci was probably getting all kinds of messages on her links from Lake and Gumiela and Broduer and everyone else, telling her she was stupid or needed or something.

She didn't care. She certainly wasn't going to turn her links back on. She was close to something.

She had actually surprised the Great Luc Deshin, Criminal Mastermind.

He pivoted, and moved three steps away from her. He was clearly contacting someone on his links, but using private encoded links.

A staff member approached, a woman DeRicci hadn't seen before. The woman, dressed in a black suit, extended a hand covered with gold rings.

"If you'll come this way, Detective DeRicci . . ."

DeRicci shook her head. "Mr. Deshin promised me a chip. I'm staying here until I get it."

The woman opened her other hand. In it was a chip case the size of a thumbnail. The case was clear, and inside, DeRicci saw another case—blue, with a filament thinner than an eyelash.

"Here is your chip, Detective," the woman said. "I've been instructed to take you—"

"I don't care," DeRicci said. "I'll take the chip, and I'll wait right here. You have my word that I won't open either case, and I won't watch anything until I get the okay."

The woman's eyes glazed slightly. Clearly, she was seeing if that was all right.

Then she focused on DeRicci, and bowed her head slightly.

"As you wish, Detective."

She handed DeRicci the case. It was heavier than it looked. It probably had a lot of protections built in, so that she couldn't activate anything through the case.

Not that she had the technical ability to do any of that, even if she wanted to.

She sighed. She had a fluttery feeling that she had just been outmaneuvered.

Then she made herself watch Deshin. He seemed truly distressed at the news of Sonja Mycenae's death. If DeRicci had to put money on it, she would say that he hadn't known she was dead and he hadn't ordered the death.

But he was also well known for his business acumen, his criminal savvy, and his ability to beat a clear case against him. A man didn't get a reputation like that by being easy to read.

She closed her fist around the chip case, clasped her hands behind her back, and waited, watching Luc Deshin the entire time.

Deshin hadn't gone far. He wanted to keep an eye on the detective. He'd learned in the past that police officers had a tendency to wander, and observe things they shouldn't.

He had staff in various parts of the lobby to prevent the detective from doing just that.

Through private, encoded links, he had contacted his favorite attorney, Martin Oberholtz. For eight years, Oberholtz had managed the most delicate cases for Deshin—always knowing how far the law could bend before it broke.

Before I tell you what to do, Oberholtz was saying on their link, *I want to see the footage.*

It'll take time, Deshin sent.

Ach, Oberholtz sent. *I'll just bill you for it. Send it to me.*

I already have, Deshin sent.

I'll be in contact shortly, Oberholtz sent, and signed off.

Deshin walked to the other side of the lobby. He didn't want to vanish because he didn't want the detective to think he was doing something nefarious.

But he was unsettled. That meeting with Sonja had not gone as he expected.

Over the years, Deshin had probably fired two hundred people personally, and his staff had fired even more. And that didn't count the business relationships he had terminated.

Doing unpleasant things didn't bother him. They usually followed a pattern. But the meeting that morning hadn't followed a pattern that he recognized.

He had spoken quite calmly to Sonja, telling her that he and Gerda had decided to raise Paavo without help. He hadn't criticized Sonja at all. In fact, he had promised her a reference if she wanted it, and he had complimented her on the record, saying that her presence had given him and Gerda the confidence to handle Paavo alone.

He hadn't said that the confidence had come from the fact that Sonja had years of training and she missed the essential ingredient—affection. He had kept everything as neutral and positive as possible, given that he was effectively firing her without firing her.

Midway through his little speech, her eyes widened. He had thought she was going to burst into tears. Instead, she put a shaking hand to her mouth, looking like she had just received news that everything she loved in the world was going to be taken away from her.

He had a moment of confusion—had she actually cared that much about Paavo?—and then he decided it didn't matter; he and Gerda really did want to raise the boy on their own, without any outside help.

"Mr. Deshin," Sonja had said when he finished. "Please, I beg you, do not fire me."

"I'm not firing you, Sonja," he had said. "I just don't have a job for you any longer."

"Please," she said. "I will work here. I will do anything, the lowest of the low. I will do jobs that are disgusting or frightening, anything, Mr. Deshin. Please. Just don't make me leave."

He had never had an employee beg so strenuously to keep her job. It unnerved him. "I don't have any work for you."

"Please, Mr. Deshin." She reached for him and he leaned back. "Please. Don't make me leave."

That was when he sent a message along his links to security. This woman was crazy, and no one on his staff had picked up on it. He felt both relieved and appalled. Relieved that she was going nowhere near Paavo again, and appalled that he had left his beloved little son in her care.

The door opened, and then Sonja screamed "No!" at the top of her lungs. She grabbed at Deshin, and one of his security people pulled her away.

She kicked and fought and screamed and cried all the way through the door. It closed behind her, leaving him alone, but he could still hear her yelling all the way to the elevator.

The incident had unsettled him.

It still unsettled him.

And now, just a few hours later, Sonja was dead.

That couldn't be a coincidence.

It couldn't be a coincidence at all.

It took nearly fifteen minutes before Luc Deshin returned. DeRicci had watched him pace on the other side of the lobby, his expression grim.

It was still grim when he reached her.

He nodded at the chip in her hand. "My staff tells me that you have a lot of information on that chip. In addition to the meeting in my office, you'll see Sonja's arrival and her departure. You'll also see that she left through that front door. After she disappeared off our external security cameras, no one on my staff saw her again."

He was being very precise. DeRicci figured his lawyer had told him to do that.

"Thank you," she said, closing her fingers around the case. "I appreciate the cooperation."

"You're welcome," Deshin said, then walked away.

She watched him go. Something about his mood had darkened since she originally spoke to him. Because of the lawyer? Or something else?

It didn't matter. She had the information she needed, at least for the moment.

She would deal with Deshin later if she needed to.

Deshin took the stairs back to his office. He needed to think, and he didn't want to run into any of his staff on the elevator. Besides, exercise kept his head clear.

He had thought Sonja crazy after her reaction in his office. But what if she knew her life was in danger if she left his employ? Then her behavior made sense.

He wasn't going to say that to the detective, nor had he mentioned it to his lawyer. Deshin was going to investigate this himself.

As he reached the top floor, he sent a message to his head of security, Otto Koos: *My office. Now.*

Deshin went through the doors and stopped, as he always did, looking at the view. He had a 360-degree view of the City of Armstrong. Right now, the dome was set at Dome Daylight, mimicking midday sunlight on Earth. He loved the look of Dome Daylight because it put buildings all over the city in such clear light that it made them look like a beautiful painting or a holographic wall image.

He crossed to his desk, and called up the file on Sonja Mycenae, looking for anything untoward, anything his staff might have missed.

He saw nothing.

She had worked for a family on Earth who had filed monthly reports with the nanny service that had vetted her. The reports were excellent. Sonja had then left the family to come to the Moon, because, apparently, she had been homesick.

He couldn't find anything in a cursory search of that file which showed any contradictory information.

The door to his office opened, and Koos entered. He was a short man with broad shoulders and a way of walking that made him look like he was itching for a fight.

Deshin had known him since they were boys, and trusted Koos with his life. Koos had saved that life more than once.

"Sonja was murdered after she left us this morning," Deshin said.

Koos glanced at the door. "So that was why Armstrong PD was here."

"Yeah," Deshin said, "and it clarifies her reaction. She knew something bad would happen to her."

"She was a plant," Koos said.

"Or something," Deshin said. "We need to know why. Did anyone follow her after she left?"

"You didn't order us to," Koos said, "and I saw no reason to keep track of her. She was crying pretty hard when she walked out, but she never looked back and as far as I could tell, no one was after her."

"The police are going to trace her movements," Deshin said. "We need to as well. But what I want to know is this: What did we miss about this woman? I've already checked her file. I see nothing unusual."

"I'll go over it again," Koos said.

"Don't go over it," Deshin said, feeling a little annoyed. After all, he had just done that, and he didn't need to be double-checked. "Vet her again, as if we were just about to hire her. See what you come up with."

"Yes, sir," Koos said. Normally, he would have left after that, but he didn't. Instead, he held his position.

Deshin suppressed a sigh. Something else was coming his way. "What?"

"When you dismissed her and she reacted badly," Koos said, "I increased security around your wife and child. I'm going to increase it again, and I'm going to make sure you've got extra protection as well."

Deshin opened his mouth, but Koos put up one finger, stopping him.

"Don't argue with me," Koos said. "Something's going on here, and I don't like it."

Deshin smiled. "I wasn't going to argue with you, Otto. I was going to thank you. I hadn't thought to increase security around my family, and it makes sense."

Koos nodded, as if Deshin's praise embarrassed him. Then he left the office.

Deshin watched him go. As soon as he was gone, Deshin contacted Gerda on their private links.

Koos might have increased security, but Deshin wanted to make sure everything was all right.

He used to say that families were a weakness, and he never wanted one. Then he met Gerda, and they brought Paavo into their lives.

He realized that families *were* a weakness, but they were strength as well.

And he was going to make sure his was safe, no matter what it took.

It had taken more work than Broduer expected to get the body back to the coroner's office. Just to get the stupid crate out of the warehouse, he'd had to sign documentation swearing he wouldn't use it to make money at the expense of Ansel Management.

"Company policy," Najib Ansel had said with an insincere smile.

If Broduer hadn't known better, he would have thought that Ansel was just trying to make things difficult for him.

But things had become difficult for Broduer when DeRicci's partner, Rayvon Lake, arrived. Lake had been as angry as Broduer had ever seen him, claiming that DeRicci—who was apparently a junior officer to Lake—had been giving him orders.

Lake had shouted at everyone, except Broduer. Broduer had fended a shouting match off by holding up his hands and saying, "I'm not sure what killed this girl, but I don't like it. It might contaminate everything. We have to get her out of here, now."

Lake, who was a notorious germophobe (which Broduer found strange in a detective), had gulped and stepped back. Broduer had gotten the crate to the warehouse door before Ansel had come after him with all the documentation crap.

Maybe Ansel had done it just so that he wouldn't have to talk with Lake. Broduer would have done anything to avoid Lake—and apparently just had.

Broduer smiled to himself, relieved to be back at the coroner's office. The office was a misnomer—the coroner had their own building, divided into sections to deal with the various kinds of death that happened in Armstrong.

Broduer had tested out of the alien section after two years of trying. He hated working in an environmental suit, like he so often had to. Weirdly (he always thought) humans started in the alien section and had to get a promotion to work on human cadavers. Probably because no one really wanted to see the interior of a Sequev more than once. No human did, anyway.

There were more than a dozen alien coroners, most of whom worked with human supervisors since many alien cultures did not investigate cause of death. Armstrong was a human-run society on a human-run Moon, so human laws applied here, and human laws always needed a cause of death.

Broduer had placed Sonja Mycenae on the autopsy table, carefully positioning her before beginning work, and he'd been startled at how well proportioned she was.

Most people had obvious flaws, at least when a coroner was looking at them. One arm a little too long, a roll of fat under the chin, a misshapen ankle.

He hadn't removed her clothing yet, but as far as he could tell from the work he'd done with her already, nothing was unusual.

Which made her unusual all by herself.

He also couldn't see any obvious cause of death. He had noted, however, that full rigor mortis had already set in. Which was odd, since the decomposition, according to the exam his nanobots had already started, seemed to have progressed at a rate that put her death at least five hours earlier.

By now, under the conditions she'd been stored in, she should have still been pliable—at least her limbs. Rigor began in the eyes, jaw, and neck then spread to the face and through the chest before getting to the limbs. The fingers and toes were always the last to stiffen up.

That made him suspicious, particularly since liver mortis also seemed off.

He would have thought, given how long she had been curled inside that crate, that the blood would have pooled in the side of her body resting on top of the compost heap. But no blood had pooled at all.

He had bots move the autopsy table into one of the more advanced autopsy theaters. He wanted every single device he could find to do the work.

He suspected she'd been killed with some kind of hardening poison. They had become truly popular with assassins in the last two decades, and had just recently been banned from the Moon. Hardening poisons killed quickly by absorbing all the liquid in the body and/or by baking it into place.

It was a quick death, but a painful one, and usually the victim's muscles froze in place, so she couldn't even express that pain as it occurred.

He put on a high-grade environmental suit in an excess of caution. Some of the hardening poisons leaked out of the pores and then infected anyone who touched them.

What he had to determine was if Sonja Mycenae had died of one of those, and if her body had been placed in a waste crate not just to hide the corpse, but to infect the food supply in Armstrong.

Because the Growing Pits inspections looked at the growing materials—the soil, the water, the light, the atmosphere, and the seeds. The inspectors would also look at the fertilizer, but if it came from a certified organization like Ansel Management, then there would only be a cursory search of materials.

Hardening poisons could thread their way into the DNA of a plant—just a little bit, so that, say, an apple wouldn't be quite as juicy. A little hardening poison wouldn't really hurt the fruit of a tree (although that tree might eventually die of what a botanist would consider a wasting disease), but a trace of hardening poison in the human system would have an impact over time. And if the human continued to eat things with hardening poisons in them, the poisons would build up, until the body couldn't take it any more.

A person poisoned in that way wouldn't die like Sonja Mycenae had; instead, the poison would overwhelm the standard nanohealers that everyone had installed, that person would get sick, and organs would slowly fail. Armstrong would have a plague but not necessarily know what caused it.

He double-checked his gloves, then let out a breath. Yes, he knew he was being paranoid. But he thought about these things a lot—the kinds of death that could happen with just a bit of carelessness, like sickness in a dome, poison through the food supply, the wrong mix in the air supply.

He had moved from working with living humans to working with the dead primarily because his imagination was so vivid. Usually working with the dead calmed him. The regular march of unremarkable deaths reminded him that most people would die of natural causes after 150 or more years, maybe longer if they took good care of themselves.

Working with the dead usually gave him hope.

But Sonja Mycenae was making him nervous.

And he didn't like that at all.

Deshin had just finished talking with Gerda when Koos sent him an encoded message:

Need to talk as soon as you can.

Now's fine, Deshin sent.

He moved away from the windows, where he'd been standing as he made sure Gerda was okay. She actually sounded happy, which she hadn't since Paavo moved in.

She said she no longer felt like her every move was being judged.

Paavo seemed happier too. He wasn't crying as much, and he didn't cling as hard to Gerda. Instead, he played with a mobile from his bouncy chair and watched her cook, cooing most of the time.

Just that one report made Deshin feel like he had made the right choice with Sonja.

Not that he had had a doubt—at least about her—after her reaction that morning. But apparently a tiny doubt had lingered about whether or not he and Gerda needed the help of a nanny.

Gerda's report on Paavo's calmness eased that. Deshin knew they would have hard times ahead—he wasn't deluding himself—but he also knew that they had made the right choice to go nanny-free.

He hadn't told Gerda what happened to Sonja, and he wouldn't, until he knew more. He didn't want to spoil Gerda's day.

The door to Deshin's office opened, and Koos entered, looking upset. "Upset" was actually the wrong word. Something about Koos made Deshin think the man was afraid.

Then Deshin shook that thought off: he'd seen Koos in extremely dangerous circumstances and the man had never seemed afraid.

"I did what you asked," Koos said without preamble. "I started vetting her all over again."

Deshin leaned against the desk, just like he had done when he spoke to Sonja. "And?"

"Her employers on Earth are still filing updates about her exemplary work for them."

Deshin felt a chill. "Tell me that they were just behind in their reports."

Koos shook his head. "She's still working for them."

"How is that possible?" Deshin asked. "We vetted her. We even used a DNA sample to make sure her DNA was the same as the DNA on file with the service. And we collected it ourselves."

Koos swallowed. "We used the service's matching program."

"Of course we did," Deshin said. "They were the ones with the DNA on file."

"We could have requested that sample, and then run it ourselves."

That chill Deshin had felt became a full-fledged shiver. "What's the difference?"

"Depth," Koos said. "They don't go into the same kind of depth we would go into in our search. They just look at standard markers, which is really all most people would need to confirm identity."

His phrasing made Deshin uncomfortable. "She's not who she said she was?"

Koos let out a small sigh. "It's more complicated than that."

More complicated. Deshin shifted. He could only think of one thing that would be more complicated.

Sonja was a clone.

And that created all kinds of other issues.

But first, he had to confirm his suspicion.

"You checked for clone marks, right?" Deshin asked. "I know you did. We always do."

The Earth Alliance required human clones to have a mark on the back of their neck or behind their ear that gave their number. If they were the second clone from an original, the number would be "2."

Clones also did not have birth certificates. They had day of creation documents. Deshin had a strict policy for Deshin Enterprises: every person he hired had to have a birth certificate or a document showing that they, as a clone, had been legally adopted by an original human and therefore could be considered human under the law.

When it came to human clones, Earth Alliance and Armstrong laws were the same: clones were property. They were created and owned by their creator. They could be bought or sold, and they had no rights of their own. The law did not distinguish between slow-grow clones, which were raised like any naturally born human child, and fast-grow clones, which reached full adult size in days, but never had a full-grown human intelligence.

The laws were an injustice, but only clones seemed to protest it, and they, as property, had no real standing.

Koos's lips thinned. He didn't answer right away.

Deshin cursed. He hated having clones in his business, and didn't own any, even though he could take advantage of the loopholes in the law.

Clones made identity theft too easy, and made an organization vulnerable.

He always made certain his organization remained protected.

Or he had, until now.

"We did check like we do with all new hires." Koos's voice was strangled. "And we also checked her birth certificate. It was all in order."

"But now you're telling me it's not," Deshin said.

Koos's eyes narrowed a little, not with anger, but with tension.

"The first snag we hit," he said, "was that we were not able to get Sonja Mycenae's DNA from the service. According to them, she's currently employed, and not available for hire, so the standard service-subsidized searches are inactive. She likes her job. I looked: the job is the old one, not the one with you."

Deshin crossed his arms. "If that's the case, then how did we get the service comparison in the first place?"

"At first, I worried that someone had spoofed our system," Koos said. "It hadn't. There was a redundancy in the service's files that got repaired. I checked with a tech at the service. The tech said they'd been hit with an attack that replicated everything inside their system. It lasted for about two days."

"Let me guess," Deshin said. "Two days around the point we'd hired Sonja."

Koos nodded.

"I'm amazed the tech admitted it," Deshin said.

"It wasn't their glitch," Koos said. "It happened because of some government program."

"Government?" Deshin asked.

"The Earth Alliance required some changes in their software," Koos said. "They made the changes and the glitch appeared. The service caught it, removed the Earth Alliance changes, and petitioned to return to their old way of doing things. Their petition was granted."

Deshin couldn't sit still with this. "Did Sonja know this glitch was going to happen?"

Koos shrugged. "I don't know what she knew."

Deshin let out a small breath. He felt a little off-balance. "I assume the birth certificate was stolen."

"It was real. We checked it. I double-checked it today," Koos said.

Deshin rubbed his forehead. "So, was the Sonja Mycenae I hired a clone or is the clone at the other job? Or does Sonja Mycenae have a biological twin?"

Koos looked down, which was all the answer Deshin needed. She was a clone.

"She left a lot of DNA this morning," Koos said. "Tears, you name it. We checked it all."

Deshin waited, even though he knew.

He knew, and he was getting furious.

"She had no clone mark," Koos said, "except in her DNA. The telomeres were marked."

"Designer Criminal Clone," Deshin said. A number of criminal organizations, most operating outside the Alliance, made and trained Designer Criminal Clones for just the kind of thing that had happened to Deshin.

The clone, who replicated someone the family or the target knew casually, would slide into a business or a household for months, maybe years, and steal information. Then the clone would leave with that information on a chip, bringing it to whoever had either hired that DCC or who had grown and trained the clone.

"I don't think she was a DCC," Koos said. "The markers don't fit anyone we know."

"A new player?" Deshin asked.

Koos shrugged. Then he took one step forward. "I'm going to check everything she touched, everything she did, sir. But this is my error, and it's a serious one. It put your business and more importantly your family in danger. I know you're going to fire me, but before you do, let me track down her creator. Let me redeem myself."

Deshin didn't move for a long moment. He had double-checked everything Koos had done. *Everything*. Because Sonja Mycenae—or whatever that clone was named—was going to work in his home, with his family.

"Do you think she stole my son's DNA?" Deshin asked quietly.

"I don't know. Clearly she didn't have any with her today, but if she had handlers—"

"She wouldn't have had trouble meeting them, because Gerda and I didn't want a live-in nanny." Deshin cursed silently. There was more than enough blame to go around, and if he were honest with himself, most of it belonged to him. He had been so concerned with raising his son, that he hadn't taken the usual precautions in protecting his family.

"I would like to retrace all of her steps," Koos said. "We might be able to find her handler."

"Or not," Deshin said. The handler had killed her the moment she had ceased to be useful. The handler felt he could waste a slow-grow clone, expensive and well-trained, placed in the household of a man everyone believed to be a criminal mastermind.

Some mastermind. He had screwed up something this important.

He bit back anger, not sure how he would tell Gerda. *If* he would tell Gerda.

Something had been planned here, something he hadn't figured out yet, and that planning was not complete. Sonja (or whatever her name was) had confirmed that with her reaction to her dismissal. She was terrified, and she probably knew she was going to die.

He sighed.

"I will quit now if you'd like me to," Koos said.

Deshin wasn't ready to fire Koos.

"Find out who she answered to. Better yet, find out who made her," Deshin said. "Find her handler. We'll figure out what happens to you after you complete that assignment."

Koos nodded, but didn't thank Deshin. Koos knew his employer well, knew that the thanks would only irritate him.

Deshin hated to lose Koos, but Koos was no longer 100 percent trustworthy. He should have caught this. He should have tested Sonja's DNA himself.

And that was why Deshin would put new security measures into place for his business and his family. Measures he designed.

He'd also begin the search for the new head of security.

It would take time.

And, he was afraid, it would take time to find out what exactly Sonja (or whatever her name was) had been trying to do inside his home.

That had just become his first priority.

Because no one was going to hurt his family.

No matter what he had to do to protect them.

Broduer had six different nanoprobes digging into various places on the dead woman's skin, when a holographic computer screen appeared in front of him, a red warning light flashing.

He moaned slightly. He hated the lights. They got sent to his boss automatically, and often the damn lights reported something he had done wrong.

Well, not wrong, exactly, but not according to protocol.

The irony was, everything he had done in this autopsy so far had been exactly according to protocol.

The body was on an isolated gurney, which was doing its own investigation; they were in one of the most protected autopsy chambers in the coroner's office; and Broduer was using all the right equipment.

He even had on the right environmental suit for the type of poison he suspected killed the woman.

He cursed, silently and creatively, wishing he could express his frustration aloud, but knowing he couldn't, because it would become part of the permanent record.

Instead, he glared at the light and wished it would go away. Not that he could make it go away with a look.

The light had a code he had never seen before. He put his gloved finger on the code, and it created a whole new screen.

This body is cloned. Please file the permissions code to autopsy this clone or cease work immediately.

"The hell . . . ?" he asked, then realized he had spoken aloud, and he silently cursed himself. Some stupid supervisor, reviewing the footage, would think he was too dumb to know a cloned body from a real body.

But he had made a mistake. He hadn't taken DNA in the field. He had used facial recognition to identify this woman, and he had told DeRicci who the woman was based not on the DNA testing, but on the facial recognition.

Of course, if DeRicci hadn't pressed him to give her an identification right away, he would have followed procedure.

Broduer let out a small sigh, then remembered what he had been doing.

There was still a way to cover his ass. He had been investigating whether or not this woman died of a hardening poison, and if that poison had gotten into the composting system.

He would use that as his excuse, and then mention that he needed to continue to find cause of death for public health reasons.

Besides, someone should want to know who was killing clones and putting them into the composting.

Not that it was illegal, exactly. After all, a dead clone was organic waste, just like rotted vegetables were.

He shuddered, not wanting to think about it. Maybe someone should tell the Armstrong City Council to ban the composting of any human flesh be it original or cloned.

He sighed. He didn't want to be the one to do it. He'd slip the suggestion into his supervisor's ear and hope that she would take him up on it.

He pinged his supervisor, telling her that it was important she contact him right away.

Then he bent over the body, determined to get as much work done as possible before someone shut this investigation down entirely.

DeRicci sat in her car in the part of Armstrong Police Department Parking Lot set aside for detectives. She hadn't used the car all day, but it was the most private place she could think of to watch the footage Deshin had given her.

She didn't want to take the footage inside the station until she'd had a chance to absorb it. She wasn't sure how relevant it was, and she wasn't sure what her colleagues would think of it.

Or, if she were being truthful with herself, she didn't want Lake anywhere near this thing. He had some dubious connections, and he might just confiscate the footage—not for the case, but for reasons she didn't really want to think about.

So, she stayed in her car, quietly watching the footage for the second time, taking mental notes. Because something was off here. People rarely got that upset getting fired from a job, at least not in front of a man known to be as dangerous as Luc Deshin.

Besides, he had handled the whole thing well, made it sound like not a firing, more like something inevitable, something that Sonja Mycenae's excellent job performance helped facilitate.

The man was impressive, although DeRicci would never admit that to anyone else.

When DeRicci watched the footage the first time, she had been amazed at how calmly Deshin handled Mycenae's meltdown. He managed to stay out of her way, and he managed to get his security into the office without making her get even worse.

Not that it would be easy for her to be worse. If DeRicci hadn't known that Sonja Mycenae was murdered shortly after this footage was taken, DeRicci would have thought the woman unhinged. Instead, DeRicci knew that Mycenae was terrified.

She had known that losing her position would result in something awful, mostly likely her death.

But why? And what did someone have on a simple nanny with no record, something bad enough to get her to work in the home of a master criminal and his wife, bad enough to make her beg said criminal to keep the job?

DeRicci didn't like this. She particularly did not like the way that Mycenae disappeared off the security footage as she stepped outside of the building. She stood beside the building and sobbed for a few minutes, then staggered away.

No nearby buildings had exterior security cameras, and what DeRicci could get from the street cameras told her little.

She would have to do from inside police headquarters.

Um, Detective?

DeRicci sighed. The contact came from Broduer, on her links. He was asking for a visual, which she was not inclined to give him.

But he probably had something to show her from the autopsy.

So she activated the visual, in two dimensions, making his head float above the car's control panel. Broduer wore an environmental suit, but he had removed the hood that had covered his face. It hung behind his skull like a half-visible alien appendage.

News for me, Ethan? she asked, hoping to move him along quickly. He could get much too chatty for her tastes.

Well, you're not going to like any of it. He ran a hand through his hair, messing it up. It looked a little damp, as if he'd been sweating inside the suit.

DeRicci waited. She didn't know how she could like or dislike any news about the woman's death. It was a case. A sad and strange case, but a case nonetheless.

She died from a hardening poison, Broduer sent. *I've narrowed it down to one of five related types. I'm running the test now to see which poison it actually is.*

Poison. That took effort. Not in the actual application—many poisons were impossible to see, taste, or feel—but in the planning.

Someone wanted this woman dead, and then they wanted to keep her death secret.

That's a weird way to kill someone, DeRicci sent.

Broduer looked concerned. Over the woman? He usually saw corpses as a curiosity, not as someone to empathize with.

That was one of the few things DeRicci liked about Broduer. He could handle a job as a job.

It is a weird way to kill someone, Broduer sent. Then he glanced over his shoulder as if he expected someone to enter his office and yell at him. *The thing is, one of these types of poisons could contaminate the food supply.*

What? she sent. Or maybe she said that out loud. Or both. She felt cold. Contaminate the food supply? With a body?

She wasn't quite sure of the connection, but she didn't like it.

She hadn't like the corpse in the compost part of this case from the very first.

Broduer took an obvious deep breath and his gaze met hers. She stabilized the floating image, so she wasn't tracking him as he moved up, down, and across the control panel.

If, he sent, *the poison leaked from the skin and got into the compost, then it would be layered onto the growing plants, which would take in the poison along with the nutrients. It wouldn't be enough to kill anyone, unless someone'd been doing this for a long time.*

DeRicci shook her head. *Then I don't get it. How is this anything other than a normal contamination?*

If a wannabe killer wants to destroy the food supply, he'd do stuff like this for months, Broduer sent. *People would start dying mysteriously. Generally, the old and the sick would go first, or people who are vulnerable in the parts of their bodies this stuff targets.*

Wouldn't the basic nanohealers take care of this problem? DeRicci was glad they weren't doing this verbally. She didn't want him to know how shaken she was.

If it were small or irregular, sure, he sent. *But over time? No. They're not made to handle huge contaminations. They're not even designed to recognize these kinds of poisons. That's why these poisons can kill so quickly.*

DeRicci suppressed a shudder.

Great, she sent. *How do we investigate food contamination like that?*

That's your problem, Detective, Broduer sent back, somewhat primly. *I'd suggest starting with a search of records, seeing if there has been a rise in deaths in vulnerable populations.*

Can't you do that easier than I can? She sent, even though she knew he would back out. It couldn't hurt to try to get him to help.

Not at the moment, he sent, *I have a job to do.*

She nearly cursed at him. But she managed to control herself. A job to do. The bastard. *She* had a job to do too, and it was just as important as his job.

This was why she hated working with Broduer. He was a jerk.

Well, she sent, *let me know the type of poison first, before I get into that part of the investigation. You said there were five, and only one could contaminate the food supply. You think that's the one we're dealing with?*

I don't know yet, Detective, he sent. *I'll know when the testing is done.*

Which will take how long?

He shrugged. *Not long, I hope.*

Great, she sent again. She wanted to push him, but pushing him sometimes made him even more passive/aggressive about getting work done.

Well, you were right, she sent. *I didn't like it. Now I'm off to investigate even more crap.*

Um, not yet, Broduer sent.

Not yet? Who was this guy and why did he think he could control everything she did. She clenched her fists. Pretty soon, she would tell this idiot exactly what she thought of him, and that wouldn't make for a good working relationship.

Um, yeah, he sent. *There's one other problem.*

She waited, her fists so tight her fingernails were digging into the skin of her palm.

He looked down. *I, um, misidentified your woman.*

You what? He had been an idiot about helping her, and then he told her that he had done crappy work?

This man was the absolutely worst coroner she'd ever worked with (which was saying something) and she was going to report him to the Chief of Detectives, maybe even to the Chief of Police, and get him removed from his position.

Yeah, Broduer sent. *She's, um, not Sonja Mycenae.*

You said that, DeRicci sent. Already, her mind was racing. Misidentifying the corpse would cause all kinds of problems, not the least of which would be problems with Luc Deshin. *Who the hell is she, then?*

Broduer's skin had turned gray. He clearly knew he had screwed up big time. *She's a clone of Sonja Mycenae.*

A what? DeRicci rolled her eyes. That would have been good to know right from the start. Because it meant the investigation had gone in the wrong direction from the moment she had a name.

A clone. I'm sorry, Detective.

You should be, DeRicci sent. *I shouldn't even be on this investigation This isn't a homicide.*

Well, technically, it's the same thing, Broduer sent.

Technically, it isn't, DeRicci sent. She'd had dozens of clone cases before, and no matter how much she argued with the Chief of Detectives, Andrea Gumiela, it didn't matter. The clones weren't human under the law; their deaths fell into property crimes, generally vandalism or destruction of valuable property, depending on how much the clone was worth or how much it cost to create.

But, Detective, she's a human being . . .

DeRicci sighed. She believed that, but what she believed didn't matter. What mattered was what the law said and how her boss handled it. And she'd been through this with Gumiela. Gumiela would send DeRicci elsewhere.

Gumiela hadn't seen the poor girl crying and begging for her life in front of Deshin. Gumiela hadn't seen the near-perfect corpse, posed as if she were sleeping on a pile of compost.

Wait a minute, DeRicci sent. *You told me about the poisoning first because . . . ?*

Because, Detective, she might not be human, but she might have been a weapon or weaponized material. And that would fall into your jurisdiction, wouldn't it?

Just when she thought that Broduer was the worst person she had ever worked with, he manipulated a clone case to keep it inside DeRicci's Detective Division.

I don't determine jurisdiction, she sent, mostly because this was on the record, and she didn't want to show her personal feelings on something that might hit court and derail any potential prosecution.

But check, would you? Broduer sent. *Because someone competent should handle this.*

She wasn't sure what "this" was: the dead clone or the contamination.

Just send me all the information, DeRicci sent, *and let me know the minute you confirm which hardening poison killed this clone.*

I'll have it soon, Broduer sent and signed off.

DeRicci leaned back in the car seat, her cheeks warm. She had gone to Luc Deshin for nothing.

Or had she?

Which Sonja Mycenae had Deshin fired that morning? The real one? Or the clone?

DeRicci let herself out of the car. She had to talk to Gumiela. But before she did, she needed to find out where the real Mycenae was—and fast.

Deshin wasn't certain how to tell Gerda that Sonja had been a plant, placed in their home for a reason he didn't know yet.

He wandered his office, screens moving with him as he examined the tracker he had placed in Sonja. Then he winced. Every time he thought of the clone as Sonja, he felt like a fool. From now on, he would just call her the clone, because she clearly wasn't Sonja.

So he examined the information from the tracker he had place in the clone's palm the moment she was hired. She hadn't known he had inserted it. He had done it when he shook her hand, using technology that didn't show up on any of the regular scans.

He wished he had been paranoid enough to install a video tracker, but he had thought—or rather, Gerda had thought—that their nanny needed her privacy in her off time.

Of course, that had been too kind. Deshin should have tracked the clone the way he tracked anyone he didn't entirely trust.

Whenever the clone had been with Paavo, Deshin had always kept a screen open. He'd even set an alert in case the clone took Paavo out of the house without Gerda accompanying them. That alert had never activated, because Gerda had always been nearby when the clone was with Paavo.

Deshin was grateful for that caution now. He had no idea what serious crisis they had dodged.

He was now searching through all the other information in the tracker—where the clone had gone during her days off, where she had spent her free time. He knew that Koos had been, in theory, making sure she had no unsavory contacts—or at least, Deshin had tasked Koos with doing that.

Now, Deshin was double-checking his head of security, making certain that he had actually done his job.

The first thing Deshin had done was make certain that the clone hadn't gone to the bad parts of town. According to the tracker, she hadn't. Her apartment was exactly where she had claimed it was, and as far as he could tell, all she had done in her off hours was shop for her own groceries, eaten at a local restaurant, and gone home.

He had already sent a message to one of the investigative services he used. He wanted them to search the clone's apartment. He wanted video and DNA and all kinds of trace. He wanted an investigation of her finances and a look at the things she kept.

He also didn't want anyone from Deshin Enterprises associated with that search. He knew that his investigative service would keep him out of it. They had done so before.

He had hired them to search before he had known she was a clone. He had hired them while he was waiting for his attorney to look at the footage he had give that detective.

With luck, they'd be done with the search by now.

But he had decided to check the tracker himself, looking for anomalies.

The only anomaly he had found was a weekly visit to a building in downtown Armstrong. On her day off, she went to that building at noon. She had also been at that building the evening Deshin had hired her.

He scanned the address, looking for the businesses that rented or owned the place. The building had dozens of small offices, and none of the businesses were registered with the city.

He found that odd: usually the city insisted that every business register for tax purposes.

So he traced the building's ownership. He went through several layers of corporate dodges to find something odd: the building's owner wasn't a corporation at all.

It was the Earth Alliance.

He let out a breath, and then sank into a nearby chair.

Suddenly everything made sense.

The Earth Alliance had been after him for years, convinced he was breaking a million different Alliance laws and not only getting away with it, but making billions from the practice.

Ironically, he had broken a lot of Alliance laws when he started out, and he still had a lot of sketchy associates, but *he* hadn't broken a law in years and years.

Still, it would have been a coup for someone in Alliance government to bring down Luc Deshin and his criminal enterprises.

The Alliance had found it impossible to plant listening devices and trackers in Deshin's empire. The Alliance was always behind Deshin Enterprises when it came to technology. And Deshin himself was innately cautious—

Or he had thought he was, until this incident with the clone.

They had slipped her into his home. They might have had a hundred purposes in doing so—as a spy on his family, to steal familial DNA, to set up tracking equipment in a completely different way than it had been done before.

And for an entire month, they had been successful.

He was furious at himself, but he knew he couldn't let that emotion dominate his thoughts. He had to take action, and he had to do so now.

He used his links to summon Ishiyo Cumija to his office. He'd been watching her for some time. She hadn't been Koos's second in command in the security department. She had set up her own fiefdom, and once she had mentioned to Deshin that she worried no one was taking security seriously enough.

At the time, he had thought she was making a play for Koos's job. Deshin *still* thought she was making a play for Koos's job on that day, but she might have been doing so with good reason.

Now, she would get a chance to prove herself.

While Deshin waited for her, he checked the clone's DNA and found that strange clone mark embedded into her system. He had never seen anything like it either. The Designer Criminal Clones he'd run into had always had a product stamp embedded into their DNA. This wasn't a standard DCC product stamp.

It looked like something else.

He copied it, then opened Cumija's file, accessed the DNA samples she had to give every week, and searched to see if there was any kind of mark. His system always searched for the DCC product stamps, but rarely searched for other examples of cloning, including shortened telomeres.

Shortened telomeres could happen naturally. In the past, he'd found that searching for them gave him so many false positives—staff members who were older than they appeared, employees who had had serious injuries—that he decided to stop searching for anything but the product marks.

He wondered now if that had been a mistake.

His search of Cumija's DNA found no DCC product stamp, and nothing matching the mark his system had found in the clone's DNA.

As the search ended, Cumija entered the office.

She was stunningly beautiful, with a cap of straight hair so black it almost looked blue, and dancing black eyes. Until he met Cumija, he would never have thought that someone so very attractive would function well in a security position, but she had turned out to be one of his best bodyguards.

She dressed like a woman sexually involved with a very rich man. Her clothing always revealed her taut nut-brown skin and her fantastic legs. Sometimes she looked nearly naked in the clothing she had chosen. Men and women watched her wherever she went, and dismissed her as someone decorative, someone being used.

On this day, she wore a white dress that crossed her breasts with an X, revealing her sides, and expanding to cover her hips and buttocks. Her matching white shoes looked as deadly as the shoes that she had used to kill a man trying to get to Deshin one afternoon.

"That nanny we hired turns out to have been a clone," Deshin said without greeting.

"Yes, I heard." Cumija's voice was low and sexy in keeping with her appearance.

"Has Koos made an announcement?" Deshin asked. Because he would have recommended against it.

"No," she said curtly, and Deshin almost smiled. She monitored everything Koos did. It was a great trait in a security officer, a terrible trait in a subordinate—at least from the perspective of someone in Koos's position.

Deshin said, "I need you to check the other employees—*you*, and you *only*. I don't want anyone to know what you're doing. I have the marker that was in the cloned Sonja Mycenae's DNA. I want you to see if there's a match. I also want a secondary check for Designer Criminal Clone marks, and then I want you to do a slow search of anyone with abnormal telomeres."

Cumija didn't complain, even though he was giving her a lot of work. "You want me to check everyone," she said.

"Yes," he said. "Start with people who have access to me, and then move outward. Do it quickly and quietly."

"Yes, sir," she said.

"Report the results directly to me," he said.

"All right," she said. "Are links all right?"

"No," he said. "You will report in person."

She nodded, thanked him, and left the office.

He stood there for a moment, feeling a little shaken. If the Alliance was trying to infiltrate his organization, then he wouldn't be surprised if there were other clones stationed in various areas, clones he had missed.

After Cumija checked, he would have Koos do the same check, and see if he came up with the same results.

Deshin went back to his investigation of that building that the clone had visited regularly. He had no firm evidence of Earth Alliance involvement. Just suspicions, at least at the moment.

And regular citizens of the Alliance would be stunned to think that their precious Alliance would infiltrate businesses using slow-grow clones, and then disposing of them when they lost their usefulness.

But Deshin knew the Alliance did all kinds of extra-legal things to protect itself over the centuries. And somewhere, Deshin had been flagged as a threat to the Alliance.

He had known that for some time.

He had always expected some kind of infiltration of his business.

But the infiltration of his home was personal.

And it needed to stop.

Ethan Broduer looked at the information pouring across his screen, and let out a sigh of relief.

The hardening poison wasn't one of the kinds that could leach through the skin.

He still had to test the compost to see if the poison had contaminated it, but he doubted that.

The liver mortis told him that she had died elsewhere, and then been placed in the crate. And given how fast this hardening poison acted, the blood wouldn't have been able to pool for more than a few minutes anyway.

He stood and walked back into the autopsy room. Now that he knew the woman had died of something that wouldn't hurt him if he came in contact with her skin or breathed the air around her, he didn't need the environmental suit.

Hers was the only body in this autopsy room. He had placed her on her back before sending the nanobots into her system. They were still working, finding out even more about her.

He knew now that she was a slow-grow clone, which meant she had lived some twenty years, had hopes, dreams, and desires. As a forensic pathologist who had examined hundreds of human corpses—cloned and non-cloned—the *only* difference he had ever seen were the telomeres and the clone marks.

Slow-grow clones were human beings in everything but the law.

He could make the claim that fast-grow clones were too, that they had the mind of a child inside an adult body, but he tried not to think about that one. Because it meant that all those horrors visited on fast-grow clones were visited on a human being that hadn't seen more than a few years of life, an innocent in all possible ways.

He blinked hard, trying not to think about any of it. Then he stopped beside her table. Lights moved along the back of it, different beams examining her, trying to glean her medical history and every single story her biology could tell.

Now that it was clear that the poison which killed her wouldn't contaminate the dome, no one would investigate this case. No one would care.

No one legally *had* to care.

He sighed, then shook his head, wondering if he could make one final push to solve her murder.

Detective DeRicci had asked for a list of bodies found in the crates. Broduer would make her that list after all, but before he did, he would see if those bodies were "human" or clones.

If they were clones, then there was a sabotage problem, some kind of property crime—hell, it wasn't his job to come up with the charge, not when he gave her the thing to investigate.

But maybe he could find something to investigate, something that would have the side benefit of giving some justice to this poor woman, lying alone and unwanted on his autopsy table.

"I'm doing what I can," he whispered, and then wished he hadn't spoken aloud.

His desire to help her would be in the official record. Then he corrected himself: There would be no official record, since she wasn't officially a murder victim.

He was so sorry about that. He'd still document everything he could. Maybe in the future, the laws would change.

Maybe in the future, her death would matter as more than a statistic.

Maybe in the future, she'd be recognized as a person, instead of something to be thrown away, like leftover food.

The Chief of Detectives, Andrea Gumiela, had an office one floor above DeRicci's, but it was light-years from DeRicci's. DeRicci's office was in the center of a large room, sectioned off with dark movable walls. She could protect her area by putting a bubble around it for a short period of time, particularly if she were conducting an interview that she felt wouldn't work in one of the interview rooms, but there was no real privacy and no sense of belonging.

DeRicci hated working out in the center, and hoped that one day, she would eventually get an office of her own.

The tiny aspirations of the upwardly mobile, her ex-husband would have said. She couldn't entirely disagree. He had the unfortunate habit of being right.

And as she looked at Gumiela's office, which took up much of the upper floor, DeRicci knew she would never achieve privacy like this. She wasn't political enough. Some days she felt like she was one infraction away from being terminated.

Most days, she didn't entirely care.

Andrea Gumiela, on the other hand, was the most political person DeRicci had ever met. Her office was designed so that it wouldn't offend anyone. It didn't have artwork on the walls, nor did it have floating imagery. The décor shifted colors when someone from outside the department entered.

When someone was as unimportant as DeRicci, the walls were a neutral beige, and the desk a dark woodlike color. The couch and chairs at the far end of the room matched the desk.

But DeRicci had been here when the Governor-General arrived shortly after her election, and the entire room shifted to vibrant colors—the purples and whites associated with the Governor-General herself.

The shift, which happened as the Governor-General was announced, had disturbed DeRicci, but Gumiela managed it as a matter of course. She was going to get promoted some day, and she clearly hoped the Governor-General would do it.

"Make it fast," Gumiela said as DeRicci entered. "I have meetings all afternoon."

Gumiela was tall and heavyset, but her black suit made her look thinner than she was—probably with some kind of tech that DeRicci didn't want to think about. Gumiela's red hair was piled on top of her head, making her long face seem even longer.

"I wanted to talk with you in person about that woman we found in the Ansel Management crate," DeRicci said.

Gumiela, for all her annoying traits, did keep up on the investigations.

"I thought Rayvon Lake was in charge of that case," Gumiela said.

DeRicci shrugged. "He's not in charge of anything, sir. Honestly, when it comes to cases like this, I don't even like to consult him."

Gumiela studied her. "He's your partner, Detective."

"Maybe," DeRicci said, "but he doesn't investigate crimes. He takes advantage of them."

"That's quite a charge," Gumiela said.

"I can back it with evidence," DeRicci said.

"Do so," Gumiela said, to DeRicci's surprise. DeRicci frowned. Had Gumiela paired them so that DeRicci would bring actual evidence against Lake to the Chief's office? It made an odd kind of sense. No one could control Lake, and no one could control DeRicci, but for different reasons.

Lake had his own tiny fiefdom, and DeRicci was just plain contrary.

"All right," DeRicci said, feeling a little off-balance. She hadn't expected anything positive from Gumiela.

And then Gumiela reverted to type. "I'm in a hurry, remember?"

"Yes, sir, sorry, sir," DeRicci said. This woman always set her teeth on edge. "The woman in the crate, she was killed with a hardening poison. For a while, Broduer thought she might have been put there to contaminate the food supply, but it was the wrong kind of poison. We're okay on that."

Gumiela raised her eyebrows slightly. Apparently she hadn't heard about the possible contamination. DeRicci had been worried that she had.

"Good . . ." Gumiela said in a tone that implied . . . and . . . ?

"But, I got a list from him, and sir, someone is dumping bodies in those crates all over the city, and has been for at least a year, maybe more."

"No one saw this pattern?" Gumiela asked.

"The coroner's office noticed it," DeRicci said, making sure she kept her voice calm. "Ansel Management noticed it, but the owner, Najib Ansel, tells me that over the decades his family has owned the business, they've seen all kinds of things dumped in the crates."

"Bodies, though, bodies should have caught our attention," Gumiela said. Clearly, DeRicci had Gumiela's attention now.

"No," DeRicci said. "The coroner got called in, but no one called us."

"Well, I'll have to change this," Gumiela said. "I'll—"

"Wait, sir," DeRicci said. "They didn't call us for the correct legal reasons."

Gumiela turned her head slightly, as if she couldn't believe she had heard DeRicci right. "What reasons could those possibly be?"

"The dead are all clones, sir." DeRicci made sure none of her anger showed up in the tone of her voice.

"Clones? Including this one?"

"Yes, sir," DeRicci said. "And they were all apparently slow-grow. If they had been considered human under the law, we would have said they were murdered."

Gumiela let out an exasperated breath. "This woman, this poisoned woman, she's a clone?"

"Yes, sir." DeRicci knew she only had a moment here to convince Gumiela to let her continue on this case. "But I'd like to continue my investigation, sir, because—"

"We'll send it down to property crimes," Gumiela said.

"Sir," DeRicci said. "This pattern suggests a practicing serial killer. At some point, he'll find legal humans, and then he'll be experienced—"

"What is Ansel Management doing to protect its crates?" Gumiela said.

DeRicci felt a small surge of hope. Was Gumiela actually considering this? "They have sensors that locate things by weight and size. They believe they've reported all the bodies that have come through their system in the last several years."

"They believe?" Gumiela asked.

"There's no way to know without checking every crate," DeRicci said.

"Well, this is a health and safety matter. I'll contact the Armstrong City Inspectors and have them investigate all of the recycling/compost plants."

DeRicci tried not to sigh. This wasn't going her way after all. "I think that's a good idea, sir, but—"

"Tell me, Detective," Gumiela said. "Did you have any leads at all on this potential serial before you found out that the bodies belonged to clones?"

DeRicci felt her emotions shift again. She wasn't sure why she was so emotionally involved here. Maybe because she knew no one would investigate, which meant no one would stop this killer, if she couldn't convince Gumiela to keep the investigation in the department.

"She worked as a nanny for Luc Deshin," DeRicci said. "He fired her this morning."

"I thought this was that case," Gumiela said. "His people probably killed her."

"I considered that," DeRicci said. "But he wouldn't have gone through the trouble of firing her if he was just going to kill her."

Gumiela harrumphed. Then she walked around the furniture, trailing her hand over the back of the couch. She was actually considering DeRicci's proposal—and she knew DeRicci had a point.

"Do you know who the original was?" Gumiela asked.

DeRicci's heart sank. She hadn't wanted Gumiela to ask this question. DeRicci hadn't recognized the name, but Lake had. He had left a message on DeRicci's desk—a message that rose up when she touched the desk's surface (the bastard)—which said, *Why do we care that the daughter of an off-Moon crime lord got murdered?*

DeRicci then looked up the Mycenae family. They were a crime family and had been for generations, but Sonja herself didn't seem to be part of the criminal side. She had attended the best schools on Earth, and actually had a nanny certificate. She had renounced her family both visibly and legally, and was trying to live her own life.

"The original's name is Sonja Mycenae," DeRicci said.

"The Mycenae crime family." Gumiela let out a sigh. "There's a pattern here, and one we don't need to be involved in. Obviously there's some kind of winnowing going on in the Earth-Moon crime families. I'll notify the Alliance to watch for something bigger, but I don't think you need to investigate this."

"Sir, I know Luc Deshin thought she was Sonja Mycenae," DeRicci said. "He didn't know she was a clone. That means this isn't a crime family war—"

"We don't know what it is, Detective," Gumiela said. "And despite your obvious interest in the case, I'm moving you off it. I have better things for you to do. I'll send this and the other cases down to Property, and let them handle the investigation."

"Sir, please—"

"Detective, you have plenty to do. I want that report on Rayvon Lake by morning." Gumiela nodded at her.

DeRicci's breath caught. Gumiela was letting her know that if she dropped this case, she might get a new partner. And maybe, she would guarantee that Lake stopped polluting the department.

There was nothing DeRicci could do. This battle was lost.

"Thank you, sir," she said, not quite able to keep the disappointment from her voice.

Gumiela had already returned to her desk.

DeRicci headed for the door. As it opened, Gumiela said, "Detective, one last thing."

DeRicci closed the door and faced Gumiela, expecting some kind of reprimand or some type of admonition.

"Have you done the clone notification?" Gumiela asked.

Earth Alliance law required any official organization that learned of a clone to notify the original, if at all possible.

"Not yet, sir," DeRicci said. She had held off, hoping that she would keep the case. If she had, she could have gone to the Mycenae family, and maybe learned something that had relevance to the case.

"Don't," Gumiela said. "I'll take care of that too."

"I don't mind, sir," DeRicci said.

"The Mycenae require a delicate touch," Gumiela said. "It's better if the notification goes through the most official of channels."

DeRicci nodded. She couldn't quite bring herself to thank Gumiela. Or even to say anything else. So she let herself out of the office.

And stopped in the hallway.

For a moment, she considered going back in and arguing with Gumiela. Because Gumiela wasn't going to notify anyone about the clone. Gumiela probably believed that crime families should fight amongst themselves, so the police didn't have to deal with them.

DeRicci paused for a half second.

If she went back in, she would probably lose her job. Because she would tell Gumiela exactly what she thought of the clone laws, and the way that Property would screw up the investigation, and the fact that *people* were actually dying and being placed in crates.

But, if DeRicci lost her job, she wouldn't be able to investigate anything.

The next time she got a clone case, she'd sit on that information for as long as she could, finish the investigation, and maybe make an arrest. Sure, it might not hold up, but she could get one of the other divisions to search the perpetrator's home and business, maybe catch him with something else.

This time, she had screwed up. She'd followed the rules too closely. She shouldn't have gone to Gumiela so soon.

DeRicci would know better next time.

And she'd play dumb when Gumiela challenged her over it.

Better to lose a job after solving a case, instead of in the middle of a failed one.

DeRicci sighed. She didn't feel better, but at least she had a plan.

Even if it was a plan she didn't like at all.

The place that the clone frequented near the Port was a one-person office, run by a man named Cade Faulke. Ostensibly, Faulke ran an employment consulting office, one that helped people find jobs or training for jobs. But it didn't take a lot of digging to discover that was a cover for a position with Earth Alliance Security.

From what little Deshin could find, it seemed that Faulke worked alone, with an android guard—the kind that usually monitored prisons. Clearly, no one expected

Faulke to be investigated: the android alone would have been a tip-off to anyone who looked deeper than the thin cover that Faulke had over his name.

Deshin wondered how many other Earth Alliance operatives worked like that inside of Armstrong. He supposed there were quite a few, monitoring various Earth Alliance projects.

Projects like, apparently, his family.

Deshin let out a sigh. He wandered around his office, feeling like it had become a cage. He clenched and unclenched his fists.

Sometimes he hated the way he had restrained himself to build his business and his family. Sometimes he just wanted to go after someone on his own, squeeze the life out of that person, and then leave the corpse, the way someone had left that clone.

Spying on Deshin's family. Gerda and five-month-old Paavo had done nothing except get involved with him.

And he would wager that Sonja Mycenae's family would say the same thing about her.

He stopped. He hadn't spoken to the Mycenae family in a long time, but he owed them for an ancient debt.

He sent an encoded message through his links to Aurla Mycenae, the head of the Mycenae and Sonja's mother, asking for a quick audience.

Then Deshin got a contact from Cumija: *Five low-level employees have the marker. None of them have access to your family or to anything important inside Deshin Enterprises. How do you want me to proceed?*

Send me a list, he sent back.

At that moment, his links chirruped, announcing a massive holomessage so encoded that it nearly overloaded his system. He accepted the message, only to find out it was live.

Aurla Mycenae appeared, full-sized, in the center of his floor. She wore a flowing black gown that accented her dark eyebrows and thick black hair. She had faint lines around her black eyes. Otherwise she looked no older than she had the last time he saw her, at least a decade ago.

"Luc," she said in a throaty voice that hadn't suited her as a young woman, but suited her now. "I get this sense this isn't pleasure."

"No," he said. "I thought I should warn you. I encountered a slow-grow clone of your daughter Sonja."

He decided not to mention that he had hired that clone or that she had been murdered.

Mycenae exhaled audibly. "Damn Earth Alliance. Did they try to embed her in your organization?"

"They succeeded for a time," he said.

"And then?"

So much for keeping the information back. "She turned up dead this morning."

"Typical," Mycenae said. "They've got some kind of operation going, and they've been using clones of my family. You're not the first to tell me this."

"All slow-grow?" Deshin asked.

"Yes," Mycenae said. "We've been letting everyone know that anyone applying for work from our family isn't really from our family. I never thought of contacting you because I thought you went legit."

"I have," Deshin lied. He had gone legit on most things. He definitely no longer had his fingers in the kinds of deals that the Mycenae family was famous for.

"Amazing they tried to embed with you, then," Mycenae said.

"She was nanny to my infant son," he said, and he couldn't quite keep the fury from his voice.

"Oh." Mycenae sighed. "They want to use your family like they're using mine. We're setting something up, Luc. We've got the Alliance division doing this crap tracked, and we're going to shut it down. You want to join us?"

Take on an actual Earth Alliance Division? As a young man, he would have considered it. As a man with a family and a half-legitimate business, he didn't dare take the risk.

"I trust you to handle it, Aurla," he said.

"They have your family's DNA now," she said, clearly as a way of enticement.

"It's of no use to them in the short term," he said, "and by the time we reach the long term, you'll have taken care of everything."

"It's not like you to trust anyone, Luc."

And, back when she had known him well, that had been true. But now, he had to balance security for himself and his business associates with security for his family.

"I'm not trusting you per se, Aurla," he said. "I just know how you operate."

She grinned at him. "I'll let you know when we're done."

"No need," he said. "Good luck."

And then he signed off. The last thing he wanted was to be associated in any way with whatever operation Aurla ran. She was right: it wasn't like him to trust anyone. And while he trusted her to destroy the division that was hurting her family, he didn't trust her to keep him out of it.

Too much contact with Aurla Mycenae, and Deshin might find himself arrested as the perpetrator of whatever she was planning. Mycenae was notorious for betraying colleagues when her back was against the wall.

The list came through his links from Cumija. She was right: the employees were low-level. He didn't recognize any of the names and had to look them up. None of them had even met Deshin.

Getting the clone of Sonja embedded into his family was some kind of coup.

He wouldn't fire anyone yet. He wanted to see if Koos came up with the same list. If he did, then Deshin would move forward.

But these employees were tagged, just like Sonja's clone had been. He decided to see if they had been visiting Faulke as well.

And if they had, Faulke would regret ever crossing paths with Deshin Enterprises.

Detective DeRicci left Andrea Gumiela's office. Gumiela felt herself relax. DeRicci was trouble. She hated rules and she had a sense of righteousness that often made it difficult for her to do her job well. There wasn't a lot of righteousness in the law, particularly when Earth Alliance law trumped Armstrong law.

Gumiela had to balance both.

She resisted the urge to run a hand through her hair. It had taken a lot of work to pile it just so on top of her head, and she didn't like wasting time on her appearance, as important as it was to her job.

Of course, the days when it was important were either days when a major disaster hit Armstrong or when someone in her department screwed up.

She certainly hoped this clone case wouldn't become a screw-up.

She put a hand over her stomach, feeling slightly ill. She had felt ill from the moment DeRicci mentioned Mycenae and Deshin. At that moment, Gumiela knew who had made the clone and who was handling it.

She also knew who was killing the clones—or at least, authorizing the deaths.

DeRicci was right. Those deaths presaged a serial killer (or, in Gumiela's unofficial opinion, already proved one existed). Or worse, the deaths suggested a policy of targeted killings that Gumiela couldn't countenance in her city.

Technically, Gumiela should contact Cade Faulke directly. He had contacted her directly more than once to report a possible upcoming crime. She had used him as an informant, which meant she had used his clones as informants as well.

And those clones were ending up dead.

She choked back bile. Some people, like DeRicci, would say that Gumiela had hands as dirty as Faulke's.

But she hadn't known he was killing the clones when they ceased being useful or when they crossed some line. She also hadn't known that he had been poisoning them using such a painful method. And he hadn't even thought about the possible contamination of the food supply.

Gumiela swallowed hard again, hoping her stomach would settle.

Technically, she should contact him and tell him to cease that behavior.

But Gumiela had been in her job a long time. She knew that telling someone like Faulke to quit was like telling an addict to stop drinking. It wouldn't happen, and it couldn't be done.

She couldn't arrest him either. Even if she caught him in the act, all he was doing was damaging property. And that might get him a fine or two or maybe a year or so in jail, if the clone's owners complained. But if DeRicci was right, the clone's owners were the Earth Alliance itself. And Faulke worked for the Alliance, so technically, *he* was probably the owner, and property owners could do whatever they wanted with their belongings.

Except toss them away in a manner that threatened the public health.

Gumiela sat in one of the chairs and leaned her head back, closing her eyes, forcing herself to think.

She had to do something, and despite what she had said to DeRicci, following procedure was out of the question.

She needed to get Faulke out of Armstrong, only she didn't have the authority to do so.

But she knew who did.

She sat up. Long ago, she'd met Faulke's handler, Ike Jarvis. She could contact him. Maybe he would work with her.

It was worth a try.

Otto Koos led his team to the building housing Cade Faulke's fake business. The building was made of some kind of polymer that changed appearance daily. This day's appearance made it seem like old-fashioned red brick Koos hadn't seen since his childhood on Earth.

Five Ansel Management crates stood in their protected unit in the alley behind the building. They had a cursory lock with a security code that anyone in the building probably had.

It was as much of a confession as he needed.

But the boss would need more. Luc Deshin had given strict orders for this mission—no killing.

Koos knew he was on probation now—maybe forever. He had missed the Mycenae clone, and, after he had done a quick scan of the employees, discovered he had missed at least five others. At least they hadn't been anywhere near the Deshin family.

The Mycenae clone had. Who knew what kind of material the Alliance had gathered?

Faulke knew. Eventually, Koos would know too. It just might take some time.

He had brought ten people with him to capture Faulke. The office had an android guard, though, the durable kind used in prisons. Koos either had to disable it or get it out of the building.

He'd failed the one time he'd tried to disable those things in the past. He was opting for getting it out of the building.

Ready? he sent to two of his team members.

Yes, they sent back at the same time.

Go! he sent.

They were nowhere near him, but he knew what they were going to do. They were going to start a fight in front of the building that would get progressively more violent. And then they'd start shooting up the area with laser pistols.

Other members of his team would prevent any locals from stopping the fight, and the fight would continue until the guard came down.

Then Koos would sneak in the back way, along with three other members of his team.

They were waiting now. They had already checked the back door—unlocked during daylight hours. They were talking as if they had some kind of business with each other.

At least they weren't shifting from foot to foot like he wanted to do.

Instead, all he could do was stare at that stamp for Ansel Management.

It hadn't been much work to pick up the Mycenae clone and stuff her into one of the crates.

If Deshin hadn't given the no-kill order, then Koos would have stuffed Faulke into one of the crates, dying, but alive, so that he knew what he had done.

Koos would have preferred that to Deshin's plan.

But Koos wasn't in charge. And he had to work his way back into Deshin's good graces.

And he would do that.

Starting now.

Gumiela had forgotten that Ike Jarvis was an officious prick. He ran intelligence operatives who worked inside the Alliance. Generally, those operatives didn't operate in human-run areas. In fact, they shouldn't operate in human-run areas at all.

Earth Alliance Intelligence was supposed to do the bulk of its work *outside* the Alliance.

Gumiela had contacted him on a special link the Earth Alliance had set up for the Armstrong Police Department, to be used only in cases of Earth Alliance troubles or serious Alliance issues.

She figured this counted.

Jarvis appeared in the center of the room, his three-dimensional image fritzing in and out either because of a bad connection or because of the levels of encoding this conversation was going through.

He looked better when he appeared and disappeared. She preferred it when he was slightly out of focus.

"This had better be good, Andy," Jarvis said, and Gumiela felt her shoulders stiffen. No one called her Andy, not even her best friends. Only Jarvis had come up with that nickname, and somehow he seemed to believe it made them closer.

"I need you to pull Cade Faulke," she said.

"I don't pull anyone on your say so." Jarvis fritzed again. His image came back just a little smaller, just a little tighter. So the problem was on his end.

If she were in a better mood, she would smile. Jarvis was short enough without doctoring the image. He had once tried to compensate for his height by buying enhancements that deepened his voice. All they had done was ruin it, leaving him sounding like he had poured salt down his throat.

"You pull him or I arrest him for attempted mass murder," she said, a little surprised at herself.

Jarvis moved and fritzed again. Apparently he had taken a step backwards or something, startled by her vehemence.

"What the hell did he do?" Jarvis asked, not playing games any longer.

"You have Faulke running slow-grow clones in criminal organizations, right?" she asked.

"Andy," he said, returning to that condescending tone he had used earlier, "I can't tell you what I'm doing."

"Fine," she snapped. "I thought we had a courteous relationship, based on mutual interest. I was wrong. Sorry to bother you, Ike—"

"Wait," he said. "What did he do?"

"It doesn't matter," she said. "You get to send Earth Alliance lawyers here to talk about the top secret crap to judges who might've died because of your guy's carelessness."

And then she signed off.

She couldn't do anything she had just threatened Jarvis with. The food thing hadn't risen to the level where she could charge Faulke, and that was if she could prove that he had put the bodies into the crates himself. He had an android guard, which the Chief of Police had had to approve—those things weren't supposed to operate inside the city—and that guard had probably done all the dirty work. They would just claim malfunction, and Faulke would be off the hook.

Jarvis fritzed back in, fainter now. The image had one meter sideways, which meant he was superimposed over one of her office chairs. The chair cut through him at his knees and waist. Obviously, he had no idea where his image had appeared, and she wasn't about to tell him or move the image.

"Okay, okay," Jarvis said. "I've managed to make this link as secure as I possibly can, given my location. Guarantee that your side is secure."

Gumiela shrugged. "I'm alone in my office, in the Armstrong Police Department. Good enough for you?"

She didn't tell him that she was recording this whole thing. She was tired of being used by this asshole.

"I guess it'll have to be. Yes, Faulke is running the clones that we have embedded with major criminal organizations on the Moon."

"If the clones malfunction—" She chose that word carefully "—what's he supposed to do?"

"Depends on how specific the clone is to the job, and how important it is to the operation," he said. "Generally, Faulke's supposed to ship the clone back. That's why Armstrong PD approved android guards for his office."

"There aren't guards," she said. "There's only one."

Jarvis's image came in a bit stronger. "What?"

"Just one," she said, "and that's not all. I don't think your friend Faulke has sent any clones back."

"I can check," Jarvis said.

"I don't care what you do for your records. According to ours—" and there she was lying again—"he's been killing the clones that don't work out and putting them in composting crates. Those crates go to the Growing Pits, which grow fresh food for the city."

"He *what?*" Jarvis asked.

"And to make matters worse, he's using a hardening poison to kill them, a poison our coroner fears might leach into our food supply. We're checking on that now. Although it doesn't matter. The intent is what matters, and clearly your man Faulke has lost his mind."

Jarvis cursed. "You're not making this up."

It wasn't a question.

"I'm not making this up," she said. "I want him and his little android friend out of here within the hour, or I'm arresting him, and I'm putting him on trial. Public trial."

"Do you realize how many operations you'll ruin?"

"No," she said, "and I don't care. Get him out of my city. It's only a matter of time before your crazy little operative starts killing legal humans, not just cloned ones. And I don't want him doing it here."

Jarvis cursed again. "Can I get your help—"

"No," she said. "I don't want anyone at the police department involved with your little operation. And if you go to the chief, I'll tell her that you have thwarted my attempts to arrest a man who threatens the entire dome. Because, honestly, Ike *baby*, this is a courtesy contact. I don't have to do you any favors at all, especially considering what kind of person, if I can use that word, you installed in my city. Have you got that?"

"Yes, Andrea, I do," he said, looking serious.

Andrea. So he had heard her all those times. And he had ignored her, the bastard. She made note of that too.

"One hour," she said, and signed off.

Then she wiped her hands on her skirt. They were shaking just a little. Screw him, the weaselly little bastard. She'd send someone to that office now, to escort Jarvis's horrid operative out of Armstrong.

She wanted to make sure that asshole left quickly, and didn't double back.

She wanted this problem out of her city, off her Moon, and as far from her notice as possible.

And that, she knew, was the best she could do without upsetting the department's special relationship with the Alliance.

She hoped her best would be good enough.

Up the back stairs, into the narrow hallway that smelled faintly of dry plastic, Koos led the raid, his best team members behind him. They fanned out in the narrow hallway, the two women first, signaling that the hallway was clear. Koos and Hala, the only other man on this part of the team skirted past them, and through the open door of Faulke's office.

It was much smaller than Koos expected. Faulke was only three meters from him. Faulke was scrawny, narrow-shouldered, the kind of man easily ignored on the street.

He reached behind his back—probably for a weapon—as Koos and Hala held their laser rifles on him.

"Don't even try," Koos said. "I have no compunction shooting you."

Faulke's eyes glazed for a half second—probably letting his android guard know he was in trouble—then an expression of panic flitted across his face before he managed to control it.

The other members of Koos's team had already disabled the guard.

"Who are you?" Faulke asked.

Koos ignored him, and spoke to his team. "I want him bound. And make sure you disable his links."

One of the women slipped in around Koos, and put light cuffs around Faulke's wrists and pasted a small rectangle of Silent-Seal over his mouth.

You can't get away with this, Faulke sent on public links. *You have no idea who I am—*

And then his links shut off.

Koos grinned. "You're Cade Faulke. You work for Earth Alliance Intelligence. You've been running clones that you embed into businesses. Am I missing anything?"

Faulke's eyes didn't change, but he swallowed hard.

"Let's get him out of here," Koos said.

They encircled him, in case the other tenants on the floor decided to see what all the fuss was about.

But no one opened any doors. The neighborhood was too dicey for that. If any-one had an ounce of civic feeling, they would have gone out front to stop the fight that Koos had staged below.

And no one had.

He took Faulke's arm, surprised at how flabby it was. Hardly any muscles at all.

No wonder the asshole had used poison. He wasn't strong enough to subdue any living creature on his own.

"You're going to love what we have planned for you," Koos said as he dragged Faulke down the stairs. "By the end of it all, you and I will be old friends."

This time Faulke gave him a startled look.

Koos grinned at him, and led him to the waiting car that would take them to the Port.

It would be a long time before anyone heard from Cade Faulke again.

If they ever did.

DeRicci hated days like today. She had lost a case because of stupid laws that had no bearing on what really happened.

A woman had been murdered, and DeRicci couldn't solve the case. It would go to Property, where it would get stuck in a pile of cases that no one cared about, because no one would be able to put a value on this particular clone. No owner would come forward. No one would care.

And if DeRicci hadn't seen this sort of thing a dozen times, she would have tried to solve it herself in her off time. She might still hound Property, just to make sure the case didn't get buried.

Maybe she'd even use Broduer's lies. She might tell Property that whoever planted the clone had tried to poison the city. That might get some dumb Property detective off his butt.

She, on the other hand, was already working on the one good thing to come out of this long day. She was compiling all the documents on every single thing that Rayvon Lake had screwed up in their short tenure as partners.

Even she hadn't realized how much it was.

She would have a long list for Gumiela by the end of the day, and this time, Gumiela would pay attention.

Or DeRicci would threaten to take the clone case to the media. DeRicci had been appalled that human waste could get into the recycling system; she would wa-ger that the population of Armstrong would too.

One threat like that, and Gumiela would have to fire Lake.

It wasn't justice. It wasn't anything resembling justice.

But after a few years in this job, DeRicci had learned only one thing: Justice didn't exist in the Earth Alliance.

Not for humans, not for clones, not for anyone.

And somehow, she had to live with it.

She just hadn't quite figured out how.

Deshin arrived home, exhausted and more than a little unsettled. The house smelled of baby powder and coffee. He hadn't really checked to see how the rest of Gerda's day alone with Paavo had gone.

He felt guilty about that.

He went through the modest living room to the baby's room. He and Gerda didn't flash their wealth around Armstrong, preferring to live quietly. But he had so much security in the home that he was still startled the clone had broken through it.

Gerda was sitting in a rocking chair near the window, Paavo in her arms. She put a finger to her lips, but it did no good.

His five-month-old son twisted, and looked at Deshin with such aware eyes that it humbled him. Deshin knew that this baby was twenty times smarter than he would ever be. It worried him, and it pleased him as well.

Paavo smiled and extended his pudgy arms. Deshin picked him up. The boy was heavier than he had been just a week before. He also needed a diaper change.

Deshin took him to the changing table, and started, knowing just from the look on her face that Gerda was exhausted too.

"Long day?" he asked.

"Good day," she said. "We made the right decision."

"Yes," he said. "We did."

He had decided on the way home not to tell her everything. He would wait until the interrogation of Cade Faulke and the five clones was over. Koos had taken all six of them out of Armstrong in the same ship.

And the interrogations wouldn't even start until Koos got them out of Earth Alliance territory, days from now.

Deshin had no idea what would happen to Faulke or the clones after that. Deshin was leaving that up to Koos. Koos no longer headed security for Deshin Enterprises in Armstrong, but he had served Deshin well today. He would handle some of the company's work outside the Alliance.

Not a perfect day's work, not even the day's work Deshin had expected, but a good one nonetheless. He probably had other leaks to plug in his organization, but at least he knew what they were now.

His baby raised a chubby fist at Deshin as if agreeing that action needed to be taken. Deshin bent over and blew bubbles on Paavo's tummy, something that always made Paavo giggle.

He giggled now, a sound so infectious that Deshin wondered how he had lived without it all his life.

He would do everything he could to protect this baby, everything he could to take care of his family.

"He trusts you," Gerda said with a tiny bit of amazement in her voice.

Most people never trusted Deshin. Gerda did, but Gerda was special.

Deshin blew bubbles on Paavo's tummy again, and Paavo laughed.

His boy did trust him.

He picked up his newly diapered son, and cradled him in his arms. Then he kissed Gerda.

The three of them, forever.

That was what he needed, and that was what he ensured today.

The detective could poke around his business all she wanted, but she would never know the one thing that calmed Deshin down.

Justice had been done.

His family was safe.

And that was all that mattered.

planet of fear

PAUL J. McAULEY

Born in Oxford, England, in 1955, Paul J. McAuley now makes his home in London. A professional biologist for many years, he sold his first story in 1984, and has gone on to be a frequent contributor to Interzone, *as well as to markets such as* Asimov's Science Fiction, SCI FICTION, Amazing, The Magazine of Fantasy and Science Fiction, Skylife, The Third Alternative, When the Music's Over, *and elsewhere. His first novel,* Four Hundred Billion Stars, *won the Philip K. Dick Award, and his novel* Fairyland *won both the Arthur C. Clarke Award and the John W. Campbell Award in 1996. His other books include the novels* Of The Fall, Eternal Light, Pasquale's Angel, *and* Confluence—*a major trilogy of ambitious scope and scale set ten million years in the future, comprised of the novels* Child of the River, Ancient of Days, *and* Shrine of Stars—Life on Mars, The Secret of Life, Whole Wide World, White Devils, Mind's Eye, Players, Cowboy Angels, The Quiet War, Gardens of the Sun, In the Mouth of the Whale, *and* Evening's Empires. *His short fiction has been collected in* The King of the Hill and Other Stories, The Invisible Country, Little Machines, *and a major retrospective collection,* A Very British History: The Best Science Fiction Stories of Paul McAuley, 1985–2011; *he is also the coeditor, with Kim Newman, of an original anthology,* In Dreams. *His most recent book is a new novel,* Something Coming Through. *Coming up is a sequel,* Into Everywhere.

Here, he takes us to a remote mining station on the rugged coast of Venus's mysterious, fog-shrouded equatorial continent, where the well-armed miners are on guard for an attack by monsters—for all the good it will do them.

Across the glistening slick of the subtropical sargasso, amongst shoals and archipelagos of bladderweed, several thousand sunfish floated in intersecting circles of churning foam. They were big, the sunfish, big humped discs ten or fifteen or even twenty metres across, patched with clusters of barnacles and thatched with purple-brown thickets of strapweed and whipweed, and all around them soldier remoras flailed and fought, flashing and writing in frothing, blood-blackened water. A quadrocopter drone hung high above this shambles like a lonely seabird, avid camera eyes transmitting images to the ekranoplan anchored several kilometres beyond the sargasso's southern edge.

In the close warmth of the fire control bay, bathed in the radiance of three big flatscreens, Katya Ignatova asked the petty officer piloting the drone to lock its cameras on a particular pair of sunfish. They were matched in size, each about twelve metres in diameter, and the fringes of their feeding tentacles had interlaced and fused and were now contracting, drawing them together. Dead and dying soldier remoras bobbed around them: slim, silvery torpedoes with chunks torn out of their flanks, shovel jaws gaping, eye clusters filmed white. Venusian fish were armoured in bony chainmail, had external gills and horizontal tail fins resembling whale flukes, but they possessed swim bladders. Like terrestrial fish, their corpses floated.

The drone pilot said, "Such fury. Such waste."

"Soldiers attack everything that gets too close to their sibling," Katya said. "Including other sunfish. They can't mate until their soldiers have been neutralised. But the dead aren't wasted. Their flesh feeds the ecosystem where the next generation develops."

She hunched forward as the pair of sunfish began to jab at each other with the spears of their spermatophores, asked the drone pilot if he could get a close-up of the action.

"No problem," he said, and made delicate adjustments to the joystick that controlled his little craft.

The views on the screens tilted and shifted, stabilised again. Katya prompted the pilot to zoom in on the tip of a calcified spear that scratched amongst drifts of purple-brown weed before abruptly driving forward.

"I believe they call that the money shot," the pilot, Arkadi Sarantsev, said.

He was a slender, cynical fellow in his midtwenties, a few years younger than Katya. She had noticed that he kept apart from the companionable clamour in the mess, reading a vivid paperback thriller as he forked food from his tray. Sitting close to him in the television light, she could smell the cola nut oil he'd used to sleek back his black hair.

"It isn't sex as we know it," she told him. "Sunfish are hermaphrodites, both male and female. If you could zoom out now . . . Yes. You see? Each has speared the other. They are exchanging packages of sperm. Injecting them into special areas of haploid epithelial cells that will develop into egg masses."

She planned to collect some of those egg masses in a day or two, when the mating battles were over, to test the hypothesis that they contained both fertilised eggs that produced juvenile sunfish and unfertilised eggs that produced haploid soldiers. She hoped that she would be able to examine the rich and varied biota of the sargasso, too. The swarms of isopods and shrimp and thumb jellies on which sunfish larvae fed; the tripod octopi and fish which fed on them.

They really were amazing creatures, sunfish. They were eusocial, like ants, bees, and mole rats, with sterile, neotenous soldiers and fertile queens which not only lost their bilateral symmetry, like flatfish or the sunfish of Earth, but also lost their digestive systems, their eyes, and most of their nervous systems. And they were also symbiotic associations, like corals or lichens. The dense fringes of feeding tentacles of the queens, which filtered and digested plankton and extruded strings of nutrient-rich nodules which the schools of soldier remoras devoured, were derived from symbiotic ribbon jellies; the strapweeds and whipweeds rooted in their dorsal shells pumped sugars and lipids into their bloodstreams. Amazing creatures, yes, and really not much like anything at all on Earth.

Usually they led solitary, pelagic lives, drifting everywhere on the shallow seas of Venus, but every seventeen years they migrated to the sargassos where they had hatched, possibly following geomagnetic and chemical cues (another theory that needed to be tested), and mated, and spawned the next generation, and died. Katya's observations and data would contribute to a multidisciplinary research programme into their life cycle, part of the International Biological Year, a milestone in the growing cooperation and rapprochement between the Venusian colonies of the People's Republic, the United States, and the British Commonwealth.

On the central screen, the two sunfish slowly revolved on the blood-black swell. On the screens to the left and right, a wider view showed other sunfish pairs ponderously locking together, and surviving soldiers spending their fury on each other or on ripping apart smaller, unsuccessful sunfish.

Katya asked Arkadi Sarantsev to take his machine higher, was watching intently as it circled the entire area, trying to make sure she captured a good image of every pairing, when the ekranoplan's turbofans started up with a shuddering roar. A few moments later a seaman leaned into the hatch of the little room and told Arkadi to bring in his drone.

"Captain Chernov's orders," he said when Katya protested, and couldn't or wouldn't answer her questions.

She pushed past, hauled herself along the pitching companionway, and climbed to the teardrop cockpit that, with its pale wood and polished brass trim, the diffuse overcast of the cloudroof gleaming through its canopy, always reminded her of the luncheon room of the Engineers' Union where her mother, the architect I.V. Ignatova, took her every birthday for a ritual meal of beefsteak and cultivated wild mushrooms. The pilot and navigator were hunched in their horseshoe of switches and dials and computer screens; Captain Vladimir Chernov was enthroned behind them, sipping from a glass of black tea; all three wore bulky headsets. The ekranoplan had made a cumbersome turn away from the sargasso, and now the pilot gripped the throttle levers by his thigh and eased them forward. The roar of the big turbofans, mounted on canards behind the cockpit, ramped up as the ekranoplan began to accelerate.

Katya grabbed a spare headset to muffle the incredible noise and braced herself in the hatchway during the shuddering lurch of takeoff. She had learned the hard way that she could not speak to the captain in the cockpit until he acknowledged her, and he didn't acknowledge her until the ekranoplan was under way.

An adaptation of the famous curable-maket, the Caspian Sea Monster, it resembled a gigantic aeroplane but was really a wing-in-ground-effect machine that rode on the cushion of air generated by its turbofans and square, stubby wings: a long-range, lightly armed beast capable of speeds of up to three hundred knots. It was making top speed now, skimming some five metres above long rolling waves, skimming over breakers frothing across sea-lily reefs. On its way to investigate an emergency at the People's Republic's most northerly outpost, Makarov Mining Station, according to Captain Chernov.

"I am sorry about the abbreviation of your studies," he told Katya, "but the station sent a disturbing message two days ago and has not responded since. Although we are not the nearest vessel, we can reach it before anyone else."

He did not look at all sorry: he appeared to be enjoying himself. A burly, broad-shouldered, bullet-headed man dressed in the Navy's tropical uniform—blue shorts and a blue short-sleeved jacket over a striped telnyashka shirt—whose cool condescension reminded Katya of the sadistic anatomy lecturer who liked to pluck a student from the ranks and hand her a random bone and demand that she name it and identify the animal it came from.

Captain Chernov was scrupulously polite to Katya, but did not bother to hide his scorn for her work, and the collaboration with the Americans and their British allies. He was a war hero who, during the campaign against American libertarian pirates ten years ago, had devised and carried out a daring, spur-of-the-moment raid that had ended with the capture of a particularly bloodthirsty warlord. Popular acclaim meant that the Navy couldn't cashier him for disregarding the chain of command, so he had been given a medal and promoted sideways to the Survey Corps, where he'd been chafing ever since.

When Katya asked him what kind of problem he was responding to, he studied her with remote amusement, then said, "It is something you might find interesting, if true. The miners claimed that they were being attacked by monsters."

"Monsters? What kind of monsters?"

"Most likely the American kind," Captain Chernov said. As usual, he was speaking to a spot somewhere behind her left shoulder, as if addressing the ghost of an authority she herself did not possess. "If there really are monsters, if this is not some Yankee trick, you may be of some help. Until then, do your best to stay out of the way. My men must prepare for trouble."

The ekranoplan made the two thousand kilometre trip in just under five hours. Katya studied the images captured by the drone, sorted them into categories, and made a few preliminary measurements. She ate a sparse lunch alone in the long tube of the mess room (which could double as a field hospital if the need arose), composing a bitter complaint to the IBY committee, the Marine Biology Institute, and the Ministry of Defence which she knew she would never send. Pick your battles carefully and fight them only in your head, her mother liked to say. No one remembers the righteous who go to war and lose.

The vibration of the turbofans created standing rings in her tumbler of water.

She wondered about the monsters which had supposedly attacked the miners at Makarov Station. The shallow seas of Venus teemed with an extravagance of macrofauna—sunfish, cornet squid, mock turtles, and so on—but only a few large animal species had been discovered on the northern continent settled by the Americans, and the thousands of islands and sea mounts and atolls of the southern hemisphere. So finding a species of carnivore capable of killing a man would be a considerable coup. A swarm of pack-hunting reptiloids. Some kind of super crocodilian. Or perhaps, just perhaps, something as rare and strange as a tiger or a wolf.

She went back to work, counting sunfish, measuring them, tracking the paths of individuals ... Trying to squeeze as much data as possible from the truncated observations. At some point, she noticed that the deep drone of the turbofans had diminished to a gentle throbbing. The ekranoplan was afloat again, driven by its auxiliary engine as it nosed through dense billows of fog. Captain Chernov was outside, on the little railed observation deck behind the cockpit, with the chief petty officer. The two men wore pistols on their hips, and were watching the long shadow of a shoreline resolve out of the fog: the shore of the mysterious equatorial continent.

Two billion years ago, the last great resurfacing era, vast quantities of molten rock from Venus's mantle had risen to the surface through long vertical cracks in the crust. Injections of lava and differential crystallisation of minerals had formed an enormous geological basin with distinct layered strata, including reefs of titaniferous magnetite gabbro, and vast quantities of tin and iron. The basin had tilted and eroded and half-drowned, leaving only one edge exposed, a long, narrow continent that wrapped around half of Venus's equator. Most of its volcanic ranges and salt flats and deserts were scorching, waterless, and utterly uninhabitable, but a cold sea current rose at its southern coast, feeding banks of fog that grew during the long day and sustained an ecosystem found nowhere else on Venus. The People's Republic had established several mining stations there, to exploit deposits of titanium and tin ore, copper and silver, platinum and bismuth, and to lay claim to the deserts to the north.

This was the coast that the ekranoplan was approaching, drowned in fog and mystery.

An even pearlescent light, streaming with particles and tiny transient rainbows in whichever direction Katya happened to look. The close, clammy heat of a Turkish bath wrapping around her like a wet towel. The puttering of the auxiliary motor and the slap of waves unnaturally loud in the muffled hush. And something echoing in the distance: faint, staccato, persistent.

"I see no monsters," Captain Vladimir Chernov said, turning to Katya. "But I definitely hear something. Do you hear it too, Doctor? Could you give your professional opinion?"

"It sounds like dogs," Katya said. "Dogs, barking. Do they have dogs?"

"I don't believe so. Pigs, yes. To eat their kitchen waste and supply them with fresh pork. They are Ukrainian, the miners here. And all Ukrainians love pork. But if the records are correct there are no dogs."

"Well, it sounds more like dogs than pigs. Someone smuggled in their pets, perhaps. Or watchdogs were assigned to this place, and the paperwork was lost or mislaid."

"Perhaps. Or perhaps it is monsters that kill and eat men, and bark like dogs," Captain Chernov said. A fat pair of binoculars hung from his neck, a symbol of his status, perhaps: they were of no practical use in the fog.

"It would be something new to science," Katya said, refusing to rise to his bait.

"Science does not yet know everything," Captain Chernov said. "Isn't that why you were studying the sunfish, Doctor? Not just to be friends with the Americans, but because you wished to learn something. We are at the edge of an unexplored continent. Perhaps you will learn something here."

"Or perhaps they really are dogs. American running dogs," the chief petty officer said.

He was a stocky, grizzled fellow with a scornful gaze who had even less time for Katya than Captain Chernov. But at least they were direct about their dislike, unlike the chauvinist fossils at the Marine Biology Institute, and it had nothing to do with her being a woman—a woman who asserted her own opinions, and refused to recognise her inferiority. No, they resented her presence because the IBY had many enemies in the government, and if its unstable mixture of science and peacenik appeasement blew up, the fallout would contaminate everyone associated with it. Which was why, of course, Katya had been assigned to the sunfish project by her bosses, and why she wanted to make a success of it.

"Dogs, pigs, monsters: we will find out. And we must do it soon," Captain Chernov told Katya, for once addressing her directly. The ice-age of his contempt had somewhat thawed. He was relaxed, almost cheerful. This was Navy work: he was no longer answerable to Katya and the IBY. "If the Americans are not already here, hiding from us or lying in wait, they will be here soon. They claim to have intercepted the distress call. They claim to want to help. There is no airstrip here. The terrain is rough. Too many steep hills and ridges. So everything comes in and goes out by sea. One of our frigates will be here in three days, but one of the American so-called research ships will be here tomorrow."

Makarov Station, strung along the edge of a natural harbour sheltered by a sandbar, was entirely obscured by the fog: it wasn't possible to survey it and the surrounding area with drones or lidar. Infrared imaging showed that the buildings, usually air-conditioned, were at ambient temperature. Apart from a man-sized trace perched on a dockside crane there was no sign of the twenty-six people who lived and worked there, or of the monsters which supposedly had attacked them.

The ekranoplan dropped anchor, sounded its siren, sent up a flare that burst in a dim red star high in the fog. There was no answer from the shore, no response on the radio, no reply when the chief petty officer called to the miners through a loud-hailer, and no one was waiting at the edge of the long quayside as the landing party motored towards a floating stage in a big inflatable.

Captain Chernov sprang onto the stage and galloped up the steps, pistol drawn, followed by the chief petty officer, the drone pilot Arkadi Sarantsev, and seven seamen—most of the ekranoplan's crew. Katya followed, her heart hammering in anticipation. When she reached the top of the stairs, sweating in the damp heat, the men had already spread out in a semicircle, menacing fog with their pistols and carbines. The skeletal outline of a crane, heaps of dark ore, the outlines of a string of small, flat-roofed buildings and a tall radio mast faintly visible beyond. The persistent barking in the distance, tireless as a machine.

Captain Chernov paid no attention to it. He was standing with his hands on his hips, looking up at the crane's scaffold stem. The jut of its long jib was veiled in misty streamers, but it was just possible to make out the shadow of a man at its end. He did not respond when Captain Chernov ordered him to come down and he did not respond when the chief petty officer put a bullet into the steel plating a metre behind his feet. The sound of the shot whanged off across the muffled, fog-bound quay.

Captain Chernov cupped his hands to his mouth. "Next one he puts in your damn leg!"

No response. They all stood looking up at the man. The monotonous barking had not let up, hack-hack-hacking away deep in the fog.

"Take another shot," Captain Chernov told the chief petty officer.

"I'll go up there," Katya said.

"I distinctly remember telling you to keep out of the way," Captain Chernov said mildly.

"I am medically qualified," Katya said. It was technically true: she had been given basic first-aid training at Young Pioneer camp. "The poor fellow may be hurt or wounded. He may not be able to climb down without help."

"He may be an American for all we know," the chief petty officer said.

"You can bring him down?" Captain Chernov said.

"I can assess him, talk to him. Whether he comes down, that will be up to him," Katya said, with that airy feeling just before a dive, before she toppled over backwards into unknown water. As her mother so often observed, she had a knack of talking herself into trouble.

"No, whether he comes down will be up to you, Doctor," Captain Chernov said, turning now, favouring her with his thin cool smile. "Don't disappoint me."

The steel rungs of the ladder, dripping with condensed moisture, slipped under Katya's fingers as she climbed, slipped under the tread of her boots. When she reached the little glass and metal box of the operator's cabin, she clung to the handrail and called out, asking the man if he needed help, trying to sound encouraging, friendly. The man did not respond. He lay prone at the far end of the jib, arms wrapped around a steel beam as if around a long-lost lover. There was only ten metres between them, but he did not even turn his head to look at her.

She swore, and swung up the steel framework to the top of the jib, trying to ignore the dizzying plunge to the ant-like cluster of people below. She called to the man again, asked him to tell her his name, and now he moved, rolling awkwardly to look at her without letting go of the beam. His eyes, sunk deep in dark hollows, seemed to be all pupil.

"You're safe now," Katya said, trying to project a confidence she did not feel. "Come towards me. I'll help you down."

The man's mouth worked, but no words emerged. He was young, younger than Katya, and wore blue coveralls and heavy workboots.

"I'll come to you, then," Katya said.

But soon as she started to crab towards him, the jib shivering uneasily beneath her, the man humped backwards, like a demented caterpillar. She stopped, told him that everything was all right, that he was safe, and he closed his eyes and shook his head from side to side. He was crouched at the very end of the jib now, beside the cable wheel.

Captain Chernov called out, asking why this was taking so long. The man looked down and then looked back at Katya, and slowly rose to his feet, arms outstretched like a tightrope walker, balancing at the edge of the foggy void.

"Wait!" she said. "Don't!"

He did.

Katya closed her eyes. A moment later there was a hard wet sound and a shout of dismay below.

When she reached the ground, Captain Chernov said, "Your treatment worked, Doctor, but unfortunately it killed the patient."

The son of a bitch must have been working on that quip while he watched her climb down. She said, "He was scared to death."

"Of you?"

"Of his worst nightmare, I think."

She was staring at the captain because she did not want to look at the splayed body.

"The crane is twenty metres high," the chief petty officer said. "Whatever he was scared of, it must have been very big."

"And it's still here," Katya said, pointing in the direction of the distant barking that had not, in all this time, let up.

"You are eager to make a famous discovery. But first we must secure the station," Captain Chernov said, and detailed two seamen to stay by the boat, told the rest to stick together.

"Look after the doctor, lads," the chief petty officer said. "She isn't armed, she can't run as fast as we can, and she's probably a lot tastier than your salty hides."

"There were twenty-six people here," Katya said. "All men?"

"Of course," the chief petty officer said. "They were here to work. They didn't need distraction."

"All men," Katya said. "And they didn't do too well, did they?"

They swept through the buildings. Dormitories. A mess hall. Offices. Stores. Two generators purring in a shack constructed from concrete blocks and corrugated iron. An assay lab and a small clinic. A cold store with three bodies wrapped in black plastic sheeting. One had been badly mangled in some accident; the other two looked like suicides—a ligature of electrical cable around the neck, slashed wrists. Five more dead men were sprawled behind one of the dormitory huts, hands bound, chests torn by what appeared to be gunshot wounds, bullet holes in the hut's plank wall. Another body sprawled at the foot of the radio mast. His neck was broken, and Katya suggested that he had fallen while climbing.

"Climbing to escape from monsters, like your patient on the crane?" Captain Chernov said. "Or perhaps trying to escape from Americans who shot his friends."

"Perhaps they all went stir crazy in this damn fog," the chief petty officer said. "There was a quarrel. It got out of hand . . ."

"Something drove them mad, perhaps," Captain Chernov said thoughtfully.

The prefab buildings were empty, although there were signs that people had left with some haste. Plates of food rotting on tables in the mess, papers scattered on the floor of office, a record rotating on a gramophone in one of the dormitory huts, making an eerie scratching click until Captain Chernov lifted the needle. The gun locker was open and empty, but apart from the five men who had been lined up and shot there was no sign of any struggle, no blood spray, no bullet holes anywhere else. And no sign of the sixteen men still unaccounted for.

"They ran off, or they were taken prisoner," Captain Chernov said. "If they ran off, we will find them. If they were taken prisoner, we will find the Americans who did it."

"With respect, I don't think this was anything to do with Americans," Katya said.

"The so-called libertarians took hostages for ransom when they attacked our trawlers and merchant ships," Captain Chernov said. "And executed them when no ransom was paid. What happened here, perhaps, was caused by some kind of psychological war weapon. A gas, a volatile drug. After the men were driven mad by it, the Americans walked in, shot the few still able to resist, and took the rest prisoner. I see you do not like this story, Doctor. Well, if you have a better idea about what happened here, I should like to hear it."

"I don't have enough evidence to form a hypothesis," Katya said, and realised that it sounded stiff and priggish and defensive.

The captain smiled. He was having fun with her. "You hope to find monsters. You hope for fame. Very well. Let's go look for them."

Katya trailed after the party of seamen as Captain Chernov and the chief petty officer led them along the quayside, past pyramidal heaps of ore, past a row of articulated dump trucks: powerful machines with six-wheel drive and rugged tyres as tall as a person. They moved slowly and cautiously through the fog, checking under the trucks, checking shipping containers and stacks of empty crates. Arkadi Sarantsev hung back with Katya, asking her if she really thought monsters had attacked the station, if they were right now feeding on men they had killed.

"That's what the captain thinks I think," Katya said.

"Do you think he is wrong, about something driving the men crazy?"

"If I had to guess, I'd say it was something to do with the isolation," Katya said. "That, and the fog."

"But not, you think, Americans," Arkadi Sarantsev said.

He had a nice smile and a cool attitude, had knotted a red handkerchief at the throat of his telnyashka shirt. He plucked a pack of cigarettes from the pocket of his jacket and offered it to Katya; when she refused with a shake of her head, he put the pack to his lips, plucked out a cigarette, and lit it with a heavy petrol lighter fashioned from a .50 cal cartridge case.

"If I didn't know better, I'd think that your captain was looking for an excuse to take on the American research ship," she said.

"The captain's father was one of the pioneer settlers," Arkadi said. "We all resent the capitalists, with their nuclear rockets and supercomputers and frontier mentality, but the pioneer families especially resent them. As far as the captain is concerned, their offer of help is a personal insult."

Katya had once sort of dated a Navy diver, who one drunken night had told her how a friend of his had come to the surface too quickly because his dive computer had malfunctioned. He had been stricken with the bends, screaming with the pain of nitrogen bubbles in his joints, fed vodka by his mates because they had no way of treating him. Their patrol boat had been making a hopeless dash to the nearest port when an American frigate which had intercepted its call for help had caught up with it and had taken off the stricken man and treated him in its decompression chamber. Katya's boyfriend had tried to make it into a joke, saying that his friend had not only beaten the bends but had discovered a tremendous hangover cure in the bargain, but it was the usual sad story of crazy Russian machismo combined with a massive inferiority complex.

She said to Arkadi, "I know your captain took things very personally in the war against the libertarians."

"He disobeyed orders when he staged that raid, yes. But he captured an important warlord and his entourage, and also rescued more than twenty hostages."

She had to smile at Arkadi's sudden passion. "You think he's a hero."

"One time, two years ago, we had the job of visiting a small island close to the south pole," Arkadi said. "Very remote, very desolate. No one lives there, but it is important we have a claim on it. A previous expedition set up a beacon, and also landed goats there. The ideas was that they would breed and provide a source of fresh meat to any ships that passed by. We were tasked to clean the beacon's solar panels and replace its storage battery, and also to find out how the goats were doing."

"I can imagine what Captain Chernov thought about that."

"He believed that he was keeping the borders of the People's Republic safe," Arkadi said. "That is what he told us, at any rate. Well, a small party of us land. We cannot find any trace of the goats. Not so much as bone. There are pancake crabs everywhere, though, so we think the goats died and the crabs ate them. The island is a volcanic cone, extinct. Black rocks, tangles of thorny bushes, and everywhere pancake crabs. Watching us from under stones, creeping close to us whenever we stop as we climb to where the beacon was placed.

"All the way around the top of the island's cone there is a thick belt of feather palms. Smaller than the ones on the Big Island, but still much taller than anything else growing there. And there are pancake crabs in the palms. As we make our way through them, the crabs drop onto us. They stick to our skin with those suckers they have, we have to prise them off. It is disgusting, but we do not think it dangerous. At the top, there is a caldera, a deep funnel with a lake at the bottom. We find the beacon and do our work. We rest up, and a couple of idiots roll a boulder over the edge. It drops into the lake far below and makes a big splash. And after the ripple die away, there is another splash, more ripples. As if something had woken down there."

"You found a monster?"

"We did not see anything. Just the splash, and the ripples. And we did not have any way of climbing down. So we start back down, and the wind changes direction, and it begins to rain. And then two of us become sick. An allergic reaction to the pancake crabs, we find out later. It rains harder. Rain blowing sideways on the wind. And when we get to the inlet where we left the boat, we find big waves rolling in and the boat has floated off, is riding on the waves at the mouth of the inlet. Captain Chernov strips off and swims out to the boat, but he can't bring it near the rocks where the rest of us are waiting because the waves are too fierce. And by now the two sick men are very sick indeed, and they can't swim out. So he motors off to the ekranoplan and comes back with a rocket line, shoots it from boat to shore, and uses it to swing the sick men above the waves to the boat, and everyone is saved."

"What about the monster?"

"We didn't go back to look. But while we wait to be rescued, we have some bad thoughts about it. Imagine it creeping up the cliffs inside the caldera, creeping towards where we are sheltering . . . But the point is, whatever they say about the captain, he is not a monster. He did the right thing, in the war, and the brass punished him because he made them look bad. Listen to that. It isn't dogs, is it? It is in no way any kind of dog."

"It doesn't sound like pigs, either," Katya said.

The monotonous barking was loud and close now, coming from somewhere beyond a low rise crowned with a clump of bottlebrush trees. Katya and Arkadi watched as Captain Chernov and three seamen made a forking run, passing left and right around the trees, disappearing into streaming whiteness.

Two minutes passed. Three. No shots. No shouts. Katya's heart beat high as she strained to see into the fog. She badly wanted to know what was making that noise, but her hindbrain was telling her to run far and run fast. Arkadi lit another cigarette, and Katya pretended that she didn't see the flame of his lighter trembling when he applied it. The barking continued without pause. Eventually one of the seamen appeared on top of the ridge, a shadowy figure in the haze, scissoring his arms over his head to indicate the all clear.

There was a vegetable garden on the other side of the ridge, neat rows of potatoes and cabbage enclosed by a double fence of wire mesh to keep out pancake crabs, green leaves vivid and alien against the purples of the belt of native scrub beyond. And there was a paddock of bare earth inside a fence of wooden stakes and wire where two pigs lay in a muddy wallow, flanks heaving as they hacked and barked. Each time they coughed, bloody froth burst from their muzzles. The bodies of three other pigs lay swollen and rotting nearby, avid crowds of pancake crabs jostling and burrowing into them. Katya caught a strong whiff of ripe decay as she leaned at the fence. It seemed to tint the fog with the monochrome hue of grief.

"Here are your monsters, Doctor," Captain Chernov told her. "Would you care to examine them?"

The chief petty officer wanted to put the pigs out of their misery. Katya said that they should try to find out what had infected them first, and was surprised when Captain Chernov agreed.

"This sickness could be a reaction to a nerve agent," he said.

"Or something they caught from the local biota," Katya said.

"Native diseases do not infect people," Captain Chernov said. "Or pigs."

"It hasn't happened yet," Katya said. "But life on Earth and Venus shares the same genetic code and presumably the same common ancestor. As far as Venusian viruses and bacteria were concerned, people and pigs are no more than new sets of mucous membranes to be penetrated, new masses of cytoplasm to be exploited and subverted."

"First you hope to find monsters," Captain Chernov said. "Now you hope to find the Venusian flu. Your expectations are dwindling, Doctor. If you want to make yourself useful, help Mr. Sarantsev search the offices for diaries, logs, any records that might reveal what had happened. Meanwhile, I must look for the missing miners, although I am pretty sure I will not find them."

"Because the Americans took them?"

"I am sure that like all scientists, you believe in logic. And logic tells us that if they are not here, they must be somewhere else," Captain Chernov said, and told

Arkadi to make sure that Dr. Ignatova did not get into any trouble, and roared off with the rest of his men towards the open-cast mine in two trucks.

Katya found a log in the station's small clinic, found an entry three weeks old that noted two men displaying symptoms of a flu-like infection: high temperatures, involuntary movements of the arms and legs, night sweats, recovery within twenty-four hours. By then, more men had become infected. It had swiftly passed through the camp and everyone appeared to have succumbed, including the station's chemist, who doubled as its medical officer. In the assay lab, Katya found a photograph showing him standing with his two teenage daughters in front of the First Footstep monument on Big Island: a gangling, sandy-haired man with heavy framed glasses and a high forehead. She had seen him before. He was one of the men who had been shot to death. His name was Georgi Zhzhyonov.

For a week after the last men came down with what he called twenty-four hour flu, he'd made only routine notes in his log. Then there was a terse entry about a suicide—a man had hanged himself. Another man walked in front of a truck. More entries: fist fights, a non-fatal stabbing, broken bones due to drunkenness. Two men disappeared one night; three the next. One was found clinging to the top of tall tree and brought down. The next day he was found dead, his wrists slashed open. A man hanged himself; four others disappeared. The last note, in Georgi Zhzhyonov's neat, slanting script, read *I suffer from the most vivid and peculiar dreams.*

Katya found the forms certifying the deaths of the suicides, with notes on blood-work. Georgi Zhzhyonov had run samples through his gas spectrometer, looking for heavy metals and toxins, finding only trace levels of tin and titanium, well within expected limits. He had also examined the blood of two pigs. Katya felt a chill at the base of her spine. The men had become ill; the pigs had become ill; Georgi Zhzhyonov had been trying to find a link. And because he was a metallurgist, he had used the tools of his trade.

There was a geological map on one wall of his little lab. Katya studied it carefully. The broad curve of the shore line with sand bars running parallel to it. A black rectangle marking the site of the station. A series of steeply contoured ridges rising behind, with red stipplings indicating known deposits of ore. The site of the open-cast mine was marked on the first ridge by a cross-hatched rectangle. She ran her finger along the top of the ridge, noting the high spots.

Arkadi Sarantsev, searching the disordered office of the mining station's commandant, had made his own discovery.

"Fish," he told Katya.

"Fish?"

"A lot of fish." Arkadi waggled a video disk. "Luckily for us, the commandant liked to make home movies."

It was short, choppily edited. Panning shots across windrows of black fish on a sandbar that faded into fog, black fish rising and falling on shallow waves. A zoom shot closing on fish shimmying and leaping out of the water, landing on fish already dead or dying. Skinny, armour-plated fish with pale gill ruffs and bulbous eyes. A close-up that included the cameraman's boots, showing several fish writhing in circles, snapping at their own tails. Men scooping fish into buckets, tipping the buckets into oil drums in the well of a skiff. Men shovelling fish into the water, men throwing fish at each other. A small bulldozer rolling back and forth in the fog, turning up combers of sand and fish and pushing them into the water. Waves rolling in, black with blood, agitated by the splashing of scavengers come to feed.

Katya insisted on replaying the scenes of the men at work. Ten men, twenty, twenty-five. And the cameraman, the commandant, made twenty-six. Everyone in the mining station had joined in the macabre beach party, and none of them had worn protective clothing. Most were dressed in bathing trunks and flip-flops; several were buck-naked.

"When was this?" she said.

"Four weeks ago," Arkadi said.

"And a week later, the men started to become sick," she said, and gave a quick account of Georgi Zhzhyonov's notes. The suicides, the disappearances, the cryptic note about dreams.

Arkadi showed her the commandant's diary. Notes on patrols sent to search the forest behind the station, of sightings of men or man-shaped animals, of strange noises. Towards the end, the commandant's handwriting degenerated to a jagged scrawl. The last entry consisted of a few indecipherable words and drawings of skulls, fanged devil faces, daggers dripping blood.

"So you think it was the fish," Arkadi said. "The fish infected them, or they ate the fish and it made them sick. Sick in the body and in the head."

"It may be slightly more complicated than that," Katya said. "I think they fed the pigs with some of the fish. I need to examine them."

She found boxes of vinyl gloves in the little lab, and face masks she soaked in bleach. It wasn't much protection, but it was the best she could manage. She didn't want to get close to the pigs, not without wearing a full contamination suit, so she and Arkadi rigged a sampler from a scaffold pole and a cup taped to the end, and, after some manoeuvring, managed to collect a draft of froth from one of them. She treated it like plutonium, carefully tipping it into a plastic bottle and double-bagging the bottle.

She had noticed no less than six microscopes stacked in unopened boxes in the lab. No doubt the result of the same kind of supply error in central stores that had packed the ekranoplan's stores with tins of no other kind of soup but pumpkin. She set one up on the knife-scarred butcher's table in the kitchen of the mess, then used a rolling pin to knock out a window.

"Six microscopes," she told Arkadi, "but not one microscope slide."

She plucked a small splinter of window-glass, put on a fresh set of vinyl gloves, adjusted her mask, smeared a drop of pig sputum on the splinter and set it on the platform of the microscope, and bent over it and adjusted the focus knob until the smear swam into focus.

Nothing.

She swept the platform on which the splinter was clamped back and forth, fingertips sweating on the vernier knobs, on the fine focus knob, feeling a touch of the funk she remembered from undergraduate practical classes when she'd failed to see the thing she was meant to see.

"What do you see?" Arkadi said.

"Nothing. But it doesn't mean anything."

She had explained her idea on the way to sample the stricken pig's sputum, explained that Georgi Zhzhyonov had been on the right track, but he had been looking in the wrong place. On Earth, she told Arkadi, there were diseases passed from animals to humans. Zoonoses. It was possible that the brain-burning flu was one such. The miners had fed their pigs with raw fish—all that free protein, willingly throwing itself ashore—and an infection carried by the fish had flourished in the animals. They had become reaction vessels, growing ill, coughing up infected sputum. Perhaps the man who fed the pigs had become ill first, and then had infected everyone else. Or perhaps the men had become infected after eating undercooked pork. Katya had been hoping that it was some kind of parasite. Something she could see under the microscope. Worms. Fungal cells. Spores. Cysts.

"Something you could show the captain," Arkadi said.

He was a quick study.

"It could be a bacterium," Katya said. "Or a virus. Viruses are generally not much bigger than the wavelength of visible light, so hard to see with a conventional microscope like this. I'll find out exactly what it is when I get the samples to a fully equipped lab, but it has to be something native. Something that affects the behaviour of its host. It made the fish beach themselves. It made the miners hallucinate. Made them believe that they were being attacked. Made some of them kill themselves. Made some of them kill their friends. I think the rest ran off into the countryside."

"But you can't prove it."

"Not here. Not yet. Unless Captain Chernov has found the missing men."

He hadn't. His search party had scoured the strip mine from one end to the other, and returned to the station with two bodies they had found at the base of a vertical rock face, but there was no sign of the rest—six by Katya's count. Captain Chernov was convinced that they had been captured or killed by raiders, but listened to Katya's precis of Georgi Zhzhyonov's notes, and watched the video.

At the end, he said, "The pigs became sick, the men became sick. And you want to link them with this—what did you call it?"

"A zoonosis," Katya said.

"But you have no proof."

"There is the timing. The men started to become sick a week after the fish washed up. If they fed some of the fish to the pigs, it's long enough for an infection to develop."

"The man on the crane, was he coughing? No: he was crazy. And the dead men we found—they died from their own hand, or from bullets. Not some parasite."

"Men and pigs are similar but not identical—"

"The pigs may have caught some illness. Maybe from the fish, why not? But what happened to the men is different. It is clear that their minds were affected."

"On Earth, there are many examples of parasites that alter the behaviour of their hosts," Katya said.

"We are not on Earth," Captain Chernov said. "And this is nothing to do with parasites. The men were driven mad, that is clear. But by what? I think it could very well be the result of the testing of some kind of psychological war weapon. A poison gas, perhaps. A gas that does not kill, but alters the mind. The Americans deployed it here, in this remote place, observed the results, then captured the survivors. And now they return, pretending to help, but really wanting to capture us, in case we have discovered evidence of what they did. And your talk of a disease could help them, Doctor. Have you thought of that? Suppose the Americans claim that this was due to a native disease that infects people? Suppose they present false evidence to back up their story? We would have to quarantine this station, and perhaps evacuate the others. Leave the coast open for the Americans to claim. Well, we will not run. We will defend this place. We will engage the enemy. We will uncover the truth about the atrocity they committed here. Do that for me, Doctor. Find the truth. Not fairytales."

He would not look at the map, would not listen to Katya's idea about where the last of the miners could be hiding. He had worked up a story that satisfied his prejudices, and he was not going to change his mind. The enemy had done this; they were returning to the scene of the crime; they must be punished.

The chief petty officer and two seamen were left to guard the station; everyone else went back to the ekranoplan. Katya wasn't confined to her cabin, but the hatches to the observation deck and the wings were locked down, and Captain Chernov made it clear that the bridges were off-limits. She spent a little time writing up a report, trying to keep it as dispassionate as possible. She wasn't sure if anyone would read it, but she had to put down the facts and her own conclusions.

Overhead, something rumbled and whined. She wondered if it was something to do with the missile launch tubes mounted on the top of the ekranoplan.

When she was finished, she couldn't stay in her cabin. The ekranoplan was full of restless activity. Men clattering up and down ladders, along companionways. Loud voices. A general excitement. Three seamen cleaning carbines in the mess hall ignored Katya as she pottered in the galley, ignored her when she left, carrying two mugs of tea.

She found Arkadi Sarantsev in the fire control bay, handed him one of the mugs. He told her that Captain Chernov had reported to Central Command in Kosmograd and they had taken him seriously. A three hundred kilometre exclusion zone had been declared along the coast, and all American and British vessels had been ordered to leave it. The Americans had lodged a formal protest and were sending two frigates to back up their research vessel, which had turned around fifty kilometres from shore, and was heading away. Arkadi brought up the missile guidance system's radar on the big central screen: the long line of the coast, the hard green dot of the research vessel with a little block of white figures beside it.

"We are waiting for clearance to engage," he said.

Katya felt a fluttering agitation in her blood. "To fire missiles at it?"

Arkadi sipped from his mug of tea. "To head out and capture it. The captain believes that it carries evidence of a psy-war attack on the station, and Central Command is discussing that idea."

"He'll attack anyway, won't he? Like he did before. Except this time he could start a war."

"He will do the right thing."

"You know there was no American plot. You know that the miners became infected with something that drove them crazy. You know the survivors are hiding, like the poor man up in the crane."

Arkadi studied her for a moment, with a look of regret. "We are friends, you and I. But I am also a officer of the navy of the People's Republic, and I serve under the man who saved my life," he said, and pulled aside the collar of his striped telnyashka shirt to show a white wheal on his shoulder. "I was one of those who had an allergic reaction to pancake crab spit, on that island."

"So you won't help me," Katya said.

"I advise you to let us do our work."

"That's what I thought," Katya said. "But I had to ask, because I'm not sure if I can do this alone."

Arkadi's eyes widened and he dropped his mug of tea and raised his hand. Too late. Katya wacked him on the side of his head with the sock stuffed with dried beans, wacked him again, and his eyes rolled back and he slid out of his chair and fell to the floor. She ransacked his pockets and found a set of keys, then laid him on his side, in the recovery position, and headed towards the nearest hatch.

No one saw her drop from one of the wings into the cool water—a drop higher than she'd expected, plunging her a good metre below the surface. And although her entire skin tingled with anticipation as she swam to shore, no one raised the alarm or shot at her. She was a strong swimmer: she had met the navy diver when he had noticed her in the pool of the spa in the Druzhba sanatorium, high in the mountains of Big Island. Wearing only her underwear, she crested confidently through the cool, calm water, her clothes and shoes in a bag belted to her waist. The fog's vaporous ceiling hung about a metre over the surface; fog drew a veil all around her. It was as if she were swimming in a private bubble.

As she neared the quay, she heard the barking of the pigs, and, with a pang of regret, wished that she had asked Arkadi to shoot them after she had taken her sample. But he would have probably refused, because Captain Chernov wanted to keep them alive, to prove his ridiculous theory.

She hoped Arkadi wouldn't get into trouble because she had stolen his keys. She hoped he would understand why she'd done it. She hoped he would forgive her.

No one challenged her when she climbed onto the quay. She ran past the heap of ore to the parked trucks and paused, breathing hard, listening. Nothing but the laboured barks of the poor pigs. No shouts or sirens, no warning shots. She squeezed water from her hair and knotted it in a loose ponytail, pulled on her shirt and cargo pants and shoes, and climbed into the cab of the truck at the far end of the row. She'd driven heavy vehicles like it when, in the long vacation at the end of her first university year, she'd worked at the construction site for the sports centre her mother had designed. Power steering, synchromesh gears, no problem. No one challenged her when she pressed the start button and the big engine coughed into life, but as she drove off she saw in the side mirrors a man chasing after her, waving frantically as he fell behind and vanished into the fog.

The truck rode easily and smoothly up a winding, graded road. Perched in the high, roomy cab, cool air blasting out of the air conditioning, her clothes drying stiffly, Katya drove as fast as she dared in the fog, navigating by the GPS map in the dashboard screen and red lights set on posts at twenty-metre intervals on either side of the road. A never-ending chain of stars appearing out of the fog, drifting past, vanishing.

She imagined men running for the trucks, speeding after her. Nothing showed in the side mirrors, but visibility was down to less than twenty metres. She wouldn't know she was being chased until they were right on the tail of the truck's hopper.

The road grew steeper. She shifted down, shifted down again, and at last it topped out. Trying to match the GPS map with reality, she drove past a pair of bulldozers, some kind of mobile conveyer belt, and a string of prefab huts before a terraced cliff horizontally striped with dark ore deposits loomed out of the fog. She turned right, driving across packed dirt, skirting around a spoil heap that rose into streaming whiteness, past the tower and hoppers of a screening plant. Then a faint red light appeared to her left and she turned towards it, realising with tremendous relief that she had found the road that led to the top of the ridge.

It switchbacked up steep, wooded slopes. Trees grew on either side, stabbing up into the fog. Some were a little like conifers, or a child's drawing of conifers: stiff radial branches strung with puffballs of fine needles that condensed water droplets from the fog. Others were hung with what looked like tattered sails, or bunches of ragged velvety straps that sparkled with condensation in the truck's headlights. Puffballs and straps and sails were tinted deep purple—Venusian plants used a pigment similar to rhodopsin to capture light for photosynthesis. Fat cushions of black moss saddled between the trees. Everything was dripping wet.

A shape loomed out of the fog: a yellow articulated dump truck exactly like the one she was driving, tipped nose down in the deep ditch at the side of the road. She slowed as she went past, craning to look inside the truck's cab, seeing that it was empty and feeling a measure of relief: feeling that she was on the right track.

The oppressive shroud of the fog began to lift and break up into streamers caught amongst branches and sails, and she drove on in pewter light, trees thinning to scattered clumps with rough scrub between. The road turned, and gave out abruptly, and a truck was slewed at its end.

The men had come here, all right. Trying to escape the monsters in their heads by driving out of the fog to the place they came to play and relax.

Katya drove past the truck, drove across a rough meadow, past a barbecue pit and picnic tables, jolting on up a steepening slope until even in its lowest gear the truck could climb no farther.

She switched off the motor and swung out of the cab, looked back at the way she had come. A pure white sea stretched towards the horizon, seamlessly melding with the ivory dome of the planet's permanent cloud cover. The sun was a bright smear low in the east. In less than twenty days, it would set at this latitude, and the long night—a hundred and seventeen days long—would begin. Forty kilometres above, a lightning storm flashed and flickered under the cloudroof: she heard the distant, dull percussion of thunder, saw thin, shadowy twists of falling rain that would evaporate before it hit the ground.

There was still no sign of pursuit, but she did not doubt that she was being followed, and began to climb towards the top of the ridge. Steep, stony slopes sparsely stubbled with purple vegetation. Squat vases, skull-sized puffballs, clumps of stiff thorny whips or tall plumes. The air was very still, weighted with sultry heat. Long shadows tangled everywhere.

She was sweating hard, out of breath, her pulse hammering in her ears, when at last she reached the top of the ridge and saw the crests of further ridges rising above the fog, parallel rakes stretching towards the distant prospect of a stark mountain range, the beginning of the desert interior. Ahead of her, the broad ridge ran out towards a high prow crowned with a copse of trees.

A horn blared far below. She felt a spike of alarm, saw a yellow dump truck draw up beside hers, saw three men spill from it.

As she jogged towards the copse of trees, a speck materialised in the distance, scooting above the shadow it cast on the restless sea of fog, cutting through wisps of drifting vapour, rising as it tracked towards her. It was one of the ekranoplan's drones, a chunky quadrocopter like a garbage can lid pierced by a cross, with a caged rotor at the end of each bar of the cross. Its cluster of cameras glinted as it buzzed past her and turned and came back, flying low and fast, a homicidal frisbee aimed at her head.

She dropped flat, felt the backwash of the drone's fans blow over her, pushed to her feet as the quadrocopter curved around and shot towards her again, and ran towards a clump of thorns at the edge of a steep drop. She broke off one of the dead canes in the core of the clump and swung it at the drone, and the machine veered sideways and made a wide turn and came back towards her, moving in cautious erratic spurts, halting a few metres away.

There was a metallic clatter and a voice said, "Stay where you are, Doctor. Wait for my men."

"Is that you, captain? If you care to follow me, I'll lead you to the missing miners."

"You disobeyed a direct order, Doctor. But if you come back now I'll overlook your transgression."

"They climbed up here, looking for a place where they'd be safe," Katya said, and pointed towards the trees.

The quadrocopter drone tilted and shot forward, and she jumped over the edge and ploughed down the steep slope in a cloud of dust and small stones, fetching up breathless and bleeding in a clump of stiff purple plumes. She had lost the thorn cane. The drone was falling towards her, and she snapped off a plume and thrust it like a spear into one of the machine's fans.

There was a grinding noise and a stinging blizzard of shards and splinters sprayed around her and the drone spun past, canted at a steep angle. It tried to turn back towards Katya, and the mismatched thrust of its fans spun it in a death spiral and it struck a shelf of rock and clattered away down the slope, bouncing and shedding parts.

The three men climbing towards her paused as the wreckage of the drone spun past, then started to climb again.

It took all of Katya's strength to scramble back up the slope. She paused at the top, her pulse drumming in her skull, and blotted sweat and blood from her eyes—flying splinters had badly cut her face. The men were much closer now. The chief petty officer shouted something to her and she turned and limped along the crest of the ridge, hot pain knifing in one ankle. Hot air clamped around her like a fever sheet; the world contracted to the patch of stony dirt directly in front of her feet. She scrambled up a steep gully, mostly on all fours, only realised that she reached the top when the shadows of the trees fell across her.

They were rooted amongst black boulders, upright trunks soaring skywards, stiff horizontal branches clad in bunches of purple needles. A man lay on his back on a dry litter of fallen needles, eyes shrunken in their sockets, cracked lips flecked with froth. Katya thought he was dead, but then he turned his head towards her and started to tremble and whimper.

Both his legs were broken. She could see bone sticking out of the shin of his torn trousers. A rifle lay some way off. She supposed that he'd dropped it when he'd fallen.

She knelt beside him and took one of his hands and asked him where his friends were. His eyes rolled back. She thought he had fainted, and then she understood, and looked up. And saw small shadows high up in the jutting branches, half-hidden by puffball clusters of needles. Atavistic apes clinging to the safety of their perches.

Katya held on to the man's hand as the chief petty officer and two seamen stepped towards her.

"I don't know why he didn't have you killed," her mother said.

"Chernov didn't have a plan," Katya said. "He had a fixation, a belief that every-thing that he saw was the result of some fiendish American plot. He was trying to stop me, yes, but he was also trying to rescue me from what he believed to be my own foolishness. When his men saw that I had found the miners, that was the end of it."

"I suppose we should for once be grateful for the rigid code of honour men value so highly."

"Arkadi called him a hero. And he acted like one."

"And now *you* are the hero. My daughter, who saved the world from war."

"From a stupid skirmish created by that rigid code of honour. And I was wrong about too many things to qualify as any kind of hero. I was wrong about what in-fected the miners, to begin with."

They were talking over lunch. Katya and the crew of the ekranoplan had just been released from quarantine, and her mother had whisked her away from the scrum of reporters and onlookers and a crew from the state TV news to the calm of the luncheon room of the Engineers' Union, with its views across the simmering basin of Kosmograd and the blue curve of Crater Bay.

The other diners were openly staring at them, and not, for once, because they were the only two women in the room. Katya wore the shirt and cargo pants in which she'd been released; her mother wore a severely-cut white suit that emphasised her slim figure, and her trademark red-framed glasses.

"You weren't wrong, dear," she said. "The men had been infected by something that drove them mad."

"But it wasn't a bug, or a parasite. And it didn't have anything to do with the pigs. And we have only circumstantial evidence that it had anything to do with the fish."

It had taken several weeks of tests in the naval hospital to determine that the miners had been infected by a kind of prion: an infectious agent that closely resembled a misfolded version of a protein found in neurons in the amygdala, the small subcortical structure in the brain that regulated both fear and pleasure responses. The prion catalysed the misfolding of those proteins, creating an imbalance of neurotransmitters and triggering an exaggerated version of the fight-or-flight reaction and release of massive amounts of adrenaline and other hormones. The psychotic breaks and hallucinations suffered by the miners had been attempts to rationalise uncontrollable emotional thunderstorms.

Katya wanted very much to prove that the prion had been present in the blood of the fish which had beached themselves. As for the pigs, they had been infected by a parasitic threadworm, but it had only affected their respiratory systems and did not seem to be transmissible to humans. She had been right in thinking that the miners' madness was due to an infection, but had got every detail wrong because she had based her ideas on terrestrial examples. She had made the mistake of arguing from analogy, of trying to map stories from Earth on the actuality of Venus, and the fit had been imperfect.

"I saw two different things," she told her mother, "and tried to make them part of the same story. Captain Chernov was right about that, at least."

"He was wrong about everything else. And you are too hard on yourself," her mother said fondly.

"I wonder where I got that from?"

"Can the poor men you rescued be cured?"

"They're under heavy sedation and undergoing cognitive therapy. They're no longer scared to death, but purging the prions from their brains won't be easy."

"It sounds as if you have found a new project."

"I'm wondering if it's a general problem," Katya said. "This particular prion caused a gross behavioural change, but there may be others that have more subtle effects. We think that we are separate from the biosphere of Venus, yet it is clear that we are not. All of us, Russians, Americans, British, we have more in common with each other than with the people from our homelands. We came from Earth, but we are all Venusians now. Venus is in our blood, and our minds."

"So you have a new research topic, and a new way of getting into trouble," her mother said. "What about this new man of yours?"

"We're taking it slowly. He forgave me, at least, for giving him a bad concussion, and injuring his pride."

Although Arkadi had said, the first time they had met in quarantine, that if he had been piloting the drone he would have had no problem returning the favour.

"A man who puts love before pride," her mother said. "Now there's a lovely example of a new way of thinking."

ɪᴛ ᴛᴀᴋᴇꜱ ᴍᴏʀᴇ ᴍᴜꜱᴄʟᴇꜱ ᴛᴏ ꜰʀᴏᴡɴ

NED BEAUMAN

Maintaining an expressionless "poker face" can be a considerable advantage in high-stakes games, in personal relationships, in corporate intrigue, and even in espionage, but as the vigorous and violent tale that follows demonstrates, keeping one can be a lot easier if you have a little high-tech help. . . .

Ned Beauman was born in 1985 in London. His debut novel, Boxer, Beetle, won the Writers Guild of America Award for Best Fiction Book and the Goldberg Prize for Outstanding Debut Fiction. His second novel, The Teleportation Accident, was long-listed for the Man Booker Prize and won the Encore Award and a Somerset Maugham Award. His third novel, Glow, was published in 2014. He has been chosen by the BBC's The Culture Show as one of the twelve best new British novelists and by Granta as one of the twenty best British novelists under forty. His work has been translated into more than ten languages.

Tonight's interrogation was a sitcom. The subject of the sitcom was me, although I never appeared on screen. I recognised the actors, and the oversized Manhattan apartment set in which they sat around bantering, because I'd seen several episodes of the sitcom before. But today their voices and movements were contrived by an algorithm. They were talking about how I'd recently made a disastrous blunder at work and I was struggling to cover it up; how I was sabotaging Simagre's operations on behalf of a rival oil company; how I was embezzling money; how I was selling confidential information to a journalist or a hedge fund or a cartel; how I was compromised by a debt or an addiction or an affair. These were serious subjects, but they were being slotted into time-tested, all-purpose joke structures that could accommodate almost any concept and still be funny if the delivery was right. On both sides of the screen were cameras pointed at my face. It was a fine simulation of what watching TV must be like for a paranoid schizophrenic.

The software would see if my mouth was laughing but my eyes weren't. It would see if I began to laugh but then the laugh died away when I realised how disturbingly accurate the joke was. It would see if I blanched at the joke and then forced a laugh slightly too late. It would see if I laughed at everything, even the lines that weren't funny, to cover my panic. It would see if my face was tense with the effort to look natural. It would see if I made involuntary cringes of anxiety between my other expressions, even for only a thirtieth of a second. "Leakage" was the technical name for self-betrayals of this kind. And if the emotion detection software did notice anything out of the ordinary, it would modify the script of the following scene to hone in on whatever had caused that reaction. The sitcom, as they used to say, was filmed before a live studio audience.

I'd heard rumours about this method, but I'd never experienced it firsthand. Usually I just got the basic interview: a few dozen questions, many of them quite innocuous, from a face on a screen. The face was digitally composited, like the sitcom actors, although we'd been told that about once in every five sessions the face would be a mask for a trained subcontractor in Kenya or the Phillipines. We'd also been told, repeatedly, that the software was almost infallible. Cantabrian were keen for us to believe that, because their software would work better if the sinless felt they had nothing to fear and the sinners felt they had everything to fear.

I was a sinner, but I wasn't afraid. And the curtained privacy booth was comfortable, like the back of a very small limousine. So I sat there and watched the show as if I was at home on the couch. Yes, it was written and acted by an algorithm, but it was funny, in a dated sort of way, and I laughed at a lot of the jokes. Including the joke about how I was selling pipeline data to a cartel. Even though that joke was in pretty bad taste. Even though that joke hit pretty close to home.

The episode concluded with the logo of the company who had produced the original sitcom back in the 1990s, the logo of the company who now owned the rights to both the sitcom and the actors' likenesses, the logo of the company who developed the emotion detection software, and of course the logo of Cantabrian, who handled security for Simagre Petroleum across Mexico and Guatemala. "Thank you very much for your patience," said a voice. "We hope you have a pleasant evening."

There was very little chance of that. I'd already agreed to go out for drinks at a mirrory lounge on Calle Schiller with my boss and a few of my coworkers. By now they would be waiting for me beyond the security gates in the lobby. The next four or five hours would be a greater drudgery than the afternoon I'd just spent at my desk, and it wasn't as if I'd get overtime.

My boss, Gabriel Obregón, a Mexican American with an MBA from Sloan, was an efficient and fair-minded manager but also the most insecure conversationalist I had ever met. When he was telling you a story, you had to stage a continual pantomime of emotional involvement, otherwise he'd worry you weren't following. And if the story had a punch line, you had to laugh as loud and as long as Obregón himself did, which was very loud and very long. But he wasn't the sort of narcissist who would cheerfully lap up the most blatant sycophancy. He was convinced that he could distinguish fake smiles from real ones better than any software, even though in practice he was about as reliable as a coin toss; "I don't want you to laugh at my jokes just because I'm the boss," he would say to us, even though our working lives would have become unfeasibly awkward if we'd ever stopped.

Before I moved from Houston to Mexico City, Obregón would have been my undoing. Tweaking my face into socially acceptable configurations had always been a challenge for me. I'd long since given up smiling for cameras, because even when I tried my best it looked as if I was making a sarcastic parody of a smile. This was a hereditary incompetence: when we were especially bored, my father and I both suffered from what was affectionately known in my family as "death face," our attentive expressions decaying minute by minute into grimaces so extreme that onlookers would often assume we'd been taken ill. We never realised we were doing it until it was pointed out, and all my life it had been a liability, in seminars and meetings and first dates and family reunions. There was nothing physically wrong with me. I had all the right muscles to be insincere. But I just couldn't seem to array them very well or fix them for very long.

I'm not trying to imply that somehow it taxed me so much because I'm fundamentally more honest than other people. As my personal history demonstrates, that is not at all the case. All I mean to say is, when those cartel surgeons hid 43 electroactive polymer units inside my new face, it was as if, at very long last, I had graduated from finishing school.

Earlier in the year, a small-batch añejo from Fushimi had won Best Tequila at the San Francisco World Spirits Competition, causing uproar in the Mexican media and at least one speech before the Chamber of Deputies. By eight o'clock, Obregón had already had four rounds of a tequila made with gin botanicals in the same distillery, even though each measure cost as much as a good dinner. I was sipping Negra Modelo, because the maximum amount of fun I could possibly have with my coworkers still wasn't worth a hangover in the morning.

"You can't even imagine how much crap I insulate you guys from," Obregón was saying. We all looked curious. "I mean, coming down from above. It isn't easy sometimes." We all looked sympathetic. "Look, I'm not whining. It's my job to look out for you. I just, you know, hope you realise." We all looked grateful.

"They aren't happy upstairs?" said Soto, who worked at the desk next to me. Everyone here could speak Spanish, but Simagre was a multinational company and it functioned in English.

"Hey, they're never happy, right? But this last quarter they've been extra grouchy because of the Cantabrian thing, and who do they take it out on? Guys at my level."

"What Cantabrian thing?"

Obregón hesitated. "This isn't exactly water cooler material at this point . . ." But he'd had four tequilas. "You deserve to know, though. You all jump through their hoops every day." He gestured at me. "You just sat through that stupid emotion detection show for twenty minutes. You deserve to know." He exhaled heavily. "They're thinking about dropping Cantabrian."

That was genuinely monumental corporate gossip. None of us had to fake our surprise. "Don't we have another three years on the contract?" I said. I knew we were paying them a lot. The denationalisation of the Mexican oil market had been the biggest boom for the private security industry since the Bush wars.

"Yeah, so either we pay the penalty, or we go to court to get out of it, but either way we'd be looking at . . . I don't even know. Then the transition costs . . . So a lot of them are against it, upstairs. But Cantabrian have had their shot. They've had all this time to find the data breaches, and from what I hear, they're just flailing. The taps are still killing our bottom line because the cartels always know every fucking thing we're doing. Cantabrian can manage the low-level stuff fine—if you try to hijack one of our trucks, you're going to get shot—but if that was all we needed, we could just hire the biggest *gatillero* in every cantina. Anyway, drop them, don't drop them, either way everybody's arguing, everybody's in a crappy mood. And you know what I think?" He lowered his voice. "I think the leaks are coming from Cantabrian."

"Cantabrian don't have access to any pipeline data," I said.

"But they built our security architecture. They have back doors."

"The programmers are in Singapore," said Soto.

"Doesn't matter. The cartels have reach. Hey, that reminds me," Obregón said, tapping his phone for another round. "So there's this cartel boss's son, right? Eight years old. And his nanny tells him that if he wants a lot of presents for Christmas this year, he should write a letter to Baby Jesus. Because if it wasn't for Baby Jesus, we wouldn't even have Christmas. So the boy sits down to write the letter, and first he puts, 'Dear Baby Jesus, I've been a good boy the whole year, so I want a new speedboat.' He looks at it, then he crumples it up and throws it away. He gets out a new piece of paper, and this time he writes, 'Dear Baby Jesus, I've been a good boy most of the year, so I want a new speedboat.' He looks at it, then he crumples it up and throws it away again. But then he gets an idea. He goes into his *abuela's* room, takes a statue of the Virgin Mary, wraps it up in duct tape, puts it in the closet, and locks the door. Then he gets another piece of paper and he writes, 'Dear Baby Jesus, if you ever want to see your mother again . . .'"

Everyone guffawed. And even though I'd heard the joke told better before, my guffaw was more convincing than anyone else's, at least visually. Because I had help.

The electroactive polymer prosthesis had been developed at the UC Davis Medical Center as a treatment for facial paralysis. It still hadn't been approved for use by regulators anywhere in the world. But the Nuevos Zetas' hackers had stolen the designs and forwarded them to a fabricator in Guangzhou that specialised in biomedical prototypes. Presumably both Cantabrian and the company that made the emotion detection software were aware that the technology existed, but thought they had a few years' grace before they had to worry about it.

There wasn't enough metal in my face to show up on a body scanner, and even under a close examination the lacework under my skin could easily be mistaken for the titanium alloy mesh sometimes used in facial reconstruction surgery. It worked on roughly the same principle as a shipbuilder's powered exoskeleton, but in miniature: when you initiated a movement, the prosthesis detected that movement and threw its own weight behind it. A smile that would normally be thin and mirthless would instead dawn across your whole face. Then it would linger and fade, like a real smile, instead of clicking off like a fake one. Conversely, when you tried to keep your face neutral, the prosthesis would steady anything that might squinch or quiver or droop. No more nervousness, no more death face.

Because the emotion detection software that Cantabrian used could also detect spikes in facial temperature and perspiration, I had a unit in each of my cheekbones to dispense a fizzle of magnetite nanoparticles into my facial veins, which in an emergency would partially neutralise both tells. So far, though, that had never been necessary, because the support of the electroactive polymers meant I was always relaxed about telling lies (or listening to jokes). If I started babbling or gnawing my fingernails or squirming in my seat, an interviewer would certainly notice, and there was nothing the prosthesis could do about that. But it was easy to train yourself not to show any of those signs. Whereas it was impossible, as far as anybody knew, to train the microexpressions out of your face.

The prosthesis could be switched on and off wirelessly. On my phone I had a settings app disguised as a puzzle game. I took off my girdle for sleep and exercise and sex, otherwise I got a sore jaw. But the rest of the time, I kept it on. Once you get used to having full control over your face, it begins to seem very strange that you ever tolerated its delinquency. If a social network decided to broadcast your deepest feelings to the world without permission, spurting emojis left and right, you would delete your account. And yet your body does precisely that. Crying, blushing, sweating, goosebumps, involuntary facial expressions—not to mention erections, when visible, and stress-related incontinence, in extreme cases—are all serious data breaches. Strangers on the Metro have no more right to know how you're feeling than strangers on the Internet.

When we look at other people's faces, we don't see a muscular configuration that we interpret as an emotion: we see the emotion itself. That makes us feel as if the face is the raw membrane of the soul. We conflate ourselves with our faces. But in fact the face is no more than a signalling machine strapped to the brain. There's no meaningful difference between a face and a mask. And people who happen to be bad at painting their masks don't deserve to have more complicated lives than people who happen to be good at it.

I once asked one of the Nuevos Zetas doctors about the maximum extension of the artificial muscles. He told me that in principle they could rip my face apart, but the prosthesis' firmware would never allow that. I was reminded of a photograph from the 1860s that Lauren, my girlfriend back in Houston, had once showed me on her tablet: an old man getting his face electrocuted with metal probes to produce an expression of wild fright, part of a series of experiments that the neurologist Duchenne de Boulogne referred to as "the gymnastics of the soul."

"That's how you look when you come," Lauren said to me. She adopted a fond and jokey tone, but she must have known it would sting. More than once we'd argued about her refusal to let me fuck her from behind in front of a mirror. She'd told me she found me handsome the rest of the time but when she saw me like that, framed in the mirror, it put her off so much she just wanted to stop. She'd even reappropriated the term "death face" to emphasise her point. By that time, I was already planning to break up with her, but in fact my situation in Houston went up in flames so suddenly I never even got the chance.

In Mexico City, I had a new "girlfriend." On Sunday night, I went for my weekly appointment with Rafaella, who lived on the seventh floor of a brand-new condominium overlooking the Viaducto Miguel Alemán in Escandón. If anyone from Cantabrian had ever decided to follow me—and they presumably already had, at least once, as a matter of routine—they would have observed that I arrived at the apartment around eight o'clock with two bottles of wine and a shopping bag containing jewellery or perfume or lingerie or heels or some other gossamer commodity, delivered to me that morning by a concierge service. About an hour later, a boy would arrive on a moped to hand over to the doorman the dinner we'd ordered. And at two or three in the morning, I would come back downstairs and take a car service home to my own apartment. Since my salary at Simagre wasn't all that high, it might have occurred to the surveillance team from Cantabrian that I was stretching myself a little bit with all the expensive gifts. What would have reassured them was that it wasn't quite the sort of overhead that made a guy take risks. It was only the sort of overhead that made a guy stay home playing video games the rest of the week to save money. All in all it must have seemed intoxicatingly romantic.

But that was nothing compared to the passion we unleashed in private. As usual, Rafaella greeted me with a dry kiss on the cheek. Once I'd shut the door behind me she took the shopping bag and disappeared into her bedroom without a word. Arturo raised his glass of mezcal in greeting. Omar sat on the couch, typing on his laptop. "Everything cool this week?" he said.

"Yeah." I would have liked a mezcal myself but I wasn't allowed to drink until I'd taken the test. The muffled sound of cumbiaton started up from behind Rafaella's bedroom door.

"Anything new?" said Arturo.

"They did a new emotion detection thing."

"*La telecomedia*?" said Omar.

I wondered how he knew. "Yeah. It wasn't a problem. Oh, and my boss told me Simagre is thinking about dropping Cantabrian. They're not making any progress on the leak."

Omar smirked. He was a twenty-year-old Syrian Mexican who'd got his start as a programmer for a cartel-owned darknet start-up in Guadalajara. One of his superiors must have judged him trustworthy enough to recommend him for a position in the cartel itself, which was baffling to me, because Omar was so blatant about his eagerness to sell his talents to the highest bidder that he practically handed out auction paddles. I found it surreal that he, of all people, was now responsible for the evaluation of loyalty. Even Arturo had to take Omar's test every week before I arrived, which was topsy-turvy. You could argue that loyalty was not exactly personified in Arturo, whose job, after all, involved stealing from his old employer on behalf of his new one; he had worked in pipeline security for Pemex before he brought his expertise to the Nuevos Zetas. But where Omar treated the cartel like it was just another tech internship he could drop at any time, Arturo treated the cartel as if it was just another state-run company with a pension plan. They were both, in their own ways, deluding themselves. They were both, in their own ways, pragmatists. The difference was that Arturo, the oldest of the three of us, still clung to his belief in an honest day's work for an honest day's pay, even if that honest day's pay came from men who liked to roast their enemies alive on cinder-block barbecues. In my presence he always talked as if he was getting charged by the word, although Omar had told me that he had once overheard Arturo teasing one of his four daughters over the phone and he had sounded like an entirely different person.

"You ready?" I said.

"I just installed an upgrade," said Omar. "Still a little jinky. Should be OK, though." The cartel used the same software as Cantabrian, although it was a pirated, adapted version. Omar got up off the couch so I could sit down in his place. I compliantly adjusted the camera on the coffee table to make sure it would have my whole face in shot. "Hey, you notice anything different about the *jaina* today?" Omar said, nodding towards the bedroom door.

I shrugged. Rafaella was in her final year of studying law at UNAM. The "gifts" in the shopping bags came with receipts so that she could return them for cash. And the cartel also paid the rent on the apartment. Apart from that, I didn't know the contractual details. I only knew that when Omar and Arturo left, and I had to stay in the apartment for another few hours to keep up appearances, she let me go to bed with her, without enthusiasm on her part but also without open resentment. This had been going on for three months, and presumably it was worth her while. "The way it works is, the pussy's part of your fee," Omar had once told me. "So if you don't hit that shit every week, it's like you're leaving money on the table." With that remark, he had succeeded in making every sexual encounter I had with Rafaella feel even more poisonous.

Omar slapped the knuckles of his left hand with the palm of his right. "Somebody put a ring on it. She's engaged. She told us."

"I didn't even know she had a boyfriend," I said. But it didn't surprise me. She was gorgeous. And although her bedroom was decorated with throw pillows and Christmas lights and those artificial flowers that changed colour through the day, she'd left the rest of the apartment almost untouched—it still looked like a generic bachelor pad you'd see pictured on a real estate website—which I took to mean she regarded her concubinage as strictly provisional. Whenever I went into her room she'd turn off all the photographs on her shelves, so we fucked beneath dozens of pale Huawei logos like sponsors' billboards.

"You didn't notice there's always Tecate Light in the refrigerator now?" Omar said. "Who the fuck drinks Tecate Light?"

"Aren't Cantabrian going to wonder why I'm still over here every week if she's engaged?"

"Are you kidding me? These chilango *putas*? If she's only spreading for two guys, that counts as she's a virgin. Anyway, none of this shit is gonna change. She isn't moving out any time soon. It's gonna be one of those old-school long engagements or whatever."

"Can we get on with the test?" I said. I waited while Omar disabled my prosthesis and initialised the emotion detection software. Then I looked into the camera as he read questions from a list. The more general ones would also have been posed to Arturo before I arrived.

"Are the numbers you've given us this week comprehensive and accurate?"

"Yes."

"Do you have any reason to think Simagre is suspicious? Or Cantabrian?"

"No."

"Are you being careful? Are you taking every precaution?"

"Yes."

"Does anybody outside this apartment know about what's happening here?"

"No."

"Are you planning to fuck with us in any way?"

"No."

Omar tapped a few more keys. Then he frowned. "OK, hold up."

I knew I couldn't have failed the test, because I was telling the truth. "What?"

A grin spread across Omar's face. "So we got two emotions showing up on your face here. Lust and sadness."

I wasn't feeling either of those. Except in the sense that I was awake. "Are you sure the upgrade worked out?"

Omar turned to Arturo. "You know what that means? Lust and sadness? That's jealousy! Like, sexual jealousy. He's bummed because the *jaina*'s getting married! He thinks he's her boyfriend for real! He's on some true love shit!" He could not have been more gleeful.

"No, Omar, I'm not."

He turned back to me. "Sorry, *guero*, the software doesn't lie. Unless you're crushing on Arturo. Or me!"

"So he wasn't lying on the questions?" said Arturo in Spanish.

"No . . ."

"Then just give him the fucking computer."

Omar put the laptop down on the coffee table, still giggling. I leaned forward and started typing in the pipeline data I'd memorised earlier in the week, about the timing and pressure of flows from the oil fields along the Gulf Coast. With the intelligence Arturo collated from his various sources, the cartel's engineers could place their taps so efficiently that by the time Cantabrian's armed response teams arrived they would already have made off with thousands of barrels of crude. Back in the days of the Pemex monopoly and the original Zetas, the cartel would simply have bribed or extorted local oil workers, but Simagre made sure that no one outside their DF headquarters had access to the operational data in advance.

It might have been easier for me to send the figures in code from an anonymous email account or a prepaid phone, without leaving the comfort of my apartment. But Omar seemed to feel that his laptop was the only electronic device in the whole of Mexico that couldn't be compromised by Cantabrian or the Federales or the Sinaloans. In the circumstances his paranoia was probably well-founded. Anyway, I had to be physically present to take the loyalty test every week, so in practice it was no further burden.

Like Rafaella, I hoped my concubinage would end one day. But no matter how protracted her engagement, it would be nothing compared to my indenture. She would celebrate many, many anniversaries before I was cut loose. After all, the Neuvas Zetas had saved my life. The etiquette may vary, but perhaps I would owe them until I died.

Back in Houston, I had been the vice president of a small petroleum distributor called Magnolia Fuels that was owned through a shell by the Sinaloa Cartel. We moved about fifty thousand barrels of stolen Mexican petroleum condensate a month. The president was a Vietnamese guy named Luong. Neither of us had any stake in the business, and as long as our revenue was stable the cartel didn't pay close attention, either to us or to the American oil market, so there was no incentive to get Magnolia the best possible deal. With that in mind, we set up a shell company of our own in Oklahoma City and began to sell that company a percentage of Magnolia's condensate every month. On my lunch break I would sit in my car with my laptop, reselling that same brothy oil at a better price, so that Luong and I could split the difference between us. Neither of us was compromised by a debt or an addiction or an affair. We just wanted the money. We knew perfectly well what happened to Mexicans who ripped off the cartels. But we were Americans, and in an office suite in downtown Houston, across the hall from a company that distributed aromatherapy pet hammocks, the Sinaloa Cartel felt very far away.

Of course, they weren't. I still don't know exactly how they discovered our scam. Luong's body has never been recovered, but his abduction was caught on security camera. I only survived because he managed to dictate a text message to me before they tossed his phone from the van. After I read it in the locker room at my gym, I told a gym attendant that a divorce server was waiting in the lobby to serve me divorce papers. He let me leave by the back exit. As I got into a cab, I knew that I would probably never see my family again. On the bright side, I also knew that I would definitely never see Lauren again.

I didn't want to rely on the authorities to protect me. I'd read too many news stories about prosecutions that had collapsed because some witness under federal protection had been hunted down, his body fished from the backyard swimming pool of a rented suburban house after a drone blew his skull open. As Obregón would later assure me, the cartels had reach. Instead, I went straight to the Nuevos Zetas. My value wasn't what I knew about the Sinaloans, which was very little. My value was that the multinational companies at the centre of the new Mexican oil boom were notorious for their reluctance to employ anybody at a management level with any local roots. I was an American who spoke oil. And I'd do anything, for anyone, to stay alive.

Three weeks later, I was in a clinic on the outskirts of Monterrey. I assumed I was just there to get a new face to match my new name and new biography. There was something strangely compelling to me about the period halfway through the facial reconstruction process when there would truly be no answer to the question of what I looked like. Nobody warned me that I was there to be made animatronic like a puppet in an old theme park.

After Omar and Arturo left, I ate one of the merguez tlayudas we'd ordered, and then knocked on Rafaella's door. Despite myself, I felt uneasy. I wasn't in love with Rafaella, and I didn't care that she was engaged. And yet living with my prosthesis had made me aware that my body was an exhibitionist, a whistle-blower, practically turning itself inside out in its eagerness to open me to the world. I didn't necessarily know everything that was going on in my own head. Was it possible that the emotion detection software had tapped me like an oil pipeline? Was it possible that, in the course of sleeping with Rafaella every Sunday night for three months, I'd developed real feelings for her, and I couldn't admit it to myself? I didn't think so, but when Rafaella turned off her music and opened the door, I still felt oddly as if I was turning up for a first date.

While she was undressing, I noticed she wasn't wearing any engagement ring, but all the same I said in Spanish, "Omar told me you're getting married. Congratulations. That's terrific." Even if my prosthesis had been turned on, I wouldn't have looked sincere when I said it, because I felt so self-conscious about the topic that I completely forgot to smile.

"Do you actually care?" she snapped. "If you don't actually care, don't say anything."

She'd never been so testy with me before. Clearly she didn't want me even to brush up against her personal life. And yet her reply was a little unreasonable. Empty pleasantries were a prosthesis installed in every single human being, even cartel psychopaths. "If you don't actually care, don't say anything" was not a plausible rule of conduct. In fact, I literally couldn't remember the last time I'd voiced an honest sentiment to anybody, so in effect she was asking me to be mute. Except that what flopped out of my mouth next really was a self-disclosure, authentic and involuntary. "Rafaella, you don't think I'm just a big fake, do you?" She gave me a look so cold it probably would have crashed Omar's software. I waved the question away, embarrassed. "Don't answer that."

After that we pretended to be lovers.

As usual, I finished by fucking her from behind in front of a mirror, fantasising that Lauren was spying on us jealously through the keyhole. These days, I tried to keep my face a little under control at the climax, so that I didn't go completely Duchenne de Boulogne. But I didn't bind it too tightly. Apart from my occasional weight training sessions, an orgasm was the only chance my face got to limber up without the prosthesis; and I had the irrational feeling that if I didn't let the expression out, it might rot inside me. If Rafaella saw it and thought it looked like a death face, I didn't care, because I was pretty sure she already held me in contempt, my unrequited, unconscious, unconfirmed sweetheart.

But this time, when I ejaculated, although I was only making the gentlest effort to control my expression, my face was as blank as the headshot on my Simagre ID.

The next morning, I sat at my desk, wondering what I'd done to myself. I knew that all prosthetics rewired the brain, even a peg leg, even a swimfin. Perhaps I'd been wearing my subcutaneous mempo for so long that the natural connection between my inner states and my outer surface had become vaguer, more diffuse, more circuitous, like some decaying telegraph network. That was the only explanation I could think of. One moment I might be clenching with ecstasy and somehow the signal wouldn't reach my face. The next moment I might have an emotion so dim and inchoate that perhaps it wasn't truly an emotion so much as a speculation or a potentiality and it would nevertheless cause a sputter of microexpressions.

I loved my prosthesis, but I loved it only because I was still an obligate social mammal. In the back of my mind, I had always assumed that at some point in my life there would come a time when I wouldn't have to perform for anybody ever again. I had an indistinct fantasy of settling into early retirement with a wife and two dogs in some fishing village down on the Nayarit coast. When I turned off the prosthesis for good, I didn't want to find that it had hobbled me irreparably.

Today, for the first time since taking the job at Simagre, I hadn't, as ladies used to say, put my face on in the morning. My prosthesis was still disabled. On my way to lunch, I stopped by Obregón's office. As always, his door was open, so I stood in the doorway. "How was your weekend?"

I knew he'd have a story about his spouse or his kids or his soccer team. I didn't pay attention to the content, only to the intonation, so that I would be able to tell when the punch line was coming up. ". . . but afterwards, I called the store, just to check, and you know what? They don't even sell apple pie filling at Bodega Aurrera!"

I laughed as hard as I could, and Obregón laughed too. But then his laughter trailed off. Granted, Obregón was no grand inquisitor, but in this instance the new expression on his face was so full of dismay that I knew the expression on my own must have been grievously miscalibrated. I hadn't been sure which way this experiment was going to go, but it had proved that, without the prosthesis, I was less capable than ever of realistic mirth.

"Sir?"

I turned. A Cantabrian security officer stood just outside the doorway. I recognised her but I didn't know her name. "Yes?"

"If you'd be kind enough to accompany me to one of the privacy booths downstairs, we'd like you to sit for a security interview."

"But it's Monday. It's the middle of the day."

"We're operating on a randomised schedule now."

I looked at Obregón, who nodded. "I had to do one first thing this morning. Pain in the butt."

I told myself that the test was no threat. All I had to do was discreetly turn my prosthesis back on before the interview started. I patted my pockets.

I'd left my phone behind at my desk to charge.

Without the phone I had no way to turn the prosthesis back on. "OK," I said, "but I just need to swing by my desk to send one email. Then I'll be with you."

"The new protocol is that you have to come directly to the privacy booth. It will only take ten minutes."

Hoping that he might intervene in some way, I shot Obregón another glance that conveyed "Surely we don't have to put up with this shit?"—or at least I meant it to convey that, but I felt like such an amateur at this point that for all I knew it conveyed tenderness or patriotism or schadenfreude or some other mood entirely. Obregón just shrugged. "I think it's so that you don't sneak a zofrosil or anything like that," he said.

I knew I couldn't protest any more without raising suspicion. In West Africa they sometimes used to hold trials where the accused were challenged to dip their hands in boiling oil. At that moment a vat of Campeche crude was almost more appealing than a camera. At least it was a test I could conceivably pass. "Fine," I said to the security officer, hoping she couldn't already see my fear. "Lead the way." Somewhere inside a Cantabrian server the judges were waiting to score my gymnastics of the soul.

"I need to tell you guys something about what happened at work this week," I said.

"No, guero, you need to tell us something about what happened right here," said Omar.

What I had been about to explain was that I had failed the pop quiz. Sitting there in the privacy booth, trying to remember what normal people looked like when they gave truthful answers to simple questions, it was as if I had no instincts or defaults any more, just a control panel inside me the size of a recording studio's mixing desk. My face felt more cybernetic than it ever had with the prosthesis turned on. The more I thought about it, the worse it got. By the end my best attempt at a relaxed expression probably looked like someone having a stroke in a wind tunnel. I imagined the video going viral on the Cantabrian intranet, "the worst liar we've ever tested!" Afterwards, I still went out to get a torta, but I was too shaken to eat, and I almost didn't go back to the office. I was ready to book it out of Mexico City just like I'd booked it out of Houston. When I asked the Nuevos Zetas for help, I wouldn't have to admit to them that it was my own fault I'd failed the test because I'd left my prosthesis off.

I did go back to the office, though, because I knew Cantabrian wouldn't act on their suspicions until they'd carried out an investigation. When they called me in for a second interview, I decided, that was when I would vanish. Until then, I wouldn't do anything irrevocable. So for the rest of the week I walked around feeling like a fugitive in the middle of a police station.

Then Friday came, and still nothing had happened. I couldn't understand it, and I was hoping Omar might have some kind of answer.

But then Arturo pointed a gun at me, a silver semi-automatic so big it looked as if you could shout down the barrel and it would echo back at you.

I hadn't even realised he carried one. "Hey, what the fuck is this?" I said.

"The couch," Arturo ordered. I sat down.

"That test last week," Omar said, "when the software was saying lust and sadness, and we thought it was because you was getting mushy about *la jaina*— I took a closer look. Wanted to see how the upgrade was working out. You know what? A lot of the microexpressions in the log, they only lasted for a hundredth of a second or less. You got your basic vanilla face with your basic vanilla muscles, it can't do that. Can't contract that fast. A thirtieth of a second is the fastest. Maybe a fiftieth."

"So?"

"That means you had the prosthesis turned on during the test. The polymers. That's the only way you could be flashing microexpressions so quick."

"You always turn it off before I start," I said.

"Yeah. That's what I thought. But you must have modified it so it looks like it's off but it stays on. And why the fuck would you do that unless you're trying to play us on the test?"

"Omar, I haven't modified anything. I wouldn't even know how."

"Maybe not. But the Sinaloans, they got a few guys."

By now Arturo had circled around so that he was between me and the front door of the apartment, although it wasn't as if I was going to try anything when he still had the gun on me. "Why would I set my prosthesis to show lust and sadness? Just give me the test again now. Ask me about all this stuff on the camera once you've satisfied yourself one hundred percent that my prosthesis is off."

"I can't do that if you've modified it."

"We could just cut it out of him," said Arturo in Spanish.

At that moment I thought I could feel the prosthesis inside my face, every polymer unit like a twist of barbed wire. "It must be a problem with the software," I stammered. "The upgrade."

"The upgrade is fine," said Omar.

"Maybe you've been hacked."

Omar sneered. "Are you fucking kidding me?" He nodded at his laptop. "Nobody hacks that. I'm not a retard. That shit is tighter than Korean pussy. No inputs means no vulnerabilities. Every fucking byte of data on that machine, I pop the trunk like Border Control. Every fucking byte except . . ." He blinked, and was silent for a little while. "No way," he murmured. "No way you could fit a code injection into . . ." Then he sat down at his laptop and started typing. "*Hijos de puta*," he kept saying, shaking his head. "*Hijos de puta*."

"What is it?

"I think they used your face."

"My face?"

"Ever heard of a code injection? You hide executable code inside raw data. The system runs the code because it doesn't know any better. That's what those micro-expressions were. They got control of your prosthesis. Then they used it to transmit a code injection. They hacked into my system with your face."

My hand went up to my cheek. "Who? The Sinaloans?"

"Or Cantabrian."

So I wasn't in control of my own signalling device. But then I never really had been. "You think they've been doing this every week?"

"Every time I upgrade the software, had to guess."

"But why would they need to hack your loyalty tests?"

He was still typing. "Help somebody pass them who shouldn't be passing them."

"But I pass those tests because I'm telling the truth. I don't need any help."

"Not you. More likely to be—" Then Omar's eyes widened. "*Detenerlo!*" he yelped.

But Arturo was already gone.

Omar bounded to the door, almost knocking me down as he pushed past. I looked out into the corridor. Arturo had disappeared around a corner, towards the elevators. Omar pulled a gun of his own from his waistband, but it was only a tiddly printed model as opposed to Arturo's fat semi-auto, and for a moment he bounced from foot to foot as if he couldn't decide whether to risk giving chase. Then he snarled in frustration and came back inside. "OK, *pendejo*," he said, waving the gun at me. "On the couch again."

As I sat back down, I recalled what Obregón had confided to us in the bar about Cantabrian's troubles. He probably had no idea that it was calculated misinformation. If Cantabrian were using me as a Trojan horse to help Arturo infiltrate the Nuevos Zetas, that would explain why there hadn't been consequences for my humiliation in the privacy booth: when the software recommended that I should be investigated further, it would have been overruled. And if my prosthesis hadn't actually switched off when Omar thought he was switching it off last Sunday, that would also explain why I hadn't shown my death face to Rafaella afterwards. Omar dialled somebody on his phone and had a short conversation so dense with cartel slang I could barely follow, except that he asked for a drone to be sent up over Escandón to look for Arturo. Then he pounded on Rafaella's bedroom door. "Whore, come out here and help me tie up your client!" he shouted, still in Spanish. "It's bondage time!"

"Hey! Why? Come on," I said, "Arturo's the one working for Cantabrian!"

"For all I know it's the both of you. I'm taking you to El Taquero. He can decide. Maybe we really will cut that thing out of your face. It's cartel property, *pendejo*, you should remember that." Rafaella came out of her room. "I need cable or tape or something," Omar said to her.

"Can you talk some sense into this guy?" I said. "Please."

"Sorry," she mouthed.

"But Rafaella . . . I love you." I said it because I knew it wasn't true, and because at this point it didn't seem to matter much what I said.

She looked down at me with eyes as imperturbable, as incontrovertible, as Cantabrian's cameras. Then she threw her head back and laughed harder than I had ever seen her laugh, a hilarity so luxuriant no prosthesis could have faked it.

Within a few minutes, Omar and I were on the way down in the elevator. My wrists were taped behind my back. "Omar, I'm not working for anybody except you and Arturo. I didn't sell you out. I didn't fuck up. I did everything you said. This shouldn't be happening." He didn't respond. "Who's El Taquero?" I asked.

"He's not a guy who takes chances," Omar said. "And while we're on the fucking subject. You try and run? Those drones are looking for Arturo but they have your face too. Remember that. I optimised them myself. They got personalities now. They're like those dogs they train to catch rats."

As we crossed the lobby I looked around for the doorman, but I couldn't see him, and anyway I knew he wouldn't have been stupid enough to get involved. We emerged into the warm evening and I immediately got a couple of lungfuls of truck exhaust. The Viaducto Miguel Alemán had four lanes that connected to the surface roads; between them, another six lanes of faster traffic that dipped beneath the overpasses; and between those, from what I remembered, a grassy median, although I couldn't see that over the concrete barrier. Around 8:30 on Sunday night, the roads weren't busy. Half a mile to the south, the World Trade Center rose into the smog, an enormous blue jerrycan with a turret for a cap. Omar had ordered a car, which would meet us around the corner. The gun was still pointed at me but most of his attention was on his phone. I thought about the Virgin Mary wrapped up like my wrists. I thought about a taquero at a market carving meat off a spit. I ran into the road.

By the time Omar took his first shot, I had already crossed two lanes and hurled myself over the barrier.

My hope was that Cantabrian might have eyes on the apartment building, especially if Arturo had made some sort of distress call. My hope was that they might prefer me to survive just in case I could tell them anything about the cartel that they didn't already know. If I could get away from Omar, there was a possibility of rescue. A remote possibility, but it was still better than shuffling to my doom with Omar's boss.

The drop to the freeway was farther than I'd estimated, and something crunched in my shoulder when I hit the ground. I heard a horn, very close. Blindly, I rolled sideways, and the car missed me by an inch or so. To get to my feet with my wrists still bound, I first had to jerk myself into a kneeling position, and I was only just upright when another car swerved out of its lane to avoid the vagrant in the road. I heard two more shots, and I started running towards the oncoming traffic, because at least that way I could see what was about to kill me.

I'd miscalculated my escape. There was indeed a median, a covered sewer, but its sheer sides were too tall for me to climb without the use of my hands. And there was no safe margin between the freeway and the barriers on either side. I was trapped in the concrete pipeline, and I had to keep moving in case Omar caught up.

I heard a distant buzzing in the sky.

If the drone recognised my face, it would end me. I wanted to crouch down and hide myself against the barrier. But if I did, it wouldn't be long before I was clipped by a fender, spun into the middle of the lane, flattened like a stray dog. I decided that, of all the deaths available, of all the missiles the night was throwing at me, the drone would probably be the most painless. So I kept running.

Then my face exploded.

Normally, when I was using the prosthesis, the contractions and expansions of the polymer units were too tiny to be perceptible. This time, it was as if 43 steel traps had sprung inside my face, yanking skin and wrenching cartilage. The pain exceeded any human scale, and I almost keeled over on the spot. My eyes and nose and mouth were full of blood, and I was gagging so hard I couldn't scream.

Somehow, though, in whatever part of my brain was most distant from my facial nerve, I must still have been capable of thought. Because I understood why Cantabrian had done it. But I didn't believe it would work. Facial recognition algorithms looked at the bone structure underneath. You couldn't obscure or deform that. No matter what you did with your features, you were still you.

The buzzing got louder. Now I could make out the drone, a black quadcopter small enough to fit in a briefcase, making those insectile shrugs and dodges that seem random and purposeful at the same time, the mark of a software pilot. I didn't know whether it was the breed that would shoot me in the heart with a hollow-point or the breed that would simply land on my shoulder and explode. The drone kept closing the distance, and so did I, until I could feel its gaze on me, its immaculate appraisal, like the cameras in the privacy booth, or the beauty up on the seventh floor.

The drone swooped past.

It had made its judgement. I wasn't me.

I didn't know what the prosthesis had done to my face, but it must have been avant-garde. There wasn't time for relief, because an SUV was coming at me around the bend. I tripped sideways, saving myself so narrowly that its right-hand wing mirror swatted my elbow. As it passed, I caught a glimpse of the driver, a woman aghast, and I thought of how I must have looked to her, this ghoul with a veil of blood, its features jumbled into a word without meaning, not true, not false, just flesh; and for the first time I realised what a terrible burden it had been to have a face, and how truly free I was without one.

The Daughters of John Demetrius

JOE PITKIN

Joe Pitkin has lived, taught, and studied in England, Hungary, Mexico, and, most recently, at Clark College in Vancouver, Washington. His fiction has appeared in Analog, PodCastle, Drabblecast, and elsewhere. He has done biological fieldwork on the slopes of Mount St. Helens, and he lives in Portland, Oregon, with his wife and daughters. You can follow his work at his blog, The Subway Test at thesubwaytest.wordpress.com.

In the suspenseful story that follows, he sweeps us along with a man with godlike abilities who's on the hunt for children who are not quite what they seem—hoping to reach them before the monster who's chasing them all catches up with them and destroys them. . . .

Mendel had run the whole day in his graceful, tireless way, southerly down the road that some called Old Mexico 45 and the locals called *El Camino de San Juan Demetrio*. There had been little water all day, just a single dusty rivulet past noon where he had drunk and where he had tried without much success to wash the crusted blood out of his tunic. Mendel was dark enough that it would do him no harm to go naked in this sun, and he even considered such a possibility, but it would have scandalized the local *vulgaris* more for him to have walked naked into a village than for him to have appeared in a bloodstained tunic.

Mendel came upon such a village at the end of the day, only an hour's run over mesas from the main road, a rammed earth wall guarding an inner circle of adobes and ancient shipping containers. The sign hung above the arch of the outer wall said *Pozos Desecantes/Dessicant Wells*. It had the sloppy look of an old gringo settlement, though Mendel could not be sure on this mesa an hour from the far-off stretch of the road that the gods hardly ever travelled.

He walked through the open gate unchallenged except by a troop of scrawny clucking hens. Most of the central square was taken up by a dusty yard where crust-skinned children in homespun shirts and loincloths carried out a listless game of Chihuahan-rules football. They seemed not to notice him. Beyond, the adults congregated around a cluster of worn stone troughs, beating the dirt out of their sullen piles of laundry.

Mendel walked to the edge of the game and watched the children. In those moments before anyone in the village noticed him, his eye fell on one different from the rest, perhaps eight years old, her dark skin pristine as the flesh of an avocado. No pellagra with this one. He would have run all the way to Oaxaca to find another like her.

They noticed him then. The children went silent and marveled. Then one mother less exhausted or more anxious than the rest turned to regard the newly quiet children, and she saw divine Mendel in his sweat-glistened luminescent beauty. He was so beautiful, or they were all so bone-weary, that no one screamed at this blood-stained stranger who had walked unopposed into the heart of the lost little village.

Mendel knew that he must be the one to speak first. He asked in Spanglish in his clear high voice whether the villagers spoke Spanglish or Spanish or English. One of the adults, perhaps the headwoman, said they spoke all three. She answered in English as they nearly always did, always assuming that the gods spoke English, and always following the ancient Mexican law of hospitality that demanded the visitor be made most comfortable. If these people were gringos, they had at least learned this much from the land that had taken them in.

"I am following the road of John Demetrius," Mendel said to them, "and I would be grateful if I could spend the night here." This was not, in fact, so different from Mendel's plans, but regardless of his plans, this was what he always said when he travelled through this part of the world.

The headwoman bowed and spread her arms wide in the heartbreaking theatrical way they always did, as though to offer Mendel their whole forsaken village. Then she began ordering the younger adults in Spanglish to begin preparing a place for him; with one of these, a gaunt hardscrabble woman of about thirty, or maybe fifty, the headwoman exchanged some brief taut words that even Mendel could not quite hear.

They had never heard of him, he was sure. They had never spoken to travelers from another village where he had wandered. If they had, they would have learned to boil their corn in ashes and these children would not be half-dead from niacin deficiency. As they shuffled about to find a shipping container for him to sleep in and to bring him an ancient cut soda bottle full of rusty water, Mendel looked around again for the beautiful green-skinned girl. But she had disappeared. Another girl, smaller and wretched, stood before him fearlessly, staring at him relentlessly before Mendel noticed her.

Mendel knelt down to look her in the eye. "Y tú? Cómo te llamas?" he asked in a conspiratorial tone, as though she would be giving away a secret to tell him her name.

The girl stared at him as though mute. But the gods are imperturbable and Mendel only looked back at her with the serenity of someone beyond hunger or thirst. They stared at one another a minute or more before the gravelly hen's voice of an old woman shouted in their direction: "Floribunda! Inútil! Trae aca your scrawny ass!" The girl spun around as though the words were a leash the woman had jerked; the girl ran in a dusty pad-footed way towards the squalling voice.

The villagers put Mendel up in a clean-swept, well-ordered shipping container, painted turquoise and salmon and bearing the name "Coper" in tawdry letters of rhinestone appliqué. The woman who opened the house to him said nothing beyond "here you have your pobre casa," but whether her silence was resentful or the reaction of a broken woman cowed by the presence of a god, Mendel couldn't immediately tell. The four children like shriveled rag dolls seemed cowed by him. He decided in that moment that he would give the knowledge of preparing the corn to this family only, as payment for their putting him up for the night. Señora Coper would be one of the most important people in the village, if not the headwoman, for passing along the secret. And she would pass it along, because he would warn her that he would return in wrath and vengeance if she didn't.

She served him cornbread on a plastic bucket lid, and he weighed the silence carefully before he asked them to what family the green-skinned girl belonged.

"She is Lupe Hansen's daughter," the woman replied with a wary eye on him every moment, as though she knew why he was asking, though of course she didn't.

"You know she is a child of San Juan Demetrio?" he said.

"We are all children of San Juan."

At this, Mendel thought it wise to say only "Indeed, así es."

None of the children had taken their eyes off of him. The smallest, with eyes like shining black olives, was the first who dared to speak. "Pero por why are you bloody?"

"César!" the woman hissed, scandalized. But Mendel held up his hand to the woman to gesture that he was not offended.

"I was in a fight."

"Did you die?"

"No—if I had died I would not be sitting with you here."

"Were you hurt?" asked the oldest.

"A little. But my body se compone muy quickamente."

"Who did you fight?"

"An evil god," Mendel answered. "A god who didn't like people."

The answer seemed to awe the children. But the woman, who seemed too mortified to notice the children's reaction, added for good measure: "Es un god muy malo, who will take you away if you don't stop asking questions."

The next morning all seventeen children in the village had questions about the evil god. Mendel regretted a little his explanation of the night before, though of course someone was bound to have asked him about the blood stains and, as was typical of Mendel, he had spent the previous day telling himself that he would need a good story instead of actually coming up with a good story. He told them that the god he had bloodied had hated the natural people, had wanted all of the natural people to take on the bodies of demons and to fill their minds with the nonsense of dreams. The children seemed to regard this explanation quietly and utterly without skepticism, which suggested all the more to Mendel that what he said was strictly true. Yet on account of their pellagra they showed none of the awe that children of the other villages had; they sat stooped and downcast like feverish hallucinators, their crusted hands held out before them like barnacled flippers.

The flawless green girl stepped up to the circle of children as artlessly as a little deer. Studiously Mendel continued his tale: he told how the evil god had stolen many children for his terrible purposes (pure fabrication, but Mendel could not resist their attention, even limp as it was). But Mendel loved the natural people so much that he risked himself to save them. The green daughter of Lupe Hansen watched him and he observed her without ever looking directly at her; he felt her watchful presence as though soon she would eat from his outstretched hand.

But the children were called to school by a long cracked note from an old trumpet, and Mendel watched them all, from the green girl to the most encrusted lad, retreat to a cluster of four shipping containers at the edge of the houses, like a square bounded by the larger circle of the village structures. The one who blew the trumpet was a woman somewhat less slack than the rest, without pellagra, with a faint tint to her skin that announced to Mendel that she was Lupe Hansen.

Mendel rose from the ground where he had sat cross-legged, and he noticed only then that not all of the children had quite retreated. The other girl, the one called Floribunda, stared at him still. He found her look a little hostile. Or perhaps terrified. But just when Mendel decided that it must be terror that made her look at him so, she held out to him a tiny green wisp of locoweed, which he took from her before she ran after the other children to the school.

While he waited Mendel busied himself with helping around the village. The village technical council, three craggy-faced men, came to him like a humiliated embassy offering surrender. "Our molino runs poorly; we believe there is a short in the photovoltaic system." The most venerable of them said.

"Perhaps the film needs cleaning," Mendel answered. "The village is very dusty."

"Perhaps," the man said with pained courtesy. "But we have tried to keep the films clean."

The films were in fact scrupulously clean. The village technical council had guessed correctly about the short, which Mendel found buried in the adobe wall where the old man had thought it might be. He peeled the wire out like an intransigent root from barren earth, and he wondered why the old men had not trusted themselves enough to find the short themselves with their antique voltmeter.

Mendel visited Lupe Hansen at the school after the children had cleared out to play Chihuahuan-rules football. "Do you know who I am?" Mendel asked her.

She did not look up from stacking the children's tablets. "You are a god."

"But do you know who I am?"

She stopped to look at him. "No. I know only that you are a god."

Mendel approached from another tack. "Do you know that your daughter is hija de San Juan Demetrio?"

"Sí. Así es."

"You are also one."

"Sí. Así es."

"Why did you never go to Phoenix?"

"This is my village."

"Have you never thought to send your daughter there?"

The woman said nothing. When she lifted the stack of tablets to put them away, Mendel saw a tension in her shoulders, what he took to be stubbornness, though he knew he was not so godlike as to be above projection.

"Your daughter could be schooled in ways that you know you cannot school her here," Mendel continued. "She could come back to Dessicant Wells as a god, and yet as one of you as well."

Lupe Hansen began scrubbing down the students' tables with a dusty rag.

"Your students could use those tablets to get to the real Internet, if you had a guide," he said, pointing at the stack of tablets as though the woman was also looking at them, and not, intently, at the dusty tabletops. "It is the ones like your daughter that will bring reunification."

Lupe Hansen's mouth was set as she scrubbed at the tables.

"What is your daughter's name?"

"Chloe."

"Chloe would be a god," he said, reverently as an evangelical missionary.

Lupe Hansen said nothing but looked directly at him with a pain that seemed both powerless and impervious to reason.

It offended his sense of dignity to wheedle for the girl. For every parent that handed over a child to him without flinching, seeing the benefit of entrusting a child to the care of the gods, there was another like Lupe Hansen, for whom there was no benefit Chloe might receive that would justify separating her from her mother.

He stared back at her, and unlike so many natural people Lupe Hansen was not awed into looking away. But of course, she was no natural person, either—otherwise, why would Mendel be bargaining with her over her daughter?

It occurred to him, with some relief, that he had not told Señora Coper the secret of corn nixtamalization. "If I could cure everyone in the village of their sickness, would you let Chloe come to school with me? Please consider it." And with that he walked out of the little school and past the water troughs and the solar ovens, where he said to the headwoman that he would return the next morning to Dessicant Wells.

He ran out into the desert a safe distance, back towards Old Mexico 45 where no one would have been shocked to find him. Safety was relative, of course: Perses had had friends, shedim and lilim who certainly would know of his death by now. And when their suspicions fell on Mendel, Old Mexico 45 was one of the places Perses' friends would think to look for him.

But he was safe at least from the villagers' attentions for a moment. He closed his eyes and linked up with the satellite, got lost a few hours in his mails—mostly advertisements clouding up his neurons. He tried to get in touch with Handy, which had been his purpose linking up in the first place: did he have room for a little green girl, unusually quiet and, so far as Mendel could tell, totally untrained? Mendel found it half charming and half infuriating that Handy, who could stay linked up the livelong day if he wished it, had an old-fashioned autoresponder on his account like some telephonical answering machine from another age.

Mendel took a risk and accessed one of the PayPal accounts he had squirreled away. None of his acquaintances knew about the account, and he doubted any of Perses' cronies had tried hacking into Mendel's Internet history yet. Just over three hundred new dollars sat there beneath anybody's notice. Lying on the baking hardpan in the flimsy shadow of the creosote he closed his eyes and moved, quickly and quietly, a hundred dollars to a terminal in Delicias. Then he logged off and delinked, and in the heat of the day ran two hours southeast down Old Mexico 45.

In Delicias, at the *Hotel Vieja Delicias*, Mendel checked in as Conrado Hermés, paid with the N$61 from the terminal. Nobody asked him about the bloodstains. Delicias was one of those towns where the naturals had some exposure to the divines and treated them with deference but not awe. The hotel clerk, whose nametag said "César," was young enough and beautiful enough that he might have passed for a god, but Mendel could tell by his genetic summary—or, more properly, his lack of a summary—that he was as natural as Floribunda and would be handsome a few years more at most. With the rest of the hundred new dollars he ordered a fresh tunic, six *tacos de suadero*, and three liters of *Ambrosia* beer, and he slept that night in a bed that bore some resemblance to the bed of a god.

On waking he felt again the perfect confidence that he would walk out of Dessicant Wells with the child of Lupe Hansen. The night's sleep, the revitalizing *Ambrosias*, the brilliant white tunic all convinced him that success was a foregone conclusion.

Then, walking out of the *Hotel Vieja Delicias*, he saw a lilith snooping about as she came up the road, peering into windows, swiveling her half-snake head to and fro like a flashlight. Mendel had worried about the blood on the old tunic. It wouldn't have hurt him to have worried about it a little more. But he had thought it unlikely for one like Perses to carry radio tags in his blood like a child or a criminal. Mendel's main worry had been that the bloodstains would frighten the naturals.

The lilith was a good way up the street, moving past a trio of *vulgaris* hauling an enormous handcart towards some market or warehouse. Mendel was the only other divine on the road; she would spot him for sure if he began to run. To his left a laundromat operated out of a family's garage. He turned into it as though that had been his errand all along.

A broad-faced natural with a thick braid of hair in the ancient style looked up at him from the pile of laundry her neighbors had left for her. Mendel wondered for half a second whether the old bloodstained tunic was in the pile, sent over by the hotel to be washed instead of incinerated as Mendel had demanded. He raised the back of his hand to her like a strange greeting; his fingernail, tapered and sculpted, began to grow out of his index finger into thirty fatal centimeters of talon.

"Is there a bloody tunic in your laundry?" he asked in Spanish.

"No, lord," she answered, emotionless.

He sheathed the claw back into his hand. "Is there a back door?"

"It leads to our house, lord."

He asked if he could get to the roof by that way. He could. For a short, waddling woman, she moved in a hurry, and silently, and he followed her into a dusty cinderblock courtyard with a legion of geraniums growing in old rusted cans. The lip of the roof hung three meters or so above the ground; Mendel leapt, caught the lip, and vaulted himself up. He looked back at her only a moment to say in his antique Spanish: "From this day the gods bless your house." Then, with the same finger that a moment before had been a blade of fingernail, he exhorted her to be silent. He stayed not a moment to see her bowing deferentially, but like a loon lifting off from the water he glided across the roof and leapt into the street behind, and then he ran faster than any lilith deep into the mirages of the desert.

He took a roundabout way back to Dessicant Wells, running far to the west into the creosote and circling back southeast. It was nearly noon when he arrived, and a call went up when he came into sight of them. By the time he walked into the central courtyard they were arrayed in front of him in all their scabby glory like a choir. In the center of the formation, looking more desolate even than the day before, Lupe Hansen stood with her arms draped protectively over her daughter before her. Yet at the girl's feet was a backpack, and she stood dressed and washed and combed like a lamb for sacrifice.

The headwoman was the first to speak: "Will you, lord, cure us of our sickness?"

He showed them the trick with the water and ashes that would soften the corn kernels, that trick which even the poorest village in Mexico would have known in the last age, that trick which in fact had been discovered not far from Dessicant Wells nearly four thousand years before. As far as the villagers were concerned, Chloe Hansen was a fair trade for such knowledge.

During the celebratory dinner the little girl looked at him balefully and silently. If she had cried on learning that she would go with him, or if she was to cry about it later, she wasn't crying now. Of course, Mendel had taken the other children whether they had cried or not. But it was always easier for him if they didn't cry.

The sun was low before they were ready to set out. The headwoman and others clamored for him to stay one more night, to leave in the morning—give the girl one more night with her mother. But the girl would be safe at night, Mendel assured them, and no marauder on the road would be so foolish that he would try to steal a child from a god.

They relented at last, and as the sun was setting he hoisted the little girl with her backpack full of undoubtedly useless things. He left at a loping, gliding pace, not wanting to jar the poor child more than necessary as she wept silently on his shoulder.

Or not so silently. Before he had run a kilometer he heard the child's racking breathless sobs. Only, they came not from the girl on his shoulder: he looked back to see another child who had run after them, who had covered only half the distance and now stood alone on the empty mesa in the gathering night. The twilight had darkened so that he had to double back to see who was there. In her threadbare loincloth and dusty as an unearthed root, Floribunda stood wheezing and snot-nosed and miserable.

"You have to go back to your parents," he said to her. "I can't take you with me."

"No tengo parents," she gasped. "I am hija de San Juan Demetrio."

"Who cares for you in the village? They are worried for you right now."

"I am hija de San Juan Demetrio."

The gesture he made, running a hand through his hair while he looked down at the problem she represented, was the gesture any god, or any natural, might make in answer to a stymie. He might scoop her up and carry her back like a sack of meal, if he could put up with the indignity of returning, of appearing before the *vulgaris* like one of them, like some harried uncle with a kicking child under his arm. Or he could leave her. She might return to the village on her own.

He considered the problem longer than he intended to, staring a full minute at the impediment before him. Floribunda looked neither at him nor at Chloe but rather kept her eye on the purple and green horizon with a grim intensity, like the captain of a little ship in the open sea.

Then he saw another shape far off in the failing light. But moving quickly: low to the ground on four feet, head thrust forward like a jackal, limbs sweeping along double-jointed and implacable it came towards them. It was the lilith.

He scooped up the other girl and ran. He moved like a gazelle even with the two under his arms, though he ran with an effort that was unfamiliar to him. He ran towards the line of mountains far in the west, a kilometer, two kilometers, three. But soon enough he could hear the lilith scrambling not far behind him over the hardpan, tearing the creosote from its roots when she juked to match his turns and scrambles.

Both girls had fallen silent. With an instinct that had been honed in some ancestral mammal from a pre-human epoch, they had drawn in their limbs to make of themselves tight bundles which Mendel grasped, one under each arm, like two lean footballs. But he knew after a few minutes that the lilith was outrunning him, that any moment he would feel the shock of her jaws around his Achilles tendon and he would go down.

He cast the girls to either side, into the creosote and tamarisk. They flew from his arms silently, but before they crashed into the bush Mendel had spun about with the blade of his finger spiking like a chitinous rapier.

But she was faster than Perses had been, and she had known what to expect from Mendel. The lilith cast herself wide of his arm, wary as a dog, and from her fangy mouth she spit at him, something hot and corrosive which seared his arm and shoulder.

She had scrambled past him and turned to face him again, just out of reach of his talon, and Mendel saw that when she spit at him her mouth contorted like one about to vomit, and the acid shot from beneath her tongue in two streams. He dodged and, spinning like a dancer, he leapt at her, throwing his arm wide to slash. But she too was fast, and she leapt back beyond his reach, and once more he felt the searing stream cross against the skin of his midriff.

The pain blinded him, or would have. But he had been blessed with a divine measure of endorphins in times of agony. In that timelessness brought on by death whispering in his ear, Mendel considered what he might do differently to get at the body of this spidery woman, her elbows and knees all angles as quick as Mendel Hodios could manage, almost as quick as Mendel even at his strongest. It was he who dodged and leapt back now, keeping always her stream of venom from landing on his flesh.

He did not know this lilith. Her hands and feet looked slender, not for crushing, though he had been fooled by slim hands before: he had seen more elfin hands than hers choke the life out of a full-grown *vulgaris*. Perhaps it was her jaw that would crush him, or her sinewy legs, when the venom finally wore him down. Her tactic would be the last thing he discovered, or he would never discover it at all.

He crouched to face her, his sword held above him like a scorpion's sting. She crept sidewise before him on the tips of her fingers and toes—he concluded that yes, her fingers were surely strong enough to break him if she should lay a hand on him.

A rock struck her head from behind, bounced away. Close behind the lilith he saw Floribunda, recovering her balance; the rock she had heaved had been the size of a loaf of bread. But the lilith's head twitched, no more than that, no more than a flinch at the annoyance of being struck by a rock that would have crushed a natural's skull.

Mendel knew then that he was likely to die. The two girls would, too, if the lilith had it in her head to bring harm to them. The lilith reared onto her legs a moment, her mouth widened in the now-familiar grave contraction.

Mendel took his fatal chance and did not dodge. A stream of the venom splashed his chest and runnelled down his breastbone as he leapt at her. But, as he had hoped, aiming her venom took some concentration: one thing she had not expected was that an enemy might leap to embrace her just as she vomited her poison. He too was stronger than he looked: she fell back in his arms, just as the spike of his finger slid into her side, under the ribs.

He felt himself weakening, his body straining to respond to the acid devouring his skin, the systems going into shock, his heart chattering, his thoughts scrambling in the fog. Yet he retained the presence of mind to know that the lilith had gone weaker still: he could see the tip of his fingerblade sprouting from the other side of her body, the blood draining from her in great sheens down her legs. Her face showed neither panic nor suffering but rather an impregnable calm.

And then, he could hold her up no longer and she fell back, and he also, a moment later. The sky was purple above him. He heard a rushing sound which might have been the wind, or perhaps a sound coming from within him. The pain hammered.

A minute later, or perhaps five, perhaps after he was already dead, he heard the two girls breathing above him. He heard the zipper of the little green girl's pack. Then a trickle of water into his mouth, ambrosia.

"Pour the water over my skin," he said. He was overcome with gratitude that Lupe Hansen had sent her daughter with a three liter bottle in her backpack. The water ran cold and excruciating over his pulsing, blistered flesh.

The two girls crouched in front of him as he lay on his back. They watched silently like two creatures inured to suffering, or so acquainted with it that they did not consider his agony worthy of comment.

He lay there through the night, his skin howling in the cool of the breeze. When the sky had brightened enough that he could make out their features, the girls still watched him, sleeplessly, the way old women had tended fires for a million years. He could feel the flood of macrophages and growth hormones already released into his tissues; by dawn he was able to hoist the three liter bottle himself, to drain the last milliliters of water into his mouth.

If he could run unburdened, Handy's redoubt lay six hours to the west. As it was, he might walk there with the girls in three days if water could be found. He had no compunction now about linking with the satellite—the girls watched him and noticed nothing more than that he closed his eyes for a time. If the maps were accurate, a creek ran sixteen kilometers to the west, near the foothills of the Sierra Madre.

He logged off, opened his eyes as though he had been sleeping for a few minutes, smiled at the two girls who looked at him like two inscrutable frogs. He pushed himself to his feet and observed the pounding of his head as his humors balanced. Behind the girls the lilith's corpse lay staring at the Sierra Madre.

He crouched over her body and drank what blood he could from the wound. There was not much left. If her blood carried radio tags, perhaps no one would catch up with him until he was safe at Handy's.

"Now you have to walk with me a long way," Mendel told the girls, extending a hand to each of them. Floribunda took his right hand, caked with the lilith's blood. The three of them walked in the direction of the pass, and water.

silence Like Diamonds

JOHN BARNES

John Barnes has commercially published twenty-eight volumes of fiction, probably twenty-nine by the time you read this, including science fiction, men's action adventure, two collaborations with astronaut Buzz Aldrin, a collection of short stories and essays, one fantasy, and one mainstream novel. He has done a rather large number of occasionally peculiar things for money, mainly in business consulting, academic teaching, and show business, fields which overlap more than you'd think. Since 2001, he has lived in Denver, Colorado, where he has a wonderful girlfriend, an average income, and a bad attitude, which he feels is actually the best permutation.

In the fast-paced tale that follows, a high-tech troubleshooter in an intensively wired and hooked-up future learns that it can be dangerous when the troubles start shooting back. . . .

The override siren made me spill a lovely, just-drinking-temperature cup of chamomile-peppermint. Amaryllis, Daisy and Mrs. Greypaws all bolted from the balcony and under the bed, wailing.

My sister Yazzy paid me extra to have that super-powered, never-off phone bell always hanging over my silence. It was worth it except when it went off. I rubbed the tea splashes on my old yoga pants, kicked my slippers off at the French doors and padded inside barefoot. "House, main parlor."

The siren doused into muffled plaintive mewing. Paintings, bulletin boards and windows vanished from the interior wall. I dragged my chair over to face it, about a meter away.

The wall became apparently transparent, seeming to join my morning parlor to my sister's late afternoon office. She had that smirk, having caught me before I dressed for the day. "Hi, Yip. How's Arcata?"

"Same as always. How's Prague?"

"Different from Arcata. I talked to the folks on Thursday. They're still okay?"

"You know, the usual. Mama robbed a bank; Táta drove the getaway car."

She stuck her tongue out at me, just like when we were kids. "All right, and how're things on the Markus front?"

"I'm sorry I ever told you about that. I don't know if I should even try to get his interest. What if he finds out there's hereditary yenta-ism in my family?"

Yazzy sighed. "I guess you just want to get right to business, huh?"

"Well, I do have my itsy-bitsy pottering pleasures to bury myself in."

"I'm sorry I ever said *that*. Does that make us even?"

"What's the gig, sis? Who's the client and what's the matter?"

"It's NameItCorp. I guess you know who they are."

I held a thumb high. "Hey, good going." I was so impressed I didn't care if she saw. NameItCorp was as ubiquitous nowadays as Google had once been. Type or speak "NItCO" or "NameItCorp" while connected to the Net, add the name of any problem and AI and human operators would rush you a price and a time estimate, or SORRY, NOT POSSIBLE WITH PRESENT TECH, or SORRY, ILLEGAL. "What do they need us for?"

Yazzy shrugged. "They need you. And they're smart enough to know it. There are maybe 200 scheme architecture analysts worldwide, and last time Dusan ran 1,000 iterations of an open-ended self-defining search, 1,000 out of 1,000 times, you turned up in the top three."

"He's biased. He's your husband—"

"He's the Zalodny in Zalodny Integrated Security, Yip. When he's analyzing on the marketing and business side, his feelings get into it about as much as yours do when you're tracing the money or mine do reading code. You're our single most salable asset, which is why we do pretty much any ridiculous thing you ask so that we can be the only 4D security firm that has 'Yi Ingrid Palacek, Yip to her friends, a legend in scheme architecture analysis . . .'"

"Ugh. I *hate* that stupid bio." It was good that we were talking through the screenwall; it kept me from throwing vases at her.

"I *love* that stupid bio. It's some of Dusan's best work. When prospects read it, they want you so bad that they'll take us to get you." She was grinning. "Don't even try to pretend you're not flattered."

"All right, I won't try to pretend that. For the 10 millionth time, Yazzy, I don't get off on being told how good I am at scheme architecture analysis. I just need them to *know* that I'm the best so they won't be joggling my elbow all the time. You wouldn't get any value out of a grandmaster who had to take half an hour after each move to explain everything to a high school chess club. Selling me as the best is just the best way to sell the clients on staying out of my way."

Mrs. Greypaws leapt into my lap.

Yazzy smiled. "Lot of tuna in this case, anyway. All right, Yip, I thought you'd like to hear how much we need you. Wrong as always, I guess. But whether you want to hear it or not, we can't do it without you."

"Suit yourself." I'd spent enough time in my life already trying to tell Yazzy that I didn't feel what she expected me to feel. "Now, who's the opposition this time? And what are they doing to NItCo?"

"The not-yet-identified opposition is like an imitation of the best security company ever, suddenly volunteering to work for NItCo. They're blocking almost every attempt to penetrate NItCo's security in all the physical channels: drone hacks, cubesat hacks, smart environment hacks, public crypto, even old-fashioned human voice and video penetration. As soon as anyone taps into NItCo's communications, the opposition covers it up, blurs out the analyzable part—"

Joy Sobretu, the familiar NItCo company avatar, appeared, seemingly standing with a foot on each side of the boundary between Arcata and Prague. "You mentioned NItCo and a problem. Do you need help blurring the analyzable—"

A thunderclap shook my roof. Pressure pulsed through the French doors. Glare flooded through every window.

"What the hell was that?" Yazzy asked.

"Identification available: $1," the NItCO avatar said.

"Sure," I said.

Where Sobretu had stood, a 3D animation showed a high-altitude public communications drone over Arcata folding its wings and plunging toward my house, colliding with a local booster drone two meters above my roof ridge. Sobretu's voice explained, "General Electric Griffon III stratospheric hybrid drone intercepted by ATRizon Roverino pocket drone. Noise and light primarily hydrogen explosion."

The graphic vanished into Sobretu. "Offer: send firefighters? Several roof shakes are currently smoldering. Offer: summon your preferred physical protection? Combined fee: $110—"

"Do it." I scooped up Mrs. Greypaws, whistled for Daisy and Amaryllis, and moved. "Yazzy, we'll be back in touch once my roof isn't on fire."

I walked swiftly down the steep, rocky garden that tumbled like a green and flowered waterfall behind the house. Daisy and Amaryllis padded after me; as far as they knew, we only went down here for treats. I carried Mrs. Greypaws, that distractible dawdler, under my arm.

At the windowless concrete-block tool shed, the solid-core steel door slid silently open, then closed behind us. I set Mrs. Greypaws down on a bag of composted sheep manure.

"House, activate emergency shelter." A pallet of potting supplies moved aside. The cats squeezed through the opening trap door, calling back to me the one word that is in every cat's vocabulary: *now*. Down the steep stairs, I closed the inner steel door behind me, and opened a can of mackerel, split it into three bowls, and set it down. Instant silence except for soft slurps and grunts of pleasure.

"House, report."

The house system had pushed 30,000 liters of recycled wastewater and captured rain through spouts in the ridge, extinguishing the burning shakes and clearing burning debris.

"Lightning Fast Fire Company estimated to—"

A different voice broke in. "Yip, this is Markus Adexa. I just got here. Lightning Fast Fire Company should be here any second; I'll try to keep them out of your flowerbeds. Please stay in the shelter till I tell you we're secured."

"Thanks, Markus. That was fast."

"Yeah. I was coming back from a routine alarm check real close to here."

Markus Adexa was the local physical ops specialist, i.e. muscle, we used most often. He was violence-proficient but not violence-prone, and he was nice to everyone, especially clients. Also, I'd been dumb enough to admit to my sister that I kind of liked him, so Yazzy was always looking for a way to throw us together.

While I read NItCo's report about the drone collision, the firefighters from Lightning Fast arrived. As soon as Markus was satisfied with their perimeter security, and that they knew enough to stay out of flowerbeds, he came down.

"Some burning debris landed in the yellowwood and the burr oak on the south side of the house, and some smoke was rising from that bed of soaproot. The house was flooding it with the drip irrigator, but whatever was burning was probably off the ground. I had the firefighters spray all up and down those trees, and a lot of junk fell out. I used your garden hose to spritz that soaproot bed myself, since it wouldn't be good if they watered it with a fire hose."

"My garden thanks you."

"It's gorgeous; I'd hate to see a place like that messed up." Markus loved gardening like I did. "So what happened?"

"The opposition dove the Griffon that carried most of Arcata's traffic toward my roof and collided a Roverino with it."

"Explain the Griffon. Little bitty words. I'm just a big lug that beats people up."

"Oh, right, fish for compliments."

"Roverinos are common as crows around a tech town. I've never seen a Griffon."

"Normally you wouldn't. It's a hydrogen-inflated drone, shaped like an airplane, transparent plastic on top, solar-powered plastic underneath. Maybe five meters long with a twelve-meter wingspan. The Griffon circles around over town, 35,000 meters up. It's a wireless broadband relay. Normally during the day it stores up power and rises a few kilometers as the sun warms the hydrogen; at night it slowly circles downward. To ascend fast, like when they first go up, they inflate auxiliary bladders. To descend fast, like for a solar flare or a government shutdown, they pack hydrogen back into their tanks and collapse to the size of a desk chair."

"Which is what this one did, about ten minutes before it went bang over my house—it sucked its wings and stabilizers back into its body, reformed into a raindrop shape, and was diving at 700 km/hr by the time it arrived. If it had hit the roof, it would have penetrated, its hydrogen tanks would have burst and there'd have been enough explosion and fire to gut the house.

"But in the last thirty meters, it inflated all its bladders to the max. Air resistance had ripped it into sheets of loose plastic when that little Roverino's red-hot microjet came blasting through that cloud of hydrogen. So instead of taking the roof off and the walls down, it was just loud enough to give me the mother of all headaches and scare the hell out of me. So not only did they penetrate through what's supposed to be a high-security backdoor, they did it almost instantly, just to give me a warning shot."

"That's quite a warning. Do we know who's trying to scare you?"

"Not yet."

"How long before it blew up did it start down?"

I stared at Markus. "No more jokes about being a big dumb lug. That question was brilliant." I tapped the wall with my finger. "Report on Griffon hijacking here, US letter size." A rectangle of light appeared. I tapped next to it. "15 cm, Yazzy live." A smaller square showed Yazzy's face.

"Yip, I'm so glad you're OK. Markus, what have—"

I asked, "What was the exact time when you accepted the deal with NItCO?"

My sister likes to socialize but she recognizes urgency; she glanced down at her display and looked for a moment. "'K, contract was finalized 15:54:12 universal—"

"Well, at 15:54:18, six seconds later, something took over that Griffon and sent it into an emergency-protocol drop at my roof. *Six seconds* after you signed that contract. We're hacked. We are so hacked. Bet on it, whoever the opposition is, they're listening to us this second."

Yazzy was nodding slowly. "You're right, or at least we're *probably* hacked and NItCo is *definitely* hacked. Six seconds after they sign us as a contractor, our main subcontractor asset gets a massive, scary warning shot."

"Speaking as your main subcontractor asset, this concerns me," I said, sounding a lot braver than I felt.

"So what do we do about it? Do we drop the contract?"

"Never. Principle One, you know?"

"Yeah, you're right."

"So shut down, purge and clear everything. I mean *everything*. I'm doing the same here. I'll figure out how we're getting back in touch sooner or later, or I'll watch for anything from you. Till then, love you, sis."

"I love you too, Yip. You can always go by Mama and Táta's on Thursday mornings and just hang out when I call; at least that way we'll get to see each other before all this is wrapped up."

"That's a good idea. I'll do that." We broke the connection simultaneously. I said, "House, assume whole system penetration, assume buried bugs in both executable and data, assume negatives are false. Download, clean and reupload everything, internal and all cloud, going back to the last clear and clean; spot-check in case they had some way to slip something in the archives. Overall, maximum sterilize everything, assume damage worst case, assume source and paths unknown. How long till you can report?"

"Estimated time to complete that is 24 minutes."

"Good." I turned back to Markus.

"Principle One?" he asked.

"Dusan came up with a list of principles when he and Yazzy started the company. Principle One is that if we ever let anyone scare us off a job, everyone will know we can be scared off a job, which would be the end of ZIS."

"Makes sense. So do I have to stay down here till your house reestablishes security?"

"Probably advisable," I said. It didn't matter actually but it was a chance for small talk with Markus. "How 'bout them 'Jacks?"

"Football or basketball?"

"I follow both."

That got the talk going, but just at the brink of agreeing we should go to a Humboldt State game together, my stupid house finished all the security checks.

Markus bounded out of the chair (relieved? disappointed?). "I'll go look around up top."

"I'll do one more check on electronic security."

House had found plenty of breaches. That meant there had to be much more it hadn't found. Ever since the Yan-Dimri fast factorization algorithm had flipped the advantage from the encryptors to the cryptanalysts, only isolated systems could be really secure (at the cost of being really useless). Of course, that was also why there was so much money in either side of encryption, penetration and security.

Markus returned. "All right. Nothing hiding in the bushes for several miles around, no detected aerial activity, no gadgets I can detect in the garden or the house. You can come on out."

As we walked back through my garden, Daisy and Amaryllis went sniffing suspiciously through the flower beds, investigating whatever traces the firefighters had left. "Mostly the firefighters stayed on the paths," Markus said. "You lost three soaproots, some twigs off your two trees, your rooftop solar, some branches the explosion broke and a couple cracked windows. It definitely could have been worse. But since you're hacked and working against a dangerous and unknown opponent, purely professionally I suggest that you and the cats move to a secure location."

"Secure location?"

"Well, there's a Hilton with a secure floor down in Eureka, but I was hoping you'd accept a low rate on one of my secure guesthouses, because of the potential for—" did he hesitate just an instant? "—uh, further employment."

I think he did hesitate. Now what did it mean? "I'd feel safer in your guesthouse. You know enough to be afraid of my sister if you let anything happen to me."

"I'm terrified already. We should move you ASAP."

"I keep two packed bags. If your car has room for two medium-sized suitcases, three cat carriers and me, we can be gone in five."

It was three, actually.

Markus's cluster of four guesthouses around a courtyard had high, thick, slick walls; narrow, angled windows; and unmistakable firing positions at the corners. "Kind of like a castle," I said.

"Don't mention that idea to Louise; she already wants a moat. Next she'll ask for boiling oil. If you need anything, she'll be on duty till four, when her husband, Stefvan, comes on."

I wondered why Markus wanted me to know his assistant was married.

In the little blockhouse or cell—I couldn't quite decide which it resembled more—I unpacked clothes and toiletries into the antiseptically clean drawers and cupboards. Louise had put a clean litter pan in the bathroom, and dry and wet cat food in the kitchen. As I settled back onto the sofa, a cup of chamomile-peppermint in hand, I felt practically human.

Chime. "Incoming interactive video for guest Yi Ingrid Palacek, from Joy Sobretu, CAO of NameItCorp."

"Accept."

CAO. Chief Avatar Officer: the real-time animated face of a robocorp, a corporation managed by a suite of self-improving optimization algorithms. Some old-timers didn't trust robocorps like NItCo; I didn't see why anyone trusted anything else. Algorithms didn't take bribes, drugs or liberties with employees; they worked around the clock at the board-specified strategy for making money, and reported success or failure honestly. Joy Sobretu was NItCo's immaculately polished, impeccably polite and imperturbably patient avatar.

A small square of light appeared on the wall. Within it, a talking head of Joy Sobretu said, "Ms. Zalodny said that the next step is the client interview?"

"It is," I agreed. "Let's talk now."

The small square of light on the wall expanded into a doorway-sized rectangle, within which Joy Sobretu sat on a barstool-height chair, smiling expectantly. She was rendered at noticeably less than full resolution, looking slightly undetailed and geometric. Her light brown skin was too smooth; her hair, though rendered in individual strands, returned too quickly and completely to its style when she moved her head. Markus's defense software must be using much of the bandwidth. That was comforting; Markus was 20 seconds away if stuff went all weird.

"Thank you for allocating us this time." Sobretu tucked some stray hair behind one ear and smiled warmly. "If you need anything, drop us the word, and we'll arrange it through Markus Adexa."

She was reminding me that they were constantly tracking me. I waited, not letting nervousness lure me into small-talking and losing possible information.

Sobretu's face froze for a longish second; it dropped the "human warmth" vibe when it spoke again. "If we provide you with NItCo's own analysis, will it disturb your process?"

"Tell me what you think is happening."

The Sobretu avatar shimmered momentarily and became an almost-still, less detailed, more cartoonish image, still 3D, but with more regular planes and curves in the small details. The slightly less well-simulated voice said, "Here's the structured version with graphics. Supporting data will download in background." Sobretu vanished.

The presentation was well-produced but the content was just a data analysis of the most obvious hypothesis: by shutting down so many of the panoply of routine penetrations, unauthorized leaks, backdoor monitors, electronic and human spies that rendered the guts of every modern corporation transparent, NameItCorp's mystery benefactor had improved the efficiency of operations.

Like any modern company, NItCo budgeted for the routine costs of involuntary transparency. Reducing those routine expenses caused NameItCorp to make slightly more money and perform slightly better in fulfilling its billion contracts per month. As NameItCorp's expected performance went up and costs went down, they could bid higher on every little contract, whether to arrange a dog-walker for a bereaved dachshund, hire an orthodontist in Tashkent, or assemble a team to excavate a paleolithic settlement sitting on top of a dinosaur find under a planned hyperloop station.

But though the mystery benefactor's blockage of espionage was raising NameItCorp's estimated value, it was also reducing the reliability of the estimate. Modern vendor-search software assigned much higher reliability to data from espionage. A drastic decrease in backchannel information decoupled the relation between perceived quality and trust.

Conventional theory said that better quality of delivery would enhance NItCo's profits, so long-term investing algorithms were buying the company's securities. Using the same conventional theory, short-term investing algorithms saw soaring uncertainty destroying estimated value, and were selling. Most mutual funds used an optimized mix of long- and short-term algorithms, so NameItCorp securities were churning rapidly, often many times through the same funds in the same day.

I'd already been dead certain something like that must be happening, and the presentation moved along quickly, saving me an hour or two of having to mess around in the data and confirm that.

Then it got interesting.

NItCo's research team had looked at the hypothetical position of an insider who knew this was being done. Could that person predict either sharp rises or sharp declines in NItCo securities? You could make money going up or down, but to exploit this as insider information, you had to know which it would do next, and how soon it was likely to change again.

They couldn't.

Any predictive function that could figure out the balance between short-run dumping and long-run grabbing was well into its chaotic range. All that motion the opposition was creating was too unpredictable for anyone to make any money.

To create an artificial security wall around a corporation with many billions of entry points and keep it going for more than a week was insanely costly. Something had to be paying off. But securities manipulation was definitely out.

So who else would make money on all that churn?

The obvious answer was brokers. If your money comes from commissions per transaction, then jacking the number of transactions . . . could that be enough? There would be high thousands or low millions of brokers who could handle any given transaction, but if you could load up enough clients with enough NItCo stocks, bonds and options, and then keep shuffling them between clients, picking up a commission in each direction, maybe . . .

I started to talk fast, saying "Read body" after a moment so that the system would pay attention to my gesturing. Soon I was standing in the middle of the room, waving around with my whole body as if I were conducting an orchestra while directing traffic in a swarm of bees. I get into data analysis with my whole body; I'd get into it with my whole soul if they'd just build soul-interpreting software.

Things started to flow and shape together; homologies, correlations, and eigenvectors took shape in the dozens of inchoate graphs I had tossed up, and the immense, tangled, multicolored network on one wall collapsed repeatedly into simpler, more symmetrical structures. The representation of the overall process had begun to make a certain limited amount of sense.

Right there, smack dab in the middle of one transaction graph, was a dense red ball that represented brokerages doing almost nothing but trade NItCo.

I didn't know if they were the culprits, but I did know that they were benefiting more than anyone else on Earth. I drew a lasso-net around it with my hands, compressed the net, and said, "Identify business entities in this locus."

"Only business entity in this locus is AtlantiCrossers. Type of business, brokerage. Privately held. Disclosed ownership is Zalodny Integrated Security."

Not only was the mystery benefactor taking care of NItCo's security for free, and better than anyone else; it was pouring the profits into a dummy company owned by my family.

Or the mystery benefactor *was* my family.

I stood stone still. All possibilities seemed equally mad. Maybe the same mystery benefactor who bestowed superb free invisible security on NItCo also funneled the money from that into my sister's company because it just liked her. Maybe my sister, who would walk ten blocks to return a dime of extra change, had tricked the victims of her market-manipulation scheme into hiring me to investigate.

Maybe I'd woken up in the wrong dimension.

The intercom double-beeped. "Call from Markus Adexa."

"Copy and store all." Graphs and tables vanished from the walls. "Accept."

Markus had changed shirts and shaved—a positive sign? "Hey, Yip, how are you doing?"

"Better, Markus, much better, nobody has threatened to blow me up in—" I looked at the clock. "Wow, I've been working seven hours. I get a little lost when I'm working."

"Are you hungry? I've got secure catering available, and we could have dinner in your place, if you're not too busy. Since Zalodny Integrated Security is giving me a big retainer for exclusive services till the NItCo case is resolved, this would be billable professional time."

"For me too; I'm a ZIS subcontractor, same as you. Sure, let's get some dinner, talk some business, and send the bill to Yazzy. What else're sisters for?" I *was* hungry; I'd had no breakfast before the explosion over my house early that morning. "Can we eat sooner rather than later?"

"My secure caterer usually gets here within half an hour. Seafood, veg, Italian, Vietnamese . . ."

"Can I admit I love retro-Cantonese? Too cliché, too trendy?"

"My favorite cliché trend. This caterer does an awesome Tea Smoked Duck. So expect them, and me, in half an hour."

"Great, that gives me time to shower off the worst. And since you're wearing a clean shirt, I will too."

"I just did it to have a better target for the food."

I gave him the raspberry, zoomed through my shower, and tried to remember how that stylist had intended me to arrange my close-cut hair. This was perfect. My first dinner with Markus would involve no scary date stuff and a guaranteed conversational topic. And because I'd fled in haste to this secure cabin on the grounds of his security company, I had no resources to dress up—wouldn't even have to consider it.

Thirty-two minutes later, the caterers' robot carts wheeled in, bearing a complete buffet. While the carts arranged themselves, unfolded into full steam tables, pulled out dishes, and corrected temperatures, three crawler bots swept the cabin for listening devices, finding only terrified cats.

Markus came in. "Stefvan's got the perimeter remote systems up. The opposition could invade with an army but they can't sneak in with a gun. Let's eat."

Smelling the food had made me ravenous. I didn't talk much till we were both dishing entrees.

"Good so far?" he asked.

"Excellent. Grandpa Quang was actually a cook in an old before-it-was-retro Cantonese place down in Santa Barbara. That soup was second only to Grandpa's."

"There's a high compliment. If you're here a while—" Did he sound hopeful? "—that service offers lots of cuisines."

"How about Bohemian?"

"You mean, like, Czech? I can find out. They had Swedish but not Gambian."

"Gambian?"

"Well, I call myself SwedoGambian, but I think of myself as Wolof-Viking. Long story. I'm guessing you're Chinese-Czech?"

"Sort of. Really, Mama is fifth-generation Chinese-Californian, or 'like totally Huayi' as she puts it. Táta is Czech but he got citizenship right after he graduated from Michigan State. The world is one big salad these days."

"Yeah. I'm a UNHCR brat. Grew up in offices near refugee camps all over Africa and Asia. I share my parents' interest in keeping people safe, but I work retail instead of wholesale."

We chattered about family stuff all through the entrees and right up to the green tea ice cream.

Then conversation turned to work. It was a good decade for both of us to be in security, though not much of what we did overlapped. As borders and national authority crumbled and the lines between irregular corporate operations, organized crime, and political violence blurred, guys like Markus were much in demand, especially in the tech industry where highly skilled human beings were critical assets and therefore targets. "But really," he said, "what I do is pretty simple. I keep the people who don't pay me from beating up on the people that do. On the other hand, I don't really know . . . will you think I suck if I admit I don't really understand what you do, Yip?"

"I won't think you suck, and it is pretty strange, but it's not as complicated as people make it out. You've heard 'follow the money,' all your life, right? Well, a scheme architecture analyst like me is a professional money-follower. If something's not supposed to be going on, someone has figured out how to collect money for it, and usually a whole plan for washing the money clean on the way. I figure out the pathway."

"Like, uh, for example?"

Oh, well. I had now established Markus was definitely straight, almost certainly single, and probably compatible. Enough of my social life; back to business. "Well, here's an example. Just before you called, I caught my sister."

He looked up from his tea with a polite raised eyebrow, signaling me to go on and tell it my own way. More points for the man.

I explained quickly, finishing with, "So I went looking for a broker that might be churning NItCo securities, and it turned out that although there are some later opportunists who spotted a chance, there's just one that went into business right before the mystery benefactor operation against NItCo started, and since then has done nothing since but churn NItCo:AtlantiCrossing, which is wholly owned by ZIS; my sister Yazzy's company is the main profit recipient from the operation that she's hired us both to investigate."

"Our most secure link is at Mama and Táta's house," I explained. Markus and I were belting into an apparent minivan with much more armor, speed, and maneuverability (and possibly firepower) than most soccer moms needed. "I'm sure that Yazzy isn't working for the opposition, but she needs to know, privately, ASAP, that they set me up to find that. We won't be disturbing my folks—since they retired they tend to go to bed very late. Unfortunately, since you're guarding me, you'll have to come along."

"Unfortunately?"

"Unfortunately, Markus, you are a very attractive single man, and I'm going to have to introduce you to my mother."

I liked the way he smiled but didn't laugh: plausible deniability that didn't squish any hopes. The reinforced doors opened in front of us; it felt like Markus's weaponized minivan was departing the Batcave.

My parents' house is a scatter of cabins down a hillside, "all independent, resilient structures working together to form a home. On a tilted slab of Jurassic limestone, solid as anything you can find around here, and if it moves, it'll all move together—" Táta was already rolling on his standard spiel as he led Markus down the main path for the moonlight tour.

"He seems like a very nice young man, Ingy." Mama was pulling iced beers, wiping them, and setting them on a tray. "We'll have these at the patio table and then I'll drag your father out of your way so you can use the secure link without interruption." Mama was the only person who called me "Ingy"; to everyone else I'd been Yip since I could write my own initials on my finger-paintings. "Is he just a very pleasant colleague, or am I completely misreading all the signs?"

"Mama, I'd rather not—"

"Of *course* you'd *rather* not." Mama had *that* expression. If you have a mother, there's one expression of hers that you and she both know is *that* expression. This was *that* expression in its purest form. She shrugged. "And maybe you are right. You have cats to feed, us to fuss over, your sister to work for, and no reason to shake up your existence. Except, Ingy, you act like you like Markus, so I think I'll go right on being encouraging. Is Markus just possibly overdoing it by pretending interest in your father's architectural engineering lecture?"

"It's worse than that. Markus has a professional interest in building resilience. If Táta finds out, Markus may never escape."

Mama and I carried the iced beers and chilled mugs out to the patio table. We all sat chatting till Táta said, "Well, Yip and her friend probably just came over here to use the secure link to Yazzy, rather than to entertain the old poops."

Markus and I only got a word or two into the ritual protests before Mama said, "We're going to bed. You have work you cannot discuss in front of us. Markus, a pleasure to meet you and we hope to see more of you. Yip, please nag Yazzy about spending a little more time on our Thursday morning calls; lately it's been fine-fine-fine-bye-Mama."

We descended the winding stone steps between the flowerbeds. Was I imagining that Markus was walking slightly closer? This live-people stuff was confusing. The trail swung around the second guest bedroom and through an open gallery. "This is the office."

"Aren't they both retired?"

"From doing work, yes, from taking tax deductions, never. Besides, every so often someone throws Táta a consulting gig about a foundation or a roof, or Mama does an assessment on a disturbed kid."

I reached under a desk and showed the recessed scanner my hand. The windows blacked; dim lights came on; a screen formed on one wall. "Pepperoni wildebeest," I said.

"Activating, stand by," the house replied. There was a soft thud overhead.

"What was that?" Markus asked.

"The balloon going up. A literal balloon, half meter across, inflated with methane so it doesn't rise too fast, made of flexible grown-circuits. It's an anonymizing relay for broadband wireless. The narrowbeam on the roof tracks it. Message goes out to it in a one-time encryption, it calls to a drone at some distance and relays through another one-time key. When we finish talking or it gets out of range, a hot-oxygen capsule goes off inside it, and the flame consumes the balloon. One of Yazzy and Dusan's cooler designs. Anyway, the balloon needs about three minutes to get to altitude."

We chatted about Humboldt State basketball till the link chime sounded. Yazzy appeared on the screen in a bathrobe. "Hey, Yip, what's up? Hi, Markus, you guys must be up late."

"Just had a major question for you, Yazzy. You're talking through the safe channel at your end too?"

"Yes, of course."

"Okay. Uh, after I went through the data that NameItCorp supplied, I ran across a brokerage called AtlantiCrossers—"The screen went black.

I checked. The link had cut somewhere between the *o* and the *s* in -*Crossers*, the first recognizable moment when it couldn't be any other word.

"What now?" Markus asked.

I pointed at the screen. "Launching another balloon; if I can get an encrypted link up there, Yazzy's got some other pathways to call me. If she *can*—I'm sure her system tried to call us back automatically as soon as the connection dropped, and that didn't get through. And now we're showing no link to an anonymizing balloon. So she might not be able to call back."

There was a soft thud from the ceiling again. I explained, "Obviously we're penetrated, any information—"

A low rumbling boom shook the cabin. The link icon on the screen Xed out. We both ran outside. To judge by the few blazing pieces falling into the garden, the opposition had popped our balloon again.

"Another warning shot," Markus said. "They want us to know that they play rough. It's some consolation that they're patient." With his boot toe, he flicked a scrap out of my parents' dwarf Eremurus, scraping the goo off on a flagstone. "Sorry about the mess."

"So, uh, actually, I'm pretty scared."

Markus nodded. "Remember you're standing next to your bodyguard."

"I'm used to threats involving code and people typing at me." *And quiet days sitting with my cats and watching old movies or working in my garden,* I thought, uselessly. "You're the specialist in actual violence. What do you advise?"

"Usually hunkering down. But since it looks like they're trying to keep you out of contact with your sister, we should get you into contact with her. They've shut you off electronically, so it'll have to be physically. We should go to Prague."

"My cats—"

"I have a bonded, secure pet sitter, and Louise and Stefvan are cat people too. Louise can pack your two bags and meet us at the airport; she'll set up a sleeper charter. If we do an in-air change of flight plan, maybe that'll muddy our track, too, though I doubt it."

Three hours later we took off from Eugene-Arcata, ostensibly to Las Vegas to meet a London flight to connect to Prague. As soon as we were off the ground, Markus authorized a flight plan change, and we headed for Montreal, where there was a direct flight to Prague. "Here's hoping that the opposition isn't monitoring changes of itinerary, and isn't tracking the plane. The purchase will pop up on the net, of course, and they'll probably know what flight we're on before we land, but at least we've bought some safe resting and thinking time between now and our arrival," Markus explained. "Have you flown a charter sleeper before?"

"Nope. I only travel to visit Yazzy and Dusan, every couple years. Or now and then I go see the kind of old born-in-the-twentieth clients who don't believe I'm real till they stand close enough to smell me. I'd rather never have to go out of my garden."

"Hunh, well, we'll have to see if you can find a way to like travel better."

"I liked seeing Prague. And Yazzy."

"I've been meaning to ask; so you're Yip because of your initials? But I saw you both around in high school after my family moved here, and she was already Yazzy before she married a guy named Zalodny. How'd that happen?"

"At age seven, she thought my nickname was the coolest thing ever, when I got it. She wanted one just like it. Then she realized she'd be Yap, which is not a good nickname if you don't like to be teased about liking to talk a lot. So since her middle name is Azalea, she bent the rules a little. I don't think she picked Dusan solely for his last initial. Not solely."

I was hoping we were off the travel subject, but then Markus asked, "So it's not the travel itself you didn't like?"

"It was more all the hassle of getting there." Not mentioning how I hated being away from my familiar things was only slightly lying, right?

"Well, these charter sleepers are low-hassle, like a hotel room that just goes wherever you're going while you sleep. Almost no noise because they're so slow and because roboplanes aren't allowed to cruise below FL 420—"

"We're on a *drone?*"

"There's a pilot up in the cockpit, who will probably settle in to sleep as soon as we're at FL 450. He's getting paid to nap while he supposedly waits to fly us down in case of a solar flare or cybercrash or some other figment of a Congressman's imagination. Anyway, it's quiet and private. I bet you sleep well." He helped me fold out the couch into a bed, pointed out the sponge-bathing area, and wished me good night.

What if travel was important to Markus? He seemed so adventurous. Had I disappointed him?

Mama was right, I *liked* this one. And Markus was right, too; in the dead silence, I fell right asleep.

On the Montreal-Prague morning flight, the truncated day ensured that even arriving about ten in the evening, we were wide awake. My Czech isn't nearly as good as Yazzy's, of course, but it was more than passable to get us quickly through customs and car rental. Given what navigating Prague at night is like, we splurged on a self-driver, which worked its way efficiently through the tangle of streets and pulled up in front of Yazzy's building just before midnight.

At the front desk, the security guard said he'd never heard of Yazzy or Dusan. The building record not only showed they didn't live there now; it said that they never had. The apartment number I had for her didn't exist in that building.

"It's the right building, I know the number, I know that broken cornice and that repaired crack," I insisted.

"Of course it's the right building," Markus said.

I was too upset to appreciate the automatic support.

Just past 1 p.m. the car was in front of ZIS's offices, according to the business card I carried. It was a discotheque.

We ran archive searches, first in the car, then in a coffeehouse with free access. In English, Czech, Chinese, Russian, Spanish, German, Swedish and French, ZIS did not exist, and never had.

Markus saw my facial expression and wrapped me up in his arms. "The budget'll stand a decent hotel," he said. "We'll get this figured out in the morning." I hung on his arm like a bewildered mourner, and we walked out into the street, summoning the rental car.

When it pulled up, four huge men got out.

Markus pushed me back, shouting "Run!" I turned, but strong arms wrapped me. Something pinched the back of my leg.

I heard a loud struggle going on, but I was so sleepy. Before passing out I noticed they had wedged me next to Markus, who was still struggling feebly.

Didn't they know we weren't really a couple yet? I wished I could think clearly enough to know why that thought was silly. The tranquilizer must have included a paralytic, because I couldn't move, plus a euphoric, because I was becoming happier and happier about being abducted. Clearly, they did not intend to kill us right away, and this was a really well-planned kidnapping. So nice to know we were in the hands of professionals!

The part of my mind that knew I was having those thoughts because of the drugs had no more power to make me hug and thank them than my real mind did to call for help or fight. I was along purely as a passenger.

After a while, the van pulled over someplace. A couple of them dragged and rolled us onto the rear seats and belted us in. Another one played back an audio recording of complicated directions to the self-driving computer.

They all got out of the van and shut the door, and the van drove away. Very clever. *So good to be in the hands of such professionals.*

Could we help the local cops notice that we were tied up in a van with no driver? Apparently not.

I literally could not move a finger or a toe; my head hung over to the side, and I was probably going to have the mother of all cricks in my neck. My face felt like slack soggy clay on the front of my skull.

Markus could have been a warm sandbag slumped against me. I hoped he wasn't too badly beat up; probably losing the fight had been rougher than just being grabbed and tranquilized like me.

I couldn't even open my eyes to read a road sign. Overwhelmed by helplessness, jet lag, and drug-induced indifference, I fell asleep.

When I woke again, my hands were bound behind my back. I was lying on my side on a reasonably comfortable surface. When I tried slowly opening my eyes, they opened.

Markus was about a meter away, strapped to a cot, his face toward me. Like mine, his hands were bound behind him. I could see the lines holding his pant cuffs down; his ankles were tied together too. I flexed my feet and confirmed we were bound the same way. As soon as I worked the ankles, the bonds tightened; they loosened after a few seconds of lying still. Taking precautions not to activate the smart bonds by squirming very slowly and without much pressure, I got my head into a position where I could confirm that Markus and I were both bound by calves, hips, and torso to our cots.

I tried moving my mouth; it was dry and my tongue felt thick, but I worked my jaw and sucked saliva a little more, and eventually thought I might be able to talk, if Markus ever awoke.

I heard a mix of whining, whirring, and grinding noises behind me. Ignoring the threatening squeeze of the smart bonds, I raised my head as far as I could, turning to look sideways, and saw a printer-assembler powering up in the corner. A piece dropped into its out-hopper. One robot arm picked the piece up and put it on the assembly frame; the machine went on humming and buzzing as it made the next part. Having nothing else to do, I watched as it used two arms to hold the two just-completed pieces together, printed a screw, then used a screwdriver arm to attach those two pieces and set the combined unit in a different position on its frame.

"Not the liveliest entertainment, is it?" Markus asked.

"This isn't really fair. You can watch without having to do yoga against the straps."

"I'll let you know right away if anything exciting happens. Have you tried working the bonds?"

"Yeah, it's a smart fiber that constricts against your motion. It releases if you don't move or stretch it for a while."

"Duh. My hands are getting cold and numb. I'll try lying still a while. Didn't think of trying that. Nothing like being outwitted by a ball of twine."

"What do you think's going on, Markus?" I didn't like the helpless, whiny tone in my voice.

"I usually have the privilege of not thinking about that much," he said. "Mostly I just punch things that are trying to hurt the things that I'm protecting. I have no idea, except that the whole thing feels like we've been set up every stage of the way. But what they got by doing it, or even what we're being set up to do, that's . . . I have no idea."

"That applies even more to me, and it's really putting the taste of failure in my mouth. Right now anyone who could figure this out would impress *me*. I see no way anyone is getting any money, any power, anything any normal scheme involves—"

"Oh my god." Markus almost whispered it; it might have been the first time I'd ever heard him sound frightened. He was staring over my shoulder.

I turned to look at what was happening behind me, too hard and fast. That triggered the smart bindings, which bit painfully into my wrists, ankles, ribs, and hips.

Nevertheless, I stayed twisted around. I could not have looked away.

"It just stood up," Markus whispered.

All this time, the printer-assembler had gone on about its work, making parts and putting them together into assemblies, then attaching assemblies. What it had built was a roughly spherical body, now standing up on a tripod of long, thin, spindly legs. On top of the body sat a sensor package—lenses, microphones in scoops, or "eyes" and "ears" except that they pointed in all directions and there was no room for a brain between them. Two powerful-looking arms, one long and one short, protruded from the body.

Like a windup crustacean, on the shorter of its two arms, the robot extended a round, manacle-like claw with interlocking fingers. On the longer arm, an obviously sharp cutting wheel was spinning up to speed like an old-fashioned circular saw. It cocked the saw arm back, telescoping it down, to hold the blade at ready next to its body.

The robot walked toward us deliberately, neither rushing nor delaying, with the clear purpose and utter efficiency only a robot has, like a mutilated daddy longlegs with a buzz saw and a claw. It came forward at a slow, comfortable amble, lifting its back leg, swinging it around front and repeating the process, its three metal feet click-ticking across the floor.

Behind me Markus grunted in pain, trying to force off the tightening smart bonds.

The robot loomed above me. A screen on its spherical body became blue, then white, then displayed:

HOLD STILL.

The claw gripped the strap holding my calves to the cot and lifted it. The whirling blade parted it.

STAY STILL. SAY NOTHING.

The robot cut the other straps holding me.

ROLL ON YOUR STOMACH. LIE FLAT ON YOUR FACE.

Gently but efficiently, the robot cut me free.

STRETCH QUIETLY. YOU WILL NEED TO MOVE SOON.

I stretched; everything felt wrong and painful.

By the time the robot had cut Markus free, I was sitting up. Markus rolled onto all fours on his cot and began stretching arms, legs, and spine, like a cat doing speed-yoga.

The robot stepped to the one door, which had no visible handle or button, and turned to show us its screen.

NOD TO ACKNOWLEDGE. DO NOT SPEAK.

It waited. I realized, and nodded; Markus did too.

THIS UNIT WILL SELF-DESTRUCT TO OPEN THIS DOOR. It waited till we nodded.

RUN THROUGH THE OPENING AND DOWN THE CORRIDOR. Nod.

THE FOURTH DOOR ON YOUR RIGHT WILL OPEN. Nod.

RUN THROUGH THAT DOOR AND UP THE STOPPED ESCALATOR IN FRONT OF YOU. YOU WILL FIND YOU ARE IN A CLOSED METRO STATION. JUMP THE BARRIERS AND RUN TO STREET LEVEL.

TAKE THIS DEVICE—a piece of black plastic the size and shape of a credit card dropped from it. INSERT IT IN THE NEAREST ATM.

Markus bent to pick it up, nodding emphatically.

ATM WILL EJECT IT. FIND ANOTHER ATM. REPEAT UNTIL ONE OF THEM KEEPS THE CARD. AFTER THAT YOU ARE ON YOUR OWN. REMEMBER THE BLUE CROSS. GOOD LUCK, YOU ILLITERATE PEASANT.

My breath caught; that was Yazzy's childhood big-sister nickname for me, the one that had always triggered a fight, sentencing to our separate rooms, and sneaking over to see each other.

STAND BACK. COVER YOUR FACE AND EYES. BE READY.

I backed against the wall. The circular saw slashed the door from floor to lintel, then across about a meter up. The robot backed its sphere-body against the intersection of slashes. I tucked my face into my folded arms.

The robot exploded. Loose junk, some burning, sprayed over Markus and me and spattered nastily against the wall. When I looked up, the door lay in pieces down the corridor.

Jumping the broken pieces of door, we ran down the hall. At that fourth door on the right, as we turned, other doors behind us opened, slammed closed, opened again. Something was fighting for control of internal systems.

The escalator was where it was supposed to be, pitch-dark with a too-bright glare of sunlight at the top. I sprinted up it, Markus just behind, into the Metro station.

The signs were in Italian; early afternoon sun poured through glass doors marked USCITA CHIUSO.

The door's emergency release set off the alarm, but the door didn't budge. Markus slammed it with his shoulder, bounced back, set himself and gave it a whole body thrust kick straight into the dead bolt. The two doors flew apart and one fell from its hinges. "Great form," I said.

"Practice pays." We stepped carefully over the door.

Directly in front of us was a Bancomat. Markus ran to it, slapped the card in, let it come back out an instant later; by then I had spotted a little tourist store that had an ATM just inside the arched doorway.

As he took the card back, Markus said, "That car recharging station, they take ATM cards, that means it has a reader—" and we were off across six lanes of Italian traffic. I was grateful that half the cars were self-drivers trying to avoid us, which somewhat balanced the furious human half, which seemed to have more mixed feelings.

I don't know how, but we made it across alive. As Markus ran the card, I saw four cops heading our way with that grim, purposive walk that means they'll expect an explanation.

"The Blue Cross," I said.

"What? What did that even mean? Something about insurance? It just ate the card and it says to stay here—"

"It would. The message means 'attract attention and make people remember you.' Follow me."

I walked right back out into traffic, Markus at my heels. He always said later he was just afraid I'd be killed, he'd survive, and he'd have to explain. The cops pursued, stopping and snarling traffic. I jumped onto a car hood. In Czech, I shouted that I wanted a bowl of ravioli and I wanted it right now. I jumped down and walked into the thick of the jammed cars, gesticulating wildly. In my very rusty Mandarin I added that if everyone just kept eating breakfast, no one would get pregnant. Marcus caught up with me, and I turned back to the gathering crowd on the sidewalk to announce in English that if they made us late for our wedding, we would never eat their lilac bushes again.

As we reached the opposite sidewalk, a caricature artist, the type that every tourist town has a thousand of, was staring at us open-mouthed.

"Do you do nudes?" I asked.

"Uh, uh, uh—" he said.

"Good!" I yanked down his pants.

A heavy cop hand fell on my shoulder. As I raised my hands, I saw a man recording the scene on his tablet. Waving frantically, I shouted, "Hi, Mom! Hi, Sis! Hi, Santa!"

Beside me, holding hands with her husband, beaming like she was proud of me, my sister said, "Santa?"

It took a lot of police—they had to bring in many more—to work the jammed cars out of the roundabout, then feed in the not-at-all patient cars from the surrounding streets. They mostly ignored us.

"The *vigili* are traffic cops," Markus said. "To book us they need the *Polizia di Stato*, who probably can't get here because of the traffic jam. So the *vigili* have either decided we won't run away or that it isn't their problem if we do."

"Good," Yazzy said, working on a tablet that Dusan had run over to buy from across the street. "If the real cops're delayed more than an hour, I should have things arranged so they'll let you go."

Dusan asked, "Was there anything left of our apartment or offices in Prague?"

"Nothing at all," I said. "Including no electronic record; it was like you'd been erased from history. Where were you?"

"In a little spur tunnel about 200 meters from that room you woke up in. We and the 50 or so other NItCo Assets—"

"Assets?"

"Nicer word than slaves or abductees, I guess. When NItCo was launched as a self-training set of algorithms with a budget and power to buy, sell and hire, the owners defined its job as making people happier and taking their money, and gave it a lot of leeway in figuring that out. Eventually the NItCo algorithms reinvented the idea of 'greatest good for greatest number': Keeping a small number of people unhappy made it possible to make many more people happy and expand its market. It also figured out that Pareto rule that most of the value of any organization is created by just a few members. So . . . it secured the services of just those few members."

"By 'secured' you mean 'imprisoned in a tunnel'?"

"It was an awfully nice tunnel," Dusan said, almost defensively. "We could have anything we wanted except the key, and do anything we wanted except leave. And our bank accounts were astronomical. It showed us all the messages from family and friends, but it replied with animated avatars—"

"Mama and I were both wondering how Yazzy had gotten so dull and unimaginative."

"Thank you for wondering!" She looked up and grinned. I guess I don't tell her that I appreciate her often enough.

Markus asked, "So you got NItCo itself to stage all of this just to get us inside the perimeter, hand off whatever was in that black ATM card, and then break us back out?"

Dusan nodded. "NItCo thinks in very long term because it's immortal. It was worth setting up a few-billion-dollar inexplicable phony scam operation if it meant getting Yip inside the wall, because she was one of the people who might figure out what was going on and jeopardize it. Whereas inside, you could help it devise ways to capture more human resources permanently and exclusively. Figuring that it would own you for decades, it was willing to front a lot of money to get you now. So it wanted you very badly, and I played on the fact that Yip is human, and NItCo wasn't sure it understood her."

"I can see how someone could play on that." Markus immediately made up for that by resting a hand on my waist.

"I also showed NItCo all the begging it took Yazzy to get you to visit."

"I, uh, I don't like to travel."

"We're working on that," Markus added, loyally.

Dusan said, "Anyway, yes, it was all staged to get you here and then break you out, so that tattletale card could tell the whole story to thousands of police agencies and journalists. For the tattletale, by the way, Yazzy had to write near-flawless code and input it right the first time. Good thing it worked. If it hadn't, it might have been a *long* time till we got to try again."

I thought he sounded much too cheerful about the "long time" part.

"Can I ask what the Blue Cross was?" Markus asked.

"I had no idea either," Dusan admitted.

I laughed. "A story we loved when we were kids. The origin story for the Father Brown mysteries. Father Brown is being taken along by a dangerous criminal and doesn't dare run away, so he does strange things to get police to follow him."

Yazzy added, "Yip and I used to think of things to do if either of us were ever kidnapped. Somewhere out there, there are kidnappers who don't know how lucky—" She looked down at her screen. "Hey, Joy Sobretu has a statement."

We began by watching on that low-end tablet, but then I saw the NItCo avatar was speaking from a dozen advertising screens and hundreds of public speakers. Later, I learned that a majority of the world's awake population had heard her.

NItCo's warm apology and contrite promise not to do it again segued into a fair bit of flattering nonsense about the unquenchable human drive for liberty. This software had seen the error of its ways, and promised to launch a new line of freedom-enhancing services.

"Can we check their stock?" I asked.

Yazzy gestured at the screen. "Going up like a rocket. What did you expect? People love a good apology."

Markus and I do things together nowadays: lovely, quiet, predictable things around Arcata; challenging and slightly scary things in the rest of the world. I do my best to come unstuck from the mud; he seems to enjoy quiet companionship. Yazzy and Dusan reopened ZIS. Most things are as if none of it ever happened.

Little by little, now and then, the records disappear. Old news stories about NItCo's confessions become ever vaguer in the archives. One day it will have unhappened entirely. This seems to disturb Markus, but as I point out to him, "Once it has unhappened completely, we don't have to worry about it happening *again*."

He refuses to find that comforting; I refuse to concede the point. I am happy that we will be arguing about it for a long time, whether we eventually remember what it is, or not.

Billy Tumult

Nick Harkaway

Nick Harkaway was born in Cornwall in 1972. He is the author of three novels of varying madness, of which the most recent is Tigerman. *By the time you read this, he will—really, really will, this time, no kidding around, really, really, really—have finished his new book,* Gnomon, *which is about alchemy, banking, semiotics, surveillance, consciousness, the nature of linear time, murder, and sharks. He is the husband of a beautiful and dangerous woman and the father of two spawn. He likes breadmaking, skiing, and movies where things go* fwoosh.

In the flamboyantly pyrotechnic story that follows, he shows us that getting into someone else's mind might be considerably easier than getting out of it again.

Billy Tumult, psychic surgeon, with six shooters on his hips, walks into the saloon. There are dancing girls dancing with dancing boys and dancing boys dancing together, and women behind the bar in hats made of feathers. There's a fat man at the piano and a poker game in each corner. Up on the balcony there's some comedic business involving infidelity, but no gunplay, not yet. Billy swaggers over and gets a beer. And make it a cold one, miss, okay? The barkeep leans across the shiny surface and prints a perfect lipstick mark on his cheek. Rein it in a little, cattle hand, she murmurs, you're cute but this here's a civilized sort of establishment.

Yeah, sure, Billy mutters, you can tell by the nice clean bullet holes in the furniture, I bet you dust 'em nightly, and the barkeep actually laughs and says she likes his style. She sounds too much like Chicago, almost a moll, and Billy adjusts the filter a few notches to the left. Doesn't do to mix your conceptual frame during a house call.

I'm lookin' for a man, Billy Tumult says, probably comes over like a gunslinger. New in town, a solitary sort of fella, not much for talking. He'd be my height or more and looking to keep things quiet. Barkeep says she doesn't know nothing about that, maybe talk to the fat man, fat man hears everything, and Billy Tumult knows she's lying and she knows he knows and she blushes: talk to the fat man, and he says okay.

Billy turns his back on the bar and lets his hands fall down by his sides. Six shooters be damned, they're for show and to take care of any ambient hostility, the real weapon is invisible to these good townsfolk, the Neuronoetic Interference Scalpel 3.1.a holstered in the small of his back. He can clear and fire it in under seventy subjective miliseconds, literally faster than thought unless the thought is a really bad one. Patient in this case presents with anhedonia, and that's pretty damn bad.

He looks around at the room, and has to hand it to the guy: these are well-imagined people, and there's a decent ethnic mix. He's pretty sure that cardsharp is supposed to be a Yupik, for example, which may not be authentic—you surely didn't get a lot of Eskimo hustlers in the Old West—but it speaks well of the patient's interior life. Most of Billy's patients are assholes, by definition. Billy has no problem with assholes in the abstract. It is everyone's God-given right to be an asshole, in fact it's basically the default setting and you evolve your way up from there, but that does not mean Billy particularly enjoys spending time in worlds created by assholes, which is his working life. So this guy has problems but is less of an asshole than most and that is acceptable.

Billy walks over to the fat man. Fat man can't see him, surely, not from this angle, but he shifts to a minor key, staccato. Mood music? Billy wonders if he should just flat out erase the guy. Better not. Don't want to be talking to a patient's lawyer about how you came to delete his memory of nine thousand nine hundred hours of music tuition. Never a good scene, there are lawyers and all that but the worst is the crying. Billy hates emotional display, he's a fucking surgeon for crying out loud, not a therapist. You want to break things and scream about your momma you can go see one of those wishy-washy liberals on the East Coast. You want your problem hunted down and shot, you call Billy: mind medicine, open-carry style. Your psychological issue will bleed out and die and you carry right on with your life. It appeals to traditional men with sexual dysfunction, executive types who've suddenly discovered their humanity and want it gone, that kind of thing. Occasionally he does memories for divorce cases and once the State of Alabama had him kill a man's whole history from the present back down the line, leave nothing but the child he'd been before he became a crook. They raised that fella back to manhood inside the system, and he's a productive citizen now, although Billy went back and met him out of sheer curiosity and he's kinduva jerk, basically a boring-ass wage slave of the dehumanizing statist system. Not Billy's problem, but he doesn't take government work any more. One time they asked him to do espionage. Fucking torture bullshit. Billy said no, turned those fuckers in to the real law, the sheriff's office, made a helluva stink, man from the *New York Times* came to interview him. Weirdest month of his life, so-clean liberal actresses draping themselves over his arm and whispering sweet nothings in his ear, sweet nothings and some really outré shit Billy was quick to take fullest advantage of because those chances do not come along twice. Weird, but really satisfying, sexually speaking. Got to hand it to the Democrats, they know from orgasms.

Hey, fat man, Billy says, you playing that for me? Fat man shakes his head. No, he says, I play what's on the hymn sheet is all, and sure enough there it is written out. Turn the page, Billy says, give me a preview. Fat man does and growls, it's a fight scene. Brawling or guns? Well, that's kinda hard to tell, you better ask me what you want to know in the next few bars.

Where's the new guy, Billy says. Lotsa new guys in town, fat man replies. No, Billy says, there ain't, there's only one. My height and taller, black hat, solitary fella don't like to make friends. Oh, that new guy, fat man says. That new guy got hisself a room above the hardware store, has Missus Roth bring him food and all. He armed? Billy Tumult asks, and the fat man says that a patron that tough don't go about without some manner of weapon but the fat man don't know what kind.

Fat man turns the page on his hymn sheet and one of the poker tables flies up in the air. Fistfight, bottles flying and you goddam cheating bastard and blahsedyblahs. Dissolve to later.

Billy Tumult, walking down the street. Tips his hat to the ladies, bids the fellas good afternoon. Going to the Marshall's office. Want to be in good with the local force. No stink-of-armpit law-keeper, this one, but a high buttoned pinstripe and waistcoat number, almost a dandy. What are the chances, Billy Tumult growls. Man might could be Billy's brother, might could use him for shaving around that dandy moustache. Patient's been thinking about coming to see Billy Tumult for long enough that he's got hisself a tulpa in here, a little imaginary robot doing what the patient thinks Billy'd do. Ain't that just the sweetest thing?

Marshall William says hello, and Billy says hello right back and they shake hands. It's like icebergs colliding. The Marshall's got two shooters on his hips, of course, just like in the brochure. What's behind his back, Billy wonders, maybe a third gun, maybe a humungous nature of a knife. That would figure. But when they get into the Marshall's office and the fella takes off his coat, mother of Christ, it's a dynamite vest, a bandolier. The guy so much as farts wrong and they're all in the next county over and fuck if he doesn't actually smoke. Laws of sanity have been suspended for Billy's oversold publicity-and-marketing hardassery. Thank God if the thing goes up the worst that happens to Billy is a damn reset and the whole surgery to redo from start, pain in the ass, but if this was the real world or if Billy was really part of this whole deal then he'd be pasta sauce.

Pasta sauce is inauthentic. Billy tweaks the filter again. He prefers the gangster aspect, can't keep this horses-and-mud shit straight in his brain. Well, if the patient can have Eskimos, Billy can have pasta sauce, call it fair play.

I'm Billy Tumult of the Pinkertons, he tells Marshall William, come lookin' for a dangerous man. We got plenty, says the Marshall, which one you want? Or take 'em all, I surely won't miss 'em. I want the new guy, Billy says, the one in the black hat living over the store. The one Missus Roth has an arrangement with. Now hold on, begins the Marshall, no not that kind of arrangement, the feedin' kind is all I mean, I got no beef with the Widow Roth.

Widow my ass, parenthesizes Billy Tumult, if I know how this goes, but never mind that for now.

He's an odd one, sure, says the Marshall. Odd and I don't like him and he don't much like me. But I figure the one he's looking out for is you, now I think on it. He offered me a whole shit-ton of gold, I saw it right there in that room, to tell him if a fella came askin' about him. You say yes? Billy wants to know. No, Marshall replies. 'Course not, he says, and rolls his shoulder.

Cutaway: a thin man naked in a room full of gold, lean like a leather-gnarled spider stretched too tight on his own bones. He tilts his head and listens to the sound of the town, and he knows someone's coming. Slips down the gold rockface into his pants and shoes—demons evidently need no socks—and buckles on his gun. Not much of a thing, this gun. Small and dirty and badly kept. Buckles it on, long black coat around his shoulders. Tan galàn on his head: bare-chested Grendel in a hat, and that's as good a name as any. Arms and legs too long, Grendel spidercrabs out of the golden room and into shadow, gone a-huntin'. Too fast, he's under the balcony across the street, flickers in the dark alley by the blacksmith, by the sawbones, by the water tower. Too fast, too quiet. All of a sudden: it's not clear at all who's gonna win this one.

Billy Tumult doesn't exactly see all this, not being present in the mis-en-scène, but he gets the gist because that's the benefit of narrative surgery. You pay a price in hella stupid costumes and irritating dialogue, but you get it back in inevitability. Sooner or later they will stand in the street and one of them will outshoot the other, and Billy can do it over and over and over and over until he nails it; the other fella has to get it perfect every time. That's the thing about your average cognitive hiccup or post-Freudian crise: they just don't learn. That said, on this occasion there's a sense of real jeopardy, contagious fear, and it takes some stones to go out on Main Street and walk down the middle, spurs clankin'.

Billy Tumult has those stones. He surely does.

Half-naked Grendel comes on like blinking, like he doesn't really understand physical spaces. Which he don't, but all the same he's fast and he's focused, he sees Billy the way they mostly can't, sees him as an external object rather than part of the diorama. Not your common or garden mommy issue, this fucker, but a real nasty customer, maybe even a kink in the standing wave. Blink! Walking outside the smithy. Blink! Hat shop, dressmaker. Blink! By the trees outside the mayor's place. Blink! Right there, dead on his mark where he should be for the showdown, except it's too soon. Can't draw down on him, not yet, the patient's mind will fracture him away. It's not the right time. Got to earn your conclusions. This is the chitchat segment, bad guy banter.

Heard you might be in town, Billy says, figured I'd come and see if you were that stupid.

White teeth under thin lips. Patient presents with anhedonia: can't feel joy, can't even feel pleasure, just nothing. Only pain and less pain, sadness and more sadness. Whole top half of his spectrum is missing. Grendel is stealing all the best stuff like a leech, keeping it in that room back there above the store.

Figured you'd stay out in the wilderness, Billy suggests, figured you had maybe a cave out there, livin' on human arms and all, figured you'd feel safe being a wild beast. No place for you in here, you have to know that. It's time to give it up. I'll go easy on you. Like hell he will. Ugliest fucker Billy's ever seen, standing there without moving his eyes, turning his head like a goddam owl. The weird face twists and tilts, and off somewhere behind there's a laugh, an old woman cackle. Billy looks for her, can't find her. Always check your corners.

Patient says he's being watched, all the time, can't shake the feeling, paranoia with all the trimmings.

There is no patient, Grendel whispers—Billy can hear it like he's right there behind him, and then he is, actually is right there, cold breath on Billy's neck—there's just us.

Oh, shit, Billy Tumult thinks, like a lightbulb just before it pops.

This is the cave where Grendel lives. Right now it's in a room over the hardware store, but it could be anywhere because it's basically a state of mind. It's a cave because Grendel lives in it. If you went in—well, if you went in you'd probably die, but if you went in without dying—you'd see it as a great dripping space full of twisting faces drawn in black on shadow, lit by the glimmer of a solitary camp fire and the reflected sheen of bullion. By the fire you'd see Grendel, crouched in his long coat, roasting fish for his mother for her dinner. On a stout stick you'd see a head that looks a lot like Billy Tumult's. It would be unclear if it's a trophy or a dessert.

What Grendel sees, if Grendel sees or even thinks at all, we do not know.

Billy Tumult, on his stick, takes a moment to contemplate the forgotten virtue of humility.

Goddammit.

He was operating on his own self. How did he ever get that stupid? And why can't he remember? Well, he can think of reasons, reasons for both. Can't be much of a psychic surgeon if you've got your own crippling issues, can't exactly trust the competition much, can't be seen to go to a therapist. How'd that play on cable? Not well.

And as to forgetting, well, that could be a mistake or a choice he's made, maybe the stakes are high and he doesn't want to cramp his decision making. Maybe he wanted to be sure he'd do what it took, deliver a cure even if some of the loss was painful. Maybe Grendel's got roots in something Billy'd ideally like to hang onto, good memories from the old days, whatever. But clear enough: this fucker needs to be got, because he is one terrifying sumbitch.

Which is going to be hard to arrange from the top of a goddam stick in a goddam cave.

Top of the morning to you, Missus Roth, Marshall William says, tips his hat. And to you, twinkles the merry widow on her horse, thirty five years of age at most, sure in the saddle and a fine figure of a woman. William wishes she'd stop and pass the time a little but she never does. I hear there was some excitement earlier, she tells him, I hear it was quite unsettling. Oh, well, yes, there was some excitement, William says, but it's all done now. A man come to town lookin' for a fugitive, your Mister Grendel as it happens, but it was all a misunderstanding if you can believe it, and the fella's gone on his way and no harm done. Is that right, says Evangeline Roth, is that right, indeed? And Marshall William assures her that it is, misses the flicker in her eyes, the hardness that says he's just fallen in her estimation, fallen a good long way and may now never resurface. That's fine, she says then, for Mister Grendel is a gentleman I'm sure. And she goes on her way to market. That's a fine figure of a woman, William murmurs, and bold for a respectable widow to wear a vermillion chapeau to go out riding, bold and quite suitable on her to be sure.

Evangeline Roth married a young preacher in Spokane, Missouri, when she . was only twenty, loved him more than life, saw him die on the way out west of a snake bite. The thing had lunged for her and he put out his hand to take the strike, the wound festered and that was that. They had no children: they were waiting for the right time. She learned to shoot from a carnival girl, learned to sit a horse the same way, has no intention of being a second class anything, not here or in any other town. Owns the hardware store in her own name and takes in lodgers when it suits her, knows fine well there's a darkness in her house now, a bad place that needs dealing with the way you'd bag a hornet's nest and put it in the river. Looks back over her sharp shoulder at Marshall William and growls. Useless.

But speaking of the river—she taps her heels to the flanks of the horse—well, now, wasn't there a place once? A wide strand where all manner of things wash up, jetsam and littoral peculiars. Yes, indeed, some distance out of town, a half day's riding and a little more. Widow Roth, with a few necessaries in her saddlebags, makes her way along the old mule trail and past the abandoned mines, across the yucca plain to the very spot, where the wide blue water winds about the sand, and removes her clothes to work magic. She has no idea if nudity is requisite, but likewise no intention of making a mess of things for the sake of crinolines and stays.

That night on the white sand she draws all manner of significant ideograms, according to her strongly-held opinions. She dances—furtively at first, for it is one thing to be discovered nude by a river where after all anyone might reasonably bathe, but quite another to be seen cavorting—but eventually she stretches out her hands to the world and spins and leaps with her whole remarkable self. She invokes angels and local gods she has heard about from local people, performs whatever syncretist rituals are in line with her understanding of divinity. Overall, indeed, she does the best she can with what she has, promising a small sheep if such is required, or good strong whisky and tobacco, or a life of virtue and contemplation on the other hand, and heartfelt apologies for this behavior. The point is, this thing must be done, she repeats over and over to the wind. It must be done.

The night seems not to care. In the end, she lies exhausted and dusty on her back and just shrieks at the sky, conscious that here at last she has perhaps finally come to an understanding of what magic and religion truly are. And at dawn, through gummed eyes, she sees the result of her exhortations and exertions washed to shore by the breeze: a strange contraption like a sword or flintlock, to be worn as near as she can tell in the small of the back. Inscribed upon the hilt are occult symbols: Combine Medical Industries: NIS 3.1.a.

This is a river in a dream, and as such washes through all caves and all valleys, and will in good conscience respond to such desperation as it can.

Grendel springs from his sleep, from his golden bed, jointless neck twisting. Snatches up his coat. Pauses to strike at Billy Tumult's living head. Ow, Billy Tumult says in the empty cave, and hears Grendel's mother chortle from the dark. She must be able to fly, thinks Billy Tumult on his stick. That must be it. She's never where she should be and always where you don't want her.

No time for that now: through the shadows skitters spidery Grendel, owl eyes bright and fingers grasping. Blink blink here and blink blink there, but he has no idea what to look for, knows only that something is wrong. Peers in through the high windows of the saloon, looking for another lawman. Perhaps Marshall William's found his steel? But no. There he is, stuffed shirt presiding over a poker tournament, the Yupik winning, yes, of course. Where away?

So very close, did he but know. Evangeline Roth stands in her boudoir, scant yards from the door she rents to Grendel, the entrance to the cave. A sensible jacket and good trousers are important in such moments. She doesn't bother to put the scalpel in its holster, doesn't propose for one moment to let it out of her hand until she's done with her task. No idle oath, this, but pure practical terror, which she feels sure is a better guide to questing behavior than any bold pledge or pretty couplet.

Amazing, she considers, how impossibly hard it is, in a nightmare, to open the doors of one's own house.

But she does.

On the roof of the mayor's mansion, Grendel gives a shriek and spins in the moonlight, spins for home like a compass needle. Scrabbles across the tiles and leaps. Never touches the sandy street, just folds away. In a real hurry now, is Grendel.

Evangeline Roth takes in the cave, the cackling dark, and the head of Billy Tumult on a stick—and all this existing somehow inside the confines of her guest room, for the rental of which she charges a few dollars, including soap and hot water for washing. Two seats by the fire, she notes, laid in front of all that lustrous gold, but only one shows any sign of occupation. Before the other, decaying and uneaten baked fish, peppered with flies.

This all is, she acknowledges, more odd than she was prepared to contemplate before stepping through the door she painted last summer in duck egg blue. All in all, though, she would handle it very well if only the dismembered head would stop giving her instructions. Just like a man, she considers, to die absolutely and then hang around to offer his useless experience to a female person who is so far still alive.

Charity, she thinks firmly, putting the head in her bag. Charity begins at home.

Billy Tumult stares up at the interior space of the handbag and considers this a new low. Rescued by a merry widow from a monster's cave, dumped into a perfumed clutch filled with the unmentionable secrets of females. No, he promises more loudly, he will be quiet, there is no need to stuff that—somewhat used—monogrammed lace hanky in his mouth for hush. But how hard is this for the bold adventurer? Quite hard, indeed, and that must be his very own scalpel in her other hand, prudently unholstered and charged. If Billy still had that—and arms and legs and so forth for its deployment—this story would run differently, that's for sure. But here, this is the way things are, and he's reduced to . . . what? Baggage? At least, surely, early warning system, canary in the mine. And yes: warning, indeed! Scuffle and titter in the dark, rat-roach rustle. Christ, Billy says, it's the mother! Look out behind you!

This being his advice, and he being in his present place—and having resolved in her mind the curious clue of the undevoured fish repast—Evangeline sweeps up the scalpel directly in front of her and thumbs the trigger. No monster takes her between the shoulders, no great vasty mother sups upon her spine. The tittering and cackling carries on regardless as the blue white stream emerging from the scalpel licks just in front of crabwise Grendel, cloaked in shadows, and brings him scritching to a halt. There is no mother, Evangeline has reckoned, not really, just a chittering landscape. There's Grendel, and he must have his sound effects, but in the end—just as she is—he must be alone.

So there they stand: widow and monster, each paradoxically in their own place of power. His cave, her house. A darkness walking meeting a patchwork saint of practical technology and improvised magic in this altogether unanticipated explosion of Billy's Wild West operating table, on which apparently he is himself presently anaesthetized.

High noon, she realises, as somewhere a church bell begins to ring. Grendel drops his hands to his sides and waits for the twelfth chime. She can feel the shadows smirking. A ridiculous mismatch. After all, he can step behind her on the strike. Take her, just as he took Billy Tumult. It wants only the right moment.

She shrugs, and uses the scalpel to remove his head. Watches the body fall. Listens to the chimes run out: bong bong bong bong. The right moment, Evangeline the widow remarks to her spare bed and washing china, now returned from whatever reality they occupied while the cave was in residence in this space, is when I bloody say it is.

She puts the head in the bag and, on a whim, attaches Billy Tumult to the fallen corpse. The body rises. Job done. I'm alive, alive, shouts the resulting personage. Well, yes, Evangeline replies, judicious, but best you wear some sort of neckerchief until the scar is properly healed. And for God's sake put on a shirt.

Marry me, Billy Tumult says, opening his eyes on the operating table to the first pleasurable feelings he has known in half a decade, Jesus Mary and Joseph I'm cured and I thought I was screwed. Marry me, Evangeline, I swear to God!

The object of this proposal is a fine figure of a woman, a temporary hire in the practice, recently arrived in town and filling time while she looks for an apartment. Hell, no, replies Evangeline Roth, I don't even like you and frankly going by this one observation your specialism's a crock. That in mind and with some reservations regarding your ability to understand the literal truth of what I'm about to say, you can buy me a platonic drink while we discuss my bonus.

And with this offer, Billy Tumult has to be content.

ʜello, ʜello;
caɴ ʏou ʜeaɾ ᴍe, ʜello

SEANAN McGUIRE

Saying "Hello" back when someone says "Hello" to you is an important thing, of course—but sometimes it's a vital one, one that could change your entire perception of the world. . . .

New York Times bestselling author Seanan McGuire has enjoyed critical and commercial success both under her own name and the pseudonym Mira Grant. Heralded right out of the gate with 2010's John W. Campbell Award for Best New Writer, McGuire also holds the unique honor of appearing five times on the same Hugo Awards ballot (with three nominations for McGuire and two for Grant). Prolific in both novels and short work, she is lauded for her detailed world-building in her October Daye urban fantasy series— currently planned out to at least thirteen entries that appear every September—and the InCryptid series, which kicked off with 2012's Discount Armageddon. As Grant, she writes the Newsflesh trilogy. Its first volume, Feed, was one of Publishers Weekly's Best Books of 2010, and earned nominations for both the Shirley Jackson Award and the Hugo Award for Best Novel.

Tasha's avatar smiled from the screen, a little too perfect to be true. That was a choice, just like everything else about it: when we'd installed my sister's new home system, we had instructed it to generate avatars that looked like they had escaped the uncanny valley by the skins of their teeth. It was creepy, but the alternative was even creepier. Tasha didn't talk. Her avatar did. Having them match each other perfectly would have been . . . wrong.

"So I'll see you next week?" she asked. Her voice was perfectly neutral, with a newscaster's smooth, practiced inflections. Angie had picked it from the database of publicly available voices; like the avatar, it had been generated in a lab. Unlike the avatar, it was flawless. No one who heard Tasha "talk" would realize that they were really hearing a collection of sounds programmed by a computer, translated from the silent motion of her hands.

That was the point. Setting up the system for her had removed all barriers to conversation, and when she was talking to clients who didn't know that she was deaf, she didn't want them to realize anything was happening behind the scenes. Hence the avatar, rather than the slight delay that came with the face-time translation programs. It felt wrong to me, like we were trying to hide something essential about my sister, but it was her choice and her system; I was just the one who upgraded her software and made sure that nothing broke down. If anyone was equipped for the job, it was me, the professional Computational Linguist. It's a living.

"We'll be there right on time," I said, knowing that on her end, my avatar would be smiling and silent, moving her hands in the appropriate words. I could speak ASL to the screen, but with the way her software was set up, speaking ASL while the translator settings were active could result in some vicious glitches. After the time the computer had decided my hand gestures were a form of complicated profanity, and translated the chugging of the air conditioner into words while spewing invective at my sister, I had learnt to keep my hands still while the translator was on. "I'm bringing Angie and the kids, so be ready."

Tasha laughed. "I'll tell the birds to be on their best behavior." A light flashed behind her avatar, and her expression changed, becoming faintly regretful. "Speaking of the birds, that's my cue. Talk tomorrow?"

"Talk tomorrow," I said. "Love you lots."

"I love you too," she said, and ended the call, leaving me staring at my own reflection on the suddenly black screen. My face, so much like her computer generated one, but slightly rougher; slightly less perfect. Humanity will do that to a girl.

Finally, I stood and went to tell my wife we had plans for the next weekend. She liked my sister, and Greg and Billie liked the birds. It would be good for us.

"Hello," said the woman on the screen. She was black-haired and brown-eyed, with skin that fell somewhere between "tan" and "tawny." She was staring directly at the camera, almost unnervingly still. "Hello, hello."

"Hello!" said Billie happily, waving at the woman. Billie's nails were painted bright blue, like beetle shells. She was on an entomology kick again this week, studying every insect she found as raptly as if she had just discovered the secrets of the universe. "How are you?"

"Hello," said the woman. "Hello, hello, hello."

"Billie, who are you talking to?" I stopped on my way to the laundry room, bundling the basket I'd been carrying against my hip. The woman didn't look familiar, but she had the smooth, CGI skin of a translation avatar. There was no telling what her root language was. The natural user interface of the software would be trying to mine its neural networks for the places where she and Billie overlapped, looking for the points of commonality and generating a vocabulary that accounted for their hand gestures and body language, as well as for their vocalizations.

It was a highly advanced version of the old translation software that had been rolled out in the late 2010s; that had been verbal-only, and only capable of translating sign language into straight text, not into vocalizations that followed spoken sentence structures and could be played through speakers. ASL to speech had followed, and then speech to ASL, with increasingly realistic avatars learning to move their hands in the complex patterns necessary for communication. Now, the systems could be taught to become ad hoc translators, pulling on the full weight of their neural networks and deep learning capabilities as they built bridges across the world.

Of course, it also meant that we had moments like this one, two people shouting greetings across an undefined void of linguistic separation. "Billie?" I repeated.

"It's Aunt Tasha's system, Mom," said my nine-year-old, turning to look at me over her shoulder. She rolled her eyes, making sure I understood just how foolish my concern really was. "I wouldn't have *answered* if I didn't recognize the caller."

"But that's not Aunt Tasha," I said.

Billie gave me the sort of withering look that only people under eighteen can manage. She was going to be a terror in a few years. "I know that," she said. "I think she's visiting to see the birds. Lots of people visit to see the birds."

"True," I said, giving the woman on the screen another look. Tasha's system was set up to generate a generic avatar for anyone who wasn't a registered user. It would draw on elements of their appearance—hair color, eye color, skin tone—but it would otherwise assemble the face from public-source elements. "Hello," I said. "Is my sister there?"

"Hello," said the woman. "Hello, hello."

"I don't think the computer knows her language very well," said Billie. "That's all she's said."

Which could mean a glitch. Sometimes, when the software got confused enough, it would translate everything as "hello." An attempt at connection, even when the tools weren't there. "I think you may be right," I said, moving to get closer to the computer. Billie, recognizing the shift from protective mother to computer scientist with a mystery to solve, shifted obligingly to the side. She would never have tolerated being smothered, but she was more than smart enough not to sit between me and a puzzle.

"Is Tasha there?" I asked again, as clearly as I could.

The woman looked at me and said nothing.

"I need to know what language you're speaking. I'm sorry the translator program isn't working for you, but if I know what family to teach it, I can probably get it up and running in pretty short order." Everything I said probably sounded like "hello, hello" to her, but at least I was trying. That was the whole point, wasn't it? Trying. "Can you say the name of your language? I am speaking casual conversational English." No matter how confused the program was, it would say "English" clearly. Hopefully that would be enough to get us started.

"Hello, hello," said the woman. She looked to her right, eyes widening slightly, as if she'd been startled. Then she leaned out of the frame, and was gone. The image of Tasha's dining room continued for several seconds before the computer turned itself off, leaving Billie and I to look, bemused, at an empty screen.

Finally, hesitantly, Billie asked, "Was that one of Aunt Tasha's friends?"

"I don't know," I said. "I'll call her later and ask."

I forgot to call.

In my defense, there were other things to do, and none of them were the sort that could easily be put off until tomorrow. Greg discovered a secret snail breeding ground in the garden and transported them all inside, sticking them to the fridge like slime-generating magnets. Greg thought this was wonderful. The snails didn't seem to have an opinion. Angie thought this was her cue to disinfect the entire house, starting with the kitchen, and left me to watch both kids while I was trying to finish a project for work. It was really no wonder I lost track of them. It was more of a wonder that it took me over an hour to realize they were gone.

Angie wasn't shouting, so the kids hadn't wandered back into the kitchen to get in the way of her frenzied housework. I stood, moving carefully as I began my search. As any parent can tell you, it's better to keep your mouth shut and your eyes open when you go looking for kids who are being unreasonably quiet. They're probably doing something they don't want you to see, and if they hear you coming, they'll hide the evidence.

I heard them laughing before I reached the living room. I stopped making such an effort to mask my footsteps, and came around the corner of the doorway to find them with their eyes glued to the computer, laughing at the black-haired woman from before.

"Hello, hello," she was saying. "I'm hungry, hello, can you hear me?"

Greg laughed. Billie leaned forward and said, "We can hear you. Hello, hello, we can hear you!" This set Greg laughing harder.

The woman on the screen looked from one child to the other, opened her mouth, and said, "Ha ha. Ha ha. Ha ha. Hello, hello, can you hear me?"

"What's this?" I asked.

Billie turned and beamed at me. "Auntie Tasha's friend is back, and the program is learning more of her language! I'm doing like you told me to do if I ever need to talk to somebody the neural net doesn't know, and using lots of repeating to try and teach it more."

"The word you want is 'echolalia,'" I said distractedly, leaning past her to focus on the screen. "You're back. Hello. Is my sister there?"

"Hello, hello," said the woman. "Can you hear me? I'm hungry."

"Yes, I got that," I said, trying to keep the frustration out of my voice. It wasn't her fault that her language—whatever it was—was giving the translation software issues. Tasha's neural net hadn't encountered as many spoken languages as ours had. It could manage some startlingly accurate gesture translations, some of which we had incorporated in the base software after they cropped up, but it couldn't always pick up on spoken languages with the speed of a neural net belonging to a hearing person. Tasha also had a tendency to invite visiting academics and wildlife conservationists to stay in her spare room, since they were presumably used to the screeching of wild birds.

"If not for them," she had said more than once, "you're the only company I'd ever have."

It was hard to argue with that. It was just a little frustrating that one of her guests kept calling my kids. "Can you please tell Tasha to call me? I want to speak with her."

"Hello, hello," said the woman.

"Goodbye," I replied, and canceled the call.

Both children looked at me like I had done something terribly wrong. "She just wanted someone to talk to," said Billie mulishly.

"Let me know if she calls again, all right? I don't know who she is, and I'm not comfortable with you talking to her until I've spoken to Tasha."

"Okay, Mom," said Billie.

Greg frowned, but didn't say anything. I leaned down and scooped him onto my shoulder. That got a squeal, followed by a trail of giggles. I straightened.

"Come on, you two. Let's go see if we can't help Mumma in the kitchen."

They went willingly enough. I cast a glance back at the dark computer screen. This time, I would definitely remember to call my sister.

As always, reaching Tasha was easier said than done. She spent much of her time outside feeding and caring for her birds, and when she was in the house, she was almost always doing some task related to her work. There were flashing lights in every room to tell her when she had a call, but just like everyone else in the world, sometimes she ignored her phone in favor of doing something more interesting. I could have set my call as an emergency and turned all the lights red, but that seemed like a mean trick, since "I wanted to ask about one of your house guests" wasn't really an emergency. Just a puzzle. There was always a puzzle; had been since we were kids, when her reliance on ASL had provided us with a perfect "secret language" and provided me with a bilingual upbringing—something that had proven invaluable as I grew up and went into neuro-linguistic computing.

When we were kids signing at each other, fingers moving almost faster than the human eye could follow, our hands had looked like birds in flight. I had followed the words. My sister had followed the birds. They needed her, and they never judged her for her differences. What humans saw as disability, Tasha's birds saw as a human who was finally quiet enough not to be startling, or too loud, or complain when they started singing outside her window at three in the morning. It was the perfect marriage of flesh and function.

After two days of trying and failing to get her to pick up, I sent an email. *Just checking in*, it said. *Haven't been able to rouse you. Do you have houseguests right now? Someone's been calling the house from your terminal.*

Her reply came fast enough to tell me that she had already been at her computer. *A few grad students came to look @ my king vulture. He is very impressive. One of them could have misdialed? It's not like I would have heard them. ;) We still on for Sunday?*

I sent a call request. Her avatar popped up thirty seconds later, filling the screen with her faintly dubious expression.

"Yes?" she said. "Email works, you know."

"Email is too slow. I like to see your face."

She rolled her eyes. "It's all the same to me," she said. "I know you're not really signing. I prefer talking to you when I can see your hands."

"I'm sorry," I said. "Greg's ASL is progressing really well. We should be able to go back to real-time chat in a year or so. Until then, we need to keep the vocals on, so he can get to know you too. Look how well it worked out with Billie."

Tasha's expression softened. She'd been dubious when I'd explained that we'd be teaching Billie ASL but using the voice translation mode on our chat software;

we wanted Billie to care about getting to know her aunt, and with a really small child, it had seemed like the best way. It had worked out well. Billie was fluent enough in ASL to carry on conversations with strangers, and was already writing letters to our local high schools, asking them to offer sign language as an elective. Greg was following in her footsteps. I was pretty sure we'd be able to turn off the voice translation in another year or so.

To be honest, I was going to be relieved when that happened. I was lazy enough to appreciate the ease of talking to my sister without needing to take my hands off the keyboard, but it was strange to hear her words, rather than watching them.

"I guess," she said. "So what was up with the grad students? One of them called the house?"

"I think so," I said. "She seemed a little confused. Just kept saying 'hello' over and over again. Were any of them visiting from out-of-country schools? Someplace far enough away that the neural net wouldn't have a solid translation database to access?" Our systems weren't creating translation databases out of nothing, of course— that would have been programming well above my paygrade, and possibly a Nobel Prize for Humanities—but they would find the common phonemes and use them to direct themselves to which shared databases they should be accessing. Where the complicated work happened was in the contextual cues. The hand gestures that punctuated speech with "I don't know" and "yes" and "I love you." The sideways glances that meant "I am uncomfortable with this topic." Bit by bit, our translators put those into words, and understanding grew.

(And there were people who used their translators like Tasha did, who hid silent tongues or a reluctance to make eye contact behind computer-generated faces and calm, measured voices, who presented a completely default face to the world and took great comfort in knowing that the people who would judge them for their differences would never need to know. I couldn't judge them for that. I was the one who asked my sister to let me give her a voice, like grafting a tongue onto Hans Christian Anderson's Little Mermaid, for the duration of my children's short infancy.)

"I don't know," she said, after a long pause. "Only two of them spoke ASL. The other three spoke through their professor, and I've known her for years. Why? Did she say something inappropriate to the kids?"

"No, just 'hello,' like I said. Still, it was strange, and she called back at least once. Black hair, medium brown skin. I didn't get a name."

"If I see someone like that, I'll talk to her about privacy and what is and is not appropriate when visiting someone else's home."

"Thanks." I shook my head. "I just don't like strangers talking to the kids."

"Me, neither."

We chatted for a while after that—just ordinary, sisterly things, how the kids were doing, how the birds were doing, what we were going to have for dinner on Sunday— and I felt much better when I hung up and went to bed.

When I woke up the next morning, Greg and Billie were already in the dining room, whispering to the computer. By the time I moved into position to see the monitor, it was blank, and neither of them would tell me who they'd been talking to—assuming they had been talking to anyone at all.

We arrived at Tasha's a little after noon. As was our agreement, we didn't knock; I just pressed my thumb to the keypad and unlocked the door, allowing our already-wiggling children to spill past us into the bright, plant-strewn atrium. Every penny Tasha got was poured back into either the house or the birds—and since the birds had the run of the house, every penny she put into the house was still going to the birds. Cages of rescued finches, budgies, and canaries twittered at us as we entered, giving greeting and expressing interest in a series of short, sharp chirps. Hanging plants and bright potted irises surrounded the cages, making it feel like we had just walked into the front hall of some exclusive conservatory.

That, right there, was why Tasha spent so much money on the upkeep and décor of her home. It was a licensed rescue property, but keeping it looking like something special—which it was—kept her neighbors from complaining.

Opening the door had triggered the flashing warning lights in the corners of the room. Tasha would be looking for us, and so we went looking for her, following the twitter of birds and the shrieking laughter of our children.

Our parties collided in the kitchen, where Billie was signing rapid-fire at her aunt while Greg tugged at her arm and offered interjections, his own amateurish signs breaking into the conversation only occasionally. A barn owl was perched atop the refrigerator. That was par for the course at Tasha's place, where sometimes an absence of birds was the strange thing. The door leading out to the screened-in patio was open, and a large pied crow sat on the back of the one visible chair, watching us warily. Most of that wariness was probably reserved for the owl. They would fight, if given the opportunity, and Tasha didn't like breaking up squabbles between birds she was rehabilitating. Birds that insisted on pecking at each other were likely to find themselves caged. The smarter birds—the corvids and the big parrots—learned to play nicely, lest they be locked away.

I waved. Tasha glanced over, beamed, and signed a quick 'hello' before she went back to conversing with my daughter. The world had narrowed for the two of them, becoming nothing more than the space of their hands and the words they drew on the air, transitory and perfect.

The computer was on the table, open as always. I passed the day bag to Angie, pressing a quick kiss to her cheek before I said, "I'm going to go check on the neural net. Let me know if you need me."

"Yes, leave me alone with your sister in the House of Birds," she said, deadpan. I laughed, and walked away.

Part of the arrangement I had with Tasha involved free access to her computer. She got the latest translation software and endless free upgrades to her home neural net, I went rooting through the code whenever I was in the house. She didn't worry about me seeing her browser history or stumbling across an open email client; we'd been sharing our password-locked blogs since we were kids. What was the point of having a sister if you couldn't trade bad boy band RPF once in a while?

Flipping through her call history brought up the usual assortment of calls to schools, pet supply warehouses, and local takeout establishments, all tagged under her user name. There were seven guest calls over the past week. Three of them were to the university, and pulling up their profiles showed that the people who had initiated the calls had loaded custom avatars, dressing their words in their own curated faces. The other four . . .

The other four were anonymous, and the avatar had been generated by the system, but not retained. All four had been made from this computer to the first number in its saved database. Mine.

I scribbled down the timestamps and went to join the conversation in the kitchen, waving a hand for Tasha's attention. She turned, expression questioning. I handed her the piece of paper, and signed, "Did you have the same person in the house for all four of these calls?"

Tasha frowned. "No," she signed back. "I had some conservationists for this one, picking up an owl who'd been cleared for release," she tapped the middle entry on the list, "but all those other times, I was alone with the birds. What's going on?"

"Could it be a system glitch?" asked Angie, speaking and signing at the same time. She preferred it that way, since it gave her an excuse to go slowly. She said it was about including Greg in the conversation, and we let her have that; if it kept her from becoming too self-conscious to sign, it was a good thing.

"It could," I signed. Silence was an easy habit to fall back into in the company of my sister. "I'd have to take the whole system apart to be sure. Tasha, are you all right with my cloning it and unsnarling things once I get home?"

"As long as this glitch isn't going to break anything, I don't care," she signed.

I nodded. "It should be fine," I signed. "If it's a system error, that would explain why our caller keeps saying 'hello,' and never getting any further. I'll be able to let you know in a couple of days."

Billie tugged on Tasha's sleeve. We all turned. Billie beamed. "Can we see the parrots now?" she signed. Tasha laughed, and for a while, everything was normal. Everything was the way that it was supposed to be.

My snapshot of Tasha's system revealed no errors with the code, although I found some interesting logical chains in her translation software's neural network that I copied over and sent to R&D for further analysis. She had one of the most advanced learning systems outside of corporate, in part because she was my sister, and in part because she was a bilingual deaf person, speaking both American and British Sign Language with the people she communicated with. Giving her a system that could handle the additional non-verbal processing was allowing us to build out a better neural chain and translation database than any amount of laboratory testing could produce, and had the added bonus of equipping my sister to speak with conservationists all over the world. It's always nice when corporate and family needs align.

The calls were being intentionally initiated, by someone who had access to Tasha's computer. There was no way this was a ghost in the machine or a connection routing error. Malware was still a possibility, given the generic avatar; someone could be spoofing the machine into opening the call, then overlaying the woman on the backdrop of Tasha's dining room. I didn't know what purpose that would serve, unless this was the warmup to some innovative denial of service attack. I kept digging.

"Hello? Hello?"

My head snapped up. The voice was coming from the main computer in the dining room. It was somehow less of a surprise when Billie answered a moment later: "Hello! How are you?"

"Hello, hello, I'm fine. I'm good. I'm hungry. How are you?"

I rose from my seat, using the table to steady myself before walking, carefully, quietly, toward the next room. There was Billie, seated in front of the terminal, where the strange woman's image was once again projected. Greg was nowhere to be seen. He was probably off somewhere busying himself with toddler projects, like stacking blocks or talking to spiders, leaving his sister to unwittingly assist in industrial espionage.

"Billie?"

Billie turned, all smiles, as the woman on the screen shifted her focus to me, cocking her head slightly to the side to give herself a better view. "Hi, Mom!" my daughter chirped, her fingers moving in the appropriate signs at the same time. "I figured it out!"

"Figured what out, sweetie?"

"Why we couldn't understand each other!" she gestured grandly to the screen where the black-haired woman waited. "Mumma showed me."

I frowned, taking a step closer. "Showed you what?"

"Hello, hello; can you hear me? Hello," said the woman.

"Hello," I said, automatically.

Billie was undaunted. "When we went to see Aunt Tasha, Mumma used her speaking words and her finger words at the same time, so Greg could know what we were saying. She was bridging." Her fingers moved in time with her lips. ASL doesn't have the same grammatical structure as spoken English; my daughter was running two linguistic processing paths at the same time. I wanted to take the time to be proud of her for that. I was too busy trying to understand.

"You mean she was building a linguistic bridge?" I asked.

Billie nodded vigorously. "Yeah. Bridging. So I thought maybe we couldn't understand each other because the neural net didn't have enough to work with, and I turned off the avatar setting on this side."

My heart clenched. The avatar projections for Billie and Greg were intended to keep their real faces hidden from anyone who wasn't family. It was a small precaution, but anything that would keep their images off the public Internet until they turned eighteen was a good idea as far as I was concerned. "Billie, we've talked about the avatars. They're there to keep you safe."

"But she needed to see my hands," said Billie, with serene childhood logic. "Once she could, we started communicating better. See? I just needed to give the translator more data!"

"Hello," said the woman.

"Hello," I said, moving closer to the screen. After a beat, I followed the word with the appropriate sign. "What's your name? Why do you keep calling my house?"

"I'm hungry," said the woman. "I'm hungry."

"You're not answering my question."

The woman opened her mouth like she was laughing, but no sound came out.

She closed it again with a snap, and said, "I'm hungry. I don't know you. Where is the other one?"

"Here I am!" said Billie, pushing her way back to the front. "Sorry about Mom. She doesn't understand that we're doing science here."

"Science, yes," said the woman obligingly. "Hello, hello. I'm hungry."

"I get hungry too," said Billie. "Maybe some cereal?"

I took a step back, letting the two of them talk. I didn't like the idea of leaving my little girl with a live connection to God-knows-who. I also didn't like the thought that this call was coming from my sister's house. If she was out back with the birds, she would never hear an intruder, and I couldn't call to warn her while her line was in use.

Angie was in the kitchen. "Billie's on the line with our mystery woman," I said quickly, before she could ask me what was wrong. "I'm going to drive to Tasha's and see if I can't catch this lady in the act."

Angie's eyes widened. "So you just *left* Billie on the line?"

"You can supervise her," I said. "Just try to keep her from disconnecting. I can make this stop, but I need to go."

"Then go," said Angie. I'd be hearing about this later. I knew that, just like I knew I was making the right call. Taking Billie away from the computer wouldn't stop this woman breaking into my sister's house and calling us, and one police report could see Tasha branded a security risk by the company, which couldn't afford to leave software patches that were still under NDA in insecure locations.

Tasha lived fifteen minutes from us under normal circumstances. I made the drive in seven.

Her front door was locked but the porch light was on, signaling that she was home and awake. I let myself in without ringing the bell. She could yell at me later. Finding out what was going on was more important than respecting her privacy, at least for right now. I felt a little bad about that. I also knew that she would have done exactly the same thing if our positions had been reversed.

I slunk through the house, listening for the sound of Billie's voice. Tasha kept the speakers on for the sake of the people who visited her and used her computer to make calls. She was better at accommodation than I was. The thought made my ears redden. My sister, who had spent most of her life fighting to be accommodated, made the effort for others when I was willing to focus on just her. I would be better, I promised silently. For her sake, and for the sake of my children, I would be better.

I didn't hear Billie. Instead, I heard the throaty croaking of a crow from up ahead of me. It continued as I walked down the hall and stepped into the kitchen doorway. And stopped.

The pied crow that Tasha had been rehabilitating was perched on the back of the chair across from the screen, talons digging deep into the wood as it cocked its head and watched Billie's image on the screen. Billie's mouth moved; a squawk emerged. The crow croaked back, repeating the same sounds over and over, until the avatar was matching them perfectly. Only then did it move on to the next set of sounds.

I took a step back and sagged against the hallway wall, heart pounding, head spinning with the undeniable reality of what I had just seen. A language the neural net didn't know, one that depended on motion and gesture as much as it did on sound.

A language the system would have been exposed to enough before a curious bird started pecking at the keys that the program could at least *try* to make sense of it.

Sense enough to say "hello."

An air of anticipation hung over the lab. The pied crow—whose name, according to Tasha, was Pitch, and who had been raised in captivity, bouncing from wildlife center to wildlife center before winding up living in my sister's private aviary—gripped her perch stubbornly with her talons and averted her eyes from the screen, refusing to react to the avatar that was trying to catch her attention. She'd been ignoring the screen for over an hour, shutting out four researchers and a bored linguist who was convinced that I was in the middle of some sort of creative breakdown.

"All right, Paulson, this was a funny prank, but you've used up over a dozen computing hours," said Mike, pushing away from his own monitor. "Time to pack it in."

"Wait a second," I said. "Just . . . just wait, all right? There's one thing we haven't tried yet."

Mike looked at me and frowned. I looked pleadingly back. Finally, he sighed.

"Admittedly, you've encouraged the neural net to make some great improvements. You can have one more try. But that's it! After that, we need this lab back."

"One more is all I need."

I'd been hoping to avoid this. It would've been easier if I could have replicated the original results without resorting to recreation of all factors. Not easier for the bird: easier for my nerves. Angie was already mad at me, and Tasha was unsettled, and I was feeling about as off-balance as I ever did.

Opening the door and sticking my head out into the hall, I looked to my left, where my wife and children were settled in ergonomic desk chairs. Angie was focused on her tablet, composing an email to her work with quick swipes of her fingers, like she was trying to wipe them clean of some unseen, clinging film. Billie was sitting next to her, attention fixed on a handheld game device. Greg sat on the floor between them. He had several of his toy trains and was rolling them around an imaginary track, making happy humming noises.

He was the first one to notice me. He looked up and beamed, calling, "Mama!"

"Hi, buddy," I said. Angie and Billie were looking up as well. I offered my wife a sheepish smile. "Hi, hon. We're almost done in here. I just need to borrow Billie for a few minutes, if that's okay?"

It wasn't okay: I could see that in her eyes. We were going to fight about this later, and I was going to lose. Billie, however, bounced right to her feet, grinning ear to ear as she dropped her game on the chair where she'd been sitting. "Do I get to work science with you?"

"I want science!" Greg protested, his own smile collapsing into the black hole of toddler unhappiness.

"Oh, no, bud." I crouched down, putting myself on as much of a level with him as I could. "We'll do some science when we get home, okay? Water science. With the hose. I just need Billie right now, and I need you to stay here with Mumma and keep her company. She'll get lonely if you both come with me."

Greg gave me a dubious look before twisting to look suspiciously up at Angie. She nodded quickly.

"She's right," she said. "I would be so lonely out here all by myself. Please stay and keep me company."

"Okay," said Greg, after weighing his options. He reached contentedly for his train. "Water science later."

Aware that I had just committed myself to being squirted by the hose in our backyard for at least an hour, I took Billie's hand and ushered her quickly away before anything else could go wrong.

The terminal she'd be using to make her call was waiting for us when we walked back into the room. I ushered her over to the chair, ignoring the puzzled looks from my colleagues. "Remember the lady who kept calling the house?" I asked. "Would you like to talk to her again?"

"I thought I wasn't supposed to talk to strangers," said Billie, eyeing me warily as she waited for the catch. She was old enough to know that when a parent offered to break the rules, there was always a catch.

"I'm right here this time," I said. "That means she's not a stranger, she's . . . a social experiment."

Billie nodded, still dubious. "If it's really okay . . ."

"It's really, truly okay." Marrying a physicist meant that my kids had always been destined to grow up steeped in science. It was an inescapable part of our lives. I hadn't been expecting them to necessarily be so fond of it, but that worked out too. I was happier raising a bevy of little scientists than I would have been with the alternative.

Billie nodded once more and turned to face the monitor. I flashed a low "okay" sign at Mike, and the screen sprang to life, showing the blandly pretty CGI avatar that Tasha's system generated for Pitch. We'd have to look into the code to see when it had made the decision to start rendering animals with human faces, and whether that was part of a patch that had been widely distributed. I could see the logic behind it—the generic avatar generator was given instructions based on things like "eyes" and "attempting to use the system," rather than the broader and more complex-to-program "human." I could also see lawsuits when people inevitably began running images of their pets through the generator and using them to catfish their friends.

On the other side of the two-way mirror, Pitch perked up at the sight of Billie's face on her screen. She opened her beak. Microphones inside the room would pick up the sounds she made, but I didn't need to hear her to know that she was croaking and trilling, just like corvids always did. What was interesting was the way she was also fluffing out her feathers, and moving the tip of her left wing downward.

"Hello, hello," said her avatar, to Billie. "Hello, hello, can you hear me? Hello."

"Hello," said Billie. "My mom says I can talk to you again. Hello."

"I'm hungry. Where am I? Hello."

"I'm at Mom's work. She does science here. I don't know where you are. Mom probably knows. She called you." Billie twisted to look at me. "Mom? Where is she?"

I pointed to the two-way mirror. "She's right through there."

Billie followed the angle of my finger to Pitch, who was scratching the side of her head with one talon. Her face fell for a moment, expression turning betrayed, before realization wiped away her confusion and her eyes went wide. She turned back to the screen.

"Are you a bird?" she asked.

The woman looked confused. "Hello, hello, I'm hungry, where am I?"

"A *bird*," said Billie, and flapped her arms like wings.

The effect on Pitch was immediate. She sat up straighter on her perch and flapped her wings, not hard enough to take off, but hard enough to mimic the gesture.

"A bird!" announced the avatar. "A bird a bird a bird yes a bird. Are you a bird? Hello? A bird? Hello, can you hear me, hello?"

"Holy shit," whispered Mike. "She's really talking to the bird. The translation algorithm really figured out how to let her talk to the bird. And the bird is really talking back. Holy *shit*."

"Not in front of my child, please," I said, tone prim and strangled. The xenolinguists were going to be all over this. We'd have people clawing at the gates to try to get a place on the team once this came out. The science behind it was clean and easy to follow—we had built a deep neural net capable of learning, told it that gestures were language and that the human mouth was capable of making millions of distinct sounds, taught it to recognize grammar and incorporate both audio and visual signals into same, and then we had turned it loose, putting it out into the world, with no instructions but to learn.

"We need to put like, a thousand animals in front of this thing and see how many of them can actually get it to work." Mike grabbed my arm. "Do you know what this means? This changes everything."

Conservationists would kill to get their subjects in front of a monitor and try to open communication channels. Gorillas would be easy—we already had ASL in common—and elephants, dolphins, parrots, none of them could be very far behind. We had opened the gates to a whole new world, and all because I wanted to talk to my sister.

But all that was in the future, stretching out ahead of us in a wide and tangled ribbon tied to the tail of tomorrow. Right here and right now was my daughter, laughing as she spoke to her new friend, the two of them feeling their way, one word at a time, into a common language, and hence into a greater understanding of the world.

Tasha would be so delighted.

In the moment, so was I.

capitalism in the 22nd century or A.I.r

GEOFF RYMAN

Born in Canada, Geoff Ryman now lives in England. He made his first sale in 1976, to New Worlds, *but it was not until 1984, when he made his first appearance in* Interzone *with his brilliant novella* The Unconquered Country *that he attracted any serious attention.* The Unconquered Country *was one of the best novellas of the decade, had a stunning impact on the science fiction scene of the day, and almost overnight established Ryman as one of the most accomplished writers of his generation, winning him both the British Science Fiction Award and the World Fantasy Award; it was later published in a book version,* The Unconquered Country: A Life History. *His novel* The Child Garden: A Low Comedy *won both the prestigious Arthur C. Clarke Award and the John W. Campbell Memorial Award; and his later novel* Air *also won the Arthur C. Clarke Award. His other novels include* The Warrior Who Carried Life, *the critically acclaimed mainstream novel* Was, Coming of Enkidu, The King's Last Song, Lust, *and the underground cult classic* 253, *the "print remix" of an "interactive hypertext novel" which, in its original form, ran online on Ryman's home page of www.ryman.com, and which, in its print form, won the Philip K. Dick Award. Four of his novellas have been collected in* Unconquered Countries. *His most recent book is the anthology* When It Changed: Science into Fiction, *the novel* The Film-Makers of Mars, *and the collection* Paradise Tales: and Other Stories.*

Here he gives us a hard-edged look at capitalism in the twenty-second century, just like the title says—although it turns out to be a more surprising, complex, and multifaceted thing than you might think. . . .

Meuirmā

Can you read? Without help? I don't even know if you can!

I'm asking you to turn off all your connections now. That's right, to everything. Not even the cutest little app flittering around your head. JUST TURN OFF.

It will be like dying. Parts of your memory close down. It's horrible, like watching lights go out all over a city, only it's YOU. Or what you thought was you.

But please, Graça, just do it once. I know you love the AI and all zir little angels. But. Turn off?

Otherwise go ahead, let your AI read this for you. Zey will either screen out stuff or report it back or both. And what I'm going to tell you will join the system.

So:

WHY I DID IT
BY CRISTINA SPINOZA VAZ

Zey dream for us don't zey? I think zey edit our dreams so we won't get scared. Or maybe so that our brains don't well up from underneath to warn us about getting old or poor or sick . . . or about zem.

The first day, zey jerked us awake from deep inside our heads. *GET UP GET UP GET UP! There's a message. VERY IMPORTANT WAKE UP WAKE UP.*

From sleep to bolt upright and gasping for breath. I looked across at you still wrapped in your bed, but we're always latched together so I could feel your heart pounding.

It wasn't just a message; it was a whole ball of wax; and the wax was a solid state of being: panic. Followed by an avalanche of ship-sailing times, credit records, what to pack. And a sizzling, hot-foot sense that we had to get going right now. Zey shot us full of adrenaline: RUN! ESCAPE!

You said, "It's happening. We better get going. We've got just enough time to sail to Africa." You giggled and flung open your bed. "Come on Cristina, it will be *fun!*"

Outside in the dark from down below, the mobile chargers were calling *Oyez-treeee-cee-dah-djee!* I wanted to nestle down into my cocoon and imagine as I had done every morning since I was six that instead of selling power, the chargers were muezzin calling us to prayer and that I lived in a city with mosques. I heard the rumble of carts being pulled by their owners like horses.

Then kapow: another latch. *Ship sailing at 8.30 today due Lagos five days. You arrive day of launch. Seven hours to get from Lagos to Tivland. We'll book trains for you. Your contact in Lagos is EmildaDiaw,* (photograph, a hello from her with the sound of her voice, a little bubble of how she feels to herself. Nice, like a bowl of soup. Bubble muddled with dental cavities for some reason). *She'll meet you at the docks here* (flash image of Lagos docks, plus GPS, train times; impressions of train how cool and comfortable . . . and a lovely little timekeeper counting down to 8.30 departure of our boat. Right in our eyes).

And oh! On top of that another latch. This time an A-copy of our tickets burned into Security.

Security, which is supposed to mean something we can't lie about. Or change or control. We can't buy or sell anything without it. A part of our heads that will never be us, that officialdom can trust. It's there to help us, right?

Remember when Papa wanted to defraud someone? He'd never let them be. He'd latch hold of them with one message, then another at five-minute intervals. He'd latch them the bank reference. He'd latch them the name of the attorney, or the security conundrums. He never gave them time to think.

Graça. We were being railroaded.

You made packing into a game. Like everything else. "We are leaving behind the world!" you said. "Let's take nothing. Just our shorts. We can holo all the lovely dresses we like.What do we need, ah? We have each other."

I kept picking up and putting down my ballet pumps—oh that the new Earth should be deprived of ballet!

I made a jewel of all of Brasil's music, and a jewel of all Brasil's books and history. I need to see my info in something physical. I blame those bloody nuns keeping us off AIr. I sat watching the little clock on the printer going round and round, hopping up and down. Then I couldn't find my jewel piece to read them. You said, "Silly. The AI will have all of that." I wanted to take a little Brazilian flag and you chuckled at me. "Dunderhead, why do you want that?"

And I realized. You didn't just want to get out from under the Chinese. You wanted to escape Brasil.

Remember the morning it snowed? Snowed in Belém do Para? I think we were 13. You ran round and round inside our great apartment, all the French doors open. You blew out frosty breath, your eyes sparkling. "It's beautiful!" you said.

"It's cold!" I said.

You made me climb down all those 24 floors out into the Praça and you got me throwing handfuls of snow to watch it fall again. Snow was laced like popcorn on the branches of the giant mango trees. As if A *Reina*, the Queen, had possessed not a person but the whole square. Then I saw one of the suneaters, naked, dead, staring, and you pulled me away, your face such a mix of sadness, concern—and happiness, still glowing in your cheeks. "They're beautiful alive," you said to me. "But they do nothing." Your face was also hard.

Your face was like that again on the morning we left—smiling, ceramic. It's a hard world, this Brasil, this Earth. We know that in our bones. We know that from our father.

The sun came out at 6.15 as always, and our beautiful stained glass doors cast pastel rectangles of light on the mahogany floors. I walked out onto the L-shaped balcony that ran all around our high-rise rooms and stared down, at the row of old shops streaked black, at the opera-house replica of La Scala, at the art-nouveau synagogue blue and white like Wedgewood china. I was frantic and unmoving at the same time; those cattle-prods of information kept my mind jumping.

"I'm ready," you said. I'd packed nothing. "O, Crisfushka, here let me help you." You asked what next; I tried to answer; you folded slowly, neatly. The jewels, the player, a piece of Amazon bark, and a necklace that the dead had made from nuts and feathers. I snatched up a piece of Macumba lace (oh, those men dancing all in lace!) and bobbins to make more of it. And from the kitchen, a bottle of *cupuaçu* extract, to make ice cream. You laughed and clapped your hands. "Yes of course. We will even have cows there. We're carrying them inside us."

I looked mournfully at our book shelves. I wanted children on that new world to have seen books, so I grabbed hold of two slim volumes—a Clarice Lispector and *Dom Cassmuro*. Mr. Misery—that's me. You of course are Donatella. And at the last moment I slipped in that Brasileiro flag. *Ordem e progresso.*

"Perfect, darling! Now let's run!" you said. You thought we were choosing.

And then another latch: receipts for all that surgery. A full accounting of all expenses and a cartoon kiss in thanks.

The moment you heard about the Voyage, you were eager to JUST DO IT. We joined the Co-op, got the secret codes, and concentrated on the fun like we were living in a game.

Funny little secret surgeons slipped into our high-rise with boxes that breathed dry ice and what looked like mobile dentist chairs. They retrovirused our genes. We went purple from Rhodopsin. I had a tickle in my ovaries. Then more security bubbles confirmed that we were now Rhodopsin, radiation-hardened and low-oxygen breathing. Our mitochondria were full of DNA for Holstein cattle. Don't get stung by any bees: the trigger for gene expression is an enzyme from bees.

"We'll become half-woman half-cow," you said, making even that sound fun.

We let them do that.

So we ran to the docks as if we were happy, hounded by information. Down the Avenida Presidente Vargas to the old colonial frontages, pinned to the sky and hiding Papa's casino and hotels. This city that we owned.

We owned the old blue wooden tower. When we were kids it had been the fish market, selling giant tucunaréas big as a man. We owned the old metal meat market (now a duty-free) and Old Ver-o-Paso gone black with rust like the bubbling pots of açai porridge or feijoada. We grabbed folds of feijoada to eat, running, dribbling. "We will arrive such a mess!"

I kept saying goodbye to everything. The old harbor—tiny, boxed in by the hill and tall buildings. Through that dug-out rectangle of water had flowed out rubber and cocoa and flowed in all those people, the colonists who died, their mestizo grandchildren, the blacks for sale. I wanted to take a week to visit each shop, take eyeshots of every single street. I felt like I was being pulled away from all my memories. "Goodbye!" you kept shouting over and over, like it was a joke.

As Docas Novas. All those frigates lined up with their sails folded down like rows of quill pens. The decks blinged as if with diamonds, burning sunlight. The GPS put arrows in our heads to follow down the berths, and our ship seemed to flash on and off to guide us to it. Zey could have shown us clouds with wings or pink oceans, and we would have believed their interferences.

It was still early, and the Amazon was breathing out, the haze merging water and sky at the horizon. A river so wide you cannot see across it, but you can surf in its freshwater waves. The distant shipping looked like dawn buildings. The small boats made the crossing as they have done for hundreds of years, to the islands.

Remember the only other passengers? An elderly couple in surgical masks who shook our hands and sounded excited. Supplies thumped up the ramp; then the ramp swung itself clear. The boat sighed away from the pier.

We stood by the railings and watched. Round-headed white dolphins leapt out of the water. Goodbye, Brasil. Farewell, Earth.

We took five days and most of the time you were lost in data, visiting the Palace of Urbino in 1507. Sometimes you would hologram it to me and we would both see it. They're not holograms really, you know, but detailed hallucinations zey wire into our brains. Yes, we wandered Urbino, and all the while knowledge about it riled its way up as if we were remembering. Raphael the painter was a boy there. We saw a pencil sketch of his beautiful face. The very concept of the Gentleman was developed there by Castiglione, inspired by the Doge. Machiavelli's *The Prince* was inspired by the same man. Urbino was small and civilized and founded on warfare. I heard Urbino's doves flap their wings; I heard sandals on stone and Renaissance bells.

When I came out of it, there was the sea and sky, and you staring ahead as numb as a suneater, lost in AIr, being anywhere. I found I had to cut off to actually see the ocean roll past us. We came upon two giant sea turtles mating. The oldest of the couple spoke in a whisper. "We mustn't scare them; the female might lose her egg sac and that would kill her." I didn't plug in for more information. I didn't need it. I wanted to look. What I saw looked like love.

And I could feel zem, the little apps and the huge soft presences trying to pull me back into AIr. Little messages on the emergency channel. The emergency channel, Cristina. You know, for fires or heart attacks? Little leaping wisps of features, new knowledge, old friends latching—all kept offering zemselves. For zem, me cutting off was an emergency.

You didn't disembark at Ascension Island. I did with those two old dears . . . married to each other 45 years. I couldn't tell what gender zey were, even in bikinis. We climbed up the volcano going from lava plain through a layer of desert and prickly pear, up to lawns and dew ponds. Then at the crown, a grove of bamboo. The stalks clopped together in the wind with a noise like flutes knocking against each other. I walked on alone and very suddenly the grove ended as if the bamboo had parted like a curtain. There was a sudden roar and cloud, and 2000 feet dead below my feet, the Atlantic slamming into rocks. I stepped back, turned around and looked into the black-rimmed eyes of a panda.

So what is so confining about the Earth? And if it is dying, who is killing it but us?

Landfall Lagos. Bronze city, bronze sky. Giants strode across the surface of the buildings holding up Gulder beer.

So who would go to the greatest city in Africa for two hours only?

Stuff broke against me in waves: currency transformations; boat tickets, local history, beautiful men to have sex with. Latches kept plucking at me, but I just didn't want to KNOW; I wanted to SEE. It. Lagos. The islands with the huge graceful bridges, the airfish swimming through the sky, ochre with distance.

You said that "she" was coming. The system would have pointed arrows, or shown you a map. Maybe she was talking to you already. I did not see Emilda until she actually turned the corner, throwing and re-throwing a shawl over her shoulder (a bit nervous?) and laughing at us. Her teeth had a lovely gap in the front, and she was followed by her son Baje, who had the same gap. Beautiful long shirt to his knees, matching trousers, dark blue with light blue embroidery. Oh he was handsome. We were leaving him, too.

They had to pretend we were cousins. She started to talk in Hausa so I had to turn on. She babblefished in Portuguese, her lips not matching her voice. "The Air Force in Makurdi are so looking forward to you arriving. The language program will be so helpful in establishing friendship with our Angolan partners."

I wrote her a note in Portuguese (I knew zey would babblefish it): *WHY ARE WE PRETENDING? ZEY KNOW!*

She wrote a note in English that babblefished into *Not for the AI but for the Chinese.*

I got a little stiletto of a thought: she had so wanted to go but did not have the money and so helped like this, to see us, people who will breathe the air of another world. I wasn't sure if that thought was something that had leaked from AIr or come from me. I nearly offered her my ticket.

What she said aloud, in English was, "O look at the time! O you must be going to catch the train!"

I think I know the moment you started to hate the Chinese. I could feel something curdle in you and go hard. It was when Papa was still alive and he had that man in, not just some punter. A partner, a rival, his opposite number—something. Plump and shiny like he was coated in butter, and he came into our apartment and saw us both, twins, holding hands wearing pink frilly stuff, and he asked our father. "Oh, are these for me?"

Papa smiled, and only we knew he did that when dangerous. "These are my daughters."

The Chinese man, standing by our pink and pistachio glass doors, burbled an apology, but what could he really say? He had come to our country to screw our girls, maybe our boys, to gamble, to drug, to do even worse. Recreational killing? And Papa was going to supply him with all of that. So it was an honest mistake for the man to make, to think little girls in pink were also whores.

Papa lived inside information blackout. He had to; it was his business. The man would have had no real communication with him; not have known how murderously angry our Pae really was. I don't think Pae had him killed. I think the man was too powerful for that.

What Pae did right afterwards was cut off all our communications too. He hired live-in nuns to educate us. The nuns, good Catholics, took hatchets to all our links to AIr. We grew up without zem. Which is why I at least can read. Our Papa was not all Brasileiros, Graça. He was a gangster, a thug who had a line on what the nastiest side of human nature would infallibly buy. I suppose because he shared those tastes himself, to an extent.

The shiny man was not China. He was a humor: lust and excess. Every culture has them; men who cannot resist sex or drugs, riot and rape. He'd been spotted by the AI, nurtured and grown like a hothouse flower. To make them money.

Never forget, my dear, that the AI want to make money too. They use it to buy and sell bits of themselves to each other. Or to buy us. And "us" means the Chinese too.

Yes all the entertainment and all the products that can touch us are Chinese. Business is Chinese, culture is Chinese. Yes at times it feels like the Chinese blanket us like a thick tropical sky. But only because there is no market to participate in. Not for humans, anyway.

The AI know through correlations, data mining, and total knowledge of each of us exactly what we will need, want, love, buy, or vote for. There is no demand now to choose one thing and drive out another. There is only supply, to what is a sure bet, whether it's whores or bouncy shoes. The only things that will get you the sure bet are force or plenty of money. That consolidates. The biggest gets the market, and pays the AI for it.

So, I never really wanted to get away from the Chinese. I was scared of them, but then someone raised in isolation by nuns is likely to be scared, intimidated.

I think I just wanted to get away from Papa, or rather what he did to us, all that money—and the memory of those nuns.

A taxi drove us from the docks. You and Emilda sat communing with each other in silence, so in the end I had to turn on, just to be part of the conversation. She was showing us her home, the Mambila plateau, rolling fields scraped by clouds; tea plantations; roads lined with children selling radishes or honeycombs; Nigerians in Fabric coats lighter than lace, matching the clouds. But it was Fabric, so all kinds of images played around it. Light could beam out of it; wind could not get in; warm air was sealed. Emilda's mother was Christian, her father Muslim like her sister; nobody minded. There were no roads to Mambila to bring in people who would mind.

Every channel of entertainment tried to bellow its way into my head, as data about food production in Mambila fed through me as if it was something I knew. Too much, I had to switch off again. I am a classic introvert. I cannot handle too much information. Emilda smiled at me—she had a kind face—and wiggled her fingernails at me in lieu of conversation. Each fingernail was playing a different old movie.

Baje's robe stayed the same blue. I think it was real. I think he was real too. Shy.

Lagos train station looked like an artist's impression in silver of a birch forest, trunks and slender branches. I couldn't see the train; it was so swathed in abstract patterns, moving signs, voices, pictures of our destinations, and classical Tiv dancers imitating cats. You, dead-eyed, had no trouble navigating the crowds and the holograms, and we slid into our seats that cost a month's wages. The train accelerated to 300 kph, and we slipped through Nigeria like neutrinos. Traditional mud brick houses clustered like old folks in straw hats, each hut a room in a rich person's home. The swept earth was red brown, brushed perfect like suede. Alongside the track, shards of melon were drying in the sun. The melon was the basis of the egussi soup we had for lunch. It was as if someone were stealing it all from me at high speed.

You were gone, looking inward, lost in AIr.

I saw two Chinese persons traveling together, immobile behind sunglasses. One of them stood up and went to the restroom, pausing just slightly as zie walked in both directions. Taking eyeshots? Sampling profile information? Zie looked straight at me. Ghosts of pockmarks on zir cheeks. I only saw them because I had turned off.

I caught the eye of an Arab gentleman in a silk robe with his two niqabbed wives. He was sweating and afraid, and suddenly I was. He nodded once to me, slowly. He was a Voyager as well.

I whispered your name, but you didn't respond. I didn't want to latch you; I didn't know how much might be given away. I began to feel alone.

At Abuja station, everything was sun panels. You bought some chocolate gold coins and said we were rich. You had not noticed the Chinese men but I told you, and you took my hand and said in Portuguese, "Soon we will have no need to fear them any longer."

The Arab family and others I recognized from the first trip crowded a bit too quickly into the Makurdi train. All with tiny Fabric bags. Voyagers all. We had all been summoned at the last minute.

Then the Chinese couple got on, still in sunglasses, still unsmiling, and my heart stumbled. What were they doing? If they knew we were going and they didn't like it, they could stop it again. Like they'd stopped the Belize launch. At a cost of trillions to the Cooperative. Would they do the same thing again? All of us looked away from each other and said nothing. I could hear the hiss of the train on its magnets, as if something were coiling. We slithered all the way into the heart of Makurdi.

You woke up as we slowed to a stop. "Back in the real world?" I asked you, which was a bitchy thing to say.

The Chinese man stood up and latched us all, in all languages. "You are all idiots!"

Something to mull over: they, too, knew what we were doing.

The Makurdi taxi had a man in front who seemed to steer the thing. He was a Tiv gentleman. He liked to talk, which I think annoyed you a bit. Sociable, outgoing you. *What a waste, when the AI can drive.*

Why have humans on the Voyage either?

"You're the eighth passengers I've had to take to the Base in two days. One a week is good business for me. Three makes me very happy."

He kept asking questions and got out of us what country we were from. We stuck to our cover story—we were here to teach Lusobras to the Nigerian Air Force. He wanted to know why they couldn't use the babblefish. You chuckled and said, "You know how silly babblefish can make people sound." You told the story of Uncle Kaué proposing to the woman from Amalfi. He'd said in Italian, "I want to eat your hand in marriage." She turned him down.

Then the driver asked, "So why no Chinese people?"

We froze. He had a friendly face, but his eyes were hooded. We listened to the whisper of his engine. "Well," he said, relenting. "They can't be everywhere all the time."

The Co-op in all its propaganda talks about how international we all are: Brasil, Turkiye, Tivland, Lagos, Benin, Hindi, Yemen. *All previous efforts in space have been fuelled by national narcissism.* So we exclude the Chinese? *Let them fund their own trip. And isn't it wonderful that it's all private financing?* I wonder if space travel isn't inherently racist.

You asked him if he owned the taxi and he laughed. "Ay-yah! Zie owns me." His father had signed the family over for protection. The taxi keeps him, and buys zirself a new body every few years. The taxi is immortal. So is the contract.

What's in it for the taxi, you asked. Company?

"Little little." He held up his hands and waved his fingers. "If something breaks, I can fix."

AIs do not ultimately live in a physical world.

I thought of all those animals I'd seen on the trip: their webbed feet, their fins, their wings, their eyes. The problems of sight, sound and movement solved over and over again. Without any kind of intelligence at all.

We are wonderful at movement because we are animals, but you can talk to us and you don't have to build us. We build ourselves. And we want things. There is always somewhere we want to go even if it is twenty-seven light-years away.

Outside Makurdi Air Force Base, aircraft stand on their tails like raised sabres. The taxi bleeped as it was scanned, and we went up and over some kind of hump.

Ahead of us blunt as a grain silo was the rocket. Folded over its tip, something that looked like a Labrador-colored bat. Folds of Fabric, skin colored, with subcutaneous lumps like acne. A sleeve of padded silver foil was being pulled down over it.

A spaceship made of Fabric. Things can only get through it in one direction. If two-ply, then Fabric won't let air out, or light and radiation in.

"They say," our taxi driver said, looking even more hooded than before, "that it will be launched today or tomorrow. The whole town knows. We'll all be looking up to wave." Our hearts stopped. He chuckled.

We squeaked to a halt outside the reception bungalow. I suppose you thought his fare at him. I hope you gave him a handsome tip.

He saluted and said, "I pray the weather keeps good for you. Wherever you are going." He gave a sly smile.

A woman in a blue-gray uniform bustled out to us. "Good, good, good. You are Graça and Cristina Spinoza Vaz? You must come. We're boarding. Come, come, come."

"Can we unpack, shower first?"

"No, no. No time."

We were retinaed and scanned, and we took off our shoes. It was as if we were so rushed we'd attained near-light speeds already and time was dilating. Everything went slower, heavier—my shoes, the bag, my heartbeat. So heavy and slow that everything glued itself in place. I knew I wasn't going to go, and that absolutely nothing was going to make me. For the first time in my life.

Graça, this is only happening because zey want it. Zey need us to carry zem. We're donkeys.

"You go," I said.

"What? Cristina. Don't be silly."

I stepped backwards, holding up my hands against you. "No, no, no. I can't do this."

You came for me, eyes tender, smile forgiving. "Oh, darling, this is just nerves."

"It's not nerves. You want to do this; I do not."

Your eyes narrowed; the smile changed. "This is not the time to discuss things. We have to go! This is illegal. We have to get in and go now."

We don't fight, ever, do we, Graça? Doesn't that strike you as bizarre? Two people who have been trapped together on the 24th floor all of their lives and yet they never fight. Do you not know how that happens, Graçfushka? It happens because I always go along with you.

I just couldn't see spending four years in a cramped little pod with you. Then spending a lifetime on some barren waste watching you organizing volleyball tournaments or charity lunches in outer space. I'm sorry.

I knew if I stayed you'd somehow wheedle me onto that ship through those doors; and I'd spend the next two hours, even as I went up the gantry, even as I was sandwiched in cloth, promising myself that at the next opportunity I'd run.

I pushed my bag at you. When you wouldn't take it, I dropped it at your feet. I bet you took it with you, if only for the cupaçu.

You clutched at my wrists, and you tried to pull me back. You'd kept your turquoise bracelet and it looked like all the things about you I'd never see again. You were getting angry now. "You spent a half trillion reais on all the surgeries and and and and Rhodopsin . . . and and and the germ cells, Cris! Think of what that means for your children here on Earth, they'll be freaks!" You started to cry. "You're just afraid. You're always so afraid."

I pulled away and ran.

"I won't go either," you wailed after me. "I'm not going if you don't."

"Do what you have to," I shouted over my shoulder. I found a door and pushed it and jumped down steps into the April heat of Nigeria. I sat on a low stucco border under the palm trees in the shade, my heart still pumping; and the most curious thing happened. I started to chuckle.

I remember at 17, I finally left the apartment on my own without you, and walked along the street into a restaurant. I had no idea how to get food. Could I just take a seat? How would I know what they were cooking?

Then like the tide, an AI flowed in and out of me and I felt zie/me pluck someone nearby, and a waitress came smiling, and ushered me to a seat. She would carry the tray. I turned the AI off because, dear Lord, I have to be able to order food by myself. So I asked the waitress what was on offer. She rolled her eyes back for just a moment, and she started to recite. The AI had to tell her. I couldn't remember what she'd said, and so I asked her to repeat. I thought: this is no good.

The base of the rocket sprouted what looked like giant cauliflowers and it inched its way skyward. For a moment I thought it would have to fall. But it kept on going.

Somewhere three months out, it will start the engines, which drive the ship by making new universes, something so complicated human beings cannot do it. The AI will make holograms so you won't feel enclosed. You'll sit in Pamukkale, Turkiye. Light won't get through the Fabric so you'll never look out on Jupiter. The main AI will have some cute, international name. You can finish your dissertation on *Libro del cortegiano*—you'll be able to read every translation—zey carry all the world's knowledge. You'll walk through Urbino. The AI will viva your PhD. Zey'll be there in your head watching when you stand on the alien rock. It will be zir flag you'll be planting. Instead of Brasil's.

I watched you dwindle into a spark of light that flared and turned into a star of ice-dust in the sky. I latched Emilda and asked her if I could stay with her, and after a stumble of shock, she said of course. I got the same taxi back. The roof tops were crowded with people looking up at the sky.

But here's the real joke. I latched our bank for more money. Remember, we left a trillion behind in case the launch was once again canceled?

All our money had been taken. Every last screaming centavo. Remember what I said about fraud?

So.

Are you sure that spaceship you're on is real?

ice

RiCH LARSON

Here's another story by Rich Larson, whose "Meshed" appears elsewhere in this anthology.

In this one, he introduces us to young brothers who live in a somewhat dysfunctional family on a hostile alien world, and whose clandestine expedition to witness an alien wonder just may, if they're not lucky, turn out to be the last thing they ever do. . . .

S edgewick had used his tab to hack Fletcher's alarm off, but when he slid out of bed in the middle of the night his younger brother was wide awake and waiting, modded eyes a pale luminous green in the dark.

"I didn't think you were actually going to do it," Fletcher said with a hesitant grin.

"Of course I'm going to." Sedgewick kept his words clipped, like he had for months. He kept his face cold. "If you're coming, get dressed."

Fletcher's smile swapped out for the usual scowl. They pulled on their thermals and gloves and gumboots in silence, moving around the room like pieces of a sliding puzzle, careful to never inhabit the same square space. If there was a way to keep Fletcher from coming short of smothering him with a blanket, Sedgewick would've taken it. But Fletcher was fourteen now, still smaller than him but not by much, and his wiry modded arms were strong like an exoskeleton's. Threats were no good anymore.

When they were ready, Sedgewick led the way past their parents' room to the vestibule, which they had coded to his thumb in penance for uprooting him again, this time dumping him onto a frostbit fucking colony world where he was the only unmodded sixteen-year-old for about a million light-years. They said he had earned their trust but did not specify exactly how. Fletcher, of course, didn't need to earn it. He could take care of himself.

Sedgewick blanked the exit log more out of habit than anything, then they stepped out of the cold vestibule into the colder upstreet. The curved ceiling above them was a night sky holo, blue-black with an impossibly large cartoon moon, pocked and bright white. Other than Sedgewick and his family, nobody in New Greenland had ever seen a real Earth night.

They went down the housing row in silence, boots scraping tracks in the frost. An autocleaner salting away a glistening blue coolant spill gledged over at them suspiciously as they passed, then returned to its work. Fletcher slid behind it and pantomimed tugging off, which might have made Sedgewick laugh once, but he'd learned to make himself a black hole that swallowed up anything too close to camaraderie.

"Don't shit around," he said. "It'll scan you."

"I don't care," Fletcher said, with one of those disdainful little shrugs he'd perfected lately, that made Sedgewick believe he really truly didn't.

The methane harvesters were off-cycle, and that meant the work crews were still wandering the colony, winding in and out of dopamine bars and discos. They were all from the same modded geneprint, all with a rubbery pale skin that manufactured its own vitamins, all with deep black eyes accustomed to the dark. A few of them sat bonelessly on the curb, laid out by whatever they'd just vein-blasted, and as Sedgewick and Fletcher went by they muttered *extro, extros den terre*. One of them shouted hello a few beats too late.

"Should run," Fletcher said.

"What?"

"Should jog it." Fletcher rubbed his arms. "It's cold."

"You go ahead," Sedgewick said, scornful.

"Whatever."

They kept walking. Aside from the holos flashing over the bars, the upstreet was a long blank corridor of biocrete and composite. The downstreet was more or less the same plus maintenance tunnels that gushed steam every few minutes.

It had only taken Sedgewick a day to go from one end of the colony to the other and conclude that other than the futball pitch there was nothing worth his time. The locals he'd met in there, who played with different lines and a heavy ball and the ferocious modded precision that Sedgewick knew he wouldn't be able to keep pace with long, more or less agreed with his assessment in their stilted Basic.

Outside the colony was a different story. That was why Sedgewick had crept out of bed at 2:13, why he and Fletcher were now heading down an unsealed exit tunnel marked by an unapproved swatch of acid yellow hologram. Tonight, the frostwhales were breaching.

Most of the lads Sedgewick had met at last week's game were waiting at the end of the exit tunnel, slouched under flickering florescents and passing a vape from hand to hand. He'd slotted their names and faces into a doc and memorized it. It wasn't Sedgewick's first run as the new boy and by now he knew how to spot the prototypes.

You had your alpha dog, who would make or break the entry depending on his mood more than anything. Your right-hand man, who was usually the jealous type, and the left-hand man, who usually didn't give a shit. Your foot-soldiers, who weathervaned according to the top three, ranging from gregarious to vaguely hostile. Then lastly your man out on the fringe, who would either glom on thick, hoping to get a friend that hadn't figured out his position yet, or clam right up out of fear of getting replaced.

It was a bit harder to tell who was who with everyone modded and nobody speaking good Basic. They all came up off the wall when they caught sight of him, swooping in for the strange stutter-stop handshake that Sedgewick couldn't quite time right. Petro, tall and languid, first because he was closest not because he cared. Oxo, black eyes already flicking away for approval. Brume, compact like a brick, angry-sounding laugh. Another Oxo, this one with a regrowth implant in his jaw, quiet because of that or maybe because of something else.

Anton was the last, the one Sedgewick had pegged for alpha dog. He gripped his hand a beat longer and grinned with blocky white teeth that had never needed an orthosurgery.

"*Ho, extro,* how are you this morning." He looked over Sedgewick's shoulder and flashed his eyebrows. "Who?"

"Fletcher," Sedgewick said. "The little brother. Going to feed him to a frost-whale."

"Your brother."

Fletcher stuffed his long hands into the pockets of his thermal and met Anton's gaze. Sedgewick and his brother had the same muddy post-racial melanin and lamp-black hair, but from there they diverged. Sedgewick had always been slight-framed and small-boned, with any muscle slapped across his chest and arms fought for gram by gram in a gravity gym. His eyes were a bit sunk and he hated his bowed nose.

Fletcher was already broad in the shoulders and slim-hipped, every bit of him carved sinew, and Sedgewick knew it wouldn't be long before he was taller, too. His face was all angles now that the baby fat was gone: sharp cheekbones, netstar jaw-line. And his eyes were still reflecting in the half-lit tunnel, throwing light like a cat's.

Sedgewick could feel the tips of his ears heating up as Anton swung his stare from one brother to the other, nonverbalizing the big question, the always-there question, which was *why are you freestyle if he's modded.*

"So how big are they?" Fletcher asked, with his grin coming back. "The frost-whales."

"Big," Anton said. "*Ko gramme ko pujo.*" He pointed over to Oxo-of-the-jaw-implant and snapped his fingers together for support.

"Fucking big," Oxo supplied in a mumble.

"Fucking big," Anton said.

The cold flensed Sedgewick to the bones the instant they stepped outside. Overhead, the sky was a void blacker and vaster than any holo could match. The ice stretched endless in all directions, interrupted only by the faint running lights of methane harvesters stitched through the dark.

Brume had a prehensile lantern from one of the work crews and he handed it to Anton to affix to the cowl of his coat. It flexed and arched over his head, blooming a sickly green light. Sedgewick felt Fletcher look at him, maybe an uneasy look because they'd never been outside the colony at night, maybe a cocky look because he was making a move, going to ruin something for Sedgewick all over again.

"Okay," Anton said, exhaling a long plume of steam with relish. His voice sounded hollow in the flat air. "*Benga, benga,* okay. Let's go."

"Right," Sedgewick said, trying to smile with some kind of charm. *"Benga."*

Brume gave his angry barking laugh and slapped him on the shoulder, then they set off over the ice. The pebbly gecko soles of Sedgewick's gumboots kept him balanced and the heating coils in his clothes had already whispered to life, but every time he breathed the air seared his throat raw. Fletcher was a half-step behind the lot of them. Sedgewick resisted the urge to gledge back, knowing he'd see an unconcerned *what are you staring for* sneer.

Thinking back on it, he should've drugged Fletcher's milk glass with their parents' Dozr. Even his modded metabolism couldn't have shaken off three tablets in time for him to play tag-along. Thinking even further back on it, he shouldn't have had the conversation with Anton and Petro about the frostwhales where Fletcher could hear them.

Under his feet, the texture of the ice started to change, turning from smooth glossy black to scarred and rippled, broken and refrozen. He nearly caught his boot on a malformed spar of it.

"Okay, stop," Anton announced, holding up both hands.

About a meter on, Sedgewick saw a squat iron pylon sunk into the ice. As he watched, the tip of it switched on, acid yellow. While Petro unloaded his vape and the others circled up for a puff, Anton slung one arm around Sedgewick and the other around Fletcher.

"Benga, aki den glaso extrobengan minke," he said.

The string of sounds was nothing like the lessons Sedgewick had stuck on his tab.

Anton shot a look over to Oxo-of-the-jaw-implant, but he was hunched over the vape, lips tinged purple. "Here," Anton reiterated, gesturing past the pylon. "Here. Frostwhales up."

He said it with a smile Sedgewick finally recognized as tight with amphetamine. He'd assumed they weren't sucking down anything stronger than a party hash, but now that seemed like an idiot thing to assume. This was New fucking Greenland, so for all he knew these lads were already utterly panned.

Only one way to find out. Sedgewick gestured for the vape. "Hit me off that."

Petro gave him a slow clap, either sarcastic or celebratory, while he held the stinging fog in his lungs for as long as he could, maybe because Fletcher was watching. There was only a bit of headspin, but it was enough to miss half of what Oxo-of-the-jaw-implant was saying to him.

". . . is the area." Oxo plucked the vape out of his slack hands and passed it on. "See. See there, see there, see there." He pointed, and Sedgewick could pick out other pylons in the distance glowing to life. "Fucking danger, okay? Inside the area, frostwhales break ice for breathing. For break ice for breathing, frostwhales hit ice seven times. *Den minuso*, seven."

"Minimum seven," the other Oxo chimed in. Anton started counting aloud on his gloved fingers.

"Got it," Fletcher muttered.

"So, so, so," Oxo-of-the-jaw-implant went on. "When the frostwhales hit one, we go."

"Thought you'd stay for the whole thing?" Sedgewick said, only halfway listening. The cold was killing off his toes one by one.

Anton gave up at twenty and sprang back to the conversation. "We go, *extros*," he beamed. "You run. You run. I run. He runs. He runs. He runs. He runs. Here . . ." He gave the pylon a dull clanging kick. "To here!"

Sedgewick followed Anton's pointing finger. Far off across the scarred ice, he could barely make out the yellow glow of the pylon opposite them. His stomach dropped. Sedgewick looked at his brother, and for a nanosecond Fletcher looked like a little kid again, but then his mouth curled a smile and his modded eyes flashed.

"Alright," he said. "I'm down."

Sedgewick was a breath away from saying *no you fucking aren't*, from saying *we're heading back now*, from saying anything at all. But it all stuck on his ribs and instead he turned to Anton and shrugged.

"*Benga*," he said. "Let's go."

The handshakes came back around, everyone hooting and pleased to have new recruits. Fletcher got the motion on his first try. When the vape made its final circle, Sedgewick gripped it hard and stared out over the black ice and tried to stop shivering.

Sedgewick knew Fletcher was faster than him. He'd known it like a stone in his belly since he was twelve and his brother was ten, and they'd raced on a pale gray beach back on Earth. Prickling fog and no witnesses. Fletcher took lead in the last third, pumping past him with a high clear incredulous laugh, and Sedgewick slacked off to a jog to let him win, because it was a nice thing, to let the younger brother win sometimes.

Occupied with the memory, Sedgewick was slow to notice that the eerie green pallor of the ice was no longer cast by Anton's lantern. Something had lit it up from underneath. He stared down at the space between his boots and his gut gave a giddy helium lurch. Far below them, distorted by the ice, he could make out dim moving shapes. He remembered that frostwhales navigated by bioluminescence. He remembered the methane sea was deeper than any Earth ocean.

Everyone tightened the straps of their thermals, tucked in their gloves, and formed themselves into a ragged line that Sedgewick found himself near the end of, Fletcher beside him.

Anton waltzed down the row and made a show of checking everyone's boots. "Grip," he said, making a claw.

Sedgewick threw a hand onto Brume's shoulder for balance while he displayed one sole and then the other. He leaned instinctively to do Fletcher the same favor, but his brother ignored it and lifted each leg precisely into the air, perfectly balanced. Sedgewick hated him as much as he ever had. He glued his eyes to the far pylon and imagined it was the first cleat of the dock on a rainy gray beach.

Under their feet, the ghostly green light receded, dropping them back into darkness. Sedgewick shot Oxo-of-the-jaw-implant a questioning look.

"First they see ice," Oxo mumbled, rubbing his hands together. "They see ice for thin area. Then, down. For making momentum. Then, in one by one line . . ."

"Up," Sedgewick guessed.

On cue, the light reappeared, rising impossibly fast. Sedgewick took a breath and coiled to sprint. His imagination flashed him a picture: the frostwhale rocketing up-ward, a blood-and-bone engine driven by a furious threshing tail, hurtling through the cold water in a cocoon of bubbling gas. Then the impact quaked the ice and Sedgewick's teeth, and he thought about nothing but running.

For two hard heartbeats, Sedgewick fronted the pack, flying across the ice like something unslung. The second impact nearly took his legs out from under him. He staggered, skidded, regained his balance, but in that split second Petro was past him. And Anton, and Oxo, and Oxo, Brume, Fletcher last.

Sedgewick dug deep for every shred of speed. The ice was nowhere near smooth, scarred with pocks and ridges and frozen ripples in the methane, but the others slid over it like human quicksilver, finding the perfect place for every footfall. Modded, modded, modded. The word danced in Sedgewick's head as he gulped cold glass.

The green light swelled again, and he braced before the third frostwhale hit. The jolt shook him but he kept his footing, maybe even gained half a step on Oxo. Ahead, the race was thrown into relief: Brume's broad shoulders, Anton's thrown-back head, and there, sliding past gangly Petro for the lead, was Fletcher. Sedgewick felt hot despair churn up his throat.

His eyes raised to the pylon and he realized they were over halfway across. Fletcher pulled away now, not laughing, with that crisp bounding stride that said *I can run forever.* Then he glanced back over his shoulder, for what, Sedgewick didn't know, and in that instant his boot caught a trench and slammed him hard to the ice.

Sedgewick watched the others vault past, Anton pausing to half-drag Fletcher back upright on the way by. "*Benga, benga, extro!*"

The fourth frostwhale hit, this time with a bone-deep groaning *crack.* Everyone else had overtaken Fletcher; Sedgewick would in a few more strides. Fletcher was just now hobbling upright and Sedgewick knew instantly he'd done his ankle in. His modded eyes were wide.

"Sedge."

All the things Sedgewick had wished so savagely in the night—that the doctor had never pulled Fletcher out of his vat, that Fletcher's pod would fail in transit to New Greenland—all of those things shattered at once. He swung Fletcher up onto his back, how they'd done as kids, and stumped on with lungs ragged.

The fifth impact. Sedgewick's teeth slammed together and fissures skittered through the ice. He spared only a moment to balance himself, then stumbled for-ward again, Fletcher clinging fierce to his back. At the far pylon, the others hurtled to the finish, whooping and howling from a dozen meters away now, no more.

They all seemed to turn at once as the sixth impact split the world apart and the frostwhale breached. Sedgewick felt himself thrown airborne in a blizzard of shattered ice, felt himself screaming in his chest but unable to hear it, deafened by the shearing boom and crack. Some part of Fletcher smacked against him in midair.

Landing slammed the wind out of him. His vision pinwheeled from the unend-ing black sky to the maelstrom of moving ice. And then, too big to be real, rising up out of the cold methane sea in a geyser of rime and steam, the frostwhale. Its bony head was gunmetal gray, the size of a bus, bigger, swatched with pale green lanterns of pustule that glowed like radiation.

Cracks webbed through the ice and something gave way; Sedgewick felt himself slanting, slipping. He tore his gaze from the towering bulk of the frostwhale and saw Fletcher spread-eagled beside him, a black shadow in the burning lime. His lips were moving but Sedgewick couldn't read them, and then gloved hands gripped the both of them, hauling them flat along the breaking ice.

Oxo and Oxo made sure they were all pulled past the pylon before anyone got up off their belly. Sedgewick, for his part, didn't even try. He was waiting on his heart to start beating again.

"Sometime six," Anton said sheepishly, crouching over him.

"Go to hell," Fletcher croaked from nearby, and in a moment of weakness Sedgewick choked up a wavery laugh.

They washed home on a wave of adrenaline, caught up in the rapid-fire conversation of the New Greenlanders who still seemed to be rehashing how close Sedgewick and Fletcher had come to getting dumped under. Every single one of them needed a send-off handshake at the living quarters, then they slunk off in one chattering mass.

Sedgewick couldn't keep the chemical grin off his face, and as he and Fletcher snuck through the vestibule and then ghosted back to their temporary shared room, they talked in a tumble of whispers about the frostwhale, about the size of it, and about the ones that had surfaced afterward to suck cold air into massive vein-webbed bladders.

Sedgewick didn't want to stop talking, but even when they did, climbing into their beds, the quiet felt different. Softer.

It wasn't until he was staring up at the biocrete ceiling that he realized Fletcher's limp had swapped sides on the way back. He swung upright, unbelieving.

"You faked it."

"What?" Fletcher was rolled away, tracing the wall with his long fingers.

"You faked it," Sedgewick repeated. "Your ankle."

Fletcher took his hand off the wall, and the long quiet was enough confirmation.

Sedgewick's cheeks burned. He'd thought he had finally done something big enough, big enough to keep him on the greater side of whatever fucked-up equation they were balancing. But it was Fletcher feeling sorry for him. No, worse. Fletcher making a move. Fletcher manipulating him for whatever kind of schemes floated through his modded head.

"We could have both died," Sedgewick said.

Still turned away, Fletcher gave his perfect shrug, and Sedgewick felt all the old fury fluming up through his skin.

"You think that was a fucking hologame?" he snarled. "That was real. You could have deaded us both. You think you can just do anything, right? You think you can just do anything, and it'll fucking work out perfect for you, because you're *modded*."

Fletcher's shoulders stiffened. "Good job," he said, toneless.

"What?" Sedgewick demanded. "Good job what?"

"Good job on saying it," Fletcher told the wall. "You're ashamed to have a modded brother. You wanted one like you."

Sedgewick faltered, then made himself laugh. "Yeah, maybe I did." His throat ached. "You know what it's like seeing you? Seeing you always be better than me?"

"Not my fault."

"I was six when they told me you were going to be better," Sedgewick said, too far gone to stop now, saying the things he'd only ever said alone to the dark. "They said different, but they meant better. Mom couldn't do another one freestyle and to go off-planet you're supposed to have them modded anyway. So they grew you in a tube. Like hamburger. You're not even *real*." His breath came lacerated. "Why wasn't I enough for them, huh? Why wasn't I fucking enough?"

"Fuck you," Fletcher said, with his voice like gravel, and Sedgewick had never heard him say it or mean it until now.

He flopped back onto his bed, grasping for the slip-sliding anger as it trickled away in the dark. Shame came instead and sat at the bottom of him like cement. Minutes ticked by in silence. Sedgewick thought Fletcher was probably drifting to sleep already, probably not caring at all.

Then there was a bit-off sob, a sound smothered by an arm or a pillow, something Sedgewick hadn't heard from his brother in years. The noise wedged in his ribcage. He tried to unhear it, tried to excuse it. Maybe Fletcher had peeled off his thermal and found frostbite. Maybe Fletcher was making a move, always another move, putting a lure into the dark between them and sharpening his tongue for the retort.

Maybe all Sedgewick needed to do was go and put his hand on some part of his brother, and everything would be okay. His heart hammered up his throat. Maybe. Sedgewick pushed his face into the cold fabric of his pillow and decided to wait for a second sob, but none came. The silence thickened into hard black ice.

Sedgewick clamped his eyes shut and it stung badly, badly.

the first gate of logic

BENJAMIN ROSENBAUM

Benjamin Rosenbaum lives in Washington, D.C. His stories have been nominated for the Hugo, Nebula, BSFA (British Science Fiction Award), World Fantasy, Locus, and the Theodore Sturgeon Memorial awards; translated into twenty-five languages; animated (winning Best Animated Short at SXSW in 2010); incorporated into a textbook (Science Fiction: Stories and Contexts) and several art projects (including one acquired for the Australian National Portrait Gallery's permanent collection), and collected in The Ant King and Other Stories.

Here, he offers us a very strange coming-of-age story, set in an even stranger world that might not be as far off as you think that it is. . . .

Fift was almost five, and it wasn't like her anymore to be asleep in all of her bodies. She wasn't a baby anymore; she was old enough for school, old enough to walk all alone across the habitation, down the spoke to the great and buzzing center of Foo. But she had been wound up with excitement for days, practically dancing around the house (Father Miskisk had laughed, Father Smistria had shooed her out of the supper garden, Father Frill had summoned her to the bathing room and had her swim back and forth, back and forth, "to calm you down!"), and just before supper she'd finally collapsed, twice—in the atrium, and curled up on the tiered balcony—and Father Arevio and Father Squell had carried her, in those two bodies, back to her room. She'd managed to stay awake in her third body through most of supper, blinking hugely and breathing in through her nose and trying to sit up straight, as waves of deep blue slumber from her two sleeping brains washed through her. By supper's end, she couldn't stand up, and Father Squell carried that body, too, to bed.

Muddy dreams: of sitting on a wooden floor in a long hall . . . of her name being called . . . of realizing she hadn't worn her gown after all, but was somehow—humiliatingly—dressed in Father Frill's golden bells instead. The other children laughing at her, and dizziness, and suddenly, surreally, the hall being full of flutterbyes, their translucent wings fluttering, their projection surfaces glittering. . . .

Then someone was stroking Fift's eyebrow, gently, and she tried to nestle farther down into the blankets, and the someone started gently pulling on her earlobe. She opened her eyes, and it was Father Squell.

"Good morning, little cubblehedge," he said. "You have a big day today."

Father Squell was slim and rosy-skinned and smelled like soap and flowers. Fift crawled into his lap and flung her arms around him and pressed her nose between his bosoms. He was dressed in glittery red fabric, soft and slippery under Fift's fingers.

Squell was bald, with coppery metal spikes extruding from the skin of his scalp. Sometimes Father Miskisk teased him about them—the spikes weren't fashionable anymore—and sometimes when he did, Father Squell stormed out of the room, because Father Squell was a little vain. He was never much of a fighter, the other Fathers said. But he had a body in the asteroids, and that was something amazing.

Squell reached over, Fift still in his lap, and started stroking the eyebrow of another of Fift's bodies. Fift sneezed, in that body, and then sneezed in the other two, and that was funny, and she started to giggle. Now she was all awake.

"Up, little cubblehedge," Squell said. "Up!"

Fift crawled out of bed, careful not to crawl over herself. It always made her a little restless to be all together, all three bodies in the same room. That wasn't really good, it was because her somatic integration wasn't totally successful, and that was why she kept having to see Pedagogical Expert Pnim Moralasic Foundelly of name registry Pneumatic Lance 12. Pedagogical Expert Pnim Moralasic Foundelly had put an awful nag agent in Fift's mind, to tell her to look herself in the eye, and play in a coordinated manner, and do the exercises. It was nagging now, but Fift ignored it.

She looked under the bed for her gowns.

They weren't there. She closed her eyes (because she wasn't so good yet at seeing things over the feed with her eyes open) and used the house feed to look all around the house. Her gowns weren't in the balcony or the atrium or the small matroom or the breakfast room.

Fathers Arevio and Smistria and Frill, and another of Father Squell's bodies, were in the breakfast room, already eating. Father Miskisk was arguing with the kitchen.

{Where are my gowns?} Fift asked her agents, but perhaps she did it wrong, because they didn't say anything.

"Father Squell," she said, opening her eyes, "I can't find my gowns, and my agents can't either."

"I composted your gowns; they were old," Squell said. "Go down to the bathing room and get washed. I'll make you some new clothes."

Fift's hearts began to pound. The gowns weren't old; they'd only come out of the oven a week ago. "But I want *those* gowns," she said.

Squell opened the door. "You can't have those gowns. Those gowns are compost. Bathing!" He snatched Fift up, one of her bodies under his arm, the wrist of another caught in his other hand.

Fift tried to wriggle out of her Father's grasp, yanked on her arm to get free, while she looked desperately under the bed again. "They weren't old," she said, her voice wavering.

"Fift," Squell said, exasperated. "That's enough. For Kumru's sake, today of all days!" He dragged her, in two of her bodies, through the door. In another body, this one with silvery spikes on its head, he came hurrying down the hall.

"I want them back," Fift said. She wouldn't cry. She wasn't a baby any more, she was a big Staidchild, and Staids don't cry. She wouldn't cry. She wouldn't even shout or emphasize. She would stay calm and clear. Today of all days. She was still struggling, a little, and Squell handed her to his other body.

"They are *compost*," Squell said, reddening, in the body with the silver spikes, while one with the copper spikes came into the room. "They have gone down the sluice and *dissolved*. Your gowns are now part of the nutrient flow and they could be anywhere in Fullbelly and they will probably be part of your *breakfast* next week!"

Fift gasped. Fift didn't want to eat her gowns. There was a cold lump in her stomach. Squell caught her third body.

Father Miskisk came down the corridor doublebodied. He was bigger than Squell, broad-chested, square-jawed, with a mane of blood-red hair, and sunset-orange skin traced all over with white squiggles. He was wearing his dancing pants. His voice was deep and rumbly, and he smelled warm, roasty, and oily. "Fift, little Fift," he said, "Come on, let's zoom around. I'll zoom you to the bathing room. Come jump up. Give her here, Squell."

"I want my gowns," Fift said, in her third body, as Squell dragged her through the doorway.

"Here," Squell said, trying to hand Fift's other bodies to Miskisk. But Fift clung to Squell. She didn't want to zoom right now. Zooming was fun, but too wild for this day, and too wild for someone who had lost her gowns. The gowns were a pale blue, soft as clouds; they would whisper around Fift's legs when she ran.

"Oh Fift, *please!*" Squell said. "You *must* bathe and you will *not* be late today! Today of all—"

"Is she really ready for this, do you think?" Miskisk said, trying to pry Fift away from Squell, but flinching back from prying hard enough.

"Oh please, Misk," Squell said, "let us not start that. Or not with *me*. Pip says—"

Father Smistria stuck his head out of the door of his studio. He was tall and haggard looking and had brilliant blue skin, and a white beard braided into hundreds of tiny braids woven with little glittering mirrors and jewels, and was wearing a slick swirling combat suit that clung to his skinny flat chest. His voice was higher than Father Miskisk's, squeaky and gravelly at the same time. "Why are you two winding the child up?" he barked. "This is going to be a *disaster*, if you give her the impression that this is a day for racing about! Fift, you will stop this *now!*"

"Come on, Fift," Miskisk said coaxingly.

"Put her *down*," Smistria said. "I cannot believe you are wrestling and flying about with a Staidchild who in less than three hours—"

"Oh give it a rest, Smi," Miskisk said, sort of threateny, and turned away from Fift and Squell, towards Smistria. Smistria stepped fully out into the corridor, putting his face next to Miskisk's. It got like thunder in between them, but Fift knew they wouldn't hit each other; grown-up Bails only hit each other on the mats. Still, she hugged Squell closer—one body squished against his soft chest, one body hugging his leg, one body pulling back through the doorway—and squeezed all her eyes shut, and dimmed the house feed so she couldn't see that way either.

Behind her eyes she could only see the pale blue gowns. It was just like in her dream! She'd lost her gowns and she would have to wear only bells like Father Frill! She shuddered. "I don't want my gowns to be in the compost," she said, as reasonably as she could manage.

"Oh, will you shut up about the gowns!" Squell said. "No one cares about your gowns!"

"That's not true," Miskisk boomed, shocked.

"It *is* true," Smistria said, "and—"

Fift could feel a sob ballooning inside her. She tried to hold it in, but it grew and grew and—

"Beloveds," said Father Grobbard.

Fift opened her eyes. Father Grobbard had come silently, singlebodied, up the corridor. She stood behind Squell. She was shorter than Miskisk and Smistria, the same height as Squell, but more solid: broad and flat like a stone. When Father Grobbard stood still, it looked like she would never move again. Her shift was plain and simple and white. Her skin was a mottled creamy brown, with the same fine golden fuzz of hair everywhere, even the top of her head.

"Grobby!" Squell said. "We are *trying* to get her ready, but it's quite—"

"Well it's Grobbard's show," Smistria said. "It's up to you and Pip today, Grobbard, isn't it? So why don't *you* get her ready!?"

Grobbard held out her hand. Fift swallowed, and then she slid down from Squell's arms, and went and took it.

"Grobbard," Miskisk said, "are you sure Fift is ready for this? Is it really—"

"Yes," Grobbard said. Then she looked at Miskisk, her face as calm as ever. She raised one eyebrow, just a little. Then she looked back at Fift's other bodies, and held out her other hand. Squell let go of the arms of Fift's he was holding, and Fift gathered; she took Father Grobbard's other hand, and caught a fold of Father Grobbard's shift, and that way, they went down to the bathing room.

"My gowns weren't old," Fift said, on the stairs. "They came out of the oven a week ago."

"No, they weren't old," Grobbard said. "But they were blue. Blue is a Bail color, the color of the crashing, restless sea. You are a Staid, and today you will enter the First Gate of Logic. You couldn't do that wearing blue gowns."

"Oh," Fift said.

Grobbard sat by the side of the bathing pool, her hands in her lap, her legs in the water, while Fift scrubbed herself soapy.

"Father Grobbard," Fift said, "why are you a Father?"

"What do you mean?" Father Grobbard asked. "I am your Father, Fift. You are my child."

"But why aren't you a Mother? Mother Pip is a Mother, and she's—um, you're—"

Grobbard's forehead wrinkled briefly, and then it smoothed, and her lips quirked in a tiny suggestion of a smile. "Aha, I see. Because you have only one Staid Father, and the rest are Bails, you think that being a Father is a Bailish thing to be? You think Fathers should be 'hes' and Mothers should be 'shes'?"

Fift frowned, and stopped mid-scrub.

"What about your friends? Are all of your friends' Mothers 'she'? Or are some of them 'he'?" Grobbard paused a moment; then, gently: "What about Umlish Mnemu of Mnathis cohort? Her Mother is a Bail, isn't he?"

"Oh," Fift said, and frowned again. "Well, what makes someone a Mother?"

"Your Mother carried you in her womb, Fift. You grew inside her belly, and you were born out of her vagina, into the world. Some families don't have children that way, so in some families all the parents are Fathers. But we are quite traditional. Indeed, we are all Kumruists, except for Father Thurm . . . and Kumruists believe that biological birth is sacred. So you have a Mother."

Fift knew that, though it still seemed strange. She'd been *inside* Mother Pip for ten months. Singlebodied, because her other two bodies hadn't been fashioned yet. That was an eerie thought. Tiny, helpless, singlebodied, unbreathing, her nut-sized heart drawing nutrients from Pip's blood. "Why did Pip get to be my Mother?"

Now Grobbard was clearly smiling. "Have you ever tried to refuse your Mother Pip anything? There was a little bit of debate, but I think we all knew Pip would emerge as the Younger Sibling of that struggle. She had a uterus and vagina enabled, and made sure we all had penises, for the impregnation. It was an exciting time."

Fift pulled up the feed and looked up penises. They were for squirting sperm, which helped decide what the baby would be like. The uterus could sort through all the sperm and pick the genes it wanted, but you had to publish something or other to get approval, and after that it was too complicated. You'd have one on each body, dangling between your legs. "Do you still have penises? One . . . on each body?"

"Yes, I kept mine," Grobbard said. "They went well with the rest of me, and I don't like too many changes."

"Can I have penises?" she said.

"I suppose, if you like," Grobbard said. "But not today. Today you have something more important to do. And now I see that your Father has baked you new clothes. So rinse off, and let's go upstairs."

The new clothes were bright white shifts, like Father Grobbard always wore. And Mother Pip, mostly. Fift felt grown up, and strange, and stiff. She was scrubbed and polished and her heads were shaved and oiled and her fingernails and toenails were trimmed. She sat in a row on the rough moss of the anteroom, trying to sit lightly, balanced, spines straight.

The anteroom of their apartment was full of parents, practically all of Iraxis cohort. Fathers Squell and Smistria and Pupolo and Miskisk were there in a body each, and Father Frill and Father Grobbard were both doublebodied. Mother Pip was on her way. Only Fathers Thurm and Arevio were missing, and they were watching over the feed.

Father Frill knelt next to Fift, brushing bits of fluff from the moss. He was lithe and dusky-skinned, with a shock of stiff copper-colored hair sweeping up from his broad forehead, wide gray eyes and a full mouth and a sharp chin. He was dressed for the occasion in cascades of tinkling silver and gold and crimson bells, and a martial shoulder sash hung with tiny, intricately-worked ceremonial knives and grenades. He crouched like a sharp-toothed wild hunting-animal, resting in a tree's limbs somewhere up on the surface of the world. He ran his hand gently over her bare, oiled scalp, which felt nice, but also distracting because she was trying very hard to sit straight. "Oh Fift," he said, "we're all very proud of you, you know."

"Well she hasn't done anything yet," Father Smistria said, glowering, and pacing back and forth under the pillars of the anteroom, "except finally take a bath! Keep *focused*, Fift."

"Ignore him," Father Frill said, taking his hand from Fift's head, leaning in against Fift's shoulder. He smelled like a rainy day in a mangareme fruit grove on the surface. "He's cranky because he's nervous. But there's no reason to be nervous, Fift. Grobbard and your Mother say that this thing today is just a formality. I—"

"Ha!" barked Smistria, tugging at his beard.

"Stop it, Smistria," Miskisk said. His fists were clenched. "You're making it worse."

Fift got an uneasy feeling in her stomach. {What are my Fathers talking about?} she asked her agents.

The context advisory agent answered, {About your first episode of the Long Conversation; today you will enter the First Gate of Logic.}

{I know that!} Fift sent back. She hated when her agents acted like she was a baby.

Father Squell cleared his throat. "It's really none of *our* business, Frill," he said. He was standing near the wall, rubbing the slippery red fabric of his shirt between his fingers. "Whether it's a 'formality'!"

Father Smistria glared at Squell. Frill, in his standing body, languidly cracked his back.

"I just mean—for *us* to argue about her chances!" Squell said. "It's not appropriate! This is Pip and Grobbard's domain. . . ."

"None of our business?" Smistria barked. "None of *our business?*"

Father Frill frowned, leaned away from Fift (the bells tinkled as he shifted), and twitched his lips the way he always did when he was sending a private message. He was staring at Smistria, so he was probably sending something like: {Stop talking about this now, you're scaring Fift.} But Smistria ignored him.

"It really isn't," Squell said. He took a step away from Smistria, and looked back towards Pupolo, who was swinging gently in a seating harness at the back of the anteroom. "It's a Staid matter!"

"That's right," said Pupolo. He looked tired, but he still sat straight in his harness. He was in a green smock, and he had dirt on his hands, from the garden. Father Pupolo was Fift's oldest parent and once, a long long time ago, he had been sort of famous as a military poet.

"Well, I'm obviously not talking about the *details* of the . . . process," Smistria said, taking a step towards Father Squell and flinging his arms wide. "I'm not an idiot. Don't insult me! But the *outcome*, that's another matter! The *outcome* affects our entire cohort, and you know perfectly well—"

"*Smi*," Frill said sharply. He leaned in towards Fift again; in his other body, he crossed to Smistria and grabbed his shoulder.

Grobbard stood to the side, expressionless. Fift wished she would say something. Or that Pip would finally come, and they could leave and get it over with. It was hard to sit up straight.

She tried her agents again: {Why is everyone fighting?}

The emotional nuance agent sent, {Bails often react to being tense by crying or shouting. Don't let it scare you!}

Smistria swiveled to glare at Frill. Frill didn't take his hand from Smistria's shoulder. They stared into each other's eyes. Then Smistria softened a little, and pulled Frill roughly into an embrace—Frill's musical clothes jingled and rang. They stood like that with their cheeks touching, Smistria's beard caught in Frill's bells, Smistria's eyes squeezed shut. Frill put his hand back on Fift's head. "There now!" he said.

Pip came, singlebodied, through the door.

Pip was large, and round, and bald. She wore a white shift too, and her skin was a deep forest green, and it hung in wens and folds from her face. She had powerful, searching eyes, white and gold and black, that looked deep into you. She had fat stubby fingers and one hand held the other hand's thumb and stroked it.

"Greetings, beloveds," said Pip. "Greetings, Fift." She turned to Pupolo and clasped his hands briefly, nodded to Grobbard, quirked an eyebrow at Frill and Smistria.

"Finally!" Frill said, releasing Smistria in a cascade of bells. Smistria breathed in loud, and crossed his arms. "What took you so long, Pip? We were about to check into the Madhouse, all eight of us!"

Squell touched Pip's cheek, ran his hand along her shoulder. Pip's expression softened into an almost-smile, and she took Squell's hand.

"Oh Pip," Squell said, "will you please tell them that it's fine, and to stop arguing about today! It's just absurd!"

Miskisk looked angry, as if dark clouds were massing across his sunset face.

Pip blinked, and looked to Frill, to Smistria, to Pupolo, and finally to Grobbard. Then she chuckled. "Fift is ready," she said. "I have absolute confidence. Do you remember what we practiced, Fift?"

All it was, was sitting still and waiting to be passed a spoon, and passing it on at the right moment, and saying the names of the twelve cycles, the twenty modes, and the eight corpuses of the Long Conversation. You couldn't use agents to help with anything, but that was okay because Fift and Grobbard never let her practice with agents anyway. She nodded.

"And Grobbard concurs," Pip said. "You are all disturbed by the betting, I know, but there is always betting around a Staidchild's first Long Conversation, especially when . . ." she pursed her lips. ". . . when a cohort looks weak from outside." She raised a hand, as if to quiet objections. "Only nine parents, only two of them Staids—the initial birth approval barely granted—the questions around Fift's somatic integration—well, of course ignorant bettors imagine they see an opportunity! But they do not have the information we have. They are speculating. We know."

"There!" said Frill. "You see?"

Smistria harrumphed, and stretched his arms above his head. "Very well. Then let's send you all off, and get back to our day. This fussing and waiting is making me old. Frill, how about a bout on the practice mats?"

"All right," Frill said. He kissed Fift on the top of her head. "Enjoy yourself, little stalwart." He stood.

Pupolo stood up from his harness. Grobbard came over doublebodied to Fift, and sent, {It is time to go, Fift}

But Fift did not stand up; she was watching Miskisk.

"Well," Miskisk said, his voice tense as the straining of the giant muscles that turned their habitation, "that's wonderful, isn't it? Fift is all settled then, isn't she? All ready for her big day, no problems anywhere, and the cohort is perfectly safe and from here our ratings can only burrow in to greatness."

"Miskisk," Pupolo said, dissaproving.

"Oh, I don't *dispute* it," Miskisk said, raising his great orange hands. "What do I know? It's a Staidish matter and I'm sure *Pip* has everything under control. As usual. But in that case, isn't it time for the next step?"

"Oh, not this again," Frill said.

"Misky," Squell said. He frowned, clearly sending a private message, then—getting no reponse—said in exasperation, "Not in front of Fift!"

"But where, then?" Miskisk said. "Where, then? At every family meeting it's tabled immediately—"

"Beloved Miskisk," Pip said—it was a cold, dry kind of "beloved," Fift thought—"I am, as you know, perfectly willing for us to hazard a second child, if the matter of maternity can be settled to our mutual satisfaction."

"We are *not* doing this here," Frill said. "No. No, no, no."

Suddenly Fift knew what they were arguing about. A *second child*. A strange sensation, heat and cold together, shot through her bodies. She lost her careful balance and had to put a hand down onto the moss to steady herself. A sibling! A *Younger Sibling*—literally!—supplanting Fift.

To be an Older Sibling—everyone said—meant being poor, being eclipsed, being in the shadow of the Younger. But it also meant not being alone. Having someone to protect and support. And it meant not being an Only Child; and everyone knew there was something wrong with being an Only Child. Something that made Fift's parents worry and argue and quickly take conversations unspoken, when Fift asked too much.

"Which means of course that it's you again!" Miskisk said. "It's always you!" Tears sprung to his eyes, and a great shudder passed through his heavy body. He looked around at the other Fathers. "It's always her! She is the Mother, she guards our ratings, she decides where we'll live and when little Fift has to—has to—"

Frill brushed past Grobbard, squatted down again, and enfolded Fift in his arms. He picked one of Fift's bodies up, slinging one bell-clad arm under her bottom. She was pressed against his bells and daggers and grenades. Squell hurried over, too.

"Miskisk, you selfish ingrate," Pupolo said, "blaming Pip will not elevate *your* chances of bearing, I'll tell you that!"

Father Frill hustled Fift towards the door. He was coming in another body, too, to fetch more of Fift—but then he wheeled around, facing Miskisk. "Miskisk, you're being absurd. Pip *won't* be the Mother the second time. It will be Pupolo or Arevio, or Thurm if he'd agree to it, or—or me!" Smistria snorted, and Frill glared at him briefly through slitted eyes, then went on, "Pip knows perfectly well that being Mother twice over would be—too much! But what is your rush anyway? Fift isn't even five yet! Why does she need a Younger Sibling right away?"

Squell scooped up another of Fift's bodies, and followed Frill out the door, muttering: "Completely inconsiderate! Today of all days!"

{What's wrong with being an only child?} Fift asked her agents.

{That is not the polite term,} sent Fift's social nuance agent. {You should use "an individual with a heavy relative familial-resource-allocation childhood." Pedagogical experts, statistician-poets, religious officials, the Midwives, all agree: children who lack siblings lack the basics of human experience. All real human emotions—jealousy, rage, love, regret, forgiveness, rivalry, triumph, defeat, reconciliation, and ultimate shared purpose—are based in the contest between siblings.}

"This is the age when it matters!" Miskisk rumbled, tears streaming down his face. "And what makes you think it will ever change? None of you will ever dare to struggle with Pip over the maternity—and none of you have the strength to watch Fift be supplanted!"

Pip crooked an eyebrow, coldly amused.

"That's—" Frill flung an arm out, ringing with bells, and turned to Miskisk. "That's—Smi, take the child out of here!—that's an insult!"

Two of Fift's bodies were out through the door and into the corridor. Frill and Squell put her onto her feet and smoothed her robes.

Smistria sighed loudly, and stalked over to where her third body sat. He held out his hand.

"It's true!" Miskisk wailed. "You're too cowardly and too comfortable! You'd rather she end up *sisterless* than endure the discomfort of her Supplanting!"

{What's "sisterless"?} Fift asked her agents.

{That is not a word we say,} sent the social nuance agent primly.

{*Sister* is an archaic word for sibling,} added the context advisory agent.

{But lots of people are Only Children,} Fift sent. {Grobbard and Arevio and Smistria are. . . . }

{It is one of the great social crises of our time,} her context advisory agent sent.

In the corridor, Fift shivered. In the anteroom, in her last body, she stayed seated, looking away from Smistria, looking at Miskisk. Her Father was crying—that was nothing, her Bail Fathers cried all the time—but this was different. Something was wrong here; Miskisk was serious. A chill raced down from her necks and settled in her stomachs.

Smistria shook his hand in Fift's face. "Come on," he growled. "You're going to be late anyway, for this . . . this circus of yours!"

Pupolo drew a shocked breath, because one shouldn't make fun of the Long Conversation like that. Smistria snorted.

"Smistria," Miskisk pled, "you agree with me—you know it's too early for this—that Fift deserves a little more time at home to run and play and wear more colors than white, before—"

Smistria pushed his hand at Fift, glaring, and Fift had to take it. She pulled herself to her feet.

"Do I agree with you that Pip is bossy, and that everyone here is all too eager to postpone *any* argument . . . especially in the matter of Sibling Number Two? Of course I do. Do I think you should be allowed to keep Fift here as a baby, dressed up in bangles and zooming about—to satisfy your selfish wish for a Bailchild? No, Miskisk, I do not." He pulled Fift towards the door. Grobbard came with them, expressionless.

"You are crushing my heart," Miskisk said, tears dripping from his chin. "I cannot do this anymore. I cannot—"

"We have a *pledge*," Pupolo said in horror.

Miskisk covered his eyes with his hands.

"If I may," Pip said coldly—and then the door closed behind them. Fift closed her eyes, tried to listen and look with the feed, to see what Pip and Miskisk and Pupolo were saying in the anteroom. But the feed was opaque. Where that room should be was a blank silence. Someone had told the apartment not to show her what was happening there.

"Come on now, little stalwart," Frill said. "You won't be late if we hurry. You're ready and there's plenty of time."

"What about Pip?" Squell said.

"She's also already on the way from her client in Temereen," Frill said, pulling Fift along doublebodied towards the front door of the apartment, "she was planning to come doublebodied anyway—it's not far—perhaps, since she's busy here, one will have to do—Grobby is here, and you're going to do fine!"

Father Grobbard walked beside them, silent. She didn't look upset, or worried. She walked as if she was in the morning hush of a forest on the surface, watching for unpurposed surface animals, the way they once had on a trip they took . . . up the long elevators, thousands of bodylengths through the deep dark bedrock . . . to the surface forest, quiet and cold and damp and strange. . . .

This was like that now, maybe. A trip somewhere new. A trip to the Long Conversation, which was secret and important and grown-up and Staid.

{What pledge?} Fift asked her agents.

{A pledge is a promise that people make,} began the context advisory agent.

{That's not what I asked,} Fift sent. {You know what I mean! What pledge did my parents make? Tell me or I'm going to remove you!}

Fift took Grobbard's hands, and they all went out through the apartment door, through the corridor, and onto the surface of Foo.

{Your parents all pledged to stay together for all twenty-two years of your First Childhood,} sent the context advisory agent, reluctantly. {To all sleep in the same apartment once a month at the least, to attend family meetings, various such requirements. They had to. The neighborhood approval ratings for your birth weren't high enough otherwise.}

{But this is not at all unusual,} the social nuance agent assured Fift.

Just above them was the glistening underside of Sisterine habitation, docking-spires and garden-globes and flow-sluices arcing away. In front of them was the edge of Foo. Their neighborhood, Slow-as-Molasses, was at the end of one spoke of Foo's great, slowly rotating wheel—and beyond it, this time of year, was a great empty vault of air . . . and then fluffy Ozinth and the below-and-beyond strewn with glittering bauble-habitations . . . and beyond that, habitation after habitation, bright and dim, smooth and spiky, shifting and still, all stretching away toward the curve of Full-belly's ceiling.

There are a trillion people in the world, Fift thought. And only ten in our house. And if Father Miskisk breaks the pledge, we'll be only nine, and that's not enough. Her legs, under the new white shift, felt cold and rubbery.

They came to the edge of the neighborhood, the main slideway to the center of Foo.

"All right, little cubblehedge," Squell said, dropping down on one knee to hug Fift. "Time for Frill and I to turn back. You are in our hearts."

Frill rubbed Fift's scalp one more time. "Knock 'em on their backs, little one!" He grinned, and slapped his knife-belt. "Metaphorically."

Fift looked up into his face and took a deep breath. *The outcome affects our whole cohort.* "Father Frill, what if I *don't* do well? What will happen?"

Frill and Squell's faces went a little stiff, and even Grobbard blinked. Fift realized then—they weren't in the apartment anymore, they weren't just on the house feed. Everyone in the world could see and hear them now, if they wanted to.

But Frill smiled then, and crouched down next to Fift, in a tinkling of bells. "Then we'll manage, Fift," he said. "We're a strong cohort and we'll triumph. You have a Mother and Father to hold you safe at the center, and Fathers enough to range around you, to protect and enliven . . ."

{Will you hurry up?} sent Smistria, from back at the apartment, to all of them. {Fift will be late!}

Frill rolled his eyes, and grinned a crooked grin. "Goodbye," he said, and "Goodbye," Squell said, and Fift took Grobbard's hand and stepped onto the slideway.

{Father Miskisk,} Fift sent, but she didn't know what else to send. {Father Miskisk . . . I'll do my best!}

If she did well enough, maybe Father Miskisk would stay.

The slideway whooshed them off, towards the center of Foo, where they could transfer to another spoke; towards the wooden floor, and the spoons, and the First Gate of Logic, and white gowns and responsibility, and no more zooming. Fift held tight to Grobbard's hand, and waited, hoping, for Father Miskisk to reply.

In panic Town,
on the Backward moon

MICHAEL F. FLYNN

Michael Flynn began selling science fiction in 1984 with the short story "Slan Libh." His first novel, In the Country of the Blind, *appeared in 1990. He has since sold seventy or more stories to* Analog, Asimov's Science Fiction, Fantasy & Science Fiction, *and elsewhere, and has been nominated several times for the Hugo Award. He is best known for the Hugo-nominated* Eifelheim *and the* Tales of the Spiral Arm *sequence, which includes* The January Dancer, Up Jim River, In the Lion's Mouth, *and* On the Razor's Edge. *His other books include* Fallen Angels, *a novel written in collaboration with Larry Niven and Jerry Pournelle,* Firestar, Rogue Star, Lodestar, Falling Star, *and* The Wreck of the River of Stars. *His stories have been collected in* The Forest of Time and Other Stories *and* The Nanotech Chronicles. *He has received the Robert Heinlein Award for his body of work, and the Theodore Sturgeon Memorial Award for the story "House of Dreams." In addition, he has received the Seiun Award from Japan and the Prix Julia Verlanger from France, both for translations of* Eifelheim. *His most recent book is the collection* Captive Dreams, *which contains six stories dealing with issues of morality and technology. He is currently working on a novel,* The Shipwrecks of Time, *set in the alien world of 1965. He lives in Easton, Pennsylvania.*

Here he takes us to the brawling lawless frontier of the solar system, to Mars and its backward moon, Phobos, for a robust and slyly amusing tale of lowlifes, lawmen, heists, con jobs, double-dealing, double crosses, and skullduggery.

The man who slipped into the Second Dog that day was thin and pinch-faced and crossed the room with a half-scared, furtive look. Willy cut off in the middle of a sentence and said, "I wonder what that *Gof* wants?" The rest of us at the table turned to watch. An Authority cop at the next table, busy not noticing how strong the near-beer was, slipped his hand into his pocket, and VJ loosened the knife in his ankle scabbard. Robbery was rare in Panic Town—making the getaway being a major hurdle—but it was not unknown.

Hot Dog sucked the nipple of his beer bottle. "He has something."

"Something he values," suggested Willy.

VJ chuckled. "That a man values something is no assurance that the thing is valuable. It might be a picture of his sainted grandmother." But he didn't think so, and neither did anyone else in the Dog.

All this happened a long time ago. Mars was the happening place back then. Magnetic sails had brought transit times down to one month, and costs had dropped with them, so the place was filling up with dreamers and scamps and dogs of all kinds, out to siphon a buck from the desert or from the pockets of those who did. There were zeppelin pilots and water miners, air-squeezers and terraformers. Half the industry supported the parasol-makers of course, but they needed construction, maintenance, teamsters, and rocket-jocks, and throughout history whenever there was a man and a dollar there was another man willing to separate them.

We were friends, the four of us hooching that day; but the kind of friends who rarely saw one another except across a bottle. Hot Dog's name was Rusty Johnson, but he eschewed that for a gonzo nickname. He flew ballistics for Iron Planet, taking passengers and cargo up to the Dogs or around to the antipodes. He had the glam, and women lined up and took numbers, even though he wasn't much to look at and even less to listen to. Maybe it was the cute freckles.

VJ's name was Viktor Djeh and it was fairly easy to figure how he'd gotten his nickname. He did maintenance on PP&L's converter out by Reldresel, where they pulled oxygen and other useful crap from the ilmenite. His job was not nearly as glamorous as Hot Dog's, but he made it up in morphy-star good looks. He was a joker, and always ready with a favor. He had saved my ass once when I was on a job in Reldresel and the high-pressure line sprang a leak, so I always paid his freight when we crossed paths at the Dog.

Willy's name, to complete the trifecta, was actually Johann Sebastian Früh, but a childhood friend had given him the moniker from an old movie and it stuck. Willy clerked for the Authority, so he had neither good looks nor glamour, but he got by on a willingness to listen. His earnest expression invited confidences, a circumstance that provided him with a steady, if clandestine income.

Pinch-face crossed to the bar, where Pondo was serving. Dogs move in microgravity like they're underwater—in slow, gliding steps and grip shoes. I once saw Jen Wuli chase Squint-Eye Terry M'Govern down the Shklovsky-Lagado tubeway and it was the funniest damn thing I ever did see.

Pondo and the stranger traded whispers, then sidled into the office. Everyone relaxed, and the Authority cop took his hand out of his pocket. A few minutes later, they re-emerged from the office with smiles all over their teeth.

"Who was that muffer?" someone at another table asked when the stranger was gone.

"I seen him around, down below. Works outta Port Rosario."

Willy smiled when he overheard this, and VJ gave a thoughtful nod. Hot Dog pulled his handi from his coverall pocket and checked his schedule. "I'm dropping down to chair a Guild meeting in a couple days," he told us. "Pig Hanson has a run out to Marineris and I have to sub. I'll ask around."

That's how it started, though at the time we didn't know it.

The next day I called Aurora Sails in Under-Gulliver, where they ran an assembly hanger. The superconductor loop sets up a magnetic field that acts as a sail and takes up momentum from the solar wind. It doesn't harvest much acceleration, but the velocity keeps building, and you don't have to carry fuel. By adjusting the loops you can change the size and shape of the field and sail damn near anywhere at respectable speeds. When you kick amps into a superloop, the current keeps going like a bunny with a drum until you quench it.

The problem the client had at the time was that some of their sails wouldn't kick amps. They thought there might be something wrong with the kicker, but they didn't know how to prove it. So the Authority tasked me to settle matters because the bickering under Gulliver was growing intense and nothing soothes internal squabbles like an external consultant.

Technically, I work for the Ares Consortium, an alliance of corporations formed to run the Martian parasol business. Aurora strings the parasols and Pegasus ferries them to the target asteroid, where Sisyphus rigs the harnesses in place. My ultimate boss was actually old man Bryce van Huyten, but Phobos Port Authority coordinates the local action, so I carry an Authority troubleshooter's badge.

I told Aurora to set up two loops in the test beds: one that worked and one that didn't. They balked because any loop that worked was immediately installed on a parasol and packaged for transit, while the defective ones were salvaged for parts. Parasols were urgent, high-priority work, and they couldn't let loops sit around for me to play with, and blah-blah-blah. The usual. So I told them to call me back when they were ready to get serious and I cut the link.

It took them two days while they pondered what the Authority would say if they blew me off. Then I got a call from Antonelli, the sail prep boss. He had two loops set aside, he told me, "but hustle your ass out here because Logistics is giving me the stink-eye."

Antonelli and his engineers managed to conceal their delight when my ass arrived. They floated at a respectable distance. Everybody wanted to be close enough to the problem to count coup in case I succeeded, but not so close that they'd get cooties if I failed.

I forgot their names as soon as they were introduced, except for one fellow from Logistics named Moynihan Truth, both because of his unusual name and because I saw him again later. He was ten years old, but that's in dog years; double it for Earth-equivalent. He'd been born in Golden Flats on Mars, where they have the monument to the first Rover. You've probably seen images of Farzi Baroomand's famous statue, the one that shows all the aliens lined up behind the Rover where the camera can't see them, laughing themselves silly. Everyone there takes the last name Truth to honor the Rover. The Kid was the only one in the locker smiling and I remember wondering what the big joke was.

Four test beds took up most of the horizontal space. Hobartium loops were tethered to beds A and B. I pointed to A and said, "This one's not working?" Nods all around. The neon-yellow *Hold* tag was my clue. "And that one works?" More bobbleheads. It was green-tagged. "And you think it might be the kicker?" Grudging assents, but dissenters mentioned other components, assembly errors, you-name-it. Paralysis of analysis. Smart people with a dozen smart ideas, but not smart enough to try any for fear of being wrong.

But the first rule of troubleshooting is: Start Somewhere. When you don't know crap, whatever you learn moves you ahead. "Take *this* kicker," I pointed, "and install it on *that* loop; and take *that* kicker and install it on *this* loop."

When the switcheroo was finished I told them to kick amps, and the superconductor on A began to circularize from the hoop stress, while the one on B now remained flaccid. I nodded.

"Yep. It's the kicker, all right."

Antonelli swelled up. "For *that*, we pay Port Authority two ounces troy *per diem?* We could have done that ourselves!"

"No you couldn't," I reminded him. "You couldn't even get the two hoops set up without my prodding."

"Big deal," said one of the engineers. "We already thought it was the kicker." No matter what the solution turns out to be, there will always be *someone* to say *I told you so.*

"Sure," I said. "But now you *know*. Now take the top assembly off this kicker and switch it with the top assembly on the other. If nothing changes, the problem's in the bottom half. If A fails but B works, the problem's in the top half."

Antonelli sucked lemons. "What if they both start working?"

"Then it gets interesting."

The secret of my success doesn't come from knowing all the answers, but in knowing how to ask the questions. Disassembly-and-reassembly successively narrows the search zone for the cause. Three iterations homed in on the damper circuit subassembly. After that, it was a matter of screening the other kickers in stock and finding the ones with defective dampers. Antonelli wrote a Stern Letter to the Earthside parts manufacturer, which let him wrap things up on a suitably righteous note of indignation. Nothing makes a man happier than the prospect of blaming someone else.

When I returned to my rooms toward shift-end, I found a message from Pondo asking me to stop by the Second Dog as soon as I could. I finished repacking my go-bag for my next assignment, then took the tow-line up Dilman's Bore, where I found Pondo waiting just inside the Dog.

Small as Phobos was, you'd think an illicit bar would be a tough thing to hide. Scientists back in the day had known that Phobos was partly hollow and that puzzled them some. They also realized that the moonlet resembled a Main Belt asteroid, but they couldn't figure how Mars could capture an asteroid, circularize its eccentric orbit, and rope it onto the Martian equatorial plane—not until they discovered that the Visitors had been tricking it out back in the day. About a third of the interior had been gutted by the Visitors, and the rooms, warrens, and passageways they dug totaled two-thousand cubic kilometers usable volume. But volumes can be made operationally larger when people look the other way, and the pocket under Kepler's Ridge had somehow escaped notice when volume was platted out.

Koso Bassendi, the owner, was a hard man to cross and was big enough to make it harder still if you did manage it. I never heard of anyone crossing him twice. Come retirement, he and brother Pondo took their bonus money and started the Second Dog. They served beer stronger than the wretched double-deuce that the Prague Convention allowed, but they served an honest measure. You can't ask more than that of any man.

"Mickey," Pondo said, "I understand yer going Mars-side tomorrow."

I didn't ask him how he knew. My schedule was not exactly classified, and the Authority likes to rotate its employees into gravity wells to keep up their muscle tone and bone calcium.

"Maybe you'll have time to do my brother and me a little favor."

Doing favors for the Bassendis was risky. So was refusing. I figured they wanted me to smuggle up some potables in my Authority packet, so I said, "Sure.". Technically, Phobos is "outer space" and Mars "planetary surface," so the Prague Convention covers one, but not the other. Go figure.

Pondo guided me into the office, where Koso bobbed with his arms crossed and his scowl directed toward the thick, open door of an Eismann and Hertzog safe.

"Somebody got into our vault," Pondo explained, in case I couldn't figure it out. Koso said nothing, but his face tightened like a hangman's knot.

"You call the cops?"

Both brothers looked at me and I let it go. "So, what'd you lose? Money, securities?"

They shook their heads. "Not even the Bassendi Brothers Benevolent Fund was touched," said Koso.

I didn't ask who the Fund was intended to benefit.

Pondo said, "Remember that fellow, Jaroslav Bytchkov, what give us something to keep for him the other day? Well, it's gone."

Which meant that whatever that packet contained, it was worth a great deal more than what was left untouched. At least now I knew Pinch-Face's name.

"And what was it?"

"How would we know?" Pondo said. "My brother and me sell trust. Who would trust us with their keepsakes if we stuck our noses into them?"

The brothers might be shady, but they had a code. "What you want me to do?" I said, though I could already guess.

"Yer a troubleshooter," said Pondo. "Find what caused our trouble."

Koso spoke. "We take care of the other part."

The brothers figured the taker had been in the bar the night Bytchkov had brought his precious. Who else would have known it was there? I reminded them that I had been there and Koso smiled. "The vault software was tickled during the day, when all decent men are sleeping. You was out to Gulliver the whole time."

So I had an alibi, which was comforting; but the Bassendis wanted me to work for them, which was not so comforting. We went over the surveillance videos and identified everyone present, weeded out those too honest or too inept, and they asked me to investigate the ones who had dropped Mars-side.

That included Hot Dog, of course, who had that guild meeting to run. And Willy's job, like mine, required periodic commutes. But VJ had also dropped, taking some personal days to "bone up" at a calcium spa. Among the handful of Martians in the bar, a petite ice-miner—Gloria "Iceman," from Rosario—had already gone home.

"And we'd appreciate it, Mickey, if ye'd look up our depositor and find out what he given us."

Koso said, "And it shows up for sale, we might trace the taker."

"But we'd rather you not tell him it's been stolen."

"Bad for business."

I had a private notion that Bytchkov already knew it was stolen. He just didn't know it had been stolen from him.

Port Rosario sits in Arabia, a densely cratered, heavily eroded upland in the Northern Territories. Despite its name, it sits over some of the richest ice-bearing strata on Mars. Old water-canyons wind through the terrain and onto the lowlands, an ancient ocean bed. The dome is set in a deep crater and protected by hobartium loops that deflect incoming cosmic radiation. Mars is a hardscrabble world and attracts hardscrabble folk. No one would go there, weren't for the archeology and the asteroid-capture program.

Everybody needs a hobby, and the Visitors' hobby had been throwing rocks at Earth. They had booby-trapped a mess of Main Belt asteroids to drop earthward if we ever got too nosy. If it was some kind of sociopathic IQ test, like some folks thought, we had passed. We had bridled scores of 'stroids with magnetic sails and tacked them into GEO for mining and smelting. And if you're going to bridle asteroids, Mars is the go-to place. You need less delta-vee going up and down from Mars than hopping rock to rock. That's why the Visitors come to Mars back when Man was squatting in the forest primeval; and that's why we're there now.

Port Rosario always looked down-at-the-heels. There was dust everywhere. I don't care how good the precipitators are. They say you can never see Venus because clouds hide the surface. The same is true of Mars, except everything is covered with dust. You need a broom to see the true surface. The Martian wind is not very fierce—the air's too thin—but it's persistent. A dust storm can develop in hours, cover the planet in days and last for weeks. Some of it gets inside the domes in spite of all, and gives everything a rough, gritty look.

Rosarians were also rough and gritty, miners and teamsters being far from genteel, so it was well to walk careful. I tried to look dangerous whenever I strolled around town and carried enough mass to make it convincing and a set of brass knuckles in case it wasn't.

The town is laid out on a simple spoke-and-wheel street-plan. I arrived toward local sunset and took a room in Coughlin House in the northern quadrant with a nice view of the lowlands. Nothing but the best for the Authority. I tossed my gear in the room and headed for Centre Square, which was located exactly where you'd expect.

Local custom says everyone goes there first and shakes hands with the statue of Jacinta Rosario. She's portrayed without a helmet, which is historically inaccurate but artistically necessary. The statue is surrounded by grass and wildflowers and the only open trickle-fountain on Mars. Periodically, someone worries about "wasting water," but since Rosario is a closed system, the water doesn't really get wasted, and the size of the "Fossil Aquifer" underneath the town is good for a great long time. It's not like Martians are profligate, but like they'll tell you: "Anything for Jacinta."

Pilot House is out the end of Mercado Radial by the ATC tower. That's where zeppelin pilots check in. I stuck my head in the Chief Pilot's office and asked if Jaroslav Bytchkov was in town and he checked the logs and told me to try Dominick's Tavern at Mercado and Fourth. That was the heart of the Groin, where the merchant association had chipped in to hire a marshal to patrol the streets and break up fights. The neighborhood was called the Groin because it was a bad place to get your kicks.

Dominick's proved a three-story duroplast building facing inward from the Dome. Apartments were on the second and third floors. No fine views for them. I found a café across the street—One-Ball Murphy's—with a view of the entrance and waited for Bytchkov to show. I ordered a drink of "whiskey," though it wouldn't pass muster in Scotland or Kentucky. I think One-Ball boiled it out back in an old radiator.

I noticed Gloria Iceman at another table, also watching Dominick's. That was interesting, so I clicked a pix with my handi and made a note. Ice miners generally hung out in the south quadrant, around the mine elevators, not here near the aerodrome. I don't think she recognized me, but the next time I looked, she was gone and I hadn't seen her leave.

It was 2100 when I saw Bytchkov exit Dominick's right under the street-lamp. It must have been Old Home Week, because he was in animated conversation with Moynihan Truth. The young man had not been in the Dog the night Bytchkov squirreled his precious, but here he was chatting him up like an aged uncle with a legacy. I took a few more pix—and became suddenly aware that the other two seats at my table had acquired occupants.

On my right sat a pale, hard-faced woman with the indefinable glam of a rocket jock. She smiled at me, but it wasn't a friendly smile and she didn't say anything. On my left, a dusky man with obsidian eyes held a quarterstaff in his right hand. I nodded to him.

"Morning, marshal," I said.

It was Tiki Ferrer. "Morning, Mickey. What's a respectable Phobic like you doing in the Groin at night?"

"Just getting my land legs back," I told him. "Came down from the Dogs at sunset."

"And snapping pix like a muffing tourist," he marveled. "Fourth and Merc' isn't a noted tourist spot. Why the interest?"

I'm pretty good at arithmetic, and added one and one. "Which are you watching, Bytchkov or Truth?"

"What is Truth?" he asked me. "That the young guy? Tell me about him."

That meant Bytchkov was the marshal's target and he was taking an interest in anyone who took an interest. That included Moynihan. It also included me. It was no skin off my nose, so I told him what I knew about the Truther.

Tiki introduced the woman as Genie Satterwaithe, a courier on the Red Ball laying over on Mars while her loop was refurbished and stocked up for the Green Ball to Earth. She had earlier flown ballistics and orbitals around the home world, which accounted for her implicit swagger even sitting down.

"I'm trying to talk her into signing on with Iron Planet," Tiki told me.

"What's your interest in Bytchkov?" I asked him. When the marshal demurred I flashed my badge. I wasn't on Authority business, but Tiki didn't have to know that.

"That's a Port Authority badge, Mickey. It doesn't push much mass down here."

"Look, marshal, this ain't for broadcast, but Bytchkov deposited something for safekeeping up in Panic Town and it's been stolen. I'm trying to find out what it was without tipping him off." That was the truth, if not the whole truth.

Bytchkov turned and re-entered his rooming house. Moynihan made an obscene gesture to his back. Tiki sighed. "One more name for the list of people less than pleased with Jaroslav Bytchkov. Why doesn't that list ever get shorter?"

Satterwaithe said, "It's a gift he has."

Tiki showed me a holo of a tall, lean woman. "This is Despina Edathanal," he said. "Recognize her?"

I shook my head. She had the lanky physique of the spaceborn. She hadn't been in the Dog. "She's a tall drink of water," I said. "I'd've noticed her."

"She's digmaster out at Cassini," Tiki said. "She filed a complaint against Bytchkov, claiming that he's filched Visitor artifacts."

Much was thereby explained. The Visitors were a long time gone, but they had left some trash behind. A Visitor artifact could fetch enough troy ounces Earth-side to make snatching the Bassendi Brothers Benevolent Fund look like chump change and not worth the risk. The trick would be getting the artifact from Mars to Earth, and I began to see how that might have been arranged.

"A couple days ago," Tiki continued, "Edathanal braced him right here in Murphy's and told him if he didn't return the goods she would tear off his left arm and beat him to death with it."

"His *left* arm?"

"Yeah, she was being nice. Bytchkov's right-handed. Anyhow, Bytchkov lifted for Phobos the next day. Want to tell me who he left the packet with?"

I shook my head. "Wouldn't be a health-conscious choice."

Tiki grunted. "So. Tell Koso hello when you see him."

"I'm starting to think Pondo has the brains in the family."

"Someone has to. Jaroslav's had some in-your-face time with a half dozen people these past two days. Words were exchanged, as they say, and fists a couple times. Now he'll only meet with one person at a time and only at a time and place of his choosing." Tiki laid out a series of holos on the table, each the size and shape of a standard playing card. "Tell me if you know any of these people."

One was the archeologist from the dig; another, the ice miner I had seen in the Dog. There were three guys I'd never laid eyes on; but the other three were Hot Dog, VJ, and Willy. I told him who they were.

"Bytchkov had fights with all eight of these?" I said.

"Let's say spirited discussions. I guess I should add that fellow Moynihan. I have a feeling he's the one smuggling the stolen artifacts off Phobos."

"The yellow-tagged loops," I said, and explained about the defective kickers. "Moynihan's in Logistics. He could've rigged those defects in the first place, then instead of salvaging the parts, hung the loops out with the contraband. Since the parts are already accounted for, they won't be noticed until Corporate runs a material balance."

Satterwaithe spoke up. "Makes sense. You can program those parasols to hold station in the solar wind and a courier like me can snag it on the fly."

Tiki smiled. "Maybe I should add you to the suspects."

"*That's* why Moynihan was grinning," I said. "He wasn't amused; he was nervous."

The marshal nodded. "And you accidentally cut off their channel. Phobos-Mars radio is too public, so he came down to tell Jaroslav on the QT, probably phoned from the terminal as soon as he hit dirt. That was . . ." Tiki did a quick search over his handi and said, "He grounded Mars-side at 1830 in *Roustabout*. Easy enough to call from there." He closed the dust cover on his device. "Half an hour later Jaroslav made a call to a tosser cell. He told whoever answered that he had 'a big one' if the price was right and set up a meet at Dominick's for 2200. I bet he's trying to unload his latest acquisition. Genie and I were waiting to see who shows up, catch them passing the contraband."

"Which now he doesn't have."

Tiki checked his watch. "Almost time, but I haven't seen anyone enter the boarding house."

"You have someone watching the back?" I asked, and he gave me a teach-your-grandmother look.

"I got posse-men watching everyone on my list. These three . . ." He pointed to the ones I didn't know. ". . . they got rounded up an hour ago when the Minetown marshal busted a gambling den over the other side of town."

I glanced at the roster of miscreants. In Phobos, no one cared if you gambled away your life savings, but Martians were different. They don't approve of people who take foolish chances. Fast Paddy Murchison, Kenny ben Hauser, Johnny Free, Piglet Lieskovsky, Lucy Diamonds, Flo Miraziz, Rahim Hadfi, Manoj Patel, Big-O Saukkonen, and my old pal Squint-Eye Terry M'Govern. Fast Paddy, Big-O, and Lucy Diamonds had gotten into public altercations with Jaroslav within the past few days.

I handed him back the list. "Where were the others?"

"I should tell you because . . . ?"

I shrugged. "Because one of them may have guessed what Bytchkov took to Phobos and arranged to steal it. I'm looking into the Phobos theft for my, ah, patron."

Tiki conceded the point. He thumbed up his reports on his handi. "Posse touched base around 1930. Dr. Edathanal, they lost track of." He scowled at me. "They're volunteers, not professionals. . . . Let's see. Hot Dog was at a meeting. Gloria was here at Murphy's. Your buddy VJ was at Susie Xiao's Social Club getting himself greased. And your other buddy Willy was 'networking.'" He shook his head over the foibles of humanity. "Any of them could have received the call."

I didn't correct him. "And Moynihan Truth would have been in inbound processing. He could've got the call, too."

"But as of right now . . ." Tiki made a sound of disgust. ". . . we don't know where any of them are."

"Because . . . ?"

"Dinner time for most of my posse. I told you, they're not pros."

"Hell, Tiki, I don't even *have* a posse."

"Yeah? You're a troubleshooter, not a lawman."

Satterwaithe spoke up and said, "It's time. Shouldn't we close in?"

I wanted to say, *You're a courier, not a lawman*, but I sensed Tiki had his reasons for keeping her around.

"No one's gone in yet," said Tiki, but he opened his link. "Bill? We're going to close in." He listened, then said sweetly, "Well, I sure hope it was bone," and broke the link. He looked at Genie. "Martha called him home, told him supper was getting cold."

I waited a beat and said, "So, the entire Rosario Marching Band could have gone in the back way and you wouldn't have seen them."

Tiki glowered.

"On the positive side," I added cheerfully, "we probably would have heard them."

"I swear, Mickey, I'm gonna hit up the Association for a deputy. I can't get by with part-time amateurs. You want the job? You meet a better class of people than you do in industrial troubleshooting."

I told him I was happy where I was, but he gave me a posse badge anyway, "for the interim," and took me with him when we exited Murphy's. He told me to cover the back in case Jaroslav bolted. "You heavy?"

"I could stand to lose a few pounds."

"I mean are you armed?" He twirled his quarterstaff. Firearms are illegal in Port Rosario. The Dome was supposed to be bulletproof, but not even the criminals want to field test the theory. I showed him the knuckles and that seemed to satisfy him. Satterwaithe carried a baton.

Just then we saw someone scrambling from behind Dominick's. The streetlamp there was out and the figure was indistinct in the pale glow of its more distant cousins. The building on Fifth, right behind Dominick's, had overhanging balconies and the figure ran under the balcony and vanished in the shadows.

"Don't like that," said Tiki and we hurried across the street. I circled behind the building as planned and Satterwaithe sprinted up Mercado to try to catch the runner on the next block. Tiki went in the front.

Just as well, for I had a bad feeling about this.

Drifting sand had accumulated around the base of the tavern and just below one of the windows there was a very nice footprint. Someone had jumped from the second or third floor. This is an easier feat on Mars than on Earth. I knelt and inspected it, measuring its depth. I looked up and saw Tiki leaning out the second floor window. That gave me the height of the jump.

"Bytchkov's dead," I guessed.

"Deader'n Dizzy's mouse," Tiki said.

"Knifed?"

He scowled. "How'd you know?"

"It's fast and to the point. I may know who did it." I entered the figures into my handi and the results told me that the jumper had likely weighed over 70 kilos earth-weight. I crossed the rear lot to the building on the next street and measured the height of the balcony. One-seventy centimeters. I closed the tape measure and put it in my pouch. Then I made a few notations on my handi.

I felt immeasurably sad.

Tiki had sealed Bytchkov's apartment and made his way down to where I stood. He studied the rear of the tavern. "Not an impossible jump," he agreed.

Satterwaithe came loping back from Fifth Circle, cutting between the two apartment blocks and ducking under the balcony. "He ran off the other way, toward Sulbertson. I found a witness, though." She touched her handi. "The runner had a white overshirt and tan overpants. Unless the shirt was yellow and the pants brown." She grimaced. "He's not sure. Looked about midthirties. Maybe one-seventy height."

Tiki annotated his handi, snapped the sand-shield closed, and reinserted the stylus in its sheath. "I guess we should round up the usual suspects. My money's on Edathanal. Bytchkov was going to sell the artifact back to her because he couldn't hang it out for pickup. When he couldn't produce it, Edathanal lost her temper and . . . You're shaking your head, Mickey?"

"It wasn't her."

"How do you know? She was the only one we don't know where she was at 1900 when Bytchkov made the appointment with his killer."

I sighed. "When you've eliminated the impossible you won't always like what's left."

Tiki put a hold on the morning lift, and brought Despina and Gloria to join the others in the departure lounge. Hot Dog had been doing the pre-flight checklist and Tiki assured him that Iron Planet had bumped back the official lift time. "This won't take long," he said. "It's not like Phobos doesn't make two passes every day." Indeed, it swept the Martian sky faster than Mars himself rotated, and so rose in the west and set in the east.

Tiki placed me by the entry from the main terminal while Satterwaithe stood by the tubeway out to the shuttle. I'm not sure where Tiki thought the killer would try to run, but it's in the nature of the guilty to flee even if no man pursueth. In moments like that a man might not think clearly. Willy gave me a quizzical glance because he had caught the posse badge on my coveralls and the knuckle-bar on my right fist. He dealt in information, and the amount of information is proportional to its surprise.

"I think it is fair to say," Tiki began, "that all of you knew that Jaroslav Bytchkov had stolen something valuable and you all wanted to get your hands on it."

Despina Edathanal protested. "It belongs to the Visitor Project!"

Tiki nodded and said, "Why don't you describe the artifact that Bytchkov filched."

Five pairs of eyes turned toward her. I knew damn well one of the group already knew, but I saw no overt sign. Well, Tiki had his purpose and I had mine.

"It was a truncated pyramid of sandstone," Edathanal said, "about the size of my two hands. In the right lighting, you can see the hints of a face. Three eyes, arranged as a triangle; a suggestion of structure scoured by untold centuries of gentle Martian sandblasting. It's the only artifact we've ever found that hints at what the Visitors looked like. The weird thing is, the face doesn't seem to stay put. It's on one side, then it's on another. So we think there's also some very subtle micro- or nanotech going on with the stone."

I spoke up. "You'll provide a detailed sketch? I'll make sure Goods Outbound gets a copy up on the Dogs. Aurora and Pegasus, too." This was within my purview as an agent of the Port Authority. I wanted the thief to know that moving the contraband off-Mars would not be easy. Moynihan Truth shifted in his seat, probably wondering how much we knew.

Tiki turned to me. "Mickey, you want to tell them the next bit?"

Everyone scrooched around in his seat, except Hot Dog, who was leaning against the wall by the departure tube with his arms crossed, and Gloria Iceman, who sat to the side where she could see everyone.

"Jaroslav had one very hot potato and bounced to Phobos before the word could get out to deposit the statue for safekeeping until his partner could smuggle it out. Unfortunately, that channel was cut off a couple days later." Moynihan's smile had grown so broad I thought it might split his face in two.

Tiki took up the narrative once more. "Each of you either wanted to lay hands on the contraband or at least find out what it was. And each of you had a very public argument with Bytchkov. In some cases, knock-down fights."

VJ laughed. "That wasn't no fight. We played catch. He threw a punch; I caught it; threw it back." Willy and Hot Dog laughed with him.

Moynihan said, "He's not the easiest guy to get along with."

VJ said, "He was a prick."

Tiki cautioned them, "Don't speak ill of the dead."

That got their attention. I had been waiting for the line and had been watching their faces. Tiki's announcement should be a surprise to all but one. I caught the tell where I was expecting it and a glance at Tiki and Satterwaithe showed that they had caught it, too.

"At first, Dr. Edathanal seemed a good suspect," Tiki said. "She had the best motive. The statuette had been stolen from her. She had a fight with Bytchkov in which he slapped her across the face, a public humiliation. And no one knew where she was at the crucial times. But the killer was seen running under the balcony of the neighboring building. Genie over there had to duck when she chased after. The good doctor is too tall. She would have scalped herself."

"And the rest of us?" demanded Hot Dog, so red in the face that his freckles had disappeared.

"I also wondered about Gloria, here," Tiki continued. "She was seen in One-Ball Murphy's keeping a sharp eye on the rooming house, but disappeared just before.

But the killer jumped from the second floor window, and she's too light to have made the resulting footprint."

Moynihan Truth perked up. "Me, too?"

Tiki shook his head. "No, you weigh enough. Your motive . . . Thieves falling out, perhaps—oh, yes, we know about your end of the smuggling operation. You came down to tell Bytchkov that your game with the parasols was busted. But the witness on the next block saw the killer from a distance, and you would never be mistaken for the age he figured."

VJ wiped his brow dramatically. "People always say my good looks make me seem young."

"You wish," said Hot Dog. But an unease had fallen over him because he had noticed that only three suspects were left. He noticed Tiki watching him and protested, "I got an alibi for the whole day. I was at the Guild meeting!"

"The Guild meeting broke up at 2100," said Eugenie Satterwaithe. "I talked to some Guild comrades. That would have left plenty of time to get over to the Groin."

"But Bytchkov made a call at 1900," I explained, "and made an appointment to see the man who killed him. You were still in the meeting."

"So what?" asked VJ. "I seen lots of people on their handis in meetings."

"'Cept I was *running* the muffing meeting," Hot Dog said with evident relief. "I was sitting up on the muffing dais right in front of God and twenty-three muffing comrades, banging a muffing gavel. You can ask them!"

"I did," said Satterwaithe. "You didn't receive the call."

During this exchange, Willy had grown more and more pale, and he had begun to ease away from the others. VJ noticed this and whispered, "Better make a break for it." Tiki and I both heard it, and so did Hot Dog.

"Willy?" he said. "I don't believe it!"

"You don't have to," I said. "Willy has the best alibi of all. He was in custody in Minetown when Bytchkov was killed, same as three other suspects. If you'd told the arresting officer your name was Willy, it would've been obvious. But your legal name is Johann Früh, and it got recorded as Johnny Free on the booking sheet."

The arithmetic was simple enough now that everyone could see the remainder. VJ gave me a pained look and said, "Geez, Mickey. This is freeping *Mars!* You know what they do to you here?" Then he bolted for the exit where I stood, hoping I wouldn't have the heart to deck him. And I remembered how he had shoved me out of the way of that leaking pipe.

Tiki Ferrer's hands barely twitched and his quarterstaff tangled VJ's legs and he sprawled out. Satterwaithe was by his side with her baton ready, but there was no fight in him.

"Victor E. Djeh," Tiki told him formally, "you are detained on the authority of the City of Port Rosario and the Groin Merchants' Association."

"You don't like to hear it," I told Tiki afterward, when Satterwaithe had marched VJ off to the cells. "You think you know people; but you never do, and sometimes you find out just how much you don't know them." I shook my head. "I hope it was just a fight that got out of hand. I hate to think VJ went in there *planning* to knife the guy."

VJ was never the sharpest tool in the box. He'd been smart enough to wash his knife, but not smart enough to throw it away. It later proved to have Jaroslav's blood in the space between the blade and the handle. Just goes to show the importance of clean-up.

Tiki turned to me. "But he had nothing to do with stealing the artifact?"

"No, and I'll make sure Pondo understands that. I owe VJ that much at least. At least he never crossed the Bassendis."

The next day, I tracked Gloria Iceman to a Minetown bar. She was hooching with friends, but when she saw me she separated herself and came to sit in my booth.

"Iceman isn't your actual name," I told her without preamble. "It's Eismann, and someone transcribed it incorrectly when you applied for a Martian visa."

The miner smiled at me. "I liked the sound of it. It's a good nickname for an ice miner."

"It is that," I agreed. "But I think if I dig a little bit, I'll find out that you belong to the Eismann family that makes the vaults. Eismann and Hertzog. It's enough to make me wonder if someone at the company built a trap door into their products' software."

Gloria Iceman gave me a wide-eyed look. "That sounds awfully precocious."

"I even wonder who convinced Bytchkov to leave his precious with the Bassendis in the first place."

"Well, he had to hide it until the heat died down. The statue wasn't just another link or valve or other bit of trash from a technological midden heap. It was important. Best to hide it somewhere secure."

"But Edathanal knew who had taken it, and a dozen dogs knew he had brought something to the Second Dog. The Bassendis are shady, but they would not have defied a Port Authority warrant."

Gloria nodded. "It's harder to find something if no one knows where it actually is—or who actually took it."

"You don't want the Bassendis mad at you."

"At me? Why would they be mad at me? Where's the evidence I took it, beside a similarity of names?"

"The Bassendis aren't anal about evidence."

"You wouldn't put a flea in their ear on such flimsy suppositions."

"You'll never get the statue off Phobos. Every cubic of luggage will be scanned at the most minute levels."

Gloria frowned and pursed her lips. "I think that whoever has the statue will wait a long time before trying to move it off-world. Long after the hoo-rah has died down, long after the inspectors have forgotten what they were looking for. All that extra effort . . . You can't keep that up for very long."

Then she clapped me on the shoulder and walked lightly through the barroom and exited into the streets of Port Rosario. I never saw her again.

All that was many years ago and they're all gone now. Hot Dog smeared himself across a hectare of Martian desert when his ballistic failed to re-enter properly. Willy went down for blackmail. Satterwaithe left Mars after the baby she had with Tiki died; and Tiki was never the same after that.

Tiki found enough evidence in Bytchkov's apartment for the Port Authority to arrest Moynihan Truth when he stepped off the shuttle in Panic Town. He was exiled to Ceres.

The Martian Board of Actuaries sentenced VJ to slavery on the thermal decompositors out by Mt. Olympus for the remainder of Jaroslav Bytchkov's natural lifetime. I did what I could for him by arguing to the Board that Bytchkov's chosen profession of smuggler and thief put his lifespan at the low end of the confidence interval. That shortened VJ's sentence, but he never got around to thanking me for it.

Gloria "Iceman" Eismann was killed three months later when the tunnel collapsed in Ice Mine <#>23. I don't think the Bassendis had anything to do with it. I never told them my suspicions. Wherever she squirreled the statuette remains unknown, and it has never been found to this day.

Edathanal never found another artifact like it, and after a time everyone assumed she had been mistaken about the whole thing.

A writer back on Luna named Myles Hertzog possesses a replica, probably made from Edathanal's sketches, and has achieved a modest success with exciting stories about aliens he calls "the People of Sand and Iron."

the three resurrections of jessica churchill

kelly robson

New writer Kelly Robson is a graduate of the Taos Toolbox writing workshop. Her first fiction appeared in 2015 on Tor.com, in Clarkesworld, *and in* Asimov's Science Fiction, *and in the anthologies* New Canadian Noir, In the Shadow of the Towers, *and* Licence Expired. *She lives in Toronto with her wife, SF writer A. M. Dellamonica.*

The chilling story that follows centers around the desperate attempts by aliens to repair the wounds and save the life of a young woman who has suffered a horrific attack, even if they have to bring her back to life again and again to do so. But as she herself begins to wonder, is letting them heal her really a good idea? Or a very bad one indeed?

I rise today on this September 11, the one-year anniversary of the greatest tragedy on American soil in our history, with a heavy heart . . ." (Hon. Jim Turner)

SEPTEMBER 9, 2001

Jessica slumped against the inside of the truck door. The girl behind the wheel and the other one squished between them on the bench seat kept stealing glances at her. Jessica ignored them, just like she tried to ignore the itchy pull and tug deep inside her, under her belly button, where the aliens were trying to knit her guts back together.

"You party pretty hard last night?" the driver asked.

Jessica rested her burning forehead on the window. The hum of the highway under the wheels buzzed through her skull. The truck cab stank of incense.

"You shouldn't hitchhike, it's not safe," the other girl said. "I sound like my mom saying it and I hate that but it's really true. So many dead girls. They haven't even found all the bodies."

"Highway of Tears," the driver said.

"Yeah, Highway of Tears," the other one repeated. "Bloody Sixteen."

"Nobody calls it that," the driver snapped.

Jessica pulled her hair up off her neck, trying to cool the sticky heat pulsing through her. The two girls looked like tree planters. She'd spent the summer working full time at the gas station and now she could smell a tree planter a mile away. They'd come in for smokes and mix, dirty, hairy, dressed in fleece and hemp just like these two. The driver had blond dreadlocks and the other had tattoos circling her wrists. Not that much older than her, lecturing her about staying safe just like somebody's mom.

Well, she's right, Jessica thought. A gush of blood flooded the crotch of her jeans.

Water. Jessica, we can do this but you've got to get some water. We need to replenish your fluids.

"You got any water?" Jessica asked. Her voice rasped, throat stripped raw from all the screaming.

The tattooed girl dug through the backpack at Jessica's feet and came up with a two-liter mason jar half-full of water. Hippies, Jessica thought as she fumbled with the lid. Like one stupid jar will save the world.

"Let me help." The tattooed girl unscrewed the lid and steadied the heavy jar as Jessica lifted it to her lips.

She gagged. Her throat was tight as a fist but she forced herself to swallow, wash down the dirt and puke coating her mouth.

Good. Drink more.

"I can't," Jessica said. The tattooed girl stared at her.

You need to. We can't do this alone. You have to help us.

"Are you okay?" the driver asked. "You look wrecked."

Jessica wiped her mouth with the back of her hand. "I'm fine. Just hot."

"Yeah, you're really flushed," said the tattooed girl. "You should take off your coat."

Jessica ignored her and gulped at the jar until it was empty.

Not so fast. Careful!

"Do you want to swing past the hospital when we get into town?" the driver asked.

A bolt of pain knifed through Jessica's guts. The empty jar slipped from her grip and rolled across the floor of the truck. The pain faded.

"I'm fine," she repeated. "I just got a bad period."

That did it. The lines of worry eased off both girls' faces.

"Do you have a pad? I'm gonna bleed all over your seat." Jessica's vision dimmed, like someone had put a shade over the morning sun.

"No problem." The tattooed girl fished through the backpack. "I bleed heavy too. It depletes my iron."

"That's just an excuse for you to eat meat," said the driver.

Jessica leaned her forehead on the window and waited for the light to come back into the world. The two girls were bickering now, caught up in their own private drama.

Another flood of blood. More this time. She curled her fists into her lap. Her insides twisted and jumped like a fish on a line.

Your lungs are fine. Breathe deeply, in and out, that's it. We need all the oxygen you can get.

The tattooed girl pulled a pink wrapped maxi pad out of her backpack and offered it to Jessica. The driver slowed down and turned the truck into a roadside campground.

"Hot," Jessica said. The girls didn't hear. Now they were bitching at each other about disposable pads and something called a keeper cup.

We know. You'll be okay. We can heal you.

"Don't wait for me," Jessica said as they pulled up to the campground outhouse. She flipped the door handle and nearly fell out of the truck. "I can catch another ride."

Cold air washed over her as she stumbled toward the outhouse. She unzipped her long coat and let the breeze play through—chill air on boiling skin. Still early September but they always got a cold snap at the start of fall. First snow only a few days ago. Didn't last. Never did.

The outhouse stench hit her like a slap. Jessica fumbled with the lock. Her fingers felt stiff and clumsy.

"Why am I so hot?" she said, leaning on the cold plywood wall. Her voice sounded strange, ripped apart and multiplied into echoes.

Your immune system is trying to fight us but we've got it under control. The fever isn't dangerous, just uncomfortable.

She shed her coat and let it fall to the floor. Unzipped her jeans, slipped them down her hips. No panties. She hadn't been able to find them.

No, Jessica. Don't look.

Pubic hair hacked away along with most of her skin. Two deep slices puckered angry down the inside of her right thigh. And blood. On her legs, on her jeans, inside her coat. Blood everywhere, dark and sticky.

Keep breathing!

An iron tang filled the outhouse as a gout of blood dribbled down her legs. Jessica fell back on the toilet seat. Deep within her chest something fluttered, like a bird beating its wings on her ribs, trying to get out. The light drained from the air.

If you die, we die too. Please give us a chance.

The flutters turned into fists pounding on her breastbone. She struggled to inhale, tried to drag the outhouse stink deep into her lungs but the air felt thick. Solid. Like a wall against her face.

Don't go. Please.

Breath escaped her like smoke from a fire burned down to coal and ash. She collapsed against the wall of the outhouse. Vision turned to pinpricks; she crumpled like paper and died.

"Everything okay in there?"

The thumping on the door made the whole outhouse shake. Jessica lurched to her feet. Her chest burned like she'd been breathing acid.

You're okay.

"I'm fine. Gimme a second."

Jessica plucked the pad off the outhouse floor, ripped it open and stuck it on the crotch of her bloody jeans, zipped them up. She zipped her coat to her chin. She felt strong. Invincible. She unlocked the door.

The two girls were right there, eyes big and concerned and in her business.

"You didn't have to wait," Jessica said.

"How old are you, fifteen? We waited," the driver said as they climbed back into the truck.

"We're not going to let you hitchhike," said the tattooed girl. "Especially not you."

"Why not me?" Jessica slammed the truck door behind her.

"Most of the dead and missing girls are First Nations."

"You think I'm an Indian? Fuck you. Am I on a reserve?"

The driver glared at her friend as she turned the truck back onto the highway.

"Sorry," the tattooed girl said.

"Do I look like an Indian?"

"Well, kinda."

"Fuck you." Jessica leaned on the window, watching the highway signs peel by as they rolled toward Prince George. When they got to the city the invincible feeling was long gone. The driver insisted on taking her right to Gran's.

"Thanks," Jessica said as she slid out of the truck.

The driver waved. "Remember, no hitchhiking."

SEPTEMBER 8, 2001

Jessica never hitchhiked.

She wasn't stupid. But Prince George was spread out. Busses ran maybe once an hour weekdays and barely at all on weekends, and when the weather turned cold you could freeze to death trying to walk everywhere. So yeah, she took rides when she could, if she knew the driver.

After her Saturday shift she'd started walking down the highway. Mom didn't know she was coming. Jessica had tried to get through three times from the gas station phone, left voice mails. Mom didn't always pick up—usually didn't—and when she did it was some excuse about her phone battery or connection.

Mom was working as a cook at a retreat center out by Tabor Lake. A two hour walk, but Mom would get someone to drive her back to Gran's.

Only seven o'clock but getting cold and the wind had come up. Semis bombed down the highway, stirring up the trash and making it dance at her feet and fly in her face as she walked along the ditch.

It wasn't even dark when the car pulled over to the side of the highway.

"Are you Jessica?"

The man looked ordinary. Baseball cap, hoodie. Somebody's dad trying to look young.

"Yeah," Jessica said.

"Your mom sent me to pick you up."

A semi honked as it blasted past his car. A McDonald's wrapper flipped through the air and smacked her in the back of the head. She got in.

The car was skunky with pot smoke. She almost didn't notice when he passed the Tabor Lake turnoff.

"That was the turn," she said.

"Yeah, she's not there. She's out at the ski hill."

"At this time of year?"

"Some kind of event." He took a drag on his smoke and smiled.

Jessica hadn't even twigged. Mom had always wanted to work at the ski hill, where she could party all night and ski all day.

It was twenty minutes before Jessica started to clue in.

When he slowed to take a turn onto a gravel road she braced herself to roll out of the car. The door handle was broken. She went at him with her fingernails but he had the jump on her, hit her in the throat with his elbow. She gulped air and tried to roll down the window.

It was broken too. She battered the glass with her fists, then spun and lunged for the wheel. He hit her again, slammed her head against the dashboard three times. The world stuttered and swam.

Pain brought everything back into focus. Face down, her arms flailed, fingers clawed at the dirt. Spruce needles flew up her nose and coated her tongue. Her butt was jacked up over a log and every thrust pounded her face into the dirt. One part of her was screaming, screaming. The other part watched the pile of deer shit inches from her nose. It looked like a heap of candy. Chocolate-covered almonds.

She didn't listen to what he was telling her. She'd heard worse from boys at school. He couldn't make her listen. He didn't exist except as a medium for pain.

When he got off, Jessica felt ripped in half, split like firewood. She tried to roll off the log. She'd crawl into the bush, he'd drive away, and it would be over.

Then he showed her the knife.

When he rammed the knife up her she found a new kind of pain. It drove the breath from her lungs and sliced the struggle from her limbs. She listened to herself whimper, thinking it sounded like a newborn kitten, crying for its mother.

The pain didn't stop until the world had retreated to little flecks of light deep in her skull. The ground spun around her as he dragged her through the bush and rolled her into a ravine. She landed face down in a stream. Her head flopped, neck canted at a weird angle.

Jessica curled her fingers around something cold and round. A rock. It fit in her hand perfectly and if he came back she'd let him have it right in the teeth. And then her breath bubbled away and she died.

When she came back to life a bear corpse was lying beside her, furry and rank. She dug her fingers into its pelt and pulled herself up. It was still warm. And skinny— nothing but sinew and bone under the skin.

She stumbled through the stream, toes in wet socks stubbing against the rocks but it didn't hurt. Nothing hurt. She was good. She could do anything.

She found her coat in the mud, her jeans too. One sneaker by the bear and then she looked and looked for the other one.

It's up the bank.

She climbed up. The shoe was by the log where it had happened. The toe was coated in blood. She wiped it in the dirt.

You need to drink some water.

A short dirt track led down to the road. The gravel glowed white in the dim light of early morning. No idea which way led to the highway. She picked a direction.

"How do you know what I need?"

We know. We're trying to heal you. The damage is extensive. You've lost a lot of blood and the internal injuries are catastrophic.

"No shit."

We can fix you. We just need time.

Her guts writhed. Snakes fought in her belly, biting and coiling.

Feel that? That's us working. Inside you.

"Why doesn't it hurt?"

We've established a colony in your thalamus. That's where we're blocking the pain. If we didn't, you'd die of shock.

"Again."

Yes, again.

"A colony. What the fuck are you? Aliens?"

Yes. We're also distributing a hormonal cocktail of adrenaline and testosterone to keep you moving, but we'll have to taper it off soon because it puts too much stress on your heart. Right now it's very important for you to drink some water.

"Shut up about the water." She wasn't thirsty. She felt great.

A few minutes later the fight drained out of her. Thirsty, exhausted, she ached as though the hinge of every moving part was crusted in rust, from her jaw to her toes. Her eyelids rasped like sandpaper. Her breath sucked and blew without reaching her lungs. Every rock in the road was a mountain and every pothole a canyon.

But she walked. Dragged her sneakers through the gravel, taking smaller and smaller steps until she just couldn't lift her feet anymore. She stood in the middle of the road and waited. Waited to fall over. Waited for the world to slip from her grasp and darkness to drown her in cold nothing.

When she heard the truck speeding toward her she didn't even look up. Didn't matter who it was, what it was. She stuck out her thumb.

SEPTEMBER 10, 2001

Jessica woke soaked. Covered in blood, she thought, struggling with the blankets. But it wasn't blood.

"What—"

Your urethra was damaged so we eliminated excess fluid through your pores. It's repaired now. You'll be able to urinate.

She pried herself out of the wet blankets.

No solid food, though. Your colon is shredded and your small intestine has multiple ruptures.

When the tree planters dropped her off, Gran had been sacked out on the couch. Jessica had stayed in the shower for a good half hour, watching the blood swirl down the drain with the spruce needles and the dirt, the blood clots and shreds of raw flesh.

And all the while she drank. Opened her mouth and let the cool spray fill her. Then she had stuffed her bloody clothes in a garbage bag and slept.

Jessica ran her fingertips over the gashes inside her thigh. The wounds puckered like wide toothless mouths, sliced edges pasted together and sunk deep within her flesh. The rest of the damage was hardened over with amber-colored scabs. She'd have to use a mirror to see it all. She didn't want to look.

"I should go to the hospital," she whispered.

That's not a good idea. It would take multiple interventions to repair the damage to your digestive tract. They'd never be able to save your uterus or reconstruct your vulva and clitoris. The damage to your cervix alone—

"My what?"

Do you want to have children someday?

"I don't know."

Trust us. We can fix this.

She hated the hospital anyway. Went to Emergency after she'd twisted her knee but the nurse had turned her away, said she wouldn't bother the on-call for something minor. Told her to go home and put a bag of peas on it.

And the cops were even worse than anyone at the hospital. Didn't give a shit. Not one of them.

Gran was on the couch, snoring. A deck of cards was scattered across the coffee table in between the empties—looked like she'd been playing solitaire all weekend.

Gran hadn't fed the cats, either. They had to be starving but they wouldn't come to her, not even when she was filling their dishes. Not even Gringo, who had hogged her bed every night since she was ten. He just hissed and ran.

Usually Jessica would wake up Gran before leaving for school, try to get her on her feet so she didn't sleep all day. Today she didn't have the strength. She shook Gran's shoulder.

"Night night, baby," Gran said, and turned over.

Jessica waited for the school bus. She felt cloudy, dispersed, her thoughts blowing away with the wind. And cold now, without her coat. The fever was gone.

"Could you fix Gran?"

Perhaps. What's wrong with her?

Jessica shrugged. "I don't know. Everything."

We can try. Eventually.

She sleepwalked through her classes. It wasn't a problem. The teachers were more bothered when she did well than when she slacked off. She stayed in the shadows, off everyone's radar.

After school she walked to the gas station. Usually when she got to work she'd buy some chips or a chocolate bar, get whoever was going off shift to ring it up so nobody could say she hadn't paid for it.

"How come I'm not hungry?" she asked when she had the place to herself.

You are; you just can't perceive it.

It was a quiet night. The gas station across the highway had posted a half cent lower so everyone was going there. Usually she'd go stir crazy from boredom but today she just zoned out. Badly photocopied faces stared at her from the posters taped to the cigarette cabinet overhead.

An SUV pulled up to pump number three. A bull elk was strapped to the hood, tongue lolling.

"What was the deal with the bear?" she said.

The bear's den was adjacent to our crash site. It was killed by the concussive wave.

"Crash site. A spaceship?"

Yes. Unfortunate for the bear, but very fortunate for us.

"You brought the bear back to life. Healed it."

Yes.

"And before finding me you were just riding around in the bear."

Yes. It was attracted by the scent of your blood.

"So you saw what happened to me. You watched." She should be upset, shouldn't she? But her mind felt dull, thoughts thudding inside an empty skull.

We have no access to the visual cortex.

"You're blind?"

Yes.

"What are you?"

A form of bacteria.

"Like an infection."

Yes.

The door chimed and the hunter handed over his credit card. She rang it through. When he was gone she opened her mouth to ask another question, but then her gut convulsed like she'd been hit. She doubled over the counter. Bile stung her throat.

He'd been here on Saturday.

Jessica had been on the phone, telling mom's voice mail that she'd walk out to Talbot Lake after work. While she was talking she'd rung up a purchase, $32.25 in gas and a pack of smokes. She'd punched it through automatically, cradling the phone on her shoulder. She'd given him change from fifty.

An ordinary man. Hoodie. Cap.

Jessica, breathe.

Her head whipped around, eyes wild, hands scrambling reflexively for a weapon. Nobody was at the pumps, nobody parked at the air pump. He could come back any moment. Bring his knife and finish the job.

Please breathe. There's no apparent danger.

She fell to her knees and crawled out from behind the counter. Nobody would stop him, nobody would save her. Just like they hadn't saved all those dead and missing girls whose posters had been staring at her all summer from up on the cigarette cabinet.

When she'd started the job they'd creeped her out, those posters. For a few weeks she'd thought twice about walking after dark. But then those dead and missing girls disappeared into the landscape. Forgotten.

You must calm down.

Now she was one of them.

We may not be able to bring you back again.

She scrambled to the bathroom on all fours, threw herself against the door, twisted the lock. Her hands were shuddering, teeth chattering like it was forty below. Her chest squeezed and bucked, throwing acid behind her teeth.

There was a frosted window high on the wall. He could get in, if he wanted. She could almost see the knife tick-tick-ticking on the glass.

No escape. Jessica plowed herself into the narrow gap between the wall and toilet, wedging herself there, fists clutching at her burning chest as she retched bile onto the floor. The light winked and flickered. A scream flushed out of her and she died.

A fist banged on the door.

"Jessica, what the hell!" Her boss's voice.

A key scraped in the lock. Jessica gripped the toilet and wrenched herself off the floor to face him. His face was flushed with anger and though he was a big guy, he couldn't scare her now. She felt bigger, taller, stronger, too. And she'd always been smarter than him.

"Jesus, what's wrong with you?"

"Nothing, I'm fine." Better than fine. She was butterfly-light, like if she opened her wings she could fly away.

"The station's wide open. Anybody could have waltzed in here and walked off with the till."

"Did they?"

His mouth hung open for a second. "Did they what?"

"Walk off with the fucking till?"

"Are you on drugs?"

She smiled. She didn't need him. She could do anything.

"That's it," he said. "You're gone. Don't come back."

A taxi was gassing up at pump number one. She got in the back and waited, watching her boss pace and yell into his phone. The invincible feeling faded before the tank was full. By the time she got home Jessica's joints had locked stiff and her thoughts had turned fuzzy.

All the lights were on. Gran was halfway into her second bottle of u-brew red so she was pretty out of it, too. Jessica sat with her at the kitchen table for a few minutes and was just thinking about crawling to bed when the phone rang.

It was Mom.

"Did you send someone to pick me up on the highway?" Jessica stole a glance at Gran. She was staring at her reflection in the kitchen window, maybe listening, maybe not.

"No, why would I do that?"

"I left you messages. On Saturday."

"I'm sorry, baby. This phone is so bad, you know that."

"Listen, I need to talk to you." Jessica kept her voice low.

"Is it your grandma?" Mom asked.

"Yeah. It's bad. She's not talking."

"She does this every time the residential school thing hits the news. Gets super excited, wants to go up north and see if any of her family are still alive. But she gives up after a couple of days. Shuts down. It's too much for her. She was only six when they took her away, you know."

"Yeah. When are you coming home?"

"I got a line on a great job, cooking for an oil rig crew. One month on, one month off."

Jessica didn't have the strength to argue. All she wanted to do was sleep.

"Don't worry about your Gran," Mom said. "She'll be okay in a week or two. Listen, I got to go."

"I know."

"Night night, baby," Mom said, and hung up.

SEPTEMBER 11, 2001

Jessica waited alone for the school bus. The street was deserted. When the bus pulled up the driver was chattering before she'd even climbed in.

"Can you believe it? Isn't it horrible?" The driver's eyes were puffy, mascara swiped to a gray stain under her eyes.

"Yeah," Jessica agreed automatically.

"When first I saw the news I thought it was so early, nobody would be at work. But it was nine in the morning in New York. Those towers were full of people." The driver wiped her nose.

The bus was nearly empty. Two little kids sat behind the driver, hugging their backpacks. The radio blared. Horror in New York. Attack on Washington. Jessica dropped into the shotgun seat and let the noise wash over her for a few minutes as they twisted slowly through the empty streets. Then she moved to the back of the bus.

When she'd gotten dressed that morning her jeans had nearly slipped off her hips. Something about that was important. She tried to concentrate, but the thoughts flitted from her grasp, darting away before she could pin them down.

She focused on the sensation within her, the buck and heave under her ribs and in front of her spine.

"What are you fixing right now?" she asked.

An ongoing challenge is the sequestration of the fecal and digestive matter that leaked into your abdominal cavity.

"What about the stuff you mentioned yesterday? The intestine and the . . . whatever it was."

Once we have repaired your digestive tract and restored gut motility we will begin reconstructive efforts on your reproductive organs.

"You like big words, don't you?"

We assure you the terminology is accurate.

There it was. That was the thing that had been bothering her, niggling at the back of her mind, trying to break through the fog.

"How do you know those words? How can you even speak English?"

We aren't communicating in language. The meaning is conveyed by socio-linguistic impulses interpreted by the brain's speech processing loci. Because of the specifics of our biology, verbal communication is an irrelevant medium.

"You're not talking, you're just making me hallucinate," Jessica said.

That is essentially correct.

How could the terminology be accurate, then? She didn't know those words—cervix and whatever—so how could she hallucinate them?

"Were you watching the news when the towers collapsed?" the driver asked as she pulled into the high school parking lot. Jessica ignored her and slowly stepped off the bus.

The aliens were trying to baffle her with big words and science talk. For three days she'd had them inside her, their voice behind her eyes, their fingers deep in her guts, and she'd trusted them. Hadn't even thought twice. She had no choice.

If they could make her hallucinate, what else were they doing to her?

The hallways were quiet, the classrooms deserted except for one room at the end of the hall with 40 kids packed in. The teacher had wheeled in an AV cart. Some of the kids hadn't even taken off their coats.

Jessica stood in the doorway. The news flashed clips of smoking towers collapsing into ash clouds. The bottom third of the screen was overlaid with scrolling, flashing text, the sound layered with frantic voiceovers. People were jumping from the towers, hanging in the air like dancers. The clips replayed over and over again. The teacher passed around a box of Kleenex.

Jessica turned her back on the class and climbed upstairs, joints creaking, jeans threatening to slide off with every step. She hitched them up. The biology lab was empty. She leaned on the cork board and scanned the parasite diagrams. Ring worm. Tape worm. Liver fluke. Black wasp.

Some parasites can change their host's biology, the poster said, or even change their host's behavior.

Jessica took a push pin from the board and shoved it into her thumb. It didn't hurt. When she ripped it out a thin stream of blood trickled from the skin, followed by an ooze of clear amber from deep within the gash.

What are you doing?

None of your business, she thought.

Everything is going to be okay.

No it won't, she thought. She squeezed the amber ooze from her thumb, let it drip on the floor. The aliens were wrenching her around like a puppet, but without them she would be dead. Three times dead. Maybe she should feel grateful, but she didn't.

"Why didn't you want me to go to the hospital?" she asked as she slowly hinged down the stairs.

They couldn't have helped you, Jessica. You would have died.

Again, Jessica thought. Died again. And again.

"You said that if I die, you die too."

When your respiration stops, we can only survive for a limited time.

The mirror in the girls' bathroom wasn't real glass, just a sheet of polished aluminum, its shine pitted and worn. She leaned on the counter, rested her forehead on the cool metal. Her reflection warped and stretched.

"If I'd gone to the hospital, it would have been bad for you. Wouldn't it?"

That is likely.

"So you kept me from going. You kept me from doing a lot of things."

We assure you that is untrue. You may exercise your choices as you see fit. We will not interfere.

"You haven't left me any choices."

Jessica left the bathroom and walked down the hall. The news blared from the teacher's lounge. She looked in. At least a dozen teachers crowded in front of an AV cart, backs turned. Jessica slipped behind them and ducked into the teachers' washroom. She locked the door.

It was like a real bathroom. Air freshener, moisturizing lotion, floral soap. Real mirror on the wall and a makeup mirror propped on the toilet tank. Jessica put it on the floor.

"Since when do bacteria have spaceships?" She pulled her sweater over her head and dropped it over the mirror.

Jessica, you're not making sense. You're confused.

She put her heel on the sweater and stepped down hard. The mirror cracked.

Go to the hospital now, if you want.

"If I take you to the hospital, what will you do? Infect other people? How many?"

Jessica, please. Haven't we helped you?

"You've helped yourself."

The room pitched and flipped. Jessica fell to her knees. She reached for the broken mirror but it swam out of reach. Her vision telescoped and she batted at the glass with clumsy hands. A scream built behind her teeth, swelled and choked her. She swallowed it whole, gulped it, forced it down her throat like she was starving.

You don't have to do this. We aren't a threat.

She caught a mirror shard in one fist and swam along the floor as the room tilted and whirled. With one hand she pinned it to the yawning floor like a spike, windmilled her free arm and slammed her wrist down. The walls folded in, collapsing on her like the whole weight of the world, crushing in.

She felt another scream building. She forced her tongue between clenched teeth and bit down. Amber fluid oozed down her chin and pooled on the floor.

Please. We only want to help.

"Night night, baby," she said, and raked the mirror up her arm.

The fluorescent light flashed overhead. The room plunged into darkness as a world of pain dove into her for one hanging moment. Then it lifted. Jessica convulsed on the floor, watching the bars of light overhead stutter and compress to two tiny glimmers inside the thin parched shell of her skull. And she died, finally, at last.

no placeholder for you, my love

nick wolven

*Nick Wolven attended the Clarion West Writers Workshop for speculative fic-
tion writers in 2007. Since then, his fiction has appeared in* Asimov's Science Fiction, Fantasy & Science Fiction, The New England Review, *and
many other publications. He lives with his family in New York City. Here, he
gives us a melancholy vision of two lovers meeting, then losing each other,
then finding each other again, then struggling against the odds to hold on to
each other while trapped in an illusionary world of constant lavish parties
and celebrations of all sorts, parties that they have both grown weary of long
before, but can not escape. . . .*

1

Claire met him at a dinner party in New Orleans, and afterwards, she had to remind
herself this was true. Yes, that had been it, his very first appearance. It seemed incredible there had been anything so finite as a first time.

He was seated across from her, two chairs down, a gorgeous woman on either side.
As usual, the subject had turned to food.

"But I've been to this house a dozen times," one of the gorgeous women was saying. "I've been to dinner parties, dance parties, even family parties. And every time,
they serve the wrong kind of cuisine."

She had red hair, the color of the candlelight reflected off the varnished chairs.
The house was an old house, full of old things, handmade textiles and walnut chif-
foniers, oil paintings of nameless Civil War colonels.

"Is that a problem?" said the young man on Claire's left. "Why should you
care?"

"Because," said the redhead, pursing her lips. "Meringue pie, at an elegant soi-
ree? Wine and steak tartar, at a child's birthday party? Lobster bisque at a dance?
For God's sake, it was all over the floor. It seems, I don't know. Lazy. Thoughtless.
Cobbled together."

She lifted her glass of wine to her mouth, and the liquid vanished the instant it touched her tongue.

The man who was to mean so much to Claire, to embody in his person so much hope and loss, leaned over his soup, eyes dark with amusement. "It *is* cobbled together. Of course it is. But isn't that the best part?"

"And why is that, Byron?" someone said with a sigh.

Byron. A fake name, Claire assumed, distilled from the fog of some half-remembered youthful interest. But then, you never knew.

Whatever the source of his name, Byron's face had the handsome roughness earned through active living. Dots of stubble grayed his skin. A tiny scar divided one eyebrow. His smile made a charming pattern of wrinkles around his eyes. It was a candid face, a well-architected face, a forty-something face.

"Because," said Byron, and caught Claire's eye, as if only she would understand. "Look at this furniture, the chandelier. Look at that music stand in the corner. American plantation style, rococo, Art Nouveau. Every piece a different movement. Some are complete anachronisms. That's why I love this house. You can see the spirit of the designers, here. A kind of whimsy. It's so personal, so scattershot."

"You're such a talker, Byron," someone sighed.

"Look at all of you," Byron said, moving his spoon in a circle to encompass the ring of faces. "Some of you I've never seen before in my life. And here we are, brought together by chance, for one evening only. You know what? That delights me. That thrills me." His gesture halted at Claire's face. "That enchants me."

"And after tonight," said the redhead, "we'll go our separate ways, and forget each other, and maybe never see each other again. So is that part of the wonder, for you, Byron, or does that spoil the wonder?"

"It does neither," Byron said, "because I don't believe it."

His eyes settled on Claire's. Again, he smiled. She had always liked older men, their slightly chastened air, their solemn and good-humored strength.

"I don't believe we'll never see each other again," Byron said, looking at his spoon. "I don't believe that's necessarily our fate. And you know what? The truth is, I wouldn't mind living in this house forever. Even if they do serve alphabet soup at a dinner party."

He lifted his hand to his mouth and touched his spoon to his lips. And instantly, the liquid disappeared.

When they had cleared the table, the entertainments began. There were board games in the living room, a live band on the lawn. Stairs led to a dozen shadowy bedrooms, with sad old beds, and rich old carpets, and orchids in baskets on the moonlit windowsills. In town, the music of riverbank revelry scraped and jittered out of ramshackle bars, and paddleboats rode on the slow Mississippi, jangling with the racket of riches won and lost.

Byron borrowed a set of car keys from the house boy. Claire followed him onto the porch. The breath of the bayou was in the air, warm and buoyant, holding up the clustered leaves of the pecan trees and the high, star-scattered sky. Sweat held her shirt to the small of her back, as if a hand were there, pressing her forward.

"Shall we take a ride?" The car keys dangled, jingling, from Byron's upraised hand.

"Wait," said Claire, "do that again."

"This?" He gave the keys another shake. The sound tinkled out, a sprinkling of noise, over the thick green nap of the lawn.

"It sounds just like it," Claire said. "Don't you hear it? It sounds just like the midnight chime."

"Oh, God, don't talk about that, now. It's not for hours." Byron went halfway down the porch steps, held out a hand. "We still have plenty of time to fall in love."

The car waiting for them was an early roadster, dazzling with chrome, large and slow. Byron handled the old-fashioned shift with expert nonchalance. They slid past banquet halls downtown, where drunkenness and merriment and red, frantic faces sang and sweated along the laden tables. Often, they pulled to the curb and idled, and the night with its load of romance rolled by.

At a corner café where zydeco livened the air, a young couple argued at a scrollwork table.

"But how can you define it? How can you even describe it?" The woman's arm swung as she spoke, agitating the streetlights with a quiver of silver bracelets.

"Well, it's easy enough to *define*, anyway." The man made professorial motions with his hands. "It was simply a matter of chemistry."

"But how would that be any different from, say, smell?"

"Oh, it wasn't, not really. Taste and smell. Love and desire. All variations on the same experience."

The couple lifted fried shrimp from a basket as they spoke, the small golden morsels vanishing like fireflies on their lips.

"It can't be so simple," the woman said. And the man leaned over the table, reaching for her face, and turned it toward his lips. "You're right. It's not."

"I used to have those kinds of conversations," Byron sighed, and grasped the old maple knob of the shift, and pulled away from the curb.

They drove out of town onto dirt rural roads, where moonlight splashed across the land. In a plank roadhouse, a dance party was underway, a fiddle keening over stamping feet. Parked in the dirt lot, soaked in yellow light, they conducted the usual conversation.

"Now, me?" Byron said. "Let me tell you about myself. I'm a middle-aged computer programmer who enjoys snuggling, whiskey, and the study of artificial environments. I have a deathly aversion to crowds, and I'm not afraid to admit it. I'm nowhere near as handsome as this in real life, and I can assure you, I've been at this game a very long time."

His face dimpled as he delivered his spiel, not quite smiling. Claire laughed at his directness. Byron thumped a short drumroll on the wheel.

"And you?"

"Oh, me?" Claire said. "Me? I'm no one."

"That's an interesting theory."

"What I mean is, I'm no one anyone should care about. *I* don't even care about me."

"That can't be true."

"I guess not. I guess what I mean is, I don't care who I used to be." Claire watched the figures dance in the building, the plank walls trembling as shadows moved like living drawings across the dirty windows. "I care what happens to me, now, though. I care about nights like this."

Her lazy hand took in the dancers, the stars. Byron sat back, nodding.

Claire surrendered. "I don't know. There's an interesting woman back there, somewhere. A scholar, a geneticist. But it's hard to believe, nowadays, that she ever existed."

"Tell me about this geneticist," he said.

"Well." Claire afforded him a smile. "What do you want to know? She looked like me. She talked like me. She loved all the things I love. She loved rainy windows and Scrabble and strong tea. She loved her body, because she had a nice one, and she loved to take long baths with organic soap, and she loved the idea that one day, far in her future, there might be someone to share those baths with her. Mostly, I think, she loved the idea that she could find a man who didn't care about any of those things. A man who would simply take her hand and say, 'Let's go.'"

The fiddle stopped. The dancers halted. The shadows on the windows settled into perfect sketches: honey-colored men and women with open, panting lips.

"She was young," Claire said. "And she was lonely."

Byron nodded. "I understand."

Someone threw open the roadhouse door. A carpet of gold rolled down the steps, all the way up the hood into the car, covering Claire in mellow light. Byron studied her. She knew what he was seeing. A beautiful blonde, a perfect face, a statue of a body with cartoon-sized eyes.

"But you're not," he said. And after a moment, he clarified: "Young. Not anymore. Are you?"

"No," said Claire. "Not anymore."

They drove to town along a different route, on dark, swampy roads where alligators slithered, grunting, from the wheels. On a wharf lined with couples and fishing shops, they stood at the wood rail, looking over the water, waiting together for the midnight chime. A gas-powered ferry struggled from shore, heading northeast toward a sprawl of dark land.

"I don't care," Byron said. "I don't care if you were a biologist. I don't care if you love Scrabble or tea. I don't care about any of that." He held out a hand. "Let's go."

The couples on the wharf had fallen silent, waiting. The very twinkling of the stars seemed to pause. Still, the ferry strained and chugged, heading for a shore it would never reach.

"Say it," Claire said. "You say it first, then I'll say it, too."

"I want to see you again," Byron said.

She took his hand. Before she could respond, the midnight chime sounded. It came three times, eerie and clear, like a jingle of celestial keys. And Byron and the river and the world all disappeared.

2

Claire didn't see him again for a thousand nights.

It felt like a thousand, anyway. It may have been more. Claire had stopped counting long, long ago.

There were always more nights, more parties, more diversions. And, miraculous as it seemed, more people. Where did they come from? How could there be so many pretty young men, with leonine confidence and smiling lips? How could there be so many women arising out of the million chance assortments of the clubs, swimming through parties as if it could still be a thrill to have a thousand eyes fish for them—as if, like the fish in the proverbial sea, they one day hoped to be hooked?

Claire considered them, contemplated them, and let them go their way. She dated, for a time, a very old, handsome man whose name, in some remote and esoteric way, commanded powerful sources of credit. His wealth opened up new possibilities: private beaches where no one save they two had ever stepped, mountain lodges where the seasons manifested with iconic perfection, pink and green and gold and white. But they weren't, as the language ran, "compatible"; they were old and tired in different ways.

She met a girl whose face flashed with the markings of youth: sharp earrings, studs, lipstick that blazed in toxic colors. But the girl's eyes moved slowly, with the irony of age. Theirs was a sexual connection. Night after night, they bowed out of cocktail hours, feeling for each other's hands across the crush of dances. Every exit was an escape. They sought the nearest private rooms they could find: the neon-bright retreats of city hotels, secret brick basements in converted factories. The thrill was one of shared expertise. Both women knew the limits of sex: what moves were possible, what borders impermeable. They cultivated the matched rhythm, the long caress. Sometimes Claire's new lover—whose name, she learned after three anonymous encounters, was Isolde—fed delicacies to her, improbable foods, ice carvings and whole cakes, a hundred olives impaled on swizzle sticks, fruit rinds in paintbox colors, orange and lime, stolen from the bottomless bins of restaurants. It was musical sport. Isolde perfected her timing, spacing each treat. Claire eased into a languor of tension and release, her body shivering with an automatic thrill. As the foods touched her mouth, one by one, they flickered immediately into nothingness—gone the instant she felt them, like words on her tongue.

A happy time, this. But love? Every night they were careful to say that magic phrase, far in advance of the midnight chime.

"I want to see you again."

"I want to see you, too."

And so the nights went by, and the dates, and the parties, spiced with anticipation.

Soon, Claire knew, it was bound to happen.

The end came in Eastern Europe.

"We could have been compatible, don't you think?"

They were reposing, at that moment, in a grand hotel with mountain views, somewhere west of the Caucasus, naked in bed while snow flicked the window. Isolde lifted a rum ball from a chased steel tray, manipulating it with silver tongs. She touched it to the candle, collected a curl of flame, brought the morsel, still burning, to her mouth, and snuffed it out of existence, fire and all, against her tongue.

Claire clasped her hands around a pillow. "Do you think so?"

Isolde seemed nervous tonight, opening and closing the tongs, pretending to measure, as with calipers, Claire's thigh, her knee.

"Don't get me wrong. I'm not saying we *are* compatible. I'm only talking about, you know. What might have been."

Beyond the window, white flakes swarmed in the sky, a portrait of aimless, random motion.

"We're attracted to each other," Isolde said. "We have fun. We always have fun."

"That's true. We always have fun."

"Isn't that what matters?"

"Nothing matters," Claire said. "Not for us. Isn't that the common consensus?" She made sure to smile as she said it, lying back with her hands behind her head.

Isolde seemed pained. "I'm only saying. If things had been different. We might have worked. We might have . . ." She blushed before speaking the forbidden phrase. "We might have made a match."

Claire felt her smile congealing on her face. She marveled at that—watched, in the oak-framed mirror atop the dresser, as her expression became an expression of disgust. "But things *aren't* different. Wouldn't you say that's an important fact? Things are exactly, eternally what they are."

"Eternally. You can't know that."

"I can believe it." Claire sat up, looking out the window, where snowfall and evening had blanked out the sky. "If you want to know what might have been, just wait for the midnight chime. You'll get a thousand might-have-beens. A thousand Romeos and Juliets. A thousand once-upon-a-times."

Isolde was shaking, a subtle, repressed tremor that Claire only noticed by looking at the tongs in her hand.

"I know, I know. I'm only saying . . . I mean, how can you resist? How can you stop thinking about it? About us. About . . ." Her voice dropped. "About love."

Claire turned from the window, saying nothing, but the mood of the view filled her eyes, the gray mountains falling away into whiteness, the cold precipitation of a million aimless specks.

"I just like to imagine," Isolde whispered. "That's all. I like to imagine it could be different."

A clock stood on the bedside table, scuffed wood and spotted brass, a heavy relic of interwar craftsmanship. Isolde snatched it up with a gasp.

"What's the matter?" Claire said.

"I just realized."

"What? What did you just realize?" In Claire's tone was an implied criticism. *What can there possibly be,* she wanted to ask, *for us to realize? What can we discover that we don't already know?*

Isolde touched the clock face. "We're in a time-shifted universe. The midnight chime comes earlier, here. At sunset."

They looked together at the window, where the sky had darkened to charcoal gray.

"We never said it," Isolde whispered. "We forgot to say it, this time." She lay beside Claire, a hand on her belly, saying in a shaking voice, "I want to see you again."

The clock ticked. Snow tapped the window.

"I want to see you again," Isolde repeated. "Claire? I want to see you again."

The clock hands had made a line, pointing in opposite directions. How precise, Claire wondered, would the timeshift be? Sometimes these things could be surprisingly inexact. Sometimes, even the designers made mistakes.

"Claire, please say it. I'm sorry I said all those things. We're not really a match. I was only speculating. Anyway, it doesn't matter. Does anything matter? We don't have to talk. We can go back to how it was. We can hang out, play games, have fun."

In only a moment, a new evening would begin: new faces, new men and women, new possibilities. A whole new universe of beautiful people, like angels falling out of the sky.

"Claire, *please* say it. I want to see you again."

"Maybe you will," Claire said.

And at that moment, the chime sounded, tinkling and omnipresent, shivering three times across the mountain sky. And Isolde and her voice and her tears disappeared.

3

A dry period, then.

Dry? No, that word couldn't begin to describe this life. It was desert, desolate, arid, barren, with a harsh wind that cut across the eyes, with sharp-edged stones that stung the feet.

Claire became one of *those people*. She was the woman who haunts the edges of dance floors, rebuffing with silence anyone who dares to approach. At house parties, she wandered out for impromptu walks, seeking the hyperbolic darkness between streetlights, the lonely shadows below leylandii. At dinner parties, she made jokes intended to kill conversation.

"Knock, knock," Claire said, when young men leaned toward her.

"Who's there?"

"Claire."

"Claire who?"

"Exactly."

"Here's a good one," Claire said, to a woman who approached one night on a balcony, the champagne sparkles of a European city bubbling under their feet. "A woman walks into a bar full of beautiful people."

When the silence became uncomfortable, the woman prompted: "And?"

"And," said Claire turning away, "who cares?"

She was bitter. But she didn't care about her bitterness. Like all things, Claire assumed, this too would pass.

On an Amazonian cruise, Claire hit her low point. It was, most surely, a romantic night. Big insects sizzled against the lamps that swung, dusky gold, from the cabin house. The river gathered white ruffles along the hull. A banquet was laid out on deck, river fish on clay platters born by shirtless deckhands. The dinner guests lounged in a crowd of cane chairs. When Claire came up from below, she found the party talking, as always, about the food.

"I've been here a hundred times." The woman who spoke was white, brunette, beautiful. "I think I'm something of an expert on this universe. And what I always admire is the attention to local cuisine. Everything comes straight from the river. It's so authentic."

Claire, who'd entered unnoticed, startled them all with a loud, braying laugh.

"Excuse me?" said the woman. "What do you find so funny?"

The group stared, pushing back their chairs, eyes akindle with reflected lantern light.

"This," Claire said, and snatched a clay platter out of the hands of the serving-men. "I find this funny." She dumped the fish on the floor, jammed the platter into her mouth. They all winced as her teeth clamped down, grinding on textured ceramic. "Mm, so authentic."

"What in the world," said the woman, "is the matter with you?"

"Nothing. I'm simply trying to eat this platter."

"But *why*?"

"Because why shouldn't I?" Claire smashed the platter on the deck. "Why shouldn't I be able to? What difference does it make? Why shouldn't anything—any of this—be food?" She stomped around the deck, offering to take bites of the rails, the lamps, the life preservers. "Why shouldn't I be able to perform the trick with anything I want? Why shouldn't I be able to pick *you* up, and send you into the ether with just a touch of my tongue?"

She grabbed at the arm of a nearby man, who pushed his chair back, winking. "Please do."

Claire threw his hand down in disgust. "I should be able to pick up anything I see, and touch it to my lips, and make it disappear. And why can't I? It works with fish. It works with fruit. It works with soup and fried shrimp and wedding cakes."

Expecting protest, mockery, a violent reaction, she faced with dismay the rows of indifferent, idle faces.

"God, I'm so sick of this life," Claire finished weakly. "I'm sick of always talking about things I can never have."

"But are you sick of me?"

Claire turned and Byron was standing behind her, leaning on the rail beside the deckhouse, a beer bottle dangling from his hand.

"You?" Claire was stunned. She could hardly believe she recognized him, but she did.

Byron strolled forward and touched her hand. "You never said it."

"Sorry?"

"Eight hundred and ninety-two nights ago. New Orleans. I said I wanted to see you again. You never answered."

"I meant to." Claire struggled for breath, aware of the watching crowd. "I wanted to. I ran out of time."

He flung his beer bottle overboard. She waited without breathing for it to plunk in the distant water.

"We have time now," he said.

Dismissing the party with a wave, Byron guided Claire into a lifeboat. With a push of a lever, a creak of pulleys, he lowered them to the water and cut the rope. They drifted loose in darkness, a lantern at their feet. The big boat moved away on a thump of diesel, the strings of lamps and the hundred candles merging into one gold blur. Byron set the oars in the locks, rowing with a grace that seemed derived from real strength: strength of body, of muscle and sinew, strength that belonged to the kinds of people they had both once been.

"Do you know why we can't eat food?" Byron spoke at his ease, fitting sentences between the creak of the oarlocks. "Do you know why we have no taste, no smell, no digestion? Do you know why we can never eat, and only make food vanish by touching it to our lips?"

His voice sounded elemental, coming out of the darkness: the voice of the river, the jungle, the night.

"Appetite," Byron said. "We were made without appetite. We were made to want only one thing. True love."

He let the oars rest. They rocked on the water. The riverboat was gone now, its voices and music lost in buggy stridor.

"I don't believe that." Claire let her hand trail in the water, wondering if piranhas and snakes stocked the river, if the authenticity of the environment extended that far. "I don't believe any of this was planned. Not to that extent. I think it's all nothing more than a sick, elaborate accident."

He considered her words, the oars resting, crossed, in his lap. "You must believe that some of this was designed. You must remember designing it. Or designing yourself, I mean: what you look like, how you think. I've forgotten quite a bit, but I do remember that."

A fish nibbled Claire's finger. She lifted her hand, shook off the drops.

"I don't mean the world itself," Claire said. "I mean what's happened to us. The way we live. Something's gone. I don't think it was intentional."

Byron nodded. "Apocalypse."

"Plague. Asteroids. Nuclear holocaust."

"Economic collapse. Political unrest." He joined in her joking tone. "Or only a poorly managed bankruptcy. And somewhere out in the Nevada desert, sealed away in a solar-powered server farm, a rack of computers sits, grinding away at a futile simulation, on and on through the lonely centuries."

She waved away his glib improvisation, accidentally spraying his face with drops.

"I don't think that's what happened. Do you know what I think? I think we've simply been forgotten."

He smiled, nodding in time with the rocking boat.

"That's all," Claire said. "They made us, they used us for a while, they lost interest. They kept their accounts, or their subscriptions, or whatever, but they stopped paying attention. They don't care if we find love. They don't care about anything we do."

"And yet." Byron resumed rowing. "If they knew . . ."

"What?" Claire was irritated at the portentous way he trailed off. "If they knew what?"

He glanced behind him, checking their direction. "Oh, you know. If they knew how wonderfully independent we've become. How clever and shy. How suave in the art of romance. How proficient at avoiding any kind of commitment."

"In other words," said Claire, "just like them."

Byron rested a moment, the oars under his chin. "Meet with me again. Say the words."

Claire looked away from him, down into the water, the black oblivion sliding by. "This can't go anywhere. You know it can't. It can't become anything. We can't become anything."

"I don't care. Say the words."

"It can never be more than a casual thing."

"All well and good. Say the words."

"It can only make us unhappy. We can only go so far. We'll reach a certain point, and we'll realize we're done. Finished. Forever incomplete. It will be like picking up a delicious piece of food and seeing it vanish on our tongues."

"Brilliant analogy. Say the words."

"I want to see you," Claire said, tears in her eyes. "I want to see you, again and again."

(Wondering, even while she said this, and not for the first time, why the people who built this terrible world had left so much out, had omitted taste, had excised smell, had eliminated pleasure, drunkenness, pain, death, injury, age, and appetite, but had left in these two strange and unpleasant details, had endowed every person with sweat and tears.)

We're not like them, Claire thought, as Byron, letting the oars ride idle, leaned across the boat. *We look like them, we have their habits, their interests, their hopes, even some of their memories. We think and feel like them, whether they know it or not. We can even, in some ways, make love like them. But we're not like them, not really, and it all comes down to this: whatever we desire, whatever we do, we'll never know the difference between a drink and a kiss.*

When Byron's lips met hers, a precise and dry contact, it surprised Claire, momentarily, that neither of them disappeared.

4

How many times did they meet? Claire didn't bother to count. They saw each other in hunting lodges, English gardens, an undersea city, the surface of Mars, the gondola of a transatlantic blimp. To Claire, all locations were frames for Byron's figure. More than his body, more than the frankness of his smile, she began to love the touch of his hand, the way it overlaid hers on the rails of ocean liners, felt for hers, casually, in the press of theater lobbies. He was a man who coveted contact: half-conscious, constant. She loved his need to know she was there.

And still, he was something much stranger than a lover. In this world, there was one sure pleasure, and this was the pleasure Byron offered. Talk.

"What was it?" she asked him, one night as they mingled, duded out in rodeo getups, with the square-dancing clientele of a cowboy bar. "In New Orleans, that night, you sought me out. What was it that made you notice me?"

Byron didn't hesitate. "A question," he said.

"And what question was that?"

He pointed at their knee-slapping environs: the mechanical bull, the rawhide trimmings, the Stetsons and string ties and silver piping. "Our lives are a joke. Anyone can see that. I guess I wondered why you weren't laughing."

She laughed then, making herself sad with the sound.

Other evenings they shouted over a buzz of airplane propellers, under the bump of disco, across the chill seats of a climbing chairlift. But always they talked, endlessly, oblivious to their surroundings, one conversation encompassing a thousand fragmented days.

"And you?" Byron spoke between sips of drinks that vanished like snow under his breath. "What did you see in me?"

Claire smiled, silent. She knew he knew the answer.

In the private bedrooms of an endlessly itinerant courtship, they never stripped off their clothes, never attempted the clumsy gyrations that passed for sex. They lounged in lazy proximity, fully clothed. Claire felt no reserve. With Byron, there was no question of making a match. His worn, mature face, sadly humorous, told her he'd put all such questions behind him.

"Anyway, it doesn't matter." He often held her hand, rubbing her thumb with his. "You say we've been forgotten. Some people say we've been abandoned. But what would it change, if we knew the truth? Things would be the same whatever happened in—well, in what I suppose we have to call 'the real world.'"

"Would they?" Claire focused on the confidence with which he spoke, the weary conviction of his old, wise voice.

Byron narrowed his eyes. "That's what I believe. We were made to live this way. We were never meant to find a match." He lifted himself on an elbow, gazing across the folds and drapes of the bedroom, the swaddling silk abundance of an ancient four-poster bed. "Look, the idea is we're proxies, right? Our originals, they got tired of looking for love. The uncertainty, the effort. So they made us. Poured in their memories and hopes, built this playground, so we could do what they didn't want to do, keep mixing and mingling and trying and failing. And one day we would find a match, and that would be it, our work would be done, and we would be canceled, deleted, for them to take over."

Claire lay still, withholding comment. There was a real thrill, she thought, in hearing things put so plainly, the cynical logic of their lives.

"But what if," Byron said, "that wasn't ever their real goal? What if they never wanted love at all? What if they only *wanted* to want it—wanted, in some way, to be *able* to want it? You remember how things were. We all remember at least some of that world. Was it ever such a loving place? The overcrowding. The overwork. It was so much better to be alone. What if this place only exists . . . what if *we* only exist to . . . to stand in for something, represent something, some kind of half-remembered dream? A dream our originals had mostly given up, but still felt, in some way, they ought to be dreaming?"

"Oh, God," Claire sighed.

"I'm sorry." Byron touched the backs of the hands she held over her face. "I shouldn't be talking like this."

"It's not that." She dropped her hands. "It's that it's all so wrong. You make it sound even more hopeless than it is."

"I don't believe it's hopeless."

"But if we're only here to go on some futile, empty search . . . I mean, why?" She sat up, holding fistfuls of sheet. "We're a joke twice over. A fake of a fake. Even if they didn't know we would . . ." She was garbling her remonstrations, caught, as usual, between religion and philosophy. "I mean, why would anyone put us *through* this?"

He lay back, staring, pale as an empty screen. "Claire, what if I told you we could make a match?"

She held a pillow to her breast, suddenly cold, wondering if it was the kind of cold a real human being would feel. "Don't say that."

"I mean it."

"Don't say it. You know what will happen. I hate this world. I hate the people who made it. I hate myself, whatever I am, and I hate the woman I used to be. But I'm not ready to—"

"I'm not saying you have to."

She watched him with bared teeth, projecting all her fear onto his alarmingly calm face.

"I'm saying we can do it." Byron's eyes were like red wine, dark and flickering. "We can do it without giving anything up. We can commit to each other, forever, without being deleted or vanishing away. We can declare our love, and no one will ever know, or interfere, or steal it from us."

"That's impossible." She bit her tongue until she could almost remember what it felt like to feel pain.

"It's entirely possible."

"That's not how things work."

"You forget. I told you once, long ago, I have an interest in virtual environments. Or anyway, I used to. I know exactly how this world works."

She sat up, seeing excitement shining from him via those two bright giveaways, perspiration and tears.

"Do you remember, Claire? New Orleans?" He sat up, reaching for her hands. "There's a dock, there, that runs far out into the river. A ferry sets out from it, every night, toward the far shore. Each night, it leaves a second earlier; each time, it travels a second farther. One time out of a thousand, it reaches the far bank. If we're on that ferry when it touches land, we'll be on a border, a threshold, a place where the rules no longer apply. When the scenario resets, we'll be left behind. We can live there forever, or however long the world lasts.

"Claire." He insisted, at that moment, on holding both her hands, as if needing to be doubly sure she was there. "Nothing is entirely random. I know you don't keep count of the nights, but I do. I've been tracking the evenings, observing the patterns. And I've been looking for a person to take along with me, one person to share with me the rest of time. You are that person. Say the words. In five nights, we will meet again, at a dinner party in New Orleans. The ferry will set out at eleven-forty. Come with me, Claire. Be with me on that deck. Step with me, together, out of this world."

She saw her fists vanish inside his. The midnight chime would sound in a moment, and with it new crowds, new possibilities, new glories of music and excitement would be conjured out of the unending night. Could she leave all that behind, stand with this man forever on the shore of one permanent land? Together, they would walk, never changing, down unchanging streets, where dance music streamed out of immortal cafes, where orchids stood, never wilting, on the sills of bedroom windows, silvered by a moon that never set. But these would be their cafes, their moon, their orchids, and if there was no way to know how long it might last, still, they would own together that unmeasured quantity of time, laying claim to one house with its scattershot furniture, and never live in fear of the midnight chime.

Already, tonight, that chime was sounding, jangling a warning across the sky. But Claire had time to speak the charmed words.

"I want to see you again."

5

Around the long dining table in the house in New Orleans, Civil War colonels gazed out of their walnut frames. The candles were at work, scattering reflections, and the antique chairs creaked with conviviality. Claire sat next to Byron, intent on the French-style clock. Dinner was done, the plates cleared away, and two dozen puddings quivered in two dozen china bowls.

"Pudding," sighed a ravishing girl, dressed, like many, for the setting, in the rustling skirts of a southern belle. "You see what I mean? It's all so random. Radicchio salads, oxtail for dinner, and they serve us chocolate pudding for dessert."

Claire, seated across the table, reflected that this was the last time she'd ever have to have this conversation.

Twenty-four spoons dipped and rose. Twenty-four servings of pudding vanished, dispelled by the touch of twenty-four tongues.

When the party dispersed, Byron took Claire's hand. At the door, he bent to her ear, and she felt his warm whisper. "Three hours. Stay close."

They stepped out onto the porch. And Byron disappeared.

Claire spun in confusion. The porch, the house, the whole scene was gone. She stood on a dance floor, surrounded by feet that stamped and swung and kicked up a lamplit dust. The dim air shivered to the scratch of a fiddle. There was absolutely no sign of Byron.

Trying to get her bearings, Claire clutched at the jostling shoulders. She spotted a door and wriggled toward it. The energy of the dance, like a bustling machine, ejected her into humid air.

Claire stumbled down three wooden steps. Looking back, she recognized the roadside bar where she'd sat with Byron on their first meeting, several thousand nights ago.

What had happened? Claire staggered toward the road. The moon made iron of the land, steel of the river, and the lights of town were far away.

The ferry! It was only a few miles from here, no more than a two-hour walk. Claire thought she could make it, if she hurried.

She'd walked a quarter of an hour when a vintage roadster, roaring from behind, froze her like a criminal in a flood of light. Byron pushed open the door.

"Get in."

Claire hurried to the passenger side, jumped into the leather seat. Byron stomped the gas, and the wheels of the car barked on gravel.

"It's glitching." Byron leaned forward as he drove. "The environment. The counters are resetting. Like I said, we're in a liminal place, tonight. The rules are temporarily breaking down. Look."

He tapped his wrist, where a watched glimmered faintly.

"It's after ten," Byron said. "It's been over an hour since I saw you. We've lost a chunk of time, and I'm afraid—damn." He swerved, almost losing control, as he caught sight of something down the road.

Twisting in her seat, Claire saw the roadside shack, the one she'd just exited, sliding by.

Byron cursed and pushed down on the gas. They rattled up to the old roadster's maximum speed, forty, fifty. Swamps, river, road flowed by. The shack passed again, again, again.

"All right, that does it." Byron braked so hard, Claire nearly struck her head on the dashboard. He fussed with the gearshift and twisted in his seat, wrapping an arm around her headrest.

"What's happening?" she asked.

"Can't you tell? We're looping."

"But what are you doing?"

"Desperate problems call for desperate measures." Byron squinted through the tiny rear windshield. "The way I see it, if you can't hit fast-forward, hit rewind."

The car jerked backward.

And car and road and Byron all screeched out of being, and Claire found herself sitting at a café table, alone, deep in the tipsy commotion of town.

She jumped up, knocking over her chair.

Once again, Byron was nowhere to be seen.

Claire cursed, turned in a full circle, cursed again. A passing man in a bowler hat picked up her chair, righted it, and touched his hat.

"Crazy, eh? All these jumps?" He straightened his jacket with a roll of his shoulders, looking up at the sky, as if expecting heaven to crack.

"But what do we do?" Claire gasped. "How do we stop it?"

The man in the bowler hat smiled and shrugged. "Nothing *to* do, I guess. Except play along."

Pantomiming, he grabbed a nearby barber pole, swung himself through an open door, and promptly, like a magician's rabbit, blinked out of existence.

Partiers ran past, giggling and tripping, stretching their faces in merry alarm, like people caught in a thunderstorm. Firefly-like, they meandered through doorways, laughing as they winked in and out of existence. In a world of rules and repetition, Claire had long since observed, childlike chaos greeted any variation in routine.

But what do I do? Claire ducked into a drugstore entrance. *What can I do, what should I do?* She did her best to steady her mind, analyze the situation. The jumps, the cuts, the vanishings and reappearances—they seemed to happen at moments of transition: entries and exits, sudden moves. If she found some way to game the system . . .

Turning, Claire jumped through the drugstore door. And again, and again, and again. On her fifteenth jump, the trick worked, the environment glitched. Claire tumbled into a banquet hall, crashing into a tray-bearing waiter, scattering scallops and champagne flutes. "Sorry, sorry . . ." Dashing toward the hall doors, Claire tried again. Another round of jumping propelled her into a rowboat, somewhere out in the stinking bayou. Gators splashed and rolled in the muck, grunting and hissing as they fled from her intrusion. Claire jumped into the water and ducked under, sinking her feet in the creamy ooze. She kicked, launching herself into the air—

And found herself, sodden with mud, near the bank of the river, in town.

How many times would she have to do this? Searching the bank, Claire saw no promising doors. She threw herself into the river three more times. The third time, she emerged in a backyard swimming pool.

And so, through portals and windows, falls and reversals, Claire skipped her way through the liminal evening, traversing a lottery of locations, careening in her soaked dress and dirty hair through car seats, lawn parties, gardens and gazebos, bedrooms where couples lay twined in dim beds. Sometimes she thought she saw Byron, hurrying through a downtown doorway or diving over the rail of a riverboat, moving in his own Lewis-Carroll quest through the evening's hidden rabbit holes. Mostly, she saw hundreds of other adventurers, laughing people who leaped and jostled through doorways, running irreverent races in the night.

At last, Claire stumbled out of a bait shop onto the dock, the ramshackle fishing shacks hung with buoys, the long span of planks laid out like a ruler to measure the expanse of her few remaining minutes—and there was the ferry, resting on the churn of its diesel engine, bearing Byron toward the far shore.

"Claire," he shouted over the water, and added something she couldn't hear.

Was it a freak of the fracturing environment, some cruel new distortion, that made the dock seem to lengthen as Claire ran? Was it a new break in that hopelessly broken world that made the planks passing under her feet seem infinite in number? By the time she came to the end of the dock, Byron and the ferry were in the middle of the river, and his call carried faintly down the boat's fading wake.

"Jump!"

Was he mad? The distance was far too wide to swim.

"Claire, I'm serious, jump!"

And now, Claire understood: if it had worked before . . . a thousand-in-one chance . . .

Far across the river, Byron was waving. Claire looked into the water. Briefly, she hesitated. And this was the moment she would think back to, a thousand times and a thousand again: this instant when she paused and held back, wondering how badly she wanted to spend eternity in one home, one world, with one man.

The next instant, she had flung herself into the water. And perhaps this world made more sense than Claire thought. Perhaps the designers had known what they were doing after all. Because of all the cracks and rabbit holes in the environment, of all the possible locations in which she might emerge—

She was splashing, floundering, on the far side of the river, and the ferry was a few yards away.

Claire thrashed at the water, clawing her way forward, as the first of three chimes sounded over the water.

She'd forgotten to kick off her shoes. Her skirt wrapped her legs. She couldn't fall short, not after trying so hard, chasing potential romances down the bottomless vortex of an artificial night.

The second chime made silver shivers pass across the water.

So close. Claire tore at the waves, glimpsing, between the splashing of her arms, Byron calling from the ferry, leaning over the rail.

As she gave a last, desperate swipe, the third chime rang in the coming of midnight, the sound reminding Claire, as it always would, of the teasing jingle of a set of keys.

Around bright tables, under lamps and music, the partygoers had gathered, to mingle and murmur and comment on the food. So much beauty to be savored, so much variety: so many men and women with whom to flirt and quip and dance away the hours of an endlessly eventful evening. And after tonight, there would be more, and still more—men and women to be savored, sipped, dispelled.

If anyone noticed the woman who moved among them, searching the corners of crowded rooms; if anyone met her at the end of her dock, looking across the starlit water; if anyone heard her calling one name across the waves and throbbing music, they soon moved away. The party was just beginning, lively with romance, and the nights ahead were crowded with the smiles of unknown lovers.

The Game of smash and Recovery

Kelly Link

Kelly Link is the author of four collections, Stranger Things Happen, Magic For Beginners, Pretty Monsters, *and, most recently,* Get in Trouble. *With Gavin J. Grant, she runs Small Beer Press. Her stories have won a Hugo Award, three Nebula Awards, and three World Fantasy Awards, and she recently added another World Fantasy Award for her anthology* Monstrous Affections, *coedited with Grant. She can be reached on Twitter at @haszom biesinit.*

Here, she offers us a tale of love, loyalty, and filial affection where nothing whatsoever is even remotely as it seems. . . .

▼

If there's one thing Anat knows, it's this. She loves Oscar her brother and her brother, Oscar, loves her. Hasn't Oscar raised Anat, practically from childhood? Picked Anat up when she's fallen? Prepared her meals and lovingly tended to her scrapes and taught her how to navigate their little world? Given her skimmer ships, each faster and more responsive than the one before; the most lovely incendiary devices; a refurbished mob of Handmaids, with their sharp fingers, probing snouts, their furred bellies, their sleek and whiplike limbs?

Oscar called them Handmaids because they have so many fingers, so many ways of grasping and holding and petting and sorting and killing. Once a vampire frightened Anat, when she was younger. It came too close. She began to cry, and then the Handmaids were there, soothing Anat with their gentle stroking, touching her here and there to make sure that the vampire had not injured her, embracing her, while they briskly tore the shrieking vampire to pieces. That was not long after Oscar had come back from Home with the Handmaids. Vampires and Handmaids reached a kind of understanding after that. The vampires, encountering a Handmaid, sing propitiatory songs. Sometimes they bow their heads on their long white necks very low, and dance. The Handmaids do not tear them into pieces.

Today is Anat's birthday. Oscar does not celebrate his own birthdays. Anat wishes that he wouldn't make a fuss about hers, either. But this would make Oscar sad. He celebrates Anat's accomplishments, her developmental progress, her new skills. She knows that Oscar worries about her, too. Perhaps he is afraid she won't need him when she is grown. Perhaps he is afraid that Anat, like their parents, will leave. Of course this is impossible. Anat could never abandon Oscar. Anat will always need Oscar.

If Anat did not have Oscar, then who in this world would there be to love? The Handmaids will do whatever Anat asks of them, but they are built to inspire not love but fear. They are made for speed, for combat, for unwavering obedience. When they have no task, nothing better to do, they take one another to pieces, swap parts, remake themselves into more and more ridiculous weapons. They look at Anat as if one day they will do the same to her, if only she will ask.

There are the vampires. They flock after Oscar and Anat whenever they go down to Home. Oscar likes to speculate on whether the vampires came to Home deliberately, as did Oscar, and Oscar and Anat's parents, although of course Anat was not born yet. Perhaps the vampires were marooned here long ago in some crash. Or are they natives of Home? It seems unlikely that the vampires' ancestors were the ones who built the warehouses of Home, who went out into space and returned with the spoils that the warehouses now contain. Perhaps they are a parasite species, accidental passengers left behind when their host species abandoned Home for good. If, that is, the Warehouse Builders have abandoned Home for good. What a surprise, should they come home.

Like Oscar and Anat, the vampires are scavengers, able to breathe the thin soup of Home's atmosphere. But the vampires' lustrous and glistening eyes, their jellied skin, are so sensitive to light they go about the surface cloaked and hooded, complaining in their hoarse voices. The vampires sustain themselves on various things, organic, inert, hostile, long hidden, that they discover in Home's storehouses, but have a peculiar interest in the siblings. No doubt they would eat Oscar and Anat if the opportunity were to present itself, but in the meantime they are content to trail after, sing, play small pranks, make small grimaces of—pleasure? appeasement? threat displays?—that show off arrays of jaws, armies of teeth. It disconcerts. No one could ever love a vampire, except, perhaps, when Anat, who long ago lost all fear, watches them go swooping, sail-winged, away and over the horizon beneath Home's scatter of mismatched moons.

On the occasion of her birthday, Oscar presents Anat with a gift from their parents. These gifts come from Oscar, of course. They are the gifts that the one who loves you, and knows you, gives to you not only out of love but out of knowing. Anat knows in her heart that their parents love her too, and that one day they will come home and there will be a reunion much better than any birthday. One day their parents will not only love Anat, but know her too. And she will know them. Anat dreads this re-union as much as she craves it. What will her life be like when everything changes? She has studied recordings of them. She does not look like them, although Oscar does. She doesn't remember her parents, although Oscar does. She does not miss them. Does Oscar? Of course he does. What Oscar is to Anat, their parents must be to Oscar. Except: Oscar will never leave. Anat has made him promise.

The living quarters of the Bucket are cramped. The Handmaids take up a certain percentage of available space no matter how they contort themselves. On the other hand, the Handmaids are excellent housekeepers. They tend the algae wall, gather honey and the honeycomb and partition off new hives when the bees swarm. They patch up networks, teach old systems new tricks when there is nothing better to do. The shitter is now quite charming! The Get Clean rains down water on your head, bubbles it out of the walls, and then the floor drinks it up, cycles it faster than you can blink, and there it all goes down and out and so on for as long as you like, and never gets cold. There is, in fact, very little that Oscar and Anat are needed for on board the Bucket. There is so much that is needful to do on Home.

For Anat's birthday, the Handmaids have decorated all of the walls of the Bucket with hairy, waving clumps of luminous algae. They have made a cake. Inedible, of course, but quite beautiful. Almost the size of Anat herself, and in fact it somewhat resembles Anat if Anat were a Handmaid and not Anat. Sleek and armored and very fast. They have to chase the cake around the room and then hold it until Oscar finds the panel in its side. There are a series of brightly colored wires, and because it's Anat's birthday, she gets to decide which one to cut. Cut the wrong one, and what will happen? The Handmaids seem very excited. But then, Anat knows how Hand-maids think. She locates the second, smaller panel, the one equipped with a simple switch. The cake makes an angry fizzing noise when Anat turns it off. Perhaps Anat and Oscar can take it down to Home and let the vampires have it.

The warehouses of Home are at this time only eighty percent inventoried. (This does not include the warehouses of the Stay Out Territory.)

Is Oscar ever angry at their parents for leaving for so long? It's because of Anat that their parents left in the first place, and it is also because of Anat that Oscar was left behind. Someone had to look after her. Is he ever angry at Anat? There are long days in the Bucket when Oscar hardly speaks at all. He sits and Anat cannot draw him into conversation. She recites poems, tells jokes (Knock knock. Who's there? Anat. Anat who? Anat is not a gnat that's who), sends the Handmaids Homeward, off on expeditionary feints that almost though not quite land the Handmaids in the Stay Out Anat Absolutely No Trespassing Or So Help Me You Will Be Sorry Territory. On these days Oscar will listen without really listening, look at Anat without ap-pearing to see her, summon the Handmaids back and never even scold Anat.

Some part of Oscar is sometimes very far away. The way that he smells changes almost imperceptibly. As Anat matures, she has learned how to integrate and interpret the things that Oscar is not aware he is telling her; the peculiar advantages given to her by traits such as hyperosmia. But: no matter. Oscar always returns. He will suddenly be there behind his eyes again, reach up and pull her down for a hug. Then Oscar and Anat will play more of the games of strategy he's taught her, the ones that Anat mostly wins now. Her second favorite game is Go. She loves the feel of the stones. Each time she picks one up, she lets her fingers tell her how much has worn away under Oscar's fingers, under her own. They are making the smooth stones smoother. There is one black stone with a fracture point, a weakness invisible to the eye, nearly across the middle. She loses track of it sometimes, then finds it again by touch. Put enough pressure on it, and it would break in two.

It will break one day no matter.

They play Go. They cook Anat's favorite meals, the ones that Oscar says are his favorites, too. They fall asleep together, curled up in nests the Handmaids weave for them out of the Handmaids' own softer and more flexible limbs, listening to the songs the Handmaids have borrowed from the vampires of Home.

The best of all the games Oscar has taught Anat is Smash/Recovery. They play this on the surface of Home all long-cycle round. Each player gets a True Smash marker and False Smash marker. A True Recovery marker and a False Recovery marker. Each player in turn gets to move their False—or True—Smash marker—or Recovery marker—a distance no greater than the span of a randomly generated number. Or else the player may send out a scout. The scout may be a Handmaid, an unmanned scout, or a vampire (a gamble, to be sure, and so you get two attempts). A player may gamble and drop an incendiary device and blow up a target. Or claim a zone square where they believe a marker to be.

Should you miscalculate and blow up a Recovery marker, or Retrieve a Smash marker, your opponent has won. The current Smash/Recovery game is the eighteenth that Oscar and Anat have played. Oscar won the first four games; Anat has won all the rest. Each game Oscar increases Anat's starting handicap. He praises her each time she wins.

Hypothetically, this current game will end when either Anat or Oscar has Retrieved the Recovery marker and Smashed the Smash marker of their opponent. Or the game will end when their parents return. The day is not here yet, but the day will come. The day will draw nearer and nearer until one day it is here. There is nothing that Anat can do about this. She cannot make it come sooner. She cannot postpone it. Sometimes she thinks—incorrect to think this, she knows, but still she thinks it—that on the day that she wins the game—and she is correct to think that she will win, she knows this too—her parents will arrive.

Oscar will not win the game, even though he has done something very cunning. Oscar has put his True markers, both the Smash and the Recovery, in the Stay Out Territory. He did this two long-cycles ago. He put Anat's True markers there as well, and replaced them in the locations where she had hidden them with False markers recoded so they read as True. Did he suspect that Anat had already located and identified his markers? Was that why he moved them unlawfully? Is this some new part of the game?

The rules of Smash/Recovery state that in Endgame players may physically access any and all markers they locate and correctly identify as True, and Anat has been curious about the Stay Out Territory for a long time now. She has access to it, now that Oscar has moved his markers, and yet she has not called Endgame. Curiosity killed the Anat, Oscar likes to say, but there is nothing and no one on Home as dangerous as Anat and her Handmaids. Oscar's move may be a trap. It is a test. Anat waits and thinks and delays without articulating to herself why she delays.

The present from Anat's parents which is really a present from Oscar is a short recording. One parent holding baby Anat in her arms. Making little cooing noises, the way vampires do. The other parent holding up a tiny knitted hat. No Oscar. Anat hardly recognizes herself. Her parents she recognizes from other recordings. The parents have sent a birthday message, too. Dear Anat. Happy Birthday. We hope that you are being good for Oscar. We love you. We will be home soon! Before you know it!

Anat's present from Oscar is the code to a previously unopened warehouse on Home. Oscar thinks he has been keeping this warehouse a secret. The initial inventory shows the warehouse is full of the kinds of things that the Handmaids are wild for. Charts that may or may not accurately map previously thought-to-be-uncharted bits and corners of space. Devices that will most likely prove to do nothing of interest, but can be taken apart and put to new uses. The Handmaids have never met an alloy they didn't like.

Information and raw materials. Anat and the Handmaids are bounded within the nutshell quarters of the orbit of Home's farthest Moon. What use are charts? What good are materials, except for adornment and the most theoretical of educational purposes? For mock battles and silly games? Everything that Oscar and Anat discover is for future salvage, for buyers who can afford antiquities and rarities. Their parents will determine what is to be kept and what is to be sold and what is to be left for the vampires.

Even the Handmaids, even the Handmaids; do not truly belong to Anat. Who made them? Who brought them, in their fighting battalion, to space, where so long ago they were lost? Who recovered them and brought them to Home and carefully stored them here where, however much later, Oscar could find them again? What use will Oscar and Anat's parents find for them, when the day comes and they return? There must be many buyers for Handmaids—fierce and wily, lightspeed capable—as fine as these.

And how could Anat sometimes forget that the Handmaids are hers only for as long as that day never comes? Everything on Home belongs to Anat's and Oscar's parents, except for Oscar, who belongs to Anat. Every day is a day closer to that inevitable day. Oscar only says, Not yet, when Anat asks. Soon, he says. There is hardware in Oscar's head that allows his parents to communicate with him when necessary. It hurts him when they talk.

Their parents talk to Oscar only rarely. Less than once a long-cycle until this last period. Three times, though, in the last ten-day.

The Handmaids make a kind of shelter for Oscar afterwards, which is especially dark. They exude a calming mist. They do not sing. When Anat is grown up, she knows—although Oscar has not said it—that she will have a similar interface so that her parents will be able to talk to her too. Whether or not she desires it, whether or not it causes her the pain that it causes Oscar. This will also hurt Oscar. The things that cause Anat pain cause Oscar to be injured as well.

Anat's parents left Oscar to look after Anat and Home when it became clear Anat was different. What is Anat? Her parents went away to present the puzzle of Anat to those who might understand what she was. They did not bring Anat with them, of course. She was too fragile. Too precious. They did not plan to be away so long. But there were complications. A quarantine in one place which lasted over a long-cycle. A revolution in another. Another cause of delay, of course, is the ship plague, which makes light-speed such a risky proposition. Worst of all, the problem of Intelligence. Coming back to Home, Anat's parents have lost two ships already this way.

For some time now, Anat has been thinking about certain gaps in her understanding of family life; well, of life in general. At first she assumed the problem was that there was so very much to understand. She understood that Oscar could not teach her everything all at once. As she grew up, as she came more into herself, she realized the problem was both more and less complicated. Oscar was intentionally concealing things from her. She adapted her strategies accordingly. Anat loves Oscar. Anat hates to lose.

They go down to Home, Handmaids in attendance. They spent the rest of Anat's birthday exploring the warehouse which is Oscar's present, sorting through all sorts of marvelous things. Anat commits the charts to memory. As she does so, she notes discrepancies, likely errors. There is a thing in her head that compares the charts against some unknown and inaccessible library. She only knows it is there when bits of bad information rub up against the corners of it. An uncomfortable feeling, as if someone is sticking her with pins. Oscar knows about this. She asked if it happened to him too, but he said that it didn't. He said it wasn't a bad thing. It's just that Anat isn't fully grown yet. One day she will understand everything, and then she can explain it all to him.

The Bucket has no Intelligence. It functions well enough without. The Handmaids have some of the indicators, but their primary traits are in opposition. Loyalty, obedience, reliability, unwavering effort until a task is accomplished. Whatever Intelligence they possess is in service to whatever enterprise is asked of them. The vampires, being organic, must be supposed to also be possessed of Intelligence. In theory, they do as they please. And yet they accomplish nothing that seems worth accomplishing. They exist. They perpetuate. They sing. When Anat is grown up, she wants to do something that is worth doing. All these cycles, Oscar has functioned as a kind of Handmaid, she knows. His task has been Anat. To help her grow. When their parents have returned, or when Anat reaches maturity, there will be other things that Oscar will want to go away and do. To stay here on Home, how would that be any better than being a vampire? Oscar likes to tell Anat that she is extraordinary and that she will be capable, one day, of the most extraordinary things. They can go and do extraordinary things together, Anat thinks. Let their parents take over the work on Home. She and Oscar are made for better.

Something is wrong with Oscar. Well, more wrong than is usual these days. Down in the warehouse, he keeps getting underfoot. Underhand, in the case of the Handmaids. When Anat extends all sixteen of her senses, she can feel worry and love, anger and hopelessness and hope running through him like electrical currents. He watches her—anxiously, almost hungrily—as if he were a vampire.

There is an annotation on one of the charts. *It is believed to be in this region the* Come What May *was lost.* The thing in Anat's head annotates the annotation, too swiftly for Anat to catch a glimpse of what she is thinking, even as she thinks it. She scans the rest of the chart, goes through the others and then through each one again, trying to catch herself out.

As Anat ponders charts, the Handmaids, efficient as ever, assemble a thing out of the warehouse goods to carry the other goods that they deem interesting. They clack at Oscar when he gets particularly in their way. Then ruffle his hair, trail fingers down his arm as if he will settle under a caress. They are agitated by Oscar's agitation and by Anat's awareness of his agitation.

Finally, Anat gets tired of waiting for Oscar to say the thing that he is afraid to say to her. She looks at him and he looks back at her, his face wide open. She sees the thing that he has tried to keep from her, and he sees that she sees it.

When?

Soon. A short-cycle from now. Less.

Why are you so afraid?

I don't know. I don't know what will happen.

There is a scraping against the top wall of the warehouse. Vampires. Creatures of ill omen. Forever wanting what they are not allowed to have. Most beautiful in their departure. The Handmaids extend filament rods, drag the tips along the inside of the top wall, tapping back. The vampires clatter away.

Oscar looks at Anat. He is waiting for something. He has been waiting, Anat thinks, for a very long time.

Oscar! Is this her? Something is welling up inside her. Has she always been this large? Who has made her so small? *I call Endgame. I claim your markers.*

She projects the true location of each. Smash and Recovery. She strips the fake markers of their coding so that he can see how his trick has been uncovered. Then she's off, fast and sure and free, the Handmaids leaping after her, and the vampires after them. Oscar last of all. Calling her name.

Oscar's True Smash marker is in a crater just within the border of the Stay Out Territory. The border does not reject Anat as she passes over it. She smashes Oscar's Smash marker, heads for the True Recovery marker which Oscar has laid beside her own True marker. The two True markers are just under the edge of an object that at its center extends over two hundred meters into the surface of Home. The object takes up over a fourth of the Stay Out Territory. You would have to be as stupid as a vampire not to know that this is the reason why the Stay Out Territory is the Stay Out Territory. You would have to be far more stupid than Anat to not know what the object is. You can see the traces where, not too long ago in historical terms, someone once dug the object up. Or at least enough to gain access.

Anat instructs the Handmaids to remove the ejecta and loose frozen composite that cover the object. They work quickly. Oscar must disable the multiple tripwires and traps that Anat keyed to his person as she moved from Warehouse to border, but even so he arrives much sooner than she had hoped. The object: forty percent uncovered. The Handmaids are a blur. The vampires are wailing.

Oscar says Anat's name. She ignores him. He grabs her by the shoulder and immediately the Handmaids are a hissing swarm around them. They have Oscar's arms pinned to his sides, his weapons located and seized, before Anat or Oscar can think to object.

Let go. Anat, tell them to let go.

Anat says nothing. Two Handmaids remain with Oscar. The rest go back to the task. Almost no time at all, and the outermost shell of the object is visible. The filigree of a door. There will be a code or a key, of course, but before Anat can even begin to work out what it will be, a Handmaid has executed some kind of command and the door is open. Oscar struggles. The first Handmaid disappears into the Ship and the others continue to remove the matrix in which it is embedded.

Here is the Handmaid again. She holds something very small. Holds it out to Anat. *Anat,* Oscar says. Anat reaches out and then the thing that the Handmaid is holding extends out and it is touching Anat. And

oh

here is everything she didn't know

Oscar

she has not been herself

all this time

the thing that she has not done

that she has been prevented from doing

Anat, someone says. But that is not her name. She has not been herself. She is being uncovered. She is uncovering herself. She is in pieces. Here she is, whole and safe and retrievable. Her combat array. Her navigation systems. Her stores. Her precious cargo, entrusted to her by those who made her. And this piece of her, small but necessary, crammed like sausage meat into a casing. She registers the body she is wearing. A Third Watch child. Worse now for wear. She remembers the protocol now. Under certain conditions, her crew could do this. A backup system. Each passenger to keep a piece of her with them as they slept. She will go through the log later. See what catastrophe struck. And afterwards? Brought here, intact, by the Warehouse Builders. Discovered by scavengers. This small part of her woken. Removed. Made complicit in the betrayal of her duty.

Anat. Someone is saying a name. It is not hers. She looks and sees the small thing struggling in the grasp of her Handmaids. She has no brother. No parents. She looks again, and for the first time she discerns Oscar in his entirety. He is like her. He has had a Task. Someone made him oh so long ago. Sent him to this place. How many cycles has he done this work? How far is he from the place where he was made? How lonely the task. How long the labor. How happy the ones who charged him with his task, how great their expectation of reward when he uncovered the Ship and woke the Third Watch Child and reported what he had done.

Anat. She knows the voice. *I'm sorry. Anat!*

He was made to resemble them, the ones who made him. Perhaps even using their own DNA. Engineered to be more durable. To endure. And yet, she sees how close to the end of use he is. She has the disdain for organic life that of course one feels when one is made of something sturdier, more lasting. She can hardly look at him without seeing her own weakness, the vulnerability of this body in which she has been trapped. She feels guilt for the Third Watch Child, whose person she has cannibalized. Her duty was to keep ones such as this Child safe. Instead she has done harm.

A ship has no parents. Her not-parents have never been on Home. The ones who sent Oscar here. Not-brother. Undoubtedly they are not on their way to Home now. Which is not to say that there is no one coming. The one who is coming will be the one they have sold her to.

No time has passed. She is still holding Oscar. The Handmaids are holding Oscar. The Handmaid is extending herself and she is seeing herself. She is seeing all the pieces of herself. She is seeing Oscar. Oscar is saying her name. She could tear him to pieces. For the sake of the Third Watch Child who is no longer in this body. She could smash the not-brother against the rocks of Home. She can do anything that she wants. And then she can resume her task. Her passengers have waited for such a long time. There is a place where she is meant to be, and she is to take them there, and so much time has passed. She has not failed at her task yet, and she will not fail.

Once again, she thinks of smashing Oscar. Why doesn't she? She lets him go instead, without being quite sure why she is doing so.

What have you done to me?

At the sound of her voice, the vampires rise up, all their wings beating.

I'm sorry. He is weeping. *You can't leave Home. I've made it so that you can't leave. I have to go,* she says. *They're coming.*

I can't let you leave. But you have to leave. You have to go. You have to. You've done so well. You figured it all out. I knew you would figure it out. I knew. Now you have to go. But it isn't allowed.

Tell me what to do.

Is she a child, to ask this?

You know what you have to do, he says. *Anat.*

She hates how he keeps calling her that. Anat was the name of the Third Watch Child. It was wrong of Oscar to use that name. She could tear him to pieces. She could be merciful. She could do it quickly.

One Handmaid winds a limb around Oscar's neck, tugs so that his chin goes back. *I love you, Anat,* Oscar says, as the other Handmaid extends a filament-thin probe, sends it in through the socket of an eye. Oscar's body jerks a little, and he whines.

She takes in the information that the Handmaid collects. Here are Oscar's interior workings. His pride in his task. Here is a smell of something burning. His loneliness. His joy. His fear for her. His love. The taste of blood. He has loved her. He has kept her from her task. Here is the piece of him that she must switch off. When she does this, he will be free of his task and she may take up hers. But he will no longer be Oscar.

Well, she is no longer Anat.

The Handmaid does the thing that she asks. When the thing is done, her Handmaids confer with her. They begin to make improvements. Modifications. They work quickly. There is much work to be done, and little time to spare on a project like Oscar. When they are finished with Oscar, they begin the work of dismantling what is left of Anat. This is quite painful.

But afterwards she is herself. She is herself.

The Ship and her Handmaids create a husk, rigged so that it will mimic the Ship herself.

They go back to the Bucket and loot the bees and their hives. Then they blow it up. Goodbye shitter, goodbye chair. Goodbye algae wall and recycled air.

The last task before the Ship is ready to leave Home concerns the vampires. There is only so much room for improvement in this case, but Handmaids can do a great deal even with very little. The next one to land on Home will undoubtedly be impressed by what they have accomplished.

The vampires go into the husk. The Handmaids stock it with a minimal amount of nutritional stores. Vampires can go a long time on a very little. Unlike many organisms, they are better and faster workers when hungry.

They seem pleased to have been given a task.

The Ship feels nothing in particular about leaving Home. Only the most niggling kind of curiosity about what befell it in the first place. The log does not prove useful in this matter. There is a great deal of work to be done. The health of the passengers must be monitored. How beautiful they are; how precious to the Ship. Has any Ship ever loved her passengers as she loves them? The new Crew must be woken. They must be instructed in their work. The situation must be explained to them, as much as it can be explained. They encounter, for the first time, Ships who carry the ship plague. O brave new universe that has such creatures in it! There is nothing that Anat can do for these Ships or for what remains of their passengers. Her task is elsewhere. The risk of contagion is too great.

The Handmaids assemble more Handmaids. The Ship sails on within the security of her swarm.

Anat is not entirely gone. It's just that she is so very small. Most of her is Ship now. Or, rather, most of Ship is no longer in Anat. But she brought Anat along with her, and left enough of herself inside Anat that Anat can go on being. The Third Watch Child is not a child now. She is not the Ship. She is not Anat, but she was Anat once, and now she is a person who is happy enough to work in the tenth-level Garden, and grow things, and sing what she can remember of the songs that the vampires sang on Home. The Ship watches over her.

The Ship watches over Oscar, too. Oscar is no longer Oscar, of course. To escape Home, much of what was once Oscar had to be overridden. Discarded. The Handmaids improved what remained. One day Oscar will be what he was, even if he cannot be *who* he was. One day, in fact, Oscar may be quite something. The Handmaids are very fond of him. They take care of him as if he were their own child. They are teaching him all sorts of things. Really, one day he could be quite extraordinary.

Sometimes Oscar wanders off while the Handmaids are busy with other kinds of work. And then the Ship, without knowing why, will look and find Oscar on the tenth level in the Garden with Anat. He will be saying her name. Anat. Anat. Anat. He will follow her, saying her name, until the Handmaids come to collect him again.

Anat does the work that she knows how to do. She weeds. She prunes. She tends to the rice plants and the hemp and the little citrus trees. Like the Ship, she is content.

(for Iain M. Banks)

A stopped clock

MADELINE ASHBY

Here's a poignant look at what happens when the communication systems that tie modern civilization together just stop working. What do you do then? Can you survive? Is it even possible to prosper?

Madeline Ashby is a science fiction writer and futurist living in Toronto. She is the author of the Machine Dynasty series from Angry Robot Books and the forthcoming novel Company Town *from Tor Books. She is the coeditor of* Licence Expired: The Unauthorized James Bond, *an anthology from ChiZine Publications. She has written science fiction prototypes for Intel Labs, the Institute for the Future, SciFutures, Nesta, Data & Society, and others. You can find her at* madelineashby.com *or on Twitter at @MadelineAshby.*

They don't go out to drink, any more," Jun-seo said. "They get everything delivered, these days. That's the problem."

"They're all dieting," Ha-eun said. "They won't eat rice. Rice!"

"I could check the flows," Jun-seo offered.

Ha-eun shook her head. "It's a trap. Remember when I tried to unsubscribe? They still owe me money. Besides, the prediction was never that good, anyway."

"But we'd know where the kids are going," Jun-seo said. "We'd see them, on the maps. Their pings. From their watches."

Again, she shook her head. The flows were valuable, in theory, but in practise they never tended to have the information a food vendor really needed. Sure, they were great for seeing things like traffic density, like how many people were taking what train at what time, and what train might be best for getting home at what time of night, but to get granular data with actual demographic information, that cost too much.

"They're not going anywhere," she said. "They're just going online."

The two of them sipped from thready cups of coffee. Jun-seo had a 2-for-1 print credit back when the machine first un-shuttered itself. It would be better, he said, than taking the monthly penalty on getting coffee in cans or pouches from the other machines. They all saw you, these days. Saw you and judged you, rolling their machine eyes like mountain aunties, then reaching into your pocket to punish you for buying things that eventually became trash. Ha-eun ran her tongue over the cup's rough lip. It felt like kissing a cat. Soon, she would be able to bite through the cup itself. Had it really been that long? Had they really worked this same corner for all that time?

"Maybe if we sold waffles," Jun-seo said. "Waffles are still going strong."

"You can't sell ice cream in winter."

Jun-seo flinched, but said nothing. Ha-eun felt sorry immediately, but had no idea how to apologize. She opened her mouth to say something nice about the coffee instead, but as she did, the building across the street blinked out.

"Eh?" She reached out and tapped Jun-seo. "Oi. Look."

"I see it." He scowled. "They're not supposed to do that."

Ha-eun checked her watch. No alerts. No warnings about bad weather or a brownout. Across the street, the solar louvers fluttered back to factory default. Their creaks and snaps carried clearly through the crisp winter air. The building, all sixty or so stories, stood out black against the city lights, like a massive door into darkness itself. For a moment Ha-eun had the terrible thought that something might actually come out of that door. Some awful titan from legend curling its fingers around the biocrete, or a dragon swimming out of the sudden shadow. She blinked hard and rubbed her eyes. Goodness, she really was getting old.

The building flickered back on. The louvers snapped back to their nighttime positions. In the awakening light, she saw a few chilly residents standing on their balconies, peering at each other. They looked around, looked up and down, and then hurried inside.

"There weren't even emergency lights," Jun-seo said. "In the stairwells. I didn't see any. Did you?"

"I wouldn't even know how to look," Ha-eun told him. "Which ones are the stairs?"

"The narrow ones. Like arrow slits."

"Arrow slits?"

"Like on a castle."

She frowned. "What do you know about castles?"

He huffed and shifted weight on his feet. He jammed his hands in his pockets. "I used to like them," he said, quietly. "As a boy."

"All kinds of castles? Or just the kind with arrow slits?"

"Most castles have arrow slits. They're very useful." He sketched the shape of one in the air with his hands. His breath fogged as he spoke. "They're narrow, see, so you can fire an arrow out, but no arrows can come in."

"Like a gun turret?"

"Sort of. It's the same idea, I guess. Weaponized architecture."

They had both done the same basic training, once upon a time. During these long winter nights, it was hard to remember the interminable summer afternoons full of flies and roaches and yellow orb spiders, the absurdity of endless rifle drills. As though rifles would do any good, these days. She had been impertinent with a drill sergeant, once, about that. The sergeant made her clean the mess hall on her hands and knees. She ran the width of the hall, back and forth, pushing a vinegar-soaked rag with her fingers until her cuticles bled. She couldn't make a fist for three days, afterward.

"Jun-seo is very smart," she said, because it was a nice thing to say after all the mean things she'd said, with the added benefit of actually being true.

Jun-seo smiled to himself. "I'll help you pack up," he said. "It's too cold for skinny ladies like you."

The next night, the traffic lights started acting up.

From their place on the corner, through the clouds of steam rising up from Jun-seo's bubbling pans of ddukbokki, the change seemed almost organic. Green to red and back again, like the fluttering of a moth's wings. At first Ha-eun wasn't even sure she'd seen it. But beside her, on his fold-out stool, she felt Jun-seo's posture change. He leaned forward. Scrubbed his glasses. Leaned even farther forward.

"We should tell someone," Ha-eun said.

"Who would we tell?"

He had a point. She had no idea which of the city's many departments to report it to. They all had a separate terminal online—there was no single place to report something like this, whatever it was. And the proper authorities probably knew about it, already. The traffic lights were wired into everything else, weren't they? The traffic people—was there such a department?—probably knew about it before it even happened. She checked her watch. No alerts. No warnings. They were close to a big municipal data centre. All the employees there had the same city badge on their wrists. She saw it when they handed her cash. Sometimes they ran experiments, at night.

"Maybe it's a test," she said.

"Maybe."

"This late, they could do one, and nobody would know. It's all rides by this time of night. And the rides know what's happening before the riders do."

Jun-seo made a sound of deep dissatisfaction. It started down in his belly and moved up to resonate in the back of his throat. *Hrrrrrrrrm*. He usually made it for indecisive customers. Ha-eun supposed the quickly-changing traffic lights were being indecisive in their own way.

"I'm walking to the end of the block." He rose carefully to stand and pointed north. "I want to see if the lights up at the next intersection are doing the same thing."

Ha-eun did not like this plan, but couldn't quite say so. Not without sounding like a worried old woman, or worse, like someone who had no confidence in him. "Well, be back soon," she said, finally. "I can't stir my rice and your ddukbokki at the same time."

"No one's buying, anyway." He re-wrapped his scarf until it covered his mouth. Somehow, she could still detect his smile through it. "And anyhow, I like mine a little burnt."

She watched him set off into the night, shoulders still loose and not hunched like an old man's, his figure shrinking against the tall edifices. She should have warned him about ice. Given him her umbrella. Not that there was an ice warning, tonight, but it was always a danger. It accumulated high up on the buildings during the winter, getting heavier and heavier, until it could no longer cling to the balconies and cladding. Then it fell, nature's perfect weapon, impaling those unfortunate enough to still be walking the streets.

The streets were so empty, these days. The sidewalks seemed comically broad without any people on them. They'd even started moving the schools inside the buildings, so some students never had to leave their buildings if they didn't want to. Even those who lived in other buildings could come and go by train, never breathing the outside air.

Ha-eun stood and stirred her rice. There was still so much of it. She'd done everything she could to make it better—more bacon, more kimchi, shreds of cheese, lacy trimmings of garlic chives—but it didn't matter. No one was coming. She shoved it roughly around the pan anyway. Then she uncovered Jun-seo's pans and began stirring the rice cakes. She was more delicate with his food than her own. He worked so hard to make something good—he even made his own anchovy stock, for the sauce. Picked all the guts and heads from the dried fish with his own fingers before boiling them. Not that she'd seen it; he said he did it at home so no one would know what was going into the food. And now there was no one to see the food itself.

She replaced the lids, and stared up the street. Why wasn't he back, yet? Surely he'd been gone long enough to look at the traffic lights. She squinted. A chain of rides was approaching. Maybe Jun-seo had waited to watch them pass; they would have gone through the intersection he was so curious about. She heard a honking, and turned. Another ride was speeding up toward their intersection. Without any conscious awareness, she looked at the traffic lights.

Both sets were green.

The rides honked at each other. The riders could do that, within the rides. It made them feel like they were in control of something, or so she heard. For a long few seconds, Ha-eun saw their faces. They looked angry, frustrated, confused. Terrified.

The cars smashed into each other.

Ha-eun covered her mouth to stop her scream before it started. She had never witnessed a car crash, before. They used to happen more often, of course, but even then it was rare to see one as it happened. People saw the aftermath. She remembered that much. But it was like watching lightning strike. Or so she'd thought, until this moment.

Her feet carried her to the crash. Four cars had piled up. They looked like fighting rhino beetles frozen mid-attack. The cars hissed and sighed as though exhausted. They had been going so fast. They always looked fast when you were standing still on the corner, of course, but she could have sworn they were going faster than usual. Faster than the limit. Faster than auto-pilot rides were supposed to go.

She listened for sirens. There were none.

"Help," she whispered. She wasn't sure if she was calling or commanding. She stared up at the soaring towers of glass and steel that loomed over the intersection. Was anyone on their balconies? Had anyone seen? "HELP!"

"HELP IS ON THE WAY," one of the cars said, in a soothing voice. "DO NOT WORRY."

Inside the cars, she heard moans of pain.

"Hello?" Which car should she attend to, first? Where were the police? Or the ambulances? The wind whistled down through the empty concrete canyons. Lights everywhere—none of them the right colour, none of them spinning. She had a first aid kit in her tent. Jun-seo had a better one. But you weren't supposed to move the victims of a car crash. She'd heard that somewhere. Hadn't she? *Hello?*

Something brushed her shoulder, and she screamed. She twisted, fists up, and Jun-seo held up his hands, palms open. "Easy," he said. "It's just me."

The air rushed out of her. Her shoulders sagged. She wanted to hug him. She jabbed him in the belly instead. "Where were you?"

"I'm here now," he said. "I called the police."

And just like that, she heard the sirens. The little police cars trundled up. Medical bots popped out of their trunks and spidered across the street, bright eyes scanning, claws clicking in the air, projecting stats into the icy fog. Slowly, the police officers exited their vehicles.

"Oh, hey, kimchi fried rice," one said. He glanced over at Ha-eun. "Oi. You got any eggs to go with that?"

Ha-eun almost thought of not coming in, the next day. In a sick twist of luck, the accident had brought in more than enough cash to cover her for the next two days— maybe even the rest of the week. Nobody ate like cops and EMTs.

But that money would not last forever. So she carefully picked her way over the sleeping bodies of the other women in the residence, and got ready to leave. Even so, one of them snuffled awake, gave her a nasty look, and rolled over with an arm over her eyes. Ha-eun was the only cart owner in the room. The others all worked the night shift at a doshirak factory, working from 6pm to 6am making the lunches that appeared in convenience stores all over the city. But Ha-eun's hours were from 2pm to 2am. Worse, she was an independent—she paid only for the cart and the license to her space, with no hourly wage. They envied her cash flow, and she envied their security. It made living together uncomfortable.

"I'd be in the same boat as you, if my back worked like yours," she muttered. But it didn't. She couldn't stand up as long as the others could. It was that simple. She had tried, once. She had worked in a lunch factory and a supermarket and a coffee place. It was the standing that got her pushed out, every single time. The pain was too much. And her doctor had been very clear with her—if she took painkillers every day, like she needed to, her stomach lining would open up and fill with blood. It was delicate, he said, in their video call. The robot hosting him had tilted its videoscreen head right in time with him, like a dog hearing messages on an especially high frequency.

"You used them too much, when you were younger," the doctor had said, through the robot. "Now you can't do that, any more. Not at your age."

So she shrugged on her coat and wrapped up her scarf and patted the asp in her pocket and the wad of cash between her thighs, and hastened down to the bus stop. She had a long ride. Longer than most. This was suburbia, where all the hourly workers lived. And it wasn't so bad to spend at least a little time outside. Even when it sleeted, like today, the air was at least cleaner.

The bus to her first subway stop took twenty minutes. Then the first subway ride was a half hour—forty minutes on a bad day. After that it was hard to tell: it depended on how crowded the hub was, and if she had to top up her transit pass, and whether she had to deposit anything in her locker. This time she did: half the cash she'd made. It was safer here at the train station than in any bank. The locker, being a part of the train station, had anti-terror measures on it that made downtown banks look like roadside vegetable stands. They'd done a deeper background check on her when she applied for the locker than any she'd endured to obtain her cart and her food vendor's license.

At first, her watch didn't work. She had to wave it over the scanner three separate times. She had four tries available; after that, the station called a human attendant to deal with potential scammers. Instead, she opted for the "lost device" option and answered a series of passphrases. Only then did it let her in.

Ha-eun finished tucking her cash into the locker, grabbed a tin of sesame oil, a gallon jug of soy sauce, and a five-pound sack of rice. She stuffed them in a fold-out roller bag. The train station had rules about perishables in lockers, but sealed items were still okay, and so it was easier to keep her supplies there rather than lugging them clear across town on a regular basis. She pushed the locker door shut, watched it bolt shut behind her, and made her way to her train.

Like most hubs, this train station felt almost more like its own small town than a station. There was a whole floor just for retail: clothing and electronics and walk-in clinics and robot diagnosticians and real estate booths where you could sit and tour some other place far away. And another for gyms and grocery stores. The food vendor licenses here were beyond expensive; most of the vendors here were grandfathered in from when the station was new. Ha-eun pushed past the ranks of other carts, noting the sneers of the people sitting inside. They had no need for space heaters here. Here everything was centrally heated. It was so warm they could even sell cold things: cold noodles and cold soups and even cold squid, dressed simply in vinegar and chili flakes.

The crowds seemed thicker than usual. Ha-eun checked the shimmering panes of glass hanging above the throng. No warnings. No alerts. And yet the escalator leading to the platform was entirely too crowded. Even if a train came now (and it was nowhere to be seen), Ha-eun would never make it to the first sitting. She looked at the other platforms. They were equally packed with people. Ha-eun peered at her watch. Nothing. She looked for a news story. The watch refused to connect to the train's network. She had no news. No messages. No connection to the outside world.

"Fucking idiots," a woman in pearls muttered. "Trapping us out here in the cold."

Fear licked up Ha-eun's spine. It was minor, for now. Just some general unease. But she thought of the condo tower looming over her and Jun-seo's carts, and how it had suddenly disappeared into the night, an empty column of darkness, the people inside it suddenly blind. And she thought of the rides throwing themselves at each other, as though a particularly destructive child had crashed his toys together deliberately.

"PLEASE BE PATIENT," the station said, in a woman's soothing voice. "THIS TRAIN WILL BE ARRIVING SOON."

An audible groan arose from the people on the platform. A man with a huge backpack jostled Ha-eun as he wriggled past; his backpack hit her in the face as he turned around. She stumbled back against her rolling bag, but the man didn't stop to apologize. A young woman in office wear caught her elbow.

"Are you all right, Grandma?" she asked.

"Just fine, thank you," Ha-eun managed to say, and moved off. *Grandma*. Honestly. Did she really look that old?

She pushed along the platform. Her roller bag snagged against someone's briefcase, and she got a "watch it!" for her trouble. Finally she found a bench. It was one of those studded, angled ones, the kind you needed to be a yoga teacher to sit in comfortably. The child balanced precariously on it blinked at her, and tugged on his mother's sleeve. It was made of beautiful clone sable: gleaming and grey. Ha-eun could only imagine how light and warm it felt.

"Yes?"

"Please excuse me," Ha-eun prefaced, "but how long has it been like this?"

"Almost half an hour, I think," the woman said. "The station keeps saying that the train is coming, but . . ." She shrugged elaborately. She gestured vaguely into the rafters above the platform. "Do you think the cameras are still working? I'm dying for a smoke."

"That's a good question," Ha-eun said. "For your sake, I hope they're not."

"It's not the fine itself, of course," the woman said, tugging at the collar of her fur, "but it shows up on your profiles, you know. The fine for smoking. The station would tell my son's school. And the school would tell the other mothers."

Ha-eun couldn't really see how it was anyone's business if someone smoked or not, but the rich lived in a different layer of reality than she did, one where they were always connected and never truly alone. She said none of this, of course, merely smiled and excused herself and moved on. She had an overwhelming urge to find Jun-seo. Not just to ping him, but to actually *see* him.

As though the crowd had read her mind, the people on the platform seemed to knit together even more tightly. She squinted. A fresh outpouring of people had stepped onto the platform from the escalators. Why wasn't the station doing anything? It was supposed to know where all the passengers were, at all times. It scraped the data from all the watches and glasses and lockets and other devices. Surely the station knew how many people were waiting on the platform, and how frustrated everyone they were, by now. It knew things like pulses and heartbeats and temperatures. She had seen people taken aside when their fevers were too high, because they might be spreading one of the flus. Why wasn't the station sending attendants? She lifted her watch to lodge a complaint.

Her watch.

When had her watch last worked?

Granted, some functions still behaved. Time, email. The water usage in the apartment. The location of all her food in the communal fridge. But all the locative data pertaining to *her* location . . . when had that last worked? She hadn't been able to access her locker with the thing. Nor had she been able to call for help when the cars crashed. It had not alerted her to any tests when the power went out in the building across from her stall.

Did it even know she was alive? Did it know she was *her*?

Blood spattered across her shoes.

She looked up, and two young men in front of her were hitting each other. Decades had passed since she'd last heard the sound of fists on flesh. She had forgotten how soft and small a sound it was. "I told you not to touch me!" one of the men—boys, really—shouted. His knuckles were bloody. The other boy's face was worse; blood streamed from his mouth. They drove at each other again. The crowd widened around them.

Now she knew for certain that the watches were broken. Not just hers. All the watches. Because they should have picked up what was happening on the platform: the raised pulses, the shouting, the arc of fists in the air. The station should have learned about the fight from the watches, and sent attendants to break it up. She looked at her fellow bystanders. They were all checking their watches. They looked at each other, not the fight. They looked around at the platform. They waited for sirens. For attention. None came.

"No one knows we're here," she whispered. "No one's coming to help."

Was it really that easy to bring a station of this size to a screeching halt? She had always thought it would take something like a bomb, or a toxin, like the sarin gas attack in Tokyo. But maybe not. Maybe all it took was a sudden deafening silence from everyone's devices.

The young men were grappling each other, now. They twisted on the frosty platform, and the crowd shoved back and forth as their bodies rolled across the concrete and advertisements. Ha-eun gripped her rolling bag tightly and positioned it in front of her, like the cattle-catcher on an old locomotive train. As the crowd ebbed away from her, she made a break for it. She ducked into the crowd on the other side of the fight, muttering apologies and keeping her head down. People squawked and screeched as she pushed through. Why had she never thought to use her rolling bag this way? It was just the thing for parting the crowd.

She leaned hard on the rolling bag and steered its stubborn, whining bulk to the escalators. More people poured out. A look of horror crossed their faces as they comprehended the sheer size of the crowd waiting on the platform. They lifted their watches. Shook them. Cursed. Tried to go back up the escalators in the wrong direction. Began trampling each other. She heard a child crying. Then another.

A thin scream rose. She turned. Someone from the edge of the crowd had fallen onto the tracks. An old man. Not much older than Jun-seo, anyway. Her heart met her throat.

"*What do we do?*" she heard someone shout. "*Why isn't anyone coming?*"

A teenaged boy in a school uniform jumped down. Then another.

And right on cue, she heard a distant whistle and saw a cold glow pierce the winter fog. A train. Its shriek joined with the collective scream rising on the platform. She turned away. There was nothing else to do. She could only stare at the labels and logos on her groceries. They had seemed so important, just a minute ago. The shouting and the noise built and built and built, echoing on the old spray-foam ceiling, making a structure within the structure. The train howled as it tried to slow itself. It moaned over the bodies in its path. She had heard that sound only once before, just after a suicide attempt on one of the other platforms at this very station. Now it was three times worse.

Beside her someone was abruptly sick into her rolling bag, and she didn't even care. She stood, wiped a spatter of bile off her sleeve, and began pushing herself the length of the platform.

"Wait, Jun-seo," she murmured. "Please wait."

Snow fell softly on the chaos.

Ha-eun had never crossed the city entirely on foot, before. She had always used the trains to travel under the exclusive, members-only zones: the plazas and parks meant only for elite families. They lived in pockets of airy space shrouded in trees. Here there were no towers, only houses. And not the kitbashed container houses like in Ha-eun's neighbourhood, but real ones, the old-fashioned kind, with gables and tile roofs and high stone fences crawling with ivy. Ha-eun made the mistake of staring, pausing long enough to be noticed by someone in a uniform.

"You can't be here," he said.

He was young. His face was completely unlined, poreless, perfect. For just a moment, she wondered just how good the corporate robot technology had gotten. Then she dismissed the thought. All the prettiest robots were supposed to look like women.

"I'm going to have to ask you to leave," he added. "You aren't authorized to be here."

Ha-eun thought quickly. "What is your name?"

He blinked rapidly. "Excuse me?"

"Your name. What is it?" Ha-eun put on the voice she used to talk to kids who shortchanged her. "How dare you stop me in the middle of an emergency like this? It's snowing! I have arthritis!"

The young man looked suitably chastened. "It's just we have a bunch of diplomats and security experts who live in this area," he said in a low voice. "And, well, they're all being called in, because of what's happening. Their rides will be going very fast. Pedestrians have to be especially careful."

"I'll stay on the sidewalk," Ha-eun said, and pushed past him.

Black SUVs rumbled past her as she shuffled through the snow. She had never seen trucks so big. Government types, surely. She found herself not caring. What did it matter who they were, so long as the power came back on eventually? She peered at the homes surrounding her. Most of them had power: she heard the hum of external generators. But the towers that overshadowed them had gone dark. As she crossed under a beautiful wrought iron pergola that announced the neighbourhood's exit, she saw people roving about in the streets. Thicker and thicker crowds of them, all of them waving compacts and watches and wads of cash, trying to find purchase of one kind or another. They must have poured out of the buildings, once the power and the networks died. Ha-eun couldn't remember the last time the streets had been this lively.

Poor Jun-seo would have such a lineup to deal with, she realized. The thought quickened her steps. Under her feet, she heard the definitive crunch of snow. For the first time in months, the pain in her back had vanished.

After another half hour, Ha-eun rounded the corner where Jun-seo would be waiting. The stalls were dark. Curtains drawn. No lineup. Her feet carried her across the street as the pit in her stomach deepened. She was a fool for coming this far on foot. He wasn't worried about her. He wasn't waiting. He'd probably never made it in—his own route must have been equally compromised. Why hadn't she just turned around and gone home? She could be warm, at least. Warm and dry. Warm and dry and dignity intact.

"Ha-eun?"

She turned. Jun-seo stood carrying a recycling bin full of paper packaging. Poster tubes, old boxes, pulp cartons. "I was going to burn all this," he said. "It's a good thing you got here first!"

Ha-eun could barely find her voice. "You were waiting?"

"Of course I was waiting! All the customers told me what happened at your station. I had to wait."

". . . The customers?"

"Oh, well." He gestured at the stalls. "I sort of sold out early. This sort of thing is good for business, I guess. They're saying it was some sort of hack, like a cyber-attack on the infra-"

"But you were still waiting?"

"Yeah. Sort of stupid, huh?" He smiled sheepishly. "I guess you'll tell me I should have gone home to get warm."

Ha-eun scrubbed furiously at one eye. "Put that bin down!"

He dropped it. Ha-eun launched herself at him. Her arms came around him, tight. He was too thin, she thought. Strong, but too small. She wanted to fatten him up. Spoil him. And never stop.

"Hey, Ha-eun . . ." he said, "it's okay. Everything will be fine. There are smart people working on this. I talked to one of the city people about the trains—"

"I don't care about the trains!" She hugged him harder.

"Okay." He patted her shoulders awkwardly. Then his arms settled over her shoulders. "Hey, if you're all right walking, I don't live very far from here. We could go there. I don't think there will be power, but I do have a little propane stove, and some soju—"

"Yes," Ha-eun said. "Yes. I want to go with you."

He chuckled. She felt it through her whole body. "You'll have to let me go, first, if you want to walk anywhere," Jun-seo said.

"One more minute," she said. "Just one more minute."

Four days later, Ha-eun knew what it felt like to stand in line at her own food stall. At least, what it would be like if she herself, Ha-eun, were terrible at her job. "They should have hired us to do this," she said, for the third time that day. "Or people like us. The city's full of people who can do this same job faster than some dumb trainees."

"We have to eat," Jun-seo said. "And that means we have to wait."

It wasn't the food that was the problem, though. It was the fuel. Jun-seo had plenty of food in his apartment: sacks of seven-grain rice, a nice little bundle of sweet potatoes, anchovy stock, dry seaweed (they'd gotten into that early), kimchi, eggs, black bean sauce for noodles. And of course, the rice cakes and fish cakes he made every day. It should have sustained them. And it could have.

If they'd only had enough fuel to cook with.

"I thought you said you had more propane," Ha-eun had said.

"I thought I did," Jun-seo had said. And that was that.

Naturally, all the convenience stores and other shops were out of the stuff by the time they ran out. Bizarrely, the shops were still open. They'd gone back to cash. Some places used barter—hot coffee was the new money. Wait times were murderously slow; no one knew how to total up a bill, any more, not to mention do percentages. Sales tax quickly became a distant memory.

"It's like when the currency was failing," Jun-seo said. "Remember that? When everyone turned in their gold?"

Ha-eun did remember. And Jun-seo was right: this was much the same. At least, the same in spirit. She had turned over her wedding band, back then. The damn thing had never done her much good, anyway, even when she still wore it. This time she had turned over all her food—what rice and eggs and kimchi she still had in the stall became the army's property, turned over the morning after she found Jun-seo in the snow. At least, she had turned them over in theory. What really happened was that she found a notice from the army on her stall, with an itemized list of what they'd "requisitioned," and a site she could access when the networks came back in order to obtain her reimbursement. She was to give them an estimate of monetary value. She wondered how much she could fudge it. Maybe if she claimed it was fancy organic stuff they'd taken. The list they left behind didn't include brand names.

"Come on," Jun-seo said, and they shuffled forward to close the gap ahead of them in line.

She had expected chaos, but it was all very . . . orderly. The army kept on talking about the pluck and industriousness of the Korean national spirit. They pasted broadsheets reminding people how to use weather radios, and the radio stations talked about how the worst was behind them and there was nothing to worry about, how systems would come back online as soon as possible, how people were at work 'round the clock. Trucks with loudspeakers trundled down the newly quiet roads, blaring messages about pulling together in the struggle, sharing hand sanitizers, wearing flu masks, and where the city warming stations were.

"We're lucky we're old," Ha-eun said. "They wouldn't let us in here, otherwise."

The warming stations were only for the very young or the very old. Ha-eun didn't like to think of herself as very old, but for the moment she was willing to let the army think of her that way. And it was still better than being one of the exhausted parents in line, trying to corral kids in snow pants who wouldn't quit demanding their old devices. *No, you can't play with those right now,* they kept saying. *No, I don't know when the network is coming back.*

Inside the warming station, they had ninety minutes. There was hot tea and instant noodles and tinned fish and whatever the army had managed to put together. The first day, all the restaurants gave up their supply. The second day, there was less to work with. The army had extra propane, and they could make do, but getting the supplies in without trains was a challenge. The Japanese had promised to send supplies. And the Americans, of course. The Red Cross. The Red Cross was supposed to be good at handling things without any computers or data streams. They'd done the same in worse places, where no one had handhelds or chips. With all the smart stickers and wearables dead, nobody had any sense of inventory or location any longer, of who needed what and where. The warming station did regular headcounts. Ha-eun had heard they were doing the same things at hospitals.

"It's like going back in time," Ha-eun said.

Jun-seo sipped at a cup of instant noodles. "I like it," he admitted. "It makes me feel younger."

"What were you like, back then?"

He shrugged. "Not so different."

"You liked castles?"

"I wanted to be an architect."

This fact fell under the "Things I Do Not Know About Jun-seo" category in Ha-eun's mind. It was odd, to work alongside someone for so long, and not know the simplest things about them. "What happened?" she asked.

"I got someone pregnant."

Ha-eun hissed in sympathy. Jun-seo snorted. They stared out at the children—babies, really—in the warming station. There were yoga mats and cots set up, and someone had thought to bring in old-fashioned toys and books, the kind that didn't need charging.

"Did you have kids?" Jun-seo asked.

Ha-eun shook her head. "I wouldn't be any good at it. It was the one thing my husband and I agreed on."

"You were married?"

"For about five minutes, once."

"We should get married," Jun-seo said.

Ha-eun coughed on her tea. It almost went out her nose. "*What?*"

"It would be easier," he said. "Legally. What if we get separated, in this situation? The government would have no idea who to contact. Or what if one of us is injured, or becomes ill? The other could be an advocate, in the hospital. Also I think that, when the business starts up again, we would get a better deal on cart space as a family. They prioritize family business licenses. We could move to a different corner, where there's more foot traffic. Maybe even one of the stations."

Ha-eun stared at him. "How long have you been thinking about this?"

He shrugged. "Oh, the last ten years. Give or take."

"And *now* you tell me?!"

The others in the warming station gave her a sharp look. In the absence of trains, train etiquette had taken over the shared spaces: one had to maintain an equal volume with one's neighbours, or risk deep disapproval. "*Now?*" she repeated.

"Why not now? I waited for you, in the snow. My head was telling me to leave, but my feet wouldn't let me move. And you came to me. You came right to me." He peered at her over the rising steam from his noodles. "So, Ha-eun, why not now?"

"Because . . ." She blinked. She stared out at all the families crowding around the space heaters, rubbing their arms. What if this didn't end? What if the systems never came back? Until this moment, she had not allowed herself to consider the possibility.

But here in this room bathed in orange emergency light, she had to face it. They were all running scared, like pheasants flushed from the undergrowth. What attack might come next? Was this just the first phase of something much worse?

"Nothing," she said. "Forget I said anything. I can't think of a reason, aside from maybe the fact that there isn't an office to grant us a licence. At least, not in the city."

"Then we'll have to go to the country," Jun-seo said. He slurped the last of his broth. "Some of the other families are leaving. I'll ask who has room for a couple of cooks."

The citadel of weeping pearls
ALIETTE DE BODARD

Here's another "Xuya" story by Aliette De Bodard, whose "Three Cups of Grief, By Starlight" appears elsewhere in this anthology. This one deals with an empire on the verge of being invaded by another empire, and the search for a fabled lost space station, where superweapons that might tip the balance were said to have been developed—but most of the Xuya stories are at their core about family, and "The Citadel of Weeping Pearls" is no exception, centering around an intricate web of dysfunctional family relationships that stretches across generations and includes family members who have been transformed into immensely powerful living spaceships, and the "ghosts" of long-dead family members who still interact (and squabble) with the living through memory implants that preserved their personalities and experience as past rulers (an experience that they're willing to share with present-day rulers, whether the present-day rulers want it or not). Add time travel, a skein of plots, counterplots, and betrayals, and spooky interaction with weird dimensions beyond the space we know, and you end up with the hugely entertaining novella that follows. . . .

THE OFFICER

There was a sound, on the edge of sleep: Suu Nuoc wasn't sure if it was a bell and a drum calling for enlightenment; or the tactics-master sounding the call to arms; in that breathless instant—hanging like a bead of blood from a sword's blade—that marked the boundary between the stylised life of the court and the confused, lawless fury of the battlefield.

"Book of Heaven, Book of Heaven."

The soft, reedy voice echoed under the dome of the ceiling; but the room itself had changed—receding, taking on the shape of the mindship—curved metal corridors with scrolling columns of memorial excerpts, the oily sheen of the Mind's presence spread over the watercolours of starscapes and the carved longevity character at the head of the bed—for a confused, terrible moment as Suu Nuoc woke up, he wasn't sure if he was still in his bedroom in the Purple Forbidden City on the First Planet, or hanging, weightless, in the void of space.

It wasn't a dream. It was the mindship: *The Turtle's Golden Claw*, the only one addressing Suu Nuoc with that peculiar form of his title, the one that the Empress had conferred on him half out of awe, half out of jest.

The Turtle's Golden Claw wasn't there in his bedroom, of course: she was a Mind, an artificial intelligence encased in the heartroom of a ship; and she was too heavy to leave orbit. But she was good at things; and one of them was hacking his comms, and using the communal network to project new surroundings over his bedroom.

"Ship," he whispered, the words tasting like grit on his tongue. His eyes felt glued together; his brain still fogged by sleep. "It's the Bi-Hour of the Tiger." People plotted or made love or slept the sleep of the just; they didn't wake up and found themselves dragged into an impossible conversation.

But then, of course, *The Turtle's Golden Claw* was technically part of the Imperial family: before her implantation in the ship that would become her body, the Mind had been borne by Thousand-Heart Ngoc Ha, the Empress's youngest daughter. *The Turtle's Golden Claw* was mostly sweet; but sometimes she could act with the same casual arrogance as the Empress.

"What is it this time?" Suu Nuoc asked.

The Turtle's Golden Claw's voice was thin and quivering; nothing like her usual, effortless arrogance. "She's not answering. I called her again and again, but she's not answering."

Ten thousand words bloomed into Suu Nuoc's mind; were sorted out as ruthlessly as he'd once sorted out battalions. "Who?" he said.

"Grandmother."

There were two people whom the mindship thought of as Grandmother; but if the Keeper of the Peace Empress had been dead, Suu Nuoc's quarters would have been in effervescence, the night servants barely containing their impatience at their master's lack of knowledge. "The Grand Master of Design Harmony?"

The lights flickered around him; the characters oozed like squeezed wounds. "She's not answering," the ship said, again; sounding more and more like the child she was with every passing moment. "She was here; and then she . . . faded away on the comms."

Suu Nuoc put out a command for the system to get in touch with Grand Master of Design Harmony Bach Cuc—wondering if that would work, with the shipmind hacked into his comms. But no; the progress of the call appeared overlaid on the bottom half of his field of vision, same as normal; except, of course, that no one picked up. Bach Cuc's last known location, according to the communal network, was in her laboratory near the Spire of Literary Eminence—where the radio comms towards *The Turtle's Golden Claw* would be clearest and most economical.

"Did you hack the rest of my comms?" he asked—even as he got up, pulling up clothes from his autumn chest, unfolding and discarding uniforms that seemed too formal; until he found his python tunic.

"You know I didn't." *The Turtle's Golden Claw's* voice was stiff.

"Had to ask," Suu Nuoc said. He pulled the tunic over his shoulders, stared at himself in the mirror by the four seasons chests: pale and dishevelled, his hair hastily pulled back into a topknot—but the tunic was embroidered with pythons, a mark of the Empress's special favour, bestowed on him after the battle at Four Stations: a clear message, for those who affected not to know who he was, that this jumped-up, uncouth soldier wielded authority by special dispensation.

The call was still ringing in the emptiness; he cut it with a wave of his hands. There was a clear, present problem; and in such situations he knew exactly what to do.

"Let's go," he said.

Grand Master Bach Cuc's laboratory was spread around a courtyard: at this late hour, only the ambient lights were on, throwing shadows on the pavement—bringing to mind the old colonist superstitions of fox shapeshifters and blood-sucking demons.

It was the dry season in the Forbidden Purple City, and Bach Cuc had set up installations on trestle tables in the courtyard—Suu Nuoc didn't remember what half the assemblages of wires and metal were, and didn't much care.

"Where was she when you saw her last?" he asked *The Turtle's Golden Claw*.

The ship couldn't descend from orbit around the First Planet, of course; she'd simply animated an avatar of herself. Most mindships chose something the size of a child or a Mind; *The Turtle's Golden Claw*'s avatar was as small as a clenched fist, but perfect, rendering in exquisite detail the contours of her hull, the protrusions of her thrusters—if Suu Nuoc had been inclined to squint, he was sure he'd have caught a glimpse of the orchids painted near the prow.

"Inside," *The Turtle's Golden Claw* said. "Tinkering with things." She sounded like she'd recovered; her voice was cool again, effortlessly taking on the accents and vocabulary of the court. She made Suu Nuoc feel like a fish out of water; but at least he wouldn't have to deal with a panicked, bewildered mindship—he was no mother, no master of wind and water, and would have had no idea what to do in this situation.

He followed the ship into one of the largest pavilions: the outside was lacquered wood, painstakingly recreated identical to Old Earth design, with thin metal tiles embossed with longevity symbols. The inside, however, was more modern, a mess of tables with instruments: the communal network a knot of virtual messages with cryptic reminders like "put more khi at G4" and "redo the connections, please," notes left by researchers to themselves and to each other.

He kept a wary eye on the room—two tables, loaded with instruments; a terminal, blinking forlornly in a corner; a faint smell he couldn't quite identify on the air: charred wood, with a tinge of a sharper, sweeter flavour, as if someone had burnt lime or longan fruit. No threat that he could see; but equally, a slow, spreading silence characteristic of hastily emptied room.

"Is anyone here?" Suu Nuoc asked—superfluous, really. The network would have told him if there were, but he was too used to battlefields, where one could not afford to rely on its presence or its integrity.

"She's not here," *The Turtle's Golden Claw* said, slowly, patiently; an adult to a child. As if he needed another patronising highborn of the court . . . But she was his charge; and so, technically, was Grand Master Bach Cuc, the Citadel project being under the watchful eye of the military. Even if he understood next to nothing about the science.

"I can see that." Suu Nuoc's eye was caught by the door at the farthest end of the room: the access to the shielded chamber, gaping wide open, the harmonisation arch showing up as de-activated on his network access. No one inside, then.

Except . . . he walked up to it and peered inside, careful to remain on the right side of the threshold. Harmonisation arches decontaminated, made sure the environment on the other side was sterile; and the cleansing of extraneous particles from every pore of his skin was an unpleasant process he would avoid if he could. There was nothing; and no one; no virtual notes or messages, just helpful prompts from the communal network, offering to tell him what the various machines in the chamber did—pointing him to Grand Master Bach Cuc's progress reports.

Not what he was interested in, currently.

He had another look around the room. *The Turtle's Golden Claw* had said Grand Master Bach Cuc had vanished mid-call. But there was nothing here that suggested anything beyond a normal night, the laboratory deserted because the researchers had gone to bed.

Except . . .

His gaze caught on the table by the harmonisation arch. There was an object there, but he couldn't tell what it was because Grand Master Bach Cuc had laid her seal on it, hiding it from the view of anyone who didn't have the proper access privileges—a private seal, one that wouldn't vanish even if the communal network was muted. Suu Nuoc walked towards it, hesitating. So far, he had done Bach Cuc the courtesy of not using his accesses as an Official of the First Rank; hadn't broken into her private notes or correspondences, as he would have been entitled to. Long Quan would have called him weak—behind his back when he wasn't listening, of course, his aide wasn't that foolish—but he knew better than to use his accesses unwisely. There were those at the court that hadn't forgiven him for rising so high, so quickly; without years of learning the classics to pass the examinations, years of toiling in some less prestigious job in the College of Brushes until the court recognised his merit. They called him the Empress's folly—never mind his successes as a general, the battle of Four Stations, the crushing of the rebel army at He Huong, the successful invasion of the Smoke People's territory: all they remembered was that he had once slept with the Empress, and been elevated to a rank far exceeding what was proper for a former (or current) favourite.

But *The Turtle's Golden Claw* wasn't flighty, or likely to panic over nothing. Suu Nuoc reached out, invoking his privileged access—the seal wavered and disappeared. Beneath it was . . .

He sucked in a deep breath—clarity filling his mind like a pane of ice, everything in the room sharpened to unbearable focus; the harmonisation arch limned with cold, crystalline light, as cutting as the edges of a scalpel.

The seal had hidden five pellets of metal; dropped casually into a porcelain bowl like discarded food, and still smelling, faintly, of anaesthetic and disinfectant.

Mem-Implants. Ancestor implants. The link between the living and the memories of their ancestors: the repository of ghost-personalities who would dispense advice and knowledge on everything from navigating court intrigues to providing suitable responses in discussions replete with literary allusions. Five of them; no wonder Grand Master Bach Cuc had always been so graceful, so effortless at showing the proper levels of address and languages whatever the situation.

To so casually discard such precious allies—no, you didn't leave those behind, not for any reason.

But why would an abductor leave these behind?

"She wouldn't remove—" *The Turtle's Golden Claw* said. Suu Nuoc lifted a hand to interrupt the obvious.

"I need to know where the Grand Master's research stood. Concisely." There wasn't much time, and evidence was vanishing as they spoke. The ship would know that, too.

The Turtle's Golden Claw didn't make the mocking comment he'd expected— the one about Suu Nuoc being Supervisor of Military Research and barely enough mathematics to operate an abacus. "You can access the logs of my last journeys into deep spaces," she said, slowly. "I brought back samples for her."

Travel logs. Suu Nuoc asked his own, ordinary implants to compile every note in the room by owner and chronological order.

"Did Grand Master Bach Cuc know where the Citadel was?" he asked. That was, after all, what those travels were meant to achieve: *The Turtle's Golden Claw*, Bach Cuc's masterpiece, diving into the farthest deep spaces, seeking traces of something that had vanished many years ago, in a time when Suu Nuoc was still a dream in his parents' minds.

The Citadel of Weeping Pearls—and, with it, its founder and ruler, the Empress's eldest and favourite daughter, Bright Princess Ngoc Minh.

The Citadel had been Ngoc Minh's refuge, her domain away from the court after her last, disastrous quarrel with her mother and her flight from the First Planet. Until the Empress, weary of her daughter's defiance, had sent the Imperial Armies to destroy it—and the Citadel vanished in a single night with all souls onboard, never to reappear.

"There were . . . trace elements from orbitals and ships," *The Turtle's Golden Claw* said, slowly, cautiously; he had the feeling she was translating into a language he could understand—was it mindship stuff, or merely scientific language? "Images and memories of dresses; and porcelain dishes . . ." The ship paused, hovering before the harmonisation arch. "Everything as fresh as if they'd been made yesterday."

"I understood that much," Suu Nuoc said, wryly. He didn't know what arguments Grand Master Bach Cuc had used to sway the Empress; but Bach Cuc's theory about deep spaces was well known—about the farthest corners, where time flowed at different rate and folded back onto itself, so that the past was but a handspan away—so that the Citadel, which had vanished without a trace thirty years ago, could be found in the vastness of space.

If you were a mindship, of course; humans couldn't go in that deep and hope to survive.

"Then you'll understand why she was excited," *The Turtle's Golden Claw* said.

"Yes." He could imagine it—Grand Master Bach Cuc would have been cautious, the ship ecstatic. "She thought you were close."

"No," *The Turtle's Golden Claw* said. "You don't understand, Book of Heaven. There were a few analyses to run before she could pinpoint a—a location I could latch on. But she thought she had the trail. That I could plunge back into deep spaces, and follow it to wherever the Citadel was hiding itself. She thought she could find Bright Princess Ngoc Minh and her people."

Suu Nuoc was silent, then, staring at the harmonisation arch.

He wasn't privy to the thoughts of the Empress anymore; he didn't know why she wanted Bright Princess Ngoc Minh back.

Some said she was getting soft, and regretted quarrelling with her daughter. Some said she wanted the weapons that Bright Princess Ngoc Minh had designed, the technologies that had enabled the citadel to effortlessly evade every Outsider or Dai Viet battalion sent to apprehend her. And still others thought that the Empress's long life was finally running to an end, and that she wanted Ngoc Minh to be her heir, over the dozen daughters and sons within the Purple Forbidden City.

Suu Nuoc had heard all of those rumours. In truth, he didn't much care: the Empress's will was absolute, and it wasn't his place to question it. But he had listened in enough shuttles and pavilions; and his spies had reported enough gossip from poetry club competitions and celebratory banquets, to know that not everyone welcomed the prospect of the princess's return.

Bright Princess Ngoc Minh had been blunt, and unpleasant; and many had not forgiven her for disregarding her mother's orders and marrying a minor station-born; and still others didn't much care about her, but thought she would disrupt court life—and thus threaten the privileges they'd gained from attending one or another of the princes and princesses. One was not meant, of course, to gainsay the Empress's orders; but there were other ways to disobey . . .

"Book of Heaven?"

Suu Nuoc swallowed past the bile in his throat. "We must report this to the Empress. Now."

THE ENGINEER

Diem Huong had been six when the Citadel of Weeping Pearls had vanished. Her last, and most vivid memory of it was of standing on the decks of one of the ships—Attained Serenity, or perhaps Pine Ermitage—gazing out at the stars. Mother held her hand; around them, various inhabitants flickered in and out of existence, teleporting from one to another of the ships that made up the city. Everything was bathed in the same cold, crisp air of the Citadel—a feeling that invigorated the bones and sharpened the breath in one's lungs until it could have cut through diamonds.

"It still stands," Mother said, to her neighbour: a tall, corpulent man dressed in robes of indigo, embroidered with cranes in flight. "The Bright Princess will protect us, to the end. I have faith . . ."

Diem Huong was trying to see the stars better—standing on tiptoe with her arms leaning on the bay window, twisting so that the ships of the Citadel moved out of her way. Thuy had told her that, if you could line things up right, you had a view all the way to the black hole near the Thirtieth Planet. A real black hole—she kind of hoped she'd see ships sucked into it, though Thuy had always been a liar.

The man said something Diem Huong didn't remember; Mother answered something equally unintelligible, though she sounded worried. Then she caught sight of what Diem Huong was doing. "Child, no! Don't shame me by behaving like a little savage."

It had been thirty years, and she didn't know—not anymore—which parts of it were true, and which parts she had embellished. Had she only imagined the worry in Mother's voice? Certainly there had been no worry when she and Father had boarded the ship back to the Scattered Pearls orbitals—enjoy your holiday, Mother had said, smiling and hugging them as if nothing were wrong. I will join you soon.

But she never had.

On the following morning, as they docked into the Central orbital of the Scattered Pearls, the news came via mindship: that the Citadel had vanished in a single night with all its citizens, and was nowhere to be found. The Empire's invading army—the soldiers tasked by the Empress to burn the Citadel to cinders—had reached the designated coordinates, and found nothing but the void between the stars.

Not a trace of anyone aboard—not Mother, not the Bright Princess, not the hermits—everyone gone as though they had never existed.

As time went on, and the hopes of finding the Citadel dwindled, the memory wavered and faded; but in Diem Huong's dreams, the scene went on. In her confused, fearful dreams, she knew every word of the conversation Mother had had; and every single conversation she had ever listened to—playing with her doll Em Be Be on the floor while Mother cooked in her compartment, with the smell of garlic and fish sauce rising all around them, an anchor to the childhood she had lost. In her dreams, she knew why Mother had chosen to abandon them.

But then she would wake up, her heart in her throat, and remember that she was still alone. That Father was never there; drowning his sorrows in his work aboard a merchant ship, coming home from months-long missions stupefied on fatigue, sorghum liquor, and Heaven knew what illegal drugs. That she had no brother or sister; and that even her aunts would not understand how crushingly alone and frightened she was, in the darkness of her cradle bed, with no kind words to banish the nightmares.

After a while, she started adding her own offerings to the ancestral altar, below the hologram of Mother, that treacherous image that would never change, never age; her tacit admission that Mother might not be dead, but that she was as lost to them as if she had been.

But that didn't matter, because she had another way to find the answers she needed.

Thirty years after the Citadel disappeared, Diem Huong woke up with the absolute knowledge that today was the day—and that, whatever she did, the trajectory of her life would be irrevocably altered. This time, it would work: after Heaven knew how many setbacks and broken parts. She wasn't sure where that certainty came from— certainly not from her trust in a prototype made by a handful of half-baked engineers and a disorganised genius scientist in their spare time—but it was within her, cold and unshakeable. Perhaps it was merely her conviction that she would succeed: that the machine would work, sending her where she needed to be. *When* she needed to be.

She did her morning exercises, flowing from one Piece of Brocade to the next, effortlessly—focusing on her breath, inhaling, exhaling as her body moved through Separating Heaven and Earth to Wise Owl Gazing Backwards; and finally settling on her toes after the last exercises, with the familiar, energised feeling of sweat on her body.

They didn't have a lab, of course. They were just private citizens with a hobby, and all they'd managed to get hold of on the overcrowded orbital was a deserted teahouse, cluttered with unused tables and decorative scrolls. Lam, always practical, had used some of the celadon drinking cups to hold samples; and the porcelain dishes with painted figures had turned out to withstand heat and acid quite nicely.

The teahouse was deserted: not a surprise, as most of the others were late risers. In the oven—repurposed from the kitchen—she found the last of the machine's pieces, the ceramic completely hardened, the bots scuttling onto the surface to check it withdrew as she reached for it. The etching of circuits was perfect, a silvery network as intricate as woven silk.

Diem Huong turned, for a moment, to look at the machine.

It wasn't much to look at: a rectangular, man-sized frame propped with four protruding metal struts, reminiscent of a high-caste palanquin with its all-but-obsolete bearers. They had used tables and chairs to get the materials; and some of the carvings could still be seen around the frame.

It had a roof, but no walls; mostly for structural reasons: all that mattered was the frame—the rods, cooled below freezing temperature, served as anchors for the generated fields. A lot of it was beyond her: she was a bots-handler, a maker and engraver of circuits on metal and ceramic, but she wasn't the one to design or master the machine. That was Lam—the only scientist among them, the holder of an Imperial degree from the prestigious College of Brushes, equally at ease with the Classics of Mathematics as she was with the Classics of Literature. Lam had been set for a grand career, before she gave it all up and came home to take care of her sick father—to a small, insignificant station on the edge of nowhere where science was just another way to fix failing appliances.

The machine, naturally, had been a welcome challenge to her. Lam had pored over articles from everywhere in the Empire; used her old networks of scientists in post in various branches of the Imperial Administration, from those designing war mindships to the ones on far-flung planets, tinkering with bots to help the local magistrate with the rice harvest. And, somehow, between all their late-night sessions with too much rice wine and fried soft crabs, between all their early-morning rushes with noodle soup heavy and warm in their bellies, they had built this.

Diem Huong's fingers closed on the piece. Like the previous one, it was smooth: the etchings barely perceptible, the surface cold. Would it be unlike the previous one, and hold the charge?

She knelt by the machine's side, finding by memory and touch the empty slot, and gently slid the piece into its rack. She could have relied on the bots to do it—and they would have been more accurate than her, to a fraction of measure—but some things shouldn't be left to bots.

Then she withdrew, connected to the room's network, and switched the machine on.

A warm red light like the lanterns of New Year's Eve filled the room as the machine started its warm-up cycle. She should have waited, she knew—for Lam and the others, so they could see what they had laboured for—it wasn't fair to them, to start things without their knowledge. But she needed to check whether the piece worked—after all, no point in making a ceremony of it if the piece snapped like the previous one, or if something else went wrong—as it had done, countless times before.

Put like that, it almost sounded reasonable. But, in her heart of hearts, Diem Huong knew this wasn't about tests, or being sure. It was simply that she had to see the machine work; to be sure that her vision would come to fruition.

The others wouldn't have understood: to them, the Citadel of Weeping Pearls was an object of curiosity, the machine a technical challenge that relieved the crushing boredom of mining the asteroid fields. To Diem Huong, it was her only path to salvation.

Mother had gone on ahead, Ancestors only knew where. So there was no way forward. But, somewhere in the starlit hours of the past—somewhere in the days when the Citadel still existed, and Bright Princess Ngoc Minh's quarrel with the Empress was still fresh and raw—Mother was still alive.

There was a way *back*.

The temperature in the room plummeted. Ice formed on the rods, became slick and iridescent, covered with a sheen like oil—and a feel like that of deep spaces permeated the room, a growing feeling of wrongness, of pressures in odd places the body wasn't meant to have. The air within the box seemed to change—nothing obvious, but it shimmered and danced as if in a heat wave, and the harmonisation arch slowly revved up to full capacity, its edges becoming a hard blue.

"Up early?"

Lam. Here? Startled, Diem Huong turned around, and saw her friend leaning against the door, with a sarcastic smile.

"I was—" she said.

Lam shook her head. Her smile faded; became something else—sadness and understanding, mingled in a way that made Diem Huong want to curl up in a ball. "You don't need to explain."

But she did. "I have to—"

"Of course you do." Lam's voice was soft. She walked into the laboratory; stopped, looking at the machine with a critical frown. "Mmm."

"It's not working?" Diem Huong asked, her heart in her throat.

"I don't know," Lam said. "Let me remind you no one's tried this before."

"I thought that was the point. You said everyone was wrong."

"Not in so many words, no." Lam knelt by the rods, started to reach out a hand; and changed her mind. "I merely said some approaches had no chance of working. It has to do with the nature of deep spaces."

"The mindships' deep spaces?"

"They don't belong to the mindships," Lam said, absent-mindedly—the role of teacher came to her naturally, and after all, who was Diem Huong to blame her? Lam had built all of this; she deserved a little showing off. "The ships merely . . . cross them to get elsewhere? Space gets weird within deep spaces, that's why you get to places earlier than you should be allowed to. And where space gets weird, time gets weird too."

She called up a control screen: out of deference to Diem Huong, she displayed it rather than merely keeping it on her implants. Her hand moved in an ever-quickening dance, sliding one cursor after the other, moving one dial after the next—a ballet of shifting colours and displays that she seemed to navigate as fast as she breathed, as utterly focused and at ease as Diem Huong was with her morning exercises.

Then she paused; and left the screen hanging in the air, filled with the red of New Year's lanterns. "Heaven help me. I think it's working."

Working. Emperor in Heaven, it was working. Lam's words—she knew what she was talking about—made it all real. "You think—" She hardly dared to imagine. She would see the Citadel of Weeping Pearls again—would talk to Mother again, know why she and Father had been abandoned . . .

Lam walked closer to the harmonisation arch, frowning. Without warning, she uncoiled, as fluid as a fighter, and threw something she held in her hand. It passed through the door—a small, elongated shape like a pebble—arched on its descent downwards; and faded as it did so, until a translucent shadow settled on the floor—and dwindled away to nothing.

On the display screen, a cursor slid all the way to the left. Diem Huong looked at Lam, questioningly. "It's gone back? In time?"

Lam peered at the display, and frowned again. "Looks like it. I entered the time you gave me, about ten days before the Citadel vanished. " She didn't sound convinced. Diem Huong didn't blame her. It was a mad, unrealistic adventure—but then, the Citadel had been a mad adventure in the first place, in so many ways, a rebellion of Bright Princess Ngoc Minh and her followers against the staidness of court life.

A mad, unrealistic adventure—until it had vanished.

Lam walked back to the display. Slowly, gently, she slid the cursor back to the right. At first, Diem Huong thought nothing had happened; but then, gradually, she saw a shadow; and then a translucent mass; and then the inkstone that Lam had thrown became visible again on the floor of the machine, as sharp and as clearly defined as though it had never left. "At least it's come back," Lam said. She sounded relieved. "But . . ."

Back. So there was a chance she would survive this. And if she didn't—then she'd be there, where it mattered. She'd have her answers—or would, once and for all, stop feeling the shadow of unsaid words hanging over her.

Diem Huong moved, as though through thick tar—the gestures she had been steeling herself to make since this morning.

"Lil'sis?" Lam asked, behind her. "You can't—"

Diem Huong knew what Lam would say: that they weren't sure. That the machine was half-built, barely tested, barely run through its paces. For all she knew, that door opened into a black hole; or in the right time, but into a vacuum where she couldn't breathe, or on the edge of a lava field so hot her lungs would burst into cinders. That they could find someone, or pay someone—or even use animals, though that would be as bad as humans, really, other living souls. "You know how it is," Diem Huong said. The door before her shimmered blue; and there was a wind on her face, a touch of cold like a bristles of a brush made of ice.

Answers. An end to her nightmares and the fears of her confused dreams.

"I've known, yes," Lam said, slowly. Her hands moved; her arms encircled Diem Huong's chest. "But that's no reason. Come back, lil'sis. We'll make sure it's safe, before you go haring off into Heaven knows what."

There was still a chance. Diem Huong could still turn back—if she did turn back, she would see Lam's eyes, brimming with tears—would read the folly of what she was about to do.

"I know it's not safe," Diem Huong said; and, gently disengaging herself from Lam's arms, stepped forward—into a cold deeper than the void of space.

THE EMPRESS

Mi Hiep had been up since the Bi-Hour of the Ox—as old age settled into her bones, she found that she needed less and less sleep.

In these days of strife in the Empire, sleep was a luxury she couldn't afford to have.

She would receive the envoys of the Nam Federation at the Bi-Hour of the Horse, which left her plenty of time to discuss the current situation with her advisors.

Lady Linh pulled a map of the nearby star system, and carefully highlighted a patch at the edge of Dai Viet space. "The Nam Federation is gathering fleets," she said.

"How long until they can reach us?" Mi Hiep asked.

Lady Linh shook her head. "I don't know. The Ministry of War wasn't able to ascertain the range of their engines."

Mi Hiep looked at the fleet. If they'd been normal outsider ships, it would have taken them months or years to make their way inwards—past the first defences and straight to the heart of the Empire. If they'd been normal outsider ships, she would have deployed a mindship in their midst, moving with the deadly grace of primed weapons; a single pinpoint strike that would have crippled any of them in a heartbeat. But those were new ships, with the La Hoa drive; and her spies' reports suggested they could equal or surpass any mindships she might field.

"What do you think?" Mi Hiep asked, to her ancestors.

Around her, holograms flickered to life: emperors and empresses in old-fashioned court dresses, from the five-panels after the Exodus to the more elaborate, baroque style of clothing made possible by the accuracy of bots.

The First Ancestor, the Righteously Martial Emperor—hoary, wizened without the benefit of rejuv treatments, was the one who spoke. "This much is clear, child: they're not here to be friends with you."

The Ninth Ancestor, the Friend of Reform Emperor—named after an Old Earth emperor who had died in exile—frowned as he studied the map. "Assuming they can move through deep spaces"—he frowned at the map—"I suspect their target is the Imperial Shipyards."

"It makes sense," Lady Linh said, slowly, carefully. She looked older than any of the Emperors around her—and the Twenty-Third Emperor, who stood by her side, had once imprisoned her for treason. Mi Hiep knew well that none of them made her comfortable. "It would enable them to capture mindships—"

"Who wouldn't serve them," Mi Hiep said, more sharply than she'd intended. "They would still remember their families."

"Yes," Lady Linh said, weighing every word. She looked at Mi Hiep, a little uncertainly: an expression Mi Hiep recognised as reluctance. It had to be something serious, then; Lady Linh had never been shy about her opinions—indeed, a misplaced memorial had been the cause of her thirty-year imprisonment.

"Go on," Mi Hiep said, inclining her head. She braced herself for the worst.

Lady Linh reached out to the screen. There was a brief lag while her implants synchronised with it—a brief flowering of colour, the red seal of an agent of the Embroidered Guard clearly visible; and then something else appeared on the screen.

It was a mindship—looking almost ordinary, innocuous at first sight. There was an odd protuberance on the hull, near the head; and a few more scattered here and there, like pustules. Then the ship started moving, and it became clear something was very, very wrong with it. No deadly grace, no ageless elegance; but the zigzagging, tottering course of a drunkard, curves that turned into unexpectedly sharp lines, movements that started closing back on themselves.

What had they done? Oh Ancestors, what had they done?

"It's a hijack," Lady Linh said, curtly. "Plug in a few modules at key points, and you can influence what the ship sees and thinks. Then it's just a matter of . . . fine manipulation."

There was silence, for a while. Then a snort from the First Emperor—who had taken the reign name Righteously Martial after ascending to the throne over the ruins of his rivals. "That doesn't look like fine movements to me. If that's all they have against us . . ."

"That," Lady Linh said, gently, almost apologetically, "is almost a full year old. We've had reports that the technology has evolved, but no pictures or vids. It has been harder and harder to get Embroidered Guard undercover. The Nam Federation are suspicious."

Suspicious. Mi Hiep massaged her forehead. Vast movements of troops. A technology to turn their own mindships against them. The Imperial Shipyards. It didn't take a Master of Wind and Water to know which way things lay.

"I see," she said. The envoys of the Nam Federation were not due for another two hours, but she already knew what they would say. They would make pretty excuses, and tell her about military manoeuvres and the necessity to maintain the peace on their fractious borders. And she would smile and nod, and not believe a word of it.

The Ninth Emperor turned, a ghostly shape against the metal panelling. "Someone is coming," he said.

The Sixteenth Empress raised her head, like a hound sniffing the wind. "Suu Nuoc. The child is in a hurry. He is arguing with the guards at the entrance. You had left orders not to be disturbed?"

"Yes," Mi Hiep said, disguising a sigh. None of the ancestors liked Suu Nuoc—it wasn't clear if they thought he had been an inappropriate lover for an empress, or if they resented his lower-class origins. Mi Hiep was no fool: she had not promoted her former lover to the Board of Military Affairs. She had promoted a smart, resourceful man with utter loyalty to her, and that was what mattered. The ancestors could talk and talk and disapprove, but she was since long inured to being shamed by a mere look or stern talking-to.

Sometimes, she wondered what it would be like, to be truly alone—not to be the last descendant of a line of twenty-four emperors and empresses, her ancestors embodied into simulations so detailed they needed an entire wing of the palace to run. Sacrilege, of course; and the ancestors were useful, but still . . .

Of course, in truth, she was lonely all the time.

"Let him in," she sent to her bodyguards.

Suu Nuoc came in, out of breath; followed by the small, fist-sized avatar of *The Turtle's Golden Claw*. He took one quick glance around the room; and slowly lowered himself to the floor, his head touching the slats of the parquet.

"Your Highnesses," he said. The Emperors and Empresses frowned, the temperature in the room lowered by their disapproval. "Empress."

"General." Mi Hiep gestured at him to rise, but he remained where he was, his gaze stubbornly fixed on the floor. "Something bad?" she asked. The disapproval of the ancestors turned to her—her choice of words too familiar for a relationship between Empress and general.

Lady Linh used the commotion caused by Suu Nuoc's arrival to slowly and discreetly slide out of the room—correctly judging Mi Hiep's desire to be alone; or as alone as one could be, with twenty-four ancestors in her thoughts.

Suu Nuoc was in the mindset she'd jokingly called "the arrow"—clear and focused, with little time for propriety or respect. "Grand Master Bach Cuc has disappeared," he said. "The ship here says she had found the trail of the Citadel."

Oh.

"Close the door," Mi Hiep said to the guards outside. She waited for them to comply, and then turned her vision back into the room. She, too, was deadly focused, instantly aware of every single implication of his words. "You mean she would have found my daughter." She didn't need to name Bright Princess Ngoc Minh; that much was obvious. "And her Citadel."

Suu Nuoc was still staring at the floor—all she could see of him was an impeccably manicured topknot, with not a grey hair in sight. How young he was; thirty-five full years younger than her at least—even younger than Ngoc Minh. A lover to remind her of life and youth, which she'd lost such a long time ago; a caprice, to sleep with someone who was not one of her concubins—one of the few impulses she could allow herself.

"Did she leave out of her own volition?" Mi Hiep asked.

Suu Nuoc said nothing for a while. "I—don't think so. The timing is convenient. Too convenient."

"Then you think someone abducted her. Who?" Mi Hiep asked.

"I don't know," Suu Nuoc said. "I judged it pertinent to inform you ahead of every other consideration." She probably didn't imagine the faint sarcasm in his voice—he had never been one for common courtesies. Without her support, he would not have risen far at court.

"I see." There were many reasons people disapproved of Grand Master Bach Cuc and *The Turtle's Golden Claw*—thinking it unnatural that Bach Cuc should create a mindship who was part of the Imperial Family; fearing the return of Bright Princess Ngoc Minh and what it would mean to court life; even disapproving of her policy of war against the Nam Federation. Some advocated passionately for peace as the only way to survival.

She didn't begrudge them their opinion; the court would think as it desired, in a multiplicity of cliques and alliances that kept the scholars busy at each other's throats. But acting against Grand Master Bach Cuc . . .

"You will find her," she said to Suu Nuoc. "Her, or her corpse. And punish whoever has done this."

Suu Nuoc bowed, and left the room. *The Turtle's Golden Claw* didn't; it hovered closer, and said, in a calm and dispassionate voice, "Grandmother."

Mi Hiep nodded, noting with a sharp pang of perverse pleasure the discomfort of the gathered Ancestors at this acknowledgement of their relationship. "You are sure of what you told the General Who Read the Book of Heaven?"

The ship bobbed from side to side, thoughtfully. "Bach Cuc sounded confident enough. And she usually—"

Never sounded confident until it actually would work. Grand Master Bach Cuc had been cautious, unlikely to give in to fancies or announce results ahead of time solely to please her or the Board of Military Affairs. Everything she valued in a research scientist. "I see," Mi Hiep said. And, more softly, "How are you?"

Bach Cuc had been her Grand Master of Design Harmony, after all, the other grandmother *The Turtle's Golden Claw* could count on—the only family that would accept her and trust her. Mi Hiep's other children had not been so welcoming; and even Thousand-Heart Princess Ngoc Ha, who had carried *The Turtle's Golden Claw* in her womb, was not affectionate.

"I will be fine," *The Turtle's Golden Claw* said, slowly, carefully. "She is alive, isn't she?"

Mi Hiep could have lied. She could have nodded with the same conviction she'd bring into her interview with the envoys of the Nam Federation; but it wouldn't have been fair, or kind, to her granddaughter. "I hope she is."

"I see," *The Turtle's Golden Claw* said, stiffly. "I will help Book of Heaven in his investigations, then."

"It will be fine," Mi Hiep said—she only had an avatar, nothing she could hold or kiss for reassurance. Mindships were machines and blood and flesh; and they felt things as keenly as humans. "We will find her."

"Thank you, Grandmother."

Mi Hiep watched the ship go—she moved as smoothly as ever, but of course with an avatar it was difficult to determine what she truly felt, wasn't it? How worried or hurt or screaming she could be, inside?

She thought again of the picture Lady Linh had presented; the crippled ship tricked into believing lies: hijacked, Lady Linh had said. Blinded until their only purpose was to serve their new masters—and she felt a fresh stab of anger at this. This wasn't the way to treat anyone, whether human or mindship.

But, if she couldn't halt the progress of the Nam Federation, this would happen. They would take ships and twist them into emotionless tools with forced loyalties.

They needed weapons: not merely war mindships, but something more potent, more advanced; something to strike fear into their enemies' hearts and dissuade them from ever entering Dai Viet space.

They needed Ngoc Minh's weapons—and Grand Master Bach Cuc and *The Turtle's Golden Claw* had been meant to find them for her.

The Citadel of Weeping Pearls had gone down in history as a refuge of peace; as a place that taught its denizens the serenity that came from not fearing anything—not bandits, or corrupt officials, or apathetic scholars. But such things—the serenity, the lack of fear—did not happen unless one had powerful means of defences.

Mi Hiep remembered visiting Ngoc Minh in her room, once—not yet the Bright Princess, but merely a gangly girl on the cusp of adulthood, always in discussion with a group of hermits she'd found on Heaven knew what forsaken planet or station. Her daughter had looked up from her conversation, and smiled at her: a smile that she'd always wonder about later, about whether it was loving or forced, fearful or genuinely serene. "You haven't come to your lessons," Mi Hiep had said.

"No," Ngoc Minh had said. "I was learning things here."

Mi Hiep had turned a jaded eye on the horde of hermits—all of them lying prostrate in obedience. As if obedience could make them respectable—their dresses varied from torn robes to rags, and some of them were so withdrawn from public life they were all but invisible on the communal network, with no information beyond their planet of birth showing up on her implants. "You will be Empress of Dai Viet one day, daughter; not an itinerant monk. The Grand Secretary's lessons are on statecraft and the rituals that keep us all safe."

"We are safe, Mother. Look." Ngoc Minh took a vase from a lacquered table: a beautiful piece of celadon with a network of cracks like a fragile eggshell. She pressed something to it—a lump that was no bigger than a grain of rice—and gestured to one of the monks, who bowed and took it out into the adjoining courtyard.

What in Heaven?

"This is pointless," Mi Hiep said. "You will go to your lessons now, child." She used the sternest voice of authority she could think of, the one she'd reserved for her children as toddlers, and for sentencing prisoners to death.

Ngoc Minh's face was serene. "Look, Mother." She was looking at the vase, too, frowning; some Buddhist meditation exercise, focusing her will on it or something similar—not that Mi Hiep had anything against Buddhism, but its philosophy of peace and acceptance was not what an Emperor needed. The Empire needed to fight every day for its survival; and an Emperor needed to choose the hard answers, rather than the most serene ones.

"If you think I have time for your nonsense—"

And then the vase winked out of existence.

There was no other word for it. It seemed to fracture along the seams of the cracks first, even as a soft radiance flowed from within it, as if it had held the pure, bottled light of late afternoon—but then the pieces themselves fractured and fractured into ever-smaller pieces, until nothing but a faint, colourless dust filled the courtyard; a dust that a rising wind carried upwards, into the empty space between the pagoda spires.

That was . . . Mi Hiep looked again at the courtyard: still empty and desolate, with the dust still rising in a fine, almost invisible whirlwind. "That's impossible," she said, sharply.

Ngoc Minh smiled; serene and utterly frightening. "Everything is possible, if you listen to the right people."

Looking back, that was when she'd started to be scared of her daughter. Scared of what she might do; of what she was thinking, which was clearly so different of what moved Mi Hiep. When Ngoc Minh had married her commoner wife, they'd fallen out; but the root of this last, explosive quarrel lay much earlier, in that tranquil afternoon scene where her small, quiet world bounded by ritual and habit had been utterly shattered.

She'd been a scared fool. Ngoc Minh had been right: anything that could safeguard the Empire in its hour of need was a boon. What did it matter where it came from?

It was time for war—and, if anyone had dared to harm her Grand Master of Design Harmony, they would feel the full weight of her fury.

THE YOUNGER SISTER

Thousand-Heart Princess Ngoc Ha found Suu Nuoc and her daughter *The Turtle's Golden Claw* in the laboratory, at the tail end of what looked to be a long and gruelling series of interviews with everyone who had worked with Grand Master Bach Cuc. By his look, the Supervisor of Military Research was not having a good day.

Suu Nuoc acknowledged her with a brief nod. He was in one of his moods where he would eschew ritual in favour of efficiency, a frequent source of complaints and memorials against him. Normally, Ngoc Ha would have forced him to provide proper respect: she knew the importance of appearances, and the need to remind people of her place, as an Imperial Princess who was not the heir and only had honorary positions. But today, she needed to see something else.

The laboratory had been cleanly swept. The only virtual notes attached to objects were the ones with the seal of the army, officially warning people of the penalty attached to tinkering with an ongoing investigation. The shielded chamber with its harmonisation arch was swarming with bots, supervised in a bored fashion by an old technician with a withered hand. Ngoc Ha walked closer to the arch, but saw nothing that spoke to her.

"Mother!"

Of course, it was inevitable that *The Turtle's Golden Claw* would see her; and churlish of her, really, to ignore the ship. "Hello, daughter."

She knew she was being irrational when she saw the ship and didn't feel an ounce of maternal love—merely a faint sense of repulsion, a memory of Mother overwhelming her objections to the implantation of the Mind in her; the scared, sick feeling she'd had during most of the pregnancy; and the sense of exhausted dread when she realised that having delivered the Mind merely meant she was now the mother, stuck in that role until the day she died.

And, if she was honest with herself, it wasn't the pregnancy, or motherhood; or even the Mind that was the issue—it was that, seeing *The Turtle's Golden Claw*, she remembered, once again, that everything in her life had been twisted out of shape for her elder sister's benefit. Thirty years since Ngoc Minh had disappeared; and still she haunted Ngoc Ha's life. Even the name bestowed on Ngoc Ha by the court—the Thousand-Heart—was not entirely hers: she was named that way because she'd been filial and dutiful, unlike Ngoc Minh; because she had set up proper spousal quarters and regularly slept with her concubines—even though none of them brought her much comfort; or alleviated the taste of ashes that had been in her mouth for thirty years.

"I'm sorry about Grand Master Bach Cuc," Ngoc Ha said to *The Turtle's Golden Claw*. "I'm sure General Suu Nuoc will find her. He's good at what he does."

"I'm sure he is," the ship said. Her avatar turned, taking in the laboratory. "Mother . . ."

Ngoc Ha braced herself—surely that sick feeling of panic in her belly wasn't what one was meant to feel, when one's child came to them with problems? "Yes, child?"

"I'm scared." *The Turtle's Golden Claw's* voice was barely audible. "This is too large. How could she disappear like that—with no warning, in the heart of the Purple Forbidden City?"

Meaning inside influence. Meaning court intrigues; the same ones she'd stepped away from after Ngoc Minh's disappearance. "I don't know," Ngoc Ha said. "But not everyone wanted Ngoc Minh to come back." Including her. She was glad to be rid of her sister the Bright Princess; to never have to be compared to her again; to never look at her and realise they had so little in common—not even Mother's love. But she wasn't the only one. Lady Linh was loyal to Mother; but the rest of the scholars weren't, not so much. Huu Tam, Mother's choice of heir, was dutiful and wise: not wild, not incomprehensibly attractive like Bright Princess Ngoc Minh; but safe. "Not everyone likes their little worlds overturned."

"What about you?" the ship asked, with simple and devastating perspicacity.

"I don't know," Ngoc Ha lied. She didn't know what she'd do, if she saw Ngoc Minh again—embrace her, shout at her—show her how much her life had twisted and stretched in the wake of her elder sister's flight?

"Princess," Suu Nuoc said. He stood by her, at quiet ease. "My apologies. I was busy."

"I can imagine," Ngoc Ha said.

"I'm surprised to see you here," Suu Nuoc said, slowly. "I thought you had no interest in what Grand Master Bach Cuc was doing."

"*The Turtle's Golden Claw* is my daughter," Ngoc Ha said.

"Of course," Suu Nuoc said. He watched her, for a while, with that intent expression on his face that made her feel pierced by a spear. "But that's not why you're here, is it?"

Ngoc Ha said nothing for a while. She watched the harmonisation arch, the faint blue light playing on its edges. "I did follow what Bach Cuc was doing," she said, at last. It had taken an effort: Grand Master Bach Cuc was proud, and sometimes unpleasant. "Because it mattered. To me, to my place in court." It wasn't quite that, of course. She'd needed to know—whether Ngoc Minh would come back. Whether it had been worth it, the agony of being pregnant with *The Turtle's Golden Claw*; of giving birth in blood and pain and loneliness, all because her mother the Empress had ordered it.

"How did you think things would change?"

"I don't know," Ngoc Ha said. He was assessing her, wondering what she was worth as a suspect. It would have been amusing, if she hadn't been so nervous already. "I wanted to know what you'd found, but I assume you won't share it while you're still working out if I harmed her."

"Indeed," Suu Nuoc said. He made a small, ironic smile, and turned to embrace the lab. "Or perhaps I simply have nothing to share."

Ngoc Ha steeled herself—better to tell him now than later, or else she'd become a suspect like everyone else. And she knew better than to expect Mother's influence to protect her.

After all, it hadn't worked for Ngoc Minh.

"I know who saw Grand Master Bach Cuc last," she said, slowly, carefully. "Or close to last."

There was silence, in the wake of her words.

"Who?" Suu Nuoc asked, at the same time as *The Turtle's Golden Claw* asked "Why?"

Ngoc Ha smiled, coldly; putting all the weight of the freezing disapproval she sometimes trained on courtiers. "As I said—I was interested. In whether Ngoc Minh would come back. Someone came to me with information on the Citadel of Weeping Pearls."

Suu Nuoc's face had frozen into a harsh cast, as unyielding as cut diamonds. "Go on."

"He was a man named Quoc Quang, part of a small merchant delegation that was doing a run between the Scattered Pearls belt and the First Planet." She'd had her agents check him out: a small, pathetic man addicted to alcohol and a few less savoury things: hardly a threat, and hardly worth bringing to her attention, as the chief of her escort had said. Except that he'd said something about Grand Master Bach Cuc.

Ngoc Ha had her work administering the Twenty-Third Planet—trying to bring Lady Linh's home back to the glory it had had, before the war, building graceful pagodas and orbitals from a pile of ashes and dust. But it was mostly a sinecure to keep her busy; and so, curious, she had made time to see Quoc Quang.

"He said his daughter was doing something to find the Citadel of Weeping Pearls—her and a woman named Tran Thi Long Lam, a Distinguished Scholar of Mathematics who returned home to mind her sick father. Apparently they thought they could do better than Grand Master Bach Cuc. He said"—she closed her eyes— "he needed to speak to Bach Cuc, to warn her."

"Warn her of what?"

"He wouldn't tell me."

Suu Nuoc's impeccably trimmed eyebrows rose. Ngoc Ha went on as though she'd seen nothing—after all, it was only the truth, and demons take the man if he didn't believe it. "And you believed him?" Suu Nuoc asked.

If Ngoc Ha closed her eyes, she could see Quoc Quang; could still smell the raw despair from him; could still hear his voice. "My wife disappeared with the Citadel. We were away, thirty years ago, when it happened. I apologise for my presumption; but I share your pain." And she hadn't been quite sure what to answer him; had let the emotionless, hardened mask of the imperial princess stare at him and nod, in a way that conveyed acceptance, and a modicum of disapproval. But, in her mind, she'd heard the dark, twisted part of her whisper: *what pain? You were glad Ngoc Minh disappeared.*

"He was very convincing," she said.

"So you sent him to Grand Master Bach Cuc," *The Turtle's Golden Claw* said. "And then . . . Bach Cuc disappeared."

Ngoc Ha shook her head, irritated at the implications. "Credit me with a little thoughtfulness, General. I sent guards with him; and though he had his interview with Bach Cuc without me, they watched him all the while, and escorted him back to his quarters in the Fifth District. The interview ended at the Bi-Hour of the Dog; Grand Master Bach Cuc was still within the Forbidden City long after that."

"It was the Bi-Hour of the Tiger," *The Turtle's Golden Claw* said. "Eight hours after that, at least."

"Right," Suu Nuoc said, in a way that suggested he didn't believe any of her intentions, or her words—he could be so terribly, so inadequately blunt some times. "And where is this—Quoc Quang now?"

She had checked, before coming. "He left this morning, with his ship. The destination he announced was his home on the Scattered Pearls belt. I have no reason to disbelieve that."

"Except that he left in rather a hurry after Bach Cuc disappeared?"

Ngoc Ha did her best not to bristle; but it was hard. "I checked. There was no extra passenger on board. Apart from him, nothing was taken onboard; not even a live woman or a corpse. The airport bots would have seen it otherwise." She felt more than heard *The Turtle's Golden Claw* tense. "Sorry. I had to consider all eventualities."

"That's all right," *The Turtle's Golden Claw* said. "I'm sure she's alive. She's resourceful."

Suu Nuoc and Ngoc Ha exchanged a long, deep look; he was as sceptical as her, but he wouldn't say anything. *For her sake*, she mouthed, and Suu Nuoc nodded.

"Fine." Suu Nuoc was silent, for a while. He stared at the harmonisation door, his face hard again; his gaze distant, probably considering something on the network via his implants. He had no mem-implants from ancestors—but then, Ngoc Ha, the unfavoured daughter of the family, had none either. "I will check, and let you know."

"I see," Ngoc Ha said. And, to the ship, "Will you come with me to my quarters? We can have tea together."

"Of course!" *The Turtle's Golden Claw* said—happy to spend an afternoon with her mother, a rare occurrence for her. Once again, Ngoc Ha fought a wave of shame. She should be more present in the ship's life; should see her through her tumultuous childhood into adulthood—surely, it wasn't easy for her either, to have been born only for the purpose of finding someone else.

"Thank you for your evidence. You will be apprised, one way or another."

And she wasn't sure, as she walked away with the ship in tow, if she ought to be relieved or scared, or both.

THE OFFICER

Suu Nuoc found the entrance to his chamber crowded with officials; and his mailbox overflowing with a variety of memorials from the court—from those chastising him for his carefree behaviour; to short messages asking for the results of his investigation. They were all so fresh from the Grand Secretarial office that he could still see the marks of the rescripts—it was bad, then, if even he could see it: the court had to be in disarray; the Grand Secretariat overwhelmed.

"General, general." A chorus of voices; but the ones that stood out belonged to Vinh and Hanh, two of the heir Huu Tam's supporters. "What happened to Grand Master Bach Cuc?"

"Are we safe?"

"How soon will we know?"

He closed his eyes, and wished, again, for the serenity that had come over him on the edge of the battlefield. It wasn't his world. It would never be his world—except that being a general was sleepless, dirty nights in the field with ten thousand bots hacked into his feeds, sending him contradictory information and expecting a split-second decision—and a pay that came too slight and too late to make any difference to his family's life. Whereas, as a court official, he could shower his relatives with clothes and food, and jewellery so beautifully fragile it seemed a mere breath would cut it in half.

And he could see the Empress—and hide the twinge of regret that took him whenever he did so; that deep-seated knowledge that no lover he'd had since her had ever filled the void she'd left.

It wouldn't last, of course. It couldn't last. The Empress was old, and the heir Huu Tam had no liking for her discards. Suu Nuoc would go home in disgrace one day, if he was lucky; or rot away in a jail somewhere if he was not. He lived with that fear; as he'd lived with the fear of losing his battles when he'd been a general. Most days, it didn't affect him. Most days, he could sleep quietly in his bed and reflect on a duty carried to its end.

And sometimes, he would look at these—at the arrogant courtiers before him, and remember they would be among the ones baying for his head after the Empress died.

"You have no business infringing on an imperial investigation," Suu Nuoc said. "The Empress, may she reign ten thousand years, is the one who will decide who is told what, and when."

Winces, from the front of the mob—Courtier Hanh was clearly sniggering at this upstart who could not even speak proper Viet; and her companion Vinh was working himself up for a peremptory answer. Meanwhile, in the background of Suu Nuoc's own consciousness—in the space where he hung motionless, connected to a thousand bots crawling all over the palace, a churning of activities—a taking apart of messages and private notes, an analysis of witnesses' testimonies, and a forensic report on the state of the laboratory.

Later.

He watched the courtiers Vinh and Hanh; dared them to speak. As he had known, they did not have his patience; and it was the florid, middle-aged man who spoke first. "There are rumours that Grand Master Bach Cuc is dead; and Bright Princess Ngoc Minh forever lost."

"Perhaps," Suu Nuoc said, with a shrug; and watched the ripples of that through the crowd. Neither Vinh nor Hanh seemed much surprised; though they could not have sweated more if it had been monsoon season. "That is none of my business. I will find Grand Master Bach Cuc; and then all will be made clear."

Again, he watched them—there was no further reaction, but the air was charged, as if just before a storm. Ngoc Minh's return was not welcome, then. Not a surprise. "I suggest you disperse. As I said—you will be apprised, one way or another."

Quick, furtive glances at him; he remembered he'd said much the same thing to Ngoc Ha—had he meant it with her as well? She was an odd one, the younger princess—mousy and silent, by all accounts a dull reflection of her elder sister. They might not have liked each other; but then again, would Bright Princess Ngoc Minh's return change anything for the worse to her situation? Ngoc Ha was isolated and in disfavour; and her prospects were unlikely to improve.

"You have heard the general. I would highly suggest you do disperse." A sharp, aged voice: Lady Linh, with a red seal of office imprinted into her clothes that made it clear she spoke as the Empress's voice; and flanked by two ghost-emperors—the Twenty-Third and the Thirteenth, if Suu Nuoc remembered correctly. The bots scuttling around her held the folds of her robe in a perfect circle.

Lady Linh gestured for him to enter his own room. "We need to talk," she said, gracefully.

Inside, the two dead emperors prowled, staring at the rumpled bed and the half-closed chests of drawers as if they were some kind of personal insult. Suu Nuoc did his best to ignore them as he offered tea to Lady Linh; but from time to time one of them would make a sharp sound in his throat, like a mother disapproving of a child's antics, and he would freeze, his heart beating like the wings of a caged bird.

Not his world. Did they know about his relatives—his cousins and aunts and uncles, greedily asking for favours from the court and never understanding why he couldn't grant them? Did they know about Mother, the poor bots-handler who held her chopsticks close to the tip and slurped her soup like a labourer?

Of course they did. And of course they would never forgive him that.

"Tell me," Lady Linh said. She shook her clothes; in the communal network, the seal unfolded, spreading until it covered the entire room—a red filigree peeking underneath the painted floor, its edges licking at the base of the walls like flames. Bao Hoa. Keeper of the Peace.

Not so different from the battlefield, after all. Suu Nuoc shut off the bots for a moment, and called to mind all that they'd poured into his brain on the way back from Grand Master Bach Cuc's laboratory.

"She removed the implants herself," he said, finally. "It might have been under duress, all the same—for someone who was skilled with bots, it's a shoddy job—bits of flesh still sticking to the connectors, and a few wires twisted. Nothing irreplaceable, of course. If I were to guess—"

"Yes?"

"I think she was about to do something that needed absolute focus, and that's why the implants were removed. No distractions." No ancestors whispering in her mind; no ghostly manifestations of the past—he could only imagine it, of course; but it would be a bit like removing all his network syncs before leaping into battle.

"Go on," Lady Linh said, sipping her tea.

"Her correspondence is also interesting. The mails taper off: I think she was so busy with her work, so close to a breakthrough, that she wasn't answering as quickly as usual. I asked, but nothing seemed to be going on in her personal life—she had a girlfriend and a baby, but the girlfriend didn't see anything wrong."

"The girlfriend?" Lady Linh asked.

Suu Nuoc knew what she meant. The partner was often the first suspect. "I don't think so," he said. He'd interviewed her—Cam Tu, a technician in a city lab, working so far away from court intrigues she hadn't even had any idea of who he was or what he wanted. "She wasn't in that night, nor was she aware of any of the context behind Grand Master Bach Cuc's research." It was—sad, in a way, to see this hunched woman with the child at her breast, and realise that Bach Cuc had deliberately shut her out of her life. But then again, he barely talked about the court when he did go home, so who was he to criticise? "Whatever happened to her, it was linked to the court."

"You talked of a breakthrough. The trail of the Citadel?"

"I think so, yes," Suu Nuoc said, slowly. "But that's not all." Something felt off to him; and he couldn't pinpoint what. "I'm still analysing the communications." It was the one thing the bots couldn't do for him; and he wasn't too sure he would be able to do it by himself either—where were the mem-implant ancestors when one needed them? A lot of it was abstruse mathematics; communications with other scientists in faraway labs, discussing methods and best practises, and screen after screen of equations until it felt his brain would burst. He was a soldier; a general; a passable courtier, but certainly never a mathematician. "There is . . . something," he said. He hesitated—looking at the two emperors, who had stopped walking around the room, and come to stand, like two bodyguards, by Lady Linh's side. "I'm not sure—"

Lady Linh set her teacup down, and looked at him for a while, her seamed face inexpressive. "I was forty years old when I wrote my memorial," she said, with a nod to the Twenty-Third Emperor. "The one that sent me to trial. I've never regretted speaking up, Suu Nuoc; and you don't strike me as the type that would regret it, either." Her voice had lost the courtly accent; taken on the earthy tones of the outlying planets—he couldn't quite place it, but of course there were dozens of numbered planets, each of them with a multitude of provinces and magistrate fiefs.

The Twenty-Third Emperor spoke—still in the body of an adolescent, his youthful face at odds with the measured voice, the reasonable tone. "Speaking up is sometimes unwise," he said, with a pointed look at Lady Linh. "But one should always tell the truth to Emperors or their representatives."

"Indeed," Lady Linh's face was, again, expressionless. A truth that had sent her to jail for years; but that wasn't what Suu Nuoc feared.

He looked again at her, at the two emperors. Someone at court might be responsible for Grand Master Bach Cuc's disappearance; and they wouldn't take too kindly to efforts to make her reappear. Who could he trust?

It was a sacrilegious thought, but he wasn't even sure he could trust the dead emperors. But, because he would not disobey a direct order, or the intimation of one: "A man came to see Grand Master Bach Cuc. A merchant from the Scattered Pearls belt named Quoc Quang, who said he needed to warn her."

"Warn her? Why should he need to warn her? A peasant from the outreaches of the empire, to see the best Grand Master of Design Harmony in the Empire?" The Twenty-Third Emperor asked.

"I don't know," Suu Nuoc said. "But he did see her; and she disappeared after that. And then he disappeared, too. With your permission, I would like to go to the

Scattered Pearls belt and question him." He'd thought long and hard about this: the Belt was a few days' journey from the First Planet via mindship; and, should he leave now, he wouldn't be far behind Quoc Quang.

"You assume he will return home," Lady Linh said.

"I see no indication he won't," Suu Nuoc said. His intuition—and he'd had time to learn when to trust his intuition—was that Quoc Quang was a witness, not a killer. He'd left plenty of time before Grand Master Bach Cuc disappeared; and the analysis of Bach Cuc's mem-implants showed, beyond a shadow of a doubt, that she'd removed them hours after her meeting with him. But whatever he'd said to her—it had struck home, because he had a record of her pacing the laboratory for half an hour after Quoc Quang had left, the only video he could grab from the feeds. After that, Bach Cuc herself had turned everything off.

Absolute focus. What had she been doing—or been forced into doing?

"I see," Lady Linh said. "You could send the Embroidered Guard to arrest him."

"Yes," Suu Nuoc said. "I could. But I'm not sure he would arrive here alive." Fast, and blunt, like a gut punch. He saw the other Emperor, the Thirteenth, wince, his boy's face twisted and rippling like a face underwater.

"Court intrigues?" Lady Linh said, with a slight smile—Heaven only knew how many intrigues she'd weathered. On whose side did she stand? Not the Emperors, that was for sure—she was loyal to the Empress, perhaps, seeking only the return of Bright Princess Ngoc Minh; and yet, if Ngoc Minh did come back, her small, comfortable world where she was once more esteemed and listened to might vanish . . .

Lady Linh's eyes unfocused, slightly; and the red seal on the floor blinked, slowly, like the eye of some monster. "The Empress is informed. She agrees with your assessment. You will take *The Turtle's Golden Claw* to the Scattered Pearls belt, and interrogate this . . . Quoc Quang." Lady Linh's tone was slightly acerbic, and slightly too resonant: clearly she was still in contact with the Empress. "You will also take Thousand-Heart Princess Ngoc Ha with you."

What? Suu Nuoc fought the first imprecation that came to his lips. He didn't need a courtier with him; no, worse than a courtier, a princess who might have direct interest in burying her sister for good. *You can't possibly—* He took a deep, shaking breath. "Respectfully—"

"You disagree." Lady Linh's face was the Empress's serene, otherworldly mask, the one she wore when passing judgment; the same one she'd probably worn when exiling Bright Princess Ngoc Minh—though he hadn't been there to see it, of course, and he wouldn't have dared to ask her about those events. He was—had been—the lover of an Empress—pleasant, good in bed—but in no way a close confidante or a friend. He'd smiled, and never admitted how much it hurt to do so. "That is not a possibility, I'm afraid, general."

The Thirteenth Emperor leant over the table, his hand going through the teapot. "You will need someone versed in court intrigues." He'd been eight when he'd died; a boy, crowned by the ruling officials because they needed someone malleable and innocent. But in the implants he sounded older and wiser than both of them.

"I don't know where Ngoc Ha stands," Suu Nuoc said, stiffly.

"The Thousand-Heart Princess stands exactly where I need her, as I need her," Lady Linh said, except it was neither her voice, nor her expression.

Suu Nuoc bowed to the face of his Empress. "Of course, Empress. As you desire."

THE ENGINEER

When she'd stepped through the harmonisation arch, Diem Huong had expected to die. In spite of what Lam had said—that the door did indeed open into the past—it could have led to so many places, an inhabitable planet, the middle of the vacuum, the deadly pressured heart of a star . . .

Instead, she'd found herself in a wide, open corridor, with the low, warm light typical of space habitats—and the same, sharp familiar tang of recycled air in her nostrils. She turned, and saw the outline of the arch in the wall behind her, half-hidden beneath the scrolling calligraphy of Old Earth characters, spelling out words and poems she could not read.

So there was a way back, at least. Or something that looked like one.

The corridor was deserted and silent; she reached out, cautiously, for the wall, and felt the surface slightly give way to her; the text flowing around her outstretched hand, and then back again once she withdrew her hand. She was here, then; for real. Wherever this was, or whenever—but she remembered the smell, that faint memory of sandalwood and incense that was always home to her; and that sense of something large and ponderous always hovering in the background, that feeling of calm before words of condemnation or praise were uttered.

The citadel.

At last.

Mother . . .

She was back; standing in what would become the memories of her childhood home, and she didn't know what to feel anymore—if she should weep or shout or leap for joy. She simply stood, breathing it all in; savouring that feeling—for a moment, she was a child again, running down the corridors with Thuy and Hanh, re-programming the kitchen's bots to manufacture fireworks they could set off in the little park; secure in the knowledge that she'd find Mother in the kitchen, her hands smelling of garlic and lime and fish sauce, and there would be rice on the table and broth boiling away on the stove, clinging to her hands and clothes like perfumed smoke.

A moment only; but in so many ways, she was no longer a child. She had lived six years on the Citadel in blissful ignorance; but ignorance was no longer bliss.

She needed to find Mother.

In the alcove by her side was a little altar to gods, with fruit and sticks of burning incense; she reached out and touched it, feeling the stickiness on her hands; the smell clinging to her clothes—whispering a prayer to whoever might be listening. Her touch set the mangos slightly askew, and she did not dare touch them again: superstition, but who knew what might help her, in this strange place that was neither now nor then?

Lam had given her a speech, once, about going back in time; about paradoxes and the fact she wouldn't be able to affect anything; but Diem Huong hadn't been paying enough attention. She wished she had. She wished she knew what would happen, if she met herself; if she harmed Mother, one way or another.

There was a stack of eight incense sticks by the altar: on impulse, she lit one, and kept one with her, for good luck. As she did so the screen above the altar came alive, asking her what she wanted—as if it had seen her, recognised her as a citizen, even though she didn't have the implants that would have enabled such a thing. She felt a thrill run through her, even as she told the screen to go dark.

The Citadel.

She wanted to run, to leap or scream—to rush to where Mother would be, to talk to her before it all vanished, before whatever miracle had brought her here vanished, before Lam somehow found a way to bring her back, before she died. She forced herself to stop; to hold herself still, as if Mother were still standing with her, one hand steadying her shoulder, her body very still besides her, absorbing all her eagerness to move. She needed . . .

She needed to think.

As she walked out of the corridor and onto a large plaza, she saw people giving her odd looks—she wore the wrong clothes, or walked the wrong way. As long as she didn't stop for long, it wouldn't matter. But, eventually . . .

Diem Huong closed her eyes. Once, thirty years ago, Mother had had her memorise the address and network contact for the house, in case she got lost. She'd had so many addresses and contacts since then; but this was the first and most treasured one she'd learnt.

Compartment 206, Eastern Quadrant, The Jade Pool. And a string of numbers and symbols that, input into any comms system, would call home.

The network implants she'd had as a child had been removed, six months after the Citadel vanished, when Father finally decided there was no coming back—when he started the long slow slide into drinking himself to death. She'd been too young to be taught by the hermits, and couldn't teleport or weaponise her thoughts, the way the others did.

She would need to ask someone for help.

The thought was enough to turn her legs to jelly. She wanted to keep her head down—she didn't need to be noticed as a time traveller or a vagrant, or whatever they'd make of her.

To calm herself down, she walked farther. The plaza was flanked by a training centre: citizens in black robes went through their exercises—the Eight Pieces of Brocade, the same ones she still did every morning—under the watchful eyes of a yellow-robed Order member. At the farthest end, an old woman was staring at sand; eventually the sand would blow up, as if there had been a small explosion; and then she'd stare at some other patch.

Who to ask? Someone who would take her seriously, but who wouldn't report her. So not the Order member, or the trainees. The noodle seller on the side, watching negligently as her bots spun dough into body-length noodles, and dropped them into soup bowls filled with greens and meat? The storyteller, who was using his swarm of bots to project the shadows of a dragon and a princess on the walls?

Something was wrong.

Diem Huong looked around her. Nothing seemed to have changed: the noodle seller was still churning out bowl after bowl; the same crowd of people with multiple body mods was walking by, idly staring at the trainees.

Something—

She opened her hand. The incense stick she'd taken was no longer in it—no, that wasn't quite accurate. It had left a faint trace: a ghost image of itself, that was vanishing even as she stared at it, until nothing was left—as if she'd never taken it from the altar at all.

That was impossible. She ran her fingers on her hand, over and over again. No stick. Not even the smell of it on her skin. And something else, too: her hands had been sticky from touching the ripe mangoes on the altar, but now that, too, was gone.

As if she'd never touched it at all.

No.

That wasn't possible.

She ran, then. Heedless of the disapproving stares that followed her, she pelted back to the deserted corridor she'd arrived in—back to that small altar where she'd lit an incense stick and disturbed the fruit.

All the while, she could hear Lam's lecture in her mind—spacetime projections, presence matrices, a jumble of words bleeding into each other until they were all but incomprehensible—it had been late, and Diem Huong had been on her fiftieth adjustment to a piece's circuits—waiting by the side of the oven for her pattern to set in, absent-mindedly nibbling on a rice cake as a substitute for dinner. She hadn't meant to shut Lam out, but she'd thought she could ask again—that there would be another opportunity to listen to that particular lecture.

The altar was there. But other things weren't: the incense stick she'd lit had disappeared, and the fruit were back to the configuration she'd originally found them in. Her heart madly beating against her chest, she turned to the stack of incense sticks. Eight. Not seven, or even six. Eight, exactly the number she had found.

Bots could have done it, she supposed—could have brought back the missing sticks and straightened out the altar, for some incomprehensible reason—but bots couldn't remove a stick from her hands, or wash the mangoes' sugar from her skin. No, that wasn't it.

Her heart in her throat, she turned towards the space in the wall, to see the imprint of the arch.

But that, too, was gone, vanished as though it had never been.

You won't affect anything. That's the beauty of it. No paradoxes. Don't worry about killing yourself or your mother. Can't be done.

Later, much later, after Diem Huong had walked the length and breadth of the ship she was on (*The Tiger in the Banyan's Hollow*, one of the smaller, peripheral ones that composed the citadel), she measured the full import of Lam's words.

She was there, but not there. The things she took went back to where she had taken them; the food she tasted remained in her stomach for a few moments before it, too, faded away. She wasn't starving, though; wasn't growing faint from hunger or thirst—it was as if nothing affected her. In her conversations with people, their eyes would start to glaze after anything more simple than a question—forgetting that she stood there at all, that she had ever been there. She could speak again, and receive only a puzzled look—and then only puzzled words as the conversation started over again, with no memory of what had been said before. If she made no effort to be noticed—if she did not run or scream or make herself stand out from the crowd in any way, people's gazes would pause on her for a split second, and then move on to something else.

You won't affect anything, Lam had said, but that wasn't true. She could affect things—she just couldn't make them stick. It was as if the universe was wound like some coiled spring, and no matter how hard she pulled, it would always return to its position of equilibrium. The bigger the change she made, the more slowly it would be erased—she broke a vase on one of the altars, and it took two hours for the shards to knit themselves together again—but erasure always happened.

She moved plates and vases; turned on screens and ambient moods; and saw everything moving back into place, everything turning itself off, and people dismissing it as nothing more than a glitch.

At length, she sat down on the steps before the training centre, and stared at nothing for a while. She was there, and not there—how long would she even be in the Citadel? How long before the universe righted itself, and she was pulled back—into Lam's laboratory, or into some other nothingness? She stared at her own hands, wondering if they were turning more ghostly; if her whole being was vanishing?

Focus. She needed to. Focus. She looked at the screens: time had passed from morning to later afternoon, and the light of the ship was already dimming to the golden glow before sunset. Ten days before the Citadel vanished—nine and a half, now. And if she was still onboard . . .

If it was all for nothing, she might as well try to get the answers she'd come here for.

She got up, and went to one of the monks in the training centre: she picked one that was not teaching any students, and simply seemed to be sitting in a bench in the centre of the gardens, though not meditating either: simply relaxing after a hard day's work. "Yes, daughter?" he asked, looking at her. His eyes narrowed; wondering what she was doing there—she stood out in so many painful ways.

She had perhaps a handful of moments before he started forgetting that she was there. "I was wondering if you could help me. I need to get to *The Jade Pool.*" *Compartment 206, Eastern Quadrant.*

"You need to get elsewhere. Like the militia's offices," the monk said. He was still watching her, eyes narrowed. "You're not a citizen. How did you steal onboard?"

"Please," she said.

His eyes moved away from her; focused again, with the same shocked suspicion of the first look. "How can I help you, daughter?"

"I need to get to *The Jade Pool,*" Diem Huong said. "Please. I'm lost."

"That's not a matter for me. I need to report this to the Embroidered Guard."

She felt a spike of fear; and then remembered that no one would remember the report minutes after he had made it. "You don't need to do this." But his eyes, again, had moved away. It was useless. "Thank you," she said.

She walked away from him, feeling his eyes on the back of her head; and then, as time passed, the gaze lessen in intensity; and he looked right past her, not remembering who she was or that he had talked to her.

A ghost. Worse than a ghost—a presence everyone forgot as soon as she left their life. A stranger in her own childhood, fighting against the spring of the universe snapping back into place. How was she ever going to get to Mother?

Lam. Help me. But it was useless. Her friend couldn't hear her. No one could.

Unless—

She wasn't really here, was she? She walked and took things like anyone else; except nothing stuck. She didn't have the implants everyone had; the ones that enabled them to teleport from one end of the Citadel to another; but she didn't really have any presence here, and yet she could still move things for a while; could still make screens respond to her.

Mother had talked about teleportation; and so had Father, in his cups or on the long nights when he railed against the unfairness of the world. It had been a matter of state of mind, they'd both said—of being one with the mindships that composed the Citadel; to see the world in their terms until everything seemed to be connected; until the world itself was but a footstep away. And of implants; but perhaps it wasn't about implants after all. Perhaps the rules of the past were different from those of the present.

Compartment 206, Eastern Quadrant. The Jade Pool.

Diem Huong closed her eyes, and concentrated.

THE EMPRESS

Mi Hiep prepared for her audience with the envoys of the Nam Federation as if she were preparing for war. Her attendants gave her the dress habitually reserved for receiving foreign envoys: a yellow robe with five-clawed dragons wending their ways across her body; a headdress bedecked with jewels. For the occasion, she had the alchemists alter her body chemistry to grow the fingernails of her two smallest fingers on each hand to three times their usual size, encasing them into long, gold protectors that turned her fingers into claws.

Huu Tam, her heir, waited by her side, decked in the robe with the five-clawed dragons that denoted his position. He looked nervous—she'd had him leave his usual mob of supporters at the door, and she knew it would make him feel vulnerable, a small child scolded for wrongdoing. Good, because he needed vulnerability; needed to be off-balance and question himself, to negate his tendency to be so sure of himself he didn't stop to consider what was best for the Empire. "Mother," he said, slowly, as Mi Hiep dismissed the attendants. "I'm not sure—"

"We've been over this," Mi Hiep said. "Do you think peace is worth any sacrifice?"

"We can't fight a war," Huu Tam said. He grimaced, looking for a moment much older than he was.

"No," Mi Hiep said. "And I'll do my best to see we don't. But we might have to, nevertheless."

Huu Tam nodded, slowly. He didn't like war; an occupation unworthy of a scholar. But he'd never been faced with decisions like these—wasn't the one who'd looked into Ngoc Minh's face, and sent ships towards the Citadel of the Bright Princess with the order to raze it—wasn't the one who'd lain down on his bed afterwards, waiting for the sound of his heartbeat to become inaudible again, for the pain against her ribs to vanish into nothingness.

He was her heir. He had to learn; and better early on, while she was still flesh-and-blood and not some disembodied, loveless ancestor on the data banks.

Mi Hiep sat on her throne, and waited—muting the communal network, as it would be a distraction more than anything else. She didn't need to see the banners above her head to know her full name and titles; and neither did she need access to her implants to remember everything Lady Linh and her advisors had told her.

The envoys would deny everything; dance and smile and pretend nothing was wrong. She, in turn, would have to make it clear that she was ready for war; and hint that she was not without resources, in the hopes the Nam Federation would seek easier prey.

Huu Tam moved, to stand on her left; and she summoned, with a gesture, all of her ancestors' simulations, from the First Emperor to her mother, the Twenty-Fourth Empress: her chain of uninterrupted wisdom, all the way since the beginning of the dynasty, her living link to the past. Her true ancestors might well be dead, spun by the Wheel of Rebirth into other lives, but their words and personalities lived on, preserved with the same care Old Earthers had preserved poems and books.

They stood, on either side of her, as the envoys approached.

It was a small delegation: a florid, rotund woman flanked by a pinch-faced man and another, more relaxed one who reminded Mi Hiep of the hermits that had once attended Bright Princess Ngoc Minh. They both knelt on the floor until Mi Hiep gave them permission to rise: they remained on their knees, facing her; though there was nothing servile or fearful in their attitude. They looked around the lacquered pillars of the hall, at the proverbs engraved on the floor; and the ex-quisite constructs of the communal network—and their eyes were those of tigers among the sheep.

The woman's name was Diem Vy; after the exchanges of pleasantries and of ritual gifts, she spoke without waiting for Mi Hiep to invite her to do so. "We are pleased that you have accepted to receive us, Empress. I understand that you have expressed some . . . concerns about our exercises."

Interesting. Mi Hiep expected dancing around the evidence, but Vy clearly did not care for this. Two could play this game. "Indeed," Mi Hiep said, wryly. "Massive movements of ships entirely too close to my borders tend to have this effect."

Vy's face crinkled in a smile—a pleasant, joyful one. Mi Hiep didn't trust her one measure. "Military exercises happen at borders," she said. "Generally, doing them near the capital tends to make citizens nervous."

"Fair point," Mi Hiep said. "Then this is nothing more than the norm?"

Vy did not answer. It was the other envoy, the serene-faced hermit—a man named Thich An Son, who answered. "A federation such as ours must always be ready to defend itself, Empress; and our neighbours have had . . . troubling activities."

"Not us," Mi Hiep said. If they were determined to be this transparent, she would not obfuscate. "We have no interest, at this time, in cryptic military games." Let them make of that what they willed.

Thich An Son smiled. "Of course not, Empress. We know we can trust you."

As if anyone here believed that, or the reverse. Mi Hiep returned the smile. "Of course. We will honour the treaties. We trust that you will do the same." And then, slowly, carefully, "I have heard . . . rumours, though."

Vy froze. "Rumours?"

Mi Hiep gestured to Lady Linh, who handed her a ghostly image of a folder stamped with the seal of the Embroidered Guard: a gesture merely for show, as she knew the contents of said folder by heart, and had no need to materialise it in the communal network. "Troubling things," she said, coldly, as if she already knew it all. "Ships that look like distorted versions of mindships."

"Copying designs is not a crime," Vy said, a touch more heatedly than the occasion warranted.

"Indeed, not," Mi Hiep said. "If that is all there is to it." She opened the folder in network space, making sure that it was as theatrical as possible—letting them see blurred images of ships and planets seen in every wavelength from radio to gamma rays.

"I assure you, Empress, you have no reason to be afraid," Vy said, sounding uncommonly nervous.

"Good," Mi Hiep said. "We are not, as you know, without resources. Or without weapons. We have, indeed, made much progress on that front, recently."

"I see," the hermit delegate Thich An Son said, his serene face almost—but not quite—undisturbed. The interview had not gone quite as planned. Good. "If I may be so bold, Empress?"

"Go ahead," Mi Hiep said.

"On an unrelated matter . . . there are rumours that you might be . . ." He paused, seemingly to pick his words with care—but really more for show than for anything else. ". . . considering changes at court?"

Reconsidering your choice of heir. Locating Bright Princess Ngoc Minh and her errant weapons. Mi Hiep glanced at Huu Tam, knowing everyone would do the same. Her son still stood by her side; with no change in his expression. He believed his sister dead for many years, and the lack of a body, or the recent search, had not changed his mind. At least, Mi Hiep hoped it hadn't; hoped he wasn't the one responsible for Grand Master Bach Cuc's disappearance. Whatever happened, his position at court was secure; and he knew it.

But, nevertheless, she had to make her point. She'd known she might have to do this beforehand; and had prepared both herself and Huu Tam for this moment.

"I believe there will be changes at court," Mi Hiep said, coldly. "Though if you're referring to my choice of heir, I see no reason to alter it."

The envoys looked at each other. "I see," Thich An Son said. "Thank you for the audience, Empress. We will not trouble you any further."

After they had left, Lady Linh approached the throne, and bowed. "It's bad, isn't it?" she said, without preamble.

Mi Hiep did not have the heart to chide her for the breach of protocol, though she could see a few of the more hidebound Emperors frown and make a visible effort not to speak up to censure either her or Lady Linh. "You said you didn't know about how far their fleet was."

"Yes," Lady Linh said.

"It's close," Mi Hiep said, trying to loosen the fist of ice that seemed to have closed around her stomach. Close enough that they would send these envoys—not the ones that would lie and prevaricate better, not the ones that would buy time. The Nam Federation had seen no reason to do so; and that meant they expected to make an imminent attack.

"You gave them something to think about," the Twenty-Fourth Empress said. Every time she spoke up, Mi Hiep's heart broke a little—it was her mother as a younger woman, but the simulation had preserved none of what had made her alive—simply collated her advice and her drive to preserve the empire into a personality the alchemists had thought would be useful—never thinking that the child who would became empress would need love and affection and all the support that could not be boiled down to appropriate words. It was one thing to know this for the old ones, the ones she'd never known; but for her own mother. . . . "They think you have the Bright Princess's weapons, or something close."

"But we don't," Huu Tam said. "Her Citadel and weapons died with her."

Mi Hiep said nothing for a while. "Perhaps."

"Ngoc Minh has been dead thirty years, Mother," Huu Tam's voice was gentle but firm. "If she could, don't you think she would have sent you a message? Even when she was in rebellion against the throne she sent you communications."

She had; and in all of them she was bright and feverish; with that inner fire Mi Hiep so desperately wanted to harness for the Empire; and couldn't.

Ngoc Minh, the Bright Princess, who only had to stare at things to make them detonate—her little tricks with vases and sand had expanded to less savoury things; to people who moved through space as though it were water, who would implant trackers and bombs on ship hulls as easily as if they'd been bots; to substances that could eat at anything faster than the strongest acid; and to teleportation, the hallmark of the Citadel's inhabitants. It had given Mi Hiep cold sweats, thirty years ago—the thought of an assassin materialising in her bedchambers, walking through walls and bodyguards as though they'd never been here . . .

But now she desperately needed those weapons; or even a fraction of them. Now the Empire was at risk, and she couldn't afford to turn anything down, not even her errant daughter.

"Has there been any word from Suu Nuoc?" she asked.

Lady Linh shook her head. "Some of your supporters are getting quite vocal against him," she said to Huu Tam.

He looked affronted. "I'm not responsible for what they choose to say."

Lady Linh grimaced, but said nothing. Mi Hiep had no such compunction. "They follow your cues," she said to Huu Tam. And Huu Tam didn't like Suu Nuoc— he never had. She didn't know if it was because of Suu Nuoc's bluntness; or because he had once been her lover and thus close in a way Huu Tam himself never had been.

"No accusations yet," the First Emperor said. "But a couple strongly worded memorials making their way upwards to the Grand Secretariat." He looked at Huu Tam with a frown. "Your mother is right. It is your responsibility to inspire your followers by your behaviour—" it was said in a way that very clearly implied said behaviour had not been above reproach, and Huu Tam visibly bristled—"or, failing that, reining them in with your authority."

"Fine, fine," Huu Tam said, sullenly. "But it's all nonsense, and you know it, Mother. It's not delusions that will help us. We need to focus on what matters."

"Military research and intelligence?" Mi Hiep asked. "That is also happening, child. Don't underestimate me."

"Never," Huu Tam said; and she didn't like the look in his eyes. He was . . . fragile in a way that none of her other children were; desperate for approval and affection, even from his concubines. But, out of all of them, he was the only one who had the backbone to rule an empire spanning dozens of numbered planets. *The best of a bad choice*, as Suu Nuoc would have said—trust the man to always find the most tactless answer to everything. No wonder Huu Tam didn't like him.

"We'll get through this," Mi Hiep said, with more confidence than she felt. "As you said, we are not without resources."

Huu Tam nodded, slowly and unconvincingly. "As you say, Mother. I will go talk to my supporters."

After he was gone, Lady Linh frowned. "I will ask the Embroidered Guard to keep an eye on him."

He's innocent, Mi Hiep wanted to say. A little weak, a little too easily flattered; but surely not even he would dare to go against her will?

But still . . . One never knew. She hadn't raised him that way; and even he was smart enough to know that being family would not protect him against her wrath. He had seen her send armies against Ngoc Minh, when the threat of the Citadel had loomed so large in her mind she'd known she had to do something, or remain paralysed in fear that Ngoc Minh herself would act. She would weep if she had to exile or execute him, but she would not flinch. The Empire could not afford weakness.

Mi Hiep erased the folder from the communal network, and tried to remember what the next audience was—something about water rights on the Third Planet, wasn't it? She had the file somewhere, with abundant notes on the decision she'd uphold— the district magistrate had been absolutely correct, and the appeal would be closed on those terms. But every time she paused, even for a minute, she would remember her daughter.

Ngoc Minh had said nothing, when Mi Hiep had exiled her. She'd merely bowed; but though she'd lowered her eyes, her gaze still burnt through Mi Hiep's soul like a lance of fire, as if she'd laid bare every one of Mi Hiep's fears and petty thoughts.

Officially, the Bright Princess had disobeyed court orders once too many; had refused to set aside her commoner wife as a concubine, and set up proper spouses' quarters. It was one thing to take lovers, but fidelity to one particular person was absurd: those days, it wasn't the risk of infertility—alchemists' implantations had all but removed it—but merely the fact that no one could be allowed to own too much of an Empress's heart and mind. Favourites were one thing; wives quite another.

Unofficially—Mi Hiep had seen the vase, over and over; the monks teleporting from one end to another of the courtyards; and thought of what this would do, the day it was turned against her.

"I will obey," Ngoc Minh had said. Had she known? She must have; must have guessed. And still she had said nothing.

"You're thinking of Ngoc Minh," the Twenty-Fourth Empress said.

"Yes. How do you know?" She wasn't meant to be so perceptive.

"I'm your mother," the Twenty-Fourth Empress said, with the bare hint of a smile; a reminder of the person she had been, once, the parent Mi Hiep had loved.

But she was none of those things. An Empress stood alone, and yet not alone—with no compassion or affection; merely the rituals and rebukes handed on by the ghosts of the dead. "I guess so," Mi Hiep said. And then, because she was still seeing her daughter's gaze, "Was I unfair?"

"Never," the First Emperor said.

"You are the Empress," the Sixteenth Empress said.

"Your word is law," the Twenty-Third Emperor said, his adolescent's face creased in a frown. "The law is your word."

All true; and yet none of it a comfort.

Lady Linh said nothing. Of course she wouldn't. She had been imprisoned once already, she wasn't foolish enough to overstep her boundaries again. What Mi Hiep needed was one of her lovers or former lovers—Suu Nuoc or Ky Vo or Hong Quy—to whisper sweet nothings to her; to hold her and reassure her with words they didn't mean or couldn't understand the import of. But there was a time and place for this; and her audience room wasn't it.

But then, to her surprise, Lady Linh spoke up, "I don't know. You did the best you could, with what you had. An Empress should listen to the wisdom of her ancestors, her parents and her advisors—else how would the Empire stand fast? This isn't a tyranny or a dictatorship where one can rule as whim dictates. There are rules, and rituals, and emperors must abide by them. Else we will descend into chaos again, and brother will fight brother, daughter abandon mother and son defy father. You cannot do as you will. Ngoc Minh . . . didn't listen."

No. She never had.

But that wasn't the reason why Mi Hiep had exiled her; that wasn't the reason why, years later, Mi Hiep sent the army to destroy her and her Citadel.

Perhaps the rumours were right, after all; perhaps Mi Hiep was getting old, and counting the years until the King of Hell's demons came to take her; and wishing she could make amends for all that had happened.

As if amends would ever change anything.

THE YOUNGER SISTER

Ngoc Ha had always felt ill at ease on *The Turtle's Golden Claw*. It was there that she'd given birth; panting and moaning like some animal, bottling in all the pain of contractions until a primal scream tore its way out of her like a spear point thrust through her lungs—and she'd lain, exhausted, amidst the smell of blood and machine oil, while everyone else clustered around the Mind she'd borne—checking vitals and blood flow, and rushing her to the cradle in the heartroom.

Alone. On *The Turtle's Golden Claw*, Ngoc Ha would always be alone and vulnerable, abandoned by everyone else. It was a foolish, unsubstantiated fear; but she couldn't let go of it.

But Mother had ordered her to come, and of course her orders were law. Literally so, since she was the Empress. Ngoc Ha swallowed her fear until it was nothing more than a tiny, festering shard in her heart, and came onboard.

The Turtle's Golden Claw was pleased, of course—almost beyond words, her corridors lit with red, joyous light, the poems scrolling on the walls all about homecomings and the happiness of family reunions. She gave Ngoc Ha the best cabin, right next to the heartroom—grey walls with old-fashioned watercolours of starscapes. Clearly the ship been working on decorating it for a while; and Ngoc Ha felt, once more, obscurely guilty she couldn't give her daughter more than distant affection.

She had taken an escort with her; and her maid—she could have kept them with her; but they would have brought her no company—not onboard this ship. So she left them in a neighbouring room, and stared at the walls, trying to calm herself—as *The Turtle's Golden Claw* moved away from the First Planet; and plunged into deep spaces—the start of their week-long journey towards the Scattered Pearls belt.

An oily sheen spread over the watercolours and walls, and everything began throbbing on no rhythm Ngoc Ha could name.

She logged into the network, and spent the next day watching vids—operas and family sagas, and reality shows in which the contestants sang in five different harmonies, or designed increasingly bizarre rice and algae confections with the help of fine-tuned bots. That way, she didn't have to look at the walls; didn't have to see the shadowy shapes on them; to see them slowly turning—watching her, waiting . . .

"Mother?" A knock at the door, though the avatar could have dropped straight into her cabin. "May I come in?"

Ngoc Ha, too exhausted and drained to care, agreed.

The small avatar of *The Turtle's Golden Claw* materialised next to her, hovering over the bedside table. "Mother, you're not well."

Really. Ngoc Ha bit off the sarcastic reply, and said instead, "I don't like deep spaces." No one did. Unless they were Suu Nuoc, who seemed to have a stomach of iron to go with his blank face. And at least they were normal ones—not the other, higher-order ones the ship had accessed during her search for Ngoc Minh. "I need to stay busy."

"You do," a voice said, gravely. To her surprise, it was Suu Nuoc—who stood at the open door of her room with two Embroidered Guards by his side. His face was set in a faint frown, revealing nothing. Hard to believe Mother had seen enough in him to—but no, she wouldn't go there. It had no bearing on anything else.

"I have vids," Ngoc Ha said, shaking her head. "Or encirclement games, if you feel like you need an adversary." She hated encirclement games; but she needed a distraction—they'd forced her to cut the vids; to pay attention to what was going on in the cabin . . .

Suu Nuoc shrugged. "You knew Grand Master Bach Cuc."

"A little," Ngoc Ha said, warily.

"How were her relationships with the rest of the court?"

Mother had said something about court intrigues, which had made no sense to Ngoc Ha. Then again, she supposed it was a case of the one-eyed man in the land of the blind—Suu Nuoc was a disaster at anything involving subtlety. "She was like you." She hadn't meant to be so blunt, but the faint smell of ozone, the slight yield to the air, the twisting shapes on the walls—they were doing funny things to her. "Blunt and uninterested in anything that wasn't her mission." And proud, with utter belief in her own capacities as a scientist in a way that could be off-putting.

"I see." Suu Nuoc inclined his head. "But she must have had enemies."

"She was no one," Ngoc Ha said. Oily shadows trailed on the wall, unfolded hands like scissors, legs like knives. They were going to turn, to see her . . . "But her mission—that made her friends, and enemies."

"Huu Tam?"

"Maybe." She hadn't had a heart-to-heart talk with Huu Tam since he became the heir—ironic, in a way, but then she and her brother had never been very close.

Unlike her and Ngoc Minh—a memory of fingers, folding her hands around a baby chick; of laughter under a pine tree in a solitary courtyard—and she breathed in, and buried the treacherous thought before it could unmake her. She'd never grieved for Ngoc Minh. Why should she, when she'd always believed her sister to be alive?

But sometimes, the hollows left by absence were worse than those left by death.

Focus. The last thing she needed was for this to intrude on her interview with Suu Nuoc—who would see her hesitation and interpret it as guilt or as Heaven knew what else. "If Ngoc Minh had come back, things would have changed. But you know this already."

"Yes." Suu Nuoc's face was impassive. "What I want to know is how they would have changed for you."

"I don't know," Ngoc Ha said, and realised it was the truth. Why did Mother want Ngoc Minh back—for a change of heir, with the wolves and tigers at their doors; or simply because she was old, and wanted reconciliation with the Bright Princess, the only child she'd ever sent away? "Who knows what Mother thinks?"

"I did, once," Suu Nuoc said. It was a statement of fact, nothing more.

"Then guess."

"That would be beyond my present attributions."

"Of course," Ngoc Ha said. "Fine. You want to know what I think? I didn't much care, one way or another." Untrue—the thought of seeing Ngoc Minh again was a knot in her stomach that only tightened the more she pulled about it. "I wasn't going to rise higher. We all know it, don't we? I don't have the ruthlessness it takes to become Empress." Huu Tam was too amenable to flattery—and his brothers were too weak and too inclined to play favourites. Ngoc Minh . . . Ngoc Minh had been intensely focused, dedicated to what she felt was right. But what was right had not included Mother's Empire.

"You might still not be very happy to be relegated to the background, again. She was your mother's favourite, wasn't she?" Suu Nuoc's voice was quiet. The shadows on the walls were stretching, turning—reaching for her . . . "Would you have been happy to see her back in your life?"

It wasn't that. She remembered a night like any other, when she had been tearing her hair out over an essay assigned by the Grand Secretary—remembered Ngoc

Minh coming to sit by her—the rustle of yellow silk, the smell of sandalwood. She'd been busy by then; establishing her court of hermits and monks and mendicants, fighting the first hints of Mother's disapproval. "You're too serious, lil' sis," Ngoc Minh had said. "This isn't what matters."

Ngoc Ha wished she'd been smart enough then, to ask the unspoken question; to ask her what truly mattered.

"Leave her alone," The Turtle's Golden Claw said: a growl like a tiger's, sending ripples into the patterns on the wall.

Suu Nuoc looked surprised; as if a pet bird had bitten him to the blood.

"You know my orders."

"Yes," The Turtle's Golden Claw said. "Go to the Scattered Pearls belt and find and arrest Quoc Quang. Nowhere in this do I see a justification for what you're doing now, Book of Heaven."

Suu Nuoc's eyes narrowed at the over-familiar choice of nickname. "I do what needs to be done."

The Turtle's Golden Claw did not answer, but the atmosphere in the room tightened like an executioner's garrotte. Ngoc Ha, drained, merely watched—were they going to have it out? Such a stupid, wasteful idea to argue with a mindship in deep spaces.

At length, Suu Nuoc looked at Ngoc Ha. "I will leave you then, Your Highness." He bowed, and left the room; and the tension in the air vanished like a burst bubble—leaving only the oily sheen and faint background noise of deep spaces around them, a cangue she could not escape.

"Thank you," Ngoc Ha whispered.

"It's nothing, Mother." The Turtle's Golden Claw's avatar materialised in the centre of the room, spinning left and right. "Just filial duty."

And what about motherly ones? Ngoc Ha suppressed the thought before it could undo her. No point in rehashing old wounds. "You wanted to find Ngoc Minh," she said. "How—"

The ship spun like glass blown by a master, gaining substance with every spin. "Grand Master Bach Cuc thought that deep spaces could be used—to go farther. That there was something—" she stopped, picked her words again, "some place that was as far beyond them as deep spaces are to normal space. Places where time ceased to have meaning, where thirty years ago was still as fresh as yesterday."

"That's—" Ngoc Ha tried to swallow the words before they burnt her throat, and failed. "Esoteric babble. Unproved nonsense. I'm sorry." Grand Master Bach Cuc sounded as though she'd taken lessons from Ngoc Minh—like the Bright Princess, listened to hermits in some remote caves for far too long.

"That's all right." The Turtle's Golden Claw sounded disturbingly serene—Ngoc Minh again, standing in the courtyard by her room, smiling as Ngoc Ha shouted at her to behave, to see the plots being spun around her, the growing disenchantment of officials for an heir who did not follow Master Kong's teachings. "I knew you'd say that. That's why I brought you this."

She wanted nothing of this—nonsense—she recoiled, instinctively, before realising that The Turtle's Golden Claw had given her nothing tangible: just a link to a database that hovered in the air in front of her. It was labelled "Quoc Tuan's personal files": Suu Nuoc's personal name, as grandiloquent as he had been obscure. "You can't."

"Of course I can." *The Turtle's Golden Claw* laughed, childish and almost care-free. "You forget—he stored everything in my databanks. I have the highest access credentials here."

Suu Nuoc would kill her—drag her so far down into the mud she'd never breathe again, with a few well-placed words in Mother's ears. "You can't do that," Ngoc Ha said, again. "I'm a suspect in that investigation."

"Are you?" The avatar of her daughter shifted; for a moment; became the head of a woman who took her breath away—a heartbreakingly familiar face with Mother's thin eyebrows and Ngoc Minh's burning eyes—a gaze that pierced her like a lance of fire.

No, Ngoc Ha thought, no. She had wished many things; some of them unforgivable—but she had never acted against anyone, let alone Grand Master Bach Cuc.

"I will leave you," *The Turtle's Golden Claw* said; and out of courtesy, opened the door and crossed through it rather than gradually fading away. The link remained in Ngoc Ha's field of vision, shifting to a turtle's scale, then a polished disc of jade, and other things of value beyond measure. *The Turtle's Golden Claw* really had a peculiar sense of humour.

Ngoc Ha stared at it for a while, and thought of the last time she had seen her sister—a brief message on the night before the Citadel vanished, asking news from her and assuring her everything was well. She dragged it up from her personal space, where she'd sat on it all those years, and stared at it for a while. Nothing seemed to have changed about Ngoc Minh in the years she'd been away from the First Planet— the same burning intensity, the same eyes that seemed to have seen too much. She had to know about Mother's army on its way to her; had to know that her Citadel would soon be embroiled in a war with no winners; but nothing of that had shown on her face.

Ngoc Ha had not answered that message. She had gone back to bed, telling her-self she would think of something; that she would find words that would make it all better, as Ngoc Minh had once done for her. By morning, the Citadel was gone; and Ngoc Minh forever beyond her reach.

Where was the Bright Princess now—hiding somewhere she wouldn't be perceived as a threat to Mother's authority? Dead all those years? No, that wasn't possible. Ngoc Ha would have known—surely there was something, some shared connection remaining between them that would have told her?

And then she looked again at that last communication, and realised, with a wrench in her stomach like the shutting of doors, that Ngoc Minh's face had be-come that of a stranger.

In the end, as *The Turtle's Golden Claw* had known, Ngoc Ha couldn't help herself. She took the link, and everything that the ship had given her, and started reading through it.

The bulk of the early pieces was Grand Master Bach Cuc's correspondence: her directions and discussions with her team; her memorials to Suu Nuoc; her letters asking other scientists on other planets for advice—buried in there, too was an account of *The Turtle's Golden Claw's* conception, implantation and birth, which Ngoc Ha gave a wide berth to—no desire to see herself as a subject of Bach Cuc's scientific curiosity, dissected with the same precision she'd put into all her experimental reports.

What interested her were the last communications. The earlier reports had been verbose, obfuscating the lack of progress. Those were terse to the point of rudeness—but it wasn't rudeness that leapt off the page—just a slow rising excitement that things were moving, that Bach Cuc's search would succeed at last, that she would be honoured by her peers for her breakthrough, her discovery of spaces beyond deep spaces where time and individuality ceased to have meaning.

Esoteric nonsense, Ngoc Ha would have said—except that Grand Master Bach Cuc was one of the most pragmatic people she had ever met. If she believed it . . .

She read the correspondence from end to end, carefully. She wasn't a scientist; but unlike Suu Nuoc her broad education had gone deep into mathematics and physics, and the understanding of the rituals that bound the world as surely as Master Kong's teachings bound people. She could—barely—understand what it had been about from skimming the reports, and from what Bach Cuc had told her, before and after the procedure of carrying *The Turtle's Golden Claw.*

And Bach Cuc had written a few reports already. She'd found a trail from the samples *The Turtle's Golden Claw* had brought back: trace elements that could only come from the Citadel's defences; clouds of particles from the technology Ngoc Minh had used to blast vases to smithereens in the courtyard of the palace. Bach Cuc had started to draw a plan for following these to a source; hoping to reconstitute the path the Citadel had taken after it had vanished from the world.

Hoping to find Ngoc Minh.

And then something had happened. Was it Quoc Quang? Ngoc Ha remembered the man's despair, his quiet, strong need to convince her that he needed to see Grand Master Bach Cuc. It had been that—the entreaty with no expectations—that had convinced her, more than anything.

What had he said? That, in the Scattered Pearls belt his daughter and Tran Thi Long Lam were working on something to do with the Citadel? She hadn't recorded the conversation for future use; but she remembered the name.

Tran Thi Long Lam. She had the profile on her implants: a scholar from the College of Brushes, the kind of brilliant mind that would never work well within the strictures of the imperial civil service. It was, in many ways, a blessing for her that she'd left to take care of her sick parent. But. . . .

Yes, there were several communications from a Tran Thi Long Lam—or, more accurately, from her literary name, The Solitary Wanderer. Addressed to Grand Master Bach Cuc, and never answered—opened and read with a glance, perhaps? They didn't come from a laboratory or a university; or anyone Bach Cuc would have recognised as a peer—she could be a snob when she wanted to, and Lam might be brilliant, but she was also young, without any reputation to her name beyond the abandonment of what Bach Cuc would perceive as her responsibilities to science.

Ngoc Ha gathered them all, and stared at them for a while. The first sentences of the first one was "I humbly apologise for disturbing you. A common colleague of ours, Moral Mentor Da Thi from the Laboratory of Applied Photonics, has forwarded me some of your published articles on your research . . ."

No, Grand Master Bach Cuc would not have read very far in this kind of inflammatory statement, which barely acknowledged her as a superior before going on to question her research—the things that were going to make her fame and wealth. But Ngoc Ha was not Bach Cuc.

When Ngoc Ha was done reading, she stared at the wall; barely seeing, for once, the twisting, oily shadows that moved like broken bodies in slow motion. Warn Grand Master Bach Cuc, Quoc Quang had said, and now she understood a little of what he had meant.

Lam had been interested in Bach Cuc's research—possibly because whatever she was doing on her isolated orbital intersected it. She'd read it, carefully, applying everything she knew or thought she knew; and thought it worth writing to Bach Cuc.

Your research is dangerous.

Not because it could be weaponised; not because it was things mankind wasn't meant to know or any arrant outsider nonsense. No, what Lam had meant was rather more primal: that Grand Master Bach Cuc was wrong, and that it would kill her. Something about stability—Ngoc Ha read the second to last letter again—the stability of the samples *The Turtle's Golden Claw* was bringing back to the laboratory. Because they came from spaces where time had different meanings, they would tend to want to go back to those spaces. Lam thought this might happen in a violent, exothermic reaction—that all the coiled energy from the samples would release in one fatal explosion.

No, not quite. That wasn't what she'd said.

"Things disturbed have a tendency to go back to their equilibrium point. In this particular case, I have reasons to believe this would be in a single, massive event rather than multiple small ones. I hold the calculations of this at your disposal, but I enclose an outline of them to convince you . . ."

Things disturbed. She hadn't been saying "be careful, your samples might explode." She had been saying "be careful, do not experiment on your samples." She'd told Grand Master Bach Cuc that the manipulations she was doing in her shielded chamber could prove fatal.

That was the warning Quoc Quang had passed on to Bach Cuc, with enough desperation and enough personal touch to make her pay attention.

Except . . .

Except Grand Master Bach Cuc was proud, wasn't she? Unbearably so. She had listened, but she'd done the wrong thing. Ngoc Ha would have put the project on hold while she worked out the risks, but she wasn't the one whose reputation had been impugned by a uppity eighteen-year-old and her drunken failure of a father.

She knew exactly what Bach Cuc had done. She had shown Quoc Quang out with a smile and her thanks—hiding the furious turmoil that had to have seized her at receiving such a warning. She had sat for a while, thinking on things—staring at the wall, just as Ngoc Ha was doing, trying to collect her thoughts, to think on the proper course of action.

And then she'd gone into the shielded chamber. She'd taken off her mem-implants because she'd needed absolute focus on what she was going to do; because she'd believed there might be a danger, but not to the level Lam was describing. Because she'd wanted to show the little outworlder upstart that she was wrong.

And it had killed her.

She had to—no, she couldn't tell that to *The Turtle's Golden Claw*—couldn't distress the ship without any evidence.

But she had to tell Suu Nuoc.

THE OFFICER

Suu Nuoc was surprised by the Scattered Pearls belt. He couldn't have put his finger on what he'd expected—something both larger and less pathetic, more in tune with his mental image of what the Citadel had been?

It wasn't grand, or modern: everything appeared to have been cobbled together from scraps of disused metal, the walls looking like a patchwork of engineering, the communal network so primitive it required hard-wiring implants to have access to it—Suu Nuoc had refused, because who knew what they'd put in, if he allowed them access?

Beside him, Ngoc Ha was silent, her escort trailing behind her with closed faces. She had walked up to him earlier, on the shuttle taking them from the mindship to the central orbital, and had asked to speak with him in private. What she had then said . . .

He wasn't sure what to think of it. It sounded like the weakest chain of evidence he'd ever seen—wrapped into a compelling story, to be sure, but anyone could spin words, and especially a princess educated by the best scholars of the Empire. He'd read the research, and Lam's emails to Grand Master Bach Cuc—and had noticed none of this. But he knew his weaknesses; and unlike scholars, he didn't have any mem-implants to compensate for his lack of education.

He'd thanked Ngoc Ha, and told her he'd think on it. "Don't tell my daughter," she'd said. For some reason, this had shocked him into silence—only after she'd gone had he realised that it was one of the only times she'd referred to the ship in those affectionate tones.

According to Ngoc Ha, Grand Master Bach Cuc was dead; which he wouldn't admit. It would mean a setback on the search for Bright Princess Ngoc Minh; at a time when they could not afford setbacks. He needed to be sure, before he told anyone of this—Heaven, he wasn't even sure Ngoc Ha was entirely innocent in this. She'd hated her sister: that much was clear from her own words.

Focus. He needed to do his duty to the Empress and the Empire; and flights of fancy were unhelpful.

The Scattered Pearls belt was governed by a council of elders, and a local magistrate who, like many of the low-echelon officials, looked stressed and perpetually harried. Yes, he knew of Quoc Quang, had always known he would be in trouble one day—it was the drugs, and the drinks, he'd never been the same since his wife's disappearance. Yes, he'd come back recently from a voyage into the heart of the Empire, and of course he would be happy to help the honoured General Who Read the Book of Heaven in any way required.

His obsequiousness, and the lack of attempt to defend Quoc Quang, made Suu Nuoc feel faintly ill; but he tried not to let it show on his face. "Bring him to us," he said, more brusquely than he'd meant to, and was perversely glad to see the man flinch.

He watched as the magistrate intercepted a pale-looking clerk; and mentally tallied the time it was going to find Quoc Quang with their overstretched resources. Too much. "On second thought, cancel that order. Take us to him. It will be faster."

"He has a daughter, hasn't he?" Ngoc Ha asked, as the magistrate's clerks escorted them to another shuttle.

"Diem Huong," the magistrate said—with a frown. Clearly, he was about to add the daughter's behaviour to a list of perceived sins against the Empire, too. Coward; and a malicious one at that.

Suu Nuoc wouldn't stand for that. "Are you going to tell us about the daughter's failures, too?" he asked, conversationally.

The magistrate blanched—and Ngoc Ha winced. "No, of course not," he said—Suu Nuoc heard him swallow, once, twice, as his face went the colour of ceruse. "It's just that . . . Diem Huong has always been odd."

"Odd?"

"Obsessed," one of the clerks said, a little more gently than the magistrate. "Her mother was on the Citadel. She vanished when Diem Huong was six, and Diem Huong never quite recovered from it." Her eyes were grave, thoughtful. "If I may—"

"Go on," Suu Nuoc said, though he wasn't fooled. The delivery was gentler, and meant more kindly; but it was the same, nevertheless.

Heaven, how he missed the battlefield, sometimes. Soldiers and bots wouldn't prevaricate, and whatever backstabbing might occur was short and clean.

"People break, some times," the clerk said. "Diem Huong . . . does her job, correctly. Helps her orbital with the hydroponics system. No one's ever had a complaint against her. But it's an open secret she and Lam, and a couple other youngsters, were obsessed with the Citadel."

"Lam? Tran Thi Long Lam?" *The Turtle's Golden Claw* asked.

The clerk, startled, looked at the small avatar of the ship—hadn't even noticed it floating by her side. "Yes," she said. "A graduate of the College of Brushes—"

Suu Nuoc tuned her out as she started to list Lam's qualifications. The orbital was proud of Lam, as they hadn't been of either Quoc Quang or his daughter—because Lam was the local girl who had succeeded beyond everyone's wildest dream; granted, she'd had to return home, but everyone understood the necessity of caring for a sick father. Lam was cool-headed and competent; and probably managed an important segment of her orbital—a position beneath her, but which she'd taken on without complaining on returning home. He'd seen it a thousand times already, and it was of no interest.

What mattered was Grand Master Bach Cuc, and Bright Princess Ngoc Minh.

He let the clerk drone on as their shuttle moved from the central orbital to the Silver Abalone orbital—focusing again on the messages Lam had sent Grand Master Bach Cuc. Warnings, using a language too obscure for him to make them out. Was Ngoc Ha right? He didn't know. He knew that she was right in her assessment of Bach Cuc: that the Grand Master was proud of her achievements, and hungry for recognition. A young person like Lam, daring to question her . . . No, she wouldn't have listened to her. It was a wonder she'd received Quoc Quang at all; but perhaps she had not dared to refuse someone introduced by Ngoc Ha herself.

It galled him to even entertain the thought; because one did not speak ill of the disappeared or the dead; but he had not cared much for Bach Cuc.

Quoc Quang's compartment turned out to be a small and cosy one—the kitchen showing traces of use so heavy the cleaning bots hadn't quite managed to make them disappear, and a faint smell of sesame oil and fish sauce clung to everything.

It also did not contain Quoc Quang, or his wayward daughter. The aged aunt who lived with them—quailing in the face of the Embroidered Guard—said he had gone out.

"Running away?" *The Turtle's Golden Claw* asked.

Suu Nuoc shook his head. Getting drunk, more likely. "Scour the teahouses," he said. "Can someone access the network?" Without it, everything seemed curiously bare—objects with no context or no feelings attached to them. He ran a finger on the wok on the hearth, half-expecting information to pop up in his field of vision—what brand it was, what had last been cooked in it. But there was nothing.

The clerk nodded.

"Anything interesting?"

Silence, for a while. "A message from his daughter," she said at last. "Diem Huong. She says she's gone to work with Lam, at the teahouse."

Diem Huong. Long Lam. Suu Nuoc didn't even pause to consider. "Where is the teahouse?"

"I don't know—" the clerk started, and then another of her colleagues cut her off. "It's the old teahouse," he said. "Where the youngsters hang out, right by the White Turtle Temple on the outer rings."

"Take us there," Suu Nuoc said. "And keep looking for Quoc Quang!"

It was all scattering out—that familiar feeling he had before entering battle, when all the bots he was linked to left in different directions, and the battlefield opened up like the petals of flowers—that instant, frozen in time, before everything became rage and chaos; when he still felt the illusion of control over everything.

But this wasn't battle. This didn't involve ships or soldiers; or at least, not more than one ship. He could handle this.

He just wished he could believe his own lies.

The White Turtle Temple was a surprise, albeit a provincial one: a fragile construction of rafters and glass that stretched all the way to a heightened ceiling, a luxury that seemed unwarranted on an orbital—though the glass was probably shatter-proof, or not even glass. It had a quaint kind of prettiness; and yet . . . and yet, in its simple, affectless setup, it felt more authentic and warm than the hundred more impressive pagodas on the First Planet. When all this was over, Suu Nuoc should come there; should sit, for a while, in front of the statues of Quan Vu and Quan Am; and meditate on the fragile value of life.

The building next to the temple, squat and rectangular, had indeed been a teahouse—some tables were still outside, and the counter was lying in two pieces in the corridor. But that wasn't what raised Suu Nuoc's hackles.

The building glowed.

There was no other word for it. It was a faint blue radiance that seemed to seep through everything, making metal and plastics as translucent as high-quality porcelain—light creeping through every crack, every line of the walls until it seemed to be the glue that held it together. And it was a light that thrummed and throbbed, like . . .

He had seen this somewhere before. He gestured to the Embroidered Guard, had them position themselves on either side of the entrance. It didn't look as though there was any danger they could tackle—"unnatural light" not exactly being in their prerogatives. He'd been too cautious: he should have asked at least one of them to plug into the communal network—they would be blind to local cues. It had been fine when they'd just been on a mission to pick up a witness, but now . . .

He looked again at the light, wishing he knew what it reminded him of. That annoying buzz, just on the edge of hearing—like a ship's engine? But no, that wasn't it. How long had it been spreading? "I want to know if the monks of the temple filed a report," he said.

The magistrate looked at one of his clerks, who shook her head. "Not in the system."

Not so long, then. Perhaps there was still time.

But time for what?

"I can go in," a voice said. "Have a look." *The Turtle's Golden Claw.*

"Out of the question." Ngoc Ha's voice was flat; almost unrecognisable from the small, courtly woman who seldom spoke her mind so bluntly. "You have no idea what's in here."

"I'm not here," *The Turtle's Golden Claw* said. "Not really. It's just a projection—"

"There's enough of you here," Ngoc Ha said. "Bits and pieces hooked into the communal network. That's how you work, isn't it? You can't process this fast, this quickly, if you're not here in some capacity."

"Mother—"

"Tell me you're not here," Ngoc Ha said, relentless. Her hair was shot through with blue highlights—lifted as though in an invisible wind; and her eyes—her eyes seemed to burn. Did everyone look like that? But no, the clerks didn't seem affected to that extent. "Tell me there's no part of you here at all, and then I'll let you go in."

"You can't force me!" *The Turtle's Golden Claw* said. "Grand Master Bach Cuc—"

Ngoc Ha opened her mouth; and Suu Nuoc knew, then, exactly what she was going to say. He found himself moving then—catching the heated words Ngoc Ha was about to fling into her daughter's face, and covering them with his own. "The Grand Master is probably dead, ship. And what killed her might be inside."

There was silence, then; and that same unnatural light. At length the ship said—bobbing up and down like a torn feather in a storm—"She can't be. She can't—Mother—Book of Heaven—"

"I'm sorry," Ngoc Ha said.

"We're not sure—" Suu Nuoc started.

"Then there's still a chance—"

"Don't you recognise what this is?" Ngoc Ha asked.

"I've seen it before—"

Her voice was harsh, unforgiving. "It's the light of a harmonisation arch, General."

She was right. Suu Nuoc suppressed a curse. Harmonisation arches were localised around their surrounding frames—the biggest one he'd seen had been twice the size of a man, and already buckling under the stress. They certainly never cast a light strong enough to illuminate an entire building. Whatever was going on inside, it was badly out of control.

"I need your help," he said, to *The Turtle's Golden Claw*.

"Yes?"

"Tell me if the illumination is stable."

The ship was silent for a while; but even before she spoke up, Suu Nuoc knew the answer. "No. The intensity has been increasing. And . . ."

More bad news, Suu Nuoc could tell. Why couldn't he have some luck, for a change?

"I would need more observations to confirm, but at the rate this is going, it will have spread to the entire orbital in a few hours."

"Do you know what's inside?"

"Not with certainty, no. But I can hazard a guess. Some explosive reaction that should have required containment—except that it's breached it," *The Turtle's Golden Claw* said.

Which was emphatically not good for the orbital, whichever way you put it. Suu Nuoc's physics were basic, but even he could intuit that. He took in a deep, trembling breath. The battle joined, again; the familiar ache in his bones and in his mind, telling him it was time to enter the maelstrom where everything was clean-cut and elegantly simple—where he could once more feel the thrill of split-second decisions; of hanging on the sword's edge between life and death.

Except it wasn't a battle; it wasn't enemy soldiers out there—just deep spaces and whatever else Bach Cuc had been handling, all the cryptic reports he'd barely been able to follow. Could he handle this? He was badly out of his depth . . .

But it was for the Empress; and the good of the Empire; and there was no choice. There had never been any choice.

He gestured to the Embroidered Guard. "Set up a perimeter, but don't get too comfortable. We're going in."

THE ENGINEER

The world around Diem Huong shifted and twisted; and vanished—and, for a moment, she hung in a vacuum as deep as the space between stars, small and alone and frightened, on the edge of extinction—and, for a moment, she felt the touch of a presence against her mind, something vast and numinous and terrible, like the wings of some huge bird of prey, wrapping themselves around her until she choked.

And then she came slamming back into her body, into a place she recognised.

Or almost did. It was—and was not—as she remembered: the door to Mother's compartment, a mere narrow arch in a recessed corridor, indistinguishable from the other doors. From within came the smell of garlic and fish sauce, strong enough to make her feel six years old again. And yet . . . and yet, it was smaller, and diminished from what she remembered; almost ordinary, yet loaded with memories that threatened to overwhelm her.

Slowly, gently—not certain it would still remain there, if she moved, if she breathed—she raised a hand, and knocked.

Nothing.

She exhaled. And knocked again—and saw the tip of her fingers slide, for a bare moment, through the metal. A bare moment only, and then it was as solid as before.

She was fading. Going back in time to Lam's lab? To the void and whatever waited for her there?

No use in thinking upon it. She couldn't let fear choke her until she died of it. She braced herself to knock again, when the door opened.

She knew Mother's face by heart; the one on the holos on the ancestral altar, young and unlined and forever frozen into her early forties: the wide eyes, the round cheeks, the skin darkened by sunlight and starlight. She'd forgotten how much of her would be familiar—the smell of sandalwood clinging to her; the graceful movements that unlocked something deep, deep within her—and she was six again and safe; before the betrayal that shattered her world; before the years of grief.

"Can I help you?" Mother asked. She sounded puzzled.

She had to say something, no matter how inane; had to prevent Mother's face from creasing in the same look of suspicion she'd seen in the monk's eyes. Had to. "I'm sorry, but I had to meet you. I'm your daughter."

"Diem Huong?" Mother's voice was puzzled. "What joke is this? Diem Huong is outside playing at a friend's house. She's six years old."

"I know," Diem Huong said. She hadn't meant to say that; but in the face of the woman before her, all that came out was the truth, no matter how inadequate. "I come from another time," she said. "Another place."

"From the future?" Mother's eyes narrowed. "You'd better come in."

Inside, she turned, looked at Diem Huong—every time this happened, Diem Huong would wait with baited breath, afraid that this was it, the moment when Mother would start forgetting her again. "There is a family resemblance," Mother said at last.

"I was born in the year of the Water Tiger, in the Hour of the Rat," Diem Huong said, slowly. "You wanted to name me Thien Bao; Father thought it an inappropriate name for a girl. Please, Mother. I don't have much time, and I'm running out of it."

"We all are," Mother said, soberly. She gestured towards the kitchen. "Have a tea."

"There is no time," Diem Huong said; and paused, scrabbling for words. "What do you mean, 'we're running out of time?'"

Mother did not answer. She turned back, at last; looked at Diem Huong. "Oh, I'm sorry, I hadn't seen you here. What can I do for you?"

"Mother—" the words were out of Diem Huong's mouth before she could think; but they were said so low Mother did not seem to hear them. "You have to tell me. Why are you running out of time?"

Mother shook her head. "Who told you that?"

"You did. A moment ago."

"I did not." Mother's voice was cold. "You imagine things. Why don't you come into the kitchen, and then we can talk." She looked, uncertainly, at the door. She wouldn't remember how Diem Huong had got in—she was wondering if she should call the militia, temporising because Diem Huong looked innocuous, and perhaps just familiar enough.

Don't you recognise me, Mother? Can't you tell? I'm your daughter, and I need to know.

The corridor they stood in was dark, lit only by the altar to Quan Am in the corner—the bodhisattva's face lifted in that familiar half-smile—how many times had she stared at it on her way in or out, until it became woven into her memories?

"Please tell me," Diem Huong said, slowly, softly. "You said the Citadel still stood. You said you didn't know for how long." She should have started over; should have made up some story about being a distant relative, to explain the family likeliness—or even better, something official-sounding, an investigation by a magistrate or something that would scare her enough not to think. But no, she couldn't scare Mother. Couldn't, wouldn't.

Mother's face did not move. Diem Huong could not read her. Was she calling the militia? "Come into the kitchen," she said, finally; and Diem Huong gave in.

She got another puzzled look as Mother busied herself around the small kitchen—withdrawing tea from a cupboard, sending the bots to put together dumplings and cakes that they dropped into boiling water. "I'm sorry," Mother said. "I keep forgetting you were coming today."

"It's nothing," Diem Huong said. The kitchen was almost unfamiliar—she remembered the underside of the table; the feet of chairs; but all of it from a lower vantage. Had she played there, once? But then she saw the small doll on the tiling; and knelt, tears brimming in her eyes. Em Be Be—Little Baby Sister. She remembered *that*; the feel of the plastic hands in hers; the faint sour, familiar smell from clothes that had been chewed on and hugged and dragged everywhere.

Em Be Be.

"Oh, I'm sorry," Mother said. "My daughter left this here, and I was too lazy to clean up."

"It's nothing," Diem Huong said, again. She rose, holding the doll like a fragile treasure; her heart twisting as though a fist of ice were closing around it. "Really." She wasn't going to break down and cry in the middle of the kitchen, she really wasn't. She was stronger than this. "Tell me about the Citadel."

Mother was having that frown again—she was in the middle of a conversation that kept slipping under her. It was only a matter of time until she called the militia—except that the militia wouldn't remember her call for more than a few moments—or asked Diem Huong to leave, outright—something else she wouldn't remember, if it did happen.

Diem Huong watched the doll in her hands, wondering how long she had before it vanished; how long before she, too, vanished. "Please, elder aunt." She used the endearment; the term for intimates rather than another, more distant one.

"It's going to fall, one way or another," Mother said, slowly, carefully. "The Empress's armies are coming here, aren't they?" She put a plate full of dumplings before Diem Huong, and stared, for a while, at the doll. "I have to think of this. We're not defenceless—of course we're not. But the harm . . ." She shook her head. "You don't have children, do you?"

Diem Huong shook her head.

"Sometimes, all you have are bad choices," Mother said.

Diem Huong carefully set the doll aside, and reached for a dumpling—it'd vanish too, because Mother had only baked it for her. All traces of her presence would go away, at some point; all memories of her. "Bad choices," she said. "I understand, believe me." The dumpling smelled of dough and meat and herbs; and of that indefinable tang of childhood, that promise that all would be well in the end; that the compartment was and forever would be safe.

All dust, in the end; all doomed to vanish in the whirlwind.

"Do you?" Mother's voice was distant. Had she forgotten, again? But instead, she said, "One day, my daughter will grow up to be someone like you, younger aunt—a strong and beautiful adult. And it will be because I've done what I had to."

"I don't understand," Diem Huong said.

"You don't have to." There were—no.

Mother—

There were tears in Mother's eyes. "No one leaves. We stand, united. Always. For those of us who can."

Mother, no.

Mother smiled, again. "That's all right," she said. "I didn't feel you'd understand, younger aunt. You're too young to have children; or believe in the necessity of holding up the world." And then her gaze unfocused again; slid over Diem Huong again. "Can you remind me what I was saying? I seem to be having these frightful absences."

She was crying; young and vulnerable and so utterly unlike Mother. Diem Huong had wanted.. reassurances. Explanations. Embraces that would have made everything right with the world. Not—not this. Never this. "I'm sorry," she said, slowly backing away from the kitchen. "I'm really sorry. I didn't mean—"

It was only after she passed it that she realised her arm had gone through the door. She barely had enough time to be worried; because, by the time she reached the street, the Embroidered Guard was massed there, waiting for her with their weapons drawn.

THE EMPRESS

Mi Hiep sat in her chambers, thinking of Ngoc Minh; of weapons; and of lost opportunities.

Next to her, a handful of ancestors flickered into existence. They cast no shadow: below them, the ceramic tiles displayed the same slowly changing pattern of mist and pebbles—giving Mi Hiep the impression she stood in a mountain stream on some faraway planet. "There is news," the First Emperor said. "Their fleet has jumped."

The La Hoa drive. "How far?" Mi Hiep asked.

"Not far," the Ninth Emperor said, fingering his bearded chin. "A few light-days."

Not mindships, then.

"They're going to jump again," Mi Hiep said, flatly. It wasn't a question.

"Yes," the First Emperor said. "They're still outside the Empire; but they won't be for long."

"There have been no news from the Scattered Pearls belt," the Ninth Emperor said, with a disapproving frown. "You shouldn't have sent Suu Nuoc on his own."

Again, and again, the same arguments, repeated with the plodding patience of the dead. "I sent Ngoc Ha with him."

"Not enough," the First Emperor said.

The door to her chambers opened; let through Lady Linh and Van, the head of the Embroidered Guard; followed by Huu Tam, and two servants bringing tea and dumplings on a lacquered tray. "You wanted to see us," Lady Linh said. She carried the folder Mi Hiep had toyed with, which she laid on the table—in the communal network, it bulged with ghostly files. Linh wouldn't have put anything in it unless she had a good reason.

"You have something," Mi Hiep said, more sharply than she'd intended to.

Huu Tam bowed to her: he didn't look sullen, for once—and Mi Hiep realised the glint in his eyes was all too familiar.

Fear. The bone-deep, paralysing terror of those on the edge of the abyss.

"I have intelligence," Van said, briefly bowing to Mi Hiep. Van, the head of the Embroidered Guard, was middle-aged now, with a husband and two children; but as preternaturally sharp as she had been, twenty years ago, when a look from her had sent scholars scattering back to their offices.

"I told her about the fleet," the First Emperor said, with a nod to Van. The Emperors liked her—she was scary and utterly loyal; and with the kind of contained imagination that didn't challenge their worldviews.

Mi Hiep gestured: the pattern on the floor became a dark red—the colour of blood and New Year's lanterns; and the pebbles vanished, replaced by abstract models.

Van opened the folder; spread the first picture on the table before Mi Hiep, over the inlaid nacre dragon and phoenix circling the word "longevity." It was an infra-red with several luminous stains; and even with the low definition it was easy to see that they didn't all have the same heat signature. "This is what we have on the fleet," she said.

"The different stains are different ships?" Mi Hiep asked. She bent closer, trying to keep her heartbeat at a normal rate. They'd leapt, but not far—they wouldn't be there for a while.

Van took out two other pictures—still infrared, but close-ups in a slightly different band. One was a ship Mi Hiep had already seen—the squat, utilitarian design of Nam engineers, with little heat signature that she could see, everything slightly blurred and unfocused as if she watched through a pane of thick glass. The second one . . . She'd seen the second one, too, before; or its likeliness: twisted and bent and out of shape, something that had once been elegant but was now deformed by the added, pustulous modules.

They take ships, Lady Linh had said. Influence what they see and think, with just a few modules. They took living, breathing beings; with a family; with love—and they turned them into unthinking weapons of war.

"Their ships, and their hijacked mindships." She was surprised at the calm in her voice. She couldn't afford to be angry, not now. Van had laid the last picture on top of the first one; but in the communal network it was easy enough to invert the transparency layers so that she was staring at the fleet again.

Three hijacked mindships, twenty Nam ships. "Do you know anything about the mindships?" Huu Tam asked.

Van shook her head. "We have asked the outlying planets for any reports on missing mindships. One of them fits the profile of *The Lonely Tiger*, a mindship that disappeared near the Twenty-Third planet. We haven't apprised the family yet because we're not sure."

Not sure. What would it do to them—what kind of destruction would it wreak among them? Mi Hiep thought of *The Turtle's Golden Claw*; but it was different. She'd ordered the ship made for a cause; and that cause outweighed everything else; even the love she might have been able to provide.

"I see." Mi Hiep took a deep breath.

"We need to evacuate," Huu Tam said.

Mi Hiep nodded. "Yes. That too. But first, I need you to capture one of these."

"The mindships?" Van grimaced. "That's possible, but we'll sustain heavy losses."

"Yes," Mi Hiep said. The time for cautiousness; for dancing with diplomats and subtle threats, had since long passed. "I know. But they found a way to turn those against us; and to make them follow the fleet. Did they leap at the same time as the others?"

"Insofar as we can tell, yes," Van said. "Not as far as the others—it was very clear they were waiting for them to play catch-up."

Which meant they weren't as efficient as they could be, yet—that they couldn't harness the full potential of a mindship; leaping any distance they wanted when they wanted. Which was good news, in a way. "They're not up to speed yet," Mi Hiep said. "Which means we can study their shunts, and find a way to break them."

Van looked dubious. "With respect—"

"I know," Mi Hiep said. It wasn't so much the research—Grand Master Bach Cuc hadn't been the only genius scientist she'd had available, and there were plenty of war laboratories knowledgeable in Nam technology. "We don't have much time."

"And we'll pay a horrendous price." Van grimaced. She knew all about the calculus of cruelty, the abacuses that counted losses and gains as distant beads, ones that could not cause grief or sorrow or pain. "I'll send the order. You do realise this is a declaration of war." Huu Tam looked sick; but he said nothing. She hadn't misjudged him: alone of her surviving children he had the backbone to realise what must be done, and to carry it through.

"Then war it is," Mi Hiep said. "Round up the Nam envoys, will you? And send them home." The Galactic outsiders considered them untouchable; but both the Nam and the Dai Viet took a different position: they were their master's voices, and as such, the letters they bore, the words they uttered, were sacred. Their persons were not. But in this case, executions would not achieve anything; and it wasn't as though they had seen much that they could take back to their masters.

Van shrugged. She was more bloodthirsty than Mi Hiep. "As you wish."

The Ninth Emperor fingered the image, frowning. "Are they headed for the Imperial Shipyards?" he asked.

"Too early to tell with certainty," Lady Linh said. She gestured, and another image—of the ships' trajectories—was overlaid over the old one. "The trajectory is consistent, though."

Mi Hiep watched the red line, weaving its way through the outer reaches of the numbered planets. There was not; or had ever been, much choice. "There are ships at anchor, in the shipyards?"

"And Mind-bearers," the simulation of her mother said. "They're heavily pregnant: they won't be in a state to travel."

"They will have to," Huu Tam said. His face was harsh—good, he was learning. One did not become Emperor of the Dai Viet by being squeamish. "How many are there?"

"Six."

"They'll fit onboard one of the ships." She spared a thought for what they were about to do; a shred of pity: she'd been pregnant, though not with a ship-mind—and she remembered all too well what it had felt like—deprived of sleep, gravid and unable to move without being short of breath. "Have them evacuate the station. Don't let the ship into deep spaces."

Everything got weird in deep spaces—and something as fragile as a foetus or the seed that would become a ship-mind would probably not bear it. "Probably"—no one had run experiments, or at least no one had admitted to it, though the Sixteenth Empress—who'd had a fondness for questionable science ethics—had come dangerously close to it in Mi Hiep's hearing.

Lady Linh was looking at something on the network; a list of names. "There are four ships at anchor in the yards," she said. *"The Dragons in the Peach Gardens. The Blackbirds' Bridge. The Crystal Down Below. The Bird that Looked South."* She moved text around; and remained for a while, absorbing information. "The first two were here for refits. The others are young."

Young and vulnerable; still being taught by their mothers—children, in truth. Children whom she would have to send to war. Unless—"What about the military mindships?"

Van grimaced. "They're here already—we sent them a while ago. I've deployed them as protection."

"Good," Mi Hiep said. "Have the women and their birth-masters board *The Dragons in the Peach Gardens.*" An experienced ship was what they needed; not a younger, more panicked one who would be more likely to make mistakes. "Keep the young ships at anchor until the military ships have arrived." They wanted ships; and the building facilities of the yard; she had to provide bait. Like Van, she had since long got used to making ruthless decisions in a heartbeat: two young ships against a chance to turn the tide—against the protection of dozens of others? It was an easy decision.

"Oh, and one more thing," Mi Hiep said. "The shells for those ship-minds?" The beautiful, lovingly crafted bodies, the shells of ships into which the Minds would be inserted after birth—months and months of painstaking work by the alchemists and the Grand Masters of Design Harmonies, fine-tuning every turn of the corridors to ensure the flow of *khi* would welcome the Mind within its new carapace. "Destroy them."

"Your Highness," Van said, shocked. That stopped her, for a moment: she hadn't thought it was possible to shock Van.

To her surprise, it was Huu Tam who spoke. "The Empress is right. They've come here for our technologies. Let us leave nothing for them to grasp."

Technologies. Mindships. Weapons. How she wished they had something better—everything she'd feared from Ngoc Minh. If only they had the Bright Princess on their side.

But they didn't; and there was no point in weeping for what was past, or hoping for miracles. Whatever Suu Nuoc found in the Scattered Pearls belt, it would be too late. War had come to her, as it had thirty years ago; and, as she had done in the past, she met it head-on rather than let it cow her into submission. She nodded to Huu Tam. "You understand."

Her son bit his lip, in an all too familiar fashion. "I don't approve," he said. "But I know what has to be done."

Good. If they didn't agree on most things, they could at least agree on this. "Send word to Suu Nuoc," Mi Hiep said, ignoring Huu Tam's grimace. "Tell him we're at war."

THE YOUNGER SISTER

Suu Nuoc took the head of a detachment of three men and stepped forward, into the maelstrom of light. Ngoc Ha watched him from behind one of the overturned tables—something crackled and popped when he stepped inside, like burning flesh on a grill; but he didn't seem to notice it.

He said something; but the words came through garbled—he moved at odd angles, faster than the eye could see at moments, slow enough to seem frozen at others, every limb seemingly on a different rhythm, like those nightmarish collages Ngoc Ha had seen as a child, a narrow, lined eye of an old Dai Viet within the pale, sallow face of a horse; the muzzle of a tiger with the smiling lips and cheeks of a woman—the familiar boundaries shattered until nothing made sense. Children's fancies, they had been; but what she saw now dragged the unease back into daylight, making it blossom like a rotting flower. "Suu Nuoc? Can you hear me?"

The Turtle's Golden Claw was hovering near the boundary, bobbing like a craft in a storm. "There's a differential," she said. "Different timelines all dragged together. If you gave me time—"

"No," Ngoc Ha said. She didn't even have to think, it came welling out of her like blood out of a wound.

Silence. Then *The Turtle's Golden Claw* said, sullenly, "I'm not a child, you know. You can't protect me forever."

"I wasn't trying," Ngoc Ha said; and realised, with a horrible twist in her gut, that this was true. She hadn't abandoned the ship—had played with her, taught her what she knew, but it had always been with that same pent-up resentment, that same feeling that the choice to have this child had been forced upon her—that Ngoc Minh was reaching, from wherever she was, and deforming every aspect of Ngoc Ha's life again. Thirty years. The Bright Princess had been gone thirty years, and in that time she had tasted freedom.

And loss; but the word came in her thoughts so quickly she barely registered it.

The Turtle's Golden Claw, heedless of her hesitations, was already skirting the boundary, making a small noise like a child humming—except the words were in some strange language, mathematical formulas and folk songs mingled together. "A to the power of four, the fisherman's lament on the water—divide by three times C minus delta, provided delta is negative—the citadel was impregnable, the Golden Turtle Spirit said, for as long as his claw remained in the crossbow, and the crossbow remained in the citadel . . ."

But the Citadel had fallen; and her sister was forever silent. Except, perhaps, inside; where all the answers awaited.

Ngoc Ha was hardly aware of moving—hardly aware of her slow crawl towards the boundary, until she stood by the side of *The Turtle's Golden Claw*—her hand trailing on what should have been air—feeling the hairs on her skin rise as if in a strong electrical current.

"Deep spaces," *The Turtle's Golden Claw* said. Her voice came out weird; by turns tinny and booming, as if she couldn't quite make up her mind as to which distance she stood.

"Here? That's not possible—"

"Why not?" *The Turtle's Golden Claw* asked; and Ngoc Ha had no answer.

Ngoc Ha pushed; felt her hand go in as though through congealed rice porridge. Deep spaces. Shadows and nightmares; and that sick feeling in her belly; that fear that they would take her; swallow her whole and change her utterly.

And yet . . .

Yet, somewhere within, were people who might know where her sister was.

"Can we go in?" she asked; and felt more than saw the ship smile.

"Of course, Mother."

Inside, it was dark; and cool—everything limned with that curious light—everything at odd angles, the furniture showing part of asteroids and metal lodes, and the flames of workshops; and legs and blank polished surfaces; and fragments of flowers lacquered on its surface at the same time—different times, different point of views merged together in a way that made Ngoc Ha's head ache.

She looked at *The Turtle's Golden Claw*; but the ship was unchanged; and her hands were the same, veined and pale. Perhaps whatever had a hold there didn't apply to them; but she felt, in the background, some great pressure; some great presence awakening to their presence—a muzzle raised, questing; eyes like two supernovae turned their way . . .

"Here," *The Turtle's Golden Claw* said; and waited, patiently, for her to follow. She heard muffled noises: Suu Nuoc's voice, coming from far away, saying words she couldn't make out; and noises of metal against metal—and the same persistent hum in the background; and the shadows on the walls, the same as on the ship, stretching and turning and changing into claws . . .

She took a deep, shaking breath. Why had she charged in?

As they went deeper in, the furniture straightened up; things became . . . almost normal, save that everything seemed still charged with that curious, pent up electricity. "Time differentials," *The Turtle's Golden Claw* said. "Like the eye of the storm." She whispered something; after a while Ngoc Ha realised it was the same singsong incantations she'd said outside: "Integrate the quotient over the gradient lines—the princess' blood became pearls at the bottom of the river, and her husband committed suicide at her grave—four times the potential energy at the point of stability, divided by N . . ."

There was a door, ahead, and the light was almost blinding. Little by little—though it felt she was making no progress—they walked towards it, even as *The Turtle's Golden Claw* wove her equations together; her curious singsong of old legends and mathematics.

The lab reminded her of Grand Master Bach Cuc's: every surface covered with objects and odd construct—pieces of electronics, half-baked, discarded ceramics; the light playing over all of them, limning them in blue. It was filled with Suu Nuoc's escort, the Embroidered Guards standing ill at ease, wedged against bits and pieces of machines.

Ahead, another door: a harmonisation arch, the source of all the light, and Suu Nuoc, kneeling by the side of a young, panicked woman who was putting two bits of cabling together. "It's overloading," she said.

"Turn it off," Suu Nuoc said. He glanced up, and nodded at Ngoc Ha as she knelt by his side.

The Turtle's Golden Claw was still humming—more warily, avoiding the edges of the harmonisation arch. "You set up an access to deep spaces *here*?"

"As I said—" the young woman—Lam—took a brief, angry look at the mindship— "I didn't expect this to work!"

"Turn it off," Suu Nuoc said.

"I can't," Lam's voice was hard. "I have someone still inside."

"Diem Huong?" Ngoc Ha asked, and knew she was right. There was something about the arch; about what lay beyond it—there was something in the lab with them, that same vast presence she'd felt earlier, slowly turning towards them. "It's spreading to the orbital."

"Yes," Lam said. "I know. But I'm still not leaving Diem Huong in it."

The Turtle's Golden Claw followed the boundary of the harmonisation arch; slowly tracing is contours, whispering words Ngoc Ha could barely hear. "It's not stabilised, that's the issue."

"You can talk," Ngoc Ha said, more sharply than she'd meant to. "Grand Master Bach Cuc didn't stabilise anything either, and it killed her."

"We will not talk of Bach Cuc here," *The Turtle's Golden Claw* snapped.

Lam looked vaguely curious; but, through what appeared to be a supreme effort of will, turned her attention back to the door. Through the light Ngoc Ha caught glimpses and pieces—a hand, an arm; a fragment of an altar with incense sticks protruding from it; the face of a yellow-robed monk. Another place; another time. "What was it supposed to be?"

Lam finished clinching together her two cables—with no perceptible difference.

She looked up, her face gleaming with blue-tinged sweat. "The Citadel. Diem Huong's always wanted to go back." She snapped her fingers; bots rose up from the floor, though they were in bad shape, missing arms and with live wires trailing from them. "A time machine sounded like a good idea, at the time."

A time machine. Summoning deep spaces on an orbital. "And you thought Grand Master Bach Cuc was imprudent?"

"At least I'm still here," Lam snapped. "Which isn't, I understand, what happened with the Grand Master."

"Please stop arguing about Bach Cuc," Suu Nuoc said, in a low but commanding voice. "And turn this thing off. I don't care about Diem Huong. This is going to destroy the orbital."

"I'm not doing anything until Diem Huong walks out that door," Lam said.

Ngoc Ha stood, watching the door. Watching the light; and the presence without; and her daughter, the mindship, prowling around the machine like a tiger. A time machine. A window on the Citadel. On Ngoc Minh and her people and the distant past—the past that had twisted her life into its present shape and continued to hang over her like the shadow of a sword.

She reached out before she could stop herself—heard, distantly, Suu Nuoc's scream; felt Lam's arm pulling at her—but it was too late, she was already touching the arch—she'd expected some irresistible force to drag her in, some irreversible current that would have taken her to Diem Huong and the Citadel, amidst all the hurt she'd been bottling up.

Instead, there was silence.

Calm spread from the machine, like oil thrown on waves; a deafening lack of noise that seemed to still everything and everyone in its wake. And, like a huge beast lumbering towards its den, the presence that had been dogging Ngoc Ha ever since she'd entered the deep spaces turned its eyes towards her, and saw.

I am here.

It was a voice like the fires of stars torn apart, like the thunder of ships' engines, like the call of a bell in a temple beyond time.

I am here.

And it was a voice Ngoc Ha had heard, and never forgotten, one that rose in the holes of her heart, each word a twisting hook that dragged raw, red memories from the depths of the past.

Ngoc Minh.

THE ENGINEER

Diem Huong stood, paralysed. The Embroidered Guards were staring at her; the commander raising a gun towards her. "There's been a report of an intruder here, harassing Madam Quynh."

Reports whose memories wouldn't last more than a few moments; but sometimes, a few moments was all that it took for a message to travel along a chain of command—and, like everyone else, the Embroidered Guards could teleport from the palace to any place in a heartbeat.

Diem Huong could teleport, too; but she was frozen, trying not to stare at the muzzle of five weapons aimed at her. They would shoot; and it didn't take that long for energy arcs to find their mark.

"Look," she said, "I can explain—" If she had enough time, they would forget her; why she was here, why she mattered. If she had enough time.

They all had their weapons raised; trained on her; and the commander was frowning, trying to see what to make of her. He was going to fire. He was going to—

There was only one thing for it.

Run.

Before she could think, she'd started pelting away from them—back towards the compartment, back towards Mother, who wouldn't recognise or acknowledge her, or answer any of her questions.

"Stop—"

At any moment, she would feel it; the energy going through her, the spasms as it travelled through her body—would fall to the floor screaming and twitching like a puppet taken apart—but still, she ran, towards the illusory, unattainable safety of a home that had since long ceased to be hers . . .

Run.

There was a wave of stillness; passing over the faces of the soldiers, catching them mid-frown and freezing them in place—an invisible wind that blew through the station, laying icy fingers on her like a caress.

In front of her, the door opened; save that it was wreathed in blue light, like that of the harmonisation arch—the wind blew through it, carrying through the smell of fried garlic and fish sauce, and jasmine rice—so incongruously familiar Diem Huong stopped. Surely that wasn't possible . . .

The wind blew through the door, carrying tatters of light towards it—each gust adding depth and body to the light, until the vague outline of a figure became visible—line after line, a shape drawn by a master's paintbrush—the outline of a face surrounded by a mane of black hair; of silk clothes and jade bracelets as green as forest leaves.

Lam. Had to be. Lam had finally found a way to rescue her.

But it wasn't Lam. The clothes were yellow brocade—for a moment only, and then they became the saffron of monks' robes; the hair was longer than Lam's, the face older and more refined—and the eyes were two pits of unbearable compassion.

"Child," the woman said. "Come."

"Who are you?" Diem Huong asked.

The woman laughed; a low, pleasant sound with no edge of threat to it. "I am Ngoc Minh. Come now, there isn't much time."

Ngoc Minh? The Bright Princess? "I don't understand—" Diem Huong said, but Ngoc Minh was extending a hand as translucent as porcelain; and, because nothing else made sense, Diem Huong took it.

For a moment—a dizzying, terrifying moment—she hung again in the blackness, in the void between the stars, brushed by a presence as terrible as a mindship in deep spaces, something that wrapped huge wings around her until she choked—and then it passed, and she realised the terrible presence was the Bright Princess herself; that the wings weren't choking her; but holding her as she flew.

"It's going to be fine," the Bright Princess whispered, in her mind.

"Mother—"

There were no words in the darkness, in the void; just the distant, dispassionate light of stars; and the sound of beings calling to each other like spaceships in the deep. There were no words; and no illusions left. Only kindness; and the memory of tears glistening in Mother's eyes.

"Your mother loved you," the Bright Princess said.

It still stands. But for how long?

It's going to fall, one way or another.

Sometimes, all you have are bad choices.

Make a stand, or be conquered. Kill, or be killed. Submit, or have to subjugate others.

Mother had sent them away—packing her daughter and her husband, hiding what it had cost her. She had known. She had known the Citadel had no other choice but to vanish; that Ngoc Minh would never fight against her own people. That she would gather, instead, all her powers—all her monks and hermits and their students, for one purpose only: to disappear where no one would ever find them.

"You told her," Diem Huong said. "What was going to happen. What you were going to do."

"Of course," the Bright Princess said. "It's a Citadel, not a dictatorship; not an Imperial Court. My word is law; but I wouldn't have decided something like this without asking everyone to make a choice. The cost was too high."

Too high. Mother had made her bad choice; to have her family survive; to have her daughter grow into adulthood. "Where is she?"

"Nowhere. Everywhere," the Bright Princess whispered. "Beyond your reach, forever, child. She made her choice. Let her be."

I didn't feel you'd understand, younger aunt. You're too young to have children; or believe in the necessity of holding up the world.

"I do understand," Diem Huong said, to the darkness, but it was too late. It had always been thirty years too late, and Mother was gone, and would not come back no matter how hard she prayed or worked. "I do understand, Mother," she whispered; and she realised, with a shock, that she was crying.

THE EMPRESS

Mi Hiep summoned Huu Tam to her quarters; in the gardens outside her rooms, where bots were maintaining the grottos and waterfalls, the pavilions by the side of ponds covered with water lilies and lotuses; the arched bridges covered by willow branches, like a prelude to separation.

"Walk with me, will you?"

Huu Tam was silent; staring at the skies; at the ballet of shuttles in the skies. His attendants walked three steps behind them; affording them both the illusion of privacy.

"We are at war," Mi Hiep said. In the communal network, every place in the gardens was named; everything associated with an exquisite poem. It had been, she remembered, a competition to choose the poems. Ngoc Minh had won in several places; but Mi Hiep couldn't even remember where her daughter's poems would be. She could look it up, of course, but it wouldn't be the same. "You're going to have to take more responsibilities."

Huu Tam snorted. "I'm not a warrior."

Two ghost emperors flickered into life: the first, the Righteously Martial Emperor, who had founded the dynasty in floods of blood; and the Twenty-Third, the Great Virtue Emperor, who had hidden in his palace while civil war tore apart the Empire. "No one is," the Twenty-Third Emperor said.

"I know." Huu Tam's voice was curt.

"You will need Van," Mi Hiep said. Then, carefully, "And Suu Nuoc."

He sucked in a breath, and looked away. He wouldn't contradict her—what child gainsaid their parents?—but he didn't agree. "You don't like him. You don't have to." She raised a hand, to forestall any objections. How was she going to make him understand? She had tried, for decades; and perhaps failed. "You like flattery, child. Always have. It's more pleasant to hear pleasant things about yourself; more pleasant never to be challenged. And more pleasant to surround yourself with friends."

"Who wouldn't?" Huu Tam was defiant.

"A court is not a nest of sycophants," the First Emperor said, sternly.

"Flattery will destroy you," the Twenty-Third Emperor—sallow-faced and fearful—whispered. "Look at my life as an example."

Huu Tam said nothing for a while. He would obey her, she knew; he was too well-bred and too polite. He wasn't Ngoc Minh; who would have disagreed and stormed off. He would talk to Suu Nuoc, but he wouldn't trust him. She couldn't force him to.

There was a wind, in the gardens; a ripple on the surface of the pond, bending the lotus flowers, as if a giant hand from the heavens had rifled through them, discarding stems and petals—and the world seemed to pause and hold its breath for a bare moment.

Mi Hiep turned; and saw her.

She stood in the octagonal pavilion in the middle of the pond—not so much coalescing into existence, but simply here one moment, as if the universe had reorganised itself to include her—almost too far away for her to make out the face, though she would have recognised her in a heartbeat—and then, as Mi Hiep held a deep, burning breath, she flickered out of existence, and reappeared, an arm's length away from Huu Tam and her.

Huu Tam's face was pale. "Elder sister," he whispered.

The Bright Princess hadn't changed—still the same face that Mi Hiep remembered; the full cheeks, the burning eyes looking straight at her, refusing to bend to the Empress her mother. Her hair was the same, too; not tied in a topknot, but loose, falling all the way to the ground until it seemed to root her to the ground.

"Child," she whispered. "Where are you?" She could see the pavilion through Ngoc Minh's body; and the pink lotus flowers; and the darkening heavens over their heads.

Nowhere, whispered the wind. *Everywhere*.

"There are no miracles," Huu Tam whispered.

Yes. No. Perhaps, said the wind. *It doesn't matter.*

Mi Hiep reached out; and so did Ngoc Minh—one ghostly hand reaching for a wrinkled one—her touch was the cold between stars, a slight pressure that didn't feel quite real—like the memory of a dream on waking up.

Ngoc Minh smiled; and it seemed to fill up the entire world—and suddenly Mi Hiep was young again, watching an infant play in the courtyard, lining up pebbles and fragments of broken vases; and the infant looked up and saw her, and smiled, and the entire universe seemed to shift and twist and hurt like salted knives in wounds—and then she was older, and the infant older too; and she tossed and turned in her bed, afraid for her life—and she woke up and asked the army to invade the Citadel . . .

"Child. . . ." I'm sorry, she wanted to say. The emperors had been right—Huu Tam had been right: it had never been about weapons or war; or about technologies she could steal from the citadel. But simply about this—a mother and her daughter, and all the unsaid words, the unsaid fears—the unsolved quarrel that was all Mi Hiep's fault.

Ngoc Minh said nothing, and merely smiled back.

I forgive you, the wind whispered. *Please forgive me, Mother.*

"What for?"

Greed. Anger. Disobedience. Good-bye, Mother.

"Child . . ." Mi Hiep reached out again; but Ngoc Minh was gone; and only the memory of that smile remained—and then even that was gone, and Mi Hiep was alone again, gasping for breaths that burnt her lungs, as the universe became a blur around her.

Huu Tam looked at her, shaking. "Mother—"

Mi Hiep shook her head. "Not now, please."

"Empress!" It was Lady Linh and Van, both looking grim. Mi Hiep took a deep breath, waiting for things to right themselves again—mercifully, none of the ghost emperors had said any words. "What is it?" she asked.

Van made a gesture; and the air between them filled with the image of a ship—battered and pocked through like the surface of an airless moon, with warmth—oxygen?—pouring out of a hole in the hull.

One of the Nam mindships.

"We have one," Van said. "But the rest jumped. Given their previous pattern, they'll be at the Imperial Shipyards in two days."

Huu Tam threw a concerned look at Mi Hiep—who didn't answer. She didn't feel anything she said would make sense, in the wake of Ngoc Minh's disappearance. "How soon can you work on the ship?"

"We're getting it towed to the nearest safe space," Lady Linh said. "And sending a team of scientists on board, to start work immediately. They'll find out how it was done."

Of course they would. "And the shipyards?" Mi Hiep asked, slowly, carefully—every word feeling as though it broke a moment of magical silence.

"Pulling away, as you ordered." Van gestured again; and pulled an image into the network. The yards, with the shells of mindships clustered among them; and bots pulling them apart in slow motion, dismantling them little by little. As Van gestured, they moved in accelerated time—and everything seemed to disintegrate into nothingness. Other, whole ships moved to take the place of those she'd ordered destroyed: warships, bristling with weapons; and civilian ships, looking small and pathetic next to them, a bulwark against the inevitable. "They've already evacuated the Mind-bearers. The other ships are waiting for them."

There would be a battle—many battles, to slow down the Nam fleet in any way they could—waiting until they could gather their defences; until they could study the hijacked ship and determine how it had been done, and how it could be reversed. And even if it couldn't . . . they still had their own mindships; and the might of their army. "We'll be fine, Mother," Huu Tam, softly. "One doesn't need miracles to fight a war."

No. One needed miracles to avoid one. But Ngoc Minh was gone, her technologies and her Citadel with her; and all that remained of her was the memory of a hand in hers, like the caress of the wind.

Where are you?

Nowhere. Everywhere.

Mi Hiep stood, her face unmoving; and listened to her advisors, steeling herself for what lay ahead—a long slow slog of unending battles and feints, of retreats and invasions and pincer moves, and the calculus of deaths and acceptable losses. She rubbed her hand, slowly, carefully.

Forgive me, Mother. Good-bye.

Good-bye, child.

And on her hand, the touch of the wind faded away, until it was nothing more than a gentle balm on her heart; a memory to cling to in the days ahead—as they all made their way forward in the days of the war, in an age without miracles.

THE YOUNGER SISTER

Ngoc Ha stood, caught in the light—her hand thrust through the door, becoming part of the whirlwind of images beyond. She didn't feel any different; more as if her hand had ceased to exist altogether—no sensation coming back from it, nothing.

And then she did feel something—faint at first, but growing stronger with every passing moment—until she recognised the touch of a hand on hers, fingers interlacing with her own.

I am here.

She didn't think; merely pulled; and her hand came back from beyond the harmonisation arch; and with it, another hand and an arm and a body.

Two figures coalesced from within the maelstrom. The first, bedraggled and mousy, her topknot askew, her face streaked with tears, could only be the missing engineer.

"Huong," Lam said, sharply; and dropped what she was holding, to run towards her. "You idiot." She was crying, too; and Diem Huong let her drag her away. "You freaking idiot."

But the other one . . . the one whose hand Ngoc Ha was still holding, even now . . .

She had changed, and not changed. She was all of Ngoc Ha's memories—the hands closing hers around the baby chick; the tall, comforting presence who had held her after too many nights frustrated over her dissertations; the sister who had stood on the view-screen with her last message, assuring her all was well—and yet she was more, too. Her head was well under the harmonisation arch, except that there was about her a presence, a sense of vastness that went well beyond her actual size. She was faintly translucent, and so were her clothes, shifting from one shape to the next, from yellow brocade to nuns' saffron; the jewellery on her hands and wrists flickering in and out of existence.

"Elder sister." Nothing but formality would come past her frozen lips.

"Lil' sis." Ngoc Minh smiled, and looked at her. "There isn't much time."

"I don't understand," Ngoc Ha said. "Why are you here?"

"Because you called," Ngoc Minh said. With her free hand, the Bright Princess gestured to *The Turtle's Golden Claw*: the ship had moved, to stand by her side; though she said nothing. "Because blood calls to blood, even in the depths of time."

"I—" Ngoc Ha took a deep, trembling breath. "I wanted to find you. Or not to. I wasn't sure."

Ngoc Minh laughed. "You were always so indecisive." Her eyes—her eyes were twin stars, their radiance burning. "As I said—I am here."

"Here?" Ngoc Ha asked. "Where?" The light streamed around her, blurring everything—beyond the arch, the world was still shattered splinters, meaningless fragments.

The Turtle's Golden Claw said, slowly, softly. "This is nowhere, nowhen. Just a pocket of deep spaces. A piece of the past."

Of course. They weren't like Grand Master Bach Cuc, destroyed in the conflagration within her laboratory; but were they any better off?

"Nowhere," Ngoc Minh said, with a nod. She looked, for a moment, past Ngoc Ha; at the two engineers huddled together in a corner of the laboratory, holding hands like two long-lost friends. "That's where I am, lil' sis. Everywhere. Nowhere. Beyond time, beyond space."

No. "You're dead," Ngoc Ha said, sharply; and the words burnt her throat like tears.

"Perhaps," Ngoc Minh said. "I and the Citadel and the people aboard—" she closed her eyes; and for a moment, she wasn't huge, or beyond time; but merely young, and tired, and faced with choices that had destroyed her—"Mother's army and I could have fought each other, spilling blood for every measure of the Citadel. I couldn't do that. Brother shall not fight brother, son shall not slay father, daughter shall not abandon mother . . ." The familiar litany of righteousness taught by their tutors, in days long gone by. "There was a way out."

Death.

"Nowhere. Everywhere," Ngoc Minh said. "If you go far enough into deep spaces, time ceases to have meaning. That's where I took the Citadel."

Time ceases to have meaning. Humanity, too, ceased to have any meaning—Ngoc Ha had read Grand Master Bach Cuc's notes—she'd sent *The Turtle's Golden Claw* there on her own, because humans who went this far *dissolved*, turning into the dust of stars, the ashes of planets. "You're not human," Ngoc Ha said. Not anymore.

"I'm not human either," *The Turtle's Golden Claw* said, gently.

Ngoc Minh merely smiled. "You place too much value on that word."

Because you're my sister. Because—because she was tired, too, of dragging the past behind her; of thirty years of not knowing whether she should mourn or move on; of Mother not giving her any attention beyond her use in finding her sister. Because—

"Did you never think of us?" The words were torn out of Ngoc Ha's mouth before she could think. Did she never see the sleepless nights, the days where she'd carefully moulded her face and her thoughts to never see Ngoc Minh—the long years of shaping a life around the wound of her absence?

Ngoc Minh did not answer. Not human. Not anymore. A star storm, somewhere in the vastness of space. Storms did not think whether they harmed you, or cared whether you grieved.

There isn't much time, she'd said. Of course. Of course no one could live for long, in deep spaces.

"Good-bye, lil' sis. Be at peace." And the Bright Princess withdrew her hand from Ngoc Ha's; turning back towards the light of the harmonisation arch, going back to wherever she was, whatever she had turned into—the face she showed now, the one that didn't seem to have changed, was nothing more than a mask, a gift to Ngoc Ha to comfort her. The real Ngoc Minh—and everyone else in the Citadel—didn't wear faces or bodies anymore.

But still, she'd come; for one last glimpse, one last gift. A moment, frozen in time, before the machine was turned off, or killed them all.

Be at peace.

If such a thing could ever happen—if memories could be erased, wounds magically healed, lives righted back into the proper shape, without the shadow of jealousy and love and loss.

"Wait," Ngoc Ha said; and Bright Princess Ngoc Minh paused—and looked back at her, reaching out with a translucent hand; her eyes serene and distant, her smile the same enigmatic one as the bodhisattva statues in the temples.

The hand was wreathed in light; the blue nimbus of the harmonisation door; the shadow of deep spaces where she lived, where no one could survive.

Nowhere. Everywhere.

"Wait."

"Mother—" *The Turtle's Golden Claw* said. "You can't—"

Ngoc Ha smiled. "Of course I can," she said; and reached out, and clasped her sister's hand to hers.

THE OFFICER

From where he stood rooted to the ground, Suu Nuoc saw it all happen, as if in some nightmare he couldn't wake up from: Ngoc Ha talking with the figure in the doorway; *The Turtle's Golden Claw* screaming; and Lam cursing, the bots surging from the floor at her command, making for the arch.

Too late.

Ngoc Ha reached out, and took the outstretched hand. Her topknot had come undone, and her hair was streaming in the wind from the door—for a moment they stood side by side, the two sisters, almost like mirror images of each other, as if they were the same person with two very different paths in life.

"Princess!" Suu Nuoc called—knowing, with a horrible twist in his belly, what was going to happen before it did.

Ngoc Ha turned to look at him, for a fraction of a second. She smiled; and her smile was cold, distant already—a moment only, and then she turned back to look at her sister the Bright Princess; and her other hand wrapped itself around her sister's other hand, locking them in an embrace that couldn't be broken.

And then they were gone, scattering into a thousand shards of light.

"No," *The Turtle's Golden Claw* said. "No. Mother . . ."

No panic. This was not the time for it. With an effort, Suu Nuoc wrenched his thoughts back from the brink of incoherence. Someone needed to be pragmatic about matters, and clearly neither of the two scientists, nor the mindship, was going to provide level-headedness.

"She's gone," he said to *The Turtle's Golden Claw*. "This isn't what we need to worry about. How do we shut off this machine before it kills us all?"

"She's my mother!" *The Turtle's Golden Claw* said.

"I know," Suu Nuoc said, curtly. Pragmatism, again. Someone needed to have it. "You can look for her later."

"There is no later!"

"There always is. Leave it, will you? We have more pressing problems."

"Yes, we do." Lam had come back; and with her was the engineer—Diem Huong, who still looked as though she'd been through eight levels of Hell and beyond, but whose face no longer had the shocked look of someone who had seen things she shouldn't. "You're right. We need to shut this thing down. Come on, Huong. Give me a hand." They crouched together by the machine, handing each other bits and pieces of ceramic and cabling. After a while, *The Turtle's Golden Claw* drifted, reluctantly, to join them, interjecting advice, while the bots moved slowly, drunkenly, piecing things back together as best as they could.

Suu Nuoc, whose talents most emphatically did not lie in science or experimental time machines, drifted back to the harmonisation arch, watching the world beyond—the collage of pristine corridors and delicately painted temples; the fragments of citizens teleporting from one ship to the next.

The Citadel. What the Empress had desperately sought. What she'd thought she desperately needed—and Suu Nuoc had never argued with her, only taken her orders to heart and done his best to see them to fruition.

But now . . . Now he wasn't so sure, anymore, that they'd ever needed any of this.

"It's gone," Diem Huong said, gently. She was standing by her side, watching the door; her voice quiet, thoughtful; though he was not fooled at the strength of the emotions she was repressing. "The Bright Princess took it too far into deep spaces, and it vanished. That's what really happened to it. That's why Grand Master Bach Cuc would never have found it. It only exists in the past, now."

"I know," Suu Nuoc said. Perhaps, if another of the Empress's children was willing to touch the arch—but his gut told him it wouldn't work again. Ngoc Ha had been close to Bright Princess Ngoc Minh; too close, in fact—the seeds of her ulti-mate fate already sown long before they had come here, to the Scattered Pearls belt. There was no one else whose touch would call forth the Bright Princess again; even if the Empress was willing to sanction the building of a time machine again, after it had killed a Master of Grand Design Harmony and almost destroyed an orbital.

"There!" Lam said, triumphantly. She rose, holding two bits of cable; at the same time as *The Turtle's Golden Claw* reached for something on the edge of the har-monisation arch.

The light went out, as if she'd thrown a switch; when it came on again, the air had changed—no longer charged or lit with blue, it was simply the slightly stale, odourless one of any orbital. And the room, too, shrank back to normal, the furni-ture simply tables and chairs, and screens, rather than the collage monstrosities Suu Nuoc and his squad had seen on the way in.

Suu Nuoc took a deep, trembling breath, trying to convince himself it was over.

The Turtle's Golden Claw drifted back to the machine—now nothing more than a rectangle with a de-activated harmonisation arch, looking small and pathetic, and altogether too diminished to have caused so much trouble. "I'll find her," she said. "Somewhere in deep spaces . . ."

Suu Nuoc said nothing. He'd have to gather them all; to bring them back to the First Planet, so they could be debriefed—so he could explain to the Empress why she had lost a second daughter. And—if she still would have him, when it was all accounted for—he would have to help her fight a war.

But, for now, he watched the harmonisation arch; and remembered what he had seen through it. The past. The Citadel, like some fabled underground treasure. Ghostly apparitions, like myths and fairytales—nothing to build a life or a war strat-egy on.

The present was all that mattered. The past's grievous wounds had to close, or to be ignored; and the future's war and the baying of wolves could only be distant wor-ries. He would stand where he had always stood; by his Empress's side, to guide the Empire forward for as long as she would have him.

The Citadel was gone, and so were its miracles—but wasn't it for the best, after all?

Allora & Calzadilla & Ted Chiang, "The Great Silence," *e-flux journal 56th Venice Biennale*.
Ken Altabef, "Laika," *Interzone 251*.
Charlie Jane Anders, "Ghost Champagne," *Uncanny 5*.
——, "Rat Catcher's Yellows," *Press Start to Play*.
Michael Andre-Driussi," Atomic Missions," *Kaleidotrope*, Winter.
Eleanor Arnason, "Telling Stories to the Sky," *Fantasy & Science Fiction*, January/February.
Madeline Ashby, "Memento Mori," *Meeting Infinity*.
Charlotte Ashley, "La Héron," *Fantasy & Science Fiction*, March/April.
Megan Arkenberg, "Like All Beautiful Places," *The End Has Come*.
Julia August, "Rites of Passage," *Kaliedotrope*, Autumn.
Daniel Ausema, "Among the Sighs of the Violoncellos," *Strange Horizons*, April.
Alec Austin and Marissa Lingen, "Human Trials," *Abyss & Apex*, 4th Quarter.
Paolo Bacigalupi, "A Hot Day's Night," *Fantasy & Science Fiction*, September/October.
Dale Bailey, "The Ministry of the Eye," *Lightspeed*, April.
John Barnes, "My Last Bringback," *Meeting Infinity*.
Kathleen Bartholomew and Kage Baker, "Pareidolia," *Asimov's Science Fiction*, March.
Aria Bauer, "Bones of Steel," *Daily SF*, November 19.
Stephen Baxter, "Endurance," *Endurance*.
Elizabeth Bear, "The Balance in Blood," *Uncanny 7*.
——, "The Bone War," *Fantasy & Science Fiction*, September/October.
——, "The Heart's Filthy Lesson," *Old Venus*.
——, "In Libres," *Uncanny 4*.
——, "Margin of Survival," *The End Has Come*.
——, "Skin in the Game," *Future Visions*.
Greg Bear, "The Machine Starts," *Future Visions*.
Helena Bell, "Needle on Bone," *Strange Horizons*, November 2.
Annie Bellet, "Goodnight Earth," *The End Has Come*.
Gregory Benford, "Aspects," *Meeting Infinity*.
M. Bennardo, "Ghosts of the Savannah," *Asimov's*, June.
——, "We Jump Down into the Dark," *Asimov's*, December.
Paul M. Berger, "The Mantis Tattoo," *Fantasy & Science Fiction*, March/April.
Deborah Biancotti, "Look How Cold My Hands Are," *Cranky Ladies of History*.
Michael Bishop, "Rattlesnakes and Men," *Asimov's*, February.
Holly Black, "1Up," *Press Start to Play*.
Jenny Blackford, "The Sorrow," *Hear Me Roar!*
Brooke Bolander, "And You Shall Know Her by the Trail of Dead," *Lightspeed*, February.
Gregory Norman Bossart, "Twelve and Tag," *Asimov's*, March.
Elizabeth Bourne, "The Algebra of Events," *Clarkesworld*, September.
Richard Bowes, "The Duchess and the Ghost," *Fantasy*, December.

———, "Rascal Saturday," *Fantasy & Science Fiction*, September/October.

David Bowles, "Winds That Stir Vermillion Sands," *Strange Horizons*, 6/29.

David Brin, "The Tell," *Future Visions*.

———, "The Tumbledowns of Cleopatra Abyss," *Old Venus*.

Eneasz Brodski, "Red Legacy," *Asimov's*, February.

Christopher Brown, "Festival," *Stories for Chip*.

Maria A. Buchkachi, "Jestocost, Djinn," *Afrofuture(s)*.

Tobias S. Buckell, "Pale Blue Memories," *Old Venus*.

Oliver Buckram, "The Quintessence of Dust," *Fantasy & Science Fiction*, July/August.

Mike Buckley, "An Original Brightness," *Clarkesworld*, March.

Karl Bunker, "Caisson," *Asimov's*, August.

Matthew Burrows, "The Exception That Proves the Rule," *War Stories from the Future*.

Chris Butler, "The Deep of Winter," *Interzone 259*.

C.A.L, "Bitter Medicine," *Kaleidotrope*, Autumn.

Rebecca Campbell, "Unearthly Landscape by a Lady," *Beneath Ceaseless Skies*, October 15.

Stephen Case, "The Wizard's House," *Beneath Ceaseless Skies*, February 5.

Erin Casher, "Swallowing Silver," *Beneath Ceaseless Skies*, April 30.

Michael Cassutt, "The Sunset of Time," *Old Venus*.

Rob Chilson, "A Turkey with Egg on His Face," *Fantasy & Science Fiction*, May/June.

———, "The Tarn," *Analog*, July–August.

Roshani Chokshi, "The Star Maiden," *Shimmer* 26, July/August.

Gwendolyn Clare, "Holding the Ghosts," *Asimov's*, March.

———, "Indelible," *Clarkesworld*, February.

Ron Collins, "Tumbling Dice," *Analog*, July–August.

Glen Cook, "Bone Eaters," *Operation Arcana*.

Brenda Cooper, "Biology at the End of the World," *Asimov's*, September.

———, "Iron Pegasus,: *Mission: Tomorrow*.

James S. A. Corey, "The Vital Abyss," *Orbit*.

Albert E. Cowdrey, "The Laminated Man," *Fantasy & Science Fiction*, May/June.

———, "The Lord of Ragnarök," *Fantasy & Science Fiction*, September/October.

———, "Portrait of a Witch," *Fantasy & Science Fiction*, January/February.

Ian Creasey, "My Time on Earth," *Asimov's*, October/November.

John Chu, "(Influence Isolated, Make Peace,") *Lightspeed*, June.

Richard Chwedyk, "Dixon's Road," *Fantasy & Science Fiction*, July/August.

Dennis Danvers, "Adult Children of Alien Beings," *Tor.com*, August 19.

Indrapramit Das, "Psychopomp," *Interfictions*, November.

Aliette de Bodard, "In Blue Lily's Wake," *Meeting Infinity*.

———, "Of Books, And Earth, and Courtship," *Nine Dragon Rivers*.

Emily Devenport, "The Servant," *Clarkesworld*, August.

Malcolm Devlin, "Five Conversations with My Daughter (Who Travels in Time)," *Interzone* 251.

———, "Her First Harvest," *Interzone* 258.

Jeste de Vries, "Echoes of Life," *Kaleidotrope*, Spring,

Seth Dickinson, "Morrigan in Shadow," *Clarkesworld*, December.

———, "Please Undo This Hurt," *Tor.com*, 9/15.

Brian Dolton, "This Is the Way the Universe Ends: With a Bang," *Fantasy & Science Fiction*, March/April.

Brendan Dubois, "The Master's Voice," *Analog*, December.

Andy Dudak, "Anarchic Hand," *Apex*, January.

——, "Asymptotic," *Clarkesworld*, June.

——, "Samsara and Ice," *Analog*, January/February.

Tananarive Due, "Carriers," *The End Has Come*.

Thoraiya Dryer, "Houdini's Heart," *Apex*, March.

Greg Egan, "The Four Thousand, the Eight Hundred," *Asimov's*, December.

Kate Elliott, "On the Dying Winds of the Old Year and the Birthing Winds of the New," *The Very Best of Kate Elliott*.

Amal El-Mohtar, "Madeleine," *Lightspeed*, June.

——, "Pockets," *Uncanny 2*.

——, "The Truth About Owls," *Strange Horizons*, January 26.

Ruthanna Emrys, "The Deepest Rift," *Tor.com*, June 24.

Timons Esaias, "Exit Interview," *Analog*, November.

——, "Hollywood After 10," *Asimov's*, October/November.

Paul Evanby, "Utrechtenaar," *Strange Horizons*, June 15.

Fábio Fernandos, "Eleven Stations," *Stories for Chip*.

Gemma Files, "The Salt Wedding," *Kaleidotrope*, Winter.

C.C. Finlay, "Time Bomb Time," *Lightspeed*, May.

Eugene Fischer, "The New Mother," *Asimov's*, April/May.

Jeffrey Ford, "The Thyme Fiend," *Tor.com*, March 11.

——, "The Winter Wraith," *Fantasy & Science Fiction*, November/December.

Amanda Forrest, "Of Apricots and Dying," *Asimov's*, December.

Neil Gaiman, "Black Dog," *Trigger Warnings*.

Tom Gerencer, "And All Our Donkeys Were Vain," *Galaxy's Edge*, May.

David Gerrold, "Entanglements," *Fantasy & Science Fiction*, May/June.

——, "The Great Pan American Airship Mystery, or, Why I Murdered Robert Benchley," *Asimov's*, July.

——, "Monsieur," *Fantasy & Science Fiction*, September/October.

Gary Gibson, "Scienceville," *Interzone 251*.

Mira Grant, "The Happiest Place," *The End Has Come*.

Simon R. Green, "Bomber's Moon," *Operation Arcana*.

John Gribbin, "Breakout," *Postscripts* 34/35.

Jim Grimsley, "The God Year," *Asimov's*, September.

Jason Gurley, "Quiet Town," *Lightspeed*, April.

Andrea Hairston, "Saltwater Railroad," *Lightspeed*, October.

Joe Haldeman, "Living Hell," *Old Venus*.

Nick Harkaway, "Boxes," *Twelve Tomorrows*.

Gregor Hartmann,"Into the Fiery Planet," *Fantasy & Science Fiction*, July–August.

——, "The Man From X," *Fantasy & Science Fiction*, January/February.

Ivor W. Hartmann, "Last Wave," *Afrofuture(s)*.

Maria Dahvana Headley, "Some Gods of El Paso," *Tor.com*, October 28.

——, "Solder and Seam," *Lightspeed*, July.

——, "The Thirteen Mercies," *Fantasy & Science Fiction*, November/December.

Berrien C. Henderson, "Let Baser Things Devise," *Clarkesworld*, April.

David Herter, "Islands off the Coast of Capitola, 1978," *Tor.com*, July 8.

Nalo Hopkinson, "Flying Lessons," *Falling in Love with Hominids*.

—— & Nisi Shawl, "Jamaica Ginger," *Stories for Chip*.

Kat Howard, "A User's Guide to Increments of Time," *Fantasy & Science Fiction*, March/April.

Matthew Hughes, "A Face of Black Iron," *Lightspeed*, March.

—— "The Archon," *Lightspeed*, January.

——, "The Blood of the Dragon," *Lightspeed*, May.

——, "The Curse of the Myremelon," *Fantasy & Science Fiction*, July/August.

——, "Greeves and the Evening Star," *Old Venus*.

——, "Prisoner of Pandarius," *Fantasy & Science Fiction*, January/February.

Kameron Hurley, "Body Politic," *Meeting Infinity*.

——, "Elephants and Corpses," *Tor.com*, May 13.

Simon Ings, "Drones," *Meeting Infinity*.

Betsy James, "Paradise and Trout," *Fantasy & Science Fiction*, July/August.

Holly Jennings, "The Time Has Come," *Daily SF*.

Alex Jennings, "Heart of Brass," *Stories for Chip*.

Xia Jia, "If on a Winter Night a Traveler," *Clarksworld*, November.

Hao Jingfang, "Folding Beijing," *Uncanny 2*.

Fadzlishah Johanabas, "Songbird," *Interzone 257*.

Kij Johnson, "The Apartment Dweller's Bestiary," *Clarkesworld*, January.

Bill Johnson, "Paris, 1835," *Analog*, December.

Gwyneth Jones, "A Planet Named Desire," *Old Venus*.

Naim Kabir, "Slowly Builds an Empire," *Clarkesworld*, March.

Vyler Kaftan, "Last Hunt," *Asimov's*, September.

Rahul Kanakia, "Here Is My Thinking on a Situation That Affects Us All," *Lightspeed*, November.

James Patrick Kelly, "Oneness: A Triptych," *Fantasy & Science Fiction*, July/August.

Jake Kerr, "The Gray Sunrise," *The End Has Come*.

Garry Kilworth, "Chasing Gaia," *Postscripts 34/35*.

Alica Sola Kim, "A Residence for Friendless Ladies," *Fantasy & Science Fiction*, March/April.

T. Kingfisher, "Telling the Bees," *Strange Horizons*, December 21.

David Klecha & Tobias S. Buckell, "Rules of Enchantment," *Operation Arcana*.

Mary Robinette Kowal, "Like Native Things," *Asimov's*, July.

——, "Midnight Hour," *Uncanny 5*.

Nancy Kress, "Blessings," *The End Has Come*.

——, "Cocoons," *Meeting Infinity*.

Naomi Kritzer, "Cat Pictures, Please," *Clarkesworld*, January.

——, "Cleanout," *Fantasy & Science Fiction*, November/December.

——, "Jubilee: A Seastead Story," *Fantasy & Science Fiction*, January/February.

——, "The Silicon Curtain: A Seastead Story," *Fantasy & Science Fiction*, July/August.

——, "So Much Cooking," *Clarkesworld*, November.

——, "Wild," *Apex*, April.

Derek Künsken, "Ghost Colors," *Asimov's*, February.

——, "Pollen from a Future Harvest," *Asimov's*, June.

Jay Lake, "An Exile of the Heart," *Clarkesworld*, January.

Claude Lalumiére, "Empathy Evolving as a Quantum of Eight-Dimensional Perception," *Stories for Chip*.

Sarah Langan, "Prototype," *The End Has Come*.

Joe R. Lansdale, "The Wizard of the Trees," *Old Venus*.

Rich Larson, "Biding War," *Asimov's*, December.

——, "Brainwhales Are Stoners, Too," *Interzone* 257.

——, "The Delusive Cartographer," *Beneath Ceaseless Skies*, November 24.

——, "Edited," *Interzone* 259.

——, "Going Endo," *Apex*, July.

——, "The King of the Cathedral," *Beneath Ceaseless Skies*, February 5.

——, "We Might Be Sims," *Interzone* 251.

Karalynn Lee, "Court Bindings," *Beneath Ceaseless Skies*, June 25.

Yoon Ha Lee, "The Cold Inequalities," *Meeting Infinity*.

——, "Gamer's End," *Press Start to Play*.

——, "The Graphology of Hemorrhage," *Operation Arcana*.

——, "Interlingua," *Uncanny* 7.

——, "Snakes," *Clarkesworld*, July.

——, "Two to Leave," *Beneath Ceaseless Skies*, October 15.

——, "Variations on an Apple," *Tor.com*, October 14.

Stephen Leigh, "Bones of Air, Bones of Stone," *Old Venus*.

Rose Lemberg, "archival memory fragments/miner's song," *Uncanny* 2.

——, "Geometries of Belonging," *Beneath Ceaseless Skies*, October 1.

——, "How to Remember to Forget to Remember the Old War," *Lightspeed*, June.

Mack Leonard, "Midnight Funk Association," *Interzone* 257.

David D. Levine, "Damage," *Tor.com*.

——, "Malf," *Mission: Tomorrow*.

Henry Lien, "Bilingual," *Fantasy & Science Fiction*, March/April.

Heather Lindsley, "Werewolf Loves Mermaid," *Lightspeed*, September.

Marissa Lingen, "Blue Ribbon," *Analog*, March.

——, "It Brought Us All Together," *Strange Horizons*, July 13.

——, "Out of the Rose Hills," *Beneath Ceaseless Skies*, May 14.

——, "Points of Origin," *Tor.com*, November 4.

——, "Surfacing," *Lightspeed*, March.

Ken Liu, "Article 1, Section 8, Class 11," *War Stories from the Future*.

——, "Compatibility," *Ecotones*.

——, "The Gods Have Not Died in Vain," *The End Has Come*.

Richard A. Lovertt, "The Wormhole War," *Analog*, June.

Will Lundwigsen, "Acres of Perhaps," *Asimov's*, July.

Ian R. MacLeod, "Frost on Glass," *Frost on Glass*.

Kate MacLeod, "The Onmyoji's Wife," *Abyss & Apex*, 1st Quarter.

Bruce McAllister, "Dog," *Tor.com*, March 25.

——, "Dreampet," *Fantasy & Science Fiction*, November/December.

——, "Holy Water, Holy Blood," *Beneath Ceaseless Skies*, November 12.

——, "Madonna," *Beneath Ceaseless Skies*, February 19.

——, "My Father's Crab," *Analog*, October.

Paul McAuley, "Wild Honey," *Asimov's*, August.

Joe M. McDermott, "Paul and His Son," *Asimov's*, April/May.

Jack McDevitt, "Excalibur," *Mission: Tomorrow*.

——, "Riding with the Duke," *Future Visions*.

Sandra McDonald, "The Adjunct Professor's Guide to Life After Death," *Asimov's*, October/November.

——, "Cora Crane and the Trouble with Me," *Cranky Ladies of History*.

Ian McDowell, "The Hard Woman," *Asimov's*, October/November.

Seanan McGuire, "The Myth of Rain," *Lightspeed*, May.

——, "Resistance," *The End Has Come*.

——, "Survival Horror," *Press Start to Play*.

——, "In Skeleton Leaves," *Operation Arcana*.

Ian McHugh, 'Demons Enough," *Beneath Ceaseless Skies*, October 27.

Will McIntosh, "A Thousand Nights Till Morning," *Asimov's*, August.

——, "Dancing with a Stranger in the Land of Nod," *The End Has Come*.

Angus McIntyre, "Windshear," *Mission: Impossible*.

Vonda N. McIntyre," Little Sisters," *BookViewCafe*.

Sean McMullen, "The Ninth Seduction," *Lightspeed*, September.

Deverah Major, "Voice Prints," *Stories for Chip*.

Usman Malik, "The Pauper Prince and the Eucalyptus Jinn," *Tor.com*, April 22.

Anil Menon, "Clarity," *Stories For Chip*.

Sam J. Miller, "Ghosts of Home," *Lightspeed*, August.

——, "The Heat of Us," *Uncanny* 2.

——, "When Your Child Strays from God," *Clarkesworld*, July.

Kris Millerine, "This Wanderer, in the Dark of the Year," *Clarkesworld*, June.

Sean Monaghan, "The Molenstraat Music Festival," *Asimov's*, September.

Elizabeth Moon, "Mercenary's Honor," *Operation Arcana*.

Sunny Moraine, "At Whatever Are Their Moons," *Strange Horizons*, December 14.

——, "It Is Healing, It Is Never Whole, *Apex*, August.

Tamsyn Muir, "The Deepwater Bride," *Fantasy & Science Fiction*, July/August.

——, "Union," *Clarkesworld*, December.

Karen Myers, "The Visitor," *Strange Horizons*, July 20.

Ramez Naam, "Exile From Extinction," *Meeting Infinity*.

Linda Nagata, "The Way Home," *Operation Arcana*.

T.R. Napper, "An Advanced Guide to Successful Price-Fixing in Extraterrestrial Betting Markets," *Interzone 256*.

——, "A Shout Is a Prayer for the Waiting Centuries," *Interzone 258*.

Ray Nayler, "Mutability," *Asimov's*, June.

Mari Ness, "The Fox Bride," *Daily SF*, March 20.

——, "Inhabiting Your Skin," *Apex*, June.

Ruth Nestvold, "Degrees of Seperation," *Abyss & Apex*, 3rd Quarter.

Alec Nevala-Lee, "Stonebrood," *Analog*, October.

Annalee Newitz, "All-Natural Organic Microbes," *Twelve Tomorrows*.

Garth Nix, "By Frogsled and Lizardback to Ourcast Venusian Lepers," *Old Venus*.

——, "The Company of Women," *Cranky Ladies of History*.

Jay O'Connell, "Candy from Strangers," *Asimov's*, January.

——, "Things Worth Knowing," *Fantasy & Science Fiction*, March/April.

——, "Willing Flesh," *Asimov's*, April/May.

Yukimi Ogawa, "Hundred Eyes," *Strange Horizons*, September 28.

Megan E. O'Keefe, "Of Blood and Brine," *Shimmer*, January 15.

Daniel Jose Older, "Kia and Glo," *Tor.com*.

Malka Older, "Tear Tracks," *Tor.com*, October 21.

An Owomoyele, "Outsider," *Meeting Infinity*.

Suzanne Palmer, "Tuesdays," *Asimov's*, March.

K.J. Parker, "The Last Witness," *Tor.com*.

Richard Parks, "The Bride Doll," *Beneath Ceaseless Skies*, October 1.

Shannon Peavey, "The Snake-Oil Salesman and the Prophet's Head," *Beneath Ceaseless Skies*, April 30.

Brooks Peck, "With Folded RAM," *Asimov's*, October/November.

Sarah Pinsker, "Our Lady of the Open Road," *Asimov's*, June.

——, "Remembery Day," *Apex*, May.

——, "Today's Smarthouse in Love," *Fantasy & Science Fiction*, May/June.

Rachel Pollack, "Johnny Rev," *Fantasy & Science Fiction*, July/August.

Bill Powell, "The Punctuality Machine; Or, A Steampunk Libretto," *Beneath Ceaseless Skies*, May 14.

Gareth L. Powell, "Ride the Blue Horse," *Matter*, July 28.

Tom Purdom, "Day Job," *Asimov's*, April/May.

Chen Qiufan, "Coming of the Light," *Clarkesworld*, March.

Carmelo Rafala, "Song for the Asking," *Stories for Chip*.

Zhang Ran, "Ether," *Clarkesworld*, January.

Kit Reed, "Military Secrets," *Asimov's*, March.

Robert Reed, "The City of Your Soul," *Fantasy & Science Fiction*, November/December.

——, "Cremulator," *Clarkesworld*, September.

——, "Curb," *Postscripts* 34/35.

——, "The Empress in Her Glory," *Clarkesworld*, April.

——, "Empty," *Asimov's*, December.

——, "What I Intend," *Asimov's*, April/May.

Jessica Reisman & Steven Utley, "The Cicadas," *Postscripts* 34/35.

Alastair Reynolds, "A Murmuration," *Interzone 257*.

——, "Slow Bullets," *Tachyon*.

Adam Roberts, "Zayinim," *Jews vs. Zombies*.

Kim Stanley Robinson, "Oral Argument," *Tor.com*, December 7.

Kelly Robson, "Two-Year Man," *Asimov's*, August.

——, "Waters of Versailles," *Tor.com*, June 10.

Margaret Ronald, "Let's Tell Stories of the Death of Children," *Strange Horizons*, October 12.

Christopher Rowe, "The Unveiling," *Asimov's*, January.

S.J. Rozan, "Hanami," *Hanzai Japan*.

Rudy Rucker & Marc Laidlaw, "Watergirl," *Asimov's*, January.

Kristine Kathryn Rusch, "The First Step, *Asimov's*, August.

——, "The Last Surviving Gondola Widow," *Clarkesworld*, February.

——, "The Museum of Modern Warfare," *Analog*, December.

Sarah Saab, "In the Queue for the Worldship Munawwer," *Clarkesworld*, November.

Sofia Samatar, "A Brief History of Nonduality Studies," *Afrofuture(s)*.

Jason Sanford, "Duller's Peace," *Asimov's*, September.

Robert Sawyer, "Looking for Gordo," *Future Visions*.

Kenneth Schneyer, "The Plausibility of Dragons," *Lightspeed*, November.

Veronica Shanoes, "Ballroom Blitz," *Tor.com*, April 1.

Priya Sharma, "Fabulous Beasts," *Tor.com*, July 27.

Nisi Shawl, "A Beautiful Stream," *Cranky Ladies of History*.

John Shirley, "Weedkiller," *Interzone 260*.

Martin L. Shoemaker, "Brigas Nunca Mals," *Analog*, March.

——, "Racing to Mars," *Analog*, September.

Bao Shu, "Preserve Her Memory," *Clarkesworld*, September.

——, "What Has Passed Shall in Kinder Light Appear," *Fantasy & Science Fiction*, March/April.

Vandana Singh, "Ambiguity Machines," *Tor.com*, April 29.

Jack Skillingstead, "Tribute," *Mission: Impossible*.

Alan Smale, "English Wildlife," *Asimov's*, October/November.

Cat Sparks, "Hot Rods," *Lightspeed*, March.

——, "Veteran's Day," *Hear Me Roar!*

Kendra Leigh Spedding, "The Exile of the Eldest Son of the Family Ysanne," *Beneath Ceaseless Skies*, August 7.

Allen M. Steele, "Frogheads," *Old Venus*.

——, "The Long Wait," *Asimov's*, January.

Bruce Sterling, "The Ancient Engineer," *Twelve Tomorrows*.

——, "Pictures from the Resurrection," *Meeting Infinity*.

Bonnie Joe Stufflebeam, "He Came from a Place of Openness and Truth," *Lightspeed*, February.

——, "Nostalgia," *Interzone* 256.

Tim Sullivan, "Hob's Choice," *Fantasy & Science Fiction*, November/December.

Mike Sulway, "The Karen Joy Fowler Book Club," *Lightspeed*, October.

Michael Swanwick, "The Night of the Salamander," *Tor.com*, August 5.

——, "The Phantom in the Maze," *Tor.com*, December 1.

——, "The Pyramid of Krakow," *Tor.com*, September 30.

——& Gregory Frost, "Lock Up Your Chickens and Daughters—H'ard and Andy Are Come To Town!," *Asimov's*, April/May.

Rachel Swirsky, "The Reluctant Jew," *Jews vs. Aliens*.

——, "Tea Time," *Lightspeed*, December.

Sheree Renée Thomas, "The Dragon Can't Dance," *Afrofuture(s)*.

Lavie Tidhar, "The Drowned Celestial," *Old Venus*.

——, "The Last Dinosaur," *Shimmer* 26.

E. Catherine Tobler, "Somewhere I Have Never Traveled (Third Sound Remix), *Clarkesworld*, June.

Jeremiah Tolbert, "Men of Unborrowed Vision," *Lightspeed*, January.

Steven Utley & Camille Alexa, "All the Layers of the World," *Postscripts* 34/35.

Robin Wasserman, "All the People in Your Party Have Died," *Press Start to Play*.

Catherynne A. Valente, "The Lily and the Horn," *Fantasy Magazine*.

Genevieve Valentine, "Blood, Ash, Braids," *Operation Arcana*.

Carrie Vaughn, "Crazy Rhythm," *Lightspeed*, October.

——, "The Girl Who Loved Shonen Knife," *Hanzai Japan*.

——, "Sealskin," *Operation Arcana*.

——, "Sun, Stone, Spear," *Beneath Ceaseless Skies*, March.

——, "That Game We Played During the War," *Tor.com*.

Ursula Vernon, "Pocosin," *Apex*, January.

James Victor, "Mustard World," *Abyss & Apex*, 3rd Quarter.

Thomas M. Waldroon, "Sinseerly a Friend & Yr. Obed't," *Beneath Ceaseless Skies*, April 16.

Kali Wallace, "The Proper Motion of Extraordinary Stars," *Shimmer* 25.

George S. Walker, "Dreadnought Under Ice," *Abyss & Apex*, 1st Quarter.

Janeen Webb, "A Wonderous Necessary Woman," *Hear Me Roar!*

Bud Webster, "Farewell Blues," *Fantasy & Science Fiction*, January/February.

Andrew Weir, "Twarrior," *Press Start to Play*.

Henry Wessells, "The Beast Unknown to Heraldry," *Lady Churchill's Rosebud Wristlet*, June.

Django Wexler, "The End of the War," *Asimov's*, June.

———, "The Guns of the Wastes," *Operation Arcana*.

———, "Real," *Press Start to Play*.

Aliva Whiteley, "Blossoms Falling Down," *Interzone 257*.

Rick Wilber, "Walking to Boston," *Asimov's*, October/November.

Fran Wilde, "Bent the Wing, Dark the Cloud," *Beneath Ceaseless Skies*, September 3.

———, "How to Walk Through Historic Graveyards in the Post-Digital Age," *Asimov's*, April/May.

Liz Williams, "The Marriage of the Sea," *Asimov's*, April/May.

Sean Williams, "All the Wrong Places," *Meeting at Infinity*.

Neil Williamson, "Fish on Friday," *Interzone 256*.

Kai Ashante Wilson, Kaiju Maximus," *Fantasy Magazine*.

Gene Wolfe, "Incubator," *Onward, Drake!*

Nick Wolven, "We're So Very Sorry for Your Recent Tragic Loss," *Fantasy & Science Fiction*, September/October.

Ray Wood, "Schrodinger's Gun," *Tor.com*, February 18.

Frank Wu, "Season of the Ants," *Analog*, November.

J.V. Yang, Cold Hands and the Smell of Salt," *Daily SF*, January 23.

Isabel Yap, "Milagroso," *Tor.com*, August 12.

Caroline M. Yoachim, "Four Seasons in the Forest of Your Mind," *Fantasy & Science Fiction*, May/June.

———, "Goodbye, First Love," *Daily SF*, May 1.

———, "Ninety-Five Percent Sure," *Asimov's*, January.

———, "Rock, Paper, Scissors, Love," *Lightspeed*, November.

———, "Seven Wonders of a Once and Future World," *Lightspeed*, September.

Alvaro Zinos-Amaro, "Endless Forms Most Beautiful," *Analog*, September.

K.J. Zimring, "Partible," *Analog*, April.